The

Complete Short Stories

of

GUY DE
MAUPASSANT

Ten Volumes in One

WALTER J. BLACK CO.
171 MADISON AVENUE · NEW YORK CITY

Contents

Volume I

BALL-OF-FAT 1

THE DIAMOND NECKLACE 28

A PIECE OF STRING 34

THE STORY OF A FARM-GIRL 38

IN THE MOONLIGHT 51

MME. TELLIER'S EXCURSION 54

LOVE 71

MME. FIFI 75

MONSIEUR PARENT 83

USELESS BEAUTY 109

AN AFFAIR OF STATE 121

BABETTE 127

A COCK CROWED 132

LILIE LALA 135

A VAGABOND 138

THE MOUNTEBANKS 146

UGLY 149

THE DEBT 152

A NORMANDY JOKE 155

THE FATHER 159

THE ARTIST 164

FALSE ALARM 167

THAT PIG OF A MORIN 172

Volume II

MISS HARRIET 181

THE HOLE 195

THE INN 199

A FAMILY 208

BELLFLOWER 212

IN THE WOOD.. 215

THE MARQUIS DE FUMEROL.. 219

SAVED 224

THE SIGNAL 227

THE DEVIL 231

THE VENUS OF BRANIZA.. 236

THE RABBIT 238

LA MORILLONNE 243

EPIPHANY 245

SIMON'S PAPA 253

WAITER, A BOCK! 259

THE SEQUEL TO A DIVORCE... 264

THE CLOWN 268

THE MAD WOMAN.. 271

MADEMOISELLE 273

Volume III

A BAD ERROR.. 277

THE PORT 280

CHÂLI 286

JEROBOAM 293

VIRTUE IN THE BALLET..296

THE DOUBLE PINS..300

HOW HE GOT THE LEGION OF HONOR...............................303

A CRISIS 307

GRAVEYARD SIRENS 311

GROWING OLD 316

A FRENCH ENOCH ARDEN..319

JULIE ROMAIN 323

AN UNREASONABLE WOMAN..328

ROSALIE PRUDENT 332

HIPPOLYTE'S CLAIM 335

BENOIST 338

FECUNDITY 342

A WAY TO WEALTH...348

AM I INSANE? 352

FORBIDDEN FRUIT 354

THE CHARM DISPELLED...358

MADAME PARISSE 361

MAKING A CONVERT..366

Volume IV

A LITTLE WALK...371

A WIFE'S CONFESSION..374

A DEAD WOMAN'S SECRET..378

LOVE'S AWAKENING 381

BED NO. 29..385

MARROCA 392

A PHILOSOPHER 398

A MISTAKE 402

FLORENTINE 406

CONSIDERATION 410

WOMAN'S WILES 414

MOONLIGHT 418

DOUBTFUL HAPPINESS 421

HUMILIATION 425

THE WEDDING NIGHT... 429

THE NONCOMMISSIONED OFFICER... 434

IN THE COURT ROOM.. 438

A PECULIAR CASE.. 441

A PRACTICAL JOKE.. 446

A STRANGE FANCY... 448

AFTER DEATH 453

ON CATS 458

ROOM NO. ELEVEN.. 462

ONE PHASE OF LOVE.. 466

GOOD REASONS 471

A FAIR EXCHANGE... 474

THE TOBACCO SHOP.. 479

A POOR GIRL.. 484

THE SUBSTITUTE 488

A PASSION 491

—————•—————

Volume V

CAUGHT 497

THE ORDERLY 499

JOSEPH 501

REGRET 506

THE DEAF-MUTE 510

MAGNETISM 516

IN VARIOUS RÔLES.. 519

THE FALSE GEMS.. 523

COUNTESS SATAN 527

A USEFUL HOUSE... 531

THE COLONEL'S IDEAS... 533

TWO LITTLE SOLDIERS... 537

GHOSTS 542

WAS IT A DREAM? 545

THE NEW SENSATION... 549

VIRTUE! 551

THE THIEF 554

THE DIARY OF A MADMAN.. 557

ON PERFUMES 560

THE WILL 562

IN HIS SWEETHEART'S LIVERY.. 565

AN UNFORTUNATE LIKENESS... 569

A NIGHT IN WHITECHAPEL.. 571

LOST 575

A COUNTRY EXCURSION.. 577

THE RELICS 584

A RUPTURE 587

MARGOT'S TAPERS 589

THE ACCENT 592

PROFITABLE BUSINESS 595

BERTHA 598

THE LAST STEP 604

Volume VI

A MÉSALLIANCE 607

AN HONEST DEAL... 612

THE LOG 615

DELILA 619

THE ILL-OMENED GROOM... 623

THE ODALISQUE OF SENICHOU.. 627

BRIC-A-BRAC 632

THE ARTIST'S WIFE.. 635

IN THE SPRING... 639

THE REAL ONE AND THE OTHER... 643

THE CARTER'S WENCH... 645

THE RENDEZVOUS 648

SOLITUDE 652

THE MAN WITH THE BLUE EYES.. 656

AN ARTIFICE 659

THE SPECTER 662

THE RELIC 667

THE MARQUIS 670

A DEER PARK IN THE PROVINCES... 674

AN ADVENTURE 677

THE BED 680

UNDER THE YOKE... 682

A FASHIONABLE WOMAN.. 685

WORDS OF LOVE... 690

THE UPSTART 692

HAPPINESS 695

CHRISTMAS EVE 699

THE AWAKENING 702

THE WHITE LADY... 705

MADAME BAPTISTE 709

REVENGE 713

AN OLD MAID... 717

COMPLICATION 722

FORGIVENESS 726

THE WHITE WOLF.. 730

TOINE 734

AN ENTHUSIAST 739

THE TRAVELER'S STORY.. 750

Volume VII

A JOLLY FELLOW.. 755

A LIVELY FRIEND... 760

THE BLIND MAN... 764

THE IMPOLITE SEX... 767

THE CORSICAN BANDIT... 771

THE DUEL 773

THE LOVE OF LONG AGO... 779

THE FARMER'S WIFE.. 782

BESIDE A DEAD MAN... 787

A QUEER NIGHT IN PARIS... 790

A DUEL 796

THE UMBRELLA 800

THE QUESTION OF LATIN... 806

MOTHER AND SON!!! 812

HE? 816

Volume VIII

THE AVENGER 821

THE CONSERVATORY 824

LETTER FOUND ON A CORPSE.. 828

THE LITTLE CASK.. 832

POOR ANDREW 836

A FISHING EXCURSION.. 840

AFTER 843

THE SPASM 847

A MEETING 852

A NEW YEAR'S GIFT... 857

MY UNCLE SOSTHENES... 861

ALL OVER 866

MY LANDLADY 870

THE HORRIBLE 874

THE FIRST SNOWFALL.. 878

THE WOODEN SHOES... 884

BOITELLE 887

SELFISHNESS 893

Volume IX

THE WATCHDOG 897

THE DANCERS 900

CHRISTENING 903

A COSTLY OUTING... 906

THE MAN WITH THE DOGS... 909

A KING'S SON... 914

MOHAMMED FRIPOULI 919

"BELL" 924

THE VICTIM 927

THE ENGLISHMAN 930

—————o—————

Volume X

SENTIMENT 935

FRANCIS 938

THE ASSASSIN 942

SEMILLANTE 945

ON THE RIVER.. 948

SUICIDES 952

A MIRACLE 955

THE ACCURSED BREAD... 959

MY TWENTY-FIVE DAYS.. 962

A LUCKY BURGLAR... 967

AN ODD FEAST... 970

SYMPATHY 972

A TRAVELER'S TALE... 975

LITTLE LOUISE ROQUE.. 979

VOLUME I

BALL-OF-FAT

For many days now the fag-end of the army had been straggling through the town. They were not troops, but a disbanded horde. The beards of the men were long and filthy, their uniforms in tatters, and they advanced at an easy pace without flag or regiment. All seemed worn-out and back-broken, incapable of a thought or a resolution, marching by habit solely, and falling from fatigue as soon as they stopped. In short, they were a mobilized, pacific people, bending under the weight of the gun; some little squads on the alert, easy to take alarm and prompt in enthusiasm, ready to attack or to flee; and in the midst of them, some red breeches, the remains of a division broken up in a great battle; some somber artillery men in line with these varied kinds of foot soldiers; and, sometimes the brilliant helmet of a dragoon on foot who followed with difficulty the shortest march of the lines.

Some legions of free-shooters, under the heroic names of "Avengers of the Defeat," "Citizens of the Tomb," "Partakers of Death," passed in their turn with the air of bandits.

Their leaders were former cloth or grain merchants, ex-merchants in tallow or soap, warriors of circumstance, elected officers on account of their escutcheons and the length of their mustaches, covered with arms and with braid, speaking in constrained voices, discussing plans of campaign, and pretending to carry agonized France alone on their swagger-ing shoulders, but sometimes fearing their own soldiers, prison-birds, that were often brave at first and later proved to be plunderers and debauchees.

It was said that the Prussians were going to enter Rouen.

The National Guard who for two months had been carefully reconnoiter-ing in the neighboring woods, shooting sometimes their own sentinels, and ready for a combat whenever a little wolf stirred in the thicket, had now returned to their firesides. Their arms, their uniforms, all the murderous accoutrements with which they had lately struck fear into the national heart for three leagues in every direction, had suddenly disappeared.

The last French soldiers finally came across the Seine to reach the Audemer bridge through Saint-Sever and Bourg-Achard; and, marching behind, on foot, between two officers of ordnance, the General, in despair, unable to do anything with these incongruous tatters, himself lost in the breaking-up of a people accustomed to conquer, and disastrously beaten, in spite of his legendary bravery.

A profound calm, a frightful, silent expectancy had spread over the city. Many of the heavy citizens, emasculated by commerce, anxiously awaited the conquerors, trembling lest their roasting spits or kitchen knives be considered arms.

All life seemed stopped; shops were closed, the streets dumb. Sometimes an inhabitant, intimidated by this silence, moved rapidly along next the walls. The agony of waiting made them wish the enemy would come.

In the afternoon of the day which followed the departure of the French troops, some uhlans, coming from one knows not where, crossed the town with celerity. Then, a little later, a black mass descended the side of St. Catharine, while two other invading bands appeared by the way of Darnetal and Boisguillaume. The advance guard of the three bodies joined one another at the same moment in Hotel de Ville square and, by all the neighboring streets, the German army continued to arrive, spreading out its battalions, making the pavement resound under their hard, rhythmic step.

Some orders of the commander, in a foreign, guttural voice, reached the houses which seemed dead and deserted, while behind closed shutters, eyes were watching these victorious men, masters of the city, of fortunes, of lives, through the "rights of war." The inhabitants, shut up in their rooms, were visited with the kind of excitement that a cataclysm, or some fatal upheaval of the earth, brings to us, against which all force is useless. For the same sensation is produced each time that the established order of things is overturned, when security no longer exists, and all that protect the laws of man and of nature find themselves at the mercy of unreasoning, ferocious brutality. The trembling of the earth crushing the houses and burying an entire people; a river overflowing its banks and carrying in its course the

drowned peasants, carcasses of beeves, and girders snatched from roofs, or a glorious army massacring those trying to defend themselves, leading others prisoners, pillaging in the name of the sword and thanking God to the sound of the cannon, all are alike frightful scourges which disconnect all belief in eternal justice, all the confidence that we have in the protection of Heaven and the reason of man.

Some detachments rapped at each door, then disappeared into the houses. It was occupation after invasion. Then the duty commences for the conquered to show themselves gracious toward the conquerors.

After some time, as soon as the first terror disappears, a new calm is established. In many families, the Prussian officer eats at the table. He is sometimes well bred and, through politeness, pities France, and speaks of his repugnance in taking part in this affair. One is grateful to him for this sentiment; then, one may be, some day or other, in need of his protection. By treating him well, one has, perhaps, a less number of men to feed. And why should we wound anyone on whom we are entirely dependent? To act thus would be less bravery than temerity. And temerity is no longer a fault of the commoner of Rouen, as it was at the time of the heroic defense, when their city became famous. Finally, each told himself that the highest judgment of French urbanity required that they be allowed to be polite to the strange soldier in the house, provided they did not show themselves familiar with him in public. Outside they would not make themselves known to each other, but at home they could chat freely, and the German might remain longer each evening warming his feet at their hearthstones.

The town even took on, little by little, its ordinary aspect. The French scarcely went out, but the Prussian soldiers grumbled in the streets. In short, the officers of the Blue Hussars, who dragged with arrogance their great weapons of death up and down the pavement, seemed to have no more grievous scorn for the simple citizens than the officers or the sportsmen who, the year before, drank in the same *cafés*.

There was nevertheless, something in the air, something subtle and unknown, a strange, intolerable atmosphere like a penetrating odor, the odor of invasion. It filled the dwellings and the public places, changed the taste of the food, gave the impression of being on a journey, far away, among barbarous and dangerous tribes.

The conquerors exacted money, much money. The inhabitants always paid and they were rich enough to do it. But the richer a trading Norman becomes the more he suffers at every outlay, at each part of his fortune that he sees pass from his hands into those of another.

Therefore, two or three leagues below the town, following the course of the river toward Croisset, Dieppedalle, or Biessart mariners and fishermen often picked up the swollen corpse of a German in uniform from the bottom of the river, killed by the blow of a knife, the head crushed with a stone, or perhaps thrown into the water by a push from the high bridge. The slime of the river bed buried these obscure vengeances, savage, but legitimate, unknown heroisms, mute attacks more perilous than the battles of broad day, and without the echoing sound of glory.

For hatred of the foreigner always arouses some intrepid ones, who are ready to die for an idea.

Finally, as soon as the invaders had brought the town quite under subjection with their inflexible discipline, without having been guilty of any of the horrors for which they were famous along their triumphal line of march, people began to take courage, and the need of trade put new heart into the commerce of the country. Some had large interests at Havre, which the French army occupied, and they wished to try and reach this port by going to Dieppe by land and there embarking.

They used their influence with the German soldiers with whom they had an acquaintance, and finally, an authorization of departure was obtained from the General-in-chief.

Then, a large diligence, with four horses, having been engaged for this journey, and ten persons having engaged seats in it, it was resolved to set out on Tuesday morning before daylight, in order to escape observation.

For some time before, the frost had been hardening the earth and on Monday, toward three o'clock, great black clouds coming from the north brought the snow which fell without interruption during the evening and all night.

At half past four in the morning, the travelers met in the courtyard of Hotel Normandie, where they were to take the carriage.

They were still full of sleep, and

shivering with cold under their wraps. They could only see each other dimly in the obscure light, and the accumulation of heavy winter garments made them all resemble fat curates in long cassocks. Only two of the men were acquainted; a third accosted them and they chatted: "I'm going to take my wife," said one. "I too," said another. "And I," said the third. The first added: "We shall not return to Rouen, and if the Prussians approach Havre, we shall go over to England." All had the same projects, being of the same mind.

As yet the horses were not harnessed. A little lantern, carried by a stable boy, went out one door from time to time, to immediately appear at another. The feet of the horses striking the floor could be heard, although deadened by the straw and litter, and the voice of a man talking to the beasts, sometimes swearing, came from the end of the building. A light tinkling of bells announced that they were taking down the harness; this murmur soon became a clear and continuous rhythm by the movement of the animal, stopping sometimes, then breaking into a brusque shake which was accompanied by the dull stamp of a sabot upon the hard earth.

The door suddenly closed. All noise ceased. The frozen citizens were silent; they remained immovable and stiff.

A curtain of uninterrupted white flakes constantly sparkled in its descent to the ground. It effaced forms, and powdered everything with a downy moss. And nothing could be heard in the great silence. The town was calm, and buried under the wintry frost, as this fall of snow, unnamable and float-

ing, a sensation rather than a sound (trembling atoms which only seem to fill all space), came to cover the earth.

The man reappeared with his lantern, pulling at the end of a rope a sad horse which would not come willingly. He placed him against the pole, fastened the traces, walked about a long time adjusting the harness, for he had the use of but one hand, the other carrying the lantern. As he went for the second horse, he noticed the travelers, motionless, already white with snow, and said to them: "Why not get into the carriage? You will be under cover, at least."

They had evidently not thought of it, and they hastened to do so. The three men installed their wives at the back and then followed them. Then the other forms, undecided and veiled, took in their turn the last places without exchanging a word.

The floor was covered with straw, in which the feet ensconced themselves. The ladies at the back having brought little copper foot stoves, with a carbon fire, lighted them and, for some time, in low voices, enumerated the advantages of the appliances, repeating things that they had known for a long time.

Finally, the carriage was harnessed with six horses instead of four, because the traveling was very bad, and a voice called out:

"Is everybody aboard?"

And a voice within answered: "Yes."

They were off. The carriage moved slowly, slowly for a little way. The wheels were imbedded in the snow; the whole body groaned with heavy cracking sounds; the horses glistened, puffed, and smoked; and the great whip of the driver snapped without ceasing, hovering about on all sides, knotting and unrolling itself like a thin serpent, lashing brusquely some horse on the rebound, which then put forth its most violent effort.

Now the day was imperceptibly dawning. The light flakes, which one of the travelers, a Rouenese by birth, said looked like a shower of cotton, no longer fell. A faint light filtered through the great dull clouds, which rendered more brilliant the white of the fields, where appeared a line of great trees clothed in whiteness, or a chimney with a cap of snow.

In the carriage, each looked at the others curiously, in the sad light of this dawn.

At the back, in the best places, Mr. Loiseau, wholesale merchant of wine, of Grand-Pont street, and Mrs. Loiseau were sleeping opposite each other. Loiseau had bought out his former patron who failed in business, and made his fortune. He sold bad wine at a good price to small retailers in the country, and passed among his friends and acquaintances as a knavish wag, a true Norman full of deceit and joviality.

His reputation as a sharper was so well established that one evening at the residence of the prefect, Mr. Tournel, author of some fables and songs, of keen, satirical mind, a local celebrity, having proposed to some ladies, who seemed to be getting a little sleepy, that they make up a game of "Loiseau tricks," the joke traversed the rooms of the prefect, reached those of the town, and then, in the months to come, made many a face in the province expand with laughter.

Loiseau was especially known for his love of farce of every kind, for his jokes, good and bad; and no one could ever talk with him without thinking: "He is invaluable, this Loiseau." Of tall figure, his balloon-shaped front was surmounted by a ruddy face surrounded by gray whiskers.

His wife, large, strong, and resolute, with a quick, decisive manner, was the order and arithmetic of this house of commerce, while he was the life of it through his joyous activity.

Beside them, Mr. Carré-Lamadon held himself with great dignity, as if belonging to a superior caste; a considerable man, in cottons, proprietor of three mills, officer of the Legion of Honor, and member of the General Council. He had remained, during the Empire, chief of the friendly opposition, famous for making the Emperor pay more dear for rallying to the cause than if he had combated it with blunted arms, according to his own story. Madame Carré-Lamadon, much younger than her husband, was the consolation of officers of good family sent to Rouen in garrison. She sat opposite her husband, very dainty, petite, and pretty, wrapped closely in furs and looking with sad eyes at the interior of the carriage.

Her neighbors, the Count and Countess Hubert de Breville, bore the name of one of the most ancient and noble families of Normandy. The Count, an old gentleman of good figure, accentuated, by the artifices of his toilette, his resemblance to King Henry IV., who, following a glorious legend of the family, had impregnated one of the

De Breville ladies, whose husband, for this reason, was made a count and governor of the province.

A colleague of Mr. Carré-Lamadon in the General Council, Count Hubert represented the Orléans party in the Department.

The story of his marriage with the daughter of a little captain of a privateer had always remained a mystery. But as the Countess had a grand air, received better than anyone, and passed for having been loved by the son of Louis Philippe, all the nobility did her honor, and her salon remained the first in the country, the only one which preserved the old gallantry, and to which the *entrée* was difficult. The fortune of the Brevilles amounted, it was said, to five hundred thousand francs in income, all in good securities.

These six persons formed the foundation of the carriage company, the society side, serene and strong, honest, established people, who had both religion and principles.

By a strange chance, all the women were upon the same seat; and the Countess had for neighbors two sisters who picked at long strings of beads and muttered some *Paters* and *Aves.* One was old and as pitted with smallpox as if she had received a broadside of grapeshot full in the face. The other, very sad, had a pretty face and a disease of the lungs, which, added to their devoted faith, illumined them and made them appear like martyrs.

Opposite these two devotees were a man and a woman who attracted the notice of all. The man, well known, was Cornudet the democrat, the terror of respectable people. For twenty years

he had soaked his great red beard in the *bocks* of all the democratic *cafés.* He had consumed with his friends and *confrères* a rather pretty fortune left him by his father, an old confectioner, and he awaited the establishing of the Republic with impatience, that he might have the position he merited by his great expenditures. On the fourth of September, by some joke perhaps, he believed himself elected prefect, but when he went to assume the duties, the clerks of the office were masters of the place and refused to recognize him, obliging him to retreat. Rather a good bachelor, on the whole, inoffensive and serviceable, he had busied himself, with incomparable ardor, in organizing the defense against the Prussians. He had dug holes in all the plains, cut down young trees from the neighboring forests, sown snares over all routes and, at the approach of the enemy, took himself quickly back to the town. He now thought he could be of more use in Havre where more entrenchments would be necessary.

The woman, one of those called a coquette, was celebrated for her *embonpoint*, which had given her the nickname of "Ball-of-Fat." Small, round, and fat as lard, with puffy fingers choked at the phalanges, like chaplets of short sausages; with a stretched and shining skin, an enormous bosom which shook under her dress, she was, nevertheless, pleasing and sought after, on account of a certain freshness and breeziness of disposition. Her face was a round apple, a peony bud ready to pop into bloom, and inside that opened two great black eyes, shaded with thick brows that cast a shadow within; and below, a charming mouth, humid for kissing, furnished with shining, microscopic baby teeth. She was, it was said, full of admirable qualities.

As soon as she was recognized, a whisper went around among the honest women, and the words "prostitute" and "public shame" were whispered so loud that she raised her head. Then she threw at her neighbors such a provoking, courageous look that a great silence reigned, and everybody looked down except Loiseau, who watched her with an exhilarated air.

And immediately conversation began among the three ladies, whom the presence of this girl had suddenly rendered friendly, almost intimate. It seemed to them they should bring their married dignity into union in opposition to that sold without shame; for legal love always takes on a tone of contempt for its free *confrère*.

The three men, also drawn together by an instinct of preservation at the sight of Cornudet, talked money with a certain high tone of disdain for the poor. Count Hubert talked of the havoc which the Prussians had caused, the losses which resulted from being robbed of cattle and from destroyed crops, with the assurance of a great lord, ten times millionaire whom these ravages would scarcely cramp for a year. Mr. Carré-Lamadon, largely experienced in the cotton industry, had had need of sending six hundred thousand francs to England, as a trifle in reserve if it should be needed. As for Loiseau, he had arranged with the French administration to sell them all the wines that remained in his cellars, on account of which the State owed him a formidable sum, which he counted on collecting at Havre.

And all three threw toward each other swift and amicable glances.

Although in different conditions, they felt themselves to be brothers through money, that grand free-masonry of those who possess it, and make the gold rattle by putting their hands in their trousers' pockets.

The carriage went so slowly that at ten o'clock in the morning they had not gone four leagues. The men had got down three times to climb hills on foot. They began to be disturbed because they should be now taking breakfast at Tôtes and they despaired now of reaching there before night. Each one had begun to watch for an inn along the route, when the carriage foundered in a snowdrift, and it took two hours to extricate it.

Growing appetites troubled their minds; and no eating-house, no wine shop showed itself; the approach of the Prussians and the passage of the troops having frightened away all these industries.

The gentlemen ran to the farms along the way for provisions, but they did not even find bread, for the defiant peasant had concealed his stores for fear of being pillaged by the soldiers who, having nothing to put between their teeth, took by force whatever they discovered.

Toward one o'clock in the afternoon, Loiseau announced that there was a decided hollow in his stomach. Everybody suffered with him, and the violent need of eating, ever increasing, had killed conversation.

From time to time some one yawned; another immediately imitated him; and each, in his turn, in accordance with his character, his knowledge of life, and his social position, opened his mouth with carelessness or modesty, placing his hand quickly before the yawning hole from whence issued a vapor.

Ball-of-Fat, after many attempts, bent down as if seeking something under her skirts. She hesitated a second, looked at her neighbors, then sat up again tranquilly. The faces were pale and drawn. Loiseau affirmed that he would give a thousand francs for a small ham. His wife made a gesture, as if in protest; but she kept quiet. She was always troubled when anyone spoke of squandering money, and could not comprehend any pleasantry on the subject. "The fact is," said the Count, "I cannot understand why I did not think to bring some provisions with me." Each reproached himself in the same way.

However, Cornudet had a flask full of rum. He offered it; it was refused coldly. Loiseau alone accepted two swallows, and then passed back the flask saying, by way of thanks: "It is good all the same; it is warming and checks the appetite." The alcohol put him in good-humor and he proposed that they do as they did on the little ship in the song, eat the fattest of the passengers. This indirect allusion to Ball-of-Fat choked the well-bred people. They said nothing. Cornudet alone laughed. The two good sisters had ceased to mumble their rosaries and, with their hands enfolded in their great sleeves, held themselves immovable, obstinately lowering their eyes, without

doubt offering to Heaven the suffering it had brought upon them.

Finally at three o'clock, when they found themselves in the midst of an interminable plain, without a single village in sight, Ball-of-Fat bending down quickly drew from under the seat a large basket covered with a white napkin.

At first she brought out a little china plate and a silver cup; then a large dish in which there were two whole chickens, cut up and imbedded in their own jelly. And one could still see in the basket other good things, some *pâtés*, fruits, and sweetmeats, provisions for three days if they should not see the kitchen of an inn. Four necks of bottles were seen among the packages of food. She took a wing of a chicken and began to eat it delicately, with one of those little biscuits called "Regence" in Normandy.

All looks were turned in her direction. Then the odor spread, enlarging the nostrils and making the mouth water, besides causing a painful contraction of the jaw behind the ears. The scorn of the women for this girl became ferocious, as if they had a desire to kill her and throw her out of the carriage into the snow, her, her silver cup, her basket, provisions and all.

But Loiseau with his eyes devoured the dish of chicken. He said: "Fortunately Madame had more precaution than we. There are some people who know how to think ahead always."

She turned toward him, saying: "If you would like some of it, sir? It is hard to go without breakfast so long."

He saluted her and replied: "Faith, I frankly cannot refuse; I can stand it no longer. Everything goes in time of war, does it not, Madame?" And then casting a comprehensive glance around, he added: "In moments like this, one can but be pleased to find people who are obliging."

He had a newspaper which he spread out on his knees, that no spot might come to his pantaloons, and upon the point of a knife that he always carried in his pocket, he took up a leg all glistening with jelly, put it between his teeth and masticated it with a satisfaction so evident that there ran through the carriage a great sigh of distress.

Then Ball-of-Fat, in a sweet and humble voice, proposed that the two sisters partake of her collation. They both accepted instantly and, without raising their eyes, began to eat very quickly, after stammering their thanks. Cornudet no longer refused the offers of his neighbor, and they formed with the sisters a sort of table, by spreading out some newspapers upon their knees.

The mouths opened and shut without ceasing, they masticated, swallowed, gulping ferociously. Loiseau in his corner was working hard and, in a low voice, was trying to induce his wife to follow his example. She resisted for a long time; then, when a drawn sensation ran through her body, she yielded. Her husband, rounding his phrase, asked their "charming companion" if he might be allowed to offer a little piece to Madame Loiseau.

She replied: "Why, yes, certainly, sir," with an amiable smile, as she passed the dish.

An embarrassing thing confronted them when they opened the first bottle of Bordeaux: they had but one cup.

Each passed it after having tasted. Cornudet alone, for politeness without doubt, placed his lips at the spot left humid by his fair neighbor.

Then, surrounded by people eating, suffocated by the odors of the food, the Count and Countess de Breville, as well as Madame and M. Carré-Lamadon, were suffering that odious torment which has preserved the name of Tantalus. Suddenly the young wife of the manufacturer gave forth such a sigh that all heads were turned in her direction; she was as white as the snow without; her eyes closed, her head drooped; she had lost consciousness. Her husband, much excited, implored the help of everybody. Each lost his head completely, until the elder of the two sisters, holding the head of the sufferer, slipped Ball-of-Fat's cup between her lips and forced her to swallow a few drops of wine. The pretty little lady revived, opened her eyes, smiled, and declared in a dying voice that she felt very well now. But, in order that the attack might not return, the sister urged her to drink a full glass of Bordeaux, and added: "It is just hunger, nothing more."

Then Ball-of-Fat, blushing and embarrassed, looked at the four travelers who had fasted and stammered: "Goodness knows! if I dared to offer anything to these gentlemen and ladies, I would—" Then she was silent, as if fearing an insult. Loiseau took up the word: "Ah! certainly, in times like these all the world are brothers and ought to aid each other. Come, ladies, without ceremony; why the devil not accept? We do not know whether we shall even find a house where we can pass the night. At the pace we are going now, we shall not reach Tôtes before noon to-morrow—"

They still hesitated, no one daring to assume the responsibility of a "Yes." The Count decided the question. He turned toward the fat, intimidated girl and, taking on a grand air of condescension, he said to her:

"We accept with gratitude, Madame."

It is the first step that counts. The Rubicon passed, one lends himself to the occasion squarely. The basket was stripped. It still contained a *pate de foie gras, a pâtè* of larks, a piece of smoked tongue, some preserved pears, a loaf of hard bread, some wafers, and a full cup of pickled gherkins and onions, of which crudities Ball-of-Fat, like all women, was extremely fond.

They could not eat this girl's provisions without speaking to her. And so they chatted, with reserve at first; then, as she carried herself well, with more abandon. The ladies De Breville and Carré-Lamadon, who were acquainted with all the ins and outs of good-breeding, were gracious with a certain delicacy. The Countess, especially, showed that amiable condescension of very noble ladies who do not fear being spoiled by contact with anyone, and was charming. But the great Madame Loiseau, who had the soul of a plebian, remained crabbed, saying little and eating much.

The conversation was about the war, naturally. They related the horrible deeds of the Prussians, the brave acts of the French; and all of them, although running away, did homage to those who stayed behind. Then personal stories began to be told, and Ball-of-Fat re-lated, with sincere emotion, and in the heated words that such girls sometimes use in expressing their natural feelings, how she had left Rouen:

"I believed at first that I could remain," she said. "I had my house full of provisions, and I preferred to feed a few soldiers rather than expatriate myself, to go I knew not where. But as soon as I saw them, those Prussians, that was too much for me! They made my blood boil with anger, and I wept for very shame all day long. Oh! if I were only a man! I watched them from my windows, the great porkers with their pointed helmets, and my maid held my hands to keep me from throwing the furniture down upon them. Then one of them came to lodge at my house; I sprang at his throat the first thing; they are no more difficult to strangle than other people. And I should have put an end to that one then and there had they not pulled me away by the hair. After that, it was necessary to keep out of sight. And finally, when I found an opportunity, I left town and—here I am!"

They congratulated her. She grew in the estimation of her companions, who had not shown themselves so hot-brained, and Cornudet, while listening to her, took on the approving, benevolent smile of an apostle, as a priest would if he heard a devotee praise God, for the long-bearded democrats have a monopoly of patriotism, as the men in cassocks have of religion. In his turn he spoke, in a doctrinal tone, with the emphasis of a proclamation such as we see pasted on the walls about town, and finished by a bit of eloquence whereby he gave that "scamp of a Badinguet" a good lashing.

Then Ball-of-Fat was angry, for she was a Bonapartist. She grew redder than a cherry and, stammering with indignation, said:

"I would like to have seen you in his place, you other people. Then everything would have been quite right; oh, yes! It is you who have betrayed this man! One would never have had to leave France if it had been governed by blackguards like you!"

Cornudet, undisturbed, preserved a disdainful, superior smile, but all felt that the high note had been struck, until the Count, not without some difficulty, calmed the exasperated girl and proclaimed with a manner of authority that all sincere opinions should be respected. But the Countess and the manufacturer's wife, who had in their souls an unreasonable hatred for the people that favor a Republic, and the same instinctive tenderness that all women have for a decorative, despotic government, felt themselves drawn, in spite of themselves, toward this prostitute so full of dignity, whose sentiments so strongly resembled their own.

The basket was empty. By ten o'clock they had easily exhausted the contents and regretted that there was not more. Conversation continued for some time, but a little more coldly since they had finished eating.

The night fell, the darkness little by little became profound, and the cold, felt more during digestion, made Ball-of-Fat shiver in spite of her plumpness. Then Madame de Breville offered her the little footstove, in which the fuel had been renewed many times since

morning; she accepted it immediately, for her feet were becoming numb with cold. The ladies Carré-Lamadon and Loiseau gave theirs to the two religious sisters.

The driver had lighted his lanterns. They shone out with a lively glimmer showing a cloud of foam beyond, the sweat of the horses; and, on both sides of the way, the snow seemed to roll itself along under the moving reflection of the lights.

Inside the carriage one could distinguish nothing. But a sudden movement seemed to be made between Ball-of-Fat and Cornudet; and Loiseau, whose eye penetrated the shadow, believed that he saw the big-bearded man start back quickly as if he had received a swift, noiseless blow.

Then some twinkling points of fire appeared in the distance along the road. It was Tôtes. They had traveled eleven hours, which, with the two hours given to resting and feeding the horses, made thirteen. They entered the town and stopped before the Hotel of Commerce.

The carriage door opened! A well-known sound gave the travelers a start; it was the scabbard of a sword hitting the ground. Immediately a German voice was heard in the darkness.

Although the diligence was not moving, no one offered to alight, fearing some one might be waiting to murder them as they stepped out. Then the conductor appeared, holding in his hand one of the lanterns which lighted the carriage to its depth, and showed the two rows of frightened faces, whose mouths were open and whose eyes were wide with surprise and fear.

Outside beside the driver, in plain

sight, stood a German officer, an excessively tall young man, thin and blond, squeezed into his uniform like a girl in a corset, and wearing on his head a flat, oilcloth cap which made him resemble the porter of an English hotel. His enormous mustache, of long straight hairs, growing gradually thin at each side and terminating in a single blond thread so fine that one could not perceive where it ended, seemed to weigh heavily on the corners of his mouth and, drawing down the cheeks, left a decided wrinkle about the lips.

In Alsatian French, he invited the travelers to come in, saying in a suave tone: "Will you descend, gentlemen and ladies?"

The two good sisters were the first to obey, with the docility of saints accustomed ever to submission. The Count and Countess then appeared, followed by the manufacturer and his wife; then Loiseau, pushing ahead of him his larger half. The last-named, as he set foot on the earth, said to the officer: "Good evening, sir," more as a measure of prudence than politeness. The officer, insolent as all powerful people usually are, looked at him without a word.

Ball-of-Fat and Cornudet, although nearest the door, were the last to descend, grave and haughty before the enemy. The fat girl tried to control herself and be calm. The democrat waved a tragic hand and his long beard seemed to tremble a little and grow redder. They wished to preserve their dignity, comprehending that in such meetings as these they represented in some degree their great country, and somewhat disgusted with the docility of her companions, the fat girl tried to show more pride than her neighbors, the honest women, and, as she felt that some one should set an example, she continued her attitude of resistance assumed at the beginning of the journey.

They entered the vast kitchen of the inn, and the German, having demanded their traveling papers signed by the General-in-chief (in which the name, the description, and profession of each traveler was mentioned), and having examined them all critically, comparing the people and their signatures, said: "It is quite right," and went out.

Then they breathed. They were still hungry and supper was ordered. A half hour was necessary to prepare it, and while two servants were attending to this they went to their rooms. They found them along a corridor which terminated in a large glazed door.

Finally, they sat down at table, when the proprietor of the inn himself appeared. He was a former horse merchant, a large, asthmatic man, with a constant wheezing and rattling in his throat. His father had left him the name of Follenvie. He asked:

"Is Miss Elizabeth Rousset here?"

Ball-of-Fat started as she answered: "It is I."

"The Prussian officer wishes to speak with you immediately."

"With me?"

"Yes, that is, if you are Miss Elizabeth Rousset."

She was disturbed, and reflecting for an instant, declared flatly:

"That is my name, but I shall not go."

A stir was felt around her; each discussed and tried to think of the cause of this order. The Count approached her, saying:

"You are wrong, Madame, for your refusal may lead to considerable difficulty, not only for yourself, but for all your companions. It is never worth while to resist those in power. This request cannot assuredly bring any danger; it is, without doubt, about some forgotten formality."

Everybody agreed with him, asking, begging, beseeching her to go, and at last they convinced her that it was best; they all feared the complications that might result from disobedience. She finally said:

"It is for you that I do this, you understand."

The Countess took her by the hand, saying: "And we are grateful to you for it."

She went out. They waited before sitting down at table.

Each one regretted not having been sent for in the place of this violent, irascible girl, and mentally prepared some platitudes, in case they should be called in their turn.

But at the end of ten minutes she reappeared, out of breath, red to suffocation, and exasperated. She stammered: "Oh! the rascal; the rascal!"

All gathered around to learn something, but she said nothing; and when the Count insisted, she responded with great dignity: "No, it does not concern you; I can say nothing."

Then they all seated themselves around a high soup tureen, whence came the odor of cabbage. In spite of alarm, the supper was gay. The cider was good, the beverage Loiseau and the good sisters took as a means of econ-omy. The others called for wine; Cornudet demanded beer. He had a special fashion of uncorking the bottle, making froth on the liquid, carefully filling the glass and then holding it before the light to better appreciate the color. When he drank, his great beard, which still kept some of the foam of his beloved beverage, seemed to tremble with tenderness; his eyes were squinted, in order not to lose sight of his tipple, and he had the unique air of fulfilling the function for which he was born. One would say that there was in his mind a meeting, like that of affinities, between the two great passions that occupied his life—Pale Ale and Revolutions; and assuredly he could not taste the one without thinking of the other.

Mr. and Mrs. Follenvie dined at the end of the table. The man, rattling like a cracked locomotive, had too much trouble in breathing to talk while eating, but his wife was never silent. She told all her impressions at the arrival of the Prussians, what they did, what they said, reviling them because they cost her some money, and because she had two sons in the army. She addressed herself especially to the Countess, flattered by being able to talk with a lady of quality.

When she lowered her voice to say some delicate thing, her husband would interrupt, from time to time, with: "You had better keep silent, Madame Follenvie." But she paid no attention, continuing in this fashion:

"Yes, Madame, those people there not only eat our potatoes and pork, but our pork and potatoes. And it must not be believed that they are at all proper—oh, no! such filthy things they do, saving the respect I owe to you! And if you could see them exercise for hours in the day! they are all there in the field, marching ahead, then marching back, turning here and turning there. They might be cultivating the land, or at least working on the roads of their own country! But no, Madame, these military men are profitable to no one. Poor people have to feed them, or perhaps be murdered! I am only an old woman without education, it is true, but when I see some endangering their constitutions by raging from morning to night, I say: "When there are so many people found to be useless, how unnecessary it is for others to take so much trouble to be nuisances! Truly, is it not an abomination to kill people, whether they be Prussian, or English, or Polish, or French? If one man revenges himself upon another who has done him some injury, it is wicked and he is punished; but when they exterminate our boys, as if they were game, with guns, they give decorations, indeed, to the one who destroys the most! Now, you see, I can never understand that, never!"

Cornudet raised his voice: "War is a barbarity when one attacks a peaceable neighbor, but a sacred duty when one defends his country."

The old woman lowered her head:

"Yes, when one defends himself, it is another thing; but why not make it a duty to kill all the kings who make these wars for their pleasure?"

Cornudet's eyes flashed. "Bravo, my country-woman!" said he.

Mr. Carré-Lamadon reflected profoundly. Although he was prejudiced as a Captain of Industry, the good sense of this peasant woman made him think of the opulence that would be brought into the country were the idle and consequently mischievous hands, and the troops which were now maintained in unproductiveness, employed in some great industrial work that it would require centuries to achieve.

Loiseau, leaving his place, went to speak with the innkeeper in a low tone of voice. The great man laughed, shook, and squeaked, his corpulence quivered with joy at the jokes of his neighbor, and he bought of him six cases of wine for spring, after the Prussians had gone.

As soon as supper was finished, as they were worn out with fatigue, they retired.

However, Loiseau, who had observed things, after getting his wife to bed, glued his eye and then his ear to a hole in the wall, to try and discover what are known as "the mysteries of the corridor."

At the end of about an hour, he heard a groping, and, looking quickly, he perceived Ball-of-Fat, who appeared still more plump in a blue cashmere negligee trimmed with white lace. She had a candle in her hand and was directing her steps toward the great door at the end of the corridor. But a door at the side opened, and when she returned at the end of some minutes Cornudet, in his suspenders, followed her. They spoke low, then they stopped. Ball-of-Fat seemed to be defending the entrance to her room with energy. Loiseau, unfortunately, could not hear all their words, but finally, as they raised their voices, he was able to catch a few. Cornudet insisted with vivacity. He said:

"Come, now, you are a silly woman; what harm can be done?"

She had an indignant air in responding: "No, my dear, there are moments when such things are out of place. Here it would be a shame."

He doubtless did not comprehend and asked why. Then she crid out, raising her voice still more:

"Why? you do not see why? When there are Prussians in the house, in the very next room, perhaps?"

He was silent. This patriotic shame of the harlot, who would not suffer his caress so near the enemy, must have awakened the latent dignity in his heart, for after simply kissing her, he went back to his own door with a bound.

Loiseau, much excited, left the aperture, cut a caper in his room, put on his pajamas, turned back the clothes that covered the bony carcass of his companion, whom he awakened with a kiss, murmuring: "Do you love me, dearie?"

Then all the house was still. And immediately there arose somewhere, from an uncertain quarter, which might be the cellar but was quite as likely to be the garret, a powerful snoring, monotonous and regular, a heavy, prolonged sound, like a great kettle under pressure. Mr. Follenvie was asleep.

As they had decided that they would set out at eight o'clock the next morning, they all collected in the kitchen. But the carriage, the roof of which was covered with snow, stood undisturbed in the courtyard, without horses and without a conductor. They sought him in vain in the stables, in the hay,

and in the coach-house. Then they resolved to scour the town, and started out. They found themselves in a square, with a church at one end and some low houses on either side, where they perceived some Prussian soldiers. The first one they saw was paring potatoes. The second, further off, was cleaning the hairdresser's shop. Another, bearded to the eyes, was tending a troublesome brat, cradling it and trying to appease it; and the great peasant women, whose husbands were "away in the army," indicated by signs to their obedient conquerors the work they wished to have done: cutting wood, cooking the soup, grinding the coffee, or what not. One of them even washed the linen of his hostess, an impotent old grandmother.

The Count, astonished, asked questions of the beadle who came out of the rectory. The old man responded:

"Oh! those men are not wicked; they are not the Prussians we hear about. They are from far off, I know not where; and they have left wives and children in their country; it is not amusing to them, this war, I can tell you! I am sure they also weep for their homes, and that it makes as much sorrow among them as it does among us. Here, now, there is not so much unhappiness for the moment, because the soldiers do no harm and they work as if they were in their own homes. You see, sir, among poor people it is necessary that they aid one another. These are the great traits which war develops."

Cornudet, indignant at the cordial relations between the conquerors and the conquered, preferred to shut himself up in the inn. Loiseau had a joke for the occasion: "They will repeople the land."

Mr. Carré-Lamadon had a serious word: "They try to make amends."

But they did not find the driver. Finally, they discovered him in a *café* of the village, sitting at table fraternally with the officer of ordinance. The Count called out to him:

"Were you not ordered to be ready at eight o'clock?"

"Well, yes; but another order has been given me since."

"By whom?"

"Faith! the Prussian commander."

"What was it?"

"Not to harness at all."

"Why?"

"I know nothing about it. Go and ask him. They tell me not to harness, and I don't harness. That's all."

"Did he give you the order himself?"

"No, sir, the innkeeper gave the order for him."

"When was that?"

"Last evening, as I was going to bed."

The three men returned, much disturbed. They asked for Mr. Follenvie, but the servant answered that that gentleman, because of his asthma, never rose before ten o'clock. And he had given strict orders not to be wakened before that, except in case of fire.

They wished to see the officer, but that was absolutely impossible, since, while he lodged at the inn, Mr. Follenvie alone was authorized to speak to him upon civil affairs. So they waited. The women went up to their rooms again

and occupied themselves with futile tasks.

Cornudet installed himself near the great chimney in the kitchen, where there was a good fire burning. He ordered one of the little tables to be brought from the *café*, then a can of beer, he then drew out his pipe, which plays among democrats a part almost equal to his own, because in serving Cornudet it was serving its country. It was a superb pipe, an admirably colored meerschaum, as black as the teeth of its master, but perfumed, curved, glistening, easy to the hand, completing his physiognomy. And he remained motionless, his eyes as much fixed upon the flame of the fire as upon his favorite tipple and its frothy crown; and each time that he drank, he passed his long, thin fingers through his scanty, gray hair, with an air of satisfaction, after which he sucked in his mustache fringed with foam.

Loiseau, under the pretext of stretching his legs, went to place some wine among the retailers of the country. The Count and the manufacturer began to talk politics. They could foresee the future of France. One of them believed in an Orléans, the other in some unknown savior for the country, a hero who would reveal himself when all were in despair: a Guesclin, or a Joan of Arc, perhaps, or would it be another Napoleon First? Ah! if the Prince Imperial were not so young!

Cornudet listened to them and smiled like one who holds the word of destiny. His pipe perfumed the kitchen.

As ten o'clock struck, Mr. Follenvie appeared. They asked him hurried questions; but he could only repeat two or three times without variation, these words:

"The officer said to me: 'Mr. Follenvie, you see to it that the carriage is not harnessed for those travelers tomorrow. I do not wish them to leave without my order. That is sufficient.'"

Then they wished to see the officer. The Count sent him his card, on which Mr. Carré-Lamadon wrote his name and all his titles. The Prussian sent back word that he would meet the two gentlemen after he had breakfasted, that is to say, about one o'clock.

The ladies reappeared and ate a little something, despite their disquiet. Ball-of-Fat seemed ill and prodigiously troubled.

They were finishing their coffee when the word came that the officer was ready to meet the gentlemen. Loiseau joined them; but when they tried to enlist Cornudet, to give more solemnity to their proceedings, he declared proudly that he would have nothing to do with the Germans; and he betook himself to his chimney corner and ordered another liter of beer.

The three men mounted the staircase and were introduced to the best room of the inn, where the officer received them, stretched out in an armchair, his feet on the mantelpiece, smoking a long, porcelain pipe, and enveloped in a flamboyant dressing-gown, appropriated, without doubt, from some dwelling belonging to a common citizen of bad taste. He did not rise, nor greet them in any way, not even looking at them. It was a magnificent display of natural blackguardism transformed into the military victor.

At the expiration of some moments, he asked: "What is it you wish?"

The Count became spokesman: "We desire to go on our way, sir."

"No."

"May I ask the cause of this refusal?"

"Because I do not wish it."

"But, I would respectfully observe to you, sir, that your General-in-chief gave us permission to go to Dieppe; and I know of nothing we have done to merit your severity."

"I do not wish it—that is all; you can go."

All three having bowed, retired.

The afternoon was lamentable. They could not understand this caprice of the German; and the most singular ideas would come into their heads to trouble them. Everybody stayed in the kitchen and discussed the situation endlessly, imagining all sorts of unlikely things. Perhaps they would be retained as hostages—but to what end?—or taken prisoners—or rather a considerable ransom might be demanded. At this thought a panic prevailed. The richest were the most frightened, already seeing themselves constrained to pay for their lives with sacks of gold poured into the hands of this insolent soldier. They racked their brains to think of some acceptable falsehoods to conceal their riches and make them pass themselves off for poor people, very poor people. Loiseau took off the chain to his watch and hid it away in his pocket. The falling night increased their apprehensions. The lamp was lighted, and as there was still two hours before dinner, Madame Loiseau proposed a game of Thirty-one. It would be a diversion. They accepted. Cornudet himself, having smoked out his pipe, took part for politeness.

The Count shuffled the cards, dealt, and Ball-of-Fat had thirty-one at the outset; and immediately .the interest was great enough to appease the fear that haunted their minds. Then Cornudet perceived that the house of Loiseau was given to tricks.

As they were going to the dinner table, Mr. Follenvie again appeared, and, in wheezing, rattling voice, announced:

"The Prussian officer orders me to ask Miss Elizabeth Rousset if she has yet changed her mind."

Ball-of-Fat remained standing and was pale; then suddenly becoming crimson, such a stifling anger took possession of her that she could not speak. But finally she flashed out: "You may say to the dirty beast, that idiot, that carrion of a Prussian, that I shall never change it; you understand, never, never, never!"

The great innkeeper went out. Then Ball-of-Fat was immediately surrounded, questioned, and solicited by all to disclose the mystery of his visit. She resisted, at first, but soon becoming exasperated, she said: "What does he want? You really want to know what he wants? He wants to sleep with me."

Everybody was choked for words, and indignation was rife. Cornudet broke his glass, so violently did he bring his fist down upon the table. There was a clamor of censure against this ignoble soldier, a blast of anger, a union of all for resistance, as if a demand had been made on each one of the party for the sacrifice exacted of her. The Count declared with disgust that those people conducted themselves after the fashion of the ancient barbarians. The women, especially, showed to Ball-of-Fat a most energetic and tender commiseration. The good sisters who only showed themselves at mealtime, lowered their heads and said nothing.

They all dined, nevertheless, when the first *furore* had abated. But there was little conversation; they were thinking.

The ladies retired early, and the men, all smoking, organized a game at cards to which Mr. Follenvie was invited, as they intended to put a few casual questions to him on the subject of conquering the resistance of this officer. But he thought of nothing but the cards and, without listening or answering, would keep repeating: "To the game, sirs, to the game." His attention was so taken that he even forgot to expectorate, which must have put him some points to the good with the organ in his breast. His whistling lungs ran the whole asthmatic scale, from deep, profound tones to the sharp rustiness of a young cock essaying to crow.

He even refused to retire when his wife, who had fallen asleep previously, came to look for him. She went away alone, for she was an "early bird," always up with the sun, while her husband was a "night owl," always ready to pass the night with his friends. He cried out to her: "Leave my creamed chicken before the fire!" and then went on with his game. When they saw that they could get nothing from him, they declared that it was time to stop, and each sought his bed.

They all rose rather early the next day, with an undefined hope of getting away, which desire the terror of passing another day in that horrible inn greatly increased.

Alas! the horses remained in the stable and the driver was invisible. For want of better employment, they went out and walked around the carriage.

The breakfast was very doleful; and it became apparent that a coldness had arisen toward Ball-of-Fat, and that the night, which brings counsel, had slightly modified their judgments. They almost wished now that the Prussian had secretly found this girl, in order to give her companions a pleasant surprise in the morning. What could be more simple? Besides, who would know anything about it? She could save appearances by telling the officer that she took pity on their distress. To her, it would make so little difference!

No one had avowed these thoughts yet.

In the afternoon, as they were almost perishing from *ennui,* the Count proposed that they take a walk around the village. Each wrapped up warmly and the little party set out, with the exception of Cornudet, who preferred to remain near the fire, and the good sisters, who passed their time in the church or at the curate's.

The cold, growing more intense every day, cruelly pinched their noses and ears; their feet became so numb that each step was torture; and when they came to a field it seemed to them frightfully sad under this limitless white, so that everybody returned immediately, with hearts hard pressed and souls congealed.

The four women walked ahead, the three gentlemen followed just behind. Loiseau, who understood the situation, asked suddenly if they thought that girl there was going to keep them long in such a place as this. The Count, always courteous, said that they could not exact from a woman a sacrifice so hard, unless it should come of her own will. Mr. Carré-Lamadon remarked that if the French made their return through Dieppe, as they were likely to, a battle would surely take place at Tôtes. This reflection made the two others anxious.

"If we could only get away on foot," said Loiseau.

The Count shrugged his shoulders: "How can we think of it in this snow? and with our wives?" he said. "And then, we should be pursued and caught in ten minutes and led back prisoners at the mercy of these soldiers."

It was true, and they were silent.

The ladies talked of their clothes, but a certain constraint seemed to disunite them. Suddenly at the end of the street, the officer appeared. His tall, wasp-like figure in uniform was outlined upon the horizon formed by the snow, and he was marching with knees apart, a gait particularly military, which is affected that they may not spot their carefully blackened boots.

He bowed in passing near the ladies and looked disdainfully at the men, who preserved their dignity by not seeing him, except Loiseau, who made a motion toward raising his hat.

Ball-of-Fat reddened to the ears, and the three married women resented the great humiliation of being thus met by this soldier in the company of this girl whom he had treated so cavalierly.

But they spoke of him, of his figure and his face. Madame Carré-Lamadon who had known many officers and considered herself a connoisseur of them, found this one not at all bad; she regretted even that he was not French, because he would make such a pretty hussar, one all the women would rave over.

Again in the house, no one knew what to do. Some sharp words, even, were said about things very insignificant. The dinner was silent, and almost immediately after it, each one went to his room to kill time in sleep.

They descended the next morning with weary faces and exasperated hearts. The women scarcely spoke to Ball-of-Fat.

A bell began to ring. It was for a baptism. The fat girl had a child being brought up among the peasants of Yvetot. She had not seen it for a year, or thought of it; but now the idea of a child being baptized threw into her heart a sudden and violent tenderness for her own, and she strongly wished to be present at the ceremony.

As soon as she was gone, everybody looked at each other, then pulled their chairs together, for they thought that finally something should be decided upon. Loiseau had an inspiration: it was to hold Ball-of-Fat alone and let the others go.

Mr. Follenvie was charged with the commission, but he returned almost immediately, for the German, who understood human nature, had put him out. He pretended that he would retain

everybody so long as his desire was not satisfied.

Then the commonplace nature of Mrs. Loiseau burst out with:

"Well, we are not going to stay here to die of old age. Since it is the trade of this creature to accommodate herself to all kinds, I fail to see how she has the right to refuse one more than another. I can tell you she has received all she could find in Rouen, even the coachmen! Yes, Madame, the prefect's coachman! I know him very well, for he bought his wine at our house. And to think that to-day we should be drawn into this embarrassment by this affected woman, this minx! For my part, I find that this officer conducts himself very well. He has perhaps suffered privations for a long time; and doubtless he would have preferred us three; but no, he is contented with common property. He respects married women. And we must remember too that he is master. He has only to say 'I wish,' and he could take us by force with his soldiers."

The two women had a cold shiver. Pretty Mrs. Carré-Lamadon's eyes grew brilliant and she became a little pale, as if she saw herself already taken by force by the officer.

The men met and discussed the situation. Loiseau, furious, was for delivering "the wretch" bound hand and foot to the enemy. But the Count, descended through three generations of ambassadors, and endowed with the temperament of a diplomatist, was the advocate of ingenuity.

"It is best to decide upon something," said he. Then they conspired.

The women kept together, the tone

of their voices was lowered, each gave advice and the discussion was general. Everything was very harmonious. The ladies especially found delicate shades and charming subtleties of expression for saying the most unusual things. A stranger would have understood nothing, so great was the precaution of language observed. But the light edge of modesty, with which every woman of the world is barbed, only covers the surface; they blossom out in a scandalous adventure of this kind, being deeply amused and feeling themselves in their element, mixing love with sensuality as a greedy cook prepares supper for his master.

Even gaiety returned, so funny did the whole story seem to them at last. The Count found some of the jokes a little off color, but they were so well told that he was forced to smile. In his turn, Loiseau came out with some still bolder tales, and yet nobody was wounded. The brutal thought, expressed by his wife, dominated all minds: "Since it is her trade, why should she refuse this one more than another?" The genteel Mrs. Carré-Lamadon seemed to think that in her place, she would refuse this one less than some others.

They prepared the blockade at length, as if they were about to surround a fortress. Each took some rôle to play, some arguments he would bring to bear, some maneuvers that he would endeavor to put into execution. They decided on the plan of attack, the ruse to employ, the surprise of assault, that should force this living citadel to receive the enemy in her room.

Cornudet remained apart from the rest, and was a stranger to the whole affair.

So entirely were their minds distracted that they did not hear Ball-of-Fat enter. The Count uttered a light "Ssh!" which turned all eyes in her direction. There she was. The abrupt silence and a certain embarrassment hindered them from speaking to her at first. The Countess, more accustomed to the duplicity of society than the others, finally inquired:

"Was it very amusing, that baptism?"

The fat girl, filled with emotion, told them all about it, the faces, the attitudes, and even the appearance of the church. She added: "It is good to pray sometimes."

And up to the time for luncheon these ladies continued to be amiable toward her, in order to increase her docility and her confidence in their counsel. At the table they commenced the approach. This was in the shape of a vague conversation upon devotion. They cited ancient examples: Judith and Holophernes, then, without reason, Lucrece and Sextus, and Cleopatra obliging all the generals of the enemy to pass by her couch and reducing them in servility to slaves. Then they brought out a fantastic story, hatched in the imagination of these ignorant millionaires, where the women of Rome went to Capua for the purpose of lulling Hannibal to sleep in their arms, and his lieutenants and phalanxes of mercenaries as well. They cited all the women who have been taken by conquering armies, making a battlefield of their bodies, making them also a weapon, and a means of success; and all those hideous and detestable beings who have conquered by their heroic caresses, and sacrificed their chastity to vengeance or a beloved cause. They even spoke in veiled terms of that great English family which allowed one of its women to be inoculated with a horrible and contagious disease in order to transmit it to Bonaparte, who was miraculously saved by a sudden illness at the hour of the fatal rendezvous.

And all this was related in an agreeable, temperate fashion, except as it was enlivened by the enthusiasm deemed proper to excite emulation.

One might finally have believed that the sole duty of woman here below was a sacrifice of her person, and a continual abandonment to soldierly caprices.

The two good sisters seemed not to hear, lost as they were in profound thought. Ball-of-Fat said nothing.

During the whole afternoon they let her reflect. But, in the place of calling her "Madame" as they had up to this time, they simply called her "Mademoiselle" without knowing exactly why, as if they had a desire to put her down a degree in their esteem, which she had taken by storm, and make her feel her shameful situation.

The moment supper was served, Mr. Follenvie appeared with his old phrase: "The Prussian officer orders me to ask if Miss Elizabeth Rousset has yet changed her mind."

Ball-of-Fat responded dryly: "No, sir."

But at dinner the coalition weakened. Loiseau made three unhappy remarks. Each one beat his wits for new examples but found nothing; when the Countess, without premeditation, perhaps feeling some vague need of rendering homage to religion, asked the elder of the good sisters to tell them some great deeds in the lives of the saints. It appeared that many of their acts would have been considered crimes in our eyes; but the Church gave absolution of them readily, since they were done for the glory of God, or for the good of all. It was a powerful argument; the Countess made the most of it.

Thus it may be by one of those tacit understandings, or the veiled complacency in which anyone who wears the ecclesiastical garb excels, it may be simply from the effect of a happy unintelligence, a helpful stupidity, but in fact the religious sister lent a formidable support to the conspiracy. They had thought her timid, but she showed herself courageous, verbose, even violent. She was not troubled by the chatter of the casuist; her doctrine seemed a bar of iron; her faith never hesitated; her conscience had no scruples. She found the sacrifice of Abraham perfectly simple, for she would immediately kill father or mother on an order from on high. And nothing, in her opinion, could displease the Lord, if the intention was laudable. The Countess put to use the authority of her unwitting accomplice, and added to it the edifying paraphrase and axiom of Jesuit morals: "The need justifies the means."

Then she asked her: "Then, my sister, do you think that God accepts intentions, and pardons the deed when the motive is pure?"

"Who could doubt it, Madame? An action blamable in itself often becomes meritorious by the thought it springs from."

And they continued thus, unraveling the will of God, foreseeing his decisions, making themselves interested in things that, in truth, they would never think of noticing. All this was guarded, skillful, discreet. But each word of the saintly sister in a cap helped to break down the resistance of the unworthy courtesan. Then the conversation changed a little, the woman of the chaplet speaking of the houses of her order, of her Superior, of herself, of her dainty neighbor, the dear sister Saint-Nicephore. They had been called to the hospitals of Havre to care for the hundreds of soldiers stricken with smallpox. They depicted these miserable creatures, giving details of the malady. And while they were stopped, *en route,* by the caprice of this Prussian officer, a great number of Frenchmen might die, whom perhaps they could have saved! It was a specialty with her, caring for soldiers. She had been in Crimea, in Italy, in Austria, and, in telling of her campaigns, she revealed herself as one of those religious aids to drums and trumpets, who seem made to follow camps, pick up the wounded in the thick of battle, and, better than an officer, subdue with a word great bands of undisciplined recruits. A true, good sister of the rataplan, whose ravaged face, marked with innumerable scars, appeared the image of the devastation of war.

No one could speak after her, so excellent seemed the effect of her words.

As soon as the repast was ended they quickly went up to their rooms, with the purpose of not coming down the next day until late in the morning.

The luncheon was quiet. They had given the grain of seed time to germinate and bear fruit. The Countess proposed that they take a walk in the afternoon. The Count, being agreeably inclined, gave an arm to Ball-of-Fat and walked behind the others with her. He talked to her in a familiar, paternal tone, a little disdainful, after the manner of men having girls in their employ, calling her "my dear child," from the height of his social position, of his undisputed honor. He reached the vital part of the question at once:

"Then you prefer to leave us here, exposed to the violences which follow a defeat, rather than consent to a favor which you have so often given in your life?"

Ball-of-Fat answered nothing.

Then he tried to reach her through gentleness, reason, and then the sentiments. He knew how to remain "The Count," even while showing himself gallant or complimentary, or very amiable if it became necessary. He exalted the service that she would render them, and spoke of her appreciation; then suddenly became gaily familiar, and said:

"And you know, my dear, it would be something for him to boast of that he had known a pretty girl; something it is difficult to find in his country."

Ball-of-Fat did not answer but joined the rest of the party. As soon as they entered the house she went to her room and did not appear again. The disquiet was extreme. What were they to do? If she continued to resist, what an embarrassment!

The dinner hour struck. They waited in vain. Mr. Follenvie finally entered and said that Miss Rousset was indisposed, and would not be at the table. Everybody pricked up his ears. The Count went to the innkeeper and said in a low voice:

"Is he in there?"

"Yes."

For convenience, he said nothing to his companions, but made a slight sign with his head. Immediately a great sigh of relief went up from every breast and a light appeared in their faces. Loiseau cried out:

"Holy Christopher! I pay for the champagne, if there is any to be found in the establishment." And Mrs. Loiseau was pained to see the proprietor return with four quart bottles in his hands.

Each one had suddenly become communicative and buoyant. A wanton joy filled their hearts. The Count suddenly perceived that Mrs. Carré-Lamadon was charming, the manufacturer paid compliments to the Countess. The conversation was lively, gay, full of touches.

Suddenly Loiseau, with anxious face and hand upraised, called out: "Silence!" Everybody was silent, surprised, already frightened. Then he listened intently and said: "S-s-sh!" his two eyes and his hands raised toward the ceiling, listening, and then continuing, in his natural voice : "All right! All goes well!"

They failed to comprehend at first, but soon all laughed. At the end of a quarter of an hour he began the same farce again, renewing it occasionally during the whole afternoon. And he pretended to call to some one in the story above, giving him advice in a double meaning, drawn from the fountain-head—the mind of a commercial traveler. For some moments he would assume a sad air, breathing in a whisper: "Poor girl!" Then he would murmur between his teeth, with an appearance of rage: "Ugh! That scamp of a Prussian." Sometimes, at a moment when no more was thought about it, he would say, in an affected voice, many times over: "Enough! enough!" and add, as if speaking to himself. "If we could only see her again, it isn't necessary that he should kill her, the wretch!"

Although these jokes were in deplorable taste, they amused all and wounded no one, for indignation, like other things, depends upon its surroundings, and the atmosphere which had been gradually created around them was charged with sensual thoughts.

At the dessert the women themselves made some delicate and discreet allusions. Their eyes glistened; they had drunk much. The Count, who preserved, even in his flights, his grand appearance of gravity, made a comparison, much relished, upon the subject of those wintering at the pole, and the joy of ship-wrecked sailors who saw an opening toward the south.

Loiseau suddenly arose, a glass of champagne in his hand, and said: "I drink to our deliverance." Everybody was on his feet; they shouted in agreement. Even the two good sisters consented to touch their lips to the froth of the wine which they had never before tasted. They declared that it tasted like charged lemonade, only much nicer.

Loiseau resumed: "It is unfortunate that we have no piano, for we might make up a quadrille."

Cornudet had not said a word, nor made a gesture; he appeared plunged in very grave thoughts, and made sometimes a furious motion, so that his great beard seemed to wish to free itself. Finally, toward midnight, as they were separating, Loiseau, who was staggering, touched him suddenly on the stomach and said to him in a stammer: "You are not very funny, this evening; you have said nothing, citizen!" Then Cornudet raised his head brusquely and, casting a brilliant, terrible glance around the company, said: "I tell you all that you have been guilty of infamy!" He rose, went to the door, and again repeated: "Infamy, I say!" and disappeared.

This made a coldness at first. Loiseau, interlocutor, was stupefied; but he recovered immediately and laughed heartily as he said: "He is very green, my friends. He is very green." And then, as they did not comprehend, he told them about the "mysteries of the corridor." Then there was a return of gaiety. The women behaved like lunatics. The Count and Mr. Carré-Lamadon wept from the force of their laughter. They could not believe it.

"How is that? Are you sure?"

"I tell you I saw it."

"And she refused—"

"Yes, because the Prussian officer was in the next room."

"Impossible!"

"I swear it!"

The Count was stifled with laughter. The industrial gentleman held his sides with both hands. Loiseau continued:

"And now you understand why he saw nothing funny this evening! No, nothing at all!" And the three started out half ill, suffocated.

They separated. But Mrs. Loiseau, who was of a spiteful nature, remarked to her husband as they were getting into bed, that "that *grisette*" of a little Carré-Lamadon was yellow with envy all the evening. "You know," she continued, "how some women will take to a uniform, whether it be French or Prussian! It is all the same to them! Oh! what a pity!"

And all night, in the darkness of the corridor, there were to be heard light noises, like whisperings and walking in bare feet, and imperceptible creakings. They did not go to sleep until late, that is sure, for there were threads of light shining under the doors for a long time. The champagne had its effect; they say it troubles sleep.

The next day a clear winter's sun made the snow very brilliant. The diligence, already harnessed, waited before the door, while an army of white pigeons, in their thick plumage, with rose-colored eyes, with a black spot in the center, walked up and down gravely among the legs of the six horses, seeking their livelihood in the manure there scattered.

The driver, enveloped in his sheepskin, had a lighted pipe under the seat, and all the travelers, radiant, were rapidly packing some provisions for the rest of the journey. They were only waiting for Ball-of-Fat. Finally she appeared.

She seemed a little troubled, ashamed. And she advanced timidly toward her companions, who all, with one motion, turned as if they had not seen her. The Count, with dignity, took the arm of his wife and removed her from this impure contact.

The fat girl stopped, half stupefied; then, plucking up courage, she approached the manufacturer's wife with "Good morning, Madame," humbly murmured. The lady made a slight bow of the head which she accompanied with a look of outraged virtue. Everybody seemed busy, and kept themselves as far from her as if she had had some infectious disease in her skirts. Then they hurried into the carriage, where she came last, alone, and where she took the place she had occupied during the first part of the journey.

They seemed not to see her or know her; although Madame Loiseau, looking at her from afar, said to her husband in a half-tone: "Happily, I don't have to sit beside her."

The heavy carriage began to move and the remainder of the journey commenced. No one spoke at first. Ball-of-Fat dared not raise her eyes. She felt indignant toward all her neighbors, and at the same time humiliated at having yielded to the foul kisses of this Prussian, into whose arms they had hypocritically thrown her.

Then the Countess, turning toward Mrs. Carré-Lamadon, broke the difficult silence:

"I believe you know Madame d'Etrelles?"

"Yes, she is one of my friends."

"What a charming woman!"

"Delightful! A very gentle nature, and well educated, besides; then she is an artist to the tips of her fingers, sings beautifully, and draws to perfection."

The manufacturer chatted with the Count, and in the midst of the rattling of the glass, an occasional word escaped such as "coupon—premium—limit—expiration."

Loiseau, who had pilfered the old pack of cards from the inn, greasy through five years of contact with tables badly cleaned, began a game of bezique with his wife.

The good sisters took from their belt the long rosary which hung there, made together the sign of the cross, and suddenly began to move their lips in a lively murmur, as if they were going through the whole of the "Oremus." And from time to time they kissed a medal, made the sign anew, then recommenced their muttering, which was rapid and continued.

Cornudet sat motionless, thinking.

At the end of three hours on the way, Loiseau put up the cards and said: "I am hungry."

His wife drew out a package from whence she brought a piece of cold veal. She cut it evenly in thin pieces and they both began to eat.

"Suppose we do the same," said the Countess.

They consented to it and she undid the provisions prepared for the two couples. It was in one of those dishes whose lid is decorated with a china hare, to signify that a *pâté* of hare is inside, a succulent dish of pork, where white rivers of lard cross the brown flesh of the game, mixed with some other viands hashed fine. A beautiful square of Gruyère cheese, wrapped in a piece of newspaper, preserved the imprint "divers things" upon the unctuous plate.

The two good sisters unrolled a big sausage which smelled of garlic; and Cornudet plunged his two hands into the vast pockets of his overcoat, at the same time, and drew out four hard eggs and a piece of bread. He removed the shells and threw them in the straw under his feet; then he began to eat the eggs, letting fall on his vast beard some bits of clear yellow, which looked like stars caught there.

Ball-of-Fat, in the haste and distraction of her rising, had not thought of anything; and she looked at them exasperated, suffocating with rage, at all of them eating so placidly. A tumultuous anger swept over her at first, and she opened her mouth to cry out at them, to hurl at them a flood of injury which mounted to her lips; but she could not speak, her exasperation strangled her.

No one looked at her or thought of her. She felt herself drowned in the scorn of these honest scoundrels, who had first sacrificed her and then rejected her, like some improper or useless article. She thought of her great basket full of good things which they had greedily devoured, of her two chickens shining with jelly, of her *pâtés*, her pears, and the four bottles of Bordeaux; and her fury suddenly falling, as a cord drawn too tightly breaks, she felt ready to weep. She made terrible efforts to prevent it, making ugly faces, swallowing her sobs as children do, but the tears came and glistened in the corners of her eyes, and then two great drops, detaching themselves from the rest, rolled slowly down like little streams of water that filter through rock, and, falling regularly, rebounded upon her breast. She sits erect, her eyes fixed, her face rigid and pale, hoping that no one will notice her.

But the Countess perceives her and tells her husband by a sign. He shrugs his shoulders, as much as to say:

"What would you have me do, it is not my fault."

Mrs. Loiseau indulged in a mute laugh of triumph and murmured:

"She weeps for shame."

The two good sisters began to pray again, after having wrapped in a paper the remainder of their sausage.

Then Cornudet, who was digesting his eggs, extended his legs to the seat opposite, crossed them, folded his arms, smiled like a man who is watching a good farce, and began to whistle the "Marseillaise."

All faces grew dark. The popular song assuredly did not please his neighbors. They became nervous and agitated, having an appearance of wishing to howl, like dogs, when they hear a barbarous organ. He perceived this but did not stop. Sometimes he would hum the words:

> "Sacred love of country
> Help, sustain th' avenging arm;
> Liberty, sweet Liberty
> Ever fight, with no alarm."

They traveled fast, the snow being harder. But as far as Dieppe, during the long, sad hours of the journey, across the jolts in the road, through the falling night, in the profound darkness of the carriage, he continued his vengeful, monotonous whistling with a ferocious obstinacy, constraining his neigh-bors to follow the song from one end to the other, and to recall the words that belonged to each measure.

And Ball-of-Fat wept continually; and sometimes a sob, which she was not able to restrain, echoed between the two rows of people in the shadows.

The Diamond Necklace ✕

SHE was one of those pretty, charm-ing young ladies, born, as if through an error of destiny, into a family of clerks. She had no dowry, no hopes, no means of becoming known, appreciated, loved, and married by a man either rich or distinguished; and she allowed herself to marry a petty clerk in the office of the Board of Education.

She was simple, not being able to adorn herself; but she was unhappy, as one out of her class; for women belong to no caste, no race; their grace, their beauty, and their charm serving them in the place of birth and family. Their inborn finesse, their instinctive elegance, their suppleness of wit are their only aristocracy, making some daughters of the people the equal of great ladies.

She suffered incessantly, feeling her-self born for all delicacies and luxuries. She suffered from the poverty of her apartment, the shabby walls, the worn chairs, and the faded stuffs. All these things, which another woman of her station would not have noticed, tortured and angered her. The sight of the little Breton, who made this humble home, awoke in her sad regrets and desperate dreams. She thought of quiet ante-chambers, with their Oriental hangings, lighted by high, bronze torches, and of the two great footmen in short trousers who sleep in the large armchairs, made sleepy by the heavy air from the heat-ing apparatus. She thought of large drawing-rooms, hung in old silks, of graceful pieces of furniture carrying bric-à-brac of inestimable value, and of the little perfumed coquettish apart-ments, made for five o'clock chats with most intimate friends, men known and sought after, whose attention all women envied and desired.

When she seated herself for dinner, before the round table where the table-cloth had been used three days, opposite her husband who uncovered the tureen with a delighted air, saying: "Oh! the good potpie! I know nothing better than that—" she would think of the elegant dinners, of the shining silver, of the tapestries peopling the walls with ancient personages and rare birds in the midst of fairy forests; she thought of the exquisite food served on marvelous dishes, of the whispered gallantries, lis-tened to with the smile of the sphinx, while eating the rose-colored flesh of the trout or a chicken's wing.

She had neither frocks nor jewels, nothing. And she loved only those things. She felt that she was made for them. She had such a desire to please, to be sought after, to be clever, and courted.

She had a rich friend, a schoolmate at the convent, whom she did not like to visit, she suffered so much when she returned. And she wept for whole days from chagrin, from regret, from despair, and disappointment.

*   *   *   *   *   *

One evening her husband returned elated bearing in his hand a large envelope.

"Here," he said, "here is something for you."

She quickly tore open the wrapper and drew out a printed card on which were inscribed these words:

"The Minister of Public Instruction and Madame George Ramponneau ask the honor of Mr. and Mrs. Loisel's company Monday evening, January 18, at the Minister's residence."

Instead of being delighted, as her husband had hoped, she threw the invitation spitefully upon the table murmuring:

"What do you suppose I want with that?"

"But, my dearie, I thought it would make you happy. You never go out, and this is an occasion, and a fine one! I had a great deal of trouble to get it. Everybody wishes one, and it is very select; not many are given to employees. You will see the whole official world there."

She looked at him with an irritated eye and declared impatiently:

"What do you suppose I have to wear to such a thing as that?"

He had not thought of that; he stammered:

"Why, the dress you wear when we go to the theater. It seems very pretty to me—"

He was silent, stupefied, in dismay, at the sight of his wife weeping. Two great tears fell slowly from the corners of his eyes toward the corners of his mouth; he stammered:

"What is the matter? What is the matter?"

By a violent effort, she had controlled her vexation and responded in a calm voice, wiping her moist cheeks:

"Nothing. Only I have no dress and consequently I cannot go to this affair. Give your card to some colleague whose wife is better fitted out than I."

He was grieved, but answered:

"Let us see, Matilda. How much would a suitable costume cost, something that would serve for other occasions, something very simple?"

She reflected for some seconds, making estimates and thinking of a sum that she could ask for without bringing with it an immediate refusal and a frightened exclamation from the economical clerk.

Finally she said, in a hesitating voice:

"I cannot tell exactly, but it seems to me that four hundred francs ought to cover it."

He turned a little pale, for he had saved just this sum to buy a gun that he might be able to join some hunting parties the next summer, on the plains at Nanterre, with some friends who went to shoot larks up there on Sunday. Nevertheless, he answered:

"Very well. I will give you four hundred francs. But try to have a pretty dress."

*   *   *   *   *   *

The day of the ball approached and Mme. Loisel seemed sad, disturbed, anxious. Nevertheless, her dress was nearly ready. Her husband said to her one evening:

"What is the matter with you? You have acted strangely for two or three days."

And she responded: "I am vexed not to have a jewel, not one stone, nothing to adorn myself with. I shall have such a poverty-laden look. I would prefer not to go to this party."

He replied: "You can wear some natural flowers. At this season they look very *chic*. For ten francs you can have two or three magnificent roses."

She was not convinced. "No," she replied, "there is nothing more humiliating than to have a shabby air in the midst of rich women."

Then her husband cried out: "How stupid we are! Go and find your friend Mrs. Forestier and ask her to lend you her jewels. You are well enough acquainted with her to do this."

She uttered a cry of joy: "It is true!" she said. "I had not thought of that."

The next day she took herself to her friend's house and related her story of distress. Mrs. Forestier went to her closet with the glass doors, took out a large jewel-case, brought it, opened it, and said: "Choose, my dear."

She saw at first some bracelets, then a collar of pearls, then a Venetian cross of gold and jewels and of admirable workmanship. She tried the jewels before the glass, hesitated, but could neither decide to take them nor leave them. Then she asked:

"Have you nothing more?"

"Why, yes. Look for yourself. I do not know what will please you."

Suddenly she discovered, in a black satin box, a superb necklace of diamonds, and her heart beat fast with an immoderate desire. Her hands trembled as she took them up. She placed them about her throat against her dress, and remained in ecstasy before them. Then she asked, in a hesitating voice, full of anxiety:

"Could you lend me this? Only this?"

"Why, yes, certainly."

She fell upon the neck of her friend, embraced her with passion, then went away with her treasure.

*   *   *   *   *   *

The day of the ball arrived. Mme. Loisel was a great success. She was the prettiest of all, elegant, gracious, smiling, and full of joy. All the men noticed her, asked her name, and wanted to be presented. All the members of the Cabinet wished to waltz with her. The Minister of Education paid her some attention.

She danced with enthusiasm, with passion, intoxicated with pleasure, thinking of nothing, in the triumph of her beauty, in the glory of her success, in a kind of cloud of happiness that came of all this homage, and all this admiration, of all these awakened desires, and this victory so complete and sweet to the heart of woman.

She went home toward four o'clock in the morning. Her husband had been half asleep in one of the little salons since midnight, with three other gentlemen whose wives were enjoying themselves very much.

He threw around her shoulders the wraps they had carried for the coming home, modest garments of everyday wear, whose poverty clashed with the elegance of the ball costume. She felt this and wished to hurry away in order not to be noticed by the other women who were wrapping themselves in rich furs.

Loisel retained her: "Wait, said he. "You will catch cold out there. I am going to call a cab."

But she would not listen and descended the steps rapidly. When they were in the street, they found no carriage; and they began to seek for one, hailing the coachmen whom they saw at a distance.

They walked along toward the Seine, hopeless and shivering. Finally they found on the dock one of those old, nocturnal *coupés* that one sees in Paris after nightfall, as if they were ashamed of their misery by day.

It took them as far as their door in Martyr street, and they went wearily up to their apartment. It was all over for her. And on his part, he remembered that he would have to be at the office by ten o'clock.

She removed the wraps from her shoulders before the glass, for a final view of herself in her glory. Suddenly she uttered a cry. Her necklace was not around her neck.

Her husband, already half undressed, asked: "What is the matter?"

She turned toward him excitedly:

"I have—I have—I no longer have Mrs. Forestier's necklace."

He arose in dismay: "What! How is that? It is not possible."

And they looked in the folds of the dress, in the folds of the mantle, in the pockets, everywhere. They could not find it.

He asked: "You are sure you still had it when we left the house?"

"Yes, I felt it in the vestibule as we came out."

"But if you had lost it in the street, we should have heard it fall. It must be in the cab."

"Yes. It is probable. Did you take the number?"

"No. And you, did you notice what it was?"

"No."

They looked at each other utterly cast down. Finally, Loisel dressed himself again.

"I am going," said he, "over the track where we went on foot, to see if I can find it."

And he went. She remained in her evening gown, not having the force to go to bed, stretched upon a chair, without ambition or thoughts.

Toward seven o'clock her husband returned. He had found nothing.

He went to the police and to the cab offices, and put an advertisement in the newspapers, offering a reward; he did everything that afforded them a suspicion of hope.

She waited all day in a state of bewilderment before this frightful disaster. Loisel returned at evening with his face harrowed and pale; and had discovered nothing.

"It will be necessary," said he, "to write to your friends that you have broken the clasp of the necklace and that you will have it repaired. That will give us time to turn around."

She wrote as he dictated.

*   *   *   *   *   *

At the end of a week, they had lost all hope. And Loisel, older by five years, declared:

"We must take measures to replace this jewel."

The next day they took the box which had inclosed it, to the jeweler whose name was on the inside. He consulted his books:

"It is not I, Madame," said he, "who sold this necklace; I only furnished the casket."

Then they went from jeweler to jeweler seeking a necklace like the other one, consulting their memories, and ill, both of them, with chagrin and anxiety.

In a shop of the Palais-Royal, they found a chaplet of diamonds which seemed to them exactly like the one they had lost. It was valued at forty thousand francs. They could get it for thirty-six thousand.

They begged the jeweler not to sell it for three days. And they made an arrangement by which they might return it for thirty-four thousand francs if they found the other one before the end of February.

Loisel possessed eighteen thousand francs which his father had left him. He borrowed the rest.

He borrowed it, asking for a thousand francs of one, five hundred of another, five louis of this one, and three louis of that one. He gave notes, made ruinous promises, took money of usurers and the whole race of lenders. He compromised his whole existence, in fact, risked his signature, without even knowing whether he could make it good or not, and, harassed by anxiety for the future, by the black misery which surrounded him, and by the prospect of all physical privations and moral torture, he went to get the new necklace, depositing on the merchant's counter thirty-six thousand francs.

When Mrs. Loisel took back the jewels to Mrs. Forestier, the latter said to her in a frigid tone:

"You should have returned them to me sooner, for I might have needed them."

She did open the jewel-box as her friend feared she would. If she should perceive the substitution, what would she think? What should she say? Would she take her for a robber?

*   *   *   *   *   *

Mrs. Loisel now knew the horrible life of necessity. She did her part, however, completely, heroically. It was necessary to pay this frightful debt. She would pay it. They sent away the maid; they changed their lodgings; they rented some rooms under a mansard roof.

She learned the heavy cares of a household, the odious work of a kitchen. She washed the dishes, using her rosy nails upon the greasy pots and the bottoms of the stewpans. She washed the soiled linen, the chemises and dishcloths, which she hung on the line to dry; she took down the refuse to the street each morning and brought up the water, stopping at each landing to breathe. And, clothed like a woman of the people, she went to the grocer's, the butcher's, and the fruiterer's, with her basket on her arm, shopping, haggling to the last sou her miserable money.

Every month it was necessary to renew some notes, thus obtaining time, and to pay others.

The husband worked evenings, putting the books of some merchants in order, and nights he often did copying at five sous a page.

And this life lasted for ten years.

At the end of ten years, they had restored all, all, with interest of the usurer, and accumulated interest besides.

Mrs. Loisel seemed old now. She had become a strong, hard woman, the crude woman of the poor household. Her hair badly dressed, her skirts awry, her hands red, she spoke in a loud tone, and washed the floors in large pails of water. But sometimes, when her husband was at the office, she would seat herself before the window and think of that evening party of former times, of that ball where she was so beautiful and so flattered.

How would it have been if she had not lost that necklace? Who knows? Who knows? How singular is life, and how full of changes! How small a thing will ruin or save one!

*　　*　　*　　*　　*　　*

One Sunday, as she was taking a walk in the Champs-Elysées to rid herself of the cares of the week, she suddenly perceived a woman walking with a child. It was Mrs. Forestier, still young, still pretty, still attractive. Mrs. Loisel was affected. Should she speak to her? Yes, certainly. And now that she had paid, she would tell her all. Why not?

She approached her. "Good morning, Jeanne."

Her friend did not recognize her and was astonished to be so familiarly addressed by this common personage. She stammered:

"But, Madame—I do not know—You must be mistaken—"

"No, I am Matilda Loisel."

Her friend uttered a cry of astonishment: "Oh! my poor Matilda! How you have changed—"

"Yes, I have had some hard days since I saw you; and some miserable ones—and all because of you—"

"Because of me? How is that?"

"You recall the diamond necklace that you loaned me to wear to the Commissioner's ball?"

"Yes, very well."

"Well, I lost it."

"How is that, since you returned it to me?"

"I returned another to you exactly like it. And it has taken us ten years to pay for it. You can understand that it was not easy for us who have nothing. But it is finished and I am decently content."

Madame Forestier stopped short. She said:

"You say that you bought a diamond necklace to replace mine?"

"Yes. You did not perceive it then? They were just alike."

And she smiled with a proud and simple joy. Madame Forestier was touched and took both her hands as she replied:

"Oh! my poor Matilda! Mine were false. They were not worth over five hundred francs!"

A Piece of String

Along all the roads around Goderville the peasants and their wives were coming toward the burgh because it was market day. The men were proceeding with slow steps, the whole body bent forward at each movement of their long twisted legs, deformed by their hard work, by the weight on the plow which, at the same time, raised the left shoulder and swerved the figure, by the reaping of the wheat which made the knees spread to make a firm "purchase," by all the slow and painful labors of the country. Their blouses, blue, "stiff-starched," shining as if varnished, ornamented with a little design in white at the neck and wrists, puffed about their bony bodies, seemed like balloons ready to carry them off. From each of them a head, two arms, and two feet protruded.

Some led a cow or a calf by a cord, and their wives, walking behind the animal, whipped its haunches with a leafy branch to hasten its progress. They carried large baskets on their arms from which, in some cases, chickens and, in others, ducks thrust out their heads. And they walked with a quicker, livelier step than their husbands. Their spare straight figures were wrapped in a scanty little shawl, pinned over their flat bossoms, and their heads were enveloped in a white cloth glued to the hair and surmounted by a cap.

Then a wagon passed at the jerky trot of a nag, shaking strangely, two men seated side by side and a woman in the bottom of the vehicle, the latter holding on to the sides to lessen the hard jolts.

In the public square of Goderville there was a crowd, a throng of human beings and animals mixed together. The horns of the cattle, the tall hats with long nap of the rich peasant, and the headgear of the peasant women rose above the surface of the assembly. And the clamorous, shrill, screaming voices made a continuous and savage din which sometimes was dominated by the robust lungs of some countryman's laugh, or the long lowing of a cow tied to the wall of a house.

All that smacked of the stable, the dairy and the dirt heap, hay and sweat, giving forth that unpleasant odor, human and animal, peculiar to the people of the field.

Maître Hauchecome, of Breaute, had just arrived at Goderville, and he was directing his steps toward the public square, when he perceived upon the ground a little piece of string. Maître Hauchecome, economical like a true Norman, thought that everything useful ought to be picked up, and he bent painfully, for he suffered from rheumatism. He took the bit of thin cord from the ground and began to roll it carefully when he noticed Maître Malandain, the harness-maker, on the threshold of his door, looking at him. They had heretofore had business together on the subject of a halter, and they were on bad terms, being both good haters. Maître Hauchecome was seized with a sort of shame to be seen thus by his enemy, picking a bit of string out of the dirt. He concealed his "find" quickly under his blouse, then in his trousers' pocket; then he pretended to be still looking on the ground for something which he did not find, and he went toward the market, his head forward, bent double by his pains.

He was soon lost in the noisy and slowly moving crowd, which was busy with interminable bargainings. The peasants milked, went and came, perplexed, always in fear of being cheated, not daring to decide, watching the vender's eye, ever trying to find the trick in the man and the flaw in the beast.

The women, having placed their great baskets at their feet, had taken out the poultry which lay upon the ground, tied together by the feet, with terrified eyes and scarlet crests.

They heard offers, stated their prices with a dry air and impassive face, or perhaps, suddenly deciding on some proposed reduction, shouted to the customer who was slowly going away: "All right, Maître Authirne, I'll give it to you for that."

Then little by little the square was deserted, and the Angelus ringing at noon, those who had stayed too long, scattered to their shops.

At Jourdain's the great room was full of people eating, as the big court was full of vehicles of all kinds, carts, gigs, wagons, dump carts, yellow with dirt, mended and patched, raising their shafts to the sky like two arms, or perhaps with their shafts in the ground and their backs in the air.

Just opposite the diners seated at the table, the immense fireplace, filled with bright flames, cast a lively heat on the backs of the row on the right. Three spits were turning on which were chickens, pigeons, and legs of mutton; and an appetizing odor of roast beef and gravy dripping over the nicely browned skin rose from the hearth, increased the jovialness, and made everybody's mouth water.

All the aristocracy of the plow ate there, at Maître Jourdain's, tavern keeper and horse dealer, a rascal who had money.

The dishes were passed and emptied, as were the jugs of yellow cider. Everyone told his affairs, his purchases, and sales. They discussed the crops. The weather was favorable for the green things but not for the wheat.

Suddenly the drum beat in the court, before the house. Everybody rose except a few indifferent persons, and ran to the door, or to the windows, their mouths still full and napkins in their hands.

After the public crier had ceased his drum-beating, he called out in a jerky voice, speaking his phrases irregularly:

"It is hereby made known to the inhabitants of Goderville, and in general to all persons present at the market, that there was lost this morning, on the road to Benzeville, between nine and ten o'clock, a black leather pocketbook containing five hundred francs and some business papers. The finder is requested to return same with all haste to the mayor's office or to Maître Fortune Houlbreque of Manneville, there will be twenty francs reward."

Then the man went away. The heavy roll of the drum and the crier's voice were again heard at a distance.

Then they began to talk of this event discussing the chances that Maître Houlbreque had of finding or not finding his pocketpook.

And the meal concluded. They were

finishing their coffee when a chief of the gendarmes appeared upon the threshold.

He inquired:

"Is Maître Hauchecome, of Breaute, here?"

Maître Hauchecome, seated at the other end of the table, replied:

"Here I am."

And the officer resumed:

"Maître Hauchecome, will you have the goodness to accompany me to the mayor's office? The mayor would like to talk to you."

The peasant, surprised and disturbed, swallowed at a draught his tiny glass of brandy, rose, and, even more bent than in the morning, for the first steps after each rest were specially difficult, set out, repeating: "Here I am, here I am."

The mayor was awaiting him, seated on an armchair. He was the notary of the vicinity, a stout, serious man, with pompous phrases.

"Maître Hauchecome," said he, "you were seen this morning to pick up, on the road to Benzeville, the pocketbook lost by Maître Houlbreque, of Manneville."

The countryman, astounded, looked at the mayor, already terrified, by this suspicion resting on him without his knowing why.

"Me? Me? Me pick up the pocketbook?"

"Yes, you, yourself."

"Word of honor, I never heard of it."

"But you were seen."

"I was seen, me? Who says he saw me?"

"Monsieur Malandain, the harness-maker."

The old man remembered, understood, and flushed with anger.

"Ah, he saw me, the clodhopper, he saw me pick up this string, here, M'sieu, the Mayor." And rummaging in his pocket he drew out the little piece of string.

But the mayor, incredulous, shook his head.

"You will not make me believe, Maître Hauchecome, that Monsieur Malandain, who is a man worthy of credence, mistook this cord for a pocketbook."

The peasant, furious, lifted his hand, spat at one side to attest his honor, repeating:

"It is nevertheless the truth of the good God, the sacred truth, M'sieu' the Mayor. I repeat it on my soul and my salvation."

The mayor resumed:

"After picking up the object, you stood like a stilt, looking a long while in the mud to see if any piece of money had fallen out."

The good, old man choked with indignation and fear.

"How anyone can tell—how anyone can tell—such lies to take away an honest man's reputation! How can anyone—"

There was no use in his protesting, nobody believed him. He was confronted with Monsieur Malandain, who repeated and maintained his affirmation. They abused each other for an hour. At his own request, Maître Hauchecome was searched, nothing was found on him.

Finally the mayor, very much perplexed, discharged him with the warning that he would consult the public prosecutor and ask for further orders.

The news had spread. As he left the mayor's office, the old man was surrounded and questioned with a serious or bantering curiosity, in which there was no indignation. He began to tell the story of the string. No one believed him. They laughed at him.

He went along, stopping his friends, beginning endlessly his statement and his protestations, showing his pockets turned inside out, to prove that he had nothing.

They said:

"Old rascal, get out!"

And he grew angry, becoming exasperated, hot, and distressed at not being believed, not knowing what to do and always repeating himself.

Night came. He must depart. He started on his way with three neighbors to whom he pointed out the place where he had picked up the bit of string; and all along the road he spoke of his adventure.

In the evening he took a turn in the village of Breaute, in order to tell it to everybody. He only met with incredulity.

It made him ill at night.

The next day about one o'clock in the afternoon, Marius Paumelle, a hired man in the employ of Maître Breton, husbandman at Ymanville, returned the pocketbook and its contents to Maître Houlbreque of Manneville.

This man claimed to have found the object in the road; but not knowing how to read, he had carried it to the house and given it to his employer.

The news spread through the neighborhood. Maître Hauchecome was informed of it. He immediately went the circuit and began to recount his story completed by the happy climax. He was in triumph.

"What grieved me so much was not the thing itself, as the lying. There is nothing so shameful as to be placed under a cloud on account of a lie."

He talked of his adventure all day long, he told it on the highway to people who were passing by, in the wine-shop to people who were drinking there, and to persons coming out of church the following Sunday. He stopped strangers to tell them about it. He was calm now, and yet something disturbed him without his knowing exactly what it was. People had the air of joking while they listened. They did not seem convinced. He seemed to feel that remarks were being made behind his back.

On Tuesday of the next week he went to the market at Goderville, urged solely by the necessity he felt of discussing the case.

Malandain, standing at his door, began to laugh on seeing him pass. Why?

He approached a farmer from Creque-tot, who did not let him finish, and giving him a thump in the stomach said to his face:

"You big rascal."

Then he turned his back on him.

Maître Hauchecome was confused, why was he called a big rascal?

When he was seated at the table, in Jourdain's tavern he commenced to explain "the affair."

A horse dealer from Monvilliers called to him:

"Come, come, old sharper, that's an old trick; I know all about your piece of string!"

Hauchecome stammered:

"But since the pocketbook was found."

But the other man replied:

"Shut up, papa, there is one that finds, and there is one that reports. At any rate you are mixed with it."

The peasant stood choking. He understood. They accused him of having had the pocketbook returned by a confederate, by an accomplice.

He tried to protest. All the table began to laugh.

He could not finish his dinner and went away, in the midst of jeers.

He went home ashamed and indignant, choking with anger and confusion, the more dejected that he was capable with his Norman cunning of doing what they had accused him of, and ever boasting of it as of a good turn. His innocence to him, in a confused way, was impossible to prove, as his sharpness was known. And he was stricken to the heart by the injustice of the suspicion.

Then he began to recount the adventures again, prolonging his history every day, adding each time, new reasons, more energetic protestations, more solemn oaths which he imagined and prepared in his hours of solitude, his whole mind given up to the story of the string. He was believed so much the less as his defense was more complicated and his arguing more subtile.

"Those are lying excuses," they said behind his back.

He felt it, consumed his heart over it, and wore himself out with useless efforts. He wasted away before their very eyes.

The wags now made him tell about the string to amuse them, as they make a soldier who has been on a campaign tell about his battles. His mind, touched to the depth, began to weaken.

Toward the end of December he took to his bed.

He died in the first days of January, and in the delirium of his death struggles he kept claiming his innocence, reiterating:

"A piece of string, a piece of string, —look—here it is, M'sieu' the Mayor."

The Story of a Farm-Girl

As THE weather was very fine, the people on the farm had dined more quickly than usual, and had returned to the fields.

The female servant, Rose, remained alone in the large kitchen, where the fire on the hearth was dying out, under the large boiler of hot water. From time to time she took some water out of it, and slowly washed her plates and dishes, stopping occasionally to look at the two streaks of light which the sun threw on to the long table through the window, and which showed the defects in the glass.

Three venturesome hens were picking up the crumbs under the chairs, while the smell of the poultry yard and the warmth from the cow-stall came in through the half open door, and a cock was heard crowing in the distance.

When she had finished her work, wiped down the table, dusted the mantelpiece, and put the plates on to the high dresser, close to the wooden clock, with its enormous pendulum, she drew a long breath, as she felt rather oppressed, without exactly knowing why. She looked at the black clay walls, the rafters that were blackened with smoke, from which spiders' webs were hanging amid pickled herrings and strings of onions, and then she sat down, rather overcome by the stale emanations from the floor, on which so many things had been spilled. With these was mingled the smell of the pans of milk, which were set out to raise the cream in the adjoining dairy.

She wanted to sew, as usual, but she did not feel strong enough for it, and so she went to get a mouthful of fresh air at the door, which seemed to do her good.

The fowls were lying on the smoking dung-hill; some of them were scratching with one claw in search of worms, while the cock stood up proudly among them. Now and then he selected one of them, and walked round her with a slight cluck of amorous invitation. The hen got up in a careless way as she received his attentions, supported herself on her legs and spread out her wings; then she shook her feathers to shake out the dust, and stretched herself out on the dung-hill again, while he crowed, in sign of triumph, and the cocks in all the neighboring farmyards replied to him, as if they were uttering amorous challenges from farm to farm.

The girl looked at them without thinking; then she raised her eyes and

was almost dazzled at the sight of the apple-trees in blossom, which looked almost like powdered heads. Just then, a colt, full of life and friskiness, galloped past her. Twice he jumped over the ditches, and then stopped suddenly, as if surprised at being alone.

She also felt inclined to run; she felt inclined to move and to stretch her limbs, and to repose in the warm, breathless air. She took a few undecided steps, and closed her eyes, for she was seized with a feeling of animal comfort; then she went to look for the eggs in the hen loft. There were thirteen of them, which she took in and put into the storeroom; but the smell from the kitchen disgusted her again and she went out to sit on the grass for a time.

The farmyard, which was surrounded by trees, seemed to be asleep. The tall grass, among which the tall yellow dandelions rose up like streaks of yellow light, was of a vivid green, the fresh spring green. The apple-trees threw their shade all round them, and the thatched houses, on which the blue and yellow iris flowers, with their swordlike leaves, grew, smoked as if the moisture of the stables and barns was coming through the straw.

The girl went to the shed where the carts and traps were kept. Close to it, in a ditch, there was a large patch of violets whose scent was perceptible all round, while beyond it could be seen the open country where the corn was growing, with clumps of trees in the distance, and groups of laborers here and there, who looked as small as dolls, and white horses like toys, who were pulling a child's cart, driven by a man as tall as one's finger.

She took up a bundle of straw, threw it into the ditch and sat down upon it; then, not feeling comfortable, she undid it, spread it out and lay down upon it at full length, on her back, with both arms under her head, and her limbs stretched out.

Gradually her eyes closed, and she was falling into a state of delightful languor. She was, in fact, almost asleep, when she felt two hands on her bosom, and then she sprang up at a bound. It was Jacques, one of the farm laborers, a tall fellow from Picardy, who had been making love to her for a long time. He had been looking after the sheep, and seeing her lying down in the shade, he had come stealthily, and holding his breath, with glistening eyes, and bits of straw in his hair.

He tried to kiss her, but she gave him a smack in the face, for she was as strong as he, and he was shrewd enough to beg her pardon: so they sat down side by side and talked amicably. They spoke about the favorable weather, of their master, who was a good fellow, then of their neighbors, of all the people in the country round, of themselves, of their village, of their youthful days, of their recollections, of their relatives, whom they had not seen for a long time, and might not see again. She grew sad, as she thought of it, while he, with one fixed idea in his head, rubbed against her with a kind of a shiver, overcome by desire.

"I have not seen my mother for a long time," she said. "It is very hard to be separated like that." And she directed her looks into the distance, toward the village in the North, which she had left.

Suddenly, however, he seized her by the neck and kissed her again! but she struck him so violently in the face with her clenched fist, that his nose began to bleed, and he got up and laid his head against the stem of a tree. When she saw that, she was sorry, and going up to him, she said:

"Have I hurt you?"

He, however, only laughed. "No, it was a mere nothing;" though she had hit him right on the middle of the nose. "What a devil!" he said, and he looked at her with admiration, for she had inspired him with a feeling of respect and of a very different kind of admiration, which was the beginning of real love for that tall, strong wench.

When the bleeding had stopped, he proposed a walk, as he was afraid of his neighbor's heavy hand, if they remained side by side like that much longer; but she took his arm of her own accord, in the avenue, as if they had been out for an evening walk, and said: "It is not nice of you to despise me like that, Jacques."

He protested, however. No, he did not despise her. He was in love with her, that was all.

"So you really want to marry me?" she asked.

He hesitated, and then looked at her aside, while she looked straight ahead of her. She had fat, red cheeks, a full, protuberant bust under her muslin dress, thick, red lips, and her neck, which was almost bare, was covered with small beads of perspiration. He felt a fresh access of desire, and putting his lips to her ear, he murmured: "Yes, of course I do."

Then she threw her arms round his neck, and kissed for such a long time, that they both of them lost their breath. From that moment the eternal story of love began between them. They plagued one another in corners; they met in the moonlight under a hay-stack, and gave each other bruises on the legs, with their heavy nailed boots. By degrees, however, Jacques seemed to grow tired of her: he avoided her; scarcely spoke to her, and did not try any longer to meet her alone, which made her sad and anxious, especially when she found that she was pregnant.

At first, she was in a state of consternation; then she got angry, and her rage increased every day, because she could not meet him, as he avoided her most carefully. At last, one night when everyone in the farmhouse was asleep, she went out noiselessly in her petticoat, with bare feet, crossed the yard and opened the door of the stable where Jacques was lying in a large box of straw, over his horses. He pretended to snore when he heard her coming, but she knelt down by his side and shook him until he sat up.

"What do you want?" he then asked of her. And she with clenched teeth, and trembling with anger, replied:

"I want—I want you to marry me, as you promised."

But he only laughed, and replied: "Oh, If a man were to marry all the girls with whom he has made a slip, he would have more than enough to do."

Then she seized him by the throat, threw him on to his back, so that he could not disengage himself from her,

and half strangling him, she shouted into his face: "I am *enceinte,* do you hear? I am *enceinte!*"

He gasped for breath, as he was nearly choked, and so they remained, both of them, motionless and without speaking, in the dark silence, which was only broken by the noise that a horse made as he pulled the hay out of the manger, and then slowly chewed it.

When Jacques found that she was the stronger, he stammered out: "Very well, I will marry you, as that is the case."

But she did not believe his promises. "It must be at once," she said. "You must have the banns put up."

"At once," he replied.

"Swear solemnly that you will."

He hesitated for a few moments, and then said: "I swear it, by heaven."

Then she released her grasp, and went away without another word.

She had no chance of speaking to him for several days, and as the stable was now always locked at night, she was afraid to make any noise, for fear of creating a scandal. One day, however, she saw another man come in at dinner-time, and so she said: "Has Jacques left?"

"Yes," the man replied; "I have got his place."

This made her tremble so violently, that she could not take the saucepan off the fire; and later when they were all at work, she went up into her room and cried, burying her head in her bolster, so that she might not be heard. During the day, however, she tried to obtain some information without exciting any suspicions, but she was so overwhelmed by the thoughts of her misfortune, that she fancied that all the people whom she asked, laughed maliciously. All she learned, however, was, that he had left the neighborhood altogether.

II.

Then a cloud of constant misery began for her. She worked mechanically, without thinking of what she was doing, with one fixed idea in her head: "Suppose people were to know."

This continual feeling made her so incapable of reasoning, that she did not even try to think of any means of avoiding the disgrace that she knew must ensue, which was irreparable, and drawing nearer every day, and which was as sure as death itself. She got up every morning long before the others, and persistently tried to look at her figure in a piece of broken looking-glass at which she did her hair, as she was very anxious to know whether anybody would notice a change in her, and during the day she stopped working every few minutes to look at herself from top to toe, to see whether the size of her abdomen did not make her apron look too short.

The months went on. She scarcely spoke now, and when she was asked a question, she did not appear to understand. She had a frightened look, with haggard eyes and trembling hands, which made her master say to her occasionally: "My poor girl, how stupid you have grown lately."

In church, she hid behind a pillar, and no longer ventured to go to confession. She feared to face the priest, to whom she attributed a superhuman power, which enabled him to read people's con-

sciences; and at meal times, the looks of her fellow-servants almost made her faint with mental agony. She was always fancying that she had been found out by the cowherd, a precocious and cunning little lad, whose bright eyes seemed always to be watching her.

One morning the postman brought her a letter, and as she had never received one in her life before, she was so upset by it, that she was obliged to sit down. Perhaps it was from him? But as she could not read, she sat anxious and trembling with that piece of paper covered with ink in her hand; after a time, however, she put it into her pocket, as she did not venture to confide her secret to anyone. She often stopped in her work to look at the lines, written at regular intervals, and terminating in a signature, imagining vaguely that she would suddenly discover their meaning. At last, as she felt half mad with impatience and anxiety, she went to the schoolmaster, who told her to sit down, and read the letter to her, as follows:

"My Dear Daughter:—I write to tell you that I am very ill. Our neighbor, Monsieur Dentu, begs you to come, if you can,

"For your affectionate mother,

"Cesaire Dentu,
"Deputy Mayor."

She did not say a word, and went away, but as soon as she was alone, her legs gave way, and she fell down by the roadside, and remained there till night.

When she got back, she told the farmer her trouble. He allowed her to go home for as long as she wanted, promised to have her work done by a charwoman, and to take her back when she returned.

Her mother died soon after she got there, and the next day Rose gave birth to a seven months' child, a miserable little skeleton, thin enough to make anybody shudder. It seemed to be suffering continually, to judge from the painful manner in which it moved its poor little limbs, which were as thin as a crab's legs, but it lived, for all that. She said that she was married, but that she could not saddle herself with the child, so she left it with some neighbors, who promised to take great care of it, and she went back to the farm.

But then, in her heart, which had been wounded so long, there arose something like brightness, an unknown love for that frail little creature which she had left behind her, but there was fresh suffering in that very love, suffering which she felt every hour and every minute, because she was parted from the child. What pained her most, however, was a mad longing to kiss it, to press it in her arms, to feel the warmth of its little body against her skin. She could not sleep at night; she thought of it the whole day long, and in the evening, when her work was done, she used to sit in front of the fire and look at it intently, like people do whose thoughts are far away.

They began to talk about her, and to tease her about her lover. They asked her whether he was tall, handsome, and rich. When was the wedding to be, and the christening? And often she ran away to cry by herself, for these questions seemed to hurt her, like the prick of a pin, and in order to forget their jokes, she began to work still more energetically, and still thinking of her child, she sought for the means of saving up money for it, and determined to work so that her master would be obliged to raise her wages.

Then, by degrees, she almost monopolized the work, and persuaded him to get rid of one servant girl, who had become useless since she had taken to working like two; she economized in the bread, oil, and candles, in the corn which they gave to the fowls too extravagantly, and in the fodder for the horses and cattle, which was rather wasted. She was as miserly about her master's money as if it had been her own, and by dint of making good bargains, of getting high prices for all their produce, and by baffling the peasants' tricks when they offered anything for sale, he at last intrusted her with buying and selling everything, with the direction of all the laborers, and with the quantity of provisions necessary for the household, so that in a short time she became indispensable to him. She kept such a strict eye on everything about her, that under her direction the farm prospered wonderfully, and for five miles round people talked of "Master Vallin's servant," and the farmer himself said everywhere: "That girl is worth more than her weight in gold."

But time passed by, and her wages remained the same. Her hard work was accepted as something that was due from every good servant, and as a mere token of her good-will; and she began to think rather bitterly, that if the farmer could put fifty or a hundred crowns extra into the bank every month, thanks to her, she was still only earning her two hundred francs a year, neither more nor less, and so she made up her mind to ask for an increase of wages. She went

to see the schoolmaster three times
about it, but when she got there, she
spoke about something else. She felt a
kind of modesty in asking for money,
as if it were something disgraceful;
but at last, one day, when the farmer
was having breakfast by himself in the
kitchen, she said to him, with some
embarrassment, that she wished to speak
to him particularly. He raised his head
in surprise, with both his hands on the
table, holding his knife, with its point
in the air, in one, and a piece of bread
in the other. He looked fixedly at the
girl, who felt uncomfortable under his
gaze, but asked for a week's holiday,
so that she might get away, as she was
not very well. He acceded to her request immediately, and then added, in
some embarrassment, himself:

"When you come back, I shall have
something to say to you, myself."

III.

The child was nearly eight months
old, and she did not know it again. It
had grown rosy and chubby all over like
a little bundle of living fat. She threw
herself on to it as if it had been some
prey, and kissed it so violently that it
began to scream with terror, and then
she began to cry herself, because it did
not know her, and stretched out its arms
to its nurse, as soon as it saw her. But
the next day, it began to get used to her,
and laughed when it saw her, and she
took it into the fields and ran about
excitedly with it, and sat down under
the shade of the trees, and then, for the
first time in her life, she opened her
heart to somebody, and told the infant
her troubles, how hard her work was,

her anxieties and her hopes, and she
quite tired the child with the violence
of her caresses.

She took the greatest pleasure in handling it, in washing and dressing it, for
it seemed to her that all this was the
confirmation of her maternity, and she
would look at it, almost feeling surprised that it was hers, and she used to
say to herself in a low voice, as she
danced it in her arms: "It is my baby,
it is my baby."

She cried all the way home as she
returned to the farm, and had scarcely
got in, before her master called her into
his room. She went in, feeling astonished and nervous, without knowing
why.

"Sit down there," he said.

She sat down, and for some moments
they remained side by side, in some
embarrassment, with their arms hanging at their sides, as if they did not
know what to do with them, and looking
each other in the face, after the manner of peasants.

The farmer, a stout, jovial, obstinate
man of forty-five, who had lost two
wives, evidently felt embarrassed, which
was very unusual with him. But at last
he made up his mind, and began to
speak vaguely, hesitating a little, and
looking out of the window as he talked.

"How is it, Rose," he said, "that you
have never thought of settling in life?"

She grew as pale as death, and seeing
that she gave him no answer, he went
on:

"You are a good, steady, active, and
economical girl, and a wife like you
would make a man's fortune."

She did not move, but looked frightened; she did not even try to compre-

hend his meaning, for her thoughts were in a whirl, as if at the approach of some great danger; so after waiting for a few seconds, he went on:

"You see, a farm without a mistress can never succeed, even with a servant like you are."

Then he stopped, for he did not know what else to say, and Rose looked at him with the air of a person who thinks that he is face to face with a murderer, and ready to flee at the slightest movement he may make; but after waiting for about five minutes, he asked her:

"Well, will it suit you?"

"Will what suit me, master?"

And he said, quickly: "Why, to marry me, by Jove!"

She jumped up, but fell back on to her chair as if she had been struck, and there she remained motionless, like a person who is overwhelmed by some great misfortune. But at last the farmer grew impatient, and said: "Come, what more do you want?"

She looked at him almost in terror; then suddenly the tears came into her eyes, and she said twice, in a choking voice: "I cannot, I cannot!"

"Why not?" he asked. "Come, don't be silly; I will give you until to-morrow to think it over."

And he hurried out of the room, very glad to have finished a matter which had troubled him a good deal. He had no doubt that she would the next morning accept a proposal which she could never have expected, and which would be a capital bargain for him, as he thus bound a woman to himself who would certainly bring him more than if she had the best dowry in the district.

Neither could there be any scruples about an unequal match between them, for in the country everyone is very nearly equal. The farmer works just like his laborers do; the latter frequently become masters in their turn, and the female servants constantly become the mistresses of the establishment, without making any change in their life or habits.

Rose did not go to bed that night. She threw herself, dressed as she was, on to her bed, and she had not even strength to cry left in her, she was so thoroughly astonished. She remained quite inert, scarcely knowing that she had a body, and without being at all able to collect her thoughts, though at moments she remembered a part of that which had happened, and then she was frightened at the idea of what might happen. Her terror increased, and every time the great kitchen clock struck the hour, she broke into a perspiration from grief. She lost her head, and had a nightmare; her candle went out, and then she began to imagine that some one had thrown a spell over her, as country people so often fancy, and she felt a mad inclination to run away, to escape and flee before her misfortune, as a ship scuds before the wind.

An owl hooted, and she shivered, sat up, put her hands to her face, into her hair, and all over her body, and then she went downstairs, as if she were walking in her sleep. When she got into the yard, she stooped down, so as not to be seen by any prowling scamp, for the moon, which was setting, shed a bright light over the fields. Instead of opening the gate, she scrambled over the fence, and as soon as she was outside, she started off. She went on straight before her, with a quick, elastic trot, and from time to time, she unconsciously uttered a piercing cry. Her long shadow accompanied her, and now and then some night-bird flew over her head, while the dogs in the farmyards barked, as they heard her pass. One even jumped over the ditch, followed her, and tried to bite her, but she turned round at it, and gave such a terrible yell that the frightened animal ran back, and cowered in silence in its kennel.

The stars grew dim, and the birds began to twitter; day was breaking. The girl was worn out and panting, and when the sun rose in the purple sky, she stopped, for her swollen feet refused to go any further. But she saw a pond in the distance, a large pond whose stagnant water looked like blood under the reflection of this new day, and she limped on with short steps and with her hand on her heart, in order to dip both her feet in it.

She sat down on a tuft of grass, took off her sabots which were full of dust, pulled off her stockings and plunged her legs into the still water, from which bubbles were rising here and there.

A feeling of delicious coolness pervaded her from head to foot, and suddenly, while she was looking fixedly at the deep pool, she was seized with giddiness, and with a mad longing to throw herself into it. All her sufferings would be over in there; over forever. She no longer thought of her child; she only wanted peace, complete rest, and to sleep forever, and she got up with raised arms and took two steps forward. She was in the water up to her thighs, and she was just about to throw herself in, when sharp, pricking pains in her ankles

made her jump back. She uttered a cry of despair, for, from her knees to the tips of her feet, long, black leeches were sucking in her life blood, and were swelling, as they adhered to her flesh. She did not dare to touch them, and screamed with horror, so that her cries of despair attracted a peasant, who was driving along at some distance, to the spot. He pulled off the leeches, one by one, applied herbs to the wounds, and drove the girl to her master's farm, in his gig.

She was in bed for a fortnight, and as she was sitting outside the door on the first morning that she got up, the farmer suddenly came and planted himself before her.

"Well," he said, "I suppose the affair is settled, isn't it?"

She did not reply at first, and then, as he remained standing and looking at her intently with his piercing eyes, she said with difficulty: "No, master, I cannot."

But he immediately flew into a rage. "You cannot, girl; you cannot? I should just like to know the reason why?"

She began to cry, and repeated: "I cannot."

He looked at her, and then exclaimed, angrily: "Then I suppose you have a lover?"

"Perhaps that is it," she replied, trembling with shame.

The man got as red as a poppy, and stammered out in a rage: "Ah! So you confess it, you slut! And pray who is the fellow? Some penniless, half-starved ragamuffin, without a roof to his head, I suppose? Who is it, I say?"

And as she gave him no answer, he

continued: "Ah! So you will not tell me. Then I will tell you; it is Jean Bauda!"

"No, not he," she exclaimed.

"Then it is Pierre Martin?"

"Oh! no, master."

And he angrily mentioned all the young fellows in the neighborhood, while she denied that he had hit upon the right one, and every moment wiped her eyes with the corner of her blue apron. But he still tried to find it out, with his brutish obstinacy, and, as it were, scratched her heart to discover her secret, as a terrier scratches at a hole to try and get at the animal which he scents in it. Suddenly, however, the man shouted: "By George! It is Jacques, the man who was here last year. They used to say that you were always talking together, and that you thought about getting married."

Rose was choking, and she grew scarlet, while her tears suddenly stopped, and dried up on her cheeks, like drops of water on hot iron, and she exclaimed: "No, it is not he, it is not he!"

"Is that really a fact?" asked the cunning farmer, who partly guessed the truth, and she replied hastily:

"I will swear it; I will swear it to you." She tried to think of something by which to swear, as she did not dare to invoke sacred things.

But he interrupted her: "At any rate, he used to follow you into every corner, and devoured you with his eyes at meal times. Did you ever give him your promise, eh?"

This time she looked her master straight in the face. "No, never, never; I will solemnly swear to you, that if he were to come to-day and ask me to marry him, I would have nothing to do with him."

She spoke with such an air of sincerity, that the farmer hesitated, and then he continued, as if speaking to himself: "What, then? You have not *had a misfortune,* as they call it, or it would have been known, and as it has no consequences, no girl would refuse her master on that account. There must be something at the bottom of it, however."

She could say nothing; she had not the strength to speak, and he asked her again: "You will not?"

"I cannot, master," she said, with a sigh, and he turned on his heel.

She thought she had got rid of him altogether, and spent the rest of the day almost tranquilly, but as worn out as if she, instead of the old white horse, had been turning the threshing machine all day. She went to bed as soon as she could, and fell asleep immediately. In the middle of the night, however, two hands touching the bed woke her. She trembled with fear, but she immediately recognized the farmer's voice, when he said to her: "Don't be frightened. Rose; I have come to speak to you."

She was surprised at first, but when he tried to take liberties with her, she understood what he wanted, and began to tremble violently. She felt quite alone in the darkness, still heavy from sleep, and quite unprotected, by the side of the man who stood near her. She certainly did not consent, but resisted carelessly, herself struggling against that instinct which is always strong in simple natures, and very imperfectly protected, by the undecided will of an exhausted body. She turned her head now to the wall, and now toward the room, in order to avoid the attentions which the farmer tried to press on her, and her body writhed under the coverlet, weakened as she was by the fatigue of the struggle, while he became brutal, intoxicated by desire.

They lived together as man and wife, and one morning he said to her: "I have put up our banns, and we will get married next month."

She did not reply, for what could she say? She did not resist, for what could she do?

IV.

She married him. She felt as if she were in a pit with inaccessible edges, from which she could never get out, and all kinds of misfortunes remained hanging over her head, like huge rocks, which would fall on the first occasion. Her husband gave her the impression of a man whom she had stolen, and who would find it out some day or other. And then she thought of her child, who was the cause of her misfortunes, but was also the cause of all her happiness on earth. She went to see him twice a year, and she came back more unhappy each time.

But she gradually grew accustomed to her life, her fears were allayed, her heart was at rest, and she lived with an easier mind, although still with some vague fear floating in her mind. So years went on, and the child was six. She was almost happy now, when suddenly the farmer's temper grew very bad.

For two or three years, he seemed to have been nursing some secret anxiety, to be troubled by some care, some men-

tal disturbance, which was gradually increasing. He remained at table a long time after dinner, with his head in his hands, sad and devoured by sorrow. He always spoke hastily, sometimes even brutally, and it even seemed as if he bore a grudge against his wife, for at times he answered her roughly, almost angrily.

One day, when a neighbor's boy came for some eggs, and she spoke rather crossly to him, for she was very busy, her husband suddenly came in, and said to her in his unpleasant voice: "If that were your own child, you would not treat him so."

She was hurt and did not reply, and then she went back into the house with all her grief awakened afresh. At dinner, the farmer neither spoke to her nor looked at her, and seemed to hate her, to despise her, to know something about the affair at last. In consequence, she lost her head and did not venture to remain alone with him after the meal was over, but left the room and hastened to the church.

It was getting dusk; the narrow nave was in total darkness, but she heard footsteps in the choir, for the sacristan was preparing the tabernacle lamp for the night. That spot of trembling light, which was lost in the darkness of the arches, looked to Rose like her last hope, and with her eyes fixed on it, she fell on her knees. The chain rattled as the little lamps swung up into the air, and almost immediately the small bell rang out the "Angelus" through the increasing mist. She went up to him, as he was going out.

"Is Monsieur le Curé at home?" she asked.

"Of course he is; this is his dinner-time."

She trembled as she rang the bell of the parsonage. The priest was just sitting down to dinner, and he made her sit down also. "Yes, yes, I know all about it; your husband has mentioned the matter to me that brings you here."

The poor woman nearly fainted, and the priest continued: "What do you want, my child?" And he hastily swallowed several spoonfuls of soup, some of which dropped on to his greasy cassock. But Rose did not venture to say anything more, but got up to go, while the priest said: "Courage."

So she went out, and returned to the farm, without knowing what she was doing. The farmer was waiting for her, as the laborers had gone away during her absence, and she fell heavily at his feet, and shedding a flood of tears, she said to him: "What have you got against me?"

He began to shout and to swear: "What have I got against you? That I have no children, by God! When a man takes a wife, he does not want to be left alone with her until the end of his days. That is what I have against you. When a cow has no calves, she is not worth anything, and when a woman has no children, she is also not worth anything."

She began to cry, and said: "It is not my fault! It is not my fault!"

He grew rather more gentle when he heard that, and added: "I do not say that it is, but it is very annoying, all the same."

V.

From that day forward, she had only one thought—to have a child, another child. She confided her wish to everybody, and in consequence of this, a neighbor told her of an infallible method. This was, to make her husband a glass of water with a pinch of ashes in it, every evening. The farmer consented to try it, but without success; so they said to each other: "Perhaps there are some secret ways?" And they tried to find out. They were told of a shepherd who lived ten leagues off, and so Vallin one day drove off to consult him. The shepherd gave him a loaf on which he had made some marks; it was kneaded up with herbs, and both of them were to eat a piece of it before and after their mutual caresses; but they ate the whole loaf without obtaining any results from it.

Next, a schoolmaster unveiled mysteries and processes of love which were unknown in the country, but infallible, so he declared; but none of them had the desired effect. Then the priest advised them to make a pilgrimage to the shrine at Fécamp. Rose went with the crowd and prostrated herself in the abbey, and mingling her prayers with the coarse wishes of the peasants around her, she prayed that she might be fruitful a second time; but it was in vain, and then she thought that she was being punished for her first fault, and she was seized by terrible grief. She was wasting away with sorrow; her husband was growing old prematurely, and was wearing himself out in useless hopes.

Then war broke out between them; he called her names and beat her. They quarreled all day long, and when they were in bed together at night he flung insults and obscenities at her, panting with rage, until one night, not being able to think of any means of making her suffer more, he ordered her to get up and go and stand out of doors in the rain, until daylight. As she did not obey him, he seized her by the neck, and began to strike her in the face with his fists, but she said nothing, and did not move. In his exasperation he knelt on her, and with clenched teeth and mad with rage began to beat her. Then in her despair she rebelled, and flinging him against the wall with a furious gesture, she sat up, and in an altered voice, she hissed: "I have had a child, I have had one! I had it by Jacques; you know Jacques well. He promised to marry me, but he left this neighborhood without keeping his word."

The man was thunderstruck, and could hardly speak, but at last he stammered out: "What are you saying? What are you saying?"

Then she began to sob, and amid her tears she said: "That was the reason why I did not want to marry you. I could not tell you, for you would have left me without any bread for my child. You have never had any children, so you cannot understand, you cannot understand!"

He said again, mechanically, with increasing surprise: "You have a child? You have a child?"

"You won me by force, as I suppose you know. I did not want to marry you," she said, still sobbing.

Then he got up, lighted the candle, and began to walk up and down, with his arms behind him. She was cowering on the bed and crying, and suddenly he stopped in front of her, and

said: "Then it is my fault that you have no children?"

She gave him no answer, and he began to walk up and down again, and then, stopping again, he continued: "How old is your child?"

"Just six," she whispered.

"Why did you not tell me about it?" he asked.

"How could I?" she replied, with a sigh.

He remained standing, motionless. "Come, get up," he said.

She got up, with some difficulty, and then when she was standing on the floor, he suddenly began to laugh, with his hearty laugh of his good days, and seeing how surprised she was, he added: "Very well, we will go and fetch the child, as you and I can have none together."

She was so scared that if she had the strength she would assuredly have run away, but the farmer rubbed his hands and said: "I wanted to adopt one, and now we have found one. I asked the Curé about an orphan, some time ago."

Then, still laughing, he kissed his weeping and agitated wife on both cheeks, and shouted out, as if she could not hear him: "Come along, mother, we will go and see whether there is any soup left; I should not mind a plateful."

She put on her petticoat, and they went downstairs; and while she was kneeling in front of the fireplace, and lighting the fire under the saucepan, he continued to walk up and down the kitchen with long strides, and said: "Well, I am really glad at this; I am not saying it for form's sake, but I am glad, I am really very glad."

In the Moonlight

WELL-MERITED was the name, "soldier of God," by the Abbé Marignan. He was a tall, thin priest, fanatical to a degree, but just, and of an exalted soul. All his beliefs were fixed, with never a waver. He thought that he understood God thoroughly, that he penetrated His designs, His wishes, His intentions.

Striding up and down the garden walk of his little country parsonage, sometimes a question arose in his mind: "Why did God make that?" Then in his thoughts, putting himself in God's place, he searched obstinately, and nearly always was satisfied that he found the reason. He was not the man to murmur in transports of pious humility, "O Lord, thy ways are past finding out!" What he said was: "I am the servant of God; I ought to know the reason of what he does, or to divine it if I do not."

Everything in nature seemed to him created with an absolute and admirable logic. The "wherefore" and the "because" were always balanced. The dawns were made to rejoice you on waking, the days to ripen the harvests, the rains to water them, the evenings to prepare for sleeping, and the nights dark for sleep.

The four seasons corresponded perfectly to all the needs of agriculture; and to him the suspicion could never have come that nature has no intention, and that all which lives has accustomed itself, on the contrary, to the hard conditions of different periods, of climates, and of matter.

But he hated women; he hated them unconsciously, and despised them by instinct. He often repeated the words of Christ, "Woman, what have I to do with thee?" and he would add, "One would almost say that God himself was ill-pleased with that particular work of his hands." Woman for him was indeed the "child twelve times unclean" of whom the poet speaks. She was the temptress who had ensnared the first man, and who still continued her damnable work; she was the being who is feeble, dangerous, mysteriously troublous. And even more than her poisonous beauty, he hated her loving soul.

He had often felt women's tenderness attack him, and though he knew himself to be unassailable, he grew exasperated at this need of loving which quivers continually in their hearts.

To his mind, God had only created woman to tempt man and to test him. Man should not approach her without those precautions for defense which he would take, and the fears he would cherish, near an ambush. Woman, indeed, was just like a trap, with her arms extended and her lips open toward a man.

He had toleration only for nuns, rendered harmless by their vow; but he treated them harshly notwithstanding, because, ever at the bottom of their chained-up hearts, their chastened hearts, he perceived the eternal tenderness that constantly went out even to him, although he was a priest.

He had a niece who lived with her mother in a little house near by. He was bent on making her a sister of charity. She was pretty and hare-

51

brained, and a great tease. When the
abbé sermonized, she laughed; when he
was angry at her, she kissed him vehemently, pressing him to her heart,
while he would seek involuntarily to
free himself from her embrace. Notwithstanding, it made him taste a certain sweet joy, awaking deep within him
that sensation of fatherhood which
slumbers in every man.

Often he talked to her of God, of his
God, walking beside her along the foot-
paths through the fields. She hardly
listened, but looked at the sky, the
grass, the flowers, with a joy of living
which could be seen in her eyes. Sometimes she rushed forward to catch some
flying creature, and bringing it back
would cry: "Look, my uncle, how
pretty it is; I should like to kiss it."
And this necessity to "kiss flies" or
sweet flowers worried, irritated, and
revolted the priest, who saw, even in
that, the ineradicable tenderness which
ever springs in the hearts of women.

One day the sacristan's wife, who
kept house for the Abbé Marignan, told
him, very cautiously, that his niece had
a lover!

He experienced a dreadful emotion,
and he stood choking, with the soap all
over his face, in the act of shaving.

When he found himself able to think
and speak once more, he cried: "It is
not true; you are lying, Melanie!"

But the peasant woman put her hand
on her heart; "May our Lord judge
me if I am lying, Monsieur le Curé
I tell you she goes to him every evening as soon as your sister is in bed.
They meet each other beside the river.
You have only to go there between ten

o'clock and midnight, and see for yourself."

He ceased scratching his chin and
commenced to pace the room quickly,
as he always did in his hours of gravest
thought. When he tried to begin his
shaving again, he cut himself three
times from nose to ear.

All day long, he remained silent,
swollen with anger and with rage. To
his priestly zeal against the mighty
power of love was added the moral indignation of a father, of a teacher, of a
keeper of souls, who has been deceived,
robbed, played with by a child. He felt
the egotistical sorrow that parents feel
when their daughter announces that she
has chosen a husband without them
and in spite of their advice.

After his dinner, he tried to read a
little, but he could not attune himself
to it; and he grew angrier and angrier.
When it struck ten, he took his cane,
a formidable oaken club which he always carried when he had to go out at
night to visit the sick. Smilingly he
regarded the enormous cudgel, holding
it in his solid, countryman's fist and
cutting threatening circles with it in the
air. Then, suddenly, he raised it, and
grinding his teeth, he brought it down
upon a chair, the back of which, split in
two, fell heavily to the ground.

He opened his door to go out; but he
stopped upon the threshold, surprised
by such a splendor of moonlight as you
seldom see.

Endowed as he was with an exalted
spirit, such a spirit as must have belonged to those dreamer-poets, the
Fathers of the Church, he felt himself
suddenly softened and moved by the

grand and serene beauty of the pale-faced night.

In his little garden, bathed in the soft brilliance, his fruit-trees, all a-row, were outlining in shadow upon the walk their slender limbs of wood scarce clothed with green; while the giant honeysuckle climbing on the house wall exhaled delicious, sugared breaths, which hovered through the warm, clear night like a perfumed soul.

He began to breathe deep, drinking the air as drunkards drink their wine, and walking slowly, ravished, surprised, and almost oblivious of his niece.

As he stepped into the open country he stopped to contemplate the whole plain, inundated by this caressing radiance, and drowned in the tender and languishing charm of the serene night. In chorus the frogs threw into space their short, metallic notes, and with the seduction of the moonlight, distant nightingales mingled that fitful music of theirs which brings no thoughts but dreams, a light and vibrant melody which seems attuned to kisses.

The abbé continued his walk, his courage failing, he knew not why. He felt, as it were, enfeebled, and suddenly exhausted; he had a great desire to sit down, to pause right there and praise God in all His works.

Below him, following the bends of the little river, wound a great line of poplars. On and about the banks, wrapping all the tortuous watercourse in a kind of light, transparent wadding, hung suspended a fine mist, a white vapor, which the moon-rays crossed, and silvered, and caused to gleam.

The priest paused yet again, penetrated to the depths of his soul by a strong and growing emotion. And a doubt, a vague uneasiness, seized on him; he felt that one of those questions he sometimes put to himself was now being born.

Why had God done this? Since the night is destined for sleep, for unconsciousness, for repose, for forgetfulness of everything, why, then, make it more charming than the day, sweeter than dawns and sunsets? And this slow, seductive star, more poetical than the sun and so discreet, that it seems designed to light up things too delicate, too mysterious, for the great luminary,—why had it come to brighten all the shades? Why did not the sweetest of all songsters go to rest like the others? Why set himself to singing in the vaguely troubling dark? Why this half-veil over the world? Why these quiverings of the heart, this emotion of the soul, this languor of the body? Why this display of seductions which mankind never sees, since night brings sleep? For whom was this sublime spectacle intended, this flood of poetry poured from heaven to earth? The abbé did not understand it at all.

But then, down there along the edge of the pasture appeared two shadows walking side by side under the arched roof of the trees all soaked in glittering mist.

The man was the taller, and had his arm about his mistress's neck; from time to time he kissed her on the forehead. They animated the lifeless landscape which enveloped them, a divine frame made, as it were, expressly for them. They seemed these two, a single being, the being for whom this calm and silent night was destined; and they approached the priest like a living answer, the answer vouchsafed by his Master to his question.

He stood stock-still, overwhelmed, and with a beating heart. He likened it to some Bible story, such as the loves of Ruth and Boaz, the accomplishment of the will of the Lord in one of those great scenes talked of in holy writ. Through his head ran the versicles of the Song of Songs, the ardent cries, the calls of the body, all the passionate poetry of that poem which burns with tenderness and love. And he said to himself, "God perhaps has made such nights as this to clothe with his ideals the loves of men."

He withdrew before the couple, who went on arm in arm. It was really his niece; and now he asked himself if he had not been about to disobey God. For does not God indeed permit love, since He surrounds it visibly with splendor such as this?

And he fled, in amaze, almost ashamed, as if he had penetrated into a temple where he had no right to enter.

Mme. Tellier's Excursion

MEN went there every evening at about eleven o'clock, just as they went to the *café*. Six or eight of them used to meet there; always the same set, not fast men, but respectable tradesmen, and young men in government or some other employ; and they used to drink their Chartreuse, and tease the girls, or else they would talk seriously with Madame, whom everybody respected, and then would go home at twelve o'clock! The younger men would sometimes stay the night.

It was a small, comfortable house, at the corner of a street behind Saint Etienne's church. From the windows one could see the docks, full of ships which were being unloaded, and on the hill the old, gray chapel, dedicated to the Virgin.

Madame, who came of a respectable family of peasant proprietors in the department of the Eure, had taken up her profession, just as she would have become a milliner or dressmaker. The prejudice against prostitution, which is so violent and deeply rooted in large towns, does not exist in the country places in Normandy. The peasant simply says: "It is a paying business," and sends his daughter to keep a harem of fast girls, just as he would send her to keep a girls' school.

She had inherited the house from an old uncle, to whom it had belonged. Monsieur and Madame who had formerly been innkeepers near Yvetot, had immediately sold their house, as they thought that the business at Fécamp was more profitable. They arrived one fine morning to assume the direction of the enterprise, which was declining on account of the absence of a head. They were good people enough in their way, and soon made themselves liked by their staff and their neighbors.

Monsieur died of apoplexy two years later, for as his new profession kept him in idleness and without exercise, he had grown excessively stout, and his health had suffered. Since Madame had been a widow, all the frequenters of the establishment had wanted her; but people said that personally she was quite virtuous, and even the girls in the house could not discover anything against her. She was tall, stout, and affable, and her complexion, which had become pale in the dimness of her house, the shutters of which were scarcely ever opened, shone as if it had been varnished. She had a fringe of curly, false hair, which gave her a juvenile look, which in turn contrasted strongly with her matronly figure. She was always smiling and cheerful, and was fond of a joke, but there was a shade of reserve about her which her new occupation had not quite made her lose. Coarse words always shocked her, and when any young fellow who had been badly brought up called her establishment by its right name, she was angry and disgusted.

In a word, she had a refined mind, and although she treated her women as friends, yet she very frequently used to say that she and they were not made of the same stuff.

Sometimes during the week she would hire a carriage and take some of her girls into the country, where they used to enjoy themselves on the grass by the side of the little river. They behaved like a lot of girls let out from a school, and used to run races, and play childish games. They would have a cold dinner on the grass, and drink cider, and go home at night with a delicious feeling of fatigue, and in the carriage kiss Madame as a kind mother who was full of goodness and complaisance.

The house had two entrances. At the corner there was a sort of low *café*, which sailors and the lower orders frequented at night, and she had two girls whose special duty it was to attend to that part of the business. With the assistance of the waiter, whose name was Frederic, and who was a short, light-haired, beardless fellow, as strong as a horse, they set the half bottles of wine and the jugs of beer on the shaky marble tables and then, sitting astride on the customers' knees, would urge them to drink.

The three other girls (there were only five in all), formed a kind of aristocracy, and were reserved for the company on the first floor, unless they were wanted downstairs, and there was nobody on the first floor. The salon of Jupiter, where the tradesmen used to meet, was papered in blue, and embellished with a large drawing representing Leda stretched out under the swan. That room was reached by a winding staircase, which ended at a narrow door opening on to the street, and above it, all night long a little lamp burned, behind wire bars, such as one still sees in some towns, at the foot of the shrine of some saint.

The house, which was old and damp, rather smelled of mildew. At times there was an odor of eau de Cologne in the passages, or a half open door downstairs allowed the noise of the common men sitting and drinking downstairs to reach the first floor, much to the disgust of the gentlemen who were there. Madame, who was quite familiar with those of her customers with whom she was on friendly terms, did not leave the salon. She took much interest in what was going on in the town, and they regularly told her all the news. Her serious conversation was a change from the ceaseless chatter of the three women; it was a rest from the doubtful jokes of those stout individuals who every evening indulged in the commonplace amusement of drinking a glass of liquor in company with girls of easy virtue.

The names of the girls on the first floor were Fernande, Raphaelle, and Rosa "the Jade." As the staff was limited, Madame had endeavored that each member of it should be a pattern, an epitome of each feminine type, so that every customer might find as nearly as possible, the realization of his ideal. Fernande represented the handsome blonde; she was very tall, rather fat, and lazy; a country girl, who could not get rid of her freckles, and whose short, light, almost colorless, tow-like hair, which was like combed-out flax, barely covered her head.

Raphaelle, who came from Marseilles, played the indispensable part of the handsome Jewess. She was thin, with high cheek-bones covered with rouge, and her black hair, which was always covered with pomatum, curled on to her forehead. Her eyes would have been handsome, if the right one had not had a speck in it. Her Roman nose came down over a square jaw, where two false upper teeth contrasted strangely with the bad color of the rest.

Rosa the Jade was a little roll of fat, nearly all stomach, with very short legs. From morning till night she sang songs, which were alternately indecent or sentimental, in a harsh voice, told silly, interminable tales, and only stopped talking in order to eat, or left off eating in order to talk. She was never still, was as active as a squirrel, in spite of her fat and her short legs; and her laugh, which was a torrent of shrill cries, resounded here and there, ceaselessly, in a bedroom, in the loft, in the *café*, everywhere, and always about nothing.

The two women on the ground floor were Louise, who was nicknamed "la Cocotte,"* and Flora, whom they called "Balançière,"† because she limped a little. The former always dressed as Liberty, with a tri-colored sash, and the other as a Spanish woman, with a string of copper coins which jingled at every step she took, in her carroty hair. Both looked like cooks dressed up for the carnival, and were like all other women of the lower orders, neither uglier nor better looking than they usually are. In fact they looked just like servants at an inn, and were generally called "the Two Pumps."

A jealous peace, very rarely disturbed, reigned among these five women, thanks to Madame's conciliatory wisdom and to her constant good humor; and the establishment, which was the only one of the kind in the little town, was very much frequented. Madame had succeeded in giving it such a respectable appearance; she was so amiable and obliging to everybody, her good heart was so well known, that she was treated with a certain amount of consideration. The regular customers spent money on her, and were delighted when she was especially friendly toward them. When they met during the day, they would

---

*Slang for a lady of easy virtue.
†Swing, or seesaw.

say: "This evening, you know where," just as men say: "At the *café*, after dinner." In a word Madame Tellier's house was somewhere to go to, and her customers very rarely missed their daily meetings there.

One evening, toward the end of May, the first arrival, Monsieur Poulin, who was a timber merchant, and had been mayor, found the door shut. The little lantern behind the grating was not alight; there was not a sound in the house; everything seemed dead. He knocked, gently at first, and then more loudly, but nobody answered the door. Then he went slowly up the street, and when he got to the market place, he met Monsieur Duvert, the gun-maker, who was going to the same place, so they went back together, but did not meet with any better success. But suddenly they heard a loud noise close to them, and on going round the corner of the house, they saw a number of English and French sailors, who were hammering at the closed shutters of the *café* with their fists.

The two tradesmen immediately made their escape, for fear of being compromised, but a low *Pst* stopped them; it was Monsieur Tournevau, the fish-curer, who had recognized them, and was trying to attract their attention. They told him what had happened, and he was all the more vexed at it, as he, a married man, and father of a family, only went there on Saturdays—*securitatis causa,* as he said, alluding to a measure of sanitary policy, which his friend Doctor Borde had advised him to observe. That was his regular evening, and now he would be deprived of it for the whole week.

The three men went as far as the quay together, and on the way they met young Monsieur Phillippe, the banker's son, who frequented the place regularly, and Monsieur Pinipesse, the collector. They all returned to the Rue aux Juifs together, to make a last attempt. But the exasperated sailors were besieging the house, throwing stones at the shutters, and shouting, and the five first-floor customers went away as quickly as possible, and walked aimlessly about the streets.

Presently they met Monsieur Dupuis, the insurance agent, and then Monsieur Vassi, the Judge of the Tribunal of Commerce, and they all took a long walk, going to the pier first of all. There they sat down in a row on the granite parapet, and watched the rising tide, and when the promenaders had sat there for some time, Monsieur Tournevau said: "This is not very amusing!"

"Decidedly not," Monsieur Pinipesse replied, and they started off to walk again.

After going through the street on the top of the hill, they returned over the wooden bridge which crosses the Retenue, passed close to the railway, and came out again on to the market place, when suddenly a quarrel arose between Monsieur Pinipesse and Monsieur Tournevau, about an edible fungus which one of them declared he had found in the neighborhood.

As they were out of temper already from annoyance, they would very probably have come to blows, if the others had not interfered. Monsieur Pinipesse went off furious, and soon another altercation arose between the ex-mayor, Monsieur Poulin, and Monsieur Dupuis, the insurance agent, on the subject of the tax-collector's salary, and the profits which he might make. Insulting remarks were freely passing between them, when a torrent of formidable cries were heard, and the body of sailors, who were tired of waiting so long outside a closed house, came into the square. They were walking arm-in-arm, two and two, and formed a long procession, and were shouting furiously. The landsmen went and hid themselves under a gateway, and the yelling crew disappeared in the direction of the abbey. For a long time they still heard the noise, which diminished like a storm in the distance, and then silence was restored. Monsieur Poulin and Monsieur Dupuis, who were enraged with each other, went in different directions, without wishing each other good-bye.

The other four set off again, and instinctively went in the direction of Madame Tellier's establishment, which was still closed, silent, impenetrable. A quiet, but obstinate, drunken man was knocking at the door of the *café;* then he stopped and called Frederic, the waiter, in a low voice, but finding that he got no answer, he sat down on the doorstep, and awaited the course of events.

. The others were just going to retire, when the noisy band of sailors reappeared at the end of the street. The French sailors were shouting the "Marseillaise," and the Englishmen, "Rule Britannia." There was a general lurching against the wall, and then the drunken brutes went on their way toward the quay, where a fight broke out between the two nations, in the course of which an Englishman had his arm broken, and a Frenchman his nose split. .

The drunken man, who had stopped outside the door, was crying by this time, as drunken men and children cry when they are vexed, and the others went away. By degrees, calm was restored in the noisy town; here and there, at moments, the distant sound of voices could be heard, only to die away in the distance.

One man was still wandering about, Monsieur Tournevau, the fish-curer, who was vexed at having to wait until the next Saturday. He hoped for something to turn up, he did not know what; but he was exasperated at the police for thus allowing an establishment of such public utility, which they had under their control, to be thus closed.

He went back to it, examined the walls, and tried to find out the reason. On the shutter he saw a notice stuck up, so he struck a wax vesta, and read the following, in a large, uneven hand: "Closed on account of the Confirmation."

Then he went away, as he saw it was useless to remain, and left the drunken man lying on the pavement fast asleep, outside the inhospitable door.

The next day, all the regular customers, one after the other, found some reason for going through the Rue aux Juifs with a bundle of papers under their arm, to keep them in countenance, and with a furtive glance they all read that mysterious notice:

"CLOSED ON ACCOUNT OF THE
CONFIRMATION."

II.

Madame had a brother, who was a carpenter in their native place, Virville, in the department of Eure. When Madame had still kept the inn at Yvetot, she had stood godmother to that brother's daughter, who had received the name of Constance, Constance Rivet; she herself being a Rivet on her father's side. The carpenter, who knew that his sister was in a good position, did not lose sight of her, although they did not meet often, as they were both kept at home by their occupations, and lived a long way from each other. But when the girl was twelve years old, and about to be confirmed, he seized the opportunity to write to his sister, and ask her to come and be present at the ceremony. Their old parents were dead, and as Madame could not well refuse, she accepted the invitation. Her brother, whose name was Joseph, hoped that by dint of showing his sister attentions, she might be induced to make her will in the girl's favor, as she had no children of her own.

His sister's occupation did not trouble his scruples in the least, and, besides, nobody knew anything about it at Virville. When they spoke of her, they only said: "Madame Tellier is living at Fécamp," which might mean that she was living on her own private income. It was quite twenty leagues from Fécamp to Virville, and for a peasant, twenty leagues on land are more than is crossing the ocean to an educated person. The people at Virville had never been further than Rouen, and nothing attracted the people from Fécamp to a village of five hundred houses, in the middle of a plain, and situated in another department. At any rate, nothing was known about her business.

But the Confirmation was coming on

and Madame was in great embarrassment. She had no under-mistress, and did not at all dare to leave her house, even for a day. She feared the rivalries between the girls upstairs and those downstairs would certainly break out; that Frederic would get drunk, for when he was in that state, he would knock anybody down for a mere word. At last, however, she made up her mind to take them all with her; with the exception of the man, to whom she gave a holiday, until the next day but one.

When she asked her brother, he made no objection, but undertook to put them all up for a night. So on Saturday morning the eight o'clock express carried off Madame and her companions in a second-class carriage. As far as Beuzeille they were alone, and chattered like magpies, but at that station a couple got in. The man, an aged peasant dressed in a blue blouse with a folding collar, wide sleeves tight at the wrist, and ornamented with white embroidery, wore an old high hat with long nap. He held an enormous green umbrella in one hand, and a large basket in the other, from which the heads of three frightened ducks protruded. The woman, who sat stiffly in her rustic finery, had a face like a fowl, and with a nose that was as pointed as a bill. She sat down opposite her husband and did not stir, as she was startled at finding herself in such smart company.

There was certainly an array of striking colors in the carriage. Madame was dressed in blue silk from head to foot, and had over her dress a dazzling red shawl of imitation French cashmere. Fernande was panting in a Scottish plaid dress, whose bodice, which her companions had laced as tight as they could, had forced up her falling bosom into a double dome, that was continually heaving up and down, and which seemed liquid beneath the material. Raphaelle, with a bonnet covered with feathers, so that it looked like a nest full of birds, had on a lilac dress with gold spots on it; there was something Oriental about it that suited her Jewish face. Rosa the Jade had on a pink petticoat with large flounces, and looked like a very fat child, an obese dwarf; while the Two Pumps looked as if they had cut their dresses out of old, flowered curtains, dating from the Restoration.

Perceiving that they were no longer alone in the compartment, the ladies put on staid looks, and began to talk of subjects which might give the others a high opinion of them. But at Bolbec a gentleman with light whiskers, with a gold chain, and wearing two or three rings, got in, and put several parcels wrapped in oil cloth into the net over his head. He looked inclined for a joke, and a good-natured fellow.

"Are you ladies changing your quarters?" he asked. The question embarrassed them all considerably. Madame, however, quickly recovered her composure, and said sharply, to avenge the honor of her corps:

"I think you might try and be polite!"

He excused himself, and said: "I beg your pardon, I ought to have said your nunnery."

As Madame could not think of a retort, or perhaps as she thought herself justified sufficiently, she gave him a dignified bow, and pinched in her lips.

Then the gentleman, who was sitting between Rosa the Jade and the old peasant, began to wink knowingly at the ducks, whose heads were sticking out of the basket. When he felt that he had fixed the attention of his public, he began to tickle them under their bills, and spoke funnily to them, to make the company smile.

"We have left our little pond, qu-ack! qu-ack! to make the acquaintance of the little spit, qu-ack! qu-ack!"

The unfortunate creatures turned their necks away to avoid his caresses, and made desperate efforts to get out of their wicker prison, and then, suddenly, all at once, uttered the most lamentable quacks of distress. The women exploded with laughter. They leaned forward and pushed each other, so as to see better; they were very much interested in the ducks, and the gentleman redoubled his airs, his wit, and his teasing.

Rosa joined in, and leaning over her neighbor's legs, she kissed the three animals on the head. Immediately all the girls wanted to kiss them in turn, and the gentleman took them on to his knees, made them jump up and down and pinched them. The two peasants, who were even in greater consternation than their poultry, rolled their eyes as if they were possessed, without venturing to move, and their old wrinkled faces had not a smile nor a movement.

Then the gentleman, who was a commercial traveler, offered the ladies braces by way of a joke and taking up one of his packages, he opened it. It was a trick, for the parcel contained garters. There were blue silk, pink silk, red silk, violet silk, mauve silk garters, and the buckles were made of two gilt metal Cupids, embracing each other. The girls uttered exclamations of delight, and looked at them with that gravity which is natural to a woman when she is hankering after a bargain. They consulted one another by their looks or in a whisper, and replied in the same manner, and Madame was longingly handling a pair of orange garters that were broader and more imposing than the rest; really fit for the mistress of such an establishment.

"Come, my kittens," he said, "you must try them on."

There was a torrent of exclamations, and they squeezed their petticoats between their legs, as if they thought he was going to ravish them, but he quietly waited his time, and said: "Well, if you will not, I shall pack them up again."

And he added cunningly: "I offer any pair they like, to those who will try them on."

But they would not, and sat up very straight, and looked dignified.

But the Two Pumps looked so distressed that he renewed the offer to them. Flora especially hesitated, and he pressed her:

"Come, my dear, a little courage! Just look at that lilac pair; it will suit your dress admirably."

That decided her, and pulling up her dress she showed a thick leg fit for a milk-maid, in a badly-fitting, coarse stocking. The commercial traveler stooped down and fastened the garter below the knee first of all and then above it; and he tickled the girl gently, which made her scream and jump. When he had done, he gave her the lilac pair, and asked: "Who next?"

"I! I!" they all shouted at once, and he began on Rosa the Jade, who uncovered a shapeless, round thing without any ankle, a regular "sausage of a leg," as Raphaelle used to say.

The commercial traveler complimented Fernande, and grew quite enthusiastic over her powerful columns.

The thin tibias of the handsome Jewess met with less flattery, and Louise Cocotte, by way of a joke, put her petticoats over the man's head, so that Madame was obliged to interfere to check such unseemly behavior.

Lastly, Madame herself put out her leg, a handsome, muscular, Norman leg, and in his surprise and pleasure the commercial traveler gallantly took off his hat to salute that master calf, like a true French cavalier.

The two peasants, who were speechless from surprise, looked askance, out of the corners of their eyes. They looked so exactly like fowls, that the man with the light whiskers, when he sat up, said "Co—co—ri—co," under their very noses, and that gave rise to another storm of amusement.

The old people got out at Motteville, with their basket, their ducks, and their umbrella, and they heard the woman say to her husband, as they went away:

"They are sluts, who are off to that cursed place, Paris."

The funny commercial traveler himself got out at Rouen, after behaving so coarsely that Madame was obliged sharply to put him into his right place. She added, as a moral: "This will teach us not to talk to the first comer."

At Oissel they changed trains, and at a little station further on Monsieur Joseph Rivet was waiting for them with a large cart and a number of chairs in it, which was drawn by a white horse.

The carpenter politely kissed all the

ladies, and then helped them into his conveyance.

Three of them sat on three chairs at the back, Raphaelle, Madame, and her brother on the three chairs in front, and Rosa, who had no seat, settled herself as comfortably as she could on tall Fernande's knees, and then they set off.

But the horse's jerky trot shook the cart so terribly, that the chairs began to dance, throwing the travelers into the air, to the right and to the left, as if they had been dancing puppets. This made them make horrible grimaces and screams, which, however, were cut short by another jolt of the cart.

They clung to the sides of the vehicle, their bonnets fell on to their backs, their noses on their shoulders, and the white horse trotted on, stretching out his head and holding out his tail quite straight, a little hairless rat's tail, with which he whisked his buttocks from time to time.

Joseph Rivet, with one leg on the shafts and the other bent under him, held the reins with elbows high and kept uttering a kind of chuckling sound, which made the horse prick up its ears and go faster.

The green country extended on either side of the road, and here and there the colza in flower presented a waving expanse of yellow, from which there arose a strong, wholesome, sweet and penetrating smell, which the wind carried to some distance.

The cornflowers showed their little blue heads among the rye, and the women wanted to pick them, but Monsieur Rivet refused to stop.

Then sometimes a whole field appeared to be covered with blood, so thickly were the poppies growing, and the cart, which looked as if it were filled with flowers of more brilliant hue, drove on through the fields colored with wild flowers, to disappear behind the trees of a farm, then to reappear and go on again through the yellow or green standing crops studded with red or blue.

One o'clock struck as they drove up to the carpenter's door. They were tired out, and very hungry, as they had eaten nothing since they left home. Madame Rivet ran out, and made them alight, one after another, kissing them as soon as they were on the ground. She seemed as if she would never tire of kissing her sister-in-law, whom she apparently wanted to monopolize. They had lunch in the workshop, which had been cleared out for the next day's dinner.

A capital omelette, followed by boiled chitterlings, and washed down by good, sharp cider, made them all feel comfortable.

Rivet had taken a glass so that he might hob-nob with them, and his wife cooked, waited on them, brought in the dishes, took them out, and asked all of them in a whisper whether they had everything they wanted. A number of boards standing against the walls, and heaps of shavings that had been swept into the corners, gave out the smell of planed wood, of carpentering, that resinous odor which penetrates the lungs.

They wanted to see the little girl, but she had gone to church, and would not be back until evening, so they all went out for a stroll in the country.

It was a small village, through which the high road passed. Ten or a dozen houses on either side of the single street had for tenants the butcher, the grocer, the carpenter, the innkeeper, the shoemaker, and the baker, and others.

The church was at the end of the street. It was surrounded by a small churchyard, and four enormous lime-trees, which stood just outside the porch, shaded it completely. It was built of flint, in no particular style, and had a slated steeple. When you got past it, you were in the open country again, which was broken here and there by clumps of trees which hid some homestead.

Rivet had given his arm to his sister, out of politeness, although he was in his working clothes, and was walking with her majestically. His wife, who was overwhelmed by Raphaelle's gold-striped dress, was walking between her and Fernande, and rotund Rosa was trotting behind with Louise Cocotte and Flora, the seesaw, who was limping along, quite tired out.

The inhabitants came to their doors, the children left off playing, and a window curtain would be raised, so as to show a muslin cap, while an old woman with a crutch, who was almost blind, crossed herself as if it were a religious procession. They all looked for a long time after those handsome ladies from the town, who had come so far to be present at the confirmation of Joseph Rivet's little girl, and the carpenter rose very much in the public estimation.

As they passed the church, they heard some children singing; little shrill voices were singing a hymn, but Madame would not let them go in, for fear of disturbing the little cherubs.

After a walk, during which Joseph Rivet enumerated the principal landed proprietors, spoke about the yield of the land, and the productiveness of the cows and sheep, he took his flock of women home and installed them in his house, and as it was very small, he had put them into the rooms, two and two.

Just for once, Rivet would sleep in the workshop on the shavings; his wife was going to share her bed with her sister-in-law, and Fernande and Raphaelle were to sleep together in the next room. Louise and Flora were put into the kitchen, where they had a mattress on the floor, and Rosa had a little dark cupboard at the top of the stairs to herself, close to the loft, where the candidate for confirmation was to sleep.

When the girl came in, she was overwhelmed with kisses; all the women wished to caress her, with that need of tender expansion, that habit of professional wheedling, which had made them kiss the ducks in the railway carriage.

They took her on to their laps, stroked her soft, light hair, and pressed her in their arms with vehement and spontaneous outbursts of affection, and the child, who was very good-natured and docile, bore it all patiently.

As the day had been a fatiguing one for everybody, they all went to bed soon after dinner. The whole village was wrapped in that perfect stillness of the country, which is almost like a religious silence, and the girls who were accustomed to the noisy evenings of their establishment, felt rather impressed by the perfect repose of the sleeping village. They shivered, not with cold, but with those little shivers of solitude which come over uneasy and troubled hearts.

As soon as they were in bed, two and

two together, they clasped each other in their arms, as if to protect themselves against this feeling of the calm and profound slumber of the earth. But Rosa the Jade, who was alone in her little dark cupboard, felt a vague and painful emotion come over her.

She was tossing about in bed, unable to get to sleep, when she heard the faint sobs of a crying child close to her head, through the partition. She was frightened, and called out, and was answered by a weak voice, broken by sobs. It was the little girl who, being used to sleeping in her mother's room, was frightened in her small attic.

Rosa was delighted, got up softly so as not to awaken anyone, and went and fetched the child. She took her into her warm bed, kissed her and pressed her to her bosom, caressed her, lavished exaggerated manifestations of tenderness on her, and at last grew calmer herself and went to sleep. And till morning, the candidate for confirmation slept with her head on Rosa's naked bosom.

At five o'clock, the little church bell ringing the "Angelus" woke these women up, who as a rule slept the whole morning long.

The peasants were up already, and the women went busily from house to house, carefully bringing short, starched, muslin dresses in bandboxes, or very long wax tapers, with a bow of silk fringed with gold in the middle, and with dents in the wax for the fingers.

The sun was already high in the blue sky, which still had a rosy tint toward the horizon, like a faint trace of dawn, remaining. Families of fowls were walking about the henhouses, and here and there a black cock, with a glistening breast, raised his head, crowned by his red comb, flapped his wings, and uttered his shrill crow, which the other cocks repeated.

Vehicles of all sorts came from neighboring parishes, and discharged tall, Norman women, in dark dresses, with neck-handkerchiefs crossed over the bosom, and fastened with silver brooches, a hundred years old.

The men had put on blouses over their new frock coats, or over their old dress coats of green cloth, the tails of which hung down below their blouses. When the horses were in the stable, there was a double line of rustic conveyances along the road; carts, cabriolets, tilburies, char-à-bancs, traps of every shape and age, resting on their shafts, or pointing them in the air.

The carpenter's house was as busy as a beehive. The ladies, in dressing jackets and petticoats, with their long, thin, light hair, which looked as if it were faded and worn by dyeing, were busy dressing the child, who was standing motionless on a table, while Madame Tellier was directing the movements of her battalion. They washed her, did her hair, dressed her, and with the help of a number of pins, they arranged the folds of her dress, and took in the waist, which was too large.

Then, when she was ready, she was told to sit down and not to move, and the women hurried off to get ready themselves.

The church bell began to ring again, and its tinkle was lost in the air, like a feeble voice which is soon drowned in space. The candidates came out of the houses, and went toward the parochial building which contained the school and the mansion house. This stood quite at one end of the village, while the church was situated at the other.

The parents, in their very best clothes, followed their children with awkward looks, and with the clumsy movements of bodies that are always bent at work.

The little girls disappeared in a cloud of muslin, which looked like whipped cream, while the lads, who looked like embryo waiters in a *café*, and whose heads shone with pomatum, walked with their legs apart, so as not to get any dust or dirt on to their black trousers.

It was something for the family to be proud of; a large number of relatives from distant parts surrounded the child, and, consequently, the carpenter's triumph was complete.

Madame Tellier's regiment, with its mistress at its head, followed Constance; her father gave his arm to his sister, her mother walked by the side of Raphaelle, Fernande with Rosa, and the Two Pumps together. Thus they walked majestically through the village, like a general's staff in full uniform, while the effect on the village was startling.

At the school, the girls arranged themselves under the Sister of Mercy, and the boys under the schoolmaster, and they started off, singing a hymn as they went. The boys led the way, in two files, between the two rows of vehicles, from which the horses had been taken out, and the girls followed in the same order. As all the people in the village had given the town ladies the precedence out of politeness, they came immediately behind the girls, and lengthened the double line of the procession still more, three on the right and three on the left,

while their dresses were as striking as a bouquet of fireworks.

When they went into the church, the congregation grew quite excited. They pressed against each other, they turned round, they jostled one another in order to see. Some of the devout ones almost spoke aloud, so astonished were they at the sight of these ladies, whose dresses were trimmed more elaborately than the priest's chasuble.

The Mayor offered them his pew, the first one on the right, close to the choir, and Madame Tellier sat there with her sister-in-law; Fernande and Raphaelle, Rosa the Jade, and the Two Pumps occupied the second seat, in company with the carpenter.

The choir was full of kneeling children, the girls on one side, and the boys on the other, and the long wax tapers which they held, looked like lances, pointing in all directions. Three men were standing in front of the lectern, singing as loud as they could.

They prolonged the syllables of the sonorous Latin indefinitely, holding on to the Amens with interminable *a—a's,* which the serpent of the organ kept up in the monotonous, long-drawn-out notes, emitted by the deep-throated pipes.

A child's shrill voice took up the reply, and from time to time a priest sitting in a stall and wearing a biretta, got up, muttered something, and sat down again. The three singers continued, with their eyes fixed on the big book of plain-song lying open before them on the outstretched wings of an eagle, mounted on a pivot.

Then silence ensued. The service went on, and toward the end of it,

Rosa, with her head in both her hands, suddenly thought of her mother, and her village church on a similar occasion. She almost fancied that that day had returned, when she was so small, and almost hidden in her white dress, and she began to cry.

First of all she wept silently, the tears dropped slowly from her eyes, but her emotion increased with her recollections, and she began to sob. She took out her pocket-handkerchief, wiped her eyes, and help it to her mouth, so as not to scream, but it was useless.

A sort of rattle escaped her throat, and she was answered by two other profound, heart-breaking sobs; for her two neighbors, Louise and Flora, who were kneeling near her, overcome by similar recollections, were sobbing by her side. There was a flood of tears, and as weeping is contagious, Madame soon found that her eyes were wet, and on turning to her sister-in-law, she saw that all the occupants of the pew were crying.

Soon, throughout the church, here and there, a wife, a mother, a sister, seized by the strange sympathy of poignant emotion, and agitated by the grief of those handsome ladies on their knees, who were shaken by their sobs, was moistening her cambric pocket-handkerchief, and pressing her beating heart with her left hand.

Just as the sparks from an engine will set fire to dry grass, so the tears of Rosa and of her companions infected the whole congregation in a moment. Men, women, old men, and lads in new blouses were soon sobbing; something superhuman seemed to be hovering over their heads—a spirit, the powerful breath of an invisible and all-powerful being.

Suddenly a species of madness seemed to pervade the church, the noise of a crowd in a state of frenzy, a tempest of sobs and of stifled cries. It passed over the people like gusts of wind which bow the trees in a forest, and the priest, overcome by emotion, stammered out incoherent prayers, those inarticulate prayers of the soul, when it soars toward heaven.

The people behind him gradually grew calmer. The cantors, in all the dignity of their white surplices, went on in somewhat uncertain voices, and the organ itself seemed hoarse, as if the instrument had been weeping. The priest, however, raised his hand, as a sign for them to be still, and went to the chancel steps. All were silent, immediately.

After a few remarks on what had just taken place, which he attributed to a miracle, he continued, turning to the seats where the carpenter's guests were sitting:

"I especially thank you, my dear sisters, who have come from such a distance, and whose presence among us, whose evident faith and ardent piety have set such a salutary example to all. You have edified my parish; your emotion has warmed all hearts; without you, this day would not, perhaps, have had this really divine character. It is sufficient, at times, that there should be one chosen to keep in the flock, to make the whole flock blessed."

His voice failed him again, from emotion, and he said no more, but concluded the service.

They all left the church as quickly as possible; the children themselves were restless, tired with such a prolonged tension of the mind. Besides, the elders were hungry, and one after another left the churchyard, to see about dinner.

There was a crowd outside, a noisy crowd, a babel of loud voices, in which the shrill Norman accent was discernible. The villagers formed two ranks, and when the children appeared, each family seized their own.

The whole houseful of women caught hold of Constance, surrounded her and kissed her, and Rosa was especially demonstrative. At last she took hold of one hand, while Madame Tellier held the other, and Raphaelle and Fernande held up her long muslin petticoat, so that it might not drag in the dust. Louise and Flora brought up the rear with Madame Rivet, and the child, who was very silent and thoughtful, set off home, in the midst of this guard of honor.

The dinner was served in the workshop, on long boards supported by trestles, and through the open door they could see all the enjoyment that was going on. Everywhere people were feasting; through every window could be seen tables surrounded by people in their Sunday clothes. There was merriment in every house—men sitting in their shirt sleeves, drinking cider, glass after glass.

In the carpenter's house the gaiety took on somewhat of an air of reserve, the consequence of the emotion of the girls in the morning. Rivet was the only one who was in good cue, and he was drinking to excess. Madame Tellier was looking at the clock every moment, for, in order not to lose two days following, they ought to take the 3:55 train, which would bring them to Fécamp by dark.

The carpenter tried very hard to distract her attention, so as to keep his guests until the next day. But he did not succeed, for she never joked when there was business to be done, and as soon as they had had their coffee she ordred her girls to make haste and get ready. Then, turning to her brother, she said:

"You must have the horse put in immediately," and she herself went to complete her preparations.

When she came down again, her sister-in-law was waiting to speak to her about the child, and a long conversation took place, in which, however, nothing was settled. The carpenter's wife finessed, and pretended to be very much moved, and Madame Tellier, who was holding the girl on her knees, would not pledge herself to anything definite, but merely gave vague promises: she would not forget her, there was plenty of time, and then, they were sure to meet again.

But the conveyance did not come to the door, and the women did not come downstairs. Upstairs, they even heard loud laughter, falls, little screams, and much clapping of hands, and so, while the carpenter's wife went to the stable to see whether the cart was ready, Madame went upstairs.

Rivet, who was very drunk and half undressed, was vainly trying to kiss Rosa, who was choking with laughter. The Two Pumps were holding him by the arms and trying to calm him, as they were shocked at such a scene after that morning's ceremony; but Raphaelle and Fernande were urging him on, writhing and holding their sides with laughter, and they uttered shrill cries at every useless attempt that the drunken fellow made.

The man was furious, his face was red, his dress disordered, and he was trying to shake off the two women who were clinging to him, while he was pulling Rosa's bodice, with all his might, and ejaculating: "Won't you, you slut?"

But Madame, who was very indignant, went up to her brother, seized him by the shoulders, and threw him out of the room with such violence that he fell against a wall in the passage, and a minute afterward, they heard him pumping water on to his head in the yard. When he came back with the cart, he was already quite calmed down.

They seated themselves in the same way as they had done the day before, and the little white horse started off with his quick, dancing trot. Under the hot sun, their fun, which had been checked during dinner, broke out again. The girls now were amused at the jolts which the wagon gave, pushed their neighbors' chairs, and burst out laughing every moment, for they were in the vein for it, after Rivet's vain attempt.

There was a haze over the country, the roads were glaring, and dazzled their eyes. The wheels raised up two trails of dust, which followed the cart for a long time along the highroad, and presently Fernande, who was fond of music, asked Rosa to sing something. She boldly struck up the "Gros Curé de Meudon," but Madame made her stop immediately as she thought it a song which was very unsuitable for such a day, and added:

"Sing us something of Béranger's."

After a moment's hesitation, Rosa began Béranger's song, "The Grandmother," in her worn-out voice, and all the girls, and even Madame herself, joined in the chorus:

"How I regret
    My dimpled arms,
My well-made legs,
    And my vanished charms!"

"That is first-rate," Rivet declared, carried away by the rhythm. They shouted the refrain to every verse, while Rivet beat time on the shafts with his foot, and on the horse's back with the reins. The animal, himself, carried away by the rhythm, broke into a wild gallop, and threw all the women in a heap, one on top of the other, in the bottom of the conveyance.

They got up, laughing as if they were crazy, and the song went on, shouted at the top of their voices, beneath the burning sky and among the ripening grain, to the rapid gallop of the little horse, who set off every time the refrain was sung, and galloped a hundred yards, to their great delight. Occasionally a stone breaker by the roadside sat up, and looked at the wild and shouting female load, through his wire spectacles.

When they got out at the station, the carpenter said:

"I am sorry you are going; we might have had some fun together."

But Madame replied very sensibly: "Everything has its right time, and we cannot always be enjoying ourselves."

And then he had a sudden inspiration: "Look here, I will come and see you at Fécamp next month." And he gave a knowing look, with his bright and roguish eyes.

"Come," Madame said, "you must be sensible; you may come if you like, but you are not to be up to any of your tricks."

He did not reply, and as they heard the whistle of the train he immediately began to kiss them all. When it came to Rosa's turn, he tried to get to her mouth, which she, however, smiling with her lips closed, turned away from him each time by a rapid movement of her head to one side. He held her in his arms, but he could not attain his object, as his large whip, which he was holding in his hand and waving behind the girl's back in desperation, interfered with his efforts.

"Passengers for Rouen, take your seats, please!" a guard cried, and they got in. There was a slight whistle followed by a loud one from the engine, which noisily puffed out its first jet of steam, while the wheels began to turn a little, with visible effort. Rivet left the station and went to the gate by the side of the line to get another look at Rosa, and as the carriage full of human merchandise passed him, he began to crack his whip and to jump, singing at the top of his voice:

> "How I regret
> My dimpled arms,
> My well-made legs,
> And my vanished charms!"

And then he watched a white pocket-handkerchief, which somebody was waving, as it disappeared in the distance.

III.

They slept the peaceful sleep of quiet consciences, until they got to Rouen. When they returned to the house, refreshed and rested, Madame could not help saying:

"It was all very well, but I was already longing to get home."

They hurried over their supper, and then, when they had put on their usual light evening costumes, waited for their usual customers. The little colored lamp outside the door told the passers-by that the flock had returned to the fold, and in a moment the news spread, nobody knew how, or by whom.

Monsieur Philippe, the banker's son, even carried his audacity so far as to send a special messenger to Monsieur Tournevau who was in the bosom of his family.

The fish-curer used every Sunday to have several cousins to dinner, and they were having coffee, when a man came in with a letter in his hand. Monsieur Tournevau was much excited; he opened the envelope and grew pale; it only contained these words in pencil:

"The cargo of fish has been found; the ship has come into port; good business for you. Come immediately."

He felt in his pockets, gave the messenger two-pence, and suddenly blushing to his ears, he said: "I must go out." He handed his wife the laconic and mysterious note, rang the bell, and when the servant came in, he asked her to bring him his hat and overcoat immediately. As soon as he was in the street, he began to run, and the way seemed to him to be twice as long as usual, in consequence of his impatience.

Madame Tellier's establishment had put on quite a holiday look. On the ground floor, a number of sailors were making a deafening noise, and Louise and Flora drank with one and the other, so as to merit their name of the Two Pumps more than ever. They were being called for everywhere at once; already they were not quite sober enough for their business, and the night bid fair to be a very jolly one.

The upstairs room was full by nine o'clock. Monsieur Vassi, the Judge of the Tribunal of Commerce, Madame's usual Platonic wooer, was talking to her in a corner, in a low voice, and they were both smiling, as if they were about to come to an understanding.

Monsieur Poulin, the ex-mayor, was holding Rosa on his knees; and she, with her nose close to his, was running her hands through the old gentleman's white whiskers.

Tall Fernande, who was lying on the sofa, had both her feet on Monsieur Pinipesse the tax-collector's stomach, and her back on young Monsieur Philippe's waistcoat; her right arm was round his neck, and she held a cigarette in her left.

Raphaelle appeared to be discussing matters with Monsieur Depuis, the insurance agent, and she finished by saying: "Yes, my dear, I will."

Just then, the door opened suddenly, and Monsieur Tournevau came in. He was greeted with enthusiastic cries of: "Long live Tournevau!" and Raphaelle, who was twirling round, went and threw herself into his arms. He seized her in a vigorous embrace, and without saying a word, lifting her up as if she had been a feather, he carried her through the room.

Rosa was chatting to the ex-mayor, kissing him every moment, and pulling both his whiskers at the same time in order to keep his head straight.

Fernande and Madame remained with the four men, and Monsieur Philippe exclaimed: "I will pay for some champagne; get three bottles, Madame Tellier." And Fernande gave him a hug, and whispered to him: "Play us a waltz, will you?" So he rose and sat down at the old piano in the corner, and managed to get a hoarse waltz out of the entrails of the instrument.

The tall girl put her arms round the tax-collector, Madame asked Monsieur Vassi to take her in his arms, and the two couples turned round, kissing as they danced. Monsieur Vassi, who had formerly danced in good society, waltzed with such elegance that Madame was quite captivated.

Frederic brought the champagne; the first cork popped, and Monsieur Philippe played the introduction to a quadrille, through which the four dancers walked in society fashion, decorously, with propriety of deportment, with bows, and curtsies, and then they began to drink.

Monsieur Philippe next struck up a lively polka, and Monsieur Tournevau started off with the handsome Jewess, whom he held up in the air, without letting her feet touch the ground. Monsieur Pinipesse and Monsieur Vassi had started off with renewed vigor and from time to time one or other couple would stop to toss off a long glass of sparkling wine. The dance was threatening to become never-ending, when Rosa opened the door.

"I want to dance," she exclaimed. And she caught hold of Monsieur Dupuis, who was sitting idle on the couch, and the dance began again.

But the bottles were empty. "I will pay for one," Monsieur Tournevau said.

"So will I," Monsieur Vassi declared.

"And I will do the same," Monsieur Dupuis remarked.

They all began to clap their hands, and it soon became a regular ball. From time to time, Louise and Flora ran upstairs quickly, had a few turns while their customers downstairs grew impatient, and then they returned regretfully to the *café*. At midnight they were still dancing.

Madame shut her eyes to what was going on, and she had long private talks in corners with Monsieur Vassi, as if to settle the last details of something that had already been agreed upon.

At last, at one o'clock, the two married men, Monsieur Tournevau and Monsieur Pinipesse, declared that they were going home, and wanted to pay. Nothing was charged for except the champagne, and that only cost six francs a bottle, instead of ten, which was the usual price, and when they expressed their surprise at such generosity, Madame, who was beaming, said to them:

"We don't have a holiday every day."

Love

THREE PAGES FROM A SPORTSMAN'S BOOK

I HAVE just read among the general news in one of the papers a drama of passion. He killed her and then he killed himself, so he must have loved her. What matters He or She? Their love alone matters to me; and it does not interest me because it moves me or astonishes me, or because it softens me or makes me think, but because it recalls to my mind a remembrance of my youth, a strange recollection of a hunting adventure where Love appeared to me, as the Cross appeared to the early Christians, in the midst of the heavens.

I was born with all the instincts and the senses of primitive man, tempered by the arguments and the restraints of a civilized being. I am passionately fond of shooting, yet the sight of the wounded animal, of the blood on its feathers and on my hands, affects my heart so as almost to make it stop.

That year the cold weather set in suddenly toward the end of autumn, and I was invited by one of my cousins, Karl de Rauville, to go with him and shoot ducks on the marshes, at daybreak.

My cousin was a jolly fellow of forty, with red hair, very stout and bearded, a country gentleman, an amiable semi-brute, of a happy disposition and endowed with that Gallic wit which makes even mediocrity agreeable. He lived in a house, half farm-house, half château, situated in a broad valley through which a river ran. The hills right and left were covered with woods, old manorial woods where magnificent trees still remained, and where the rarest feathered game in that part of France was to be found. Eagles were shot there occasionally, and birds of passage, such as rarely venture into our over-populated part of the country, invariably lighted amid these giant oaks, as if they knew or recognized some little corner of a primeval forest which had remained there to serve them as a shelter during their short nocturnal halt.

In the valley there were large meadows watered by trenches and separated by hedges; then, further on, the river, which up to that point had been kept between banks, expanded into a vast marsh. That marsh was the best shooting ground I ever saw. It was my cousin's chief care, and he kept it as a preserve. Through the rushes that covered it, and made it rustling and rough, narrow passages had been cut, through which the flat-bottomed boats, impelled and steered by poles, passed along silently over dead water, brushing up against the reeds and making the swift fish take refuge in the weeds, and the wild fowl, with their pointed, black heads, dive suddenly.

I am passionately fond of the water: of the sea, though it is too vast, too full of movement, impossible to hold; of the rivers which are so beautiful, but which pass on, and flee away; and above all of the marshes, where the whole unknown existence of aquatic animals palpitates. The marsh is an entire world in itself on the world of earth—a different world, which has its own life, its settled inhabitants and its passing travelers, its voices, its noises, and above all its mystery. Nothing is more impressive, nothing more disquieting, more terrifying occasionally, than a fen. Why should a vague terror hang over these low plains covered with water? Is it the low rustling of the rushes, the strange will-o'-the-wisp lights, the silence which prevails on calm nights, the still mists which hang over the surface like a shroud; or is it the almost inaudible splashing, so slight and so gentle, yet sometimes more terrifying than the cannons of men or the thunders of the skies, which make these marshes resemble countries one has dreamed of, terrible countries holding an unknown and dangerous secret?

No, something else belongs to it— another mystery, perhaps the mystery of the creation itself! For was it not in stagnant and muddy water, amid the heavy humidity of moist land under the heat of the sun, that the first germ of life pulsated and expanded to the day?

I arrived at my cousin's in the evening. It was freezing hard enough to split the stones.

During dinner, in the large room whose sideboards, walls, and ceiling were covered with stuffed birds, with wings extended or perched on branches to which they were nailed,—hawks, herons, owls, nightjars, buzzards, tiercels, vultures, falcons,—my cousin who, dressed in a sealskin jacket, himself resembled some strange animal from a cold country, told me what preparations he had made for that same night.

We were to start at half past three in the morning, so as to arrive at the place which he had chosen for our watching-place at about half past four. On that spot a hut had been built of lumps of ice, so as to shelter us somewhat from the trying wind which precedes daybreak, a wind so cold as to tear the flesh like a saw, cut it like the blade of a knife, prick it like a poisoned sting, twist it like a pair of pincers, and burn it like fire.

My cousin rubbed his hands: "I have never known such a frost," he said; "it is already twelve degrees below zero at six o'clock in the evening."

I threw myself on to my bed immediately after we had finished our meal, and went to sleep by the light of a bright fire burning in the grate.

At three o'clock he woke me. In my turn, I put on a sheepskin, and found my cousin Karl covered with a bearskin. After having each swallowed two cups of scalding coffee, followed by glasses of liqueur brandy, we started, accompanied by a gamekeeper and our dogs, Plongeon and Pierrot.

From the first moment that I got outside, I felt chilled to the very marrow. It was one of those nights on which the earth seems dead with cold. The frozen air becomes resisting and palpable, such pain does it cause; no breath of wind moves it, it is fixed and motionless; it bites you, pierces through you, dries you, kills the trees, the plants, the insects, the small birds themselves, who fall from the branches on to the hard ground, and become stiff themselves under the grip of the cold.

The moon, which was in her last quarter and was inclining all to one side, seemed fainting in the midst of space, so weak that she was unable to wane, forced to stay up yonder, seized and paralyzed by the severity of the weather. She shed a cold, mournful light over the world, that dying and wan light which she gives us every month, at the end of her period.

Karl and I walked side by side, our backs bent, our hands in our pockets and our guns under our arms. Our boots, which were wrapped in wool so that we might be able to walk without slipping on the frozen river, made no sound, and I looked at the white vapor which our dogs' breath made.

We were soon on the edge of the marsh, and entered one of the lanes of dry rushes which ran through the low forest.

Our elbows, which touched the long, ribbonlike leaves, left a slight noise behind us, and I was seized, as I had never been before, by the powerful and singular emotion which marshes cause in me. This one was dead, dead from cold, since we were walking on it, in the middle of its population of dried rushes.

Suddenly, at the turn of one of the lanes, I perceived the ice-hut which had been constructed to shelter us. I went in, and as we had nearly an hour to wait before the wandering birds would awake, I rolled myself up in my rug in order to try and get warm. Then, lying on my back, I began to look at the misshapen moon, which had four horns through the vaguely transparent walls of this polar house. But the frost of the frozen marshes, the cold of these walls, the cold from the firmament penetrated me so terribly that I began to cough. My cousin Karl became uneasy.

"No matter if we do not kill much to-day," he said: "I do not want you to catch cold; we will light a fire." And he told the gamekeeper to cut some rushes.

We made a pile in the middle of our hut which had a hole in the middle of the roof to let out the smoke, and when the red flames rose up to the clear, crystal blocks they began to melt, gently, imperceptibly, as if they were sweating. Karl, who had remained outside, called out to me: "Come and look here!" I went out of the hut and remained struck with astonishment. Our hut, in the shape of a cone, looked like an enormous diamond with a heart of fire, which had been suddenly planted there in the midst of the frozen water of the marsh. And inside, we saw two fantastic forms, those of our dogs, who were warming themselves at the fire.

But a peculiar cry, a lost, a wandering cry, passed over our heads, and the light from our hearth showed us the wild birds. Nothing moves one so much as the first clamor of a life which one does not see, which passes through the somber air so quickly and so far off, just before the first streak of a winter's day appears on the horizon. It seems to me, at this glacial hour of dawn, as if that passing cry which is carried away by the wings of a bird is the sigh of a soul from the world!

"Put out the fire," said Karl, "it is getting daylight."

The sky was, in fact, beginning to grow pale, and the flights of ducks made long, rapid streaks which were soon obliterated on the sky.

A stream of light burst out into the night; Karl had fired, and the two dogs ran forward.

And then, nearly every minute, now he, now I, aimed rapidly as soon as the shadow of a flying flock appeared above the rushes. And Pierrot and Plongeon, out of breath but happy, retrieved the bleeding birds, whose eyes still, occasionally, looked at us.

The sun had risen, and it was a bright day with a blue sky, and we were thinking of taking our departure, when two birds with extended necks and outstretched wings, glided rapidly over our heads. I fired, and one of them fell almost at my feet. It was a teal, with a silver breast, and then, in the blue space above me, I heard a voice, the voice of a bird. It was a short, repeated, heart-rending lament; and the bird, the little animal that had been spared began to turn round in the blue sky, over our heads, looking at its dead companion which I was holding in my hand.

Karl was on his knees, his gun to his shoulder watching it eagerly, until it should be within shot. "You have killed the duck," he said, "and the drake will not fly away."

He certainly did not fly away; he circled over our heads continually, and continued his cries. Never have any groans of suffering pained me so much as that desolate appeal, as that lamentable reproach of this poor bird which was lost in space.

Occasionally he took flight under the menace of the gun which followed his movements, and seemed ready to continue his flight alone, but as he could not make up his mind to this, he returned to find his mate.

"Leave her on the ground," Karl said to me, "he will come within shot by and by." And he did indeed come near us, careless of danger, infatuated by his animal love, by his affection for his mate, which I had just killed.

Karl fired, and it was as if somebody had cut the string which held the bird suspended. I saw something black descend, and I heard the noise of a fall among the rushes. And Pierrot brought it to me.

I put them—they were already cold—into the same game-bag, and I returned to Paris the same evening.

Mademoiselle Fifi

THE Major Graf* von Farlsberg, the Prussian commandant, was reading his newspaper, lying back in a great armchair, with his booted feet on the beautiful marble fireplace, where his spurs had made two holes, which grew deeper every day, during the three months that he had been in the château of Urville.

A cup of coffee was smoking on a small, inlaid table, which was stained with liquors, burnt by cigars, notched by the penknife of the victorious officer, who occasionally would stop while sharpening a pencil, to jot down figures, or to make a drawing on it, just as it took his fancy.

When he had read his letters and the German newspapers, which his baggage-master had brought him, he got up, and after throwing three or four enormous pieces of green wood on to the fire—for these gentlemen were gradually cutting down the park in order to keep themselves warm—he went to the window. The rain was descending in torrents, a regular Normandy rain, which looked as if it were being poured out by some furious hand, a slanting rain, which was as thick as a curtain, and which formed a kind of wall with oblique stripes, and which deluged everything, a regular rain, such as one frequently experiences in the neighborhood of Rouen, which is the watering-pot of France.

For a long time the officer looked at the sodden turf, and at the swollen Andelle beyond it, which was overflowing its banks, and he was drumming a waltz from the Rhine on the window-panes, with his fingers, when a noise made him turn round; it was his second in command, Captain Baron von Kelweinstein.

The major was a giant, with broad shoulders, and a long, fair beard, which hung like a cloth on to his chest. His whole, solemn person suggested the idea of a military peacock, a peacock who was carrying his tail spread out on to his breast. He had cold, gentle, blue eyes, and the scar from a sword-cut, which he had received in the war with Austria; he was said to be an honorable man, as well as a brave officer.

The captain, in short, red-faced man, who was tightly girthed in at the waist, had his red hair cropped quite close to his head, and in certain lights almost looked as if he had been rubbed over with phosphorus. He had lost two front

---

*Count.

teeth one night, though he could not quite remember how. This defect made him speak so that he could not always be understood, and he had a bald patch on the top of his head, which made him look rather like a monk, with a fringe of curly, bright, golden hair round the circle of bare skin.

The commandant shook hands with him, and drank his cup of coffee (the sixth that morning) at a draught, while he listened to his subordinate's report of what had occurred; and then they both went to the window, and declared that it was a very unpleasant outlook. The major, who was a quiet man, with a wife at home, could accommodate himself to everything; but the captain, who was rather fast, being in the habit of frequenting low resorts, and much given to women, was mad at having been shut up for three months in the compulsory chastity of that wretched hole.

There was a knock at the door, and when the commandant said, "Come in," one of their automatic soldiers appeared, and by his mere presence announced that breakfast was ready. In the dining-room, they met three other officers of lower rank: a lieutenant, Otto von Grossling, and two sub-lieutenants, Fritz Scheunebarg, and Count von Eyrick, a very short, fair-haired man, who was proud and brutal toward men, harsh toward prisoners, and very violent.

Since he had been in France, his comrades had called him nothing but "Mademoiselle Fifi." They had given him that nickname on account of his dandified style and small waist, which looked as if he wore stays, from his pale face, on which his budding mus-

tache scarcely showed, and on account of the habit he had acquired of employing the French expression, *fi, fi donc,* which he pronounced with a slight whistle, when he wished to express his sovereign contempt for persons or things.

The dining-room of the château was a magnificent long room, whose fine old mirrors, now cracked by pistol bullets, and Flemish tapestry, now cut to ribbons and hanging in rags in places, from sword-cuts, told too well what Mademoiselle Fifi's occupation was during his spare time.

There were three family portraits on the walls; a steel-clad knight, a cardinal, and a judge, who were all smoking long porcelain pipes, which had been inserted into holes in the canvas, while a lady in a long, pointed waist proudly exhibited an enormous pair of mustaches, drawn with a piece of charcoal.

The officers ate their breakfast almost in silence in that mutilated room, which looked dull in the rain, and melancholy under its vanquished appearance, although its old, oak floor had become as solid as the stone floor of a public-house.

When they had finished eating, and were smoking and drinking, they began, as usual, to talk about the dull life they were leading. The bottle of brandy and of liquors passed from hand to hand, and all sat back in their chairs, taking repeated sips from their glasses, and scarcely removing the long, bent stems, which terminated in china bowls painted in a manner to delight a Hottentot, from their mouths.

As soon as their glasses were empty, they filled them again, with a gesture of resigned weariness, but Mademoiselle Fifi emptied his every minute, and a soldier immediately gave him another. They were enveloped in a cloud of strong tobacco smoke; they seemed to be sunk in a state of drowsy, stupid intoxication, in that dull state of drunkenness of men who have nothing to do, when suddenly, the baron sat up, and said: "By heavens! This cannot go on; we must think of something to do." And on hearing this, Lieutenant Otto and Sub-lieutenant Fritz, who pre-eminently possessed the grave, heavy German countenance, said: "What, Captain?"

He thought for a few moments, and then replied: "What? Well, we must get up some entertainment, if the commandant will allow us."

"What sort of an entertainment, captain?" the major asked, taking his pipe out of his mouth.

"I will arrange all that, commandant," the baron said: "I will send Le Devoir to Rouen, who will bring us some ladies. I know where they can be found. We will have supper here, as all the materials are at hand, and, at least, we shall have a jolly evening."

Graf von Farlsberg shrugged his shoulders with a smile: "You must surely be mad, my friend."

But all the other officers got up, surrounded their chief, and said: "Let captain have his own way, commandant; it is terribly dull here."

And the major ended by yielding. "Very well," he replied, and the baron immediately sent for Le Devoir.

The latter was an old corporal who had never been seen to smile, but who carried out all orders of his superiors

to the letter, no matter what they might be. He stood there, with an impassive face, while he received the baron's instructions, and then went out; five minutes later a large wagon belonging to the military train, covered with a miller's tilt, galloped off as fast as four horses could take it, under the pouring rain, and the officers all seemed to awaken from their lethargy, their looks brightened, and they began to talk.

Although it was raining as hard as ever, the major declared that it was not so dull, and Lieutenant von Grossling said with conviction, that the sky was clearing up, while Mademoiselle Fifi did not seem to be able to keep in his place. He got up, and sat down again, and his bright eyes seemed to be looking for something to destroy. Suddenly, looking at the lady with the mustaches, the young fellow pulled out his revolver, and said: "You shall not see it." And without leaving his seat he aimed, and with two successive bullets cut out both the eyes of the portrait.

"Let us make a mine!" he then exclaimed, and the conversation was suddenly interrupted, as if they had found some fresh and powerful subject of interest. The mine was his invention, his method of destruction, and his favorite amusement.

When he left the château, the lawful owner, Count Fernand d'Amoys d'Urville, had not had time to carry away or to hide anything, except the plate, which had been stowed away in a hole made in one of the walls, so that, as he was very rich and had good taste, the large drawing-room, which opened into the dining-room, had looked like the gallery in a museum, before his pre-cipitate flight.

Expensive oil-paintings, water-colors, and drawings hung upon the walls, while on the tables, on the hanging shelves, and in elegant glass cupboards, there were a thousand knickknacks: small vases, statuettes, groups in Dresden china, grotesque Chinese figures, old ivory, and Venetian glass, which filled the large room with their precious and fantastical array.

Scarcely anything was left now; not that the things had been stolen, for the major would not have allowed that, but Mademoiselle Fifi *would have a mine,* and on that occasion all the officers thoroughly enjoyed themselves for five minutes. The little marquis went into the drawing-room to get what he wanted, and he brought back a small, delicate china teapot, which he filled with gun-powder, and carefully introduced a piece of German tinder into it, through the spout. Then he lighted it, and took this infernal machine into the next room; but he came back immediately, and shut the door. The Germans all stood expectantly, their faces full of childish, smiling curiosity, and as soon as the explosion had shaken the château, they all rushed in at once.

Mademoiselle Fifi, who got in first, clapped his hands in delight at the sight of a terra-cotta Venus, whose head had been blown off, and each picked up pieces of porcelain, and wondered at the strange shape of the fragments, while the major was looking with a pa-ternal eye at the large drawing-room which had been wrecked in such a Ne-ronic fashion, and which was strewn with the fragments of works of art. He

went out first, and said, with a smile: "He managed that very well!"

But there was such a cloud of smoke in the dining-room mingled with the to-bacco smoke, that they could not breathe, so the commandant opened the window, and all the officers, who had gone into the room for a glass of cognac, went up to it.

The moist air blew into the room, and brought a sort of spray with it, which powdered their beards. They looked at the tall trees which were dripping with the rain, at the broad valley which was covered with mist, and at the church spire in the distance, which rose up like a gray point in the beating rain.

The bells had not rung since their ar-rival. That was the only resistance which the invaders had met with in the neighborhood. The parish priest had not refused to take in and to feed the Prussian soldiers; he had several times even drunk a bottle of beer or claret with the hostile commandant, who often employed him as a benevolent in-termediary; but it was no use to ask him for a single stroke of the bells; he would sooner have allowed himself to be shot. That was his way of protest-ing against the invasion, a peaceful and silent protest, the only one, he said, which was suitable to a priest, who was a man of mildness, and not of blood; and everyone, for twenty-five miles round, praised Abbé Chantavoine's firm-ness and heroism, in venturing to pro-claim the public mourning by the ob-stinate silence of his church bells.

The whole village grew enthusiastic over his resistance, and was ready to back up their pastor and to risk any-thing, as they looked upon that silent protest as the safeguard of the national honor. It seemed to the peasants that thus they had deserved better of their country than Belfort and Strassburg, that they had set an equally valuable example, and that the name of their little village would become immortalized by that; but with that exception, they refused their Prussian conquerors nothing.

The commandant and his officers laughed among themselves at that inoffensive courage, and as the people in the whole country round showed themselves obliging and compliant toward them, they willingly tolerated their silent patriotism. Only little Count Wilhelm would have liked to have forced them to ring the bells. He was very angry at his superior's politic compliance with the priest's scruples, and every day he begged the commandant to allow his to sound "ding-dong, ding-dong," just once, only just once, just by way of a joke. And he asked it like a wheedling woman, in the tender voice of some mistress who wishes to obtain something, but the commandant would not yield, and to console *herself,* Mademoiselle Fifi made a *mine* in the château.

The five men stood there together for some minutes, inhaling the moist air, and at last, Lieutenant Fritz said, with a laugh: "The ladies will certainly not have fine weather for their drive." Then they separated, each to his own duties, while the captain had plenty to do in seeing about the dinner.

When they met again, as it was growing dark, they began to laugh at seeing each other as dandified and smart as on the day of a grand review. The commandant's hair did not look as gray as it did in the morning, and the captain had shaved—had only kept his mustache on, which made him look as if he had a streak of fire under his nose.

In spite of the rain, they left the window open, and one of them went to listen from time to time. At a quarter past six the baron said he heard a rumbling in the distance. They all rushed down, and soon the wagon drove up at a gallop with its four horses, splashed up to their backs, steaming and panting. Five women got out at the bottom of the steps, five handsome girls whom a comrade of the captain, to whom *Le Devoir* had taken his card, had selected with care.

They had not required much pressing, as they were sure of being well treated, for they had got to know the Prussians in the three months during which they had had to do with them. So they resigned themselves to the men as they did to the state of affairs. "It is part of our business, so it must be done," they said as they drove along; no doubt to allay some slight, secret scruples of conscience.

They went into the dining-room immediately, which looked still more dismal in its dilapidated state, when it was lighted up; while the table covered with choice dishes, the beautiful china and glass, and the plate, which had been found in the hole in the wall where its owner had hidden it, gave to the place the look of a bandits' resort, where they were supping after committing a robbery. The captain was radiant; he took hold of the women as if he were familiar with them; appraising them, kissing them, valuing them for what they were worth as *ladies of pleasure;* and when the three young men wanted to appropriate one each, he opposed them authoritatively, reserving to himself the right to apportion them justly, according to their several ranks, so as not to wound the hierarchy. Therefore, so as to avoid all discussion, jarring, and suspicion of partialty, he placed them all in a line according to height, and addressing the tallest, he said in a voice of command:

"What is your name?"

"Pamela," she replied, raising her voice.

Then he said: "Number One, called Pamela, is adjudged to the commandant."

Then, having kissed Blondina, the second, as a sign of proprietorship, he proffered stout Amanda to Lieutenant Otto, Eva, "the Tomato," to Sub-lieutenant Fritz, and Rachel, the shortest of them all, a very young, dark girl, with eyes as black as ink, a Jewess, whose snub nose confirmed by exception the rule which allots hooked noses to all her race, to the youngest officer, frail Count Wilhelm von Eyrick.

They were all pretty and plump, without any distinctive features, and all were very much alike in look and person, from their daily dissipation, and the life common to houses of public accommodation.

The three younger men wished to carry off their women immediately, under the pretext of finding them brushes and soap; but the captain wisely opposed this, for he said they were quite fit to sit down to dinner, and that those who went up would wish for a change when they came down, and so would disturb the other couples, and his experience in such matters carried the day. There were only many kisses; expectant kisses.

Suddenly Rachel choked, and began to cough until the tears came into her eyes, while smoke came through her nostrils. Under pretense of kissing her, the count had blown a whiff of tobacco into her mouth. She did not fly into a rage, and did not say a word, but she looked at her possessor with latent hatred in her dark eyes.

They sat down to dinner. The commandant seemed delighted; he made Pamela sit on his right, and Blondina on his left, and said, as he unfolded his table napkin: "That was a delightful idea of yours, captain."

Lieutenants Otto and Fritz, who were as polite as if they had been with fashionable ladies, rather intimidated their neighbors, but Baron von Kelweinstein gave the reins to all his vicious propensities, beamed, made doubtful remarks, and seemed on fire with his crown of red hair. He paid them compliments in French from the other side of the Rhine, and sputtered out gallant remarks, only fit for a low pothouse, from between his two broken teeth.

They did not undertsand him, however, and their intelligence did not seem to be awakened until he uttered nasty words and broad expressions, which were mangled by his accent. Then all began to laugh at once, like mad women, and fell against each other, repeating the words, which the baron then began to say all wrong, in order that he might have the pleasure of hearing them say doubtful things. They gave him as much of that stuff as he wanted, for they were drunk after the first bottle of wine, and, becoming themselves once more, and opening the door to their usual habits, they kissed the mustaches on the right and left of them, pinched their arms, uttered furious cries, drank out of every glass, and sang French couplets, and bits of German songs, which they had picked up in their daily intercourse with the enemy.

Soon the men themselves, intoxicated by that which was displayed to their sight and touch, grew very amorous, shouted and broke the plates and dishes, while the soldiers behind them waited on them stolidly. The commandant was the only one who put any restraint upon himself.

Mademoiselle Fifi had taken Rachel on to his knees, and, getting excited, at one moment kissed the little black curls on her neck, inhaling the pleasant warmth of her body, and all the savor of her person, through the slight space there was between her dress and her skin, and at another pinched her furiously through the material, and made her scream, for he was seized with a species of ferocity, and tormented by his desire to hurt her. He often held her close to him, as if to make her part of himself, and put his lips in a long kiss on the Jewess's rosy mouth, until she lost her breath; and at last he bit her until a stream of blood ran down her chin and on to her bodice.

For the second time, she looked him full in the face, and as she bathed the wound, she said: "You will have to pay for that!"

But he merely laughed a hard laugh, and said: "I will pay."

At dessert, champagne was served,

and the commandant rose, and in the same voice in which he would have drunk to the health of the Empress Augusta, he drank: "To our ladies!" Then a series of toasts began, toasts worthy of the lowest soldiers and of drunkards, mingled with filthy jokes, which were made still more brutal by their ignorance of the language. They got up, one after the other, trying to say something witty, forcing themselves to be funny, and the women, who were so drunk that they almost fell off their chairs, with vacant looks and clammy tongues, applauded madly each time.

The captain, who no doubt wished to impart an appearance of gallantry to the orgy, raised his glass again, and said: "To our victories over hearts!" Thereupon Lieutenant Otto, who was a species of bear from the Black Forest, jumped up, inflamed and saturated with drink, and seized by an access of alcoholic patriotism, cried: "To our victories over France!"

Drunk as they were, the women were silent, and Rachel turned round with a shudder, and said: "Look here, I know some Frenchmen, in whose presence you would not dare to say that." But the little count, still holding her on his knees, began to laugh, for the wine had made him very merry, and said: "Ha! ha! ha! I have never met any of them, myself. As soon as we show ourselves, they run away!"

The girl, who was in a terrible rage, shouted into his face: "You are lying, you dirty scoundrel!"

For a moment, he looked at her steadily, with his bright eyes upon her, as he had looked at the portrait before he destroyed it with revolver bullets, and then he began to laugh: "Ah! yes, talk about them, my dear! Should we be here now, if they were brave?" Then getting excited, he exclaimed: "We are the masters! France belongs to us!" She jumped off his knees with a bound, and threw herself into her chair, while he rose, held out his glass over the table, and repeated: "France and the French, the woods, the fields, and the houses of France belong to us!"

The others, who were quite drunk, and who were suddenly seized by military enthusiasm, the enthusiasm of brutes, seized their glasses, and shouting, "Long live Prussia!" emptied them at a draught.

The girls did not protest, for they were reduced to silence, and were afraid. Even Rachel did not say a word, as she had no reply to make, and then the little count put his champagne glass, which had just been refilled, on to the head of the Jewess, and exclaimed: "All the women in France belong to us, also!"

At that she got up so quickly that the glass upset, spilling the amber colored wine on to her black hair as if to baptize her, and broke into a hundred fragments as it fell on to the floor. With trembling lips, she defied the looks of the officer, who was still laughing, and she stammered out, in a voice choked with rage: "That—that—that —is not true,—for you shall certainly not have any French women."

He sat down again, so as to laugh at his ease, and trying effectually to speak in the Parisian accent, he said: "That is good, very good! Then what did you come here for, my dear?"

She was thunderstruck, and made no reply for a moment, for in her agitation she did not understand him at first; but as soon as she grasped his meaning, she said to him indignantly and vehemently: "I! I! am not a woman; I am only a strumpet, and that is all that Prussians want."

Almost before she had finished, he slapped her full in her face; but as he was raising his hand again, as if he would strike her, she, almost mad with passion, took up a small dessert knife from the table, and stabbed him right in the neck, just above the breastbone. Something that he was going to say, was cut short in his throat, and he sat there, with his mouth half open, and a terrible look in his eyes.

All the officers shouted in horror, and leaped up tumultuously; but throwing her chair between Lieutenant Otto's legs, who fell down at full length, she ran to the window, opened it before they could seize her, and jumped out into the night and pouring rain.

In two minutes, Mademoiselle Fifi was dead. Fritz and Otto drew their swords and wanted to kill the women, who threw themselves at their feet and clung to their knees. With some difficulty the major stopped the slaughter, and had the four terrified girls locked up in a room under the care of two soldiers. Then he organized the pursuit of the fugitive, as carefully as if he were about to engage in a skirmish, feeling quite sure that she would be caught.

The table, which had been cleared immediately, now served as a bed on which to lay Fifi out, and the four officers made for the window, rigid and sobered, with the stern faces of soldiers on duty, and tried to pierce through the darkness of the night, amid the steady torrent of rain. Suddenly, a shot was heard, and then another, a long way off; and for four hours they heard, from time to time, near or distant reports and rallying cries, strange words uttered as a call, in guttural voices.

In the morning they all returned. Two soldiers had been killed and three others wounded by their comrades in the ardor of that chase, and in the confusion of such a nocturnal pursuit, but they had not caught Rachel.

Then the inhabitants of the district were terrorized, the houses were turned topsy-turvy, the country was scoured and beaten up, over and over again, but the Jewess did not seem to have left a single trace of her passage behind her.

When the general was told of it, he gave orders to hush up the affair, so as not to set a bad example to the army, but he severely censured the commandant, who in turn punished his inferiors. The general had said: "One does not go to war in order to amuse oneself, and to caress prostitutes." And Graf von Farlsberg, in his exasperation, made up his mind to have his revenge on the district, but as he required a pretext for showing severity, he sent for the priest, and ordered him to have the bell tolled at the funeral of Count von Eyrick.

Contrary to all expectation, the priest showed himself humble and most respectful, and when Mademoiselle Fifi's body left the Château d'Urville on its way to the cemetery, carried by soldiers, preceded, surrounded, and followed by soldiers, who marched with loaded rifles, for the first time the bell sounded its funereal knell in a lively manner, as if a friendly hand were caressing it. At night it sounded again, and the next day, and every day; it rang as much as anyone could desire. Sometimes even, it would start at night, and sound gently through the darkness, seized by strange joy, awakened, one could not tell why. All the peasants in the neighborhood declared that it was bewitched, and nobody, except the priest and the sacristan would now go near the church tower, and they went because a poor girl was living there in grief and solitude, secretly nourished by those two men.

She remained there until the German troops departed, and then one evening the priest borrowed the baker's cart, and himself drove his prisoner to Rouen. When they got there, he embraced her, and she quickly went back on foot to the establishment from which she had come, where the proprietress, who thought that she was dead, was very glad to see her.

A short time afterward, a patriot who had no prejudices, who liked her because of her bold deed, and who afterward loved her for herself, married her, and made a lady of her.

Monsieur Parent

LITTLE George was piling hills of sand in one of the walks. He scooped the sand up with both his hands, made it into a pyramid, and then put a chestnut leaf on the top, and his father, sitting on an iron chair, was looking at him with concentrated and affectionate attention, seeing nobody else in the small public garden, which was full of people. All along the circular road other children were busy in the same manner, or were indulging in other childish games, while nursemaids were strolling two and two, with their bright cap-ribbons floating behind them, and carrying something wrapped up in lace, in their arms. Here and there little girls in short petticoats and bare legs were talking seriously together, while resting from trundling their hoops.

The sun was just disappearing behind the roofs of the Rue Saint-Lazare, but still shed its rays obliquely on that little overdressed crowd. The chestnut trees were lighted up with its yellow rays, and the three fountains before the lofty porch of the church shone like molten silver.

Monsieur Parent looked at his boy sitting there in the dusk; he followed his slightest movements with affection in his glance; but accidentally looking up at the church clock, he saw that he was five minutes late, so he got up, took the child by the arm and shook his sand-covered dress, wiped his hands and led him in the direction of the Rue Blanche. He walked quickly, so as not to get in after his wife, but as the child could not keep up the pace, he took him up and carried him, though it made him pant when he had to walk up the steep street. Parent was a man of forty, turning gray already, rather stout. He had married, a few years previously, a young woman whom he dearly loved, but who now treated him with the severity and authority of an all-powerful despot. She found fault with him continually for

everything that he did or did not do, reproached him bitterly for his slightest acts, his habits, his simple pleasures, his tastes, his movements and walk, and for having a round stomach and a placid voice.

He still loved her, however, but above all he loved the boy she had borne him, and George, who was now three, had become the greatest joy, in fact the preoccupation, of his heart. He himself had a modest private fortune, and lived without doing anything on his twenty thousand francs* a year, and his wife, who had been quite portionless, was constantly angry at her husband's inactivity.

At last he reached his house, put down the child, wiped his forehead and walked upstairs. When he got to the second floor, he rang. An old servant who had brought him up, one of those mistress-servants who are the tyrants of families, opened the door to him, and he asked her anxiously: "Has Madame come in yet?"

The servant shrugged her shoulders: "When have you ever known Madame to come home at half past six, Monsieur?"

And he replied with some embarrassment: "Very well; all the better; it will give me time to change my things, for I am very hot."

The servant looked at him with angry and contemptuous pity, and grumbled: "Oh! I can see that well enough, you are covered with perspiration, Monsieur. I suppose you walked quickly and carried the child, and only to have to wait until half past seven, perhaps, for Ma-

---

*About $4000.

dame. I have made up my mind not to have it ready at the time, but shall get it for eight o'clock, and if you have to wait, I cannot help it; roast meat ought not to be burnt!"

Monsieur Parent, however, pretended not to hear, and only said: "All right! all right. You must wash George's hands, for he has been making sand pits. I will go and change my clothes; tell the maid to give the child a good washing."

And he went into his own room, and as soon as he got in he locked the door, so as to be alone, quite alone. He was so used now to being abused and badly treated, that he never thought himself safe, except when he was locked in. He no longer ventured even to think, reflect and reason with himself unless he had secured himself against her looks and insinuations, by locking himself in. Having thrown himself into a chair, in order to rest for a few minutes before he put on clean linen, he remembered that Julie was beginning to be a fresh danger in the house. She hated his wife —that was quite plain; but she hated still more his friend Paul Limousin, who had continued to be the familiar and intimate friend of the house, after having been the inseparable companion of his bachelor days, which is very rare. It was Limousin who acted as a buffer between his wife and himself, and who defended him ardently, and even severely, against her undeserved reproaches, against crying scenes, and against all the daily miseries of his existence.

But now for six months, Julie had constantly been saying things against her mistress. She would repeat twenty times a day: "If I were you, Monsieur,

I should not allow myself to be led by the nose like that. Well, well! But there — everyone according to his nature." And one day, she had even ventured to be insolent to Henriette, who, however, merely said to her husband, at night: "You know, the next time she speaks to me like that, I shall turn her out of doors." But she, who feared nothing, seemed to be afraid of the old servant, and Parent attributed her mildness to her consideration for the old domestic who had brought him up, and who had closed his mother's eyes. Now, however, Henriette's patience was exhausted, matters could not go on like that much longer, and he was frightened at the idea of what was going to happen. What could he do? To get rid of Julie seemed to him to be such a formidable undertaking, that he hardly ventured to think of it; but it was just as impossible to uphold her against his wife, and before another month could pass, the situation between the two would become unbearable. He remained sitting there, with his arms hanging down, vaguely trying to discover some means to set matters straight, but without success, and he said to himself: "It is lucky that I have George; without him I should be very miserable."

Then he thought he would consult Limousin, but the recollection of the hatred that existed between his friend and the servant made him fear lest the former should advise him to turn her away, and again he was lost in doubt and sad uncertainty. Just then the clock struck seven, and he started up. Seven o'clock, and he had not even changed his clothes! Then, nervous and breathless, he undressed, put on a clean shirt, and hastily finished his toilette, as if he had been expected in the next room for some event of extreme importance; then he went into the drawing-room, happy at having nothing to fear. He glanced at the newspaper, went and looked out of the window, and then sat down on a sofa again. The door opened, and the boy came in, washed, brushed, and smiling, and Parent took him up in his arms and kissed him passionately; then he tossed him into the air, and held him up to the ceiling, but soon sat down again, as he was tired with all his efforts, and taking George on to his knee, he made him "ride a cock-horse." The child laughed and clapped his hands, and shouted with pleasure, as his father did, laughing until his big stomach shook, for it amused him almost more than it did the child.

Parent loved the boy with all the heart of a weak, resigned, ill-used man. He loved with mad bursts of affection, with caresses and with all the bashful tenderness which was hidden in him, and which had never found an outlet, even at the early period of his married life, for his wife had always shown herself cold and reserved. Just then, however, Julie came to the door, with a pale face and glistening eyes, and said in a voice which trembled with exasperation: "It is half past seven, Monsieur." Parent gave an uneasy and resigned look at the clock and replied: "Yes, it certainly is half past seven."

"Well, my dinner is quite ready, now."

Seeing the storm which was coming, he tried to turn it aside. "But did you not tell me when I came in that it would not be ready before eight?"

"Eight! what are you thinking about? You surely do not mean to let the child dine at eight o'clock? It would ruin his stomach. Just suppose that he only had his mother to look after him! She cares a great deal about her child. Oh! yes, we will speak about her; she is a mother. What a pity it is that there should be any mothers like her!"

Parent thought it was time to cut short a threatened scene, and so he said: "Julie, I will not allow you to speak like that of your mistress. You understand me, do you not? Do not forget it for the future."

The old servant, who was nearly choked with surprise, turned round and went out, slamming the door so violently after her, that the lusters on the chandelier rattled, and for some seconds it sounded as if a number of little invisible bells were ringing in the drawing-room.

George, who was surprised at first, began to clap his hands merrily, and blowing out his cheeks, he gave a great *boom* with all the strength of his lungs, to imitate the noise of the door banging. Then his father began telling him stories, but his mind was so preoccupied that he continually lost the thread of his story, and the child, who could not understand him, opened his eyes wide, in astonishment.

Parent never took his eyes off the clock; he thought he could see the hands move, and he would have liked to have stopped them until his wife's return. He was not vexed with her for being late, but he was frightened, frightened of her and of Julie, frightened at the thought of all that might happen. Ten minutes more would suffice to bring about an irreparable catastrophe, words and acts of violence that he did not dare to picture to himself. The mere idea of a quarrel, of loud voices, of insults flying through the air like bullets, of two women standing face to face, looking at each other and flinging abuse at each other, made his heart beat, and his tongue feel as parched as if he had been walking in the sun. He felt as limp as a rag, so limp that he no longer had the strength to lift up the child and dance him on his knee.

Eight o'clock struck, the door opened once more and Julie came in again. She had lost her look of exasperation, but now she put on an air of cold and determined resolution, which was still more formidable.

"Monsieur," she said, "I served your mother until the day of her death, and I have attended to you from your birth until now, and I think it may be said that I am devoted to the family."

She waited for a reply, and Parent stammered:

Why yes, certainly, my good Julie."

She continued: "You know quite well that I have never done anything for the sake of money, but always for your sake; that I have never deceived you nor lied to you, that you have never had to find fault with me."

"Certainly, my good Julie."

"Very well then, Monsieur, it cannot go on any longer like this. I have said nothing, and left you in your ignorance, out of respect and liking for you, but it is too much, and everyone in the neighborhood is laughing at you. Everybody knows about it, and so I must tell you also, although I do not like to repeat it. The reason why Madame comes in at any time she chooses is that she is doing abominable things."

He seemed stupefied, unable to understand, and could only stammer out: "Hold your tongue, you know I have forbidden you—" But she interrupted him with irresistible resolution.

"No, Monsieur, I must tell you everything, now. For a long time Madame has been doing wrong with Monsieur Limousin, I have seen them kiss scores of times behind the doors. Ah! you may be sure that if Monsieur Limousin had been rich, Madame would never have married Monsieur Parent. If you remember how the marriage was brought about, you would understand the matter from beginning to end."

Parent had risen, and stammered out, deadly pale: "Hold your tongue—hold your tongue or—"

She went on, however: "No, I mean to tell you everything. She married you from interest, and she deceived you from the very first day. It was all settled between them beforehand. You need only reflect for a few moments to understand it, and then, she was not satisfied with having married you, as she did not love you, she has made your life miserable, so miserable that it has almost broken my heart when I have seen it—"

He walked up and down the room with his hands clenched, repeating: "Hold your tongue—hold your tongue —" for he could find nothing else to say; the old servant, however, would not yield; she seemed resolved on everything, but George who had been at first astonished, and then frightened at those angry voices, began to utter shrill screams. He hid behind his father, and roared, with his face puckered up and his mouth open.

His son's screams exasperated Parent, and filled him with rage and courage. He rushed at Julie with both arms raised, ready to strike her, and exclaiming: "Ah! you wretch! you will send the child out of his senses." He was almost touching her, when she said:

"Monsieur, you may beat me if you like, me who reared you, but that will not prevent your wife' from deceiving you, or alter the fact that your child is not yours!"

He stopped suddenly, and let his arms fall, and he remained standing opposite to her, so everwhelmed that he could understand nothing more, and she added: "You need only look at the child to know who is its father! He is the very image of Monsieur Limousin, you need only look at his eyes and forehead, why, a blind man could not be mistaken in him."

But he had taken her by the shoulders, and was now shaking her with all his might, while he ejaculated: "Viper! viper! Go out the room, viper! Go out, or I shall kill you! Go out! Go out!"

And with a desperate effort he threw her into the next room. She fell on to the table which was laid for dinner, breaking the glasses. Then, getting up, she put it between her master and herself, and while he was pursuing her, in order to take hold of her again, she flung terrible words at him: "You need only go out this evening after dinner, and come in again immediately, and you

will see—you will see whether I have been lying! Just try it—and you will see." She had reached the kitchen door and escaped, but he ran after her, up the backstairs to her bedroom into which she had locked herself, and knocking at the door, he said: "You will leave my house this very instant."

"You may be certain of that, Monsieur," was her reply. "In an hour's time I shall not be here any longer."

He then went slowly downstairs again, holding on to the banister, so as not to fall, and went back to the drawing-room, where little George was sitting on the floor, crying; he fell into a chair, and looked at the child with dull eyes. He understood nothing, he knew nothing more, he felt dazed, stupefied, mad, as if he had just fallen on his head, and he scarcely even remembered the dreadful things the servant had told him. Then, by degrees his reason grew clearer, like muddy water settling, and the abominable revelation began to work in his heart.

Julie had spoken so clearly, with so much force, assurance, and sincerity, that he did not doubt her good faith, but he persisted in not believing her penetration. She might have been deceived, blinded by her devotion to him, carried away by unconscious hatred for Henriette. However, in measure as he tried to reassure and to convince himself, a thousand small facts recurred to his recollection, his wife's words, Limousin's looks, a number of unobserved, almost unseen trifles, her going out late, their simultaneous absence, and even some almost insignificant, but strange gestures, which he could not understand, now assumed an extreme importance for him and established a con-nivance between them. Everything that had happened since his engagement, surged through his over-excited brain, in his misery, and he doggedly went through his five years of married life, trying to recollect every detail month by month, day by day, and every disquieting circumstance that he remembered stung him to the quick like a wasp's sting.

He was not thinking of George any more, who was quiet now and on the carpet, but seeing that no notice was being taken of him, the boy began to cry. Then his father ran up to him, took him into his arms, and covered him with kisses. His child remained to him at any rate! What did the rest matter? He held him in his arms and pressed his lips on to his light hair, and relieved and composed, he whispered: "George,—my little George,—my dear little George!" But he suddenly remembered what Julie had said! Yes! she had said that he was Limousin's child. Oh! It could not be possible, surely! He could not believe it, could not doubt, even for a moment, that George was his own child. It was one of those low scandals which spring from servants' brains! And he repeated: "George—my dear little George." The youngster was quiet again, now that his father was fondling him.

Parent felt the warmth of the little chest penetrate to his through their clothes, and it filled him with love, courage, and happiness; that gentle heat soothed him, fortified him, and saved him. Then he put the small, curly head away from him a little and looked at it affectionately, still repeating: "George!

Oh! my little George!" But suddenly he thought: "Suppose he were to resemble Limousin, after all!"

There was something strange working within him, a fierce feeling, a poignant and violent sensation of cold in his whole body, in all his limbs, as if his bones had suddenly been turned to ice. Oh! if the child were to resemble Limousin—and he continued to look at George, who was laughing now. He looked at him with haggard, troubled eyes, and tried to discover whether there was any likeness in his forehead, in his nose, mouth, or cheeks. His thoughts wandered like they do when a person is going mad and his child's face changed in his eyes, and assumed a strange look, and unlikely resemblances.

Julie had said: "A blind man could not be mistaken in him." There must, therefore, be something striking, an undeniable likeness! But what? The forehead? Yes, perhaps; Limousin's forehead, however, was narrower. The mouth, then? But Limousin wore a beard, and how could anyone verify the likeness between the plump chin of the child, and the hairy chin of that man? Parent thought: "I cannot see anything now, I am too much upset; I could not recognize anything at present. I must wait; I must look at him well to-morrow morning, when I am getting up." And immediately afterward, he said to himself: "But if he is like me, I shall be saved! saved!" And he crossed the drawing-room in two strides, to examine the child's face by the side of his own in the looking-glass. He had George on his arm so that their faces might be close together, and he spoke out loud almost without knowing. "Yes—we have the same nose—the same nose perhaps, but that is not sure—and the same look. But no, he has blue eyes. Then—good heavens! I shall go mad. I cannot see anything more—I am going mad!"

He went away from the glass, to the other end of the drawing-room, and putting the child into an easy-chair, he fell into another and began to cry. He sobbed so violently that George, who was frightened at hearing him, immediately began to scream. The hall bell rang, and Parent gave a bound as if a bullet had gone through him.

"There she is," he said. "What shall I do?" And he ran and locked himself up in his room, so at any rate to have time to bathe his eyes. But in a few moments another ring at the bell made him jump again, and then he remembered that Julie had left without the housemaid knowing it, and so nobody would go to open the door. What was he to do? He went himself, and suddenly he felt brave, resolute, ready for dissimulation and the struggle. The terrible blow had matured him in a few moments, and then he wished to know the truth, he wished it with the rage of a timid man, with the tenacity of an easy-going man who has been exasperated.

But nevertheless he trembled! Was it fear? Yes. Perhaps he was still frightened of her? Does one know how much excited cowardice there often is in boldness? He went to the door with furtive steps, and stopped to listen; his heart beat furiously, and he heard nothing but the noise of that dull throbbing in his chest, and of George's shrill voice, who was still crying in the draw-

ing-room. Suddenly, however, the noise of the bell over his head startled him like an explosion; then he seized the lock, turned the key, and, opening the door, saw his wife and Limousin standing before him on the steps.

With an air of astonishment, which also betrayed a little irration she said: "So *you* open the door now? Where is Julie?" His throat felt tight and his breathing was labored, and he tried to reply without being able to utter a word, so she continued:

"Are you dumb? I asked you where Julie is?"

And then he managed to say: "She —she—has—gone."

Whereupon his wife began to get angry. "What do you mean by *gone.* Where has she gone? Why?"

By degrees he regained his coolness, and he felt rising in him an immense hatred for that insolent woman who was standing before him. "Yes, she has gone altogether. I sent her away."

"You have sent away Julie? Why, you must be mad."

"Yes, I sent her away because she was insolent—and because, because she was ill-using the child."

"Julie?"

"Yes, Julie."

"What was she insolent about?"

"About you."

"About me?"

"Yes, because the dinner was burnt, and you did not come in."

"And she said?"

"She said offensive things about you, which I ought not—which I could not listen to."

"What did she say?"

"It is no good repeating them."

"I want to hear them."

"She said it was unfortunate for a man like me to be married to a woman like you, unpunctual, careless, disorderly, a bad mother, and a bad wife."

The young woman had gone into the anteroom followed by Limousin, who did not say a word at this unexpected position of things. She shut the door quickly, threw her cloak on to a chair, and going straight up to her husband, she stammered out:

"You say?—you say?—that I am—?"

He was very pale and calm and replied:

"I say nothing, my dear. I am simply repeating what Julie said to me, as you wanted to know what it was, and I wish you to remark that I turned her off just on account of what she said."

She trembled with a violent longing to tear out his beard and scratch his face. In his voice and manner she felt that he was asserting his position as master, although she had nothing to say by way of reply, and she tried to assume the offensive, by saying something unpleasant:

"I suppose you have had dinner?" she asked.

"No, I waited for you."

She shrugged her shoulders impatiently. "It is very stupid of you to wait after half past seven," she said. "You might have guessed that I was detained, that I had a good many things to do, visits and shopping."

And then, suddenly, she felt that she wanted to explain how she had spent her time, and she told him in abrupt, haughty words, that having to buy some furniture in a shop a long distance off, very far off, in the Rue de Rennes, she had met Limousin at past seven o'clock on the Boulevard Saint-Germain, and that then she had gone with him to have something to eat in a restaurant, as she did not like to go to one by herself, although she was faint with hunger. That was how she had dinner, with Limousin, if it could be called dining, for they had only had some soup and half a fowl, as they were in a great hurry to get back, and Parent replied simply:

"Well, you were quite right. I am not finding fault with you."

Then Limousin, who had not spoken till then, and who had been half hidden behind Henriette, came forward, and put out his hand, saying: "Are you very well?"

Parent took his hand, and shaking it gently, replied: "Yes, I am very well."

But the young woman had felt a reproach in her husband's last words: "Finding fault! Why do you speak of finding fault? One might think that you meant to imply something."

"Not at all," he replied, by way of excuse. "I simply meant, that I was not at all anxious although you were late, and that I did not find fault with you for it." She, however, took the high hand, and tried to find a pretext for a quarrel.

"Although I was late? One might really think that it was one o'clock in the morning, and that I spent my nights away from home."

"Certainly not, my dear. I said *late*, because I could find no other word. You said you should be back at half past six, and you returned at half past eight. That was surely being late! I understand it perfectly well. I am not at all surprised, even. But—but—I can hardly use any other word."

"But you pronounce them, as if I had been out all night."

"Oh! no; oh! no!"

She saw that he would yield on every point, and she was going into her own room, when at last she noticed that George was screaming, and then she asked, with some feeling: "Whatever is the matter with the child?"

"I told you, that Julie had been rather unkind to him."

"What has the wretch been doing to him?"

"Oh! Nothing much. She gave him a push, and he fell down."

She wanted to see her child, and ran into the dining-room, but stopped short at the sight of the table covered with spilt wine, with broken decanters and glasses and overturned saltcellars. "Who did all that mischief?" she asked.

"It was Julie who—"

But she interrupted him furiously: "That is too much, really; Julie speaks of me as if I were a shameless woman, beats my child, breaks my plates and dishes, turns my house upside down, and it appears that you think it all quite natural."

"Certainly not, as I have got rid of her."

"Really!—you have got rid of her! But you ought to have given her in charge. In such cases, one ought to call in the Commissary of Police!"

"But, my dear—I really could not—there was no reason. It would have been very difficult."

She shrugged her shoulders, disdainfully: "There, you will never be anything but a poor, wretched fellow, a man without a will, without any firmness or energy. Ah! she must have said some nice things to you, your Julie, to make you turn her off like that. I should like to have been here for a minute, only for a minute." Then she opened the drawing-room door and ran to George, took him into her arms and kissed him, and said: "Georgie, what is it, my darling, my pretty one, my treasure?" But as she was fondling him he did not speak, and she repeated: "What is the matter with you?" And he, having seen with his child's eyes that something was wrong, replied "Julie beat papa."

Henriette turned toward her husband, in stupefaction at first, but then an irresistible desire to laugh shone in her eyes, passed like a slight shiver over her delicate cheeks, made her upper lip curl and her nostrils dilate, and at last a clear, bright burst of mirth came from her lips, a torrent of gaiety which was lively and sonorous as the song of a bird. With little mischievous exclamations which issued from between her white teeth, and hurt Parent as much as a bite would have done she laughed: "Ha!—ha!—ha!—ha! she beat—she beat—my husband — ha! — ha! — ha! How funny! Do you hear, Limousin? Julie has beaten—has beaten—my—husband. Oh! dear—oh! dear—how very funny!"

But Parent protested: "No—no—it is not true, it is not true. It was I, on the contrary, who threw her into the dining-room so violently that she knocked the table over. The child did not see clearly, I beat her!"

"Here, my darling," Henriette said to her boy; "did Julie beat papa?"

"Yes, it was Julie," he replied. But

then, suddenly turning to another idea, she said: "But the child has had no dinner? You have had nothing to eat, my pet?"

"No, mamma."

Then she again turned furiously on to her husband: "Why, you must be mad, utterly mad! It is half past eight, and George has had no dinner!"

He excused himself as best he could, for he had nearly lost his wits by the overwhelming scene and the explanation, and felt crushed by this ruin of his life.

"But, my dear, we were waiting for you, as I did not wish to dine without you. As you come home late every day, I expected you every moment."

She threw her bonnet, which she had kept on till then, into an easy-chair, and in an angry voice she said: "It is really intolerable to have to do with people who can understand nothing, who can divine nothing, and do nothing by themselves. So I suppose, if I were to come in at twelve o'clock at night, the child would have had nothing to eat? Just as if you could not have understood that, as it was after half past seven, I was prevented from coming home, that I had met with some hindrance!"

Parent trembled, for he felt that his anger was getting the upper hand, but Limousin interposed and turning toward the young woman, he said: "My dear friend, you are altogether unjust. Parent could not guess that you would come here so late, as you never do so, and then, how could you expect him to get over the difficulty all by himself, after having sent away Julie?"

But Henriette was very angry and replied: "Well, at any rate, he must get over the difficulty himself, for I will not help him. Let him settle it!" And she went into her own room, quite forgetting that her child had not had anything to eat.

Then Limousin immediately set to work to help his friend. He picked up the broken glasses which strewed the table, and took them out; he replaced the plates and knives and forks and put the child into his high chair, while Parent went to look for the lady's maid to wait at table. She came in, in great astonishment, as she had heard nothing in George's room, where she had been working. She soon, however, brought in the soup, a burnt leg of mutton, and mashed potatoes.

Parent sat by the side of the child, very much upset and distressed at all that had happened. He gave the boy his dinner, and endeavored to eat something himself, but he could only swallow with an effort, as if his throat had been paralyzed. By degrees he was seized by an insane desire to look at Limousin, who was sitting opposite to him and making bread pellets, to see whether George was like him. He did not venture to raise his eyes for some time; at last, however, he made up his mind to do so, and gave a quick, sharp look at the face which he knew so well. He almost fancied that he had never looked at it carefully, since it looked so different to what he had anticipated. From time to time he scanned him, trying to find a likeness in the smallest lines of his face, in the slightest features, and then he looked at his son, under the pretext of feeding him.

Two words were sounding in his ears: "His father! his father! his father!"

They buzzed in his temples at every beat of his heart. Yes, that man, that tranquil man who was sitting on the other side of the table was, perhaps, the father of his son, of George, of his little George. Parent left off eating; he could not manage any more; a terrible pain, one of those attacks of pain which make men scream, roll on the ground, and bite the furniture, was tearing at his entrails, and he felt inclined to take a knife and plunge it into his stomach. It would ease him and save him, and all would be over.

For how could he live now? Could he get up in the morning, join in the meals, go out into the streets, go to bed at night and sleep with that idea dominating him: "Limousin is little George's father!" No, he would not have the strength to walk a step, to dress himself, to think of anything, to speak to anybody! Every day, every hour, every moment, he would be trying to know, to guess, to discover this terrible secret. And the little boy—his dear little boy—he could not look at him any more without enduring the terrible pains of that doubt, of being tortured by it to the very marrow of his bones. He would be obliged to live there, to remain in that house, near a child whom he might love and yet hate! Yes, he should certainly end by hating him. What torture! Oh! If he were sure that Limousin was George's father, he might, perhaps, grow calm, become accustomed to his misfortune and his pain; but ignorance was intolerable.

Not to know—to be always trying to find out, to be continually suffering, to kiss the child every moment, another man's child, to take him out for walks, to carry him, to caress him, to love him, and to think continually: "Perhaps he is not my child?" Wouldn't it be better not to see him, to abandon him,—to lose him in the streets, or to go away, far away, himself, so far away that he should never hear anything more spoken about, never!

He started when he heard the door open. His wife came. "I am hungry," she said; "are not you also, Limousin?"

He hesitated a little, and then said: "Yes, I am, upon my word." And she had the leg of mutton brought in again, while Parent asked himself: "Have they had dinner? Or are they late- because they have had a lover's meeting?"

They both ate with a very good appetite. Henriette was very calm, but laughed and joked, and her husband watched her furtively. She had on a pink dressing gown trimmed with white lace, and her fair head, her white neck, and her plump hands stood out from that coquettish and perfumed dress, as from a seashell edged with foam. What had she been doing all day with that man? Parent could see them kissing, and stammering out words of ardent love! How was it that he could not manage to know everything, to guess the whole truth, by looking at them, sitting side by side, opposite to him?

What fun they must be making of him, if he had been their dupe since the first day? Was it possible to make a fool of a man, of a worthy man, because his father had left him a little money? Why could one not see these things in people's souls? How was it that nothing revealed to upright souls the deceit of infamous hearts? How was it that voices had the same sound for adoring as for lying—why was a false, deceptive look the same as a sincere one? And he watched them, waiting to catch a gesture, a word, an intonation. Then suddenly he thought: "I will surprise them this evening," and he said: "My dear, as I have dismissed Julie, I will see about getting another this very day, and I shall go out immediately to procure one by to-morrow morning, so I may not be in until late."

"Very well," she replied; "go, I shall not stir from here. Limousin will keep me company. We will wait for you." And then, turning to the maid, she said: "You had better put George to bed, and then you can clear away and go up to your own room."

Parent had got up; he was unsteady on his legs, dazed and giddy, and saying: "I shall see you again later on," he went out, holding on to the wall, for the floor seemed to roll, like a ship. George had been carried out by his nurse, while Henriette and Limousin went into the drawing-room.

As soon as the door was shut, he said: "You must be mad, surely, to torment your husband as you do." She immediately turned on him: "Ah! Do you know that I think the habit you have got into lately, of looking upon Parent as a martyr, is very unpleasant."

Limousin threw himself into an easy-chair, and crossed his legs: "I am not setting him up as a martyr in the least, but I think that, situated as we are, it is ridiculous to defy this man as you do, from morning till night."

She took a cigarette from the mantelpiece, lighted it, and replied: "But I do not defy him, quite the contrary;

only, he irritates me by his stupidity, and I treat him as he deserves."

Limousin continued impatiently: "What you are doing is very foolish! However, all women are alike. Look here: Parent is an excellent, kind fellow, stupidly confiding and good, who never interferes with us, who does not suspect us for a moment, who leaves us quite free and undisturbed, whenever we like, and you do all you can to put him into a rage and to spoil our life."

She turned to him: "I say, you worry me. You are a coward, like all other men are! You are frightened of that poor creature!" He immediately jumped up, and said, furiously: "I should like to know what he does, and why you are so set against him? Does he make you unhappy? Does he beat you? Does he deceive you and go with another woman? No, it is really too bad to make him suffer, merely because he is too kind, and to hate him, merely because you are unfaithful to him."

She went up to Limousin, and looking him full in the face, she said: "And you reproach me with deceiving him? You? You? What a filthy heart you must have?"

He felt rather ashamed, and tried to defend himself: "I am not reproaching you, my dear, I am only asking you to treat your husband gently, because we both of us require him to trust us. I think that you ought to see that."

They were close together—he, tall, dark, with long whiskers, and the rather vulgar manners of a good-looking man, who is very well satisfied with himself; she, small, fair, and pink, a little Parisian, half shopkeeper, half one of those girls of easy virtue, born in a shop, brought up at its door to entice customers by her looks, and married, accidentally, in consequence, to a simple, unsophisticated man, who saw her outside the door every morning when he went out, and every evening when he came home.

"But do you not understand, you great booby," she said, "that I hate him just because he married me, because he bought me, in fact, because everything that he says and does, everything that he thinks, reacts on my nerves? He exasperates me every moment by his stupidity, which you call kindness—by his dullness, which you call his confidence, and then, above all, because he is my husband, instead of you! I feel him between us, although he does not interfere with us much. And then? And then? No, after all, it is too idiotic of him not to guess anything! I wish he would at any rate be a little jealous. There are moments when I feel inclined to say to him, 'Don't you see, you stupid fool, that Paul is my lover?' "

Limousin began to laugh: "Meanwhile, it would be a good thing if you were to keep quiet, and not disturb our life."

"Oh! I shall not disturb it, you may be sure! There is nothing to fear, with such a fool. But it is quite incomprehensible that you cannot understand how hateful he is to me, how he irritates me. You always seem to like him, and you shake hands with him cordially. Men are very surprising at times."

"One must know how to dissimulate, my dear."

"It is no question of dissimulation, but of feeling. One might think that, when you men deceive another, you liked him

all the more on that account, while we women hate a man from the moment that we have betrayed him."

"I do not see why I should hate an excellent fellow, because I love his wife."

"You do not see it? You do not see it? You, all of you, are wanting in that fineness of feeling! However, that is one of those things which one feels, and which one cannot express. And then, moreover, one ought not. No, you would not understand, it is quite useless! You men have no delicacy of feeling."

And smiling, with the gentle contempt of a debauched woman, she put both her hands on to his shoulders and held up her lips to him, and he stooped down and clasped her closely in his arms, and their lips met. And as they stood in front of the mirror, another couple exactly like them, embraced behind the clock.

They had heard nothing—neither the noise of the key, nor the creaking of the door, but suddenly Henriette, with a loud cry, pushed Limousin away with both her arms, and they saw Parent who was looking at them, livid with rage, without his shoes on, and his hat over his forehead. He looked at them, one after the other, with a quick glance of his eyes without moving his head. He seemed possessed, and then, without saying a word, he threw himself on Limousin, seized him as if he were going to strangle him, and flung him into the opposite corner of the room so violently, that the lover lost his balance, and clutching at the air with his hands, banged his head against the wall.

But when Henriette saw that her husband was going to murder her lover, she threw herself on to Parent, seized him by the neck, and digging her ten delicate and rosy fingers into his neck, she squeezed him so tightly, with all the vigor of a desperate woman, that the blood spurted out under her nails, and she bit his shoulder, as if she wished to tear it with her teeth. Parent, half-strangled and choked, loosened his hold on Limousin in order to shake off his wife, who was hanging on to his neck; and putting his arms round her waist, he flung her also to the other end of the drawing-room.

Then, as his passion was short-lived, like that of most good-tempered men, and as his strength was soon exhausted, he remained standing between the two, panting, worn out, not knowing what to do next. His brute fury had expended itself in that effort, like the froth of a bottle of champagne, and his unwonted energy ended in a want of breath. As soon as he could speak, however, he said: "Go away—both of you—immediately—go away!"

Limousin remained motionless in his corner, against the wall, too startled to understand anything as yet, too frightened to move a finger; while Henriette, with her hands resting on a small, round table, her head bent forward, with her hair hanging down, the bodice of her dress unfastened and bosom bare, waited like a wild animal which is about to spring. Parent went on, in a stronger voice: "Go away immediately. Get out of the house!"

His wife, however, seeing that he had got over his first exasperation, grew bolder, drew herself up, took two steps toward him, and grown almost insolent already, she said: "Have you lost your head? What is the matter with you? What is the meaning of this unjustifiable violence?" But he turned toward her, and raising his fist to strike her, he stammered out: "Oh! Oh! this is too much—too much! I heard everything! Everything! Do you understand? Everything! you wretch—you wretch; you are two wretches! Get out of the house—both of you! Immediately—or I shall kill you! Leave the house!"

She saw that it was all over, and that he knew everything, that she could not prove her innocence, and that she must comply, but all her impudence had returned to her, and her hatred for the man, which was aroused now, drove her to audacity, making her feel the need of bravado, and of defying him. So she said in a clear voice: "Come, Limousin, as he is going to turn me out of doors, I will go to your lodgings with you."

But Limousin did not move; and Parent, in a fresh access of rage cried out: "Go, will you!—go, you wretches! —or else!—or else!" and he seized a chair and whirled it over his head.

Then Henriette walked quickly across the room, took her lover by the arm, dragged him from the wall, to which he appeared fixed, and led him toward the door, saying: "Do come, my friend. You see that the man is mad. Do come!"

As she went out, she turned round to her husband, trying to think of something that she could do, something that she could invent to wound him to the heart as she left the house. An idea struck her, one of those venomous deadly ideas in which all a woman's perfidy shows itself, and she said reso-

lutely: "I am going to take my child
with me."

Parent was stupefied and stammered:
"Your—your child? You dare to talk
of your child? You venture—you venture to ask for your child—after—
after— Oh! oh! that is too much! Go,
you horrid wretch! Go!" She went up
to him again, almost smiling, avenged
already, and defying him, standing close
to him, and face to face, she said: "I
want my child, and you have no right
to keep him, because he is not yours.
Do you understand? He is not yours—
he is Limousin's."

And Parent cried out in bewilderment: "You lie—you lie—you wretch!"

But she continued: "You fool! Everybody knows it, except you. I tell you,
this is his father. You need only look
at him, to see it—"

Parent staggered back from her, and
then he suddenly turned round, took a
candle and rushed into the next room.
Almost immediately, however, he returned, carrying little George wrapped
up in his bedclothes, and the child, who
had been suddenly awakened, was crying from fright. Parent threw him into
his wife's arms, and then, without saying
anything more he pushed her roughly
out, toward the stairs, where Limousin
was waiting, from motives of prudence.

Then he shut the door again, double-
locked it, and bolted it, and he had
scarcely got into the drawing-room,
when he fell full length on the floor.

II.

Parent lived alone, quite alone. During the five weeks that followed their
separation, the feeling of surprise at his
new life prevented him from thinking
much. He had resumed his bachelor
life, his habits of lounging about, and
he took his meals at a restaurant, as he
had done formerly. As he had wished
to avoid any scandal, he made his wife
an allowance, which was settled by their
lawyers. By degrees, however, the
thoughts of the child began to haunt
him. Often, when he was at home alone
at night, he suddenly thought he heard
George calling out "Papa," and his heart
would begin to beat. One night he got
up quickly and opened the door to see
whether, by chance, the child might have
returned, like dogs or pigeons do. Why
should a child have less instinct than an
animal?

After finding that he was mistaken, he
went and sat down in his armchair again
and thought of the boy. Finally he
thought of him for hours, and whole
days. It was not only a moral, but still
more a physical obsession, a nervous
longing to kiss him, to hold and fondle
him, to take him on to his knees and
dance him. He felt the child's little
arms around his neck, the little mouth
pressing a kiss on his beard, the soft
hair tickling his cheeks, and the remembrance of all those childish ways made
him suffer like the desire for some loved
woman who has run away. Twenty or
a hundred times a day he asked himself
the question, whether he was or was not
George's father, and at night, especially,
he indulged in interminable speculations
on the point, and almost before he was
in bed. Every night he recommenced
the same series of despairing arguments.

After his wife's departure, he had at
first not felt the slightest doubt; certainly the child was Limousin's, but by

degrees he began to waver. Henriette's words could not be of any value. She had merely braved him, and tried to drive him to desperation, and calmly weighing the *pros* and *cons*, there seemed to be every chance that she had lied, though perhaps only Limousin could tell the truth. But how was he to find it out, how could he question him or persuade him to confess the real facts?

Sometimes Parent would get up in the middle of the night, fully determined to go and see Limousin and to beg him, to offer him anything he wanted, to put an end to this intolerable misery. Then he would go back to bed in despair, reflecting that her lover would, no doubt, also lie! He would in fact be sure to lie, in order to avoid losing the child, if he were really his father. What could he, Parent, do then? Absolutely nothing!

And he began to feel sorry that he had thus suddenly brought about the crisis, that he had not taken time for reflection, that he had not waited and dissimulated for a month or two, so as to find out for himself. He ought to have pretended to suspect nothing, and have allowed them to betray themselves at their leisure. It would have been enough for him, to see the other kiss the child, to guess and to understand. A friend does not kiss a child as a father does. He should have watched them behind the doors. Why had he not thought of that? If Limousin, when left alone with George, had not at once taken him up, clasped him in his arms and kissed him passionately, if he had looked on indifferently while he was playing, without taking any notice of him, no doubt or hesitation could have been possible; in

that case he would not have been the father, he would not have thought that he was, would not have felt that he was. Thus Parent would have kept the child, while he got rid of the mother, and he would have been happy, perfectly happy.

He tossed about in bed, hot and unhappy, trying to recollect Limousin's ways with the child. But he could not remember anything suspicious, not a gesture, not a look, neither word nor caress. And then the child's mother took very little notice of him; if she had him by her lover, she would, no doubt, have loved him more.

They had, therefore, separated him from his son, out of vengeance, from cruelty, to punish him for having surprised them, and he made up his mind to go the next morning and obtain the magistrate's assistance to gain possession of George, but almost as soon as he had formed that resolution, he felt assured of the contrary. From the moment that Limousin had been Henriette's lover, her adored lover, she would certainly have given herself up to him, from the very first, with that ardor of self-abandonment which belongs to women who love. The cold reserve which she had always shown in her intimate relations with him, Parent, was surely also an obstacle to her bearing him a son.

In that case he would be claiming, he would take with him, constantly keep and look after, the child of another man. He would not be able to look at him, kiss him, hear him say "Papa" without being struck and tortured by the thought, "He is not my child." He was going to condemn himself to that torture, and that wretched life every moment! No, it would be better to live alone, to grow old alone, and to die alone.

And every day and every night, these dreadful doubts and sufferings, which nothing could calm or end, would recommence. Especially did he dread the darkness of the evening, the melancholy feeling of the twilight. A flood of sorrow would invade his heart, a torrent of despair, which threatened to overwhelm him and drive him mad. He was as frightened of his own thoughts as men are of criminals, and he fled before them as one does from wild beasts. Above all things he feared his empty, dark, horrible dwelling, and the deserted streets, in which, here and there, a gas lamp flickers, where the isolated foot passenger whom one hears in the distance seems to be a night-prowler, and makes one walk faster or slower, according to whether he is coming toward you or following you.

And in spite of himself, and by instinct, Parent went in the direction of the broad, well-lighted, populous streets. The light and the crowd attracted him, occupied him mind and distracted his thoughts, and when he was tired walking aimlessly about among the moving crowd, when he saw the foot passengers becoming more scarce, and the pavements less crowded, the fear of solitude and silence drove him into some large *café* full of drinkers and of light. He went there as a fly comes to a candle; he used to sit down at one of the little round tables and ask for a *bock*,* which he used to drink slowly, feeling uneasy every time that a customer got up to go. He would have liked to take him by the arm, hold him back and beg him

to stay a little longer, so much did he dread the time when the waiter would come up to him and say angrily: "Come, Monsieur, it is closing time!'

Every evening he would stop till the very last. He saw them carry in the tables, turn out the gas jets one by one, except his and that at the counter. He looked unhappily at the cashier counting the money and locking it up in the drawer, and then he went, being usually pushed out by the waiters, who murmured: "Another one who has too much! One would think he had no place to sleep in."

And each night as soon as he was alone in the dark street, he began to think of George again, and to rack his brains in trying to discover whether or not he was this child's father.

He thus got into the habit of going to the beer houses, where the continual elbowing of the drinkers brings you in contact with a familiar and silent public, where the clouds of tobacco smoke lull disquietude, while the heavy beer dulls the mind and calms the heart. He almost lived there. He was scarcely up, before he went there to find people to occupy his looks and his thoughts, and soon, as he became too listless to move, he took his meals there. About twelve o'clock he used to rap on the marble table, and the waiter would quickly bring a plate, a glass, a table napkin, and his lunch, when he had ordered it. When he had finished, he would slowly drink his cup of black coffee, with his eyes fixed on the decanter of brandy, which would soon procure him an hour or two of forgetfulness. First of all he

---

*Glass of Bavarian beer.

would dip his lips into the cognac, as if to get the flavor of it with the tip of his tongue. Then he would throw his head back and pour it into his mouth, drop by drop, and turn the strong liquor over on his palate, his gums, and the mucous membrane of his cheeks; then he would swallow it slowly, to feel it going down his throat, and into his stomach.

Thus, after every meal, he, during more than an hour, sipped three or four small glasses of brandy which stupefied him by degrees; then, having drunk it, he used to raise himself up on the seat covered with red velvet, pull his trousers up, and his waistcoat down, so as to cover the linen which appeared between the two, draw down his shirt cuffs and take up the newspapers again, which he had already read in the morning, and read them all through again, from beginning to end. Between four and five o'clock he would go for a walk on the boulevards, to get a little fresh air, as he used to say, and then come back to the seat which had been reserved for him, and ask for his absinthe. He used to talk to the regular customers, whose acquaintance he had made. They discussed the news of the day, and political events, and that carried him on till dinner-time, and he spent the evening as he had the afternoon, until it was time to close.

It was a terrible moment for him, when he was obliged to go out into the dark, and into the empty room full of dreadful recollections, of horrible thoughts, and of mental agony. He no longer saw any of his old friends, none of his relations, nobody who might remind him of his past life. But as his apartments were a hell to him, he took a room in a large hotel, a good room on the ground floor, so as to see the passers-by. He was no longer alone in that great building; he felt people swarming round him, he heard voices in the adjoining rooms, and when his former sufferings revived at the sight of his bed which was turned back, and of his solitary fireplace, he went out into the wide passages and walked up and down them like a sentinel, before all the closed doors, and looked sadly at the shoes standing in couples outside each, women's little boots by the side of men's thick ones, and he thought that no doubt all these people were happy, and were sleeping sweetly side by side or in each other's arms, in their warm beds.

Five years passed thus; five miserable years with no other events except from time to time a passing love affair. But one day when he was taking his usual walk between the Madeleine and the Rue Drouot, he suddenly saw a lady, whose bearing struck him. A tall gentleman and a child were with her, and all three were walking in front of him. He asked himself where he had seen them before, when suddenly he recognized a movement of her hand; it was his wife, his wife with Limousin and his child, his little George.

His heart beat as if it would suffocate him, but he did not stop, for he wished to see them and he followed them. They looked like a family of the better middle class. Henriette was leaning on Paul's arm and speaking to him in a low voice and looking at him sideways occasionally. Parent saw her side face, and recognized its graceful outlines, the movements of her lips, her smile, and her caressing looks, but the child chiefly took up his attention. How tall and strong he was! Parent could not see his face, but only his long, fair curls. That tall boy with bare legs, who was walking by his mother's side like a little man, was George.

He saw them suddenly all three, as they stopped in front of a shop. Limousin had grown very gray, had aged, and was thinner; his wife, on the contrary, was as young looking as ever, and had grown stouter; George he would not have recognized, he was so different to what he had been formerly.

They went on again, and Parent followed them, then walked on quickly, passed them and then turned round, so as to meet them face to face. As he passed the child he felt a mad longing to take him into his arms and run off with him, and he knocked against him, accidentally as it were. The boy turned round and looked at the clumsy man angrily, and Parent went off hastily, struck and hurt by the look. He slunk off like a thief, seized by a horrible fear lest he should have been seen and recognized by his wife and her lover, and he went to his *café* without stopping, fell breathless into his chair, and that evening he drank three absinthes.

For four months he felt the pain of that meeting in his heart. Every night he saw the three again, happy and tranquil, father, mother, and child walking on the boulevard before going in to dinner, and that new vision effaced the old one. It was another matter, another hallucination, now, and also a fresh pain. Little George, his little George, the child he had so much loved and so often kissed formerly, disappeared in the far distance and he saw a new one, like a brother of the first, a little boy with bare legs, who did not know him! He suffered terribly at that thought. The child's love was dead; there was no bond between them; the child would not have held out his arms when he saw him. He had even looked at him angrily.

Then by degrees he grew calmer, his mental torture diminished, the image that had appeared to his eyes and which haunted his nights became more indistinct and less frequent. He began once more to live like everybody else, like all those idle people who drink beer off marble-topped tables and wear out the seats of their trousers on the threadbare velvet of the couches.

He grew old amid the smoke from pipes, lost his hair under the gas lights, looked upon his weekly bath, on his fortnightly visit to the barber's to have his hair cut, and on the purchase of a new coat or hat, as an event. When he got to his *café* after buying a new hat he used to look at himself in the glass for a long time before sitting down, and would take it off and put it on again several times following, and at last ask his friend, the lady at the bar, who watched him with interest, whether she thought it suited him.

Two or three times a year he went to the theater, and in the summer he sometimes spent his evenings at one of the open air concerts in the Champs-Elysées. He brought back from them some airs which ran in his head for several weeks, and which he even hummed, beating time with his foot, while he was drinking his beer, and so the years followed each other, slow, monotonous, and long, because they were quite uneventful.

He did not feel them glide past him. He went on toward death without fear or agitation, sitting at a table in a *café*, and only the great glass against which he rested his head, which was every day becoming balder, reflected the ravages of time, which flies and devours men, poor men.

He only very rarely now thought of the terrible drama which had wrecked his life, for twenty years had passed since that terrible evening, but the life he had led since then had worn him out, and the landlord of his *café* would often say to him: "You ought to pull yourself together a little, Monsieur Parent; you should get some fresh air and go into the country! I assure you that you have changed very much within the last few months." And when his customer had gone out, he used to say to the barmaid: "That poor Monsieur Parent is booked for another world; it is no good never to go out of Paris. Advise him to go out of town for a day occasionally, he has confidence in you. It is nice weather, and will do him good." And she, full of pity and good-will for such a regular customer, said to Parent every day: "Come, Monsieur, make up your mind to get a little fresh air, it is so charming in the country when the weather is fine. Oh! if I could, I would spend my life there."

And she told him her dreams, the simple and poetical dreams of all the poor girls who are shut up from one year's end to the other in a shop and who see the noisy life of the streets go by while they think of the calm and pleasant life in the country, under the bright sun shining on the meadows, of deep woods and clear rivers, of cows lying in the grass and of all the different flowers, blue, red, yellow, purple, lilac, pink, and white, which are so pretty, so fresh, so sweet, all the wild flowers which one picks as one walks.

She liked to speak to him frequently of her continual, unrealized and unrealizable longing, and he, an old man without hope, was fond of listening to her; and used to go and sit near the counter to talk to Mademoiselle Zoé and to discuss the country with her. Then, by degrees he was seized by a vague desire to go just once and see whether it was really so pleasant there, as she said, outside the walls of the great city, and so one morning he said to her: "Do you know where one can get a good lunch in the neighborhood of Paris?"

"Go to the 'Terrace' at Saint-Germain."

He had been there formerly, just after he had got engaged, and so he made up his mind to go there again, and he chose a Sunday, without any special reason, but merely because people generally do go out on Sundays, even when they have nothing to do all the week. So one Sunday morning he went to Saint-Germain. It was at the beginning of July, on a very bright and hot day. Sitting by the door of the railway-carriage, he watched the trees and the strangely built little houses in the outskirts of Paris fly past. He felt low-spirited, and vexed at having yielded to that new longing, and at having broken through his usual habits. The view, which was continually changing, and always the same, wearied him. He was thirsty; he would have liked to get out at every station and sit down

in the *café* which he saw outside and
drink a *bock* or two, and then take the
first train back to Paris. And then, the
journey seemed very long to him. He
used to remain sitting for whole days,
as long as he had the same motionless
objects before his eyes, but he found
it very trying and fatiguing to remain
sitting while he was being whirled along,
and to see the whole country fly by,
while he himself was motionless.

.. However, he found the Seine interesting, every time he crossed it. Under the
bridge at Chatou he saw some skiffs going at great pace under the vigorous
strokes of the bare-armed oarsmen, and
he thought: "There are some fellows
who are certainly enjoying themselves!"
And then the train entered the tunnel
just before you get to the station at
Saint-Germain, and soon stopped at the
arrival platform, where Parent got out,
and walked slowly, for he already felt
tired, toward the Terrace, with his hands
behind his back, and when he got to the
iron balustrade, he stopped to look at
the distant horizon.

. The vast plain spread out before him
like the sea, green, and studded with
large villages, almost as populous as
towns. White roads crossed it, and it
was well wooded in places; the ponds at
Vesinet glistened like plates of silver,
and the distant ridges of Sannois and
Argenteuil were covered with light, bluish mist, so that they could scarcely be
distinguished. The sun bathed the
whole landscape in its full warm light,
and the Seine, which twined like an endless serpent through the plain, flowed
round the villages and along the slopes.
Parent inhaled the warm breeze which
seemed to make his heart young again,

to enliven his spirits, and to vivify his
blood, and said to himself: "It is very
nice here."

Then he went on a few steps, and
stopped again to look about him, and
the utter misery of his existence seemed
to be brought out into full relief by the
intense light which inundated the country. He saw his twenty years of *café*-
life, dull, monotonous, heart-breaking.
He might have traveled like others did,
have gone among foreigners, to unknown
countries beyond the sea, have interested
himself somewhat in everything which
other men are passionately devoted to,
in arts and sciences, he might have enjoyed life in a thousand forms, that
mysterious life which is either charming or painful, constantly changing, always inexplicable and strange.

Now, however, it was too late. He
would go on drinking *bock* after *bock*
until he died, without any family, without friends, without hope, without any
curiosity about anything, and he was
seized with a feeling of misery and a
wish to run away, to hide himself in
Paris, in his *café* and his befuddlement!
All the thoughts, all the dreams, all the
desires which are dormant in the sloth
of the stagnating hearts, had reawak-
ened, brought to life by those rays of
sunlight on the plain.

. He felt that if he were to remain there
any longer, he should lose his head, and
so he made haste to get to the Pavilion
Henri IV. for lunch, to try and forget
his troubles under the influence of wine
and alcohol, and at any rate to have
some one to speak to.

He took a small table in one of the
arbors, from which one can see all the
surrounding country, ordered his lunch

and asked to be served at once. Then some more people arrived and sat down at tables near him and he felt more comfortable; he was no longer alone. Three persons were lunching near him, and he looked at them two or three times without seeing them clearly, as one looks at total strangers. But suddenly a woman's voice sent a shiver through him which seemed to penetrate to his very marrow. "George," it had said, "will you carve the chicken?" Another voice replied: "Yes, mamma."

Parent looked up, and he understood, he guessed immediately who those people were! He should certainly not have known them again. His wife had grown quite white and very stout, an old, serious, respectable lady, and she held her head forward as she ate, for fear of spotting her dress, although she had a table napkin tucked under her chin. George had become a man; he had a slight beard, that unequal and almost colorless beard which fringes the cheeks of youths. He wore a high hat, a white waistcoat, and a monocle—because it looked dandified, no doubt. Parent looked at him in astonishment! Was that George, his son? No, he did not know that young man; there could be nothing in common between them. Limousin had his back to him, and was eating, with his shoulders rather bent.

Well, all three of them seemed happy and satisfied; they came and dined in the country, at well-known restaurants. They had had a calm and pleasant existence, a family existence in a warm and comfortable house, filled with all those trifles which make life agreeable, with affection, with all those tender words which people exchange continually when they love each other. They had lived thus, thanks to him, Parent, on his money, after having deceived him, robbed him, ruined him! They had condemned him, the innocent, the simpleminded, the jovial man to all the miseries of solitude, to that abominable life which he had led between the pavement and the counter, to every moral torture and every physical misery! They had made him a useless being, who was lost and wretched among other people, a poor old man without any pleasures, or anything to look forward to, and who hoped for nothing from anyone. For him, the world was empty, because he loved nothing in the world. He might go among other nations or go about the streets, go into all the houses in Paris, open every room, but he would not find the beloved face, the face of wife or child, that he was in search of, which smiles when it sees you, behind any door. And that idea worked upon him more than any other, the idea of a door which one opens, to see and to embrace somebody behind it.

And that was the fault of those three wretches! the fault of that worthless woman, of that infamous friend, and of that tall, light-haired lad who put on insolent airs. Now, he felt as angry with the child as he did with the other two! Was he not Limousin's son? Would Limousin have kept him and loved him, otherwise? Would not Limousin very quickly have got rid of the mother and of the child if he had not felt sure that it was his, certainly his? Does anybody bring up other people's children? And now they were there, quite close to him, those three who had made him suffer so much.

Parent looked at them, irritated and excited at the recollection of all his sufferings and of his despair, and was especially exasperated at their placid and satisfied looks. He felt inclined to kill them, to throw his siphon of Seltzer water at them, to split open Limousin's head, which he every moment bent over his plate and raised up again immediately. And they continued to live like that, without cares or anxiety of any kind. No! no! That was really too much, after all! He would avenge himself, he would have his revenge now, on the spot, as he had them under his hand. But how? He tried to think of some means, he pictured such dreadful things as one reads of in the newspapers occasionally, but could not hit on anything practical. And he went on drinking to excite himself, to give himself courage not to allow such an occasion to escape him, as he should certainly not meet with it again.

Suddenly an idea struck him, a terrible idea, and he left off drinking to mature it. A smile rose to his lips, and he murmured: "I have got them, I have got them. We will see; we will see."

A waiter asked him: "What would you like now, Monsieur?"

"Nothing. Coffee and cognac. The best." And he looked at them, as he sipped his brandy. There were too many people in the restaurant for what he wanted to do, so he would wait and follow them, for they would be sure to walk on the terrace or in the forest. When they had got a little distance off, he would join them, and then he would have his revenge, yes, he would have his revenge! It was certainly not too soon, after twenty-three years of suffering.

Ah! They little guessed what was to happen to them.

They finished their luncheon slowly, and they talked in perfect security. Parent could not hear what they were saying, but he saw their calm movements, and his wife's face, especially, exasperated him. She had assumed a haughty air, the air of a stout, devout woman, of an irreproachably devout woman, sheathed in principles, iron-clad in virtue. Then they paid the bill and got up, and then he saw Limousin. He might have been taken for a retired diplomatist, for he looked a man of great importance with his soft, white whiskers, the tips of which fell on to the facings of his coat.

They went out. George was smoking a cigar and had his hat on one side, and Parent followed them. First of all they went up and down the terrace, and calmly admired the landscape, like people who have well satisfied their hunger, and then they went into the forest, and Parent rubbed his hands and followed them at a distance, hiding himself, so as not to excite their suspicion too soon. They walked slowly, enjoying the fresh green foliage, and the warm air. Henriette was holding Limousin's arm and walked upright at his side, like a wife who is contented, and proud of herself. George was cutting off the leaves with his stick, and occasionally jumped over the ditches by the roadside, like a fiery young horse ready to gallop off through the trees.

Parent came up to them by degrees, panting rather from excitement and fatigue, for he never walked now. He soon came up to them, but he was seized by fear, an inexplicable fear, and he passed them, so as to turn round and meet them face to face. He walked on, his heart beating, for he knew that they were just behind him now, and he said to himself: "Come, now is the time. Courage! courage! Now is the moment!"

He turned around. They were all three sitting on the grass, at the foot of a huge tree, and were still talking. He made up his mind, and came back rapidly, and then stopping in front of them in the middle of the road, he said abruptly, in a voice broken by emotion: "It is I! Here I am! I suppose you did not expect me?" They all three looked at him carefully, for they thought that he was mad, and he continued: "One might think that you did not know me again. Just look at me! I am Parent, Henri Parent. You did not expect me, eh? You thought it was all over, and that you would never see me again. Ah! But here I am once more, you see, and now we will have an explanation."

Henriette was terrified and hid her face in her hands, murmuring: "Oh! Good Heavens!" And seeing this stranger who seemed to be threatening his mother, George sprang up, ready to seize him by the collar, while Limousin, who was thunderstruck, looked at this specter in horror, who, after panting for a few moments, continued: "So now we will have an explanation; the proper moment for it has come! Ah! you deceived me, you condemned me to the life of a convict, and you thought that I should never catch you!"

But the young man took him by the shoulders and pushed him back: "Are you mad?" he asked. "What do you

want? Go on your way immediately, or I shall give you a thrashing!" But Parent replied: "What do I want? I want to tell you who these people are." George, however, was in a rage and shook him; was even going to strike him, but the other said: "Just let me go. I am your father. There, look whether they recognize me now, the wretches!" And the alarmed young man removed his hands, and turned to his mother, while Parent, as soon as he was released, went toward her.

"Well," he said, "tell him who I am, you! Tell him that my name is Henri Parent; that I am his father because his name is George Parent; because you are my wife, because you are all three living on my money, on the allowance of ten thousand francs* which I have made you, since I drove you out of my house. Will you tell him also why I drove you out? Because I surprised you with this beggar, this wretch, your lover! Tell him what I was, an honorable man, whom you married for my money, and whom you deceived from the very first day. Tell him who you are, and who I am."

He stammered and panted for breath, in his rage, and the woman exclaimed in heartrending voice: "Paul, Paul, stop him; make him be quiet; do not let him say this before my son!"

Limousin had also got up, and he said in a quite low voice: "Hold your tongue! Do understand what you are doing!"

But Parent continued furiously: "I quite know what I am doing, and that is not all. There is one thing that I

---

*About $2000.

will know, something that has tormented me for twenty years."

And then turning to George, who was leaning against a tree in consternation, he said: "Listen to me. When she left my house, she thought it was not enough to have deceived me, but she also wanted to drive me to despair. You were my only consolation, and she took you with her, swearing that I was not your father, but that he was your father! Was she lying! I do not know, and I have been asking myself the question for the last twenty years."

He went close up to her, tragic and terrible, and pulling away her hands with which she had covered her face he continued: "Well, I call upon you now to tell me which of us two is the father of this young man; he or I, your husband or your lover. Come! Come! tell us." Limousin rushed at him, but Parent pushed him back, and sneering in his fury he said: "Ah! you are brave now! You are braver than you were the day you ran out of doors because I was going to half murder you. Very well! If she will not reply, tell me yourself. You ought to know as well as she. Tell me, are you this young fellow's father? Come! Come! Tell me!"

Then he turned to his wife again: "If you will not tell me, at any rate tell your son. He is a man, now, and he has the right to know who is his father. I do not know, and I never did know, never, never! I canot tell you, my boy." He seemed to be losing his senses, his voice grew shrill and he worked his arms about as if he had an epileptic attack. "Come! Give me an answer. She does not know. I will make a bet

that she does not know. No—she does not know, by Jove! She used to go to bed with both of us! Ha! ha! ha! Nobody knows—nobody. How can one know such things? You will not know either, my boy, you will not know any more than I do—never. Look here. Ask her—you will find that she does not know. I do not know either. You can choose—yes, you can choose—him or me. Choose. Good evening. It is all over. If she makes up her mind to tell you, come and let me know, will you, I am living at the Hôtel des Continents. I should be glad to know. Good evening; I hope you will enjoy yourselves very much."

And he went away gesticulating and talking to himself under the tall trees, into the empty, cool air, which was full of the smell of the sap. He did not turn round to look at them, but went straight on, walking under the stimulus of his rage, under a storm of passion, with that one fixed idea in his mind, and presently he found himself outside the station. A train was about to start and he got in. During the journey, his anger calmed down, he regained his senses and returned to Paris, astonished at his own boldness, and feeling as full of aches and fatigue, as if he had broken some bones, but nevertheless he went to have a *bock* at his *café*.

When she saw him come in, Mademoiselle Zoé was surprised and said: "What! back already? Are you tired?"

"I am tired—very tired. You know, when one is not used to going out—but I have done with it. I shall not go into the country again. I had better have stopped here. For the future, I shall not stir out again."

But she could not persuade him to tell her about his little excursion, although she wanted very much to hear all about it, and for the first time in his life he got thoroughly drunk that night, and had to be carried home.

————•————   *read*

Useless Beauty

A VERY elegant victoria, with two beautiful black horses, was drawn up in front of the mansion. It was a day in the latter end of June, about half past five in the afternoon, and the sun shone warm and bright into the large courtyard.

The Countess de Mascaret came down just as her husband, who was coming home, appeared in the carriage entrance. He stopped for a few moments to look at his wife and grew rather pale. She was very beautiful, graceful, and distinguished looking, with her long oval face, her complexion like gilt ivory, her large gray eyes, and her black hair; and she got into her carriage without looking at him, without even seeming to have noticed him, with such a particularly high-bred air, that the furious jealousy by which he had been devoured for so long again gnawed at his heart. He went up to her and said: "You are going for a drive?"

She merely replied disdainfully: "You see I am!"

"In the Bois de Boulogne?"

"Most probably."

"May I come with you?"

"The carriage belongs to you."

Without being surprised at the tone of voice in which she answered him, he got in and sat down by his wife's side, and said: "Bois de Boulogne." The footman jumped up by the coachman's side, and the horses as usual pawed the ground and shook their heads until they were in the street. Husband and wife sat side by side, without speaking. He was thinking how to begin a conversation, but she maintained such an obstinately hard look, that he did not venture to make the attempt. At last, however, he cunningly, accidentally as it were, touched the Countess's gloved hand with his own, but she drew her arm away, with a movement which was so expressive of disgust, that he remained thoughtful, in spite of his usual authoritative and despotic character. "Gabrielle!" said he at last.

"What do you want?"

"I think you are looking adorable."

She did not reply, but remained lying back in the carriage, looking like an irritated queen. By that time they were driving up the Champs-Elysées, toward the Arc de Triomphe. That immense monument, at the end of the long avenue, raised its colossal arch against the red sky, and the sun seemed to be sinking on to it, showering fiery dust on it from the sky.

The stream of carriages, with the sun reflecting from the bright, plated harness and the shining lamps, were like a double current flowing, one toward the town and one toward the wood, and the

Count de Mascaret continued: "My dear Gabrielle!"

Then, unable to bear it any longer, she replied in an exasperated voice: "Oh! do leave me in peace, pray! I am not even at liberty to have my carriage to myself, now." He, however, pretended not to hear her, and continued: "You have never looked so pretty as you do to-day."

Her patience was decidedly at an end, and she replied with irrepressible anger: "You are wrong to notice it, for I swear to you that I will never have anything to do with you in that way again." He was stupefied and agitated, and his violent nature gaining the upper hand, he exclaimed: "What do you mean by that?" in such a manner as revealed rather the brutal master than the amorous man. But she replied in a low voice, so that the servants might not hear, amid the deafening noise of the wheels:

"Ah! What do I mean by that? What do I mean by that? Now I recognize you again! Do you want me to tell everything?"

"Yes."

"Everything that has been on my heart, since I have been the victim of your terrible selfishness?"

He had grown red with surprise and anger, and he growled between his closed teeth: "Yes, tell me everything."

He was a tall, broad-shouldered man, with a big, red beard, a handsome man, a nobleman, a man of the world, who passed as a perfect husband and an excellent father, and now for the first time since they had started she turned toward him, and looked him full in the face: "Ah! You will hear some disagreeable

things, but you must know that I am prepared for everything, that I fear nothing, and you less than anyone, to-day."

He also was looking into her eyes, and already was shaking with passion; then he said in a low voice: "You are mad."

"No, but I will no longer be the victim of the hateful penalty of maternity, which you have inflicted on me for eleven years! I wish to live like a woman of the world, as I have the right to do, as all women have the right to do."

He suddenly grew pale again, and stammered: "I do not understand you."

"Oh! yes; you understand me well enough. It is now three months since I had my last child, and as I am still very beautiful, and as, in spite of all your efforts you cannot spoil my figure, as you just now perceived, when you saw me on the outside flight of steps, you think it is time that I should become *enceinte* again."

"But you are talking nonsense!"

"No, I am not; I am thirty, and I have had seven children, and we have been married eleven years, and you hope that this will go on for ten years longer, after which you will leave off being jealous."

He seized her arm and squeezed it, saying: "I will not allow you to talk to me like that, for long."

"And I shall talk to you till the end, until I have finished all I have to say to you, and if you try to prevent me, I shall raise my voice so that the two servants, who are on the box, may hear. I only allowed you to come with me for that object, for I have these witnesses, who will oblige you to listen to me, and to contain yourself; so now, pay attention to what I say. I have always felt an antipathy for you, and I have always let you see it, for I have never lied, Monsieur. You married me in spite of myself; you forced my parents, who were in embarrassed circumstances, to give me to you, because you were rich, and they obliged me to marry you, in spite of my tears.

"So you bought me, and as soon as I was in your power, as soon as I had become your companion, ready to attach myself to you, to forget your coercive and threatening proceedings, in order that I might only remember that I ought to be a devoted wife and to love you as much as it might be possible for me to love you, you became jealous—you—as no man has ever been before, with the base, ignoble jealousy of a spy, which was as degrading for you as it was for me. I had not been married eight months, when you suspected me of every perfidiousness, and you even told me so. What a disgrace! And as you could not prevent me from being beautiful, and from pleasing people, from being called in drawing-rooms, and also in the newspapers, one of the most beautiful women in Paris, you tried everything you could think of to keep admirers from me, and you hit upon the abominable idea of making me spend my life in a constant state of motherhood, until the time when I should disgust every man. Oh! do not deny it! I did not understand it for some time, but then I guessed it. You even boasted about it to your sister, who told me of it, for she is fond of me and was disgusted at your boorish coarseness.

"Ah! Remember our struggles, doors smashed in, and locks forced! For eleven years you have condemned me to the existence of a brood mare. Then as soon as I was pregnant, you grew disgusted with me, and I saw nothing of you for months, and I was sent into the country, to the family mansion, among fields and meadows, to bring forth my child. And when I reappeared, fresh, pretty, and indestructible, still seductive and constantly surrounded by admirers, hoping that at last I should live a little like a young rich woman who belongs to society, you were seized by jealousy again, and you recommenced to persecute me with that infamous and hateful desire from which you are suffering at this moment, by my side. And it is not the desire of possessing me— for I should never have refused myself to you—but it is the wish to make me unsightly.

"Beside this, that abominable and mysterious circumstance took place, which I was a long time in penetrating (but I grew acute by dint of watching your thoughts and actions). You attached yourself to your children with all the security which they gave you while I bore them in my womb. You felt affection for them, with all your aversion for me, and in spite of your ignoble fears, which were momentarily allayed by your pleasure in seeing me a mother.

"Oh! how often have I noticed that joy in you! I have seen it in your eyes and guessed it. You loved your children as victories, and not because they were of your own blood. They were victories over me, over my youth, over my beauty, over my charms, over the compliments which were paid me, and over those who whispered round me, without paying them to me. And you are proud of them, you make a parade of them, you take them out for drives in your coach in the Bois de Boulogne, and you give them donkey rides at Montmorency. You take them to theatrical matinées so that you may be seen in the midst of them, and that people may say: 'What a kind father!' and that it may be repeated."

He had seized her wrist with savage brutality, and squeezed it so violently that she was quiet, though she nearly cried out with the pain. Then he said to her in a whisper:

"I love my children, do you hear? What you have just told me is disgraceful in a mother. But you belong to me; I am master—your master. I can exact from you what I like and when I like—and I have the law on my side."

He was trying to crush her fingers in the strong grip of his large, muscular hand, and she, livid with pain, tried in vain to free them from that vise which was crushing them; the agony made her pant, and the tears came into her eyes. "You see that I am the master, and the stronger," he said. And when he somewhat loosened his grip, she asked him: "Do you think that I am a religious woman?"

He was surprised and stammered: "Yes."

"Do you think that I could lie, if I swore to the truth of anything to you, before an altar on which Christ's body is?"

"No."

"Will you go with me to some church?"

"What for?"

"You shall see. Will you?"

"If you absolutely wish it, yes."

She raised her voice and said: "Philip!" And the coachman, bending down a little, without taking his eyes from his horses, seemed to turn his ear alone toward his mistress, who said: "Drive to St. Philip-du-Roule's." And the victoria, which had reached the entrance of the Boise de Boulogne, returned to Paris.

Husband and wife did not exchange a word during the drive. When the carriage stopped before the church, Madame de Mascaret jumped out, and entered it, followed by the Count, a few yards behind her. She went, without stopping, as far as the choir-screen, and falling on her knees at a chair, she buried her face in her hands. She prayed for a long time, and he, standing behind her, could see that she was crying. She wept noiselessly, like women do weep when they are in great and poignant grief. There was a kind of undulation in her body, which ended in a little sob, hidden and stifled by her fingers.

But Count de Mascaret thought that the situation was long drawn out, and he touched her on the shoulder. That contact recalled her to herself, as if she had been burned, and getting up, she looked straight into his eyes.

"This is what I have to say to you. I am afraid of nothing, whatever you may do to me. You may kill me if you like. One of your children is not yours, and one only; that I swear to you before God, who hears me here. That is the only revenge which was possible for me, in return for all your abominable male tyrannies, in return for the penal servitude of childbearing to which you have condemned me. Who was my lover? That you will never know! You may suspect everyone, but you will never find out. I gave myself up to him, without love and without pleasure, only for the sake of betraying you, and he made me a mother. Which is his child? That also you will never know. I have seven; try and find out! I intended to tell you this later, for one cannot completely avenge oneself on a man by deceiving him, unless he knows it. You have driven me to confess it to-day; now I have finished."

She hurried through the church, toward the open door, expecting to hear behind her the quick steps of her husband, whom she had defied, and to be knocked to the ground by a blow of his fist, but she heard nothing, and reached her carriage. She jumped into it at a bound, overwhelmed with anguish, and breathless with fear; she called out to the coachman, "Home!" and the horses set off at a quick trot.

II.

The Countess de Mascaret was waiting in her room for dinner time, like a criminal sentenced to death awaits the hour of his execution. What was he going to do? Had he come home? Despotic, passionate, ready for any violence as he was, what was he meditating, what had he made up his mind to do? There was no sound in the house, and every moment she looked at the clock. Her maid had come and dressed her for the evening, and had then left the room again. Eight o'clock struck; almost at the same moment there were two knocks at the door, and the butler came in and told her that dinner was ready.

"Has the Count come in?"

"Yes, Madame la Comtesse; he is in the dining-room."

For a moment she felt inclined to arm herself with a small revolver, which she had bought some weeks before, foreseeing the tragedy which was being rehearsed in her heart. But she remembered that all the children would be there, and she took nothing except a smelling-bottle. He rose somewhat ceremoniously from his chair. They exchanged a slight bow, and sat down. The three boys, with their tutor, Abbé Martin, were on her right, and the three girls, with Miss Smith, their English governess, were on her left. The youngest child, who was only three months old, remained upstairs with his nurse.

The Abbé said grace, as was usual when there was no company, for the children did not come down to dinner when there were guests present; then they began dinner. The Countess, suffering from emotion which she had not at all calculated upon, remained with her eyes cast down, while the Count scrutinized, now the three boys, and now the three girls with uncertain, unhappy looks, which traveled from one to the other. Suddenly, pushing his wineglass from him, it broke, and the wine was spilt on the table-cloth, and at the slight noise caused by this little accident, the Countess started up from her chair; and for the first time they looked at each other. Then, almost every moment, in spite of themselves, in spite of the irritation of their nerves caused by every glance, they did not cease to exchange looks, rapid as pistol shots.

The Abbé, who felt that there was some cause for embarrassment which he could not divine, tried to get up a conversation, and started various subjects, but his useless efforts gave rise to no ideas and did not bring out a word. The Countess, with feminine tact and obeying the instincts of a woman of the world, tried to answer him two or three times, but in vain. She could not find words, in the perplexity of her mind, and her own voice almost frightened her in the silence of the large room, where nothing else was heard except the slight sound of plates and knives and forks.

Suddenly, her husband said to her, bending forward: "Here, amid your children, will you swear to me that what you told me just now is true?"

The hatred which was fermenting in her veins suddenly roused her, and replying to that question with the same firmness with which she had replied to his looks, she raised both her hands, the right pointing toward the boys and the left toward the girls, and said in a firm, resolute voice, and without any hesitation: "On the heads of my children, I swear that I have told you the truth."

He got up and throwing his table napkin on to the table with an exasperated movement, turned round and flung his chair against the wall. Then he went out without another word, while she, uttering a deep sigh, as if after a first victory, went on in a calm voice: "You must not pay any attention to what your father has just said, my darlings; he was very much upset a short time ago, but he will be all right again, in a few days."

Then she talked with the Abbé and with Miss Smith, and had tender, pretty words for all her children; those sweet spoiling mother's ways which unlock little hearts.

When dinner was over, she went into the drawing-room with all her little following. She made the elder ones chatter, and when their bedtime came she kissed them for a long time, and then went alone into her room.

She waited, for she had no doubt that he would come, and she made up her mind then, as her children were not with her, to defend her human flesh, as she defended her life as a woman of the world; and in the pocket of her dress she put the little loaded revolver which she had bought a few weeks before. The hours went by, the hours struck, and every sound was hushed in the house. Only cabs continued to rumble through the streets, but their noise was only heard vaguely through the shuttered and curtained windows.

She waited, energetic and nervous, without any fear of him now, ready for anything, and almost triumphant, for she had found means of torturing him continually, during every moment of his life.

But the first gleams of dawn came in through the fringe at the bottom of her curtains, without his having come into her room, and then she awoke to the fact, much to her surprise, that he was not coming. Having locked and bolted her door, for greater security, she went to bed at last, and remained there, with her eyes open, thinking, and barely understanding it all, without being able to guess what he was going to do.

When her maid brought her tea, she

at the same time gave her a letter from her husband. He told her that he was going to undertake a longish journey, and in a postscript he added that his lawyer would provide her with such money as she might require for her expenses.

It was at the opera, between two of the acts in "Robert the Devil." In the stalls, the men were standing up, with their hats on, their waistcoats cut very low so as to show a large amount of white shirt front, in which the gold and precious stones of their studs glistened. They were looking at the boxes crowded with ladies in low dresses, covered with diamonds and pearls, women who seemed to expand like flowers in that illuminated hothouse, where the beauty of their faces and the whiteness of their shoulders seemed to bloom for inspection, in the midst of the music and of human voices.

Two friends, with their backs to the orchestra, were scanning those parterres of elegance, that exhibition of real or false charms, of jewels, of luxury, and of pretension which showed itself off all round the Grand Theater. One of them, Roger de Salnis, said to his companion, Bernard Grandin: "Just look how beautiful Countess de Mascaret still is."

Then the elder, in turn, looked through his opera glasses at a tall lady in a box opposite, who appeared to be still very young, and whose striking beauty seemed to appeal to men's eyes in every corner of the house. Her pale complexion, of an ivory tint, gave her the appearance of a statue, while a small, diamond coronet glistened on her black hair like a cluster of stars.

When he had looked at her for some time, Bernard Grandin replied with a jocular accent of sincere conviction: "You may well call her beautiful!"

"How old do you think she is?"

"Wait a moment. I can tell you exactly, for I have known her since she was a child, and I saw her make her *début* into society when she was quite a girl. She is—she is—thirty—thirty-six."

"Impossible!"

"I am sure of it."

"She looks twenty-five."

"She has had seven children."

"It is incredible."

"And what is more, they are all seven alive, as she is a very good mother. I go to the house, which is a very quiet and pleasant one, occasionally, and she presents the phenomenon of the family in the midst of the world."

"How very strange! And have there never been any reports about her?"

"Never."

"But what about her husband? He is peculiar, is he not?"

"Yes and no. Very likely there has been a little drama between them, one of those little domestic dramas which one suspects, which one never finds out exactly, but which one guesses pretty nearly."

"What is it?"

"I do not know anything about it. Mascaret leads a very fast life now, after having been a model husband. As long as he remained a good spouse, he had a shocking temper and was crabbed and easily took offense, but since he has been leading his present, rackety life, he has become quite indifferent; but one would guess that he has some trouble, a worm gnawing somewhere, for he has aged very much."

Thereupon the two friends talked philosophically for some minutes about the secret, unknowable troubles, which differences of character or perhaps physical antipathies, which were not perceived at first, give rise to in families. Then Roger de Salnis, who was still looking at Madame de Mascaret through his opera-glasses, said.

"It is almost incredible that that woman has had seven children!"

"Yes, in eleven years; after which, when she was thirty, she put a stop to her period of production in order to enter into the brilliant period of entertaining, which does not seem near coming to an end."

"Poor women!"

"Why do you pity them?"

"Why? Ah! my dear fellow, just consider! Eleven years of maternity, for such a woman! What a hell! All her youth, all her beauty, every hope of success, every poetical ideal of a bright life, sacrificed to that abominable law of reproduction which turns the normal woman into a mere machine for maternity."

"What would you have? It is only nature!"

"Yes, but I say that Nature is our enemy, that we must always fight against Nature, for she is continually bringing us back to an animal state. You may be sure that God has not put anything on this earth that is clean, pretty, elegant, or accessory to our ideal, but the human brain has done it. It is we who have introduced a little grace, beauty, unknown charm, and

mystery into creation by singing about it, interpreting it, by admiring it as poets, idealizing it as artists, and by explaining it as learned men who make mistakes, who find ingenious reasons, some grace and beauty, some unknown charm and mystery in the various phenomena of nature.

"God only created coarse beings, full of the germs of disease, and who, after a few years of bestial enjoyment, grow old and infirm, with all the ugliness and all the want of power of human decrepitude. He only seems to have made them in order that they may reproduce their species in a repulsive manner, and then die like ephemeral insects. I said, *reproduce their species in a repulsive manner,* and I adhere to that expression. What is there as a matter of fact, more ignoble and more repugnant than that ridiculous act of the reproduction of living beings, against which all delicate minds always have revolted, and always will revolt? Since all the organs which have been invented by this economical and malicious Creator serve two purposes, why did he not choose those that were unsullied, in order to intrust them with that sacred mission, which is the noblest and the most exalted of all human functions? The mouth which nourishes the body by means of material food, also diffuses abroad speech and thought. Our flesh revives itself by means of itself, and at the same time, ideas are communicated by it. The sense of smell, which gives the vital air to the lungs, imparts all the perfumes of the world to the brain: the smell of flowers, of woods, of trees, of the sea. The ear, which enables us to communicate with our fellowmen, has also allowed us to invent music, to create dreams, happiness, the infinite, and even physical pleasure, by means of sounds!

"But one might say that the Creator wished to prohibit man from ever ennobling and idealizing his commerce with women. Nevertheless, man has found love, which is not a bad reply to that sly Deity, and he has ornamented it so much with literary poetry, that woman often forgets the contact she is obliged to submit to. Those among us who are powerless to deceive themselves have invented vice and refined debauchery, which is another way of laughing at God, and of paying homage, immodest homage, to beauty.

"But the normal man makes children; just a beast that is coupled with another by law.

"Look at that woman! Is it not abominable to think that such a jewel, such a pearl, born to be beautiful, admired, fêted, and adored, has spent eleven years of her life in providing heirs for the Count de Mascaret?"

Bernard Grandin replied with a laugh: "There is a great deal of truth in all that, but very few people would understand you."

Salnis got more and more animated. "Do you know how I picture God myself?" he said. "As an enormous, creative organ unknown to us, who scatters millions of worlds into space, just as one single fish would deposit its spawn in the sea. He creates, because it is His function as God to do so, but He does not know what He is doing, and is stupidly prolific in His work, and is ignorant of the combinations of all kinds which are produced by His scat-

tered germs. Human thought is a lucky little local, passing accident, which was totally unforeseen, and is condemned to disappear with this earth, and to recommence perhaps here or elsewhere, the same or different, with fresh combinations of eternally new beginnings. We owe it to this slight accident which has happened to His intellect, that we are very uncomfortable in this world which was not made for us, which had not been prepared to receive us, to lodge and feed us, or to satisfy reflecting beings, and we owe it to Him also that we have to struggle without ceasing against what are still called the designs of Providence, when we are really refined and civilized beings."

Grandin, who was listening to him attentively, as he had long known the surprising outbursts of his fancy, asked him: "Then you believe that human thought is the spontaneous product of blind, divine parturition?"

"Naturally. A fortuitous function of the nerve-centers of our brain, like some unforeseen chemical action which is due to new mixtures, and which also resembles a product of electricity, caused by friction or the unexpected proximity of some substance, and which, lastly, resembles the phenomena caused by the infinite and fruitful fermentations of living matter.

"But, my dear fellow, the truth of this must be evident to anyone who looks about him. If human thought, ordained by an omniscient Creator, had been intended to be what it has become, altogether different from mechanical thoughts and resignation, so exacting, inquiring, agitated, tormented, would the world which was created to receive the beings which we now are have been this unpleasant little dwelling place for poor fools, this salad plot, this rocky, wooded, and spherical kitchen garden where your improvident Providence has destined us to live naked, in caves or under trees, nourished on the flesh of slaughtered animals, our brethren, or on raw vegetables nourished by the sun and the rain?

"But it is sufficient to reflect for a moment, in order to understand that this world was not made for such creatures as we are. Thought, which is developed by a miracle in the nerves of the cells and our brain, powerless, ignorant, and confused as it is, and as it will always remain, makes all of us who are intellectual beings eternal and wretched exiles on earth.

"Look at this earth, as God has given it to those who inhabit it. Is it not visibly and solely made, planted and covered with forests, for the sake of animals? What is there for us? Nothing. And for them? Everything. They have nothing to do but to eat, or go hunting and eat each other, according to their instincts, for God never foresaw gentleness and peaceable manners; He only foresaw the death of creatures which were bent on destroying and devouring each other. Are not the quail, the pigeon, and the partridge the natural prey of the hawk? the sheep, the stag, and the ox that of the great flesh-eating animals, rather than meat that has been fattened to be served up to us with truffles, which have been unearthed by pigs, for our special benefit?

"As to ourselves, the more civilized, intellectual, and refined we are, the more we ought to conquer and subdue that animal instinct, which represents the will of God in us. And so, in order to mitigate our lot as brutes, we have discovered and made everything, beginning with houses, then exquisite food, sauces, sweetmeats, pastry, drink, stuffs, clothes, ornaments, beds, mattresses, carriages, railways, and innumerable machines, besides arts and sciences, writing and poetry. Every ideal comes from us as well as the amenities of life, in order to make our existence as simple reproducers, for which divine Providence solely intended us, less monotonous and less hard.

"Look at this theater. Is there not here a human world created by us, unforeseen and unknown by Eternal destinies, comprehensible by our minds alone, a sensual and intellectual distraction, which has been invented solely by and for that discontented and restless little animal that we are.

"Look at that woman, Madame de Mascaret. God intended her to live in a cave naked, or wrapped up in the skins of wild animals, but is she not better as she is? But, speaking of her, does anyone know why and how her brute of a husband, having such a companion by his side, and especially after having been boorish enough to make her a mother seven times, has suddenly left her, to run after bad women?"

Grandin replied: "Oh! my dear fellow, this is probably the only reason. He found that always living with her was becoming too expensive in the end, and from reasons of domestic economy, he has arrived at the same principles which you lay down as a philosopher."

Just then the curtain rose for the

third act, and they turned round, took off their hats, and sat down.

IV.

The Count and Countess Mascaret were sitting side by side in the carriage which was taking them home from the opera, without speaking. But suddenly the husband said to his wife: "Gabrielle!"

"What do you want?"

"Don't you think that this has lasted long enough?"

"What?"

"The horrible punishment to which you have condemned me for the last six years."

"What do you want? I cannot help it."

"Then tell me which of them it is?"

"Never."

"Think that I can no longer see my children or feel them round me, without having my heart burdened with this doubt. Tell me which of them it is, and I swear that I will forgive you, and treat it like the others."

"I have not the right to."

"You do not see that I can no longer endure this life, this thought which is wearing me out, or this question which I am constantly asking myself, this question which tortures me each time I look at them. It is driving me mad."

"Then you have suffered a great deal?" she said.

"Terribly. Should I, without that, have accepted the horror of living by your side, and the still greater horror of feeling and knowing that there is one among them whom I cannot recognize, and who prevents me from loving the others?"

She repeated: "Then you have really suffered very much?" And he replied in a constrained and sorrowful voice:

"Yes, for do I not tell you every day that it is intolerable torture to me? Should I have remained in that house, near you and them, if I did not love them Oh! You have behaved abominably toward me. All the affection of my heart I have bestowed upon my children, and that you know. I am for them a father of the olden time, as I was for you a husband of one of the families of old, for by instinct I have remained a natural man, a man of former days. Yes, I will confess it, you have made me terribly jealous, because you are a woman of another race, of another soul, with other requirements. Oh! I shall never forget the things that you told me, but from that day, I troubled myself no more about you. I did not kill you, because then I should have had no means on earth of ever discovering which of our—of your children is not mine. I have waited, but I have suffered more than you would believe, for I can no longer venture to love them, except, perhaps, the two eldest; I no longer venture to look at them, to call them to me, to kiss them; I cannot take them on to my knee without asking myself: 'Can it be this one?' I have been correct in my behavior toward you for six years, and even kind and complaisant; tell me the truth, and I swear that I will do nothing unkind."

He thought, in spite of the darkness of the carriage, that he could perceive that she was moved, and feeling certain that she was going to speak at last, he said: "I beg you, I beseech you to tell me."

"I have been more guilty than you think perhaps," she replied; "but I could no longer endure that life of continual pregnancy, and I had only one means of driving you from my bed. I lied before God, and I lied, with my hand raised to my children's heads, for I have never wronged you."

He seized her arm in the darkness, and squeezing it as he had done on that terrible day of their drive in the Bois de Boulogne, he stammered: "Is that true?"

"It is true."

But he in terrible grief said with a groan: "I shall have fresh doubts that will never end! When did you lie, the last time or now? How am I to believe you at present? How can one believe a woman after that? I shall never again know what I am to think. I would rather you had said to me: 'It is Jacques, or, it is Jeanne.'"

The carriage drove them into the courtyard of their mansion, and when it had drawn up in front of the steps, the Count got down first as usual, and offered his wife his arm, to help her up. And then, as soon as they had reached the first floor he said: "May I speak to you for a few moments longer?"

And she replied: "I am quite willing."

They went into a small drawing-room, while a footman in some surprise, lit the wax candles. As soon as he had left the room and they were alone, he continued: "How am I to know the truth? I have begged you a thousand times to speak, but you have remained dumb, impenetrable, inflexible, inexorable, and now to-day, you tell me that you have been lying. For six years you have

actually allowed me to believe such a thing! No, you are lying now, I do not know why, but out of pity for me, perhaps?"

She replied in a sincere and convincing manner: "If I had not done so, I should have had four more children in the last six years!"

And he exclaimed: "Can a mother speak like that?"

"Oh!" she replied, "I do not at all feel that I am the mother of children who have never been born, it is enough for me to be the mother of those that I have, and to love them with all my heart. I am—we are—women who belong to the civilized world, Monsieur, and we are no longer, and we refuse to be, mere females who restock the earth."

She got up, but he seized her hands. "Only one word, Gabrielle. Tell me the truth!"

"I have just told you. I have never dishonored you."

He looked her full in the face, and how beautiful she was, with her gray eyes, like the cold sky. In her dark hair dress, on that opaque night of black hair, there shone the diamond coronet, like a cluster of stars. Then he suddenly felt, felt by a kind of intuition, that this grand creature was not merely a being destined to perpetuate his race, but the strange and mysterious product of all the complicated desires which have been accumulating in us for centuries but which have been turned aside from their primitive and divine object, and which have wandered after a mystic, imperfectly seen, and intangible beauty. There are some women like that, women who blossom only for our dreams, adorned with every poetical attribute of civilization, with that ideal luxury, coquetry, and æsthetic charm which should surround the living statue who brightens our life.

Her husband remained standing before her, stupefied at the tardy and obscure discovery, confusedly hitting on the cause of his former jealousy, and understanding it all very imperfectly. At last he said: "I believe you, for I feel at this moment that you are not lying, and formerly, I really thought that you were."

She put out her hand to him: "We are friends then?"

He took her hand and kissed it, and replied: "We are friends. Thank you, Gabrielle."

Then he went out, still looking at her, and surprised that she was still so beautiful, and feeling a strange emotion arising in him, which was, perhaps, more formidable than antique and simple love.

An Affair of State

PARIS had just heard of the disaster of Sedan. The Republic was proclaimed. All France was panting from a madness that lasted until the time of the Commonwealth. Everybody was playing at soldier from one end of the country to the other.

Capmakers became colonels, assuming the duties of generals; revolvers and daggers were displayed on large rotund bodies, enveloped in red sashes; common citizens turned warriors, commanding battalions of noisy volunteers, and swearing like troopers to emphasize their importance.

The very fact of bearing arms and handling guns with a system excited a people who hitherto had only handled scales and measures, and made them formidable to the first comer, without reason. They even executed a few innocent people to prove that they knew how to kill; and, in roaming through virgin fields still belonging to the Prussians, they shot stray dogs, cows chewing the cud in peace, or sick horses put out to pasture. Each believed himself called upon to play a great rôle in military affairs. The cafès of the smallest villages, full of tradesmen in uniform, resembled barracks or field hospitals.

Now, the town of Canneville did not yet know the exciting news of the army and the Capital. It had, however, been greatly agitated for a month over an encounter between the rival political parties. The mayor, Viscount de Varnetot, a small, thin man, already old, remained true to the Empire, especially since he saw rising up against him a powerful adversary, in the great, sanguine form of Doctor Massarel, head of the Republican party in the district, venerable chief of the Masonic lodge, president of the Society of Agriculture and the Fire Department, and organizer of the rural militia designed to save the country.

In two weeks he had induced sixty-three men to volunteer in defense of their country—married men, fathers of families, prudent farmers and merchants of the town. These he drilled every morning in front of the mayor's window.

Whenever the mayor happened to appear, Commander Massarel, covered with pistols, passing proudly up and down in front of his troops, would make them shout, "Long live our country!" And this, they noticed, disturbed the little viscount, who no doubt heard in it menace and defiance, and perhaps some odious recollection of the great Revolution.

On the morning of the fifth of September, in uniform, his revolver on the table, the doctor gave consultation to an old peasant couple. The husband had suffered with a varicose vein for seven years, but had waited until his wife had one too, so that they might go and hunt up a physician together, guided by the postman when he should come with the newspaper.

Dr. Massarel opened the door, grew pale, straightened himself abruptly and, raising his arms to heaven in a gesture of exaltation, cried out with all his might, in the face of the amazed rustics:

"Long live the Republic! Long live the Republic! Long live the Republic!"

Then he dropped into his armchair weak with emotion.

When the peasant explained that this sickness commenced with a feeling as if ants were running up and down in his legs, the doctor exclaimed: "Hold your peace. I have spent too much time with you stupid people. The Republic is proclaimed! The Emperor is a prisoner! France is saved! Long live the Republic!" And, running to the

door, he bellowed: "Celeste! Quick! Celeste!"

The frightened maid hastened in. He stuttered, so rapidly did he try to speak: "My boots, my saber—my cartridge box—and—the Spanish dagger, which is on my night table. Hurry now!"

The obstinate peasant, taking advantage of the moment's silence, began again: "This seemed like some cysts that hurt me when I walked."

The exasperated physician shouted: "Hold your peace! For Heaven's sake! If you had washed your feet oftener, it would not have happened." Then, seizing him by the neck, he hissed in his face: "Can you not comprehend that we are living in a Republic, stupid?"

But professional sentiment calmed him suddenly, and he let the astonished old couple out of the house, repeating all the time:

"Return to-morrow, return to-morrow, my friends; I have no more time to-day."

While equipping himself from head to foot, he gave another series of urgent orders to the maid:

"Run to Lieutenant Picard's and to Sub-lieutenant Pommel's and say to them that I want them here immediately. Send Torcheboeuf to me, too, with his drum. Quick, now! Quick!" And when Celeste was gone, he collected his thoughts and prepared to surmount the difficulties of the situation.

The three men arrived together. They were in their working clothes. The Commander, who had expected to see them in uniform, had a fit of surprise.

"You know nothing, then? The Emperor has been taken prisoner. A Republic is proclaimed. My position is delicate, not to say perilous."

He reflected for some minutes before the astonished faces of his subordinates and then continued:

"It is necessary to act, not to hesitate. Minutes now are worth hours at other times. Everything depends upon promptness of decision. You, Picard, go and find the curate and get him to ring the bell to bring the people together, while I get ahead of them. You, Torcheboeuf, beat the call to assemble the militia in arms, in the square, from even as far as the hamlets of Gerisaie and Salmare. You, Pommel, put on your uniform at once, that is, the jacket and cap. We, together, are going to take possession of the mairie and summon M. de Varnetot to transfer his authority to me. Do you understand?"

"Yes."

"Act, then, and promptly. I will accompany you to your house, Pommel, since we are to work together."

Five minutes later, the Commander and his subaltern, armed to the teeth, appeared in the square, just at the moment when the little Viscount de Varnetot, with hunting gaiters on and his rifle on his shoulder, appeared by another street, walking rapidly and followed by three guards in green jackets, each carrying a knife at his side and a gun over his shoulder.

While the doctor stopped, half stupefied, the four men entered the mayor's house and the door closed behind them.

"We are forestalled," murmured the doctor; "it will be necessary now to wait for re-enforcements; nothing can be done for a quarter of an hour."

Here Lieutenant Picard appeared:

"The curate refuses to obey," said he; "he has even shut himself up in the church with the beadle and the porter."

On the other side of the square, opposite the white, closed front of the mairie, the church, mute and black, showed its great oak door with the wrought-iron trimmings.

Then, as the puzzled inhabitants put their noses out of the windows, or came out upon the steps of their houses, the rolling of a drum was heard, and Torcheboeuf suddenly appeared, beating with fury the three quick strokes of the call to arms. He crossed the square with disciplined step, and then disappeared on a road leading to the country.

The Commander drew his sword, advanced alone to the middle distance between the two buildings where the enemy was barricaded and, waving his weapon above his head, roared at the top of his lungs: "Long live the Republic! Death to traitors!" Then he fell back where his officers were. The butcher, the baker, and the apothecary, feeling a little uncertain, put up their shutters and closed their shops. The grocery alone remained open.

Meanwhile the men of the militia were arriving, little by little, variously clothed, but all wearing caps, the cap constituting the whole uniform of the corps. They were armed with their old, rusty guns, guns that had hung on chimney-pieces in kitchens for thirty years, and looked quite like a detachment of country soldiers.

When there were about thirty around him, the Commander explained in a few words, the state of affairs. Then, turning toward his major, he said: "Now, we must act."

While the inhabitants collected, talked over and discussed the matter, the doctor quickly formed his plan of campaign:

"Lieutenant Picard, you advance to the windows of the mayor's house and order M. de Varnetot to turn over the townhall to me, in the name of the Republic."

But the lieutenant was a master-mason and refused.

"You are a scamp, you are. Trying to make a target of me! Those fellows in there are good shots, you know that. No, thanks! Execute your commissions yourself!"

The Commander turned red: "I order you to go in the name of discipline," said he.

"I am not spoiling my features without knowing why," the lieutenant returned.

Men of influence, in a group near by, were heard laughing. One of them called out: "You are right, Picard, it is not the proper time." The doctor, under his breath, muttered: "Cowards!" And, placing his sword and his revolver in the hands of a soldier, he advanced with measured step, his eye fixed on the windows, as if he expected to see a gun or a cannon pointed at him.

When he was within a few steps of the building the doors at the two extremities, affording an entrance to two schools, opened, and a flood of little creatures, boys on one side, girls on the other, poured out and began playing in the open space, chattering around the doctor like a flock of birds. He scarcely knew what to make of it.

As soon as the last were out, the doors closed. The greater part of the little monkeys finally scattered, and then the Commander called out in a loud voice:

"Monsieur de Varnetot?" A window in the first story opened and M. de Varnetot appeared.

The Commander began: "Monsieur, you are aware of the great events which have changed the system of Government. The party you represent no longer exists. The side I represent now comes into power. Under these sad, but decisive circumstances, I come to demand you, in the name of the Republic, to put in my hand the authority vested in you by the out-going power."

M. de Varnetot replied: "Doctor Massarel, I am mayor of Canneville, so placed by the proper authorities, and mayor of Canneville I shall remain until the title is revoked and replaced by an order from my superiors. As mayor, I am at home in the mairie, and there I shall stay. Furthermore, just try to put me out." And he closed the window.

The Commander returned to his troops. But, before explaining anything, measuring Lieutenant Picard from head to foot, he said:

"You are a numskull, you are,—a goose, the disgrace of the army. I shall degrade you."

The Lieutenant replied: "I'll attend to that myself." And he went over to a group of muttering civilians.

Then the doctor hesitated. What should he do? Make an assault? Would his men obey him? And then, was he surely in the right? An idea burst upon him. He ran to the telegraph office, on the other side of the square, and hurriedly sent three dispatches:

"To the Members of the Republican Government, at Paris"; "To the New Republican Prefect of the Lower Seine, at Rouen"; "To the New Republican Sub-Prefect of Dieppe."

He exposed the situation fully; told of the danger run by the commonwealth from remaining in the hands of the monarchistic mayor, offered his devout services, asked for orders and signed his name, following it up with all his titles. Then he returned to his army corps and, drawing ten francs out of his pocket, said:

"Now, my friends, go and eat and drink a little something. Only leave here a detachment of ten men, so that no one leaves the mayor's house."

Ex-Lieutenant Picard chatting with the watch-maker, overheard this. With a sneer he remarked: "Pardon me, but if they go out, there will be an opportunity for you to go in. Otherwise, I can't see how you are to get in there!"

The doctor made no reply, but went away to luncheon. In the afternoon, he disposed of offices all about town, having the air of knowing of an impending surprise. Many times he passed before the doors of the mairie and of the church, without noticing anything suspicious; one could have believed the two buildings empty.

The butcher, the baker, and the apothecary reopened their shops, and stood gossiping on the steps. If the Emperor had been taken prisoner, there must be a traitor somewhere. They did not feel sure of the revenue of a new Republic.

Night came on. Toward nine o'clock, the doctor returned quietly and alone to the mayor's residence, persuaded that his adversary had retired. And, as he was trying to force an entrance with a few blows of a pickaxe, the loud voice of a guard demanded suddenly: "Who goes there?" Monsieur Massarel beat a retreat at the top of his speed.

Another day dawned without any change in the situation. The militia in arms occupied the square. The inhabitants stood around awaiting the solution. People from neighboring villages came to look on. Finally, the doctor, realizing that his reputation was at stake, resolved to settle the thing in one way or another. He had just decided that it must be something energetic, when the door of the telegraph office opened and the little servant of the directress appeared, holding in her hand two papers.

She went directly to the Commander and gave him one of the dispatches; then, crossing the square, intimidated by so many eyes fixed upon her, with lowered head and mincing steps, she rapped gently at the door of the barricaded house, as if ignorant that a part of the army was concealed there.

The door opened slightly; the hand of a man received the message, and the girl returned, blushing and ready to weep, from being stared at.

The doctor demanded, with stirring voice: "A little silence, if you please." And, after the populace became quiet, he continued proudly:

"Here is a communication which I have received from the Government." And raising the dispatch, he read:

"Old mayor deposed. Advise us what is most necessary. Instructions later.

"For the Sub-Prefect,
"SAPIN, *Counselor.*"

He had triumphed. His heart was beating with joy. His hand trembled, when Picard, his old subaltern, cried out to him from a neighboring group: "That's all right; but if the others in there won't go out, your paper hasn't a leg to stand on." The doctor grew a little pale. If they would not go out —in fact, he must go ahead now. It was not only his right, but his duty. And he looked anxiously at the house of the mayoralty, hoping that he might see the door open and his adversary show himself. But the door remained closed. What was to be done? The crowd was increasing, surrounding the militia. Some laughed.

One thought, especially, tortured the doctor. If he should make an assault, he must march at the head of his men; and as, with him dead, all contest would cease, it would be at him, and at him alone that M. de Varnetot and the three guards would aim. And their aim was good, very good! Picard had reminded him of that.

But an idea shone in upon him, and turning to Pommel, he said: "Go, quickly, and ask the apothecary to send me a napkin and a pole."

The Lieutenant hurried off. The doctor was going to make a political banner, a white one, that would perhaps, rejoice the heart of that old legitimist, the mayor.

Pommel returned with the required linen and a broom handle. With some pieces of string, they improvised a standard, which Massarel seized in both hands. Again, he advanced toward the house of mayoralty, bearing the standard before him. When in front of the door, he called out: "Monsieur de Varnetot!"

The door opened suddenly, and M. de Varnetot and the three guards appeared on the threshold. The doctor recoiled, instinctively. Then, he saluted his enemy courteously, and announced, almost strangled by emotion: "I have come, sir, to communicate to you the instructions I have just received."

That gentleman, without any salutation whatever, replied: "I am going to withdraw, sir, but you must understand that it is not because of fear, or in obedience to an odious government that has usurped the power." And, biting off each word, he declared: "I do not wish to have the appearance of serving the Republic for a single day. That is all."

Massarel, amazed, made no reply; and M. de Varnetot, walking off at a rapid pace, disappeared around the corner, followed closely by his escort. Then the doctor, slightly dismayed, returned to the crowd. When he was near enough to be heard, he cried: "Hurrah! Hurrah! The Republic triumphs all along the line!"

But no emotion was manifested. The doctor tried again: "The people are free! You are free and independent! Do you understand? Be proud of it!"

The listless villagers looked at him with eyes unlit by glory. In his turn, he looked at them, indignant at their indifference, seeking for some word that could make a grand impression, electrify this placid country and make good his mission. The inspiration came, and turning to Pommel, he said: "Lieutenant, go and get the bust of the ex-Emperor, which is in the Council Hall, and bring it to me with a chair."

And soon the man reappears, carrying on his right shoulder, Napoleon III. in plaster, and holding in his left hand a straw-bottomed chair.

Massarel met him, took the chair, placed it on the ground, put the white image upon it, fell back a few steps and called out, in sonorous voice:

"Tyrant! Tyrant! Here do you fall! Fall in the dust and in the mire. An expiring country groans under your feet. Destiny has called you the Avenger. Defeat and shame cling to you. You fall conquered, a prisoner to the Prussians, and upon the ruins of the crumbling Empire the young and radiant Republic arises, picking up your broken sword."

He awaited applause. But there was no voice, no sound. The bewildered peasants remained silent. And the bust, with its pointed mustaches extending beyond the cheeks on each side, the bust, so motionless and well groomed as to be fit for a hairdresser's sign, seemed to be looking at M. Massarel with a plaster smile, a smile ineffaceable and mocking.

They remained thus face to face, Napoleon on the chair, the doctor in front of him about three steps away. Suddenly the Commander grew angry. What was to be done? What was there that would move this people, and bring about a definite victory in opinion? His hand happened to rest on his hip and to

come in contact there with the butt end of his revolver, under his red sash. No inspiration, no further word would come. But he drew his pistol, advanced two steps, and, taking aim, fired at the late monarch. The ball entered the forehead, leaving a little, black hole, like a spot, nothing more. There was no effect. Then he fired a second shot, which made a second hole, then, a third; and then, without stopping, he emptied his revolver. The brow of Napoleon disappeared in white powder, but the eyes, the nose, and the fine points of the mustaches remained intact. Then, exasperated, the doctor over-turned the chair with a blow of his fist and, resting a foot on the remainder of the bust in a position of triumph, he shouted: "So let all tyrants perish!"

Still no enthusiasm was manifest, and as the spectators seemed to be in a kind of stupor from astonishment, the Commander called to the militiamen: "You may now go to your homes." And he went toward his own house with great strides, as if he were pursued.

His maid, when he appeared, told him that some patients had been waiting in his office for three hours. He hastened in. There were the two varicose-vein patients, who had returned at daybreak, obstinate but patient.

The old man immediately began his explanation: "This began by a feeling like ants running up and down the legs."

----●----

Babette

Chaff

I WAS not very fond of inspecting that asylum for old, infirm people officially, as I was obliged to go over it in

company of the superintendent, who was talkative and a statistician. But then the grandson of the foundress accompanied us, and was evidently pleased at that minute inspection. He was a charming man, and the owner of a large forest, where he had given me permission to shoot, and I was of course obliged to pretend to be interested in his grandmother's philanthropic work. So with a smile on my lips, I endured the superintendent's interminable discourse, punctuating it here and there, as best as I could by:

"Ah! really! Very strange indeed! I should never have believed it!"

I was absolutely ignorant of the remark to which I replied thus, for my thoughts were lulled to repose by the constant humming of our loquacious guide. I was vaguely conscious that the persons and things might have appeared worthy of attention to me, if I had been there alone as an idler, for in that case, I should certainly have asked the superintendent: "What is this Babette, whose name appears so constantly in the complaints of so many of the inmates."

Quite a dozen men and women had spoken to us about her, now to complain of her, now to praise her; and especially the women, as soon as they saw the superintendent, cried out:

"M'sieur, Babette has again been—"

"There! that will do, that will do!" he interrupted them, his gentle voice suddenly becoming harsh.

At other times he would amicably question some old man with a happy countenance, and say:

"Well, my friend! I suppose you are very happy here?"

Many replied with fervent expressions of gratitude, with which Babette's name was frequently mingled. When he heard them speak so, the superintendent put

on an ecstatic air, looked up to heaven with clasped hands, and said, slowly shaking his head: "Ah! Babette is a very precious woman, very precious!"

Yes, it would certainly interest one to know who that creature was, but not under present circumstances, and so, rather than to undergo any more of this, I made up my mind to remain in ignorance of who Babette was, for I could pretty well guess what she would be like. I pictured her to myself as a flower that had sprung up in a corner of these dull courtyards, like a ray of sun shining through the sepulchral gloom of these dismal passages.

I pictured her so clearly to myself, that I did not even feel any wish to know her. Yet she was dear to me, because of the happy expression which they all put on when they spoke of her, and I was angry with the old women who spoke against her. One thing, certainly, puzzled me, and that was, that the superintendent was among those who went into ecstasies over her, and this made me strongly disinclined to question him about her, though I had no other reason for the feeling.

But all this passed through my mind in rather a confused manner, without my taking the trouble to fix or to formulate any ideas or explanations. I continued to dream rather than to think effectively, and it is very probable that, when my visit was over, I should not have remembered much about it, not even with regard to Babette, if I had not been suddenly awakened by the sight of her in the flesh, and been quite upset by the difference that there was between my fancy and the reality.

We had just crossed a small back

yard, and had gone into a very dark passage, when a door suddenly opened at the other end of it, and an unexpected apparition appeared. We could indistinctly see that it was the figure of a woman. At the same moment, the superintendent called out in a furious voice:

"Babette! Babette!"

He had mechanically quickened his pace, and almost ran. We followed him, and he quickly opened the door through which the apparition had vanished. It led on to a staircase, and he again called out, but a burst of stifled laughter was the only reply. I looked over the balustrade, and saw a woman down below, who was looking at us fixedly.

She was an old woman—there could be no doubt of that, from her wrinkled face, and the few straggling gray locks which appeared under her cap. But one did not think of that when one saw her eyes, which were wonderfully youthful, in fact, one saw nothing but them. They were profound eyes, of a deep, almost violet blue; the eyes of a child.

Suddenly the superintendent called out to her: "You have been with *La Frieze* again!"

The old woman did not reply, but shook with laughter, as she had done just before; and then she ran off, giving the superintendent a look, which said as plainly as words could have done: "Do you think I care a fig for you?"

Those insulting words were clearly written in her face, and at the same time I noticed that the old woman's eyes had utterly changed, for during that short moment of bravado, the childish eyes had become the eyes of a monkey, of some ferocious, obstinate baboon.

This time, in spite of my dislike to question him further, I could not help saying to him: "That is Babette, I suppose?"

"Yes," he replied, growing rather red, as if he guessed that I understood the old woman's insulting looks.

"Is she the woman who is so precious?" I added, with a touch of irony, which made him grow altogether crimson.

"That is she," he said, walking on quickly, so as to escape my further questions.

But I was egged on by curiosity, and I made a direct appeal to our host's complaisance: "I should like to see this *Frieze*," I said. "Who is *Frieze?*"

He turned round, and said: "Oh! nothing, nothing, he is not at all interesting. What is the good of seeing him? It is not worth while."

And he ran downstairs, two steps at a time. He who was usually so minute, and so very careful to explain everything, was now in a hurry to get finished, and our visit was cut short.

The next day I had to leave that part of the country, without hearing anything more about Babette, but I came back about four months later, when the shooting season began. I had not forgotten her during that time, for nobody could ever forget her eyes, and so I was very glad to have as my traveling companion, on my three hours' diligence journey from the station to my friend's house, a man who talked to me about her all the time.

He was a young magistrate whom I had already met, and who had much interested me by his wit, by his close manner of observing things, by his singularly refined casuistry, and, above all, by the contrast between his professional severity and his tolerant philosophy.

But he never appeared so attractive to me as he did on that day, when he told me the history of the mysterious Babette.

He had inquired into it, and had applied all his facilities as an examining magistrate to it, for, like me, his visit to the asylum had roused his curiosity. This is what he had learned and what he told me.

When she was ten years old, Babette had been violated by her own father, and at thirteen had been sent to the house of correction for vagabondage and debauchery. From the time she was twenty until she was forty, she had been a servant in the neighborhood, frequently changing her situations, and being nearly everywhere her employer's mistress. She had ruined several families without getting any money herself, and without gaining any definite position. A shopkeeper had committed suicide on her account, and a respectable young fellow had turned thief and incendiary, and had finished at the hulks.

She had been married twice, and had twice been left a widow, and for ten years, until she was fifty, she had been the only courtesan in the district.

"She was very pretty, I suppose?"

"No, she never was that. It seems she was short, thin, with no bust or hips, at her best, I am told, and nobody can remember that she was pretty, even when she was young."

"Then how can you explain?"

"How?" the magistrate exclaimed.

"Well! what about the eyes? You could not have looked at them?"

"Yes, yes, you are right," I replied. "Those eyes explain many things, certainly. They are the eyes of an innocent child."

"Ah!" he exclaimed again, enthusiastically, "Cleopatra, Diana of Poitiers, Ninon de L'Enchlos, all the queens of love who were adored when they were growing old, must have had eyes like hers. A woman who has such eyes can never grow old. But if Babette lives to be a hundred, she will always be loved as she has been, and as she is."

"As she is! Bah! By whom, pray?"

"By all the old men in the asylum, by Jove; by all those who have preserved a fiber that can be touched, a corner of their heart that can be inflamed, or the least spark of desire left."

"Do you think so?"

"I am sure of it. And the superintendent loves her more than any of them."

"Impossible!"

"I would stake my head on it."

"Well, after all it is possible, and even probable; it is even certain. I now remember."

And I again saw the insulting, ferocious, familiar look which she had given the superintendent.

"And who is *La Frieze?*" I asked the magistrate suddenly. "I suppose you know that also?"

"He is a retired butcher, who had both his legs frozen in the war of 1870, and of whom she is very fond. No doubt he is a cripple, with two wooden legs, but still a vigorous man enough, in spite of his fifty-three years. The loins of a Hercules, and the face of a satyr. The superintendent is quite jealous of him!"

I thought the matter over again, and it seemed very probable to me. "Does she love *La Frieze?*"

"Yes, he is the chosen lover."

When we arrived at the host's house a short time afterward, we were surprised to find everybody in a terrible state of excitement. A crime had been committed in the asylum; the gendarmes were there and our host was with them, so we instantly joined them. *La Frieze* had murdered the superintendent, and they gave us the details, which were horrible. The former butcher had hidden behind a door, and catching hold of the other, had rolled on to the ground with him and bitten him in the throat, tearing out his carotid artery, from which the blood spurted into the murderer's face.

I saw him, *La Frieze*. His fat face, which had been badly washed, was still blood stained; he had a low forehead, square jaws, pointed ears, sticking out from his head, and flat nostrils, like the muzzle of some wild animal; but above all, I saw Babette.

She was smiling, and at that moment, her eyes had not their monkey-like and ferocious expression; they were pleading and tender, full of the sweetest childlike candor.

"You know," my host said to me in a low voice, "that the poor woman has fallen into senile imbecility, and that is the cause of her looks, which are strange, considering the terrible sight she has seen."

"Do you think so?" the magistrate said. "You must remember that she is not yet sixty, and I do not think that it is a case of senile imbecility, but that she is quite conscious of the crime that has been committed."

"Then why should she smile?"

"Because she is pleased at what she has done."

"Oh! no, you are really too subtle!"

The magistrate suddenly turned to Babette, and, looking at her steadily, he said:

"I suppose you know what has happened, and why this crime was committed?"

She left off smiling, and her pretty, childlike eyes became abominable monkey's eyes again, and then the answer was suddenly to pull up her petticoats and to show us the lower part of her limbs. Yes, the magistrate had been quite right. That old woman had been a Cleopatra, a Diana, a Ninon de l'Enclos, and the rest of her body had remained like a child's even more than her eyes. We were thunderstruck at the sight.

"Pigs! pigs!" *La Frieze* shouted to us, "you also want to have something to do with her!"

And I saw that actually the magistrate's face was pale and contracted, and that his hands and lips trembled like those of a man caught in the act of doing wrong.

———•———

A Cock Crowed

MADAME BERTHA D'AVANCELLES had up till that time resisted all the prayers of her despairing adorer, Baron Joseph de Croissard. He had pursued her ardently in Paris during the winter, and now he was giving fêtes and shooting parties in her honor at his château at Carville, in Normandy.

Monsieur d'Avancelles, her husband, saw nothing and knew nothing, as usual. It was said that he lived apart from his wife on account of a physical weakness for which Madame d'Avancelles would not pardon him. He was a short, stout, bald man, with short arms, legs, neck, nose, and very ugly, while Madame d'Avancelles, on the contrary, was a tall, dark, and determined young woman, who laughed in her husband's face with sonorous peals, while he called her openly "Mrs. Housewife." She looked at the broad shoulders, strong build, and fair mustaches of her titled admirer, Baron Joseph de Croissard, with a certain amount of tenderness.

She had not, however, granted him anything as yet. The baron was ruining himself for her, and there was a constant round of fêting, hunting parties, and new pleasures, to which he invited the neighboring nobility. All day long the hounds gave tongue in the woods, as they followed the fox or the wild boar, and every night dazzling fireworks mingled their burning plumes with the stars, while the illuminated windows of the drawing-room cast long rays of light on to the wide lawns, where shadows were moving to and fro.

It was autumn, the russet-colored season of the year, and the leaves were whirling about on the grass like flights of birds. One noticed the smell of damp earth in the air, of the naked earth, like one scents the odor of the bare skin, when a woman's dress falls off her, after a ball.

One evening, in the previous spring, during an entertainment, Madame d'Avancelles had said to Monsieur de Croissard, who was worrying her by his importunities: "If I do succumb to you, my friend, it will not be before the fall of the leaf. I have too many things to do this summer to have any time for it." He had not forgotten that bold and amusing speech, and every day he became more pressing, every day he pushed his approaches nearer,—to use a military phrase,—and gained a hold on the heart of the fair, audacious woman, who seemed only to be resisting for form's sake.

It was the day before a large wild-boar hunt, and in the evening Madame Bertha said to the baron with a laugh: "Baron, if you kill the brute, I shall have something to say to you." And so at dawn he was up and out, to try and discover where the solitary animal had its lair. He accompanied his huntsmen, settled the places for the relays, and organized everything personally to insure his triumph. When the horns gave the signal for setting out, he appeared in a closely fitting coat of scarlet and gold, with his waist drawn in tight, his chest expanded, his eyes radiant, and as fresh and strong as if he had just got out of bed. They set off; the wild boar bolted through the underwood as soon as he was dislodged, followed by the hounds in full cry, while the horses set off at a gallop through the narrow

132

side-cuts in the forest. The carriages which followed the chase at a distance drove noiselessly along the soft roads.

From mischief, Madame d'Avancelles kept the baron by her side, lagging behind at a walk in an interminably long and straight drive, over which four rows of oaks hung, so as to form almost an arch, while he, trembling with love and anxiety, listened with one ear to the young woman's bantering chatter, and with the other to the blast of the horns and to the cry of the hounds as they receded in the distance.

"So you do not love me any longer?" she observed.

"How can you say such things?" he replied.

And she continued: "But you seem to be paying more attention to the sport than to me."

He groaned, and said: "Did you not order me to kill the animal myself?"

And she replied gravely: "Of course I reckon upon it. You must kill it under my eyes."

Then he trembled in his saddle, spurred his horse until it reared and, losing all patience, exclaimed: "But, by Jove, Madame, that is impossible if we remain here."

Then she spoke tenderly to him, laying her hand on his arm, or stroking his horse's mane, as if from abstraction, and said with a laugh: "But you must do it—or else, so much the worse for you."

Just then they turned to the right, into a narrow path which was overhung by trees, and suddenly, to avoid a branch which barred their way, she leaned toward him so closely, that he felt her hair tickling his neck. Suddenly he threw his arms brutally round her, and putting his heavily mustached mouth to her forehead, he gave her a furious kiss.

At first she did not move, and remained motionless under that mad caress; then she turned her head with a jerk, and either by accident or design her little lips met his, under their wealth of light hair, and a moment afterward, either from confusion or remorse, she struck her horse with her riding-whip, and went off at full gallop, and they rode on like that for some time, without exchanging a look.

The noise of the hunt came nearer, the thickets seemed to tremble, and suddenly the wild boar broke through the bushes, covered with blood, and trying to shake off the hounds who had fastened on to him, and the baron, uttering a shout of triumph exclaimed: "Let him who loves me follow me!" And he disappeared in the copse, as if the wood had swallowed him up.

When she reached an open glade a few minutes later, he was just getting up, covered with mud, his coat torn, and his hands bloody, while the brute was lying stretched out at full length, with the baron's hunting-knife driven into its shoulder up to the hilt.

The quarry was cut at night by torchlight. It was a warm and dull evening, and the wan moon threw a yellow light on to the torches which made the night misty with their resinous smoke. The hounds devoured the wild boar's entrails, and snarled and fought for them, while the prickers and the gentlemen, standing in a circle round the spoil, blew their horns as loud as they could. The flourish of the hunting-horns resounded beyond the woods on that still night and was repeated by the echoes of the distant valleys, awaking the timid stags, rousing the yelping foxes and disturbing the little rabbits in their gambols at the edge of the rides.

The frightened nightbirds flew over the eager pack of hounds, while the women, who were moved by all these strangely picturesque things, leaned rather heavily on the men's arms, and turned aside into the forest rides, before the hounds had finished their meal. Madame d'Avancelles, feeling languid after that day of fatigue and tenderness, said to the baron: "Will you take a turn in the park, my friend?" And without replying, but trembling and nervous, he went with her, and immediately they kissed each other. They walked slowly under the almost leafless trees through which the moonbeams filtered, and their love, their desires, their longing for a closer embrace became so vehement, that they nearly yielded to it at the foot of a tree.

The horns were not sounding any longer, and the tired hounds were sleeping in the kennels. "Let us return," the young woman said, and they went back.

When they got to the château and before they went in, she said in a weak voice: "I am so tired that I shall go to bed, my friend." And as he opened his arms for a last kiss, she ran away, saying as a last good-bye: "No—I am going to sleep. Let him who loves me follow me!"

An hour later, when the whole silent château seemed dead, the baron crept stealthily out of his room, and went and scratched at her door. As she did not reply, he tried to open it, and found that it was not locked.

She was in a reverie, resting her arms against the window ledge. He threw himself at her knees, which he kissed madly, through her dress. She said nothing, but buried her delicate fingers caressingly in his hair, and suddenly, as if she had formed some great resolution, whispered with a daring look: "I shall come back, wait for me." And stretching out her hand, she pointed with her finger to an indistinct white spot at the end of the room; it was her bed.

Then, with trembling hands and scarcely knowing what he was doing, he quickly undressed, got into the cool sheets, and stretching himself out comfortably, almost forgot his love in the pleasure he found, tired out as he was, in the contact of the linen. She did not return, however, no doubt finding amusement in making him languish. He closed his eyes with a feeling of exquisite comfort, and reflected peaceably while waiting for what he so ardently longed for. But by degrees his limbs grew languid and his thoughts became indistinct and fleeting, until his fatigue gained the upper hand and he fell asleep.

He slept that unconquerable, heavy sleep of the worn-out hunter, slept through until daylight. Then, as the window had remained half open, the crowing of a cock suddenly woke him. The baron opened his eyes, and feeling a woman's body against his—finding himself, much to his surprise, in a strange bed, and remembering nothing for the moment—he stammered:

"What? Where am I? What is the matter?"

Then she, who had not been asleep at all, looking at this unkempt man with red eyes and swollen lips replied in the haughty tone of voice in which she occasionally spoke to her husband:

"It is nothing; it is only a cock crowing. Go to sleep again Monsieur, it has nothing to do with you."

Lilie Lala

"WHEN I saw her for the first time," Louis d'Arandel said, with the look of a man who was dreaming and trying to recollect something, "I thought of some slow and yet passionate music that I once heard, though I do not remember who was the composer. It told of a fair-haired woman, whose hair was so silky, so golden, and so vibrating that her lover had it cut off after her death, and had the strings of the magic bow of a violin made out of it, which afterward emitted such superhuman complaints and love melodies, that they made its hearers love until death.

"In her eyes there lay the mystery of deep waters; one was lost in them, drowned in them like in fathomless depths, and at the corners of her mouth there lurked the despotic and merciless smile of those women who do not fear that they may be conquered, who rule over men like cruel queens, whose hearts remain as virgin as those of the strictest Carmelite nuns, amid a flood of lewdness.

"I have seen her angelic head, the bands of her hair which looked like plates of gold, her tall, gracefull figure, her white, slender, childish hands, in stained glass windows in churches. She suggested pictures of the Annunciation, where the Archangel Gabriel descends with ultramarine colored wings, and Mary is sitting at her spinning wheel and spinning, while uttering pious prayers, seemingly a tall sister to the white lilies that are growing beside her and the roses.

"When she went through the acacia alley, she appeared on some first night in the stage box at one of the theaters, nearly always alone, and apparently feeling life a great burden, and angry because she could not change the eternal, dull round of human enjoyment, nobody would have believed that she went in for a fast life—that in the annals of gallantry she was catalogued under the strange name of "Lilie Lala," and that no man could rub against her without being irretrievably caught, and spending his last halfpenny on her.

"But with all that, Lilie had the voice of a school-girl, of some little innocent creature who still uses a skipping rope and wears short dresses, and had that clear, innocent laugh which reminds people of wedding bells. Sometimes, for fun, I would kneel down before her, like before the statue of a saint, and clasping my hands as if in prayer, I used to say: *'Sancta Lilie, ora pro nobis!'*

"One evening, at Biarritz. when the

sky had the dull glare of intense heat and the sea was of a sinister, inky black, and was swelling and rolling in enormous phosphorescent waves on the beach at Port-Vieux, Lilie, who was listless and strange, and was making holes in the sand with the heels of her boots, suddenly exclaimed in one of those confidences which women sometimes bestow, and for which they are sorry as soon as the story is told:

" 'Ah! My dear fellow, I do not deserve to be canonized, and my life is rather a subject for a drama than a chapter from the Gospels or the "Golden Legend:" As long as I can remember anything, I can remember being wrapped in lace, being carried by a woman, and continually being fussed over, as are children who have been long waited for, and who are consequently spoiled more than usual.

" 'Those kisses were so nice, that I still seem to feel their sweetness, and I shrine the remembrance of them in a little place in my heart, as one preserves some lucky talisman in a reliquary. I still seem to remember an indistinct landscape lost in the mist, outlines of trees which frightened me as they creaked and groaned in the wind, and ponds on which swans were sailing. And when I look in the glass for a long time, merely for the sake of seeing myself, it seems to me as if I recognize the woman who, formerly, used to kiss me most frequently, and speak to me in a more loving voice than anyone else did. But what happened afterward?

" 'Was I carried off, or sold to some strolling circus owner by a dishonest servant? I do not know, I have never been able to find out; but I remember

that my whole childhood was spent in a circus which traveled from fair to fair, and from place to place, with files of vans, processions of animals, and noisy music.

" 'I was as tiny as an insect, and they taught me difficult tricks, to dance on the tight-rope and to perform on the slack-rope. I was beaten as if I had been a bit of plaster, and more frequently I had a piece of dry bread to gnaw than a slice of meat. But I remember that one day I slipped under one of the vans, and stole a basin of soup as my share, which one of the clowns was carefully making for his three learned dogs.

" 'I had neither friends nor relations; I was employed on the dirtiest jobs, like the lowest stable-help, and I was tattooed with bruises and scars. Of the whole company, however, the one who beat me the most, who was the least sparing of his thumps, and who continually made me suffer, as if it gave him pleasure, was the manager and proprietor, a kind of old, vicious brute, whom everybody feared like the plague, a miser who was continually complaining of the receipts, who hid away the crown pieces in his mattress, invested his money in the funds, and cut down the salaries of all, as far as he could.

" 'His name was Rapha Ginestous. Any other child but myself would have succumbed to such a constant martyrdom, but I grew up, and the more I grew, the prettier and more desirable I became; so that when I was fifteen, men were already beginning to write love-letters to me, and to throw bouquets to me in the arena. I felt also that all the men in the company were watching me, and were coveting me as their prey; that their lustful looks rested on my pink tights, and followed the graceful outlines of my body when I was posing on the rope that stretched from one end of the circus to the other, or jumped through the paper hoops at full gallop.

"They were no longer the same, and spoke to me in a totally different tone of voice. They tried to come into my dressing-room when I was changing my dress, and Rapha Ginestous seemed to have lost his head, and his heart throbbed audibly when he came near me. Yes, he had the audacity to propose bargains to me which covered my cheeks and forehead with blushes, and which filled me with disgust; and as I felt a fierce hatred for him, and detested him with all my soul and all my strength —as I wished to make him suffer the tortures which he had inflicted on me, a hundredfold, I used him as the target at which I was constantly aiming.

" 'Instinctively, I employed every cunning perfidy, every artful coquetry, every lie, every artifice that can unset the strongest and most sceptical, and place them at our mercy, like submissive animals. He loved me, he really loved me, that lascivious goat, who had never seen anything in a woman except a soft couch, and an instrument of convenience and of forgetfulness. He loved me like old men do love, with frenzy, with degrading transports, and with the prostration of his will and of his strength. I held him as in a leash, and did whatever I liked with him.

" 'I was much more manageress than he was manager, and the poor wretch wasted away in vain hopes and in useless transports; he had not even touched the tips of my fingers, and was reduced to bestowing his caresses on my columbine shoes, my tights, and my wigs. And I cared not *that* for it, you understand! Not the slightest familiarity did I allow, and he began to grow thin and ill, and became idiotic. And while he implored me, and promised to marry me, with his eyes full of tears, I shouted with laughter; I reminded him of how he had beaten, abused, and humiliated me, and had often made me wish for death. And as soon as he left me, he would swill bottles of gin and whiskey, and constantly got so abominably drunk that he rolled under the table, and all to drown his sorrow and forget his desire.

" 'He covered me with jewels, and tried everything he could to tempt me to become his wife. In spite of my inexperience in life, he consulted me with regard to everything he undertook, and one evening, after I had stroked his face with my hand, I persuaded him without any difficulty, to make his will, by which he left me all his savings, and the circus and everything belonging to it.

" 'It was in the middle of winter, near Moscow; it snowed continually, and one almost burnt oneself at the stoves in trying to keep warm. Rapha Ginestous had had supper brought into the largest van, which was his, after the performance, and for hours we ate and drank. I was very nice toward him, and filled his glass every moment; I even sat on his knee and kissed him. And all his love, and the fumes of the alcohol of the wine, mounted to his head, and gradually made him so helplessly intoxicated, that he fell from his chair inert, as if he had been struck by lightning, without opening his eyes or saying a word.

" 'The rest of the troupe were asleep, the lights were out in all the little windows, and not a sound was to be heard, while the snow continued to fall in large flakes. So having put out the petroleum lamp, I opened the door, and taking the drunkard by the feet, as if he had been a bale of goods, I threw him out into that white shroud.

" 'The next morning the stiff and convulsed body of Rapha Ginestous was picked up, and as everybody knew his inveterate drinking habits, no one thought of instituting an inquiry, or of accusing me of a crime. Thus was I avenged, and gained a yearly income of nearly fifteen thousand francs.* What, after all, is the good of being honest, and of pardoning our enemies, as the Gospel bids us?'

"And now," Louis d'Arandel said in conclusion, "suppose we go and have a cocktail or two at the Casino, for I do not think that I have ever talked so much in my life before."

*About $3000.

A Vagabond

FOR more than a month Randel had been walking, seeking for work everywhere. He had left his native place, Ville-Avary, in the department of La Manche, because there was no work to be had. He was a journeyman carpenter, twenty-seven years old, a steady fellow and good workman, but for two months, he, the eldest son, had been obliged to live on his family, with nothing to do but loaf in the general stoppage of work. Bread was getting scarce with them; the two sisters went out as charwomen, but earned little, and he, Jacques Randel, the strongest of them all, did nothing because he had nothing to do, and ate the others' bread.

Then he went and inquired at the town-hall, and the mayor's secretary told him that he would find work at the Labor-Center. So he started, well provided with papers and certificates, and carrying another pair of shoes, a pair of trousers, and a shirt in a blue handkerchief at the end of his stick.

He had walked almost without stopping, day and night, along interminable roads, in the sun and rain, without ever reaching that mysterious country where workmen find work. At first he had the fixed idea that he must only work at his own trade, but at every carpenter's shop where he applied he was told that they had just dismissed men on account of work being so slack, and finding himself at the end of his resources, he made up his mind to undertake any job that he might come across on the road. And so by turns he was a navvy, stableman, stone-sawyer; he split wood, lopped the branches of trees, dug wells, mixed mortar, tied up faggots, tended goats on a mountain, and all for a few pence, for he only obtained two or three days' work occasionally, by offering himself at a shamefully low price, in order to tempt the avarice of employers and peasants.

And now for a week he had found nothing and he had no money left. He was eating a piece of bread, thanks to the charity of some women from whom he had begged at house-doors, on the road. It was getting dark, and Jacques Randel, jaded, his legs failing him, his stomach empty, and with despair in his heart, was walking barefoot on the grass by the side of the road, for he was taking care of his last pair of shoes, the other pair having already ceased to exist for a long time. It was a Saturday, toward the end of autumn. The heavy gray clouds were being driven rapidly among the trees, and one felt that it would rain soon. .The country was deserted at that time of the evening, and on the eve of Sunday. Here and there in the fields there rose up stacks of thrashed-out corn, like huge yellow mushrooms, and the fields looked bare, as they had already been sown for the next year.

Randel was hungry, with the hunger of some wild animal, such a hunger as drives wolves to attack men. Worn out and weakened with fatigue, he took longer strides, so as not to take so many steps, and with heavy head, the blood throbbing in his temples, with red eyes and dry mouth, he grasped his stick tightly in his hand, with a longing to strike the first passer-by whom he should meet, and who might be going home to supper, with all his force.

He looked at the sides of the road, with the image of potatoes dug up and lying on the ground, before his eyes; if he had found any, he would have gathered some dead wood, made a fire in the ditch, and have had a capital supper off the warm, round tubers, which he would first of all have held burning hot in his cold hands. But it was too late in the year and he would have to gnaw a raw beet-root, as he had done the day before, having picked one up in a field.

For the last two days he had spoken aloud as he quickened his steps, under the influence of his thoughts. He had never done much thinking, hitherto, as he had given all his mind, all his simple faculties, to his industrial requirements. But now fatigue, and this desperate search for work which he could not get, refusals and rebuffs, nights spent in the open air lying on the grass, long fasting, the contempt which he knew people with a settled abode felt for a vagabond, the question which he was continually asked: "Why did you not remain at home?" distress at not being able to use his strong arms which he felt so full of vigor, the recollection of his relations who had remained at home and who also had not a half-penny, filled him by degrees with a rage which was accumulating every day, every hour, every minute, and which now escaped his lips in spite of himself in short, growling sentences.

As he stumbled over the stones which rolled beneath his bare feet, he grumbled: "How wretched! how miserable! A set of hogs, to let a man die of hunger, a carpenter. A set of hogs—not twopence—not twopence. And now it is raining—a set of hogs!"

He was indignant at the injustice of fate, and cast the blame on men, on all men, because Nature, that great, blind mother, is unjust, cruel and perfidious, and he repeated through his clenched teeth, "A set of hogs," as he looked at the thin gray smoke which rose from the roofs, for it was the dinner hour. And without thinking about that other injustice, which is human, and which is called robbery and violence, he felt inclined to go into one of those houses to murder the inhabitants, and to sit down to table, in their stead.

He said to himself: "I have a right to live, and they are letting me die of hunger—and yet I only ask for work— a set of hogs!" And the pain in his limbs, the gnawing in his heart, rose to his head like terrible intoxication, and gave rise to this simple thought in his brain: "I have the right to live because I breathe, and because the air is the common property of everybody, and so nobody has the right to leave me without bread!"

A thick, fine, icy cold rain was coming down, and he stopped and murmured: "How miserable! another month of walking before I get home." He was indeed returning home then; for he saw that he should more easily find work in his native town where he was known—and he did not mind what he did—than on the highroads, where everybody suspected him. As the carpentering business was not going well he would turn day-laborer, be a mason's hodman, ditcher, break stones on the road. If he only earned tenpence a day, that would at any rate find him something to eat.

He tied the remains of his last pocket handkerchief round his neck to prevent the cold water from running down his back and chest; but he soon found that it was penetrating the thin material of which his clothes were made, and he glanced round him with the agonized look of a man who does not know where to hide his body and to rest his head, and has no place of shelter in the whole world.

Night came on and wrapped the country in obscurity, and in the distance, in a meadow, he saw a dark spot on the grass; it was a cow, and so he got over the ditch by the roadside and went up to her, without exactly knowing what he was doing. When he got close to her, she raised her great head to him, and he thought: "If I only had a jug, I could get a little milk." He looked at the cow, and the cow looked at him, and then suddenly giving her a violent kick in the side, he said: "Get up!"

The animal got up slowly, letting her heavy udder hang down below her; then the man lay down on his back between the animal's legs, and drank for a long time, squeezing the warm swollen teats which tasted of the cow-stall, with both hands, and drank as long as any milk remained in that living well. But the icy rain began to fall more heavily, and he saw no place of shelter on the whole of that bare plain. He was cold, and he looked at a light which was shining among the trees, in the window of a house.

The cow had lain down again, heavily, and he sat down by her side and stroked her head, grateful for the nourishment she had give him. The animal's strong, thick breath, which came out of her nostrils like two jets of steam in the evening air, blew on to the workman's face, who said: "You are not cold, inside there!" He put his hands on to her chest and under her legs, to find some warmth there, and then the idea struck him that he might pass the night against that large, warm stomach. So he found a comfortable place and laid his forehead against the great udder from which he had quenched his thirst just previously, and then, as he was worn out with fatigue, he fell asleep immediately.

He woke up, however, several times, with his back or his stomach half frozen, according as he put one or the other to the animal's flank. Then he turned over to warm and dry that part of his body which had remained exposed to the night air, and he soon went soundly to sleep again.

The crowing of a cock woke him; the day was breaking, it was no longer raining and the sky was bright. The cow was resting with her muzzle on the ground, and he stooped down, resting on his hands, to kiss those wide nostrils of moist flesh, and said: "Good-bye, my beauty, until next time. You are a nice animal! Good-bye." Then he put on his shoes and went off, and for two hours he walked straight on before him, always following the same road, and then he felt so tired that he sat down on the grass. It was broad daylight by that time, and the church bells were ringing; men in blue blouses, women in white caps, some on foot, some in carts, began to pass along the road, going to the neighboring villages to spend Sunday with friends or relations.

A stout peasant came in sight, driving a score of frightened, bleating sheep in front of him, whom an active dog kept together, so Randel got up and raising his cap, he said: "You do not happen to have any work for a man who is dying of hunger?" But the other, giving an angry look at the vagabond, replied: "I have no work for fellows whom I meet on the road."

And the carpenter went back and sat down by the side of the ditch again. He waited there for a long time, watching the country people pass, and looking for a kind, compassionate face before he renewed his request, and finally selected a man in an overcoat, whose stomach was adored with a gold chain. "I have been looking for work," he said, "for the last two months and cannot find any, and I have not a halfpenny in my pocket."

But the semi-gentleman replied: "You should have read the notice which is stuck up at the beginning of the village: 'Begging is prohibited within the boundaries of this parish.' Let me tell you that I am the mayor, and if you do not get out of here pretty quickly, I shall have you arrested."

Randel, who was getting angry, replied: "Have me arrested if you like; I should prefer it, for at any rate I should not die of hunger." And he went back and sat down by the side of his ditch again, and in about a quarter of an hour two gendarmes appeared on the road. They were walking slowly, side by side, well in sight, glittering in the sun with their shining hats, their yellow accouterments and their metal buttons, as if to frighten evildoers, and to put them to flight at a distance. He knew that they were coming after him, but he did not move, for he was seized with a sudden desire to defy them, to be arrested by them, and to have his revenge later.

They came on without appearing to have seen him, walking with military steps, heavily, and balancing themselves as if they were doing the goose-step; and then suddenly as they passed him, they noticed him and stopped, looking at him angrily and threateningly. The brigadier came up to him and asked: "What are you doing here?"

"I am resting," the man replied, calmly.

"Where do you come from?"

"If I had to tell you all the places I have been to, it would take me more than an hour."

"Where are you going to?"

"To Ville-Avary."

"Where is that?"

"In La Manche."

"Is that where you belong to?"

"It is."

"Why did you leave it?"

"To try for work."

The brigadier turned to his gendarme, and said, in the angry voice of a man who is exasperated at last by the same trick: "They all say that, these scamps. I know all about it." And then he continued: "Have you any papers?"

"Yes, I have some."

"Give them to me."

Randal took his papers out of his pocket, his certificates, those poor, worn-out, dirty papers which were falling to pieces, and gave them to the soldier, who spelled them through, hemming and hawing and then having seen that they were all in order, he gave them back to Randel with the dissatisfied look of a man whom some one cleverer than himself has tricked.

After a few moments further reflection, he asked him: "Have you any money on you?"

"No."

"None whatever?"

"None."

"Not even a sou?"

"Not even a sou!"

"How do you live then?"

"On what people give me."

"Then you beg?"

And Randel answered resolutely: "Yes, when I can."

Then the gendarme said: "I have caught you on the highroad in the act of vagabondage and begging, without any resources or trade, and so I command you to come with me."

The carpenter got up and said: "Wherever you please." And placing himself between the two soldiers, even before he had received the order to do so, he added: "Come, lock me up; that will at any rate put a roof over my head when it rains."

And they set off toward the village, whose red tiles could be seen through the leafless trees, a quarter of a league off. Service was just going to begin when they went through the village. The square was full of people, who immediately formed two hedges to see the criminal, who was being followed by a crowd of excited children, pass. Male and female peasants looked at the prisoner between the two gendarmes, with hatred in their eyes, and a longing to throw stones at him, to tear his skin with their nails, to trample him under their feet. They asked each other whether he had committed murder or robbery. The butcher, who was an ex-Spahi declared that he was a deserter. The tobacconist thought that he recognized him as the man who had that very morning passed a bad half-franc piece off on him, and the ironmonger declared that he was the murderer of widow Malet, for whom the police had been looking, for six months.

In the hall of the municipal council, into which his custodians took him, Randel saw the mayor again, sitting on the magisterial bench, with the school-master by his side.

"Ah! ah!" the magistrate exclaimed, "so here you are again, my fellow. I told you I should have you locked up. Well, brigadier, what is he charged with?"

"He is a vagabond without house or home, Monsieur le Maire, without any resources or money, so he says, who was arrested in the act of begging, but he is provided with good testimonials, and his papers are all in order."

"Show me his papers," the mayor said. He took them, read them, re-read, re-turned them, and then said: "Search him"; they searched him, but found nothing, and the mayor seemed per-plexed, and asked the workman:

"What were you doing on the road this morning?"

"I was looking for work."

"Work? On the highroad?"

"How do you expect me to find any if I hide in the woods?"

They looked at each other, with the hatred of two wild beasts which belong to different, hostile species, and the magistrate continued: "I am going to have you set at liberty, but do not be brought up before me again."

To which the carpenter replied: "I would rather you locked me up; I have had enough running about the country."

But the magistrate replied severely: "Be silent." And then he said to the two gendarmes: "You will conduct this man two hundred yards from the village, and let him continue his journey."

"At any rate, give me something to eat," the workman said; but the other grew indignant: "It only remains for us to feed you! Ah! ah! ah! that is rather strong!"

But Randel went on, firmly: "If you let me nearly die of hunger again, you will force me to commit a crime, and then, so much the worse for you other fat fellows."

The mayor had risen, and he re-peated: "Take him away immediately, or I shall end by getting angry."

The two gendarmes thereupon seized the carpenter by the arms and dragged him out. He allowed them to do it without resistance, passed through the village again, and found himself on the highroad once more; and when the men had accompanied him two hundred yards beyond the village, the brigadier said: "Now off with you, and do not let me catch you about here again, for if I do, you will know it."

Randel went off without replying, or knowing where he was going. He walked on for a quarter of an hour or twenty minutes, so stupefied that he no longer thought of anything. But sud-denly, as he was passing a small house, where the window was half open, the smell of the soup and boiled meat stopped him suddenly in front of it, and hunger, fierce, devouring, madden-ing hunger seized him, and almost drove him against the walls of the house, like a wild beast.

He said aloud, in a grumbling voice: "In Heaven's name they must give me some, this time." And he began to knock at the door vigorously with his stick, and as nobody came he knocked louder and called out: "Hallo! you people in there, open the door!" And then, as nothing moved, he went up to the window, and pushed it open with his hand, and the close warm air of the kitchen, full of smell of hot soup, meat, and cabbage escaped into the cold, outer air, and with a bound the carpenter was in the house. Two covers were laid on the table; no doubt the proprietors of the house, on going to church, had left their dinner on the fire, their nice, Sunday boiled beef and vegetable soup, while there was a loaf of new bread on the chimney-piece, between two bottles which seemed full.

Randel seized the bread first of all, and broke it with as much violence as if he were strangling a man, and then he began to eat it voraciously, swallowing great mouthfuls quickly. But almost immediately the smell of the meat attracted him to the fireplace, and having taken off the lid of the sauce-pan, he plunged a fork into it and brough out a large piece of beef, tied with a string. Then he took more cabbage, carrots, and onions until his plate was full, and having put it on the table, he sat down before it, cut the meat into four pieces, and dined as if he had been at home. When he had eaten nearly all the meat, besides a quantity of vegetables, he felt thirsty, and took one of the bottles off the mantelpiece.

Scarcely had he poured the liquor into his glass than he saw it was brandy. So much the better; it was warming; it would instill some fire into his veins, and that would be all right, after being so cold; and he drank some. He found it very good, certainly, for he

had grown unaccustomed to it, and he poured himself out another glassful, which he drank at two gulps. And then, almost immediately he felt quite merry and light-hearted from the effect of the alcohol, just as if some great happiness were flowing through his system.

He continued to eat, but more slowly, dipping his bread into the soup. His skin had become burning, and especially his forehead, where the veins were throbbing. But suddenly the church bells began to ring. Mass was over, and instinct rather than fear, the instinct of prudence which guides all beings, and makes them clear-sighted in danger, made the carpenter get up. He put the remains of the loaf into one pocket, and the brandy bottle into the other, and he furtively went to the window and looked out into the road. It was still deserted, so he jumped out and set off walking again, but instead of following the highroad, he ran across the fields toward a wood which he saw a little way off.

He felt alert, strong, light-hearted, glad of what he had done, and so nimble that he sprang over the inclosures of the fields, at a single bound, and as soon as he was under the trees, he took the bottle out of his pocket again, and began to drink once more, swallowing it down as he walked, and then his ideas began to get confused, his eyes grew dim, and his legs elastic as springs, and he started singing the old popular song:

"Oh! how nice, how nice it is,
  To pick the sweet, wild strawberries."

He was now walking on thick, damp, cool moss, and the soft carpet under his feet made him feel absurdly inclined to turn head over heels, like he used to do as a child; so he took a run, turned a somersault, got up, and began over again. And between each time, he began to sing again:

"Oh! how nice, how nice it is,
To pick the sweet, wild strawberries."

Suddenly he found himself on the edge of a sunken road, and in the road he saw a tall girl, a servant who was returning to the village with two pails of milk. He watched, stooping down and with his eyes as bright as those of a dog who scents a quail, but she saw him, raised her head and said: "Was that you singing like that?" He did not reply, however, but jumped down into the road, although it was at least six feet down, and when she saw him suddenly standing in front of her, she exclaimed: "Oh! dear, how you frightened me!"

But he did not hear her, for he was drunk, he was mad, excited by another requirement which was more imperative than hunger, more feverish than alcohol; by the irresistible fury of the man who has been in want of everything for two months, and who is drunk; who is young, ardent, and inflamed by all the appetites which nature has implanted in the flesh of vigorous men.

The girl started back from him, frightened at his face, his eyes, his half-open mouth, his outstretched hands, but he seized her by the shoulders, and without a word threw her down in the road. She let her two pails fall, and they rolled over noisily, and all the milk was spilt, and then she screamed, but comprehending that it would be of no use to call for help in that lonely spot, and

seeing that he was not going to make an attempt on her life, she yielded without much difficulty, and not very angrily either, for he was a strong, handsome young fellow, and really not rough.

When she got up, the thought of her overturned pails suddenly filled her with fury, and taking off one of her wooden clogs, she threw it, in her turn, at the man to break his head, since he did not pay her for her milk.

But he, mistaking the reason for this sudden violent attack, somewhat sobered, and frightened at what he had done, ran off as fast as he could while she threw stones at him, some of which hit him in the back.

He ran for a long time, very long, until he felt more tired than he had ever been before. His legs were so weak that they could scarcely carry him; all his ideas were confused, he lost the recollection of everything, and could no longer think about anything; and so he sat down at the foot of a tree, and in five minutes was fast asleep. He was soon awakened, however, by a rough shake and, on opening his eyes he saw two cocked hats of polished leather bending over him, and the two gendarmes of the morning, who were holding him and binding his arms.

"I knew I should catch you again," said the brigadier, jeeringly. But Randel got up without replying. The two men shook him, quite ready to ill treat him if he made a movement, for he was their prey now, he had become a jailbird, caught by hunters of criminals who would not let him go again.

"Now, start!" the brigadier said, and they set off. It was getting evening, and the autumn twilight was settling, heavy and dark, over the land, and in half an hour they reached the village, where every door was open, for the people had heard what had happened. Peasants and peasant women and girls, excited with anger, as if every man had been robbed, and every woman violated, wished to see the wretch brought back, so that they might overwhelm him with abuse. They hooted him from the first house in the village until they reached the mansion-house, where the mayor was waiting for him. Eager to avenge himself on this vagabond as soon as he saw him, he cried:

."Ah! my fine fellow! here we are!" And he rubbed his hands, more pleased than he usually was, and continued: "I said so. I said so, the moment I saw him in the road." And then with increased satisfaction:

"Oh! you blackguard! Oh! you dirty blackguard! You will get your twenty years, my fine fellow!"

The Mountebanks

COMPARDIN, the clever manager of the Eden Réunis Theater, as the theater critics invariably called him, was reckoning on a great success, and had invested his last franc in the affair, without thinking of the morrow, or of the bad luck which had been pursuing him so inexorably for months past. For a whole week, the walls, the kiosks, shopfronts, and even the trees, had been placarded with flaming posters, and from one end of Paris to the other carriages were to be seen which were covered with fancy sketches by Chéret, representing two strong, well-built men who looked like ancient athletes. The younger of them, who was standing with his arms folded, had the vacant smile of an itinerant mountebank, and the other, who was dressed in what was supposed to be the costume of a Mexican trapper, held a revolver in his hand. There were large-type advertisements in all the papers that the Montefiores would appear without fail at the Eden Réunis, the next Monday.

Nothing else was talked about, for the puff and humbug attracted people. The Montefiores, like fashionable knickknacks, succeeded that whimsical jade Rose Péché, who had gone off the preceding autumn, between the third and fourth acts of the burlesque, "Ousca Iscar," in order to make a study of love in company of a young fellow of seventeen, who had just entered the university. The novelty and difficulty of their performance revived and agitated the curiosity of the public, for there seemed to be an implied threat of death, or, at any rate, of wounds and of blood in it, and it seemed as if they defied danger with absolute indifference. And that always pleases women; it holds them and masters them, and they grow pale with emotion and cruel enjoyment. Consequently, all the seats in the large theater were let almost immediately, and were soon taken for several days in advance. And stout Compardin, losing his glass of absinthe over a game of dominoes, was in high spirits, seeing the future through rosy glasses, and exclaimed in a loud voice: "I think I have turned up trumps, by George!"

*   *   *   *   *   *   *

The Countess Regina de Villégby was lying on the sofa in her boudoir, languidly fanning herself. She had only received three or four intimate friends that day, Saint Mars Montalvin, Tom Sheffield, and her cousin Madame de Rhouel, a Creole, who laughed as incessantly as a bird sings. It was growing dusk, and the distant rumbling of the carriages in the Avenue of the Champs-Elysées sounded like some somnolent rhythm. There was a delicate perfume of flowers; the lamps had not been brought in yet, and chatting and laughing filled the room with a confused noise.

"Would you pour out the tea?" the Countess said, suddenly, touching Saint Mars's fingers, who was beginning an amorous conversation in a low voice, with her fan. And while he slowly filled the little china cup, he continued: "Are the Montefiores as good as the lying newspapers make out?"

Then Tom Sheffield and the others all joined in. They had never seen anything like it, they declared; it was most exciting, and made one shiver unpleasantly, as when the *espada* comes to close quarters with the infuriated brute at a bull fight.

Countess Regina listened in silence, and nibbled the petals of a tea rose.

"How I should like to see them!" giddy Madame de Rhouel exclaimed.

"Unfortunately, cousin," the Countess said, in the solemn tones of a preacher, "a respectable woman dare not let herself be seen in improper places."

They all agreed with her. Nevertheless, Madame de Villégby was present at the Montefiores' performance, two days later, dressed all in black, and wearing a thick veil, at the back of a stage box.

Madame de Villégby was as cold as a steel buckler. She had married as soon as she left the convent in which she had been educated, without any affection or even liking for her husband; the most sceptical respected her as a saint, and she had a look of virgin purity on her calm face as she went down the steps of the Madeleine on Sundays, after high mass.

Countess Regina stretched herself nervously, grew pale, and trembled like the strings of a violin, on which an artist had been playing some wild symphony. She inhaled the nasty smell of the sawdust, as if it had been the perfume of a bouquet of unknown flowers; she clenched her hands, and gazed eagerly at the two mountebanks, whom the public applauded rapturously at every feat. And contemptuously and haughtily she compared those two men, who were as vigorous as wild animals that have grown up in the open air, with the rickety limbs that look so awkward in the dress of an English groom.

*   *   *   *   .   *   *   *

Count de Villégby had gone back to the country, to prepare for his election as Councillor-General, and the very evening that he started, Regina again took the stage box at the Eden Réunis. Consumed by sensual ardor as if by some love philter, she scribbled a few words on a piece of paper—the eternal formula that women write on such occasions.

"A carriage will be waiting for you at the stage door after the performance —*An unknown woman who adores you."*

And then she gave it to a box opener, who handed it to the Montefiore who was the champion pistol shot.

Oh! that interminable waiting in a malodorous cab, the overwhelming emotion, and the nausea of disgust, the fear, the desire of waking the coachman who was nodding on the box, of giving him her address, and telling him to drive her home. But she remained with her face against the window, mechanically watching the dark passage illuminated by a gas lamp, at the "actors' entrance," through which men were continually hurrying, who talked in a loud voice, and chewed the end of cigars which had gone out. She sat as if she were glued to the cushions, and tapped impatiently on the bottom of the cab with her heels.

When the actor, who thought it was a joke, made his appearance, she could hardly utter a word, for evil pleasure is as intoxicating as adulterated liquor. So face to face with this immediate surrender, and this unconstrained immodesty, he at first thought that he had to do with a street-walker.

Regina felt various sensations, and a morbid pleasure throughout her whole person. She pressed close to him, and raised her veil to show how young, beautiful, and desirable she was. They did not speak a word, like wrestlers before a combat. She was eager to be locked up with him, to give herself to him, and, at last, to know that moral uncleanness, of which she was, of course, ignorant as a chaste wife; and when they left the room in the hotel together, where they had spent hours like amorous deer, the man dragged himself along, and almost groped his way like a blind man, while Regina was smiling, though she exhibited the serene candor of an unsullied virgin, like she did on Sundays, after mass.

Then she took the second. He was very sentimental, and his head was full of romance. He thought the unknown woman, who merely used him as her plaything, really loved him, and he was not satisfied with furtive meetings. He questioned her, besought her, and the Countess made fun of him. Then she chose the two mountebanks in turn. They did not know it, for she had forbidden them ever to talk about her to each other, under the penalty of never seeing her again, and one night the younger of them said with humble tenderness, as he knelt at her feet:

"How kind you are, to love me and to want me! I thought that such happiness only existed in novels, and that ladies of rank only made fun of poor strolling mountebanks, like us!"

Regina knitted her golden brows.

"Do not be angry," he continued, "because I followed you and found out where you lived, and your real name, and that you are a countess, and rich, very rich."

"You fool!" she exclaimed, trembling with anger. "People make you believe things, as easily as they can a child!"

She had had enough of him; he knew her name, and might compromise her. The Count might possibly come back from the country before the elections, and then the mountebank began to love her. She no longer had any feeling, any desire for those two lovers, whom a fillip from her rosy fingers could bend to her will. It was time to go on to the next chapter, and to seek for fresh pleasures elsewhere.

"Listen to me," she said to the champion shot, the next night, "I would rather not hide anything from you. I like your comrade; I have given myself to him, and I do not want to have anything more to do with you."

"My comrade!" he repeated.

"Well, what then? The change amuses me!"

He uttered a furious cry, and rushed at Regina with clenched fists. She thought he was going to kill her, and closed her eyes, but he had not the courage to hurt that delicate body, which he had so often covered with caresses, and in despair, and hanging his head, he said hoarsely:

"Very well, we shall not meet again, since it is your wish."

The house at the Eden Réunis was as full as an overfilled basket. The violins were playing a soft and delightful waltz of Gungl's, which the reports of a revolver accentuated.

The Montefiores were standing opposite to one another, as in Chéret's picture, and about a dozen yards apart. An electric light was thrown on the younger, who was leaning against a large white target, and very slowly the other traced his living outline with bullet after bullet. He aimed with prodigious skill, and the black dots showed on the cardboard, and marked the shape of his body. The applause drowned the orchestra, and increased continually, when suddenly a shrill cry of horror resounded from one end of the hall to the other. The women fainted, the violins stopped, and the spectators jostled each other. At the ninth ball, the younger brother had fallen to the ground, an inert mass, with a gaping wound in his forehead. His brother did not move, and there was a look of madness on his face, while the Countess de Villégby leaned on the ledge of her box, and fanned herself calmly, as implacably as any cruel goddess of ancient mythology.

The next day, between four and five, when she was surrounded by her usual friends in her little, warm, Japanese drawing-room, it was strange to hear in what a languid and indifferent voice she exclaimed:

"They say that an accident happened to one of those famous clowns, the Monta—the Monte—what is the name, Tom?"

"The Montefiores, Madame!"

And then they began to talk about Angèle Velours, who was going to buy the former Folies, at the Hôtel Drouot, before marrying Prince Storbeck.

Ugly

CERTAINLY, at this blessed epoch of the equality of mediocrity, of rectangular abomination, as Edgar Allan Poe says—at this delightful period, when everybody dreams of resembling everybody else, so that it has become impossible to tell the President of the Republic from a waiter—in these days which are the forerunners of that promising, blissful day, when everything in this world will be of a dull, neutral uniformity, certainly at such an epoch, one has the right, or rather it is one's duty, to be ugly.

Lebeau, however, assuredly exercised that right with the most cruel vigor. He fulfilled that duty with the fiercest heroism, and to make matters worse, the mysterious irony of fate had caused him to be born with the name of Lebeau, while an ingenious god-father, the unconscious accomplice of the pranks of destiny, had given him the Christian name of Antinous.*

Even among our contemporaries, who were already on the highroad to the coming ideal of universal hideousness, Antinous Lebeau was remarkable for his ugliness, and one might have said that he positively threw zeal, too much zeal, into the matter, though he was not hideous like Mirabeau, who made people exclaim, "Oh! the beautiful monster!"

Alas! No. He was without any beauty of ugliness. He was ugly, that was all, nothing more nor less; in short, he was uglily ugly. He was not humpbacked, nor knock-kneed, nor potbellied; his legs were not like a pair of tongs, and his arms were neither too long nor too short, and yet, there was an utter lack of uniformity about him, not only in painters' eyes, but also in everybody's, for nobody could meet him in the street without turning to look after him, and thinking: "Good heavens! what an object."

His hair was of no particular color; a light chestnut, mixed with yellow. There was not much of it; still, he was not absolutely bald, but just bald

enough to allow his butter-colored pate to show. Butter-colored? Hardly! The color of margarine would be more applicable, and such pale margarine!

His face was also like margarine, but of adulterated margarine, certainly. His cranium, the color of unadulterated margarine, looked almost like butter, in comparison.

There was very little to say about his mouth! Less than little; the sum total was—nothing. It was a chimerical mouth.

But take it that I have said nothing about him, and let us replace this vain description by the useful formula: "Impossible to describe." But you must not forget that Antinous Lebeau was ugly, that the fact impressed everybody as soon as they saw him, and that nobody remembered ever having seen an uglier person; and let us add, as the climax of his misfortune, that he thought so himself.

From this you will see that he was not a fool, and not ill-natured either; but, of course, he was unhappy. An unhappy man thinks only of his wretchedness, and people take his nightcap for a fool's cap, while, on the other hand, goodness is only esteemed when it is cheerful. Consequently, Antinous Lebeau passed for a fool, and an ill-tempered fool; he was not even pitied because he was so ugly!

He had only one pleasure in life, and

---

*A youth of extraordinary beauty, page to the Emperor Hadrian (A. D. 117-138), and the object of his extravagant affection. He was drowned in the Nile, whether by accident, or in order to escape from the life he was leading, is uncertain.

that was to go and roam about the darkest streets on dark nights, and to hear the street-walkers say:

"Come home with me, you handsome, dark man!"

It was, alas! a furtive pleasure, and he knew that it was not true. For, occasionally, when the woman was old or drunk and he profited by the invitation, as soon as the candle was lighted in the garret, they no longer murmured the fallacious "handsome, dark man." When they saw him, the old women grew still older, and the drunken women get sober. And more than one, although hardened against disgust and ready for all risks, said to him, in spite of liberal payment:

"My little man, I must say, you are most confoundedly ugly."

At last, however, he renounced even that lamentable pleasure, when he heard the still more lamentable words which a wretched woman could not help uttering when he went home with her:

"Well, I must have been very hungry!"

Alas! It was he was hungry, unhappy man; hungry for something that should resemble love, were it ever so little; he longed not to live like a pariah any more, not to be exiled and proscribed by his ugliness. And the ugliest, the most repugnant woman would have appeared beautiful to him, if she would only not think him ugly, or, at any rate, not tell him so, and not let him see that she felt horror at him on that account.

The consequence was, that, when he one day met a poor, blear-eyed creature, with her face covered with scabs, and bearing evident signs of alcoholism, with a driveling mouth, and ragged and filthy petticoats, to whom he gave liberal alms, for which she kissed his hand, he took

her home with him, had her cleansed, dressed, and taken care of, made her his servant, and then his housekeeper. Next he raised her to the rank of his mistress, and, finally, of course, he married her.

She was almost as ugly as he was! Almost, but certainly not quite; for she was hideous, and her hideousness had its charm and its beauty, no doubt; that something by which a woman can attract a man. And she had proved that by deceiving him, and she let him see it better still, by seducing another man.

That other man was actually uglier than he was.

He was certainly uglier, a collection of every physical and moral ugliness, a companion of beggars whom she had picked up among her former vagrant associates, a jail-bird, a dealer in little girls, a vagabond covered with filth, with legs, like a toad's, with a mouth like a lamprey's, and a death's head, in which the nose had been replaced by two holes.

"And you have wronged me with a wretch like that," the poor cuckold said. "And in my own house! and in such a manner that I might catch you in the very act! And why, why, you wretch? Why, seeing that he is uglier than I am?"

"Oh! no," she exclaimed. "You may say what you like, that I am a dirty slut and a strumpet; but do not say that he is uglier than you are."

And the unhappy man stood there, vanquished and overcome by her last words, which she uttered without understanding all the horror which he would feel at them.

"Because, you see, he has his own particular ugliness, while you are merely ugly like everybody else is."

The Debt

"Pst! Pst! Come with me, you handsome dark fellow. I am very nice, as you will see. Do come up. At any rate you will be able to warm yourself, for I have a capital fire at home."

But nothing enticed the foot-passengers, neither being called a handsome, dark fellow, which she applied quite impartially to old or fat men also, nor the promise of pleasure which was emphasized by a caressing ogle and smile, nor even the promise of a good fire, which was so attractive in the bitter December wind. And tall Fanny continued her useless walk, and the night advanced and foot-passengers grew scarcer. In another hour the streets would be absolutely deserted, and unless she could manage to pick up some belated drunken man, she would be obliged to return home alone.

And yet tall Fanny was a beautiful woman! With the head of a Bacchante, and the body of a goddess, in all the full splendor of her twenty-three years, she deserved something better than this miserable pavement, where she could not even pick up the five francs which she wanted for the requirements of the next day. But there! In this infernal Paris, in this swarming crowd of competitors who all jostled each other, courtesans, like artists, did not attain to eminence until their later years. In that they resembled precious stones, as the most valuable of them are those that have been set the oftenest.

And that was why tall Fanny, who was later to become one of the richest and most brilliant stars of Parisian gallantry, was walking about the streets on this bitter December night without a half-penny in her pocket, in spite of the head of a Bacchante, and the body of a goddess, and in all the full splendor of her twenty-three years.

However, it was too late now to hope to meet anybody; there was not a single foot-passenger about; the street was decidedly empty, dull, and lifeless. Nothing was to be heard, except the whistling of sudden gusts of wind, and nothing was to be seen, except the flickering gas lights, which looked like dying butterflies. Well! The only thing was to return home alone.

But suddenly, tall Fanny saw a human form standing on the pavement at the next crossing. It seemed to be hesitating and uncertain which way to go. The figure, which was very small and slight, was wrapped in a long cloak, which reached almost to the ground.

"Perhaps he is a hunchback," the girl said to herself. "They like tall women!" And she walked quickly toward him, from habit already saying: *"Pst! Pst!* Come home with me, you handsome, dark fellow!" What luck! The man did not go away, but came toward Fanny, although somewhat timidly, while she went to meet him, repeating her wheedling words, so as to reassure him. She went all the quicker, as she saw that he was staggering with the zigzag walk of a drunken man, and she thought to herself: "When once they sit down, there is no possibility of getting these beggars up again, for they want to go to sleep just where they are. I only hope I shall get to him before he tumbles down."

Luckily she reached him just in time to catch him in her arms, but as soon as she had done so, she almost let him fall, in her astonishment. It was neither a drunken man, nor a hunchback, but a child of twelve or thirteen in an overcoat, who was crying, and who said in a weak voice: "I beg your pardon, Madame, I beg your pardon. If you only knew how hungry and cold I am! I beg your pardon! Oh! I am so cold."

"Poor child!" she said, putting her arms around him and kissing him. And she carried him off, with a full, but happy heart, and while he continued to sob, she said to him mechanically: "Don't be frightened, my little man. You will see how nice I can be! And then, you can warm yourself; I have a capital fire."

But the fire was out; the room, however, was warm, and the child said, as soon as they got in: "Oh! How comfortable it is here! It is a great deal better than in the streets, I can tell you! And I have been living in the streets for six days." He began to cry again, and added: "I beg your pardon, Madame. I have eaten nothing for two days."

Tall Fanny opened her cupboard, which had glass doors. The middle shelf held all her linen, and on the upper one there was a box of Albert biscuits, a drop of brandy at the bottom of a bottle, and a few small lumps of sugar in a cup. With that and some water out of a jug, she concocted a sort of broth, which he swallowed ravenously, and when he had done, he wished to tell his story, which he did, yawning all the time.

His grandfather (the only one of his relatives whom he had ever known), who had been a painter and decorator at Soisson, had died about a month before; but before his death he had said to him:

"When I am gone, little man, you will find a letter to my brother, who is in business in Paris, among my papers. You must take it to him, and he will be certain to take care of you. However, in any case you must go to Paris, for you have an aptitude for painting, and only there can you hope to become an artist."

When the old man was dead (he died in the hospital), the child started, dressed in an old coat of his grandfather's, and with thirty francs, which was all that the old man had left behind him, in his pocket. But when he got to Paris, there was nobody of the name at the address mentioned on the letter. The dead man's brother had left there six months before; nobody knew where he had gone to, and so the child was alone. For a few days he managed to exist on what he had over, after paying for his journey. After he had spent his last franc, he had wandered about the streets, as he had no money with which to pay for a bed, buying his bread by the half-penny-worth, until for the last forty-eight hours he had been without anything, absolutely without anything.

He told her all this while he was half asleep, amid sobs and yawns, so that the girl did not venture to ask him any more questions, in spite of her curiosity, but, on the contrary, cut him short, and undressed him while she listened, and only interrupted him to kiss him, and to say to him: "There, there, my poor child! You shall tell me the rest tomorrow. You cannot go on now, so go to bed and have a good sleep." And as soon as he had finished, she put him to bed, where he immediately fell into a profound sleep. Then she undressed herself quickly got into bed by his side, so that she might keep him warm, and went to sleep, crying to herself, without exactly knowing why.

The next day they breakfasted and dined together at a common eating-house, on money that she had borrowed, and when it was dark, she said to the child: "Wait for me here; I will come for you at closing time." She came back sooner, however, about ten o'clock. She had twelve francs, which she gave him, telling him that she had *earned them,* and she continued, with a laugh: "I feel that I shall make some more. I am in luck this evening, and you have brought it me. Do not be impatient, but have some milk-posset while you are waiting for me."

She kissed him, and the kind girl felt real maternal happiness as she went out. An hour later, however, she was arrested by the police for having been found in a prohibited place, and off she went, food for St. Lazare.*

And the child, who was turned out by the proprietor at closing time, and then driven from the furnished lodgings the next morning, where they told him that *tall Fanny was in jail,* began his wretched vagabond life in the streets again, with only the twelve francs to depend on.

*   *   *   *   *   *   *

Fifteen years afterward, the newspapers announced one morning that the famous Fanny Clariet, the celebrated "horizontal," whose caprices had caused a revolution in high life, that queen of frail beauties for whom three men had

committed suicide, and so many others had ruined themselves, that incomparable living statue, who had attracted all Paris to the theater where she impersonated Venus in her transparent skin tights, made of woven air and a knitted nothing, had been shut up in a lunatic asylum. She had been seized suddenly; it was an attack of general paralysis, and as her debts were enormous, when her estate had been liquidated, she would have to end her days at La Salpêtrière.

"No, certainly not!" François Guerland, the painter, said to himself, when he read the notice of it in the papers. "No, the great Fanny shall certainly not end like that." For it was certainly she; there could be no doubt about it. For a long time after she had shown him that act of charity, which he could never forget, the child had tried to see his benefactress again. But Paris is a very mysterious place, and he himself had had many adventures before he grew up to be a man, and, eventually, almost somebody! But he only found her in the distance; he had recognized her at the theater, on the stage, or as she was getting into her carriage, which was fit for a princess. And how could he approach her then? Could he remind her of the time when her price was five francs? No, assuredly not; and so he had followed her, thanked her, and blessed her, from a distance.

But now the time had come for him to pay his debt and he paid it. Although tolerably well known as a painter with a future in store for him, he was not rich. But what did that matter? He

*A prison in Paris.

mortgaged that future which people prophesied for him, and gave himself over, hand and foot, to a picture-dealer. Then he had the poor woman taken to an excellent asylum where she could have not only every care, but every necessary comfort and even luxury. Alas! however, general paralysis never forgives. Sometimes it releases its prey, like the cruel cat releases the mouse, for a brief moment only to lay hold of it again later, more fiercely than ever. Fanny had that period of abatement in her symptoms, and one morning the physician was able to say to the young man: "You are anxious to remove her? Very well! But you will soon have to bring her back, for the cure is only apparent, and her present state will only endure for a month, at most, and then only if the patient is kept free from every excitement and excess!"

"And without that precaution?" Guerland asked him.

"Then," the doctor replied; "the final crisis will be all the nearer; that is all. But whether it would be nearer or more remote, it will not be the less fatal."

"You are sure of that?"

"Absolutely sure."

François Guerland took tall Fanny out of the asylum, installed her in splendid apartments, and went to live with her there. She had grown old, bloated, with white hair, and sometimes wandered in her mind, and she did not recognize in him the poor little lad on whom she had taken pity in the days gone by, nor did he remind her of the circumstances. He allowed her to believe that she was adored by a rich young man, who was passionately devoted to her. He was young, ardent, and caressing. Never had a mistress such a lover, and for three weeks before she relapsed into the horrors of madness, which were happily soon terminated by her death, she intoxicated herself with the ecstasy of his kisses, and thus bade farewell to conscient life in an apotheosis of love.

*   *   *   *   *   *   *

The other day at dessert, after an artists' dinner, they were speaking of François Guerland, whose last picture at the Salon had been so deservedly praised.

"Ah! yes," one of them said with a contemptuous voice and look—"That handsome fellow Guerland!"

And another, accentuating the insinuation, added boldly: "Yes, that is exactly it! That handsome, too handsome fellow Guerland, the man who allows himself to be kept by women."

A Normandy Joke ✕

THE procession came in sight in the hollow road which was shaded by the tall trees which grew on the slopes of the farm. The newly-married couple came first, then the relations, then the invited guests, and lastly the poor of the neighborhood while the village urchins, who hovered about the narrow road like flies, ran in and out of the ranks, or climbed up the trees to see it better.

The bridegroom was a good-looking young fellow, Jean Patu, the richest farmer in the neighborhood. Above all things, he was an ardent sportsman who seemed to lose all common sense in order to satisfy that passion, who spent large sums on his dogs, his keepers, his ferrets, and his guns. The bride, Rosalie Roussel, had been courted by all the likely young fellows in the district, for they all thought her prepossessing and they knew that she would have a good dowry, but she had chosen Patu—partly, perhaps, because she liked him better than she did the others, but still more, like a careful Normandy girl, because he had more crown pieces.

When they went in at the white gateway of the husband's farm, forty shots resounded without any one seeing those who fired. The shooters were hidden in the ditches, and the noise seemed to please the men, who were sprawling about heavily in their best clothes, very much. Patu left his wife, and running up to a farm servant whom he perceived behind a tree, he seized his gun, and fired a shot himself, kicking his heels about like a colt. Then they went on, beneath the apple-trees heavy with fruit, through the high grass and through the herd of calves, who looked at them with their great eyes, got up slowly and remained standing with their muzzles turned toward the wedding party.

The men became serious when they came within measurable distance of the wedding-dinner. Some of them, the rich ones, had on tall, shining silk hats, which seemed altogether out of place there; others had old head-coverings with a long nap, which might have been taken for moleskin, while the humbler among them wore caps. All the women had on shawls, which they wore as loose wraps, holding the ends daintily under their arms. They were red, parti-colored, flaming shawls, and their brightness seemed to astonish the black fowls on the dung-heap, the ducks on the side of the pond, and the pigeons on the thatched roofs.

The extensive farm-buildings awaited the party at the end of that archway of apple-trees, and a sort of vapor came out of open door and windows, an almost overwhelming smell of eatables, which permeated the vast building, issuing from its openings and even from its very walls. The string of guests extended through the yard; when the foremost of them reached the house, they broke the chain and dispersed, while behind they were still coming in at the open gate. The ditches were now lined with urchins and poor curious people. The shots did not cease, but came from every side at once, injecting a cloud of smoke, and that powdery smell which has the same intoxicating effects as absinthe, into the atmosphere.

The women were shaking their dresses outside the door to get rid of the dust, were undoing their cap strings and folding their shawls over their arms. Then they went into the house to lay them aside altogether for the time. The table was laid in the great kitchen, which could hold a hundred persons; they sat down to dinner at two o'clock and at eight o'clock they were still eating; the men, in their shirt sleeves, with their waistcoats unbuttoned, and with red faces, were swallowing the food and drink as if they were insatiable. The cider sparkled merrily, clear and golden in the large glasses, by the side of the dark, blood-colored wine, and between every dish they made the *trou,* the Normandy *trou,* with a glass of brandy which inflamed the body, and put foolish notions into the head.

From time to time, one of the guests, being as full as a barrel, would go out for a few moments to get a mouthful of fresh air, as they said, and then return with redoubled appetite. The farmers' wives, with scarlet faces and their corsets nearly bursting, did not like to follow their example, until one of them, feeling more uncomfortable than the others, went out. Then all the rest followed her example, and came back quite ready for any fun, and the rough jokes began afresh. Broadsides of doubtful jokes were exchanged across the table, all about the wedding-night, until the whole arsenal of peasant wit was exhausted. For the last hundred years, the same broad jokes had served for similar occasions, and although everyone knew them, they still hit the mark, and made both rows of guests roar with laughter.

At the bottom of the table four young fellows, who were neighbors, were preparing some practical jokes for the newly-married couple, and they seemed to have got hold of a good one, by the way they whispered and laughed. Suddenly, one of them profiting by a moment of silence, exclaimed: "The poachers will have a good time to-night with this moon! I say, Jean, you will not be looking at the moon, will you?" The bridegroom turned to him quickly

and replied: "Only let them come, that's all!" But the other young fellow began to laugh, and said: "I do not think you will neglect your duty for them!"

The whole table was convulsed with laughter, so that the glasses shook, but the bridegroom became furious at the thought that anybody should profit by his wedding to come and poach on his land, and repeated: "I only say: just let them come!"

Then there was a flood of talk with a double meaning which made the bride blush somewhat, although she was trembling with expectation, and when they had emptied the kegs of brandy they all went to bed. The young couple went into their own room, which was on the ground floor, as most rooms in farmhouses are. As it was very warm, they opened the windows and closed the shutters. A small lamp in bad taste, a present from the bride's father, was burning on the chest of drawers, and the bed stood ready to receive the young people, who did not stand upon all the ceremony which is usual among refined people.

The young woman had already taken off her wreath and her dress, and was in her petticoat, unlacing her boots, while Jean was finishing his cigar, and looking at her out of the corners of his eyes. It was an ardent look, more sensual than tender, for he felt more desire than love for her. Suddenly with a brusque movement, like a man who is going to set to work, he took off his coat. She had already taken off her boots, and was now pulling off her stockings; then she said to him: "Go and hide yourself behind the curtains while I get into bed."

He seemed as if he were going to refuse, but with a cunning look went and hid himself with the exception of his head. She laughed and tried to cover up his eyes, and they romped in an amorous and happy manner, without shame or embarrassment. At last he did as she asked him, and in a moment she unfastened her petticoat which slipped down her legs, fell at her feet and lay on the floor in a circle. She left it there, stepped over it, naked with the exception of her floating chemise, and slipped into the bed, whose springs creaked beneath her weight. He immediately went up to her, without his shoes and in his trousers, and stopping over his wife sought her lips, which she hid beneath the pillow, when a shot was heard in the distance, in the direction of the forest of Râpées, as he thought.

He raised himself anxiously, and running to the window, with his heart beating, he opened the shutters. The full moon flooded the yard with yellow light, and the silhouettes of the apple-trees made black shadows at his feet, while in the distance the fields gleamed, covered with the ripe corn. But as he was leaning out, listening to every sound in the still night, two bare arms were put round his neck, and his wife whispered, trying to pull him back: "Do leave them alone; it has nothing to do with you. Come to bed."

He turned round, put his arms round her, and drew her toward him, feeling her warm skin through the thin material, and lifting her up in his vigorous arms, he carried her toward their couch, but just as he was laying her on the bed, which yielded beneath her weight, they heard another report, considerably nearer this time. Jean, giving way to his tumultuous rage, swore aloud: "Good God! Do you think I shall not go out and see what it is, because of you? Wait, wait a few minutes!" He put on his shoes again, took down his gun, which was always hanging within reach upon the wall, and, as his wife threw herself on her knees in her terror to implore him not to go, he hastily freed himself, ran to the window and jumped into the yard.

She waited one hour, two hours, until daybreak, but her husband did not return. Then she lost her head, aroused the house, related how angry Jean was, and said that he had gone after the poachers, and immediately all the male farm-servants, even the boys, went in search of their master. They found him two leagues from the farm, tied hand and foot, half dead with rage, his gun broken, his trousers turned inside out, three dead hares hanging round his neck, and a placard on his chest, with these words:

"Who goes on the chase, loses his place."

And later on when he used to tell this story of his wedding night, he generally added: "Ah! As far as a joke went, it was a good joke. They caught me in a snare, as if I had been a rabbit, the dirty brutes, and they shoved my head into a bag. But if I can only catch them some day, they had better look out for themselves!"

That is how they amuse themselves in Normandy, on a wedding day.

The Father

I.

As HE lived at Batignolles and was a clerk in the Public Education Office, he took the omnibus every morning to the center of Paris, sitting opposite a girl with whom he fell in love.

She went to the shop where she was employed at the same time every day. She was a little brunette, one of those dark girls whose eyes are so dark that they look like spots, and whose complexion has a look like ivory. He always saw her coming at the corner of the same street. She generally ran to catch the heavy vehicle, and would spring upon the steps before the horses had quite stopped. Then getting inside, rather out of breath, and sitting down, she would look round her.

The first time that he saw her, François Tessier felt that her face pleased him extremely. One sometimes meets a woman whom one longs to clasp madly in one's arms immediately, without even knowing her. That girl answered to his inward desires, to his secret hopes, to that sort of ideal of love which one cherishes in the depths of the heart, without knowing it.

He looked at her intently, in spite of himself, and she grew embarrassed at his looks and blushed. He saw it and tried to turn away his eyes; but he involuntarily fixed them upon her again every moment, although he tried to look in another direction, and in a few days they knew each other without having spoken. He gave up his place to her when the omnibus was full, and got outside, though he was very sorry to do it. By this time she had gone so far as to greet him with a little smile; and although she always dropped her eyes under his looks, which she felt were too ardent, yet she did not appear offended at being looked at in such a manner.

They ended by speaking. A kind of rapid intimacy had become established between them, a daily intimacy of half an hour, which was certainly one of the most charming half hours in his life to him. He thought of her all the rest of the time, saw her continually during the long office hours, for he was haunted and bewitched by that floating and yet tenacious recollection which the image of a beloved woman leaves in us, and it seemed to him that the entire possession of that little person would be maddening happiness to him, almost above human realization.

Every morning now she shook hands with him, and he preserved the feeling of that touch, and the recollection of the gentle pressure of her little fingers, until the next day. He almost fancied that he preserved the imprint of it on his skin, and he anxiously waited for this short omnibus ride all the rest of the time, while Sundays seemed to him heartbreaking days. However, there was no doubt that she loved him, for one Sunday in spring, she promised to go and lunch with him at Maison-Lafitte the next day.

II.

She was at the railway station first, which surprised him, but she said: "Before going, I want to speak to you. We have twenty minutes, and that is more than I shall take for what I have to say."

She trembled as she hung on his arm, and looked down, while her cheeks were pale, but she continued: "I do not want you to be deceived in me, and I shall not go there with you unless you promise, unless you swear—not to do—not to do anything that is at all improper—"

She had suddenly become as red as a poppy, and said no more. He did not know what to reply, for he was happy and disappointed at the same time. At the bottom of his heart, he perhaps preferred that it should be so, and yet—during the night he had indulged in anticipations that sent the hot blood flowing through his veins. He should love her less, certainly, if he knew that her conduct was light, but then it would be so charming, so delicious for him! And he made all a man's usual selfish calculations in love affairs.

As he did not say anything she began to speak again in an agitated voice, and with tears in her eyes: "If you do not promise to respect me altogether, I shall return home."

And so he squeezed her arm tenderly and replied: "I promise, you shall only do what you like." She appeared relieved in mind, and asked with a smile: "Do you really mean it?"

And he looked into her eyes and replied. "I swear it."

"Now you may take the tickets," she said.

During the journey they could hardly speak, as the carriage was full, and when they got to Maison-Lafitte they went toward the Seine. The sun, which shone full upon the river, upon the leaves, and upon the turf, seemed to reflect in them his brightness, and they went, hand in hand, along the bank, looking at the shoals of little fish swimming near the bank, brimming over with happiness, as if they were raised from earth in their lightness of heart.

At last she said: "How foolish you must think me!"

"Why?" he asked.

"To come out like this, all alone with you."

"Certainly not; it is quite natural."

"No, no, it is not natural for me—because I do not wish to commit a fault, and yet this is how girls fall. But if you only knew how wretched it is, every day, the same thing, every day in the month, and every month in the year. I live quite alone with mamma, and as she has had a great deal of trouble, she is not very cheerful. I do the best I can and try to laugh in spite of everything, but I do not always succeed. But all the same, it was wrong in me to come, though you, at any rate, will not be sorry."

By the way of an answer he kissed her ardently on the ear that was nearest him, but she started away from him with an abrupt movement, and getting suddenly angry exclaimed: "Oh! Monsieur François, after what you swore to me!" And they went back to Maison-Lafitte.

They had lunch at the Petit-Havre, a low house, buried under four enormous poplar trees, by the side of the river. The air, the heat, the small bottle of white wine, and the sensation of being so close together, made them red and silent, with a feeling of oppression, but after the coffee they regained their high spirits, and having crossed the Seine, started off along the bank toward the

village of La Frette. Suddenly he asked:
"What is your name?"

"Louise."

"Louise," he repeated, and said nothing more.

The river, which described a long curve, bathed a row of white houses in the distance, which were reflected in the water. The girl picked the daisies and made them into a great bunch, while he sang vigorously, as intoxicated as a colt that has been turned into a meadow. On their left, a vine-covered slope followed the river. Suddenly François stopped motionless with astonishment: "Oh! look there!" he said.

The vines had come to an end, and the whole slope was covered with lilac bushes in flower. It was a violet-colored wood! A kind of great carpet stretched over the earth, reaching as far as the village, more than two miles off. She also stood surprised and delighted, and murmured: "Oh! how pretty!" And crossing a meadow they walked toward that curious low hill, which every year furnishes all the lilac which is sold through Paris on the carts of the flower-peddlers.

A narrow path went beneath the trees, so they took it, and when they came to a small clearing, they sat down.

Swarms of flies were buzzing around them, and making a continuous, gentle sound, and the sun, the bright sun of a perfectly still day, shone over the bright slopes, and from that wood of flowers a powerful aroma was borne toward them, a wave of perfume, the breath of the flowers.

A church clock struck in the distance. They embraced gently, then clasped each other close, lying on the grass,

without the knowledge of anything except of that kiss. She had closed her eyes and held him in her arms, pressing him to her closely, without a thought, with her reason bewildered, and from head to foot in passionate expectation. And she surrendered herself altogether without knowing that she had given herself to him. But she soon came to herself with the feeling of a great misfortune, and she began to cry and sob with grief, with her face buried in her hands.

He tried to console her, but she wanted to start, to return and go home immediately, and she kept saying as she walked along, quickly: "Good heavens! good heavens!"

He said to her: "Louise! Louise! Please let us stop here." But now her cheeks were red and her eyes hollow, and as soon as they got to the railway station in Paris, she left him, without even saying good-bye.

III.

When he met her in the omnibus next day, she appeared to him to be changed and thinner, and she said to him: "I want to speak to you; we will get down at the Boulevard."

As soon as they were on the pavement, she said: "We must bid each other good-bye; I cannot meet you again after what has happened."

"But why?" he asked.

"Because I cannot; I have been culpable, and I will not be so again."

Then he implored her, tortured by desire, maddened by the wish of having her entirely, in the absolute freedom of nights of love, but she replied firmly: 'No, I cannot, I cannot."

He, however, only grew all the more excited, and promised to marry her, but she said: "No," and left him.

For over a week he did not see her. He could not manage to meet her, and as he did not know her address, he thought he had lost her altogether. On the ninth day, however, there was a ring at his bell, and when he opened it, she was there. She threw herself into his arms, and did not resist any longer, and for three months she was his mistress. He was beginning to grow tired of her, when she told him a woman's most precious secret, and then he had one idea and wish—to break with her at any price. As, however, he could not do that, not knowing how to begin or what to say, full of anxiety, he took a decisive step. One night he changed his lodgings, and disappeared.

The blow was so heavy that she did not look for the man who had abandoned her, but threw herself at her mother's knees, confessed her misfortune, and some months after gave birth to a boy.

IV.

Years passed, and François Tessier grew old, without there having been any alteration in his life. He led the dull, monotonous life of bureaucrats, without hopes and without expectations. Every day he got up at the same time, went through the same streets, went through the same door, past the same porter, went into the same office, sat in the same chair, and did the same work. He was alone in the world, alone, during the day, in the midst of his different colleagues, and alone at night in his bache-lor's lodgings, and he laid by a hundred francs a month, against old age.

Every Sunday he went to the Champs-Elysées to watch the elegant people, the carriages, and the pretty women, and the next day he used to say to one of his colleagues: "The return of the carriages from the Bois de Boulogne was very brilliant yesterday." One fine Sunday morning, however, he went into the Parc Monceau where the mothers and nurses, sitting on the sides of the walks, watched the children playing, and suddenly François Tessier started. A woman passed by, holding two children by the hand: a little boy of about ten and a little girl of four. It was she.

He walked another hundred yards, and then fell into a chair, choking with emotion. She had not recognized him, and so he came back, wishing to see her again. She was sitting down now and the boy was standing by her side very quietly, while the little girl was making sand castles. It was she, it was certainly she, but she had the serious looks of a lady, was dressed simply, and looked self-possessed and dignified. He looked at her from a distance, for he did not venture to go near, but the little boy raised his head, and François Tessier felt himself tremble. It was his own son, there could be no doubt of that. And as he looked at him, he thought he could recognize himself as he appeared in an old photograph taken years ago. He remained hidden behind a tree, waiting for her to go, that he might follow her.

He did not sleep that night. The idea of the child especially harassed him. His son! Oh! If he could only have known, have been sure? But what could he have done? However, he went to the house where she had once lived and asked about her. He was told that a neighbor, an honorable man of strict morals had been touched by her distress and had married her; he knew the fault she had committed and had married her, and had even recognized the child, his, François Tessier's child, as his own.

He returned to the Parc Monceau every Sunday, for then he always saw her, and each time he was seized with a mad, an irresistible longing to take his son into his arms, cover him with kisses and to steal him, to carry him off.

He suffered horribly in his wretched isolation as an old bachelor, with nobody to care for him, and he also suffered atrocious mental torture, torn by paternal tenderness springing from remorse, longing, and jealousy, and from that need of loving one's own children which nature has implanted in all. And so at last he determined to make a despairing attempt, and going up to her, as she entered the park, he said, standing in the middle of the path, pale and with trembling lips: "You do not recognize me." She raised her eyes, looked at him, uttered an exclamation of horror, of terror, and taking the two children by the hand she rushed away, dragging them after her, while he went home and wept, inconsolably.

Months passed without his seeing her again. He suffered, day and night, for he was a prey to his paternal love. He would gladly have died, if he could only have kissed his son; he would have committed murder, performed any task, braved any danger, ventured anything. He wrote to her, but she did not reply, and after writing her some twenty let-

ters he saw that there was no hope of altering her determination. Then he formed the desperate resolution of writing to her husband, being quite prepared to receive a bullet from a revolver, if need be. His letter only consisted of a few lines, as follows:

"MONSIEUR:
"You must have a perfect horror of my name, but I am so miserable, so overcome by misery, that my only hope is in you, and therefore I venture to request you to grant me an interview of only five minutes.
"I have the honor, etc."

The next day he received the reply:

"MONSIEUR:
"I shall expect you to-morrow, Tuesday, at five o'clock."

V.

As he went up the staircase, François Tessier's heart beat so violently that he had to stop several times. There was a dull and violent noise in his breast, the noise as of some animal galloping; he could only breathe with difficulty, and had to hold on to the banisters in order not to fall.

He rang the bell on the third floor, and when a maidservant had opened the door, he asked: "Does Monsieur Flamel live here?"

"Yes, Monsieur. Kindly come in."

He was shown into the drawing-room; he was alone and waited, feeling bewildered, as in the midst of a catastrophe, until a door opened and a man came in. He was tall, serious, and rather stout, he wore a black frock-coat, and pointed to a chair with his hand.

François Tessier sat down, and said, panting: "Monsieur—Monsieur—I do not know whether you know my name—whether you know—"

Monsieur Flamel interrupted him: "You need not tell it me, Monsieur, I know it. My wife has spoken to me about you."

He spoke it in the dignified tone of voice of a good man who wishes to be severe,—with the commonplace stateliness of an honorable man, and François Tessier continued: "Well, Monsieur, I want to say this. I am dying of grief, of remorse, of shame, and I would like once, only once, to kiss the child."

Monsieur Flamel rose and rang the bell, and when the servant came in, he said: "Will you bring Louis here?" When she had gone out, they remained face to face, without speaking, having nothing more to say to one another, and waited. Then, suddenly, a little boy of ten rushed into the room, and ran up to the man whom he believed to be his father, but he stopped when he saw a stranger, and Monsieur Flamel kissed him and said: "Now go and kiss that gentleman, my dear." And the child went up to Tessier nicely, and looked at him.

François Tessier had risen, he let his hat fall and was ready to fall himself as he looked at his son, while Monsieur Flamel had turned away, from a feeling of delicacy, and was looking out of the window.

The child waited in surprise, but he picked up the hat and gave it to the stranger. Then François, taking the child up in his arms, began to kiss him wildly all over his face, on his eyes, his cheeks, on his mouth, on his hair, and the youngster, frightened at the shower of kisses tried to avoid them, turned away his head and pushed away the man's face with his little hands. But suddenly François Tessier put him down, cried: "Good-bye! Good-bye!" and rushed out of the room as if he had been a thief.

The Artist

"BAH! Monsieur," the old mountebank said to me; "it is a matter of exercise and habit, that is all! Of course, one requires to be a little gifted that way and not to be butter-fingered, but what is chiefly necessary is patience and daily practice for long, long years."

His modesty surprised me all the more, because of all performers who are generally infatuated with their own skill, he was the most wonderfully clever one I had met. Certainly I had frequently seen him, for everybody had seen him in some circus or other, or even in traveling shows, performing the trick that consists of putting a man or woman with extended arms against a wooden target, and in throwing knives between their fingers and round their heads, from a distance. There is nothing very extraordinary in it, after all, when one knows *the tricks of the trade,* and that the knives are not the least sharp, and stick into the wood at some distance from the flesh. It is the rapidity of the throws, the glitter of the blades, and the curve which the handles make toward their living object, which give an air of danger to an exhibition that has become commonplace, and only requires very middling skill.

But here there was no trick and no deception, and no dust thrown into the eyes. It was done in good earnest and in all sincerity. The knives were as sharp as razors, and the old mountebank planted them close to the flesh, exactly in the angle between the fingers. He surrounded the head with a perfect halo of knives, and the neck with a collar from which nobody could have extricated himself without cutting his carotid artery, while, to increase the difficulty, the old fellow went through the performance without seeing, his whole face being covered with a close mask of thick oilcloth.

Naturally, like other great artists, he was not understood by the crowd, who confounded him with vulgar tricksters, and his mask only appeared to them a trick the more, and a very common trick into the bargain.

"He must think us very stupid," they said. "How could he possibly aim without having his eyes open?"

And they thought there must be imperceptible holes in the oilcloth, a sort of latticework concealed in the material. It was useless for him to allow the public to examine the mask for themselves before the exhibition began. It was all very well that they could not discover any trick, but they were only all the more convinced that they were

being tricked. Did not the people know that they ought to be tricked?

I had recognized a great artist in the old mountebank, and I was quite sure that he was altogether incapable of any trickery. I told him so, while expressing my admiration to him; and he had been touched by my open admiration and above all by the justice I had done him. Thus we became good friends, and he explained to me, very modestly, the real trick which the crowd do not understand, the eternal trick contained in these simple words: "To be gifted by nature and to practice every day for long, long years."

He had been especially struck by the certainty which I expressed that any trickery must become impossible to him. "Yes," he said to me; "quite impossible! Impossible to a degree which you cannot imagine. If I were to tell you! But where would be the use?"

His face clouded over, and his eyes filled with tears. I did not venture to force myself into his confidence. My looks, however, were not so discreet as my silence, and begged him to speak; so he responded to their mute appeal.

"After all," he said; "why should I not tell you about it? You will understand me." And he added, with a look of sudden ferocity: "She understood it, at any rate!"

"Who?" I asked.

"My strumpet of a wife," he replied. "Ah! Monsieur, what an abominable creature she was—if you only knew! Yes, she understood it too well, too well, and that is why I hate her so; even more on that account, than for having deceived me. For that is a natural fault, is it not, and may be pardoned? But the other thing was a crime, a horrible crime."

The woman, who stood against the wooden target every night with her arms stretched out and her fingers extended, and whom the old mountebank fitted with gloves and with a halo formed of his knives, which were as sharp as razors and which he planted close to her, was his wife. She might have been a woman of forty, and must have been fairly pretty, but with a perverse prettiness; she had an impudent mouth, a mouth that was at the same time sensual and bad, with the lower lip too thick for the thin, dry upper lip.

I had several times noticed that every time he planted a knife in the board, she uttered a laugh, so low as scarcely to be heard, but which was very significant when one heard it, for it was a hard and very mocking laugh. I had always attributed that sort of reply to an artifice which the occasion required. It was intended, I thought, to accentuate the danger she incurred and the contempt that she felt for it, thanks to the sureness of the thrower's hands, and so I was very much surprised when the mountebank said to me:

"Have you observed her laugh, I say? Her evil laugh which makes fun of me, and her cowardly laugh which defies me? Yes, cowardly, because she knows that nothing can happen to her; nothing, in spite of all she deserves, in spite of all that I ought to do to her, in spite of all that I *want* to do to her."

"What do you want to do?"

"Confound it! Cannot you guess? I want to kill her."

"To kill her, because she has—"

"Because she has deceived me? No,

no, not that, I tell you again. I have forgiven her for that a long time ago, and I am too much accustomed to it! But the worst of it is that the first time I forgave her, when I told her that all the same I might some day have my revenge by cutting her throat, if I choose, without seeming to do it on purpose, as if it were an accident, mere awkwardness—"

"Oh! So you said that to her?"

"Of course I did, and I meant it. I thought I might be able to do it, for you see I had the perfect right to do so. It was so simple, so easy, so tempting! Just think! A mistake of less than half an inch, and her skin would be cut at the neck where the jugular vein is, and the jugular would be severed. My knives cut very well! And when once the jugular is cut—good-bye. The blood would spurt out, and one, two, three red jets, and all would be over; she would be dead, and I should have had my revenge!"

"That is true, certainly, horribly true!"

"And without any risk to me, eh? An accident, that is all; bad luck, one of those mistakes which happen every day in our business. What could they accuse me of? Whoever would think of accusing me, even? Homicide through imprudence, that would be all! They would even pity me, rather than accuse me. 'My wife! My poor wife!' I should say, sobbing. 'My wife, who is so necessary to me, who is half the breadwinner, who takes part in my performance!' You must acknowledge that I should be pitied!"

"Certainly; there is not the least doubt about that."

"And you must allow that such a revenge would be a very nice revenge, the best possible revenge which I could have with assured impunity."

"Evidently that is so."

"Very well! But when I told her so, as I have told you, and more forcibly still; threatening her, as I was mad with rage and ready to do the deed that I had dreamed of on the spot, what do you think she said?"

"That you were a good fellow, and would certainly not have the atrocious courage to—"

"Tut! tut! tut! I am not such a good fellow as you think. I am not frightened of blood, and that I have proved already, though it would be useless to tell you how and where. But I had no necessity to prove it to her, for she knows that I am capable of a good many things; even of crime; especially of one crime."

"And she was not frightened?"

"No. She merely replied that I could not do what I said; you understand. That I could not do it!"

"Why not?"

"Ah! Monsieur, so you do not understand? Why do you not? Have I not explained to you by what constant, long, daily practice I have learned to plant my knives without seeing what I am doing?"

"Yes, well, what then?"

"Well! Cannot you understand what she has understood with such terrible results, that now my hand would no longer obey me if I wished to make a mistake as I threw?"

"Is it possible?"

"Nothing is truer, I am sorry to say. For I really have wished to have the revenge which I have dreamed of, and which I thought so easy. Exasperated by that bad woman's insolence and confidence in her own safety, I have several times made up my mind to kill her, and have exerted all my energy and all my skill to make my knives fly aside when I threw them to make a border round her neck. I have tried with all my might to make them deviate half an inch, just enough to cut her throat. I wanted to, and I have never succeeded, never. And always the slut's horrible laugh makes fun of me, always, always."

And with a deluge of tears, with something like a roar of unsatiated and muzzled rage, he ground his teeth as he wound up: "She knows me, the jade; she is in the secret of my work, of my patience, of my trick, routine, whatever you may call it! She lives in my innermost being, and sees into it more closely than you do, or than I do myself. She knows what a faultless machine I have become, the machine of which she makes fun, the machine which is too well wound up, the machine which cannot get out of order—and she knows that I *cannot* make a mistake."

———•———

False Alarm

"I HAVE a perfect horror of pianos," said Frémecourt, "of those hateful boxes which fill up a drawing-room, and have

not even the soft sound and the queer shape of the mahogany or veneered spinets, to which our grandmothers sighed out exquisite, long-forgotten ballads, allowing their fingers to run over the keys, while around them there floated a delicate odor of powder and muslin, and some little Abbé or other turned over the leaves, continually making mistakes as he looked at the patches close to the lips on the white skin of the player instead of at the music. "I wish there were a tax upon them, or that some evening during a riot, the people would make huge bonfires of them, which would illuminate the whole town. They simply exasperate me, and affect my nerves, and make me think of the tortures those poor girls must suffer, who are condemned not to stir for hours, but to keep on constantly strumming away at the chromatic scales and monotonous arpeggios, and to have no other object in life except to win a prize at the Conservatoire.

"Their incoherent music suggests to me the sufferings of those who are ill, abandoned, wounded. It proceeds from every floor of every house, it irritates you, nearly drives you mad, and makes you break out into ironical fits of laughter.

"And yet when that madcap Lâlie Spring honored me with her love—I never can refuse anything to a woman who smells of rare perfume, and who has a large store of promises in her looks, and who puts out her red, smiling lips immediately, as if she were going to offer you handsel money—I bought a piano, so that she might strum upon it to her heart's content. I got it, however, on the hire-purchase system, and paid so much a month, as *grisettes** do for their furniture.

"At that time I had the apartments I had so long dreamed of: warm, elegant, light, well-arranged, with two entrances, and an incomparable porter's wife, who had been canteen-keeper in a Zouave regiment, and knew everything and understood everything at a wink.

"It was the kind of apartment from which a woman has not the courage to escape, so as to avoid temptation, where she becomes weak, and rolls herself up on the soft, eider-down cushions like a cat, where she is appeased, and in spite of herself, thinks of love at the sight of the low, wide couch, so suitable for caresses, rooms with heavy curtains, which quite deaden the sound of voices and of laughter, and filled with flowers that scent the air, whose smell lingers on the folds of the hangings.

"They were rooms in which a woman forgets time, where she begins by accepting a cup of tea and nibbling a sweet cake, and abandons her fingers timidly and with regret to other fingers which tremble, and are hot, and so by degrees loses her head and succumbs.

"I do not know whether the piano brought us ill luck, but Lâlie had not even time to learn four songs before she disappeared like the wind, just as she had come—*flick-flack,* good-night, goodbye. Perhaps it was from spite, because she had found letters from other women on my table; perhaps to change her companion, as she was not one of those to hang on to one man and become a fixture.

"I had not been in love with her, certainly, but yet such breakings have always some effect on a man. Some

*Work-girl, a name applied to those whose virtue is not too rigorous.

string breaks when a woman leaves you, and you think that you must start all over again, and take another chance in that forbidden sport in which one risks so much, the sport that one has been through a hundred times before, and which leaves you nothing to show in the end.

"Nothing is more unpleasant than to lend your apartments to a friend, to realize that some one is going to disturb the mysterious intimacy which really exists between the actual owner and his fortune, and violate the soul of those past kisses which float in the air; that the room whose tints you connect with some recollection, some dream, some sweet vision, and whose colors you have tried to make harmonize with certain fair-haired, pink-skinned girls, is going to become a commonplace lodging, like the rooms in an ordinary lodging house, fit only for hidden crime and for evanescent love affairs.

"However, poor Stanis had begged me so urgently to do him that service; he was so very much in love with Madame de Fréjus. Among the characters in this comedy there was a brute of a husband who was terribly jealous and suspicious; one of those Othellos who have always a flea in their ear, and come back unexpectedly from shooting or the club, who pick up pieces of torn paper, listen at doors, smell out meetings with the nose of a detective, and seem to have been sent into the world only to be cuckolds, but who know better than most how to lay a snare, and to play a nasty trick. So when I went to Venice, I consented to let him have my rooms.

"I will leave you to guess whether they made up for lost time, although,

after all, it is no business of yours. My journey, however, which was only to have lasted a few weeks, — just long enough for me to benefit by the change of air, to rid my brain of the image of my last mistress, and perhaps to find another, among that strange mixture of society which one meets there, a medley of American, Slav, Viennese, and Italian women, who instill a little artificial life into that old city, asleep amid the melancholy silence of the lagoons, —was prolonged, and Stanis was as much at home in my rooms as he was in his own.

"Madame Piquignolles, the retired canteen-keeper, took great interest in this adventure, watched over their little love affair, and, as she used to say, was on guard as soon as they arrived one after the other, the marchioness covered with a thick veil, and slipping in as quickly as possible, always uneasy, and afraid that Monsieur de Fréjus might be following her, and Stanis with the assured and satisfied look of an amorous husband, who is going to meet his little wife after having been away from home for a few days.

"Well, one day during one of those delicious moments when his beloved one, fresh from her bath, and invigorated by the coolness of the water, was pressing close to her lover, reclining in his arms, and smiling at him with half-closed eyes, during one of those moments when people do not speak, but continue their dream, the sentinel, without even asking leave, suddenly burst into the room, for worthy Madame Piquignolles was in a terrible fight.

"A few minutes before, a well-dressed gentleman, followed by two others of seedy appearance, but who looked very strong, and fit to knock anybody down, had questioned and cross-questioned her in a rough manner, and tried to turn her inside out, as she said, asking her whether Monsieur de Frémecourt lived on the first floor, without giving her any explanation. When she declared that there was nobody occupying the apartments then, as her lodger was not in France, Monsieur de Fréjus—for it could certainly be nobody but he—had burst out into an evil laugh, and said: 'Very well; I shall go and fetch the Police Commissary of the district, and he will make you let us in!'

"And as quickly as possible, while she was telling her story, now in a low, and then in a shrill voice, the woman picked up the marchioness's dress, cloak, lace-edged drawers, silk petticoat, and little varnished shoes, pulled her out of bed, without giving her time to let her know what she was doing, or to moan, or to have a fit of hysterics, and carried her off, as if she had been a doll, with all her pretty toggery, to a large, empty cupboard in the dining-room, that was concealed by Flemish tapestry. 'You are a man. Try to get out of the mess,' she said to Stanis as she shut the door; 'I will be answerable for Madame.' And the enormous woman, who was out of breath by hurrying upstairs as she had done, and whose kind, large, red face was dripping with perspiration, while her ample bosom shook beneath her loose jacket, took Madame de Fréjus on to her knees as if she had been a baby, whose nurse was trying to quiet her.

"She felt the poor little culprit's heart beating as if it were going to burst, while shivers ran over her skin, which was so soft and delicate that the porter's wife was afraid that she might hurt it with her coarse hands. She was struck with wonder at the cambric chemise, which a gust of wind would have carried off as if it had been a pigeon's feather, and by the delicate odor of that scarce flower which filled the narrow cupboard, and which rose up in the darkness from that supple body, which was impregnated with the warmth of the bed.

"She would have liked to be there, in that profaned room, and to tell them in a loud voice—with her hands upon her hips as at the time when she used to serve brandy to her comrades at Daddy l'Arbi's—that they had no commonsense, that they were none of them good for much, neither the Police Commissary, the husband nor the subordinates, to come and torment a pretty young thing, who was having a little bit of fun, like that. It was a nice job, to get over the wall in that way, to be absent from the second call of names, especially when they were all of the same sort, and were glad of five francs an hour! She had certainly done quite right to get out sometimes and to have a sweetheart, and she was a charming little thing, and that she would say, if she were called before the Court as a witness.

"And she took Madame de Fréjus in her arms to quiet her, and repeated the same thing a dozen times, whispered pretty things to her, and interrupted her occasionally to listen whether they were not searching all the nooks and corners of the apartment. 'Come, come,' she said; 'do not distress yourself. Be calm, my dear. It hurts me to hear you cry like that. There will be no mischief done, I will vouch for it.'

"The marchioness, who was nearly fainting and who was prostrate with terror, could only sob out: 'Good heavens! Good heavens!'

"She scarcely seemed to be conscious of anything; her head seemed vacant, her ears buzzed, and she felt benumbed, like one who goes to sleep in the snow.

"Ah! Only to forget everything, as her love dream was over, to go out quickly like those little rose-colored tapers at Nice, on Shrove Tuesday evening.

"Oh! Not to awake any more, as the to-morrow would come in black and sad, because a whole array of barristers, ushers, solicitors, and judges would be against her, and disturb her usual quietude, would torment her, cover her with mud, as her delicious, amorous adventure—her first—which had been so carefully enveloped in mystery, and had been kept so secret behind closed shutters and thick veils, would become an everyday episode of adultery which would get wind and be discussed from door to door. The lilac had faded, and she was obliged to bid farewell to happiness, as if to an old friend who was going far, very far away, never to return!

"Suddenly, however, she started and sat up, with her neck stretched out and her eyes fixed, while the ex-canteen-keeper, who was trembling with emotion, put her hands to her left ear, which was her best, like a speaking trumpet, and tried to hear the cries which succeeded each other from room to room, amid a noise of opening and shutting of doors.

"'Ah! upon my word, I am not blind. It is Monsieur de Stanis who is looking for me, and making all that noise. Don't you hear: "M'ame Piquignolles, M'me Piquignolles!" Saved, saved!'

"Stanis was still quite pale, and in a panting voice he cried out to them: 'Nothing serious, only that fool Frémecourt, who lent me the rooms, has forgotten to pay for his piano for the last five months, a hundred francs* a month. You understand; they came to claim it, and as we did not reply, why, they fetched the Police Commissary, and gained entrance in the name of the law.'

"'A nice fright to give one!' Madame Piquignolles said, throwing herself on to a chair. 'Confound the nasty piano!'

"It may be useless to add, that the marchioness has quite renounced *trifles*, as our forefathers used to say, and would deserve a prize for virtue, if the Academy would only show itself rather more gallant toward pretty women, who take crossroads in order to become virtuous.

"Emotions like that cure people of running risks of that kind!"

_____

$20.

That Pig of a Morin

"THERE, my friend," I said to Labarbe, "you have just repeated those five words, 'That pig of a Morin.' Why on earth do I never hear Morin's name mentioned without his being called a *pig?*"

Labarbe, who is a Deputy, looked at me with eyes like an owl's, and said: "Do you mean to say that you do not know Morin's story, and yet come from La Rochelle?" I was obliged to declare that I did not know Morin's story, and then Labarbe rubbed his hands, and began his recital.

"You knew Morin, did you not, and you remember his large linen-draper's shop on the Quai de la Rochelle?"

"Yes, perfectly."

"All right, then. You must know that in 1862 or '63 Morin went to spend a fortnight in Paris for pleasure, or for his pleasures, but under the pretext of renewing his stock, and you also know what a fortnight in Paris means for a country shopkeeper; it makes his blood grow hot. The theater every evening, women's dresses rustling up against you, and continual excitement; one goes almost mad with it. One sees nothing but dancers in tights, actresses in very low dresses, round legs, fat shoulders, all nearly within reach of one's hands, without daring or being able to touch, and one scarcely ever tastes an inferior dish. And one leaves it, with heart still all in a flutter, and a mind still exhilarated by a sort of longing for kisses which tickle one's lips.

"Morin was in that state when he took his ticket for La Rochelle by the 8:40 night express. And he was walking up and down the waiting-room at the station, when he stopped suddenly in front of a young lady who was kissing an old one. She had her veil up, and Morin murmured with delight: 'By Jove, what a pretty woman!'

"When she had said 'Good-bye' to the old lady, she went into the waiting-room, and Morin followed her; then she went on to the platform and Morin still followed her; then she got into an empty carriage, and he again followed her. There were very few travelers by the express, the engine whistled, and the train started. They were alone. Morin devoured her with his eyes. She appeared to be about nineteen or twenty, and was fair, tall, and with demure looks. She wrapped a railway rug round her legs and stretched herself on the seat to sleep.

"Morin asked himself: 'I wonder who she is?' And a thousand conjectures, a thousand projects went through his head. He said to himself: 'So many adventures are told as happening on railway journeys, that this may be one that is going to present itself to me. Who knows? A piece of good luck like that happens very quickly, and perhaps I need only be a little venturesome. Was it not Danton who said: "Audacity, more audacity, and always audacity." If it was not Danton it was Mirabeau, but that does not matter. But then, I have no audacity, and that is the difficulty. Oh! If one only knew, if one could only read people's minds! I will bet that every day one passes by magnificent opportunities without knowing it, though a gesture would be enough to let me know that she did not ask for anything better.

172

"Then he imagined to himself combinations which led him to triumph. He pictured some chivalrous deed, or merely some slight service which he rendered her, a lively, gallant conversation which ended in a declaration, which ended in—in what you think.

"But he could find no opening; had no pretext, and he waited for some fortunate circumstance, with his heart ravaged, and his mind topsy-turvy. The night passed, and the pretty girl still slept, while Morin was meditating his own fall. The day broke and soon the first ray of sunlight appeared in the sky, a long, clear ray which shone on the face of the sleeping girl, and woke her, so she sat up, looked at the country, then at Morin and smiled. She smiled like a happy woman, with an engaging and bright look, and Morin trembled. Certainly that smile was intended for him, it was a discreet invitation, the signal which he was waiting for. That smile meant to say: 'How stupid, what a ninny, what a dolt, what a donkey you are, to have sat there on your seat like a post all night.

'Just look at me, am I not charming? And you have sat like that for the whole night, when you have been alone with a pretty woman, you great simpleton!'

"She was still smiling as she looked at him, she even began to laugh; and he lost his head trying to find something suitable to say, no matter what. But he could thing of nothing, nothing, and then, seized with a coward's courage, he said to himself: 'So much the worse, I will risk everything,' and suddenly, without the slightest warning, he went toward her, his arms extended, his lips protruding and seizing her in his arms kissed her.

"She sprang up with a bound, crying out: 'Help! help!' and screaming with terror; then she opened the carriage door, and waved her arm outside; then mad with terror she was trying to jump out, while Morin, who was almost distracted, and feeling sure that she would throw herself out, held her by her skirt and stammered: 'Oh! Madame! Oh! Madame!'

"The train slackened speed, and then stopped. Two guards rushed up at the young woman's frantic signals, and she threw herself into their arms, stammering: 'That man wanted—wanted—to—to—' And then she fainted.

"They were at Mauzé station, and the gendarme on duty arrested Morin. When the victim of his brutality had regained her consciousness, she made her charge against him, and the police drew it up. The poor linen-draper did not reach home till night, with a prosecution hanging over him for an outrage on morals in a public place.

II.

"At that time I was editor of the 'Fanal des Charentes,' and I used to meet Morin every day at the Café du Commerce. The day after his adventure he came to see me, as he did not know what to do. I did not hide my opinion from him, but said to him: 'You are no better than a pig. No decent man behaves like that.'

"He cried. His wife had given him a beating, and he foresaw his trade ruined, his name dragged through the mire and dishonored, his friends outraged and taking no more notice of him. In the end he excited my pity, and I sent for my colleague Rivet, a bantering, but very sensible little man, to give us his advice.

"He advised me to see the Public Prosecutor, who was a friend of mine, and so I sent Morin home, and went to call on the magistrate. He told me that the woman who had been insulted was a young lady, Mademoiselle Henriette Bonnel, who had just received her certificate as governess in Paris, and spent her holidays with her uncle and aunt, who were very respectable tradespeople in Mauzé, and what made Morin's case all the more serious was, that the uncle had lodged a complaint. But the public official had consented to let the matter drop if this complaint were withdrawn, so that we must try and get him to do this.

"I went back to Morin's and found him in bed, ill with excitement and distress. His wife, a tall, rawboned woman with a beard, was abusing him continually, and she showed me into the room, shouting at me: 'So you have come to see that pig of a Morin. Well, there he is, the darling!' And she planted herself in front of the bed, with her hands on her hips. I told him how matters stood, and he begged me to go and see her uncle and aunt. It was a delicate mission, but I undertook it, and the poor devil never ceased repeating: 'I assure you I did not even kiss her, no, not even that. I will take my oath to it!'

"I replied: 'It is all the same; you are nothing but a pig.' And I took a thousand francs which he gave me, to employ them as I thought best, but as

I did not care venturing to her uncle's house alone, I begged Rivet to go with me, which he agreed to do, on the condition that we went immediately, for he had some urgent business at La Rochelle that afternoon. So two hours later we rang at the door of a nice countryhouse. A pretty girl came and opened the door to us, who was assuredly the young lady in question, and I said to Rivet in a low voice: 'Confound it! I begin to understand Morin!'

"The uncle, Monsieur Tonnelet, subscribed to 'The Fanal,' and was a fervent political co-religionist of ours. He received us with open arms, and congratulated us and wished us joy; he was delighted at having the two editors in his house, and Rivet whispered to me: 'I think we shall be able to arrange the matter of that pig of a Morin for him.'

"The niece had left the room, and I introduced the delicate subject. I waved the specter of scandal before his eyes; I accentuated the inevitable depreciation which the young lady would suffer if such an affair got known, for nobody would believe in a simple kiss. The good man seemed undecided, but could not make up his mind about anything without his wife, who would not be in until late that evening. But suddenly he uttered an exclamation of triumph: 'Look here, I have an excellent idea. I will keep you here to dine and sleep, and when my wife comes home, I hope we shall be able to arrange matters.'

"Rivet resisted at first, but the wish to extricate that pig of a Morin decided him, and we accepted the invitation. So the uncle got up radiant, called his niece, and proposed that we should take a stroll in his grounds, saying: 'We will leave serious matters until the morning.' Rivet and he began to talk politics, while I soon found myself lagging a little behind with the girl, who was really charming! charming! and with the greatest precaution I began to speak to her about her adventure, and try to make her my ally. She did not, however, appear the least confused, and listened to me like a person who was enjoying the whole thing very much.

"I said to her: 'Just think, Mademoiselle, how unpleasant it will be for you. You will have to appear in court, to encounter malicious looks, to speak before everybody, and to recount that unfortunate occurrence in the railway-carriage, in public. Do you not think, between ourselves, that it would have been much better for you to have put that dirty scoundrel back into his place without calling for assistance, and merely to have changed your carriage?' She began to laugh, and replied: 'What you say is quite true! but what could I do? I was frightened, and when one is frightened, one does not stop to reason with oneself. As soon as I realized the situation, I was very sorry that I had called out, but then it was too late. You must also remember that the idiot threw himself upon me like a madman, without saying a word and looking like a lunatic. I did not even know what he wanted of me.'

"She looked me full in the face, without being nervous or intimidated, and I said to myself: 'She is a funny sort of girl, that: I can quite see how that pig Morin came to make a mistake,' and I went on, jokingly: 'Come, Mademoi-

selle, confess that he was excusable, for after all, a man cannot find himself opposite such a pretty girl as you are, without feeling a legitimate desire to kiss her.'

"She laughed more than ever, and showed her teeth, and said: 'Between the desire and the act, Monsieur, there is room for respect.' It was a funny expression to use, although it was not very clear, and I asked abruptly: 'Well now, supposing I were to kiss you now, what would you do?' She stopped to look at me from head to foot, and then said calmly: 'Oh! you? That is quite another matter.'

"I knew perfectly well, by Jove, that it was not the same thing at all, as everybody in the neighborhood called me 'Handsome Labarbe.' I was thirty years old in those days, but I asked her: 'And why, pray?'

"She shrugged her shoulders, and replied: 'Well, because you are not so stupid as he is.' And then she added, looking at me slyly: 'Nor so ugly, either.'

"Before she could make a movement to avoid me, I had implanted a hearty kiss on her cheek. She sprang aside, but it was too late, and then she said: 'Well, you are not very bashful, either! But don't do that sort of thing again.'

"I put on a humble look and said in a low voice: 'Oh! Mademoiselle, as for me, if I long for one thing more than another, it is to be summoned before a magistrate on the same charge as Morin.'

"'Why?' she asked.

"Looking steadily at her, I replied: 'Because you are one of the most beautiful creatures living; because it would be an honor and a glory for me to have offered you violence, and because people would have said, after seeing you: "Well, Labarbe has richly deserved what he has got, but he is a lucky fellow, all the same." '

"She began to laugh heartily again, and said: 'How funny you are!' And she had not finished the word *funny*, before I had her in my arms and was kissing her ardently wherever I could find a place, on her forehead, on her eyes, on her lips occasionally, on her cheeks, in fact, all over her head, some part of which she was obliged to leave exposed, in spite of herself, in order to defend the others. At last she managed to release herself, blushing and angry. 'You are very unmannerly, Monsieur,' she said, 'and I am sorry I listened to you.'

"I took her hand in some confusion, and stammered out: 'I beg your pardon, Mademoiselle. I have offended you; I have acted like a brute! Do not be angry with me for what I have done. If you knew—'

"I vainly sought for some excuse, and in a few moments she said: 'There is nothing for me to know, Monsieur.' But I had found something to say, and I cried: 'Mademoiselle, I love you!'

"She was really surprised, and raised her eyes to look at me, and I went on: 'Yes, Mademoiselle, and pray listen to me. I do not know Morin, and I do not care anything about him. It does not matter to me the least if he is committed for trial and locked up meanwhile. I saw you here last year, and I was so taken with you, that the thought of you has never left me since, and it does not matter to me whether you be-

lieve me or not. I thought you adorable, and the remembrance of you took such a hold on me that I longed to see you again, and so I made use of that fool Morin as a pretext, and here I am. Circumstances have made me exceed the due limits of respect, and I can only beg you to pardon me.'

"She read the truth in my looks, and was ready to smile again; then she murmured: 'You humbug!' But I raised my hand, and said in a sincere voice (and I really believe that I was sincere): 'I swear to you that I am speaking the truth.' She replied quite simply: 'Really?'

"We were alone, quite alone, as Rivet and her uncle had disappeared in a side walk, and I made her a real declaration of love, while I squeezed and kissed her hands, and she listened to it as to something new and agreeable, without exactly knowing how much of it she was to believe, while in the end I felt agitated, and at last really myself believed what I said. I was pale, anxious, and trembling, and I gently put my arm round her waist, and spoke to her softly, whispering into the little curls over her ears. She seemed dead, so absorbed in thought was she.

"Then her hand touched mine, and she pressed it, and I gently circled her waist with a trembling, and gradually a firmer, grasp. She did not move now, and I touched her cheeks with my lips, and suddenly, without seeking them mine met hers. It was a long, long kiss, and it would have lasted longer still, if I had not heard a *Hum! Hum!* just behind me. She made her escape through the bushes, and I turning round saw Rivet coming toward me, and walking in the middle of the path. He said without even smiling: 'So that is the way in which you settle the affair of that pig Morin.'

"I replied, conceitedly: 'One does what one can, my dear fellow. But what about the uncle? How have you got on with him? I will answer for the niece.'

—" 'I have not been so fortunate with him,' he replied. Whereupon I took his arm, and we went indoors.

III.

"Dinner made me lose my head altogether. I sat beside her, and my hand continually met hers under the tablecloth, my foot touched hers, and our looks encountered each other.

"After dinner we took a walk by moonlight, and I whispered all the tender things I could think of to her. I held her close to me, kissed her every moment, moistening my lips against hers, while her uncle and Rivet were disputing as they walked in front of us. We went in, and soon a messenger brought a telegram from her aunt, saying that she would return by the first train the next morning, at seven o'clock.

" 'Very well, Henriette,' her uncle said, 'go and show the gentlemen their rooms.' She showed Rivet his first, and he whispered to me: 'There was no danger of her taking us into yours first.' Then she took me to my room, and as soon as she was alone with me, I took her in my arms again and tried to excite her senses and overcome her resistance, but when she felt that she was near succumbing, she escaped out of the room, and I got between the sheets, very much put out and excited and feeling rather foolish, for I knew that I should not sleep much. I was wondering how I could have committed such a mistake, when there was a gentle knock at my door, and on my asking who was there, a low voice replied: 'I.'

"I dressed myself quickly and opened the door, and she came in: 'I forgot to ask you what you take in the morning,' she said, 'chocolate, tea, or coffee?' I put my arms around her impetuously and said, devouring her with kisses: 'I will take—I will take—' But she freed herself from my arms, blew out my candle, and disappeared, and left me alone in the dark, furious, trying to find some matches and not able to do so. At last I got some and I went into the passage, feeling half mad, with my candlestick in my hand.

"What was I going to do? I did not stop to reason, I only wanted to find her, and I would. I went a few steps without reflecting, but then I suddenly thought to myself: 'Suppose I should go into the uncle's room, what should I say?' And I stood still, with my head a void, and my heart beating.

"But in a few moments, I thought of an answer: 'Of course, I shall say that I was looking for Rivet's room, to speak to him about an important matter,' and I began to inspect all the doors, trying to find hers, and at last I took hold of a handle at a venture, turned it and went in. There was Henriette, sitting on her bed and looking at me in tears. So I gently turned the key, and going up to her on tiptoe, I said: 'I forgot to ask you for something to read, Mademoiselle.' I will not tell you the book I read, but it is the most wonderful of romances, the most divine of poems. And when once I had turned the first page, she let me turn over as many leaves as l liked, and I got through so many chapters that our candles were quite burned out.

"Then, after thanking her, I was stealthily returning to my room, when a rough hand seized me, and a voice— it was Rivet's—whispered in my ear: 'So you have not yet quite settled that affair of Morin's?'

"At seven o'clock the next morning, she herself brought me a cup of chocolate. I have never drunk anything like it, soft, velvety, perfumed, delicious. I could scarcely take away my lips from the cup, and she had hardly left the room when Rivet came in. He seemed nervous and irritable like a man who had not slept, and he said to me crossly: 'If you go on like this, you will end by spoiling the affair of that pig of a Morin!'

"At eight o'clock the aunt arrived. Our discussion was very short, for they withdrew their complaint, and I left five hundred francs for the poor of the town. They wanted to keep us for the day, and they arranged an excursion to go and see some ruins. Henriette made signs to me to stay, behind her uncle's back, and I accepted, but Rivet was determined to go, and though I took him aside, and begged and prayed him to do this for me he appeared quite exasperated and kept saying to me: 'I have had enough of that pig of a Morin's affair, do you hear?'

"Of course I was obliged to go also, and it was one of the hardest moments of my life. I could have gone on arranging that business as long as I lived, and when we were in the railway carriage, after shaking hands with her

in silence, I said to Rivet: 'You are a mere brute!' And he replied: 'My dear fellow, you were beginning to excite me confoundedly.'

"On getting to the 'Fanal' office, I saw a crowd waiting for us, and as soon as they saw us, they all exclaimed: 'Well, have you settled the affair of that pig of a Morin?' All La Rochelle was excited about it, and Rivet, who had got over his ill humor on the journey, had great difficulty in keeping himself from laughing as he said: 'Yes, we have managed it, thanks to Labarbe.' And we went to Morin's.

"He was sitting in an easy-chair, with mustard plasters on his legs, and cold bandages on his head, nearly dead with misery. He was coughing with the short cough of a dying man, without anyone knowing how he had caught it, and his wife seemed like a tigress ready to eat him. As soon as he saw us he trembled violently as to make his hands and knees shake, so I said to him immediately: 'It is all settled, you dirty scamp, but don't do such a thing again.'

"He got up choking, took my hands and kissed them as if they had belonged to a prince, cried, nearly fainted, embraced Rivet, and even kissed Madame Morin, who gave him such a push as to send him staggering back into his chair. But he never got over the blow; his mind had been too much upset. In all the country round, moreover, he was called nothing but that pig of a Morin, and the epithet went through him like a sword-thrust every time he heard it. When a street-boy called after him: 'Pig!' he turned his head instinctively. His friends also overwhelmed him with horrible jokes, and used to chaff him, whenever they were eating ham, by saying: 'It's a bit of you!' He died two years later.

"As for myself, when I was a candidate for the Chamber of Deputies in 1875, I called on the new notary at Foncerre, Monsieur Belloncle, to solicit his vote, and a tall, handsome, and evidently wealthy lady received me. 'You do not know me again?' she said.

"I stammered out: 'But—no, Madame.'

" 'Henriette Bonnel?'

" 'Ah!' And I felt myself turning pale, while she seemed perfectly at her ease, and looked at me with a smile.

"As soon as she had left me alone with her husband, he took both my hands, and squeezing them as if he meant to crush them, he said: 'I have been intending to go and see you for a long time, my dear sir, for my wife has very often talked to me about you. I know under what painful circumstances you made her acquaintance, and I know also how perfectly you behaved, how full of delicacy, tact, and devotion you showed yourself in the affair—' He hesitated, and then said in a lower tone, as if he had been saying something low and coarse: 'In the affair of that pig of a Morin.' "

VOLUME II

Miss Harriet ✕—

THERE were seven of us in a four-in-hand, four women and three men, one of whom was on the box seat beside the coachman. We were following, at a foot pace, the broad highway which serpentines along the coast.

Setting out from Etretat at break of day, in order to visit the ruins of Tancarville, we were still asleep, chilled by the fresh air of the morning. The women, especially, who were but little accustomed to these early excursions, let their eyelids fall and rise every moment, nodding their heads or yawning, quite insensible to the glory of the dawn.

It was autumn. On both sides of the road the bare fields stretched out, yellowed by the corn and wheat stubble which covered the soil like a bristling growth of beard. The spongy earth seemed to smoke. Larks were singing high up in the air, while other birds piped in the bushes.

At length the sun rose in front of us, a bright red on the plane of the horizon; and as it ascended, growing clearer from minute to minute, the country seemed to awake, to smile, to shake and stretch itself, like a young girl who is leaving her bed in her white airy chemise. The Count d'Etraille, who was seated on the box, cried:

"Look! look! a hare!" and he pointed toward the left, indicating a piece of hedge. The leveret threaded its way along, almost concealed by the field, only its large ears visible. Then it

swerved across a deep rut, stopped, again pursued its easy course, changed its direction, stopped anew, disturbed, spying out every danger, and undecided as to the route it should take. Suddenly it began to run, with great bounds from its hind legs, disappearing finally in a large patch of beet-root. All the men had woke up to watch the course of the beast.

René Lemanoir then exclaimed:

"We are not at all gallant this morning," and looking at his neighbor, the little Baroness of Stérennes, who was struggling with drowsiness, he said to her in a subdued voice: "You are thinking of your husband, Baroness. Reassure yourself; he will not return before Saturday, so you have still four days."

She responded to him with a sleepy smile:

"How rude you are." Then, shaking off her torpor, she added: "Now, let somebody say something that will make us all laugh. You, Monsieur Chenal, who have the reputation of possessing a larger fortune than the Duke of Richelieu, tell us a love story in which you have been mixed up, anything you like."

Léon Chenal, an old painter, who had once been very handsome, very strong, who was very proud of his physique and very amiable, took his long white beard in his hand and smiled; then, after a few moments' reflection, he became suddenly grave.

"Ladies, it will not be an amusing

181

tale; for I am going to relate to you the most lamentable love affair of my life, and I sincerely hope that none of my friends has ever passed through a similar experience.

I.

"At that time I was twenty-five years old, and was making daubs along the coast of Normandy. I call 'making daubs' that wandering about, with a bag on one's back, from mountain to mountain, under the pretext of studying and of sketching nature. I know nothing more enjoyable than that happy-go-lucky wandering life, in which you are perfectly free, without shackles of any kind, without care, without pre-occupation, without thought even of to-morrow. You go in any direction you please, without any guide save your fancy, without any counselor save your eyes. You pull up, because a running brook seduces you, or because you are attracted, in front of an inn, by the smell of potatoes frying. Sometimes it is the perfume of clematis which decides you in your choice, or the naïve glance of the servant at an inn. Do not despise me for my affection for these rustics. These girls have soul as well as feeling, not to mention firm cheeks and fresh lips; while their hearty and willing kisses have the flavor of wild fruit. Love always has its price, come whence it may. A heart that beats when you make your appearance, an eye that weeps when you go away, these are things so rare, so sweet, so precious, that they must never be despised.

"I have had rendezvous in ditches in which cattle repose, and in barns among the straw, still steaming from the heat of the day. I have recollections of canvas spread on rude and creaky benches, and of hearty, fresh, free kisses, more delicate, free from affectation, and sincere than the subtle attractions of charming and distinguished women.

"But what you love most amid all these varied adventures are the country, the woods, the risings of the sun, the twilight, the light of the moon. For the painter these are honeymoon trips with Nature. You are alone with her in that long and tranquil rendezvous. You go to bed in the fields amid marguerites and wild poppies, and, with eyes wide open, you watch the going down of the sun, and descry in the distance the little village, with its pointed clock-tower, which sounds the hour of midnight.

"You sit down by the side of a spring which gushes out from the foot of an oak, amid a covering of fragile herbs, growing and redolent of life. You go down on your knees, bend forward, and drink the cold and pellucid water, wetting your mustache and nose; you drink it with a physical pleasure, as though you were kissing the spring, lip to lip. Sometimes, when you encounter a deep hole, along the course of these tiny brooks, you plunge into it, quite naked, and on your skin, from head to foot, like an icy and delicious caress, you feel the lovely and gentle quivering of the current.

"You are gay on the hills, melancholy on the verge of pools, exalted when the sun is crowned in an ocean of blood-red shadows, and when it casts on the rivers its red reflection. And at night, under the moon, as it passes the vault of heaven, you think of things, singular things, which would never have occurred to your mind under the brilliant light of day.

"So, in wandering through the same country we are in this year, I came to the little village of Benouville, on the Falaise, between Yport and Etretat. I came from Fécamp, following the coast, a high coast, perpendicular as a wall, with projecting and rugged rocks falling sheer down into the sea. I had walked since the morning on the close clipped grass, as smooth and as yielding as a carpet. Singing lustily, I walked with long strides, looking sometimes at the slow and lazy flight of a gull, with its short, white wings, sailing in the blue heavens, sometimes at the green sea, or at the brown sails of a fishing bark. In short, I had passed a happy day, a day of listlessness and of liberty.

"I was shown a little farmhouse, where travelers were put up, a kind of inn, kept by a peasant, which stood in the center of a Norman court, surrounded by a double row of beeches.

"Quitting the Falaise, I gained the hamlet, which was hemmed in by trees, and I presented myself at the house of Mother Lecacheur.

"She was an old, wrinkled, and austere rustic, who always seemed to yield to the pressure of new customs with a kind of contempt.

"It was the month of May: the spreading apple-trees covered the court with a whirling shower of blossoms which rained unceasingly both upon people and upon the grass.

"I said:

"'Well, Madame Lecacheur, have you a room for me?'

"Astonished to find that I knew her name, she answered:

"'That depends; everything is let; but, all the same, there will be no harm in looking.'

"In five minutes we were in perfect accord, and I deposited my bag upon the bare floor of a rustic room, furnished with a bed, two chairs, a table, and a washstand. The room opened into the large and smoky kitchen, where the lodgers took their meals with the people of the farm and with the farmer himself, who was a widower.

"I washed my hands, after which I went out. The old woman was fricasseeing a chicken for dinner in a large fireplace, in which hung the stew-pot, black with smoke.

"'You have travelers, then, at the present time?' said I to her.

"She answered in an offended tone of voice:

"'I have a lady, an English lady, who has attained to years of maturity. She is occupying my other room.'

"By means of an extra five sous a day, I obtained the privilege of dining out in the court when the weather was fine.

"My cover was then placed in front of the door, and I commenced to gnaw with hunger the lean members of the Normandy chicken, to drink the clear cider, and to munch the hunk of white bread, which, though four days old, was excellent.

"Suddenly, the wooden barrier which opened on to the highway was opened, and a strange person directed her steps toward the house. She was very slender, very tall, enveloped in a Scotch shawl with red borders. You would have believed that she had no arms, if you had not seen a long hand appear just above the hips, holding a white tourist umbrella. The face of a mummy, surrounded with sausage rolls of plaited gray hair, which bounded at every step she took, made me think, I know not why, of a sour herring adorned with curling papers. Lowering her eyes, she passed quickly in front of me, and entered the house.

"This singular apparition made me curious. She undoubtedly was my neighbor, the aged English lady of whom our hostess had spoken.

"I did not see her again that day. The next day, when I had begun to paint at the end of that beautiful valley, which you know extends as far as Etretat, lifting my eyes suddenly, I perceived something singularly attired standing on the crest of the declivity; it looked like a pole decked out with flags. It was she. On seeing me, she suddenly disappeared. I re-entered the house at midday for lunch, and took my seat at the common table, so as to make the acquaintance of this old and original creature. But she did not respond to my polite advances, was insensible even to my little attentions. I poured water out for her with great alacrity, I passed her the dishes with great eagerness. A slight, almost imperceptible movement of the head, and an English word, murmured so low that I did not understand it, were her only acknowledgments.

"I ceased occupying myself with her, although she had disturbed my thoughts. At the end of three days, I knew as much about her as did Madame Lecacheur herself.

"She was called Miss Harriet. Seeking out a secluded village in which to pass the summer, she had been attracted to Benouville, some six months before, and did not seem disposed to quit it. She never spoke at table, ate rapidly, reading all the while a small book, treating of some Protestant propaganda. She gave a copy of it to everybody. The curé himself had received no less than four copies, at the hands of an urchin to whom she had paid two sous' commission. She said sometimes to our hostess, abruptly, without preparing her in the least for the declaration:

"'I love the Saviour more than all; I worship him in all creation; I adore him in all nature; I carry him always in my heart.'

And she would immediately present the old woman with one of her brochures which were destined to convert the universe.

"In the village she was not liked. In fact, the schoolmaster had declared that she was an atheist, and that a sort of reproach attached to her. The curé, who had been consulted by Madame Lecacheur, responded:

"'She is a heretic, but God does not wish the death of the sinner, and I believe her to be a person of pure morals.'

"These words, 'atheist,' 'heretic,' words which no one can precisely define, threw doubts into some minds. It was asserted, however, that this Englishwoman was rich, and that she had passed her life in traveling through every country in the world, because her family had thrown her off. Why had her family thrown her off? Because of her natural impiety?

"She was, in fact, one of those people of exalted principles, one of those opinionated puritans of whom England produces so many, one of those good and insupportable old women who haunt the *tables d'hôte* of every hotel in Europe, who spoil Italy, poison Switzerland, render the charming cities of the Mediterranean uninhabitable, carry everywhere their fantastic manias, their petrified vestal manners, their indescribable toilettes, and a certain odor of indiarubber, which makes one believe that at night they slip themselves into a case of that material. When I meet one of these people in a hotel, I act like birds which see a manikin in a field.

"This woman, however, appeared so singular that she did not displease me.

"Madame Lecacheur, hostile by instinct to everything that was not rustic, felt in her narrow soul a kind of hatred for the ecstatic extravagances of the old girl. She had found a phrase by which to describe her, I know not how, but a phrase assuredly contemptuous, which had sprung to her lips, invented probably by some confused and mysterious travail of soul. She said: 'That woman is a demoniac.' This phrase as uttered by that austere and sentimental creature, seemed to me irresistibly comic. I, myself, never called her now anything else but 'the demoniac,' feeling a singular pleasure in pronouncing this word on seeing her.

"I would ask Mother Lecacheur: 'Well, what is our demoniac about today?' To which my rustic friend would respond, with an air of having been scandalized:

"'What do you think, sir? She has picked up a toad which has had its leg battered, and carried it to her room,

and has put it in her washstand, and dressed it up like a man. If that is not profanation, I should like to know what is!'

"On another occasion, when walking along the Falaise, she had bought a large fish which had just been caught, simply to throw it back into the sea again. The sailor, from whom she had bought it, though paid handsomely, was greatly provoked at this act—more exasperated, indeed, than if she had put her hand into his pocket and taken his money. For a whole month he could not speak of the circumstance without getting into a fury and denouncing it as an outrage. Oh yes! She was indeed a demoniac, this Miss Harriet, and Mother Lecacheur must have had an inspiration of genius in thus christening her.

"The stable-boy, who was called Sapeur, because he had served in Africa in his youth, entertained other aversions. He said, with a roguish air: 'She is an old hag who has lived her days.' If the poor woman had but known!

"Little kind-hearted Céleste did not wait upon her willingly, but I was never able to understand why. Probably her only reason was that she was a stranger, of another race, of a different tongue, and of another religion. She was in good truth a demoniac!

"She passed her time wandering about the country, adoring and searching for God in nature. I found her one evening on her knees in a cluster of bushes. Having discovered something red through the leaves, I brushed aside the branches, and Miss Harriet at once rose to her feet, confused at having been found thus, looking at me with eyes as terrible as those of a wild cat surprised in open day.

"Sometimes, when I was working among the rocks, I would suddenly descry her on the banks of the Falaise standing like a semaphore signal. She gazed passionately at the vast sea, glittering in the sunlight, and the boundless sky empurpled with fire. Sometimes I would distinguish her at the bottom of an alley, walking quickly, with her elastic English step; and I would go toward her, attracted by I know not what, simply to see her illuminated visage, her dried-up features, which seemed to glow with an ineffable, inward, and profound happiness.

"Often I would encounter her in the corner of a field sitting on the grass, under the shadow of an apple-tree, with her little Bible lying open on her knee, while she looked meditatively into the distance.

"I could no longer tear myself away from that quiet country neighborhood, bound to it as I was by a thousand links of love for its soft and sweeping landscapes. At this farm I was out of the world, far removed from everything, but in close proximity to the soil, the good, healthy, beautiful green soil. And, must I avow it, there was something besides curiosity which retained me at the residence of Mother Lecacheur. I wished to become acquainted a little with this strange Miss Harriet, and to learn what passes in the solitary souls of those wandering old, English dames.

II.

"We became acquainted in a rather singular manner. I had just finished a study which appeared to me to display genius and power; as it must have, since it was sold for ten thousand francs, fifteen years later. It was as simple, however, as that two and two make four, and had nothing to do with academic rules. The whole of the right side of my canvas represented a rock, an enormous rock, covered with seawrack, brown, yellow, and red, across which the sun poured like a stream of oil. The light, without which one could see the stars concealed in the background, fell upon the stone, and gilded it as if with fire. That was all. A first stupid attempt at dealing with light, with burning rays, with the sublime.

"On the left was the sea, not the blue sea, the slate-colored sea, but a sea of jade, as greenish, milky, and thick as the overcast sky.

"I was so pleased with my work that I danced from sheer delight as I carried it back to the inn. I wished that the whole world could have seen it at one and the same moment. I can remember that I showed it to a cow which was browsing by the wayside, exclaiming, at the same time: 'Look at that, my old beauty; you will not often see its like again.'

"When I had reached the front of the house, I immediately called out to Mother Lecacheur, shouting with all my might:

"'Ohé! Ohé! my mistress, come here and look at this.'

"The rustic advanced and looked at my work with stupid eyes, which distinguished nothing, and did not even recognize whether the picture was the representation of an ox or a house.

"Miss Harriet came into the house, and passed in rear of me just at the moment when, holding out my canvas at arm's length, I was exhibiting it to the female innkeeper. The 'demoniac' could not help but see it, for I took care to exhibit the thing in such a way that it could not escape her notice. She stopped abruptly and stood motionless, stupefied. It was her rock which was depicted, the one which she usually climbed to dream away her time undisturbed.

"She uttered a British 'Oh,' which was at once so accentuated and so flattering, that I turned round to her smiling, and said:

" 'This is my last work, Mademoiselle.'

"She murmured ecstatically, comically, and tenderly:

" 'Oh! Monsieur, you must understand what it is to have a palpitation.'

"I colored up, of course, and was more excited by that compliment than if it had come from a queen. I was seduced, conquered, vanquished. I could have embraced her—upon my honor.

"I took my seat at the table beside her, as I had always done. For the first time, she spoke, drawling out in a loud voice:

" 'Oh! I love nature so much.'

"I offered her some bread, some water, some wine. She now accepted these with the vacant smile of a mummy. I began to converse with her about the scenery.

"After the meal, we rose from the table together and walked leisurely across the court; then, attracted by the fiery glow which the setting sun cast over the surface of the sea, I opened the outside gate which faced in the direction of the Falaise, and we walked on side by side, as satisfied as any two persons could be who have just learned to understand and penetrate each other's motives and feelings.

"It was a misty, relaxing evening, one of those enjoyable evenings which impart happiness to mind and body alike. All is joy, all is charm. The luscious and balmy air, loaded with the perfumes of herbs, with the perfumes of grass-wrack, with the odor of the wild flowers, caresses the soul with a penetrating sweetness. We were going to the brink of the abyss which overlooked the vast sea and rolled past us at the distance of less than a hundred meters.

"We drunk with open mouth and expanded chest, that fresh breeze from the ocean which glides slowly over the skin, salted as it is by long contact with the waves.

"Wrapped up in her square shawl, inspired by the balmy air and with teeth firmly set, the English-woman gazed fixedly at the great sun-ball, as it descended toward the sea. Soon its rim touched the waters, just in rear of a ship which had appeared on the horizon, until, by degrees, it was swallowed up by the ocean. We watched it plunge, diminish, and finally disappear.

"Miss Harriet contemplated with passionate regard the last glimmer of the flaming orb of day.

"She muttered: 'Oh! love—I love —' I saw a tear start in her eye. She continued: 'I wish I were a little bird, so that I could mount up into the firmament.'

"She remained standing as I had

often before seen her, perched on the river bank, her face as red as her flaming shawl. I should have liked to have sketched her in my album. It would have been an ecstatic caricature. I turned my face away from her so as to be able to laugh.

"I then spoke to her of painting, as I would have done to a fellow-artist, using the technical terms common among the devotees of the profession. She listened attentively to me, eagerly seeking to divine the sense of the obscure words, so as to penetrate my thoughts. From time to time, she would exclaim: 'Oh! I understand, I understand. This is very interesting.' We returned home.

"The next day, on seeing me, she approached me eagerly, holding out her hand; and we became firm friends immediately.

"She was a brave creature, with an elastic sort of a soul, which became enthusiastic at a bound. She lacked equilibrium, like all women who are spinsters at the age of fifty. She seemed to be pickled in vinegary innocence, though her heart still retained something of youth and of girlish effervescence. She loved both nature and animals with a fervent ardor, a love like old wine, mellow through age, with a sensual love that she had never bestowed on men.

"One thing is certain: a mare roaming in a meadow with a foal at its side, a bird's nest full of young ones, squeaking, with their open mouths and enormous heads, made her quiver with the most violent emotion.

"Poor solitary beings! Sad wanderers from *table d'hôte* to *table d'hôte*, poor beings, ridiculous and lamentable, I love you ever since I became acquainted with Miss Harriet!

"I soon discovered that she had something she would like to tell me, but dared not, and I was amused at her timidity. When I started out in the morning with my box on my back, she would accompany me as far as the end of the village, silent, but evidently struggling inwardly to find words with which to begin a conversation. Then she would leave me abruptly, and, with jaunty step, walk away quickly.

"One day, however, she plucked up courage:

" 'I would like to see how you paint pictures? Will you show me? I have been very curious.'

"And she colored up as though she had given utterance to words extremely audacious.

"I conducted her to the bottom of the Petit-Val, where I had commenced a large picture.

"She remained standing near me, following all my gestures with concentrated attention. Then, suddenly, fearing, perhaps, that she was disturbing me, she said to me: 'Thank you,' and walked away.

But in a short time she became more familiar, and accompanied me every day, her countenance exhibiting visible pleasure. She carried her folding stool under her arm, would not consent to my carrying it, and she sat always by my side. She would remain there for hours immovable and mute, following with her eye the point of my brush in its every movement. When I would obtain, by a large splatch of color spread on with a knife, a striking and unexpected effect, she would, in spite of herself, give vent to a half-suppressed 'Oh!' of astonishment, of joy, of admiration. She had the most tender respect for my canvases, an almost religious respect for that human reproduction of a part of nature's work divine. My studies appeared to her to be pictures of sanctity, and sometimes she spoke to me of God, with the idea of converting me.

"Oh! He was a queer good-natured being, this God of hers. He was a sort of village philosopher without any great resources, and without great power; for she always figured him to herself as a being quivering over injustices committed under his eyes, and helpless to prevent them.

"She was, however, on excellent terms with him, affecting even to be the confidant of his secrets and of his whims. She said:

"'God wills, or God does not will,' just like a sergeant announcing to a recruit: 'The colonel has commanded.'

"At the bottom of her heart she deplored my ignorance of the intention of the Eternal, which she strove, nay, felt herself compelled, to impart to me.

"Almost every day, I found in my pockets, in my hat when I lifted it from the ground, in my box of colors, in my polished shoes, standing in the mornings in front of my door, those little pious brochures, which she, no doubt, received directly from Paradise.

"I treated her as one would an old friend, with unaffected cordiality. But I soon perceived that she had changed somewhat in her manner; but, for a while, I paid little attention to it.

"When I walked about, whether to the bottom of the valley, or through some country lanes, I would see her suddenly appear, as though she were returning from a rapid walk. She would then sit down abruptly, out of breath, as though she had been running or overcome by some profound emotion. Her face would be red, that English red which is denied to the people of all other countries; then, without any reason, she would grow pale, become the color of the ground, and seem ready to faint away. Gradually, however, I would see her regain her ordinary color, whereupon she would begin to speak.

"Then, without warning, she would break off in the middle of a sentence, spring up from her seat, and march off so rapidly and so strongly, that it would, sometimes, put me to my wits' end to try and discover whether I had done or said anything to displease or offend her.

"I finally came to the conclusion that this arose from her early habits and training, somewhat modified, no doubt, in honor of me, since the first days of our acquaintanceship.

"When she returned to the farm, after walking for hours on the wind-beaten coast, her long curled hair would be shaken out and hanging loose, as though it had broken away from its bearings. It was seldom that this gave her any concern; though sometimes she looked as though she had been dining *sans cérémonie;* her locks having become disheveled by the breezes.

"She would then go up to her room in order to adjust what I called her glass lamps. When I would say to her, in familiar gallantry, which, however, always offended her:

" 'You are as beautiful as a planet to-day, Miss Harriet,' a little blood would immediately mount into her cheeks, the blood of a young maiden, the blood of sweet fifteen.

"Then she would become abruptly savage and cease coming to watch me paint. But I always thought:

" 'This is only a fit of temper she is passing through.'

"But it did not always pass away. When I spoke to her sometimes, she would answer me, either with an air of affected indifference, or in sullen anger; and she became by turns rude, impatient, and nervous. For a time I never saw her except at meals, and we spoke but little. I concluded, at length, that I must have offended her in something: and, accordingly, I said to her one evening:

" 'Miss Harriet, why is it that you do not act toward me as formerly? What have I done to displease you? You are causing me much pain!'

"She responded, in an angry tone, in a manner altogether *sui generis:*

" 'I am always with you the same as formerly. It is not true, not true,' and she ran upstairs and shut herself up in her room.

"At times she would look upon me with strange eyes. Since that time I have often said to myself that those condemned to death must look thus when informed that their last day has come. In her eye there lurked a species of folly, a folly at once mysterious and violent—even more, a fever, an exasperated desire, impatient, at once incapable of being realized and unrealizable!

"Nay, it seemed to me that there was also going on within her a combat, in which her heart struggled against an unknown force that she wished to overcome—perhaps, even, something else. But what could I know? What could I know?

III

"This was indeed a singular revelation.

"For some time I had commenced to work, as soon as daylight appeared, on a picture, the subject of which was as follows:

"A deep ravine, steep banks dominated by two declivities, lined with brambles and long rows of trees, hidden, drowned in milky vapor, clad in that misty robe which sometimes floats over valleys at break of day. At the extreme end of that thick and transparent fog, you see coming, or rather already come, a human couple, a stripling and a maiden embraced, interlaced, she, with head leaning on him, he, inclined toward her, and lip to lip.

"A ray of the sun, glistening through the branches, has traversed the fog of dawn and illuminated it with a rosy reflection, just behind the rustic lovers, whose vague shadows are reflected on it in clear silver. It was well done, yes, indeed, well done.

"I was working on the declivity which led to the Val d'Etretat. This particular morning, I had, by chance, the sort of floating vapor which was necessary for my purpose. Suddenly, an object appeared in front of me, a kind of phantom; it was Miss Harriet. On seeing me, she took to flight. But I called after her saying: 'Come here, come here, Mademoiselle, I have a nice little picture for you.'

"She came forward, though with seeming reluctance. I handed her my sketch. She said nothing, but stood for a long time motionless, looking at it. Suddenly she burst into tears. She wept spasmodically, like men who have been struggling hard against shedding tears, but who can do so no longer, and abandon themselves to grief, though unwillingly. I got up, trembling, moved myself by the sight of a sorrow I did not comprehend, and I took her by the hand with a gesture of brusque affection, a true French impulse which impels one quicker than one thinks.

"She let her hands rest in mine for a few seconds and I felt them quiver, as if her whole nervous system was twisting and turning. Then she withdrew her hands abruptly, or, rather, tore them out of mine.

"I recognized that shiver as soon as I had felt it; I was deceived in nothing. Ah! the love shudder of a woman, whether she is fifteen or fifty years of age, whether she is one of the people or one of the *monde,* goes so straight to my heart that I never had any difficulty in understanding it!

"Her whole frail being trembled, vibrated, yielded. I knew it. She walked away before I had time to say a word, leaving me as surprised as if I had witnessed a miracle, and as troubled as if I had committed a crime.

"I did not go in to breakfast. I took a walk on the banks of the Falaise, feeling that I could just as soon weep as laugh, looking on the adventure as both comic and deplorable, and my position

as ridiculous, fain to believe that I had lost my head.

"I asked myself what I ought to do. I debated whether I ought not to take my leave of the place and almost immediately my resolution was formed.

"Somewhat sad and perplexed, I wandered about until dinner time, and entered the farmhouse just when the soup had been served up.

"I sat down at the table, as usual. Miss Harriet was there, munching away solemnly, without speaking to anyone, without even lifting her eyes. She wore, however her usual expression, both of countenance and manner.

"I waited, patiently, till the meal had been finished. Then, turning toward the landlady, I said: 'Madame Lecacheur, it will not be long now before I shall have to take my leave of you.'

"The good woman, at once surprised and troubled, replied in a quivering voice: 'My dear sir, what is it I have just heard you say? Are you going to leave us, after I have become so much accustomed to you?'

"I looked at Miss Harriet from the corner of my eye. Her countenance did not change in the least; but the underservant came toward me with eyes wide open. She was a fat girl, of about eighteen years of age, rosy, fresh, strong as a horse, yet possessing a rare attribute in one in her position—she was very neat and clean. I had kissed her at odd times, in out of the way corners, in the manner of a mountain guide, nothing more.

"The dinner being over, I went to smoke my pipe under the apple-trees, walking up and down at my ease, from one end of the court to the other. All the reflections which I had made during the day, the strange discovery of the morning, that grotesque and passionate attachment for me, the recollections which that revelation had suddenly called up, recollections at once charming and perplexing, perhaps, also, that look which the servant had cast on me at the announcement of my departure—all these things, mixed up and combined, put me now in an excited bodily state, with the tickling sensation of kisses on my lips, and in my veins something which urged me on to commit some folly.

"Night having come on, casting its dark shadows under the trees, I descried Céleste, who had gone to shut the hencoops, at the other end of the inclosure. I darted toward her, running so noiselessly that she heard nothing, and as she got up from closing the small traps by which the chickens went in and out, I clasped her in my arms and rained on her coarse, fat face a shower of kisses. She made a struggle, laughing all the same, as she was accustomed to do in such circumstances. What made me suddenly loose my grip of her? Why did I at once experience a shock? What was it that I heard behind me?

"It was Miss Harriet who had come upon us, who had seen us, and who stood in front of us, as motionless as a specter. Then she disappeared in the darkness.

"I was ashamed, embarrassed, more annoyed at having been surprised by her than if she had caught me committing some criminal act.

"I slept badly that night; I was worried and haunted by sad thoughts. I seemed to hear loud weeping; but in this I was no doubt deceived. Moreover, I thought several times that I heard some one walking up and down in the house, and that some one opened my door from the outside.

"Toward morning, I was overcome by fatigue, and sleep seized on me. I got up late and did not go downstairs until breakfast time, being still in a bewildered state, not knowing what kind of face to put on.

"No one had seen Miss Harriet. We waited for her at table, but she did not appear. At length, Mother Lecacheur went to her room. The Englishwoman had gone out. She must have set out at break of day, as she was wont to do, in order to see the sun rise.

"Nobody seemed astonished at this and we began to eat in silence.

"The weather was hot, very hot, one of those still sultry days when not a leaf stirs. The table had been placed out of doors, under an apple-tree; and from time to time Sapeur had gone to the cellar to draw a jug of cider, everybody was so thirsty. Céleste brought the dishes from the kitchen, a ragout of mutton with potatoes, a cold rabbit, and a salad. Afterward she placed before us a dish of strawberries, the first of the season.

"As I wanted to wash and freshen these, I begged the servant to go and bring a pitcher of cold water.

"In about five minutes she returned, declaring that the well was dry. She had lowered the pitcher to the full extent of the cord, and had touched the bottom, but on drawing the pitcher up again, it was empty. Mother Lecacheur, anxious to examine the thing for herself, went and looked down the hole.

She returned announcing that one could see clearly something in the well, something altogether unusual. But this, no doubt, was pottles of straw, which, out of spite, had been cast down it by a neighbor.

"I wished also to look down the well, hoping to clear up the mystery, and perched myself close to its brink. I perceived, indistinctly, a white object. What could it be? I then conceived the idea of lowering a lantern at the end of a cord. When I did so, the yellow flame danced on the layers of stone and gradually became clearer. All four of us were leaning over the opening, Sapeur and Céleste having now joined us. The lantern rested on a black and white, indistinct mass, singular, incomprehensible. Sapeur exclaimed:

"'It is a horse. I see the hoofs. It must have escaped from the meadow, during the night, and fallen in headlong.'

"But, suddenly, a cold shiver attacked my spine, I first recognized a foot, then a clothed limb; the body was entire, but the other limb had disappeared under the water.

"I groaned and trembled so violently that the light of the lamp danced hither and thither over the object, discovering a slipper.

"'It is a woman! who—who—can it be? It is Miss Harriet.'

"Sapeur alone did not manifest horror. He had witnessed many such scenes in Africa.

"Mother Lecacheur and Céleste began to scream and to shriek, and ran away.

"But it was necessary to recover the corpse of the dead. I attached the boy securely by the loins to the end of the pulley-rope; then I lowered him slowly, and watched him disappear in the darkness. In the one hand he had a lantern, and held on to the rope with the other. Soon I recognized his voice, which seemed to come from the center of the earth, crying:

"'Stop.'

"I then saw him fish something out of the water. It was the other limb. He bound the two feet together, and shouted anew:

"'Haul up.'

"I commenced to wind him up, but I felt my arms strain, my muscles twitch, and was in terror lest I should let the boy fall to the bottom. When his head appeared over the brink, I asked:

"'What is it?' as though I only expected that he would tell me what he had discovered at the bottom.

"We both got on to the stone slab at the edge of the well, and, face to face, hoisted the body.

"Mother Lecacheur and Céleste watched us from a distance, concealed behind the wall of the house. When they saw, issuing from the well, the black slippers and white stockings of the drowned person, they disappeared.

"Sapeur seized the ankles of the poor chaste woman, and we drew it up, inclined, as it was, in the most immodest posture. The head was in a shocking state, bruised and black; and the long, gray hair, hanging down, was tangled and disordered.

"'In the name of all that is holy, how lean she is!' exclaimed Sapeur, in a contemptuous tone.

"We carried her into the room, and

as the women did not put in an appearance, I, with the assistance of the lad, dressed the corpse for burial.

"I washed her disfigured face. By the touch of my hand an eye was slightly opened; it seemed to scan me with that pale stare, with that cold, that terrible look which corpses have, a look which seems to come from the beyond. I plaited up, as well as I could, her disheveled hair, and I adjusted on her forehead a novel and singularly formed lock. Then I took off her dripping wet garments, baring, not without a feeling of shame, as though I had been guilty of some profanation, her shoulders and her chest, and her long arms, slim as the twigs of branches.

"I next went to fetch some flowers, corn poppies, blue beetles, marguerites, and fresh and perfumed herbs, with which to strew her funeral couch.

"Being the only person near her, it was necessary for me to perform the usual ceremonies. In a letter found in her pocket, written at the last moment, she asked that her body be buried in the village in which she had passed the last days of her life. A frightful thought then oppressed my heart. Was it not on my account that she wished to be laid at rest in this place?

"Toward the evening, all the female gossips of the locality came to view the remains of the defunct; but I would not allow a single person to enter; I wanted to be alone; and I watched by the corpse the whole night.

"By the flickering light of the candles, I looked at the body of this miserable woman, wholly unknown, who had died so lamentably and so far away from home. Had she left no friends, no relatives behind her? What had her infancy been? What had been her life? When had she come thither, all alone, a wanderer, like a dog driven from home? What secrets of suffering and of despair were sealed up in that disagreeable body, in that spent and withered body, that impenetrable hiding place of a mystery which had driven her far away from affection and from love?

"How many unhappy beings there are! I felt that upon that human creature weighed the eternal injustice of implacable nature! Life was over with her, without her ever having experienced, perhaps, that which sustains the most miserable of us all—to wit, the hope of being once loved! Otherwise, why should she thus have concealed herself, have fled from the face of others? Why did she love everything so tenderly and so passionately, everything living that was not a man?

"I recognized, also, that she believed in a God, and that she hoped for compensation from him for the miseries she had endured. She had now begun to decompose, and to become, in turn, a plant. She who had blossomed in the sun was now to be eaten up by the cattle, carried away in herbs, and in the flesh of beasts, again to become human flesh. But that which is called the soul had been extinguished at the bottom of the dark well. She suffered no longer. She had changed her life for that of others yet to be born.

"Hours passed away in this silent and sinister communion with the dead. A pale light at length announced the dawn of a new day, and a bright ray glistened on the bed, shedding a dash of fire on the bedclothes and on her hands. This was the hour she had so much loved, when the waking birds began to sing in the trees.

"I opened the window to its fullest extent, I drew back the curtains, so that the whole heavens might look in upon us. Then bending toward the glassy corpse, I took in my hands the mutilated head, and slowly, without terror or disgust, imprinted a long, long kiss upon those lips which had never before received the salute of love."

*   *   *   *   *   *

Léon Chenal remained silent. The women wept. We heard on the box seat Count d'Etraille blow his nose, from time to time. The coachman alone had gone to sleep. The horses, which felt no longer the sting of the whip, had slackened their pace and dragged softly along. And the four-in-hand, hardly moving at all, became suddenly torpid, as if laden with sorrow.

The Hole

CUTS AND WOUNDS WHICH CAUSED DEATH.

That was the heading of the charge which brought Leopold Rénard, upholsterer, before the Assize Court.

Round him were the principal witnesses, Madame Flamèche, widow of the victim, Louis Ladureau, cabinetmaker, and Jean Durdent, plumber.

Near the criminal was his wife, dressed in black, a little ugly woman, who looked like a monkey dressed as a lady.

This is how Renard described the drama:

"Good heavens, it is a misfortune of which I am the first and last victim, and with which my will has nothing to do. The facts are their own commentary, Monsieur le Président. I am an honest man, a hard-working man, an upholsterer in the same street for the last sixteen years, known, liked, respected, and esteemed by all, as my neighbors have testified, even the porter, who is not *folâtre* every day. I am fond of work, I am fond of saving, I like honest men, and respectable pleasures. That is what has ruined me, so much the worse for me; but as my will had nothing to do with it, I continue to respect myself.

"Every Sunday for the last five years, my wife and I have spent the day at Passy. We get fresh air, not to say that we are fond of fishing—as fond of it as we are of small onions. Mélie inspired me with that passion, the jade; she is more enthusiastic than I am, the scold, and all the mischief in this business is her fault, as you will see immediately.

"I am strong and mild-tempered, without a pennyworth of malice in me. But she! oh! la! la! she looks insignificant, she is short and thin, but she does more mischief than a weasel. I do not deny that she has some good qualities; she has some, and those very important to a man in business. But her character! Just ask about it in the neighborhood; even the porter's wife, who has just sent me about my business—she will tell you something about it.

"Every day she used to find fault with my mild temper: 'I would not put up with this! I would not put up with that.' If I had listened to her, Monsieur le Président, I should have had at least three bouts of fisticuffs a month."

Madame Renard interrupted him: "And for good reasons too; they laugh best who laugh last."

He turned toward her frankly: "Oh! very well, I can blame you, since you were the cause of it."

Then, facing the President again he said:

"I will continue. We used to go to Passy every Saturday evening, so as to be able to begin fishing at daybreak the next morning. It is a habit which has become second nature with us, as the saying is. Three years ago this summer I discovered a place, oh! such a spot! There, in the shade, were eight feet of water at least and perhaps ten, a hole with a *retour* under the bank, a regular retreat for fish and a paradise for any fisherman. I might look upon that hole as my property, Monsieur le Président, as I was its Christopher Columbus. Everybody in the neighborhood knew it, without making any opposition. They used to say: 'That is Renard's place'; and nobody would have gone to it, not even Monsieur Plumsay, who is renowned, be it said without any offense, for appropriating other people's places.

"Well, I went as usual to that place, of which I felt as certain as if I had owned it. I had scarcely got there on Saturday, when I got into 'Delila,' with my wife. 'Delila' is my Norwegian boat, which I had built by Fourmaise, and which is light and safe. Well, as I said, we got into the boat and we were going to bait, and for baiting there is nobody to be compared with me, and they all know it. You want to know with what I bait? I cannot answer that question; it has nothing to do with the accident; I cannot answer, that is my secret. There are more than three hundred people who have asked me; I have been offered glasses of brandy and liquors, fried fish, matelots,* to make me tell! But just go and try whether the chub will come. Ah! they have patted my stomach to get at my secret, my recipe. Only my wife knows, and she will not tell it, any more than I shall! Is not that so, Mélie?"

The President of the Court interrupted him:

"Just get to the facts as soon as you can."

The accused continued: "I am getting to them; I am getting to them. Well, on Saturday, July 8, we left by the five twenty-five train, and before dinner we went to ground-bait as usual. The weather promised to keep fine, and I said to Mélie: 'All right for tomorrow!' And she replied: 'It looks like it.' We never talk more than that together.

"And then we returned to dinner. I was happy and thirsty, and that was the cause of everything. I said to

---

*A preparation of several kinds of fish, with a sharp sauce.

Mélie: 'Look here, Mélie, it is fine weather, so suppose I drink a bottle of *Casque à mèche.* That is a little white wine which we have christened so, because if you drink too much of it it prevents you from sleeping and is the opposite of a night cap. Do you understand me?

"She replied: 'You can do as you please, but you will be ill again, and will not be able to get up to-morrow.' That was true, sensible, prudent, and clearsighted, I must confess. Nevertheless, I could not withstand it, and I drank my bottle. It all comes from that.

"Well, I could not sleep. By Jove! It kept me awake till two o'clock in the morning, and then I went to sleep so soundly that I should not have heard the angel shouting at the Last Judgment.

"In short, my wife woke me at six o'clock and I jumped out of bed, hastily put on my trousers and jersey, washed my face and jumped on board 'Delila.' But it was too late, for when I arrived at my hole it was already taken! Such a thing had never happened to me in three years, and it made me feel as if I were being robbed under my own eyes. I said to myself, 'Confound it all! confound it!' And then my wife began to nag at me. 'Eh! What about your *Casque à mèche!* Get along, you drunkard! Are you satisfied, you great fool?' I could say nothing, because it was all quite true, and so I landed all the same near the spot and tried to profit by what was left. Perhaps after all the fellow might catch nothing, and go away.

"He was a little thin man, in white linen coat and waistcoat, and with a large straw hat, and his wife, a fat woman who was doing embroidery, was behind him.

"When she saw us take up our position close to their place, she murmured: 'I suppose there are no other places on the river!' And my wife, who was furious, replied: 'People who know how to behave make inquiries about the habits of the neighborhood before occupying reserved spots.'

"As I did not want a fuss, I said to her: 'Hold your tongue, Mélie. Let them go on, let them go on; we shall see.'

"Well, we had fastened 'Delila' under the willowtrees, and had landed and were fishing side by side, Mélie and I, close to the two others; but here, Monsieur, I must enter into details.

"We had only been there about five minutes when our male neighbor's float began to go down two or three times, and then he pulled out a chub as thick as my thigh, rather less, perhaps, but nearly as big! My heart beat, and the perspiration stood on my forehead, and Mélie said to me: 'Well, you sot, did you see that?'

"Just then, Monsieur Bru, the grocer of Poissy, who was fond of gudgeon fishing, passed in a boat, and called out to me: 'So somebody has taken your usual place, Monsieur Renard?' And I replied: 'Yes, Monsieur Bru, there are some people in this world who do not know the usages of common polite-|ness.'

"The little man in linen pretended not to hear, nor his fat lump of a wife, either."

Here the President interrupted him a second time: "Take care, you are insulting the widow, Madame Flamèche, who is present."

Renard made his excuses: "I beg your pardon, I beg your pardon, my anger carried me away. Well, not a quarter of an hour had passed when the little man caught another chub and another almost immediately, and another five minutes later.

"The tears were in my eyes, and then I knew that Madame Renard was boiling with rage, for she kept on nagging at me: 'Oh, how horrid! Don't you see that he is robbing you of your fish? Do you think that you will catch anything? Not even a frog, nothing whatever. Why, my hands are burning, just to think of it.'

"But I said to myself: 'Let us wait until twelve o'clock. Then this poaching fellow will go to lunch, and I shall get my place again.' As for me, Monsieur le Président, I lunch on the spot every Sunday; we bring our provisions in 'Delila.' But there! At twelve o'clock, the wretch produced a fowl out of a newspaper, and while he was eating, actually he caught another chub!

"Mélie and I had a morsel also, just a mouthful, a mere nothing, for our heart was not in it.

"Then I took up my newspaper, to aid my digestion. Every Sunday I read the 'Gil Blas' in the shade like that, by the side of the water. It is Columbine's day, you know, Columbine who writes the articles in the 'Gil Blas.' I generally put Madame Renard into a passion by pretending to know this Columbine. It is not true, for I do not know her, and have never seen her, but that does not matter; she writes very well, and then she says things straight

out for a woman. She suits me, and there are not many of her sort.

"Well, I began to tease my wife, but she got angry immediately, and very angry, and so I held my tongue. At that moment our two witnesses, who are present here, Monsieur Ladureau and Monsieur Durdent, appeared on the other side of the river. We knew each other by sight. The little man began to fish again, and he caught so many that I trembled with vexation, and his wife said: 'It is an uncommonly good spot, and we will come here always, Désiré.' As for me, a cold shiver ran down my back, and Madame Renard kept repeating: 'You are not a man; you have the blood of a chicken in your veins'; and suddenly I said to her: 'Look here, I would rather go away, or I shall only be doing something foolish.'

"And she whispered to me as if she had put a red-hot iron under my nose: 'You are not a man. Now you are going to run away, and surrender your place! Off you go, Bazaine!'

"Well, I felt that, but yet I did not move, while the other fellow pulled out a bream, Oh! I never saw such a large one before, never! And then my wife began to talk aloud, as if she were thinking, and you can see her trickery. She said: 'That is what one might call stolen fish, seeing that we baited the place ourselves. At any rate, they ought to give us back the money we have spent on bait.'

"Then the fat woman in the cotton dress said in turn: 'Do you mean to call us thieves, Madame?' And they began to explain, and then they came to words. Oh! Lord! those creatures know some good ones. They shouted so loud, that our two witnesses, who were on the other bank, began to call out by way of a joke: 'Less noise over there; you will prevent your husbands from fishing.'

"The fact is that neither of us moved any more than if we had been two tree-stumps. We remained there, with our noses over the water, as if we had heard nothing, but by Jove, we heard all the same. 'You are a mere liar.'

" 'You are nothing better than a street-walker.'

" 'You are only a trollop.'

" 'You are a regular strumpet.'

"And so on, and so on; a sailor could not have said more.

"Suddenly I heard a noise behind me, and turned round. It was the other one, the fat woman who had fallen on to my wife with her parasol. *Whack! whack!* Mélie got two of them, but she was furious, and she hits hard when she is in a rage, so she caught the fat woman by the hair and then, *thump, thump.* Slaps in the face rained down like ripe plums. I should have let them go on—women among themselves, men among themselves—it does not do to mix the blows, but the little man in the linen jacket jumped up like a devil and was going to rush at my wife. Ah! no, no, not that, my friend! I caught the gentleman with the end of my fist, *crash, crash,* one on the nose, the other in the stomach. He threw up his arms

and legs and fell on his back into the river, just into the hole.

"I should have fished him out most certainly, Monsieur le Président, if I had had the time. But unfortunately the fat woman got the better of it, and she was drubbing Mélie terribly. I know that I ought not to have assisted her while the man was drinking his fill, but I never thought that he would drown, and said to myself: 'Bah, it will cool him.'

"I therefore ran up to the women to separate them, and all I received was scratches and bites. Good Lord, what creatures! Well, it took me five minutes, and perhaps ten, to separate those two viragoes. When I turned around, there was nothing to be seen, and the water was as smooth as a lake. The others yonder kept shouting: 'Fish him out!' It was all very well to say that, but I cannot swim and still less dive!

"At last the man from the dam came, and two gentlemen with boat-hooks, but it had taken over a quarter of an hour. He was found at the bottom of the hole in eight feet of water, as I have said, but he was dead, the poor little man in his linen suit! There are the facts, such as I have sworn to. I am innocent, on my honor."

The witnesses having deposed to the same effect, the accused was acquitted.

————————

The Inn

LIKE all the little wooden inns in the higher Alps, tiny auberges situated in the bare and rocky gorges which intersect the white summits of the mountains, the inn of Schwarenbach is a refuge for travelers who are crossing the Gemmi.

It is open six months in the year, and is inhabited by the family of Jean Hauser. As soon as the snow begins to fall, and fills the valley so as to make the road down to Loëche impassable, the father, with mother, daughter, and the three sons depart, leaving the house in charge of the old guide, Gaspard Hari, with the young guide, Ulrich Kunsi, and Sam, the great mountain dog.

The two men and the dog remain till spring in their snowy prison, with nothing before their eyes except immense, white slopes of the Balmhorn, surrounded by light, glistening summits, and shut up, blocked up, and buried by the snow which rises around them, enveloping and almost burying the little house up to the eaves.

It was the day on which the Hauser family were going to return to Loëche, as winter was approaching, and the descent was becoming dangerous. Three mules started first, laden with baggage and led by the three sons. Then the mother, Jeanne Hauser, and her daughter Louise mounted a fourth mule, and set off in their turn. The father followed them, accompanied by the two men in charge, who were to escort the family as far as the brow of the descent. First of all they skirted the small lake, now frozen over, at the foot of the mass of rocks which stretched in front of the inn; then they followed the valley, which was dominated on all sides by snow-covered peaks.

A ray of sunlight glinted into that little white, glistening, frozen desert, illuminating it with a cold and dazzling flame. No living thing appeared among this ocean of hills; there was no stir in that immeasurable solitude, no noise disturbed the profound silence.

By degrees the young guide, Ulrich Kunsi, a tall, long-legged Swiss, left daddy Hauser and old Gaspard behind, in order to catch up with the mule which carried the two women. The younger one looked at him as he approached, as if she would call him with her sad eyes. She was a young, light-haired peasant girl, whose milk-white cheeks and pale hair seemed to have lost their color by long dwelling amid the ice. When Ulrich had caught up with the animal which carried the women, he put his hand on the crupper, and relaxed his speed. Mother Hauser began to talk to him, and enumerated with minutest detail all that he would have to attend to during the winter. It was the first winter he would spend up there, while old Hari had already spent fourteen winters amid the snow, at the inn of Schwarenbach.

Ulrich Kunsi listened, without appearing to understand, and looked incessantly at the girl. From time to time he replied: "Yes, Madame Hauser"; but his thoughts seemed far away, and his calm features remained unmoved.

They reached Lake Daube, whose broad, frozen surface reached to the bottom of the valley. On the right, the Daubenhorn showed its black mass, rising up in a peak above the enormous moraines of the Lömmeon glacier, which soared above the Wildstrubel. As they approached the neck of the Gemmi, where the descent to Loëche begins, the immense horizon of the Alps of the Valais, from which the broad, deep valley of the Rhône separated them, came in view.

In the distance, there was a group of white, unequal, flat or pointed mountain summits, which glistened in the sun; the Mischabel with its twin peaks, the huge group of the Weisshorn, the heavy Brunegghorn, the lofty and formidable pyramid of Mont Cervin, slayer of men, and the Dent Blanche, that terrible coquette.

Then beneath them, as at the bottom of a terrible abyss, they saw Loëche, its houses looking like grains of sand which had been thrown into that enormous crevice which finishes and closes the Gemmi, and which opens, down below, on to the Rhône.

The mule stopped at the edge of the path, which turns and twists continually, zigzagging fantastically and strangely along the steep side of the mountain, as far as the almost invisible little village at its feet. The women jumped into the snow, and the two old men joined them.

"Well," father Hauser said, "goodbye, and keep up your spirits till next year, my friends," and old Hari replied: "Till next year."

They embraced each other, and then Madame Hauser in her turn, offered her cheek, and the girl did the same. When Ulrich Kunsi's turn came, he whispered in Louise's ear:

"Do not forget those up yonder," and she replied: "No," in such a low voice, that he guessed what she had said, without hearing it.

"Well, adieu," Jean Hauser repeated, "and don't fall in." Then, going before the two women, he commenced the descent, and soon all three disappeared at the first turn in the road, while the two men returned to the inn at Schwarenbach.

They walked slowly side by side, without speaking. The parting was over, and they would be alone together for four or five months. Then Gaspard Hari began to relate his life last winter. He had remained with Michael Canol, who was too old now to stand it; for an accident might happen during that long solitude. They had not been dull, however; the only thing was to be resigned to it from the first, and in the end one would find plenty of distraction, games and other means of whiling away the time.

Ulrich Kunsi listened to him with his eyes on the ground, for in thought he was with those who were descending to the village. They soon came in sight of the inn, which was scarcely visible, so small did it look, a mere black speck at the foot of that enormous billow of snow. When they opened the door, Sam, the great curly dog, began to romp round them.

"Come, my boy," old Gaspard said, "we have no women now, so we must get our own dinner ready. Go and peel the potatoes." And they both sat down on wooden stools, and began to put the bread into the soup.

The next morning seemed very long to Kunsi. Old Hari smoked and smoked beside the hearth, while the young man looked out of the window at the snow-covered mountain opposite the house. In the afternoon he went out, and going over the previous day's ground again, he looked for the traces of the mule that had carried the two women; then when he had reached the neck of the

Gemmi, he laid himself down on his stomach, and looked at Loëche.

The village, in its rocky pit, was not yet buried under the snow, although the white masses came quite close to it, balked, however, of their prey by the pine woods which protected the hamlet. From his vantage point the low houses looked like pavingstones in a large meadow. Hauser's little daughter was there now in one of those gray-colored houses. In which? Ulrich Kunsi was too far away to be able to make them out separately. How he would have liked to go down while he was yet able!

But the sun had disappeared behind the lofty crest of the Wildstrubel, and the young man returned to the chalet. Daddy Hari was smoking, and, when he saw his mate come in, proposed a game of cards to him. They sat down opposite each other for a long time and played the simple game called *brisque;* then they had supper and went to bed.

The following days were like the first, bright and cold, without any more snow. Old Gaspard spent his afternoons in watching the eagles and other rare birds which ventured on to those frozen heights, while Ulrich journeyed regularly to the neck of the Gemmi to look at the village. In the evening they played at cards, dice, or dominoes, and lost and won trifling sums, just to create an interest in the game.

One morning Hari, who was up first, called his companion. A moving cloud of white spray, deep and light, was falling on them noiselessly, and burying them by degrees under a dark, thick coverlet of foam. This lasted four days and four nights. It was necessary to free the door and the windows, to dig out a passage, and to cut steps to get over this frozen powder, which a twelve-hours' frost had made as hard as the granite of the moraines.

They lived like prisoners, not venturing outside their abode. They had divided their duties and performed them regularly. Ulrich Kunsi undertook the scouring, washing, and everything that belonged to cleanliness. He also chopped up the wood, while Gaspard Hari did the cooking and attended to the fire. Their regular and monotonous work was relieved by long games at cards or dice, but they never quarreled, and were always calm and placid. They were never even impatient or ill-humored, nor did they ever use hard words, for they had laid in a stock of patience for this wintering on the top of the mountain.

Sometimes old Gaspard took his rifle and went after chamois, and occasionally killed one. Then there was a feast in the inn at Schwarenbach, and they reveled in fresh meat. One morning he went out as usual. The thermometer outside marked eighteen degrees of frost, and as the sun had not yet risen, the hunter hoped to surprise the animals at the approaches to the Wildstrubel. Ulrich, being alone, remained in bed until ten o'clock. He was of a sleepy nature, but would not have dared to give way like that to his inclination in the presence of the old guide, who was ever an early riser. He breakfasted leisurely with Sam, who also spent his days and nights in sleeping in front of the fire; then he felt low-spirited and even frightened at the solitude, and was seized by a longing for his daily game of cards, as one is by the domination of an invincible habit. So he went out to meet his companion, who was to return at four o'clock.

The snow had leveled the whole deep valley, filled up the crevasses, obliterated all signs of the two lakes and covered the rocks, so that between the high summits there was nothing but an immense, white, regular, dazzling, and frozen surface. For three weeks, Ulrich had not been to the edge of the precipice, from which he had looked down on to the village, and he wanted to go there before climbing the slopes which led to the Wildstrubel. Loëche was now covered by the snow, and the houses could scarcely be distinguished, hidden as they were by that white cloak.

Turning to the right, Ulrich reached the Lämmern glacier. He strode along with a mountaineer's long swinging pace, striking the snow, which was as hard as a rock, with his iron-shod stick, and with piercing eyes looking for the little black, moving speck in the distance, on that enormous, white expanse.

When he reached the end of the glacier he stopped, and asked himself whether the old man had taken that road, and then he began to walk along the moraines with rapid and uneasy steps. The day was declining; the snow was assuming a rosy tint, and a dry, frozen wind blew in rough gusts over its crystal surface. Ulrich uttered a long, shrill, vibrating call. His voice sped through the deathlike silence in which the mountains were sleeping; it reached into the distance, over the profound and motionless waves of glacial foam, like the cry of a bird over the waves of the sea; then it died away and nothing answered him.

He started off again. The sun had sunk behind the mountain tops, which still were purpled with the reflection from the heavens, but the depths of the valley were becoming gray, and suddenly the young man felt frightened. It seemed to him as if the silence, the cold, the solitude, the wintry death of these mountains were taking possession of him, were stopping and freezing his blood, making his limbs grow stiff, and turning him into a motionless and frozen object; and he began to run rapidly toward the dwelling. The old man, he thought, would have returned during his absence. He had probably taken another road; and would, no doubt, be sitting before the fire, with a dead chamois at his feet.

He soon came in sight of the inn, but no smoke rose from it. Ulrich ran faster. Opening the door he met Sam who ran up to him to greet him, but Gaspard Hari had not returned. Kunsi, in his alarm, turned round suddenly, as if he had expected to find his comrade hidden in a corner. Then he relighted the fire and made the soup; hoping every moment to see the old man come in. From time to time he went out to see if Gaspard were not in sight. It was night now, that wan night of the mountain, a livid night, with the crescent moon, yellow and dim, just disappearing behind the mountain tops, and shining faintly on the edge of the horizon.

Then the young man went in and sat down to warm his hands and feet, while he pictured to himself every possible sort of accident. Gaspard might have broken a leg, have fallen into a crevasse, have taken a false step and dislocated his ankle. Perhaps he was lying on the snow, overcome and stiff with the cold, in agony of mind, lost and perhaps shouting for help, calling with all his might, in the silence of the night.

But where? The mountain was so vast, so rugged, so dangerous in places, especially at that time of the year, that it would have required ten or twenty guides walking for a week in all directions, to find a man in that immense space. Ulrich Kunsi, however, made up his mind to set out with Sam, if Gaspard did not return by one in the morning; and he made his preparations.

He put provisions for two days into a bag, took his steel climbing-irons, tied a long, thin, strong rope round his waist and looked to see that his iron-shod stick and his ax, which served to cut steps in the ice, were in order. Then he waited. The fire was burning on the hearth, the great dog was snoring in front of it, and the clock was ticking in its case of resounding wood, as regularly as a heart beating.

He waited, his ears on the alert for distant sounds, and shivered when the wind blew against the roof and the walls. It struck twelve, and he trembled. Then, as he felt frightened and shivery, he put some water on the fire, so that he might have hot coffee before starting. When the clock struck one he got up, woke Sam, opened the door and went off in the direction of the Wildstrubel. For five hours he ascended, scaling the rocks by means of his climbing-irons, cutting into the ice, advancing continually, and occasionally hauling up the dog, who remained below at the foot of some slope that was too steep for him, by means of the rope. About six o'clock he reached one of the summits to which old Gaspard often came after chamois, and he waited till it should be daylight.

The sky was growing pale overhead, and suddenly a strange light, springing, nobody could tell whence, suddenly illuminated the immense ocean of pale mountain peaks, which stretched for many leagues around him. It seemed as if this vague brightness arose from the snow itself, in order to spread itself into space. By degrees the highest and most distant summits assumed a delicate, fleshlike rose color, and the red sun appeared behind the ponderous giants of the Bernese Alps.

Ulrich Kunsi set off again, walking like a hunter, stooping and looking for any traces, and saying to his dog: "Seek old fellow, seek!"

He was descending the mountain now, scanning the depths closely, and from time to time shouting, uttering a loud, prolonged familiar cry which soon died away in that silent vastness. Then, he put his ear to the ground, to listen. He thought he could distinguish a voice, and so he began to run and shout again. But he heard nothing more and sat down, worn out and in despair. Toward midday he breakfasted and gave Sam, who was as tired as himself, something to eat also; then he recommenced his search.

When evening came he was still walking, having traveled more than thirty miles over the mountains. As he was too far away to return home, and too tired to drag himself along any further, he dug a hole in the snow and crouched in it with his dog, under a blanket which he had brought with him. The man and the dog lay side by side, warming themselves one against the other, but frozen to the marrow nevertheless. Ulrich scarcely slept, his mind haunted by visions and his limbs shaking with cold.

Day was breaking when he got up. His legs were as stiff as iron bars, and his spirits so low that he was ready to weep, while his heart was beating so that he almost fell with excitement whenever he thought he heard a noise.

Suddenly he imagined that he *also* was going to die of cold in the midst of this vast solitude. The terror of such a death roused his energies and gave him renewed vigor. He was descending toward the inn, falling down and getting up again, and followed at a distance by Sam, who was limping on three legs. They did not reach Schwarenbach until four o'clock in the afternoon. The house was empty, and the young man made a fire, had something to eat, and went to sleep, worn-out that he did not think of anything more.

He slept for a long time, for a very long time, the unconquerable sleep of exhaustion. But suddenly a voice, a cry, a name: "Ulrich," aroused him from his profound slumber, and made him sit up in bed. Had he been dreaming? Was it one of those strange appeals which cross the dreams of disquieted minds? No, he heard it still, that reverberating cry,—which had entered at his ears and remained in his brain,—thrilling him to the tips of his sinewy fingers. Certainly, somebody had cried out, and called: "Ulrich!" There was somebody there, near the house; there could be no doubt of that,

and he opened the door and shouted: "Is it you, Gaspard?" with all the strength of his lungs. But there was no reply, no murmur, no groan, nothing. It was quite dark, and the snow looked wan.

The wind had risen, that icy wind which cracks the rocks, and leaves nothing alive on those deserted heights. It came in sudden gusts, more parching and more deadly than the burning wind of the desert, and again Ulrich shouted: "Gaspard! Gaspard! Gaspard!" Then he waited again. Everything was silent on the mountain! Then he shook with terror, and with a bound he was inside the inn. He shut and bolted the door, and then fell into a chair, trembling all over, for he felt certain that his comrade had called him at the moment of dissolution.

He was certain of that, as certain as one is of conscious life or of taste when eating. Old Gaspard Hari had been dying for two days and three nights somewhere, in some hole, in one of those deep, untrodden ravines whose whiteness is more sinister than subterranean darkness. He had been dying for two days and three nights and he had just then died, thinking of his comrade. His soul, almost before it was released, had taken its flight to the inn where Ulrich was sleeping, and it had called him by that terrible and mysterious power which the spirits of the dead possess. That voiceless soul had cried to the wornout soul of the sleeper; it had uttered its last farewell, or its reproach, or its curse on the man who had not searched carefully enough.

And Ulrich felt that it was there, quite close to him, behind the wall, be-

hind the door which he had just fastened. It was wandering about, like a
night bird which skims a lighted window
with his wings, and the terrified young
man was ready to scream with horror.
He wanted to run away, but did not
dare go out; he did not dare, and would
never dare in the future, for that phantom would remain there day and night,
round the inn, as long as the old man's
body was not recovered and deposited
in the consecrated earth of a churchyard.

Daylight came, and Kunsi recovered
some of his courage with the return of
the bright sun. He prepared his meal,
gave his dog some food, and then remained motionless on a chair, tortured
at heart as he thought of the old man
lying on the snow. Then, as soon as
night once more covered the mountains,
new terrors assailed him. He now
walked up and down the dark kitchen,
which was scarcely lighted by the flame
of one candle. He walked from one end
of it to the other with great strides,
listening, listening to hear the terrible
cry of the preceding night again break
the dreary silence outside. He felt himself alone, unhappy man, as no man had
ever been alone before! Alone in this
immense desert of snow, alone five
thousand feet above the inhabited earth,
above human habitations, above that
stirring, noisy, palpitating life, alone
under an icy sky! A mad longing impelled him to run away, no matter
where, to get down to Loëche by flinging himself over the precipice; but he
did not even dare to open the door, as
he felt sure that the other, the *dead,*
man would bar his road, so that he

might not be obliged to remain up there
alone.

Toward midnight, tired with walking,
worn-out by grief and fear, he fell into
a doze in his chair, for he was afraid of
his bed, as one is of a haunted spot.
But suddenly the strident cry of the
preceding evening pierced his ears, so
shrill that Ulrich stretched out his arms
to repulse the ghost, and he fell on to
his back with his chair.

Sam, who was awakened by the noise,
began to howl as frightened dogs do,
and trotted all about the house trying
to find out where the danger came from.
When he got to the door, he sniffed
beneath it, smelling vigorously, with his
coat bristling and his tail stiff while
he growled angrily. Kunsi, who was
terrified, jumped up, and holding his
chair by one leg, cried: "Don't come
in, don't come in, or I shall kill you."
And the dog, excited by this threat,
barked angrily at that invisible enemy
who defied his master's voice. By degrees, however, he quieted down, came
back and stretched himself in front of
the fire. But he was uneasy, and kept
his head up, and growled between his
teeth.

Ulrich, in turn, recovered his senses,
but as he felt faint with terror, he went
and got a bottle of brandy out of the
sideboard, and drank off several glasses,
one after another, at a gulp. His ideas
became vague, his courage revived, and
a feverish glow ran through his veins.

He ate scarcely anything the next
day, and limited himself to alcohol;
so he lived for several days, like a
drunken brute. As soon as he thought
of Gaspard Hari he began to drink
again, and went on drinking until he

fell on to the floor, overcome by intoxication. And there he remained on his face, dead drunk, his limbs benumbed, and snoring with his face to the ground. But scarcely had he digested the maddening and burning liquor, than the same cry, "Ulrich," woke him like a bullet piercing his brain, and he got up, still staggering, stretching out his hands to save himself from falling, and calling to Sam to help him. And the dog, who appeared to be going mad like his master, rushed to the door, scratched it with his claws, and gnawed it with his long white teeth, while the young man, his neck thrown back, and his head in the air, drank the brandy in gulps, as if it were cold water, so that it might by and by send his thoughts, his frantic terror, and his memory, to sleep again.

In three weeks he had consumed all his stock of ardent spirits. But his continual drunkenness only lulled his terror, which awoke more furiously than ever, as soon as it was impossible for him to calm it by drinking. His fixed idea, which had been intensified by a month of drunkenness, and which was continually increasing in his absolute solitude, penetrated him like a gimlet. He now walked about his house like a wild beast in its cage, putting his ear to the door to listen if the other were there, and defying him through the wall. Then as soon as he dozed, overcome by fatigue, he heard the voice which made him leap to his feet.

At last one night, as cowards do when driven to extremity, he sprang to the door and opened it, to see who was calling him, and to force him to keep quiet. But such a gust of cold wind blew into his face that it chilled him to the bone. He closed and bolted the door again immediately, without noticing that Sam had rushed out. Then, as he was shivering with cold, he threw some wood on the fire, and sat down in front of it to warm himself. But suddenly he started, for somebody was scratching at the wall, and crying. In desperation he called out: "Go away!" but was answered by another long, sorrowful wail.

Then all his remaining senses forsook him, from sheer fright. He repeated: "Go away!" and turned round to find some corner in which to hide, while the other person went round the house still crying, and rubbing against the wall. Ulrich went to the oak sideboard, which was full of plates and dishes and of provisions, and lifting it up with superhuman strength, he dragged it to the door, so as to form a barricade. Then piling up all the rest of the furniture, the mattresses, paillasses, and chairs, he stopped up the windows as men do when assailed by an enemy.

But the person outside now uttered long, plaintive, mournful groans, to which the young man replied by similar groans, and thus days and nights passed without their ceasing to howl at each other. The one was continually walking round the house and scraped the walls with his nails so vigorously that it seemed as if he wished to destroy them, while the other, inside, followed all his movements, stooping down, and holding his ear to the walls, and replying to all his appeals with terrible cries. One evening however, Ulrich heard nothing more, and he sat down, so overcome by fatigue that he went to sleep immediately, and awoke in the morning without a thought, without any recollection of what had happened, just as if his head had been emptied during his heavy sleep. But he felt hungry, and he ate.

The winter was over, and the Gemmi pass was practicable again, so the Hauser family started off to return to their inn. As soon as they had reached the top of the ascent, the women mounted their mule, and spoke about the two men who they would meet again shortly. They were, indeed, rather surprised that neither of them had come down a few days before, as soon as the road became passable, in order to tell them all about their long winter sojourn. At last, however, they saw the inn, still covered with snow, like a quilt. The door and the windows were closed, but a little smoke was coming out of the chimney, which reassured old Hauser; on going up to the door, however, he saw the skeleton of an animal which had been torn to pieces by the eagles, a large skeleton lying on its side.

They all looked closely at it, and the mother said: "That must be Sam." Then she shouted: "Hi! Gaspard!" A cry from the interior of the house answered her, so sharp a cry that one might have thought some animal uttered it. Old Hauser repeated: "Hi! Gaspard!" and they heard another cry, similar to the first.

Then the three men, the father and the two sons, tried to open the door, but it resisted their efforts. From the empty cow-stall they took a beam to serve as a battering-ram, and hurled it against the door with all their might. The wood gave way, and the boards flew into splinters; then the house was shaken by a loud voice, and inside, behind the sideboard which was overturned, they saw a man standing upright, his hair falling on to his shoulders and a beard descending to his breast, with shining eyes and nothing but rags to cover him. They did not recognize him, but Louise Hauser exclaimed: "It is Ulrich, mother." And her mother declared that it was Ulrich, although his hair was white.

He allowed them to go up to him, and to touch him, but he did not reply to any of their questions, and they were obliged to take him to Loëche, where the doctors found that he was mad. Nobody ever knew what had become of his companion.

Little Louise Hauser nearly died that summer of decline, which the medical men attributed to the cold air of the mountains.

A Family

I was going to see my friend Simon Radevin once more, for I had not seen him for fifteen years. Formerly he was my most intimate friend, and I used to spend long, quiet, and happy evenings with him. He was one of those men to whom one tells the most intimate affairs of the heart, and in whom one finds, when quietly talking, rare, clever, ingenious, and refined thoughts—thoughts which stimulate and capture the mind.

For years we had scarcely been separated: we had lived, traveled, thought, and dreamed together; had liked the same things with the same liking, admired the same books, comprehended the same works, shivered with the same sensations, and very often laughed at the same individuals, whom we understood completely, by merely exchanging a glance.

Then he married—quite unexpectedly married a little girl from the provinces, who had come to Paris in search of a husband. How ever could that little, thin, insipidly fair girl, with her weak hands, her light, vacant eyes, and her clear, silly voice who was exactly like a hundred thousand marriageable dolls, have picked up that intelligent, clever young fellow? Can anyone understand these things? No doubt he had hoped for happiness, simple, quiet, and long-enduring happiness, in the arms of a good, tender, and faithful woman; he had seen all that in the transparent looks of that schoolgirl with light hair.

He had not dreamed of the fact that an active, living, and vibrating man grows tired as soon as he has comprehended the stupid reality of a commonplace life, unless indeed, he becomes so brutalized as to be callous to externals.

What would he be like when I met him again? Still lively, witty, light-hearted, and enthusiastic, or in a state of mental torpor through provincial life? A man can change a great deal in the course of fifteen years!

The train stopped at a small station, and as I got out of the carriage, a stout, a very stout man with red cheeks and a big stomach rushed up to me with open arms, exclaiming: "George!"

I embraced him, but I had not recognized him, and then I said, in astonishment: "By jove! You have not grown thin!"

And he replied with a laugh: "What did you expect? Good living, a good table, and good nights! Eating and sleeping, that is my existence!"

I looked at him closely, trying to find the features I held so dear in that broad face. His eyes alone had not altered, but I no longer saw the same looks in them, and I said to myself: "If looks be the reflection of the mind, the thoughts in that head are not what they used to be—those thoughts which I knew so well."

Yet his eyes were bright, full of pleasure and friendship, but they had not that clear, intelligent expression which tells better than do words the value of the mind. Suddenly he said to me:

"Here are my two eldest children." A girl of fourteen, who was almost a woman, and a boy of thirteen, in the dress of a pupil from a lycée, came forward in a hesitating and awkward manner, and I said in a low voice: "Are they yours?"

"Of course they are," he replied laughing.

"How many have you?"

"Five! There are three more indoors."

He said that in a proud, self-satisfied, almost triumphant manner, and I felt profound pity, mingled with a feeling of vague contempt for this vain-glorious. and simple reproducer of his species, who spent his nights in his country house in uxorious pleasures.

I got into a carriage, which he drove himself, and we set off through the town, a dull, sleepy, gloomy town where nothing was moving in the streets save a few dogs and two or three maidser-vants. Here and there a shopkeeper standing at his door took off his hat, and Simon returned the salute and told me the man's name—no doubt to show me that he knew all the inhabitants per-sonally. The thought struck me that he was thinking of becoming a candi-date for the Chamber of Deputies, that dream of all who have buried them-selves in the provinces.

We were soon out of the town; the carriage turned into a garden which had some pretensions to a park, and stopped in front of a turreted house, which tried to pass for a château.

"That is my den," Simon said, so that he might be complimented on it, and I replied that it was delightful.

A lady appeared on the steps, dressed up for a visitor, her hair done for a visitor, and with phrases ready prepared for a visitor. She was no longer the light-haired, insipid girl I had seen in church fifteen years previously, but a stout lady in curls and flounces, one of those ladies of uncertain age, without intellect, without any of those things which constitute a woman. In short she was a mother, a stout, commonplace mother, a human layer and brood mare, a machine of flesh which procreates, without mental care save for her chil-dren and her housekeeping book.

She welcomed me, and I went into the hall, where three children, ranged according to their height, were ranked for review, like firemen before a mayor. "Ah! ah! so there are the others?" said I. And Simon, who was radiant with pleasure, named them: "Jean, Sophie, and Gontran."

The door of the drawing-room was open. I went in, and in the depths of an easy-chair I saw something trem-bling, a man, an old, paralyzed man. Madame Radevin came forward and said: "This is my grandfather, Mon-sieur; he is eighty-seven." And then she shouted into the shaking old man's ears: "This is a friend of Simon's, grand-papa."

The old gentleman tried to say "Good day" to me, and he muttered: "Oua, oua, oua," and waved his hand.

I took a seat saying: "You are very kind, Monsieur."

Simon had just come in, and he said with a laugh: "So! You have made grandpapa's acquaintance. He is price-less, is that old man. He is the delight of the children, and he is so greedy that he almost kills himself at every meal. You have no idea what he would eat if he were allowed to do as he pleased. But you will see, you will see. He looks all the sweets over as if they were so many girls. You have never seen any-thing funnier; you will see it presently."

I was then shown to my room to change my dress for dinner, and hearing a great clatter behind me on the stairs, I turned round and saw that all the children were following me behind their father—to do me honor, no doubt.

My windows looked out on to a plain, a bare, interminable plain, an ocean of grass, of wheat, and of oats without a clump of trees or any rising ground, a striking and melancholy picture of the life which they must be leading in that house.

A bell rang; it was for dinner, and so I went downstairs. Madame Radevin took my arm in a ceremonious manner, and we went into the dining-room. A footman wheeled in the old man's arm-chair, who gave a greedy and curious look at the dessert, as with difficulty he turned his shaking head from one dish to the other.

Simon rubbed his hands, saying: "You will be amused." All the children understood that I was going to be indulged with the sight of their greedy grandfather and they began to laugh accordingly, while their mother merely smiled and shrugged her shoulders. Simon, making a speaking trumpet of his hands, shouted at the old man: "This evening there is sweet rice-cream," and the wrinkled face of the grandfather brightened, he trembled violently all over, showing that he had understood and was very pleased. The dinner began.

"Just look!" Simon whispered. The grandfather did not like the soup, and refused to eat it; but he was made to, on account of his health. The footman forced the spoon into his mouth, while the old man blew energetically, so as not to swallow the soup, which was thus scattered like a stream of water on to the table and over his neighbors. The children shook with delight at the spectacle, while their father, who was also amused, said: "Isn't the old man funny?"

During the whole meal they were all taken up solely with him. With his eyes he devoured the dishes which were put on the table, and with trembling hands tried to seize them and pull them to him. They put them almost within his reach to see his useless efforts, his trembling clutches at them, the piteous appeal of his whole nature, of his eyes, of his mouth, and of his nose as he smelled them. He slobbered on to his table napkin with eagerness, while uttering inarticulate grunts, and the whole family was highly amused at this horrible and grotesque scene.

Then they put a tiny morsel on to his plate, which he ate with feverish gluttony, in order to get something more as soon as possible. When the rice-cream was brought in, he nearly had a fit, and groaned with greediness. Gontran called out to him: "You have eaten too much already; you will have no more." And they pretended not to give him any. Then he began to cry— cry and tremble more violently than ever, while all the children laughed. At last, however, they gave him his help-ing, a very small piece. As he ate the first mouthful of the pudding, he made a comical and greedy noise in his throat, and a movement with his neck like ducks do, when they swallow too large a morsel, and then, when he had done, he began to stamp his feet, so as to get more.

I was seized with pity for this pitiable and ridiculous Tantalus, and interposed on his behalf: "Please, will you not give him a little more rice?"

But Simon replied: "Oh! no my dear fellow, if he were to eat too much, it might harm him at his age."

I held my tongue, and thought over these words. Oh! ethics! Oh! logic!

Oh! wisdom! At his age! So they deprived him of his only remaining pleasure out of regard for his health! His health! What would he do with it, inert and trembling wreck that he was? They were taking care of his life, so they said: His life? How many days? Ten, twenty, fifty, or a hundred? Why? For his own sake? Or to preserve for some time longer, the spectacle of his impotent greediness in the family.

There was nothing left for him to do in this life, nothing whatever. He had one single wish left, one sole pleasure; why not grant him that last solace constantly, until he died?

After playing cards for a long time, I went up to my room and to bed; I was low-spirited and sad, sad, sad! I sat at my window, but I heard nothing but the beautiful warbling of a bird in a tree, somewhere in the distance. No doubt the bird was singing thus in a low voice during the night, to lull his mate, who was sleeping on her eggs.

And I thought of my poor friend's five children, and to myself pictured him snoring by the side of his ugly wife.

Bellflower*

How strange are those old recollections which haunt us, without our being able to get rid of them!

This one is so very old that I cannot understand how it has clung so vividly and tenaciously to my memory. Since then I have seen so many sinister things, either affecting or terrible, that I am astonished at not being able to pass a single day without the face of Mother Bellflower recurring to my mind's eye, just as I knew her formerly long, long ago, when I was ten or twelve years old.

She was an old seamstress who came to my parents' house once a week, every Thursday, to mend the linen. My parents lived in one of those country houses called châteax, which are merely old houses with pointed roofs, to which are attached three or four adjacent farms.

The village, a large village, almost a small market town, was a few hundred yards off, and nestled round the church, a red brick church, which had become black with age.

Well, every Thursday Mother Bellflower came between half past six and seven in the morning, and went immediately into the linen-room and began to work. She was a tall, thin, bearded or rather hairy woman, for she had a beard all over her face, a surprising, an unexpected beard, growing in improbable tufts, in curly bunches which looked as if they had been sown by a madman over that great face, the face of a gendarme in petticoats. She had them on her nose, under her nose, round her nose, on her chin, on her cheeks; and her eyebrows, which were extraordinarily thick and long, and quite gray, bushy and bristling, looked

---

*Clochette.

exactly like a pair of mustaches stuck on there by mistake.

She limped, but not like lame people generally do, but like a ship pitching. When she planted her great, bony, vibrant body on her sound leg, she seemed to be preparing to mount some enormous wave, and then suddenly she dipped as if to disappear in an abyss, and buried herself in the ground. Her walk reminded one of a ship in a storm, and her head, which was always covered with an enormous white cap, whose ribbons fluttered down her back, seemed to traverse the horizon from North to South and from South to North, at each limp.

I adored Mother Bellflower. As soon as I was up I used to go into the linenroom, where I found her installed at work, with a foot-warmer under her feet. As soon as I arrived, she made me take the foot-warmer and sit upon it, so that I might not catch cold in that large, chilly room under the roof.

"That draws the blood from your head," she would say to me.

She told me stories, while mending the linen with her long, crooked, nimble fingers; behind her magnifying spectacles, for age had impaired her sight, her eyes appeared enormous to me, strangely profound, double.

As far as I can remember from the things which she told me and by which my childish heart was moved, she had the large heart of a poor woman. She told me what had happened in the village, how a cow had escaped from the cowhouse and had been found the next morning in front of Prosper Malet's mill, looking at the sails turning, or about a hen's egg which had been found in the church belfry without anyone being able to understand what creature had been there to lay it, or the queer story of Jean Pila's dog, who had gone ten leagues to bring back his master's breeches which a tramp had stolen while they were hanging up to dry out of doors, after he had been caught in the rain. She told me these simple adventures in such a manner that in my mind they assumed the proportions of never-to-be-forgotten dramas, of grand and mysterious poems; and the ingenious stories invented by the poets, which my mother told me in the evening, had none of the flavor, none of the fullness or of the vigor of the peasant woman's narratives.

Well, one Thursday when I had spent all the morning in listening to Mother Clochette, I wanted to go upstairs to her again during the day, after picking hazelnuts with the manservant in the wood behind the farm. I remember it all as clearly as what happened only yesterday.

On opening the door of the linenroom, I saw the old seamstress lying on the floor by the side of her chair, her face turned down and her arms stretched out, but still holding her needle in one hand and one of my shirts in the other. One of her legs in a blue stocking, the longer one no doubt, was extended under her chair, and her spectacles glistened by the wall, where they had rolled away from her.

I ran away uttering shrill cries. They all came running, and in a few minutes I was told that Mother Clochette was dead.

I cannot describe the profound, poignant, terrible emotion which stirred my childish heart. I went slowly down into the drawing-room and hid myself in a dark corner, in the depths of a great, old armchair, where I knelt and wept. I remained there for a long time no doubt, for night came on. Suddenly some one came in with a lamp—without seeing me, however—and I heard my father and mother talking with the medical man, whose voice I recognized.

He had been sent for immediately, and he was explaining the cause of the accident, of which I understood nothing, however. Then he sat down and had a glass of liqueur and a biscuit.

He went on talking, and what he then said will remain engraved on my mind until I die! I think that I can give the exact words which he used.

"Ah!" said he, "the poor woman! she broke her leg the day of my arrival here. I had not even had time to wash my hands after getting off the diligence before I was sent for in all haste, for it was a bad case, very bad.

"She was seventeen, and a pretty girl, very pretty! Would anyone believe it? I have never told her story before, in fact no one but myself and one other person, who is no longer living in this part of the country, ever knew it. Now that she is dead, I may be less discreet.

"A young assistant teacher had just come to live in the village; he was good-looking and had the bearing of a soldier. All the girls ran after him, but he was disdainful. Besides that, he was very much afraid of his superior, the schoolmaster, old Grabu, who occasionally got out of bed the wrong foot first.

"Old Grabu already employed pretty Hortense, who has just died here, and who was afterward nicknamed Clochette. The assistant master singled out the pretty young girl, who was no doubt flattered at being chosen by this disdainful conqueror; at any rate, she fell in love with him, and he succeeded in persuading her to give him a first meeting in the hayloft behind the school, at night after she had done her day's sewing.

"She pretended to go home, but instead of going downstairs when she left the Grabus', she went upstairs and hid among the hay, to wait for her lover. He soon joined her, and he was beginning to say pretty things to her, when the door of the hayloft opened and the schoolmaster appeared, and asked: "What are you doing up there, Sigisbert?" Feeling sure that he would be caught, the young schoolmaster lost his presence of mind and replied stupidly: 'I came up here to rest a little among the bundles of hay, Monsieur Grabu.'

"The loft was very large and absolutely dark. Sigisbert pushed the frightened girl to the further end and said: 'Go there and hide yourself. I shall lose my situation, so get away and hide yourself.'

"When the schoolmaster heard the whispering, he continued: 'Why, you are not by yourself.'

" 'Yes I am, Monsieur Grabu!'

" 'But you are not, for you are talking.'

" 'I swear I am, Monsieur Grabu.'

" 'I will soon find out,' the old man replied, and double-locking the door, he went down to get a light.

"Then the young man, who was a coward such as one sometimes meets, lost his head, and he repeated, having grown furious all of a sudden: 'Hide yourself, so that he may not find you. You will deprive me of my bread for my whole life; you will ruin my whole career! Do hide yourself!'

"They could hear the key turning in the lock again, and Hortense ran to the window which looked out on to the street, opened it quickly, and then in a low and determined voice said: 'You will come and pick me up when he is gone,' and she jumped out.

"Old Grabu found nobody, and went down again in great surprise. A quarter of an hour later, Monsieur Sigisbert came to me and related his adventure. The girl had remained at the foot of the wall unable to get up, as she had fallen from the second story, and I went with him to fetch her. It was raining in torrents, and I brought the unfortunate girl home with me, for the right leg was broken in three places, and the bones had come out through the flesh. She did not complain, and merely said, with admirable resignation: 'I am punished, well punished!'

"I sent for assistance and for the workgirl's friends and told them a made-up story of a runaway carriage which had knocked her down and lamed her, outside my door. They believed me, and the gendarmes for a whole month tried in vain to find the author of this accident.

"That is all! Now I say that this woman was a heroine, and had the fiber of those who accomplish the grandest deeds in history.

"That was her only love affair, and she died a virgin. She was a martyr, a noble soul, a sublimely devoted woman! And if I did not absolutely admire her, I should not have told you this story, which I would never tell anyone during her life: you understand why."

The doctor ceased; mamma cried and papa said some words which I did not catch; then they left the room, and I remained on my knees in the armchair and sobbed, while I heard a strange noise of heavy footsteps and something knocking against the side of the staircase.

They were carrying away Clochette's body.

In the Wood

THE mayor was just going to sit down to breakfast, when he was told that the rural policeman was waiting for him at the *mairie,* with two prisoners. He went there immediately, and found old Hochedur standing up and watching a middle-class couple of mature years with stern looks.

The man, a fat old fellow with a red nose and white hair, seemed utterly dejected; while the woman, a little roundabout, stout creature, with shining cheeks, looked at the agent who had arrested them with defiant eyes.

"What is it? What is it, Hochedur?"

The rural policeman made his deposition. He had gone out that morning at his usual time, in order to patrol his beat from the forest of Champioux as far as the boundaries of Argenteuil. He had not noticed anything unusual in the country except that it was a fine day, and that the wheat was doing well, when the son of old Bredel, who was going over his vines a second time, called out to him: "Here, daddy Hochedur, go and have a look into the skirts of the wood, in the first thicket, and you will catch a pair of pigeons there who must be a hundred and thirty years old between them!"

He went in the direction that had been indicated to him, and had gone into the thicket. There he heard words and gasps, which made him suspect a flagrant breach of morality. Advancing, therefore, on his hands and knees as if to surprise a poacher, he had arrested this couple, at the very moment when they were going to abandon themselves to their natural instincts.

The mayor looked at the culprits in astonishment, for the man was certainly sixty, and the woman fifty-five at least. So he began to question them, beginning with the man, who replied in such a weak voice, that he could scarcely be heard.

"What is your name?"

"Nicolas Beaurain."

"Your occupation?"

"Haberdasher, in the Rue des Martrys, in Paris."

"What were you doing in the wood?"

The haberdasher remained silent, with his eyes on his fat stomach, and his hands resting on his thighs, and the mayor continued:

"Do you deny what the officer of the municipal authorities states?"

"No, Monsieur."

"So you confess it?"

"Yes, Monsieur."

"What have you to say in your defense?"

"Nothing, Monsieur."

"Where did you meet the partner in your misdemeanor?"

"She is my wife, Monsieur."

"Your wife?"

"Yes, Monsieur."

"Then—then—you do not live together in Paris?"

"I beg your pardon, Monsieur, but we are living together!"

"But in that case you must be mad, altogether mad, my dear sir, to get caught like that in the country at ten o'clock in the morning."

The haberdasher seemed ready to cry with shame, and he murmured: "It was she who enticed me! I told her it was stupid, but when a woman has got a thing into her head, you know, you cannot get it out."

The mayor, who liked open speaking, smiled and replied:

"In your case, the contrary ought to have happened. You would not be here, if she had had the idea only in her head."

Then Monsieur Beaurain was seized with rage, and turning to his wife, he said: "Do you see to what you have brought us with your poetry? And now we shall have to go before the Courts, at our age, for a breach of morals! And we shall have to shut up the shop, sell our good-will, and go to some other neighborhood! That's what it has come to!"

Madame Beaurain got up, and without looking at her husband, explained herself without any embarrassment, without useless modesty, and almost without hesitation.

"Of course, Monsieur, I know that we have made ourselves ridiculous. Will you allow me to plead my cause like an advocate, or rather like a poor woman; and I hope that you will be kind enough to send us home, and to spare us the disgrace of a prosecution.

"Years ago, when I was young, I made Monsieur Beaurain's acquaintance on Sunday in this neighborhood. He was employed in a draper's shop, and I was a saleswoman in a ready-made clothing establishment. I remember it, as if it were yesterday. I used to come and spend Sundays here occasionally with a friend of mine, Rose Levèque, with whom I lived in the Rue Pigalle, and Rose had a sweetheart, while I had not. He used to bring us here, and one Saturday, he told me laughing, that he should bring a friend with him the next day. I quite understood what he meant, but I replied that it would be no good; for I was virtuous, Monsieur.

"The next day we met Monsieur Beaurain at the railway station. In those days he was good-looking, but I had made up my mind not to yield to him, and I did not yield. Well, we arrived at Bezons. It was a lovely day, the sort of day that tickles your heart. When it is fine even now, just as it used to be formerly, I grow quite foolish, and when I am in the country, I utterly lose my head. The verdure, the swallows flying so swiftly, the smell of the grass, the scarlet poppies, the daisies, all that makes me quite excited!

It is like champagne when one is not used to it!

"Well, it was lovely weather, warm and bright, and it seemed to penetrate into your body by your eyes when you looked, and by your mouth when you breathed. Rose and Simon hugged and kissed each other every minute, and that gave me something to look at! Monsieur Beaurain and I walked behind them, without speaking much, for when people do not know each other well, they cannot find much to talk about. He looked timid, and I liked to see his embarrassment. At last we got to the little wood; it was as cool as in a bath there, and we all four sat down. Rose and her lover joked me because I looked rather stern, but you will understand that I could not be otherwise. And then they began to kiss and hug again, without putting any more restraint upon themselves than if we had not been there. Then they whispered together, and got up and went off among the trees without saying a word. You may fancy how I felt, alone with this young fellow whom I saw for the first time. I felt so confused at seeing them go that it gave me courage and I began to talk. I asked him what his business was, and he said he was a linen draper's assistant, as I told you just now. We talked for a few minutes and that made him bold, and he wanted to take liberties with me, but I told him sharply to keep his own place. Is not that true, Monsieur Beaurain?"

Monsieur Beaurain, who was looking at his feet in confusion, did not reply, and she continued: "Then he saw that I was virtuous, and he began to make love to me nicely, like an honorable man, and from that time he came every Sunday, for he was very much in love with me. I was very fond of him also, very fond of him! He was a good-looking fellow, formerly, and in short he married me the next September, and we started business in the Rue des Martyrs.

"It was a hard struggle for some years, Monsieur. Business did not prosper, and we could not afford many country excursions, and then we became unaccustomed to them. One has other things in one's head and thinks more of the cash box than of pretty speeches when one is in business. We were growing old by degrees without perceiving it, like quiet people who do not think much about love. But one does not regret anything as long as one does not notice what one has lost.

"And after that, Monsieur, business went better, and we became tranquil as to the future! Then, you see, I do not exactly know what passed within me— no, I really do not know, but I began to dream like a little boarding-school girl. The sight of the little carts full of flowers which are peddled about the streets made me cry; the smell of violets sought me out in my easy-chair, behind my cash box, and made my heart beat! Then I used to get up and go on to the doorstep to look at the blue sky between the roofs. When one looks at the sky from a street, it seems like a river flowing over Paris, winding as it goes, and the swallows pass to and fro in it like fish. These sort of things are very stupid at my age! But what can one do, Monsieur, when one has worked all one's life? A moment comes in

which one perceives that one could have done something else, and then, one regrets, oh! yes, one feels great regret! Just think that for twenty years I might have gone and had kisses in the woods, like other women. I used to think how delightful it would be to lie under the trees, loving some one! And I thought of it every day and every night! I dreamed of the moonlight on the water, until I felt inclined to drown myself.

"I did not venture to speak to Monsieur Beaurain about this at first. I knew that he would make fun of me, and send me back to sell my needles and cotton! And then, to speak the truth, Monsieur Beaurain never said much to me, but when I looked in the glass, I also understood quite well that I also no longer appealed to anyone!

"Well, I made up my mind, and I proposed an excursion into the country to him, to the place where we had first become acquainted. He agreed without any distrust, and we arrived here this morning, about nine o'clock.

"I felt quite young again when I got among the corn, for a woman's heart never grows old! And really, I no longer saw my husband as he is at present, but just like he was formerly! That I will swear to you, Monsieur. As true as I am standing here, I was intoxicated. I began to kiss him, and he was more surprised than if I had tried to murder him. He kept saying to me: 'Why, you must be mad this morning! What is the matter with you—' I did not listen to him, I only listened to my own heart, and I made him come into the wood with me. There is the story.

I have spoken the truth, Monsieur le Maire, the whole truth."

The mayor was a sensible man. He rose from his chair, smiled, and said: "Go in peace, Madame, and sin no more—under the trees."

The Marquis de Fumerol

ROGER DE TOUMEVILLE was sitting astride a chair in the midst of his friends and talking; he held a cigar in his hand, and from time to time took a whiff and blew out a small cloud of smoke.

"We were at dinner when a letter was brought in, and my father opened it. You know my father, who thinks that he is king of France *ad interim*. I call him Don Quixote, because for twelve years he has been running a tilt against the windmill of the Republic, without quite knowing whether it was in the name of Bourbon or of Orléans. At present he is holding the lance in the name of Orléans alone, because there is nobody else left. In any case, he thinks himself the first gentleman in France, the best known, the most influential, the head of the party; and as he is an irremovable senator, he thinks that the neighboring kings' thrones are very insecure.

"As for my mother, she is my father's inspiration, the soul of the kingdom and of religion, the right arm of God on earth, and the scourge of evil-thinkers.

"Well, this letter was brought in while we were at dinner. My father opened and read it, and then he said to my mother: 'Your brother is dying.' She grew very pale. My uncle was scarcely ever mentioned in the house, and I did not know him at all; all I knew from public talk was that he had led, and was still leading, the life of a buffoon. After having spent his fortune with an incalculable number of women, he had only retained two mistresses, with whom he was living in small apartments in the Rue des Martyrs.

"An ex-peer of France and ex-colonel of cavalry, it was said that he believed in neither God nor devil. Having no faith, therefore, in a future life he had abused this present life in every way, and had become a living wound to my mother's heart.

"'Give me that letter, Paul,' she said, and when she had read it, I asked for it in my turn. Here it is:

"'MONSIEUR LE COMTE: I think I ought to let you know that your brother-in-law, Count Fumerol, is going to die. Perhaps you would make preparations and not forget that I told you.

"Your servant, MÉLANI.'

"'We must think,' my father murmured. 'In my position, I ought to watch over your brother's last moments.'

"My mother continued: 'I will send for Abbé Poivron and ask his advice, and then I will go to my brother's with him and Roger. Stop here, Paul, for you must not compromise yourself; but a woman can, and ought, to do these things. For a politician in your position, it is another matter. It would be a fine thing for one of your opponents to be able to bring one of your most laudable actions up against you.'

" 'You are right!' my father said. 'Do as you think best, my dear wife.'

"A quarter of an hour later, the Abbé Poivron came into the drawing-room, and the situation was explained to him, analyzed, and discussed in all its bearings. If the Marquis de Fumerol, one of the greatest names in France, were to die without the succor of religion, it would assuredly be a terrible blow to the nobility in general, to the Count de Tourneville in particular, and the free thinkers. would be triumphant. The evilly disposed newspapers would sing songs of victory for six months; my mother's name would be dragged through the mire and brought into the slander of Socialistic journals, and my father's would be bespattered. It was impossible that such a thing should occur.

"A crusade was therefore immediately decided upon, which was to be led by the Abbé Poivron, a little fat, clean, slightly-scented priest, the faithful vicar of a large church in a rich and noble quarter.

"The landau was ordered and we three started, my mother, the curé, and I, to administer the last sacraments to my uncle.

"It had been decided that first of all we should see Madame Mélani who had written the letter, and who was most likely the porter's wife or my uncle's servant, and I got down as a scout in front of a seven-storied house and went into a dark passage, where I had great difficulty in finding the porter's den. He looked at me distrustfully, and I said:

" 'Madame Mélani, if you please.'

" 'Don't know her!'

" 'But I have received a letter from her.'

" 'That may be, but I don't know her. Are you asking for some kept woman?'

" 'No, a servant probably. She wrote me about a place.'

" 'A servant—a servant? Perhaps it is the Marquis's. Go and see, the fifth story on the left.'

"As soon as he found I was not asking for a kept woman, he became more friendly and came as far as the passage with me. He was a tall, thin man with white whiskers, the manners of a beadle, and majestic in movement.

"I climbed up a long spiral staircase, whose balusters I did not venture to touch, and I gave three discreet knocks at the left-hand door on the fifth story. It opened immediately, and an enormous dirty woman appeared before me, who barred the entrance with her open arms, which she placed upon the two doorposts, and grumbled out:

" 'What do you want?'

" 'Are you Madame Mélani?'

" 'Yes.'

" 'I am the Viscount de Tourneville.'

" 'Ah! All right! Come in.'

" 'Well, the fact is, my mother is downstairs with a priest.'

" 'Oh! All right; go and bring them up; but take care of the porter.'

"I went downstairs and came up again with my mother, who was followed by the abbé, and I fancied that I heard other footsteps behind us. As soon as we were in the kitchen, Mélani offered us chairs, and we all four sat down to deliberate.

" 'Is he very ill?' My mother asked.

" 'Oh! yes, Madame; he will not be here long.'

" 'Does he seem disposed to receive a visit from a priest?'

" 'Oh! I do not think so.'

" 'Can I see him?'

" 'Well—yes—Madame—only — only —those young ladies are with him.'

" 'What young ladies?'

" 'Why—why—his lady friends, of course.'

" 'Oh!' Mamma had grown scarlet, and the Abbé Poivron had lowered his eyes.

"The affair began to amuse me, and I said: 'Suppose I go in first? I shall see how he receives me, and perhaps I shall be able to prepare his heart for you.'

"My mother, who did not suspect any trick, replied: 'Yes, go my dear.'

"But a woman's voice cried out: 'Mélani!'

"The fat servant ran out and said: 'What do you want, Mademoiselle Claire?'

" 'The omelet, quickly.'

" 'In a minute, Mademoiselle.' And coming back to us, she explained this summons.

" 'They ordered a cheese omelet at two o'clock as a slight collation.' And immediately she began to break eggs into a salad bowl, and began to whip them vigorously, while I went out on to the landing and pulled the bell, so as to announce my official arrival. Mélani opened the door to me, and made me sit down in an anteroom, while she went to tell my uncle that I had come. Then she came back and asked me to go in,

while the abbé hid behind the door, so that he might appear at the first sign.

"I was certainly very much surprised at seeing my uncle, for he was very handsome, very solemn, and very elegant—the old rake.

"Sitting, almost lying in a large armchair, his legs wrapped in blankets, with his hands, his long, white hands over the arms of the chair, he was waiting for death with Biblical dignity. His white beard fell on his chest, and his hair, which was also white, mingled with it on his cheeks.

"Standing behind his armchair, as if to defend him against me, were two young women, two stout young women, who looked at me with the bold eyes of prostitutes. In their petticoats and morning wrappers, with bare arms, with coal-black hair twisted up on to the napes of their necks, with embroidered Oriental slippers which showed their ankles and silk stockings, they looked like the immoral figures of some symbolical painting, by the side of the dying man. Between the easy-chair and the bed, there was a table covered with a white cloth, on which two plates, two glasses, two forks, and two knives, were waiting for the cheese omelet which had been ordered some time before of Mélani.

"My uncle said in a weak, almost breathless, but clear voice: 'Good morning, my child: it is rather late in the day to come to see me; our acquaintanceship will not last long.'

"I stammered out: 'It was not my fault, uncle'; and he replied: 'No; I know that. It is your father's and mother's fault more than yours. How are they?'

" 'Pretty well, thank you. When they heard that you were ill, they sent me to ask after you.'

" 'Ah! Why did they not come themselves?'

"I looked up at the two girls and said gently: 'It is not their fault if they could not come, uncle. But it would be difficult for my father, and impossible for my mother to come in here.' The old man did not reply, but raised his hand toward mine, and I took the pale, cold hand and kept it in my own.

"The door opened, Mélani came in with the omelet and put it on the table, and the two girls immediately sat down in front of their plates and began to eat without taking their eyes off me.

"Then I said: 'Uncle, it would be a great pleasure for my mother to embrace you.'

" 'I also—' he murmured, 'should like—' He said no more, and I could think of nothing to propose to him, and nothing more was heard except the noise of the plates and the slight sound of eating mouths.

"Now the abbé, who was listening behind the door, seeing our embarrassment, and thinking we had won the game, thought the time had come to interpose, and showed himself. My uncle was so stupefied at that apparition, that at first he remained motionless; then he opened his mouth as if he meant to swallow up the priest, and cried out in a strong, deep, furious voice: 'What are you doing here?'

"The abbé, who was used to difficult situations, came forward, murmuring: 'I have come in your sister's name, Monsieur le Marquis; she has sent me —she would be so happy, Monsieur—'

"But the Marquis was not listening. Raising one hand, he pointed to the door with a proud and tragic gesture, and said angrily and gasping for breath: 'Leave this room—go out—robber of souls. Go out from here, you violator of consciences! Go out from here, you picklock of dying men's doors!'

"The abbé went backward, and I too, went to the door, beating a retreat with him; and the two little women, who were avenged, got up, leaving their omelet half eaten, and stood on either side of my uncle's armchair, putting their hands on his arms to calm him, and to protect him against the criminal enterprises of the Family and of Religion.

"The abbé and I rejoined my mother in the kitchen, and Mélani again offered us chairs. 'I knew quite well that you would fail that way; we must try some other means, otherwise he will escape us.' And we began deliberating afresh, my mother being of one opinion and the abbé of another, while I held a third.

"We had been discussing the matter in a low voice for half an hour, perhaps, when a great noise of furniture being moved and of cries uttered by my uncle, more vehement and terrible even than the former had been, made us all jump up.

"Through the doors and walls we could hear him shouting: 'Go out—out —rascals—humbugs; get out, scoundrels—get out—get out!'

"Mélani rushed in, but came back immediately to call me to help her, and I hastened in. Opposite to my uncle who was terribly excited by anger, almost standing up and vociferating, two men, one behind the other, seemed to be waiting till he should be dead with rage.

"By his long, ridiculous coat, his pointed English shoes, by his manners, —like those of a tutor out of a situation,—by his high collar, white necktie and straight hair, by his humble face, I immediately recognized the first as a Protestant minister.

"The second was the porter of the house, who belonged to the Reformed religion and had followed us. Having known of our defeat he had gone to fetch his own pastor, in hope of a better fate. My uncle seemed mad with rage! If the sight of the Catholic priest, of the priest of his ancestors, had irritated the Marquis de Fumerol, who had become a freethinker, the sight of his porter's minister made him altogether beside himself. I therefore took the two men by the arm and threw them out of the room so violently that they fell up against each other twice, between the two doors which led to the staircase; then I disappeared in my turn and returned to the kitchen, which was our headquarters, in order to take counsel with my mother and the abbé.

"But Mélani came back in terror, sobbing out: 'He is dying—he is dying —come immediately—he is dying.'

"My mother rushed out. My uncle had fallen on to the carpet, full length along the floor, and did not move. I fancy he was already dead. My mother was superb at that moment! She went straight up to the two girls who were kneeling by the body and trying to raise it up, and pointing to the door with irresistible authority, dignity, and majesty, she said: 'Now it is for you to go out.'

"And they went out without a pro-
test, and without saying a word. I must add that I was getting ready to turn them out as unceremoniously as I had done the parson and the porter.

"Then the Abbé Poivron administered extreme unction to my uncle with all the customary prayers and remitted all his sins, while my mother sobbed, kneeling near her brother. Suddenly, however, she exclaimed: 'He recognized me; he pressed my hand; I am sure he recognized me and thanked me! Oh, God, what happiness!'

"Poor mamma! If she had known or guessed to whom those thanks ought to have been addressed!

"They laid my uncle on his bed; he was certainly dead that time.

"'Madame,' Mélani said, 'we have no sheets to bury him in; all the linen belongs to those two young ladies,' and when I looked at the omelet which they had not finished, I felt inclined to laugh and to cry at the same time. There are some strange moments and some strange sensations in life, occasionally!

"We gave my uncle a magnificent funeral, with five speeches at the grave. Baron de Croiselles, the Senator, showed in admirable terms, that God always returns victorious into well-born souls which have gone astray for a moment. All the members of the Royalist and Catholic party followed the funeral procession with triumphant enthusiasm, speaking of that beautiful death, after a somewhat restless life."

Viscount Roger ceased speaking, and those around him laughed. Then somebody said: "Bah! That is the story of all conversions *in extremis*."

Saved

THE little Maquise de Rennedon came rushing in like a ball through the window. She began to laugh before she spoke, to laugh till she cried, like she had done a month previously, when she had told her friend that she had betrayed the Marquis in order to have her revenge, but only once, just because he was really too stupid and too jealous.

The little Baroness de Grangerie had thrown the book which she was reading on to the sofa, and looked at Annette, curiously. She was already laughing herself, and at last she asked:

"What have you been doing now?"

"Oh! my dear!—my dear! it is too funny—too funny. Just fancy—I am saved!—saved!—saved!"

"How do you mean, saved?"

"Yes, saved!"

"From what?"

"From my husband, my dear, saved! Delivered! free! free! free!"

"How free? In what?"

"In what? Divorce! yes a divorce! I have my divorce!"

"You are divorced?"

"No, not yet; how stupid you are! One does not get divorced in three hours! But I have my proofs that he has deceived me—caught in the very act —just think!—in the very act. I have got him tight."

"Oh! do tell me all about it! So he deceived you?"

"Yes, that is to say no—yes and no— I do not know. At any rate, I have proofs, and that is the chief thing."

"How did you manage it?"

"How did I manage it? This is how! I have been energetic, very energetic. For the last three months he has been odious, altogether odious, brutal, coarse, a despot—in one word, vile. So I said to myself: This cannot last, I must have a divorce! But how?—for it is not very easy. I tried to make him beat me, but he would not. He vexed me from morning till night, made me go out when I did not wish to, and to remain at home when I wanted to dine out; he made my life unbearable for me from one week's end to the other, but he never struck me.

"Then I tried to find out whether he had a mistress Yes, he had one, but he took a thousand precautions in going to see her, and they could never be caught together. Guess what I did then?"

"I cannot guess."

"Oh! you could never guess. I asked my brother to procure me a photograph of the creature."

"Of your husband's mistress?"

"Yes. It cost Jacques fifteen louis,* the price of an evening, from seven o'clock till midnight, including a dinner, at three louis an hour, and he obtained the photograph into the bargain.'

"It appears to me that he might have obtained it anyhow by means of some artifice and without—without—without being obliged to take the original at the same time."

"Oh! she is pretty, and Jacques did not mind the least. And then, I wanted some details about her, physical details about her figure, her breast, her complexion, a thousand things, in fact."

"I do not understand you."

"You shall see. When I had learned all that I wanted to know, I went to a

---

*60.

224

—how shall I put it—to a man of business—you know—one of those men who transact business of all sorts—agents of—of—of publicity and complicity—one of those men—well, you understand what I mean."

"Pretty nearly, I think. And what did you say to him?"

"I said to him, showing the photograph of Clarisse (her name is Clarisse): 'Monsieur, I want a lady's maid who resembles this photograph. I require one who is pretty, elegant, neat, and sharp. I will pay her whatever is necessary, and if it costs me ten thousand francs* so much the worse. I shall not require her for more than three months.'

"The man looked extremely astonished, and said: 'Do you require a maid of an irreproachable character, Madame?' I blushed and stammered: 'Yes of course, for honesty.' He continued: 'And—then—as regards morals?' I did not venture to reply, so I only made a sign with my head which signified *No.* Then suddenly, I comprehended that he had a horrible suspicion and losing my presence of mind, I exclaimed: 'Oh! Monsieur,—it is for my husband, in order that I may surprise him.'

"Then the man began to laugh, and from his looks I gathered that I had regained his esteem. He even thought I was brave, and I would willingly have made a bet that at that moment he was longing to shake hands with me. However, he said to me: 'In a week Madame, I shall have what you require; I will answer for my success, and you shall not pay me until I have succeeded. So this is a photograph of your husband's mistress?'

" 'Yes, Monsieur.'

" 'A handsome woman, and not too stout. And what scent?'

"I did not understand, and repeated: 'What scent?'

"He smiled: 'Yes, Madame, perfume is essential in tempting a man, for it unconsciously brings to his mind certain reminiscences which dispose him to action; the perfume creates an obscure confusion in his mind, and disturbs and energizes him by recalling his pleasures to him. You must also try to find out what your husband is in the habit of eating when he dines with his lady, and you might give him the same dishes the day you catch him. Oh! we have got him, Madame, we have got him.'

"I went away delighted, for here I had lighted on a very intelligent man.

"Three days later, I saw a tall, dark girl arrive at my house; she was very handsome, and her looks were modest and bold at the same time, the peculiar look of a female rake. She behaved very properly toward me, and as I did not exactly know what she was, I called her Mademoiselle, but she said immediately: 'Oh! pray, Madame, only call me Rose.' And she began to talk.

" 'Well, Rose, you know why you have come here?'

" 'I can guess it, Madame.'

" 'Very good, my girl—and that will not be too much bother for you?'

" 'Oh! Madame, this will be the eighth divorce that I shall have caused; I am used to it.'

" 'Why, that is capital. Will it take you long to succeed?'

" 'Oh! Madame, that depends en-

*$2000.

tirely on Monsieur's temperament. When I have seen Monsieur for five minutes alone, I shall be able to tell you exactly.'

" 'You will see him soon, my child, but I must tell you that he is not handsome.'

" 'That does not matter to me, Madame; I have already separated some very ugly ones. But I must ask you Madame, whether you have discovered his favorite perfume?'

" 'Yes, Rose—verbena.'

" 'So much the better, Madame, for I am also very fond of that scent! Can you also tell me, Madame, whether Monsieur's mistress wears silk underclothing and nightdresses?'

" 'No, my child, cambric and lace.'

" 'Oh! then she is altogether of superior station, for silk underclothing is getting quite common.'

" 'What you say is quite true!'

" 'Well, Madame, I will enter your service.' And so as a matter of fact she did immediately, and as if she had done nothing else all her life.

"An hour later my husband came home. Rose did not even raise her eyes to him, but he raised his eyes to her. She already smelled strongly of verbena. In five minutes she left the room, and he immediately asked me: 'Who is that girl?'

" 'Why—my new lady's maid.'

" 'Where did you pick her up?'

" 'Baroness de Grangerie got her for me with the best references.'

" 'Ah! she is rather pretty!'

" 'Do you think so?'

" 'Why, yes—for a lady's maid.'

"I was delighted, for I felt that he was already biting, and that same eve-

ning Rose said to me: 'I can now promise you that it will not take more than a fortnight, Monsieur is very easily caught!'

" 'Ah! you have tried already?'

" 'No, Madame, he only asked what my name was, so that he might hear what my voice was like.'

" 'Very well, my dear Rose. Get on as quick as you can.'

" 'Do not be alarmed, Madame; I shall only resist long enough not to make myself depreciated.'

"At the end of a week, my husband scarcely ever went out; I saw him roaming about the house the whole afternoon, and what was most significant in the matter was that he no longer prevented me from going out. And I, I was out of doors nearly the whole day long—in order—in order to leave him at liberty.

"On the ninth day, while Rose was undressing me, she said to me with a timid air: 'It happened this morning, Madame.'

"I was rather surprised, or rather overcome even, not at the part itself, but at the way in which she told me, and I stammered out: 'And—and—it went off well?'

" 'Oh! yes, very well, Madame. For the last three days he has been pressing me, but I did not wish matters to proceed too quickly. You will tell me when you want us to be caught, Madame.'

" 'Yes, certainly. Here! let us say Thursday.'

" 'Very well, Madame, I shall grant nothing more till then, so as to keep Monsieur on the alert.'

" 'You are sure not to fail?'

" 'Oh! quite sure, Madame. I will excite him, so as to make him be there at the very moment which you may appoint.'

" 'Let us say five o'clock then.'

" 'Very well, Madame, and where?'

" 'Well—in my bedroom.'

" 'Very good, Madame, in your bedroom.'

" 'You will understand what I did then, my dear. I went and fetched mamma and papa first of all, and then my uncle d'Orvelin, the President, and Monsieur Raplet, the Judge, my husband's friend. I had not told them what I was going to show them, but I made them all go on tiptoe as far as the door of my room. I waited till five o'clock exactly, and oh! how my heart beat! I had made the porter come upstairs as well, so as to have an additional witness! And then—and then at the moment when the clock began to strike, I opened the door wide. Ah! ah! ah!

Here he was evidently—it was quite evident, my dear. Oh! what a head! If you had only seen his head! And he turned round, the idiot! Oh! how funny he looked—I laughed, I laughed. And papa was angry and wanted to give my husband a beating. And the porter, a good servant helped him to dress himself before us—before us. He buttoned his braces for him—what a joke it was! As for Rose, she was perfect, absolutely perfect. She cried—oh! she cried very well. She is an invaluable girl. If you ever want her, don't forget!

"And here I am. I came immediately to tell you of the affair directly. I am free. Long live divorce!"

And she began to dance in the middle of the drawing-room, while the little Baroness, who was thoughtful and put out, said:

"Why did you not invite me to see it?"

The Signal

THE little Marchioness de Rennedon was still asleep in her dark and perfumed bedroom.

In her soft, low bed, between sheets of delicate cambric, fine as lace and caressing as a kiss, she was sleeping alone and tranquil, the happy and profound sleep of divorced women.

She was awakened by loud voices in the little blue drawing-room, and she recognized her dear friend, the little Baroness de Grangerie, who was disputing with the lady's maid, because the latter would not allow her to go into the Marchioness's room. So the little Marchioness got up, opened the door, drew back the door-hangings and showed her head, nothing but her fair head, hidden under a cloud of hair.

"What is the matter with you, that you have come so early?" she asked. "It is not nine o'clock yet."

The little Baroness, who was very pale, nervous, and feverish, replied: "I must speak to you. Something horrible has happened to me."

"Come in, my dear."

She went in, they kissed each other and the little Marchioness got back into her bed, while the lady's maid opened the windows to let in light and air. Then when she had left the room, Madame de Rennedon went on: "Well, tell me what it is."

Madame de Grangerie began to cry, shedding those pretty bright tears which make women more charming. She sobbed out, without wiping her eyes, so as not to make them red: "Oh, my dear, what has happened to me is abominable, abominable. I have not slept all night, not a minute; do you hear, not a minute. Here, just feel my heart, how it is beating."

And taking her friend's hand, she put it on her breast, on that firm, round covering of women's hearts which often suffices men, and prevents them from seeking beneath. But her heart was really beating violently.

She continued: "It happened to me yesterday during the day, at about four o'clock—or half past four; I cannot say exactly. You know my apartments, and you know that my little drawing-room, where I always sit, looks on to the Rue Saint-Lazare, and that I have a mania for sitting at the window to look at the people passing. The neighborhood of the railway station is very gay; so full of motion and lively—just what I like! So, yesterday, I was sitting in the low chair which I have placed in my window recess; the window was open and I was not thinking of anything, simply breathing the fresh air. You remember how fine it was yesterday!

"Suddenly, I remarked a woman sitting at the window opposite—a woman in red. I was in mauve, you know, my pretty mauve costume. I did not know the woman, a new lodger, who had been there a month, and as it has been raining for a month, I had not yet seen her, but I saw immediately that she was a bad girl. At first I was very much shocked and disgusted that she should be at the window just as I was; and then by degrees, it amused me to watch her. She was resting her elbows on the window ledge, and looking at the men, and the men looked at her also, all or nearly all. One might have said that they knew of her presence by some means as they got near the house, that they scented her, as dogs scent game, for they suddenly raised their heads, and exchanged a swift look with her, a sort of freemason's look. Hers said: 'Will you?' Theirs replied: 'I have no time,' or else: 'Another day'; or else: 'I have not got a sou'; or else: 'Hide yourself, you wretch!'

"You cannot imagine how funny it was to see her carrying on such a piece of work, though after all it is her regular business.

"Occasionally she shut the window suddenly, and I saw a gentleman go in. She had caught him like a fisherman hooks a gudgeon. Then I looked at my watch, and I found that they never stopped longer than from twelve to twenty minutes. In the end she really infatuated me, the spider! And then the creature is so ugly.

"I asked myself: 'How does she manage to make herself understood so quickly, so well and so completely? Does she add a sign of the head or a motion of the hands to her looks?' And

I took my opera-glasses to watch her proceedings. Oh! they were very simple: first of all a glance, then a smile, then a slight sign with the head which meant: 'Are you coming up?' But it was so slight, so vague, so discreet, that it required a great deal of knack to succeed as she did. And I asked myself: 'I wonder if I could do that little movement, from below upward, which was at the same time bold and pretty, as well as she does,' for her gesture was very pretty.

"I went and tried it before the looking-glass, and my dear, I did it better than she, a great deal better! I was enchanted, and resumed my place at the window.

"She caught nobody more then, poor girl, nobody. She certainly had no luck. It must really be very terrible to earn one's bread in that way, terrible and amusing occasionally, for really some of these men one meets in the street are rather nice.

"After that they all came on my side of the road and none on hers; the sun had turned. They came one after the other, young, old, dark, fair, gray, white. I saw some who looked very nice, really very nice, my dear, far better than my husband or than yours—I mean than your late husband, as you have got a divorce. Now you can choose.

"I said to myself: 'If I give them the sign, will they understand me, who am a respectable woman?' And I was seized with a mad longing to make that sign to them. I had a longing, a terrible longing; you know, one of those longings which one cannot resist! I have some like that occasionally. How silly

such things are, don't you think so? I believe that we women have the souls of monkeys. I have been told (and it was a physician who told me) that the brain of a monkey is very like ours. Of course we must imitate some one or other. We imitate our husbands when we love them, during the first months after our marriage, and then our lovers, our female friends, our confessors when they are nice. We assume their ways of thought, their manners of speech, their words, their gestures, everything. It is very foolish.

"However, as for me, when I am much tempted to do a thing I always do it, and so I said to myself: 'I will try it once, on one man only, just to see. What can happen to me? Nothing whatever! We shall exchange a smile and that will be all and I shall deny it, most certainly.'

"So I began to make my choice, I wanted some one nice, very nice, and suddenly I saw a tall, fair, very good-looking fellow coming alone. I like fair men, as you know. I looked at him, he looked at me; I smiled, he smiled, I made the movement, oh! so faintly; he replied *yes* with his head, and there he was, my dear! He came in at the large door of the house.

"You cannot imagine what passed through my mind then! I thought I should go mad. Oh! how frightened I was. Just think, he will speak to the servants! To Joseph, who is devoted to my husband! Joseph would certainly think that I had known that gentleman for a long time.

"What could I do, just tell me? And he would ring in a moment. What could I do, tell me? I thought I would go and meet him, and tell him he had made a mistake, and beg him to go away. He would have pity on a woman, on a poor woman: So I rushed to the door and opened it, just at the moment when he was going to ring the bell, and I stammered out, quite stupidly: 'Go away, Monsieur, go away; you have made a mistake, a terrible mistake; I took you for one of my friends whom you are very like. Have pity on me, Monsieur.'

"But he only began to laugh, my dear, and replied: 'Good morning, my dear, I know all about your little story, you may be sure. You are married, and so you want forty francs instead of twenty, and you shall have them, so just show the way.'

"And he pushed me in, closed the door, and as I remained standing before him, horror-struck, he kissed me, put his arm round my waist and made me go back into the drawing-room, the door of which had remained open. Then he began to look at everything like an auctioneer, and continued: 'By Jove, it is very nice in your rooms, very nice. You must be very down on your luck just now, to do the window business!'

"Then I began to beg him again: 'Oh! Monsieur, go away, please go away, my husband will be coming in soon, it is just his time. I swear that you have made a mistake!' But he answered quite coolly: 'Come, my beauty, I have had enough of this nonsense, and if your husband comes in, I will give him five francs to go and have a drink at the *café* opposite.' And then seeing Raoul's photograph on the chimney-piece, he asked me: 'Is that your—your husband?'

" 'Yes, that is he.'

" 'He looks like a nice, disagreeable sort of fellow. And who is this? One of your friends?'

"It was your photograph, my dear, you know, the one in ball dress. I did not know any longer what I was saying and I stammered: 'Yes, it is one of my friends.'

" 'She is very nice; you shall introduce me to her.'

"Just then the clock struck five, and Raoul comes home every day at half past! Suppose he were to come home before the other had gone, just fancy what would have happened! Then—then—I completely lost my head—altogether—I thought—I thought—that—that—the best thing would be—to get rid—of—of this man—as quickly as possible— The sooner it was over—you understand."

*   *   *   *   *   *

The little Marchioness de Rennedon had begun to laugh, to laugh madly, with her head buried in her pillow, so that the whole bed shook, and when she was a little calmer she asked:

"And—and—was he good-looking?"

"Yes."

"And yet you complain?"

"But—but—don't you see, my dear, he said—he said—he should come again to-morrow—at the same time—and I—I am terribly frightened— You have no idea how tenacious he is and obstinate— What can I do—tell me—what can I do?"

The little Marchioness sat up in bed to reflect, and then she suddenly said: "Have him arrested!"

The little Baroness looked stupefied,

and stammered out: "What do you say? What are you thinking of? Have him arrested? Under what pretext?"

"That is very simple. Go to the Commissary of Police and say that a gentleman has been following you about for three months; that he had the insolence to go up to your apartments yesterday; that he has threatened you with another visit to-morrow, and that you demand the protection of the law, and they will give you two police officers who will arrest him."

"But, my dear, suppose he tells—"

"They will not believe him, you silly thing, if you have told your tale cleverly to the commissary, but they will believe you, who are an irreproachable woman, and in society."

"Oh! I shall never dare to do it."

"You must dare, my dear, or you are lost."

"But think that he will—he will insult me if he is arrested."

"Very well, you will have witnesses, and he will be sentenced."

"Sentenced to what?"

"To pay damages. In such cases, one must be pitiless!"

"Ah! speaking of damages—there is one thing that worries me very much— very much indeed. He left me two twenty-franc pieces on the mantelpiece."

"Two twenty-francs pieces?"

"Yes."

"No more?"

"No."

"That is very little. It would have humiliated me. Well?"

"Well! What am I to do with that money?"

The little Marchioness hesitated for a few seconds, and then she replied in a serious voice:

"My dear—you must make—you must make your husband a little present with it. That will be only fair!"

The Devil

THE peasant was standing opposite the doctor, by the bedside of the dying old woman, and she, calmly resigned and quite lucid, looked at them and listened to their talking. She was going to die, and she did not rebel at it, for her life was over—she was ninety-two.

The July sun streamed in at the window and through the open door and cast its hot flames on to the uneven brown clay floor, which had been stamped down by four generations of clodboppers. The smell of the fields came in also, driven by the brisk wind, and parched by the noontide heat. The grasshoppers chirped themselves hoarse, filling the air with their shrill noise, like that of the wooden crickets which are sold to children at fair time.

The doctor raised his voice and said: "Honoré, you cannot leave your mother in this state; she may die at any moment." And the peasant, in great distress, replied: "But I must get in my wheat, for it has been lying on the ground a long time, and the weather is just right for it; what do you say about it, mother?" And the dying woman, still possessed by her Norman avariciousness, replies *yes* with her eyes and her forehead, and so urged her son to get in his wheat, and to leave her to die alone. But the doctor got angry, and stamping his foot he said: "You are no better than a brute, do you hear, and I will not allow you to do it. Do you understand? And if you must get in your wheat to-day, go and fetch Rapet's wife and make her look after your mother. I *will* have it. And if you do not obey me, I will let you die like a dog, when you are ill in your turn; do you hear me?"

The peasant, a tall, thin fellow with slow movements, who was tormented by indecision, by his fear of the doctor and his keen love for saving, hesitated, calculated, and stammered out: "How much does La Rapet charge for attending sick people?"

"How should I know?" the doctor cried. "That depends upon how long she is wanted for. Settle it with her, by Jove! But I want her to be here within an hour, do you hear."

So the man made up his mind. "I will go for her," he replied; "don't get angry, doctor." And the latter left, calling out as he went: "Take care, you know, for I do not joke when I am angry!" And as soon as they were alone, the peasant turned to his mother, and said in a resigned voice: "I will go and fetch La Rapet, as the man will have it. Don't go off while I am away."

And he went out in his turn.

La Rapet, who was an old washerwoman, watched the dead and the dying of the neighborhood, and then, as soon as she had sewn her customers into that linen cloth from which they would emerge no more, she went and took up her irons to smooth the linen of the living. Wrinkled like a last year's apple, spiteful, envious, avaricious with a phenomenal avarice, bent double, as if she had been broken in half across the loins, by the constant movement of the iron over the linen, one might have said that she had a kind of monstrous and cynical affection for a death struggle. She never spoke of anything but of the people she had seen die, of the various kinds of deaths at which she had been present, and she related, with the greatest minuteness, details which were always the same, just like a sportsman talks of his shots.

When Honoré Bontemps entered her cottage, he found her preparing the starch for the collars of the village women, and he said: "Good evening; I hope you are pretty well, Mother Rapet."

She turned her head round to look at him and said: "Fairly well, fairly well, and you?"

"Oh! as for me, I am as well as I could wish, but my mother is very sick."

"Your mother?"

"Yes, my mother!"

"What's the matter with her?"

"She is going to turn up her toes, that's what's the matter with her!"

The old woman took her hands out of the water and asked with sudden sympathy: "Is she as bad as all that?"

"The doctor says she will not last till morning."

"Then she certainly is very bad!" Honoré hesitated, for he wanted to make a few preliminary remarks before coming to his proposal, but as he could hit upon nothing, he made up his mind suddenly.

"How much are you going to ask to stop with her till the end? You know that I am not rich, and I cannot even afford to keep a servant-girl. It is just that which has brought my poor mother to this state, too much work and fatigue! She used to work for ten, in spite of her ninety-two years. You don't find any made of that stuff nowadays!"

La Rapet answered gravely: "There are two prices: Forty sous by day and three francs by night for the rich, and twenty sous by day, and forty by night for the others. You shall pay me the twenty and forty." But the peasant reflected, for he knew his mother well. He knew how tenacious of life, how vigorous and unyielding she was. He knew, too, that she might last another week, in spite of the doctor's opinion, and so he said resolutely: "No, I would rather you would fix a price until the end. I will take my chance, one way or the other. The doctor says she will die very soon. If that happens, so much the better for you, and so much the worse for me, but if she holds out till to-morrow or longer, so much the better for me and so much the worse for you!"

The nurse looked at the man in astonishment, for she had never treated a death as a speculative job, and she hesitated, tempted by the idea of the possible gain. But almost immediately she suspected that he wanted to juggle her. "I can say nothing until I have seen your mother," she replied.

"Then come with me and see her."

She washed her hands, and went with

him immediately. They did not speak on the road; she walked with short, hasty steps, while he strode on with his long legs, as if he were crossing a brook at every step. The cows lying down in the fields, overcome by the heat, raised their heads heavily and lowed feebly at the two passers-by, as if to ask them for some green grass.

When they got near the house, Honoré Bontemps murmured: "Suppose it is all over?" And the unconscious wish that it might be so showed itself in the sound of his voice.

But the old woman was not dead. She was lying on her back, on her wretched bed, her hands covered with a pink cotton counterpane, horribly thin, knotty paws, like some strange animal's, or like crabs' claws, hands closed by rheumatism, fatigue, and the work of nearly a century which she had accomplished.

La Rapet went up to the bed and looked at the dying woman, felt her pulse, tapped her on the chest, listened to her breathing, and asked her questions, so as to hear her speak: then, having looked at her for some time longer, she went out of the room, followed by Honoré. His decided opinion was, that the old woman would not last out the night, and he asked: "Well?" And the sick-nurse replied: "Well, she may last two days, perhaps three. You will have to give me six francs, everything included."

"Six francs! six francs!" he shouted. "Are you out of your mind? I tell you that she cannot last more than five or six hours!" And they disputed angrily for some time, but as the nurse said she would go home, as the time was slipping away, and as his wheat would not come to the farmyard of its own accord, he agreed to her terms at last:

"Very well, then, that is settled; six francs including everything, until the corpse is taken out."

"That is settled, six francs."

And he went away, with long strides, to the wheat, which was lying on the ground under the hot sun which ripens the grain, while the sick-nurse returned to the house.

She had brought some work with her, for she worked without stopping by the side of the dead and dying, sometimes for herself, sometimes for the family, who employed her as seamstress also, paying her rather more in that capacity. Suddenly she asked:

"Have you received the last sacrament, Mother Bontemps?"

The old peasant woman said "No" with her head, and La Rapet, who was very dévout, got up quickly: "Good heavens, is it possible? I will go and fetch the curé"; and she rushed off to the parsonage so quickly, that the urchins in the street thought some accident had happened, when they saw her trotting off like that.

The priest came immediately in his surplice, preceded by a choir-boy, who rang a bell to announce the passage of the Host through the parched and quiet country. Some men, working at a distance, took off their large hats and remained motionless until the white vestment had disappeared behind some farm buildings; the women who were making up the sheaves stood up to make the sign of the cross; the frightened black hens ran away along the ditch until they reached a well-known hole through

which they suddenly disappeared, while a foal, which was tied up in a meadow, took fright at the sight of the surplice and began to gallop round at the length of its rope, kicking violently. The choir-boy, in his red cassock, walked quickly, and the priest, the square biretta on his bowed head, followed him, muttering some prayers. Last of all came La Rapet, bent almost double, as if she wished to prostrate herself; she walked with folded hands, as if she were in church.

Honoré saw them pass in the distance, and he asked: "Where is our priest going to?" And his man, who was more acute, replied: "He is taking the sacrament to your mother, of course!"

The peasant was not surprised and said: "That is quite possible," and went on with his work.

Mother Bontemps confessed, received absolution and extreme unction, and the priest took his departure, leaving the two women alone in the suffocating cottage. La Rapet began to look at the dying woman, and to ask herself whether it could last much longer.

The day was on the wane, and a cooler air came in stronger puffs, making a view of Epinal, which was fastened to the wall by two pins, flap up and down. The scanty window curtains, which had formerly been white, but were now yellow and covered with fly-specks, looked as if they were going to fly off, and seemed to struggle to get away, like the old woman's soul.

Lying motionless, with her eyes open, the old mother seemed to await the death which was so near, and which yet delayed its coming, with perfect indifference. Her short breath whistled in her throat. It would stop altogether soon, and there would be one woman less in the world, one whom nobody would regret.

At nightfall Honoré returned, and when he went up to the bed and saw that his mother was still alive he asked: "How is she?" just as he had done formerly, when she had been sick. Then he sent La Rapet away, saying to her: "To-morrow morning at five o'clock, without fail." And she replied: "To-morrow at five o'clock."

She came at daybreak, and found Honoré eating his soup, which he had made himself, before going to work.

"Well, is your mother dead?" asked the nurse.

"She is rather better, on the contrary," he replied, with a malignant look out of the corner of his eyes. Then he went out.

La Rapet was seized with anxiety, and went up to the dying woman, who was in the same state, lethargic and impassive, her eyes open and her hands clutching the counterpane. The nurse perceived that this might go on thus for two days, four days, eight days, even, and her avaricious mind was seized with fear. She was excited to fury against the cunning fellow who had tricked her, and against the woman who would not die.

Nevertheless, she began to sew and waited with her eyes fixed on the wrinkled face of Mother Bontemps. When Honoré returned to breakfast he seemed quite satisfied, and even in a bantering humor, for he was carrying in his wheat under very favorable circumstances.

La Rapet was getting exasperated; every passing minute now seemed to her so much time and money stolen from her. She felt a mad inclination to choke this old ass, this headstrong old fool, this obstinate old wretch—to stop that short, rapid breath, which was robbing her of her time and money, by squeezing her throat a little. But then she reflected on the danger of doing so, and other thoughts came into her head, so she went up to the bed and said to her: "Have you ever seen the Devil?" Mother Bontemps whispered: "No."

Then the sick-nurse began to talk and to tell her tales likely to terrify her weak and dying mind. "Some minutes before one dies the Devil appears," she said, "to all. He has a broom in his hand, a saucepan on his head and he utters loud cries. When anybody had seen him, all was over, and that person had only a few moments longer to live"; and she enumerated all those to whom the Devil had appeared that year: Josephine Loisel, Eulalie Ratier, Sophie Padagnau, Séraphine Grospied.

Mother Bontemps, who was at last most disturbed in mind, moved about, wrung her hands, and tried to turn her head to look at the other end of the room. Suddenly La Rapet disappeared at the foot of the bed. She took a sheet out of the cupboard and wrapped herself up in it; then she put the iron pot on to her head, so that its three short bent feet rose up like horns, took a broom in her right hand and a tin pail in her left, which she threw up suddenly, so that it might fall to the ground noisily.

Certainly when it came down, it made a terrible noise. Then, climbing on to a chair, the nurse showed herself, gesticulating and uttering shrill cries into the pot which covered her face, while she menaced the old peasant woman, who was nearly dead, with her broom.

Terrified, with a mad look on her face, the dying woman made a super-human effort to get up and escape; she even got her shoulders and chest out of bed; then she fell back with a deep sigh. All was over, and La Rapet calmly put everything back into its place; the broom into the corner by the cupboard, the sheet inside it, the pot on to the hearth, the pail on to the floor, and the chair against the wall. Then with a professional air, she closed the dead woman's enormous eyes, put a plate on the bed and poured some holy water into it, dipped the twig of boxwood into it, and kneeling down, she fervently repeated the prayers for the dead, which she knew by heart, as a matter of business.

When Honoré returned in the evening, he found her praying. He calculated immediately that she had made twenty sous out of him, for she had only spent three days and one night there, which made five francs altogether, instead of the six which he owed her.

The Venus of Braniza

SOME years ago there lived in Braniza a celebrated Talmudist, renowned no less on account of his beautiful wife, than for his wisdom, his learning, and his fear of God. The Venus of Braniza deserved that name thoroughly; she deserved it for herself, on account of her singular beauty, and even more as the wife of a man deeply versed in the Talmud, for the wives of the Jewish philosophers are, as a rule, ugly or possess some bodily defect.

The Talmud explains this in the following manner: It is well known that marriages are made in heaven, and at the birth of a boy a divine voice calls out the name of his future wife, and vice versâ. But just as a good father tries to get rid of his good wares out of doors, and only uses the damaged stuff at home for his children, so God bestows on the Talmudists those women whom other men would not care to have.

Well, God made an exception in the case of our Talmudist, and had bestowed a Venus on him, perhaps only in order to confirm the rule by means of this exception, and to make it appear less hard. This philosopher's wife was a woman who would have done honor to any king's throne, or to a pedestal in any sculpture gallery. Tall, and with a wonderfully voluptuous figure, she carried a strikingly beautiful head, surmounted by thick, black plaits, on her proud shoulders. Two large, dark eyes languished and glowed beneath long lashes, and her beautiful hands looked as if they were carved out of ivory.

This glorious woman, who seemed to have been designed by nature to rule, to see slaves at her feet, to provide occupation for the painter's brush, the sculptor's chisel, and the poet's pen, lived the life of a rare and beautiful flower shut up in a hothouse. She would sit the whole day long wrapped up in her costly furs looking down dreamily into the street.

She had no children; her husband, the philosopher, studied and prayed and studied again from early morning until late at night; his mistress was "the Veiled Beauty," as the Talmudists call the Kabbalah. She paid no attention to her house, for she was rich, and everything went of its own accord like a clock which has only to be wound up once a week; nobody came to see her, and she never went out of the house; she sat and dreamed and brooded and—yawned.

*   *   *   *   *   *

One day when a terrible storm of thunder and lightning had spent its fury over the town, and all windows had been opened in order to let the Messias in, the Jewish Venus was sitting as usual in her comfortable easy-chair, shivering in spite of her furs, and thinking. Suddenly she fixed her glowing eyes on her husband who was sitting before the Talmud, swaying his body backward and forward, and said suddenly:

"Just tell me, when will Messias, the son of David, come?"

"He will come," the philosopher replied, "when all the Jews have become either altogether virtuous or altogether vicious, says the Talmud."

"Do you believe that all the Jews will ever become virtuous?" the Venus continued.

"How am I to believe that?"

"So Messias will come when all the Jews have become vicious?"

The philosopher shrugged his shoulders, and lost himself again in the labyrinth of the Talmud, out of which, so it is said, only one man returned in perfect sanity. The beautiful woman at the window again looked dreamily out into the heavy rain, while her white fingers played unconsciously with the dark furs of her splendid robe.

*   *   *   *   *   *

One day the Jewish philosopher had gone to a neighboring town, where an important question of ritual was to be decided. Thanks to his learning, the question was settled sooner than he had expected, and instead of returning the next morning, as he had intended, he came back the same evening with a friend who was no less learned than himself. He got out of the carriage at his friend's house and went home on foot. He was not a little surprised when he saw his windows brilliantly illuminated, and found an officer's servant comfortably smoking his pipe in front of his house.

"What are you doing here?" he asked in a friendly manner, but with some curiosity, nevertheless.

"I am on guard, lest the husband of the beautiful Jewess should come home unexpectedly."

"Indeed? Well, mind and keep a good lookout."

Saying this, the philosopher pretended to go away, but went into the house through the garden entrance at the back. When he got into the first room, he found a table laid for two, which had evidently only been left a short time previously. His wife was sitting as usual at her bedroom window wrapped in her furs, but her cheeks were suspiciously red, and her dark eyes had not their usual languishing look, but now rested on her husband with a gaze which expressed at the same time satisfaction and mockery. At that moment his foot stuck against an object on the floor, which gave out a strange sound. He picked it up and examined it in the light. It was a pair of spurs.

"Who has been here with you?" asked the Talmudist.

The Jewish Venus shrugged her shoulders contemptuously, but did not reply.

"Shall I tell you? The Captain of Hussars has been with you."

"And why should he not have been here with me?" she said, smoothing the fur on her jacket with her white hand.

"Woman! are you out of your mind?"

"I am in full possession of my senses," she replied, and a knowing smile hovered round her red voluptuous lips. "But must I not also do my part, in order that Messias may come and redeem us poor Jews?"

The Rabbit

OLD LECACHEUR appeared at the door of his house at his usual hour, between five and a quarter past five in the morning, to look after his men who were going to work.

With a red face, only half awake, his right eye open and the left nearly closed, he was buttoning his braces over his fat stomach with some difficulty, all the time looking into every corner of the farmyard with a searching glance. The sun was darting his oblique rays through the beech-trees by the side of the ditch and the apple-trees outside, making the cocks crow on the dung-hill, and the pigeons coo on the roof. The smell of the cow stalls came through the open door, mingling in the fresh morning air with the pungent odor of the stable where the horses were neighing, with their heads turned toward the light.

As soon as his trousers were properly fastened, Lecacheur came out, and went first of all toward the hen-house to count the morning's eggs, for he had been suspecting thefts for some time. But the servant girl ran up to him with lifted arms and cried:

"Master! Master! they have stolen a rabbit during the night."

"A rabbit?"

"Yes, Master, the big gray rabbit, from the hutch on the left." Whereupon the farmer quite opened his left eye, and said, simply:

"I must see that."

And off he went to inspect it. The hutch had been broken open and the rabbit was gone. Then he became thoughtful, closed his left eye again, scratched his nose, and after a little consideration, said to the frightened girl, who was standing stupidly before him:

"Go and fetch the gendarmes; say I expect them as soon as possible."

Lecacheur was mayor of the village, Pairgry-le Gras, and ruled it like a tyrant, on account of his money and position. As soon as the servant had disappeared in the direction of the village, which was only about five hundred yards off, he went into the house to have his morning coffee and to discuss the matter with his wife. He found her on her knees in front of the fire, trying to get it to burn up quickly. As soon as he got to the door, he said:

"Somebody has stolen the gray rabbit."

She turned round so quickly that she found herself sitting on the floor, and looking at her husband with distressed eyes, she said:

"What is it, Cacheux! Somebody has stolen a rabbit?"

"The big gray one."

She sighed: "How sad! Who can have done it?"

She was a little, thin, active, neat woman, who knew all about farming. But Lecacheur had his own ideas about the matter.

"It must be that fellow Polyte."

His wife got up suddenly and said in a furious voice:

"He did it! he did it! You need not look for any one else. He did it! You have said it, Cacheux!"

All her peasant's fury, all her avarice, all the rage of a saving woman against the man of whom she had always been suspicious, and against the girl whom she had always suspected, could be seen in the contraction of her mouth, in the wrinkles in her cheeks, and in the forehead of her thin, exasperated face.

"And what have you done?" she asked.

"I have sent for the gendarmes."

This Polyte was a laborer, who had been employed on the farm for a few days, and had been dismissed by Lecacheur for an insolent answer. He was an old soldier, and was supposed to have retained his habits of marauding and debauchery from his campaigns in Africa. He did anything for a livelihood, but whether working as a mason, a navvy, a reaper, whether he broke stones or lopped trees, he was always lazy. So he remained in no position long, and had, at times, to change his neighborhood to obtain work.

From the first day that he came to the farm, Lecacheur's wife had detested him, and now she was sure that he had committed the robbery.

In about half an hour the two gendarmes arrived. Brigadier Sénateur was very tall and thin, and Gendarme Lenient, short and fat. Lecacheur made them sit down and told them the affair, and then they went and saw the scene of the theft, in order to verify the fact that the hutch had been broken open, and to collect all the proofs they could. When they got back to the kitchen, the mistress brought in some wine, filled their glasses and asked with a distrustful look:

"Shall you catch him?"

The brigadier, who had his sword between his legs, appeared thoughtful. Certainly, he was sure of taking him, if he was pointed out to him, but if not, he could not himself answer for being able to discover him. After reflecting for a long time, he put this simple question:

"Do you know the thief?"

And Lecacheur replied, with a look of Normandy slyness in his eyes:

"As for knowing him, I do not, as I did not see him commit the robbery. If I had seen him, I should have made him eat it raw, skin and flesh, without a drop of cider to wash it down. As for saying who it is, I cannot, although I believe it is that good-for-nothing Polyte."

Then he related at length his troubles with Polyte, his leaving his service, his bad reputation, things which had been told him, accumulating insignificant and minute proofs. Then the brigadier, who had been listening very attentively while he emptied his glass and filled it again, turned to his gendarme with an indifferent air, and said:

"We must go and look in the cottage of Severin's wife." At which the gendarme smiled and nodded three times.

Then Madame Lecacheur came to them, and very quietly, with all a peasant's cunning, questioned the brigadier in her turn. The shepherd Severin, a simpleton, a sort of brute who had been brought up from youth among his bleating flocks, and who knew of scarcely anything besides them in the world, had nevertheless preserved the peasant's instinct for saving, at the bottom of his heart. For years and years he had hidden in hollow trees and crevices in the rocks, all that he earned, either as shepherd, or by curing the fractures of animals (for the bonesetter's secret had been handed down to him by the old shepherd whose place he took), by touch or advice, for one day he bought a small proprety consisting of a cottage and a field, for three thousand francs.

A few months later it became known that he was going to marry a servant notorious for her bad morals, the innkeeper's servant. The young fellows said that the girl, knowing that he was pretty well off, had been to his cottage every night, and had taken him, bewitched him, led him on to matrimony, little by little, night by night.

And then, having been to the mayor's office and to church, she lived in the house which her man had bought, while he continued to tend his flocks, day and night, on the plains.

And the brigadier added:

"Polyte has been sleeping with her for three weeks, for the thief has no place of his own to go to!"

The gendarme made a little joke:

"He takes the shepherd's blankets."

Madame Lecacheur, seized by a fresh access of rage, of rage increased by a married woman's anger against debauchery, exclaimed:

"It is she, I am sure. Go there. Ah! the blackguard thieves!"

But the brigadier was quite unmoved.

"A minute," he said. "Let us wait until twelve o'clock; as Polyte goes and dines there every day I shall catch them with it under their noses."

The gendarme smiled, pleased at his chief's idea, and Lecacheur also smiled now, for the affair of the shepherd struck him as very funny: deceived husbands are always amusing.

*   *   *   *   *   *

Twelve o'clock had just struck when the brigadier, followed by his man, knocked gently three times at the door of a small lonely house, situated at the corner of a wood, some five hundred yards from the village.

They stood close against the wall, so as not to be seen from within, and waited. As nobody answered, the brigadier knocked again in a minute or two. It was so quiet that the house seemed uninhabited; but Lenient, the gendarme, who had very quick ears, said that he heard somebody moving about inside. Sénateur got angry. He would not allow anyone to resist the authority of the law for a moment, and, knocking at the door with the hilt of his sword, he cried out:

"Open the door, in the name of the law."

As this order had no effect, he roared out:

"If you do not obey, I shall smash the lock. I am the brigadier of the gendarmerie, by G—d! Here, Lenient."

He had not finished speaking when the door opened and Sénateur saw before him a fat girl, with a very red color, blowsy, with pendent breasts, big stomach, and broad hips, a sort of sanguine and sensual female, the wife of the shepherd Severin. He entered the cottage.

"I have come to pay you a visit, as I want to make a little search," he said, and he looked about him. On the table there was a plate, a jug of cider and a glass half full, which proved that a meal had been going on. Two knives were lying side by side, and the shrewd gendarme winked at his superior officer.

"It smells good," the latter said.

"One might swear that it was stewed rabbit," Lenient added, much amused.

"Will you have a glass of brandy?" the peasant woman asked.

"No, thank you; I only want the skin of the rabbit that you are eating."

She pretended not to understand, but she was trembling.

"What rabbit?"

The brigadier had taken a seat, and was calmly wiping his forehead.

"Come, come, you are not going to try and make us believe that you live on couch grass. What were you eating there all by yourself for your dinner?"

"I? Nothing whatever, I swear to you. A mite of butter on my bread."

"You are a novice, my good woman —*a mite of butter on your bread.* You are mistaken; you ought to have said: a mite of butter on the rabbit. By G—d, your butter smells good! It is special butter, extra good butter, butter fit for a wedding; certainly not household butter!"

The gendarme was shaking with laughter, and repeated:

"Not household butter, certainly."

As Brigadier Sénateur was a joker, all the gendarmes had grown facetious, and the officer continued:

"Where is your butter?"

"My butter?"

"Yes, your butter."

"In the jar."

"Then where is the butter jar."

"Here it is."

Sht brought out an old cup, at the bottom of which there was a layer of rancid, salt butter. The brigadier smelled it, and said, with a shake of his head:

"It is not the same. I want the butter that smells of the rabbit. Come, Lenient, open your eyes; look under the sideboard, my good fellow, and I will look under the bed."

Having shut the door, he went up to the bed and tried to move it; but it was fixed to the wall, and had not been moved for more than half a century, apparently. Then the brigadier stooped, and made his uniform crack. A button had flown off.

"Lenient," he said.

"Yes, brigadier?"

"Come here, my lad, and look under the bed; I am too tall. I will look after the sideboard."

He got up and waited while his man executed his orders.

Lenient, who was short and stout, took off his kepi, laid himself on his stomach, and putting his face on the floor looked at the black cavity under the bed. Then, suddenly, he exclaimed:

"All right, here we are!"

"What have you got? The rabbit?"

"No, the thief."

"The thief! Pull him out, pull him out!"

The gendarme had put his arms under the bed and laid hold of something. He pulled with all his might, and at last a foot, shod in a thick boot, appeared, which he was holding in his right hand. The brigadier grabbed it, crying:

"Pull, pull!"

And Lenient, who was on his knees by that time, was pulling at the other leg. But it was a hard job, for the prisoner kicked out hard, and arched up his back across the bed.

"Courage! courage! pull! pull!" Sénateur cried, and they pulled with all their strength—so hard that the wooden bar gave way, and the victim came out as far as his head. At last they got that out also, and saw the terrified and furious face of Polyte, whose arms remained stretched out under the bed.

"Pull away!" the brigadier kept on exclaiming. Then they heard a strange noise as the arms followed the shoulders and the hands the arms. In the hands was the handle of a saucepan, and at the end of the handle the pan itself, which contained stewed rabbit.

"Good Lord! good Lord!" the brigadier shouted in his delight, while Lenient took charge of the man. The rabbit's skin, an overwhelming proof, was discovered under the mattress, and the gendarmes returned in triumph to the village with their prisoner and their booty.

*   *   *   *   *   *

A week later, as the affair had made much stir, Lecacheur, on going into the *mairie* to consult the schoolmaster, was told that the shepherd Severin had been waiting for him for more than an hour. He found him sitting on a chair in a corner with his stick between his legs. When he saw the mayor, he got up, took off his cap, and said:

"Good morning, Maître Cacheux"; and then he remained standing, timid and embarrassed.

"What do you want?" the former said.

"This is it, Monsieur. Is it true that somebody stole one of your rabbits last week?"

"Yes, it is quite true, Severin."

"Who stole the rabbit?"

"Polyte Ancas, the laborer."

"Right! right! And is it also true that it was found under my bed?"

"What do you mean, the rabbit?"

"The rabbit and then Polyte."

"Yes, my poor Severin, quite true, but who told you?"

"Pretty well everybody. I understand! And I suppose you know all about marriages, as you marry* people?"

"What about marriage?"

"With regard to one's rights."

"What rights?"

"The husband's rights and then the wife's rights."

"Of course I do."

"Oh! Then just tell me, M'sieu Cacheux, has my wife the right to go to bed with Polyte?"

"What do you mean by going to bed with Polyte?"

"Yes, has she any right before the law, and seeing that she is my wife, to go to bed with Polyte?"

"Why of course not, of course not."

"If I catch him there again, shall I have the right to thrash him and her also?"

"Why—why—why, yes."

"Very well, then; I will tell you why I want to know. One night last week, as I had my suspicions, I came in suddenly, and they were not behaving properly. I chucked Polyte out, to go and sleep somewhere else; but that was all, as I did not know what my rights were. This time I did not see them; I only heard of it from others. That is over, and we will not say any more about it; but if I catch them again, by G—d! if I catch them again, I will make them lose all taste for such nonsense, Maître Cacheux, as sure as my name is Severin."

*In France, the civil marriage is compulsory.

La Morillonne

THEY called her "La Morillonne,"* not only on account of her black hair and of a complexion which resembled autumnal leaves, but because of her thick purple lips which were like blackberries, when she curled them.

That she should be as dark as this in a district where everybody was fair, and born of parents who had tow-colored hair and butter-like complexions was one of the mysteries of atavism. A female ancestor must have had intimacy with one of those traveling tinkers who have gone about the country from time immemorial, with faces the color of bister and indigo, crowned by a wisp of light hair.

From that ancestor she derived not only her dark complexion, but also her dark soul and her deceitful eyes, whose depths were at times illuminated by flashes of every vice, the eyes of an obstinate and malicious animal.

Handsome? Certainly not, nor even pretty. Ugly, with an absolute ugliness! Such a false look! Her nose was flat, having been smashed by a blow, while her unwholesome-looking mouth was always slobbering with greediness, or uttering something vile. Her hair was thick and untidy, a regular nest for vermin, and she had a thin, feverish

*A sort of black grape.—EDITOR.

body, with a limping walk. In short, she was a perfect monster, and yet all the young men of the neighborhood had made love to her, and whoever had been so honored longed for her society again.

From the time that she was twelve, she had been the mistress of every fellow in the village. She had corrupted boys of her own age in every conceivable manner and place.

Young men at the risk of imprisonment, and even steady, old, notable, and venerable men, such as the farmer at Eclausiaux, Monsieur Martin, the ex-mayor, and other highly respectable citizens, had been taken by the manners of that slut. The reason why the rural policeman was not severe upon them, in spite of his love for summoning people before the magistrates, was, so people said, that he would have been obliged to take out a summons against himself.

The consequence was that she had grown up without being interfered with, and was the mistress of every fellow in the village, as said the schoolmaster, who had himself been one of *the fellows.*. But the most curious part of the business was that no one was jealous. They handed her on from one to the other, and when some one expressed his astonishment at this to her one day, she said to this unintelligent stranger:

"Is everybody not satisfied?"

And then, how could any one of them, even if he had been jealous, have monopolized her? They had no hold on her. She was not selfish, and though she accepted all gifts, whether in kind or in money, she never asked for anything, and she even appeared to prefer paying herself after her own fashion, by

stealing. All she seemed to care about as her reward was pilfering, and a crown put into her hand gave her less pleasure than a half penny which she had stolen. Neither was it any use to dream of ruling her, of being the sole male, or proud master of the henroost, for none of them, no matter how broad-shouldered he was, would have been capable of it. Some had tried to vanquish her, but in vain.

How, then, could any of them claim to be her master? It would have been the same as wishing to have the sole right of baking bread in the common oven, in which the whole village baked.

But there was one exception, and that was Bru, the shepherd.

He lived in the fields in a movable hut, feeding on cakes made of unleavened dough, which he kneaded on a stone and baked in the hot ashes, now here, now there, in a hole dug out in the ground, and heated with dead wood. Potatoes, milk, hard cheese, blackberries, and a small cask of old gin distilled by himself, were his daily food. He knew nothing about love, although he was accused of all sorts of horrible things. But nobody dared abuse him to his face; in the first place, because Bru was a spare and sinewy man, who handled his shepherd's crook like a drum-major does his staff; secondly, because of his three sheep dogs, who had teeth like wolves, and obeyed nobody but their master; and lastly, for fear of the evil eye. For Bru, it appeared, knew spells which would blight the corn, give the sheep foot-rot, cattle the rinderpest, make cows die in calving, and set fire to the ricks and stacks.

But as Bru was the only one who did

not thirst after La Morillonne, naturally one day she began to think of him, and declared that she, at any rate, was not afraid of his evil eye. So she went after him.

"What do you want?" he said, and she replied boldly:

"What do I want? I want you."

"Very well," he said, "but then you must belong to me alone."

"All right," was her answer, "if you think you can please me."

He smiled and took her into his arms, and she was away from the village for a whole week. She had, in fact, become Bru's exclusive property.

The village grew excited. They were not jealous of one another, but they were of him. What! Could she not resist him? Of course he had charms and spells against every imaginable thing. Then they grew furious; next they grew bold, and watched from behind a tree. She was still as lively as ever, but he, poor fellow, seemed to have suddenly fallen ill, and required nursing at her hands. The villagers, however, felt no compassion for the poor shepherd, and one of them, more courageous than the rest, advanced toward the hut with his gun in his hand:

"Tie up your dogs," he cried out from a distance; "fasten them up, Bru, or I shall shoot them."

"You need not be frightened of the dogs," Le Morillonne replied; "I will be answerable for it that they will not hurt you"; and she smiled as the young man with the gun went toward her.

"What do you want?" the shepherd said:

"I can tell you," she replied. "He wants me and I am very willing. There!"

Bru began to cry, and she continued:

"You are a good-for-nothing."

And she went off with the lad. Bru seized his crook, seeing which the young fellow raised his gun.

"Seize him! seize him!" the shepherd shouted, urging on his dogs, while the other had already got his finger on the trigger to fire at them. But La Morillonne pushed down the muzzle and called out:

"Here, dogs! here! *Prr, prr*, my beauties!"

And the three dogs rushed up to her, licked her hands and frisked about as they followed her, while she called to the shepherd from the distance:

"You see, Bru, they are not at all jealous!"

And then, with a short and evil laugh, she added:

"They are my property now."

Epiphany

"AH!" said Captain the Count de Garens, "I should rather think that I do remember that Epiphany supper, during the war!

"At the time I was quartermaster of cavalry, and for a fortnight, I had been lurking about as a scout in front of the German advanced guard. The evening before we had cut down a few Uhlans and had lost three men, one of whom was that poor little Raudeville. You remember Joseph de Raudeville well, of course.

"Well, on that day my captain ordered me to take six troopers and occupy the village of Porterin, where there had been five fights in three weeks, and to hold it all night. There were not twenty houses left standing, nay, not a dozen, in that wasp's nest. So I took ten troopers, and set out at about four o'clock; at five o'clock, while it was still pitch dark, we reached the first houses of Porterin. I halted and ordered Marchas—you know Pierre de Marchas, who afterward married little Martel-Auvelin, the daughter of the Marquis de Martel-Auvelin—to go alone into the village and to report to me what he saw.

"I had chosen nothing but volunteers, and all of good family. When on service it is pleasant not to be forced into intimacy with unpleasant fellows. This Marchas was as sharp as possible, as cunning as a fox, and as supple as a serpent. He could scent the Prussians as well as a dog can scent a hare, could find victuals where we should have died of hunger without him, and could obtain information from everybody—information which was always reliable—with incredible cleverness.

"In ten minutes he returned. 'All right,' he said; 'there have been no Prussians here for three days. It is a sinister place, is this village. I have been talking to a Sister of Mercy, who is attending to four or five wounded men in an abandoned convent.'

"I ordered them to ride on, and we penetrated into the principal street. On the right and left we could vaguely see roofless walls, hardly visible in the profound darkness. Here and there a light was burning in a room; some family had remained to keep its house standing as long as they were able; a family of brave, or of poor, people. The rain began to fall, a fine, icy-cold rain, which froze us before it wetted us through, by merely touching our cloaks. The horses stumbled against stones, against beams, against furniture. Marchas guided us, going before us on foot, and leading his horse by the bridle.

" 'Where are you taking us to?' I asked him. And he replied: 'I have a place for us to lodge in, and a rare good one.' And soon we stopped before a small house, evidently belonging to some person of the middle class, completely shut up, built on to the street with a garden in the rear.

"Marchas broke open the lock by means of a big stone, which he picked up near the garden gate; then he mounted the steps, smashed in the front door with his feet and shoulders, lighted a bit of wax candle, which he was never without and preceded us into the comfortable apartments of some rich private individual, guiding us with admirable assurance, just as if he had lived in this house which he now saw for the first time.

"Two troopers remained outside to take care of our horses; then Marchas said to stout Ponderel, who followed him: 'The stables must be on the left; I saw that as we came in; go and put the animals up there, for we do not want them,' and then turning to me he said: 'Give your orders, confound it all!'

"Marchas always astonished me, and I replied with a laugh: 'I shall post my sentinels at the country approaches and I will return to you here.'

"'How many men are you going to take?'

"'Five. The others will relieve them at five o'clock in the evening.'

"'Very well. Leave me four to look after provisions, to do the cooking, and to set the table. I will go and find out where the wine is hidden away.'

"I went off to reconnoiter the deserted streets, until they ended in the open country, so as to post my sentries there.

"Half an hour later I was back, and found Marchas lounging in a great armchair, the covering of which he had taken off, from love of luxury as he said. He was warming his feet at the fire and smoking an excellent cigar, whose perfume filled the room. He was alone, his elbows resting on the arms of the chair, his cheeks flushed, his eyes bright, and looking delighted.

"I heard the noise of plates and dishes in the next room, and Marchas said to me, smiling in a beatific manner: 'This is famous; I found the champagne under the flight of steps outside, the brandy—fifty bottles of the very finest—in the kitchen garden under a pear-tree, which did not look to me to be quite straight, when I looked at it by the light of my lantern. As for solids, we have two fowls, a goose, a duck, and three pigeons. They are being cooked at this moment. It is a delightful part of the country.'

"I had sat down opposite to him, and

the fire in the grate was burning my nose and cheeks.

"'Where did you find this wood?' I asked.

"'Splendid wood,' he replied. 'The owner's carriage. It is the paint which is causing all this flame, an essence of alcohol and varnish. A capital house!'

"I laughed, for I found the creature was funny, and he went on: 'Fancy this being the Epiphany! I have had a bean put into the goose, but there is no queen; it is really very annoying!' And I repeated like an echo: 'It is annoying, but what do you want me to do in the matter?'

"'To find some, of course.'

"'Some women. Women? — you must be mad!'

"'I managed to find the brandy under the pear-tree, and the champagne under the steps; and yet there was nothing to guide me, while as for you, a petticoat is a sure sign. Go and look, old fellow.'

"He looked so grave, so convinced, that I could not tell whether he was joking or not. So I replied: 'Look here, Marchas, are you having a joke with me?'

"'I never joke on duty.'

"'But where the devil do you expect me to find any women?'

"'Where you like; there must be two or three remaining in the neighborhood, so ferret them out and bring there here.'

"I got up, for it was too hot in front of the fire, and Marchas went on: 'Do you want an idea?'

"'Yes.'

"'Go and see the priest.'

"'The priest? What for?'

" 'Ask him to supper, and beg him to bring a woman with him.'

" 'The priest! A woman! Ha! ha! ha!'

"But Marchas continued with extraordinary gravity: 'I am not laughing; go and find the priest and tell him how we are situated, and, as he must be horribly dull, he will come. But tell him that we want one woman at least, a lady, of course, since we are all men of the world. He is sure to have the names of his female parishioners on the tips of his fingers, and if there is one to suit us, and you manage it well, he will indicate her to you.'

" 'Come, come, Marchas, what are you thinking of?'

" 'My dear Garens, you can do this quite well. It will be very funny. We are well bred, by Jove! and we will put on our most distinguished manners and our grandest style. Tell the abbé who we are, make him laugh, soften him, seduce him, and persuade him!'

" 'No, it is impossible.'

"He drew his chair close to mine, and as he knew my weak side, the scamp continued: 'Just think what a swagger thing it will be to do, and how amusing to tell about; the whole army will talk about it, and it will give you a famous reputation.'

"I hesitated, for the adventure rather tempted me. He persisted: 'Come, my little Garens. You are in command of this detachment, and you alone can go and call on the head of the church in this neighborhood. I beg of you to go, and I promise you that after the war, I will relate the whole affair in verse in the "Revue des Deux Mondes." You owe this much to your men, for you

have made them march enough during the last month.'

"I got up at last and asked: 'Where is the parsonage?'

" 'Take the second turning at the end of the street; you will then see an avenue, and at the end of the avenue you will find the church. The parsonage is beside it.' As I departed he called out: 'Tell him the bill of fare, to make him hungry!'

"I discovered the ecclesiastic's little house without any difficulty; it was by the side of a large, ugly, brick church. As there was neither bell nor knocker, I knocked at the door with my fist, and a loud voice from inside asked: 'Who is there?' to which I replied: 'A quartermaster of hussars.'

"I heard the noise of bolts, and a key being turned. Then I found myself face to face with a tall priest with a large stomach, the chest of a prize-fighter, formidable hands projecting from turned-up sleeves, a red face, and the looks of a kind man. I gave him a military salute and said: 'Good day, Monsieur le Curé.'

"He had feared a surprise, some marauders' ambush, and he smiled as he replied: 'Good day, my friend; come in.' I followed him into a small room, with a red tiled floor, in which a small fire was burning, very different to Marchas's furnace. He gave me a chair and said: 'What can I do for you?'

" 'Monsieur, allow me first of all to introduce myself'; and I gave him my card, which he took and read half aloud: 'The Comte de Garens.'

"I continued: 'There are eleven of us here Monsieur l'Abbé, five on grand guard, and six installed at the house of an unknown inhabitant. The names of the six are, Garens (that is I), Pierre de Marchas, Ludovic de Ponderel, Baron d'Etreillis, Karl Massouligny, the painter's son, and Joseph Herbon, a young musician. I have come to ask you, in their name and my own, to do us the honor of supping with us. It is an Epiphany supper, Monsieur le Curé, and we should like to make it a little cheerful.'

"The priest smiled and murmured: 'It seems to me to be hardly a suitable occasion for amusing oneself.'

"I replied: 'We are fighting every day, Monsieur. Fourteen of our comrades have been killed in a month, and three fell as late as yesterday. That is war. We stake our life every moment: have we not, therefore, the right to amuse ourselves freely? We are Frenchmen, we like to laugh, and we can laugh everywhere. Our fathers laughed on the scaffold! This evening we should like to brighten ourselves up a little, like gentlemen, and not like soldiers; you understand me, I hope. Are we wrong?'

"He replied quickly: 'You are quite right, my friend, and I accept your invitation with great pleasure.' Then he called out: 'Hermance!'

"An old, bent, wrinkled, horrible, peasant woman appeared and said: 'What do you want?'

" 'I shall not dine at home, my daughter.'

" 'Where are you going to dine then?'

" 'With some gentlemen, hussars.'

"I felt inclined to say: 'Bring your servant with you,' just to see Marchas's face, but I did not venture to, and continued: 'Do you know anyone among your parishioners, male or female, whom I could invite as well?' He hesitated, reflected, and then said: 'No, I do not know anybody!'

"I persisted: 'Nobody? Come, Monsieur, think; it would be very nice to have some ladies, I mean to say, some married couples! I know nothing about your parishioners. The baker and his wife, the grocer, the—the—the—watchmaker — the — shoemaker — the — the chemist with his wife. We have a good spread, and plenty of wine, and we should be enchanted to leave pleasant recollections of ourselves behind us with the people here.'

"The priest thought again for a long time and then said resolutely: 'No, there is nobody.'

"I began to laugh. 'By Jove, Monsieur le Curé, it is very vexing not to have an Epiphany queen, for we have the bean. Come, think. Is there not a married mayor, or a married deputy-mayor, or a married municipal councilor, or schoolmaster?'

" 'No, all the ladies have gone away.'

" 'What, is there not in the whole place some good tradesman's wife with her good tradesman, to whom we might give this pleasure, for it would be a pleasure to them, a great pleasure under present circumstances?'

"But suddenly the curé began to laugh, and he laughed so violently that he fairly shook, and exclaimed: 'Ha! ha! ha! I have got what you want, yes. I have got what you want! Ha! ha! ha! We will laugh and enjoy ourselves, my children, we will have some fun. How pleased the ladies will be, I say, how delighted they will be. Ha! ha! Where are you staying?'

"I described the house, and he understood where it was. 'Very good,' he said. 'It belongs to Monsieur Bertin-Lavaille. I will be there in half an hour, with four ladies. Ha! ha! ha! four ladies!'

"He went out with me, still laughing, and left me, repeating: 'That is capital; in half an hour at Bertin-Lavaille's house.'

"I returned quickly, very much astonished and very much puzzled. 'Covers for how many?' Marchas asked, as soon as he saw me.

" 'Eleven. There are six of us hussars besides the priest and four ladies.'

"He was thunderstruck, and I triumphant, and he repeated: 'Four ladies! Did you say, four ladies?'

" 'I said four women.'

" 'Real women?'

" 'Real women.'

" 'Well, accept my compliments!'

" 'I will, for I deserve them.'

"He got out of his armchair, opened the door, and I saw a beautiful, white tablecloth on a long table, round which three hussars in blue aprons were setting out the plates and glasses. 'There are some women coming!' Marchas cried. And the three men began to dance and to cheer with all their might.

"Everything was ready, and we were waiting. We waited for nearly an hour, while a delicious smell of roast poultry pervaded the whole house. At last, however, a knock against the shutters made us all jump up at the same moment. Stout Ponderel ran to open the door, and in less than a minute a little Sister of Mercy appeared in the doorway. She was thin, wrinkled, and timid, and successively saluted the four bewildered hussars who saw her enter. Behind her, the noise of sticks sounded on the tiled floor in the vestibule. As soon as she had come into the drawing-room I saw three old heads in white caps, following each other one by one, balancing themselves with different movements, one canting to the right, while the other canted to the left. Then three worthy women showed themselves, limping, dragging their legs behind them, crippled by illness and deformed through old age, three infirm old women, past service, the only three pensioners who were able to walk in the establishment which Sister Saint-Benedict managed.

"She had turned round to her invalids, full of anxiety for them, and then seeing my quartermaster's stripes, she said to me: 'I am much obliged to you for thinking of these poor women. They have very little pleasure in life, and you are at the same time giving them a great treat and doing them a great honor.'

"I saw the priest, who had remained in the obscurity of the passage, and who was laughing heartily, and I began to laugh in my turn, especially when I saw Marchas's face. Then, motioning the nun to the seats, I said: 'Sit down, Sister: we are very proud and very happy that you have accepted our unpretentious invitation.'

"She took three chairs which stood against the wall, set them before the fire, led her three old women to them, settled them on them, took their sticks and shawls which she put into a corner, and then, pointing to the first, a thin woman with an enormous stomach, who was evidently suffering from the dropsy, she said: 'This is Mother Paumelle, whose husband was killed by falling from a roof, and whose son died in Africa; she is sixty years old.' Then she pointed to another, a tall woman, whose head shook unceasingly: 'This is Mother Jean-Jean, who is sixty-seven. She is nearly blind, for her face was terribly singed in a fire, and her right leg was half burned off.'

"Then she pointed to the third, a sort of drawf, with protruding, round, stupid eyes, which she rolled incessantly in all directions. 'This is La Putois, an idiot. She is only forty-four.'

"I bowed to the three women as if I were being presented to some Royal Highness, and turning to the priest I said: 'You are an excellent man, Monsieur l'Abbé, and we all owe you a debt of gratitude.'

"Everybody was laughing, in fact, except Marchas, who seemed furious, and just then Karl Massouligny cried: 'Sister Saint-Benedict, supper is on the table!'

"I made her go first with the priest, then I helped up Mother Paumelle, whose arm I took and dragged her into the next room, which was no easy task, for her swollen stomach seemed heavier than a lump of iron.

"Stout Ponderel gave his arm to Mother Jean-Jean, who bemoaned her crutch, and little Joseph Herbon took the idiot, La Putois, to the dining-room, which was filled with the odor of the viands.

"As soon as we were opposite our plates, the Sister clapped her hands three times, and, with the precision of soldiers presenting arms, the women made a rapid sign of the cross, and then the priest slowly repeated the 'Benedictus' in Latin. Then we sat down, and the two fowls appeared, brought in by Marchas, who chose to wait rather than to sit down as a guest at this ridiculous repast.

"But I cried: 'Bring the champagne at once!' and a cork flew out with the noise of a pistol, and in spite of the resistance of the priest and the kind Sister, the three hussars sitting by the side of the three invalids, emptied their three full glasses down their throats by force.

"Massouligny, who possessed the faculty of making himself at home, and of being on good terms with everyone, wherever he was, made love to Mother Paumelle, in the drollest manner. The dropsical woman, who had retained her cheerfulness in spite of her misfortunes, answered him banteringly in a high falsetto voice which seemed to be assumed, and she laughed so heartily at her neighbor's jokes that her large stomach looked as if it were going to rise up and get on to the table. Little Herbon had seriously undertaken the task of making the idiot drunk, and Baron d'Etreillis whose wits were not always particularly sharp, was questioning old Jean-Jean about the life, the habits, and the rules in the hospital.

"The nun said to Massouligny in consternation: 'Oh! oh! you will make her ill; pray do not make her laugh like that, Monsieur. Oh! Monsieur.' Then she got up and rushed at Herbon to take a full glass out of his hands which he was hastily emptying down La Putois's throat, while the priest shook with laughter, and said to the Sister:

'Never mind, just this once, it will not hurt her. Do leave them alone.'

"After the two fowls they ate the duck, which was flanked by the three pigeons and a blackbird, and then the goose appeared, smoking, golden-colored, and diffusing a warm odor of hot, browned fat meat. La Paumelle who was getting lively, clapped her hands; La Jean-Jean left off answering the Baron's numerous questions, and La Putois uttered grunts of pleasure, half cries and half sighs, like little children do when one shows them sweets. 'Allow me to carve this bird,' the curé said. 'I understand these sort of operations better than most people.'

" 'Certainly, Monsieur l'Abbé,' and the Sister said: 'How would it be to open the window a little; they are too warm, and I am afraid they will be ill.'

"I turned to Marchas: 'Open the window for a minute.' He did so; the cold outer air as it came in made the candles flare, and the smoke from the goose—which the curé was scientifically carving, with a table napkin round his neck — whirl about. We watched him doing it, without speaking now, for we were interested in his attractive handiwork, and also seized with renewed appetite at the sight of that enormous golden-colored bird, whose limbs fell one after another into the brown gravy at the bottom of the dish. At that moment, in the midst of greedy silence which kept us all attentive, the distant report of a shot came in at the open window.

"I started to my feet so quickly that my chair fell down behind me, and I shouted: 'Mount, all of you! You,

Marchas, will take two men and go and see what it is. I shall expect you back here in five minutes.' And while the three riders went off at full gallop through the night, I got into the saddle with my three remaining hussars, in front of the steps of the villa, while the curé, the Sister, and the three old women showed their frightened faces at the window.

"We heard nothing more, except the barking of a dog in the distance. The rain had ceased, and it was cold, very cold. Soon I heard the gallop of a horse, of a single horse, coming back. It was Marchas, and I called out to him: 'Well?'

" 'It is nothing; François has wounded an old peasant who refused to answer his challenge and who continued to advance in spite of the order to keep off. They are bringing him here, and we shall see what is the matter.'

"I gave orders for the horses to be put back into the stable, and I sent my two soldiers to meet the others, and returned to the house. Then the curé, Marchas and I took a mattress into the room to put the wounded man on; the Sister tore up a table napkin in order to make lint, while the three frightened women remained huddled up in a corner.

"Soon I heard the rattle of sabers on the road, and I took a candle to show a light to the men who were returning. They soon appeared, carrying that inert, soft, long, and sinister object which a human body becomes when life no longer sustains it.

"They put the wounded man on the mattress that had been prepared for him, and I saw at the first glance that he was dying. He had the death rattle, and was spitting up blood which ran out of the corners of his mouth, forced out of his lungs by his gasps. The man was covered with it! His cheeks, his beard, his hair, his neck, and his clothes seemed to have been rubbed, to have been dipped in a red tub; the blood had congealed on him, and had become a dull color which was horrible to look at.

"The old man, wrapped up in a large shepherd's cloak, occasionally opened his dull, vacant eyes. They seemed stupid with astonishment, like the eyes of hunted animals which fall at the sportsman's feet, half dead before the shot, stupefied with fear and surprise.

"The curé exclaimed: 'Ah! there is old Placide, the shepherd from Les Marlins. He is deaf, poor man, and heard nothing. Ah! Oh, God! they have killed the unhappy man!' The Sister had opened his blouse and shirt, and was looking at a little blue hole in the middle of his chest, which was not bleeding any more. 'There is nothing to be done,' she said.

"The shepherd was gasping terribly and bringing up blood with every breath. In his throat to the very depth of his lungs, they could hear an ominous and continued gurgling. The curé, standing in front of him, raised his right hand,

made the sign of the cross, and in a slow and solemn voice pronounced the Latin words which purify men's souls. But before they were finished, the old man was shaken by a rapid shudder, as if something had broken inside him; he no longer breathed. He was dead.

"When I turned round I saw a sight which was even more horrible than the death struggle of this unfortunate man. The three old women were standing up huddled close together, hideous, and grimacing with fear and horror. I went up to them, and they began to utter shrill screams, while La Jean-Jean, whose leg had been burned and could not longer support her, fell to the ground at full length.

"Sister Saint-Benedict left the dead man, ran up to her infirm old women, and without a word or a look for me wrapped their shawls round them, gave them their crutches, pushed them to the door, made them go out, and disappeared with them into the dark night.

"I saw that I could not even let a hussar accompany them, for the mere rattle of a sword would have sent them mad with fear.

"The curé was still looking at the dead man; but at last he turned to me and said:

" 'Oh! What a horrible thing.' "

Simon's Papa

Noon had just struck. The schooldoor opened and the youngsters streamed out tumbling over one another in their haste to get out quickly. But instead of promptly dispersing and going home to dinner as was their daily wont, they stopped a few paces off, broke up into knots and set to whispering.

The fact was that that morning Simon, the son of La Blanchotte, had, for the first time, attended school.

They had all of them in their families heard of La Blanchotte; and although in public she was welcome enough, the mothers among themselves treated her with compassion of a somewhat disdainful kind, which the children had caught without in the least knowing why.

As for Simon himself, they did not know him, for he never went abroad, and did not play around with them through the streets of the village or along the banks of the river. So they loved him but little; and it was with a certain delight, mingled with astonishment, that they gathered in groups this morning, repeating to each other this sentence, concocted by a lad of fourteen or fifteen who appeared to know all about it, so sagaciously did he wink: "You know Simon — well, he has no papa."

La Blanchotte's son appeared in his turn upon the threshold of the school.

He was seven or eight years old, rather pale, very neat, with a timid and almost awkward manner.

He was making his way back to his mother's house when the various groups of his schoolfellows, perpetually whispering, and watching him with the mischievous and heartless eyes of children bent upon playing a nasty trick, gradually surrounded him and ended by inclosing altogether. There he stood amid them, surprised and embarrassed, not understanding what they were going to do with him. But the lad who had brought the news, puffed up with the success he had met with, demanded:

"What do you call yourself?"

He answered: "Simon."

"Simon what?" retorted the other.

The child, altogether bewildered, repeated: "Simon."

The lad shouted at him: "You must be named Simon something! That is not a name—Simon indeed!"

And he, on the brink of tears, replied for the third time:

"I am named Simon."

The urchins began laughing. The lad triumphantly lifted up his voice: "You can see plainly that he has no papa."

A deep silence ensued. The children were dumfounded by this extraordinary, impossibly monstrous thing—a boy who had not a papa; they looked upon him as a phenomenon, an unnatural being, and they felt rising in them the hitherto inexplicable pity of their mothers for La Blanchotte. As for Simon, he had propped himself against a tree to avoid falling, and he stood there as if paralyzed by an irreparable disaster. He sought to explain, but he could think of no answer for them, no way to deny this horrible charge that he had no papa. At last he shouted at them quite recklessly: "Yes, I have one."

"Where is he?" demanded the boy.

Simon was silent, he did not know. The children shrieked, tremendously excited. These sons of toil, nearly related to animals, experienced the cruel craving which makes the fowls of a farmyard destroy one of their own kind as soon as it is wounded. Simon suddenly spied a little neighbor, the son of a widow, whom he had always seen, as he himself was to be seen, quite alone with his mother.

"And no more have you," he said, "no more have you a papa."

"Yes," replied the other, "I have one."

"Where is he?" rejoined Simon.

"He is dead," declared the brat with superb dignity, "he is in the cemetery, is my papa."

A murmur of approval rose amid the scapegraces, as if the fact of possessing a papa dead in a cemetery made their comrade big enough to crush the other one who had no papa at all. And these rogues, whose fathers were for the most part evil-doers, drunkards, thieves, and ill-treaters of their wives hustled each other as they pressed closer and closer to Simon as though they, the ligitimate ones, would stifle in their pressure one who was beyond the law.

The lad next Simon suddenly put his tongue out at him with a waggish air and shouted at him:

"No papa! No papa!"

Simon seized him by the hair with both hands and set to work to demolish his legs with kicks, while he bit his cheek ferociously. A tremendous struggle ensued between the two boys, and Simon found himself beaten, torn, bruised, rolled on the ground in the middle of the ring of applauding little vagabonds. As he arose, mechanically brushing his little blouse all covered with dust with his hand, some one shouted at him:

"Go and tell your papa."

He then felt a great sinking in his heart. They were stronger than he, they had beaten him and he had no answer to give them, for he knew it was true that he had no papa. Full of pride he tried for some moments to struggle against the tears which were suffocating him. He had a choking fit, and then without cries he began to weep with great sobs which shook him incessantly. Then a ferocious joy broke out among his enemies, and, just like savages in fearful festivals, they took one another by the hand and danced in a circle about him as they repeated in refrain:

"No papa! No papa!"

But suddenly Simon ceased sobbing. Frenzy overtook him. There were stones under his feet; he picked them up and with all his strength hurled them at his tormentors. Two or three were struck and ran away yelling, and so formidable did he appear that the rest became panic-stricken. Cowards, like a jeering crowd in the presence of an exasperated man, they broke up and fled. Left alone, the little thing without a father set off running toward the fields, for a recollection had been awakened which nerved his soul to a great determination. He made up his mind to drown himself in the river.

He remembered, in fact, that eight days ago a poor devil who begged for his livelihood had thrown himself into the water because he had no more money. Simon had been there when they fished him out again; and the sight of the fellow, who had seemed to him so miserable and ugly, had then impressed him—his pale cheeks, his long drenched beard, and his open eyes being full of calm. The bystanders had said:

"He is dead."

And some one had added:

"He is quite happy now."

So Simon wished to drown himself

also because he had no father, just as the wretched being did who had no money.

He reached the water and watched it flowing. Some fishes were rising briskly in the clear stream and occasionally made little leaps and caught the flies on the surface. He stopped crying in order to watch them, for their feeding interested him vastly. But, at intervals, as in the lulls of a tempest, when tremendous gusts of wind snap off trees and then die away, this thought would return to him with intense pain:

"I am about to drown myself because I have no papa."

It was very warm and fine weather. The pleasant sunshine warmed the grass; the water shone like a mirror; and Simon enjoyed for some minutes the happiness of that languor which follows weeping, desirous even of falling asleep there upon the grass in the warmth of noon.

A little green frong leaped from under his feet. He endeavored to catch it. It escaped him. He pursued it and lost it three times following. At last he caught it by one of its hind legs and began to laugh as it saw the efforts the creature made to escape. It gathered itself up on its large legs and then with a violent spring suddenly stretched them out as stiff as two bars.

Its eyes stared wide open in their round, golden circle, and it beat the air with its front limbs, using them as though they were hands. It reminded him of a toy made with straight slips of wood nailed zigzag one on the other, which by a similar movement regulated the exercise of the little soldiers fastened thereon. Then he thought of his home

and of his mother, and overcome by great sorrow he again began to weep. His lips trembled; and he placed himself on his knees and said his prayers as before going to bed. But he was unable to finish them, for such hurried and violent sobs overtook him that he was completely overwhelmed. He thought no more, he no longer heeded anything around him but was wholly given up to tears.

Suddenly a heavy hand was placed upon his shoulder, and a rough voice asked him:

"What is it that causes you so much grief, my fine fellow?"

Simon turned round. A tall workman, with a black beard and hair all curled, was staring at him good-naturedly. He answered with his eyes and throat full of tears:

"They have beaten me because—I—I have no papa—no papa."

"What!" said the man smiling, "why, everybody has one."

The child answered painfully amid his spasms of grief:

"But I—I—I have none."

Then the workman became serious. He had recognized La Blanchotte's son, and although a recent arrival to the neighborhood he had a vague idea of her history.

"Well," said he, "console yourself, my boy, and come with me home to your mother. She will give you a papa."

And so they started on the way, the big one holding the little one by the hand. The man smiled afresh, for he was not sorry to see this Blanchotte, who by popular report was one of the prettiest girls in the country-side—and, perhaps, he said to himself, at the bottom of his heart, that a lass who had erred once might very well err again.

They arrived in front of a very neat little white house.

"There it is," exclaimed the child, and he cried: "Mamma."

A woman appeared, and the workman instantly left off smiling, for he at once perceived that there was no more fooling to be done with the tall pale girl, who stood austerely at her door as though to defend from one man the threshold of that house where she had already been betrayed by another. Intimidated, his cap in his hand, he stammered out:

"See, Madame, I have brought you back your little boy, who had lost himself near the river."

But Simon flung his arms about his mother's neck and told her, as he again began to cry:

"No, mamma, I wished to drown myself, because the others had beaten me —had beaten me—because I have no papa."

A burning redness covered the young woman's cheeks, and, hurt to the quick, she embraced her child passionately, while the tears coursed down her face. The man, much moved, stood there, not knowing how to get away. But Simon suddenly ran to him and said:

"Will you be my papa?"

A deep silence ensued. La Blanchotte, dumb and tortured with shame, leaned against the wall, her hands upon her heart. The child, seeing that no answer was made him, replied:

"If you do not wish it, I shall return to drown myself."

The workman took the matter as a jest and answered laughing:

"Why, yes, I wish it certainly."

"What is your name, then," went on the child, "so that I may tell the others when they wish to know your name?"

"Philip," answered the man.

Simon was silent a moment so that he might get the name well into his memory; then he stretched out his arms, quite consoled, and said:

"Well, then, Philip, you are my papa."

The workman, lifting him from the ground, kissed him hastily on both cheeks, and then strode away quickly.

When the child returned to school next day he was received with a spiteful laugh, and at the end of school, when the lads were on the point of recommencing, Simon threw these words at their heads as he would have done a stone: "He is named Philip, my papa."

Yells of delight burst out from all sides.

"Philip who? Philip what? What on earth is Philip? Where did you pick up your Philip?"

Simon answered nothing; and immovable in faith he defied them with his eye, ready to be martyred rather than fly before them. The schoolmaster came to his rescue and he returned home to his mother.

For a space of three months, the tall workman, Philip, frequently passed by La Blanchotte's house, and sometimes made bold to speak to her when he saw her sewing near the window. She answered him civilly, always sedately, never joking with him, nor permitting him to enter her house. Notwithstanding this, being, like all men, a bit of a coxcomb, he imagined that she was often rosier than usual when she chatted with him.

But a fallen reputation is so difficult to recover, and always remains so fragile that, in spite of the shy reserve La Blanchotte maintained, they already gossiped in the neighborhood.

. As for Simon, he loved his new papa much, and walked with him nearly every evening when the day's work was done. He went regularly to school and mixed in a dignified way with his schoolfellows without ever answering them back.

One day, however, the lad who had first attacked him said to him:

"You have lied. You have not a papa named Philip."

"Why do you say that?" demanded Simon, much disturbed.

The youth rubbed his hands. He replied:

"Because if you had one he would be your mamma's husband."

Simon was confused by the truth of this reasoning; nevertheless he retorted:

"He is my papa all the same."

"That can very well be," exclaimed the urchin with a sneer, "but that is not being your papa altogether."

La Blanchotte's little one bowed his head and went off dreaming in the direction of the forge belonging to old Loizon, where Philip worked.

This forge was entombed in trees. It was very dark there, the red glare of a formidable furnace alone lit up with great flashes five blacksmiths, who hammered upon their anvils with a terrible din. Standing enveloped in flame, they worked like demons, their eyes fixed on the red-hot iron they were pounding;

and their dull ideas rising and falling with their hammers.

Simon entered without being noticed and quietly plucked his friend by the sleeve. Philip turned round. All at once the work came to a standstill and the men looked on very attentively. Then, in the midst of this unaccustomed silence, rose the little slender pipe of Simon:

"Philip, explain to me what the lad at La Michande has just told me, that you are not altogether my papa."

"And why that?" asked the smith.

The child replied in all innocence:

"Because you are not my mamma's husband."

No one laughed. Philip remained standing, leaning his forehead upon the back of his great hands, which held the handle of his hammer upright upon the anvil. He mused. His four companions watched him, and, like a tiny mite among these giants, Simon anxiously waited. Suddenly, one of the smiths, voicing the sentiment of all, said to Philip:

"All the same La Blanchotte is a good and honest girl, stalwart and steady in spite of her misfortune, and one who would make a worthy wife for an honest man."

"That is true," remarked the three others.

The smith continued:

"Is it the girl's fault if she has fallen? She had been promised marriage, and I know more than one who is much respected to-day and has sinned every bit as much."

"That is true," responded the three men in chorus.

He resumed:

"How hard she has toiled, poor thing,

to educate her lad all alone, and how much she has wept since she no longer goes out, save to church, God only knows."

"That also is true," said the others.

Then no more was heard save the roar of the bellows which fanned the fire of the furnace. Philip hastily bent himself down to Simon:

"Go and tell your mamma that I shall come to speak to her."

Then he pushed the child out by the shoulders. He returned to his work and in unison the five hammers again fell upon their anvils. Thus they wrought the iron until nightfall, strong, powerful, happy, like Vulcans satisfied. But as the great bell of a cathedral resounds upon feast days above the jingling of the other bells, so Philip's hammer, dominating the noise of the others, clanged second after second with a deafening uproar. His eye on the fire, he plied his trade vigorously, erect amid the sparks.

The sky was full of stars as he knocked at La Blanchotte's door. He had his Sunday blouse on, a fresh shirt, and his beard was trimmed. The young woman showed herself upon the threshold and said in a grieved tone:

"It is ill to come thus when night has fallen, Mr. Philip."

He wished to answered, but stammered and stood confused before her. She resumed:

"And you understand quite well that it will not do that I should be talked about any more."

Then he said all at once:

"What does that matter to me, if you will be my wife!"

No voice replied to him, but he believed that he heard in the shadow of the room the sound of a body falling. He entered very quickly; and Simon, who had gone to his bed, distinguished the sound of a kiss and some words that his mother said very softly. Then he suddenly found himself lifted up by the hands of his friend, who, holding him at the length of his herculean arms, exclaimed to him:

"You will tell your school-fellows that your papa is Philip Remy, the blacksmith, and that he will pull the ears of all who do you any harm."

On the morrow, when the school was full and lessons about to begin, little Simon stood up quite pale with trembling lips:

"My papa," said he in a clear voice, "is Philip Remy, the blacksmith, and he has promised to box the ears of all who do me any harm."

This time no one laughed any longer, for he was very well known, was Philip Remy, the blacksmith, and he was a papa of whom anyone in the world would be proud.

Waiter, a Bock! *

WHY on this particular evening, did I enter a certain beer shop? I cannot explain it. It was bitterly cold. A fine rain, a watery mist floated about, veiling the gas jets in a transparent fog, making the pavements under the shadow

*Bavarian beer.

of the shop fronts glitter, which revealed the soft slush and the soiled feet of the passers-by.

I was going nowhere in particular; was simply having a short walk after dinner. I had passed the Credit Lyonnais, the Rue Vivienne, and several other streets. Suddenly I descried a large *café*, which was more than half full. I walked inside, with no object in mind. I was not the least thirsty.

By a searching glance I detected a place where I would not be too much crowded. So I went and sat down by the side of a man who seemed to me to be old, and who smoked a half-penny clay pipe, which had become as black as coal. From six to eight beer saucers were piled up on the table in front of him, indicating the number of "bocks" he had already absorbed. With that same glance I had recognized in him a "regular toper," one of those frequenters of beer-houses, who come in the morning as soon as the place is open, and only go away in the evening when it is about to close. He was dirty, bald to about the middle of the cranium, while his long gray hair fell over the neck of his frock coat. His clothes, much too large for him, appeared to have been made for him at a time when he was very stout. One could guess that his pantaloons were not held up by braces, and that this man could not take ten paces without having to pull them up and readjust them. Did he wear a vest? The mere thought of his boots and the feet they enveloped filled me with horror. The frayed cuffs were as black at the edges as were his nails.

As soon as I had sat down near him,

this queer creature said to me in a tranquil tone of voice:

"How goes it with you?"

I turned sharply round to him and closely scanned his features, whereupon he continued:

"I see you do not recognize me."

"No, I do not."

"Des Barrets."

I was stupefied. It was Count Jean des Barrets, my old college chum.

I seized him by the hand, so dumfounded that I could find nothing to say. I, at length, managed to stammer out:

"And you, how goes it with you?"

He responded placidly:

"With me? Just as I like."

He became silent. I wanted to be friendly, and I selected this phrase:

"What are you doing now?"

"You see what I am doing," he answered, quite resignedly.

I felt my face getting red. I insisted:

"But every day?"

"Every day is alike to me," was his response, accompanied with a thick puff of tobacco smoke.

He then tapped on the top of the marble table with a sou, to attract the attention of the waiter, and called out:

"Waiter, two 'bocks.' "

A voice in the distance repeated:

"Two 'bocks,' instead of four."

Another voice, more distant still, shouted out:

"Here they are, sir, here they are."

Immediately there appeared a man with a white apron, carrying two "bocks," which he set down foaming on the table, the foam running over the edge, on to the sandy floor.

Des Barrets emptied his glass at a single draught and replaced it on the table, sucking in the drops of beer that had been left on his mustache. He next asked:

"What is there new?"

"I know of nothing new, worth mentioning, really," I stammered: "But nothing has grown old for me; I am a commercial man."

In an equable tone of voice, he said: "Indeed—does that amuse you?"

"No, but what do you mean by that? Surely you must do something!'

"What do you mean by that?"

"I only mean, how do you pass your time!"

"What's the use of occupying myself with anything. For my part, I do nothing at all, as you see, never anything. When one has not got a sou one can understand why one has to go to work. What is the good of working? Do you work for yourself, or for others? If you work for yourself you do it for your own amusement, which is all right; if you work for others, you reap nothing but ingratitude."

Then sticking his pipe into his mouth, he called out anew:

"Waiter, a 'bock.' It makes me thirsty to keep calling so. I am not accustomed to that sort of thing. Yes, I do nothing; I let things slide, and I am growing old. In dying I shall have nothing to regret. If so, I should remember nothing, outside this public-house.. I have no wife, no children, no cares, no sorrows, nothing. That is the very best thing that could happen to one."

He then emptied the glass which had been brought him, passed his tongue over his lips, and resumed his pipe.

I looked at him stupefied and asked him:

"But you have not always been like that?"

"Pardon me, sir; ever since I left college."

"It is not a proper life to lead, my dear sir; it is simply horrible. Come, you must indeed have done something, you must have loved something, you must have friends."

"No; I get up at noon, I come here, I have my breakfast, I drink my 'bock'; I remain until evening, I have my dinner, I drink 'bock.' Then about one in the morning, I return to my couch, because the place closes up. And it is this latter that embitters me more than anything. For the last ten years, I have passed six-tenths of my time on this bench, in my corner; and the other four-tenths in my bed, never changing. I talk sometimes with the *habitués*."

"But on arriving in Paris what did you do at first?"

I paid my *devoirs* to the Café de Medicis."

"What next?"

"Next? I crossed the water and came here."

"Why did you take even that trouble?"

"What do you mean? One cannot remain all one's life in the Latin Quarter. The students make too much noise. But I do not move about any longer. Waiter, a 'bock.' "

I now began to think that he was making fun of me, and I continued:

"Come now, be frank. You have been

the victim of some great sorrow; despair in love, no doubt! It is easy to see that you are a man whom misfortune has hit hard. What age are you?"

"I am thirty years of age, but I look to be forty-five at least."

I looked him straight in the face. His shrunken figure, badly cared for, gave one the impression that he was an old man. On the summit of his cranium, a few long hairs shot straight up from a skin of doubtful cleanness. He had enormous eyelashes, a large mustache, and a thick beard. Suddenly I had a kind of vision, I know not why—the vision of a basin filled with noisome water, the water which should have been applied to that poll. I said to him:

"Verily, you look to be more than that age. Of a certainty you must have experienced some great dissappointment."

He replied:

"I tell you that I have not. I am old because I never take air. There is nothing that vitiates the life of a man more than the atmosphere of a *café*."

I could not believe him.

"You must surely have been married as well? One could not get baldheaded as you are without having been much in love."

He shook his head, sending down his back little hairs from the scalp:

"No, I have always been virtuous."

And raising his eyes toward the luster, which beat down on our heads, he said:

"If I am baldheaded, it is the fault of the gas. It is the enemy of hair. Waiter, a 'bock.' You must be thirsty also?"

"No, thank you. But you certainly interest me. When did you have your first discouragement? Your life is not normal, is not natural. There is something under it all."

"Yes, and it dates from my infancy. I received a heavy blow when I was very young. It turned my life into darkness, which will last to the end."

"How did it come about?"

"You wish to know about it? Well, then, listen. You recall, of course, the castle in which I was brought up, seeing that you used to visit it for five or six months during the vacations? You remember that large, gray building in the middle of a great park, and the long avenues of oaks, which opened toward the four cardinal points! You remember my father and my mother, both of whom were ceremonious, solemn, and severe.

"I worshiped my mother; I was suspicious of my father; but I respected both, accustomed always as I was to see everyone bow before them. In the country, they were Monsieur le Comte and Madame la Comtesse; and our neighbors, the Tannemares, the Ravelets, the Brennevilles, showed the utmost consideration for them.

"I was then thirteen years old, happy, satisfied with everything, as one is at that age, and full of joy and vivacity.

"Now toward the end of September, a few days before entering the Lycée, while I was enjoying myself in the mazes of the park, climbing the trees and swinging on the branches, I saw crossing an avenue my father and mother, who were walking together.

"I recall the thing as though it were yesterday. It was a very windy day.

The whole line of trees bent under the pressure of the wind, moaned and seemed to utter cries—cries dull, yet deep—so that the whole forest groaned under the gale.

"Evening had come on, and it was dark in the thickets. The agitation of the wind and the branches excited me, made me skip about like an idiot, and howl in imitation of the wolves.

"As soon as I perceived my parents, I crept furtively toward them, under the branches, in order to surprise them, as though I had been a vertible wolf. But suddenly seized with fear, I stopped a few paces from them. My father, a prey to the most violent passion, cried:

"'Your mother is a fool; moreover, it is not your mother that is the question, it is you. I tell you that I want money, and I will make you sign this.'

"My mother responded in a firm voice:

"'I will not sign it. It is Jean's fortune, I shall guard it for him and I will not allow you to devour it with strange women, as you have your own heritage.'

"Then my father, full of rage, wheeled round and seized his wife by the throat, and began to slap her full in the face with the disengaged hand.

"My mother's hat fell off, her hair became disheveled and fell down her back: she essayed to parry the blows, but could not escape from them. And my father, like a madman, banged and banged at her. My mother rolled over on the ground, covering her face in both her hands. Then he turned her over on her back in order to batter her still more, pulling away the hands which were covering her face.

"As for me, my friend, it seemed as though the world had come to an end, that the eternal laws had changed. I experienced the overwhelming dread that one has in presence of things supernatural, in presence of irreparable disaster. My boyish head whirled round and soared. I began to cry with all my might, without knowing why, a prey to terror, to grief, to a dreadful bewilderment. My father heard me. I believed that he wanted to kill me, and I fled like a hunted animal, running straight in front of me through the woods.

"I ran perhaps for an hour, perhaps for two, I know not. Darkness had set in, I tumbled over some thick herbs, exhausted, and I lay there lost, devoured by terror, eaten up by a sorrow capable of breaking forever the heart of a child. I became cold, I became hungry. At length day broke. I dared neither get up, walk, return home, nor save myself, fearing to encounter my father whom I did not wish to see again.

"I should probably have died of misery and of hunger at the foot of a tree if the guard had not discovered me and led me by force.

"I found my parents wearing their ordinary aspect. My mother alone spoke to me:

"'How you have frightened me, you naughty boy; I have been the whole night sleepless.'

"I did not answer, but began to weep. My father did not utter a single word.

"Eight days later I entered Lycée.

"Well, my friend, it was all over with me. I had witnessed the other side of things, the bad side; I have not been able to perceive the good side since that day. What things have passed in my mind, what strange phenomena have warped my ideas, I do not know. But I no longer have a taste for anything, a wish for anything, a love for anybody, a desire for anything whatever, no ambition, no hope. And I always see my poor mother lying on the ground, in the avenue, while my father was maltreating her. My mother died a few years after; my father lives still. I have not seen him since. Waiter, a 'bock.' "

A waiter brought him his "bock," which he swallowed at a gulp. But, in taking up his pipe again, trembling as he was, he broke it. Then he made a violent gesture:

"Zounds! This is indeed a grief, a real grief. I have had it for a month, and it was coloring so beautifully!"

Then he went off through the vast saloon, which was now full of smoke and of people drinking, calling out:

"Waiter, a 'bock'—and a new pipe."

The Sequel to a Divorce

CERTAINLY, although he had been engaged in the most extraordinary, most unlikely, most extravagant, and funniest cases, and had won legal games without a trump in his hand—although he had worked out the obscure law of divorce, as if it had been a Californian gold mine, Maître* Garrulier, the celebrated, the only Garrulier, could not check a movement of surprise, nor a disheartening shake of the head, nor a smile, when the Countess de Baudémont explained her affairs to him for the first time.

He had just opened his correspondence, and his slender hands, on which he bestowed the greatest attention, buried themselves in a heap of female letters, and one might have thought oneself in the confessional of a fashionable preacher, so impregnated was the atmosphere with delicate perfumes.

Immediately — even before she had said a word—with the sharp glance of a practised man of the world, that look which made beautiful Madame de Serpenoise say: "He strips your heart bare!" the lawyer had classed her in the third category. Those who suffer came into his first category, those who love, into the second, and those who are bored, into the third—and she belonged to the latter.

She was a pretty windmill, whose sails turned and flew round, and fretted the blue sky with a delicious shiver of joy, as it were, and had the brain of a bird, in which four correct and healthy ideas cannot exist side by side, and in which all dreams and every kind of folly are engulfed, like a great kaleidoscope.

Incapable of hurting a fly, emotional, charitable, with a feeling of tenderness for the street girl who sells bunches of violets for a penny, for a cab horse which a driver is ill-using, for a melancholy pauper's funeral, when the body, without friends or relations to follow it, is being conveyed to the common grave, doing anything that might afford five minutes' amusement, not

*Title given to advocates in France.

caring if she made men miserable for the rest of their days, and taking pleasure in kindling passions which consumed men's whole being, looking upon life as too short to be anything else than one uninterrupted round of gaiety and enjoyment, she thought that people might find plenty of time for being serious and reasonable in the evening of life, when they are at the bottom of the hill, and their looking-glasses reveal a wrinkled face, surrounded with white hair.

A thorough-bred Parisian, whom one would follow to the end of the world, like a poodle; a woman whom one adores with the head, the heart, and the senses until one is nearly driven mad, as soon as one has inhaled the delicate perfume that emanates from her dress and hair, or touched her skin, and heard her laugh; a woman for whom one would fight a duel and risk one's life without a thought; for whom a man would remove mountains, and sell his soul to the devil several times over, if the devil were still in the habit of frequenting the places of bad repute on this earth.

She had perhaps come to see this Garrulier, whom she had so often heard mentioned at five o'clock teas, so as to be able to describe him to her female friends subsequently in droll phrases, imitating his gestures and the unctuous inflections of his voice, in order, perhaps, to experience some new sensation, or, perhaps, for the sake of dressing like a woman who was going to try for a divorce; and, certainly, the whole effect was perfect. She wore a splendid cloak embroidered with jet — which gave an almost serious effect to her golden hair, to her small slightly turned-up nose,

with its quivering nostrils, and to her large eyes, full of enigma and fun—over a dark stuff dress, which was fastened at the neck by a sapphire and a diamond pin.

The barrister did not interrupt her, but allowed her to get excited and to chatter, to enumerate her causes for complaint against poor Count de Baudémont, who certainly had no suspicion of his wife's escapade, and who would have been very much surprised if anyone told him of it at that moment, when he was taking his fencing lesson at the club.

When she had quite finished, he said coolly, as if he were throwing a pail of water on some burning straw:

"But, Madame, there is not the slightest pretext for a divorce in anything that you have told me here. The judges would ask me whether I took the Law Courts for a theater, and intended to make fun of them."

And seeing how disheartened she was, —that she looked like a child whose favorite toy had been broken, that she was so pretty that he would have liked to kiss her hands in his devotion, and as she seemed to be witty, and very amusing, and as, moreover, he had no objection to such visits being prolonged, when papers had to be looked over, while sitting close together,—Maître Garrulier appeared to be considering. Taking his chin in his hand, he said:

"However, I will think it over; there is sure to be some dark spot that can be made out worse. Write to me, and come and see me again."

In the course of her visits, that black spot had increased so much, and Madame de Baudémont had followed her lawyer's advice so punctually, and had played on the various strings so skillfully that a few months later, after a lawsuit, which is still spoken of in the course of which the President had to take off his spectacles, and to use his pocket-handkerchief noisily, the divorce was pronounced in favor of the Countess Marie Anne Nicole Bournet de Baudémont, *née* de Tanchart de Peothus.

The Count, who was nonplussed at such an adventure turning out so seriously, first of all flew into a terrible rage, rushed off to the lawyer's office and threatened to cut off his knavish ears for him. But when his access of fury was over, and he thought of it, he shrugged his shoulders and said:

"All the better for her, if it amuses her!"

Then he bought Baron Silberstein's yacht, and with some friends, got up a cruise to Ceylon and India.

Marie Anne began by triumphing, and felt as happy as a schoolgirl going home for the holidays; she committed every possible folly, and soon, tired, satiated, and disgusted, began to yawn, cried, and found out that she had sacrificed her happiness, like a millionaire who has gone mad and has cast his banknotes and shares into the river, and that she was nothing more than a disabled waif and stray. Consequently, she now married again, as the solitude of her home made her morose from morning till night; and then, besides she found a woman requires a mansion when she goes into society, to race meetings, or to the theater.

And so, while she became a marchioness, and pronounced her second "Yes," before a very few friends, at the office of the mayor of the English urban district, malicious people in the Faubourg were making fun of the whole affair, and affirming this and that, whether rightly or wrongly, and comparing the present husband to the former one, even declaring that he had partially been the cause of the former divorce. Meanwhile Monsieur de Baudémont was wandering over the four quarters of the globe trying to overcome his homesickness, and to deaden his longing for love, which had taken possession of his heart and of his body, like a slow poison.

He traveled through the most out-of-the-way places, and the most lovely countries, and spent months and months at sea, and plunged into every kind of dissipation and debauchery. But neither the supple forms nor the luxurious gestures of the bayaderes, nor the large passive eyes of the Creoles, nor flirtations with English girls with hair the color of new cider, nor nights of waking dreams, when he saw new constellations in the sky, nor dangers during which a man thinks it is all over with him, and mutters a few words of prayer in spite of himself, when the waves are high, and the sky black, nothing was able to make him forget that little Parisian woman who smelled so sweet that she might have been taken for a bouquet of rare flowers; who was so coaxing, so curious, so funny; who never had the same caprice, the same smile, or the same look twice, and who, at bottom, was worth more than many others, either saints or sinners.

He thought of her constantly, during long hours of sleeplessness. He carried her portrait about with him in the breast pocket of his pea-jacket — a charming portrait in which she was smiling, and showing her white teeth between her half-open lips. Her gentle eyes with their magnetic look had a happy, frank expression, and from the mere arrangement of her hair, one could see that she was fair among the fair.

He used to kiss that portrait of the woman who had been his wife as if he wished to efface it, would look at it for hours, and then throw himself down on the netting and sob like a child as he looked at the infinite expanse before him, seeming to see their lost happiness, the joys of their perished affections, and the divine remembrance of their love, in the monotonous waste of green waters. And he tried to accuse himself for all that had occurred, and not to be angry with her, to think that his grievances were imaginary, and to adore her in spite of everything and always.

And so he roamed about the world, tossed to and fro, suffering and hoping he knew not what. He ventured into the greatest dangers, and sought for death just as man seeks for his mistress, and death passed close to him without touching him, perhaps amused at his grief and misery.

For he was as wretched as a stonebreaker, as one of those poor devils who work and nearly break their backs over the hard flints the whole day long, under the scorching sun or the cold rain; and Marie Anne herself was not happy, for she was pining for the past and remembered their former love.

At last, however, he returned to France, changed, tanned by exposure, sun, and rain, and transformed as if by some witch's philter.

Nobody would have recognized the elegant and effeminate clubman in this corsair with broad shoulders, a skin the color of tan, with very red lips, who rolled a little in his walk; who seemed to be stifled in his black dress-coat, but who still retained the distinguished manners and bearing of a nobleman of the last century, one of those who, when he was ruined, fitted out a privateer, and fell upon the English wherever he met them, from St. Milo to Calcutta. And wherever he showed himself his friends exclaimed:

"Why! Is that you? I should never have known you again!"

He was very nearly starting off again immediately; he even telegraphed orders to Havre to get the steam-yacht ready for sea directly, when he heard that Marie Anne had married again.

He saw her in the distance, at the Théâtre Français one Tuesday, and when he noticed how pretty, how fair, how desirable she was,—looking so melancholy, with all the appearance of an unhappy soul that regrets something,—his determination grew weaker, and he delayed his departure from week to week, and waited, without knowing why, until, at last, worn out with the struggle, watching her wherever she went, more in love with her than he had ever been before, he wrote her long, mad, ardent letters in which his passion overflower like a stream of lava.

He altered his handwriting, as he remembered her restless brain, and her many whims. He sent her the flowers which he knew she liked best, and told her that she was his life, that he was dying of waiting for her, of longing for her, for her his idol.

At last, very much puzzled and surprised, guessing — who knows? — from the instinctive beating of her heart, and her general emotion, that it must be he this time, he whose soul she had tortured with such cold cruelty, and knowing that she could make amends for the past and bring back their former love, she replied to him, and granted him the meeting that he asked for. She fell into his arms, and they both sobbed with joy and ecstasy. Thier kisses were those which lips give only when they have lost each other and found each other again at last, when they meet and exhaust themselves in each other's looks, thirsting for tenderness, love, and enjoyment.

*　　*　　*　　*　　*　　*

Last week Count de Baudémont carried off Marie Anne quietly and coolly, just like one resumes possession of one's house on returning from a journey, and drives out the intruders. And when Maître Garrulier was told of this unheard of scandal, he rubbed his hands —the long, delicate hands of a sensual prelate—and exclaimed:

"That is absolutely logical, and I should like to be in their place."

The Clown

THE hawkers' cottage stood at the end of the Esplanade, on the little promontory where the jetty is, and where all the winds, all the rain, and all the spray met. The hut, both walls and roof, was built of old planks, more or less covered with tar; its chinks were stopped with oakum, and dry wreckage was heaped up against it. In the middle of the room an iron pot stood on two bricks, and served as a stove, when they had any coal, but as there was no chimney, it filled the room, which was ventilated only by a low door, with acrid smoke, and there the whole crew lived, eighteen men and one woman. Some had undergone various terms of imprisonment, and nobody knew what the others had done, but though they were all, more or less, suffering from some physical defect and were virtually old men, they were still all strong enough for hauling. For "Chamber of Commerce" tolerated them there, and allowed them that hovel to live in, on condition that they should be ready to haul, by day and by night.

For every vessel they hauled, each got a penny by day, and twopence by night. It was not certain, however, on account of the competition of retired sailors, fishermen's wives, laborers who had nothing to do, people who were all stronger than those half-starved wretches in the hut.

And yet they lived there, those eighteen men and one woman. Were they happy? Certainly not. Hopeless? Not that, either; for they occasionally got a little beside their scanty pay, and then they stole occasionally, fish, lumps of coal, things without any value to those who lost them, but of great value to the poor, beggarly thieves.

The eighteen supported the woman, and there was no jealousy on her account! She had no special favorite among them.

She was a fat woman of about forty, chubby-faced and puffy, of whom daddy La Bretagne, who was one of the eighteen, used to say: "She does us honor."

If she had had a favorite among them, daddy La Bretagne would certainly have had the greatest right to that privilege, for although he was one of the most crippled among them, being partially paralyzed in his legs, he showed himself as skillful and strong-armed as any of them, and in spite of his infirmities, he always managed to secure a good place in the row of haulers. None of them knew as well as he how to inspire visitors with pity during the season, and to make them put their hands into their pockets. He was a past master at cadging, so that among those empty stomachs and penniless rascals he had windfalls of victuals and coppers more frequently than fell rightly to his share. But he did not make use of them in order to monopolize their common mistress.

"I am just," he used to say. "Let each of us have his spoonful in turn, and no more, when we are all eating out of the same dish."

With the coal he picked up, he used to make a good fire for the whole band in the iron pot, over which he cooked whatever he brought home with him, without anyone complaining about it, for he used to say:

"It gives you a good fire at which to warm yourselves, for nothing, and the smell of my stew into the bargain."

As for his money, he spent it in drink with the trollop, and afterward, what was left of it, with the others.

"You see," he used to say, "I am just, and more than just. I give her up to you, because it is your right."

The consequence was, that they all liked daddy La Bretagne, so that he gloried in it, and said proudly:

"What a pity that we are living under the Republic! These fellows would think nothing of making me king."

And one day, when he said this, his trollop replied: "The king is here, old fellow!" And at the same time she presented a new comrade to them, who was no less ragged or wretched looking than the eighteen, but quite young by the side of him. He was a tall, thin fellow of about forty, and without a gray streak in his long hair. He was dressed only in a pair of trousers and a shirt, which he wore outside them, like a blouse, and the trollop said:

"Here, daddy La Bretagne, you have two knitted vests on, so just give him one."

"Why should I?" the hauler asked.

"Because I choose you to," the woman replied. "I have been living with you set of old men for a long time, so now I want to have a young one; there he is, so you must give him a vest, and keep him here, or I shall throw you up. You may take it or leave it, as you like; do you understand me?"

The eighteen looked at each other open-mouthed, and good daddy La Bretagne scratched his head, and then said:

"What she asks is quite right, and we must give way," he replied.

Then they explained themselves, and

came to an understanding. The poor devil did not come like a conqueror, for he was a wretched clown who had just been released from prison, where he had undergone three years' hard labor for an attempted outrage on a girl, but with one exception, the best fellow in the world, so people declared.

"And something nice for me," the trollop said; "for I can assure you that I mean him to reward me for anything I may do for him."

From that time, the household of eighteen persons was increased to nineteen, and at first all went well. The clown was very humble, and tried not to be burdensome to them. Fed, clothed, and supplied with tobacco, he tried not to be too exacting in the other matter; and if needful, he would have hauled like the others, but the woman would not allow it.

"You shall not fatigue yourself, my little man," she said. "You must reserve yourself entirely for home."

And he did as she wished.

And soon the eighteen, who had never been jealous of each other, grew jealous of the favored lover. Some tried to pick a quarrel with him. He resisted. The best fellow in the world, no doubt, but he was not going to be taken for a mussel shut up in its shell, for all that. Let them call him as lazy as a priest if they liked; he did not mind that, but when they put hairs into his coffee, armfuls of rushes among his wreckage, and filth into his soup, they had better look out!

"None of that, all the lot of you, or you will see what I can do," he used to say.

They repeated their practical jokes, however, and he thrashed them. He did not try to find out who the culprits were, but attacked the first one he met, so much the worse for him. With a kick from his wooden clog (it was his specialty) he smashed their noses into a pulp, and having thus acquired the knowledge of his strength, and urged on by his trollop, he soon became a tyrant. The eighteen felt that they were slaves, and their former paradise, where concord and perfect equality had reigned, became a hell, and that state of things could not last.

"Ah!" daddy La Bretagne growled, "if only I were twenty years younger, I would nearly kill him! I have my Breton's hot head still, but my confounded legs are no good any longer."

And he boldly challenged the clown to a duel, in which the latter was to have his legs tied, and then both of them were to sit on the ground and hack at each other with knives.

"Such a duel," he said, "would be perfectly fair!" he replied, kicking him in the side with one of his clogs; and the woman burst out laughing, and said:

"At any rate you cannot compete with him on equal terms as regards myself, so do not worry yourself about it."

Daddy La Bretagne was lying in his corner and spitting blood, and none of the rest spoke. What could the others do, when he, the blusterer of them all, had been served so? The jade had been right when she had brought in the intruder, and said:

"The king is here, old fellow."

Only, she ought to have remembered that, after all, she alone kept his subjects in check, and as daddy La Bretagne said, by a right object. With her to console them, they would no doubt have borne anything, but she was foolish enough to cut down their food, and not to fill their common dish as full as it used to be. She wanted to keep everything for her lover, and that raised the exasperation of the eighteen to its height. So one night when she and the clown were asleep, among all these fasting men, the eighteen threw themselves on them. They wrapped the despot's arms and legs up in tarpaulin, and in the presence of the woman who was firmly bound, they flogged him till he was black and blue.

"Yes," old Bretagne said to me himself. "Yes, Monsieur, that was our revenge. The king was guillotined in 1793, and so we guillotined our king also."

And he concluded with a sneer, saying: "But we wished to be just, and as it was not his head that had made him our king, by Jove, we settled him."

———————

The Mad Woman

"I CAN tell you a terrible story about the Franco-Prussian war," Monsieur d'Endolin said to some friends assembled in the smoking-room of Baron de Ravot's château. "You know my house in the Faubourg de Cormeil. I was living there when the Prussians came, and I had for a neighbor a kind of mad woman, who had lost her senses in consequence of a series of misfortunes. At the age of seven and twenty she had lost her father, her husband, and her newly born child, all in the space of a month.

"When death has once entered into a house, it almost invariably returns immediately, as if it knew the way, and the young woman, overwhelmed with grief, took to her bed and was delirious for six weeks. Then a species of calm lassitude succeeded that violent crisis, and she remained motionless, eating next to nothing, and only moving her eyes. Every time they tried to make her get up, she screamed as if they were about to kill her, and so they ended by leaving her continually in bed, and only taking her out to wash her, to change her linen, and to turn her mattress.

"An old servant remained with her, to give her something to drink, or a little cold meat, from time to time. What passed in that despairing mind? No one ever knew, for she did not speak at all now. Was she thinking of the dead? Was she dreaming sadly, without any precise recollection of anything that had happened? Or was her memory as stagnant as water without any current? But however this may have been, for fifteen years she remained thus inert and secluded.

"The war broke out, and in the beginning of December the Germans came to Cormeil. I can remember it as if it were but yesterday. It was freezing hard enough to split the stones, and I myself was lying back in an armchair, being unable to move on account of the gout, when I heard their heavy and regular tread, and could see them pass from my window.

"They defiled past interminably, with that peculiar motion of a puppet on wires, which belongs to them. Then the officers billeted their men on the inhabitants, and I had seventeen of them. My neighbor, the crazy woman, had a dozen, one of whom was the Commandant, a regular violent, surly swashbuckler.

"During the first few days, everything went on as usual. The officers next door had been told that the lady was ill, and they did not trouble themselves about that in the least, but soon that woman whom they never saw irritated them. They asked what her illness was, and were told that she had been in bed for fifteen years, in consequence of terrible grief. No doubt they did not believe it, and thought that the poor mad creature would not leave her bed out of pride, so that she might not come near the Prussians, or speak to them or even see them.

"The Commandant insisted upon her receiving him. He was shown into the room and said to her roughly: 'I must beg you to get up, Madame, and come downstairs so that we may all see you.' But she merely turned her vague eyes on him, without replying, and so he continued: 'I do not intend to tolerate any insolence, and if you do not get up of your own accord, I can easily find means to make you walk without any assistance.'

"But she did not give any signs of having heard him, and remained quite motionless. Then he got furious, taking that calm silence for a mark of supreme contempt; so he added: 'If you do not

come downstairs to-morrow —' And then he left the room.

"The next day the terrified old servant wished to dress her, but the mad woman began to scream violently, and resisted with all her might. The officer ran upstairs quickly, and the servant threw herself at his feet and cried: 'She will not come down, Monsieur, she will not. Forgive her, for she is so unhappy.'

"The soldier was embarrassed, as in spite of his anger, he did not venture to order his soldiers to drag her out. But suddenly he began to laugh, and gave some orders in German, and soon a party of soldiers was seen coming out supporting a mattress as if they were carrying a wounded man. On that bed, which had been unmade, the mad woman, who was still silent, was lying quite quietly, for she was quite indifferent to anything that went on, as long as they let her lie. Behind her, a soldier was carrying a parcel of feminine attire, and the officer said, rubbing his hands: 'We will just see whether you cannot dress yourself alone, and take a little walk.'

"And then the procession went off in the direction of the forest of Imauville; in two hours the soldiers came back alone, and nothing more was seen of the mad woman. What had they done with her? Where had they taken her to? No one knew.

"The snow was falling day and night, and enveloped the plain and the woods in a shroud of frozen foam, and the wolves came and howled at our very doors.

"The thought of that poor lost woman

haunted me, and I made several applications to the Prussian authorities in order to obtain some information, and was nearly shot for doing so. When spring returned, the army of occupation withdrew, but my neighbor's house remained closed, and the grass grew thick in the garden walks. The old servant had died during the winter, and nobody troubled any longer about the occurrence; I alone thought about it constantly. What had they done with the woman? Had she escaped through the forest? Had somebody found her, and taken her to a hospital, without being able to obtain any information from her? Nothing happened to relieve my doubts; but by degrees, time assuaged my fears.

"Well, in the following autumn the woodcock were very plentiful, and as my gout had left me for a time, I dragged my self as far as the forest. I had already killed four or five of the long-billed birds, when I knocked over one which fell into a ditch full of branches, and I was obliged to get into it, in order to pick it up, and I found that it had fallen close to a dead, human body. Immediately the recollection of the mad woman struck me like a blow in the chest. Many other people had perhaps died in the wood during that disastrous year, but though I do not know why, I was sure, sure, I tell you, that I should see the head of that wretched maniac.

"And suddenly I understood, I guessed everything. They had abandoned her on that mattress in the cold, deserted wood; and, faithful to her fixed idea, she had allowed herself to perish under that thick and light counterpane of snow, without moving either arms or legs.

"Then the wolves had devoured her, and the birds had built their nests with the wool from her torn bed, and I took charge of her bones. I only pray that our sons may never see any wars again."

Mademoiselle

He had been registered under the names of Jean Marie Mathieu Valot, but he was never called anything but "Mademoiselle." He was the idiot of the district, but not one of those wretched, ragged idiots who live on public charity. He lived comfortably on a small income which his mother had left him, and which his guardian paid him regularly, so he was rather envied than pitied. And then, he was not one of those idiots with wild looks and the manners of an animal, for he was by no means an unpleasing object, with his half-open lips and smiling eyes, and especially in his constant makeup in female dress. For he dressed like a girl, and showed by that how little he objected to being called Mademoiselle.

And why should he not like the nickname which his mother had given him affectionately, when he was a mere child, so delicate and weak, and with a fair complexion—a poor little diminutive lad not as tall as many girls of the same age? It was in pure love that, in his earlier years, his mother whispered that tender Mademoiselle to him, while his old grandmother used to say jokingly:

"The fact is, that as for the male element in him it is really not worth mentioning in a Christian—no offense to God in saying so." And his grandfather, who was equally fond of a joke, used to add: "I only hope it will not disappear as he grows up."

And they treated him as if he had really been a girl and coddled him, the more so as they were very prosperous and did not require to toil to keep things together.

When his mother and grandparents were dead, Mademoiselle was almost as happy with his paternal uncle, an unmarried man, who had carefully attended the idiot, and who had grown more and more attached to him by dint of looking after him; and the worthy man continued to call Jean Marie Mathieu Valot, Mademoiselle.

He was called so in all the country round as well, not with the slightest intention of hurting his feelings, but, on the contrary, because all thought they would please the poor gentle creature who harmed nobody in doing so.

The very street boys meant no harm by it, accustomed as they were to call the tall idiot in a frock and cap by the nickname; but it would have struck them as very extraordinary, and would have led them to rude fun, if they had seen him dressed like a boy.

Mademoiselle, however, took care of that, for his dress was as dear to him as his nickname. He delighted in wearing it, and, in fact, cared for nothing else, and what gave it a particular zest was that he knew that he was not a girl, and that he was living in disguise. And this was evident by the exaggerated feminine bearing and walk he put on, as if to show that it was not natural to him. His enormous, carefully filled cap was adorned with large variegated ribbons. His petticoat, with numerous flounces, was distended behind by many hoops. He walked with short steps, and with exaggerated swaying of the hips, while his folded arms and crossed hands were distorted into pretensions of comical coquetry.

On such occasions, if anybody wished to make friends with him, it was necessary to say:

"Ah! Mademoiselle, what a nice girl you make."

That put him into a good humor, and he used to reply, much pleased:

"Don't I? But people can see I only do it for a joke."

But, nevertheless, when they were dancing at village festivals in the neighborhood, he would always be invited to dance as Mademoiselle, and would never ask any of the girls to dance with him; and one evening when somebody asked him the reason for this, he opened his eyes wide, laughed as if the man had said something very stupid, and replied:

"I cannot ask the girls, because I am not dressed like a lad. Just look at my dress, you fool!"

As his interrogator was a judicious man, he said to him:

"Then dress like one, Mademoiselle."

He thought for a moment, and then said with a cunning look:

"But if I dress like a lad, I shall no

longer be a girl; and then, I am a girl"; and he shrugged his shoulders as he said it.

But the remark seemed to make him think.

For some time afterward, when he met the same person, he would ask him abruptly:

"If I dress like a lad, will you still call me Mademoiselle?"

"Of course, I shall," the other replied. "You will always be called so."

The idiot appeared delighted, for there was no doubt that he thought more of his nickname than he did of his dress, and the next day he made his appearance in the village square, without his petticoats and dressed as a man. He had taken a pair of trousers, a coat, and a hat from his guardian's clothespress. This created quite a revolution in the neighborhood, for the people who had been in the habit of smiling at him kindly when he was dressed as a woman, looked at him in astonishment and almost in fear, while the indulgent could not help laughing, and visibly making fun of him.

The involuntary hostility of some, and the too evident ridicule of others, the disagreeable surprise of all, were too palpable for him not to see it, and to be hurt by it, and it was still worse when a street urchin said to him in a jeering voice, as he danced round him:

"Oh! oh! Mademoiselle, you wear trousers! Oh! oh! Mademoiselle!"

And it grew worse and worse, when a whole band of these vagabonds were on his heels, hooting and yelling after him, as if he had been somebody in a masquerading dress during the Carnival.

It was quite certain that the unfor- tunate creature looked more in disguise now than he had formerly. By dint of living like a girl, and by even exaggerating the feminine walk and manners, he had totally lost all masculine looks and ways. His smooth face, his long flax-like hair, required a cap with ribbons, and became a caricature under the high chimney-pot hat of the old doctor, his grandfather.

Mademoiselle's shoulders, and especially her swelling stern, danced about wildly in this old-fashioned coat and wide trousers. And nothing was as funny as the contrast between his quiet dress and slow trotting pace, the winning way he used his head, and the conceited movements of his hands, with which he fanned himself like a girl.

Soon the older lads and the girls, the old women, men of ripe age and even the Judicial Councilor, joined the little brats, and hooted Mademoiselle, while the astonished idiot ran away, and rushed into the house with terror. There he took his poor head between both hands, and tried to comprehend the matter. Why were they angry with him? For it was quite evident that they were angry with him. What wrong had he done, and whom had he injured, by dressing as a boy? Was he not a boy, after all? For the first time in his life, he felt a horror for his nickname, for had he not been insulted through it? But immediately he was seized with a horrible doubt.

"Suppose that, after all, I am a girl?"

He would have liked to ask his guardian about it but he did not like to, for he somehow felt, although only obscurely, that he, worthy man, might not tell him the truth, out of kindness.

And, besides, he preferred to find out for himself, without asking anyone.

All his idiot's cunning, which had been lying latent up till then, because he never had any occasion to make use of it, now came out and urged him to a solitary and dark action.

The next day he dressed himself as a girl again, and made his appearance as if he had perfectly forgotten his escapade of the day before, but the people, especially the street boys, had not forgotten it. They looked at him sideways, and, even the best of them, could not help smiling, while the little blackguards ran after him and said:

"Oh! oh! Modemoiselle, you had on a pair of breeches!"

But he pretended not to hear, or even to guess to what they were alluding. He seemed as happy and glad to look about him as he usually did, with half-open lips and smiling eyes. As usual, he wore an enormous cap with variegated ribbons, and the same large petticoats; he walked with short, mincing steps, swaying and wriggling his hips and gesticulating like a coquette, and licked his lips when they called him Mademoiselle, while really he would have liked to have jumped at the throat of those who called him so.

Days and months passed, and by degrees those about him forgot all about his strange escapade. But he had never left off thinking about it, or trying to find out—for which he was ever on the alert—how he could ascertain his qualities as a boy, and how to assert them victoriously. Really innocent, he had reached the age of twenty without knowing anything or without ever having any

natural impulse, but being tenacious of purpose, curious and dissembling, he asked no questions, but observed all that was said and done.

Often at their village dances, he had heard young fellows boasting about girls whom they had seduced, and girls praising such and such a young fellow, and often, also, after a dance, he saw the couples go away together, with their arms round each other's waists. They had no suspicions of him, and he listened and watched, until, at last, he discovered what was going on.

And then, one night, when dancing was over, and the couples were going away with their arms round each other's waists, a terrible screaming was heard at the corner of the woods through which those going to the next village had to pass. It was Josephine, pretty Josephine, and when her screams were heard, they ran to her assistance, and arrived only just in time to rescue her, half strangled, from Mademoiselle's clutches.

The idiot had watched her and had thrown himself upon her in order to treat her as the other young fellows did the girls, but she resisted him so stoutly that he took her by the throat and squeezed it with all his might until she could not breathe, and was nearly dead.

In rescuing Josephine from him, they had thrown him on the ground, but he jumped up again immediately, foaming at the mouth and slobbering, and exclaimed:

"I am not a girl any longer, I am a young man, I am a young man, I tell you."

VOLUME III

A Bad Error

I MADE Mrs. Jadelle's acquaintance in Paris, this winter. She pleased me infinitely at once. You know her as well as I—no—pardon me—nearly as well as I. You know that she is poetic and fantastic at one and the same time. You know she is free in her manner and of impressionable heart, impulsive, courageous, venturesome, audacious—above all, prejudiced, and yet, in spite of that, sentimental, delicate, easily hurt, tender, and modest.

She was a widow, and I adore widows, from sheer laziness. I was on the lookout for a wife, and I paid her my court. I knew her, and more than that, she pleased me. The moment came when I believed it would do to risk my proposal. I was in love with her and in danger of becoming too much so. When one marries, he should not love his wife too much, or he is likely to make himself foolish; his vision is distorted, and he becomes silly and brutal at the same time. A man must assert himself. If he loses his head at first, he risks being a nobody a year later.

So one day I presented myself at her house with light gloves on, and I said to her; "Madame, I have the honor of loving you, and I have come to ask you if there is any hope of my pleasing you enough to warrant your placing your happiness in my care and taking my name."

She answered quietly: "What a question, sir! I am absolutely ignorant of whether you will please me sooner or later, or whether you will not; but I ask nothing better than to make a trial of it. As a man, I do not find you bad. It remains to be seen how you are at heart and in character and habits. For the most part marriages are tempestuous or criminal because people are not careful enough in yoking themselves together. Sometimes a mere nothing to sufficient, a mania or tenacious opinion upon some moral or religious point, no matter what, a gesture which displeases, or some little fault or disagreeable quality, to turn an affianced couple, however tender and affectionate, into a pair of irreconcilable enemies, incensed with, but chained to, each other until death. I will not marry sir, without knowing the depths and corners and recesses of the soul of the man with whom I am to share my existence. I wish to study him at leisure, at least for some months.

"Here is what I propose. You will come and pass the summer in my house at De Lauville, my country place, and we shall see then if we are fitted to live side by side—I see you laugh! You have a bad thought. Oh! sir, if I were not sure of myself, I would never make this proposition. I have for love, what you call love, you men, such a scorn, such a disgust that a fall is impossible for me. Well, do you accept?"

I kissed her hand.

"When shall we start, Madame?"

"The tenth of May."

"It is agreed."

A month later I was installed at her house. She was truly a singular woman. From morning until evening she was studying me. As she was fond of horses, we passed each day in riding through the woods, talking about everything; but she was always trying to probe my innermost thoughts, to which end she observed my slightest movement.

277

As for me, I became foolishly in love, and did not trouble myself about the fitness of our characters. But I soon perceived that even my sleep was put under inspection. Some one slept in a little room adjoining mine, entering very late and with infinite precaution. This espionage for every instant finally made me impatient. I wished to hasten the conclusion, and one evening thought of a way of bringing it about. She had received me in such a way that I had abstained from any new essay, but a violent desire invaded me to make her pay, in some fashion, for this restricted *régime* to which I had submitted, and I thought I knew a way.

You know Cesarine, her chambermaid, a pretty girl from Granville, where all the women are pretty, and as blond as her mistress was brunette? Well, one afternoon I drew the little soubrette into my room and, putting a hundred francs in her hand, I said to her:

"My dear child, I do not wish you to do anything villainous, but I desire the same privilege toward your mistress that she takes toward me."

The little maid laughed, with a sly look, as I continued:

"I am watched day and night, I know. I am watched as I eat, drink, dress myself, shave, and put on my socks, and I know it."

The little girl stammered: "Yes, sir —" then she was silent. I continued:

"You sleep in the room next to mine to see if I snore, or if I dream aloud, you cannot deny it!"

"Yes, sir—" Then she was silent again.

I became excited: "Oh! well, my girl," said I, "you understand that it is not fair for everything to be known about me while I know nothing of the person who is to be my wife. I love her with all my soul. She has the face, the heart, and mind that I have dreamed of, and I am the happiest of men on this account; nevertheless there are some things I would like to know better—"

Cesarine decided to put my bank-note in her pocket. I understood that the bargain was concluded.

"Listen, my girl," said I. "We men— we care much for certain—certain details—physical details, which do not hinder a woman from being charming, but which can change her price in our eyes. I do not ask you to say anything bad of your mistress, nor even to disclose to me her defects, if she has any. Only answer me frankly four or five questions, which I am going to put to you. You know Mrs. Jadelle as well as you do yourself, since you dress and undress her every day. Now then, tell me this: Is she as plump as she has the appearance of being?"

The little maid did not answer.

I continued: "You cannot, my child, be ignorant of the fact that women put cotton, padding, you know, where— where—where they nourish their infants and also where they sit. Tell me, does she use padding?"

Cesarine lowered her eyes. Finally she said timidly: "Ask whatever you want to, sir, I will answer all at one time."

"Well, my girl, there are some women whose knees meet, so much so that they touch with each step that they take; and there are others who have them far apart, which makes their limbs like the arches of a bridge, so that one might view the landscape between them. This is the prettier of the two fashions. Tell me, how are your mistress's limbs?"

Still the maid said nothing.

I continued: "There are some who have necks so beautiful that they form a great fold underneath. And there are some that have large arms with a thin figure. There are some that are very large before and nothing at all behind, and there are some large behind and nothing at all in front. All this is very pretty, very pretty, but I wish to know just how your mistress is made. Tell me frankly, and I will give you much more money—"

Cesarine looked at me out of the corner of her eye and, laughing with all her heart, answered: "Sir, aside from being dark, mistress is made exactly like me."

Then she fled.

I had been made sport of. This was the time I found myself ridiculous, and I resolved to avenge myself, at least, upon this impertinent maid.

An hour later I entered the little room with precaution where she listened to my sleeping, and unscrewed the bolts.

Toward midnight she arrived at her post of observation. I followed her immediately. On perceiving me, she was going to cry out, but I put my hand over her mouth, and, without too great effort, I convinced myself that, if she had not lied, Mrs. Jadelle was very well made.

I even put much zest into this authentication which, though pushed a little far, did not seem to displease Cesarine. She was, in very fact, a ravishing specimen of the Norman peasant race, strong and fine at the same time. She was

wanting perhaps in certain delicate attentions that Henry VI. would have scorned, but I revealed them to her quickly, and as I adore perfumes, I gave her a box the next evening, with a flask of lavender-water.

We were soon more closely bound to each other than I could have believed, almost friends. She became an exquisite mistress, naturally *spirituelle* and broken to pleasure. She had been a courtesan of great merit in Paris.

The delights which she brought me enabled me to await Mrs. Jadelle's conclusion of proof without impatience. I became an incomparable character, supple, docile, and complacent. My *fianceé* found me delightful beyond a doubt, and I judged, from certain signs, that I was soon to be accepted. I was certainly the happiest man in the world, awaiting tranquilly the legal kiss of the woman I loved, in the arms of a young and beautiful girl for whom I had much fondness.

It is here, Madame, that I must ask your forbearance a little; I have arrived at a delicate point.

One evening, as we were returning from a horseback ride, Mrs. Jadelle complained sharply that her grooms had not taken certain measures prescribed by her for the horse she rode. She repeated many times: "Let them take care, I have a way of surprising them."

I passed a calm night in my bed. I awoke early, full of ardor and energy. Then I dressed msyelf.

I was in the habit of going up on the tower of the house each morning to smoke a cigarette. This was reached by a limestone staircase, lighted by a large window at the top of the first story.

I advanced without noise, my feet encased in morocco slippers with wadded soles, and was climbing the first steps when I perceived Cesarine bending out the window, looking down below.

Not that I saw Cesarine entirely, but only a part of Cesarine, and that the lower part. I loved this part just as much; of Mrs. Jadelle, I would have preferred, perhaps the upper. She was thus so charming, so round, this part which offered itself to me, and only slightly clothed in a white skirt.

I approached so softly that the girl heard nothing. I put myself on my knees; with infinite precaution I took hold of the two sides of the skirt and, quickly, I raised it. I recognized there the full, fresh, plump, sweet, ischial tuberosities of my mistress, and threw there, your pardon, Madame,—I threw there a tender kiss, a kiss of a lover who dares anything.

I was surprised. It was verbena! But

I had no time for reflection. I received a sudden blow, or rather a push in the face which seemed to break my nose. I uttered a cry that made my hair rise. The person had turned around—it was Mrs. Jadelle!

She was fighting the air with her hands, like a woman who had lost consciousness. She gasped for some seconds, made a gesture of using a horsewhip, and then fled.

Ten minutes later, Cesarine, stupefied, brought me in a letter. I read:

"Mrs. Jadelle hopes that M. de Brives will immediately rid her of his presence."

I departed. Well, I am not yet consoled. I have attempted every means and all explanations to obtain a pardon for my misunderstanding, but all proceedings have been nipped in the bud.

Since that moment, you see, I have in my—in my heart a scent of verbena which gives me an immoderate desire to smell the perfume again.

The Port

I.

HAVING sailed from Havre on the third of May, 1882, for a voyage in the China seas, the square-rigged three-master, "Notre Dame des Vents," made her way back into the port of Marseilles on the eighth of August, 1886, after an absence of four years. When she had discharged her first cargo in the Chinese port for which she was bound, she had immediately found a new freight for Buenos Ayres, and from that place had conveyed goods to Brazil.

Other passages, then damage repairs, calms ranging over several months, gales which knocked her out of her course— all the accidents, adventures, and misadventures of the sea, in short—had kept far from her country this Norman three-master, which had come back to Marseilles with her hold full of tin boxes containing American preserves.

At her departure she had on board, besides the captain and the mate, fourteen sailors, eight Normans, and six Britons. On her return there were left only five Britons and four Normans, the other Briton had died while on the way; the four Normans, having disappeared under various circumstances, had been replaced by two Americans, a negro, and a Norwegian carried off, one evening, from a tavern in Singapore.

The big vessel, with reefed sails and yards crossed over her masts, drawn by a tug from Marseilles, rocking over a sweep of rolling waes which subsided gently into calm water, passed in front of the Chateau d'If, and then under all the gray rocks of the roadstead, which the setting sun covered with a golden vapor. She entered the ancient port, in which are packed together, side by side, ships from every part of the world, pellmell, large and small, of every shape and every variety of rigging, soaking like a *bouillabaisse* of boats in this basin too limited in extent, full of putrid water where shells touch each other, rub against each other, and seem to be pickled in the juice of the vessels.

"Notre Dame des Vents" took up her station between an Italian brig and an English schooner, which made way to let this comrade slip in between them; then, when all the formalities of the customhouse and of the port had been complied with, the captain authorized two-thirds of his crew to spend the night on shore.

It was already dark. Marseilles was lighted up. In the heat of this summer's evening, a flavor of cooking with garlic floated over the noisy city, filled with the clamor of voices, of rolling vehicles, of the crackling of whips, and of southern mirth.

As soon as they felt themselves on shore, the ten men, whom the sea had been tossing about for some months past,

proceeded along quite slowly with the hesitating steps of persons who are out of their element, unaccustomed to cities, two by two, in procession.

They swayed from one side to another as they walked, looked about them, smelling out the lanes opening out on the harbor, rendered feverish by the amorous appetite which had been growing to maturity in their bodies during their last sixty-six days at sea. The Normans strode on in front, led by Célestin Duclos, a tall young fellow, sturdy and waggish, who served as a captain for the others every time they set forth on land. He divined the places worth visiting, found out byways after a fashion of his own, and did not take much part in the squabbles so frequent among sailors in seaport towns. But, once he was caught in one, he was afraid of nobody.

After some hesitation as to which of the obscure streets that lead down to the waterside, and from which arise heavy smells, a sort of exhalation from closets, they ought to enter, Célestin gave the preference to a kind of winding passage, where gleamed over the doors projecting lanterns bearing enormous numbers on their rough colored glass. Under the narrow arches at the entrance to the houses, women wearing aprons, like servants, seated on straw chairs, rose up on seeing them coming near, taking three steps toward the gutter which separated the street into halves, and so cutting off the path from this file of men, who sauntered along at their leisure, humming and sneering, already getting excited by the vicinity of those dens of prostitutes.

Sometimes, at the end of a hall, behind a second open door, which presented itself unexpectedly, covered over with dark leather, would appear a big wench, undressed, whose heavy thighs and fat calves abruptly outlined themselves under her coarse white cotton wrapper. Her short petticoat had the appearance of a puffed-out girdle; and the soft flesh of her breast, her shoulders, and her arms made a rosy stain on a black velvet corsage with edgings of gold lace. She kept calling out from her distant corner, "Will you come here, my pretty boys?" and sometimes she would go out herself to catch hold of one of them, and to drag him toward her door with all her strength, fastening on him like a spider drawing forward an insect bigger than itself. The man, excited by the struggle, would offer a mild resistance, and the rest would stop to look on, undecided between the longing to go in at once and that of lengthening this appetizing promenade. Then when the woman, after desperate efforts, had brought the sailor to the threshold of her abode, in which the entire band would be swallowed up after him, Célestin Duclos, who was a judge of houses of this sort, suddenly exclaimed: Don't go in there, Marchand! That's not the place."

The man thereupon, obeying this direction, freed himself with a brutal shake; and the comrades formed themselves into a band once more, pursued by the filthy insults of the exasperated wench, while other women, all along the alley in front of them, came out past their doors, attracted by the noise, and in hoarse voices threw out to them invitations coupled with promises. They went on, then, more and more stimu-lated by the combined effects of the coaxings and the seductions held out as baits to them by the choir of portresses of love all over the upper part of the street, and the ignoble maledictions hurled at them by the choir at the lower end—the despised choir of disappointed wenches. From time to time, they met another band—soldiers marching along with spurs jingling at their heels— sailors marching again—isolated citizens —clerks in business houses. On all sides might be some fresh streets, narrow, and studded all over with those equivocal lanterns. They pursued their way still through this labyrinth of squalid habitation, over those greasy pavements through which putrid water was oozing, between those walls filled with women's flesh.

At last, Duclos made up his mind, and, drawing up before a house of rather attractive exterior, made all his companions follow him in there.

II.

Then followed a scene of thorough-going revelry. For four hours the six sailors gorged themselves with love and wine. Six months' pay was thus wasted.

In the principal room in the tavern they were installed as masters, gazing with malignant glances at the ordinary customers, who were seated at the little tables in the corners, where one of the girls, who was left free to come and go, dressed like a big baby or a singer at a *café* concert, went about serving them, and then seated herself near them. Each man, on coming in, had selected his partner, whom he kept all the evening, for the vulgar taste is not changeable.

They had drawn three tables close up to them; and, after the first bumper, the procession divided into two parts, increased by as many women as there were seamen, had formed itself anew on the staircase. On the wooden steps the four feet of each couple kept tramping from time to time, while the several files of lovers were swallowed up behind the narrow doors leading into the different rooms.

Then they came down again to have a drink, and after they had returned to the rooms, descended the stairs once more.

Now, almost intoxicated, they began to howl. Each of them, with bloodshot eyes, and his chosen female companion on his knee, sang or bawled, struck the table with his fist, shouted while swilling wine down his throat, setting free the brute within. In the midst of them, Célestin Duclos pressing close to him a big damsel with red cheeks, who sat astirde over his legs, gazed at her ardently. Less tipsy than the others, not that he had taken less drink, he was as yet occupied with other thoughts, and, more tender than his comrades, he tried to get up a chat. His thoughts wandered a little, escaped him, and then came back, and disappeared again, without allowing him to recollect exactly what he meant to say.

"What time—what time—how long are you here?"

"Six months," the girl answered.

He seemed to be satisfied with her, as this were a proof of good conduct, and he went on questioning her:

"Do you like this life?"

She hesitated, then in a tone of resignation:

"One gets used to it. It is not more worrying than any other kind of life. To be a servant-girl or else a scrub is always a nasty occupation."

He looked as if he also approved of this truthful remark.

"You are not from this place?" said he.

She answered merely by shaking her head.

"Do you come from a distance?"

She nodded, still without opening her lips.

"Where is it you come from?"

She appeared to be thinking, to be searching her memory, then said falteringly:

"From Perpignan."

He was once more perfectly satisfied, and said:

"Ah! yes."

In her turn she asked:

"And you, are you a sailor?"

"Yes, my beauty."

"Do you come from a distance?"

"Ah! yes. I have seen countries, ports, and everything."

"You have been round the world, perhaps?"

"I believe you, twice rather than once."

Again she seemed to hesitate, to search in her brain for something that she had forgotten, then, in a tone somewhat different, more serious:

"Have you met many ships in your voyages?"

"I believe you, my beauty."

"You did not happen to see the 'Notre Dame des Vents'?"

He chuckled:

"No later than last week."

She turned pale, all the blood leaving her cheeks, and asked:

"Is that true, perfectly true?"

"'Tis true as I tell you."

"Honor bright! you are not telling me a lie?"

He raised his hand.

"Before God, I'm not!" said he.

"Then do you know whether Célestin Duclos is still on her?"

He was astonished, uneasy, and wished, before answering, to learn something further.

"Do you know him?"

She became distrustful in turn.

"Oh! 'tis not myself—'tis a woman who is acquainted with him."

"A woman from this place?"

"No, from a place not far off."

"In the street? What sort of a woman?"

"Why, then, a woman—a woman like myself."

"What has she to say to him, this woman?"

"I believe she is a countrywoman of his."

They stared into one another's eyes, watching one another, feeling, divining that something of a grave nature was going to arise between them.

He resumed:

"I could see her there, this woman."

"What would you say to her?"

"I would say to her—I would say to her—that I had seen Célestin Duclos."

"He is quite well—isn't he?"

"As well as you or me—he is a strapping young fellow."

She became silent again, trying to collect her ideas; then slowly.

"Where has the 'Notre Dame des Vents' gone to?"

"Why, just to Marseilles."

She could not repress a start.

"Is that really true?"

"'Tis really true."

"Do you know Duclos?"

"Yes, I do know him."

She still hesitated; then in a very gentle tone:

"Good! That's good!"

"What do you want with him?"

"Listen!—you will tell him—nothing!"

He stared at her, more and more perplexed. At last he put this question to her:

"Do you know him, too, yourself?"

"No," said she.

"Then what do you want with him?"

Suddenly, she made up her mind what to do, left her seat, rushed over to the bar where the landlady of the tavern presided, seized a lemon, which she tore open and shed its juice into a glass, then she filled this glass with pure water, and carrying it across to him:

"Drink this!"

"Why?"

"To make it pass for wine. I will talk to you afterward."

He drank it without further protest, wiped his lips with the back of his hand, then observed:

"That's all right. I am listening to you."

"You will promise not to tell him you have seen me, or from whom you learned what I am going to tell you. You must swear not to do so."

He raised his hand.

"All right. I swear I will not."

"Before God?"

"Before God."

"Well, you will tell him that his father

died, that his mother died, that his brother died, the whole three in one month, of typhoid fever, in January, 1883— three years and a half ago."

In his turn he felt all his blood set in motion through his entire body, and for a few seconds he was so much overpowered that he could make no reply; then he began to doubt what she had told him, and asked:

"Are you sure?"

"I am sure."

"Who told it to you?"

She laid her hands on his shoulders, and looking at him out of the depths of her eyes:

"You swear not to blab?"

"I swear that I will not."

"I am his sister!"

He uttered that name in spite of himself:

"Françoise?"

She contemplated him once more with a fixed stare, then, excited by a wild feeling of terror, a sense of profound horror, she faltered in a very low tone, almost speaking into his mouth:

"Oh! oh! it is you, Célestin."

They no longer stirred, their eyes riveted in one another.

Around them, his comrades were still yelling. The sounds made by glasses, by fists, by heels keeping time to the choruses, and the shrill cries of the women, mingled with the roar of their songs.

He felt her leaning on him, clasping him, ashamed and frightened, his sister. Then, in a whisper, lest anyone might hear him, so hushed that she could scarcely catch his words:

"What a misfortune! I have made a nice piece of work of it!"

The next moment her eyes were filled with tears, and she faltered:

"Is that my fault?"

But, all of a sudden, he said:

"So then, they are dead?"

"They are dead."

"The father, the mother, and the brother?"

"The three in one month, as I told you. I was left by myself with nothing but my clothes, for I was in debt to the apothecary and the doctor and for the funeral, of the three, and had to pay what I owed with the furniture.

"After that I went as a servant to the house of Maître Cacheux,— you know him well,— the cripple. I was just fifteen at the time, for you went away when I was not quite fourteen. I tripped with him. One is so senseless when one is young. Then I went as a nursery-maid to the notary, who debauched me also, and brought me to Havre, where he took a room for me. After a little while he gave up coming to see me. For three days I lived without eating a morsel of food; and then, not being able to get employment, I went to a house, like many others. I, too, have seen different places—ah! and dirty places! Rouen, Evreux, Lille, Bordeaux, Perpignan, Nice, and then Marseilles, where I am now!"

The tears started from her eyes, flowed over her nose, wet her cheeks, and trickled into her mouth.

She went on:

"I thought you were dead, too?—my poor Célestin."

He said:

"I would not have recognized you myself—you were such a little thing then, and here you are so big!—but how is it that you did not recognize me?"

She answered with a despairing movement of her hands:

"I see so many men that they all seem to me alike."

He kept his eyes still fixed on her intently, oppressed by an emotion that dazed him and filled him with such pain as to make him long to cry like a little child that has been whipped. He still held her in his arms, while she sat astride on his knees, with his open hands against the girl's back; and now by sheer dint of looking continually at her, he at length recognized her, the little sister left behind in the country with all those whom she had seen die, while he had been tossing on the seas. Then, suddenly taking between his big seaman's paws this head found once more, he began to kiss her, as one kisses kindred flesh. And after that, sobs, a man's deep sobs, heaving like great billows, rose up in his throat, resembling the hiccoughs of drunkenness.

He stammered:

"And this is you—this is you, Françoise—my little Françoise!"

Then, all at once, he sprang up, began swearing in an awful voice, and struck the table such a blow with his fist that the glasses were knocked down and smashed. After that, he advanced three steps, staggered, stretched out his arms, and fell on his face. And he rolled on the floor, crying out, beating the boards with his hands and feet, and uttering such groans that they seemed like a death rattle.

All those comrades of his stared at him, and laughed.

"He's not a bit drunk," said one.

"He ought to be put to bed," said another.

"If he goes out, we'll all be run in together."

Then, as he had money in his pockets, the landlady offered to let him have a bed, and his comrades, themselves so much intoxicated that they could not stand upright, hoisted him up the narrow stairs to the apartment of the woman who had just been in his company, and who remained sitting on a chair, at the foot of that bed of crime, weeping quite as freely as he had wept, until the morning dawned.

Châli

ADMIRAL DE LA VALLÉE, who seemed to be half asleep in his armchair, said in a voice which sounded like an old woman's:

"I had a very singular little love adventure once; would you like to hear it?"

He spoke from the depths of his great armchair, with that everlasting dry, wrinkled smile on his lips, that smile à la Voltaire, which made people take for a terrible sceptic.

I.

"I was thirty years of age and a first lieutenant in the navy, when I was intrusted with an astronomical expedition to Central India. The English Government provided me with all the necessary means for carrying out my enterprise, and I was soon busied with a few followers in that vast, strange, surprising country.

"It would take me ten volumes to relate that journey. I went through wonderfully magnificent regions, was received by strangely handsome princes, and was entertained with incredible magnificence. For two months it seemed to me as if I were walking in a fairy kingdom, on the back of imaginary elephants. In the midst of wild forests I discovered extraordinary ruins, delicate and chiseled like jewels, fine as lace and enormous as mountains, those fabulous, divine monuments which are so graceful that one falls in love with their form as with a woman, feeling a physical and sensual pleasure in looking at them. As Victor Hugo says, 'Whilst wide-awake, I was walking in a dream.'

"Toward the end of my journey I reached Ganhard, which was formerly one of the most prosperous towns in Central India, but is now much decayed. It is governed by a wealthy, arbitrary, violent, generous, and cruel prince. His name is Rajah Maddan, a true Oriental potentate, delicate and barbarous, affable and sanguinary, combining feminine grace with pitiless ferocity.

"The city lies at the bottom of a valley, on the banks of a little lake surrounded by pagodas, which bathe their walls in the water. At a distance the city looks like a white spot, which grows larger as one approaches it, and by degrees you discover the domes and spires, the slender and graceful summits of Indian monuments.

"At about an hour's distance from the gates, I met a superbly caparisoned elephant, surrounded by a guard of honor which the sovereign had sent me, and I was conducted to the palace with great ceremony.

"I should have liked to have taken the time to put on my gala uniform, but royal impatience would not admit of it. He was anxious to make my acquaintance, to know what he might expect from me.

"I was ushered into a great hall surrounded by galleries, in the midst of bronze-colored soldiers in splendid uniforms, while all about were standing men dressed in striking robes, studded with precious stones.

"I saw a shining mass, a kind of setting sun reposing on a bench like our garden benches, without a back; it was the rajah who was waiting for me, motionless, in a robe of the purest canary color. He had some ten or fifteen million francs' worth of diamonds on him, and by itself, on his forehead, glistened the famous star of Delhi, which has always belonged to the illustrious dynasty of the Pariharas of Mundore, from whom my host was descended.

"He was a man of about five-and-twenty, who seemed to have some negro blood in his veins, although he belonged to the purest Hindoo race. He had large, almost motionless, rather vague eyes, fat lips, a curly beard, low forehead, and dazzling sharp white teeth, which he frequently showed with a mechanical smile. He got up and gave me his hand in the English fashion, and then made me sit down beside him on a bench which was so high that my feet hardly touched the ground, and on which I was very uncomfortable.

"He immediately proposed a tiger hunt for the next day; war and hunting were his chief occupations, and he could hardly understand how one could care for anything else. He was evidently fully persuaded that I had only come all that distance to amuse him a little, and to be the companion of his pleasures.

"As I stood greatly in need of his assistance, I tried to flatter his tastes, and he was so pleased with me that he immediately wished to show me how his trained boxers fought, and led the way into a kind of arena situated within the palace.

"At his command two naked men appeared, their hands covered with steel claws. They immediately began to attack each other, trying to strike one another with these sharp weapons, which left long cuts, from which the blood flowed freely down their dark skins.

"It lasted for a long time, till their bodies were a mass of wounds, and the combatants were tearing each other's flesh with these pointed blades. One of them had his jaw smashed, while the ear of the other was split into three pieces.

"The prince looked on with ferocious pleasure, uttered grunts of delight, and imitated all their movements with careless gestures, crying out constantly:

" 'Strike, strike hard!'

"One fell down unconscious and had to be carried out of the arena, covered with blood, while the rajah uttered a sigh of regret because it was over so soon.

"He turned to me to know my opinion; I was disgusted, but I congratulated

him loudly. He then gave orders that I was to be conducted to Kuch-Mahal (the palace of pleasure), where I was to be lodged.

"This *bijou* palace was situated at the extremity of the royal park, and one of its walls was built into the sacred lake of Vihara. It was square, with three rows of galleries with colonnades of most beautiful workmanship. At each angle there were light, lofty, or low towers, standing either singly or in pairs; no two were alike, and they looked like flowers growing out of that graceful plant of Oriental architecture. All were surmounted by fantastic roofs, like coquettish ladies' caps.

"In the middle of the edifice a large dome raised its round cupola, like a woman's bosom, beside a beautiful clock-tower.

"The whole building was covered with sculpture from top to bottom, with exquisite arabesques which delighted the eye, motionless processions of delicate figures whose attitudes and gestures in stone told the story of Indian manners and customs.

"The rooms were lighted by windows with dentelated arches, looking on to the gardens. On the marble floor were designs of graceful bouquets in onyx, lapis-lazuli, and agate.

"I had scarcely had time to finish my toilette when Haribada, a court dignitary who was specially charged to communicate between the prince and me, announced his sovereign's visit.

"The saffron-colored rajah appeared, again shook hands with me, and began to tell me a thousand different things, constantly asking me for my opinion, which I had great difficulty in giving him.

Then he wished to show me the ruins of the former palace at the other extremity of the gardens.

"It was a real forest of stones inhabited by a large tribe of apes. On our approach the males began to run along the walls, making the most hideous faces at us, while the females ran away, carrying off their young in their arms. The rajah shouted with laughter and pinched my arm to draw my attention, and to testify his own delight, and sat down in the midst of the ruins, while around us, squatting on the top of the walls, perching on every eminence, a number of animals with white whiskers put out their tongues and shook their fists at us.

"When he had seen enough of this, the yellow rajah rose and began to walk sedately on, keeping me always at his side, happy at having shown me such things on the very day of my arrival, and reminding me that a grand tiger-hunt was to take place the next day, in my honor.

"I was present at it, at a second, a third, at ten, twenty in succession. We hunted all the animals which the country produces in turn; the panther, the bear, elephant, antelope, and the crocodile—half the beasts in creation I should say. I was disgusted at seeing so much blood flow, and tired of this monotonous pleasure.

"At length the prince's ardor abated and, at my urgent request, he left me a little leisure for work, contenting himself by loading me with costly presents. He sent me jewels, magnificent stuffs, and well-broken animals of all sorts, which Haribada presented to me with apparently as grave respect as if I had been the sun himself, although he heartily despised me at the bottom of his heart.

"Every day a procession of servants brought me, in covered dishes, a portion of each course that was served at the royal table. Every day he seemed to take an extreme pleasure in getting up some new entertainment for me—dances by the bayaderes, jugglers, reviews of the troops, and I was obliged to pretend to be most delighted with it, so as not to hurt his feelings when he wished to show me his wonderful country in all its charm and all its splendor.

"As soon as I was left alone for a few moments I either worked or went to see the monkeys, whose company pleased me a great deal better than that of their royal master.

"One evening, however, on coming back from a walk, I found Haribada outside the gate of my palace. He told me in mysterious tones that a gift from the king was waiting for me in my abode, and he said that his master begged me to excuse him for not having sooner thought of offering me that of which I had been deprived for such a long time.

"After these obscure remarks the ambassador bowed and withdrew.

"When I went in I saw six little girls standing against the wall, motionless, side-by-side, like smelts on a skewer. The eldest was perhaps ten and the youngest eight years old. For the first moment I could not understand why this girls' school had taken up its abode in my rooms; then, however, I divined the prince's delicate attention: he had made me a present of a harem, and had chosen it very young from an excess of generosity. There, the more unripe the fruit is, in the higher estimation it is held.

"For some time I remained confused, embarrassed, and ashamed in the presence of these children, who looked at me with great grave eyes which seemed already to divine what I might want of them.

"I did not know what to say to them; I felt inclined to send them back; but I could not return the presents of a prince; it would have been a mortal insult. I was obliged, therefore, to install this troop of children in my palace.

"They stood motionless, looking at me, waiting for my orders, trying to read my thoughts in my eyes. Confound such a present! How absurdly it was in my way. At last, thinking that I must be looking rather ridiculous, I asked the eldest her name.

" 'Châli,' she replied.

"This little creature, with her beautiful skin, which was slightly yellow, like old ivory, was a marvel, a perfect statue, with her face and its long and severe lines.

"I then asked, in order to see what she would reply, and also, perhaps, to embarrass her:

" 'What have you come here for?'

"She replied in her soft, harmonious voice: 'I have come to be altogether at my lord's disposal, and to do whatever he wishes.' She was evidently quite resigned.

"I put the same question to the youngest, who answered immediately in her shrill voice:

" 'I am here to do whatever you ask me, my master.'

"This one was like a little mouse, and was very taking, just as they all were,

so I took her in my arms and kissed her. The others made a movement to go away, thinking, no doubt, that I had made my choice; but I ordered them to stay, and sitting down in the Indian fashion, I made them all sit round me and began to tell them fairy-tales, for I spoke their language tolerably well.

"They listened very attentively, and trembled, wringing their hands in agony. Poor little things, they were not thinking any longer of the reason why they were sent to me.

"When I had finished my story, I called Latchmân, my confidential servant, and made him bring sweetmeats and cakes, of which they ate enough to make themselves ill. Then, as I began to find the adventure rather funny, I organized games to amuse my wives.

"One of these diversions had an enormous success. I made a bridge of my legs and the six children ran underneath, the smallest beginning and the tallest always knocking against them a little, because she did not stoop enough. It made them shout with laughter, and these young voices sounding through the low vaults of my sumptuous palace seemed to wake it up and to people it with childlike gaiety and life.

"Next I took great interest in seeing to the sleeping apartments of my innocent concubines, and in the end I saw them safely locked up under the surveillance of four female servants, whom the prince had sent me at the same time in order to take care of my sultanas.

"For a week I took the greatest pleasure in acting the part of a father toward these living dolls. We had capital games of hide-and-seek and puss-in-the-corner, which gave them the greatest pleasure. Every day I taught them a new game, to their intense delight.

"My house now seemed to be one large nursery, and my little friends, dressed in beautiful silk stuffs, and in materials embroidered with gold and silver, ran up and down the long galleries and the quiet rooms like little human animals.

"Chăli was an adorable little creature, timid and gentle, who soon got to love me ardently, with some degree of shame, with hesitation as if afraid of European morality, with reserve and scruples, and yet with passionate tenderness. I cherished her as if I had been her father.

"The others continued to play in the palace like a lot of happy kittens, but Chăli never left me except when I went to the prince.

"We passed delicious hours together in the ruins of the old castle, among the monkeys, who had become our friends.

"She used to lie on my knees, and remain there, turning all sorts of things over in her little sphinx's head, or perhaps not thinking of anything, retaining that beautiful, charming, hereditary pose of that noble and dreamy people, the hieratic pose of the sacred statues.

"In a large brass dish I had one day brought provisions, cakes, fruits. The apes came nearer and nearer, followed by their young ones, who were more timid; at last they sat down round us in a circle, without daring to come any nearer, waiting for me to distribute my delicacies. Then, almost invariably, a male more daring than the rest would come to me with outstretched hand, like a beggar, and I would give him something, which he would take to his wife. All the others immediately began to utter furious cries, cries of rage and jealousy; and I could not make the terrible racket cease except by throwing each one his share.

"As I was very comfortable in the ruins I had my instruments brought there, so that I might be able to work. As soon, however, as they saw the copper fittings on my scientific instruments, the monkeys, no doubt taking them for some deadly engines, fled on all sides, uttering the most piercing cries.

"I often spent my evenings with Chăli on one of the external galleries that looked on to the lake of Vihara. One night in silence we looked at the bright moon gliding over the sky, throwing a mantle of trembling silver over the water, and, on the further shore, upon the row of small pagodas like carved mushrooms with their stalks in the water. Taking the thoughtful head of my little mistress between my hands, I printed a long, soft kiss on her polished brow, on her great eyes, which were full of the secret of that ancient and fabulous land, and on her calm lips which opened to my caress. I felt a confused, powerful above all a poetical, sensation, the sensation that I possessed a whole race in this little girl, that mysterious race from which all the others seem to have taken their origin.

"The prince, however, continued to load me with presents. One day he sent me a very unexpected object, which excited a passionate admiration in Chăli. It was merely one of those cardboard boxes covered with shells stuck on outside, which can be bought at any European seaside resort for a penny or two. But there it was a jewel beyond price, and no doubt was the first that had found its way into the kingdom. I put it on a table and left it there, wondering at the value which was set upon this trumpery article out of a bazaar.

"But Châli never got tired of looking at it, of admiring it ecstatically. From time to time she would say to me, 'May I touch it?' And when I had given her permission she raised the lid, closed it again with the greatest precaution, touched the shells very gently, and the contact seemed to give her real physical pleasure.

"However, I had finished my scientific work, and it was time for me to return. I was a long time in making up my mind, kept back by my tenderness for my little friend, but at last I was obliged to fix the day of my departure.

"The prince got up fresh hunting excursions and fresh wrestling matches, and after a fortnight of these pleasures I declared that I could stay no longer, and he gave me my liberty.

"My farewell from Châli was heartrending. She wept, lying beside me, with her head on my breast, shaken with sobs. I did not know how to console her; my kisses were no good.

"All at once an idea struck me, and getting up I went and got the shell-box, and putting it into her hands, I said, 'That is for you; it is yours.'

"Then I saw her smile at first. Her whole face was lighted up with internal joy, with that profound joy which comes when impossible dreams are suddenly realized, and she embraced me ardently.

"All the same, she wept bitterly when I bade her a last farewell.

"I gave paternal kisses and cakes to all the rest of my wives, and then I left for home.

II.

"Two years had passed when my duties again called me to Bombay, and because I knew the country and the language well, I was left there to undertake another mission.

"I finished what I had to do as quickly as possible, and as I had a considerable amount of spare time on my hands I determined to go and see my friend Rajah Maddan and my dear little Châli once more, though I expected to find her much changed.

"The rajah received me with every demonstration of pleasure, and hardly left me for a moment during the first day of my visit. At night, however, when I was alone, I sent for Haribadà, and after several misleading questions I said to him:

"Do you know what has become of little Châli, whom the rajah gave me?'

"He immediately assumed a sad and troubled look, and said, in evident embarrassment:

" 'We had better not speak of her.'

" 'Why? She was a dear little woman.'

" 'She turned out badly, sir.'

" 'What — Châli? What has become of her? Where is she?'

" 'I mean to say that she came to a bad end.'

" 'A bad end! Is she dead?'

" 'Yes. She committed a very dreadful action.'

"I was very much distressed. I felt my heart beat; my breast was oppressed with grief and I insisted on knowing what she had done and what had happened to her.

"The man became more and more embarrassed, and murmured: 'You had better not ask about it.'

" 'But I want to know.'

" 'She stole—'

" 'Who—Châli? What did she steal?'

" 'Something that belonged to you.'

" 'To me? What do you mean?'

" 'The day you left she stole that little box which the prince had given you; it was found in her hands.'

" 'What box are you talking about?'

" 'The box covered with shells.'

" 'But I gave it to her.'

"The Hindoo looked at me with stupefaction, and then replied: 'Well, she declared with the most sacred oaths that you had given it to her, but nobody could believe that you could have given a king's present to a slave, and so the rajah had her punished.'

" 'How was she punished? What was done to her?'

" 'She was tied up in a sack and thrown into the lake from this window, from the window of the room in which we are, where she had committed the theft.'

"I felt the most terrible grief that I ever experienced, and made a sign to Haribada to go away so that he might not see my tears. I spent the night on the gallery which looked on to the lake, on the gallery where I had so often held the poor child on my knees, and pictured to myself her pretty little body lying decomposed in a sack in the dark waters beneath me.

"The next day I left again, in spite of the rajah's entreaties and evident vexation; and I now still feel as if I had never loved any woman but Châli."

Jeroboam

ANYONE who said, or even insinuated, that the Reverend William Greenfield, vicar of St. Sampson's, Tottenham, did not make his wife Anna perfectly happy, would certainly have been very malicious. In their twelve years of married life he had honored her with twelve children, and could anybody ask more of a saintly man?

Saintly even to heroism, in truth! For his wife Anna, who was endowed with invaluable virtues, which made her a model among wives and a paragon among mothers, had not been equally endowed physically. In one word, she was hideous. Her hair, which though thin was coarse, was the color of the national half-and-half, but of thick half-and-half which looked as if it had been already swallowed several times. Her complexion, which was muddy and pimply, looked as if it were covered with sand mixed with brick-dust. Her teeth, which were long and protruding seemed to start out of their sockets in order to escape from that almost lipless mouth whose sulphurous breath had turned them yellow. Evidently Anna suffered from bile.

Her china-blue eyes looked different ways, one very much to the right and the other very much to the left, with a frightened squint; no doubt in order that they might not see her nose, of which they felt ashamed. They were quite right! Thin, soft, long, pendent, sallow, and ending in a violet knob, it irresistibly reminded those who saw it of something both ludicrous and indescribable. Her body, through the inconceivable irony of nature, was at the same time thin and flabby, wooden and chubby, without either the elegance of slimness or the rounded curves of stoutness. It might have been taken for a body which had formerly been fat, but which had now grown thin, while the covering had remained stretched on the framework.

She was evidently nothing but skin and bone, but had too much bone and too little skin.

It will be seen that the reverend gentleman had done his duty, his whole duty, in fact more than his duty, in sacrificing a dozen times on this altar. Yes, a dozen times bravely and loyally! His wife could not deny it, or dispute the number, because the children were there to prove it. A dozen times, and not one less!

And, alas! not once more. This was the reason why, in spite of appearances, Mrs. Anna Greenfield ventured to think, in the depths of her heart, that the Reverend William Greenfield, vicar of St. Sampson's, Tottenham, had not made her perfectly happy. She thought so all the more as, for four years now, she had been obliged to renounce all hope of that annual sacrifice, which had been so easy and so regular formerly, but which had now fallen into disuse. In fact, at the birth of her twelfth child, the reverend gentleman had expressly said to her:

"God has greatly blessed our union, my dear Anna. We have reached the sacred number of the Twelve Tribes of Israel. Were we now to persevere in the works of the flesh it would be mere debauchery, and I cannot suppose that you would wish me to end my exemplary life in lustful practices."

His wife blushed and looked down, and the holy man, with that legitimate pride of virtue which is its own reward, audibly thanked Heaven that he was "not as other men are."

A model among wives and a paragon of mothers, Anna lived with him for four years on those terms, without complaining to anyone. She contented herself by praying fervently to God that He would inspire her husband with the desire to begin a second series of the Twelve Tribes. At times even, in order to make her prayers more efficacious, she tried to compass that end by culinary means. She spared no pains, and gorged the reverend gentleman with highly seasoned dishes—hare soup, oxtails stewed in sherry, the green fat in turtle soup, stewed mushrooms, Jerusalem artichokes, celery, and horseradish; hot sauces, truffles, hashes with wine and cayenne pepper in them, curried lobsters, pies made of cocks' combs, oysters, and the soft roe of fish. These dishes were washed down by strong beer and generous wines, Scotch ale, Burgundy, dry champagne, brandy, whisky, and gin—in a word, by that numberless array of alcholic drinks with which the English people love to heat their blood.

As a matter of fact, the reverend gentleman's blood became very heated, as was shown by his nose and cheeks.

But in spite of this, the powers above were inexorable, and he remained quite indifferent as regards his wife, who was unhappy and thoughtful at the sight of that protruding nasal appendage, which, alas! was alone in its glory.

She became thinner, and, at the same time, flabbier than ever. She almost began to lose her trust in God, when, suddenly, she had an inspiration: was it not, perhaps, the work of the devil?

She did not care to inquire too closely into the matter, as she thought it a very good idea. It was this:

"Go to the Universal Exhibition in Paris, and there, perhaps, you will discover how to make yourself loved."

Decidedly luck favored her, for her husband immediately gave her permission to go. As soon as she got into the Esplanade des Invalides she saw the Algerian dancers and said to herself:

"Surely this would inspire William with the desire to be the father of the thirteenth tribe!"

But how could she manage to get him to be present at such abominable orgies? For she could not hide from herself that it was an abominable exhibition, and she knew how scandalized he would be at their voluptuous movements. She had no doubt that the devil had led her there, but she could not take her eyes off the scene, and it gave her an idea. So for nearly a fortnight you might have seen the poor, unattractive woman sitting and attentively and curiously watching the swaying hips of the Algerian women. She was learning.

The evening of her return to London she rushed into her husband's bedroom, disrobed herself in an instant, retaining only a thin gauze covering, and for the first time in her life appeared before him in all the ugliness of semi-nudity.

"Come, come," the saintly man stammered out, "are you—are you mad, Anna! What demon possesses you? Why inflict the disgrace of such a spectacle on me?"

But she did not listen to him, did not reply, and suddenly began to sway her hips about like an *almah*.* The reverend gentleman could not believe his eyes; in his stupefaction, he did not think of covering them with his hands or even of shutting them. He looked at her stupefied and dumfounded, a prey to the hypnotism of ugliness. He watched her as she advanced and retired, as she swayed and skipped and wriggled and postured in extraordinary attitudes. For a long time he sat motionless and almost unable to speak. He only said in a low voice:

"Oh, Lord! To think that twelve times—twelve times—a whole dozen!"

Then she fell into a chair, panting and worn out, and saying to herself:

"Thank Heaven! William looks as he used to do formerly on the days that he honored me. Thank Heaven! There will be a thirteenth tribe, and then a fresh series of tribes, for William is very methodical in all that he does!"

But William merely took a blanket off the bed and threw it over her, saying in a voice of thunder:

"Your name is no longer Anna, Mrs. Greenfield; for the future you shall be called Jezebel. I only regret that I have twelve times mingled my blood with your impure blood." And then, seized by pity, he added: "If you were

*Egyptian dancing girl.—(TRANSLATOR.)

only in a state of inebriety, of intoxication, I could excuse you."

"Oh, William!" she exclaimed, repentantly, "I am in that state. Forgive me, William—forgive a poor drunken woman!"

"I will forgive you, Anna," he replied, and he pointed to a wash-basin, saying: "Cold water will do you good, and when your head is clear, remember the lesson which you must learn from this occurrence."

"What lesson?" she asked, humbly.

"That people ought never to depart from their usual habits."

"But why, then, William," she asked, timidly, "have you changed your habits?"

"Hold your tongue!" he cried, "hold your tongue, Jezebel! Have you not got over your intoxication yet? For twelve years I certainly followed the divine precept: 'increase and multiply,' once a year. But since then, I have grown accustomed to something else, and I do not wish to alter my habits."

And the Reverend William Greenfield vicar of St. Sampson's, Tottenham, the saintly man whose blood was inflamed by heating food and liquor, whose ears were like full-blown poppies, and who had a nose like a tomato, left his wife and, as had been his habit for four years, went to make love to Polly, the servant.

"Now, Polly," he said, "you are a clever girl, and I mean, through you, to teach Mrs. Greenfield a lesson she will never forget. I will try and see what I can do for you."

And to accomplish this, he took her to Mrs. Greenfield, called the latter his little Jezebel, and said to her, with an unctuous smile:

"Call me Jeroboam! You don't understand why? Neither do I, but that does not matter. Take off all your things, Polly, and show yourself to Mrs. Greenfield."

The servant did as she was bidden, and the result was that Mrs. Greenfield never again hinted to her husband the desirability of laying the foundations of a thirteenth tribe.

Virtue in the Ballet

IT is a strange feeling of pleasure that the writer about the stage and about theatrical characters in general feels when he occasionally discovers a good, honest human heart in the twilight behind the scenes. Of all the witches and semi-witches of that eternal Walpurgis Night, whose boards represent the world, the ladies of the ballet have at all times and in all places been regarded as least like saints, although Hacklän-

der repeatedly tried in vain, in his earlier novels, to convince us that true virtue appears in tights and short petticoats, and is only to be found in ballet girls. I fear that the popular voice is right as a general rule, but it is equally true that here and there one finds a pearl in the dust, and even in the dirt. The short story that I am about to tell will best justify my assertion.

Whenever a new, youthful dancer

appeared at the Vienna Opera House, the *habitués* began to go after her, and did not rest until the fresh young rose had been plucked by some hand or other though often it was old and trembling. For how could those young and pretty, sometimes even beautiful, girls—with every right to life, love, and pleasure, but poor and on a very small salary—resist the seduction of the smell of flowers and of the flash of diamonds? And if one resisted it, it was love, some real, strong passion, that gave her the strength; generally, however, only to go after luxury all the more shamelessly and selfishly, when her lover forsook her.

At the beginning of the winter season of 185— the pleasing news was spread among the *habitués,* that a girl of dazzling beauty was going to appear very shortly in the ballet at the Court Theater. When the evening came, nobody had yet seen the much discussed phenomenon, but report spread her name from mouth to mouth: it was Satanella. The moment the troop of elastic figures in fluttering petticoats jumped on to the stage, every opera-glass in the boxes and stalls was directed on the stage, and at the same instant the new dancer was discovered, although she timidly kept in the background.

She was one of those girls who seem crowned with the bright halo of virginity, but at the same time present a splendid type of womanhood. She had the voluptuous form of Ruben's second wife, whom they called, not untruly, a reincarnated Helen, and her head with its delicate nose, its small, full mouth, and its dark, enquiring eyes reminded people of the celebrated picture of the Flemish Venus in the Belvedere in Vienna.

She took the old guard of the Vienna Court Theater by storm, and the very next morning a perfect shower of *billets-doux,* jewels, and bouquets fell into the poor ballet-girl's attic. For a moment she was dazzled by all this splendor, and looked at the gold bracelets, the brooches set with rubies and emeralds, and at the sparkling earrings, with flushed cheeks. Then an unspeakable terror of being lost and of sinking into degradation seized her, and she pushed the jewels away and was about to send them back. But as is usual in such cases, her mother intervened in favor of the generous gentlemen, and so the jewels were accepted, but the notes which accompanied them were not answered. A second and a third discharge of Cupid's artillery followed without making any impression on that virtuous girl; in consequence a great number of her admirers grew quiet, though some continued to send her presents and to assail her with love letters. One had the courage to go still further.

He was a wealthy banker who had called on the mother of Henrietta, as we will call the fair-haired ballet-girl, and then one evening, quite unexpectedly, on the girl herself. He by no means met with the reception which he had expected from the pretty girl in the faded, cotton gown. Henrietta treated him with a certain amount of good-humored respect, which had a much more unpleasant effect on him than that coldness and prudery which is often coexistent with coquetry and selfish speculation among a certain class of women. In spite of everything, however, he soon went to see her daily, and lavished his wealth on the beautiful dancer, without request on her part and gave her no chance of refusing, for he relied on the mother for everything. The mother took pretty, small apartments for her daughter and herself in the Kärntner-strasse and furnished them elegantly, hired a cook and housemaid, made an arrangement with a fly-driver, and lastly clothed her daughter's lovely lines in silk, velvet, and valuable lace.

Henrietta persistently held her tongue at all this; only once she said to her mother, in the presence of the Stock Exchange Jupiter:

"Have you won a prize in the lottery?"

"Of course, I have," her mother replied with a laugh.

The girl, however, had given away her heart long before, and, contrary to all precedent, to a man of whose very name she was ignorant, who sent her no diamonds, and not even flowers. But he was young and good-looking, and stood, so retiringly and so evidently in love, at the small side door of the Opera House every night, when she got out of her antediluvian and rickety fly, and also when she got into it again after the performance, that she could not help noticing him. Soon, he began to follow her wherever she went, and once he summoned up courage to speak to her, when she had been to see a friend in a remote suburb. He was very nervous, but she thought all that he said very clear and logical, and she did not hesitate for a moment to confess that she returned his love.

"You have made me the happiest, and at the same time, the most wretched of men," he said after a pause.

"What do you mean?" she said innocently.

"Do you not belong to another man?" he asked her in a sad voice.

She shook her abundant, light curls.

"Up till now I have belonged to myself alone, and I will prove it to you, by requesting you to call upon me frequently and without restraint. Everyone shall know that we are lovers. I am not ashamed of belonging to an honorable man, but I will not sell myself."

"But your splendid apartments, and your dresses," her lover interposed shyly; "you cannot pay for them out of your salary."

"My mother has won a large prize in the lottery, or made a hit on the Stock Exchange." And with these words, the determined girl cut short all further explanations.

That same evening the young man paid his first visit, to the horror of the girl's mother, who was so devoted to the Stock Exchange, and he came again the next day, and nearly every day. Her mother's reproaches were of no more avail than Jupiter's furious looks, and when the latter one day asked for an explanation as to certain visits, the girl said proudly:

"That is very soon explained. He loves me as I love him, and I presume you can guess the rest."

And he certainly did guess the rest and disappeared, and with him the shower of gold ceased.

The mother cried and the daughter laughed. "I never gave the wornout old rake any hopes, and what does it matter to me what bargain you made with him? I always thought that you had been lucky on the Stock Exchange. Now, however, we must seriously consider about giving up our apartments, and make up our minds to live as we did before."

"Are you really capable of making such a sacrifice for me, to renounce luxury and to have my poverty?" her lover said.

"Certainly I am! Is not that a matter of course when one loves?" the ballet-girl replied in surprise.

"Then let me inform you, my dear Henrietta," he said, "that I am not so poor as you think; I only wished to find out whether I could make myself loved for my own sake, and I have done so. I am Count L——, and though I am a minor and dependent on my parents, yet I have enough to be able to retain your pretty rooms for you, and to offer you, if not a luxurious, at any rate a comfortable existence."

On hearing this the mother dried her tears immediately. Count L—— became the girl's acknowledged lover, and they passed the happiest hours together. Unselfish as the girl was, she was yet such a thoroughly ingenuous Viennese, that, whenever she saw anything that took her fancy, whether it was a dress, a cloak, or one of those pretty little ornaments for a side table, she used to express her admiration in such terms as forced her lover to make her a present of the object in question. In this way Count L—— incurred enormous debts, which his father paid repeatedly; at last, however, he inquired into the cause of all this extravagance, and when he discovered it he gave his son the choice

of giving up his connection with the dancer, or of relinquishing all claims on the paternal money box.

It was a sorrowful evening, when Count L—— told his mistress of his father's determination.

"If I do not give you up I shall be able to do nothing for you," he said at last, "and I shall not even know how I should manage to live myself, for my father is just the man to allow me to want, if I defy him. That, however, is a very secondary consideration; but as a man of honor, I cannot bind you, who have every right to luxury and enjoyment, to myself, from the moment when I cannot even keep you from want, and so I must set you at liberty."

"But I will not give you up," Henrietta said proudly.

The young Count shook his head sadly.

"Do you love me?" the ballet-girl said quickly.

"More than my life."

"Then we will not separate, as long as I have anything," she continued.

And she would not give up her connection with him, and when his father actually turned Count L—— into the street, she took her lover into her own lodgings. He obtained a situation as a copying clerk in a lawyer's office, and she sold her valuable dresses and jewels. Thus they lived for more than a year.

The young man's father did not appear to trouble his head about them, but nevertheless he knew everything that went on in their small home, and knew every article that the ballet-girl sold. At last, softened by such love and strength of character, he himself made the first advances to a reconciliation with his son.

At the present time Henrietta wears the diamonds which formerly belonged to the old Countess, and it is long since she was a ballet-girl. Now she sits by the side of·her husband in a carriage on whose panels their armorial bearings are painted.

———————

The Double Pins

Ah! my dear fellow, what jades women are!"

"What makes you say that?"

"Because they have played me an abominable trick."

"You?"

"Yes, me."

"Women, or a woman?"

"Two women."

"Two women at once?"

"Yes."

"What was the trick?"

The two young men were sitting outside a *café* on the Boulevards, and drinking liqueurs mixed with water, those aperients which look like infusions of all the tints in a box of water-colors. They were nearly the same age: twenty-five to thirty. One was dark and the other fair, and they had the same semi-elegant look of stockjobbers, of men who go to the Stock Exchange, and into drawing-rooms, who are to be seen everywhere, who live everywhere, and love everywhere. The dark one continued.

"I have told you of my connection with that little woman, a tradesman's wife, whom I met on the beach at Dieppe?"

"Yes."

"My dear fellow, you know how it is. I had a mistress in Paris whom I love dearly, an old friend, a good friend, who is virtually a habit, in fact—one I value very much."

"Your habit?"

"Yes, my habit, and hers also. She is married to an excellent man, whom I also value very much, a very cordial fellow and a capital companion! I may say that my life is bound up with that house."

"Well?"

"Well! they could not manage to leave Paris, and I found myself a widower at Dieppe."

"Why did you go to Dieppe?"

"For change of air. One cannot remain on the Boulevards the whole time."

"And then?"

"Then I met the little woman I mentioned to you on the beach there."

"The wife of that head of a public office?"

"Yes, she was dreadfully dull; her husband only came every Sunday, and he is horrible! I understood her perfectly, and we laughed and danced together."

"And the rest?"

"Yes, but that came later. However, we met, and we liked each other. I told her I liked her, and she made me repeat it, so that she might understand it better, and she put no obstacles in my way."

"Did you love her?"

"Yes a little! she is very nice."

"And what about the other?"

"The other was in Paris! Well, for six weeks it was very pleasant, and we returned here on the best of terms. Do you know how to break with a woman, when that woman has not wronged you in any way?"

"Yes, perfectly well."

"How do you manage it?"

"I give her up."

"How do you do it?"

"I do not see her any longer."

"But supposing she comes to you?"

"I am not at home."

"And if she comes again?"

"I say I am not well."

"If she looks after you?"

"I play her some dirty trick."

"And if she puts up with it?"

"I write her husband anonymous letters, so that he may look after her on the days that I expect her."

"That is serious! I cannot resist, and do not know how to bring about a rupture, and so I have a collection of mistresses. There are some whom I do not see more than once a year, others every ten months, others on those days when they want to dine at a restaurant, those whom I have put at regular intervals do not worry me, but I often have great difficulty with the fresh ones, so as to keep them at proper intervals."

"And then?"

"And then—then, this little woman was all fire and flame, without any fault of mine, as I told you! As her husband spends all the whole day at the office, she began to come to me unexpectedly, and

twice she nearly met my regular one on the stairs."

"The devil!"

"Yes; so I gave each of them her days, regular days, to avoid confusion, Saturday and Monday for the old one, Tuesday, Friday, and Sunday for the new one."

"Why did you show her the preference?"

"Ah! My dear friend, she is younger."

"So that only gave you two days to yourself in a week."

"That is enough for one."

"Allow me to compliment you on that."

"Well, just fancy that the most ridiculous and most annoying thing in the world happened to me. For four months everything had been going on perfectly; I felt quite safe, and I was really very happy, when suddenly, last Monday, the crash came.

"I was expecting my regular one at the usual time, a quarter past one, and was smoking a good cigar, dreaming, very well satisfied with myself, when I suddenly saw that it was past the time. I was much surprised for she is very punctual, but I thought that something might have accidentally delayed her. However, half an hour passed, then an hour, an hour and a half, and then I knew that something must have detained her—a sick headache, perhaps, or some annoying visitor. That sort of waiting is very vexatious, very annoying, and enervating. At last I made up my mind to go out, and not knowing what to do, I went to her and found her reading a novel.

" 'Well,' I said to her. And she replied quite calmly.

" 'My dear, I could not come, I was hindered.'

" 'How?'

" 'By something else.'

" 'What was it?'

" 'A very annoying visit.'

"I saw she would not tell me the true reason, and as she was very calm, I did not trouble myself any more about it, hoping to make up for lost time with the other next day. On the Tuesday I was very excited and amorous in expectation of the public official's little wife, and I was surprised that she did not come before the appointed time. I looked at the clock every moment, and watched the hands impatiently, but the quarter passed, then the half hour, then two o'clock. I could not sit still any longer, and walked up and down very soon in great strides, putting my face against the window, and my ears to the door, to listen whether she was not coming upstairs.

"Half past two, three o'clock! I seized my hat, rushed to her house. She was reading a novel, my dear fellow! 'Well!' I said anxiously, and she replied as calmly as usual:

" 'I was hindered, and could not come.'

" 'By what?'

" 'An annoying visit.'

"Of course I immediately thought that they both knew everything, but she seemed so calm and quiet that I set aside my suspicions, and thought it was only some strange coincidence, as I could not believe in such dissimulation on her part. And so, after half-an-hour's friendly talk, which was, however, interrupted a dozen times by her little girl coming in and out of the room, I

went away very much annoyed. Just imagine the next day."

"The same thing happened?"

"Yes, and the next also. And that went on for three weeks without any explanation, without anything explaining such strange conduct to me, the secret of which I suspected, however."

"They knew everything?"

"I should think so, by George. But how? Ah! I had a great deal of anxiety before I found it out."

"How did you manage it at last?"

"From their letters, for on the same day they both gave me their dismissal in identical terms."

"Well?"

"This is how it was: You know that women always have an array of pins about them. I know hairpins, I doubt them, and look after them, but the others are much more treacherous, those confounded little black-headed pins which look all alike to us, great fools that we are, but which they can distinguish, just as we can distinguish a horse from a dog.

"Well, it appears that one day my official's little wife left one of those telltale instruments pinned to the paper, close to my looking-glass. My usual one had immediately seen this little black speck, no bigger than a flea, had taken it out without saying a word and had left one of her pins, which was also black, but of a different pattern, in the same place.

"The next day, the official's wife wished to recover her property, and immediately recognized the substitution. Then her suspicions were aroused, and she put in two and crossed them. My original one replied to this telegraphic signal by three black pellets, one on the top of the other, and as soon as this method had begun, they continued to communicate with one another, without saying a word, just to spy on each other. Then it appears that the regular one, being bolder, wrapped a tiny piece of paper round the little wire point, and wrote upon it:

"'C. D., Poste Restante, Boulevard Malherbes.'

"Then they wrote to each other. You understand that was not everything that passed between them. They set to work with precaution, with a thousand stratagems, with all the prudence that is necessary in such cases, but the regular one made a bold stroke, and made an appointment with the other. I do not know what they said to each other, all that I know is that I had to pay the costs of their interview. There you have it all!"

"Is that all?"

"Yes."

"And you do not see them any more?"

"I beg your pardon, I see them as friends, for we have not quarreled altogether."

"And have they met again?"

"Yes, my dear fellow, they have become intimate friends."

"And has not that given you an idea?"

"No, what idea?"

"You great booby! The idea of making them put back the pins where they found them."

How He Got the Legion of Honor

SOME people are born with a predominant instinct, with some vocation or some desire which demands recognition as soon as they begin to speak or to think.

Ever since he was a child Monsieur Caillard had only had one idea in his head—to be decorated. When he was still quite a small boy he used to wear a zinc Cross of the Legion of Honor in his tunic, just like other children wear a soldier's cap, and he took his mother's hand in the street with a proud look, sticking out his little chest with its red ribbon and metal star so that it might show to advantage.

His studies were not a success, and he failed in his examination for Bachelor of Arts; so, not knowing what to do, he married a pretty girl, for he had plenty of money of his own.

They lived in Paris, like many rich middle-class people do, mixing with their own particular set, without going among other people, proud of knowing a Deputy, who might perhaps be a Minister some day, while two Chiefs of Division were among their friends.

But Monsieur Caillard could not get rid of his one absorbing idea, and he felt constantly unhappy because he had not the right to wear a little bit of colored ribbon in his buttonhole.

When he met any men who were

decorated on the Boulevards, he looked at them askance, with intense jealousy. Sometimes, when he had nothing to do in the afternoon, he would count them, and say to himself: "Just let me see how many I shall meet between the Madeleine and the Rue Drouot."

. Then he would walk slowly, looking at every coat, with a practiced eye, for the little bit of red ribbon, and when he had got to the end of his walk he always said the numbers out loud. "Eight officers and seventeen knights. As many as that! It is stupid to sow the Cross broadcast in that fashion. I wonder how many I shall meet going back?"

And he returned slowly, unhappy when the crowd of passers-by interfered with his seeing them.

He knew the places where most of them were to be found. They swarmed in the Palais Royal. Fewer were seen in the Avenue de l'Opera than in the Rue de la Paix, while the right side of the Boulevard was more frequented by them than the left.

They also seemed to prefer certain *cafés* and theaters. Whenever he saw a group of white-haired old gentlemen standing together in the middle of the pavement, interfering with the traffic, he used to say to himself: "They are officers of the Legion of Honor," and he felt inclined to take off his hat to them.

He had often remarked that the officers had a different bearing from mere knights. They carried their heads higher, and you felt that they enjoyed greater official consideration, and a more widely-extended importance.

Somtimes again the worthy man would be seized with a furious hatred for everyone who was decorated; he felt like a Socialist toward them. Then, when he got home, excited at meeting so many Crosses,—just like a poor hungry wretch is on passing some dainty provision-shop,—he used to ask in a loud voice:

"When shall we get rid of this wretched government?" And his wife would be surprised, and ask:

"What is the matter with you to-day?"

"I am indignant," he would reply, "at the injustice I see going on around us. Oh! the Communards were certainly right!"

After dinner he would go out again and look at the shops where all the decorations were sold, and examine all the emblems of various shapes and colors. He would have liked to possess them all, and to have walked gravely at the head of a procession with his crush-hat under his arm and his breast covered with decorations, radiant as a star, amid a buzz of admiring whispers and a hum of respect. But, alas! he had no right to wear any decoration whatever.

He used to say to himself: "It is really too difficult for any man to obtain the Legion of Honor unless he is some public functionary. Suppose I try to get appointed an officer of the Academy!"

But he did not know how to set about it, and spoke to his wife on the subject, who was stupefied.

"Officer of the Academy! What have you done to deserve it?"

He got angry. "I know what I am

talking about; I only want to know how to set about it. You are quite stupid at times."

She smiled. "You are quite right; I don't understand anything about it."

An idea struck him: "Suppose you were to speak to M. Rosselin, the Deputy, he might be able to advise me. You understand I cannot broach the subject to him directly. It is rather difficult and delicate, but coming from you it might seem quite natural."

Mme. Caillard did what he asked her, and M. Rosselin promised to speak to the Minister about it. Then Caillard began to worry him, till the Deputy told him he must make a formal application and put forward his claims.

"What were his claims?" he said. "He was not even a Bachelor of Arts."

However, he set to work and produced a pamphlet, with the title, "The People's Right to Instruction," but he could not finish it for want of ideas.

He sought for easier subjects, and began several in succession. The first was, "The Instruction of Children by Means of the Eye." He wanted gratuitous theaters to be established in every poor quarter of Paris for little children. Their parents were to take them there when they were quite young, and by means of a magic-lantern, all the notions of human knowledge were to be imparted to them. There were to be regular courses. The sight would educate the mind, while the pictures would remain impressed on the brain, and thus science would, so to say, be made visible. What could be more simple than to teach universal history, natural history, geography, botany, zoölogy, anatomy, etc., etc., thus?

He had his ideas printed in tract form, and sent a copy to each Deputy, ten to each Minister, fifty to the President of the Republic, ten to each Parisian, and five to each provincial newspaper.

Then he wrote on "Street Lending-Libraries." His idea was to have little carts full of books drawn about the streets, like orange-carts are. Every householder or lodger would have a right to ten volumes a month by means of a half-penny subscription.

"The people," M. Caillard said, "will only disturb itself for the sake of its pleasures, and since it will not go to instruction, instruction must come to it," etc., etc.

His essays attracted no attention, but he sent in his application, and he got the usual formal official reply. He thought himself sure of success, but nothing came of it.

Then he made up his mind to apply personally. He begged for an interview with the Minister of Public Instruction, and he was received by a young subordinate, already very grave and important, who kept touching the buttons of electric-bells to summon ushers, and footmen, and officials inferior to himself. He declared to M. Caillard that his matter was going on quite favorably, and advised him to continue his remarkable labors. So M. Caillard set at it again.

M. Rosselin, the Deputy, seemed now to take a great interest in his success, and gave him a lot of excellent, practical advice. Rosselin was decorated, although nobody knew exactly what he had done to deserve such a distinction.

He told Caillard what new studies he ought to undertake; he introduced him to learned Societies which took up particularly obscure points of science, in the hope of gaining credit and honors thereby; and he even took him under his wing at the Ministry.

One day, when he came to lunch with his friend (for several months past he had constantly taken his meals there), he said to him in a whisper as he shook hands: "I have just obtained a great favor for you. The Committee on Historical Works is going to intrust you with a commission. There are some researches to be made in various libraries in France."

Caillard was so delighted that he could scarcely eat or drink, and a week later he set out. He went from town to town, studying catalogues, rummaging in lofts full of dusty volumes, and was a bore to all the librarians.

One day, happening to be at Rouen, he thought he should like to embrace his wife, whom he had not seen for more than a week, so he took the nine o'clock train, which would land him at home by twelve at night.

He had his latchkey, so he went in without making any noise, delighted at the idea of the surprise he was going to give her. She had locked herself in. How tiresome! However, he cried out through the door:

"Jeanne, it is I."

She must have been very frightened, for he heard her jump out of bed and speak to herself, as if she were in a dream. Then she went to her dressing-room, opened and closed the door, and

went quickly up and down her room barefoot two or three times, shaking the furniture till the vases and glasses sounded. Then at last she asked:

"Is it you, Alexander?"

"Yes, yes," he replied; "make haste and open the door."

As soon as she had done so she threw herself into his arms, exclaiming:

"Oh! what a fright! What a surprise! What a pleasure!"

He began to undress himself methodically, like he did everything, and from a chair he took his overcoat, which he was in the habit of hanging up in the hall. But, suddenly, he remained motionless, struck dumb with astonishment—there was a red ribbon in the buttonhole!

"Why," he stammered, "this—this—this overcoat has got the rosette in it!"

In a second his wife threw herself on him, and, taking it from his hands, she said:

"No! you have made a mistake—give it to me."

But he still held it by one of the sleeves, without letting it go, repeating, in a half-dazed manner:

"Oh! Why? Just explain. Whose overcoat is it? It is not mine, as it has the Legion of Honor on it."

She tried to take it from him, terrified, and hardly able to say:

"Listen—listen—give it me—I must not tell you—it is a secret—listen to me."

But he grew angry, and turned pale:

"I want to know how this overcoat comes to be here? It does not belong to me."

Then she almost screamed at him:

"Yes it does; listen—swear to me—well—you are decorated."

She did not intend to joke at his expense.

He was so overcome that he let the overcoat fall, and dropped into an armchair.

"I am—you say I am—decorated?"

"Yes, but it is a secret, a great secret."

She had put the glorious garment into a cupboard, and came to her husband pale and trembling.

"Yes," she continued, "it is a new overcoat that I have had made for you. But I swore that I would not tell you anything about it, as it will not be officially announced for a month or six weeks, and you were not to have known till your return from your business journey. M. Rosselin managed it for you."

"Rosselin!" he contrived to utter in his joy; "he has obtained the decoration for me? He— Oh!"

And he was obliged to drink a glass of water.

A little piece of white paper had fallen to the floor out of the pocket of the overcoat. Caillard picked it up; it was a visiting-card, and he read out:

"Rosselin—Deputy."

"You see how it is," said his wife.

He almost cried with joy, and, a week later, it was announced in the "Journal Officiel" that M. Caillard had been awarded the Legion of Honor on account of his exceptional services.

———•———

A Crisis

A BIG fire was burning and the tea-table was set for two. The Count de Sallure threw his hat, gloves, and fur coat on a chair, while the Countess, who had removed her opera-cloak, was smiling amiably at herself in the glass and arranging a few stray curls with her jeweled fingers. Her husband had been looking at her for the past few minutes, as if on the point of saying something, but hesitating; finally he said:

"You have flirted outrageously to-night!" She looked him straight in the eyes, with an expression of triumph and defiance on her face.

"Why, certainly," she answered. She sat down, poured out the tea and her husband took his seat opposite her.

"It made me look quite—ridiculous!"

"Is this a scene?" she asked, arching her brows. "Do you mean to criticise my conduct?"

"Oh, no, I only meant to say that M. Burel's attentions to you were positively improper and if I had the right—I—would not tolerate it."

"Why, my dear boy, what has come over you? You must have changed your views since last year. You did not seem to mind who courted me and who did not a year ago. When I found out that you had a mistress, a mistress whom you loved passionately, I pointed out to you then, as you did me to-night (but I had good reasons), that you were compromising yourself and Mme. de Servy, that your conduct grieved me, and made me look ridiculous, what did you answer me? That I was perfectly free, that marriage between two intelligent people was simply a partnership, a sort of social bond, but not a moral bond. Is it not true? You gave me to understand that your mistress was far more captivating than I, that she was more womanly; that is what you said: 'more womanly.' Of course, you said all this in a very nice way and I acknowledge that you did your very best to spare my feelings, for which I am very grateful to you, I assure you; but I understand perfectly what you meant.

"We then decided to live practically separated; that is, under the same roof, but apart from each other. We had a child, and it was necessary to keep up appearances before the world, but you intimated that if I chose to take a lover you would not object in the least, providing it was kept secret. You even made a long and very interesting discourse on the cleverness of women in such cases; how well they could manage such things, etc., etc. I understood perfectly, my dear boy. You loved Mme. de Servy very much at that time and my conjugal—legal—affection was an impediment to your happiness; but since then, we have lived on the very best of terms. We go out in society together, it is true, but here in our own house we are complete strangers. Now, for the past month or two, you act as if you were jealous, and I do not understand it."

"I am not jealous, my dear, but you are so young, so impulsive, that I am afraid you will expose yourself to the world's criticisms."

"You make me laugh! Your conduct would not bear a very close scrutiny. You had better not preach what you do not practice."

"Do not laugh, I pray. This is no laughing matter. I am speaking as a friend, a true friend. As to your remarks, they are very much exaggerated."

"Not at all. When you confessed to me your infatuation for Mme. de Servy, I took it for granted that you authorized me to imitate you. I have not done so—"

"Allow me to—"

"Do not interrupt me. I have not done so. I have no lover—as yet. I am looking for one, but I have not found one to suit me. He must be very nice—nicer than you are—that is a compliment, but you do not seem to appreciate it."

"This joking is entirely uncalled for."

"I am not joking at all; I am in dead earnest. I have not forgotten a single word of what you said to me a year ago and when it pleases me to do so, no matter what you may say or do, I shall take a lover. I shall do it without your even suspecting it—you will be none the wiser—like a great many others."

"How can you say such things!"

"How can I say such things? But, my dear boy, you were the first one to laugh when Mme. de Gers joked about poor, unsuspecting M. de Servy."

"That might be, but it is not becoming language for you."

"Indeed! You thought it a good joke when it concerned M. de Servy, but you do not find it so appropriate when it concerns you. What a queer lot men are! However, I am not fond of talking about such things; I simply mentioned it to see if you were ready."

"Ready—for what?"

"Ready to be deceived. When a man gets angry on hearing such things he is not quite ready. I wager that in two months you will be the first one to laugh if I mention a deceived husband to you. It is generally the case when you are the deceived one."

"Upon my word you are positively rude to-night; I have never seen you that way."

"Yes—I have changed—for the worse, but it is your fault."

"Come, my dear, let us talk seriously. I beg of you, I implore you not to let M. Burel court you as he did to-night."

"You are jealous; I knew it."

"No, no; but I do not wish to be looked upon with ridicule, and if I catch that man devouring you with his eyes, like he did to-night—I—I will thrash him!"

"Could it be possible that you are in love with me?"

"Why not? I am sure I could do much worse."

"Thanks. I am sorry for you—because I do not love you any more."

The Count gets up, walks around the tea-table, and going behind his wife, he kisses her quickly on the neck. She springs up and with flashing eyes says:

"How dare you do that? Remember, we are absolutely nothing to each other; we are complete strangers."

"Please do not get angry, I could not help it; you look so lovely to-night."

"Then I must have improved wonderfully."

"You look positively charming; your arms and shoulders are beautiful and your skin—"

"Would captivate M. Burel—"

"How mean you are!—but really, I do not recall ever having seen a woman as captivating as you are."

"You must have been fasting lately."

"What's that?"

"I say, you must have been fasting lately."

"Why—what do you mean?"

"I mean just what I say. You must have fasted for some time and now you are famished. A hungry man will eat things which he will not eat at any other time. I am the neglected—dish, which you would not mind eating to-night."

"Marguerite! Who ever taught you to say those things?"

"You did. To my knowledge, you have had four mistresses. Actresses, society women, gay women, etc., so how can I explain your sudden fancy for me, except by your long fast?"

"You will think me rude, brutal, but I have fallen in love with you for the second time. I love you madly!"

"Well, well! Then you—wish to—"

"Exactly."

"To-night?"

"Oh, Marguerite!"

"There, you are scandalized again. My dear boy, let us talk quietly. We are strangers, are we not? I am your wife, it is true, but I am—free. I intended to engage my affection elsewhere, but I will give you the preference; providing—I receive the same compensation."

"I do not understand you; what do you mean?"

"I will speak more clearly. Am I as good-looking as your mistresses?"

"A thousand times better."

"Better than the nicest one?"

"Yes, a thousand times."

"How much did she cost you in three months?"

"Really—what on earth do you mean?"

"I mean, how much did you spend on the costliest of your mistresses, in jewelry, carriages, suppers, etc., in three months?"

"How do I know!"

"You ought to know. Let us say for instance, five thousand francs a month —is that about right?"

"Yes—about that."

"Well, my dear boy, give me five thousand francs and I will be yours for a month, beginning from to-night."

"Marguerite! Are you crazy?"

"No, I am not; but just as you say. Good night!"

The Countess entered her boudoir. A vague perfume permeated the whole room. The Count appeared in the doorway:

"How lovely it smells in here!"

"Do you think so? I always use Peau d'Espagne; I never use any other perfume."

"Really? I did not notice—it is lovely."

"Possibly, but be kind enough to go; I want to go to bed."

"Marguerite!"

"Will you please go?"

The Count came in and sat on a chair. Said the Countess: "You will not go? Very well."

She slowly takes off her waist, revealing her white arms and neck, then she lifts her arms above her head to loosen her hair.

The Count took a step toward her.

The Countess: "Do not come near me or I shall get real angry, do you hear?"

He caught her in his arms and tried to kiss her. She quickly took a tumbler of perfumed water standing on the toilette-table and dashed it into his face.

He was terribly angry. He stepped back a few paces and murmured:

"How stupid of you!"

"Perhaps—but you know my conditions—five thousand francs!"

"Preposterous!"

"Why, pray?"

"Why? Because—who ever heard of a man paying his wife!"

"Oh!—how horribly rude you are!"

"I suppose I am rude, but I repeat, the idea of paying one's wife is preposterous! Positively stupid!"

"Is it not much worse to pay a gay woman? It certainly would be stupid when you have a wife at home."

"That may be, but I do not wish to be ridiculous."

The Countess sat down on the bed and took off her stockings, revealing her bare, pink feet.

The Count approached a little nearer and said tenderly:

"What an odd idea of yours, Marguerite!"

"What idea?"

"To ask me for five thousand francs!"

"Odd? Why should it be odd? Are we not strangers? You say you are in love with me; all well and good. You cannot marry me, as I am already your wife, so you buy me. *Mon dieu!* have you not bought other women? Is it not much better to give me that money than to a strange woman who would squander it? Come, you will acknowledge that it is a novel idea to actually pay your own wife! An intelligent man like you ought to see how amusing it is; besides, a man never really loves anything unless it costs him a lot of money. It would add new zest to our—conjugal love, by comparing it with your—illegitimate love. Am I not right?"

She goes toward the bell.

"Now then, sir, if you do not go I will ring for my maid!"

The Count stands perplexed, displeased, and suddenly, taking a handful of bank-notes out of his pocket, he throws them at his wife saying:

"Here are six thousand, you witch, but remember—"

The Countess picked up the money, counted it, and said:

"What?"

"You must not get used to it."

She burst out laughing and said to him:

"Five thousand francs each month, or else I shall send you back to your actresses, and if you are pleased with me—I shall ask for more."

Graveyard Sirens

THE five friends had finished their dinner; there were two bachelors and three married men, all middle-aged and wealthy. They assembled thus once a month, in memory of old times, and lingered to gossip over their coffee till late at night. Many a happy evening was spent in this way, for they were fond of one another's society, and had remained closely united. Conversation among them was a sort of review of the daily papers, commenting on everything that interests and amuses Parisians. One of the cleverest, Joseph de Bardon, was a bachelor. He lived the life of a boulevardier most thoroughly and fantastically, without being debauched or depraved. It interested him, and as he was still young, being barely forty, he enjoyed it keenly. A man of the world in the broadest and best sense of the

word, he possessed a great deal of wit without much depth, a general knowledge without real learning, quick perception without serious penetration; but his adventures and observations furnished him many amusing stories, which he told with so much philosophy and humor that society voted him very intellectual.

He was a favorite after-dinner speaker, always having some story to relate to which his friends looked forward. Presently he began to tell a story without being asked. Leaning on the table with a half-filled glass of brandy in front of his plate, in the smoky atmosphere filled with the fragrance of coffee, he seemed perfectly at ease, just as some beings are entirely at home in certain places and under certain conditions—as a goldfish in its aquarium, for instance, or a nun in her cloister.

Puffing at his cigar, he said:

"A rather curious thing happened to me a little while ago."

All exclaimed at once: "Tell us about it!"

Presently he continued:

"You all know how I love to roam around the city, like a collector in search of antiquities. I enjoy watching people and things. About the middle of September, the weather being very fine, I went for a walk one afternoon, without a definite purpose. Why do we men always have the vague impulse to call on some pretty woman? We review them in our mind, compare their respective charms, the interest they arouse in us, and finally decide in favor of the one that attracts us most.

"But when the sun shines brightly and the air is balmy, sometimes we altogether lose the desire for calling.

"That day the sun was bright and the air balmy, so I simply lighted a cigar and started for the Boulevard Extérieur. As I was sauntering along, I thought I would take a look around the cemetery at Montmartre. Now, I have always liked cemeteries because they sadden and rest me; and I need that influence at times. Besides, many of my friends are laid to rest there, and I go to see them once in a while.

"As it happens, I once buried a romance in this particular cemetery,—an old love of mine, a charming little woman whose memory awakens all kinds of regrets in me—I often dream beside her grave. All is over for her now!

"I like graveyards because they are such immense, densely populated cities. Just think of all the bodies buried in that small space, of the countless generations of Parisians laid there forever, eternally entombed in the little vaults of their little graves marked by a cross or a stone, while the living—fools that they are!—take up so much room and make such a fuss.

"Cemeteries have some monuments quite as interesting as those to be seen in the museums. Cavaignac's tomb I liken, without comparing it, to that masterpiece of Jean Gonjon, the tombstone of Louis de Brézé in the subterranean chapel in the cathedral of Rouen. My friends, all so-called modern and realistic art originated there. That reproduction of Louis de Brézé is more life-like and terrible, more convulsed with agony, than any one of the statues that decorate modern tombs.

"In Montmartre is Baudin's monument, and it is quite imposing; also the tombs of Gautier and Mürger, where the other day I found a solitary wreath of yellow immortelles, laid there—by whom do you suppose? Perhaps by the last *grisette,* grown old, and possibly become a janitress in the neighborhood! It's a pretty little statue by Millet, but it is ruined by neglect and accumulated filth. Sing of youth, O Mürger!

"Well, I entered the cemetery, filled with a certain sadness, not too poignant, a feeling suggesting such thoughts as this: The place is not very cheerful, but I'm not to be put here yet.

"The impression of autumn, a warm dampness smelling of dead leaves, the pale, anæmic rays of the sun, intensified and poetized the solitude of this place, which reminds one of death and of the end of all things.

"I walked slowly along the alleys of graves where neighbors no longer visit, no longer sleep together, nor read the papers. I began reading the epitaphs. There is nothing more amusing in the world. Labiche and Meilhac have never made me laugh as much as some of these tombstone inscriptions. I tell you these crosses and marble slabs on which the relatives of the dead have poured out their regrets and their wishes for the happiness of the departed, their hopes of reunion—the hypocrites!—make better reading than Balzac's funniest tales! But what I love in Montmartre are the abandoned plots filled with yewtrees and cypress, the resting-place of those departed long ago. However, the green trees nourished by the bodies will soon be felled to make room for those that have recently passed away, whose graves will be there, under little marble slabs.

"After loitering awhile, I felt tired, and decided to pay my faithful tribute to my little friend's memory. When I reached the grave, my heart was very sad. Poor child! she was so sweet and loving, so fair and white—and now—should her grave be reopened—

"Bending over the iron railing I murmured a prayer, which she probably never heard, and I turned to leave, when I caught sight of a woman in deep mourning kneeling beside a neighboring grave. Her crape veil was thrown back, disclosing her blond hair, which seemed illumined under the darkness of her hat. I forgot to leave.

"She seemed bowed with sorrow. She had buried her face in her hands, apparently lost in deep thought. With closed lids, as rigid as a statue, she was living over torturing memories and seemed herself a corpse mourning a corpse. Presently I saw that she was weeping, as there was a convulsive movement of her back and shoulders. Suddenly she uncovered her face. Her eyes, brimming with tears, were charming. For a moment she gazed around as if awakening from a nightmare. She saw me looking at her and quickly hid her face again, greatly abashed. Now, with convulsive sobs she bent her head slowly over the tombstone. She rested her forehead against it, and her veil, falling around her, covered the whiteness of the beloved sepulcher with a dark shroud. I heard her moan and then saw her fall to the ground in a faint.

"I rushed to her side and began slapping her hands and breathing on her temples, while reading this simple inscription on the tombstone:

" 'Here lies Louis-Théodore Carrel, Captain in the Marine Infantry, killed by the enemy in Tonkin. Pray for his soul.'

"This death was quite recent. I was moved almost to tears, and renewed my efforts to revive the poor girl. At last she came to. I am not so very bad-looking, and my face must have shown how upset I was, for her very first glance showed me that she was likely to be grateful for my care. Between sobs she told me of her marriage to the officer who had been killed in Tonkin within a year after their wedding. He had married her for love, she being an orphan and possessing nothing above the required dowry.

"I consoled her, comforted her, and assisted her to her feet, saying:

" 'You must not stay here. Come away.'

" 'I am unable to walk,' she whispered.

" 'Let me help you,' I said.

" 'Thank you, you are very kind,' she murmured. 'Did you also come to mourn some one?'

" 'Yes, Madame.'

" 'A woman?'

" 'Yes, Madame.'

" 'Your wife?'

" 'A friend.'

" 'One may love a friend just as much as a wife, for passion knows no law,' said the lady.

" 'Yes, Madame,' I replied.

"And so we left the spot together, she leaning on me and I almost carrying her through the alleys. As we came out, she murmured:

" 'I'm afraid that I'm going to faint.'

" 'Wouldn't you like to take something, Madame?' I inquired.

" 'Yes,' she said, 'I would.'

"I discovered a restaurant near at hand, where the friends of the dead gather to celebrate the end of their painful duty. We went in, and I made her drink a cup of hot tea, which appeared to give her renewed strength.

"A faint smile dawned on her lips and she began telling me about herself: how terrible it was to go through life all alone, to be alone at home day and night, to have no one on whom to lavish love, confidence, and intimacy.

"It all seemed sincere and sounded well coming from her. I was softened. She was very young, perhaps twenty. I paid her several compliments that appeared to please her, and as it was growing dark I offered to take her home in a cab. She accepted. In the carriage we were so close to each other that we could feel the warmth of our bodies through our clothing, which really is the most intoxicating thing in the world.

"When the cab stopped in front of her home she said:

" 'I hardly feel able to walk upstairs, for I live on the fourth floor. You have already been so kind, that I am going to ask you to assist me to my rooms.'

"I consented gladly. She walked up slowly, breathing heavily at each step. In front of her door she added:

" 'Do come in for a few minutes, so that I can thank you again for your kindness.'

"And I, of course, followed her.

"Her apartment was modest, even a trifle poor, but well-kept and in good taste.

"We sat down side by side on a small divan, and she again began to speak of her loneliness.

"Then she rang for the maid, so as to offer me some refreshments. But the girl failed to appear, and I joyfully concluded that this maid probably came only in the morning, and was a sort of scrub-woman.

"She had taken off her hat. How pretty she was! Her clear eyes looked steadily at me, so clear and so steady that a great temptation came to me, to which I promptly yielded. Clasping her in my arms, I kissed her again and again on her half-closed lids.

"She repelled me, struggling to free herself and repeating:

" 'Do stop—do end it—'

"What did she mean to imply by this word? Under such conditions, to 'end' could have at least two meanings. In order to silence her, I passed from her eyes to her lips, and gave to the word 'end' the conclusion I preferred. She did not resist very much, and as our eyes met after this insult to the memory of the departed captain, I saw that her expression was one of tender resignation, which quickly dispelled my misgivings.

"Then I grew attentive and gallant. After an hour's chat I asked her:

" 'Where do you dine?'

" 'In a small restaurant near by.'

" 'All alone?'

" 'Why, yes.'

" 'Will you take dinner with me?'

" 'Where?' "

" 'In a good restaurant on the Boulevard.'

"She hesitated a little, but at last consented, consoling herself with the argument that she was so desperately lonely, and adding, 'I must put on a lighter gown.'

"She retired to her room, and when she emerged she was dressed in a simple gray frock that made her look exquisitely slender. She apparently had different costumes for street and for cemetery wear!

"Our dinner was most pleasant and cordial. She drank some champagne, thereby becoming very animated and lively, and we returned to her apartment together.

"This *liaison*, begun among tombstones, lasted about three weeks. But man tires of everything and especially of women. So I pleaded an urgent trip and left her. Of course, I managed to be generous, for which she was duly

thankful, making me promise and even swear that I would come back, for she really seemed to care a little for me.

"In the meantime I formed other attachments, and a month or so went by without the memory of this love being vivid enough to bring me back to her. Still, I had not forgotten her. She haunted me like a mystery, a psychological problem, an unsolved question.

"I can't tell why, but one day I imagined that I should find her in the cemetery. So I went back. I walked around a long time without meeting anyone but the usual visitors of the place, mourners who had not broken off all relations with their dead. The grave of the captain killed in Tonkin was deserted, without flowers, or wreaths.

"As I was passing through another part of this great city of Death, I suddenly saw a couple in deep mourning coming toward me through one of the narrow paths hedged with crosses. When they drew near, Oh, surprise! I recognized—her! She saw me and blushed. As I brushed past her, she gave me a little wink that meant clearly: Don't recognize me, and also seemed to say: Do come back.

"The man who accompanied her was about fifty years old, fine-looking and distinguished, an officer of the Legion of Honor. He was leading her just as I had, when we left the cemetery together.

"I was utterly nonplussed, reluctant to believe what my eyes had just seen, and I wondered to what strange tribe of creatures this graveyard huntress belonged. Was she merely a clever courtesan, an inspired prostitute, who haunted cemeteries for men disconsolate at the loss of some woman, a mistress or a wife, and hungering for past caresses? Is it a profession? Are the cemeteries worked like the streets? Are there graveyard sirens? Or had she alone the idea—wonderful for its deep philosophy—to profit by the amorous regrets awakened in these awful places? I would have given a great deal to know whose widow she was that day!"

Growing Old

THE two friends had finished dinner. From the window of the *café* they saw the Boulevard full of people. They felt the warm zephyrs which prevail in Paris on sweet summer nights and make travelers raise their heads and desire to go out, to go down, one knows not where, under the leaves, and dream of rivers lighted by the moon, of glowworms, and of nightingales.

One of them, Henry Simon, sighed profoundly and said:

"Ah! I am getting old. It is sad. Formerly on evenings like this I felt the devil in my body. Now, I feel only regrets. How quickly life goes!"

He was already a little stout and very bald; he was perhaps forty-five years old.

The other, Peter Carnier, was older, but thinner and more lively; he replied:

"As for me, my friend, I have grown old without perceiving it the least in the world. I was always gay, a jolly fellow, vigorous and all the rest. Now, as one looks at himself each day in the mirror, he does not perceive the work that age is accomplishing, because it is slow and regular, and modifies his visage so gradually that the transition is unseen. Only for this we should die of chagrin after but two or three years'

ravages. But we are not able to appreciate them. In order to take a reckoning it would be necessary to go six months without looking at ourselves; and then, what a blow!

"And the women, my dear, how I pity them, the poor beings. All their happiness, all their power, all their life is in their beauty, which lasts but ten years.

"I, then, grew old without suspecting it; I believed myself a young man, although I was nearly fifty years old. Never having felt an infirmity of any sort, I went along happy and tranquil.

"The revelation of my decadence came to me in a simple but terrible fashion, which made me downcast for nearly six months. Since then I have accepted the part.

"I have often been in love, like all men, but once in particular. I met her at the seashore at Etretat, about twelve years ago, a little after the war. There is nothing so pretty as this shore in the morning at the bathing hour. It is small, rounded like a horseshoe, incased in those high, white cliffs, pierced with those singular holes they call ports, one enormous one, extending into the sea like a giant's leg, the other opposite squat and round. A crowd of women assembles here on the right side of the shuffleboard, which they cover like a bright garden with their brilliant costumes—this box between the high rocks. The sun falls full upon the coast, upon umbrellas of all shades, upon the sea of a greenish blue. And all is gay, charming, smiling to the eyes. You seat yourself near the water to watch the bathers. They descend in a bathrobe of flannel which they throw off with a pretty motion upon reaching the fringe of the foam from the short waves; they go into the sea with a little rapid step which is arrested sometimes by a delicious cold shiver, or a slight suffocation.

"Few can stand this trial of the bath. It is there that one can judge them from the calf to the throat. The going out especially reveals the weak, although salt water may be a powerful help to flabby flesh.

"The first time that I saw this young woman thus, I was delighted, ravished. She held good, she held firm. Then there are some faces whose charm enters into us suddenly, invades us at a single blow. It seemed to me that I had found the woman that I was born to love. I had that sensation and it was like a shock.

"I had myself presented and was immediately captured as I never was before. She ravaged my heart. It is a frightful and delicious thing, the undergoing thus the domination of a woman. It is almost a punishment, and at the same time, an unbelievable happiness. Her look, her smile, her hair at the nape of the neck when the breeze moved it, all the little lines of her face, the least movement of her features delighted me, and made me extremely fond of her.

She took possession of me through all my being, by her gestures, her attitudes, even by the things she carried, which became bewitching to me. I would wait to see her veil thrown upon some piece of furniture, her gloves upon an armchair. Her costumes seemed to me inimitable. No one had hats like hers.

"She was married and the husband came every Saturday to remain until Monday. He seemed to me very indifferent. I was not at all jealous of him; I know not why, but never a being seemed to have less importance in life, or attract less of my attention than this man.

"How I loved her! And how beautiful she was, and gracious and young! She was youth, elegance, and freshness, even. Never before had I felt what a pretty being a woman is, so distinguished and delicate, so full of charm and grace! Never had I understood what a seducing beauty there is in the curve of her cheek, in the movement of her lips, in the round folds of her little ear, in the form of that simple organ which we call the nose.

"This lasted three months and then I departed for America, my heart bruised and full of despair. But the thought of her remained in me persistent, triumphant. She possessed me at a distance as she had when I was near her.

"Some years passed. I had not forgotten her. Her charming image remained before my eyes and in my heart. My tenderness remained faithful to her, a tranquil tenderness now, something like a much-loved memory of the most beautiful, most attractive thing I had met in life.

"Twelve years are such a little thing in a man's existence! One scarcely feels them pass! They go one after another these years, gently and quickly, slowly or hurriedly, each long but so soon finished! And they add so rapidly and leave so little trace behind them; they vanish so completely that in looking back over the time passed one cannot perceive anything, and cannot comprehend how it is that they have made him old. It seemed to me truly, that only a few months separated me from that charming season on the beach at Etretat.

"Last spring I went to dine at Maisons-Lafitte at the house of some friends. Just as the train was starting, a large woman got into my car, followed by four little girls. I scarcely glanced at this large, round mother, with a face like a full moon incased in a be-ribboned hat.

"She breathed heavily, being out of breath from a quick walk. The children began to babble. I opened my newspaper and began to read.

"We were just passing Asnières, when my neighbor said to me suddenly:

" 'Pardon me, sir, but are you not Mr. Carnier?'

" 'Yes, Madame.'

"Then she began to laugh, the laugh of a contented, brave woman, but a little sad, nevertheless.

" 'You do not recognize me?' said she.

"I hesitated. I fully believed that I had somewhere seen that face; but where? and when? I answered:

" 'Yes—and no—I certainly do recognize you, but cannot recall your name.'

"She blushed a little as she said: 'Mrs. Julie Lefevre.'

"Never have I received such a blow. For a second it seemed to me that all was finished for me. I felt that a veil had been torn away from before my eyes and that I was about to discover something frightful and wounding.

"It was she! That great, gross, common woman, she? And she had borne these four girls since I had seen her. And these four beings astonished me as much as the mother herself. They had come from her; they were tall already, had taken her place in life. She no longer counted, she, that marvel of coquettish, refined grace. I had seen her yesterday, it seemed to me, and I found her again like this! Was it possible? A violent grief attacked my heart, and also a revolt against Nature, even, an unreasonable indignation against her brutal work, so infamous and destructive.

"I looked at her aghast. Then I took her by the hand, and the tears mounted to my eyes. I wept for her young, I wept for her dead. For I was not acquainted with this large lady.

"She, also affected, stammered:

" 'I am much changed, am I not? What can we expect after so long? You see I have become a mother, nothing but a mother, a good mother. Adieu to all else, it is finished. Oh! I never thought that you would not recognize me if we met! And you, too, are changed; it took me some time to be sure that I was not deceived. You are quite gray. Think of it. Twelve years! twelve years! My eldest daughter is already ten years old.'

"I looked at the child. I found in her something of the former charm of her mother, but something still undecisive, not yet formed, but near at hand. And life appeared as rapid to me as a train which passes.

"We arrived at Masions-Lafitte. I kissed the hand of my old friend. I had found nothing to say to her but the most frightful commonplaces. I was too upset to talk.

"That evening, all alone in my room, I looked at myself for a long time in my glass. And I ended by recalling myself as I was, of looking back in thought to my brown mustache and my black hair and the physiognomy of my young face. Now I was old. Adieu!"

A French Enoch Arden

THE sea lashes the shore with its short and monstrous waves. Little white clouds are scudding quickly across the great blue sky, swept by a rapid wind, like birds; and the village, in the fold of the valley which runs down to the ocean, lies broiling in the sun.

Quite at the entrance is the house of the Martin-Levesques, alone, at the side of the road. It is a little fisherman's cottage, with clay walls and a thatched roof adorned with blue iris flowers. A garden as big as a handkerchief, where sprout some onions, a few cabbages, some parsley, some chervil, squares itself before the door. A hedge hems it in along the roadside.

The man has gone fishing. and the woman, before the lodge, is repairing the meshes of a big brown net hung on the wall like a great spider's web. A little girl of fourteen at the garden entrance, seated in a cane chair, leaning backward and resting her arm on the fence, is mending linen, the linen of the poor, already pieced and patched.

Another small girl, a year younger, is rocking in her arms a very little baby, yet without gestures or words; and the two youngsters of two or three years sitting on the ground are playing garden with their clumsy hands and throwing fistfuls of dust in each other's face.

No one speaks. Only the little rascal whom the girl is trying to put to sleep cries steadily, with a sharp, weak little voice. A cat is sleeping at the window, and some blooming gillyflowers make, at the foot of the wall, a fine cushion of white blossoms, over which flies are buzzing.

The little girl who is sewing near the entrance calls suddenly:

"Mamma."

"What is the matter with you?" replied the mother.

"There he is again."

She had been uneasy since morning because there was a man prowling about the house; an old man who seemed to be poor. They had observed him as they were going with their father to the boat to see him embark. He was seated on the edge of the ditch opposite their gate, and when they came back they found him still there, looking at the house.

He seemed ill and very wretched. He

had not stirred for more than an hour; then, seeing he would be considered a malefactor he had risen and departed, dragging one leg.

But soon they had seen him return with his slow and weary step; and again he had sat down, a little further away this time, as if to watch them.

The mother and daughters were afraid. The mother especially because she was of a timorous nature, and because her husband Levesque was not expected to come from the sea until nightfall.

Her husband's name was Levesque, hers was Martin, and they were called the Martin-Levesques. This is why: she had married for her first husband a man named Martin, who went to Newfoundland every summer fishing for cod.

After two years of married life she had a little girl by him; and another three months after the craft which carried her husband, the "Two Sisters," a three-masted bark from Dieppe, disappeared.

No news was ever received from it; none of its crew ever came back; it was considered to be a total wreck.

The Martin woman waited for her second husband ten years, bringing up her children with great difficulty; then, as she was a good, strong woman, a fisherman of the neighborhood, Levesque, a widower with a boy, asked her in marriage. She married him and had two children by him in three years.

They lived painfully, laboriously. Bread was dear, and meat almost unknown in the household. They ran in debt at times with the baker, in winter, during the stormy months. The little

ones were well, nevertheless. People said:

"They are brave folk, the Martin-Levesques. The wife is a hard worker and Levesque has not his equal for fishing."

The little girl seated at the gate repeated: "You would think that he knew us. Perhaps it is some poor man from Epreville or from Auzebogo."

But the mother was not deceived. No, no, it wasn't anyone of the country, surely!

As he moved no more than a stake, and as he kept his eyes glued to the Martin-Levesques' cottage, the woman became furious, and fear making her brave she seized a shovel and went out of the door.

"What are you doing there?" she called to the vagabond.

He answered in a gruff voice:

"I am taking the fresh air! Does that do you any harm?"

She replied:

"Why are you spying like this on my house?"

The man replied:

"I am not injuring anybody. Isn't it permitted to sit down by the roadside?"

Not finding an answer ready, she went back into the house.

The day passed slowly. Toward noon the man disappeared, but he came by again toward five o'clock. They did not see any more of him during the evening.

Levesque returned at dusk. They told him about it. He remarked:

"It is some skulker or good-for-nothing."

He went to bed undisturbed, while his

wife dreamed of this prowler who had looked at her so strangely.

When day came, there was a great wind, and the sailor, seeing that he could not start out to sea, helped his wife at mending nets.

About nine o'clock, the eldest daughter, a Martin, who had gone out to get some bread, came back running with a frightened air, and cried:

"Ma, there he is again!"

The mother was startled and, very pale, said to her husband:

"Go, and speak to him, Levesque, so that he won't watch us like this, because it worries me to death."

And Levesque, a big sailor with a complexion like a brick, a thickened beard, blue eyes, strong neck, always wearing woolen garments, on account of the wind and rain at sea, walked out quietly and approached the straggler.

And they began to talk.

The mother and the children looked on from the distance, anxious and trembling.

Suddenly the unknown rose and came toward the house with Levesque.

The wife, terrified, drew back.

Her husband said to her:

"Give him a piece of bread and a glass of cider. He hasn't eaten anything since the day before yesterday."

They both entered the house, followed by the woman and the children. The vagabond sat down and began to eat, with his head lowered beneath the glances.

The mother, standing up, scrutinized him. The two big girls, the Martins, leaning against the door, one of them holding the latest baby, fixed their eager eyes upon him, and the two boys, seated in the ashes of the fireplace, had stopped playing with the black kettle to look at this stranger, too.

Levesque, having taken a chair, asked him:

"Do you come from a distance?"

"I have come from Cette."

"On foot as far as that?"

"Yes, on foot. A man has to walk when he cannot afford to ride."

"And where are you going?"

"I was coming here."

"You know some one here?"

"That might be."

They were silent. He ate slowly, although he was famished, and he took a sip of cider after each mouthful of bread. He had a worn, wrinkled face and seemed to have suffered much.

Levesque brusquely asked him:

"What is your name?"

"My name is Martin."

A strange shudder shook the mother. She took a step forward, as if to scan the vagabond more closely, and stood opposite him, with her arms hanging down and her mouth open. Nobody said anything further. Levesque finally resumed:

"Are you from here?"

He answered: "I am from here." And as he raised his head the woman's eyes and his met and remained fixed upon each other, as if their glances were fastened.

She suddenly said, in a changed voice, low and trembling:

"It is you, my husband?"

He slowly replied:

"Yes, it is I."

He did not move, continuing to masticate the bread.

Levesque more surprised than moved stammered:

"It is you, Martin?"

The other man said simply:

"Yes, it is I."

And the second husband asked:

"Where have you come from?"

He first told his story.

"From the coast to Africa, I was wrecked on a reef. Three of us were saved, Picard, Vatinel, and me. And then we were captured by savages who held us twelve years. Picard and Vatinel are dead. An English traveler passing that way took me and brought me to Cette, and here I am."

The woman began to weep, her face in her apron.

Levesque said:

"What shall we do now?"

Martin asked:

"You are her husband?"

Levesque replied:

"Yes, I am."

They looked at each other and were silent.

Then Martin gazing at the children in a circle around him nodded toward two little girls.

"Those are mine."

Levesque said:

"They are yours."

He did not rise, he did not kiss them; he merely remarked:

"Good God! how tall they are."

Levesque repeated:

"What shall we do?"

Martin perplexed, could not tell. Finally he decided:

"I will do as you wish. I don't want to injure you. It is vexing all the same, considering the house. I have two children, you have three, each his own. But the mother, is she yours or mine? I will consent to whatever you wish, but the house is mine, since my father left it to me, since I was born here, and since there are papers for it at the notary's."

The woman still wept, with little sobs stifled in the blue cloth of her apron. The two tall girls drew near and looked at their father with uneasiness.

He had finished eating. But Levesque had an idea:

"We must go the the priest, he will decide."

Martin rose, and as he approached his wife, she threw herself sobbing upon his breast.

My husband! you are here! Martin, my poor Martin, you are here!"

And she held him in her arms, suddenly pierced by a breath of olden times, by a great shock of memories which recalled to her the days when she was twenty and their first embraces.

Martin, himself moved, kissed her on the cap. The two children, in the corner, began to howl together, seeing their mother weep, and the last born, in the arms of the second Martin girl, shrieked with the sharp sound of a cracked fife.

Levesque, standing up, waited:

"Come," he said, "we must get this straightened out."

Martin released his wife, and as he looked at his two daughters, their mother said to them:

"Kiss your father, at least."

They approached him together, astonished, and a little afraid. And he kissed them one after the other, on both cheeks, with a big peasant's smack. And seeing this unknown approach, the little child uttered such piercing cries that it almost went into convulsions.

Then the two men went out together. As they passed the *Café du Commerce,* Levesque asked:

"Shall we have a little drop?"

"I would like it very much," said Martin.

They entered and sat down in a room which was vacant,

"Ho! Chicot, two bottles of wine, good wine. This is Martin who has come back, Martin of the 'Two Sisters,' which was lost."

And the tavern-keeper, three glasses in one hand and a *carafe* in the other, approached, large of paunch, ruddy, fat, and asked with a quiet air:

"What, you here, Martin?"

Martin replied: "I am here."

Julie Romain

IN the springtime two years ago, I was walking along the shores of the Mediterranean. What is more charming than to dream while walking over a lonely road? One enjoys the sunlight and the caressing wind when climbing the mountains, or strolling by the seashore. And in his day-dreams, what illusions, what love-poems, what adventures pass in two hours through the mind of one who idles along a road. Every possible hope, confused and joyous, penetrates him with the warm, light air, he inhales them with the breeze, and they give birth in his being to an appetite for happiness that increases like the hunger he acquires in walking. Sweet and fleeting thoughts sing in his soul as he comes closer to nature.

I followed the road that leads from Saint Raphael to Italy, or rather, I made my way through that superb and changing scenery which seems made to be celebrated in all the love-poems of the earth. It seemed to me a pity to think that, from Cannes to Monaco, scarcely anyone comes into this part of country save to make trouble, to juggle with money, or to display, under this delicious sky and in this garden of roses and oranges, base vanities, stupid pretensions, and vile covetousness, and to show the human mind as it is—servile, ignorant, arrogant, and grasping.

Suddenly, in one of the curves of the ravishing bays I saw a group of villas, four or five only, fronting on the sea at the foot of the mountain. Behind them was a wild forest of pines, which covered two great valleys apparently without roads or outlet. Involuntarily I stopped in front of the gate of one of these châlets, so pretty was it,—a little white cottage with brown decorations, covered with roses that climbed to the roof. The garden was filled with flowers of all colors and every size, coquettishly arranged in studied disorder. The lawn was dotted with flower-beds; a vase with trailing vines stood on the step of the veranda, and over the windows hung clusters of purple grapes, while the stone ballustrade that surrounded this charming dwelling was covered with enormous red morning-glories, that looked like spots of blood. Behind the house stretched a long alley of orange-trees in flower, which reached as far as the foot of the mountain.

On the door of the villa, in small, gilt letters, I read this name: "Villa d'Antan." I asked myself what poet or fairy inhabited the place, what inspired recluse had discovered it and created this dream of a dwelling, that appeared to spring from masses of flowers.

A workman was breaking stones on the road at a short distance. I asked him the name of the proprietor of the châlet. He replied that it belonged to the famous Madame Julie Romain.

Julie Romain! In my childhood I had often heard her spoken of,—the great actress, the rival of Rachel! No woman had been more applauded, or more loved,—more loved, above all! How many duels had been fought and how many suicides had been committed because of her, and how many wild adventures had been undertaken for her sake! What was her age now, that seductress? Sixty,—no, seventy—seventy-five years. Julie Romain! Here, in this house! I recalled again the emotion created throughout France (I was twelve years old then) by her flight to Sicily with one lover, a poet, after her notorious quarrel with another adorer.

She fled with her new love one evening, after a first-night representation, during which the audience had applauded her for half an hour and called her out eleven times in succession. She went away with the poet in a post-chaise, as was the custom then; they had crossed the sea in order to love in that antique island, daughter of Greece, under the

immense grove of orange-trees that surrounds Palermo, which is called the "Conque d'Ov."

Their ascent of Ætna was gossiped about, and also how they hung over the immense crater, arm in arm, cheek against cheek, as if they desired to throw themselves into the gulf of fire.

He was dead now, the writer of affecting verses, of poems so brilliant that they dazzled a whole generation, and so subtle and mysterious that they opened a new world to other poets.

The other lover was dead also, the abandoned one, who created for her those musical expressions that remain in all hearts,—expressions of triumph and despair that are at once intoxicating and heartrending.

She lived here, in this house veiled with flowers!

I hesitated no longer. I range the bell. A domestic came to open the door, a boy of eighteen years, awkward and shy, with hands that appeared to be in his way. I wrote on my card a gallant compliment to the old actress, and an ardent prayer that she would receive me. Perhaps she might know my name and allow me to see her.

The young valet disappeared, but soon returned and asked me to follow him. He showed me into a neat drawing-room, correct in every detail in the style of Louis Philippe, with furniture of a cold and cumbersome fashion, the coverings of which were being removed in my honor by a little maid of about sixteen years, with a slender figure but not much beauty.

Then the servants left me alone. I looked around the room with interest. On the walls hung three portraits, one was of the actress in a celebrated rôle, another was of the poet-lover, wearing a long frock-coat, tight at the waist, and the ruffled shirt of those days, and the third was of the musician, seated before a clavichord. The lady was blond and charming in her portrait, but her pose was a little affected, as was the fashion of that day. Her charming mouth and blue eyes smiled graciously; and the technique of the painting was of a high degree of excellence. Those three remarkable faces seemed to be looking already at the next generation, and their surroundings had an air of a day that was past and of individualities that were no more.

A door opened and a little woman entered. She was very old, very small, with eyebrows and bands of white hair. Somehow she reminded me of a white mouse, quick and furtive in her movements. She gave me her hand, and, with a voice that was still fresh, vibrating, and sonorous, she said graciously: "Thank you, Monsieur. It is very kind of the men of to-day to remember the women of yesterday! Be seated!"

I told her that her house had attracted me, that I had tried to learn the name of the proprietor, and, having learned it, I could not resist the desire to ring her bell.

"Your visit gives me the greater pleasure, Monsieur," she said, "as it is the first time such an event has happened. When your card was handed to me, with the gracious compliment it carried, I was as startled as if some one had announced an old friend who had been gone these twenty years. I am forgotten, truly forgotten, no one remembers me, no one will think of me until the day

of my death; then, all the papers will talk for three days of Julie Romain, telling anecdotes, giving details, and souvenirs and scandals, and, perhaps, pompous eulogies. Then that will be the end of me!"

She was silent a moment and then resumed: "And that will not be long now. In a few months, in a few days, perhaps, the little woman who is now alive will be nothing but a corpse!"

She raised her eyes to her portrait, which met her gaze as if smiling at that withered caricature of itself; then she looked at the two men, the scornful poet and the inspired musician, both of whom seemed to say: "What does that ruin ask of us?"

An indescribable, keen, irresistible sadness seized my heart, the sadness that overwhelms those whose lives are finished and who struggle still with memories as a drowning man struggles in deep water.

From the place where I sat I could see brilliant and swiftly moving carriages passing along the road, going from Nice to Monte Carlo. And seated inside were beautiful young women, rich and happy, and men, smiling and satisfied. She followed my glance, and, comprehending my thought, murmured with a resigned smile: "It is not possible to be and to have been at the same time."

"How beautiful life must have been for you!" I said.

She sighed deeply: "Yes, beautiful and sweet! It is for that reason that I regret it so much."

I saw that she was disposed to talk of herself; so, softly and with delicate precautions, as one would touch a painful wound, I began to question her.

She spoke of her success, of her intoxicating joys, of her friends, of her whole triumphant existence.

"Your greatest joy and your deepest happiness—did you owe them to the theater, Madame?" I asked.

"Oh! no," she replied quickly.

I smiled and she added, raising her eyes, with a sad look, to the portraits of the two men:

"I owed my greatest happiness to them."

I could not refrain from asking her to which one she owed it.

"To both, Monsieur! I even confuse them in my mind sometimes, and besides, I feel remorse toward one of them to this day."

"Then, Madame, it is not to them but to the act of love itself that you owe your gratitude. They have merely been love's instruments."

"That is possible. But, ah! what wonderful instruments!"

"Are you certain that you have not been loved—that you would not have been loved as well, and perhaps better, by a simple man, one who was not great, but who would have offered you his whole life, his whole heart, his whole being, every thought and every hour? With those two you had two formidable rivals—music and poetry."

She cried out with force, with that youthful voice, which could still thrill the soul: "No, Monsieur, no! A simpler man might have loved me better, perhaps, but he would not have loved me as those two did. Ah! but they knew how to sing the music of love, as no other man in the world could have sung it.

"How they intoxicated me! Is it possible that any other man could have found that which they found in words and in sounds? Is it enough to love, if one does not know how to put into love all the poetry and all the music of the sky and the earth? They knew, those two, how to make a woman ecstatic with joy and with their songs and their words as well as with their deeds. Yes, there was perhaps more of illusion than reality in our passion; but those illusions lift you to the clouds, whereas realities, alone, always leave you on the earth. If others loved me more, it was through them alone that I learned, felt, and adored love!"

Suddenly she began to weep, noiselessly, tears of bitter sorrow. I appeared not to notice it and looked far away out of the window. After a few moments she went on:

"You see, Monsieur, with most people the heart grows old with the body. With me that has not happened. My poor body is sixty-nine years old, but my heart is only twenty. And that is the reason why I live all alone, with my flowers and my dreams."

Again a long silence fell between us. After a time she calmed herself, and again spoke smilingly:

"How you would laugh at me, Monsieur, if you knew how I pass my evenings when the weather is fine! I am ashamed of my folly and pity myself at the same time."

It was useless for me to beg her to tell me; she would not do so; then I rose to go, at which she cried, "What! so soon?"

I told her that I had intended to dine at Monte Carlo, and at once she asked, a little timidly: "Would you not like to dine with me? It would give me very much pleasure."

I accepted her invitation immediately. She appeared delighted and rang the bell; then, when she had given a few orders to the little maid, she said she would like to show me her house.

A kind of glass-covered veranda, full of plants, opened from the dining-room, and permitted one to see, from one end to the other, the long alley of orange-trees, extending to the foot of the mountains. A low seat, hidden under the shrubbery, indicated that the aged actress often came to sit there.

Then we went into the garden to look at the flowers. Evening came on softly, one of those calm, warm evenings that bring forth all the perfumes of the earth. It was almost dark when we placed ourselves at the table. The dinner was excellent and we sat long over it. We became quite intimate friends. A profound sympathy for her had sprung up in my heart. She drank a glass of wine and became more friendly and confidential.

"Let us go out and look at the moon," she said at last. "I adore the moon, the lovely moon! It has been the witness of my greatest joys. It seems to me that all my sweetest memories are treasured there, and that I have only to look at it in order to have them come back to me. And sometimes, in the evening, I arrange for myself a pretty scene, so pretty—if you only knew! But no, you would laugh at me too much—I cannot tell you—I don't dare —no,—no, I cannot tell you!"

"Ah, Madame, continue, I pray!" I begged of her. "What is your little

secret? Tell me! I promise you not to laugh—I swear it!"

She hesitated; I took her hands, her poor little hands, so thin and cold, and kissed them one after the other many times, as her lovers were wont to do in former days. She was moved, though she still hesitated.

"You promise me not to laugh?" she said timidly.

"Yes, I swear it, Madame!"

"Well, then come!" she said with a smile.

We rose from the table, and as the awkward youth in green livery drew back the chair behind her, she spoke a few low, quick words in his ear.

He replied, respectfully, "Yes, Madame, immediately."

She took my arm and led me upon the veranda. The orange-tree walk was a beautiful sight. The moon cast a slender line of silver among the trees,—a long line of light that fell on the yellow sand between the dense and rounded branches. As the trees were in bloom, their delicious and penetrating perfume filled the air, and among the dark foliage were thousands of fireflies, whose tiny flames looked like the seed of stars.

"Oh, what an ideal environment for a scene of love!" I cried.

She smiled. "Is it not? Is it not? You will see presently!"

She made me sit down beside her, and murmured:

"The memory of such scenes is what makes me regret life. But you hardly dream of those things, you men of to-day. You are merely money-makers, business men. You don't know how to talk to us even. When I say 'us,' I mean women who are young. Love affairs have become merely *liaisons*, which originate often in an unacknowledged bill of the dressmaker. If you find the bill more important than the woman, you disappear; but if you esteem the woman of greater value than the bill, you pay! Nice manners, and charming affections!"

She took my hand. "Look!" she said.

I was astonished and transported with pleasure at the charming picture that appeared. Below us, at the end of the alley and in the full moonlight, a youth and a maiden were coming toward us, clasping each other around the waist. They advanced, their arms entwined, walking slowly in the moon's rays, the soft effulgence of which bathed them completely.

They disappeared in the darkness for a moment, then reappeared further down the avenue.

The youth was dressed in a white satin costume of the last century, with a broad hat, over which hung an ostrich feather. The maiden wore a skirt with wide hoops, and her head was dressed with the high, powdered coiffure affected by beautiful dames in the days of the Regency.

At last they came to a halt, about a hundred steps away from us, and, standing in the middle of the alley, they embraced, after saluting each other gracefully.

Suddenly I recognized the two little servants! Then I was seized with one of those irresistible desires to laugh that shake one all over. I did not laugh, however. I resisted the impulse, and waited to see the next scene in this extraordinary comedy.

The lovers now returned toward the end of the alley, and distance again made them appear charming. They withdrew farther and farther away, and at last disappeared like figures in a dream. The alley seemed lovely without them.

I took my departure also. I left immediately, so that I should not see them again; for I thought it probable that the spectacle was made to last a long time, in order to recall all the past,—that past of love and scenic effect; that fictitious past, deceiving and seductive, falsely yet truly charming,—to cause the tender heart to throb again in the romantic breast of the old actress, and to use me as a final instrument.

An Unreasonable Woman

A GREAT wind was whistling outside, an autumn wind, groaning and galloping; one of those winds which kill the last leaves and carry them away to the clouds.

The hunters had finished their dinner and were still booted, red, animated and lighted up. They were those demi-Norman lords, half country squire, half peasant, rich and vigorous, shaped for cutting the horns of beeves when they stopped them in the market.

They had hunted all day on Mr. Blondel's estate, Mr. Blondel, the mayor of Eparville, and they were eating now around the great table, in a kind of farm-villa of which their host was the proprietor.

They were talking like a whirlwind, laughing like a roar of wild animals, and drinking like cisterns, their legs stretched out, their elbows on the cloth, their eyes shining under the flame of the lamps, heated by a hearth fire so formidable as to send to the ceiling its ruddy glow. They chatted of hunting and dogs. But they had come to the hour when other ideas come to men half tipsy, and all eyes followed the strong girl with plump cheeks who carried at the end of her red wrists great platters filled with food.

Suddenly a devil of a fellow, who had become a veterinary after having studied for a priest, and who looked after all the animals of the district, by name Sejour, said:

"My eyes! Monsieur Blondel, you have a girl there who is not starved."

And a laugh made the echoes ring. Then an old nobleman, declassed, ruined by alcohol, M. de Varnetot, raised his voice.

"I once had a droll adventure with a girl like that. Wait, I must tell it to you. Every time I think of her it recalls Mirza, my dog which I sold to Count d'Haussonel and which returned every day when she was let out, because she was unable to leave me. Finally, I got angry and begged the Count to keep her chained. Do you know what the beast did? She died of grief.

"But, to return to my maid; here is the story:

"I was then twenty-five years old, and lived as a bachelor in my castle at

Villebon. You know that when one is young and has an income, and makes a beast of himself every evening, he has his eye on all sides.

"I discovered a young girl who was in service at the house of Deboultot of Cauville. You know Deboultot well, you, Blondel. To be brief, she pleased me so much, the hussy, that I went one day to her master and made a business proposition to him. He gave me his servant and I sold him my black mare, Cocotte, which he had sought of me for two years. He extended his hand to me and said: 'It is agreed M. De Varnetot.' It was a bargain. The little one came to the castle and I took my black mare to Cauville myself, and I let him have her for three hundred crowns.

"At first everything went as if on wheels. No one mistrusted anything. Only Rose loved me a little too much for my taste. The child, you see, was not a nobody. She had something out of the common in her veins. She came from some girl who committed some error with her master.

"Briefly, she adored me. There were cajolings, endearments, little pet names, and heaps of caresses—enough to make it a matter of reflection.

"I said to myself: 'This cannot last, or I would allow myself to be caught.' But they do not catch me easily. I am not one of those to be taken in with a couple of kisses. So, I had my eyes opened when she announced to me that she was large.

"Pif! Pif! it was as if some one had put two shots from a gun into my breast. And she embraced me, she embraced me, I say, and laughed and danced as if she were mad. What! I said nothing the first day; but at night I reasoned with myself; I thought: 'It is just here; it is necessary to parry the blow and cut the thread; it is the only time.' You understand, I had my father and mother at Barneville, and my sister married to the Marquis of Yspare, at Rollebec, two leagues from Villebon. There must not be any stories.

"But how was I to draw myself out of the affair? If she left the house, something would be suspected and people would talk. If I kept here there, the condition would soon be recognized, and then I could not turn her away.

"I spoke to my uncle about it, the Baron de Creteuil, an old buck who has known more than one such case, and asked his advice. He responded tranquilly:

" 'You must marry, my boy.'

"I made a leap. 'Marry, uncle,' said I, 'marry whom?'

"He shrugged his shoulders gently as he replied:

" 'Whom you wish; that is your affair, not mine. If one is not stupid there is always somebody to be found.'

"I reflected for two weeks upon this idea, and ended by saying to myself: 'My uncle is right.'

Then I commenced to rack my brain to think of some one, when one evening the justice of the peace, with whom I was dining, said to me:

" 'Mother Paumelle's son is into mischief again; it is true that a good dog shows his race.'

"This Mother Paumelle was a sly old gypsy of whom the youth could have all they desired. For six francs she would certainly have sold her soul, and her rake of a son followed in her footsteps.

"I went and found her, and very gently made her understand the state of affairs. As I was somewhat embarrassed in my explanations, she demanded, all at once:

" 'Well, how much will you give to this little one?'

"She was malicious, this old woman, but as I was not stupid, I was prepared for business. I owned three pieces of waste land beyond Sasseville, which belong to my three farms in Villebon. The farmers were always complaining that it was too far away; in short, I took back the three fields, six acres in all, and, as my farmers found fault, I returned to them, up to the end of each lease, all their rents in poultry. In this way the thing was settled. Then, having bought a piece on one side from my neighbor, M. Aumonte, I had a little house constructed down there, the whole thing for about fifteen hundred francs in all. In this way I had got together a little farm which had not cost me very much, that I could give to the little girl for a marriage portion.

"The old woman cried out: "It is not enough; but I will wait; we will leave it without deciding anything.'

"The next day at daybreak the lad came to find me. I could scarcely recall his face, but when I saw him I was reassured; he was not bad for a peasant, but had the air of a rude fellow.

"He looked at the affair from a distance, as if he were buying a cow. When we had agreed, he wished to see the property, and we set out together over the fields. The scamp kept me going for three hours over the land; he surveyed it, measured it, took up the earth and crumbled it in his hands, as if he were afraid of being deceived in the merchandise. The house was not yet roofed; he exacted slate instead of thatch, because it needed less repairs! Then he said to me:

"'And the furniture; you must give that.'

"I protested: 'No. It is enough to give you a farm.'

"He sneered: 'Yes, a farm and a child.'

"I colored, in spite of myself. He went on:

"'Come, now, you must give a bed, a table, the chest of drawers, three chairs, and the kitchen dishes, or nothing can be done.'

"I consented to it.

"Then we started to return. He had not yet said a word about the girl. But suddenly, with a sly, constrained air, he asked:

"'But if she should die, who would it go to, this farm?'

"I answered: 'To you, naturally.'

"That was what he had wanted to know since morning. Immediately he extended his hand to me with a satisfied appearance. We were of one accord.

"Oh! but I had difficulty in making Rose consent. She dragged herself at my feet, sobbed, and kept repeating: 'It was you proposed it to me! It was you! it was you!' For more than a week she resisted in spite of my reasoning and my prayers. They are stupid, these women! As soon as they get love into their heads, they understand nothing else. Wisdom is nothing; it is love above all, and all for love!

"Finally, I got angry and threatened to throw her out. Then she yielded, little by little, on the condition that I would allow her to come and see me from time to time.

"I myself conducted her to the altar, paid for the ceremony, and gave the wedding dinner. I did the thing up grandly, in short. Then, 'Good-bye, my children!' I went to pass six months with my brother in Touraine.

"When I returned I learned that she had been at the house every week asking for me. And I had scarcely been home an hour before I saw her coming with a baby in her arms. Believe me if you will, but it affected me in some way to see this little monkey. I believe I even embraced it.

"As for the mother, she was a wreck, a skeleton, a shadow. She looked thin and old. Ye gods! it was evident this marriage was not to her liking. I said to her mechanically:

"'Are you happy?'

"Then she began to weep like a fountain, and, with hiccoughs and sobs, she cried:

"'I can never, never leave you now. I would rather die; I cannot.'

"She made a devil of a noise. I consoled her as well as I could and conducted her back to the gate.

"I learned that her husband beat her, and that her mother-in-law made life hard for her, the old cabbage-head.

"Two days later she returned. She took me in her arms and dragged herself upon the earth. 'Kill me,' she said, 'but I will never go back down there.'

"This is exactly what Mirza would have said could she have spoken! These stories began to be very tiresome to me and I went away again for another six months.

"When I returned—when I returned,

I learned that she had died three weeks before, having visited the castle every Sunday—just like Mirza. The child had also died eight days before.

"As for the husband, the cunning rascal, he inherited the property. He has turned out well since, it appears, and is now municipal counselor."

M. de Varnetot added, laughing:

"It is a fact that I made the fortune of that man!"

And M. Sejour, the veterinary, concluded gravely, carrying a glass of brandy to his lips:

"Say what you will, but with women like that, such things should not be."

Rosalie Prudent

THERE was a mystery in that affair about Rosalie Prudent, which neither the jury, nor the judge, nor the prosecuting attorney of the republic himself could understand.

The girl Rosalie was a servant at the house of the Varambot family, of Mantes. She became *enceinte,* and, unknown to her employers, had given birth to a child in the garret, during the night, and had then killed the child and buried it in the garden.

It was the ordinary story of most of the infanticides commited by servants. But one act remained inexplicable. The examination of the girl's room had resulted in the discovery of a complete *layette* for an infant, made by Rosalie herself, who had passed her nights during three months in cutting out the garments and sewing them. The grocer where she had bought her candles (paid for out of her wages), in order to perform this long task, came forward and testified to the fact of their purchase. In addition it was learned that the midwife of the town, informed by Rosalie of her condition, had given her all the advice and information necessary in case the child should be born at a time when aid was impossible to obtain. She had found a place also, at Poissy, for Rosalie Prudent, who foresaw her loss of situation, as the Varambots were severe on the subject of morality.

They appeared in court, the man and his wife, small provincials of moderate means, exasperated against the vulgar creature who had besmirched the immaculateness of their house. They would have liked to see her guillotined at once, without trial, and they overwhelmed her with insults which in their mouths became accusations.

The guilty one, a tall, handsome girl of lower Normandy, fairly well educated for her station, wept without ceasing, and made no reply to them or to anyone. The Court came to the conclusion that she had accomplished that act of barbarity in a moment of despair and insanity, since everything indicated that she had hoped to keep her infant and bring it up.

The judge tried once more to make her speak, to get her to acknowledge her crime, and having asked her with great kindness to do so, he made her understand at last that the jury sitting there to judge her did not wish her death, but were ready to pity her.

The girl appeared to be making up her mind to speak at last.

"Tell us now at first who is the father of that child," said the judge.

Until that moment she had refused obstinately to divulge this fact. Now she replied suddenly, looking straight at her employers, who had come there in a rage to calumniate her.

"It is Monsieur Joseph, the nephew of Monsieur Varambot!"

Varambot and his wife started, and both cried at the same time:

"It is false! She lies! It is infamous!"

The judge bade them be silent, and said:

"Continue, I beg of you, and tell us how it happened."

Then the girl began to speak hurriedly, seeming to find some comfort for her poor, solitary, bruised heart in giving vent to her sorrow before these severe-looking men, whom she had taken until then for enemies and inflexible judges.

"Yes it was Monsieur Joseph Varambot—it happened when he came for his vacation last summer."

"What is the occupation of this Monsieur Joseph Varambot?"

"He is underofficer in the artillery, Monsieur. He was two months at the house—two months of the summer. I wasn't thinking of anything when he began to look at me, and then to say things to me, and finally to make love to me the whole day long. I was easy, Monsieur! He told me I was a handsome girl, that I pleased him, that I was

to his taste. For myself, he pleased me, to be sure. What would you have? Anyone listens to those things, when one is alone—as I am. I am alone on the earth, Monsieur. There is no one to whom I can talk—no one to whom I can tell my troubles. I have neither father, nor mother, nor brother, nor sister—no one! He seemed like a brother who had come to me when he began to talk to me. And then he asked me to go down to the river one evening, so that we might talk without making so much noise. And I went down there. Could I have known what would happen? He put his arms around my waist—of course I didn't want to,—no, no! I couldn't help it. I wanted to cry, the air was so soft and warm—it was clear moonlight — I couldn't help it! No, I swear it to you, I couldn't help it—he did what he pleased. That lasted three weeks, as long as he remained. I would have followed him to the end of the world. But he went away, and I didn't know that I was *enceinte*—I didn't! I didn't know it until the month afterward."

She began to weep so violently that they were obliged to give her time to compose herself. Then the judge spoke, in the tone of a father confessor: "Go on, my girl, go on."

She continued: "When I knew that I was *enceinte*, I told Madame Boudin, the midwife, to whom one can tell these things; and I asked her what to do in case that happened without her. And then I made the clothes, night after night, until one o'clock in the morning; and then I looked for another place, for I knew very well I should be discharged; but I wished to remain in that house until the end, in order to economize the pennies, seeing that I had no money and that I would need it for the little one."

"Then you did not wish to kill him?"

"Oh! surely not, Monsieur."

"Why did you kill him, then?"

"Here's how it happened. It came sooner than I thought it would. It took me in the kitchen as I was washing my dishes. Monsieur and Madame Varambot had retired already, so I went upstairs, without trouble, holding to the banisters. I lay down on the floor in my room, so as not to soil the bed. That lasted perhaps one hour—but it may have been two or three—I can't tell, so much pain did I have,—and then—and then it was over, and I took up my baby!

"Oh, yes! I was happy, for sure! I did everything that Madame Boudin told me, everything! Then I laid him on the bed,—and then another pain began, and it was a pain to kill anyone. If you knew what that was, you others, you wouldn't do as much I'm sure! I fell on my knees, and then on my back on the floor, and then it began all over again, and that, too, lasted one hour, or perhaps two and there I was all alone. Finally there came another little one, yes, another, two of them, like that! I took it up as I took the first one, and I put it on the bed by the side of the other. One—two! Can it be possible, I said? Two babies! And I, who earn twenty francs a month! Say—was it possible for me to take care of them? To care for one—yes, I might do that by depriving myself, but not two!

"The thought of that turned my head.

What do I know about it, I? Could I choose, say? Do I know? I saw myself come to, my last day! I couldn't keep two, so I put the pillow on them without knowing what I was doing—and I threw myself on the bed and upon them, too. And I stayed there, rolling and crying, until daylight, which I saw through the window. I looked at them—they were both dead under the pillow, quite dead. Then I took them under my arm, I went down the stairs, and out in the garden; I took the gardener's spade and I buried them in the ground, as deep as I could, one here and the other there, not together, so that they could not talk of their mother, if they do talk, the little dead children. Do I know?

"And then I went back to my bed, and I was so sick that I could not get up. They made the doctor come, and he understood everything. That is the truth, Monsieur the judge. Do what you want to me. I am ready."

During her speech half of the jurymen had been wiping their eyes over and over again, trying to hide their emotion. All the women in the court room were sobbing.

"At what spot in the garden did you bury the other infant?" asked the judge.

"Which one did you find?" Rosalie inquired.

"The one that was under the artichokes."

"Ah! the other is buried under the strawberries beside the well!" The poor girl began again to sob so loud that it was enough to break one's heart to hear her. The jury acquitted her.

Hippolyte's Claim

THE fat Justice of the Peace, with one eye closed and the other half-open, is listening with evident displeasure to the plaintiffs. Once in a while he gives a sort of grunt that foretells his opinion, and in a thin voice resembling that of a child, he interrupts them to ask questions. He has just rendered judgment in the case of Monsieur Joly against Monsieur Petitpas, the contestants having come to court on account of the boundary of a field which had been accidentally over-stepped by Monsieur Petitpas's farmhand, while the latter was plowing.

Now he calls the case of Hippolyte Lacour, vestryman and ironmonger, against Madame Céleste Césarine Luneau, widow of Anthime Isidore Luneau.

Hippolyte Lacour is forty-five years old; he is tall and gaunt, with a clean-shaven face and long hair, and he speaks in a slow, singsong voice.

Madame Luneau appears to be about forty years of age. She is built like a prize-fighter, and her plain dress is stretched tightly over her portly form. Her enormous hips hold up her over-flowing bosom in front, while in the back they support the great rolls of flesh that cover her shoulders. Her face, with strongly-cut features, rests on a short, fat neck, and her strong voice is pitched at a key that makes the windows and the eardrums of her auditors vibrate. She is about to become a mother and her huge form protrudes like a mountain.

The witnesses for the defense are waiting to be called.

His Honor begins: Hippolyte Lacour, state your complaint.

The plaintiff speaks: Your Honor, it will be nine months on Saint-Michael's day that the defendant came to me one evening, after I had rung the Angelus, and began an explanation relating to her barrenness.

The Justice of the Peace: Kindly be more explicit.

Hippolyte: Very well, your Honor. Well, she wanted to have a child and desired my participation. I didn't raise any objection, and she promised to give me one hundred francs. The thing was all cut and dried, and now she refuses to acknowledge my claim, which I renew before your Honor.

The Justice: I don't understand in the least. You say that she wanted a child! What kind of child? Did she wish to adopt one?

Hippolyte: No, your Honor, she wanted a new one.

The Justice: What do you mean by a new one?

Hippolyte: I mean a newborn child, one that we were to beget as if we were man and wife.

The Justice: You astonish me. To what end did she make this abnormal proposition?

Hippolyte: Your Honor, at first I could not make out her reasons, and was taken a little aback. But as I don't do anything without thoroughly investigating beforehand, I called on her to explain matters to me, which she did. You see, her husband, Anthime Isidore, whom you knew as well as you know me, had died the week before, and his money reverted to his family. This greatly displeased her on account of the loss it meant, so she went to a lawyer who told her all about what might happen if a child should be born to her after ten months. I mean by this that if she gave birth to a child inside of the ten months following the death of Anthime Isidore, her offspring would be considered legitimate and would entitle her to the inheritance. She made up her mind at once to run the risk, and came to me after church, as I have already had the honor of telling you, seeing that I am the father of eight living children, the eldest of whom is a grocer in Caen, department of Calvados, and legitimately married to Victoire-Elisabeth Rabou—

The Justice: These details are superfluous. Go back to the subject.

Hippolyte: I am getting there, your Honor. So she said to me: "If you succeed, I'll give you one hundred francs as soon as I get the doctor's report." Well, your Honor, I made ready to give entire satisfaction, and after eight weeks or so I learned with pleasure that I had succeeded. But when I asked her for the hundred francs she refused to pay me. I renewed my demands several times, never getting so much as a pin. She even called me a liar and a weakling, a libel which can be destroyed by glancing at her.

The Justice: Defendant, what have you to say?

Madame Luneau: Your Honor, I say that this man is a liar.

The Justice: How can you prove this assertion?

Madame Luneau [red in the face, choking and stammering]: How can I

prove it? What proofs have I? I haven't a single real proof that the child isn't his. But, your Honor, it isn't his, I swear it on the head of my dead husband.

The Justice: Well, whose is it, then?

Madame Luneau [stammering with rage]: How do I know? How do—do I know? Everybody's, I suppose. Here are my witnesses, your Honor, they're all here, the six of them. Now make them testify, make them testify. They'll tell—

The Justice: Collect yourself, Madame Luneau, collect yourself and reply calmly to my questions. What reasons have you to doubt that this man is the father of the child you are carrying?

Madame Luneau: What reasons? I have a hundred to one, a hundred? No, two hundred, five hundred, ten thousand, a million and more reasons to believe he isn't. After the proposal I made to him, with the promise of one hundred francs, didn't I learn that he wasn't the father of his own children, your Honor, not the father of one of 'em?

Hippolyte [calmly]: That's a lie.

Madame Luneau [exasperated]: A lie! A lie, is it? I guess his wife has been seen by everybody around here. Call my witnesses, your Honor, and make them testify?

Hippolyte [calmly]: It's a lie.

Madame Luneau: It's a lie, is it? How about the red-haired ones, then? I suppose they're yours, too?

The Justice: Kindly refrain from personal attacks, or I shall be obliged to call you to order.

Madame Luneau: Well, your Honor, I had my doubts about him, and said I to myself, two precautions are better than one, so I explained my position to Césaire Lepic, the witness who is present. Says he to me, "At your disposal, Madame Luneau," and he lent me his assistance in case Hippolyte should turn out to be unreliable. But as soon as the other witnesses heard that I wanted to make sure against any disappointment, I could have had more than a hundred, your Honor, if I had wanted them. That tall one over there, Lucas Chandelier, swore at the time that I oughtn't to give Hippolyte Lacour a cent, for he hadn't done more than the rest of them who had obliged me for nothing.

Hippolyte: What did you promise for? I expected the money, your Honor. No mistake with me,—a promise given, a promise kept.

Madame Luneau [beside herself]: "One hundred francs! One hundred francs! One hundred francs for that, you liar! The others there didn't ask a red cent! Look at 'em, all six of 'em! Make them testify, your Honor, they'll tell sure. [To Hippolyte.] Look at 'em, you liar! they're as good as you. They're only six, but I could have had one, two, three, five hundred of 'em for nothing, too, you robber!

Hippolyte: Well, even if you'd had a hundred thousand—

Madame Luneau: I could, if I'd wanted 'em.

Hippolyte: I did my duty, so it doesn't change matters.

Madame Luneau [slapping her protuberant form with both hands]: Then prove that it's you that did it, prove it, you robber! I defy you to prove it!

Hippolyte [calmly]: Maybe I didn't do any more than anybody else. But you promised me a hundred francs for it. What did you ask the others for, afterward? You had no right to. I guess I could have done it alone.

Madame Luneau: It is not true, robber! Call my witnesses, your Honor; they'll answer, sure.

The Justice called the witnesses in behalf of the defense. Six red, awkward individuals appeared.

The Justice: Lucas Chandelier, have you any reason to suppose that you are the father of the child Madame Luneau is carrying.

Lucas Chandelier: Yes, sir.

The Justice: Célestin-Pierre Sidoine, have you any reason to suppose that you are the father of the child Madame Luneau is carrying?

Célestin-Pierre Sidoine: Yes, sir.

The four other witnesses testified to the same effect.

The Justice, after a pause, pronounced judgment: Whereas the plaintiff has reasons to believe himself the father of the child which Madame Luneau desired, Lucas Chandelier, Célestin-Pierre Sidoine, and others, have similar, if not conclusive reasons to lay claim to the child.

But whereas Mme. Luneau had previously asked the assistance of Hippolyte Lacour for a duly stated consideration:

And whereas one may not question the absolute good faith of Hippolyte Lacour, though it is questionable whether he had a perfect right to enter into such an agreement, seeing that the plaintiff is married, and compelled by the law to remain faithful to his lawful spouse:

Therefore the Court condemns Madame Luneau to pay an indemnity of twenty-five francs to Hippolyte Lacour for loss of time and unjustifiable abduction.

Benoist

It all came over him one Sunday after mass. He went out of church and followed the crossroad that led to his house, when he found himself behind the Martin girl who was also returning home.

The father walked beside his daughter with the important step of a rich farmer. Disdaining the blouse, he wore a kind of waistcoat of gray cloth, and had on his head a melon-shaped hat with a wide brim. She, laced in a corset which she only wore once a week, walked very straight, her waist drawn in, her shoulders large, hips projecting, switching a little. Her hat was all flowers, the confection of an Yvetot milliner, and she showed her round, strong, supple neck, where little tendrils of hair were fluttering, moistened by the air and sun.

Benoist saw only her back; but he knew her face well, which was the reason he had noticed her still further. Suddenly he said to himself: "My! but she is pretty, just the same, that Martin girl!"

He looked at her as she walked along, admiring her crudely, and feeling himself moved with desire. He had no need of seeing her face, none at all. He planted his eyes upon her figure, repeating to himself, as if he were speaking: "She is a pretty girl!"

The Martin girl turned to the right to enter "Martinère" the farm of John Martin, her father. As she turned, she looked back and saw Benoist who looked queer to her. She cried out: "Good morning, Benoist. He answered: "Good morning, Miss Martin, good morning, Mr. Martin," and passed on.

When he entered his house, the soup was on the table. He seated himself opposite his mother, beside the hired man and boy, while the maidservant went to draw the cider. He ate a few spoonfuls, then pushed his plate aside. His mother asked:

"What is the matter, don't you feel well?"

He answered: "No, I have something like a burning in my stomach and I have no appetite."

He watched the others eat, breaking off from time to time a mouthful of bread which he carried slowly to his lips and masticated a long time. He kept thinking of the Martin girl: "All the same, she is a pretty girl." And strange to say, he had never perceived it until this time, and now it had come to him so suddenly and so strongly that he was unable to eat any more. He scarcely touched the stew.

His mother said to him: "Come, now, Benoist, do eat a little; it is a side of mutton, and very good. When one has no appetite, it is well to force oneself a little sometimes."

He swallowed a mouthful, then pushed back his plate: "No, I cannot, decidedly."

Upon rising, he made a tour of the farm and gave the boy a half-holiday, promising to drive up the cattle in passing. The country was empty, it was a day of repose. From place to place, in a field of clover, the cows moved slowly, with bodies expanded, ruminating under the full sun. Some detached plows were standing in a corner of a plowed field; and the upturned earth, ready for the seed, displayed its large brown ridges in the midst of patches of yellow where bits of wheat and oat straw were left to decay after a late reaping.

An autumn wind, somewhat dry, was blowing over the plain, announcing a cool evening after sunset. Benoist sat down beside a ditch, put his hat on his knees as if he needed the air on his head, and said aloud, in the silence of the field: "When it comes to pretty girls, there is a pretty girl!"

He thought of her still in the evening in his bed, and again on waking the next day. He was not sad, he was not discontented; he could not have told what was the trouble with him. But there was something which held him, something that fastened to his soul, an idea which would not leave him and which made a kind of tickling in his heart.

Sometimes we find a large fly shut up in a room. We hear it flying around and buzzing until the noise possesses us, irritates us. Suddenly it stops; we forget about it; but again it starts,

forcing our attention. We can neither catch it nor kill it nor make it stay in place. Finally, we resign ourselves to its humming. So the remembrance of the Martin girl agitated Benoist's mind; it was like an imprisoned fly.

Then a desire to see her again took possession of him, and he passed and repassed before the Martin farm. He saw her at last, hanging some linen upon a line between two apple-trees.

It was warm and she was only protected by a short skirt and a chemise, which showed to advantage the white arch made by her arms, as she pinned up the napkins. He lay flat beside the ditch for more than an hour after she had gone. He returned to find himself more haunted than before.

For a month his mind was full of her, so that he trembled when her name was mentioned before him. He could not eat, and had night sweats which hindered his sleeping. On Sunday, at mass, he could not keep his eyes away from her. She perceived it and smiled at him, flattered at being appreciated.

Then one evening, he suddenly met her in the road. She stopped on seeing him approach. He walked straight to her, suffocated by a fear that seized him, but resolved to speak to her. He commenced stammering:

"See here, Miss Martin, I can't endure this any longer."

And she answered him, mockingly: "What is it that you cannot endure, Benoist?"

He replied: "That I think about you as long as there are hours in the day."

Placing her hands on her hips, she answered: "It is not I who force you to."

He murmured: "Yes, it is you; and I can neither sleep nor eat, nor rest, nor nothing."

Very low she said: "What do you think-is necessary to cure you of it?"

He was struck dumb, his arms twitching, his eyes round, his mouth open. She struck him a sharp blow in the chest and ran away as fast as she could.

From this day they often met by the ditches or in the crossroad, generally at the close of day, when he was returning with his horses and she was driving the cows to the stable. He felt himself drawn, thrown toward her, by some great impulse of heart and body. He felt a desire to press her close, to strangle her, to eat her and make her a part of himself. And he had tremblings from powerlessness, from impatience, and rage, from the fact that she was his complement, making together but one being.

There began to be gossip in the country. It was said they were promised to one another. Indeed, he had asked her if she would be his wife, and she had answered: "Yes." They were only waiting for an opportunity to speak of it to their parents.

Then, suddenly, she no longer came at certain hours to meet him. He could only get a glimpse of her at mass, on Sunday. And then, one Sunday, after the sermon, the curate announced from the high pulpit that there was a promise of marriage between Victoire Adelaide Martin and Joseph Isidore Vallin.

Benoist felt as if he had raised blood. His ears buzzed; he could no longer hear anything, and he perceived, after some time, that he was weeping into his prayer book.

For a month he kept his room. Then he began to work again. But he was not cured and still thought of her always. He shunned passing along the roads that surrounded her dwelling, not wishing to see even the trees of her yard, and this forced him to make a large circuit morning and evening.

She was now married to Vallin, the richest farmer in the district. Benoist no longer spoke to him, although they had been comrades since infancy.

Then, one evening, as Benoist was passing across the common, he learned that she was *enceinte*. Instead of resenting this, or its affecting him with a great grief, he found in it a kind of solace. It was finished now, well finished. They were more separated by this than by marriage. Truly, it was best so.

Some months passed, and still some months. He saw her sometimes, walking to the village with slow step. She blushed on seeing him, lowered her head, and hastened her steps. And he turned out of his way in order not to cross her and look into her eyes.

But he thought, with the same terror as on that first morning, of finding himself face to face with her and obliged to speak to her. What could he say, after all he had said to her in former times holding her hands and kissing the locks about her cheeks? He still often thought of their meeting place by the side of the ditch. It was villainous to do as she did, after so many promises.

However, little by little, anger left his heart; there was no longer anything but sadness. And, one day, he took his old way by the farm where she lived. He saw the roof of the house from afar. She was in there! Living there with another! The apple-trees were in blossom, the fowls were singing about the barnyard. The whole place seemed empty, the folk having gone to the fields for the spring work. He stopped near the fence and looked into the yard. The dog lay sleeping before his kennel. Three calves were walking slowly, one behind the other, toward the pool. A large turkey-cock was wheeling about before the door, parading before the poultry after the manner of a stage singer.

Benoist leaned against a post and suddenly felt himself seized with a desire to weep. But just then he heard a cry, a great, appealing cry coming from the house. He stood lost in amazement, his hands clinched upon the bars, ever listening. Another cry, prolonged, piercing, came to his ears, and entered his soul and his flesh. It was she who was in trouble! She!

Finally he started hurriedly across the inclosure, pushed open the door and saw her stretched out upon the floor, in agony, her face livid, her eyes haggard, seized with the pains of childbirth.

He stood there, paler and trembling more than she, murmuring:

"I am here, my friend; here I am."

And she replied, in gasps: "Oh, do not leave me, Benoist, do not leave me!"

He looked at her, not knowing what to say or what to do. She began to cry out again: "Oh! oh! this tears me in two! Oh! Benoist!"

And she seemed frightfully tortured. Suddenly a furious desire to help her came over Benoist; he must appease her suffering, free her from this agony. He bent over and took her up and carried her to her bed. And, although she groaned continually, he then undressed her, taking off her kerchief, her frock, and her skirt. She began to bite her hands in order not to cry out. Then he did for her as he was accustomed to do for beasts, cows, sheep, and mares: he aided her and received into his hands a large infant, which began to squall.

He wiped it and wrapped it in a cloth which was drying before the fire, then placed it on a pile of linen that lay on the table and returned to the mother. He put her on the floor again, changed the bed, and put her in it. She whispered: "Thanks, Benoist, you have a brave heart." And she wept a little, as if some regret had seized her.

As for him, he loved her no longer, not at all. It was finished. Why? How? He could not have told. What had come to pass had cured him better than ten years of absence.

She asked, weak and trembling: "What is it?"

He answered in a calm voice: "It is a girl, and a handsome one."

They were again silent. At the end of a few seconds, the mother, in a feeble voice, said: "Show her to me, Benoist."

He went and got the little one and was presenting it to her as if it were bread that had been blessed, when the door opened and Isidore Vallin appeared. He could not understand at first, then suddenly, he guessed it all.

Benoist, somewhat disconcerted, murmured: "I was passing, I was just passing when I heard a cry—and I came—here is your child, Vallin!"

Then the husband, with tears in his eyes, took the frail little monkey that was held out to him, embraced it, and stood for some seconds overcome; then he placed the child on the bed, and extended both hands to Benoist, saying: "Done now, Benoist; you see, between us all is said. If you wish, we shall from this time be friends; just that, a pair of friends—"

And Benoist replied: "I am willing, certainly—I am willing."

Fecundity

THEY were walking, these two old friends, in the garden all in blossom, where the gay springtime stirred with life.

One was a senator and the other a member of the French Academy, grave, both of them, full of reason and logic, but solemn,—people of mark and reputation.

They were speaking at first of politics, exchanging thoughts, not upon ideas but men, personalities, which in these matters, always precede reason. Then they rose to reminiscences, then they were silent, continuing to walk side by side, both softened by the sweetness of the air.

A great basket of radishes sent forth their odor, fresh and delicate. A heap of flowers, of every kind and color, threw their sweetness to the breeze, while a radiant ebony-tree full of yellow berries, scattered to the wind its fine powder, a golden smoke which reminded one of honey, and which carried, like the caressing powder of the perfumer, its embalmed seed across space.

The senator stopped, breathed in the fertile sweetness that was floating by him, looked at the blossoming tree, resplendent as a sun from which the pollen was now escaping. And he said:

"When one thinks that these imperceptible atoms, which smell good, can bring into existence in a hundred places, miles from here, plants of their own kind, can start the sap and fiber of the female trees, creating from a germ, as we mortals do, they seem mortal, and they will be replaced by other beings of the same essence forever, like us!"

Then, planted before the radiant ebony-tree whose vivifying perfume permeated every breath of air, the senator added, as if addressing it:

"Ah! my jolly fellow, if you were to count your children you would be woefully embarrassed. And behold! here is one that accomplishes them easily, who lets himself go without remorse and disturbs himself little about it afterward."

The Academician replied: "We do as much, my friend."

The senator answered: "Yes, I do not deny that; we do forget ourselves sometimes, but we know it, at least, and that constitutes our superiority."

The other man shook his head: "No, that is not what I mean; you see, my dear, there is scarcely a man who does not possess some unknown children, those children labeled *of unknown father,* whom he has created, as this tree reproduces itself, almost unconsciously.

"If it became necessary to establish the count of the women we have had, we should be, should we not, as embarrassed as this ebony-tree, which you call upon to enumerate his descendants?

"From eighteen to forty perhaps, bringing into line all our passing encounters and contacts of an hour, it can easily be admitted that we have had intimate relations with two or three hundred women. Ah, well! my friend, among this number are you sure that you have not made fruitful at least one, and that you have not, upon the streets or in prison, some blackguard son, who robs and assassinates honest people, that is to say, people like us? or perhaps a daughter, in some bad place? or perhaps, if she chanced to be abandoned by her mother, a cook in somebody's kitchen?

"Think further that nearly all women that we call 'public' possess one or two children whose father they do not know, children caught in the hazard of their embraces at ten or twenty francs. In every trade, there is profit and loss. These castaways constitute the 'loss' of their profession. Who were their generators? You—I—all of us, the men who are 'all right!' These are the results of our joyous dinners to friends, of our evenings of gaiety, of the hours when our flesh contents us and pushes us on to the completion of adventure.

"Robbers, rovers, all these miserable creatures, in short, are our children. And how much better that is for us than if we were theirs, for they reproduce also, these beggars!

"For my part I have a villainous story upon my conscience, which I would like to tell you. It brings me incessant remorse, and more than that, continual doubt and an unappeasable uncertainty which at times tortures me horribly.

"At the age of twenty-five I had undertaken, with one of my friends, now counselor of state, a journey through Brittany, on foot.

"After fifteen or twenty days of forced march, after having visited the coasts of the north, and a part of Finisterre, we arrived at Douarnenez; from there, in a day's march, we reached the wildest point of the Raz, by the bay of Trepasses, where we slept in some village whose name ends in *of*. When the morning came a strange fatigue held my comrade in bed. I say bed from habit, since our bed was composed simply of two boxes of straw.

"It was impossible to remain in such a place. I forced him to get up, and we came into Audierne toward four or five o'clock in the evening. The next day he was a little better. We set out again, but on the way he was taken with intolerable weariness, and it was with great difficulty that we were able to reach Pont-Labbe.

"There at least there was an inn. My friend went to bed, and the doctor, whom we called from Quimper, found a high fever without quite determining the nature of it.

" 'Do you know Pont-Labbe? No.' Well, it is the most characteristic Breton town from Point Raz to Morbihan —a region which contains the essence of Breton morals, and legends, and costumes. To-day, even, this corner of the country has scarcely changed at all. I say 'to-day, even,' because I return there now every year, alas!

"An old castle bathes the foot of its towers in a dismal pond, sad with the call of wild birds. A river, deep enough for coasters, comes up to the town. In the streets, narrowed by the old houses, the men wear great hats and embroidered waistcoats and the four coats, one above the other; the first, about the size of the hand, covers at least the shoulder blades, while the last stops just below the breeches.

"The girls, who are large, pretty, and fresh looking, wear a bodice of thick cloth which forms a breast-plate and corset, constraining and leaving scarcely a suspicion of their swelling, martyrized busts. Their headdresses are also of strange fashion: over the temples two embroidered bands in color frame the face, binding the hair which falls in a sheet behind the head and is mounted by a singular bonnet on the very summit, often of tissue of gold or silver.

"The servant at our inn was eighteen years old or more, with blue eyes, a pale blue which were pierced with the two little black dots of the pupils; and with teeth short and white, which she showed always in laughing and which seemed made for biting granite.

"She did not know a word of French, speaking only the Breton patois, as do most of her compatriots.

"Well, my friend was no better, and, although no malady declared itself, the doctor forbade his setting out, ordering complete rest. I spent the days near him, the little maid coming in frequently, bringing perhaps my dinner or some drink for him.

"I teased her a little, which seemed to amuse her, but we did not talk, naturally, since we could not understand each other.

"But one night, when I had remained near the sick man very late, I met, in going to my chamber, the girl entering hers. It was just opposite my open door. Then brusquely, without reflecting upon what I was doing, and more in the way of a joke than anything, I seized her around the waist, and before she was over her astonishment I had taken her and shut her in my room. She looked at me, startled, excited, terrified, not daring to cry out for fear of scandal, and of being driven out by her master at first and her father afterward.

"I had done this in laughter; but when I saw her there, the desire to possess her carried me away. There was a long and silent struggle, a struggle of body against body after the fashion of athletes, with arms drawn, contracted, twisted, respiration short, skin moist with perspiration. Oh! she fought valiantly; and sometimes we would hit a piece of furniture, a partition, or a chair; then always clutching each other we would remain immovable for some seconds in the fear of some noise that would awaken some one; then we would commence again our exciting battle, I attacking, she resisting. Exhausted, finally, she fell; and I took her brutally, upon the ground, upon the floor.

"As soon as she was released, she ran to the door, drew the bolts, and fled. I scarcely met her for some days following. She would not allow me to approach her. Then, when my comrade was strong and we were to continue our journey, on the eve of our departure, she entered my apartment at midnight, barefooted, in her chemise, just as I was about to retire.

"She threw herself in my arms, drew me to her passionately, and, until daylight, embraced me, caressed me, weeping and sobbing giving me all the assurances of tenderness and despair that a woman can give when she does not know a word of our language.

"A week after this I had forgotten this adventure, so common and frequent when on a journey, the servants of the inns being generally destined to divert travelers thus.

"Thirty years passed without my thinking of, or returning to, Pont-Labbe. Then, in 1876, in the course of an excursion through Brittany, I happened to go there, as I was compiling a document which required statistics from the various parts of the country.

"Nothing seemed to have changed. The castle still soaked its gray walls in the pond at the entrance of the little town; the inn was there, too, although repaired, remodeled, with a modern air. On entering I was received by two young Bretons, of about eighteen, fresh and genteel, enlaced in their straight girdles of cloth, and encapped with silver embroidery over their ears.

"It was about six o'clock in the evening. I had sat down to dine when, the host coming to serve me himself, fatality, without doubt, led me to ask him: 'Did you know the former master of this house? I passed a fortnight here once, thirty years ago. I seem to be speaking to you from afar.'

"He answered: 'Those were my parents, sir.'

"Then I recounted the occasion of my stopping there, recalling my being detained by the illness of my comrade. He did not allow me to finish:

" 'Oh! I remember that perfectly,' said he; 'I was fifteen or sixteen then. You slept in the room at the end of the hall and your friend in the one that is now mine, upon the street.'

"Then for the first time, a lively remembrance of the pretty maid comes back to me. I asked: 'You recall a genteel, pretty servant that your father had, who had, if I remember, sparkling eyes and fine teeth?'

"He replied: 'Yes, sir; she died in childbed some time after.'

"And, pointing toward the courtyard where a thin, lame man was taking out some manure, he added: 'That is her son.'

"I began to laugh. 'He is not beautiful, and does not resemble his mother at all. Takes after his father, no doubt.'

"The innkeeper replied: 'It may be; but they never knew who his father was. She died without telling, and no one here knew she had a lover. It was a famous surprise when we found it out. No one was willing to believe it.'

"A kind of disagreeable shiver went over me, one of those painful suggestions that touch the heart, like the approach of a heavy vexation. I looked at the man in the yard. He came now to draw some water for the horses and carried two pails, limping, making grievous effort with the limb that was shorter. He was ragged and hideously dirty, with long yellow hair, so matted that it hung in strings on his cheeks.

"The innkeeper added: 'He doesn't amount to anything, but is taken care of by charity in the house. Perhaps he would have turned out better if he had been brought up like anybody.. But, you see how it is, sir? No father, no mother, no money! My parents took pity on him as a child, but after all—he was not theirs, you see.'

"I said nothing.

"I went to bed in my old room, and all night I could think of nothing but that frightful hostler, repeating to myself: 'What if that were my son! Could I have killed that girl and brought that creature into existence?'

"It was possible, surely. I resolved to speak to this man and to find out exactly the date of his birth. A difference of two months would arrest my doubts.

"I had him come to me the next day. But he could not speak French at all. He had the appearance of understanding nothing. Besides, he was absolutely ignorant of his age, which one of the maids asked him for me. And he held himself with the air of an idiot before me, rolling his cap in his knotty paws, laughing stupidly, with something of the old laugh of the mother in the corners of his mouth and eyes.

"But the host, becoming interested, went to look up his birth on the records. He entered into life eight months and twenty-six days after my departure from Pont-Labbe, because I recalled perfectly arriving at Lorient on the fifteenth of August. The record said: 'Father unknown.' The mother was called Jeanne Karradec.

"Then my heart began to beat with pressing blows. I could not speak, so suffocated did I feel. And I looked at that brute, whose long yellow hair seemed dirty and more tangled than that of beasts. And the beggar, constrained by my look, ceased to laugh, turned his head, and took himself off.

"Every day I would wander along the little river, sadly reflecting. But to what good? Nothing could help me. For hours and hours I would weigh all the reasons, good and bad, for and against the chances of my paternity, placing myself in inextricable positions, only to return again to the horrible suspicion, then to the conviction, more atrocious still, that his man was my son.

"I could not dine and I retired to my room. It was a long time before I could sleep. Then. sleep came, a sleep haunted with insupportable visions. I could see this ninny laughing in my face and calling me 'Papa.' Then he would change into a dog and bite me in the calf of my leg, in vain I tried to free myself, he would follow me always, and, in place of barking, he would speak, abusing me. Then he would go before my colleagues at the Academy called together for the purpose of deciding whether I was his father. And one of them cried: 'It is indubitable! See how he resembles him!'

"And in fact, I perceived that the monster did resemble me. And I awoke with this idea planted in my brain, and with the foolish desire to see the man again and decide whether he did or did not have features in common with my own.

"I joined him as he was going to mass (it was on Sunday) and gave him a hundred sous, scanning his face anxiously. He began to laugh in ignoble fashion, took the money, then, again constrained by my eye, he fled, after having blurted out a word almost inarticulate, which meant to say 'Thank you,' without doubt.

"That day passed for me in the same agony as the preceding. Toward evening I went to the proprietor and, with much caution, clothing of words, finesse, and roundabout conversation, I told him that I had become interested in this poor being so abandoned by everybody and so deprived of everything, and that I wished to do something for him.

"The man replied: 'Oh, don't worry about him, sir. He wants nothing; you will only make trouble for yourself. I employ him to clean the stable, and it is all that he can do. For that, I feed him and he sleeps with the horses. He needs nothing more. If you have some old clothes, give them to him, but they will be in pieces in a week.'

"I did not insist, reserving my opinion.

"The beggar returned that evening, horribly drunk, almost setting fire to the house, striking one of the horses a blow with a pickax, and finally ended the score by going to sleep in the mud out in the rain, thanks to my generosity. They begged me, the next day, not to give him any more money. Liquor made him furious, and when he had two sous in his pocket he drank it. The innkeeper added: 'To give him money is the same as wishing to kill him.' This man had absolutely never had any money, save a few centimes thrown to him by travelers, and he knew no other destination for it but the alehouse.

"Then I passed some hours in my room with an open book which I made a semblance of reading, but without accomplishing anything except to look at this brute. My son! my son! I was trying to discover if he was anything like me. By force of searching I believed I recognized some similar lines in the brow and about the nose. And I was immediately convinced of a resemblance which only different clothing and the hideous mane of the man disguised.

"I could not stay there very long without becoming suspected, and I set out with breaking heart, after having left with the innkeeper some money to sweeten the existence of his valet.

"For six years I lived with this thought, this horrible uncertainty, this abominable doubt. And each year I condemned myself to the punishment of seeing this brute wallow in his filth, imagining that he resembles me, and of seeking, always in vain, to be helpful to him.

"And each year I come back more undecided, more tortured, more anxious. I have tried to have him instructed, but he is an idot without resource. I have tried to render life less painful to him, but he is an irremediable drunkard and uses all the money that is given him for drink. And he knows very well how to sell his clothes and procure liquor.

"I have tried to arouse pity in his employer for him, that he might treat him more gently, offering him money always. The innkeeper, astonished, finally remarked very sagely: 'All this that you would like to do for him only ruins him. He must be kept like a prisoner. As soon as he has time given him or favors shown, he becomes unmanageable. If you wish to do good to abandoned children, choose one that will respond to your trouble.'

"What could I say to that?

"And if I should disclose a suspicion of the doubts which torture me, this creature would certainly turn rogue and exploit me, compromise me, ruin me. He would cry out to me 'Papa,' as in my dream.

"And I tell myself that I have killed the mother and ruined this atrophied being, larva of the stable, hatched and bred of vileness, this man who, treated as others are, might have been like others.

"And you will not understand the sensation strange, confused, and intolerable, the fear I have in his presence, from thinking that this has come from me, that he belongs to me by that intimate bond which binds father to son, that, thanks to the terrible laws of heredity, he is a part of me in a thousand things, by his blood and his hair and his flesh, and that he has the same germs of sickness and the same ferments of passion.

"And I have ever an unappeasable need of seeing him, and the sight of him makes me suffer horribly; and from my window down there I look at him as he works in the dung-hill of the beasts, repeating to myself: 'That is my son!'

"And I feel, sometimes, an intolerable desire to embrace him. But I have never even touched his sordid hand."

The Academician was silent. And his companion, the political man, murmured: "Yes, indeed; we ought to occupy ourselves a little more with the children who have no father."

Then a breath of wind traversing the great tree shook its berries, and enveloped with a fine, odorous cloud the two old men, who took long draughts of the sweet perfume.

And the senator added: "It is good to be twenty-five years old, and it is even good to have children like that."

A Way to Wealth

"Do you know what has become of Leremy?"

"He is captain of the Sixth Dragoons."

"And Pinson?"

"Subprefect."

"And Racollet?"

"Dead."

We hunted up other names which recalled to us young figures crowned with caps trimmed with gold braid. Later, we found some of these comrades, bearded, bald, married, the fathers of many children; and these meetings, these changes, gave us some disagreeable shivers, as they showed us how short life is, how quickly everything changes and passes away.

My friend asked: "And Patience, the great Patience?"

I roared.

"Oh! If you want to hear about him, listen to me: Four or five weeks ago, as traveling inspector at Limoges, I was awaiting the dinner hour. Seated before the *Grand Café* in Theater Square, I closed my eyes wearily. The tradesmen were coming in, in twos, or threes, or fours, taking their absinthe or vermouth, talking in a loud voice of their business and that of others, laughing violently, or lowering their voices when they communicated something important or delicate.

"I said to myself: 'What am I going to do after dinner?' And I thought of the long evening in this provincial town, of the slow, uninteresting walks through the unknown streets, of the overwhelming sadness which takes possession of the solitary traveler, of the people who pass, strangers in all things and through all things, the cut of their provincial coats, their hats, their trousers, their customs, local accent, their houses, shops and carriages of singular shape. And then the ordinary sounds to which one is not accustomed; the harassing sadness which presses itself upon you little by little until you feel as if you were lost in a dangerous country, which oppresses you and makes you wish yourself back at the hotel, the hideous hotel, where your room preserves a thousand suspicious odors, where the bed makes one hesitate and the basin has a hair glued in the dirt at the bottom.

"I thought about all this as I watched them light the gas, feeling my isolated distress increase by the falling of the shadows. What was I going to do after dinner? I was alone, entirely alone, and lamentably lonesome.

"A big man came in, seated himself at a neighboring table, and commanded in a formidable voice:

" 'Waiter, my bitters.'

"The 'my' in the phrase sounded like the report of a cannon. I understood immediately that everything in existence was his, belonged to him and not to any other, that he had his character, and, by Jove! his appetite, his pantaloons, his no matter what, after his own fashion, absolute, and more complete than important. He looked about him with a satisfied air. They brought him his bitters and he called:

" 'My paper.'

"I asked myself: 'Which is his paper, I wonder?' The name of that would certainly reveal to me his opinions, his theories, his hobbies, and his nature.

"The writer brought the 'Times.' I was surprised. Why the 'Times,' a grave, somber, doctrinal, heavy journal? I thought:

" 'He is then a wise man, of serious ways, regular habits, in short, a good commoner.'

"He placed on his nose some gold eyeglasses, turned around and, before commencing to read, cast another glance all around the room. He noticed me and immediately began to look at me in a persistent, uneasy fashion. I was on the point of asking him the reason for his attention, when he cried out from where he sat:

" 'By my pipe, if it is not Gontran Lardois!'

"I answered: 'Yes, sir, you have not deceived yourself.'

"Then he got up brusquely and came toward me with outstretched hands.

" 'Ah! my old friend, how are you?' asked he.

"My greeting was constrained, not knowing him at all. Finally I stammered:

" 'Why—very well—and you?'

"He began to laugh: 'It appears that you do not know me.'

" 'No, not quite— It seems to me—however—'

"He tapped me on the shoulder:

" 'There, there! Not to bother you any longer, I am Patience, Robert Patience, your chum, your comrade.'

"I recognized him. Yes, Robert Patience, my comrade at college. It was no other. I pressed the hand he extended to me and said:

" 'Everything going well with you?'

" 'With me? Like a charm.'

"His laugh rang with triumph. He inquired:

" 'What has brought you here?'

"I explained to him that I was inspector of finances, making the rounds.

"He replied, observing my badge: 'Then you are successful?'

"I replied: 'Yes, rather; and you?'

" 'Oh! I? Very, very!'

" 'What are you doing now?'

" 'I am in business.'

" 'Then you are making money?'

" 'Lots of it. I am rich. But, come to lunch with me to-morrow at noon, No. 17 Coq-qui-chante street; then you will see my place.'

"He appeared to hesitate a second, then continued:

" 'You are still the good rounder of former times?'

" 'Yes,—I hope so.'

" 'Not married?'

" 'No.'

" 'So much the better. And you are still as fond of fun and potatoes?'

"I commenced to find him deplorably commonplace. I answered, nevertheless: 'Yes.'

" 'And pretty girls?'

" 'As to that, yes.'

"He began to laugh, with a good, hearty laugh:

" 'So much the better, so much the better,' said he. 'You recall our first farce at Bordeaux, when we had supper at the Roupie coffeehouse? Ha! what a night!'

"I recalled that night, surely; and the memory of it amused me. Other facts were brought to mind, and still others. One would say:

"Do you remember the time we shut up the fawn in Father Latoque's cellar?'

"And he would laugh, striking his fist upon the table, repeating:

" 'Yes—yes—yes—and you remember the mouth of the professor in geography, M. Marin, when we sent off a cracker on the map of the world just as he was orating on the principal volcanoes of the earth?'

"Then brusquely, I asked him:

" 'And you, are you married?'

"He cried: 'For ten years, my dear fellow, and I have four children most astonishing monkeys; but you will see them and their mother.'

"We were talking loud; the neighbors were looking around at us in astonishment. Suddenly my friend looked at his watch, a chronometer as large as a citron, and cried out:

" 'Thunder! It is rude, but I shall have to leave you; I am not free this evening.'

"He rose, took both my hands and shook them as if he wished to break off my arms, and said:

" 'To-morrow at noon, you remember?'

" 'I remember.'

"I passed the morning at work at the house of the General-Treasurer. He wished to keep me for luncheon, but I told him that I had an appointment with a friend. He accompanied me out. I asked him:

" 'Do you know where Coq-qui-chante street is?'

"He answered: 'Yes, it is five minutes from here. As I have nothing to do, I will conduct you there.'

"And we set out on the way. Soon, I noticed the street we sought. It was wide, pretty enough, at the border of the town and the country. I noticed the houses and perceived number 17. It was a kind of hotel with a garden at the back. The front, ornamented with frescoes in the Italian fashion, appeared to me in bad taste. There were goddesses hanging to urns, and others whose secret beauties a cloud concealed. Two stone Cupids held up the number.

"I said to the Treasurer: 'Here is where I am going.'

"And I extended my hand by way of leaving him. He made a brusque and singular gesture, but said nothing, pressing the hand held out to him. I rang. A maid appeared. I said:

" 'M. Patience, if you please. Is he at home?'

"She replied: 'He is here, sir—Do you wish to speak with him?'

" 'Yes.'

"The vestibule was ornamented with paintings from the brush of some local artist. Paul and Virginia were embracing under some palms drowned in a rosy light. A hideous Oriental lantern hung from the ceiling. There were many doors, masked by showy hangings. But that which struck me particularly was the odor—a permeating, perfumed odor, recalling rice powder and the moldiness of cellars—an indefinable odor in a heavy atmosphere, as overwhelming as stifling, in which the human body becomes petrified. I ascended, behind the maid, a marble staircase which was covered by a carpet of some Oriental kind, and was led into a sumptuous drawing-room.

"Left alone, I looked about me.

"The room was richly furnished, but with the pretension of an ill-bred parvenu. The engravings of the last century were pretty enough, representing women with high, powdered hair and very low-cut bodices surprised by gallant gentlemen in interesting postures. Another lady was lying on a great bed, toying with her foot with a little dog drowned in draperies. Another resisted her lover complacently, whose hand was in a suspicious place. One design showed four feet whose bodies could be divined, although concealed behind a curtain. The vast room, surrounded by soft divans, was entirely impregnated with this enervating odor, which had already taken hold of me. There was something suspicious about these walls, these stuffs, this exaggerated luxury, in short, the whole place.

"I approached the window to look into the garden, of which I could see but the trees. It was large, shady, superb. A broad path was outlined on the turf, where a jet of water was playing in the air, brought in under some masonry some distance off. And suddenly three women appeared down there, at the end of the garden, between two shapely shrubs. They were walking slowly, taking hold of each other's arms, clothed in long white dresses clouded with lace. Two of them were blonde and the other a brunette.

"They disappeared immediately among the trees. I remained transfixed, charmed, before this short but delightful apparition, which brought surging to my mind a whole poetic world. They were scarcely to be seen at all in that bower of leaves, at the end of the park, so secluded and delicious. I must have dreamed, and these were the beautiful ladies of the last century wandering under the elmtree hedge, the ladies whose light loves the clever gravures on the walls recalled. And I thought of those happy times, flowery, incorporeal, tender, when customs were so sweet and lips so easy—

"A great voice behind me made me leap back into the room. Patience had come in, radiant, extending both his hands.

"He looked at me out of the end of his eyes with the sly air of some amorous confidence and, with a large, comprehensive gesture, a Napoleonic gesture, pointed out his sumptuous drawing-room, his park, with the three women passing again at the back, and in a triumphant voice that sang of pride, said:

" 'And when you think that I commenced with nothing—my wife and my sisters-in-law!' "

Am I Insane

AM I insane or jealous? I know not which, but I suffer horribly. I committed a crime it is true, but is not insane jealousy, betrayed love, and the terrible pain I endure enough to make anyone commit a crime, without actually being a criminal?

I have loved this woman to madness —and yet, is it true? Did I love her? No, no! She owned me body and soul, I was her plaything, she ruled me by her smile, her look, the divine form of her body. It was all those things that I loved but the woman contained in that body, I despise her; hate her. I always have hated her, for she is but an impure, perfidious creature, in whom there was no soul; even less than that, she is but a mass of soft flesh in which dwells infamy!

The first few months of our union were deliciously strange. Her eyes were three different colors. No, I am not insane, I swear they were. They were gray at noon, shaded green at twilight, and blue at sunrise. In moments of love they were blue; the pupils dilated and nervous. Her lips trembled and often the tip of her pink tongue could be seen, as that of a reptile ready to hiss. When she raised her heavy lids and I saw that ardent look, I shuddered, not only for the unceasing desire to possess her, but for the desire to kill this beast.

When she walked across the room each step resounded in my heart. When she disrobed and emerged infamous but radiant from the white mass of linen and lace, a sudden weakness seized me, my limbs gave way beneath me, and my chest heaved; I was faint, coward that I was!

Each morning when she awakened I waited for that first look, my heart filled with rage, hatred, and disdain for this beast whose slave I was; but when she fixed those limpid blue eyes on me, that languishing look showing traces of lassitude, it was like a burning, unquenchable fire within me, inciting me to passion.

When she opened her eyes that day I saw a dull, indifferent look; a look devoid of desire, and I knew then she was tired of me. I saw it, knew it, felt right away that it was all over, and each hour and minute proved to me that I was right. When I beckoned her with my arms and lips she shrank from me.

"Leave me alone," she said. "You are horrid!"

Then I became suspicious, insanely jealous; but I am not insane, no indeed! I watched her slyly; not that she had betrayed me, but she was so cold that I knew another would soon take my place.

At times she would say:

"Men disgust me!" Alas! it was too true.

Then I became jealous of her indifference, of her thoughts, which I knew to be impure, and when she awakened sometimes with that same look of lassitude I suffocated with anger, and an irresistible desire to choke her and make her confess the shameful secrets of her heart took hold of me.

Am I insane? No.

One night I saw that she was happy. I felt, in fact I was convinced, that a new passion ruled her. As of old, her eyes shone, she was feverish and her whole self fluttered with love.

I feigned ignorance, but I watched her closely. I discovered nothing however. I waited a week, a month, almost a year. She was radiantly, ideally happy; as if soothed by some ephemeral caress.

At last I guessed. No, I am not insane, I swear I am not. How can I explain this inconceivable, horrible thing? How can I make myself understood? This is how I guessed.

She came in one night from a long ride on horseback and sank exhausted in a seat facing me. An unnatural flush tinted her cheeks and her eyes,—those eyes that I knew so well,—had such a look in them. I was not mistaken, I had seen her look like that; she loved! But whom? What? I almost lost my head, and so as not to look at her I turned to the window. A valet was leading her horse to the stable and she stood and watched him disappear; then she fell asleep almost immediately. I thought and thought all night. My mind wandered through mysteries too deep to conceive. Who can fathom the perversity and strange caprices of a sensual woman?

Every morning she rode madly through hills and dales and each time came back languid; exhausted. At last I understood. It was of the horse I was jealous—of the wind which caressed her face, of the drooping leaves and of the dewdrops, of the saddle which carried her! I resolved to be revenged. I became very attentive. Every time she came back from her ride I helped her down and the horse made a vicious rush at me. She would pat him on the neck, kiss his quivering nostrils, without even wiping her lips. I watched my chance.

One morning I got up before dawn and went to the path in the woods she loved so well. I carried a rope with me, and my pistols were hidden in my breast as if I were going to fight a duel. I drew the rope across the path, tying it to a tree on each side, and hid myself in the grass. Presently I heard her horse's hoofs, then I saw her coming at a furious pace; her cheeks flushed, an insane look in her eyes. She seemed enraptured; transported into another sphere.

As the animal approached the rope he struck it with his fore feet and fell. Before she had struck the ground I caught her in my arms and helped her to her feet. I then approached the horse, put my pistol close to his ear, and shot him—as I would a man.

She turned on me and dealt me two terrific blows across the face with her riding-whip which felled me, and as she rushed at me again, I shot her!

Tell me, Am I insane?

Forbidden Fruit

BEFORE marriage they had loved each other chastely, in the starlight. At first there was a charming meeting on the shore of the ocean. He found her delicious, the rosy young girl who passed him with her bright umbrellas and fresh costumes on the marine background. He loved this blond, fragile creature in her setting of blue waves and immense skies. And he confounded the tenderness which this scarcely fledged woman caused to be born in him with the vague and powerful emotion awakened in his soul, in his heart, and in his veins by the lovely salt air and the great seascape full of sun and waves.

She loved him because he paid her attention, because he was young and rich enough, genteel and delicate. She loved him because it is natural for young ladies to love young men who say tender words to them.

Then for three months they lived side by side, eye to eye, and hand to hand. The greeting which they exchanged in the morning, before the bath, in the freshness of the new day, and the adieu of the evening, upon the sand under the stars, in the warmth of the calm night, murmured low and still lower, had already the taste of kisses, although their lips had never met.

They dreamed of each other as soon as they were asleep, thought of each other as soon as they awoke, and, without yet saying so, called for and desired each other with their whole soul and body.

After marriage they adored each other above everything on earth. It was at first a kind of sensual, indefatigable rage; then an exalted tenderness made of palpable poesy, of caresses already refined, and of inventions both genteel and ungenteel. All their looks signified something impure, and all their gestures recalled to them the ardent intimacy of the night.

Now, without confessing it, without realizing it, perhaps, they commenced to weary of one another. They loved each other, it is true; but there was nothing more to reveal, nothing more to do that had not often been done, nothing 'more to learn from each other, not even a new word of love, an unforeseen motion, or an intonation, which sometimes is more expressive than a known word too often repeated.

They forced themselves, however, to relight the flame, enfeebled from the first embraces. They invented some new and tender artifice each day, some simple or complicated ruse, in the vain attempt to renew in their hearts the unappeasable ardor of the first days, and in their veins the flame of the nuptial month.

From time to time, by dint of whipping their desire, they again found an hour of factitious excitement which was immediately followed by a disgusting lassitude.

They tried moonlight walks under the leaves in the sweetness of the night, the poesy of the cliffs bathed in mist, the excitement of public festivals.

Then, one morning, Henrietta said to Paul:

"Will you take me to dine at an inn?"

"Why, yes, my dearie."

"In a very well-known inn?"

"Yes."

He looked at her, questioning with his eye, understanding well that she had something in mind which she had not spoken.

She continued: "You know, an inn—how shall I explain it?—in a gallant inn, where people make appointments to meet each other?"

He smiled: "Yes. I understand, a private room in a large *café?*"

"That is it. But in a large *café* where you are known, where you have already taken supper—no, dinner—that is — I mean—I want—no, I do not dare say it!"

"Speak out, *chérie;* between us what can it matter? We are not like those who have little secrets from each other."

"No, I dare not."

"Oh! come, now! Don't be so innocent. Say it."

"Well—oh! well—I wish—I wish to be taken for your mistress—and that the waiters, who do not know that you are married, may look upon me as your mistress, and you too—that for an hour, you believe me your mistress, in that very place where you have remembrances of—That's all! And I myself will believe that I am your mistress— —I want to commit a great sin—to deceive you—with yourself—there! It is very bad but that is what I want to do— Do not make me blush—I feel that I am blushing—imagine—my wanting to take the trouble to dine with you in a place not quite the thing—in a private room where people devote themselves to love every evening—every evening— It is very bad—I am as red as a peony! Don't look at me!"

He laughed, very much amused, and responded:

"Yes, we will go, this evening, to a very *chic* place where I am known."

Toward seven o'clock they mounted

the staircase of a large *café* on the Boulevard, he, smiling, with the air of a conqueror, she timid, veiled, but delighted. When they were in a little room furnished with four armchairs and a large sofa covered with red velvet, the steward, in black clothes, entered and presented the bill of fare. Paul passed it to his wife.

"What do you wish to eat?' said he.

"I don't know; what do they have that is good here?"

Then he read off the list of dishes while taking off his overcoat, which he handed to a waiter. Then he said :

"Serve this *menu:* Bisque soup— deviled chicken—sides of hare—duck, American style,—vegetable salad, and dessert. We will drink champagne."

The steward smiled and looked at the young lady. He took the card, murmuring: "Will M. Paul have a cordial or some champagne?"

"Champagne, very dry."

Henrietta was happy to find that this man knew her husband's name. They sat down side by side upon the sofa and began to eat.

Ten candles lighted the room, reflected in a great mirror, mutilated by the thousands of names traced on it with a diamond, making on the clear crystal a kind of huge cobweb.

Henrietta drank glass after glass to animate her, although she felt giddy from the first one. Paul, excited by certain memories, kissed his wife's hand repeatedly. Her eyes were brilliant.

She felt strangely moved by this suspicious situation; she was excited and happy, although she felt a little defiled. Two grave waiters, mute, accustomed to seeing everything and forgetting all, en-

tered only when it was necessary, and going out in the moments of overflow, going and coming quickly and softly.

Toward the middle of the dinner, Henrietta was tipsy, completely tipsy, and Paul, in his gaiety, pressed her knee with all his force. She prattled now, boldly, her cheeks red, her look lively and dizzy.

"Oh! come Paul," she said, "confess now, won't you; I want to know all."

"What do you mean, *chérie?*"

"I dare not say it."

"But you must always—"

"Have you had mistresses—many of them—before me?"

He hesitated, a little perplexed, not knowing whether he ought to conceal his good fortunes or boast of them.

She continued: "Oh! I beg you to tell me, have you had many?"

"Why some."

"How many?"

"I don't know. How can one know such things?"

"You cannot count them?"

"Why, no!"

"Oh! then you have had very many?"

"Yes."

"How many, do you suppose—somewhere near—"

"I don't know at all, my dear. Some years I had many and some only a few."

"How many a year, should you say?"

"Sometimes twenty or thirty, sometimes four or five only."

"Oh! that makes more than a hundred women in all."

"Yes, somewhere near."

"Oh! how disgusting!"

"Why disgusting?"

"Because it is disgusting—when one

thinks of all those women—bare—and always—always the same thing— Oh! it is disgusting all the same—more than a hundred women."

He was shocked that she thought it disgusting, and responded with that superior air which men assume to make women understand that they have said something foolish:

"Well, that is curious! If it is disgusting to have a hundred women, it is equally disgusting to have one."

"Oh, no, not at all!"

"Why not?"

"Because with one woman there is intrigue, there is a love that attaches you to her, while with a hundred women there is filthiness, misconduct. I cannot understand how a man can meddle with all those girls who are so foul—"

"No, they are very neat."

"One cannot be neat carrying on a trade like that."

"On the contrary, it is because of their trade that they are neat."

"Oh! pshaw! when one thinks of the nights they pass with others! It is ignoble!"

"It is no more ignoble than drinking from a glass from which I know not who drank this morning, and that has been less thoroughly washed—you may be certain of it—"

"Oh! be still, you are revolting."

"But why ask me then if I have had mistresses?"

"Then tell me, were your mistresses all girls, all of them—the whole hundred?"

"Why, no—no—"

"Some were actresses—some little working girls—and some—women of the world—"

"How many of them were women of the world?"

"Six."

"Only six?'

"Yes."

"Were they pretty?"

"Yes, of course."

"Prettier than the girls?"

"No."

"Which did you prefer, girls or women of the world?"

"Girls."

"Oh! how filthy! Why?"

"Because I do not care much for amateur talent."

"Oh! horror! You are abominable, do you know it? But tell me, is it very amusing to pass from one to another like that?"

"Yes, rather."

"Very?"

"Very."

"What is there amusing about it? Is it because they do not resemble each other?"

"They do not."

"Ah! the women do not resemble each other."

"Not at all."

"In nothing?"

"In nothing."

"That is strange! In what respect do they differ?"

"In every respect."

"In body?"

"Yes, in body."

"In the whole body?"

"Yes, in the whole body."

"And in what else?"

"Why, in the manner of—of embracing, of speaking, of saying the least thing."

"Ah! and it is very amusing, this changing?"

"Yes."

"And are men different too?"

"That I do not know."

"You do not know?"

"No."

"They must be different."

"Yes, without doubt.'"

She remained pensive, her glass of champagne in her hand. It was full and she drank it at a draught; then placing the glass upon the table, she threw both arms around her husband's neck, and murmured in his mouth:

"Oh! my dear, how I love you!" He seized her in a passionate embrace—

A waiter who was entering, drew back, closing the door; and the service was interrupted for about five minutes.

When the steward again appeared, with a grave, dignified air, bringing in the fruits for the dessert, she was holding another glassful between her fingers and, looking to the bottom of the yellow, transparent liquid, as if to see there things unknown and dreamed of, she murmured, with a thoughtful voice:

"Oh! yes! It must be very amusing, all the same!"

The Charm Dispelled

THE boat was filled with people. As the passage promised to be good, many people of Havre were making a trip to Trouville.

They loosed the moorings, a last whistle announced the departure, and immediately the entire body of the vessel shook, while a sound of stirring water was heard all along the sides. The wheels turned for some seconds, stopped, and then started gently. The captain, upon his bridge, having cried, "Go ahead!" through the tube which extends into the depths of the machinery, they now began to beat the waves with great rapidity.

We passed along the pier, covered with people. Some that were on the boat waved their handkerchiefs, as if they were setting out for America, and the friends who remained behind responded in the same fashion.

The great July sun fell upon the red umbrellas, the bright costumes, the joyous faces, and upon the ocean, scarcely moved by any undulations. As soon as they had left the port, the little vessel made a sharp turn, pointing its nose directly for the far-off coast rising to meet the foam.

On our left was the mouth of the Seine, more than twelve miles wide. Here and there great buoys pointed out banks of sand, and one could see at a distance the fresh, muddy water of the river, which had not yet mingled with the salt brine, outlined in broad, yellow stripes upon the immense, pure green sheet of the open sea.

As soon as I boarded the boat I felt

the need of walking up and down, like a sailor on his watch. Why? That I cannot say. But I began to circulate among the crowd of passengers on deck.

Suddenly some one called my name. I turned around. It was Henry Sidonie, whom I had not seen for ten years.

After we had shaken hands we resumed the walk of a bear in his cage which I had been taking alone, while we talked of people and things. And we looked at the two lines of travelers seated on both sides of the boat, chatting all the while.

All at once, Sidonie exclaimed, with a veritable expression of rage: "It is crowded with English here! Nasty people!"

The boat was full of English, in fact. Men standing about scanned the horizon with an important air which seemed to say: "It is the English who are masters of the sea! Boom! boom! here we are!"

And the white veils upon their white hats had the air of flags in their self-sufficiency.

The thin young girls, whose boots recalled the naval construction of their country, wrapping their straight figures and thin arms in multicolored shawls, smiled vaguely at the radiant landscape. Their little heads, perched on the top of their long bodies, wearing the peculiarly shaped English hat, were finished, at the back of the neck, by their thin hair, coiled around to resemble sleeping adders.

And the old spinsters, still more lank, opening to the wind their national jaw, appeared to threaten space with their enormous yellow teeth. In passing near them, one smells an odor of caoutchouc or some kind of dentifrice.

Sidonie repeated, with an increasing anger:

"Nasty people! Why couldn't they be hindered from coming to France?"

I inquired, laughingly: "Why, what do you care? As for me, I am perfectly indifferent to them."

He answered: "Yes, you are, indeed! But I—I married an Englishwoman. And there you have it!"

I stopped and laughed in his face. "The devil!" said I; "tell me about it. Has she made you so unhappy?"

He shrugged his shoulders, as he replied: "No, not precisely."

"Then she—she has—deceived you?"

"Unfortunately, no. That would give me a cause for divorce, and I should be free."

"But I do not understand."

"You do not understand? That is not astonishing. Well, she simply learned the French language, nothing more! Listen:

"I had never had the least desire to marry when I went to pass the summer at Etretat, two years ago. But there is nothing more dangerous than watering-places. One cannot imagine to what an advantage young girls are seen there. Paris may be for women, but the country is for young girls.

"The idiotic promenades, the morning baths, lunches upon the grass, all are so many snares for marriage. And, truly, there is nothing prettier than a girl of eighteen running across a field or picking flowers along the road.

"I made the acquaintance of an English family living at the same hotel as myself. The father resembled the men you see there, and the mother all other Englishwomen. They had two sons, boys, all bones, who played at violent games, with balls, sticks, or rackets, from morning until evening; then, two girls, the elder a lean, well-preserved English-woman of maturity, the younger a wonder. She was a blonde, or rather a blondine, with a head that came from the skies. When they do undertake to be pretty, these wretches, they are divine. She had blue eyes, of the blue which seems to contain all the poetry, dreams, hopes, and happiness of the world!

"What a horizon of infinite thought opens before you in the two eyes of a woman like that! How well she responds to the eternal, vague expectation of our hearts!

"It is only necessary to remember that Frenchmen always adore foreigners. As soon as we meet a Russian, an Italian, a Swede, a Spanish, or an English-woman at all pretty, we fall in love with her immediately. Everything that comes from abroad fills us with enthusiasm, whether it be trouser cloth, hats, gloves, guns, or—women. We are wrong nevertheless.

"But I believe the most seductive thing about these exotics is their faulty pronunciation of our language. As soon as a woman speaks French badly, she is charming. If she uses a wrong word, she is exquisite, and if she jabbers in a manner quite unintelligible, she becomes irresistible.

"You cannot imagine how pretty it is to hear a sweet, red mouth say: '*J'aime beaucoup la gigotte*' (I like mutton so much!).

"My little English Kate spoke a most unlikely tongue. I could understand nothing of it in the first days, she invented so many unheard-of words. That was when I became absolutely in love with the comical, gay little monkey. All these crippled, strange, ridiculous terms took on a delicious charm upon her lips; and, on the Casino terrace, in the evening, we had many long conversations, resembling spoken enigmas.

"I married her! I loved her foolishly, as one can love a dream. For the true lover adores naught but a dream which takes the shape of a woman. You recall Louis Bouilhet's admirable verse:

" 'You only were, in those rarest days,
    A common instrument under my art;
    Like the bow, on the *viol d'amour* it plays,
    I dreamed my dream o'er your empty heart.'

"Well, my dear, the greatest mistake I made was to give my wife a teacher of French. As long as she made a martyr of the dictionary and punished the grammar, I was fond of her. Our talks were very simple. She showed a surprising grace of mind, an incomparable elegance in her actions. She seemed to be a marvelous speaking jewel, a doll of flesh made to kiss, knowing how to make known, or at least indicate the things she desired, uttering at times the strangest exclamations, and expressing rather complicated sensations and emotions in a coquettish fashion, with a force as incomprehensible as it was unforeseen. She much resembled those pretty playthings which say 'papa' and 'mamma,' pronouncing them 'Baba' and 'Bamban.'

"Could I have believed that—

"She speaks now—she speaks—badly —very badly— She makes just as many mistakes—but I can understand her— yes, I understand—I know— and I know her—

"I have opened my doll to see what was inside. I have seen. And one must talk, my dear!

"Ah! you don't know, you could never imagine the theories, the ideas, the opinions of a young Englishwoman, well brought up, in whom there is nothing to reproach, who repeats to me morning and evening all the phrases in the dictionary of conversation in use at the schools for young people.

"You have seen those favors for a cotillon, those pretty gilt-paper-covered execrable bonbons? I had one of them. I tore it open. I wished to taste what was inside, and became so disgusted that now there is a rebellion in my feelings if I but see one of her compatriots.

"I have married a paroquet to whom an old-time instructress had taught French. Do you understand?"

The port of Trouville now showed its wooden piers, covered with people. I said:

"Where is your wife?"

He answered: "I have just taken her back to Etretat."

"And where are you going?"

"I? I am going to try and divert myself at Trouville."

Then, after a silence, he added: "You cannot imagine hom irksome a wife can become sometimes."

Madame Parisse

I WAS seated on the mole of the little port of Obernon, near the hamlet of La Salis, watching Antibes in the setting sun. I have never seen anything so wonderfully beautiful. The little town, inclosed within its heavy fortifications of masonry (constructed by Monsieur de Vauban), was situated in the middle of the Gulf of Nice. The great waves rolled in from afar to throw themselves at its feet, surrounding it with a garland of foam; and, above the ramparts, the houses could be seen, climbing one above another up to the two towers pointing to the sky like two horns on an ancient helmet, and standing out against the milky whiteness of the Alps—an enormous, illimitable wall of snow that appeared to shut off the entire horizon. Between the white foam at the foot of the walls and the white snow on the border of the sky, the little city, sparkling and upright on the blue background of the nearest mountain, shone in the rays of the setting sun, looking like a pyramid of red-roofed houses, the *façades* of which were white, yet of such different shades of white that they seemed to be of many hues.

The sky above the Alps was of a pale blue that was almost white, as if the snow had given to it some of its own whiteness. A few silvery clouds floated near the pale summit; and, on the other side of the gulf, Nice lay on the edge of the water like a white ribbon between the sea and the mountains. Two great lateen sails, forced onward by a strong breeze, appeared to run before the waves. I gazed at the scene, enchanted with its beauty. It was one of those sights so charming, so rare, so exquisite, which seem to take possession of you, and become one of those moments never to be forgotten, like certain happy memories. We think, we enjoy, we suffer, we are moved, from various causes, but we love by seeing! He that can feel deep emotion through the power of sight experiences the same keen joy refined and profound, felt by the man with a sensitive and nervous ear when listening to music that stirs the heart.

I said to my companion, Monsieur Martini, a pure-blooded southerner, "That is certainly one of the rarest spectacles that it ever has been my good fortune to admire. I have seen Mont-Saint-Michel, that enormous jewel of granite, spring forth from the sands at sunrise. I have seen, in the Sahara, Lake Raianecherqui, fifty kilometers in length, shine under a moon as brilliant as our sun, and exhale toward the clouds a vapor as white as milk. I have seen in the Lipari Islands the fantastic sulphur crater of Volcanello, a giant flower, the center of which is a volcano that smokes and burns with a limitless yellow flame that spreads out over the ocean. But I have seen nothing more impressive than Antibes, standing before the Alps in the setting sun. And I cannot tell why, at this moment, souvenirs of olden days haunt me. Verses of Homer come into my mind. It is a city of the old Orient, Antibes, it is a city of the 'Odyssey,' it is a western Troy—even though Troy was far from the sea."

Monsieur Martini drew from his pocket a Sarty guide, and read:

"The city was originally a colony founded by the Phœnicians of Marseilles, about the year 340 B. C. It received from them the Greek name of Antipolis, that is to say, 'city over against,' 'city in front of another,' because, in reality, it was situated opposite Nice, another colony of Marseilles. After the conquest of the Gauls, the Romans made of Antibes a municipal city, and her inhabitants enjoyed the privileges of a Roman city."

"We know," he continued, "by an epigram of Martial, that in his time—"

I interrupted him, saying: "I don't care what it was! I tell you I have before my eyes a city of the 'Odyssey.' Coast of Asia or coast of Europe—they are alike; and there is nothing on the other shore of the Mediterranean that awakens in me the memory of heroic days as does this."

The sound of an approaching step caused me to turn my head; a tall, dark woman was passing along the road that follows the sea in the direction of the cape.

Monsieur Martini murmured, emphasizing the last words: "It is Madame Parisse—you know!"

No, I did not know, but this name thrown out, the name of the shepherd of Troy, confirmed me in my dream.

I said, however, "Who is this Madame Parisse?"

He appeared surprised that I did not know her story. I reaffirmed that I did not know it, and I looked at the woman, who went on without seeing us, dreaming, walking with a slow, stately step, like the dames of antiquity, without doubt. She was about thirty-five years old, and beautiful yet, very beautiful, though perhaps a trifle too plump.

After she had passed out of sight, Monsieur Martini told me this story.

"Madame Parisse, a Mademoiselle Combelombe, had married, a year before the war of 1870, Monsieur Parisse, an employee of the government. She was then a beautiful young girl, as slender and gay as she has since become stout and sad. She had accepted Monsieur Parisse reluctantly; he was one of those little red-tape men, with short legs, who make a great fuss in a pint measure, which is yet too large for them.

"After the war, Antibes was occupied by a single battalion of line commanded by Monsieur Jean de Carmelin, a young officer who had been decorated during the campaign, and had only recently received the four stripes. As he was greatly bored with the life in that fortress, in that suffocating mole-hill shut in by enormous double walls, the commander went quite often for a walk on the Cape, a sort of park or forest, where there was a fine, fresh breeze.

"There he met Madame Parisse, who used also to come on summer evenings to breathe the fresh air under the trees. How was it that they loved? Can one tell? They met, they looked at each other, and when they could not meet, they thought of each other, without doubt. The image of the young woman with the brown eyes, black hair, and pale face, the image of that fresh and beautiful southern girl, who showed her pretty white teeth in smiling, remained floating before the eyes of the officer, who would continue his promenade lost in thought, biting his cigar instead of smoking it. And the image of the commander in his close-fitting coat and red trousers, covered with gold lace, whose blond moustache curled on his lip, must have remained before the eyes of Madame Parisse when her husband, unshaved, badly dressed, short of limb, and with pursy stomach, returned home for supper.

"From meeting so often, they smiled at seeing each other, perhaps; and from that they came to think they knew each other. He bowed to her, certainly. She was surprised, and inclined her head slightly, only just enough to escape being impolite. But at the end of two weeks she returned his salutations from afar, before coming face to face.

"He talked to her! Of what? Of the setting sun, without any doubt! And they admired it together, looking deep into each other's eyes more often than at the horizon. And every day during two weeks there was some simple pretext for a little chat of several minutes. Then they dared to take a few steps together in talking of something or other; but their eyes spoke of a thousand things more intimate, of secret and charming things, the reflection of which in the softness and emotion of a look causes the heart to beat, because they reveal the soul better than words. Then he must have taken her hand and murmured those words which a woman divines without appearing to have heard them.

"It was admitted between them that they loved, without submitting their mutual knowledge to the proof of sensuality or passion. She would have been content to remain indefinitely at the stage of romantic tenderness, but not he—he wished to go further. And he pressed her, every day more ardently, to give herself entirely to him. She resisted, did not wish it, and even seemed resolved never to yield.

"One evening, however, she said to him, as if by chance: 'My husband has just gone to Marseilles, and is going to remain there four days.'

"Jean de Carmelin threw himself at her feet, begging her to open her door that very evening near eleven o'clock. But she would not listen to him, and returned home as if angry. The commandant was in a bad humor all the evening; and the next day beginning at daybreak he walked on the ramparts in a rage, going from the drum-school to the platoon-school, and meting out reprimands to officers and men like one throwing stones into a crowd. But on returning for breakfast, he found under his napkin a note containing these four words: 'This evening, ten o'clock.' And he gave five francs, without any apparent reason, to the boy who served him.

"The day seemed long. He passed a part of it in prinking and perfuming himself. At the moment when he placed himself at the table for dinner, another envelope was handed to him. He found inside this telegram:

" 'My darling, business terminated. I return this evening: train at nine.
PARISSE.'

"The commandmant gave vent to an oath so violent that the boy let the soup-toureen fall on the floor. What should he do? Certainly, he wanted her, and that very night, too, let it cost what it might, and he would have her. He would have her by some means or another, if he had to arrest and imprison her husband. Suddenly an insane idea

crossed his mind. He called for paper and wrote:

" 'MADAME: He will not return this evening. I swear it to you, and I will be at ten o'clock at the place you know. Fear nothing, I guarantee everything on my honor as an officer.
" 'JEAN DE CARMELIN.'

"And, having sent this letter, he dined tranquilly. About eight o'clock he summoned Captain Gribois, who was next in command, and said to him, while rolling between his fingers the rumpled dispatch of Monsieur Parisse: 'Captain, I have received a telegram of a singular character, which it is impossible for me to communicate to you. You must go immediately and guard the gates of the city, in such a way that no one —you understand, no one—either comes in or goes out before six o'clock to-morrow morning. You must place guards in the streets also, and compel the inhabitants to go into their houses at nine o'clock. Anyone who is found outside after that hour will be conducted to his domicile *manu militari*. If your men meet me during the night they must retire at once with an air of not recognizing me. Do you understand me thoroughly?'

" 'Yes, commandant.'

" 'I make you responsible for the execution of these orders, captain.'

" 'Yes, commandant.'

" 'Would you like a glass of Chartreuse?'

" 'With pleasure, commandant.'

"They touched glasses, drank the yellow liquor, and Captain Gribois departed.

"The train from Marseilles came into

the station at exactly nine o'clock, and left on the platform two travelers, then went on its way toward Nice.

"One of the travelers was tall and thin. He was a Monsieur Saribe, merchant in oils. The other passenger was short and stout,—it was Monsieur Parisse. They started on their way together, their traveling bags in their hands, to reach the town, a kilometer distant. But on arriving at the gate the sentinels crossed their bayonets and ordered them off.

"Alarmed, amazed, and filled with astonishment they drew aside and deliberated; then, after taking counsel together, they returned with precaution to parley, and to make known their names. But the soldiers must have received peremptory orders, for they threatened to shoot, and the two travelers, greatly frightened, took flight at the top of their speed, leaving behind them their bags, which impeded their flight.

"The two unfortunate travelers made the circle of the ramparts and presented themselves at the Porte de Cannes. This also was closed and guarded as well by a menacing sentinel. Messieurs Saribe and Parisse, like prudent men, insisted no longer, but returned to the station to find a shelter, for the road around the fortifications was not very safe after sunset.

"The employee at the station, surprised and sleepy, gave them permission to remain until daylight in the waiting-room. They sat there, without light, side by side, on the green velvet-covered bench, too frightened to think of sleeping. The night was long for them.

"Toward half past six they learned that the gates were open and that one

could at last enter Antibes. They started for the town, but did not find their bags along the way. When they had passed through the gates, still a little uneasy, the Commandant de Carmelin, with a sly look and his head in the air, came himself to meet and question them. He bowed to them politely, and made excuses for having caused them to pass a bad night, but said he had been obliged to execute orders.

"The people of Antibes were mystified. Some talked of a surprise meditated by the Italians; others of the landing of the imperial prince; and still others imagined an Orléanist plot. The truth was not guessed until later, when they learned that the battalion of the commandant had been sent far away, and that Monsieur de Carmelin had been severely punished."

Monsieur Martini ceased speaking, and soon after Madame Parisse reappeared, her walk being finished. She passed sedately near me, her eyes on the Alps, the summits of which were ruddy with the last rays of the setting sun.

I desired to salute her, that poor, saddened woman who must think always of that one night of love now so far in the past, and of the bold man who had dared, for a kiss from her, to put a whole city in a state of siege and compromise his future. To-day he had probably forgotten her, unless sometimes, after drinking, he relates that audacious farce, so comic and so tender.

Had she ever seen him again? Did she love him still? And I thought: Here, indeed, is a trait of modern love, grotesque and yet heroic. The Homer who will sing of this Helen, and of the adventures of her Menelaus, must have the soul of a Merimée. And yet, the captain, this lover of that deserted woman, was valiant, bold, beautiful, strong as Achilles, and more cunning than Ulysses.

Making a Convert

WHEN Sabot entered the Martinville Inn, they all laughed in advance. This rascal of a Sabot, how farcical he was! See how he disliked curates, for example! Ah! yes, yes! He was ready to eat them, this merry fellow.

Sabot (Théodule), master carpenter, represented the progressive party at Martinville. He was a tall, thin man, with gay, cunning eyes, hair glued to his temples, and thin lips. When he said: "Our holy father, the priest," in a certain fashion, everybody was convulsed. He made it a point to work on Sunday during mass. Every year he would kill his pig on Monday of Holy Week in order to have blood pudding until Easter, and when he passed the curate he would always say, in a way of a joke:

"Here's a man who finds his good God upon the roof."

The priest, a large man, very tall also, dreaded him because of his talk, which made partisans. Father Maritime was a politic man, a friend of ease. The struggle between them had gone on for ten years, a secret struggle, provoking and incessant. Sabot was municipal counselor. It was believed that he would be mayor, which would be decidedly bad for the church.

The elections were about to take place. The religious camp in Martinville trembled. Then, one morning the curate set out for Rouen, announcing to his servant that he was going to see the Archbishop.

Two days later he returned. He had a joyous, triumphant air. The next day everybody knew that the choir of the church was to be remodeled. A sum of six hundred francs had been given by Monsieur from his private cashbox.

All the old pine stalls were to be removed and be replaced by new ones of heart of oak. It was a considerable piece of carpenter work, and they were talking about it in every house that evening.

Théodule Sabot did not laugh. The next day, when he went through the village, his neighbors, friends, and enemies said to him in a joking manner:

"Is it you who is to make over the choir of the church?"

He found nothing to answer, but he raged, and raged silently. The rogues would add:

"It is a good job; not less than two or three hundred clear profit."

Two days later it was known that the repairs had been given to Celestin Chambrelan, the carpenter of Percheville. Then the news was contradicted; then it was said that all of the benches of the church were also to be renewed. This would be worth two thousand francs, as some one had found out from the administration. The excitement was great.

Théodule Sabot was not asleep. Never, within the memory of man had a carpenter of the country executed a like piece of work. Then a rumor was heard that the curate was desolate at having to give this work to an out-of-town workman, but that Sabot's opinions were so opposed to his that it was impossible to give it to him.

Sabot knew it. He betook himself to the priest's house at nightfall. The servant told him that the curate was in the church. He went there. Two Ladies of the Virgin, sourish old maids, were decorating the altar for the month of Mary under the direction of the priest. There he was, in the middle of the choir, swelling out his enormous front, as he directed the work of the two women who, mounted on chairs, disposed of bouquets about the tabernacle.

Sabot felt under restraint in there, as if he were on the enemy's ground, but the desire of gain was ever pricking at his heart. He approached, cap in hand, without even noticing the Ladies of the Virgin, who remained standing, stupefied and immovable upon the chairs. He stammered:

"Good evening, Mr. Curate."

The priest responded without looking at him, all occupied with the altar:

"Good evening, Mr. Carpenter.

Sabot, out of his element, could say nothing further. After a silence, he said, however, "You are going to make some repairs?"

Father Maritime answered: "Yes, we are approaching the month of Mary."

Sabot repeated: "That's it, that's it," and then he was silent.

He felt now like withdrawing without saying anything more, but a glance of the eye around the choir restrained him. He perceived that there were sixteen stalls to be made, six to the right, and eight to the left, the door of the sacristy occupying two places more. Sixteen stalls in oak would be worth three hundred francs and, in round numbers, there ought to be two hundred francs' profit on the work if it was managed well. Then he stammered:

"I—I've come for the work."

The curate appeared surprised. He asked:

"What work?"

"The work of the repairs," murmured Sabot, desperately.

Then the priest turned toward him and, looking him straight in the eye, said: "And you speak to me of working on the choir stalls of my church!"

The tone of Father Maritime's voice caused a cold chill to run down the back of Théodule Sabot, and gave him a furious desire to scamper away. Nevertheless, he responded with humility.

"Why, yes, Mr. Curate."

Then the priest folded his arms across his ample front, and, as if powerless from surprise, replied:

"You—you—you—Sabot, come to ask that from me— You—the only impious soul in my parish! Why, it would be a scandal, a public scandal. The Archbishop would reprimand me and send me to another place, perhaps."

He breathed hard for some seconds, then in a calmer tone he continued:

"I understand that it would be hard for you to see a work of so much importance go to a carpenter in a neighboring parish. But I could not do otherwise, at least not unless—no—it is impossible. You would never consent—and without that—never."

Sabot regarded critically the line of benches that came almost up to the door of the sacristy. Christopher! If one might be able to make this alteration! And he asked: "What is it you consider necessary? Say it."

The priest, in a firm tone, replied: "It would be necessary for me to have a statement of your goodwill."

Sabot murmured: "I should say nothing—I should say nothing—that would be understood."

The curate declared: "It would be necessary to take public communion at high mass, next Sunday—"

The carpenter grew pale and, without answering, asked:

"And the church benches, are they going to be replaced with new ones too?"

The priest responded with assurance: "Yes, but that will come later."

Sabot repeated: "I would say nothing, I say nothing. In fact, I feel nothing derogatory to religion, and I believe in it certainly; what ruffles me is the practice of it, but in this case, I should not show myself contrary."

The Ladies of the Virgin, having got down from their chairs, concealed themselves behind the altar; they were listening, pale with emotion.

The curate seeing himself victorious, suddenly became friendly and familiar: "Well and good! well and good!" said he. "You have spoken wisely instead of being foolish, you understand. We shall see. We shall see."

Sabot smiled in a constrained way as he asked: "Isn't there some way of giving this communion the slip?"

The priest, with severe countenance, replied:

"At the moment that this work is given to you, I wish to be certain of your conversion." Then he continued more gently: "You will come to confess to-morrow; for it will be necessary for me to examine you at least twice."

Sabot repeated: "At least twice?"

"Yes."

The priest smiled: "You understand that it will be necessary to have a general clearing out, a complete cleansing. I shall expect you then, to-morrow."

The carpenter, much moved, asked: "Where do you do this?"

"Why, in the confessional."

"In—that box. there—in the corner? That is—scarcely—big enough for me, your box."

"Why so?"

"Seeing that—seeing that I am not accustomed to it. And seeing that I'm a little hard of hearing."

The curate showed himself lenient: "Ah! well, you can come to my house, in my dining-room. There we shall be all alone, face to face. How will that suit you?"

"That's it. That suits me, but your box, no."

"Well, to-morrow then, after the day's work, at six o'clock."

"It is understood, all plain and agreed upon; till to-morrow, then, Mr. Curate, and the rack for him who retracts."

And he extended his great rude hand, into which the priest let fall his own, heartily. The smack of this hand-shake ran along. under the arches and died away back in the organ pipes.

Théodule Sabot was not tranquil while he was at work the next day. The apprehension he felt was something like what one feels when he is going to have a tooth pulled. Every moment this thought would come to him: "I must go to confession this evening." And his troubled soul, the soul of an atheist not wholly convinced, became excited from the confused and powerful fear of some divine mystery.

He directed his steps toward the rectory, when he had finished his day's work. The curate was waiting for him in the garden, reading his breviary as he walked up and down a narrow path. He seemed radiant, and said with a great laugh:

"Ah! well! here you are! Come in, come in, Mr. Sabot, nobody is going to eat you."

And Sabot passed in first. He stammered:

"If you are not too busy I should be pleased to finish up our little business, right away."

The curate answered: "At your service. I will get my surplice. One minute and I will listen to you."

The carpenter, so disturbed that he no longer had two ideas, watched him cover himself with the white garment with its pressed folds. The priest made a sign to him.

"Put your knees on this cushion."

Sabot remained standing, ashamed to have to kneel. He muttered:

"What's the use?"

But the priest became majestic: "One can only approach the tribunal of penitence on the knees."

And Sabot kneeled.

The priest said: "Recite the 'Confiteor.'"

Sabot asked: "What's that?"

"The 'Confiteor.' If you do not know it, repeat one by one, after me, the words I pronounce."

And the curate articulated the sacred prayer, in a deliberate voice, scanning the words for the carpenter to repeat; then he said:

"Now, confess."

But Sabot said nothing more, not knowing how to commence.

Then Father Maritime came to his aid:

"My child, I will ask you some questions until you become a little more familiar with the customs. We will take up, one by one, the commandments of God. Listen to me and be not troubled. Speak very frankly, and never fear to say too much.

" 'One God alone you shall adore
And you shall love him perfectly.'

Have you ever loved some one or something more than God? Do you love Him with all your soul, with all your heart, and all the energy of your love?"

Sabot was sweating from the effort of his thought. Finally he said:

"No. Oh! no, Mr. Curate. I love the good God as much as I can. That is—yes—I love Him well. To say that I love Him better than my children, no, I cannot. To say that, if it was necessary to choose between Him and my children, I would choose the good God, that I could not. To say that I would be willing to lose a hundred francs for the love of the good God, no, I could not. But I love Him well, be sure, I love Him well, all the same."

The priest, very grave, declared: "It is necessary that you love Him before anything."

And Sabot, full of good-will, answered: "I will do my best, Mr. Curate."

Father Maritime continued: "God will not have you take His name in vain. Have you sometimes made use of an oath?"

"No. Oh! no, indeed! I never swear. Sometimes, in a moment of anger, I speak the sacred name of God. That's all. I do not swear."

The priest cried: "But that is swearing." And then gravely: "Do it no more. I will continue: You will remember the Sabbath to keep it holy. What do you do on Sunday?"

This time Sabot scratched his ear. Finally he said: "I serve the good God in my own way, Mr. Curate. I serve Him —at home. I work on Sunday—"

The curate was magnanimous in interrupting him: "I know you will be more proper in the future. I pass the commandments following, sure that you have not failed in the first two. Let us see the sixth and the ninth. I repeat: The goods of another thou shalt not take, nor retain them knowingly.' Have you turned to your own use by any means, the goods belonging to another?"

Théodule Sabot answered indignantly: "No! Ah! no! I am an honest man, Mr. Curate. I swear to that. Not to say that I have not sometimes counted more hours of work than I have done— I have sometimes done that. And I could not say that I have not put a few more centimes on notes, only a few sometimes. But as for robbing, no, no, indeed, no!"

The curate answered severely: "Take not a single centime, for that is robbery. Do it no more. 'False witness shalt thou not bear, nor lie about anything.' Have you lied?"

"No, not that: I am no liar. I am not that kind. If you ask if I have not told some stories for the sake of talking, I could not deny it. And to say that I had not made people believe what was not so, when it was for my interest to do so, I could not. But as for lies, I tell no lies."

The priest simply said: "Be a little more careful." Then he pronounced:

" 'Things of the flesh thou shalt not desire, except in marriage alone.'

"Have you desired or possessed another woman than your own?'

Sabot exclaimed with sincerity: "Oh! no. As for that, no, Mr. Curate. Deceive my poor wife? No! no! Not as much as the end of your finger. Not in thought, say nothing of action! That's true."

He was very silent for some seconds, then, very low, as if some doubt had come over him, he said: "When I go to town, to say that I never go into a house, you know, one of the houses of license, for the sake of a bit of laughter and frolic and see another kind of skin, that I could not say—but I always pay, Mr. Curate, I always pay; but I won't embarrass you with this that you have neither seen nor known."

The curate did not insist, but gave the absolution.

Théodule Sabot executed the work of the choir stalls, and received the sacrament in the months following.

VOLUME IV

A Little Walk

WHEN father Leras, bookkeeper with Messrs. Labuze and Company, went out of the store, he stood for some minutes dazzled by the brilliancy of the setting sun.

He had toiled all day under the yellow light of the gas jet, at the end of the rear shop, on the court which was as narrow and deep as a well. The little room in which for forty years he had spent his days was so dark that even in the middle of summer they could hardly dispense with the gas from eleven to three o'clock.

It was always cold and damp there; and the emanations from that sort of hole on which the window looked came into the gloomy room, filling it with an odor moldy and sewer-like.

Monsieur Leras, for forty years, arrived at eight o'clock in the morning at this prison; and the remained till seven at night bent over his books, writing with the faithfulness of a good employee.

He now earned three thousand francs per year, having begun with fifteen hundred francs. He had remained unmarried, his means not permitting him to take a wife. And never having enjoyed anything he did not desire much. From time to time, nevertheless, weary of his monotonous and continuous work, he made a Platonic vow:

"Cristi, if I had five thousand livres income I would enjoy life!"

He had never enjoyed life, never having had more than his monthly salary.

His existence passed without events, without emotion, and almost without hopes. The faculty of dreaming, which everyone has in him, had never developed in the mediocrity of his ambitions.

He had entered the employ of Messrs. Labuze and Company at twenty-one years of age. And he had never left it.

In 1856 he had lost his father, then his mother in 1859. And since then he had experienced nothing but a removal, his landlord having wanted to raise his rent.

Every day his morning alarm exactly at six o'clock made him jump out of bed by its fearful racket.

Twice, however, this machine had run down, in 1866 and in 1874, without his ever knowing why.

He dressed, made his bed, swept his room, dusted his armchair and the top of his commode. All these duties required an hour and a half.

Then he went out, bought a roll at the Lahure bakery, which had had a dozen different proprietors without losing its name, and he set out for the office eating the bread on the way.

His whole existence was thus accomplished in the narrow dark office, which was adorned with the same wall-paper. He had entered the employ young, an assistant to Monsieur Burment and with the desire of taking his place.

He had taken his place and expected nothing further.

All that harvest of memories which other men make during their lives, the unforeseen events, the sweet or tragic love affairs, the adventurous journeys, all the hazards of a free existence, had been strange to him.

The days, the weeks, the months, the seasons, the years were all alike. At the

371

same hour every day he rose, left the house, arrived at the office, took his luncheon, went away, dined, and retired without ever having interrupted the monotony of the same acts, the same deeds, and the same thoughts.

Formerly he looked at his blond mustache and curly hair in the little round glass left by his predecessor. He now looked every morning, before going out, at his white mustache and his bald head in the same glass. Forty years had flown, long and rapid, empty as a day of sorrow and like the long hours of a bad night—forty years, of which nothing remained, not even a memory, not even a misfortune, since the death of his parents, nothing.

That day Monsieur Leras stood dazzled at the street door by the brilliancy of the setting sun; and instead of returning to his house he had the idea of taking a little walk before dinner, something which he did four or five times a year.

He reached the Boulevard, where many people were passing under the budding trees. It was an evening in springtime, one of those first soft warm evenings which stir the heart with the intoxication of life.

M. Leras walked along with his mincing old man's step, with a gaiety in his eye, happy with the unusual joy and the mildness of the air.

He reached the Champs-Elysées and proceeded reanimated by the odors of youth which filled the breeze.

The whole sky glowed; and the Triumphal Arch stood with its dark mass against the shining horizon like a giant struggling in a conflagration. When he had nearly reached the stupendous monument the old bookkeeper felt hungry and went into a wine-shop to dine.

They served him in front of the shop, on the sidewalk, a sheep's foot stew, a salad, and some asparagus, and Monsieur Leras made the best dinner he had made in a long while. He washed down his Brie cheese with a small bottle of good Bordeaux; he drank a cup of coffee, which seldom occurred to him, and finally a tiny glass of brandy.

When he had paid he felt quite lively and brisk, even a little perturbed. He said: "I will continue my walk as far as the entrance to the Bois de Boulogne. It will do me good."

He started. An old air which one of his neighbors used to sing long ago came to his mind:

"When the park grows green and gay
Then doth my brave lover say
Come with me, my sweet and fair,
To get a breath of air."

He hummed it continually, beginning it over again and again. Night had fallen upon Paris, a night without wind, a night of sweet calm. Monsieur Leras followed the Avenue de Bois de Boulogne and watched the cabs pass. They came with their bright lamps, one after another, giving a fleeting glimpse of a couple embracing, the woman in light colored dress and the man clad in black.

It was a long procession of lovers, driving under the starry and sultry sky. They kept arriving continually. They passed, reclining in the carriages, silent, pressed to one another, lost in the hallucination, the emotion of desire, in the excitement of the approaching culmination. The warm darkness seemed full of floating kisses. A sensation of tenderness made the air languishing and stifling. All these embracing people, all these persons intoxicated with the same intention, the same thought, caused a fever around them. All these carriages full of caresses diffused as they passed, as it were, a subtile and disturbing emanation.

Monsieur Leras, a little wearied, finally, by walking, took a seat on a bench to watch these carriages loaded with love. And almost immediately a woman came near to him and took her place at his side.

"Good evening, my little man," she said.

He did not reply. She continued: "Don't you want a sweetheart?"

"You are mistaken, Madame."

And she took his arm.

"Come, don't be a fool, listen—"

He had risen and gone away, his heart oppressed.

A hundred steps further on another woman approached him:

"Won't you sit down a moment with me, my fine boy?"

He said to her:

"Why do you lead such a life?"

"Name of God, it isn't always for my pleasure."

He continued in a soft voice:

"Then what compels you?"

She: "Must live, you know." And she went away singing.

Monsieur Leras stood astonished. Other women passed near him, similarly accosting him. It seemed to him that something dark was setting upon his head, something heartbreaking. And he

seated himself again upon a bench. The carriages kept hurrying by.

"Better not to have come here," he thought, "I am all unsettled."

He began to think on all this love, venal or passionate, on all these kisses, bought or free, which streamed before him.

Love, he hardly knew what it meant. He never had had more than two or three sweethearts in all his life, his means not permitting. And he thought of that life which he had led, so different from the life of all, his life so dark, so dull, so flat, so empty.

There are beings who truly never have any luck. And all at once, as if a thick veil had been lifted, he perceived the misery, the infinite monotonous misery of his existence: the past misery, the present misery, the future misery; the last days like the first, with nothing before him, nothing behind him, nothing around him, nothing in his heart, nothing anywhere.

The carriages kept passing. He saw appearing and disappearing in the rapid flight of the open *fiacre*, the two beings, silent and embracing. It seemed to him that the whole of humanity was filing before him, intoxicated with joy, with pleasure, with happiness. And he was alone, looking on at it, all alone. He would be still alone to-morrow, alone always, alone as no one else is alone.

He rose, took a few steps, and suddenly fatigued, as if he had walked for many miles, he sat down on the next bench.

What was awaiting him? What did he hope for? Nothing. He thought how good it must be when a man is old to find on getting home, little prattling children there. To grow old is sweet when a person is surrounded by those beings who owe him their life, who love him, who caress him, saying those charming foolish words which warm the heart and console him for everything.

And thinking of his empty room, neat and sad, where never a person entered but himself, a feeling of distress overwhelmed his soul. It seemed to him that room was more lamentable even than his little office.

No one came to it; no one spoke in it. It was dead, silent, without the echo of a human voice. One would say that the walls had something of the people who lived within, something of their look, their face, their words.

The houses inhabited by happy families are more gay than the habitations of the wretched. His room was empty of memories, like his life, and the thought of going back into that room, all alone, of sleeping in his bed, of doing over again all his actions and all his duties of evening terrified him. And as if to put himself further away from this gloomy lodging and from the moment when he would have to return to it he rose and, finding all at once the first pathway of the park, he entered a clump of woods to sit upon the grass.

He heard round about him, above him, every where, a confused sound, immense and continuous, made of innumerable different voices, near and far, a vague and enormous palpitation of life —the breath of Paris respiring like some colossal being.

The sun already high cast a flood of light upon the Bois de Boulogne. Some carriages began to circulate, and the horseback riders gaily arrived.

A couple were going at a walk through a lonely bridle path.

Suddenly the young woman, raising her eyes, perceived something brown among the branches: she raised her hand astonished and disturbed.

"Look—what is that?"

Then uttering a scream, she let herself fall into the arms of her companion, who placed her on the ground.

The guards quickly summoned, unfastened an old man, hanging to a branch by his braces.

It was agreed that the deceased had hanged himself the evening before.

The papers found upon him disclosed the fact that he was the bookkeeper for Messrs. Labuze and Company and that his name was Leras.

They attributed his death to suicide, for which the cause could not be determined. Perhaps a sudden attack of madness.

A Wife's Confession

My FRIEND, you have asked me to relate to you the liveliest recollections of my life. I am very old, without relatives, without children; so I am free to make a confession to you. Promise me one thing—never to reveal my name.

I have been much loved, as you know; I have often myself loved. I was very beautiful; I may say this to-day, when my beauty is gone. Love was for me the life of the soul, just as the air is the life of the body. I would have preferred to die rather than exist without affection, without having somebody always to care for me. Women often pretend to love only once with all the strength of their hearts; it has often happened to be so violent in one of my attachments that I thought it would be impossible for my transports ever to end. However, they always died out in a natural fashion, like a fire when it has no more fuel.

I will tell you to-day the first of my adventures, in which I was very innocent, but which led to the others. The horrible vengeance of that dreadful chemist of Pecq recalls to me the shocking drama of which I was, in spite of myself, a spectator.

I had been a year married to a rich man, Comte Hervé de Ker—a Breton of ancient family, whom I did not love, you understand. True love needs, I believe at any rate, freedom and impediments at the same time. The love which is imposed, sanctioned by law, and blessed by the priest—can we really call that love? A legal kiss is never as good as a stolen kiss. My husband was tall in stature, elegant, and a really fine gentleman in his manners. But he lacked intelligence. He spoke in a downright fashion, and uttered opinions that cut like the blade of a knife. He created the impression that his mind was full of ready-made views instilled into him by his father and mother, who had themselves got them from their ancestors.

He never hesitated, but on every subject immediately made narrow-minded suggestions, without showing any embarrassment and without realizing that there might be other ways of looking at things. One felt that his head was closed up, that no ideas circulated in it, none of those ideas which renew a man's mind and make it sound, like a breath of fresh air passing through an open window into a house.

The château in which we lived was situated in the midst of a desolate tract of country. It was a large melancholy structure, surrounded by enormous trees, with tufts of moss on it resembling old men's white beards. The park, a real forest, was inclosed in a deep trench, called the ha-ha; and at its extremity, near the moorland, we had big ponds full of reeds and floating grass. Between the two, at the edge of a stream which connected them, my husband had got a little hut built for shooting wild ducks.

We had, in addition to our ordinary servants, a keeper, a sort of brute devoted to my husband to the death, and a chambermaid, almost a friend, passionately attached to me. I had brought her back from Spain with me five years before. She was a deserted child. She might have been taken for a gypsy with her dusky skin, her dark eyes, her hair thick as a wood and always clustering around her forehead. She was at the time sixteen years old, but she looked twenty.

The autumn was beginning. We hunted much, sometimes on neighboring estates, sometimes on our own; and I noticed a young man, the Baron de C—, whose visits at the château became singularly frequent. Then, he ceased to come; I thought no more about it; but I perceived that my husband changed in his demeanor toward me.

He seemed taciturn and preoccupied; he did not kiss me; and, in spite of the fact that he did not come into my room, as I insisted on separate apartments in order to live a little alone, I often at night heard a furtive step drawing near my door, and withdrawing a few minutes after.

As my window was on the ground floor, I thought I had also often heard some one prowling in the shadow around the château. I told my husband about it, and, having looked at me intensely for some seconds, he answered:

"It is nothing—it is the keeper."

* * *

Now, one evening, just after dinner, Hervé, who appeared to be extraordinarily gay, with a sly sort of gaiety, said to me:

"Would you like to spend three hours out with the guns, in order to shoot a fox who comes every evening to eat my hens?"

I was surprised. I hesitated; but, as he kept staring at me with singular persistency, I ended by replying:

"Why, certainly, my friend." I must tell you that I hunted like a man the wolf and the wild -boar. So it was quite natural that he should suggest this shooting expedition to me.

But my husband, all of a sudden, had a curiously nervous look; and all the evening he seemed agitated, rising up and sitting down feverishly.

About ten o'clock he suddenly said to me:

"Are you ready?"

I rose; and, as he was bringing me my gun himself, I asked:

"Are we to load with bullets or with deershot?"

He showed some astonishment; then he rejoined:

"Oh! only with deershot; make your mind easy! that will be enough."

Then, after some seconds, he added in a peculiar tone:

"You may boast of having splendid coolness."

I burst out laughing.

"I? Why, pray? Coolness because I go to kill a fox? What are you thinking of, my friend?"

And we quietly made our way across the park. All the household slept. The full moon seemed to give a yellow tint to the old gloomy building, whose slate roof glittered brightly. The two turrets that flanked it had two plates of light on their summits, and no noise disturbed the silence of this clear, sad night, sweet and still, which seemed in a death-trance. Not a breath of air, not a shriek from a toad, not a hoot from an owl; a melancholy numbness lay heavy on everything. When we were under the trees in the park, a sense of freshness stole over me, together with the odor of fallen leaves. My husband said nothing; but he was listening, he was watching, he seemed to be smelling about in the shadows, possessed from head to foot by the passion for the chase.

We soon reached the edges of the ponds.

Their tufts of rushes remained motionless; not a breath of air caressed them; but movements which were scarcely perceptible ran through the water.

Sometimes the surface was stirred by something, and light circles gathered around, like luminous wrinkles enlarging indefinitely.

When we reached the hut, where we were to lie in wait, my husband made me go in first; then he slowly loaded his gun, and the dry cracking of the powder produced a strange effect on me. He saw that I was shuddering and asked:

"Does this trial happen to be quite enough for you? If so, go back."

I was much surprised, and I replied:

"Not at all. I did not come to go back without doing anything. You seem queer this evening."

He murmured:

"As you wish." And we remained there without moving.

At the end of about half an hour, as nothing broke the oppressive stillness of this bright autumn night, I said, in a low tone:

"Are you quite sure he is passing this way?"

Hervé winced as if I had bitten him, and, with his mouth close to my ear, he said:

"Make no mistake about it! I am quite sure."

And once more there was silence.

I believe I was beginning to get drowsy when my husband pressed my arm, and his voice, changed to a hiss, said:

"Do you see him there under the trees?"

I looked in vain; I could distinguish nothing. And slowly Hervé now cocked his gun, all the time fixing his eyes on my face.

I was myself making ready to fire, and suddenly, thirty paces in front of us, appeared in the full light of the moon a man who was hurrying forward with rapid movements, his body bent, as if he were trying to escape.

I was so stupefied that I uttered a loud cry; but, before I could turn round, there was a flash before my eyes; I heard a deafening report; and I saw the man rolling on the ground, like a wolf hit by a bullet.

I burst into dreadful shrieks, terrified, almost going mad; then a furious hand —it was Hervé's—seized me by the throat. I was flung down on the ground, then carried off by his strong arms. He ran, holding me up, till he reached the body lying on the grass, and he threw me on top of it violently, as if he wanted to break my head.

I thought I was lost; he was going to kill me; and he had just raised his heel up to my forehead when, in his turn, he was gripped, knocked down, before I could yet realize what had happened.

I rose up abruptly, and I saw kneeling on top of him Porquita, my maid, clinging like a wild cat to him with desperate energy, tearing off his beard, his mustache, and the skin of his face.

Then, as if another idea had suddenly taken hold of her mind, she rose up, and, flinging herself on the corpse, she threw her arms around the dead man, kissing his eyes and his mouth, opening the dead lips with her own lips, trying to find in them a breath and the long, long kiss of lovers.

My husband, picking himself up, gazed at me. He understood, and, falling at my feet, said:

"Oh! forgive me, my darling, I suspected you, and I killed this girl's lover. It was my keeper that deceived me."

But I was watching the strange kisses of that dead man and that living woman, and her sobs and her writhings of sorrowing love, and at that moment I understood that I might be unfaithful to my husband.

A Dead Woman's Secret

SHE had died painlessly, tranquilly, like a woman whose life was irreproachable; and she now lay on her back in bed, with closed eyes, calm features, her long white hair carefully arranged, as if she had again made her toilette ten minutes before her death. Her pale physiognomy was so composed, now that she had passed away, so resigned, that one felt sure a sweet soul had dwelt in that body, that this serene grandmother had spent an untroubled existence, that this virtuous woman had ended her life without any shock, without any remorse.

On his knees, beside the bed, her son, a magistrate of inflexible principles, and her daughter Marguerite—in religion, Sister Eulalie—were weeping distractedly. She had from the time of their infancy armed them with an inflexible code of morality, teaching them a religion without weakness and a sense of duty without any compromise. He, the son, had become a magistrate, and, wielding the weapon of the law, struck down without pity the feeble and the erring. She, the daughter, quite penetrated with the virtue that had bathed her in this austere family, had become the spouse of God through disgust with men.

They had scarcely known their father; all they knew was that he had made their mother unhappy without learning any further details. The nun passionately kissed one hand of her dead mother, which hung down, a hand of ivory like that of Christ in the large crucifix which lay on the bed. At the opposite side of the prostrate body, the other hand seemed still to grasp the rumpled sheet with that wondering movement which is called the fold of the dying, and the lines had retained little creases as a memento of those last motions which precede the eternal motionlessness. A few light taps at the door caused the two sobbing heads to look up, and the priest, who had just dined, entered the apartment. He was flushed, a little puffed, from the effects of the process of digestion which had just commenced; for he had put a good dash of brandy into his coffee in order to counteract the fatigue caused by the last nights he had remained up and that which he anticipated from the night that was still in store for him. He had put on a look of sadness, that simulated sadness of the priest to whom death is a means of livelihood. He made the sign of the cross, and, coming over to them with his professional gestures, said:

"Well, my poor children, I have come to help you to pass these mournful hours."

But Sister Eulalie suddenly rose up.

"Thanks, Father; but my brother and

I would like to be left alone with her. These are the last moments that we now have for seeing her; so we want to feel ourselves once more, the three of us, just as we were years ago when we— we—we were only children, and our poor—poor mother—" She was unable to finish with the flood of tears that gushed from her eyes and the sobs that were choking her.

But the priest bowed, with a more serene look on his face, for he was thinking of his bed. "Just as you please, my children."

Then, he kneeled down, again crossed himself, prayed, rose up, and softly stole away murmuring as he went: "She was a saint."

They were left alone, the dead woman and her children. A hidden timepiece kept regularly ticking in its dark corner, and through the open window the soft odors of hay and of woods penetrated, with faint gleams of moonlight. No sound in the fields outside, save the wandering croak of toads and now and then the humming of some nocturnal insect darting in like a ball and knocking itself against the wall.

An infinite peace, a divine melancholy, a silent serenity surrounded this dead woman, seemed to emanate from her, to evaporate from her into the atmosphere outside and to calm Nature herself.

Then the magistrate, still on his knees his head pressed against the bedclothes, in a far-off, heart-broken voice that pierced through the sheets and the coverlet, exclaimed:

"Mamma, mamma, mamma!" And the sister, sinking down on the floor, striking the wood with her forehead fanatically, twisting herself about

and quivering like a person in an epileptic fit, groaned: "Jesus, Jesus—mamma —Jesus!"

And both of them, shaken by a hurricane of grief, panted with a rattling in their throats.

Then the fit gradually subsided, and they now wept in a less violent fashion, like the rainy calm that follows a squall on a storm-beaten sea. Then, after some time, they rose and fixed their glances on the beloved corpse. And memories, those memories of the past, so sweet, so torturing to-day, came back to their minds with all those little forgotten details, those little details so intimate and familiar, which make the being who is no more live over again. They recalled circumstances, words, smiles, certain intonations of voice which belonged to one whom they should never hear speaking to them again. They saw her once more happy and calm, and phrases she used in ordinary conversation rose to their lips. They even remembered a little movement of the hand peculiar to her, as if she were keeping time when she was saying something of importance.

And they loved her as they had never before loved her. And by the depth of their despair they realized how strongly they had been attached to her, and how desolate they would find themselves now.

She had been their mainstay, their guide, the best part of their youth, of that happy portion of their lives which had vanished; she had been the bond that united them to existence, the mother, the mamma, the creative flesh, the tie that bound them to their ancestors. They would henceforth be solitary, isolated; they would have nothing on earth to look back upon.

The nun said to her brother:

"You know how mamma used always to read over her old letters. They are all there in her desk. Suppose we read them in our turn, and so revive all her life this night by her side. It would be like a kind of road of the cross, like making the acquaintance of her mother, of grandparents whom we never knew, whose letters are there, and of whom she has so often talked to us, you remember?"

*   *   *

And they drew forth from the drawer a dozen little packets of yellow paper, carefully tied up and placed close to one another. They flung these relics on the bed, and selecting one of them on which the word "Father" was written, they opened and read what was in it.

It consisted of those very old letters which are to be found in old family writing-desks, those letters which have the flavor of another century. The first said, "My darling"; another, "My beautiful little girl"; then others, "My dear child"; and then again, "My dear daughter." And suddenly the nun began reading aloud, reading for the dead her own history, all her tender souvenirs. And the magistrate listened, while he leaned on the bed, with his eyes on his mother's face. And the motionless corpse seemed happy.

Sister Eulalie, interrupting herself, said: "We ought to put them into the grave with her, to make a winding-sheet of them, and bury them with her."

And then she took up another packet, on which the descriptive word did not appear.

And in a loud tone she began:

"My adored one, I love you to distraction. Since yesterday I have been suffering like a damned soul burned by the recollection of you. I feel your lips on mine, your eyes under my eyes, your flesh under my flesh. I love you! I love you! You have made me mad! My arms open! I pant with an immense desire to possess you again. My whole body calls out to you, wants you. I have kept in my mouth the taste of your kisses."

The magistrate rose up; the nun stopped reading. He snatched the letter from her and sought for the signature. There was none, save under the words, "He who adores you," the name "Henry." Their father's name was René. So then he was not the man.

Then, the son, with rapid fingers, fumbled in the packet of letters, took another of them, and read:

"I can do without your caresses no longer."

And, standing up, with the severity of a judge passing sentence, he gazed at the impassive face of the dead woman.

The nun, straight as a statue, with teardrops standing at each corner of her eyes, looked at her brother, waiting to see what he meant to do. Then he crossed the room, slowly reached the window, and looked out thoughtfully into the night.

When he turned back, Sister Eulalie, her eyes quite dry, still remained standing near the bed, with a downcast look.

He went over to the drawer and flung in the letters which he had picked up from the floor. Then he drew the curtain round the bed.

And when the dawn made the candles on the table look pale, the son rose from his armchair, and, without even a parting glance at the mother whom he had separated from them and condemned, he said slowly:

"Now, my sister, let us leave the room."

Love's Awakening

No ONE was surprised at the marriage of Mr. Simon Lebrument and Miss Jean Cordier. Mr. Lebrument came to buy out the office of Mr. Papillon; he needed, it was understood, money with which to pay for it; and Miss Jean Cordier had three hundred thousand francs clear, in stocks and bonds.

Mr. Lebrument was a handsome bachelor, who had style, the style of a notary, a provincial style, but, after all, some style, which was a rare thing at Boutigny-le-Rebours.

Miss Cordier had grace and freshness, grace a little awkward and freshness a little fixed up; but she was nevertheless, a pretty girl, desirable and entertaining.

The wedding ceremonies turned Boutigny topsy-turvy. The married couple was much admired when they returned to the conjugal domicile to conceal their happiness, having resolved to make a little, simple journey to Paris, after they had spent a few days together.

It was charming, these few days together, as Mr. Lebrument knew how to manage his early relations with his wife with a delicacy, a directness, and sense of fitness that was remarkable He took for his motto: "Everything comes to him who waits." He knew how to be patient and energetic at the same time. His success was rapid and complete.

At the end of four days Mrs. Lebrument adored her husband. She could not bear to be a moment away from him. He must be near her all day long, that she might caress his hands, his beard, his nose, etc. She would sit upon his knees and, taking him by the ears, would say: "Open your mouth and shut your eyes." He opened his mouth with confidence, shut his eyes halfway, and then would receive a very long, sweet kiss that made great shivers in his back. And in his turn, he never had enough caresses, enough lips, enough hands, enough of anything with which to enjoy his wife from morning until evening, and from evening until morning.

As soon as the first week had slipped away he said to his young companion:

"If you wish, we might leave for Paris Tuesday of next week. We shall be like lovers who are not married; go about to the theaters, the restaurants, the concert *cafés*, and everywhere, everywhere."

She jumped for joy. "Oh! yes, yes," she replied, "let us go as soon as possible."

"And as we must not forget anything, you might ask your father to have your dowry ready; I will take it with me, and at the same time pay Mr. Papillon."

She answered: "I will speak to him about it to-morrow morning."

Then he seized her in his arms and began again the little tendernesses she loved so much, and had reveled in now for eight days.

The Tuesday following, the father-in-law and the mother-in-law accompanied their daughter and son-in-law to the station, whence they set out for the capital. The father-in-law remarked:

"I tell you it is imprudent to carry so much money in your pocketbook." And the young notary smiled.

"Do not be disturbed, father-in-law," he answered, "I am accustomed to these things. You know that in my profession it often happens that I have nearly a million about me. By carrying it with me, we escape a lot of formalities and delays, to say the least. Do not give yourself any uneasiness."

Then the trainman cried out, "All aboard!" and they hurried into a compartment where they found themselves with two old ladies.

Lebrument murmured in his wife's ear: "How annoying! Now I cannot smoke."

She answered in a low tone: "I am sorry too, but not on account of your cigar."

The engine puffed and started. The journey lasted an hour, during which they could not say anything of importance, because the two old ladies did not go to sleep.

When they were in the Saint-Lazare station, in Paris, Mr. Lebrument said to his wife:

"If you wish, my dear, we will first go and breakfast on the Boulevard, then return at our leisure to find our trunk

and give it to the porter of some hotel."

She consented immediately: "Oh! yes," said she, "let us breakfast in some restaurant. Is it far from here?"

"Yes, rather far, but we will take an omnibus."

She was astonished: "Why not a cab?" she asked.

He groaned as he said smilingly: "And you are economical! A cab for five minutes' ride, at six sous per minute! You do not deprive yourself of anything!"

"That is true," said she, a little confused.

A large omnibus was passing, with three horses at a trot. Lebrument hailed it: "Conductor! eh, conductor!"

The heavy carriage stopped. The young notary pushed his wife inside, saying hurriedly, in a low voice:

"You get in while I climb up on the outside to smoke at least a cigarette before breakfast."

She had not time for any answer. The conductor, who had seized her by the arm to aid her in mounting the steps, pushed her into the 'bus, where she landed, half-frightened, upon a seat, and in a sort of stupor watched the feet of her husband through the windows at the back, as he climbed to the top of the imperial.

There she remained immovable between a large gentleman who smelled of a pipe and an old woman who smelled of a dog. All the other travelers, in two mute lines,—a grocer's boy, a workman, a sergeant of infantry, a gentleman with gold-rimmed spectacles and a silk cap with enormous visors, like gutters, and two ladies with an important, mincing air, which seemed to say:

We are here, although wo should be in a better place. Then there were two good sisters, a little girl in long hair, and an undertaker. The assemblage had the appearance of a collection of carica-tures in a freak museum, a series of ex-pressions of the human countenance, like a row of grotesque puppets which one knocks down at a fair.

The jolts of the carriage made them toss their heads a little, and as they shook, the flesh of their cheeks trem-bled; and the disturbance of the rolling wheels gave them an idiotic or sleepy look.

The young woman remained inert: "Why did he not come with me?" she asked herself. A vague sadness op-pressed her. He might, indeed, have de-prived himself of his cigar!

The good sisters gave the signal to stop. They alighted, one after the other, leaving an odor of old and faded skirts.

Soon after they were gone another stopped the 'bus. A cook came in, red and out of breath. She sat down and placed her basket of provisions upon her knees. A strong odor of dishwater pervaded the omnibus.

"It is further than I thought," said the young woman to herself.

The undertaker got out and was re-placed by a coachman who smelled of a stable. The girl in long hair was suc-ceeded by an errand-boy who exhaled the perfume of his walks.

The notary's wife perceived all these things, ill at ease and so disheartened that she was ready to weep without knowing why.

Some others got out, still others came in. The omnibus went on through the interminable streets, stopped at the sta-tion, and began its route again.

"How far it is!" said Jean. "Espe-cially when one has nothing for diver-sion and cannot sleep!" She had not been so much fatigued for many days.

Little by little all the travelers got out. She remained alone, all alone. The conductor shouted:

"Vaugirard!"

As she blushed he again repeated: "Vaugirard!"

She looked at him not understand-ing that this must be addressed to her as all her neighbors had gone. For the third time the man said: "Vaugirard!"

Then she asked: "Where are we?"

He answered in a gruff voice: "We are at Vaugirard Miss; I've told you twenty times already."

"Is it far from the Boulevard?" she asked.

"What Boulevard?"

"The Italian Boulevard."

"We passed that a long time ago."

"Ah! Will you be kind enough to tell my husband?"

"Your husband? Where is he?"

"On the outside."

"On the outside! It has been a long time since there was anybody there."

She made a terrified gesture. Then she said:

"How can it be? It is not possible. He got up there when I entered the omnibus. Look again; he must be there."

The conductor became rude: "Come, little one, this is talk enough. If there is one man lost, there ar ten to be found. Scamper out now! You will find another in the street."

The tears sprang to her eyes. She

insisted: "But, sir, you are mistaken, I assure you that you are mistaken. He had a large pocketbook in his hand."

The employee began to laugh: "A large pocketbook? I remember. Yes, he got out at the Madeleine. That's right! He's left you behind! Ha! ha!"

The carriage was standing still. She got down and looked up, in spite of herself to the roof, with an instinctive movement of the eye. It was totally deserted.

Then she began to weep aloud, without thinking that anyone was looking at or listening to her. Finally she said:

"What is going to become of me?"

The inspector came up and inquired: "What's the matter?"

The conductor answered in a jocose fashion:

"This lady's husband has left her on the way."

The other replied: "Now, now, that is nothing. I am at your service." And he turned on his heels.

Then she began to walk ahead, too much frightened, too much excited to think even where she was going. Where was she going? What should she do? How could such an error have occurred? Such an act of carelessness, of disregard, of unheard of distraction!

She had two francs in her pocket. To whom could she apply? Suddenly she remembered her cousin Barral, who was a clerk in the office of Naval Affairs.

She had just enough to hire a cab; she would go to him. And she met him just as he was starting for his office. Like Lebrument, he carried a large pocketbook under his arm.

She leaned out of the carriage and called: "Henry!"

He stopped, much surprised.

"Jeanne," said he, "here?—and alone? Where do you come from? What are you doing?"

She stammered, with her eyes full of tears: "My husband is lost somewhere—"

"Lost? where?"

"On the omnibus."

"On the omnibus! Oh!"

And she related to him the whole story, weeping much over the adventure.

He listened reflectively, and then asked:

"This morning? And was his head perfectly clear?"

"Oh! yes! And he had my dowry."

"Your dowry? The whole of it?"

"Yes, the whole of it—in order to pay for his office."

"Well, my dear cousin, your husband, whoever he is, is probably watching the wheel—this minute."

She did not yet comprehend. She stammered: "My husband—you say—"

"I say that he has run off with your —your capital—and that's all about it."

She remained standing there, suffocated with grief, murmuring:

"Then he is—he is—a wretch!"

Then, overcome with emotion, she fell on her cousin's shoulder, sobbing violently.

As people were stopping to look at them, he guided her gently into the entrance of his house, supporting her body. They mounted the steps, and as the maid came to open the door he ordered her:

"Sophie, run to the restaurant and bring breakfast for two persons. I shall not go to the office this morning."

Bed No. 29

WHEN Captain Epivent passed in the street all the ladies turned to look at him. He was the true type of a handsome officer of hussars. He was always on parade, always strutted a little and seemed preoccupied and proud of his leg, his figure, and his mustache. He had superb ones, it is true, a superb leg, figure, and mustache. The last-named was blond, very heavy, falling martially from his lip in a beautiful sweep the color of ripe wheat, carefully turned at the ends, and falling over both sides of his mouth in two powerful sprigs of hair cut square across. His waist was thin as if he wore a corset, while a vigorous masculine chest, bulged and arched, spread itself above his waist. His leg was admirable, a gymnastic leg, the leg of a dancer whose muscular flesh outlined each movement under the clinging cloth of the red pantaloon.

He walked with muscles taut with feet and arms apart, and with the slightly balanced step of the cavalier, who knows how to make the most of his limbs and his carriage, and who seems a conqueror in a uniform, but looks commonplace in a mufti.

Like many other officers, Captain Epivent carried a civil costume badly. He had no air of elegance as soon as he was clothed in the gray or black of the shop clerk. But in his proper setting he was a triumph. He had besides a handsome face, the nose thin and curved, blue eyes, and a good forehead. He was bald, without ever being able to comprehend why his hair had fallen off. He consoled himself with thinking that, with a heavy moustache, a head a little bald was not so bad.

He scorned everybody in general, with a difference in the degrees of his scorn.

In the first place, for him the middle class did not exist. He looked at them as he would look at animals, without according them more of his attention than he would give to sparrows or chickens. Officers, alone, counted in his world; but he did not have the same esteem for all officers. He only respected handsome men; an imposing presence, the true, military quality being first. A soldier was a merry fellow, a devil, created for love and war, a man of brawn, muscle and hair, nothing more. He classed the generals of the French army according to their figure, their bearing, and the stern look of their faces. Bourbaki appeared to him the greatest warrior of modern times.

He often laughed at the officers of the line who were short and fat, and puffed while marching. And he had a special scorn for the poor recruits from the polytechnic schools, those thin, little men with spectacles, awkward and unskillful, who seemed as much made for a uniform as a wolf for saying mass, as he often asserted. He was indignant that they should be tolerated in the army, those abortions with the lank limbs, who marched like crabs, did not drink, ate little, and seemed to love equations better than pretty girls.

Captain Epivent himself had constant successes and triumphs with the fair sex.

Every time he took supper in company with a woman he thought himself certain of finishing the night with her upon the same mattress, and, if unsurmountable obstacles hindered that evening, his victory was sure at least the following day. His comrades did not like him to meet their mistresses, and the merchants in the shops, who had their pretty wives at the counter, knew him, feared him, and hated him desperately. When he passed, the merchants' wives in spite of themselves exchanged a look with him through the glass of the front windows, one of those looks that avail more than tender words, which contain an appeal and a response, a desire and an avowal. And the husbands, who turned away with a sort of instinct, returned brusquely, casting a furious look at the proud, arched silhouette of the officer. And, when the captain had passed, smiling and content with his impression, the merchants, handling with nervous hands the objects spread out before them, declared:

"There's a great dandy. When shall we stop feeding all these good-for-nothings who go dragging their tinware through the streets? For my part, I would rather be a butcher than a soldier. Then if there's blood on my table, it is

the blood of beasts, at least. And he is useful, is the butcher; and the knife he carries has not killed men. I do not understand how these murderers are tolerated walking on the public streets, carrying with them their instruments of death. It is necessary to have them, I suppose, but at least, let them conceal themselves, and not dress up in masquerade, with their red breeches and blue coats. The executioner doesn't dress himself up, does he?"

The woman, without answering, would shrug her shoulders, while the husband, divining the gesture without seeing it, would cry:

"Anybody must be stupid to watch those fellows parade up and down."

Nevertheless, Captain Epivent's reputation for conquests was well established in the whole French army.

Now, in 1868, his regiment, the One Hundred and Second Hussars came into garrison at Rouen.

He was soon known in the town. He appeared every evening, toward five o'clock, upon the Boieldieu mall, to take his absinthe and coffee at the Comedy; and, before entering the establishment, he would always take a turn upon the promenade, to show his leg, his figure, and his moustaches.

The merchants of Rouen who also promenaded there with their hands behind their backs, preoccupied with business affairs, speaking in high and low voices, would sometimes throw him a glance and murmur:

"Egad! that's a handsome fellow!"

But when they knew him, they remarked:

"Look! Captain Epivent! But he's a rascal all the same!"

The women on meeting him had a very queer little movement of the head, a kind of shiver of modesty, as if they felt themselves grow weak or unclothed before him. They would lower their heads a little, with a smile upon their lips, as if they had a desire to be found charming and have a look from him. When he walked with a comrade the comrade never failed to murmur with jealous envy, each time that he saw the sport:

"This rascal of an Epivent has the chances!"

Among the licensed girls of the town it was a struggle, a race, to see who would carry him off. They all came at five o'clock, the officers' hour, to the Boieldieu mall, and dragged their skirts up and down the length of the walk, two by two, while the lieutenants, captains, and commanders, two by two, dragged their swords along the ground before entering the *café*.

One evening the beautiful Irma, the mistress, it was said, of M. Templier-Papon, the rich manufacturer, stopped her carriage in front of the Comedy and, getting out, made a pretense of buying some paper or some visiting cards of M. Paulard, the engraver, in order to pass before the officers' tables and cast a look at Captain Epivent which seemed to say: "When you will," so clearly that Colonel Prune, who was drinking the green liquor with his lieutenant-colonel, could not help muttering:

"Confound that fellow! He has the chances, that scamp!"

The remark of the Colonel was repeated, and Captain Epivent, moved by this approbation of his superior, passed the next day and many times after that under the windows of the beauty, in his most captivating attitude.

She saw him, showed herself, and smiled.

That same evening he was her lover.

They attracted attention, made an exhibition of their attachment, and mutually compromised themselves, both of them proud of their adventure.

Nothing was so much talked of in town as the beautiful Irma and the officer. M. Templier-Papon alone was ignorant of their relation.

Captain Epivent beamed with glory; every instant he would say:

"Irma happened to say to me—Irma told me to-night—or, yesterday at dinner Irma said—"

For a whole year they walked with and displayed in Rouen this love like a flag taken from the enemy. He felt himself aggrandized by this conquest, envied, more sure of the future, surer of the decoration so much desired, for the eyes of all were upon him, and he was satisfied to find himself well in sight, instead of being forgotten.

But here war was declared, and the Captain's regiment was one of the first to be sent to the front. The adieux were lamentable. They lasted the whole night long.

Sword, red breeches, cap, and jacket were all overturned from the back of a chair upon the floor; robes, skirts, silk stockings, also fallen down, were spread around and mingled with the uniform in distress upon the carpet; the room upside down as if there had been a battle; Irma wild, her hair unbound, threw her despairing arms around the officer's neck, straining him to her; then, leaving him, rolled upon the floor, overturning the furniture, catching the fringes of the armchairs, biting their feet, while the Captain much moved, but not skillful at consolation, repeated:

"Irma, my little Irma, do not cry so, it is necessary."

He occasionally wiped a tear from the corner of his eye with the end of his finger. They separated at daybreak. She followed her lover in her carriage as far as the first stopping-place. Then she kissed him before the whole regiment at the moment of separation. They even found this very genteel, worthy, and very romantic; and the comrades pressed the Captain's hand and said to him:

"Confound you, rogue, she has a heart, all the same, the little one."

They seemed to see something patriotic in it.

The regiment was sorely proved during the campaign. The Captain conducted himself heroically and finally received the cross of honor. Then, the war ended, he returned to Rouen and the garrison.

Immediately upon his return he asked of news of Irma, but no one was able to give him anything exact. Some said she was married to a Prussian major. Others, that she had gone to her parents who were farmers in the suburbs of Yvetot.

He even sent his orderly to the mayor's office to consult the registry of deaths. The name of his mistress was not to be found.

He was very angry, which fact he paraded everywhere. He even took the enemy to task for his unhappiness, attributing to the Prussians, who had occupied Rouen, the disappearance of the young girl, declaring:

"In the next war, they shall pay well for it, the beggars!"

Then, one morning as he entered the mess-room at the breakfast hour, an old porter, in a blouse and an oilcloth cap, gave him a letter, which he opened and read:

"MY DEARIE: I am in the hospital, very ill, very ill. Will you not come and see me? It would give me so much pleasure!   "IRMA."

The Captain grew pale and, moved with pity, declared:

"It's too bad! The poor girl! I will go there as soon as breakfast."

And during the whole time at the table, he told the officers that Irma was in the hospital and that he was going to see her that blessed morning. It must be the fault of those unspeakable Prussians. She had doubtless found herself alone without a sou, broken down with misery, for they must certainly have stolen her furniture.

"Ah! the dirty whelps."

Everybody listened with great excitement. Scarcely had he slipped his napkin in his wooden ring, when he rose and, taking his sword from the peg, and swelling out his chest to make him thin, hooked his belt and set out with hurried step to the city hospital.

But entrance to the hospital building, where he expected to enter immediately, was sharply refused him, and he was obliged to find his Colonel and explain his case to him in order to get a word from him to the director.

This man, after having kept the handsome Captain waiting some time in his anteroom, gave him an authorized pass and a cold and disapproving greeting.

Inside the door he felt himself constrained in this asylum of misery and suffering and death. A boy in the service showed him the way. He walked upon tiptoe, that he might make no noise, through the long corridors, where floated a slight, moist odor of illness and medicines. A murmur of voices alone disturbed the silence of the hospital.

At times, through an open door, the Captain perceived a dormitory, with its rows of beds whose clothes were raised by the forms of the bodies.

Some convalescents were seated in chairs at the foot of their couches, sewing, and clothed in the uniform gray cloth dress with white cap.

His guide suddenly stopped before one of these corridors filled with patients. He read on the door, in large letters: "Syphilis." The Captain started: then he felt that he was blushing. An attendant was preparing a medicine at a little wooden table at the door.

"I will show you," she said, "it is bed 29."

And she walked ahead of the officer. She indicated a bed: "There it is."

There was nothing to be seen but a bundle of bedclothes. Even the head was concealed under the coverlet. Everywhere faces were to be seen on the couches, pale faces, astonished at the sight of a uniform, the faces of women, young women and old women, but all seemingly plain and common in the humble, regulation garb.

The Captain, very much disturbed, supporting his sword in one hand and carrying his cap in the other, murmured: "Irma."

There was a sudden motion in the bed and the face of his mistress appeared, but so changed, so tired, so thin, that he would scarcely have known it.

She gasped, overcome by emotion and then said:

"Albert!—Albert! It is you! Oh! I am so glad—so glad." And the tears ran down her cheeks.

The attendant brought a chair. "Be seated, sir," she said.

He sat down and looked at the pale, wretched countenance, so little like that of the beautiful, fresh girl he had left. Finally he said:

"What seems to be the matter with you?"

She replied, weeping: "You know well enough, it is written on the door." And she hid her eyes under the edge of the bedclothes.

Dismayed and ashamed, he continued: "How have you caught it, my poor girl?"

She answered: "It was those beasts of Prussians. They took me almost by force and then poisoned me."

He found nothing to add. He looked at her and kept turning his cap around on his knees.

The other patients gazed at him, and he believed that he detected an odor of putrefaction, of contaminated flesh, in this corridor full of girls tainted with this ignoble, terrible malady.

She murmured: "I do not believe

that I shall recover. The doctor says it is very serious.".

Then she perceived the cross upon the officer's breast and cried: ·

"Oh! you have been honored; now I am content. How contented I am! If I could only embrace you!"

A shiver of fear and disgust ran along the Captain's skin at the thought of this kiss. He had a desire to make his escape, to be in the clear air and never see this woman again. He remained, however, not knowing how to make the adieux, and finally stammered:

"You took no care of yourself, then."

A flame flashed in Irma's eyes: "No, the desire to avenge myself came to me when I should have broken away from it. And I poisoned them too, all, all that I could. As long as there were any of them in Rouen, I had no thought for myself."

He declared, in a constrained tone in which there was a little note of gaiety: "So far, you have done some good."

Getting animated, and her cheek-bones getting red, she answered:

"Oh! yes, there will more than one of them die from my fault. I tell you I had my vengeance."

Again he said: "So much the better." Then rising, he added: "Well, I must leave you now, because I have only time to meet my appointment with the Colonel—"

She showed much emotion, crying out: "Already! You leave me already! And when you have scarcely arrived!"

But he wished to go at any cost, and said:

"But you see that I came immediately; and it is absolutely necessary that I be at the Colonel's at an appointed time."

She asked: "Is it still Colonel Prune?"

"Still Colonel Prune. He was twice wounded."

She continued: "And your comrades? Have some of them been killed?"

"Yes. Saint-Timon, Savagnat, Poli, Saprival, Robert, De Courson, Pasafil, Santal, Caravan, and Poivrin are dead. Sahel had an arm carried off and Courvoisin a leg amputated. Paquet lost his right eye."

She listened, much interested. Then suddenly she stammered:

"Will you kiss me, say? before you leave me; Madame Langlois is not there."

And, in spite of the disgust which came to his lips, he placed them against the wan forehead, while she, throwing her arms around him, scattered random kisses over his blue jacket.

Then she said: "You will come again? Say that you will come again—Promise me that you will."

"Yes, I promise."

"When, now. Can you come Thursday?"

"Yes, Thursday—"

"Thursday at two o'clock?"

"Yes, Thursday at two o'clock."

"You promise?"

"I promise."

"Adieu, my dearie."

"Adieu."

And he went away, confused by the staring glances of those in the dormitory, bending his tall form to make himself seem smaller. And when he was in the street he took a long breath.

That evening his comrades asked him: "Well, how is Irma?"

He answered in a constrained voice: "She has a trouble with the lungs; she is very ill."

But a little lieutenant, scenting something from his manner, went to headquarters, and, the next day, when the Captain went into mess he was welcomed by a volley of laughter and jokes. They had found vengeance at last.

It was learned further that Irma had made a spite marriage with the staff-major of the Prussians, that she had gone through the country on horseback with the colonel of the Blue Hussars, and many others, and that, in Rouen, she was no longer called anything but the "wife of the Prussians."

For eight days the Captain was the victim of his regiment. He received by post and by messenger, notes from those who can reveal the past and the future, circulars of specialists, and medicines, the nature of which was inscribed on the package.

And the Colonel, catching the drift of it, said in a severe tone:

"Well, the Captain had a pretty acquaintance! I send him my compliments."

At the end of twelve days he was appealed to by another letter from Irma. He tore it up with rage and made no reply to it.

A week later she wrote him again that she was very ill and wished to see him to say farewell.

He did not answer.

After some days more he received a note from a chaplain of the hospital.

"The girl Irma Pavolin is on her deathbed and begs you to come."

He dared not refuse to oblige the chaplain, but he entered the hospital with a heart swelling with wicked anger, with wounded vanity, and humiliation.

He found her scarcely changed at all and thought that she had deceived him. "What do you wish of me?" he asked.

"I wish to say farewell. It appears that I am near the end."

He did not believe it.

"Listen," said he, "you have made me the laughing stock of the regiment, and I do not wish it to continue."

She asked: "What have I done?"

He was irritated at not knowing how to answer. But he said:

"Is it nothing that I return here to be joked by everybody on your account?"

She looked at him with languid eyes, where shone a pale light of anger, and answered:

"What can I have done? I have not been genteel with you, perhaps! Is it because I have sometimes asked for something? But for you, I would have remained with M. Templier-Papon, and would not have found myself here today. No, you see, if anyone has reproaches to make it is not you."

He answered in a clear tone: "I have not made reproaches, but I cannot continue to come to see you, because your conduct with the Prussians has been the shame of the town."

She sat up, with a little shake, in the bed, as she replied:

"My conduct with the Prussians? But when I tell you that they took me, and when I tell you that if I took no thought of myself, it was because I wished to poison them! If I had wished to cure myself, it would not have been so difficult, I can tell you! But I wished to kill them, and I have killed them, come now! I have killed them!"

He remained standing: "In any case," said he, "it was a shame."

She had a kind of suffocation, and then replied:

"Why is it a shame for me to cause them to die and try to exterminate them, tell me? You did not talk that way when you used to come to my house in Jeanne-d'Arc street. Ah! it is a shame! You have not done as much, with your cross of honor! I deserve more merit than you, do you understand, more than you, for I have killed more Prussians than you!"

He stood stupefied before her trembling with indignation. He stammered: "Be still—you must—be still—because those things—I cannot allow—anyone to touch upon—"

But she was not listening: "What harm have you done the Prussians? Would it ever have happened if you had kept them from coming to Rouen? Tell me! It is you who should stop and listen. And I have done more harm than you, I, yes, more harm to them than you, and I am going to die for it while you are singing songs and making yourself fine to inveigle women—"

Upon each bed a head was raised and all eyes looked at this man in uniform who stammered again:

"You must be still—more quiet—you know—"

But she would not be quiet. She cried out:

"Ah! yes, you are a pretty *poser!* I know you well. I know you. And I tell you that I have done them more harm than you—I—and that I have killed more than all your regiment together—come now, you coward.

He went away, in fact he fled, stretching his long legs as he passed between the two rows of beds where the syphilitic patients were becoming excited. And he heard the gasping, stifled voice of Irma pursuing him:

"More than you—yes—I have killed more than you—"

He tumbled down the staircase four steps at a time, and ran until he was shut fast in his room.

The next day he heard that she was dead.

———•———

Marroca

You ask me, my dear friend, to send you my impressions of Africa, and an account of my adventures, especially of my love affairs in this seductive land. You laughed a great deal beforehand at my dusky sweethearts, as you called them, and declared that you could see me turning to France followed by a tall, ebony-colored woman, with a yellow silk handkerchief round her head, and wearing voluminous bright-colored trousers.

No doubt the Moorish dames will have their turn, for I have seen several who made me feel very much inclined to fall in love with them. But by way of making a beginning, I came across something better and very original.

In your last letter to me, you say: "When I know how people love in a country, I know that country well enough to describe it, although I may never have seen it." Let me tell you, then, that here they love furiously. From the very first moment one feels a sort of trembling ardor, of constant desire, to the very tips of the fingers, which overexcites the powers and faculties of physical sensation, from the simple contact of the hands down to the requirement which makes us commit so many follies.

Do not misunderstand me. I do not know whether you call love of the heart a love of the soul; whether sentimental idealism, Platonic love, in a word, can exist on this earth; I doubt it, myself. But that other love, sensual love, which has something good, a great deal of good about it, is really terrible in this climate. The heat, the burning atmosphere which makes you feverish, the suffocating blasts of wind from the south, waves of fire from the desert which is so near us, that oppressive sirocco which is more destructive and withering than fire, a perpetual conflagration of an entire continent, burned even to its stones by a fierce and devouring sun, inflame the blood, excite the flesh, and make brutes of us.

But to come to my story. I shall not dwell on the beginning of my stay in Africa. After visiting Bona, Constantine, Biskara, and Stéif, I went to Bougie through the defiles of Chabet, by an excellent road cut through a large forest, which follows the sea at a height of six hundred feet above it and leads to that wonderful bay of Bougie, which is as beautiful as that of Naples, of Ajaccio, or of Douarnenez, which are the most lovely that I know of.

Far away in the distance, before one rounds the large inlet where the water is perfectly calm, one sees Bougie. It is built on the steep sides of a high hill covered with trees, and forms a white spot on that green slope; it might almost be taken for the foam of a cascade falling into the sea.

I had no sooner set foot in that small, delightful town, than I knew that I should stay for a long time. In all directions the eye rests on rugged, strangely shaped hilltops, so close together that you can hardly see the open sea, so that the gulf looks like a lake. The blue water is wonderfully transparent, and the azure sky, a deep azure, as if it had received two coats of color, expands its wonderful beauty above it. They seem to be looking at themselves in a glass, a veritable reflection of each other.

Bougie is a town of ruins, and on the quay is such magnificent ruin that you might imagine you were at the opera. It is the old Saracen Gate, overgrown with ivy, and there are ruins in all directions on the hills round the town, fragments of Roman walls, bits of Saracen monuments, and remains of Arabic buildings.

I had taken a small, Moorish house, in the upper town. You know those dwellings, which have been described so often. They have no windows on the outside; but they are lighted from top to bottom by an inner court. On the first floor, they have a large, cool room, in which one spends the days, and a terrace on the roof, on which one spends the nights.

I at once fell in with the custom of all hot countries, that is to say, of taking a *siesta* after lunch. That is the hottest time in Africa, the time when one can scarcely breathe; when the streets, the fields, and the long, dazzling, white roads are deserted, when everyone is asleep or at any rate, trying to sleep, attired as scantily as possible.

In my drawing-room, which had columns of Arabic architecture, I had placed a large, soft couch, covered with a carpet from Djebel Amour. There, very nearly in the costume of Assan, I sought to rest, but I could not sleep, as I was tortured by continence. There are two forms of torture on this earth which I hope you will never know: the want of water, and the want of women, and I do not know which is the worst. In the desert, men would commit any infamy for the sake of a glass of clean, cold water, and what would one not do in some of the towns of the littoral for the companionship of a handsome woman? There is no lack of girls in Africa; on the contrary, they abound, but, to continue my comparison, they are as unwholesome as the muddy water in the pools of Sahara.

Well one day when I was feeling more enervated than usual, I was trying in vain to close my eyes. My legs twitched as if they were being pricked, and I tossed about uneasily on my

couch. At last, unable to bear it any longer, I got up and went out. It was a terribly hot day, in the middle of July, and the pavement was hot enough to bake bread on. My shirt, which was soaked with perspiration, clung to my body; on the horizon there was a slight, white vapor, which seemed to be palpable heat.

I went down to the sea, and circling the port, walked along the shore of the pretty bay where the baths are. There was nobody about, and nothing was stirring; not a sound of bird or of beast was to be heard, the very waves did not lap, and the sea appeared to be asleep in the sun.

Suddenly, behind one of the rocks, which were half covered by the silent water, I heard a slight movement. Turning round, I saw a tall, naked girl, sitting up to her bosom in the water, taking a bath; no doubt she rockoned on being alone at that hot period of the day. Her head was turned toward the sea, and she was moving gently up and down, without seeing me.

Nothing could be more surprising than that picture of a beautiful woman in the water, which was as clear as crystal, under a blaze of light. She was a statue. She turned round, uttered a cry, and half swimming, half walking, hid herself altogether behind her rock. I knew she must necessarily come out, so I sat down on the beach and waited. Presently, she just showed her head, which was covered with thick black plaits of hair. She had a rather large mouth, with full lips, large, bold eyes, and her skin, which was tanned by the climate, looked like a piece of old, hard, polished ivory.

She called out to me: "Go away!" and her full voice, which corresponded to her strong build, had a guttural accent. As I did not move, she added: "It is not right of you to stop there, Monsieur." I did not move, however, and her head disappeared. Ten minutes passed, and then her hair, then her forehead, and then her eyes reappeared, but slowly and prudently, as if she were playing at hide-and-seek, and were looking to see who was near. This time she was furious, and called out: "You will make me catch a chill, for I shall not come out as long as you are there." Thereupon, I got up and went away, but not without looking round several times. When she thought I was far enough off, she came out of the water. Bending down and turning her back to me, she disappeared in a cavity of the rock, behind a petticoat that was hanging up in front of it.

I went back the next day. She was bathing again but she had a bathing costume and she began to laugh, and showed her white teeth. A week later we were friends, and in another week we were eager lovers. Her name was Marroca, and she pronounced it as if there were a dozen *rs* in it. She was the daughter of Spanish colonists, and had married a Frenchman, whose name was Pontabèze. He was in government employ, though I never exactly knew what his functions were. I found out that he was always very busy, and I did not care for anything else.

She then altered her time for having her bath, and came to my house every day, to take her *siesta* there. What a *siesta*! It could scarcely be called reposing! She was a splendid girl, of a somewhat animal but superb type. Her eyes were always glowing with passion; her half-open mouth, her sharp teeth, and even her smiles, had something ferociously loving about them; and her curious, long and conical breasts gave her whole body something of the animal, made her a sort of inferior yet magnificent being, a creature destined for unbridled love, and roused in me the idea of those ancient deities who gave expression to their tenderness on the grass and under the trees.

And then, her mind was as simple as two and two are four, and a sonorous laugh served her instead of thought.

Instinctively proud of her beauty, she hated the slightest covering, and ran and frisked about my house with daring and unconscious immodesty. When she was at last overcome and worn out by her cries and movements, she used to sleep soundly and peacefully, while the overwhelming heat brought out minute spots of perspiration on her brown skin.

Sometimes she returned in the evening, when her husband was on duty somewhere, and we used to lie on the terrace, scarcely covered by some fine, gauzy, Oriental fabric. When the full moon lit up the town and the gulf, with its surrounding frame of hills, we saw on all the other terraces a recumbent army of silent phantoms, who would occasionally get up, change their places, and lie down again, in the languorous warmth of the starry night.

In spite of the brightness of African nights, Marroca would insist upon stripping herself almost naked in the clear rays of the moon; she did not trouble herself much about anybody who might see us, and often, in spite of my fears and entreaties, she uttered long, resounding cries, which made the dogs in the distance howl.

One night, when I was sleeping under the starry sky, she came and kneeled down on my carpet, and putting her lips, which curled slightly, close to my face, she said:

"You must come and stay at my house."

I did not understand her, and asked: "What do you mean?"

"Yes, when my husband has gone away you must come and be with me."

I could not help laughing, and said: "Why, as you come here?"

And she went on, almost talking into my mouth, sending her hot breath into my throat, and moistening my mustache with her lips:

"I want it as a remembrance."

Still I did not grasp her meaning. Then she put her arms around my neck and said: "When you are no longer here, I shall think of it."

I was touched and amused at the same time and replied: "You must be mad. I would much rather stop here."

As a matter of fact, I have no liking for assignations under the conjugal roof; they are mouse-traps, in which the unwary are always caught. But she begged and prayed, and even cried, and at last said: "You shall see how I will love you there."

Her wish seemed so strange that I could not explain it to myself; but on thinking it over, I thought I could discern a profound hatred for her husband, the secret vengeance of a woman who takes a pleasure in deceiving him, and who, moreover, wishes to deceive him in his own house.

"Is you husband very unkind to you?" I asked her. She looked vexed, and said:

"Oh, no, he is very kind."

"But you are not fond of him?"

She looked at me with astonishment in her large eyes. "Indeed, I am very fond of him, very; but not so fond as I am of you."

I could not understand it all, and while I was trying to get at her meaning, she pressed one of those kisses, whose power she knew so well, on to my lips, and whispered: "But you will come, will you not?"

I resisted, however, and so she got up immediately, and went away; nor did she come back for a week. On the eighth day she came back, stopped gravely at the door of my abode, and said: "Are you coming to my house to-night? If you refuse, I shall go away."

Eight days is a very long time, my friend, and in Africa those eight days are as good as a month. "Yes," I said, and opened my arms, and she threw herself into them.

At night she waited for me in a neighboring street, and took me to their house, which was very small, and near the harbor. I first of all went through the kitchen, where they had their meals, and then into a very tidy, whitewashed room, with photographs on the walls and paper flowers under a glass case. Marroca seemed beside herself with pleasure, and she jumped about and said: "There, you are at home, now." And I certainly acted as though

I were, though I felt rather embarrassed and somewhat uneasy.

Suddenly a loud knocking at the door made us start, and a man's voice called out: "Marroca, it is I."

She started: "My husband! Here, hide under the bed, quickly."

I was distractedly looking for my coat, but she gave me a push, and panted out: "Come along, come along."

I lay down flat on my stomach, and crept under the bed without a word, while she went into the kitchen. I heard her open a cupboard and then shut it again, and she came back into the room carrying some object which I could not see, but which she quickly put down. Then, as her husband was getting impatient, she said calmly: "I cannot find the matches." Suddenly she added: "Oh, here they are; I will come and let you in."

The man came in, and I could see nothing of him but his feet, which were enormous. If the rest of him was in proportion, he must have been a giant.

I heard kisses, a little pat on her naked flesh, and a laugh, and he said, in a strong Marseilles accent: "I forgot my purse, so I was obliged to come back; you were sound asleep, I suppose."

He went to the cupboard, and was a long time in finding what he wanted; and as Marroca had thrown herself on to the bed, as if she were tired out, he went up to her, and no doubt tried to caress her, for she flung a volley of angry *rs* at him. His feet were so close to me that I felt a stupid, inexplicable longing to catch hold of them, but I restrained myself. When he saw that

he could not succeed in his wish, he got angry, and said: "You are not at all nice, to-night. Good-bye."

I heard another kiss, then the big feet turned, and I saw the nails in his shoes as he went into the next room, the front door was shut, and I was saved!

I came slowly out of my retreat, feeling rather humiliated, and while Marroca danced a jig around me, shouting with laughter, and clapping her hands, I threw myself heavily into a chair. But I jumped up with a bound, for I had sat down on something cold, and as I was no more dressed than my accomplice was, the contact made me start. I looked round. I had sat down on a small ax, used for cutting wood, and as sharp as a knife. How had it got there? I had certainly not seen it when I went in; but Marroca seeing me jump up, nearly choked with laughter, and coughed with both hands on her sides.

I thought her amusement rather out of place; we had risked our lives stupidly, I still felt a cold shiver down my back, and I was rather hurt at her foolish laughter.

"Supposing your husband had seen me?" I said.

"There was no danger of that," she replied.

"What do you mean? No danger? That is a good joke! If he had stooped down, he must have seen me."

She did not laugh any more, she only looked at me with her large eyes, which were bright with merriment.

"He would not have stooped."

"Why?" I persisted. "Just suppose that he had let his hat fall, he would have been sure to pick it up, and then

—I was well prepared to defend my-self, in this costume!"

She put her two strong, round arms about my neck, and, lowering her voice, as she did when she said "I *adorre* you," she whispered:

"Then he would *never* have got up again."

I did not understand her, and said: "What do you mean?"

She gave me a cunning wink, and put out her hand to the chair on which I had sat down, and her outstretched hands, her smile, her half-open lips, her white, sharp, and ferocious teeth, all drew my attention to the little ax which was used for cutting wood, the sharp blade of which was glistening in the candle-light. While she put out her hand as if she were going to take it, she put her left arm round me, and drawing me to her, and putting her lips against mine, with her right arm she made a motion as if she were cutting off the head of a kneeling man!

This, my friend, is the manner in which people here understand conjugal duties, love, and hospitality!

A Philosopher Mead

BLEROT had been my most intimate friend from childhood; we had no se-crets from each other, and were united heart and soul by a brotherly intimacy and a boundless confidence in each other. I had been intrusted with the secret of all his love affairs, as he had been with mine.

When he told me that he was going to get married I was hurt, just as if he had been guilty of a treacherous act with regard to me. I felt that it must interfere with that cordial and absolute affection which had united us hitherto. His wife would come between us. The intimacy of the marriage-bed establishes a kind of complicity, a mysterious al-liance between two persons, even when they have ceased to love each other. Man and wife are like two discreet part-ners who will not let anyone else into their secrets. But that close bond which the conjugal kiss fastens is widely loosened on the day on which the woman takes a lover.

I remember Blérot's wedding as if it were but yesterday. I would not be present at the signing of the marriage contract, as I have no particular liking for such ceremonies. I only went to the civil wedding and to the church.

His wife, whom I had never seen be-fore, was a tall, slight girl, with pale hair, pale cheeks, pale hands, and eyes to match. She walked with a slightly undulating motion as if she were on board a ship, and seemed to advance with the succession of long graceful courtesies.

Blérot seemed very much in love with her. He looked at her constantly, and I felt a shiver of an immoderate desire for her pass through my frame. I went to see him in a few days, and he said to me:

"You do not know how happy I am;

I am madly in love with her; but then she is—she is—" He did not finish his sentence, but he put the tips of his fingers to his lips with a gesture which signified "divine! delicious! perfect!" and a good deal more besides.

I asked laughing, "What! all that?"

"Everything that you can imagine," was his answer.

He introduced me to her. She was very pleasant, on easy terms with me, as was natural, and begged me to look upon their house as my own. I felt that he, Blérot, did not belong to me any longer. Our intimacy was altogether checked, and we hardly found a word to say to each other.

I soon took my leave, and shortly afterward went to the East, returning by way of Russia, Germany, Sweden, and Holland, after an absence of eighteen months from Paris.

The morning after my arrival, as I was walking along the boulevards to breathe the air once more, I saw a pale man with sunken cheeks coming toward me, who was as much like Blérot as it was possible for a physical, emaciated man to resemble a strong, ruddy, rather stout man. I looked at him in surprise, and asked myself: "Can it possibly be he?" But he saw me, and came toward me with outstretched arms, and we embraced in the middle of the boulevard.

After we had gone up and down once or twice from the Rue Drouot to the Vaudeville Theatre, just as we were taking leave of each other,—for he already seemed quite done up with walking,—I said to him:

"You don't look at all well. Are you ill?"

"I do feel rather out of sorts," was all he said.

He looked like a man who was going to die, and I felt a flood of affection for my old friend, the only real one that I had ever had. I squeezed his hands.

"What is the matter with you? Are you in pain?"

"A little tired; but it is nothing."

"What does your doctor say?"

"He calls it anæmia, and has ordered me to eat no white meat and to take tincture of iron."

A suspicion flashed across me.

"Are you happy?" I asked him.

"Yes, very happy; my wife is charming, and I love her more than ever."

But I noticed that he grew rather red and seemed embarrassed, as if he was afraid of any further questions, so I took him by the arm and pushed him into a *café*, which was nearly empty at that time of day. I forced him to sit down, and looking him straight in the face, I said:

"Look here, old fellow, just tell me the exact truth."

"I have nothing to tell you," he stammered.

"That is not true," I replied, firmly. "You are ill, mentally perhaps, and you dare not reveal your secret to anyone. Something or other is doing you harm, and I mean you to tell me what it is. Come, I am waiting for you to begin."

Again he got very red, stammered, and turning his head away, he said:

"It is very idiotic—but I—I am done for!"

As he did not go on, I said:

"Just tell me what it is."

"Well, I have got a wife who is kill•

ing me, that is all," he said abruptly, almost desperately.

I did not understand at first. "Does she make you unhappy? How? What is it?"

"No," he replied in a low voice, as if he were confessing some crime; "I love her too much, that is all."

I was thunderstruck at this singular avowal, and then I felt inclined to laugh, but at length I managed to reply:

"But surely, at least so it seems to me, you might manage to—to love her a little less."

He had got very pale again, and at length made up his mind to speak to me openly, as he used to do formerly.

"No," he said, "that is impossible; and I am dying from it, I know; it is killing me, and I am really frightened. Some days, like to-day, I feel inclined to leave her, to go away altogether, to start for the other end of the world, so as to live for a long time; and then, when the evening comes, I return home in spite of myself, but slowly, and feeling uncomfortable. I go upstairs hesitatingly and ring, and when I go in I see her there sitting in her easy-chair, and she will say, 'How late you are,' I kiss her, and we sit down to dinner. During the meal I make this resolve: 'I will go directly it is over, and take the train for somewhere, no matter where'; but when we get back to the drawing-room I am so tired that I have not the courage to get up out of my chair, and so I remain, and then—and then—and then—I succumb again."

I could not help smiling again. He saw it, and said: "You may laugh, but I assure you it is very horrible."

"Why don't you tell your wife?" I asked him. "Unless she be a regular monster she would understand."

He shrugged his shoulders. "It is all very well for you to talk. I don't tell her because I know her nature. Have you ever heard it said of certain women, 'She has just married a third time?' Well, and that makes you laugh like you did just now, and yet it is true. What is to be done? It is neither her fault nor mine. She is so, because nature has made her so; I assure you, my dear old friend, she has the temperament of a Messalina. She does not know it, but I do; so much the worse for me. She is charming, gentle, tender, and thinks that our conjugal intercourse, which is wearing me out and killing me, is natural and quite moderate. She seems like an ignorant schoolgirl, and she really is ignorant, poor child.

"Every day I form energetic resolutions, for you must understand that I am dying. But one look of her eyes, one of those looks in which I can read the ardent desire of her lips, is enough for me, and I succumb at once, saying to myself: 'This is really the end; I will have no more of her death-giving kisses,' and then, when I have yielded again, like I have to-day, I go out and walk and walk, thinking of death, and saying to myself that I am lost, that all is over.

"I am mentally so ill that I went for a walk to Père Lachaise cemetery yesterday. I looked at all the graves, standing in a row like dominoes, and I thought to myself: 'I shall soon be there,' and then I returned home, quite determined to pretend to be ill, and so escape, but I could not.

"Oh! You don't know what it is. Ask a smoker who is poisoning himself with nicotine whether he can give up his delicious and deadly habit. He will tell you that he has tried a hundred times without success, and he will, perhaps, add: 'So much the worse, but I would rather die than go without tobacco.' That is just the case with me. When once one is in the clutches of such a passion or such a habit, one must give oneself up to it entirely."

He got up and gave me his hand. I felt seized with a tumult of rage, and with hatred for this woman, this careless, charming, terrible woman; and as he was buttoning up his coat to go out I said to him, brutally perhaps:

"But, in God's name, why don't you let her have a lover, rather than kill yourself like that?"

He shrugged his shoulders without replying, and went off.

For six months I did not see him. Every morning I expected a letter of invitation to his funeral, but I would not go to his house from a complicated feeling of contempt for him and for that woman; of anger, of indignation, of a thousand sensations.

One lovely spring morning I was in the Champs-Elysées. It was one of those warm days which make our eyes bright and stir up in us a tumultuous feeling of happiness from the mere sense of existence. Some one tapped me on the shoulder, and turning round I saw my old friend, looking well, stout, and rosy.

He gave me both hands, beaming with pleasure, and exclaimed:

"Here you are, you erratic individual!"

I looked at him, utterly thunderstruck.

"Well, on my word—yes. By Jove! I congratuate you; you have indeed changed in the last six months!"

He flushed scarlet, and said, with an embarrassed laugh:

"One can but do one's best."

I looked at him so obstinately that he evidently felt uncomfortable, so I went on:

"So — now — you are — completely cured?"

He stammered, hastily:

"Yes, perfectly, thank you." Then changing his tone, "How lucky that I should have come across you, old fellow. I hope we shall often meet now."

But I would not give up my idea; I wanted to know how matters really stood, so I asked:

"Don't you remember what you told me six months ago? I suppose—I—eh —suppose you resist now?"

"Please don't talk any more about it," he replied, uneasily; "forget that I mentioned it to you; leave me alone. But, you know, I have no intention of letting you go; you must come and dine at my house."

A sudden fancy took me to see for myself how matters stood, so that I might understand all about it, and I accepted.

His wife received me in a most charming manner, and she was, as a matter of fact, a most attractive woman. Her long hands, her neck, and cheeks were beautifully white and delicate, and marked her breeding, and her walk was undulating and delightful.

René gave her a brotherly kiss on the forehead and said:

"Has not Lucien come yet?"

"Not yet," she replied, in a clear, soft voice; "you know he is almost always rather late."

At that moment the bell rang, and a tall man was shown in. He was dark, with a thick beard, and looked like a modern Hercules. We were introduced to each other; his name was Lucien Delabarre.

René and he shook hands in a most friendly manner, and then we went to dinner.

It was a most enjoyable meal, without the least constraint. My old friend spoke with me constantly, in the old familiar cordial manner, just as he used to do. It was: "You know, old fellow!"—"I say, old fellow!"—"Just listen a moment, old fellow!" Suddenly he exclaimed:

"You don't know how glad I am to see you again; it takes me back to old times."

I looked at his wife and the other man. Their attitude was perfectly correct, though I fancied once or twice that they exchanged a rapid and furtive look.

As soon as dinner was over René turned to his wife, and said:

"My dear, I have just met Pierre again, and I am going to carry him off for a walk and chat along the boulevards to remind us of old times. I am leaving you in very good company."

The young woman smiled, and said to me, as she shook hands with me:

"Don't keep him too long."

As we went along, arm-in-arm, I could not help saying to him, for I was determined to know how matters stood:

"What has happened? Do tell me!"

He, however, interrupted me roughly, and answered like a man who has been disturbed without any reason.

"Just look here, old fellow; leave one alone with your questions."

Then he added, half aloud, as if talking to himself:

"After all, it would have been too stupid to have let oneself go to perdition like that."

I did not press him. We walked on quickly and began to talk. All of a sudden he whispered in my ear:

"I say, suppose we go and have a bottle of 'fizz' with some girls! Eh?"

I could not prevent myself from laughing heartily.

"Just as you like; come along, let us go."

A Mistake

THAT day Boniface, the letter-carrier, found in leaving the postoffice that his route would not be so long, and therefore felt a lively delight.

He had charge of the country around Vireville and, when he returned in the evening, he often found he had covered over twenty miles in his long march.

To-day the distribution would be easy; he could even stroll along a little and be home by three o'clock in the afternoon. What luck!

He went out along the Sennemare road and commenced his work. It was June, the month of verdure and flowers, the true month of the fields and meadows.

The man, in his blue blouse and black cap with red braid, crossed through by-paths, fields of millet, oats, and wheat, buried to the shoulders in their depths; and his head moving along above the feathery waves, seemed to float upon a calm and verdant sea, which a light breeze caused to undulate gently. He entered the farms through wooden gateways built on the slopes and shaded by two rows of beech trees, greeted the farmer by name: "Good morning, M. Chicot," and passed him his newspaper, "The Little Norman."

The farmer would wipe his hand on his trousers, receive the paper and slide in into his pocket to read at his ease after the midday meal. The dogs, asleep in barrels under the drooping apple trees, yapped with fury, pulling at their chains; but the carrier without turning, proceeded, at his military gait, stretching his long limbs, the left arm over him bag, the right manipulating his cane which marched like himself, in a continuous, hurried fashion.

He distributed his printed matter and his letters in the hamlet of Sennemare, then set out across the fields with a paper for the tax-collector who lived in a little isolated house a quarter of a mile from the village.

He was a new collector, this M. Chapatis, arrived but the week before and lately married.

He took a Paris paper and, sometimes, carrier Boniface, when he had

time, would take a look at it before delivering it at its destination.

Now, he opened his bag, took out the paper, slipped it out of its wrapper, unfolded it, and began to read while walking. The first page did not interest him; politics did not arouse him; the finance he always passed over but the general facts of the day he read eagerly.

That day they were very exciting. He became so much interested in the story of a crime executed in a game-keeper's lodge that he stopped in the middle of a cloverfield to read it more slowly. The details were frightful. A woodcutter, in passing the forester's house the morning after, had noticed a little blood upon the sill as if some one had been bleeding from the nose. "The keeper must have killed a wolf last night," he thought; but coming nearer, he perceived that the door was left open and that the lock had been broken. Then, seized with fear, he ran to the village, notified the mayor, who took with him as a re-enforcement, the keeper of fields and the school-master; these four men returned together. They found the forester with his throat cut before the chimney-piece, his wife strangled on the bed, and their little daughter, aged six years, stifled under two mattresses.

Carrier Boniface became so wrought up over the thought of this assassination, whose horrible details had been revealed to him one by one, that he felt a weakness in his limbs and said aloud:

"Christopher! But some of the people in this world are brutes!"

Then he replaced the journal in its wrapper and went on, his head full of visions of the crime. He arrived shortly at M. Chapatis's. He opened the gate of the little garden and approached the house. It was of low construction, containing only one story and a mansard roof. It was at least five hundred feet from its nearest neighbor.

The carrier mounted the two front steps, placed his hand upon the knob, trying to open the door, but found it locked. Then he perceived that the shutters had not been opened, and that no one had come out that morning.

A feeling of alarm took possession of him, for M. Chapatis, since his arrival, had always been up rather early. It was then only ten minutes after seven, nearly an hour earlier than he usually got there. No matter. The tax-collector ought to be up before that.

He made a tour around the house, walking with much precaution, as if he himself might be in some danger. He noticed nothing suspicious except a man's footprints on a strawberry bed.

But suddenly he remained motionless as he was passing a window, powerless from fright. A groan came from the house.

He approached nearer and stepping over a border of thyme, glued his ear to the opening in order to hear better; assuredly some one was groaning. He could plainly hear long, dolorous sighs, a kind of rattle, a noise of struggle. Then the groans become louder, and oft repeated, finally being accentuated and changing into cries.

Then Boniface, no longer doubtful that a crime was being committed, took to his legs, recrossed the little garden, flew across the field and the meadow, running until he was out of breath, his bag shaking and hitting against his hip, and arrived gasping and in dismay at the door of the police headquarters.

Brigadier Malautour was mending a broken chair by means of some brads and a hammer. Gendarme Rauter held the damaged piece of furniture between his knees and placed a nail at the edge of the crack; then the Brigadier, chewing his mustache, his eyes round and moist with interest in his work, would pound,—blows which fell on the fingers of his subordinate.

When the letter-carrier perceived them, he cried out:

"Come quick; some one is assassinating the tax-collector. Quick! Quick!"

The two men ceased their work and raised their heads, the astonished heads of people surprised and perplexed.

Boniface, seeing more surprise than haste, repeated:

"Quick! quick! the robbers are in the house. I heard the cries. There is no time to be lost."

The Brigadier, placing his hammer on the ground, remarked: "How was it you found out about this?"

The carrier answered: "I went to carry the paper and two letters when I noticed that the door was locked and that the collector had not been out. I walked around the house, trying to account for it, when suddenly, I heard some one groan, as if he were being strangled, as if his throat were being cut—and then I started as soon as I could to get you. There's no time to be lost."

"And you didn't try to help any?"

The carrier, much frightened, replied:

"I was afraid that one was too small a number."

Then the Brigadier, convinced, said:

"Give me time to get into my uniform and I will follow you."

And he went into the building followed by his subordinate who carried the chair. They reappeared almost immediately and all three started, in quick, trained step, for the scene of the crime.

Arriving near the house, they slackened their pace through precaution, and the Brigadier drew his revolver; then they went softly into the garden and approached the walls of the dwelling. There was nothing to indicate that the malefactors had gone away. The door remained locked, the windows closed.

"Let us wait for them," murmured the Brigadier.

But Boniface, palpitating with emotion, made them pass around to the other side and showed them an opening: "It is there," said he.

The Brigadier advanced alone and fixed his ear against the board. The two others waited, ready for anything, watching him closely.

He remained a long time motionless, listening. The better to bring his head near the wooden shutter, he had removed his three-cornered hat and held it in his right hand.

What did he hear? His face revealed nothing for some time, then, suddenly, his mustache rose at the corners, his cheeks took on folds as in a silent laugh, and, stepping over the border of thyme, he came toward the two men who were looking at him in a kind of stupor.

Walking along on the tips of his toes, he made the sign for them to follow, and when they came to the gate he advised Boniface to slip the paper and the letters under the door.

Th amazed carrier obeyed with perfect docility.

"And now, back again," said the Brigadier.

When they had gone a little way, he turned to the letter-carrier with a jocose air, his eyes upturned and shining with fun, and said, in a bantering tone:

"Well, you are a rogue, you are!"

The old fellow asked: "Why? I heard something. I swear to you I heard something."

Then the Brigadier, no longer able to restrain himself, laughed aloud. He laughed to suffocation, his two hands holding his sides, doubling himself up, his eyes full of tears, and making frightful grimaces about the nose. Both of them were frightened to look at him.

As he could neither speak, nor cease laughing, nor make them understand, he made a gesture, a popular, meaning gesture. As they could not comprehend that either, he kept repeating it, motioning back always, with his head.

Finally, his subordinate caught the meaning suddenly, and in his turn broke into formidable laughter. The old fellow remained stupefied between these two men who were twisting themselves into all shapes.

The Brigadier, finally, became calm, and giving the old man a great tap on his waistcoat, like a jolly good fellow, he cried:

"What a farce! A holy farce! I shall record it as the Crime of Father Boniface!"

The carrier opened his enormous eyes, and repeated:

"I swear to you that I heard something."

The Brigadier began to laugh. His subordinate sat down on the grass beside the ditch and laughed at his ease.

"Ah! you heard something. And your wife, do you assassinate her that way, hey, you old joker?"

"My wife?"

And he stood reflecting a long time, then he continued.

"My wife. Yes, she bawls if I strike her—and bawls that are bawls, why? Was M. Chapatis beating his wife?"

Then the Brigadier, in a delirium of humor, turned him around by the shoulders as if he had been a puppet and whispered in his ear something that caused him to look besotted with astonishment.

Then the old man murmured pensively:

"No?—not that—not that—she said nothing—mine—I would never have believed—is it possible?—one would swear that a murder—"

And, confused, disconcerted, and ashamed, he went on his way across the fields, while the two policemen, laughing continually and calling back to him from afar, with barrack-room wit, watched his black cap as it disappeared in the tranquil sea of grain.

Florentine

WE were talking about girls, for what else is there to talk about, among men? One of us said:

"Wait! A strange story occurs to me on this subject."

And he related it:

"One evening of last winter, I was suddenly taken with one of those desolate lassitudes which are overwhelming in their attack upon soul and body, from time to time. I was at home alone, and I knew well that if I remained there I should have a frightful fit of despondency, of the kind that leads to suicide when they return often.

"I put on my coat and went out, without knowing at all what I was going to do. Having descended to the Boulevard, I began to walk along past the *cafés,* nearly empty, for it was raining. One of those thin rains was falling that dampens the spirits as much as the clothes; not one of those good showers, striking one in a cascade and driving passers under the *porte-cochères* out of breath, but a rain that unceasingly deposits upon you imperceptible droplets and covers your clothing with a glistening, penetrating moisture.

"What should I do? I went up and returned, seeking some place to pass a couple of hours, and discovering, for the first time, that there was not a place of diversion in all Paris in the evening. Finally, I decided to enter the Folies-Bergères, that theater so amusing to street girls.

"There were very few in the great hall. The long, semicircular promenade contained but a few individuals, of a race usually known by their walk, their clothing, the cut of their hair and beard, their hats, and their complexion. It is not often that one sees among them a man who seems clean, perfectly clean, and whose clothing has altogether the same air. As for the girls they are always the same, as you know, plain, weary, drooping, walking with that quick step and that air of imbecile disdain which they assume, I know not why.

"I said to myself that truly not one of these flagging creatures, greasy rather than fat, either bloated or very thin, with the paunch of a prelate and their long legs bowed, was worth the louis that they obtained with much difficulty after having demanded five.

"But suddenly I perceived one of them, a little one that appeared genteel; not at all young, but fresh, droll, and provoking. I stopped her and, in beastly fashion, without thinking, set my price for the night. I did not wish to return home alone, all alone; I preferred rather the company and embrace of this worthless woman.

"And so I followed her. She lived in a big, big house in Martyr street. The gas was already extinguished on the staircase. I mounted slowly, constantly lighting taper-matches, striking the steps with my feet, stumbling and ill at ease, following a petticoat, the rustle of which I heard before me.

"She stopped at the fourth story, and having shut again the inside door, she asked:

" 'And you wish to remain until to-morrow?'

" 'Yes. You know that was the agreement.'

" 'All right, my dear, I only wanted to know. Wait for me here a minute, I will return immediately.'

"And she left me in the darkness. I heard her close two doors, then it seemed to me she was speaking with somebody. I was surprised and disturbed. The idea of blackmail occurred to me. But I have fists and solid muscles. 'We shall see,' thought I.

"I listened with all attention, both of ear and mind. Some one was moving, walking about, but with great precaution. Then another door was opened, and it seemed to me that I still heard talking, but in a very low voice.

"She returned, bringing a lighted candle. 'You can enter now,' she said.

"She spoke familiarly, as a sign of possession. I entered, and after having crossed a dining-room, where it was evident nobody ever dined, I entered a chamber like that of all these girls, a furnished room, with rep curtains, and eider-down silk quilt with suspicious, poppy-red spots.

"She continued: 'Put yourself at ease, my dear.'

"I inspected the apartment with an eye of suspicion. There seemed nothing disquieting, however. She undressed herself so quickly that she was in bed before I had my overcoat off. Then she began to laugh:

" 'Well, what is the matter with you? Are you changed into a pillar of salt? Come! Make haste!'

"I imitated her and joined her. Five minutes later I had a foolish desire to dress again and go out. But the overwhelming lassitude which had seized me at my house, returned to me, depriving me of all strength to move, and I remained, in spite of the disgust which I had for this public bed. The sensual charm which I believed I saw down there, under the lights of the theater, had disappeared in my arms, and I had with me, flesh to flesh, only a vulgar girl, like all the rest, whose indifferent and complaisant kiss had an after-taste of garlic.

"I began to talk to her:

" 'Have you been here long?' said I.

" 'Six months the fifteenth of January.'

" 'Where were you before that?'

" 'I was in Clauzel street. But the janitor made me so miserable that I left.'

"And she began to relate an interminable story of the *concierge* who had made some scandal about her.

"Suddenly I heard something moving near us. At first there was a sigh, then a light noise, but distinct, as if some one had fallen from a chair.

"I sat up quickly in bed and demanded: 'What was that noise?'

"She answered with assurance and composure: 'Don't disturb yourself, my dear, it is my neighbor. The partition is so thin that we hear all as if they were here. These are dirty boxes. They are made of pasteboard.'

"My indolence was so strong that I got down under the clothes again. We continued our talk. Incited by the curiosity which drives all men to question these creatures upon their first adventure, to wish to raise the veil from their first fault in order to find in them some far-off trace of innocence, that we may find something to love, perhaps, in the rapid recital evoked by their candor and the shame of long ago, I asked her about her first lover.

"I knew that she lied. What did it matter? Among all the lies I might discover, perhaps, some sincere or touching incident.

" 'Come,' said I, 'tell me who he was.'

" 'He was an oarsman.'

" 'Ah! Tell me about it. Where were you?'

" 'I was at Argenteuil.'

" 'What were you doing there?'

" 'I was maid in a restaurant.'

" 'What restaurant?'

" 'At the Freshwater Sailors, do you know it?'

" 'Well, yes; Bonanfan's.'

" 'Yes, that's the one.'

" 'And how did he pay his court, this oarsman?'

" 'While I was making his bed. He forced me.'

"But suddenly I recalled the theory of a doctor of my acquaintance, an observing, philosophic doctor who, in his practice in a great hospital, had daily examples of these girl-mothers and public girls, and knew all the shame and misery of women, the poor women who become the hideous prey of the wandering male with money in his pocket.

" 'Invariably,' he told me, 'is a girl debauched by a man of her own class and station in life. I have made volumes of observations upon it. It is customary to accuse the rich of culling the flower of innocence from the children of the people. That is not true. The rich pay for the culled bouquet. They cull also, but at the second flowering; they never cut the first.'

"Then turning toward my companion, I began to laugh:

" 'You may as well know that I know all about your story. The oarsman was not the first, as you well know.'

" 'Oh! yes, my dear, I swear it!'

" 'You are lying.'

" 'Oh! no, I promise you I am not.'

" 'You lie. Come, tell me the truth.'

"She seemed to hesitate, astonished. I continued:

" 'I am a sorcerer, my good child, a hypnotist. If you do not tell me the truth, I shall put you to sleep, and then I can find it out.'

"She was afraid, being stupid like her kind. She murmured:

" 'How did you ever guess it?'

"I replied: 'Come, speak.'

" 'Oh! the first time, that amounted to nothing. It was at a festival in the country. They called in a chef for the occasion, Mr. Alexander. After he came he had it all his own way in the house. He ordered everybody, even to the master and mistress, as if he had been a king. He was a large, handsome man who would not stay in place before his stove. He was always crying out: "Here, some butter—some eggs—some Madeira!" And it was necessary to carry him everything on the run, or he would get angry and say things to you that would make you blush under the skirts.

" 'When the day was finished, he would smoke his pipe before the door. And, as I passed him with a pile of plates, he said to me this: "Come, little goose, come down to the edge of the lake and show me the country." As for me, I went, like a fool; and scarcely had we arrived at the bank when he forced me so quickly that I did not even know that it was done. And then he went away by the nine o'clock train, and I never saw him again after that.'

"I asked: 'Is that all?'

"She stammered: 'Oh! I believe Florentine belongs to him.'

" 'Who is Florentine?'

" 'He is my little boy.'

" 'Ah! very well. And you made the oarsman believe that he was the father, did you not?'

" 'Yes.'

" 'He had money, this oarsman?'

" 'Yes, he left me an income of three hundred francs for Florentine's support.'

"I commenced to be amused. I continued:

" 'Very well, my girl, very well. You are all less sensual than one would believe. And how old is Florentine now?'

"She answered: 'Twelve years old. He will take his first communion in the spring.'

" 'That is good; and since that you have made a trade with your conscience.'

"She sighed resignedly: 'One must do what she can.'

"But a great noise in another part of the room made me leap out of bed with a bound; it was the noise of one falling, then rising and groping with his hands upon the wall. I had seized the candle and was looking about, frightened and furious. She got up also and tried to hold me back, saying:

" 'It is nothing, my dear, I assure you it is nothing.'

"But I had discovered on which side of the wall this strange noise was. I went straight toward a concealed door at the head of the bed and opened it suddenly—and perceived there a poor little boy, trembling and staring at me with frightened eyes, a pale, thin little boy beside a large chair filled with straw, from which he had fallen.

"When he saw me, he began to cry and, opening his arms to his mother:

" 'It was not my fault, mamma, it was not my fault. I was asleep and I fell. You mustn't scold me, for it was not my fault.'

"I turned toward the woman and said:

" 'What does he mean?'

"She seemed confused and disheartened. . But finally she said in a broken voice:

" 'What can you expect? I do not earn enough to put the child in school! I must take care of him somehow, and I cannot afford to hire another room. He sleeps with me when I have no one. When some one comes for an hour or two, he can stay in the closet very well and keep quiet; he knows how. But when one remains all night, as you have, his muscles are fatigued from sleeping on the chair—and it is not the child's fault. I would like to see you—you— sleep all night on a chair—you would sing another song—'

"She was angry, wrought up, and was crying.

"The child wept too. A poor child, pitiful and timid, a good child of the closet, of the cold, dark closet, a child who came from time to time to get a little warmth in the bed a moment empty.

"I, too, had a desire to weep.

"And I returned home to my own bed."

Consideration

SIMON BOMBARD often found life very bad! He was born with an unbelievable aptitude for doing nothing and with an immoderate desire to follow this vocation. All effort, whether moral or physical, each movement accomplished for a purpose, appeared to him beyond his strength. As soon as he heard anyone speak of anything serious he became confused, his mind being incapable of tension or even attention.

The son of a novelty merchant of Caen, he glided along smoothly, as they said in the family, until he was twenty-five years of age. But as his parents were always nearer bankruptcy than fortune, he suffered greatly for want of money.

He was a tall, large, pretty youth with red whiskers, worn Norman fashion, of florid complexion, blue eyes, sensual and gay, corpulence already apparent, and dressed with the swagger elegance of a provincial at a festival. He laughed, cried, and gesticulated at the same time, displaying a storm of good nature with all the assurance of the seasoned traveler. He considered that life was made principally for joys and pleasures, and as soon as it became necessary to curb his noisy enjoyment, he fell into a kind of chronic somnolence, being incapable of sadness.

His need for money harassed him until he formed the habit of repeating a phrase now celebrated in his circle of acquaintance: "For ten thousand francs a year, I would become an executioner."

Now, he went each year to Trouville to pass two weeks. He called this "spending the season." He would install himself at the house of his cousins who gave him the use of a room, and from the day of his arrival to that of his departure he would promenade along the board walk which extends along the great stretch of seashore.

He walked with an air of confidence, his hands in his pockets or crossed behind his back, always clothed in ample garments, with light waistcoats and showy cravats, his hat somewhat over his ear and a cheap cigar in one corner of his mouth.

He went along, brushing by the elegantly dressed women and eying contemptuously the merry men who were ready to make a disturbance for the sake of it, and seeking—seeking—what he was seeking.

He was after a wife, counting entirely upon his face and his physique. He said to himself: "Why the devil, in all the crowd that comes here, should I not be able to find my fate?" And he hunted with the scent of a dog in the chase, with the Norman scent, sure that he should recognize her, the woman who would make him rich, the moment he perceived her.

It was one Monday morning that he murmured: "Wait! wait! wait!" The weather was superb, one of those yellow and blue days of the month of July, when one might say that the sky wept from the heat. The vast shore covered with people, costumes, colors, had the air of a garden of women; and

the fishing boats with their brown sails, almost immovable upon the blue water which reflected them upside down, seemed asleep under the great sun at ten o'clock in the morning. There they remained opposite the wooden pier, some near, some further off, some still further, as if overcome by a summer day idleness, too indifferent to seek the high sea or even to return to port. And down there one could vaguely perceive in the mist the coast of Havre, showing two white points on its summit, the lighthouses of Sainte-Adresse.

He said to himself: "Wait, wait, wait!" For he had passed her now for the third time and perceived that she had noticed him, this mature woman, experienced and courageous, who was making a bid for his attention. He had noticed her before on the days preceding, because she seemed also in quest of some one. She was an Englishwoman, rather tall, a little thin, an audacious Englishwoman whom circumstances and much journeying had made a kind of man. Not bad, on the whole, walking along slowly with short steps, soberly and simply clothed, but wearing a queer sort of hat as Englishwomen always do. She had rather pretty eyes, high cheekbones, a little red, teeth that were too long and always visible.

When he came to the pier, he returned upon his steps to see if she would meet him again. He met her and she threw him a knowing glance, a glance which seemed to say: "Here I am!"

But how should he speak to her? He returned a fifth time, and when he was again face to face with her she dropped her umbrella. He threw himself forward, picked it up and presented it to her, saying:

"Permit me, Madame—"

She responded: "Oh, you are very kind!"

And then they looked at each other. They knew nothing more to say. But she blushed. Then becoming courageous, he said:

"We are having beautiful weather here."

And she answered: "Oh, delicious!"

And then they remained opposite each other embarrassed, neither thinking of going away. It was she who finally had the audacity to ask: "Have you been about here long?"

He answered laughing: "Oh! yes, about as long as I care about it." Then brusquely he proposed: "Would you like to go down to the pier? It is pretty there such days as this."

She simply said: "I should be much pleased."

And they walked along side by side, she with her harsh, direct allurement, he alluring her with his dandyism, which makes for rakishness later on.

Three months later the notables in the commercial world of Caen received one morning a square white card which said:

"*Mr. and Mrs. Prosper Bombard have the honor to announce the marriage of their son, Mr. Simon Bombard, to Mrs. Kate Robertson.*"

and on the other side:

"*Mrs. Kate Robertson has the honor or announcing her marriage to Mr. Simon Bombard.*"

They went to live in Paris. The fortune of the wife amounted to fifteen thousand francs a year income, free and clear. Simon wished to have four hundred francs a month for his personal expenses. He had to prove that his tenderness merited this amount; he did prove it easily and obtained what he asked for.

At first everything went well. Young Mrs. Bombard was no longer young, assuredly, and her freshness had undergone some wear; but she had a way of exacting things which made it impossible for anyone to refuse her. She would say, with her grave, willful, English accent: "Oh! Simon, now we must go to bed," which made Simon start toward the bed like a dog that had been ordered, "To your kennel." And she knew how to have her way by day and night, in a manner there was no resisting.

She did not get angry; she made no scenes; she never cried; she never had the appearance of being irritated or hurt, or even disturbed. She knew how to talk, that was all; and she spoke to the point, and in a tone that admitted no contradiction.

More than once Simon was on the point of rebelling; but before the brief and imperious desires of this singular woman he found himself unable to stand out. Nevertheless, when the conjugal kisses began to be meager and monotonous, and he had in his pocket what would bring him something greater, he paid for satiety, but with a thousand precautions.

Mrs. Bombard perceived all this, without his surmising it; and one evening she announced to him that she had rented a house at Mantes where they would live in the future.

Then existence became harder. He tried various kinds of diversion which did not at all compensate for the conquests he had a taste for.

He fished with a line, learned how to tell the places which the gudgeon liked, which the roach and carp preferred, the favorite spots of the bream and the kinds of bait that divers fishes will take.

But in watching his bob as it trembled on the surface of the water, other visions haunted his mind. Then he became the friend of the chief of the office of the subprefect and the captain of the police; and they played whist of evenings, at the Commerce *café;* but his sorrowful eye would disrobe the queen of clubs, or the lady of the diamonds, while the problem of the absent legs on these two-headed figures would bring up images suddenly that confused his thoughts.

Then he conceived a plan, a true Norman plan of deceit. He would have his wife take a maid who would be a convenience to him; not a beautiful girl, a coquette, adorned and showy, but a gawky woman, rough and strong-backed, who would not arouse suspicions and whom he would acquaint beforehand with his plans.

She was recommended to them by the director of the city farm, his accomplice and obliging friend, who guaranteed her under all relations and conditions. And Mrs. Bombard accepted with confidence the treasure they brought to her.

Simon was happy, happy with precaution, with fear, and with unbelievable difficulties. He could never undress beyond the watchful eye of his wife, except for a few short moments from time to time, and then without tranquillity. He sought some plan, some stratagem, and he ended by finding one that suited him perfectly.

Mrs. Bombard, who had nothing to do, retired early, while Bombard, who played whist at the Commerce *café,* returned each evening at half past nine, exactly. He got Victorine to wait for him in the passageway of his house, under the vestibule steps, in the darkness.

He only had five minutes or more for he was always in fear of a surprise; but five minutes from time to time sufficed for his ardor, and he slid a louis into the servant's hand, for he was generous in his pleasures, and she would quickly remount to her garret.

And he laughed, he triumphed all alone, and repeated aloud, like King Midas's barber fishing for the gold-fish from the reeds on the river bank: "The mistress is safe within."

And the happiness of having Mrs. Bombard safely fixed within made up for him in great part for the imperfection and incompleteness of his conquest.

One evening he found Victorine waiting for him as was her custom, but she appeared to him more lively, more animated than usual, and he remained perhaps ten minutes in the rendezvous in the corridor.

When he entered the conjugal chamber, Mrs. Bombard was not there. He felt a cold chill run down his back and sunk into a chair, tortured with fear.

She appeared with a candlestick in her hand. He asked trembling:

"You have been out?"

She answered quietly: "I went to the kitchen for a glass of water."

He forced himself to calm his suspicions of what she might have heard; but she seemed tranquil, happy, confident, and he was reassured.

When they entered the dining-room for breakfast the next morning, Victorine put the cutlets on the table. As she turned to go out, Mrs. Bombard handed her a louis which she held up delicately between her two fingers, and said to her, with her calm, serious accent:

"Wait, my girl, here are twenty francs which I deprived you of last night. I wish to give them to you."

And the girl, amazed, took the piece of gold which she looked at with a stupid air, while Bombard, frightened, opened his eyes wide at his wife.

Woman's Wiles

"WOMEN?"

"Well, what do you say about women?"

"Well, there are no conjurors more subtle in taking us in at every available opportunity with or without reason, often for the sole pleasure of playing tricks on us. And they play these tricks with incredible simplicity, astonishing audacity, unparalleled ingenuity. They play tricks from morning till night, and they all do it—the most virtuous, the most upright, the most sensible of them. You may add that sometimes they are to some extent driven to do these things. Man has always idiotic fits of obstinacy and tyrannical desires. A husband is continually giving ridiculous orders in his own house. He is full of caprices; his wife plays on them even while she makes use of them for the purpose of deception. She persuades him that a thing costs so much because he would kick up a row if its price were higher. And she always extricates herself from the difficulty cunningly by means so

simple and so sly that we gape with amazement when by chance we discover them. We say to ourselves in a stupefied state of mind, 'How is it we did not see this till now?'"

* * * * * *

The man who uttered the words was an ex-Minister of the Empire, the Comte de L——, thorough profligate, it was said, and a very accomplished gentleman. A group of young men were listening to him.

He went on:

"I was outwitted by an ordinary uneducated woman in a comic and thorough-going fashion. I will tell you about it for your instruction.

"I was at the time Minister for Foreign Affairs, and I was in the habit of taking a long walk every morning in the Champs-Elysées. It was the month of May; I walked along, sniffing in eagerly that sweet odor of budding leaves.

"Ere long, I noticed that I used to meet every day a charming little woman, one of those marvelous, graceful creatures, who bear the trade-mark of Paris. Pretty? Well, yes and no. Well-made? No, better than that: her waist was too slight, her shoulders too narrow, her breast too full, no doubt; but I prefer those exquisite human dolls to that great statuesque corpse, the Venus of Milo.

"And then this sort of woman trots along in an incomparable fashion, and the very rustle of her skirt fills the marrow of your bones with desire. She seemed to give me a side-glance as she passed me. But these women give you all sorts of looks—you never can tell— "One morning I saw her sitting on a bench with an open book between her hands. I came across, and sat down beside her. Five minutes later, we were friends. Then, each day, after the smiling salutation: 'Good day, Madame,' 'Good day, Monsieur,' we begin to chat. She told me that she was the wife of a government clerk, that her life was a sad one, that in it pleasures were few and cares numerous, and a thousand other things.

"I told her who I was, partly through thoughtlessness, and partly perhaps through vanity. She pretended to be much astonished.

"Next day she called at the Ministry to see me; and she came again there so often that the ushers, having their attention drawn to her appearance, used to whisper to one another, as soon as they saw her, the name with which they had christened her: 'Madame Léon'—that is my Christian name.

"For three months I saw her every morning without growing tired of her for a second, so well was she able incessantly to give variety and piquancy

to her physical attractiveness. But one day I saw that her eyes were bloodshot and glowing with suppressed tears, that she could scarcely speak, so much was she preoccupied with secret troubles.

"I begged of her, I implored of her, to tell me what was the cause of her agitation.

"She faltered out, at length, with a shudder: 'I am—I am *enceinte!*'

"And she burst out sobbing. Oh! I made a dreadful grimace, and I have no doubt I turned pale, as men generally do at hearing such a piece of news. You cannot conceive what an unpleasant stab you feel in your breast at the announcement of an unexpected paternity of this kind. But you are sure to know it sooner or later. So, in my turn, I gasped: 'But—but—you are married, are you not?'

"She answered: 'Yes, but my husband has been away in Italy for the last two months, and he will not be back for some time.'

"I was determined at any cost to get out of my responsibility.

"I said: 'You must go and join him immediately.'

"She reddened to her very temples, and with downcast eyes, murmured: 'Yes—but—' She either dared not or would not finish the sentence.

"I understood, and I prudently inclosed her in an envelope the expenses of the journey.

* * * * * *

"Eight days later, she sent me a letter from Genoa. The following week I received one from Florence. Then letters reached me from Leghorn, Rome, and Naples.

"She said to me:

" 'I am in good health, my dear love, but I am looking frightful. I would not care to have you see me till it is all over; you would not love me. My husband suspects nothing. As his business in this country will require him to stay there much longer. I will not return to France until after my confinement.'

"And, at the end of about eight months, I received from Venice these few words:

" 'It is a boy.'

"Some time after she suddenly entered my study one morning, fresher and prettier than ever, and flung herself into my arms. And our former connection was renewed.

"I left the Ministry, and she came to live in my house in the Rue de Grenelle. She often spoke to me about the child, but I scarcely listened to what she said about it; it did not concern me. Now and then I placed a rather large sum of money in her hand, saying: 'Put that by for him.'

"Two more years glided by; and she was more and more eager to tell me some news about the youngster—'about Léon.'

"Sometimes she would say in the midst of tears: 'You don't care about him; you don't even wish to see him. If you could know what grief you cause me!'

"At last I was so much harassed by her that I promised, one day, to go, next morning, to the Champs-Elysées when she took the child there for an airing.

"But at the moment when I was leaving the house, I was stopped by a sudden apprehension. Man is weak and foolish. What if I were to get fond of this tiny being of whom I was the father —my son?

"I had my hat on my head, my gloves in my hands. I flung down the gloves on my desk, and my hat on a chair:

" 'No, decidedly I will not go; it is wiser not to go.'

"My door flow open. My brother entered the room. He handed me an anonymous letter he had received that morning:

" 'Warn the Comte de L——, your brother, that the little woman of the Rue Casette is impudently laughing at him. Let him make some inquiries about her.'

"I had never told anybody about this intrigue, and I now told my brother the history of it from the beginning to the end. I added:

" 'For my part, I don't want to trouble myself any further about the matter; but will you, like a good fellow, go and find out what you can about her?'

"When my brother had left me, I said to myself: 'In what way can she have deceived me? She has other lovers? What does it matter to me? She is young, fresh, and pretty; I ask nothing more from her. She seems to love me, and as a matter of fact, she does not cost me much. Really, I don't understand this business.'

"My brother speedily returned. He had learned from the police all that was to be known about her husband: A clerk in the Home Department, of regular habits and good repute, and, moreover, a thinking man, but married to a very pretty woman, whose expenses seemed somewhat extravagant for her modest position. That was all.

"Now, my brother, having sought for her at her residence, and finding that she was gone out, succeeded, with the assistance of a little gold, in making the doorkeeper chatter: 'Madame D——, a very worthy woman, and her husband a very worthy man, not proud, not rich, but generous.'

"My brother asked, for the sake of saying something:

" 'How old is her little boy now?'

" 'Why, she has not got any little boy, Monsieur.'

" 'What? Little Léon?'

" 'No, Monsieur, you are making a mistake.'

" 'I mean the child she had while she was in Italy two years ago?'

" 'She has never been in Italy, Monsieur; she has not quitted the house she is living in for the last five years.'

"My brother, in astonishment, questioned the doorkeeper anew, and then he pushed his investigation of the matter further. No child, no journey.

"I was prodigiously astonished, but without clearly understanding the final meaning of this comedy.

" 'I want,' said I to him, 'to have my mind perfectly clear about the affair. I will ask her to come here to-morrow. You shall receive her instead of me. If she has deceived me, you will hand her these ten thousand francs, and I will never see her again. In fact, I am beginning to find I have had enough of her.'

"Would you believe it? I had been grieved the night before because I had a child by this woman; and I was now irritated, ashamed, wounded at having no more of her. I found myself free, released from all responsibil-ity, from all anxiety; and yet I felt my-self raging at the position in which I was placed.

"Next morning my brother awaited her in my study. She came in as quickly as usual, rushing toward him with outstretched arms, but when she saw who it was she at once drew back.

"He bowed, and excused himself.

" 'I beg your pardon, Madame, for being here instead of my brother; but he has authorized me to ask you for some explanations which he would find it painful to seek from you himself.'

"Then, fixing on her face a search-ing glance, he said abruptly:

" 'We know you have not a child by him.'

"After the first moment of stupor, she regained her composure, took a seat, and gazed with a smile at this man who was sitting in judgment on her.

"She answered simply:

" 'No; I have no child.'

" 'We know also that you have never been in Italy.'

"This time she burst out laughing in earnest.

" 'No; I have never been in Italy.'

"My brother, quite stunned, went on:

" 'The Comte has requested me to give you this money, and to tell you that it is broken off.'

"She became serious again, calmly putting the money into her pocket, and, in an ingenuous tone, asked:

" 'And I am not, then, to see the Comte any more?'

" 'No, Madame.'

"She appeared to be annoyed, and in a passionless voice she said:

" 'So much the worse; I was very fond of him.'

"Seeing that she had made up her mind on the subject so resolutely, my brother, smiling in his turn, said to her:

" 'Look here, now, tell me why you invented all this long, tricky yarn, complicating it by bringing in the sham journey to Italy and the child?'

"She gazed at my brother in amazement, as if he had asked her a stupid question, and replied:

" 'Well, I declare! How spiteful you are! Do you believe a poor little woman of the people such as I am—nothing at all—could have for three years kept on my hands the Comte de L——, Minister, a great personage, a man of fashion, wealthy, and seductive, if she had not taken a little trouble about it? Now it is all over. So much the worse. It couldn't last forever. None the less I succeeded in doing it for three years. You will say many things to him on my behalf.'

"She rose up. My brother continued questioning her:

" 'But—the child? You had one to show him?'

" 'Certainly—my sister's child. She lent it to me. I'd bet it was she gave you the information.'

" 'Good! And all those letters from Italy?'

"She sat down again so as to laugh at her ease.

" 'Oh! those letters—well, they were a bit of poetry. The Comte was not a Minister of Foreign Affairs for nothing.'

" 'But—another thing?'

" 'Oh! the other thing is my secret. I don't want to compromise anyone.'

"And bowing to him with a rather mocking smile she left the room without any emotion, an actress who had played her part to the end."

And the Comte de L—— added by way of moral:

"So take care about putting your trust in that sort of turtledove!"

Moonlight

MADAME JULIE ROUBÈRE was awaiting her elder sister, Madame Henriette Letore, who had just returned after a trip to Switzerland.

The Letore household had left nearly five weeks ago. Madame Henriette had allowed her husband to return alone to their estate in Calvados, where some matters of business required his attention, and came to spend a few days in Paris with her sister. Night came on. In the quiet parlor darkened by twilight shadows, Madame Roubère was reading in an absent-minded fashion, raising her eyes whenever she heard a sound.

At last she heard a ring at the door, and presently her sister appeared, wrapped in a traveling cloak. And immediately, without any formal greeting, they clasped each other ardently, only desisting for a moment to begin embracing each other over again. Then they talked, asking questions about each other's health, about their respective families, and a thousand other things, gossiping, jerking out hurried, broken sentences, and rushing about while Madame Henriette was removing her hat and veil.

It was now quite dark. Madame Roubère rang for a lamp, and as soon as it was brought in, she scanned her sister's face, and was on the point of embracing her once more. But she held back, scared and astonished at the other's appearance. Around her temples, Madame Letore had two long locks of white hair. All the rest of her hair was of a glossy, raven-black hue; but there alone, at each side of her head, ran, as it were, two silvery streams which were immediately lost in the black mass surrounding them. She was, nevertheless, only twenty-four years old, and this change had come on suddenly since her departure for Switzerland.

Without moving, Madame Roubère gazed at her in amazement, tears rising to her eyes, as she thought that some mysterious and terrible calamity must have fallen on her sister. She asked:

"What is the matter with you, Henriette?"

Smiling with a sad smile, the smile of one who is heartsick, the other replied:

"Why, nothing, I assure you. Were you noticing my white hair?"

But Madame Roubère impetuously seized her by the shoulders, and with a searching glance at her, repeated:

"What is the matter with you? Tell me what is the matter with you. And if you tell me a falsehood I'll soon find it out."

They remained face to face, and

Madame Henriette, who became so pale that she was near fainting, had two pearly tears at each corner of her drooping eyes.

Her sister went on asking:

"What has happened to you? What is the matter with you? Answer me!"

Then, in a subdued voice, the other murmured:

"I have—I have a lover."

And, hiding her forehead on the shoulder of her younger sister, she sobbed.

Then, when she had grown a little calmer, when the heaving of her breast had subsided, she commenced to unbosom herself, as if to cast forth this secret from herself, to empty this sorrow of hers into a sympathetic heart.

Thereupon, holding each other's hands tightly grasped, the two women went over to a sofa in a dark corner of the room, into which they sank, and the younger sister, passing her arm over the elder one's neck and drawing her close to her heart, listened.

*   *   *   *   *   *

"Oh! I recognize that there was no excuse for one; I do not understand myself, and since that day I feel as if I were mad. Be careful, my child, about yourself—be careful! If you only knew how weak we are, how quickly we yield, a moment of tenderness, one of those sudden fits of melancholy which steal into your soul, one of those longings to open your arms, to love, to embrace, which we all have at certain moments.

"You know my husband, and you know how fond of him I am; but he is mature and sensible, and cannot even comprehend the tender vibrations of a woman's heart. He is always, always the same, always good, always smiling, always kind, always perfect. Oh! how I sometimes have wished that he would roughly clasp me in his arms, that he would embrace me with those slow, sweet kisses which make two beings intermingle, which are like mute confidences! How I wished that he was self-abandoned and even weak, so that he should have need of me, of my caresses, of my tears!

"This all seems very silly; but we women are made like that. How can we help it?

"And yet the thought of deceiving never came near me. To-day, it has happened, without love, without reason, without anything, simply because the moon shone one night on the Lake of Lucerne.

"During the month when we were traveling together, my husband, with his calm indifference, paralyzed my enthusiasm, extinguished my poetic ardor. When we were descending the mountain paths at sunrise, when as the four horses galloped along with the diligence, we saw, in the transparent morning haze, valleys, woods, streams, and villages, I clasped my hands with delight, and said to him: 'What a beautiful scene, darling! Kiss me now!' he only answered, with a smile of chilling kindliness, 'There is no reason why we should kiss each other because you like the landscape.'

"And his words froze me to the heart. It seems to me that when people love each other, they ought to feel more moved by love than ever in the presence of beautiful scenes.

"Indeed, he prevented the effervescent poetry that bubbled up within me from gushing out. How can I express it? I was almost like a boiler, filled with steam, and hermetically sealed.

"One evening (we had been for four days staying in the Hotel de Fluelen), Robert, having got one of his sick headaches, went to bed immediately after dinner; and I went to take a walk all alone along the edge of the lake.

"It was a night such as one might read of in a fairy tale. The full moon showed itself in the middle of the sky; the tall mountains, with their snowy crests, seemed to wear silver crowns; the waters of the lake glittered with tiny rippling motions. The air was mild, with that kind of penetrating freshness which softens us till we seem to be swooning, to be deeply affected without any apparent cause. But how sensitive, how vibrating, the heart is at such moments! How quickly it leaps up, and how intense are its emotions!

"I sat down on the grass, and gazed at that vast lake so melancholy and so fascinating; and a strange thing passed into me; I became possessed with an insatiable need of love, a revolt against the gloomy dullness of my life. What! would it never be my fate to be clasped in the arms of a man whom I loved on a bank like this under the glowing moonlight? Was I never then, to feel on my lips those kisses so deep, delicious, and intoxicating which lovers exchange on nights that seem to have been made by God for passionate embraces? Was I never to know such ardent, feverish love in the moonlit shadows of a summer's night?

"And I burst out weeping like a woman who has lost her reason. I heard some person stirring behind me.

A man was intently gazing at me. When I turned my head round, he recognized me, and, advancing, said:

" 'You are weeping, Madame?'

"It was a young barrister who was traveling with his mother, and whom we had often met. His eyes had frequently followed me.

"I was so much confused that I did not know what answer to give or what to think of the situation. I told him I felt ill.

"He walked on by my side in a natural and respectful fashion, and began talking to me about what we had seen during our trip. All that I had felt he translated into words; everything that made me thrill he understood perfectly, better even than I did myself. And all of a sudden he recited some verses of Alfred de Musset. I felt myself choking, seized with indescribable emotion. It seemed to me that the mountains themselves, the lake, the moonlight, were singing to me about things ineffably sweet.

"And it happened, I don't know how, I don't know why, in a sort of hallucination.

"As for him, I did not see him again till the morning of his departure.

"He gave me his card!"

* * * * * *

And, sinking into her sister's arms, Madame Letore broke into groans—almost into shrieks.

Then Madame Roubère, with a self-contained and serious air, said very gently:

"You see, sister, very often it is not a man that we love, but love. And your real lover that night was the moonlight."

Doubtful Happiness

I CAN neither tell you the name of the country nor of the man. It was far, far from here, upon a hot, fertile coast. We followed, since morning, the shore and the wheat fields and the sea covered with the sun. Flowers grew down very near the waves, the light waves, so sweet and sleepy. It was very warm; but a gentle heat, perfumed with the fat, humid, fruitful earth; one could believe that he was breathing germs.

I had been told that this evening I would find hospitality in the house of a Frenchman who lived at the end of the promontory, in a grove of orange-trees. Who was he? I do not know yet. He had arrived one morning, ten years before this, bought the land, planted his vines, and sown his seed; he had worked, had this man, with passion and fury. Month after month and year after year he had added to his domains, making the fertile, virgin soil yield without ceasing, and amassing a fortune by his indefatigable labor.

It was said that he worked constantly. Up with the dawn, going through his fields until night, superintending everything without rest, he seemed harassed by a fixed idea, tortured by an insatiable desire for money which noth-satiable desire for money which noth-

Now he seemed to be very rich.

The sun was setting when I reached his dwelling. This dwelling was at the end of a point in the midst of orange-trees. It was a large, square house, very simple, overlooking the sea.

As I approached, a large, bearded man appeared in the doorway. Having saluted him, I asked for shelter for the night. He extended his hand and said, smiling:

"Enter, sir, you are at home."

He led me to a room, gave some orders to a servant with the perfect ease and good grace of a man of the world, then he left me saying:

"We will dine when you are ready to come down."

We dined, *tête-à-tête*, upon a terrace opposite the sea. At first, I spoke of his country, so rich, so far away, so little known! He smiled, answering in an abstracted way:

"Yes, this is a pretty country. But no country pleases one much when it is far from those they love."

"You regret France?"

"I—I long for Paris."

"Why not return there?"

"Oh! I am going to return there."

And gradually we begin to talk of the French world, of the boulevards, and of the many features of Paris. He asks me about men he has known, cites names, all of them familiar names upon the vaudeville stage.

"Who does one see at Tortoni's these days?"

"The same ones, except the dead."

I looked at him with marked interest,

pursued by some vague remembrance. Certainly I had seen that head somewhere! But where? And when? He seemed fatigued, although vigorous, sad, though resolute. His great blond beard fell upon his breast, and sometimes he would take it near his chin and draw it through his closed hand, slipping it along to the very end. He was a little bald but had thick eyebrows and a heavy mustache which mingled with the hair of his beard.

Behind us the sun was disappearing in the sea, throwing upon the coast a cloud of fire. The orange-trees, in flower, exhaled a powerful, delicious fragrance on the evening air. Seeing nothing but me, and fixing his look upon me, he seemed to discover in my eyes, to see at the depth of my soul, the well-known, much loved image of the broad walk, so far away, that extends from the Madeleine to the Rue Drouot.

"Do you know Bourtelle?" he asked.

"Yes, certainly."

"Is he much changed?"

"Yes, he is all white."

"And the Ridamie?"

"Always the same."

"And the women? Tell me about the women. Let us see. Did you know Suzanne Verner?"

"Yes, very well, to the end."

"Ah! And Sophie Astier?"

"Dead!"

"Poor girl! Can it be— Did you know—"

He was suddenly silent. Then, in a changed voice, his face growing pale, he continued:

"No, it is better not to speak of her, it disturbs me so."

Then, as if to change the trend of his thought, he rose and said:

"Do you wish to go in?"

"I am willing to go." And I followed him into the house.

The rooms downstairs were enormous, bare, sad, and seemed abandoned. Some glass dishes were set upon the table by the tawny-skinned servants who constantly roamed around this dwelling. Two guns hung upon two nails on the wall; and, in the corners, were to be seen some spades, some fish lines, dried palm leaves, and objects of every kind placed there at random by those entering, that they might find them at hand should they chance to have need of them on going out.

My host smiled:

"This is a lodge, or rather the lodging place of an exile," said he, "but my chamber is more as it should be. Let us go in there."

I thought, on entering, that I was in a curiosity shop, so filled was the room with all kinds of things, things disconnected, strange, and varied, that one felt to be souvenirs of something. Upon the walls were two pretty engravings of well-known paintings, some stuffs, some arms, swords, pistols; then, in the middle of the principal panel, a square of white satin in a gold frame.

Surprised, I approached to look at it, when I perceived a pin which held a hair in the middle of the shining silk.

My host placed his hand on my shoulder and said, smiling:

"That is the only thing that I see here and the only thing I have seen for ten years. Mr. Prudhomme exclaims: 'This sword is the most beautiful day in my life.' But I say: 'This pin is all of my life.' "

I sought for a commonplace phrase and ended by saying:

"You have suffered through some woman?"

He replied brusquely: "You may say I have suffered, miserably, — but come out on my balcony. A name has suddenly come to my lips that I have not dared to pronounce, because, if you had answered 'dead' as you did when I spoke of Sophie Astier, my brain would be on fire, even to-day."

We were upon a large balcony where we could see two gulfs, one on the right and the other on the left, shut in by high, gray mountains. It was the hour of twilight, when the sun, entirely out of sight, no longer lights the earth, except by reflection from the sky.

He continued: "Do you know if Jeanne de Limours still lives?"

His eye, fixed on mine, was full of trembling anxiety. I smiled and answered:

"Yes, indeed, and prettier than ever."

"You know her?"

"Yes."

He hesitated. Then asked: "Completely?"

"No."

He took my hand. "Tell me about her," said he.

"I have nothing to tell; she is one of the most charming women, or rather girls, in Paris, and the most courted. She leads an agreeable, princess-like existence, that is all."

He murmured: "I love her," as if he had said: "I am going to die." Then, brusquely: "Ah! for three years that was a frightful but delicious existence of ours. I was very near killing her five or six times and she tried to put out my eyes with that pin you were just looking at. Wait! Do you see the little white point under my left eye? That shows how we loved each other! How can I explain this passion? You could never comprehend it.

"There should be such a thing as a simple love, born of the force of two hearts and two souls; and assuredly there is such a thing as an atrocious love, cruelly torturing, born of the invincible rapture of two beings totally unlike, who detest while they adore each other.

"This girl ruined me in three years. I possessed four millions which she squandered in her calm way, tranquilly, and destroyed with a sweet smile which seemed to fall from her eyes upon her lips.

"You know her? Then you know that there is something irresistible about her! What is it! I do not know. Is it those gray eyes, whose look enters into you and remains there like the barb of an arrow? Or is it rather that sweet smile, indifferent and seductive, which stays on her face like a mask? Her slow manner penetrates, little by little, and takes hold of you like a perfume, as does her tall figure, which seems to balance itself as she passes, for she glides instead of walking, and her sweet voice, which drags a little and is so pretty that it seems to be the music of her smile; her gestures too, her always moderate gestures, always right, which intoxicate the eye, so harmonious are they.

"For three years, I saw only her upon the earth! How I suffered! Because she deceived me as well as everybody

else. Why? For no reason, only for the sake of deceiving. And when I found it out and accused her of being a street girl, a bad woman, she said tranquilly: 'Well, we are not married, are we?'

"Since I have come here, I have thought much about her, and have succeeded in understanding her, that girl is Manon Lescaut over again. Manon could never love without deceiving, and for her love, pleasure and money were all."

He was silent. Then, after some minutes he added:

"When I had squandered my last sou for her, she simply said to me: 'You understand, my dear, that I cannot live on air and weather. I love you very much, I love you more than anyone, but I must live. Misery and I can never dwell in the same house.'

"And if I could only tell you what an atrocious life I led by her side! Whenever I looked at her I had as much desire to kill her as I had to embrace her. Whenever I looked at her there came to me a furious desire to open my arms, press her to me until I strangled her. There was something about her, behind her eyes, something perfidious and unseizable which made me furious against her; and perhaps it was for that very reason that I loved her so much. In her the Feminine, the odious, frightful Feminine, was more prominent than in any other woman. She was charged and surcharged with it, as with a venomous fluid. She was Woman, more than anyone else has ever been.

"And whenever I went out with her, she would cast her eyes over all men in such a fashion that she seemed to give herself to each one with only a look. This exasperated me, but attached me more strongly to her, nevertheless. This creature belonged to everybody from merely passing through the street, in spite of me, in spite of herself, from her very nature, although the allurement was most modest and sweet. Do you understand?

"And what torment! At the theater, in a restaurant, it seemed to me that everyone possessed her before my eyes. And whenever I left her alone, others did, in fact, possess her.

"It is ten years now since I saw her, and I love her now more than ever."

Night had spread over the earth. A powerful perfume of orange flowers in the air.

I said to him: "Will you try to see her again?"

He answered: "Surely! I have here now, in money and land, seven or eight hundred thousand francs. When the million is completed, I shall sell all and set out. With that I can have one year with her, one good, entire year. And then—adieu; my life will be finished."

I asked: "And after that?"

"After that," he answered, "I don't know. It will be finished. Perhaps I shall ask her to take me as a *valet de chambre*."

Humiliation

THE two young women have the appearance of being buried in a bed of flowers. They are alone in an immense landau filled with bouquets like a giant basket. Upon the seat before them are two small hampers full of Nice violets, and upon the bear-skin which covers their knees is a heap of roses, gilly-flowers, marguerites, tuberoses, and orange flowers, bound together with silk ribbons, which seem to crush the two delicate bodies, only allowing to appear above the spread-out, perfumed bed the shoulders, arms, and a little of their bodices, one of which is blue and the other lilac.

The coachman's whip bears a sheath of anemones, the horses' heads are decorated with wallflowers, the spokes of the wheels are clothed in mignonette, and in place of lanterns, there are two round, enormous bouquets, which seem like the two eyes of this strange, rolling, flowery beast.

The landau goes along Antibes street at a brisk trot, preceded, followed, and accompanied by a crowd of other gar-landed carriages full of women concealed under a billow of violets. For it is the Flower Festival at Cannes.

They arrived at the Foncière Boulevard where the battle takes place. The whole length of the immense avenue, a doubl line of bedecked equipages was going and coming, like a ribbon without end. They threw flowers from one to the other. Flowers passed in the air like balls, hit the fair faces, hovered and fell in the dust where an army of street urchins gathered them.

A compact crowd, clamorous but orderly, looked on, standing in rows upon the sidewalks, and held in place by policemen on horseback who passed along, pushing back the curious brutally with their feet, in order that the villains might not mingle with the rich.

Now, the people in the carriages recognize each other, call to each other, and bombard one another with roses. A chariot full of pretty young women, clothed in red like devils, attracts and holds all eyes. One gentleman, who resembles the portraits of Henry IV., throws repeatedly, with joyous ardor, a huge bouquet retained by an elastic. At the threat of the blow the women lower their heads and hide their eyes, but the gracious projectile only describes a curve and again returns to its master, who immediately throws it again to a new face.

The two young women empty their arsenal with full hands and receive a shower of bouquets; then, after an hour of battle, a little wearied at the last, they order the coachman to take the road to the Juan gulf, which skirts the sea.

The sun disappeared behind the Esterel, outlining in black, upon a background of fire, the lacey silhouette of the stretched-out mountain. The calm sea was spread out blue and clear as far as the horizon, where it mingled with the sky and with the squadron anchored in the middle of the gulf, having the appearance of a troop of monstrous beasts, immovable upon the water, apocalyptic animals, hump-backed and clothed in coats-of-mail, capped with thin masts like plumes, and with eyes that lighted up when night came on.

The young women, stretched out under the fur robe, looked upon it languidly. Finally one of them said:

"How delicious these evenings are! Everything seems good. Is it not so, Margot?"

The other replied: "Yes, it is good. But there is always something lacking."

"What is it? For my part, I am completely happy. I have need of nothing."

"Yes? You think so, perhaps. But whatever well-being surrounds our bodies, we always desire something more —for the heart."

Said the other, smiling: "A little love?"

"Yes."

They were silent, looking straight before them; then the one called Marguerite said: "Life does not seem supportable to me without that. I need to be loved, if only by a dog. And we are all so, whatever you may say, Simone."

"No, no, my dear. I prefer not to be loved at all than to be loved by no one of importance. Do you think, for example, that it would be agreeable to me to be loved by—by—"

She looked for some one by whom she could possibly be loved, casting her eyes over the neighboring country. Her eyes, after having made the tour of the whole horizon, fell upon the two metal buttons shining on the coachman's back, and she continued, laughing, "By my coachman?"

Miss Marguerite scarcely smiled as she replied:

"I can assure you it is very amusing to be loved by a domestic. This has happened to me two or three times.

They roll their eyes so queerly that one is dying to laugh. Naturally, the more one is loved, the more severe she becomes, since otherwise, one puts herself in the way of being made ridiculous for some very slight cause, if anyone happened to observe it."

Miss Simone listened, her look fixed straight before her; then she declared:

"No, decidedly, the heart of my valet at my feet would not appear to me sufficient. But tell me how you perceived that you were loved."

"I perceived it in them as I do in other men, they become so stupid!"

"But others do not appear so stupid to me, when they are in love."

"Idiots, my dear, incapable of chatting, of answering, of comprehending anything."

"And you? What effect did it have on you to be loved by a domestic? Were you moved—flattered?"

"Moved? No. Flattered? Yes, a little. One is always flattered by the love of a man, whoever he may be."

"Oh! now, Margot!"

"Yes, my dear. Wait! I will tell you a singular adventure that happened to me. You will see what curious things take place among us in such cases.

"It was four years ago in the autumn, when I found myself without a maid. I had tried five or six, one after the other, all of them incompetent, and almost despaired of finding one, when I read in the advertisements of a newspaper of a young girl, knowing how to sew, embroider, and dress hair, who was seeking a place and could furnish the best of references. She could also speak English.

"I wrote to the address given, and the next day the person in question presented herself. She was rather tall, thin, a little pale, with a very timid air. She had beautiful black eyes, a charming color, and she pleased me at once. I asked for her references; she gave me one written in English, because she had come, she said, from the house of Lady Ryswell, where she had been for ten years.

"The certificate attested that the girl was returning to France of her own will, and that she had nothing to reproach her for during her long service with her, except a little of the *French coquettishness*.

"The modest turn of the English phrase made me smile a little and I engaged the maid immediately. She came to my house the same day; she called herself Rose.

"At the end of a month, I adored her. She was a treasure, a pearl, a phenomenon.

"She could dress my hair with exquisite taste; she could flute the lace of a cap better than the best of the professionals, and she could make frocks. I was amazed at her ability. Never had I been so well served.

"She dressed me rapidly with an astonishing lightness of hand. I never felt her fingers upon my skin, and nothing is more disagreeable to me than contact with a maid's hand. I immediately got into excessively idle habits, so pleasant was it to let her dress me from head to foot, from chemise to gloves—this tall, timid girl, always blushing a little and never speaking. After my bath, she would rub me and massage me while I slept a little while on my divan; indeed, I came to look upon her more as a friend in poorer circumstances, than a servant.

"One morning the *concierge*, with some show of mystery, said he wished to speak to me. I was surprised but let him enter. He was an old soldier, once orderly for my husband.

"He appeared to hesitate at what he was going to say. Finally, he said stammeringly: 'Madame, the police captain for this district is downstairs.'

"I asked: 'What does he want?'

"'He wants to search the house.'

"Certainly the police are necessary, but I do detest them. I never can make it seem a noble profession. And I answered, irritated as well as wounded:

"'Why search here? For what purpose? There has been no burglary.'

"He answered:

"'He thinks that a criminal is concealed somewhere here.'

"I began to be a little afraid and ordered the police captain to be brought that I might have some explanation. He was a man rather well brought up and decorated with the Legion of Honor. He excused himself, asked my pardon, then asserted that I had among my servants a convict!

"I was thunderstruck, and answered that I could vouch for every one of them and that I would make a review of them for his satisfaction.

"'There is Peter Courtin, an old soldier.'

"It was not he.

"'The coachman, Francis Pingau, a peasant, son of my father's farmer.'

"It was not he.

"'A stable boy, also from Champagne, and also a son of peasants I had

known, and no more except the footman whom you have seen.'

"It was not any of them.

"'Then, sir, you see that you have been deceived.'

"'Pardon me, Madame, but I am sure I am not deceived. As he has not at all the appearance of a criminal, will you have the goodness to have all your servants appear here before you and me, all of them?'

"I hesitated at first, then I yielded, summoning all my people, men and women.

"He looked at them all for an instant, then declared.

"'This is not all.'

"'Your pardon, sir,' I replied, 'this is all except my own maid who could not possibly be confounded with a convict.'

"He asked: 'Could I see her too?'

"'Certainly.'

"I rang and Rose appeared immediately. Scarcely had she entered when he gave a signal and two men, whom I had not seen, concealed behind the door, threw themselves upon her, seized her hands, and bound them with cords.

"I uttered a cry of fury, and was going to try and defend her. The captain stopped me:

"'This girl, Madame, is a man who calls himself John Nicholas Lecapet, condemned to death in 1879 for assassination preceded by violation. His sentence was changed to life imprisonment. He escaped four months ago. We have been on the search for him ever since.'

"I was dismayed, struck dumb. I

could not believe it. The policeman continued, laughing:

"'I can only give you one proof. His right arm is tattooed.'

"His sleeve was rolled up. It was true. The policeman added, certainly in bad taste:

"'Doubtless you will be satisfied without the other proofs.'

"And he led away my maid!

"Well, if you will believe it, the feeling which was uppermost in me was that of anger at having been played with in this way, deceived and made ridiculous; it was not shame at having been dressed, undressed, handled, and touched by this man, but — a — profound humiliation— the humiliation of a woman. Do you understand?"

"No, not exactly."

"Let us see. Think a minute— He had been condemned—for violation, this young man—and that—that humiliated me—there! Now do you understand?"

And Miss Simone did not reply. She looked straight before her, with her eyes singularly fixed upon the two shining buttons of the livery, and with that sphinx's smile that women have sometimes.

The Wedding Night

My DEAR Genevieve, you ask me to tell you about my wedding journey. How do you think I dare? Ah! sly one, who had nothing to tell me, who even allowed me to guess at nothing— but there! nothing from nothing!

Now, you have been married eighteen months, yes, eighteen months, you, my best friend, who formerly said you could conceal nothing from me, and you had not the charity to warn me! If you had only given the hint! If you had only put me on my guard! If you had put one little simple suspicion in my soul, you might have hindered me from making the egregious blunder for which I still blush, and which my husband will laugh at until his death. You alone are responsible for it! I have rendered myself frightfully rediculous forever; I have committed one of those errors of which the memory is never effaced—

and by your fault, wicked one! Oh! if I had known!

Wait! I take courage from writing, and have decided to tell you all. But promise me not to laugh too much. And do not expect a comedy. It is a drama.

You recall my marriage. I was to start the same evening on my wedding journey. Certainly I did not at all resemble Paulette, whom "Gyp" tells us about in that droll account of her spiritual romance, called, "About Marriage." And if my mother had said to me, as Mrs. d'Hautretan did to her daughter: "Your husband will take you in his arms —and—" I should certainly not have responded as Paulette did, laughing: "Go no farther, mamma, I know all that as well as you—"

As for me, I knew nothing at all, and mamma, my poor mamma who is always-frightened, dared not broach the delicate subject.

Well, then, at five o'clock in the evening, after the collation, they told us that the carriage was waiting. The guests had gone, I was ready. I can still hear the noise of the trunks on the staircase and the blowing of papa's nose, which seemed to indicate that he was weeping. In embracing me, the poor man said: "Good courage!" as if I were going to have a tooth pulled. As for mamma, she was a fountain. My husband urged me to hasten these painful adieux, and I was myself all in tears, although very happy. That is not easy to explain but is entirely true. All at once, I felt something pulling at my dress. It was Bijou, wholly forgotten since morning. The poor beast was saying adieu to me after his fashion. This gave my heart a little blow, and I felt a great desire to embrace my dog. I seized him (you remember he is as large as a fist) and began to devour him with kisses. I love to caress animals. It gives me a sweet pleasure, causing a kind of delicious shiver.

As for him, he was like a mad creature; he waved his paws, licked me, and nibbled, as he does when he is perfectly content. Suddenly, he took my nose in his teeth, and I felt that he had really bitten me. I uttered a little cry and put the dog down. He had bitten, although only in play. Everybody was disturbed. They brought water, vinegar, and some pieces of linen. My husband himself attended to it. It was nothing after all but three little holes which his teeth had made. At the end of five minutes the blood was stopped and we went away.

It had been decided that we should go on a journey through Normandy for about six weeks.

That evening we arrived at Dieppe. When I say evening, I mean midnight.

You know how I love the sea. I declared to my husband that I could not retire until I had seen it. He appeared very contrary. I asked him laughing, if he was sleepy.

He answered: "No, my dear, but you must understand that I would like to be alone with you."

I was surprised. "Alone with me?" I replied, "but you have been alone with me all the way from Paris, in the train."

He laughed: "Yes — but, — in the train,—that is not the same thing as being in our room."

I would not give up. "Oh, well," said I, "we shall be alone on the beach, and that is all there is to it!"

Decidedly he was not pleased. He said: "Very well; as you wish."

The night was magnificent, one of those nights which bring grand, vague ideas to the soul,—more sensations than thoughts, perhaps,—that bring a desire to open the arms as if they were wings and embrace the heavens—but how can I express it? One always feels that these unknown things can be comprehended.

There was a dreaminess, a poesy in the air, a happiness of another kind than that of earth, a sort of infinite intoxication which comes from the stars, the moon, the silver, glistening water. These are the best moments of life. They are a glimpse of a different existence, an embellished, delicious existence; they are the revelation of what could be, of what will be, perhaps.

Nevertheless, my husband appeared impatient to return. I said to him: "Are you cold?"

"No."

"Then look at the little boat down there, which seems asleep on the water. Could anything be better than this! I would willingly remain here until daybreak. Tell me, shall we wait and see aurora?"

He seemed to think that I was mocking him, and very soon took me back to the hotel by force! If I had known! Oh! the poor creature!

When we were once alone, I felt ashamed, constrained, without knowing why. I swear it. Finally, I made him go into the bath-room while I got into bed.

Oh! my dear, how can I go further? Well, here it is! He took without doubt, my extreme innocence for mischief, my extreme simplicity for profligacy, my confident, credulous abandon for some kind of tactics, and paid no regard to the delicate management that is necessary in order to make a soul wholly unprepared comprehend and accept such mysteries.

All at once, I believe he lost his head. Then fear seized me; I asked him if he wished to kill me. When terror invades, one does not reason nor think further, one is mad. In one second I had imagined frightful things. I thought of various stories in the newspapers, of mysterious crimes, of all the whispered tales of young girls married to miserable men! I fought, repulsed him, was overcome with fright. I even pulled a wisp of hair from his mustache, and

relieved by this effort, I arose, shouting: "Help! help!" I ran to the door, drew the bolts, and hurried, nearly naked, downstairs.

Other doors opened. Men, in night apparel, appeared with lights in their hands. I fell into the arms of one of them, imploring his protection. He made an attack upon my husband.

I knew no more about it. They fought and they cried; then they laughed, but laughed in a way you could never imagine. The whole house laughed, from the cellar to the garret. I heard in the corridors and in the rooms about us explosions of gaiety. The kitchen maids laughed under the roof, and the bellboy was in contortions on his bench in the vestibule.

Think of it! In a hotel!

Soon, I found myself alone with my husband, who made me some summary explanations, as one explains a surgical operation before it is undertaken. He was not at all content. I wept until daylight, and we went away at the opening of the doors.

That is not all. The next day we arrived at Pourville, which is only an embryo station for baths. My husband overwhelmed me with little attentions and tender care. After a first misunderstanding, he appeared enchanted. Ashamed, and much cast down, over my adventure of the evening before, I was also amiable as could be, and docile. But you cannot figure the horror, the disgust, almost the hatred that Henry inspired in me, when I knew the infamous secret that they conceal from young girls. I was in despair, as sad as death, mindful of everything, and harassed by the need of being near my poor parents. The next day after we arrived at Etretat. All the bathers were in a flurry of excitement. A young woman had been bitten by a little dog, and had just died of rabies. A great shiver ran down my back when I heard this story told at the hotel table. It seemed to me immediately, that I was suffering in the nose, and I had strange feelings all along my limbs.

That night I could not sleep; I had completely forgotten my husband. What if I were going to die too from rabies? I asked for some details, the next day, from the proprietor of the hotel. He gave me some frightful ones. I passed the day in walking upon the shore. I thought I could no longer speak. Hydrophobia! What a horrible death!

Henry asked me: "What is the matter? You seem sad."

I answered: "Oh! Nothing! Nothing!"

My staring eyes were fixed upon the sea without seeing it, upon farms, upon the fields, without my ever being able to say what came under my gaze. For nothing in the world would I have confessed the thought that tortured me. Some pain, true pain was felt in my nose. I wished to return.

As soon as I was back in the hotel, I shut myself up in order to examine the wound. There was nothing to be seen. Nevertheless, I could not doubt that it was working me great harm. I wrote immediately to my mother, a short letter which probably sounded strange. I asked an immediate reply to some insignificant questions. After having signed my name, I wrote: "Especially, do not forget to give me some news of Bijou."

The next day I could not eat, but I refused to see a physician. All day long I remained seated upon the beach looking at the bathers in the water. They came, the thin and the stout, all hideous in their frightful costumes; but I never thought of laughing. I thought: "They are happy, these people! They have not been bitten! They are going to live! They have nothing to fear. They can amuse themselves at will, because they are at peace!"

At that instant I carried my hand to my nose, touching it; was it not swollen? And soon I entered the hotel, shut myself in, and looked at it in the glass. Oh! it had changed color. I should die now very soon.

That evening I felt all at once a sort of tenderness for my husband, a tenderness of despair. He appeared good to me; I leaned upon his arm. Twenty times I was on the point of telling him my distressing secret, but ended in keeping silent.

He abused odiously my listlessness and the weakness of my soul. I had not the force to resist him, nor even the will. I would bear all, suffer all!

The next day I received a letter from my mother. She replied to my questions, but said not a word about Bijou. I immediately thought: "He is dead and they are concealing it from me." I wished to run to the telegraph office and send a dispatch. One thought stopped me: "If he really is dead, they will not tell me." I then resigned myself to two more days of anguish. I wrote again. I asked them to send me the dog, for diversion, because I was a little lonesome.

A trembling fit took me in the afternoon. I could not raise a full glass without spilling half. The state of my soul was lamentable. I escaped from my husband at twilight and ran to the church. I prayed a long time. On returning, I felt anew the pains in my nose and consulted a druggist whose shop was lighted. I spoke to him as if one of my friends had been bitten, asking his advice in the matter. He was an amiable man, very obliging. He advised me freely. But I forgot to notice what he said, my mind was so troubled. I only remember this: "Purging is often recommended." I bought many bottles of I know not what, under pretext of sending them to my friend.

The dogs that I met filled me with horror, creating in me a desire to flee at top of my speed. It seemed to me many times, also, that I had a desire to bite them. My night was horribly disturbed. My husband profited by it.

The next day I received a response from my mother. "Bijou," said she, "is very well, but it would expose him too much to send him alone on a railroad train." Then they would not send him to me. He was dead.

I could not yet sleep. As for Henry, he snored. He awoke many times. I was annihilated.

The next day I took a bath in the sea. I was almost overcome in entering the water, I was so frightfully cold. I was more than ever shocked by this frigid sensation. I trembled in every limb, but felt no more pain in the nose.

By chance, they presented me to the medical inspector of the baths, a charming man. I led up to my subject with extreme skill. I then said to him that my little dog had bitten me several days

before, and asked him what was necessary to be done if we discovered any inflammation. He laughed and answered: "In your situation, Madame, I see only one remedy, which would be for you to make a new nose."

And as I did not comprehend, he added: "Your husband will see to that." And I was no better informed on leaving him than I was before.

Henry, that evening, seemed very gay, very happy. We went to the Casino, but he did not wait for the end of the play before proposing to me to return. As there was nothing of interest to me, I followed him. But I could not remain in bed; all my nerves were unstrung and vibrating. Neither could he sleep. He embraced me, caressed me, became all sweetness and tenderness, as if he had finally guessed how much I was suffering. I accepted his caresses without even comprehending them or thinking about them.

But suddenly an extraordinary, fearful crisis seized me. I uttered a frightful cry, pushed back my husband who took hold of me, ran into my room, and began to beat my head and face against the door. It was rage! Horrible rage! I was lost!

Henry raised me up, himself frightened and trying to understand the trouble. I kept silent. I was resigned now. I awaited death. I knew that after some hours of respite, another crisis would seize me, even to the last which would be mortal.

I allowed them to put me in the bed. At the point of day, the irritating obsessions of my husband caused a new paroxyism, which was longer than the first. I had a desire to tear and bite and howl; it was terrible and nevertheless, not so painful as I had believed.

Toward eight o'clock in the morning, I slept for the first time in four nights. At eleven o'clock, a beloved voice awoke me. It was mamma, whom my letters had frightened and who had hastened to see me. She had in her hand a great basket, from whence came some little barks. I seized it, foolish in hope. I opened it, and Bijou jumped upon the bed, embraced me, gamboled about, rolled himself upon my pillow, frenzied with joy,

Ah! well, my dearie, you may believe me if you will, I did not comprehend all until the next day! Oh! the imagination, how it works! And to think that I believed— Tell me, was it not too foolish?

I have never confessed to anyone, you will understand why, the tortures of those four days. Think, if my husband had known! He has teased enough already about my adventures at Pourville. For my part, I cannot be too angry at his jests.

I am done. We have to accustom ourselves to everything in life.

The Noncommissioned Officer

QUARTERMASTER VARAJOU had obtained permission to pass eight days with his sister, Madame Padoie. Varajou, who was in garrison at Rennes and led a jolly life there, finding himself high and dry with his family, had written to his sister that he would devote his week of liberty to her. Not that he loved Madame Padoie so much, for she was a little moralist, devout and always irritating; but he was in need of money, in great need, and he remembered that of all his relatives, the Padoies were the only ones from whom he had never borrowed.

Father Varajou, an old horticulturist of Angers, now retired from business, had closed his purse to his rake of a son and had scarcely seen him for ten years. His daughter had married Padoie, a former employee of the Treas-

ury, who had since become collector at Vannes.

Varajou, then, on getting out of the train, took himself to the house of his brother-in-law. He found him in his office, in process of discussion with some Breton peasants of the neighborhood. Padoie raised himself from his chair, extended his hand across the table, which was covered with papers and said: "Take a seat; I will be with you in a moment." Then he seated himself again and continued his discussion.

The peasants could not understand his explanations, teh collector could not comprehend their reasoning; he spoke French, they spoke Breton, and the deputy who acted as interpreter seemed not to understand anyone.

It was long, very long. Varajou looked at his brother-in-law, thinking: "What an idiot!" Padoie must have been about fifty. He was tall, thin, bony, slow, hairy, with his eyebrows arching until they made spears of hair above his eyes. He wore on his head a velvet cap ornamented with gold braid, and his look had the tameness which his action showed. His words, his gestures, his thoughts were all slow. Varajou kept repeating: "What an idiot!"

He was himself one of those noisy brawlers for whom life has no greater pleasures than those of the café and the public woman. Outside these two poles of existence, he understood nothing. Boasting, blustering, full of disdain for everybody, he despised the whole universe from the height of his ignorance. When he had said: "What a devil of a holiday!" he had expressed the highest degree of admiration of which his mind was capable.

Padoie, having finished with his peasants, turned to him and asked:

"You are well?"

"Not bad, as you see. And you?"

"Very well, thank you. It is amiable of you to think of coming to see us."

"Oh! I have thought of it for a long time; but you know in the military profession one doesn't have much liberty."

"Oh! I know, I know; and that is why it is very amiable of you."

"And Josephine is well?"

"Yes, yes, thank you; you shall see her very soon."

"Where is she?"

"She has gone to pay some visits; we have so many relatives here, and this is a very exacting, proper town."

"I have no doubt of it."

Then the door opened and Madame Padoie appeared. She went toward her brother without eagerness, held up her cheek, and asked:

"Have you been here long?"

"No, scarcely half an hour."

"Ah! I thought the train would be late. If you are ready, come into the parlor."

They passed into a neighboring room, leaving Padoie to his accounts and his collections. When they were alone, she said:

"I have heard of some of your fine actions."

"What, for instance?"

"It appears that you have been conducting yourself like a blackguard; that you get tipsy and have been getting into debt."

He appeared very much astonished. "I," said he, "never in my life."

"Oh! you needn't deny it, I know all about it."

He still tried to defend himself, but she closed his mouth with so violent a lecture that he was forced to silence.

Then she said: "We dine at six o'clock; you are free until dinner. I cannok ask your company because I, not unfortunately, have some things to do." Left alone, he hesitated between sleeping and taking a walk. He looked for a door leading to his room and found one to the street. He decided in favor of the street.

He began to wander around slowly, his sword hitting against his legs, through the sad Breton town, so sleepy, so calm, so dead that on the border of its inner sea, they call it "The Morbihan." He looked at the little gray houses, the few passers, the empty shops, and said to himself: "Not gay, surely, nor amusing, is Vannes. A sad idea, coming here!"

He sought the port, so dreary, returned by a solitary, desolate boulevard and was back before five o'clock. Then he threw himself upon his bed to sleep until dinner.

The maid woke him by knocking on the door and saying: "Dinner is served, sir!"

He descended. In the humid dining-room, where the paper was nearly all unglued by the sun, a supper was waiting upon a round table without a cloth, for which three melancholy plates were set.

Mr. and Mrs. Padoie entered at the same time as Varajou. They were seated, then the husband and wife made the sign of the cross upon the pit of their stomachs, after which Padoie served the soup, a thick soup. It was the day for potpie. After the soup came the beef, beef too much cooked, melted and fat, which had fallen apart in boiling. The noncommissioned officer masticated it slowly, with disgust, with fatigue and rage.

Madame Padoie said to her husband: "Are you going to the President's house this evening?"

"Yes, my dear."

"Do not stay late. You are all worn out every time you go out. You are not made for the world, with your bad health."

Then she spoke of the society of Vannes, of the excellent society where the Padoies were received with consideration, thanks to their religious sentiments.

Then they served a *purée* of pota-

toes with a dish of pork, in honor of the new arrival. Then some cheese and it was finished. Not even coffee.

When Varajou understood that he was to pass the evening face to face with his sister, forced to undergo her reproaches, listen to her sermons, without even a solacing glass to cool his throat or to aid the remonstrances in slipping down, he concluded that the punishment was more than he could bear, and declared that he must go the armory to execute some commission under his leave of absence.

And he escaped at seven o'clock.

Scarcely was he in the street when he began to shake himself, like a dog just out of the water. He murmured: "What a blankety-blank-blank life of drudgery!" And he began to search for a *cafe*, the best *café* in town. He found it over a room, behind two gas jets. Inside, five or six men, some semi-gentlemen, a little noisy, were seated around some little tables drinking and chatting, while two billiard players were walking around the green cloth on which the ivory balls were hitting each other. They were counting: "Eighteen,—nineteen.—No luck. —Oh! good shot! Well played! — Eleven.—You must play on the red.— Twenty. — Froze! Froze! Twelve. — There! was I right?"

Varajou ordered a *demi-tasse* and a small glass of brandy, of the best. Then he sat down and waited its coming.

He was accustomed to pass his evenings at liberty with his comrades in the clatter of glasses and the smoke of pipes. This silence, this calm exasperated him. He began to drink, first his coffee then his brandy and then he gave a second order. Now he had a desire to laugh, then to cry, then to sing, and then of fighting some one.

He said to himself: "Jove! How this sets me up! I must make a feast of it." And the idea came to him of finding some girls to amuse himself with.

He called one of the employees: "Hey! waiter!"

"Yes, sir!"

"Say, waiter, where can one go here to have a merry time?"

The man looked stupid at this question. Finally he answered: " I don't know, sir. Only here!"

"Here! And what do you call a merry time, I should like to know!"

"Oh! I don't know, sir, drinking beer, or some good wine."

"Go on, you oyster! And the girls, where are they?"

"The girls! Ha! ha! ha!"

"Yes, the girls, where are they to be found here?"

"Girls?"

"Yes, yes, girls!"

The waiter came nearer to him and said in a low voice: "You want to know where there is a house?"

"Yes, of course!"

"You take the second street to the left and then the first to the right. It is number fifteen."

"Thanks, old man. Here is something for you."

"Thanks, sir."

And Varajou went out repeating: "Second to the left, first to the right, fifteen." At the end of a few seconds he thought: "Second to the left,— yes. But in coming out of the *café*,

did I turn to the left or to the right? Bah! It doesn't make any difference. I shall soon find out."

And he walked on, turning into the second street at the left, then into the first at the right, and looked for number fifteen. It was a house of very good appearance, where he saw the windows of the first story lighted behind the closed shutters. The vestibule door was half open and a lamp was burning in there.

"This is the place," thought the noncommissioned officer.

Then he entered and, as no one came, he called: "Hey there! hey!"

A little maid appeared and was struck dumb on seeing a soldier. He said to her: "Good evening, my child. The ladies are upstairs?"

"Yes, sir."

"In the salon?"

"Yes, sir."

"And I can go right up?"

"Yes, sir."

"The first door I come to?"

"Yes, sir."

He went up and perceived in a room well lighted with two large lamps, a luster, and two candelabra containing wax candles, four ladies in evening gowns, who seemed to be waiting for some one.

Three of them, the younger, were seated, with a somewhat starched appearance, upon a garnet velvet sofa, while the fourth, a woman about forty-five years of age, was arranging flowers in a vase; she was very large and wore a green silk frock which seemed like the envelope of a monstrous flower, her enormous arms and neck being like a rice-powdered rose.

The noncommissioned officer saluted: "Good evening, ladies."

The eldest one turned, appeared surprised, but bowed: "Good evening, sir."

He sat down. But seeing that he did not seem to be welcomed with any enthusiasm, he thought that, without doubt, only officers were admitted there, and the idea troubled him. Then he said to himself: "Bah! If one of them comes, we shall see." And then he said: "Well, everything goes well?"

The large lady, the mistress of the house, doubtless, answered:

"Very well, thank you."

He found nothing more to say, and everybody was silent. Finally, he began to be ashamed of his timidity and, laughing with a constrained laugh said: "Oh! well, there is nothing very merry about this—I'll pay for a bottle of wine—"

He had not finished his sentence when the door opened and Padoie, in evening clothes, appeared.

Varajou uttered a howl of joy and, jumping up, rushed at his brother-in-law, seized him in his arms, and made him dance all around the room, crying: "Well, if here isn't Padoie! It is Padoie! It's Padoie!"

Then, releasing the collector, who was lost in surprise, he said mockingly, in his face: "Ah! ah! ah! joker! joker!

You do break away then sometimes— Ah! what a joker— And my sister! You let her loose too—say!—"

Realizing all the benefits from this unlooked-for situation, so impressed was he with the full force of it, that he threw himself upon a sofa and began to laugh so loud that the very furniture seemed to crack.

The three young ladies arose with one accord and escaped, while the elderly one repaired toward the door, ready to flee if it became necessary.

Then two gentlemen appeared, both in evening clothes, and decorated. Padoie rushed toward them saying: "Oh! Mr. President—he is mad—surely he is mad— They sent him to us to convalesce—you can see at once that he is mad."

Varajou seated himself, comprehending nothing about him, but guessing that he had done something monstrously foolish. Finally, he arose and turning toward his brother-in-law asked: "Where are we?"

And Padoie, seized suddenly with a foolish anger stammered:

"Where are—where—where are we? Unfortunate—miserable—infamous fellow—where are we? In the house of the President—of the President of Mortemain — of Mortemain—of—of—of— Mortemain. Ah! ah — you scamp — scamp—you scamp!—"

In the Court Room

THE hall of the Justice of the Peace of Gorgeville is full of peasants who, seated in rows along the walls, are awaiting the opening of the session.

There are tall and short, stout and thin, all with the trim appearance of a row of fruit-trees. They have placed their baskets on the floor and remain silent, tranquil, preoccupied with their own affairs. They have brought with them the odor of the stable, of sweat, of sour milk, and of the manure-heap. Flies are buzzing under the white ceiling. Through the open door the crowing of cocks is heard.

Upon a sort of platform is a long table covered with green cloth. An old, wrinkled man sits there writing at the extreme left. A policeman, tipped back upon his chair, is gazing into the air, at the extreme right. And upon the bare wall, a great Christ, in wood, twisted into a pitiable pose, seems to offer his eternal suffering for the cause of these brutes with the odor of beasts.

The Justice of the Peace enters, finally. He is corpulent, high colored, and rustles his magistrate's black robe as he walks with the rapid step of a large man in a hurry; he seats himself, places his cap upon the table, and looks at the assemblage with an air of profound scorn.

He is a scholarly provincial, a bright mind of the district, one of those who translate Horace, relish the little verses of Voltaire, and know by heart Vert-Vert as well as the snuffy poetry of Parny.

He pronounced officially, the words:

"Now, Mr. Potel, call the cases."

Then smiling, he murmured:

"Quidquid tentabam dicere versus erat."

Then the clerk of the court, in an unintelligible voice, jabbered:

"Madame Victoire Bascule *vs.* Isidore Paturon."

An enormous woman came forward, a lady of the country town of the canton, with a much beribboned hat, a watch-chain festooned upon her breast, rings on her fingers, and earrings shining like lighted candles.

The Justice greeted her with a look of recognition, which savored of jest, and said:

"Madame Bascule, state your troubles."

The opposing party stands on the other side. It is represented by three persons. Among them is a young peasant of twenty-five, as fat-cheeked as an apple and as red as a poppy. At his right is his wife, very young, thin, small, like a bantam chicken, with a narrow, flat head covered, as in Crete, with a pink bonnet. She has a round eye, astonished and angry, which looks sidewise like that of poultry. At the left of the boy sits his father, an old, bent man, whose twisted body disappears in his starched blouse as if it were under a bell.

Madame Bascule explains:

"Mr. Justice, for fifteen years I have treated this boy kindly. I brought him up and loved him like a mother, I have done everything for him, I have made a man of him. He promised me, he swore to me that he would never leave me, he even took an oath, on account of which I gave him a little property, my land at Bec-de-Mortin, which is worth about six thousand. Then, this little thing, little nothing, this brat—"

The Justice: "Moderate your language, Madame Bascule."

Madame Bascule: "A little—a little —I think I am understood—turns his head, does, I know not what to him, neither do I know why,—and he goes and marries her, this fool, this great beast, and gives her my property, my property at Bec-de-Mortin. Ah! no, ah! no—I have a paper, here it is—which gives me back my property, now. We had a statement drawn up at the notary's for the property and a statement on paper for the sake of friendship. One is worth as much as the other. Each to his right, is it not so?"

She held toward the Justice a stamped paper, wide open.

Isidore Paturon: "It is not true."

The Justice: "Keep silent. You shall speak in your turn." [He reads.]

" 'I, the undersigned, Isidore Paturon, do, by this present, promise Madame Bascule, my benefactress, never to leave her while I live, and to serve her with devotion.

" 'GORGEVILLE, August 5, 1883.' "

The Justice: "There is a cross here for the signature. Do you not know how to write?"

Isidore: "No. I don't."

The Justice: "And is it you who made this cross?"

Isidore: "No, it was not I."

The Justice: "Who did make it then?"

Isidore: "She did."

The Justice: "You are ready to swear that you did not make this cross?"

Isidore [earnestly]: "Upon the head of my mother and my father, my grandmother and grandfather, and of the good God who hears me, I swear that it was not I." [He raises his hand and strikes it against his side to emphasize his oath.]

The Justice [laughing]: "What have been your relations with Madame Bascule, the lady here present?"

Isidore: "I have helped to amuse her." [Grinning at the audience.]

The Justice: "Be careful of your expressions. Do you mean to say that your connections have not been as pure as she pretends?"

Father Paturon [taking up the narrative]: "He wasn't fifteen years old yet, not fifteen years old, Mr. Judge, when she debauched—"

The Justice: "Do you mean debauched?"

The Father: "You understand me. He was not fifteen years old, I say. And for four years before that already, she had nursed him with the greatest care, feeding him like a chicken she was fattening, until he was ready to split, saving your respect. And then, when the time had come that she thought was just right, then she depraved him—"

The Justice: "Depraved— And you allowed it?"

The Father: "Her as well as another. It has to come—"

The Justice: "Then what have you to complain of?"

The Father: "Nothing! Oh! I complain of nothing, of nothing, only that he cannot get free of her when he wants to. I ask the protection of the law."

Madame Bascule: "These people weary me with their lies, Mr. Judge. I made a man of him—"

The Justice: "I see!"

Madame Bascule: "And now he denies me, leaves me, robs me of my property—"

Isidore: "It is not true, Mr. Judge.

I wanted to leave her five years ago, seeing that she had fleshed up with excess, and that didn't suit me. It troubled me much. Why? I don't know. Then I told her I was going away. She wept like a gutter and promised me her property at Bec-de-Mortin to stay a few more years, if only four or five. As for me, I said 'Yes,' of course. And what would you have done? I stayed then five years day by day and hour by hour. I was free. Each to his own. I had paid well." [Isidore's wife, quiet up to this time, cries out with a piercing, parrot-like voice:]

"Look at her, look at her, Mr. Judge, the millstone, and see if it wasn't well paid for?"

The Father [raising his head with a convinced air]: "Indeed, yes, well paid for." [Madame Bascule sinks back upon her seat and begins to weep.]

The Justice [paternally]: "What can you expect, dear Madame? I can do nothing. You have given your land at Bec-de-Mortin away in a perfectly regular manner. It is his, it belongs to him. He had the incontestable right to do what he has done, and to give it as a marriage gift to his wife. I have not entered into the question of—of—delicacy. I can only lay bare the facts from the point of view of the law. There is nothing more for me to do."

The Father [in a fierce voice]: "Then I can go home again?"

The Justice: "Certainly." [They go out under the sympathetic gaze of the peasants, as people do who win their case. Madame Bascule sits in her seat sobbing.]

The Justice [smiling]: "Come, come, dear Madame, go home, now. And if I had any counsel to give you, I should say find another—another pupil—"

Madame Bascule [through her tears]: "I cannot—cannot find one—"

The Justice: "I regret not being able to point one out to you." [She throws a despairing look toward Christ being tortured on the cross, then arises and walks away with little steps, hiccoughing with chagrin and concealing her face in her handkerchief.] The Justice adds in a bantering voice: "Calypso would not be consoled at the departure of Ulysses." Then in a grave tone, turning toward his clerk: "Call the next case."

The Clerk [mumbling]: "Celestin Polyte Lecacheur *vs.* Prosper Magloire Dieulafait—"

A Peculiar Case

WHEN Captain Hector Marie de Fontenne married Miss Laurine d'Estelle the parents and friends feared it would be a bad match.

Miss Laurine, pretty, thin, blond and confident, had at twelve the assurance of a woman of thirty. She was one of those precocious little Parisians who seem born with a full knowledge of life and of feminine tricks, with that audacity of thought, with that profound astuteness and suppleness of mind which make certain beings seem destined by fate to play with and deceive others, as they do. All their actions seem premeditated, their manner calculated, their words weighed with care, their whole existence a rôle which they are playing with people like themselves.

She was very charming and lively, with the liveliness that cannot restrain itself nor be calm, when something seems amusing or queer. She would laugh in the face of people in almost an impudent fashion, but with so much grace that they were never angered. Then she was rich, very rich.

A priest served as intermediary when she married Captain de Fontenne. Brought up in a religious house, in a most austere fashion, this officer brought to his regiment the morals of the cloister, and very strict, intolerant principles. He was one of those men who invariably become either a saint or a nihilist, in whom ideas install themselves as absolute mistresses, whose beliefs are inflexible, whose resolutions are not to be shaken.

He was a large, dark, young man, serious, severe, ingenuous, of simple mind, curt, and obstinate, one of those men who pass through life without comprehending anything beneath them in variety or subtlety, who divine nothing, suspect nothing, and admit only what they think, what they judge, and what they believe, when some one differs from them.

Miss Laurine saw him, understood him immediately, and accepted him for her husband. They made an excellent pair. She was yielding, skillful, and wise, knowing how to show herself to best advantage, always ready in good works and at festivals, assiduous at church and at the theater, at once worldly and religious, with a little air of irony, and a twinkle in her eye when chatting gravely with her grave husband. She would relate to him all her charitable enterprises with all the priests of the parish and the vicinity, and she made use of these pious occupations in order to remain away from morning until night.

But sometimes, in the midst of the recital of some act of beneficence, a foolish laugh would seize her suddenly, a nervous laugh impossible to check. The captain would look surprised, then disturbed, then a little shocked, as his wife would continue to laugh. When she became a little calm, he would ask: "What is the matter, Laurine?" And she would answer: "Nothing. It is only the memory of such a funny thing that happened to me!" And she would relate some story.

Then, during the summer of 1883, Captain Hector de Fontenne took part in the grand maneuvers of the thirty-second regiment of the army. One evening, as they camped on the edge of a town, after ten days of tent and open field, ten days of fatigue and privation, the comrades of the captain resolved to have a good dinner.

At first, Captain de Fontenne refused to accompany them; then, as his refusal surprised them, he consented. His neighbor at table, the governor of Favré, talking continually of military operations, the only thing that interested the captain, turned to him to drink glass after glass with him. It had been very hot, a heavy, parching, thirst-inspiring heat; and the captain drank without thinking or perceiving that a new gaiety had entered into him, a certain lively, burning joy, a happiness of being, full of awakened desires, of unknown appetites, and undefined hopes.

At the dessert he was tipsy. He talked and laughed and moved about, seized by a noisy drunkenness, the foolish drunkenness of a man ordinarily wise and tranquil.

Some one proposed to finish the evening at the theater. He accompanied his comrades. One of them recognized one of the actresses as some one he had formerly loved, and a supper was planned where a part of the feminine *personnel* of the troupe assisted.

The captain awoke the next day in an unknown room, in the arms of a pretty little blond woman who said to him, on seeing him open his eyes: "Good morning, sweetheart!"

He could not comprehend, at first; then, little by little his memory returned, somewhat cloudy, however. Then he got up without saying a word, dressed himself, and emptied his purse on the chimney-piece. A shame seized him when he found himself standing up in position, his sword at his side, in this furnished room, where the rumpled curtains and sofa, marbleized with spots, had a suspicious appearance, and he dared not go out, since in descending the staircase he might meet some one, nor dared he pass before the *concierge* nor go out in the street in the eyes of neighbors and passers-by.

The woman kept saying: "What has come over you? Have you lost your tongue? You had it fast enough last evening! Oh! what a muzzle!"

He bowed to her ceremoniously and, deciding upon flight, reached his abode with great steps, persuaded that one could guess from his manner and his bearing and his countenance that he had come out of the house of some girl.

And then remorse tortured him; the harassing remorse of a rigid, scrupulous man. He confessed and went to communion, but he still was ill at ease, followed ever by the memory of his fall and by feeling of debt, a sacred debt contracted against his wife.

He did not see her again until the end of the month, because she went to visit her parents during the encampment of the troops. She came back to him with open arms and a smile upon her lips. He received her with an embarrassed attitude, the attitude of a guilty man; and until evening, he scarcely talked with her.

When they found themselves alone, she asked him: "What is the matter with you, my dear; I find you very much changed."

He answered in a constrained tone: "Oh! nothing, my dear, absolutely nothing."

"Pardon me, but I know you so well, and I feel sure there is something, some care, some angry feeling, something, I know not what!"

"Oh! well, yes, there is something."

"And what is it?"

"It is impossible for me to tell you."

"To tell me? Why so? You disturb me."

"I have no reasons to give you. It is impossible for me to tell you."

She was seated upon a divan and he

walked up and down before her with his hands behind his back, avoiding the look of his wife.

Then she said: "Let us see. It is necessary for me to make you confess; it is my duty that I exact from you the truth; it is also my right. You should no more have a secret from me than I should from you."

His back was turned to her, framed in the high window, as he said:

"My dear, there are some things which are better not told. That which vexes me is one of them."

She got up, crossed the room, took him by the arm, and, having forced him to turn around, placed her two hands upon his shoulders, then, smiling and cajoling, raised her eyes as she said:

"You see, Marie [she called him Marie in moments of tenderness] you could never conceal anything from me. I should believe you had done something bad."

He answered: "I have done something very bad."

She said gaily: "Oh! is it so bad as that? I am very much astonished at you!"

He responded quickly: "I shall say nothing further. It is useless to insist."

But she drew him to an armchair, forced him to sit down in it, then seated herself on his right knee and began kissing him with light, rapid kisses which just brushed the curled end of his mustache. Then she said:

"If you don't tell me, we shall always be angry."

Pierced by remorse and tortured by his anguish, he answered: "If I should tell you what I have done, you would never pardon me."

"On the contrary, my friend, I would pardon you immediately.'

"No, it is impossible."

"I promise you."

"I tell you it is impossible!"

"I swear that I will pardon you."

"No, my dear Laurine, you never could."

"How simple you are, my friend, you cannot deny it! In refusing to tell me what you have done, you allow me to think you have done something abominable, and I shall think constantly about it, regretting your silence as much as your unknown crime. While, if you speak frankly, I shall forget it all by to-morrow."

"It is because—"

"What?"

He blushed up to the ears and said: "I shall confess to you as I would to a priest, Laurine."

On her lips was the sudden smile that she had sometimes in listening, and with a little mocking tone she said: "I am all ears."

He began: "You know, my dear, that I am a sober man. I drink only red wine, and never liquors, as you know."

"Yes, I know."

"Well, imagine how I allowed myself to drink a little, one evening toward the end of our encampment, when I was very thirsty, very much worn out with fatigue, weary, and—"

"And you got tipsy? Oh! how hideous!"

"Yes, I was intoxicated," he replied, with a severe air.

"And now, were you wholly intoxicated, so that you couldn't walk?"

"Oh! no, not so much as that. But

I lost my reason if not my equilibrium. I talked and laughed and made a fool of myself."

As he kept silent, she asked: "Is that all?"

"No."

"Ah! and after that?"

"After that I committed an infamous deed."

She looked at him, disturbed and troubled as well as somewhat excited.

"What then, my friend?"

"We had supped with—with some actresses—and I do not know how it was done, but—I have deceived you, Laurine!"

He made the statement in a grave, solemn tone. She gave a little toss to her head and her eye brightened with a sudden gaiety, a profound, irresistible gaiety. Then she said:

"You—you—you have—"

And a little dry, nervous laugh broke forth and glided between her teeth two or three times and prevented her from speaking. She tried to take him seriously, but each time she tried to pronounce a word, the laugh trembled at the bottom of her throat, leaped forth, was quickly stopped, but constantly reappeared, like gas in a bottle of champagne, pushing for escape until the froth can no longer be retained. She put her hands on her lips to calm herself, that she might restrain this unfortunate gaiety. But the laugh ran through her fingers, shaking her chest and bursting forth in spite of her. She stammered: "You — you — have deceived me— Ha!—ha! ha!—ha! ha! —ha! ha!"

And then she looked at him with a singular air, so mocking in spite of herself, that he was speechless, stupefied. And suddenly, as if able to contain herself no longer, she burst forth again, laughing with the kind of laugh that seemed like an attack of nerves. Little jerking cries issued from her mouth, coming, it seemed, from the depths of her lungs. His two hands supported her bosom, and she was almost suffocated with long whoops like the cough in whooping-cough.

With each effort that she made to calm herself a new paroxysm would begin, and each word that she tried to utter was only a greater contortion.

"My—my—my—poor friend—ha! ha! —ha! ha! ha!—ha!"

He got up, leaving her alone upon the armchair, and becoming suddenly very pale, he said: "Laurine, this is more than unbecoming."

She stammered, in a delirium of laughter:

"What—do you want—I—I—I cannot—but—but you are so funny—ha! ha! ha!—ha! ha!"

He became livid and looked at her now with fixed eye, a strange thought awakening within him. Suddenly he opened his mouth as if to say something, but said nothing, then, turning on his heel, he went out and shut the door.

Laurine, doubled up, weak, and fainting, still laughed with a dying laugh, which occasionally took on new life, like the flame of a candle almost ready to go out.

A Practical Joke

THE jokes that are played nowadays are somewhat dismal. They are not like the inoffensive, laughable jokes of our forefathers; still, there is nothing more amusing than to play a good joke on some one; to force them to laugh at their own foolishness and if they get angry, to punish them by playing a new joke on them.

I have played many a joke in my lifetime and I have had some played on me; some very good ones, too. I have played some very laughable ones and some terrible ones. One of my victims died of the consequences; but it was no loss to anyone. I will tell about it some day, but it will not be an easy task, as the joke was not at all a nice one. It happened in the suburbs of Paris and those who witnessed it are laughing yet at the recollection of it; though the victim died of it. May he rest in peace!

I will narrate two to-day. One in which I was the victim and another in which I was the instigator. I will begin with the former, as I do not find it so amusing, being the victim myself.

I had been invited by some friends in Picardie to come and spend a few weeks. They were fond of a joke like myself (I would not have known them had they been otherwise).

They gave me a rousing reception on my arrival. They fired guns, they kissed me, and made such a fuss over me that I became suspicious.

"Be careful, old fox," I said to myself, "there is something up."

During dinner they all laughed immoderately. I thought to myself, they are certainly projecting some good joke and intend to play it on me, for they laugh at nothing apparently. I was on my guard all evening and looked at everybody suspiciously, even at the servants.

When bedtime came, everybody escorted me to my room and bid me good night. I wondered why, and after shutting my door, I stood in the middle of the room with the candle in my hand. I could hear them outside in the hall, whisper and laugh; they were watching me no doubt. I looked at the walls, inspected the furniture, the ceiling, the floor, but I found nothing suspicious. I heard footsteps close to my door; surely they were looking through the keyhole. Then it struck me that perhaps my light would go out suddenly and I would be left in the dark, so I lighted all the candles and looked around once more; but I discovered nothing. After having inspected the windows and the shutters, I closed the latter with care, then I drew the curtains and placed a chair against them. If some one should try to come in that way, I would be sure to hear them, I thought. Then I sat down cautiously. I thought the chair would give way beneath me, but it was solid enough. I did not dare to go to bed, but as it was getting late I realized that I was ridiculous. If they were watching me, as I supposed they were, they certainly must laugh heartily at my uneasiness, so I resolved to go to bed. Having made up my mind, I approached the alcove. The bed looked particularly suspicious to me and I drew the heavy curtains back, pulled on them, but they held fast. Perhaps a bucket of water is hidden on

446

the top all ready to fall on me, or else the bed may fall apart as soon as I lie on it. I thought. I racked my brain to try and remember all the different jokes I had played on others, so as to guess what might be in store for me; I was not going to be caught, not I!

Suddenly, an idea struck me which I thought capital. I gently pulled the mattress off the bed and it came toward me, along with the sheets and blankets. I dragged them in the middle of the room, near the door, and made my bed up again the best way I could, put out all the lights, and felt my way into bed. I laid awake at least another hour, starting at every little sound, but everything seemed quiet, so I at last went to sleep.

I must have slept profoundly for some time, when suddenly I woke up with a start. Something heavy had fallen on me and at the same time, a hot liquid streamed all over my neck and chest, which made me scream with pain. A terrible noise filled my ears; as if a whole sideboard full of dishes had fallen in them. I was suffocating under the weight, so I reached out my hand to feel the object and I felt a face, a nose, and whiskers. I gave that face a terrible blow with my fist; but instantaneously, I received a shower of blows which drove me out of bed in a hurry and out into the hall.

To my amazement, I found it was broad daylight and everybody coming up the stairs to find out the cause of the noise. What we found was the valet, sprawled out on the bed, struggling among the broken dishes and tray. He had brought me some breakfast and having encountered my improvised couch, had very unwillingly dropped the breakfast as well as himself on my face!

The precautions I had taken to close the shutters and curtains and to sleep in the middle of the room had been my undoing. The very thing I had so carefully avoided had happened.

They certainly had a good laugh on me that day!

The other joke I speak of dates back to my boyhood days. I was spending my vacation at home as usual, in the old castle in Picardie.

I had just finished my second term at college and had been particularly interested in chemistry and especially in a compound called *phosphure de calcium* which, when thrown in water, would catch fire, explode, followed by fumes of an offensive odor. I had brought a few handfuls of this compound with me, so as to have fun with it during my vacation.

An old lady named Mme. Dufour often visited us. She was a cranky, vindictive, horrid old thing. I do not know why, but somehow she hated me. She misconstrued everything I did or said and she never missed a chance to tattle about me, the old hag! She wore a wig of beautiful brown hair, although she was more than sixty, and the most ridiculous little caps adorned with pink ribbons. She was well thought of because she was rich, but I hated her to the bottom of my heart, and I resolved to revenge myself by playing a joke on her.

A cousin of mine, who was of the same age as I, was visiting us and I communicated my plan to him; but my audacity frightened him.

One night, when everybody was downstairs, I sneaked into Mme. Dufour's room, secured a receptacle into which I deposited a handful of the calcium phosphate, having assured myself beforehand that it was perfectly dry, and ran to the garret to await developments.

Pretty soon I heard everybody coming upstairs to bed. I waited until everything was still, then I came downstairs barefooted, holding my breath, until I came to Mme. Dufour's door and looked at my enemy through the keyhole.

She was putting her things away, and having taken her dress off, she donned a white wrapper. She then filled a glass with water and putting her whole hand in her mouth as if she were trying to tear her tongue out, she pulled out something pink and white which she deposited in the glass. I was horribly frightened, but soon found it was only her false teeth she had taken out. She then took off her wig and I perceived a few straggling white hairs on the top of her head. They looked so comical that I almost burst out laughing. She kneeled down to say her prayers, got up and approached my instrument of vengeance. I waited awhile, my heart beating with expectation.

Suddenly, I heard a slight sound; then a series of explosions. I looked at Mme. Dufour; her face was a study.

She opened her eyes wide, then shut them, then opened them again and looked. The white substance was crackling, exploding at the same time, while a thick, white smoke curled up mysteriously toward the ceiling.

Perhaps the poor woman thought it was some satanic fireworks, or perhaps that she had been suddenly afflicted with some horrible disease; at all events, she stood there speechless with fright, her gaze riveted on the supernatural phenomenon. Suddenly, she screamed and fell swooning to the floor. I ran to my room, jumped into bed, and closed my eyes trying to convince myself that I had not left my room and had seen nothing.

"She is dead," I said to myself; "I have killed her," and I listened anxiously to the sound of footsteps. I heard voices and laughter and the next thing I knew my father was soundly boxing my ears.

Mme. Dufour was very pale when she came down the next day and she drank glass after glass of water. Perhaps she was trying to extinguish the fire which she imagined was in her, although the doctor had assured her that there was no danger. Since then, when anyone speaks of disease in front of her, she sighs and says:

"Oh, if you only knew! There are such strange diseases."

A Strange Fancy

It was at the end of the dinner opening the hunting season, at the house of Marquis de Bertrans. Eleven hunters, eight young women, and the doctor of the neighborhood were seated around the great illuminated table covered with fruits and flowers.

They came to speak of love, and a great discussion arose, the eternal discussion, as to whether one could love truly but once or many times. They cited examples of people who had never had but one serious love; they also cited other examples of others who had loved often, violently. The men, generally, pretended that the passion, like a malady, could strike the same person many times, and strike to kill if an obstacle appeared in his path. Although the point of view was not contestable, the women, whose opinion depended upon poesy more than on observation, affirmed that love, true love, the great love, could only fall once upon a mortal; that it was like a thunderbolt, this love, and that a heart touched by it remained ever after so vacant, ravaged, and burned out that no other powerful sentiment, even a dream, could again take root.

The Marquis, having loved much, combated this belief in lively fashion:

"I will tell you that one can love many times with all his strength and all his soul. You cite to me people who have killed themselves for love as proof of the impossibility of a second passion. I answer that if they had not been guilty of this foolishness of suicide, which removed them from all chance of another fall, they would have been healed; and they would have recommenced, again and again, until their natural death. It is with lovers as it is with drunkards. He who has drunk will drink—he who has loved will love. It is simply a matter of temperament."

They chose the doctor as arbitrator, an old Paris physician retired to the country, and begged him to give his opinion.

To be exact, he had none. As the Marquis had said, it is an affair of temperament.

"As for myself," he continued, "I have known of one passion which lasted fifty-five years without a day of respite, and which was terminated only by death."

The Marquis clapped his hands.

"This is beautiful," said a lady. "And what a dream to be so loved! What happiness to live fifty-five years enveloped in a deep, living affection! How happy and benign must be the life of one who is adored like that!"

The doctor laughed:

"In fact, Madame," said he, "you are deceived on that point, because the one loved was a man. You know him, it is Mr. Chouquet, the village pharmacist. And as for the woman, you knew her too, it is the old woman who put cane seats in chairs, and came every year to this house. But how can I make you comprehend the matter?"

The enthusiasm of the women fell. On their faces a look of disgust said: "Pooh!"—as if love could only strike those fine and distinguished creatures who were worthy of the interest of fashionable people.

The doctor continued:

"I was called, three months ago, to the bedside of this old woman. She was dying. She had come here in the old carriage that served her for a house, drawn by the nag that you have often seen, and accompanied by her two great black dogs, her friends and guard. The curate was already there. She made us the executors of her will, and in order to unveil the meaning of her testament, she related the story of her life. I have never heard anything more singular or more affecting.

"Her father made chair seats and so did her mother. She had never known a home in any one place upon the earth. As a little girl, she went around ragged and dirty. They would stop beside the road at the entrance to towns, unharness the horse and let him browse; the dog would go to sleep with his nose in his paws; the little one would play in the grass while the father and mother, under the shade of the elms bordering the roadside, would reseat all the old chairs in the neighborhood.

"No one ever talked in this ambulance dwelling. After the necessary words to decide who should make the tour of the houses and who should call out the well-known: 'Chairs to mend!' they would sit down to plait the straw, face to face or side by side.

"When the child went too far away or struck up an acquaintance with some urchin in the village, the angry voice of the father would call her: 'You come back here, you brat!' And these were the only words of tenderness she ever heard.

"When she grew larger they sent her around to collect the worn-out chairs to be rebottomed. Then she made some acquaintances from place to place among the street children. Then it would be the parents of her new friends who would call brutally to their children: 'Will you come here, you scamp! Let me catch you talking to that barefoot again!'

"Often the boys would throw stones at her. Sometimes ladies would give her a few pennies and look at her closely.

"One day—she was then eleven years old—as they were passing through this place, she met the little Chouquet behind the cemetery, weeping because some comrade had stolen two sous from him. The tears of this little well-to-do citizen, one of those fortunate ones from whom in her queer noddle she had imagined herself cut off, one of those beings always content and joyous, quite upset her. She went up to him, and when she learned the cause of his trouble, she poured into his hands all her savings, seven sous, which he took quite naturally, drying his tears. Then, mad with joy, she had the audacity to embrace him. As he was counting the money attentively, he allowed her to do it. Seeing that she was not repulsed nor beaten, she did the same thing again. She embraced him with arms and heart. Then she ran away.

"What could have taken place in her miserable head after that? Did she attach herself to this booby because she had sacrificed for him her vagabond fortune, or because she had given to him her first tender kiss? The mystery is the same for the small as for the great.

"For months she dreamed of this corner of the cemetery and of this boy. In the hope of seeing him again, she robbed her parents, keeping back a sou here and there, either from a chair seat or upon the provisions which she was sent to buy.

"When she returned here she had two francs in her pocket, but she only saw the little druggist very properly behind the big colored bottle of his father's shop, between a red decanter and a tapeworm. She loved him there still more, charmed, aroused to ecstasy by this glory of colored water, this apotheosis of shining crystal.

"This picture became an ineffaceable memory, and when she saw him, the following year, playing marbles near the school with his comrades, she threw herself upon him, seized him in her arms, and kissed him with such violence that he began to howl with fear. Then, in order to appease him, she gave him all her money—seventy cents, a real treasure which he looked at with bulging eyes.

"He took it and let her caress him as much as she wished.

"During the next four years she turned into his hand all her surplus, which he pocketed with a clear conscience, in exchange for permitted kisses. There was sometimes fifteen cents, sometimes forty, and once only five and one-half—and she wept with pain and humiliation at this, but it had been a bad year. The last time there was a five-franc piece, a great round piece that made him laugh with content.

"She thought of nothing but him; and he waited her return with a certain impatience, running to meet her, which made the heart of the girl leap with joy.

"Then he disappeared. They sent him away to college. She found it out by skillful questioning. Then she used her diplomacy to change her parents' itinerary and make them pass through there in vacation. She succeeded but for one year; then for two years she did not see him; then she scarcely recognized him, so much was he changed;

he was so large and handsome in his coat with the brass buttons, and so imposing. He feigned not to see her and passed proudly by near her.

"She wept over it for two days, and after that she suffered without ceasing.

"Every year she returned here, passing him without daring to bow, and without his deigning to raise his eyes to her. She loved him passionately. She said to me: 'Doctor, he is the only man I have seen on earth; I have not known that there are others existing.'

"Her parents died. She continued their trade, but took with her two dogs instead of one, two terrible dogs that no one would dare encounter.

"One day in entering this village, where her heart still remained, she perceived a young woman coming out of the Chouquet shop on the arm of her well-beloved. It was his wife. He was married.

"That evening she threw herself into the pond on the mayor's estate. A drunken man got her out and took her to the pharmacy. Chouquet, the son, came down in his dressing-gown, to care for her; and, without appearing to recognize her, loosed her clothing and rubbed her, then said, in a hard voice: 'My! But you are foolish! It is not necessary to make a beast of yourself like this!'

"That was sufficient to cure her. He had spoken to her! She was happy for a long time.

"He wanted no remuneration for his services, but she insisted upon paying him well. And all her life was spent like this. She made chair seats and thought of Chouquet. Every year she saw him behind his large windows. She had the habit of buying from him all her medical needs. In this way she could see him near to, and speak to him, and still give him a little money.

"As I told you in the beginning, she died this spring. After having related her sad history, she begged me to give to him she had so patiently loved all the savings of her life, because she had worked only for him, she said, fasting even, in order to put aside, and to be sure that he would think of her at least once after she was dead.

"She then gave me two thousand three hundred and twenty-seven francs. I allowed the curate twenty-seven for burial, and carried off the rest when she had drawn her last breath.

"The next day, I took myself to the house of the Chouquets. They had just finished breakfast, sitting opposite each other, large and red, smelling of their pharmaceutical products, important and satisfied.

"They made me be seated; they offered me a *kirsch* which I accepted; then I commenced my discourse in an emotional voice, persuaded that they were going to weep.

"When they understood that he had been loved by this vagabond, this chair mender, this rover, Chouquet bounced with indignation, as if she had robbed him of his reputation, of the esteem of honest people, of his honor, of something of that delicacy that was dearer to him than life.

"His wife, also exasperated, kept repeating: 'The beggar! The beggar! The beggar!' without being able to find any other word.

"He got up and walked around the table with long strides. his Greek cap tipped over his ear. He muttered: 'Think of it, Doctor! This is a horrible thing to happen to a man! What is to be done? Oh! if I had known this while she was alive I would have had her arrested and shut up in prison. And she wouldn't have got out, I can tell you!'

"I was stupefied at the result of my pious proceedings. I neither knew what to say nor what to do. But I had to complete my mission. I said: 'She has charged me to give you all her savings, which amount to two thousand three hundred francs. As what I have told you seems to be so very disagreeable to you, perhaps it would be better to give this money to the poor.'

"They looked at me, the man and the woman, impotent from shock. I drew the money from my pocket, miserable money from all the country and of every mark, gold and sous mixed. Then I asked: 'What do you decide?'

"Mrs. Chouquet spoke first. She said: 'But since it was the last wish of this woman—it seems to me that it would be difficult to refuse it.'

"The husband, somewhat confused, answered: 'We could always buy with that money something for our children.'

"I remarked, dryly: 'As you wish.'

"He continued: 'Yes, give it to us, since she has put it in your charge. We can always find means of using it in some good work.'

"I laid down the money, bowed, and went out.

"The next day Chouquet came to me and said brusquely: 'She must have left a wagon here, that—that woman. What are you going to do with this wagon?'

" 'Nothing,' said I, 'take it if you wish.'

" 'Exactly. Just what I want. I will make a lean-to of it for my kitchen stove.'

"He was going, but I recalled him. 'She also left an old horse and her two dogs. Do you want them?'

"He stopped, surprised: 'Ah! no,' he answered, 'what could I do with them? Dispose of them as you wish.'

"Then he laughed and extended his hand which I took. What else could I do? In our country, a medical man and a druggist should not be enemies.

"I have kept the dogs at my house. The curate, who has a large yard, took the horse. The wagon serves Chouquet as a cabin, and he has bought five railroad bonds with the money.

"This is the only profound love that I have met in my life."

The doctor was silent. Then the Marquis, with tears in his eyes, sighed: "Decidedly, it is only women who know how to love."

✕ After Death

ALL Veziers-le-Rethel had assisted at the funeral and interment of M. Badon-Leremince, and the last words of the discourse of the delegate of the district remained in the memory of all:

"He was an honest man, at least."

Honest man he had been in all the appreciable acts of his life; in his words, in his example, in his attitude, in his bearing, in his step, in the cut of his beard, and the form of his hats. He had never said a word that did not contain an example, never gave alms without accompanying it with advice, never held a hand without having the air of giving it a kind of benediction.

He left two children, a son and a daughter. His son was General Counselor, and his daughter, having married a notary, M. Poirel de la Voulte, held a high place in Veziers.

They were inconsolable at the death of their father, for they loved him sincerely.

As soon as the ceremonies were over, they returned to the house of death, and all three together, the son, the daughter, and the son-in-law, opened the will, whose seal was to be broken by them alone, and that only after the coffin had been placed in the earth. A direction upon the envelope expressed this wish.

It was M. Poirel de la Voulte who opened the paper, being accustomed to these things in the capacity of notary, and, having adjusted his eyeglasses over his eyes, he read, in a dull voice, made for particularizing contracts:

"My children, my dear children, I could not sleep tranquilly the eternal sleep if I did not make a confession to you from the other side of the tomb, the confession of a crime, remorse of which has rent my life. Yes, I have committed a crime, a frightful, abominable crime.

"I was twenty-six years old, had just been called to the bar in Paris, and was living the life of young people from the provinces, stranded, without acquaintances, friends, or parents in the city.

"I took a mistress. There are people who are indignant at this word, 'mistress,' but there are also beings who cannot live alone. I am one of these. Solitude fills me with a horrible agony, especially solitude in a lodging, before the fire in the evening. It seems to me then that I am alone upon earth, frightfully alone, surrounded by vague dangers, and terrible, unknown things; and the partition which separates me from my neighbor, from my neighbor whom I do not know, makes him as far removed as the stars that I see from my window. A sort of fever invades me, a fever of impatience and fear; and the silence of the walls overpowers me. It is so profound, so sad, this silence of a room where one lives alone! It is a silence about the soul, and when the furniture cracks or starts, the courage wanes, for one expects no sound in this mournful dwelling-place.

"How many times, unnerved, frightened by this mute immobility, have I begun to speak, to pronounce some words, without sequence, without reason, in order to make some noise. My voice then appeared to me so strange that I was afraid of that also. Is there anything more frightful than talking alone in an empty house? The voice seems like that of another, an unknown voice, speaking without cause, to no one, into the hollow air, with no ear to listen, for one knows, before the words are uttered into the space of the apartment, what the lips are about to say. And when they resound lugubriously in the silence, they seem more like an echo, the echo of singular words pronounced low by the thoughts.

"I took a mistress, a young girl like all those young girls who live in Paris at some trade insufficient to support them. She was sweet, good, and simple. Her parents lived at Poissy. She went to stay a few days with them from time to time.

"For a year I lived tranquilly enough with her, fully decided to leave her when I should see some young person with whom I was well enough pleased to want to marry. I would leave to this one a small income, since it is admitted in our society that the love of a woman ought to be paid for, in money when she is poor, in jewels if she is rich.

"But behold there came a day when she announced to me that she was *enceinte*. I was struck down, and perceived in an instant the ruin of my whole existence. The chain was apparent that I must drag to my dying day, in the near future, in my old age, always, the chain of a woman bound to my life by a child, the chain of a child whom it would be necessary to bring up, watch over, and protect, always concealing myself from him and him from the world. My mind was overturned by this news, and a confused desire, which I did not formulate, but which I felt in my heart, took to showing itself, like people concealed behind portières waiting until some one tells them to appear; a criminal desire that roamed around at the bottom of my thoughts: If some accident could happen! There are so many of these little beings who die before birth!

"Oh! I did not desire the death of my mistress. Poor girl, I loved her well! But I wished, perhaps, the death of the other before I had seen it.

"It was born. I had a household in my bachelor's quarters, a false household with a child—a horrible thing. It resembled all infants. I could scarcely love it. Fathers, you see, do not love until later. They have not the instinctive, surpassing love and tenderness of mothers; their affection is awakened little by little, as their mind is drawn toward their children each day in the bonds which unite living beings together.

"A year passed away. I now fled from my too small dwelling, where linen and blankets and stockings, the size of a pair of gloves, were dragging around and a thousand things of this kind were left upon the furniture, especially upon the arm of the easy-chair. I fled particularly to escape from hearing him cry; for he cried at all times, when he was changed, when he was washed, when one touched him, when he was put to bed, when he was taken up, without ceasing.

"I had made some acquaintances, and had met her who was to become your mother. I came to love her and a desire to marry her was awakened in me. I paid her my court; I asked her in marriage; she accepted me.

"And now I found myself in 'this predicament: To marry, having a child, this young girl whom I adored,—or, to tell the truth and renounce her and happiness, the future, everything'; for her parents, rigid and scrupulous people, would never give her to me if they knew.

"I passed one month of horrible anguish, of moral torture; a month where a thousand thoughts frightened and haunted me; and I felt growing in me a hate against my son, against this little piece of living, crying flesh who barred my way, ruined my life, and condemned me to an existence without hope, those vague hopes so charming to youth.

"At this time the mother of my companion fell ill and I remained alone with the infant. It was in December. It was terribly cold. What a night! My mistress had gone. I had dined in my narrow dining-room and then entered softly into the chamber where the little one slept.

"I seated myself in an armchair before the fire. The wind sighed, making the glass crack, a wind dry with frost, and I saw out of the window the stars scintillating with that bright light which they have on frosty nights.

"Then the besetting thought which had haunted me for a month entered my head again. Whenever I remained still, it descended upon me, entered into me, and roamed about. It gnawed me as fixed ideas gnaw, as a cancer gnaws into the flesh. It was there, in my head, in my heart, in my entire body, it seemed to me, and it devoured me as if it had been a beast. I tried to drive it, push it away, to open my thoughts to other things, to new hopes, as one opens a window to the fresh air of morning to drive out the vitiated air of night; but I could not, even for a second, get it out of my brain. I know not how to express this torture. It gnawed at my soul; and I felt with a frightful grief, a physical and moral grief, each succeeding pang.

"My existence was ended! How could I ever get out of the situation? How draw away, or how confess?

"And I loved her who was to become your mother with a mad passion which this insurmountable obstacle further exaggerated.

"A terrible anger grew in me which tightened my throat, an anger which approached madness — mania! Surely, I was mad that night!

"The child slept. I arose and went and looked at him sleeping. There he was, this abortion, this larva, this nothing, who condemned me to a life of unhappiness without appeal.

"He slept, his mouth open, buried in the bedclothes, in a cradle near my bed, where I could not sleep myself!

"How did I accomplish what I did? Do I know? What force drove me, what power of malice possessed me? Oh! the temptation of the crime came to me, without announcing itself. I only recall that my heart was beating furiously. It beat so strongly that I heard it as one hears the blows of a hammer behind a partition wall. I only recall that! my heart beating! In my head there was a strange confusion, a tumult, a derangement of reason, of complete cold-bloodedness. I was in one of those frightful hours of hallucination when a man is no longer conscious of his acts, either in direction or will.

"I gently raised the covers which concealed the body of my child; I threw them upon the foot of the cradle, and looked at him all bare. He did not wake. Then I went toward the window very gently and opened it.

"A breath of cold air came in like an assassin, so cold that I drew back before it. The two candles flickered. And I remained there near the window for a long time, not daring to turn and see what was behind me, and feeling ever upon my forehead, my cheeks, my hands, the fatal air that was constantly gliding it. This lasted a long time.

"I did not reflect. I was thinking of nothing. Suddenly a little cough made a frightful shiver pass through me from head to foot, a shiver which I can feel at this moment at the roots of my hair. With a startled movement I closed brusquely the two sides of the window, and turning hastened to the cradle.

"He still slept, his mouth open, all bare. I touched his limbs; they were icy and I covered him again. My heart seemed suddenly to break and to be filled with pity and tenderness for this poor little innocent being whom I had wished to kill. I kissed him over and over again upon his fine hair. Then I returned and seated myself before the fire.

"I thought with horror of what I had done, and asked myself whence came these tempests of the soul when man loses all notion of things, all control of himself, and moves in a sort of fearful drunkenness, without knowing what he does, without knowing where he goes, like a ship in a hurricane.

"The child coughed once again and I felt torn to the heart. If he should die! My God, my God! what would become of me?

"I got up and went to look at him; and, with a candle in my hand, I bent over him. Seeing him breathe tranquilly,

I was reassured, even when he coughed for the third time. But I felt such a shock, and made such a movement to arrest it (as one does at the sight of some frightful thing) that I let the candle fall.

"And, straightening myself, after having picked it up, I perceived that my temples were moistened with sweat, with a sweat hot and cold at the same time, which produced an agony of the soul like that of some frightful moral suffering, or some unnamable torture, burning like fire, and cold as ice, piercing the bones and the skin of my head.

"I remained bending over my son until daybreak, calming myself when he was quiet and transfixed by an abominable grief when a feeble cough came from his mouth.

"He awoke with red eyes, an inflamed throat, and difficult breathing. When my wife entered the house and saw him, we sent immediately for a physician. He came in an hour and asked, after having examined him:

" 'Has he taken cold?'

"I began to tremble as very old people tremble, and stammered:

" 'No, I think not.' Then I asked:

" 'What is the matter? It is anything grave?'

"He answered:

" 'I cannot say yet. I will return this evening.'

"He returned in the evening. My son had passed nearly the whole day in an invincible sleepiness, coughing from time to time. A congestion of the lungs now showed itself.

"This lasted ten days. I cannot express what I suffered during those interminable hours which separate the morning from evening and the evening from the morning.

"He died—

"And since—since that moment, I have not passed an hour, no, not an hour without that atrocious, cutting memory, a memory which gnaws, which tortures and rends the mind, and stirs in me like a writhing beast chained up in the bottom of my soul.

"Oh! if I could have become mad!"

M. Poirel de la Voulte put up his glasses, a movement which was usual with him when he had finished reading a contract, and the three heirs of the dead man looked at each other without saying a word, pale and immovable. At the end of a minute the notary said:

"This must be destroyed."

The two others lowered their head in sign of assent. He lighted a candle, separated carefully the pages which contained the dangerous confession from the pages which contained the disposition of the money, then he presented them to the flame and threw them into the fireplace.

And they watched the white leaves as they were consumed. Soon they were nothing more than a lot of little black heaps. And as they still perceived some letters which were legible on the paper, the daughter crushed it with the end of her foot, mixing it with the old ashes.

Then they all three remained quiet for some time looking at it, as if they feared that the charred secret might fly away up the chimney.

On Cats

SEATED on a bench, the other day at my door, in the full sunlight, with a cluster of anemones in flower before me, I read a book recently published, an honest book, something uncommon and charming, — "The Cooper" by George Duval. A large white cat that belonged to the gardener jumped upon my lap, and by the shock closed the book, which I placed at my side in order to caress the animal.

The weather was warm; a faint suggestive odor of new flowers was in the air, and at times came little cool breezes from the great white summits that I could see in the distance. But the sun was hot and sharp, and the day was one of those that stir the earth, make it alive, break open the seed in order to animate the sleeping germs, and cleave the buds so that the young leaves may spring forth. The cat rolled itself on my knees, lying on its back, its paws in the air, with claws protruding, then receding. The little creature showed its pointed teeth beneath its lips, and its green eyes gleamed in the half-closed slit of its eyelids. I caressed and rubbed the soft, nervous animal, supple as a piece of silk, smooth, warm, delicious, dangerous. She purred with satisfaction, yet was quite ready to scratch, for a cat loves to scratch as well as to be petted. She held out her neck and rolled again, and when I took my hand from her, she raised herself and pushed her head against my lifted hand.

I made her nervous, and she made me nervous also, for, although I like cats in a certain way, I detest them at the same time,—those animals so charming and so treacherous. It gives me pleasure to fondle them, to rub under my hand their silky fur that sometimes crackles, to feel their warmth through this fine and exquisite covering. Nothing is softer, nothing gives to the skin a sensation more delicate, more refined, more rare, than the warm, living coat of a cat. But this living coat also communicates to me, through the ends of my fingers, a strange and ferocious desire to strangle the animal I am caressing. I feel in her the desire she has to bite and scratch me. I feel it,—that same desire, as if it were an electric current communicated from her to me. I run my fingers through the soft fur and the current passes through my nerves from my finger-tips to my heart, even to my brain; it tingles throughout my being and causes me to shut my teeth hard.

And if the animal begins to bite and scratch me, I seize her by the neck, I give her a turn and throw her far from me, as I would throw a stone from a sling, so quickly and so brutally that she never has time to revenge herself.

I remember that when I was a child I loved cats, yet I had even then that strange desire to strangle them with my little hands; and one day at the end of the garden, at the beginning of the woods, I perceived suddenly something gray rolling in the high grass. I went to see what it was, and found a cat caught in a snare, strangling, suffocating, dying. It rolled, tore up the ground with its claws, bounded, fell inert, then began again, and its hoarse, rapid breathing made a noise like a pump, a frightful noise which I hear yet. I could have taken a spade and cut the snare, I could have gone to find the servant or tell my father. No, I did not move, and with beating heart I watched it die with a trembling and cruel joy. It was a cat! If it had been a dog, I would rather have cut the copper wire with my teeth than let it suffer a second more. When the cat was quite dead, but yet warm, I went to feel of it and pull its tail!

These little creatures are delicious, nothwithstanding, delicious above all, because in caressing them, while they are rubbing against our skin, purring and rolling on us, looking at us with their yellow eyes which seem never to see us, we realize the insecurity of their tenderness, the perfidious selfishness of their pleasure.

Some women, also, give us that sensation,—women who are charming, tender, with clear yet false eyes, who have chosen us entirely for their gratification. Near them, when they open their arms and offer their lips, when a man folds them to his heart with bounding pulses, when he tastes the joy of their delicate caress, he realizes well that he holds a perfidious, tricky cat, with claws and fangs, an enemy in love, who will bite him when she is tired of kisses.

Many of the poets have loved cats. Baudelaire has sung to them divinely.

I had one day the strange sensation of having inhabited the enchanted palace of the White Cat, a magic castle where reigned one of those undulant, mysterious, troubling animals, the only one, perhaps, of all living creatures that one never hears walk.

This adventure occurred last year on this same shore of the Mediterranean. At Nice there was atrocious heat, and I asked myself as to whether there was not, somewhere in the mountains above us, a fresh valley where one might find a breath of fresh air.

Thorence was recommended to me, and I wished to see it immediately. To get there I had first to go to Grasse, the town of perfumes, concerning which I shall write some day, and tell how the essences and quintessences of flowers are manufactured there, costing up to two thousand francs the liter. I passed the night in an old hotel of the town, a poor kind of inn, where the quality of the food was as doubtful as the cleanliness of the rooms. I went on my way in the morning.

The road went straight up into the mountains, following the deep ravines, which were overshadowed by sterile peaks, pointed and savage. I thought that my advisers had recommended to me a very extraordinary kind of summer excursion, and I was almost on the point of returning to Nice the same day, when I saw suddenly before me, on a mountain which appeared to close the entrance to the entire valley, an immense and picturesque ruined castle, showing towers and broken walls, of a strange architecture, in profile against the sky. It proved to be an ancient castle that had belonged to the Templars, who, in bygone days, had governed this country of Thorence.

I made a detour of this mountain, and suddenly discovered a long, green valley, fresh and reposeful. Upon its level were meadows, running waters, and willows; and on its sides grew tall pines-trees. In front of the ruins, on the other side of the valley, but standing lower, was an inhabited castle, called the Castle of the Four Towers, which was built about the year 1530. One could not see any trace of the Renaissance period, however. It was a strong and massive square structure, apparently possessing tremendous powers of resistance, and it was supported by four defensive towers, as its name would indicate.

I had a letter of introduction to the owner of this manor, who would not permit me to go to the hotel. The whole valley is one of the most charming spots in summer that one could dream of. I wandered about there until evening, and after dinner I went to the apartment that had been reserved for me. I first passed through a sort of sitting-room, the walls of which were covered by old Cordova leather; then I went through another room, where, by the light of my candle, I noticed rapidly, in passing, several old portraits of ladies—those paintings of which Théophile Gautier has written.

I entered the room where my bed was, and looked around me. The walls where hung with antique tapestries, where one saw rose-colored donjons in blue landscapes, and great fantastic birds sitting under foliage of precious stones! My dressing-room was in one of the towers. The windows wide on the inside and narrowed to a mere slit on the outside, going through the entire thickness of the walls, were, in reality, nothing but loopholes, through which one might kill an approaching enemy.

I shut my door, went to bed, and slept. Presently I dreamed; usually one dreams a little of something that

has passed during the day. I seemed to be traveling; I entered an inn, where I saw at a table before the fire a servant in complete livery, and a mason,—a strange association which did not astonish me. These people spoke of Victor Hugo, who had just died, and I took part in their conversation. At last I went to bed in a room, the door of which I could not shut; and suddenly, I saw the servant and the mason, armed with sabers, coming softly toward my bed.

I awoke at once, and a few moments passed before I could recollect where I was. Then I recalled quickly my arrival of the day before at Thorence, the occurrences of the evening, and my pleasant reception by the owner. I was just about to close my eyes, when I saw distinctly in the darkness, in the middle of my room, at about the height of a man's head, two fiery eyes watching me.

I seized a match, and while striking it I heard a noise, a light, soft noise, like the sound of a wet rag thrown on the floor, but after I had lighted the candle I saw nothing but a tall table in the middle of the room. I rose, went through both apartments, looked under the bed and into the closets, and found nothing. I thought then that perhaps I had continued dreaming after I was awake, and so I went to sleep again, but not without trouble.

I dreamed again. This time I traveled once more, but in the Orient, in the country that I love. I arrived at the house of a Turk, who lived in the middle of a desert. He was a superb Turk,—not an Arab, but a Turk, fat, friendly, and charming. He was dressed in Turkish attire, with a turban on his head, and a whole shopful of silk on his back,—a real Turk of the Théâtre Français, who made me compliments while offering me sweetmeats, sitting on a voluptuous divan.

Then a little black boy took me to a room—all my dreams ended in this fashion in those days! It was a perfumed room decorated in sky blue, with skins of wild beasts on the floor, and before the fire,—the idea of fire pursued me even in the desert,—on a low chair, was a woman, lightly clothed, who was waiting on me. She was of the purest Oriental type, with stars tattooed on her cheeks and forehead and chin; she had immense eyes, a beautiful form, and slightly brown skin,—a warm and exciting skin.

She looked at me, and I thought: "This is what I understand to be the true meaning of the word hospitality. In our stupid and prudish northern countries, with their hateful mawkishness of ideas, and silly notions of morality, a man would never receive a stranger in this fashion."

I went up to the woman and spoke to her, but she replied only by signs, not knowing a word of my language, which the Turk, her master, understood so well. All the happier that she would be silent, I took her by the hand and led her toward my couch, where I placed myself by her side. . . .

But one always awakens at those moments! So I opened my eyes and was not greatly surprised to feel beneath my hand something soft and warm, which I caressed lovingly. Then, my mind clearing, I recognized that it was a cat, a big cat rolled up against my cheek, sleeping there with confidence. I left it there and composed myself to sleep once more. When daylight appeared he was gone; and I really thought I had dreamed he had been with me; for I could not understand how he could have come in and gone out, as my door was locked.

When I related my dream and my adventure to my agreeable host (not the whole of it!) he began to laugh, and said: "He came in through his own door," and raising a curtain, he showed me a little round hole in the wall. I learned then that the old habitations of this country have long narrow runways through the walls, which go from the cellar to the garret, from the servants' rooms to the rooms of the *seigneur,* and these passages render the cat king and master of the interior of the house. He goes where it pleases him, visits his domain at his pleasure, sleeps in all the beds, sees all, hears all, knows all the secrets, all the habits, all the shames of the house. Everywhere he is at home, the animal that moves without noise, the silent prowler, the nocturnal rover of the hollowed walls. And I thought of Baudelaire.

Room No. Eleven

"WHAT! You do not know why President Amandon was removed?"

"No, not at all."

"As far as he is concerned, it would never have been known. But it is a story of the strangest sort."

"Relate it to me."

"You remember Mrs. Amandon, that pretty brunette, thin, and so distinguished and pretty that she was called Madame Marguerite in all Perthuis-le-Long?"

"Yes, perfectly."

"Very well, then. You recall also how much she was respected and considered, and better loved than anyone in the town; she knew how to receive, how to organize a festival or a charity fair, how to find money for the poor, and how to please the young people in a thousand ways.

"She was very elegant and very coquettish, nevertheless, but in a Platonic fashion, and with the charming elegance of the provinces, for she was a provincial, this pretty little woman, an exquisite provincial.

"The poets and writers who are all Parisian sing to us of the Parisian woman and of her charm, because they know only her; but I declare here that the provincial is worth a hundred times more when she is of superior quality.

"The provincial has an attraction all her own; she is more discreet than the Parisian, more humble, promising nothing and giving much, while the Parisian for the most part, promises much and gives nothing but deshabille.

"The Parisian is a triumph in the elegant effrontery of falseness; the provincial, an example of the modesty of truth.

"Yet the provincial, with her air of homely alertness, her deceitful, schoolgirl candor, her smile which means nothing, and her good little passions, direct and tenacious, is capable of a thousand times more deceit, artifice, and feminine invention than all the Parisians together, for gratifying her own tastes or vices, and that without awakening suspicion, or scandal, or gossip in the little town which watches her with all its eyes from all its windows.

"Mrs. Amandon was a type of this rare race, but charming. Never had anyone suspected her, never had anyone thought that her life was not as limpid as her look, a sly look, transparent and warm, but seemingly so honest—you should have seen it!

"Then she had admirable tact, a marvelous ingenuity and power of invention, and unbelievable simplicity.

"She picked all her lovers from the army and kept them three years, the time of their sojourn in the garrison. In short, she not only had love, she had sense.

"When some new regiment arrived at Perthuis-le-Long, she carefully observed all the officers between thirty and forty years of age—for, before thirty one is not discreet, and after forty, one is often feeble.

"Oh! she knew the list of officers as well as the colonel. She knew all, all the habits, manners, instruction, education, physical qualities, the power of resistance to fatigue, the character, whether patient or violent, the fortune, and the tendency to closeness or prod-

462

igality of each of them. Then she made her choice. She gave the preference to men of calm allurement, like herself, but they must be handsome. She also wished them to have had no previous entanglements, any passion having the power to leave traces, or that had made any trouble. Because the man whose loves are mentioned is never a very discreet man.

"After having decided upon the one she would love for the three years of his regulation sojourn, it only remained to throw down the gauntlet.

"While some women would find themselves embarrassed, would have taken ordinary means, following the way of others, having court paid them in marked-off stages of conquest and resistance, allowing her fingers to be kissed one day, her wrist the next, her cheek the following, then the lips, then the rest, she had a method more prompt, more discreet, and more sure. She gave a ball.

"The chosen officer was invited to dance with the mistress of the house. Then, in waltzing, led on by the rapid movement, bewildered by the intoxication of the dance, she would throw herself against him as if giving herself, and hold his hand with a nervous, continued pressure.

"If he did not comprehend, he was only a fool, and she passed on to the next, classed as number two, on the list of her desires.

"If he comprehended, the thing was done, without fuss, without compromising gallantries, without numerous visits.

"What could be more simple or more practical?

"How women might make use of a process similar to this to make us understand their pleasure! How much it would suppress difficulties, hesitations, and trouble from misunderstandings! How often we pass by, without knowing it, a possible happiness,—without suspecting it, because we are unable to penetrate the mystery of thought, the secret abandon of the will, the mute appeal of the flesh, the unknown soul of a woman whose mouth preserves silence, whose eye is impenetrable and clear.

"When the chosen one comprehended, he asked for a rendezvous. But she always made him wait a month or six weeks in order to watch and be sure that he had no dangerous faults.

"During this time he was racking his brain to think of some place where they could meet without peril, and imagining combinations difficult and unsafe.

"Then, at some official feast, she would say to him in a low voice:

" 'Come Tuesday evening, at nine o'clock, to the Golden Horse hotel near the ramparts, on the Vouziers road, and ask for Miss Clarisse. I shall be waiting for you. And be sure to be in civil dress.'

"For eight years she had in fact rented this furnished room by the year, in this obscure inn. It was an idea of her first lover which she found practical, and after the man departed, she kept the nest.

"Oh! it was a mediocre nest; four walls covered with gray paper adorned with blue flowers, a pine bedstead under muslin curtains, an armchair bought at her order by the innkeeper's wife, two chairs, and some necessary articles for the toilette,—what more was needed?

"Upon the walls · were three large photographs. Three colonels on horseback; the colonels of her lovers! Why not? It would not do to preserve the true likeness, the exact likeness, but she could perhaps keep some souvenirs by proxy.

"And she had never been recognized by anyone in all these visits to the Golden Horse, you ask?

"Never, by anyone!

"The means she employed were admirable and simple. She had thought out and organized some charity reunions and religious meetings, some of which she attended, others she did not. Her husband, knowing her good works, which cost him dear, lived without suspicions. Then, when a rendezvous had been agreed upon, she would say at dinner, before the servants:

" 'I am going this evening to the Association for making flannel bandages for old paralytics.'

"And she went out about eight o'clock, went straight to the Association, came out again very soon, passed through divers streets, and, finding herself alone in some little street, in some somber corner without a light, she would take off her hat, replace it by a maid's cap which she carried under her mantle, fold a kerchief after the same fashion and tie it over her shoulders, carrying her hat and the garment she had worn in a napkin; she would go trotting along, full of courage, the hips uncovered, like a good little maid that had been sent upon some errand; and sometimes she would even run, as if she were in a great hurry.

"Who could have recognized in this trim servant the lively wife of President Amandon?

"She would arrive at the Golden Horse, go up to her room, of which she had the key, and the big proprietor, master Trouveau, seeing her pass his desk, would murmur:

" 'There is Miss Clarisse coming to meet some lover.'

"He had indeed guessed something, the rogue, but did not try to learn more, and he would certainly have been much surprised to find that his client was Mrs. Amandon, or Madame Marguerite, as she was called in Perthuis-le-Long. And this is how the horrible discovery took place.

"Never had Miss Clarisse come to her meeting place two evenings in succession, never! being too nice and too prudent for that. And master Trouveau knew this well, since not once in eight years had he seen her come the next day after a visit. Often, therefore, in days of need, he had disposed of her room for a night.

"Now, sometime last summer, Mr. Amandon, the trustful president, absented himself from home for a week. It was in July. Madame was ardently in love, and as there was no fear of being surprised, she asked her lover, the handsome Commander Varangelles, one Tuesday evening on leaving him, if he wished her to return the next day.

"He replied: 'With all my heart!'

"And it was agreed that they should return at the usual hour on Wednesday. She said to him in a low tone:

" 'If you arrive first, my dear, you can wait for me in bed.'

"Then they embraced and separated.

The next day, as master Trouveau sat reading the 'Perthuis Tablet,' the Republican organ of the town, he cried out to his wife, who was plucking a fowl in the courtyard:

" 'Here! the cholera has broken out in the country. There was a man died yesterday of it in Vauvigny.' But he thought no more about it, his inn being full of people, and business very good.

"Toward noon a traveler presented himself on foot, a kind of tourist, who ordered a good breakfast, after having drank two absinthes. And, as he was very warm, he absorbed a bottle of wine and two bottles of water at least. Then he took his coffee and his little glass, or rather three little glasses. And feeling a little heavy, he asked for a room where he might sleep for an hour or two. There was no longer a vacant room, and the proprietor, after consulting his wife, gave him Miss Clarisse's.

"The man went in there and, toward five o'clock as he had not been seen to come out, the landlord went to wake him. What was his astonishment to find him dead!

"The innkeeper descended to find his wife: 'Say,' he whispered to her, 'the tourist I put in number 11, I believe is dead.'

"She raised her arms, crying: 'It's not possible! Lord God! It is the cholera!'

Master Trouveau shook his head:

" 'I should sooner believe that it was a cerebral congestion, seeing that he is as black as the dregs of wine.'

"But the mistress was frightened and kept repeating:

" 'It is not necessary to say, it is not necessary to say that we think it is

cholera. Go and make the report and say nothing. They will take him away in the night, and no one will know about it. What is neither seen nor heard perplexes nobody.'

"The man murmured: 'Miss Clarisse was here yesterday, the room will be free this evening.'

"And he found the doctor who made out the certificate, 'From congestion after a copious repast.' Then he made an agreement with the commissioner of police to remove the dead body toward midnight, that there might be no suspicion about the hotel.

"It was scarcely nine o'clock when Madame Amandon went secretly up the staircase of the Golden Horse, without being seen by anyone. She reached her room, opened the door, and entered. A candle was burning upon the chimney-piece. She turned toward the bed. The Commander, she thought, was already there and had closed the curtains.

"She said to him: 'One minute, dearie, and I will be there.'

"And she disrobed with a feverish haste, throwing her boots upon the floor and her corset upon the armchair. Then, her black dress and skirts having fallen in a circle around her, she stood in her red silk chemise like a flower that is ready to blossom.

"As the Commander said not a word, she asked:

" 'Are you asleep, my big fellow?'

"He did not answer, and she began to laugh, murmuring:

" 'Wait! He is asleep. It is too funny!'

"She kept on her black silk stockings and, running to the bed, glided in quickly, seizing him full in the arms and kissing him on the lips, in order to wake him suddenly. It was the cold dead body of the traveler.

"For one second she remained immovable, too frightened to comprehend anything. But the cold of this inert flesh penetrated her own, giving her an atrocious fright before her mind had time to reflect.

"She made a bound out of the bed, trembling from head to foot; then running to the chimney-piece, she seized the candle, returned, and looked! And she perceived a frightful visage that she had never before seen, black, swollen, with eyes closed, and a horrible grimace of the jaw.

"She uttered a cry, one of those piercing interminable cries which women utter in their fright, and, letting fall the candle, she opened the door and fled, unclothed, down the passage, continuing to scream in frightful fashion. A commercial traveler, in his socks, who occupied room number 4, came out immediately and received her in his arms.

"He asked, much startled: 'What is the matter, pretty child?'

"She stammered out, terrified: 'Some one has been killed—in—my room!'

"Other guests appeared. The landlord himself ran out.

"And suddenly the Commander showed his tall figure at the end of the corridor. When she saw him, she threw herself toward him, crying:

" 'Save me, save me, Gontran— Some one has been killed in our room.'

"Explanations were difficult. Master Trouveau however, told the truth and demanded that they release Miss Clarisse, for whom he vouched with his own head. But the commercial traveler in socks, having examined the dead body, declared that a crime had been committed, and he convinced the other strangers that Miss Clarisse and her lover should not be allowed to depart.

"They were obliged to await the arrival of the police commissioner, who gave them their liberty, but was not discreet.

"The following month, President Amandon received promotion with a new place of residence."

———•———

One Phase of Love

THE walls of the cell were bare and whitewashed. A narrow, barred window, so high that it could not easily be reached, lighted this little room; the crazy man, seated on a straw chair, looked at us with a fixed eye, vague and haunting. He was thin, with wrinkled cheeks and almost white hair that one would think had grown white in a few months. His clothes seemed too large for his dried-up limbs, his shrunken chest, and hollow body. One felt that this man had been ravaged by his thoughts, by a thought, as fruit is by a worm. His madness, his idea, was there in his head, obstinate, harassing, devouring. It was eating his body, little by little. It, the Invisible, the Impalpable, the Unseizable, the Immaterial Idea gnawed his flesh, drank his blood, and extinguished his life.

What a mystery, that this man should be killed by a Thought! He is an object of fear and pity, this madman! What strange dream, frightful and deadly, can dwell in his forehead, to fold such profound and ever-changing wrinkles in it?

The doctor said to me: "He has terrible paroxysms of rage, and is one of the most singularly demented people I have ever seen. His madness is of an amorous, erotic kind. He is a sort of necrophile. He has written a journal which shows as plainly as daylight the malady of his mind. His madness is visible, so to speak. If you are interested, you may run through this document."

I followed the doctor into his office and he gave me the journal of this miserable man.

"Read it," said he, "and give me your opinion about it."

Here is what the little book contained:

"Up to the age of thirty-two years I lived tranquilly without love. Life appeared to me very simple, very good, and very easy. I was rich. I had a taste for some things, but had never felt a passion for anything. It was good to live! I awoke happy each day, to do things which it pleased me to do, and I went to bed satisfied with calm hope for the next day and a future without care.

"I had had some mistresses without ever having my heart torn by desire or my soul bruised by love after the possession. It is good so to live. It is better to love, but terrible. Still those who love like everybody else should find happiness, less than mine, perhaps, for love has come to me in an unbelievable manner.

"Being rich, I collected ancient furniture and antiques. Often I thought of the unknown hands which had touched these things, of the eyes that had admired them, and the hearts that had loved them—for one does love such things! I often remained for hours and hours looking at a little watch of the last century. It was so dainty, so pretty with its enamel and gold embossing. And it still went, as on the day when some woman had bought it, delighted in the possession of so fine a jewel. It had not ceased to palpitate, to live its mechanical life, but had ever continued its regular ticktack, although a century had passed. Who then had first carried it upon her breast, in the warmth of the dress — the heart of the watch beating against the heart of the woman? What hand had held it at the ends of its warm fingers, then wiped the enameled shepherds, tarnished a little by the moisture of the skin? What eyes had looked upon this flowered dial awaiting the hour, the dear hour, the divine hour?

"How I wished to see her, to know her, the woman who had chosen this rare and exquisite object. But she is dead! I am possessed by a desire for women of former times; I love all those who have loved long ago. The story of past tenderness fills my heart with regrets. Oh! beauty, the smiles, the caresses of youth, the hopes! These things should be eternal!

"How I have wept, during whole nights, over the women of old, so beautiful, so tender, so sweet, whose lips have opened to the kiss, and who are now dead! The kiss is immortal! It goes form lip to lip, from century to century, from age to age! Men take it and give it and die.

"The past attracts me, the present frightens me, because the future is death. I regret all that which is gone, I weep for those who have lived; I wish to stop the hour, to arrest time. But it goes, it goes, it passes away, and it takes me, from second to second, a little of me for the annihilation of tomorrow. And I shall never live again.

"Adieu, women of yesterday, I love you.

"And yet I have nothing to complain of. I have found her whom I awaited, and I have tasted through her of inconceivable pleasure.

"I was roaming around Paris on a sunny morning, with joyous foot and happy soul, looking in the shops with the vague interest of a stroller. All at once I saw in a shop of antiquities, an Italian piece of furniture of the XVIIth century. It was very beautiful, very rare. I attributed it to a Venetian artist, named Vitelli, who belonged to that epoch. Then I passed along.

"Why did the remembrance of this piece of furniture follow me with so much force that I went back over my steps? I stopped again before the shop to look at it, and felt that it tempted me.

"What a singular thing is temptation! One looks at an object, and, little by little, it seduces you, troubles you, takes possession of you like the face of a woman. Its charm enters into you, a strange charm which comes from its form, its color, and its physiognomy. Already one loves it, wishes it, desires it. A need of possession takes you, a pleasant need at first, because timid, but increasing, becoming violent and irresistible. And the merchants seem to suspect, from the look in the eye, this secret, increasing desire. I bought that piece of furniture and had it carried to my house immediately. I placed it in my room.

"Oh! I pity those who do not know this sweet hobby of the collector with the trinket which he finally buys. He caresses it with his eye and hand as if it were flesh; he returns every moment to it, thinks of it continually, wherever he goes and whatever he may be doing. The thought of it follows him into the street, into the world, everywhere. And when he re-enters his house, before even removing his gloves or his hat, he goes to look at it with the tenderness of a lover.

"Truly, for eight days I adored that piece of furniture. I kept opening its doors and drawers; I handled it with delight and tasted all the intimate joys of possession.

"One evening, in feeling the thickness of a panel, I perceived that there might be a hiding-place there. My heart began to beat and I passed the night in searching out the secret, without being able to discover it.

"I came upon it the next day by forcing a piece of metal into a crevice in the paneling. A shelf slipped, and I saw, exposed upon a lining of black velvet, a marvelous head of hair that had belonged to some woman.

"Yes, a head of hair, an enormous twist of blond hair, also red, which had been cut off near the skin and tied together with a golden cord.

"I stood there stupefied, trembling and disturbed! An almost insensible perfume, so old that it seemed like the soul of an odor, arose from this mysterious drawer and this most surprising relic.

"I took it gently, almost religiously, and lifted it from its resting-place. Immediately it unwound, spreading out its golden billows upon the floor, where it fell, thick and light, supple and brilliant, like the fiery tail of a comet.

"A strange emotion seized me. To whom had this belonged? When? Under what circumstances? Why had it been shut up in this piece of furniture? What adventure, what drama was connected with this souvenir? Who had cut it off? Some lover, on a day of parting? Some husband, on a day of vengeance? Or, perhaps, some woman herself, who bore on her brow the look of despair? Was it at the hour of entering the cloister that she had thrown there this fortune of love, as a token left to the world of the living? Was it the hour closing the tomb upon the young and beautiful dead, that he who adored her took this diadem of her head, the only thing he could preserve of her, the only living part of her body that would not perish, the only thing that he could still love and caress and kiss, in the transport of his grief?

"Was it not strange that this hair should remain there thus, when there was no longer any vestige of the body with which she was born?

"It curled about my fingers and touched my skin with a singular caress, the caress of death. I felt myself affected, as if I were going to weep.

"I kept it a long time in my hands, then it seemed to me that it had some effect upon me, as if something of the soul still remained in it. And I laid it upon the velvet again, the velvet blemished by time, then pushed in the drawer, shut the doors of the closet, and betook myself to the street to dream.

"I walked straight ahead, full of sadness, and full of trouble, of the kind of trouble that remains in the heart after the kiss of love. It seemed to me I had lived in former times, and that I had known this woman.

"And Villon's lines came to my lips, bringing with them a sob:

" 'Tell me in what far-off land
    The Roman beauty, Flora, lives;
Hipparchia, Thais' cousin, and
    All the beauty nature gives;
Echo speak, thy voice awake
Over river, stream, and lake,
Where are beauty's smiles and tears?
And where the snows of other years?

" 'Blanche, as fair as lily's chalice,
    Singing sweet, with voice serene,
Bertha Broadfoot, Beatrice, Alice,
    Ermengarde, Le Mayne's dear
    queen?
Where is Joan, the good Lorraine,
Whom th' English brought to death
    and fame?
Where are all, O wisest seers,
And where the snows of other years?'

"When I returned to my house I had a strange desire to see my strange treasure again. I took it up and felt it, and in touching it a long shiver ran through my body.

"For some days, however, I remained in my ordinary state, although the thought of this hair never left· me. Whenever I came in, it was my first desire to look at it and handle it. I would turn the key of the secretary with the same trembling that one has· in opening the door of his well-beloved, for I had in two hands and in my heart a confused, singular, continued, sensual need of burying my fingers in this charming rivulet of dead hair.

"Then, when I had finished caressing it, when I had returned it to its resting-place, I always felt that it was there, as if it were something alive, concealed, imprisoned; I felt it and I still desired it; again I had the imperious need of touching it, of feeling it, of enervating myself to the point of weariness from contact with this cold, glistening, irritating, exciting, delicious hair.

"I lived thus a' month or two, I know not how long, with this thing possessing me, haunting me. I was happy and tortured, as in the expectation of love, as one is after the avowal which precedes the embrace.

"I would shut myself up alone with it in order to feel it upon my skin, to bury my lips in it, to kill it, and bite it. I would roll it around my face, drink it in, drown my eyes in its golden waves, and finally see the blond life beyond it.

"I loved it! Yes, I loved it. I could no longer live away from it, nor be contented an hour without seeing it. I expected — I expected — what? I know not—her!

"One night I was suddenly awakened with a feeling that I was not alone in my room. I was alone, however. But I could not go to sleep again; and, as I was tossing in the fever of insomnia, I rose and went to look at the twist of hair. It appeared to me sweeter than usual, and more animated.

"Could the dead return? The kisses with which I had warmed it failed to give me happiness, and I carried it to my bed and lay down with it, pressing it to my lips, as one does a mistress he hopes to enjoy.

"The dead returned! She came! ⸺Yes, I saw her, touched her, posesssed her as she was when alive in former times, large, blond, plump, with cool breasts, and with hips in form of a lyre. And I followed that divine, undulating line from the throat to the feet, in all the curves of the flesh with my caresses.

"Yes, I possessed her, every day and every night. She had returned, Death, Death the Beautiful, the Adorable, the Mysterious, the Unknown, and returned every night.

"My happiness was so great that I could not conceal it. I found near her a superhuman delight, and in possessing this Unseizable, Invisible Death, knew a profound, inexplicable joy. No lover ever tasted joys more ardent or more terrible.

"I knew not how to conceal my happiness. I loved this possession so much that I could not bear to leave it. I carried it with me always, everywhere. I walked with it through the city, as if it were my wife, conducting it to the theater and to restaurants as one would a mistress. But they saw it, — and guessed—they took me, and threw me into prison, like a malefactor. They took it away—oh! misery!—"

The manuscript stopped there. And suddenly, as I raised my wondeirng eyes to the doctor, a frightful cry, a howl of fury and exasperated desire filled the asylum.

"Listen," said the doctor, "it is necessary to douse that obscene maniac with water five times a day. It is only Sergeant Bertrand, the man who fell in love with the dead."

I stammered, moved with astonishment, horror, and pity: "But that hair —did it really exist?"

The doctor got up, opened a closet full of vials and instruments, and threw toward me, across his office, a long thick rope of blond hair, which flew toward me like a bird of gold.

I trembled at feeling upon my hands its caressing, light touch. And I stood there, my heart beating with disgust and desire, the disgust we have in coming in contact with objects connected with crimes, and the desire like that which comes with the temptation to test some infamous and mysterious thing.

Shrugging his shoulders, the doctor added: "The mind of man is capable of anything."

Good Reasons

Solles Villa, July 30, 1883.
My dear Lucy:

There is nothing new. We still live in the parlor, looking out to see the rain fall. One can scarcely go out at all in this frightful weather. We can only play comedies. And how stupid they are, my dear, these pieces in a drawing-room repertory. So forced, so heavy, and gross! The jokes are like bullets from a cannon, always hitting some one. Nothing bright, nothing natural, good natured, or elegant. These writers, truly, can know nothing of the world. They are entirely ignorant of how people think or speak among us. I could easily forgive them for scorning our customs or our manners, but I cannot forgive them for being ignorant of them. In order to be pointed, they make a play upon words that a barracks would do well to deride; in order to be gay, they serve us the wit they have culled outside the Boulevard, in the beer-shops of so-called artists, where the same studied paradoxes have been repeated for fifty years.

Yes, we play a comedy. As there are only two women, my husband takes the part of a soubrette, shaving his face for it. You cannot imagine, my dear Lucy, how it changed him! I should not have known him—either by day or night. If he had not allowed his mustache to grow again immediately I believe that I should have become unfaithful, so much did I dislike it.

Truly, a man without a mustache is not a man. I do not care much for a beard; it always gives an appearance of neglect; but the mustache, oh! the mustache is indispensable to a manly physiognomy. No, one never could imagine how useful this little brush of hair upon the lip is to the eye and—to the relation of married people. There have come to me many reflections upon this subject, which I scarcely dare write to you. I could say them to you easily—in a low voice. But it is difficult to find words to express certain things, and some of these, which it would be hard to replace, cut a villainous figure upon paper, so that I can scarcely pen them. Then, the subject is so delicate, so difficult, so awkward, that an infinite knowledge is necessary to approach it without danger.

Well! so much the worse if you do not understand. And now, my dear, try to read a little between the lines.

When my husband came to me shaved, I understood for the first time that I could never have a weakness for a strolling player, nor for a preacher, were he Father Didon himself, the most seductive of all! Then, when I found myself alone with him (my husband), it was much worse.

Oh! my dear Lucy, never allow yourself to be embraced by a man without mustaches; his lips have no taste, none whatever! There is no longer that charm, that softness, and that—pepper, yes, that pepper of the true kiss. The mustache is the spice of it.

Imagine a piece of dry, or even humid parchment applied to your lips. That is the caress of the shaven man. One wants very few of them, assuredly.

But whence comes the seduction of the mustache, you ask me? How do I know? At first it tickles in delicious fashion. One feels it before the mouth and it makes a charming shiver pass through the whole body, even to the tips of the toes. It is that which ca-resses, which makes the flesh tremble and start, which gives the nerves that exquisite vibration and causes the utterance of that little "ah!" as if one had received a sudden chill.

And upon the neck! Yes, have you never felt a mustache upon your neck? It intoxicates and makes you shiver, runs down your back and to the ends of your fingers. You turn, shake your shoulders, twist your head; you wish to go and to stay; it is adorable yet irritating! But it is good!

And then again—truly, do I dare say more? A husband who loves you, yes, entirely, knows how to find spots and little corners for concealing kisses, little corners one would scarcely dream of alone. Well, without a mustache these kisses lose much of their zest, without saying that they are unbecoming! Explain that as you will! For my part, here is the reason I find for it. A lip without mustaches is bare, like a body without clothes; and it is necessary to have clothes, very few if you wish, but still some!

The Creator (I dare not use any other word in speaking of these things), the Creator saw the need of veiling the nooks of our flesh where love is concealed. A shaven mouth appears to me to resemble a forest, cut down, which sheltered a fountain where one came to drink and sleep.

This recalls to me the saying of a political man, which has been in my head for three months now. My husband, who reads the newspapers, read a very singular thing to me one evening, by our Minister of Agriculture, who was then called M. Meline. Is there another one by this time? I am sure I do not know.

I was not listening, but this name, Meline, struck me. It recalled, I know not why, "Scenes of Bohemian Life." I believed at once that he lived with a *grisette*. Only certain scraps of this piece entered my head. But M. Meline made to the inhabitants of Amiens, I believe, this statement, the meaning of which I have sought until now: "There is no patriotism without agriculture!" Well, this means, I have found out recently, and now declare to you in my turn, that there is no love without a mustache. If one should tell him that, it would seem strange, would it not?

There is no love without a mustache!

"There is no patriotism without agriculture," asserts M. Meline; he is right, this minister, I know it now!

From another point of view the mustache is essential. It determines the physiognomy. It gives it a sweet, tender, violent, foolish, rakish, or enterprising air! The bearded man, really bearded, he who carries all his hair (oh! villainous word) upon his cheeks never has any delicacy of expression, because his features are concealed. And the form of the jaw and the chin show many things to him who can see.

In a mustache, a man preserves at the same time his attraction and his finesse. And of what varied appearance they are, these mustaches! Some are curved, curled, and coquettish. These seem to love women above all things!

Some are pointed, sharp as a needle, wicked. These have a preference for wine, horses, and fights.

Some are enormous, drooping, frightful. These great ones generally conceal an excellent character, a goodness that approaches weakness and a gentleness that borders on timidity.

And then, above all else, why I adore a mustache is because it is French. It has descended to us from our fathers, the Gauls, and has continued as a sign of our national character.

It is romantic, gallant, and brave. It dips itself daintily in wine and knows how to laugh with elegance, while large bearded jaws are heavy in all that they do.

Wait! I recall something which made me weep bitter tears, and which also made me love a mustache upon a man's lip, as I now plainly see.

It was during the war, when I was at home in papa's house. I was a young girl then. One day there was a battle near the house. Since morning I had heard cannons and guns and, in the evening, a German colonel entered our house and installed himself there. He went away the next day. They came to tell my father that there had been many deaths on the field. He went to find them and bring them home, in order to bury them together. They laid them all along the avenue of pines, on both sides, from the stretcher on which they brought them. And, as they commenced to smell badly, they threw some earth on the bodies to await the digging of the great ditch. In this way only their heads were to be seen, which seemed to come up out of the soil, yellow as the soil itself, with their eyes closed.

I wished to see them; but when I perceived these two lines of frightful faces, I thought it would make me ill. I began to examine them, however, one by one, seeking to find out to what nation they belonged. Their uniforms were buried, concealed by the earth, but immediately, yes, immediately, my dear, I recognized them as Frenchmen by their mustaches!

Some had been shaved the day of the battle, as if wishing to be attractive to the last moment! Their beard, nevertheless, had grown a little, for you know it grows a little even after death. Others seemed to have gone a week without shaving; but all wore the French mustache, distinctly, the proud mustache which seemed to say: "Do not confound me with my bearded friend, little one, I am your brother."

And I wept, oh! I wept more than if I had not thus recognized them, the poor dead men!

I did wrong to tell you this story. Here I am now, sad and incapable of chatting any more. Adieu, then, my dear Lucy; I embrace you with all my heart. Long live the mustache!

JEANNE.

Submitted to GUY DE MAUPASSANT.

A Fair Exchange

M. BONTRAM, the celebrated Parisian advocate who for the last ten years had obtained many separations between badly matched husbands and wives, opened the door of his office and stood back to allow a new client to enter.

He was a large, red man, with close, blond whiskers, a corpulent man, full-blooded and vigorous. He bowed.

"Take a seat," said the advocate.

The client was seated and, after some hemming, said:

"I came to ask you, sir, to plead a divorce case for me."

"Speak, sir," said the advocate, "I am listening."

"I am, sir, an old notary."

"Already!"

"Yes, already. I am thirty-seven years of age."

"Continue."

"Sir, I have made an unfortunate marriage, very unfortunate."

"You are not the only one."

"I know it, and I pity the others. But my case is entirely different, and my complaint against my wife is of a very particular nature. I will commence at the marriage rite. I was married in strange fashion. Do you believe in dangerous ideas?"

"What do you mean by that?"

"Do you believe that certain ideas are as dangerous for the mind as poison is to the body?"

"Well, yes, perhaps."

"It is certain. There are ideas which enter into us, corrode us, and kill us or render us mad, if we do not know how to resist them. They are a sort of poison to the soul. If we have the misfortune to allow one of these thoughts to glide in upon us, if we do not perceive at the beginning that it is an invader, a mistress, a tyrant, then it will extend itself hour by hour and day by day, will keep returning and finally install itself, driving out all ordinary occupation of our minds, absorbing our attention, changing our views and our judgment until we are lost.

"That is what happened to me, sir. As I have told you, I am a notary at Rouen, not poor but in straitened circumstances, full of care, forced to a constant economy, obliged to limit my tastes, yes, in everything! And it is hard, at my age.

"As a notary, I read, with great care, the advertisements on four pages of the newspapers, the wants, offers, little correspondence, etc., etc., and I had been enabled sometimes by this means to make advantageous marriages for my clients.

One day, I fell upon this:

"'A pretty girl, fashionable, well brought up, would marry honorable gentleman and bring him two million five hundred thousand francs, clear. No agencies.'

"On that very day I dined with two friends, one an attorney and the other the proprietor of a spinning mill. I don't know how the conversation turned to marriages, but I told them, laughing, about the pretty young lady with the two million five hundred thousand francs.

"The spinner said: 'What can these women be thinking of?'

"The attorney affirmed that he had several times seen excellent marriages made under these conditions, and gave some details. Then he added, turning to me: 'Why the devil don't you look this up for yourself? Jove! that would drive away care, two million five hundred thousand francs.'

"We all three laughed over it and then spoke of other things. An hour later I returned home.

"It grew cold that night. Besides, I lived in an old house, one of those old houses of the provinces which resemble mushroom-beds. In taking hold of the iron balustrade of the staircase, a coldness penetrated my arm, and as I put out the other to find the wall, in coming in contact with it, a second shiver enveloped me, joining with the other in my lungs, filling me with pain, with sadness, and weakness. And, seized by a sudden remembrance, I murmured: 'Gad! if I only had the two million five hundred thousand!'

"My room was dreary, the room of a bachelor in Rouen, which is taken care of by a maid who is also in charge of the kitchen. You know that kind of room! A great bed without curtains, a wardrobe, a commode, and a dressing table; no fire. Some coats were on the chairs, papers on the floor. I began to sing, to the air of a concert-hall tune that I frequently heard about that time:

> "'Two millions, two millions
>   Are fine,
> With five hundred thousand
>   And woman divine.'

"In fact I had not yet thought about the woman, but I thought of her then as I was sliding into my bed. I even thought of her so much that I was a long time getting to sleep.

"The next day, on opening my eyes, I remembered that I ought to be at Darnetal at eight o'clock on important business. To do this I must be up at six—and it was cold! Only think of two million five hundred thousand!

"I returned to my study about ten o'clock. In it was the odor of the red-hot stove, of old papers, with the papers of advance proceedings,—nothing can equal these,—and an odor of clerks —boots, overcoats, hair, and skin, skin in winter, too little bathed, and all heated to seventy degrees.

"I breakfasted, as I do every day, on a cutlet and a piece of cheese. Then I put myself to work. For the first time, I then began to think seriously of the pretty young lady with the two million five hundred thousand. Who was she? Why not write to her? Why not find out?

"Finally, sir, to abridge, for two weeks this idea haunted me, possessed me, and tortured me. All my little cares and troubles, of which I had plenty but had thought little about before this time, began to sting me now like the sharp points of needles, and each of my sufferings made me think still more of the pretty young lady with the two millions.

"I ended by imagining all her history. When one desires a thing, sir, he is very apt to figure it as he hopes it to be. Certainly it was not natural that a young girl of good family, dowered in such a generous fashion, should be seeking a husband by means of the newspapers. Yet, it might be that this girl was honorable but unhappy.

"Then, at first this fortune of two million five hundred thousand had not struck me as anything fairylike. We are accustomed, we who read the offers of this nature, to propositions of marriage accompanied by six, eight, ten, or even twelve millions. The figure of twelve millions is common enough. It pleases.

I know well that we can scarcely believe the validity of these promises. They, however, make us enter into the spirit of fantastic numbers, render probable, up to a certain point in our listless credulity, the prodigious sums which they represent and dispose us to consider a dowry of two million five hundred thousand as very possible and right.

"Then a young girl, the natural child of a rich man and a chambermaid, having suddenly inherited from her father, could have learned at the same time of the stain upon her birth, and in order not to have to reveal it to some man whom she might have loved, she might make an appeal to the unknown by this means, which carries in itself a sort of avowal of defect.

"My supposition was stupid. I believed in it, nevertheless. We notaries ought never to read romances, but I read one in this, sir.

"Then I wrote, as a notary, in the name of a client, and I waited. Five days later, toward three o'clock in the afternoon, when I was hard at work in my office, the chief clerk announced:

" 'Mlle. Chantefrise.'

" 'Let her come in.'

"There appeared a woman about thirty, a little stout, dark, and somewhat embarrassed.

" 'Be seated, Mademoiselle.'

"She sat down, and murmured: 'It is I, sir.'

" 'But I have not the honor of knowing you.'

" 'The person to whom you wrote.'

" 'About a marriage?'

" 'Yes, sir.'

" 'Ah! very well!'

" 'I have come myself because I thought it better to attend to those things in person.'

" 'I am of your opinion, Mademoiselle. And so you desire to marry?'

" 'Yes, sir.'

" 'You have some family?'

"She hesitated, lowered her eyes, and stammered: 'No, sir. My mother and my father—are dead.'

"I started. Then I had guessed right —and a lively sympathy was suddenly awakened in my heart for this poor creature. I could not altogether spare her delicacy of feeling and I inquired:

" 'Your fortune is in your own right?'

"She responded this time without hesitating: 'Oh! yes, sir!'

"I looked at her with close attention and truly she did not displease me, only a little hard, harder than I would have liked. She was a beautiful person, a strong person, a masterly woman. And the idea came to me of playing with her a little comedy of sentiment, of becoming her lover, of supplanting my imaginary client, when I was once assured that the dowry was not illusory. I spoke to her of this client whom I depicted as a sad man, very honorable, but a little of an invalid.

"She said vivaciously: 'Oh! sir, I love people to be well.'

" 'But you will see him—only not for three or four days, because he left for England yesterday.'

" 'Oh! how annoying,' she replied.

" 'Well, yes and no. Are you in a hurry to return home?'

" 'Not at all.'

" 'Then stay here, and I will attempt to make the time pass pleasantly for you.'

" 'You are very amiable, sir.'

" 'You are at some hotel?'

"She named the best hotel in Rouen.

" 'Well, then, Madmoiselle Chantefrise, will you permit your future— notary to offer to take you to dinner this evening?'

"She appeared to hesitate, seemed disturbed, and undecided. Then she said: 'Yes, sir.'

" 'I will be at your hotel at seven o'clock.'

" 'Yes, sir.'

" 'Then until this evening, Mademoiselle?'

" 'Yes, sir.'

"And I conducted her as far as my door.

"At seven o'clock I was at her hotel. She had made a fresh toilette for me and received me in a very coquettish fashion. I took her to dine in a restaurant where I was known and ordered a troublesome *menu*. An hour later we were very friendly and she had told me her story.

"She was the daughter of a great lady seduced by a gentleman, and she had been brought up among peasants. She was rich now, having inherited large sums from her father and from her mother, whose name she would never divulge, never. It was useless to ask it of her, useless to beg, she would never tell it. As I cared little to know these things, I asked about her fortune. She spoke about it like a practical woman, sure of herself, sure of her figures, of her titles, of her income, her interest, and investments. Her understanding of these matters gave me great confidence in her, and I became gallant, with some reserve, nevertheless. But I showed her clearly that I had a liking for her.

"She affected an excessive refinement, not without grace. I offered her some champagne, and I drank some, which blurred my ideas. I then felt clearly that I was going to be entrapped, and I was afraid, afraid of myself and afraid of her, afraid that she was not moved and that she would not succumb. In order to calm myself, I began again to speak to her of her fortune, saying that it would be necessary to precisely understand matters, since my client was a man of affairs.

"She answered with gaiety: 'Oh! I know. I have brought all the proofs.'

" 'Here, to Rouen?'

" 'Yes, to Rouen.'

" 'You have them at the hotel?'

" 'Yes, I have them all there.'

" 'Could you show them to me?'

" 'Yes, indeed.'

" 'This evening?'

" 'Yes, indeed.'

"That pleased me in every way. I paid the score and we went back to the hotel. She had, in fact, brought all her certificates. I could not doubt them, for I held them in my hands, felt them, and read them. They put such a joy in my heart that I suddenly felt a violent desire to embrace her. I understood this as a chaste desire, the desire of a contented man. And I did embrace her, in fact, once, twice, ten times—so much that—with the aid of the champagne—I succumbed—or rather—no—she succumbed.

"Ah! sir, I had a head after that, and she! She wept like a fountain, begging me not to expose her or she should be lost. I promised all that she wished, and I myself got into a terrible state of mind.

"What was to be done? I had abused my client's confidence. That would not have been so bad if I had had a client for her, but I had none. I was the client, the simple client, the deceived client, and deceived by herself. What a situation! I could let her go, it is true. But the dowry, the handsome dowry, the good dowry, palpable and sure! And then, had I the right to let her go, the poor girl, after having thus surprised her? But what of the disquiet later on? How much security would one have with a woman who thus yielded?

"I passed a terrible night of indecision, tortured by remorse, ravaged by fears, buffeted by every scruple. But in the morning, my reason cleared. I dressed myself with care, and, as eleven o'clock struck, presented myself at the hotel where she was staying.

"On seeing me, she blushed to the eyes. I said to her: 'Mademoiselle Chantefrise, there is only one thing to do to repair our wrong. I ask your hand in marriage.'

"She murmured: 'I give it to you.'

"I married her and all went well for six months. I had given up my office and lived as a stockholder, and truly I had not a reproach, not a single fault to find with my wife.

"Then I noticed that, from time to time, she made long visits. This happened on a certain day, one week Tuesday, the next week Wednesday. I began to believe myself deceived and I followed her. It was on a Tuesday. She went out on foot about one o'clock into Republic street, turned to the right, by the street which follows the archiepiscopal palace, and took Great-Bridge street to the Seine, followed the wharf up to Peter's bridge and crossed the water. From this moment she appeared disturbed, turning around often and looking sharply at all passers.

"As I was dressed like a coal driver she did not know me. Finally, she entered a dock on the left bank. I no longer doubted that her lover would arrive on the one-forty-five train.

"I seated myself behind a dray and waited. A blow of the whistle—a crowd of passengers. She advanced, rushed forward, seized in her arms a little girl of three years, whom a large peasant accompanied, and embraced her with passion. Then she turned, perceived another child, younger, either girl or boy, it might be, carried by another nurse, threw herself upon it, drew it to her with violence, and went along escorted by the two monkeys and the two nurses toward the long, somber, deserted promenade of the Queen's Course.

"I returned home dismayed, distressed in mind, comprehending and still not comprehending, nor daring to guess. When she returned for dinner, I threw these words at her:

"'Whose children are those?'

"'What children?' she asked.

"'Those that you waited at the Saint-Sever train for.'

"She gave a great cry and fainted. When she returned to consciousness she confessed to me, in a deluge of tears, that she had four. Yes, sir, two for Tuesday, two girls, and two for Wednesday, two boys.

"And this was—what shame! this was the origin of her fortune. The four fathers! She had amassed her dowry! Now sir, what do you advise me to do?"

The advocate replied with gravity: "Recognize your children, sir."

The Tobacco Shop

I WENT down to Barviller alone because I saw in the guidebook (I do not remember which one): "A beautiful museum, two Rubens, one Tenier, and a Ribera." I thought to myself: "I will see that. Then I will dine at the Hotel Europe, which the guidebook affirms excellent, and return to-morrow."

The museum was closed. They only opened it at the request of travelers. It was opened for my benefit and I was able to look upon some daubs attributed by a whimsical collector to the first masters of painting.

After that, I found myself alone with absolutely nothing to do. I was in a long street of a little unknown town, a kind of artery, through which I wandered, examining some of the poor little shops. I found it was only four o'clock, and I was suddenly seized with that feeling of discouragement which makes simpletons of the most energetic.

What could I do? Great heavens! what was there to do? I would have paid five hundred francs for some distracting idea. Finding myself barren of invention, I simply decided to smoke a good cigar, and looked about for a tobacco shop. I soon recognized one by its red lantern and entered it. The saleswoman held out several boxes for me to choose from. Having looked carefully at the cigars, all of which appeared detestable, I turned by chance and glanced at the proprietress.

She was a woman of about forty-five, strong and gray-haired. She had a fat, respectable face, in which I seemed to see something familiar. Could I have known this woman somewhere; No, assuredly not. But it might be that I had seen her somewhere? Yes, that was possible. The face before me must be an acquaintance of my eyes, some old acquaintance lost to sight and, without doubt, changed by being enormously fattened.

I murmured: "Excuse, me, Madame, for looking at you so closely, but it seems to me that I have seen you before, long ago."

She responded, blushing a little: "It is strange—but I also—"

I exclaimed: "Ah! so it goes!"

She raised both hands in a comical despair, frightened by the sound of the old name, and stammered: "Oh! oh!— if anyone should hear you—" Then suddenly she cried out, in her turn: "Wait! It is you—George!?" Then she looked around in terror to see if anyone were listening. But we were alone, all alone!

"So-it-Goes!" How had I ever recognized her! "So-it-Goes," the poor "So-it-Goes," the thin, the desolate "So-it-Goes," transformed into this fat, tranquil functionary of the government?

"So-it-Goes!" How many memories this name awakened in me: Bougival, "The Frog," Chatou, the Fournaise restaurant, long journeys in a yawl along the steep banks, in short, ten years of my life, passed in that corner of the country, upon that delicious part of the river.

There was a band of a dozen of us inhabiting the Galopois house, at Chatou, living a queer kind of life, half nude and half tipsy. The customs of canoeists have changed since then. Now, these gentlemen wear monocles.

Our band was composed of twenty canoeists, regular and irregular. On certain Sundays there would only be four of them, on others, all. That is to say, some there were there to stay, others came when they had nothing better to do. Five or six of them lived together, after the fashion of men without wives, and among them dwelt "So-it-Goes."

She was a poor, thin girl who limped. This gave her some of the attractions of a grasshopper. She was timid, awkward, and unskillful in all that she did. With fear, she attached herself to the humblest, the most unnoticed of us, anyone who would keep her a day or a month, according to his means. How she ever came to be among us, nobody knew. Some one had met her one evening at poker-dice, at a riverside ball, and had been led into one of those raffles for wives that were so much the fashion. We invited her to lunch, seeing her seated alone at a little table in the corner. No one could have asked her, but she made a part of our band.

We baptized her "So-it-Goes" (*Ça Ira*), because she was already complaining of her destiny, of her misfortune, and her sorrows. Each Sunday morning they would say to her: "Well, 'So-it-Goes,' how goes it?" And she would always answer: "Not so bad, but we must always hope that it will be better some day."

How this poor, ungraceful, awkward being came to adopt the trade which demands the most grace, tact, cleverness, and beauty, was a mystery. However, Paris is full of girls of love that are ugly enough to disgust a policeman.

What did she do the other six days of the week? She told us many times that she worked. At what? We were as ignorant of it as we were indifferent to her existence.

After that, I nearly lost sight of her. Our group had dispersed, little by little, leaving its place to another generation, to whom we also left *"Ça Ira."* I heard of her in going to breakfast at the Fournaise from time to time.

Our successors, not knowing why we had christened her as we did, believed her name to be Oriental and called her Zaïra; then they bestowed her, with all their canoes and some of the canoeists, to the following generation. (A generation of canoeists generally lives three years upon the water, then leaves the Seine to enter the law, medicine, or politics.)

Zaïra had now become Zara, and later Zara was modified into Sarah. Then they thought she was an Israelite.

The last ones, those with the monocles, called her simply "the Jewess." Then she disappeared. And behold! I had found her in Barviller, selling tobacco.

I said to her: "Well, how goes it now?"

She answered: "A little better."

I had a curiosity to know the life of this woman. At any other time I would not have cared; to-day I felt interested, puzzled, attracted. I asked her: "How did you come to get this place?"

"I don't know," said she, "it came to me when I was expecting the least."

"Was it at Chatou that you came upon it?"

"Oh! no."

"Then where?"

"At Paris, in a hotel where I lived."

"Ah! then you had a place in Paris?"

"Yes, I was with Madame Ravelet."

"Who is she, this Madame Ravelet?"

"And you don't know who Madame Ravelet is? Well!"

"No, I do not."

"The dressmaker, the great dress-maker of Rivoli street."

And then she told me a thousand things of her former life, a thousand things of the secret life of the Parisian woman, the interior workings of a great dressmaking establishment, the life of the young ladies there, their adventures, their ideas, the whole story of the heart of a working girl, that sparrow-hawk of the sidewalk who haunts the streets—in the morning in going to the shop, at midday, strolling along bareheaded after her luncheon, and in the evening when she comes out to show herself.

Happy to speak of other days, she said: "You don't know what a mob it is, nor what raids they make. We used to tell each other about them every day. Truly one can make a fool of a man, you know.

"The first tale I have to tell is on the subject of an umbrella. I had an old alpaca one, an umbrella to be ashamed of. As I was closing it upon my arrival one day, there was the tall Louise before me, saying:

" 'What! You dare to go out with that?"

" 'But I have no other, and at this moment funds are low.'

"They were always low, funds were.

"She said to me: 'Go and get one at the Madeleine.'

"I was astonished. She continued: 'That is where we all get ours; one can get all one wants there.' And then she explained the thing to me. It was very simple.

"I went with Irma to the Madeleine. We found the sexton and explained to him how we had forgotten an umbrella the week before. He asked us to describe the handle and I gave him a description of a handle with an agate apple on it. He took us into a room where there were more than fifty lost umbrellas; we looked them all over but I did not find mine; I had, however, chosen a beauty, a perfect beauty with a carved ivory handle. A few days after, Louise went and reclaimed it. She described it before seeing it, and he gave it to her without a suspicion.

"In order to do that sort of thing, one has to dress very stylish."

And she laughed, opening the cover of a large box of tobacco and letting it fall again upon its hinges. She continued:

"Oh! we each had our turn at it and we did have some queer experiences. There were five of us living in the studio, four ordinaries and one very pretty, Irma, the beautiful Irma. She was very distinguished; as she had a lover in the Cabinet Council, but that did not hinder her from making him support her prettily. And one winter she said to us: 'You don't know what a way I have thought of to make a good thing?' And she told us her idea.

"You know, Irma had such a face to trouble the heads of all men, and such a figure! and hips that would make the water come in your mouth. So she thought of a way for each of us to make a hundred francs to buy some rings with, and she arranged the thing like this:

"You must know that I was not rich at that moment, any more than the others; and we were scarcely making a hundred francs in a month at the shop, certainly not more. We wished to know her plan. We each had two or three lovers who gave a little, but not much; and it sometimes happened that in the noonday walk we nabbed a gentleman who would come the next day; we would keep him for two weeks and then give him up. Such men as that never give very much. Those at Chatou—that was for pleasure. Oh! if you only knew some of the sly things we did; truly you would die from laughter. So, when Irma proposed to us to make a hundred francs, we were all on fire. It is very bad, what I am going to tell you, but that makes no difference; you know what life is, and when one has stayed four years at Chatou—

"Well, she said to us: 'At the Opera Ball, we are going to get hold of some of the best men in Paris, the most distinguished and the richest. I know who they are.'

"We did not believe it at first; because such men are not made for dressmakers; for Irma, yes, but not for us. Oh! she was so stylish, that Irma! Do you know, we had the habit at the studio of saying that if the Emperor had seen her, he would certainly have married her.

"She made us dress ourselves in our best, and said to us: 'You, none of you will enter the ballroom, but will stay outside in cabs in the neighboring streets. A gentleman will come and get into your carriage. When he has entered, you will embrace him as prettily as you can; and then, you will utter a great cry to show that you have made a mistake and that you expected some one else. This will excite the pigeon to take the place of another, and he will try to remain by force; you will resist, you will give him a hundred blows to drive him away—and then— you will go to supper with him—and you ought to get good damages.'

"You do not quite understand it yet, do you? Well, here is what she did, the rogue!

"She made all four of us get into carriages, four carriages of the circle, that were just as they should be, then she placed us in streets near the Opera. She went to the ball alone. As she knew by name the most conspicuous men in Paris, because our establishment catered to their wives, she chose them for her intrigue. She could talk with them about anything, for she had a mind also. When she saw that one was half drunk, she threw off her mask, and he was taken as in a net. He wished to take her away immediately, but she preferred to make an appointment with him in half an hour, in a carriage opposite

No. 20 Taitbout street. It was I who was in that carriage! I was well wrapped up and my face veiled. Suddenly a gentleman put his head in the door and asked: "Is it you?'

"And I answered in a low tone: 'Yes, it is I; get in quickly.'

"He does so and I seize him in my arms and embrace him, until his breath is almost gone; then I say:

" 'Oh! I am so happy! I am so happy!'

"But suddenly I cry out: 'But it is not you! Oh! dear! oh! dear!' And I begin to weep.

"You can judge whether the man is embarrassed or not! He tries to console me; he excuses himself and protests that he is also mistaken. As for me, I keep on weeping, but less and less; and I utter great sighs. Then he says very sweet things to me.

"He was a man that was a man; and it pleased him to see me weeping less and less. To put a short thread in the needle, he proposed to take me to supper. I refused; I tried to leap from the carriage; he held me by taking me around the waist; then he embraced me, as I had him upon his entrance.

"And then— and then—we had supper—you understand—and he gave me —think of it—he gave me five hundred francs! Would you believe that there are such generous men?

"And the thing was a success for everybody. Louise, who received the least, got two hundred francs. But you know, Louise—truly, she was very thin!"

The woman of the tobacco shop went on thus, emptying her heart of all the memories amassed in the long time that she had been shut up with her official duties. The past, poor and queer though it was, moved her soul. She regretted this gallant, Bohemian life of the Parisian sidewalk, made up of privations and paid-for caresses, of laughter and misery, and moments of stratagem and true love.

I said to her: "But how did you get into the tobacco business?"

She smiled, saying: "Oh! that is a story, too. You must know that I had for a neighbor in my apartment, exactly opposite my door, a student—but one of those students who amount to nothing. This one lived at the *café* from morning until evening; he loved billiards, as I have never seen anyone love the game.

"When I was alone, we sometimes passed the evening together. It is by him that I had Roger."

"Who is Roger?"

"My son."

"Ah!"

"He—he gave me a little pension for the boy's education, but I did not think that man would ever amount to anything, as I had never seen a man so idle, never. At the end of ten years, he was still in his first examinations. When his family saw that he would do nothing, they called him home to the provinces; but we remained in correspondence on account of the child. And then, imagine at the last elections, two years ago, I learned that he had been made a deputy in his county. And then he made some speeches in the Assembly. Truly, in a kingdom of blind men, as the saying is—But, to finish, I went to find him, and immediately he obtained this tobacco business for me, as the daughter of an exile—It is true my father was exiled, but I never thought of this fact serving me in any way.

"Briefly—wait! here is Roger."

A tall, young man entered, grave, correct, and proper.

He kissed his mother on the brow and she said: "This, sir, is my son, head-clerk at the mayor's office. You know, he may be a future subprefect."

I saluted this functionary in a worthy manner, and went back to my hotel, after having pressed with gravity the extended hand of "So-it-Goes."

A Poor Girl

YES, the memory of that evening can never be effaced. For half an hour I had the sinister sensation of invincible fatality; I had the same shivers that one has in descending the shaft of a mine. I touched the black depths of human misery; I seemed to comprehend fully how impossible an honest life is under some conditions.

It was just past midnight. I was going from the Vaudeville to Drouot street, following a crowd on the Boulevard, all carrying umbrellas. A deluge of water poured rather than fell, veiling the gas jets and giving the street a sad appearance. The sidewalk glittered, more sticky than wet. The mass of people pressed on, seeing nothing.

Girls, with skirts raised, showed their ankles, allowing a white stocking to peep out in the dim nocturnal light, and waited in shadowed doorways. Some called to and some, bolder, jostled the passers, pronouncing in their ears two obscene, stupid words. They would follow a man some seconds, and push against him, breathing in his face their putrid breath. Then, seeing their beguilements useless, they would leave him with an abrupt, discontented motion and start on again, swinging their hips.

I went along, spoken to by all, taken by the sleeve, harassed and moved with disgust. Suddenly, I saw three of them running as if frightened, talking to each other in rapid fashion. Others also began to run, to flee, holding their robes with both hands, in order to run more quickly. That day a blow had been given to the network of prostitution.

All at once I felt an arm under mine, while a terrified voice murmured in my ear: "Save me, sir, save me; do not leave me."

I looked at the girl. She was not twenty years old, yet faded already. I said to her: "Remain with me." And she murmured: "Oh! thank you!"

We arrived at the line of agents. She disclosed herself in order to let me pass. I met her farther on in Drouot street.

My companion asked: "Will you come home with me?"

"No."

"Why not? You have rendered me a service that I shall not forget."

I answered, so not to embarrass her: "Because I am married."

"What difference does that make?"

"You see, my child, that is sufficient.

I have helped you out of your difficulty, leave me quietly now."

The street was deserted and dark, truly unpleasant. And this woman, who held me by the arm, rendered more frightful still the sensation of sadness which enveloped me. She wished to embrace me. I recoiled with horror. And in a hard voice she said: "Once, for peace, won't you?"

And she made a movement of rage, then abruptly began to sob. I stood lost in wonder, not quite comprehending. Finally I said:

"Tell me, what is the matter with you?"

She murmured through her tears: "If you only knew it, it is not gay, this isn't."

"What is not gay?"

"This kind of life."

"Why have you chosen it, then?"

"It was not my fault."

"Whose fault was it?"

"I know whose, I do."

A kind of interest in this abandoned creature took me and I said:

"Tell me your story."

And she told it to me.

"I was sixteen years old and in service at Yvetot at the house of Mr. Lerable, a grain dealer. My parents were dead. I had no one. I saw, of course, that my master looked at me in a queer way, and that he pinched my cheeks; and I had not long to ask myself what he meant. I knew things, certainly. In the country, one is sharpened. But Mr. Lerable was old and devout, going to mass every Sunday. I somehow never believed him capable! But the day came when he wished to take me in my kitchen. I resisted him, but it was done.

"There was opposite us a grocer, Mr. Dunstan, who had a very pleasant boy in his shop; so much so that I allowed myself to be cajoled by him. That happens to everybody, does it not? I would leave the door open evenings that he might come in.

"But one night M. Lerable heard some noise. He went up and found Antoine and tried to kill him. It was a battle with chairs, jugs of water, and everything. As for me, I found my courage and fled into the street. That was how I started out.

"I was afraid, afraid of the world. But I dressed myself under a doorway and began to walk straight on. I believed of a truth that some one had been killed and that the policemen were after me already. I reached the highway to Rouen. I told myself that at Rouen I should be concealed well enough.

"It was so dark I could not see the ditches, and I heard the dogs barking on the farms. Do you know all the things one hears at night? There are birds that cry like a man being murdered, beasts that yap and beasts that whistle, and many other things that I do not understand. I was all goose flesh. Each step I made the sign of the cross. One cannot imagine how the heart can be helped by that. When the day appeared, the idea of the policemen always took me by force, and I ran all that I could. Then I tried to calm myself.

"I felt hungry, all the same, in spite of my fear; but I had not anything, not one sou, for I had forgotten my money, all that I had on earth, which was

eighteen francs. So I was obliged to walk with an empty stomach.

"It was hot. The sun burned. Midday was past, and I kept going on. Suddenly I heard some horses behind me. I turned to look. The mounted policemen! My blood gave a leap; I thought I should fall; but I went on. They would catch me. They were looking at me now. Then one of them, the elder said:

" 'Good day, Mademoiselle.'

" 'Good day, sir.'

" 'Where are you going to?'

" 'I am going to Rouen, in service at a place that has been offered me.'

" 'Walking, like this?'

" 'Yes, walking.'

"My heart beat, sir, so that I could say no more. I kept thinking to myself: 'Now they will take me.' And I had such a desire to run that my legs danced. But they would have caught me immediately, you see.

"The old one began: 'We can journey together as far as Barantin, Mademoiselle, since we are taking the same route.'

" 'With pleasure, sir,' I said.

"And we chatted a little. I made myself as pleasant as I could, you see; so much so that they believed what was not so. Then, as we passed into a wood, the old one said: 'Would you like to stop and rest a little on this moss?'

"And I, without thinking, said: 'As you wish, sir.'

"Then he dismounted and gave his horse to the other, and we two went away in the wood. There was nothing to be said. What could you have done in my place? He took what he wished and then said to me: 'It won't do to forget the comrade.'

"He returned to the horses and the other rejoined me. I was so much ashamed that I could have wept, sir. But I dared not resist, you understand. Then we went on our way. I could speak no more, I had too much grief in my heart. And then I could no longer walk, I was so hungry. But in the village they gave me a glass of wine, which gave me new force for some time. And then they took to the trot, so not to go through Barantin in my company. And I seated myself by a ditch and wept until I had no more tears.

"I walked then for three hours more before reaching Rouen. It was seven o'clock in the evening when I arrived there. At first all the lights dazzled me. And then, I did not know where I could sit down to rest. On the way there were the ditches and the grass where I could even lie down and sleep. But in the city, nothing.

"My limbs refused to hold my body, and I felt as if I were going to fall. And then it began to rain, a little fine rain, like this evening, which goes through you without your knowing it. I have no luck when it rains. I commenced to walk the streets. I looked at all the houses, saying to myself: 'There are beds and bread in there; but I cannot find as much as a crust or a bed of straw.'

"I went through some streets where women were speaking to men along the way. In such cases, sir, one must do what one can. I took my place with the others, inviting everybody. But no one answered me. I wished I was dead.

This must have been near midnight. I no longer knew what I did. Finally, a man listened to me. He asked me: 'Where do you live? Some kind of ruse was necessary, and I answered: 'I cannot take you to my house for I live with mamma. But are there not some houses where we could go?'

"He answered. 'It is not often that I spend twenty sous for a room.' Then he added: 'Come along. I know a quiet spot where we shall not be interrupted.'

"He made me pass over a bridge, then led me to the end of the town, into a meadow near the river. I could do nothing but follow him. He made me sit down and then began to ask why we had come there. As he was long in his affair, I found myself so worn out with fatigue that I fell asleep. He went away without giving me anything. I could not see a single step. Since that day I have had troubles that I can never be cured of, because I slept all that night in the wet.

"I was awakened by two officers who took me to the station house and then to prison, where I stayed eight days, while they tried to find out who I was and where I had come from. I would not tell for fear of the consequences. They found out, however, and released me, after a verdict of innocence.

"Then it was necessary for me to make my living. I tried to find a place, but I could not because I had come out of prison. Then I recalled the old judge, who had a turn to his eye, while he was judging me, like that of father Lerable of Yvetot. And I went to find him. I was not deceived. He gave me a hundred sous when I left him saying: ' You shall have as much every time; but don't come too often; not more than twice a week.' I understood that well, because of his age. But it gave me a reflection: I said to myself: 'Young people make merry and amuse themselves, but they are never fat, while with the old it is the other way.' And since then I can always tell them, these old apes with their eyes in a groove and a little ghost of a head.

"Do you know what I did, sir? I dressed up like a country girl who had come to market and I walked the streets for my living. Oh! I could pinch them at the first blow. I would say to myself: 'Here is one who will bite.' He would approach. And then commence:

" 'Good day, Mademoiselle.'

" 'Good day, sir.'

" 'Where are you going, like this?'

" 'I am returning home to master's.'

" 'Do they live far, your people?'

" 'Rather far, but not so very.'

"Then he would not know what to say, and I would make my step a little slower to allow him to explain. Then he would give me some compliments, in a low voice, and then ask me to go home with him. I would refuse at first, you understand, and then yield. I had two or three of that sort each morning, and all my afternoons free. That was

the good time of my life. I was not made of spleen.

"But it seems one can never be quiet for a long time. It was my misfortune to make the acquaintance of a rich man of the world, an old president, who was all of seventy-five years old. One evening he took me to dine in a restaurant of the neighborhood. And then, you understand, he did not know how to be moderate. He was dead at the dessert.

"I had three months in prison, because I was not under superintendence. Then I came to Paris. And, oh! sir, it is hard here! hard to live! One cannot expect to eat every day, there are too many. But that is only so much the worse. Each to his trouble, don't you say so?"

She was silent. I walked along by her side, my heart touched. Suddenly she began to be familiar with me, saying:

"So you will not go home with me, my dear?"

"No, I have told you so already."

"Oh! well, good-bye, and thanks all the same, without any hard feeling; but I assure you that you are wrong."

And she went away, plunging into the rain which was as fine as a veil. I watched her pass under a gas jet and then disappear in a shadow. Poor girl!

The Substitute

"MADAME BONDEROI?"

"Yes, Madame Bonderoi."

"Impossible."

"I tell you it is."

"Madame Bonderoi, the old lady in a

lace cap, the devout, the holy, the honorable Madame Bonderoi, whose little false curls look as if they were glued round her head."

"That is the very woman."

"Oh! Come you must be mad."

"I swear to you that it is Madame Bonderoi."

"Then please give me the details."

"Here they are: During the life of Monsieur Bonderoi, the lawyer, people said that she utilized his clerks for her own particular service. She is one of these respectable middle-class women, with secret vices and inflexible principles, of whom there are so many. She liked good-looking young fellows, and I should like to know what is more natural than that? Do not we all like pretty girls?

"As soon as old Bonderoi was dead, his widow began to live the peaceful and irreproachable life of a woman with a fair, fixed income. She went to church assiduously, and spoke evil of her neighbors, but gave no chance to anyone to speak ill of her, and when she grew old she became the little wizened, sour-faced mischievous woman whom you know. Well, this adventure, which you would scarcely believe, happened last Friday.

"My friend, Jean d'Anglemare, is, as you know, a captain in a dragoon regiment, which is quartered in the barracks in the Rue de la Rivette. When he got to his quarters the other morning, he found that two men of his squadron had had a terrible quarrel. The duel took place between them. After the duel they became reconciled, and when their officer questioned them, they told him what their quarrel had been about. They had fought on Madame Bonderoi's account."

"Oh!"

"Yes, my dear fellow, about Madame Bonderoi. But I will let trooper Siballe speak":

" 'This is how it was, Captain. About a year and a half ago, I was lounging about the barrack-yard, between six and seven o'clock in the evening, when a woman came up and spoke to me, and said, just as if she had been asking her way: "Soldier, would you like to earn ten francs a week, honestly?" Of course I told her that I should, and so she said: "Come and see me at twelve o'clock to-morrow morning. I am Madame Bonderoi, and my address is No. 6, Rue de la Tranchée.

" ' "You may rely upon my being there, Madame." And then she went away, looking very pleased, and added: "I am very much obliged to you, soldier."

" ' "I am obliged to you, Madame," I replied. But I plagued my head about the matter, until the time came, all the same.

" 'At twelve o'clock, exactly, I rang the bell, and she let me in herself. She had a lot of ribbons on her head.

" ' "We must make haste," she said; "as my servant might come in."

" ' "I am quite willing to make haste," I replied, "but what am I to do?"

" 'But she only laughed, and replied: "Don't you understand, you great stupid?"

" 'I was no nearer her meaning, I give you my word of honor, Captain, but she came and sat down by me, and said:

" ' "If you mention this to anyone, I will have you put in prison, so swear that you will never open your lips about it."

" 'I swore whatever she liked, though

I did not at all understand what she meant. My forehead was covered with perspiration, so I took my pocket-handkerchief out of my helmet. She took it and wiped my brow with it; then she kissed me, and whispered: "Then you will?"

" ' "I will do anything you like, Madame," I replied; "as that is what I came for."

" 'Then she made herself clearly understood by her actions, and when I saw what it was, I put my helmet on a chair and showed her that in the dragoons a man never retires, Captain.

" 'Not that I cared much about is, for she was certainly not in her prime, but it is no good being too particular in such a matter, as francs are scarce, and then I have relations whom I like to help. I said to myself: "There will be five francs for my father, out of that."

" 'When I had finished my allotted task, Captain, I got ready to go, though she wanted me to stop longer, but I said to her:

" ' "To everyone their due, Madame. A small glass of brandy costs two sous, and two glasses cost four."

" 'She understood my meaning, and put a gold ten-franc piece into my hand. I do not like that coin. It is so small that if your pockets are not very well made, and come at all unsewn, one is apt to find it in one's boots, or not to find it at all, and so, while I was looking at it, she was looking at me. She got red in the face, as she had misunderstood my looks, and said: "Is not that enough?"

" ' "I did not mean that, Madame," I replied; "but if it is all the same to you, I would rather have two five-franc

pieces." And she gave them to me, and I took my leave.

" 'This has been going on for a year and a half, Captain. I go every Tuesday evening, when you give me leave to go out of barracks; she prefers that, as her servant has gone to bed then, but last week I was not well, and I had to go into the infirmary. When Tuesday came I could not get out, and I was very vexed, because of the ten francs which I had been receiving every week, and I said to myself:

" ' "If anybody goes there, I shall be done for; and she will be sure to take an artilleryman," and that made me angry. So I sent for Paumelle, who comes from my part of the country, and I told him how matters stood:

" ' "There will be five francs for you, and five for me," I said. He agreed, and went, as I had given him full instructions. She opened the door as soon as he knocked, and let him in, and as she did not look at his face, she did not perceive that it was not I, for you know, Captain, one dragoon is very like another with a helmet on.

" 'Suddenly, however, she noticed the change, and she asked, angrily: "Who are you? What do you want? I do not know you."

" 'Then Paumelle explained matters, he told her that I was not well, and that I had sent him as my substitute; so she looked at him, made him also swear to keep the matter secret, and then she accepted him, as you may suppose, for Paumelle is not a bad-looking fellow, either. But when he came back, Captain, he would not give me my five francs. If they had been for myself, I should not have said a word; but they were for my father; and on that score I would stand no nonsense, and said to him:

"'"You are not particular in what you do, for a dragoon; you are a discredit to your uniform."

"'He raised his fist, Captain, saying that fatigue duty like that was worth double. Of course, everybody has his own ideas, and he ought not to have accepted it. You know the rest.'

"Captain d'Anglemare laughed until he cried as he told me the story, but he also made me promise to keep the matter a secret, just as he had promised the two soldiers. So, above all, do not betray me, but promise me to keep it to yourself."

"Oh! You may be quite easy about that. But how was it all arranged in the end?"

"How? It is a joke in a thousand! Mother Bonderoi keeps her two dragoons, and reserves his own particular day for each of them, and in that way, everybody is satisfied."

"Oh! That is capital! Really capital!"

"And he can send his old father and mother the money as usual, and thus morality is satisfied."

A Passion

The sea was brilliant and unruffled, scarcely stirred, and on the pier the entire town of Havre watched the ships as they came on.

They could be seen at a distance, in great numbers, some of them, the steamers, with plumes of smoke; the others, the sailing vessels, drawn by almost invisible tugs, lifting toward the sky their bare masts, like leafless trees.

They hurried from every end of the horizon toward the narrow mouth of the jetty which devoured these monsters; and they groaned, they shrieked, they hissed while they spat out puffs of steam like animals panting for breath.

Two young officers were walking on the landing-stage, where a number of people were waiting, saluting or returning salutes, and sometimes stopping to chat.

Suddenly, one of them, the taller, Paul d'Henricol, pressed the arm of his comrade, Jean Renoldi, then, in a whisper, said:

"Hallo, here's Madame Poincot; give a good look at her. I assure you that she's making eyes at you."

She was moving along on the arm of her husband. She was a woman of about forty, very handsome still, slightly stout, but, owing to her graceful fullness of figure, as fresh as she was at twenty. Among her friends she was known as the Goddess, on account of her proud gait, her large black eyes, and the air of nobility attached to her person. She remained irreproachable; never had the least suspicion cast a breath on her life's purity. She was regarded as the very type of a virtuous, uncorrupted woman—so upright that no man had ever dared to think of her.

And yet for the last month Paul d'Henricol had been assuring his friend Renoldi that Madame Poincot was in love with him, and he maintained that there was no doubt of it.

"Be sure I don't deceive myself. I see it clearly. She loves you—she loves you passionately, like a chaste woman who had never loved. Forty years is a terrible age for virtuous women when they possess senses; they become foolish, and commit utter follies. She is hit, my dear fellow; she is falling like a wounded bird, and is ready to drop into your arms. I say—just look at her!"

The tall woman, preceded by her two daughters, aged twelve and fifteen years, suddenly turned pale, on her approach, as her eyes lighted on the officer's face. She gave him an ardent glance, concentrating her gaze upon him, and no longer seemed to have any eyes for her children, her husband, or any other person around her. She returned the salutation of the two young men without lowering her eyes, glowing with such a flame that a doubt, at last, forced its way into Lieutenant Renoldi's mind.

His friend said, in the same hushed voice: "I was sure of it. Did you not notice her this time? By Jove, she is a nice woman!"

*   *   *   *   *   *   *

But Jean Renoldi had no desire for a society intrigue. Caring little for love, he longed, above all, for a quiet life, and contented himself with occasional amours such as a young man can always have. All the sentimentality, the attentions, and the tenderness which a well-bred woman exacts bored him. The

chain, however slight it might be, which is always formed by an adventure of this sort, filled him with fear. He said: "At the end of a month I'll have had enough of it, and I'll be forced to wait patiently for six months through politeness."

Then a rupture would exasperate him, with the senses, the illusions, the clinging attachment, of the abandoned woman.

He avoided meeting Madame Poincot.

But one evening he found himself by her side at a dinner-party, and he felt on his skin, in his eyes, and even in his heart, the burning glance of his fair neighbor. Their hands met, and almost involuntarily were pressed together in a warm clasp. Already the intrigue was almost begun.

He saw her again, always in spite of himself. He realized that he was loved. He felt himself moved by a kind of pitying vanity when he saw what a violent passion for him swayed this woman's breast. So he allowed himself to be adored, and merely displayed gallantry, hoping that the affair would be only sentimental.

But, one day, she made an appointment with him for the ostensible purpose of seeing him and talking freely to him. She fell, swooning, into his arms; and he had no alternative but to be her lover.

And this lasted six months. She loved him with an unbridled, panting love. Absorbed in this frenzied passion, she no longer bestowed a thought on anything else. She surrendered herself to it utterly; her body, her soul her reputation, her position, her happiness,—she had cast all into that fire of her heart, as one casts, as a sacrifice, every precious object into a funeral pyre.

He had for some time grown tired of her, and deeply regretted his easy conquest as a fascinating officer; but he was bound, held prisoner. At every moment she said to him: "I have given you everything. What more would you have?" He felt a desire to answer:

"But I have asked nothing from you, and I beg of you to take back what you gave me."

Without caring about being seen, compromised, ruined she came to see him every evening, her passion becoming more inflamed each time they met. She flung herself into his arms, strained him in a fierce embrace, fainted under the force of rapturous kisses which to him were now terribly wearisome.

He said in a languid tone: "Look here! be reasonable!"

She replied:

"I love you," and sank on her knees gazing at him for a long time in an attitude of admiration. At length, exasperated by her persistent gaze, he tried to make her rise.

"Sit down. Let us talk," he said.

She murmured: "No, leave me"; and remained there, her soul in a state of ecstasy.

He said to his friend D'Henricol:

"You know, 'twill end by my beating her. I won't have any more of it! It must end, and that without further delay!" Then he went on: "What do you advise me to do?"

The other replied: "Break it off."

And Renoldi added, shrugging his shoulders:

"You speak indifferently about the matter; you believe that it is easy to break with a woman who tortures you with attention, who annoys you with kindness, who persecutes you with her affection, whose only care is to please you, and whose only wrong is that she gave herself to you in spite of you."

But suddenly, one morning the news came that the regiment was about to be removed from the garrison. Renoldi began to dance with joy. He was saved! Saved without scenes, without cries! Saved! All he had to do now was to wait patiently for two months more. Saved!

In the evening she came to him more excited than she had ever been before. She had heard the dreadful news, and, without taking off her hat, she caught his hands and pressed them nervously, with her eyes fixed on his and her voice vibrating and resolute.

"You are leaving," she said; "I know it. At first, I felt heartbroken; then, I understood what I had to do. I don't hesitate about doing it. I have come to give you the greatest proof of love that a woman can offer. I follow you. For you I am abandoning my husband, my children, my family. I am ruining myself, but I am happy. It seems to me that I am giving myself to you over again. It is the last and the greatest sacrifice. I am yours forever!"

He felt a cold sweat down his back, and was seized with a dull and violent rage, the anger of weakness. However, he became calm, and, in a disinterested tone, with a show of kindness, he refused to accept her sacrifice, tried to appease her, to bring her to reason, to make her see her own folly! She listened to him, staring at him with her great black eyes and with a smile of disdain on her lips, and said not a word in reply. He went on talking to her, and when, at length, he stopped, she said merely:

"Can you really be a coward? Can you be one of those who seduce a woman and then throw her over, through sheer caprice?"

He became pale, and renewed his arguments; he pointed out to her the inevitable consequences of such an action to both of them as long as they lived—how their lives would be shattered and how the world would shut its doors against them. She replied obstinately: "What does it matter when we love each other?" Then, all of a sudden, he burst out furiously:

"Well, then, I will not. No—do you understand? I will not do it, and I forbid you to do it." Then carried away by the rancorous feeling which had seethed within him so long, he relieved his heart:

"Ah! damn it all, you have now been sticking on to me for a long time in spite of myself, and the best thing for you now is to take yourself off. I'll be much obliged if you do so, upon my honor!"

She did not answer him, but her livid countenance began to look shriveled up, as if all her nerves and muscles had been twisted out of shape. And she went away without saying good-bye.

The same night she poisoned herself.

For a week she was believed to be in a hopeless condition. And in the city people gossiped about the case, and pitied her, excusing her sin on account of the violence of her passion, for overstrained emotions, becoming heroic through their intensity, always obtain forgiveness for whatever is blameworthy in them. A woman who kills herself is, so to speak, not an adulteress. And ere long there was a feeling of general reprobation against Lieutenant Renoldi for refusing to see her again—a unanimous sentiment of blame.

It was a matter of common talk that he had deserted her, betrayed her, ill treated her. The Colonel, overcome by compassion, brought his officer to book in a quiet way. Paul d'Henricol called on his friend: "Deuce take it, Renoldi, it's a damnable shame to let a woman die; it's not the right thing anyhow."

The other, enraged, told him to hold his tongue, whereupon D'Henricol made use of the word "infamy." The result was a duel, Renoldi was wounded, to the satisfaction of everybody, and was for some time confined to his bed.

She heard about it, and only loved him the more for it, believing that it was on her account he had fought the duel; but, as she was too ill to move, she was unable to see him again before the departure of the regiment.

He had been three months in Lille when he received, one morning, a visit from the sister of his former mistress.

After long suffering and a feeling of dejection, which she could not conquer, Madame Poincot's life was now despaired of, and she merely asked to see him for a minute, only for a minute, before closing her eyes forever.

Absence and time had appeased the young man's satiety and anger; he was touched, moved to tears, and he started at once for Havre.

She seemed to be in the agonies of death. They were left alone together; and by the bedside of this woman whom he now believed to be dying and whom he blamed himself for killing, though it was not by his own hand, he was fairly crushed with grief. He burst out sobbing, embraced her with tender, passionate kisses, more lovingly than he had ever done in the past. He murmured in a broken voice:

"No, no, you shall not die! You shall get better! We shall love each other forever—forever!"

She said in faint tones:

"Then it is true. You do love me, after all?"

And he, in his sorrow for her misfortunes, swore, promised to wait till she had recovered, and full of loving pity, kissed again and again the emaciated hands of the poor woman whose heart was panting with feverish, irregular pulsations.

The next day, he returned to the garrison.

Six weeks later she went to meet him, quite old-looking, unrecognizable, and more enamored than ever.

In his condition of mental prostration, he consented to live with her. Then, when they remained together as if they had been legally united, the same colonel who had displayed indignation with him for abandoning her, objected to this irregular connection as being incompatible with the good example officers ought to give in a regiment. He warned the lieutenant on the subject, and then furiously denounced his conduct, so Renoldi retired from the army.

He went to live in a village on the shore of the Mediterranean, the classic sea of lovers.

And three years passed. Renoldi, bent under the yoke, was vanquished,

and became accustomed to the woman's unchanging devotion. His hair had now turned white.

He looked upon himself as a man done for, gone under. Henceforth, he had no hope, no ambition, no satisfaction in life, and he looked forward to no pleasure in existence.

But one morning a card was placed in his hand, with the name—"Joseph Poincot, Shipowner, Havre."

The husband! The husband, who had said nothing, realizing that there was no use in struggling against the desperate obstinacy of women. What did he want?

He was waiting in the garden, having refused to come into the house. He bowed politely, but would not sit down, even on a bench in a gravel-path, and he commenced talking clearly and slowly.

"Monsieur, I did not come here to address reproaches to you. I know too well how things happened. I have been the victim of—we have been the victims of—a kind of fatality. I would never have disturbed you in your retreat if the situation had not changed. I have two daughters, Monsieur. One of them, the elder, loves a young man, and is loved by him. But the family of this young man is opposed to the marriage, basing their objection on the situation of —my daughter's mother. I have no feeling of either anger or spite, but I love my children, Monsieur. I have, therefore, come to ask my wife to return home. I hope that to-day she will consent to go back to my house—to her own house. As for me, I will make a show of having forgotten, for—for the sake of my daughters."

Renoldi felt a wild movement in his heart, and he was inundated with a delirium of joy like a condemned man who receives a pardon.

He stammered: "Why, yes—certainly, Monsieur—I myself—be assured of it—no doubt—it is right, it is only quite right."

This time M. Poincot no longer declined to sit down.

Renoldi then rushed up the stairs, and pausing at the door of his mistress's room, to collect his senses, entered gravely.

"There is somebody below waiting to see you," he said. " 'Tis to tell you something about your daughters."

She rose. "My daughters? What about them? They are not dead?"

He replied: "No; but a serious situation has arisen, which you alone can settle."

She did not wait to hear more, but rapidly descended the stairs.

Then he sank down on a chair, greatly moved, and waited.

He waited a long, long time. Then he heard angry voices below stairs, and made up his mind to go down.

Madame Poincot was standing up exasperated, just on the point of going away, while her husband had seized hold of her dress, exclaiming: "But remember that you are destroying our daughters, your daughters, our children!"

She answered stubbornly:

"I will not go back to you!"

Renoldi understood everything, came over to them in a state of great agitation, and gasped:

"What, does she refuse to go?"

She turned toward him, and, with a kind of shamefacedness, addressing him without any familiarity of tone in the presence of her legitimate husband, said:

"Do you know what he asks me to do? He wants me to go back, and live under one roof with him!"

And she tittered with a profound disdain for this man, who was appealing to her almost on his knees.

Then Renoldi with the determination of a desperate man playing his last card began talking to her in his turn, and pleaded the cause of the poor girls, the cause of the husband, his own cause. And when he stopped, trying to find some fresh argument, M. Poincot, at his wits' end, murmured, in the affectionate style in which he used to speak to her in days gone by:

"Look here, Delphine! Think of your daughters!"

Then she turned on both of them a glance of sovereign contempt, and, after that, flying with a bound toward the staircase, she flung at them these scornful words:

"You are a pair of wretches!"

Left alone, they gazed at each other for a moment, both equally crestfallen, equally crushed. M. Poincot picked up his hat, which had fallen down near where he sat, dusted off his knees the signs of kneeling on the floor, then raising both hands sorrowfully, while Renoldi was seeing him to the door, remarked with a parting bow:

"We are very unfortunate, Monsieur."

Then he walked away from the house with a heavy step.

VOLUME V

Caught

A YOUNG and charming lady, who was a member of the Viennese aristocracy, went last summer, without her husband, as many young and charming ladies do, to a fashionable Austrian watering place, Karlsbad, much frequented by foreigners.

As is usually the case in their rank of life, she had married from family considerations and for money; and the short spell of love after marriage was not sufficient to take deep root. After she had satisfied family traditions and her husband's wishes by giving birth to a son and heir, they both went their way; the young, handsome, and fascinating man to his clubs, to the racecourse, and behind the scenes at the theaters, and his charming, coquettish wife to her box at the opera, to the south in winter, and to some fashionable watering-place in the summer.

On the present occasion she brought with her from one of the latter resorts a young, very highly-connected Pole who enjoyed all the rights and the liberty of an avowed favorite, and performed all the duties of a slave.

As is usual in such cases, the lady rented a small house in one of the suburbs of Vienna, had it beautifully furnished, and received her lover there. She was always dressed very attractively, sometimes as "La Belle Hélène" in Offenbach's opera, only rather more after the ancient Greek fashion; another time as an *odalisque* in the Sultan's harem, and another time as a lighthearted Suabian girl, and so forth. In winter, however, she grew tired of such meetings, and as she wanted to have matters arranged more comfortably she took it into her head to receive her lover in her own house. But how was it to be done?

That, however, gave her no particular difficulty, as is the case with every woman, when once she has made up her mind to a thing. After thinking it over for a day or two she went to the next rendezvous, with a fully prepared plan of war.

The Pole was one of those types of handsome men which are rare. He was almost womanly in the delicacy of his features, of middle height, slim, and well-made, and resembled a youthful Bacchus who might very easily be made to pass for a Venus by the help of false locks—the more so as there was not even the slightest down on his lips. The lady, therefore, who was very fertile in resources, suggested to the handsome Pole that he might just as well transform himself into a handsome Polish lady, so that he might, under cover of the feminine, be able to visit her undisturbed. As it was winter, a thick, heavy, voluminous dress assisted the metamorphosis.

The lady, accordingly, bought a number of very beautiful costumes for her lover, and in the course of a few days told her husband that a charming young Polish lady, whose acquaintance she had made in the summer at Karlsbad, was going to spend the winter in Vienna, and would very frequently come and see her. Her husband listened to her with the greatest indifference, for it was one of his fundamental rules never to make love to any of his wife's female friends. He went to his club as usual at night, and the next day had forgotten all about the Polish lady.

Half an hour after the husband had left the house, a cab drove up, and a tall, slim, heavily veiled lady got out and went up the thickly carpeted stairs, only to be metamorphosed into the most ardent lover in the young woman's boudoir. The young Pole grew accustomed to his female attire so quickly that he even ventured to appear in the streets in it, and when he began to make conquests, and aristocratic gentlemen and successful speculators on the Stock Exchange looked at him significantly and even followed him, he took a real pleasure in the part he was playing, beginning to understand the pleasure a coquette feels in tormenting men.

The young Pole became more and more daring, until one evening he went to a private box at the opera, wrapped in an ermine cloak, on to which his dark, false curls fell in heavy waves.

A handsome young man in a box opposite to him ogled him incessantly from the first moment, and the young Pole responded in a manner which made the other bolder every minute. At the end of the third act the box-opener brought the fictitious Venus a small bouquet with a card concealed in it, on which was written in pencil:

"You are the most lovely woman in the world, and I implore you on my knees to grant me an interview."

The young Pole read the name of the man who had been captivated so quickly, and, with a peculiar smile, wrote on a card on which nothing but the name "Valeska" was printed: "After the theater," and sent Cupid's messenger back with it.

When the spurious Venus was about to enter her carriage after the performance, thickly veiled and wrapped in her ermine cloak, the handsome young man was standing by it with his hat off, and he opened the door for her. She was kind enough to allow him to get in with her, and during their drive she talked to him in the most charming manner, but she was cruel enough to dismiss him without pity before they reached her house. She went to the theater each night now, and every evening received an ardent note. Each evening she allowed the amorous swain to accompany her as far as her house, and men were beginning to envy him his brilliant conquest, when a catastrophe happened which was very surprising for all concerned.

The husband of the lady in whose eyes the Pole had found favor surprised the loving couple one day under circumstances which made any justification impossible. But while he, trembling with rage and jealousy, was drawing a small Circassian dagger which hung against the wall from its sheath, and as his wife threw herself, half fainting on to a couch, the young Pole had hastily put the false curls on to his head and had slipped into the silk dress and the sable cloak which he had been wearing when he came into his mistress's boudoir.

"What does this mean," the husband stammered, "Valeska?"

"Yes, sir" the young Pole replied; "Valeska, who has come here to show your wife a few love letters, which—"

"No, no," the deceived, but nevertheless guilty, husband said in imploring accents; "no that is quite unnecessary." And at the same time he put the dagger back into its sheath.

"Very well, then, there is a truce between us," the Pole observed coolly, "but do not forget what weapons I possess, and which I mean to retain against all contingencies."

Then the gentlemen bowed politely to each other, and the unexpected meeting came to an end.

From that time forward the terms on which the young married couple lived together assumed the character of that everlasting peace which President Grant once promised the whole world in his message to all nations. The young woman did not find it necessary to make her lover put on petticoats, and the husband constantly accompanies the real Valeska a good deal further than he did the false one on that memorable occasion.

The Orderly

THE cemetery, filled with officers, looked like a field covered with flowers. The *kêpis* and the red trousers, the stripes and the gold buttons, the shoulder-knots of the staff, the braid of the chasseurs and the hussars, passed through the midst of the tombs, whose crosses, white or black, opened their mournful arms—their arms of iron, marble, or wood—over the vanished race of the dead.

Colonel Limousin's wife had just been buried. She had been drowned, two days before, while taking a bath. It was over. The clergy had left; but the Colonel, supported by two brother-officers, remained standing in front of the pit, at the bottom of which he saw still the oaken coffin, wherein lay, already decomposed, the body of his young wife.

He was almost an old man, tall and thin, with white mustaches; and, three years ago, he had married the daughter of a comrade, left an orphan on the death of her father, Colonel Sortis.

The Captain and the Lieutenant, on whom their commanding officer was leaning, attempted to lead him away. He resisted, his eyes full of ears, which he heroically held back, and murmuring, "No, no, a little while longer!" he persisted in remaining there, his legs bending under him, at the side of that pit, which seemed to him bottomless, an abyss into which had fallen his heart and his life, all that he held dear on earth.

Suddenly, General Ormont came up, seized the Colonel by the arm, and dragging him from the spot almost by force, said: "Come, come, my old comrade! you must not remain here."

The Colonel thereupon obeyed, and went back to his quarters. As he opened the door of his study, saw a letter on the table, when he took it in his hands, he was near falling with surprise and emotion: he recognized his wife's handwriting. And the letter bore the postmark and the date of the same day. He tore open the envelope and read:

"Father: Permit me to call you still father as in days gone by. When you receive this letter, I shall be dead, and under the clay. Therefore, perhaps, you may forgive me.

"I do not want to excite your pity or to extenuate my sin. I only want to tell the entire and complete truth, with all the sincerity of a woman who, in an hour's time, is going to kill herself.

"When you married me through generosity, I gave myself to you through gratitude, and I loved you with all my girlish heart. I loved you as I loved my own father—almost as much; and one day, while I sat on your knee, and you were kissing me, I called you 'Father' in spite of myself. It was a cry of the heart, instinctive, spontaneous. Indeed, you were to me a father, nothing but a father. You laughed, and said to me, 'Address me always in that way, my child; it gives me pleasure.'

"We came to the city; and—forgive me, father—I fell in love. Ah! I resisted long, well, nearly two years—and then I yielded, I sinned, I became a fallen woman.

"And as to him? You will never guess who he is. I am easy enough about that matter, since there were a dozen officers always around me and with me, whom you called my twelve constellations.

"Father, do not seek to know him, and do not hate him. He only did what any man, no matter whom, would have done in his place, and then I am sure that he loved me, too, with all his heart.

"But listen! One day we had an appointment in the isle of Bécasses—you know the little isle, close to the mill. I had to get there by swimming, and he had to wait for me in a thicket, and then

to remain there till nightfall so that nobody should see him going away. I had just met him when the branches opened, and we saw Philippe, your orderly, who had surprised us. I felt that we were lost, and I uttered a great cry. Thereupon he said to me,—he, my lover, —'Go, swim back quietly, my darling, and leave me here with this man.'

"I went away so excited that I was near drowning myself, and I came back to you expecting that something dreadful was about to happen.

"An hour later, Philippe said to me in a low tone, in the lobby outside the drawing-room where I met him: 'I am at Madame's orders, if she has any letters to give me.' Then I knew that he had sold himself and that my lover had bought him.

"I gave him some letters, in fact—all my letters — he took them away, and brought me back the answers.

"This lasted about two months. We had confidence in him, as you had confidence in him yourself.

"Now, father, here is what happened. One day, in the same isle which I had to reach by swimming, but this time alone, I found your orderly. This man had been waiting for me; and he informed me that he was going to reveal everything about us to you, and deliver to you letters he had kept, stolen, if I did not yield to his desires.

"Oh! father, father, I was filled with fear—a cowardly fear, an unworthy fear, a fear above all of you, who had been so good to me, and whom I had deceived—fear on his account too—you would have killed him—for myself also perhaps! I cannot tell; I was mad, desperate; I thought of once more buying this wretch, who loved me, too—how shameful!

"We are so weak, we women, we lose our heads more easily than you do. And then, when a woman once falls, she always falls lower and lower. Did I know what I was doing? I understood only that one of you two and I were going to die—and I gave myself to this brute.

"You see, father, that I do not seek to excuse myself. Then, then—then what I should have foreseen happened—he had the better of me again and again, when he wished, by terrifying me. He, too, has been my lover, like the other, every day. Is not this abominable? And what punishment, father?

"So then it is all over with me. I must die. While I lived, I could not confess such a crime to you. Dead, I dare everything. I could not do otherwise than die — nothing could have washed me clean—I was too polluted. I could no longer love or be loved. It seemed to me that I stained everyone by merely allowing my hand to be touched.

"Presently I am going to take my bath, and I will never come back. This letter for you will go to my lover. It will reach him when I am dead, and without anyone knowing anything about it, he will forward it to you, accomplishing my last wishes. And you shall read it on your return from the cemetery.

"Adieu, father! I have no more to tell you. Do whatever you wish, and forgive me."

The Colonel wiped his forehead, which was covered with perspiration. His coolness, the coolness of days when he had stood on the field of battle suddenly came back to him. He rang.

A manservant made his appearance. "Send in Philippe to me," said the Colonel. Then he opened the drawer of his table.

The man entered almost immediately —a big soldier with red mustaches, a malignant look, and a cunning eye.

The Colonel looked him straight in the face.

"You are going to tell me the name of my wife's lover."

"But, my Colonel—"

The officer snatched his revolver out of the half-open drawer.

"Come! quick! You know I do not jest!"

"Well—my Colonel—it is Captain Saint-Albert."

Scarcely had he pronounced this name when a flame flashed between his eyes, and he fell on his face, his forehead pierced by a ball.

------●------

Joseph

THEY were both of them drunk, quite drunk, tiny Baroness Andrée de la Fraisières and little Countess Noëmi de Gardens. They had dined alone together, in the large room facing the sea. The soft breeze of a summer evening blew in at the open window, soft and fresh at the same time, a breeze that smelled of the sea. The two young women, stretched at length in their lounging chairs, sipped their Chartreuse as they smoked their cigarettes, talking most confidentially, telling each other details which nothing but this charming intoxication could have permitted their pretty lips to utter.

Their husbands had returned to Paris that afternoon, leaving them alone in that little watering-place which they had chosen so as to avoid those gallant marauders who are constantly encountered at fashionable seaside resorts. As they were absent for five days in the week, they objected to country excursions, luncheons on the grass, swimming lessons, and those sudden familiarities which spring up in the idle life of similar resorts. To them Dieppe, Etretat, Trouville seemed places to be avoided, and they had rented a house which had been built and abandoned by an eccentric individual in the valley of Roqueville, near Fécamp, and there they buried their wives for the whole summer.

The two ladies were drunk. Not knowing what to hit upon to amuse themselves, the little Baroness had suggested a good dinner and champagne. To begin with, they had found great amusement in cooking this dinner themselves; then they had eaten it merrily, and had imbibed freely, in order to allay the thirst excited by the heat of the fire. Now they were chattering and talking nonsense, from time to time gently moistening their throats with Chartreuse. In fact they did not in the least know any longer what they were saying.

The Countess, with her feet in the air on the back of a chair, was further gone than her friend.

"To complete an evening like this," she said, "we ought to have a gallant apiece. Had I foreseen this some time ago, I would have sent to Paris for two men I know, and would have let you have one."

"I can always find one," the other replied; "I could have one this very evening, if I wished."

"What nonsense! At Roqueville, my dear? It would have to be some peasant, then."

"No, not altogether."

"Well, tell me all about it."

"What do you want me to tell you?"

"About your lover."

"My dear, I do not want to live without being loved, for I should fancy I was dead if I were not loved."

"So should I."

"Is not that so?"

"Yes. Men cannot understand it! And especially our husbands!"

"No, not in the least. How can you expect it to be different? The love which we want is made up of being spoiled, of gallantries, and of pretty words and actions. That is the nourishment of our hearts; it is indispensable to our life, indispensable, indispensable."

"True, dear."

"I must feel that somebody is thinking of me, always, everywhere. When I go to sleep and when I wake up, I must know that somebody loves me somewhere, that I am being dreamed of, longed for. Without that, I should be wretched, wretched! Oh! yes, unhappy enough to do nothing but cry."

"I am just the same."

"You must remember that anything else is impossible. After a husband has been nice for six months, or a year, or two years, he usually degenerates into a brute, yes, a regular brute. He won't put himself out for anything, but shows his real self; he makes a scene on the slightest provocation, and sometimes without any provocation whatever. One cannot love a man with whom one lives constantly."

"That is quite true."

"Isn't it? What was I saying? I cannot in the least remember?"

"You were saying that all husbands are brutes!"

"Yes, brutes. All of them."

"That is true."

"And then?"

"What do you mean?"

"What was I saying just then?"

"I don't know, because you did not say it!"

"But I had something to tell you."

"Oh! yes; well, go on."

"Oh! I have got it."

"Well, I am listening."

"I was telling you that I can find lovers everywhere."

"How do you manage it?"

"Like this. Now follow me carefully. When I get to some fresh place, I take notes and make my choice."

"You make your choice?"

"Yes, of course I do. First of all, I take notes. I ask questions. Above all, a man must be discreet, rich, and generous; is not that so?"

"Quite true!" –

"And then he must please me, as a man."

"Of course."

"Then I bait the hook for him."

"Bait the hook?"

"Yes, just as one does to catch fish. Have you never fished with a hook and line?"

"No, never."

"You've lost some fun, then; it is very amusing, and besides that, instructive. Well, then, I bait the hook."

"How do you do it?"

"How dense you are. Don't we catch the men we want to catch, without their having any choice? And they really think that they choose—the fools—but it is we who choose—always. Just think, when one is not ugly, or stupid, as is the case with us, all men run after us, all—without exception. We look them over from morning till night, and when we have selected one, we fish for him."

"But that does not tell me how you do it."

"How I do it! Why, I do nothing; I allow myself to be looked at, that is all."

"Only allow yourself to be looked at?"

"Why yes; that is quite enough. When you have allowed yourself to be looked at several times, a man immediately thinks you the most lovely, the most seductive of women, and then he begins to make love to you. You give him to understand that he is not bad looking, without actually saying anything to him, of course, and he falls in love, like a log. You have him fast, and it lasts a longer or a shorter time, according to his qualities."

"And do you catch all whom you please like that?"

"Nearly all."

"Oh! So there are some who resist?"

"Sometimes."

"Why?"

"Oh! A man is a Joseph for three reasons: First, because he is in love with another woman; secondly, because he is excessively timid, or thirdly, because he is—how shall I say it?—incapable of carrying out the conquest of a woman to the end."

"Oh! my ear! Do you really believe—"

"I am sure of it. There are many of this latter class, many, many, many more than people think. Oh! they look just like everybody else—they strut like peacocks. No, when I said peacocks, I made a mistake, for they have not a peacock's virility."

"Oh! my dear!"

"As to the timid, they are sometimes unspeakably stupid. They are the sort of men who ought not to undress themselves, even when they are going to bed alone, where there is a looking-glass in the room. With them, one must be energetic, make use of looks, and squeeze their hands, and even that is useless sometimes. They never know how or where to begin. When one faints in their presence—as a last resource—they try to bring you round; and if you do not recover your senses immediately they go and get assistance.

"For myself I confess to a preference for other women's lovers. I carry them by assault at the point of the bayonet, my dear!"

"That is all very well, but when there are no men, as in this place, for instance?"

"I find them!"

"You find them. But where?"

"Everywhere. But that reminds me of my story.

"Now listen. Just two years ago my husband made me pass the summer on his estate at Bougrolles. There was nothing there—you know what I mean, nothing, nothing, nothing whatever! In the neighboring country houses there were a few disgusting boors, men who cared for nothing but shooting, and lived in country houses which had not even a bathroom. They were the sort of men who go to bed covered with perspiration, men you can't improve, because their daily lives are dirty. Now just guess what I did!"

"I cannot possibly."

"Ha! ha! ha! I had just been reading a number of George Sand's novels which exalt the man of the people, novels in which the workmen are sublime, and the men of the world are criminals. In addition to this I had seen "Ruy Blas" the winter before, and it had impressed me very much. Well, one of our farmers had a son, a good-looking young fellow of two-and-twenty who had studied for the priesthood, but had left the seminary in disgust. Well, I took him as footman!"

"Oh! And then? What afterward?"

"Then—then, my dear, I treated him very haughtily, but let him see a good deal of my person. I did not entice this rustic on, I simply inflamed him!"

"Oh! Andrée!"

"Yes, and I enjoyed the fun very much. People say that servants count for nothing! Well he did not count for much. I used to give him his orders every morning while my maid was dressing me, and every evening as well, while she was undressing me."

"Oh! Andrée!"

"My dear, he caught fire like a thatched roof. Then, at meals, I used continually to talk about cleanliness, about taking care of one's person, about baths and shower baths, until at the end of a fortnight he bathed in the river morning and night, and used so much scent as to poison the whole château. I had to forbid him to use perfume, telling him, with furious looks, that men ought never to use any scent but Eau de Cologne."

"Oh! Andrée!"

"Then, I took it into my head to get together a library suitable to the country. I sent for a few hundred moral novels, which I lent to all our peasants, and all my servants. A few books—a few poetical books, such as excite the minds of schoolboys and schoolgirls, had found their way into my collection. These, I gave to my footman. That taught him life—a funny sort of life."

"Oh! Andrée!"

"Then I grew familiar with him, and used to 'thou' * him. I had given him the name of Joseph. My dear, he was in a terrible state. He got as thin as a barn-door cock, and rolled his eyes like an idiot. I was extremely amused; it was one of the most delightful summers I ever spent."

"And then?"

"Then? Oh! yes, one day when my husband was away from home, I told him to order the basket carriage and to drive me into the woods. It was warm, very warm. There!"

"Oh! Andrée, do tell me all about it. It is so amusing."

"Here, have a glass of Chartreuse, otherwise I shall empty the decanter myself. Well, I felt ill on the road."

"How?"

"You are dense. I told him that I was not feeling well and that he must lay me on the grass, and when I was lying there, I told him I was choking and that he must unlace me. And then when I was unlaced, I fainted."

"Did you go right off?"

"Oh! dear no, not the least."

"Well?"

"Well, I was obliged to remain unconscious for nearly an hour, as he could find no means of bringing me round. But I was very patient, and did not open my eyes."

"Oh! Andrée!"

"And what did you say to him?"

"I? Nothing at all! How was I to know anything, as I was unconscious? I thanked him, and told him to help me into the carriage, and he drove me back to the château; but he nearly upset us in turning into the gate!"

"Oh! Andrée! And is that all?"

"That is all."

"You did not faint more than that once?"

"Only once, of course! I did not want to take such a fellow for my lover."

"Did you keep him long after that?"

"Yes, of course. I have him still. Why should I have sent him away? I had nothing to complain of."

---

*The second person singular is used in French—as in German—among relations and intimate friends, and to servants.

"Oh! Andrée! And is he in love with you still?"

"Of course he is."

"Where is he?"

The little Baroness put out her hand to the wall and touched the electric bell. The door opened almost immediately, and a tall footman came in who diffused a scent of Eau de Cologne all round him.

"Joseph," said the Baroness to him, "I am afraid I am going to faint; send my lady's maid to me."

The man stood motionless, like a soldier before his officer, looking ardently at his mistress, who continued: "Be quick, you great idiot, we are not in the woods to-day, and Rosalie will attend to me better than you can." He turned on his heels and went, and the Countess asked nervously: "What shall you say to your maid?"

"I shall tell her what we have been doing! No, I shall merely get her to unlace me; it will relieve my chest, for I can scarcely breathe. I am drunk, my dear—so drunk that I should fall, if I were to get up from my chair."

Regret

MONSIEUR SAVEL, who was called in Mantes "Father Savel," had just risen from bed. He wept. It was a dull autumn day; the leaves were falling. They fell slowly in the rain, resembling another rain, but heavier and slower. M. Savel was not in good spirit. He walked from the fireplace to the window, and from the window to the fireplace. Life has its somber days. It will no longer have any but somber days of sixty-two. He is alone, an old bachelor, with nobody about him. How sad it is to die alone, all alone, without the disinterested affection of anyone!

He pondered over his life, so barren, so void. He recalled the days gone by, the days of his infancy, the house, the house of his parents; his college days, his follies, the time of his probation in Paris, the illness of his father, his death. He then returned to live with his mother. They lived together, the young man and the old woman, very quietly, and desired nothing more. At last the mother died. How sad a thing is life! He has lived always alone, and now, in his turn, he too, will soon be dead. He will disappear, and that will be the finish. There will be no more of Savel upon the earth. What a frightful thing! Other people will live, they will live, they will laugh. Yes, people will go on amusing themselves, and he will no longer exist! Is it not strange that people can laugh, amuse themselves, be joyful under that eternal certainty of death! If this death were only probable, one could then have hope; but no, it is inevitable, as inevitable as that night follows the day.

If, however, his life had been complete! If he had done something; if he had had adventures grand pleasures, successes, satisfaction of some kind or another. But now, nothing. He had done nothing, never anything but rise from bed, eat, at the same hours, and go to bed again. And he has gone on like that to the age of sixty-two. He had not even taken unto himself a wife, as other men do. Why? Yes, why was it that he was not married? He might have been, for he possessed considerable means. Was it an opportunity which had failed him? Perhaps! But one can create opportunities. He was indifferent; that was all. Indifference had been his greatest drawback, his defect, his vice. How some men miss their lives through indifference! To certain natures, it is so difficult to get out of bed, to move about, to take long walks, to speak, to study any question.

He had not even been in love. No woman had reposed on his bosom, in a complete abandon of love. He knew nothing of this delicious anguish of expectation, of the divine quivering of the pressed hand, of the ecstasy of triumphant passion.

What superhuman happiness must inundate your heart when lips encounter lips for the first time, when the grasp of four arms makes one being of you, a being unutterably happy, two beings infatuated with each other.

M. Savel was sitting down, his feet on the fender, in his dressing gown. Assuredly his life had been spoiled, completely spoiled. He had however, loved. He had loved secretly, dolorously, and indifferently, just as was characteristic of him in everything. Yes, he had loved his old friend, Madame Saudres, the wife of his old companion, Saudres. Ah! if he had known her as a young girl! But he had encountered her too late; she was already married. Unquestionably he would have asked her hand; that he would! How he had loved her, nevertheless, without respite, since the first day he had set eyes on her!

He recalled, without emotion, all the times he had seen her, his grief on leaving her, the many nights that he could not sleep because of his thinking of her.

In the mornings he always got up somewhat less amorous than in the evening.

Why? Seeing that she was formerly pretty and plump, blond and joyous. Saudres was not the man she would have selected. She was now fifty-two years of age. She seemed happy. Ah! if she had only loved him in days gone by! yes, if she had only loved him! And why should she not have loved him, he, Savel, seeing that he loved her so much, yes, her, Madame Saudres!

If only she could have divined something— Had she not divined anything, had she not seen anything, never comprehended anything? But then, what would she have thought? If he had spoken what would she have answered?

And Savel asked himself a thousand other things. He reviewed his whole life, seeking to grasp again a multitude of details.

He recalled all the long evenings spent at the house of Saudres, when the latter's wife was young and so charming.

He recalled many things that she had said to him, the sweet intonations of her voice, the little significant smiles that meant so much.

He recalled the walks that the three of them had had, along the banks of the Seine, their lunches on the grass on the Sundays, for Saudres was employed at the subprefecture. And all at once the distinct recollection came to him of an afternoon spent with her in a little plantation on the banks of the river.

They had set out in the morning, carrying their provisions in baskets. It was a bright spring morning, one of those days which inebriate one. Everything smelled fresh, everything seemed happy. The voices of the birds sounded more joyous, and the flapping of their wings more rapid. They had lunch on the grass, under the willow-trees, quite close to the water, which glittered in the sun's rays. The air was balmy, charged with odors of fresh vegetation; they had drunk the most delicious wines. How pleasant everything was on that day!

After lunch, Saudres went to sleep on the broad of his back, "The best nap he had in his life," said he, when he woke up.

Madame Saudres had taken the arm of Savel, and they had started to walk along the river's bank.

She leaned tenderly on his arm. She laughed and said to him: "I am intoxicated, my friend, I am quite intoxicated." He looked at her, his heart beating rapidly. He felt himself grow pale, hoping that he had not looked too boldly at her, and that the trembling of his hands had not revealed his passion.

She had decked her head with wild flowers and water-lilies, and she had asked him: "Do you not like to see me appear thus?"

As he did not answer—for he could find nothing to say, he should rather have gone down on his knees—she burst out laughing, a sort of discontented laughter which she threw straight in his face, saying: "Great goose, what ails you? You might at least speak!"

He felt like crying, and could not even yet find a word to say.

All these things came back to him now, as vividly as on the day when they took place. Why had she said this to him, "Great goose, what ails you? You might at least speak!"

And he recalled how tenderly she had leaned on his arm. And in passing under a shady tree he had felt her ear leaning against his cheek, and he had tilted his head abruptly, for fear that she had not meant to bring their flesh into contact.

When he had said to her: "Is it not time to return?" she darted at him a singular look. "Certainly," she said, "certainly," regarding him at the same time, in a curious manner. He had not thought of anything then; and now the whole thing appeared to him quite plain.

"Just as you like, my friend. If you are tired let us go back."

And he answered:

"It is not that I am fatigued; but Saudres has perhaps waked up now."

And she had said: "If you are afraid of my husband's being awake, that is another thing. Let us return."

In returning she remained silent and leaned no longer on his arm. Why?

At this time it had never occurred to him to ask himself, "Why." Now he seemed to apprehend something that he had not then understood.

What was it?

M. Savel felt himself blush, and he got up at a bound, feeling thirty years younger, believing that he now understood Madame Saudres then to say, "I love you."

Was it possible? That suspicion

which had just entered into his soul, tortured him. Was it possible that he could not have seen, not have dreamed?

Oh! if that could be true, if he had rubbed against such good fortune without laying hold of it!

He said to himself: "I wish to know. I cannot remain in this state of doubt. I wish to know!" He put on his clothes quickly, dressed in hot haste. He thought: "I am sixty-two years of age, she is fifty-eight; I may ask her that now without giving offense."

He started out.

The Saudres' house was situated on the other side of the street, almost directly opposite his own. He went up to it, knocked, and a little servant came to open the door.

"You there at this hour, M. Savel? Has some accident happened to you?"

M. Savel responded:

"No, my girl; but go and tell your mistress that I want to speak to her at once."

"The fact is, Madame is preparing her stock of pear-jams for the winter, and she is standing in front of the fire. She is not dressed, as you may well understand."

"Yes, but go and tell her that I wish to see her on an important matter."

The little servant went away and Savel began to walk, with long, nervous strides, up and down the drawing-room. He did not feel himself the least embarrassed, however. Oh! he was merely going to ask her something, as he would have asked her about some cooking receipt, and that was: "Do you know that I am sixty-two years of age?"

The door opened and Madame appeared. She was now a gross woman, fat and round, with full cheeks, and a sonorous laugh. She walked with her arms away from her body, and her sleeves tucked up to the shoulders, her bare arms all smeared with sugar juice. She asked, anxiously:

"What is the matter with you, my friend; you are not ill, are you?"

"No, my dear friend; but I wish to ask you one thing, which to me is of the first importance, something which is torturing my heart, and I want you to promise that you will answer me candidly."

She laughed, "I am always candid. Say on."

"Well, then. I have loved you from the first day I ever saw you. Can you have any doubt of this?"

She responded laughing, with something of her former tone of voice:

"Great goose! what ails you? I knew it well from the very first day!"

Savel began to tremble. He stammered out: "You knew it? Then—"

He stopped.

She asked:

"Then? What?"

He answered:

"Then — what would you think? — what—what—what would you have answered?"

She broke forth into a peal of laughter, which made the sugar juice run off the tips of her fingers on to the carpet.

"I? But you did not ask me anything. It was not for me to make a declaration."

He then advanced a step toward her.

"Tell me—tell me— You remember the day when Saudres went to sleep on the grass after lunch—when we had walked together as far as the bend of the river, below—"

He waited, expectantly. She had ceased to laugh, and looked at him, straight in the eyes.

"Yes, certainly. I remember it."

He answered, shivering all over.

"Well,—that day—if I had been—if I had been—enterprising—what would you have done?"

She began to laugh as only a happy woman can laugh, who has nothing to regret, and responded frankly, in a voice tinged with irony:

"I would have yielded, my friend."

She then turned on her heels and went back to her jam-making.

Savel rushed into the street, cast down, as though he had encountered some great disaster. He walked with giant strides, through the rain, straight on, until he reached the river, without thinking where he was going. When he reached the bank he turned to the right and followed it. He walked a long time, as if urged on by some instinct. His clothes were running with water, his hat was crushed in, as soft as a piece of rag and dripping like a thatched roof. He walked on, straight in front of him. At last, he came to the place where they had lunched so long, long ago, the recollection of which had tortured his heart. He sat down under the leafless trees, and wept.

The Deaf-Mute

MY DEAR friend, you ask me why I do not return to Paris; you will be astonished, and almost angry, I suppose, when I give you the reason, which will without doubt be revolting to you: "Why should a hunter return to Paris at the height of the woodcock season?"

Certainly I understand and like life in the city very well, that life which leads from the chamber to the sidewalk; but I prefer a freer life, the rude life of the hunter in autumn.

In Paris, it seems to me that I am never out of doors; for, in fact, the streets are only great, common apartments without a ceiling. Is one in the air between two walls, his feet upon stone or wooden pavement, his view shut in everywhere by buildings, without any horizon of verdure, fields, or woods? Thousands of neighbors jostle you, push you, salute you, and talk with you; but the fact of receiving water upon an umbrella when it rains is not sufficient to give me the impression or the sensation of space.

Here, I perceive clearly and deliciously the difference between in doors and out. But it was not of that that I wish to speak to you.

Well, then, the woodcock are flying.

And it is necessary to tell you that I live in a great Norman house, in a valley, near a little river, and that I hunt nearly every day.

Other days, I read; I even read things that men in Paris have not the time to become acquainted with; very serious things, very profound, very curious, written by a brave, scholarly genius, a foreigner who has spent his life studying the subject and observing the facts relative to the influence of the functions of our organs upon our intelligence.

But I was speaking to you of woodcock.

My two friends, the D'Orgemol brothers, and myself remain here during the hunting season awaiting the first frost. Then, when it freezes, we set out for their farm in Cannetot, near Fécamp, because there is a delicious little wood there, a divine wood, where every woodcock that flies comes to lodge.

You know the D'Orgemols, those two giants, those Normans of ancient times, those two males of the old, powerful conquering race which invaded France, took England and kept it, established itself on every coast of the world, made towns everywhere, passed like a flood over Sicily, creating there an admirable art, struck down kings, pillaged the proudest cities, matched popes in their priestly tricks and ridiculed them, more sly than the Italian pontiffs themselves, and above all, left children in all the beds of the world. These D'Orgemols are two Normans of the best stamp, and are all Norman — voice, accent, mind, blond hair, and eyes which are the color of the sea.

When we are together we talk the patois, we live, think, and act in Norman, we become Norman landowners, more peasants than farmers.

For two weeks now, we have been waiting for woodcock. Every morning, Simon, the elder, will say: "Hey! Here's the wind coming round to the east, and it's going to freeze. In two days they will be here."

The younger, Gaspard, more exact, waits for the frost to come before he announces it.

But, last Thursday he entered my room at dawn, crying out:

"It has come! The earth is all white. Two days more and we shall go to Cannetot."

Two days later, in fact, we do set out for Cannetot. Certainly you would have laughed to see us. We take our places in a strange sort of hunting wagon that my father had constructed long ago. Constructed is the only word that I can use in speaking of this monstrous carriage, or rather this earthquake on wheels. There was room for everything inside: a place for provisions, a place for the guns, place for the trunks, and places of clear space for the dogs. Everything is sheltered except the men, perched on seats as high as a third story, and all this supported by four gigantic wheels. One mounted as best he could, making his feet, hands, and even his teeth serve him for the occasion, for there was no step to give access to the edifice.

Now, the two D'Orgemols and myself scaled this mountain, clothed like Laplanders. We have on sheepskins, wear enormous, woolen stockings outside our pantaloons, and gaiters outside our woolen stockings; we also have some black fur caps and white fur gloves. When we are installed, John, my servant, throws us our three terriers, Pif, Paf, and Moustache. Pif belongs to Simon, Paf to Gaspard, and Moustache to me. They look like three crocodiles covered with hair. They are long, low, and crooked, with bent legs, and so hairy that they have the look of a yellow thicket. Their eyes can scarcely be seen under their eyebrows, or their teeth through their beards. One could never shut them into the rolling kennels of the carriage. Each one puts his own dog under his feet to keep him warm.

And now we are off, shivering abominably. It is cold, and freezing hard. We are contented. Toward five o'clock we arrive. The farmer, master Picot, is expecting us, waiting before the door. He is also a jolly fellow, not tall, but round, squat, vigorous as a bulldog, sly as a fox, always laughing, always contented, knowing how to make money out of all of us.

It is a great festival for him when the woodcock arrives. The farm is large, and on it an old building set in an apple orchard, surrounded by four rows of beech-trees, which battle against the winds from the sea all the year.

We enter the kitchen where a bright fire is burning in our honor. Our table is set against the high chimney, where a large chicken is turning and roasting before the clear flame, and whose gravy is running into an earthen dish beneath.

The farmer's wife salutes us, a tall, quiet woman, wholly occupied with the cares of her house, her head full of accounts, the price of grain, of poultry, of mutton, and beef. She is an orderly woman, set and severe, known for her worth in the neighborhood.

At the end of the kitchen is set the long table where all the farm hands, drivers, laborers, stableboys, shepherds, and woman servants sit down. They eat in silence under the active eye of the mistress, watching us dine with master

Picot, who says witty things to make us laugh. Then, when all her servants are fed, Madame Picot takes her repast alone at one corner of the table, a rapid and frugal repast, watching the serving maid meanwhile. On ordinary days she dines with all the rest.

We all three sleep, the D'Orgemols and myself, in a bare, white room, whitewashed with lime, containing only our three beds, three chairs, and three basins.

Gaspard always wakes first and sounds the echoing watchword. In half an hour everybody is ready, and we set out with master Picot who hunts with us.

Mr. Picot prefers me to his masters. Why? Without doubt because I am not his master. So we two reach the woods by the right, while the two brothers come to the attack by the left. Simon has the care of the dogs, all three attached to the end of a rope.

For we are not hunting woodcock but the wolf. We are convinced that it is better to find the woodcock than to seek it. If one falls upon one and kills it, there you are! But when one specially wishes to meet one, he can never quite bring him down. It is truly a beautiful and curious thing, hearing the loud report of a gun, in the fresh morning air, and then, the formidable voice of Gaspard filling the space as he howls:

"Woodcock— There it is."

As for me, I am sly. When I have killed a woodcock, I cry out: "Wolf!" And then I triumph in my success when we go to a clear place for the midday lunch.

Here we are then, master Picot and I, in the little woods, where the leaves fall with a sweet and continued murmur, with a dry murmur, a little sad, for they are dead. It is cold, a light cold which stings the eyes, the nose, and the ears, and powders with a fine, white moss the limbs of the trees and the brown, plowed earth. But there is warmth through all our limbs under the great sheepskin. The sun is gay in the blue air which it warms scarcely at all, but it is gay. It is good to hunt in the woods on fresh mornings in winter.

Down below, a dog is loudly baying. It is Pif. I know his thin voice, but it ceases. Then there is another cry, and then another; and Paf in his turn begins to bark. And what has become of Moustache? Ah! there is a little cry like that of a chicken being strangled! They have stirred up a wolf. Attention, master Picot!

They separate, then approach each other, scatter again, and then return; we follow their unforeseen windings, coming out into little roads, the mind on the alert, finger on the trigger of the gun.

They turn toward the fields again, and we turn also. Suddenly, there is a gray spot, a shadow, crossing the bypath. I aim and fire. The light smoke rises in the blue air and I perceive under a bush a bit of white hair which moves. Then I shout, with all my force, "Wolf, wolf! There he is!" And I show him to the three dogs, the three hairy crocodiles, who thank me by wagging their tails. Then they go off in search of another.

Master Picot joins me. Moustache begins to yap. The farmer says: "There must be a hare there at the edge of the field."

The moment that I came out of the woods, I perceived, not ten steps from me, enveloped in his immense yellowish mantle and wearing his knitted, woolen cap such as shepherds wear at home, master Picot's herdsman Gargan, the deaf-mute. I said "Good morning," to him, according to our custom, and he raised his hand to salute me. He had not heard my voice, but had seen the motion of my lips.

For fifteen years I had known this shepherd. For fifteen years I had seen him each autumn, on the border, or in the middle of the field, his body motionless, and always knitting in his hands. His flock followed him like a pack of hounds, seeming to obey his eye.

Master Picot now took me by the arm, saying:

"Did you know that the shepherd killed his wife?"

I was stupefied. "What Gargan—the deaf-mute?"

"Yes, this winter, and his case was tried at Rouen. I will tell you about it."

And he led me into the underbrush, for the shepherd knew how to catch words from his master's lips, as if he heard them spoken. He could understand only him; but, watching his face closely, he was no longer deaf; and the master, on the other hand, seemed to divine, like a sorcerer, the meaning of all the mute's pantomime, the gestures of his fingers, the expression of his face, and the motion of his eyes.

Here is his simple story, the various, somber facts as they came to pass:

Gargan was the son of a marl digger, one of those men who go down into the marlpit to extract that kind of soft, dissolving stone, sown under the soil. A deaf-mute by birth, he had been brought up to watch the cows along the ditches by the side of the roads.

Then, picked up by Picot's father, he had become the shepherd on his farm. He was an excellent shepherd, devout, upright, knowing how to find the lost members of his flock, although nobody had taught him anything.

When Picot took the farm, in his turn, Gargan was thirty years old and looked forty. He was tall, thin, and bearded—bearded like a patriarch.

About this time a good woman of the country, Mrs. Martel, died very poor, leaving a girl fifteen years old who was called "Drops," because of her immoderate love for brandy.

Picot took in this ragged waif, employed her in light duties, giving her a home without pay in return for her work. She slept under the barn, in the stable, or the cow-house, upon straw, or on the manure-heap, anywhere, it mattered not where, for they could not give a bed to this barefoot. She slept, then, no matter where, with no matter whom, perhaps with the plowman or the stable boy. But it happened soon that she gave her attention to the deaf-mute and coupled herself with him in a continued fashion. What united these two miserable beings? How have they understood each other? Had he ever known a woman before this barn rover, he who had never talked with anyone? Was it she who found him in his wheeled hut and seduced him, like an Eve of the rut, at the edge of the road? No one knows. They only know that one day they were living together as husband and wife.

No one was astonished by it, and

Picot found it a very natural coupling. But the curate heard of this union without a mass and was angry. He reproached Mrs. Picot, disturbed her conscience, and threatened her with mysterious punishments. What was to be done? It was very simple. They must go and be married at the church and at the mayor's. They had nothing, either one of them: he, not a whole pair of pantaloons, she, not a petticoat of a single kind of cloth. So there was nothing to oppose what the law and religion required. They were united, in an hour, before the mayor and the curate, and believed that all was regulated for the best.

Now, it soon became a joke in the country (pardon the villainous word) to make a deceived husband of this poor Gargan. Before she was married, no one thought of sleeping with "Drops," but now each one wished his turn, for the sake of a laughable story. Everybody went there for a little glass behind the husband's back. The affair made so much noise that even some of the Goderville gentlemen came to see her.

For a half pint "Drops" would finish the spectacle with no matter whom, in a ditch, behind a wall, anywhere, while the silhouette of the motionless Gargan could be seen knitting a stocking not a hundred feet from there, surrounded by his bleating flock. And they laughed about it enough to make themselves ill in all the *cafés* of the country. It was the only thing talked of in the evening before the fire; and upon the road, the first thing one would ask:—"Have you paid your drop to 'Drops'?" Everyone knew what that meant.

The shepherd never seemed to see

anything. But one day the Poirot boy, of Sasseville, called to Gargan's wife from behind the mill, showing her a full bottle. She understood and ran to him laughing. Now, scarcely were they engaged in their criminal deed when the herdsman fell upon them as if he had come out of a cloud. Poirot fled at full speed, his breeches about his heels, while the deaf-mute, with the cry of a beast, sprang at his wife's throat.

The people working in the fields ran toward them. It was too late; her tongue was black, her eyes were coming out of her head, the blood was flowing from her nose. She was dead.

The shepherd was tried by the Judge at Rouen. As he was a mute, Picot served as interpreter. The details of the affair amused the audience very much. But the farmer had but one idea: his herdsman must be acquitted. And he went about it in earnest.

At first, he related the deaf-mute's whole story, including that of his marriage; then, when he came to the crime, he himself questioned the assassin.

The assemblage was very quiet.

Picot pronounced the words slowly: "Did you know that she had deceived you?" and at the same time he asked the question with his eyes in pantomime.

The other answered "No" with his head.

"Were you asleep in the mill when you surprised her?" And he made a gesture of a man seeing some disgusting thing.

The other answered "Yes" with his head.

Then the farmer, imitating the signs of the mayor who married them, and of the priest who united them in the name of God, asked his servant if he had killed his wife because she was bound to him before men and before heaven.

The shepherd answered "Yes" with his head.

Picot then said to him: "Come, tell us how it happened."

Then the deaf-mute reproduced the whole scene in pantomime. He showed how he was asleep in the mill; that he was awakened by feeling the straw move; that he had watched quietly and had seen the whole thing.

He rose, between the two policemen, and brusquely imitated the obscene movement of the criminal couple entangled before him.

A tumultuous laugh went through the hall, then stopped short; for the herdsman, with haggard eyes, moving his jaw and his great beard as if he had bitten something, with arms extended, and head thrown forward, repeated the terrible action of a murderer who strangles a being.

And he howled frightfully, so excited with anger that one would think he believed he still held her in his grasp; and the policemen were obliged to seize him and seat him by force in order to calm him.

A great shiver of agony ran through the assembly. Then master Picot, placing his hand upon his servant's shoulder, said simply: "He knows what honor is, this man does."

And the shepherd was acquitted.

As for me, my dear friend, I listened to this adventure to its close, much moved, and have related it to you in gross terms in order not to change the farmer's story. But now there is a report of a gun from the woods, and the formidable voice of Gaspard is heard growling in the wind, like the sound of a cannon:

"Woodcock! There is one."

And this is how I employ my time, watching for the woodcock to pass, while you are also going to the Bois to see the first winter costumes.

Magnetism

It was at the close of a dinner-party of men, at the hour of endless cigars and incessant sips of brandy, amid the smoke and the torpid warmth of digestion, and the slight confusion of heads generated by such a quantity of eatables and by the absorption of so many different liquors.

Those present were talking about magnetism, about Donato's tricks, and about Doctor Charcot's experiences. All of a sudden, those men, so sceptical, so happy-go-lucky, so indifferent to religion of every sort, began telling stories about strange occurrences, incredible things which nevertheless had really happened, they contended, falling back into superstitions, beliefs, clinging to these last remnants of the marvelous, becoming devotees to this mystery of magnetism, defending it in the name of science. There was only one person who smiled, a vigorous young fellow, a great pursuer of girls of light behavior, and a hunter also of frisky matrons, in whose mind there was so much incredulity about everything that he would not even enter upon a discussion of such matters.

He repeated with a sneer:

"Humbug! humbug! humbug! We need not discuss Donato, who is merely a very smart juggler. As for M. Charcot, who is said to be a remarkable man of science, he produces on me the effect of those story-tellers of the school of Edgar Allan Poe, who go mad through constantly reflecting on queer cases of insanity. He has set forth some nervous phenomena, which are unexplained and inexplicable; he makes his way into that unknown region which men explore every day, and not being able to comprehend what he sees, he remembers perhaps too well the explanations of certain mysteries given by priests. Besides, I would like to hear him speaking on these subjects; that would be quite a different thing from your repetition of what he says."

The words of the unbeliever were listened to with a kind of pity, as if he had blasphemed in the midst of an assembly of monks.

One of these gentlemen exclaimed:

"And yet miracles were performed in former days."

But the other replied: "I deny it. Why cannot they be performed any longer?"

Thereupon, each man referred to some fact, or some fantastic presentiment, or some instance of souls communicating with each other across space, or some use of secret influences produced by one being or another. And they asserted, they maintained, that these things had actually occurred, while the sceptic went on repeating energetically: "Humbug! humbug! humbug!"

At last he rose up, threw away his cigar, and with his hands in his pockets said: "Well, I, too, am going to relate to you two stories, and then I will explain them to you. Here they are:

"In the little village of Etretat, the men, who are all seafaring folk, go every year to Newfoundland to fish for cod. Now, one night the little son of one of these fishermen woke up with a start, crying out that his father was dead. The child was quieted, and again he woke up exclaiming that his father was drowned. A month later the news came that his father had, in fact, been swept off the deck of his smack by a billow. The widow then remembered how her son had awaked and spoken of his father's death. Everyone said it was a miracle, and the affair caused a great sensation. The dates were compared, and it was found that the accident and the dream had very nearly coincided, whence they drew the conclusion that they had happened on the same night and at the same hour. And there is the mystery of magnetism."

The story-teller stopped suddenly.

Thereupon, one of those who had heard him much affected by the narrative, asked:

"And can you explain this?"

"Perfectly, Monsieur. I have discovered the secret. The circumstance surprised me and even embarrassed me very much; but I, you see, do not believe on principle. Just as others begin by believing, I begin by doubting; and when I don't at all understand, I continue to deny that there can be any telegraphic communication between souls, certain that my own sagacity will be enough to explain it. Well, I have gone on inquiring into the matter, and I have ended, by dint of questioning all the wives of the absent seamen, in convincing myself that not a week passes without one of themselves or their children dreaming and declaring when they wake that the father was drowned. The horrible and continual fear of this accident makes them always talk about it. Now, if one of these frequent predictions coincides, by a very simple chance, with the death of the person referred to, people at once declare it to be a miracle; for they suddenly lose sight of all the other predictions of misfortune that have remained unconfirmed. I have myself known fifty cases where the persons who made the prediction forgot all about it in a week afterward. But if, in fact, the man was dead, then the recollection of the thing immediately revived, and people will be ready to believe in the intervention of God, according to some, and in magnetism, according to others."

One of the smokers remarked:

"What you say is right enough; but what about your second story?"

"Oh! my second story is a very delicate matter to relate. It is to myself it happened, and so I don't place any great value on my own view of the matter. One is never a good judge in a case where he is one of the parties concerned. At any rate, here it is:

"Among my acquaintances in society there was a young woman on whom I had never bestowed a thought, whom I had never even looked at attentively, never taken any notice of, as the saying is.

"I classed her among the women of no importance, though she was not quite bad-looking; in fact, she appeared to me to possess eyes, a nose, a mouth, some sort of hair—just a colorless type of countenance. She was one of those beings on whom one only thinks by accident, without taking any particular interest in the individual, and who never excites desire.

"Well, one night, as I was writing some letters by my own fireside before going to bed, I was conscious, in the midst of that train of sensual images that sometimes float before one's brain in moments of idle reverie, while I held the pen in my hand, of a kind of light breath passing into my soul, a little shudder of the heart and immediately, without reason, without any logical connection of thought, I saw distinctly, saw as if I had touched her, saw from head to foot, uncovered, this young woman for whom I had never cared save in the most superficial manner when her name happened to recur to my mind. And all of a sudden I discovered in her a heap of qualities which I had never before observed, a sweet charm, a fascination that made me languish; she awakened in me that sort of amorous uneasiness which sends you in pursuit of a woman. But I did not remain thinking of her long. I went to bed and was soon asleep. And I dreamed.

"You have all had these strange dreams which render you masters of the impossible, which open to you doors that cannot be passed through, unexpected joys, impenetrable arms!

"Which of us in these agitated, exciting palpitating slumbers, has not held, clasped, embraced, possessed with an extraordinary acuteness of sensation, the woman with whom our minds were occupied? And have you ever noticed what superhuman delight these good fortunes of dreams bestow upon us? Into what mad intoxication they cast you! With what passionate spasms they shake you! With what infinite, caressing, penetrating tenderness they fill your heart for her whom you hold fainting and hot in that adorable and sensual illusion which seems so like reality!

"All this I felt with unforgetable violence. This woman was mine, so much mine that the pleasant warmth of her skin remained between my fingers, the odor of her skin remained in my brain, the taste of her kisses remained on my lips, the sound of her voice lingered in my ears, the touch of her clasp still clung to my side, and the burning charm of her tenderness still gratified my senses long after my exquisite but disappointing awakening.

"And three times the same night I had a renewal of my dream.

"When the day dawned, she beset me, possessed me, haunted my brain and my flesh to such an extent that I no longer remained one second without thinking of her.

"At last, not knowing what to do, I dressed myself and went to see her. As I went up the stairs to her apartment, I was so much overcome by emotion that I trembled and my heart panted; I was seized with vehement desire from head to foot.

"I entered the apartment. She rose up the moment she heard my name pronounced; and suddenly our eyes met in a fixed look of astonishment.

"I sat down.

"I uttered in a faltering tone some common-places which she seemed not to hear. I did not know what to say or to do. Then, abruptly, I flung myself upon her, seizing her with both arms; and my entire dream was accomplished so quickly, so easily, so madly, that I suddenly began to doubt whether I was really awake. She was, after this, my mistress for two years."

"What conclusion do you draw from it?" said a voice.

The story-teller seemed to hesitate.

"The conclusion I draw from it—well, by Jove, the conclusion is that it was just a coincidence! And, in the next place, who can tell? Perhaps it was some glance of hers which I had not noticed and which came back that night to me—one of those mysterious and unconscious evocations of memory which often bring before us things ignored by our own consciousness, unperceived by our minds!"

"Let that be just as you wish it," said one of his table-companions, when the story was finished, "but if you don't believe in magnetism after that, you are an ungrateful fellow, my dear boy!"

In Various Rôles

In the following reminiscences will frequently be mentioned a lady who played a great part in the annals of the police from 1848 to 1866. We will call her "Wanda von Chabert." Born in Galicia of German parents, and carefully brought up in every way, when only sixteen she married, from love, a rich and handsome officer of noble birth. The young couple, however, lived beyond their means, and when the husband died suddenly, two years after they were married, she was left anything but well off.

As Wanda had grown accustomed to luxury and amusement, a quiet life in her parents' house did not suit her any longer. Even while she was still in mourning for her husband, she allowed a Hungarian magnate to make love to her. She went off with him at a venture,

and continued the same extravagant life which she had led when her husband was alive, of her own volition. At the end of two years, however, her lover left her in a town in North Italy, almost without means. She was thinking of going on the stage, when chance provided her with another resource, which enabled her to reassert her position in society. She became a secret police agent, and soon was one of their most valuable members. In addition to the proverbial charm and wit of a Polish woman, she also possessed high linguistic attainments, and spoke Polish, Russian, French, German, English, and Italian, with almost equal fluency and correctness. Then she had that encyclopedic polish which impresses people much more than the most profound learning of the specialist. She was very attractive in appearance, and she knew how to set off her good looks by all the arts of dress and coquetry.

In addition to this, she was a woman of the world in the widest sense of the term; pleasure-loving, faithless, unstable; and therefore never in any danger of really losing her heart, and consequently her head. She used to change the place of her abode, according to what she had to do. Sometimes she lived in Paris among the Polish emigrants, in order to find out what they were doing, and maintained intimate relations with the Tuileries and the Palais Royal at the same time; sometimes she went to London for a short time, or hurried off to Italy to watch the Hungarian exiles, only to reappear suddenly in Switzerland, or at one of the fashionable German watering-places.

In revolutionary circles, she was looked upon as an active member of the great League of Freedom, and diplomatists regarded her as an influential friend of Napoleon III.

She knew everyone, but especially those men whose names were to be met with every day in the journals, and she counted Victor Emmanuel, Rouher, Gladstone, and Gortschakoff among her friends as well as Mazzini, Kossuth, Garibaldi, Mieroslawsky, and Bakunin.

In the spring of 185— she was at Vevey on the lovely lake of Geneva, and went into raptures when talking to an old German diplomatist about the beauties of nature, and about Calame, Stifter, and Turgenev, whose "Diary of a Hunter," had just become fashionable. One day a man appeared at the *table d'hôte*, who excited unusual attention, and hers especially, so that there was

nothing strange in her asking the proprietor of the hotel what his name was. She was told that he was a wealthy Brazilian, and that his name was Don Escovedo.

Whether it was an accident, or whether he responded to the interest which the young woman felt for him, at any rate she constantly met him wherever she went, whether taking a walk, or on the lake or looking at the newspapers in the reading-room. At last she was obliged to confess to herself that he was the handsomest man she had ever seen. Tall, slim, and yet muscular, the young, beardless Brazilian had a head which any woman might envy, features not only beautiful and noble, but also extremely delicate, dark eyes which possessed a wonderful charm, and thick, auburn, curly hair, which completed the attractiveness and the strangeness of his appearance.

They soon became acquainted, through a Prussian officer whom the Brazilian had asked for an introduction to the beautiful Polish lady—for Frau von Chabert was taken for one in Vevey. She, cold and designing as she was, blushed when he stood before her for the first time; and when he gave her his arm, he could feel her hand tremble slightly on it. The same evening they went out riding together, the next he was lying at her feet, and on the third she was his. For four weeks the lovely Wanda and the Brazilian lived together as if they had been in Paradise, but he could not deceive her searching eyes any longer.

Her sharp and practiced eye had already discovered in him that indefinable something which makes a man appear a suspicious character. Any other woman would have been pained and horrified at such a discovery, but she found the strange consolation in it that her handsome adorer promised also to become a very interesting object for pursuit, and so she began systematically to watch the man who lay unsuspectingly at her feet.

She soon found out that he was no conspirator; but she asked herself in vain whether she was to look for a common swindler, an impudent adventurer, or perhaps even a criminal in him. The day that she had foreseen soon came; the Brazilian's banker "unaccountably" had omitted to send him any money, and so he borrowed some of her. "So he is a male courtesan," she said to herself. The handsome man soon required money again, and she lent it to him again. Then at last he left suddenly and nobody knew where he had gone to; only this much, that he had left Vevey as the companion of an old but wealthy Wallachian lady. So this time clever Wanda was duped.

A year afterward she met the Brazilian unexpectedly at Lucca, with an insipid-looking, light-haired, thin Englishwoman on his arm. Wanda stood still and looked at him steadily; but he glanced at her quite indifferently; he did not choose to know her again.

The next morning, however, his valet brought her a letter from him, which contained the amount of his debt in Italian hundred-lire notes, accompanied by a very cool excuse. Wanda was satisfied, but she wished to find out who the lady was, in whose company she constantly saw Don Escovedo.

"Don Escovedo."

An Austrian count, who had a loud and silly laugh, said:

"Who has saddled you with that yarn? The lady is Lady Nitingsdale, and his name is Romanesco."

"Romanesco?"

"Yes, he is a rich Boyar from Moldavia, where he has extensive estates."

Romanesco ran a faro bank in his apartments, and certainly cheated, for he nearly always won; it was not long, therefore, before other people in good society at Lucca shared Madame von Chabert's suspicions, and, consequently, Romanesco thought it advisable to vanish as suddenly from Lucca as Escovedo had done from Vevey, and without leaving any more traces behind him.

Some time afterward, Madame von Chabert was on the island of Heligoland, for the sea-bathing; and one day she saw Escovedo-Romanesco sitting opposite to her at the *table d'hôte,* in very animated conversation with a Russian lady; only his hair had turned black since she had seen him last. Evidently his light hair had become too compromising for him.

"The sea-water seems to have a very remarkable effect upon your hair," Wanda said to him spitefully in a whisper.

"Do you think so?" he replied, condescendingly.

"I fancy that at one time your hair was fair."

"You are mistaking me for somebody else," the Brazilian replied, quietly.

"I am not."

"For whom do you take me, pray?" he said with an insolent smile.

"For Don Escovedo."

"I am Count Dembizki from Valkynia," the former Brazilian said with a bow; "perhaps you would like to see my passport."

"Well, perhaps—"

And he had the impudence to show her his false passport.

A year afterward Wanda met Count Dembizki in Baden, near Vienna. His hair was still black, but he had a magnificent, full, black beard; he had become a Greek prince, and his name was Anastasio Maurokordatos. She met him once in one of the side walks in the park, where he could not avoid her. "If it goes on like this," she called out to him in a mocking voice, "the next time I see you, you will be king of some negro tribe or other."

That time, however, the Brazilian did not deny his identity; on the contrary, he surrendered at discretion, and implored her not to betray him. As she was not revengeful she pardoned him, after enjoying his terror for a time, and promised him that she would hold her tongue, as long as he did nothing contrary to the laws.

"First of all, I must beg you not to gamble."

"You have only to command; and we do not know each other in the future."

"I must certainly insist on that," she said maliciously.

The "Exotic Prince" had, however, made a conquest of the charming daughter of a wealthy Austrian count, and had cut out an excellent young officer, who was wooing her. The latter, in his despair, began to make love to Frau von Chabert, and at last told her he loved her. But she only laughed at him.

"You are very cruel," he stammered in confusion.

"I? What are you thinking about?" Wanda replied, still smiling; "all I mean is that you have directed your love to the wrong address, for Countess—"

"Do not speak of her; she is engaged to another man."

"As long as I choose to permit it," she said; "but what will you do if I bring her back to your arms? Will you still call me cruel?"

"Can you do this?" the young officer asked, in great excitement.

"Well supposing I can do it, what shall I be then?"

"An angel, whom I shall thank on my knees."

A few days later, the rivals met at a coffee-house; the Greek prince began to lie and boast, and the Austrian officer gave him the lie direct. In consequence, it was arranged that they should fight a duel with pistols next morning in a wood close to Baden. But as the officer was leaving the house with his seconds the next morning, a Police Commissary came up to him and begged him not to trouble himself any further about the matter, but another time to be more careful before accepting a challenge.

"What does it mean?" the officer asked, in some surprise.

"It means that this Maurokordatos is a dangerous swindler and adventurer, whom we have just taken into custody."

"He is not a prince?"

"No; a circus rider."

An hour later, the officer received a letter from the charming Countess, in which she humbly begged for pardon,

The happy lover set off to go and see her immediately, but on the way a sudden thought struck him, and so he turned back in order to thank beautiful Wanda, as he had promised, on his knees.

The False Gems

M. LANTIN had met the young woman at a *soirée*, at the home of the assistant chief of his bureau, and at first sight had fallen madly in love with her.

She was the daughter of a country physician who had died some months previously. She had come to live in Paris, with her mother, who visited much among her acquaintances, in the hope of making a favorable marriage for her daughter. They were poor and honest, quiet and unaffected.

The young girl was a perfect type of the virtuous woman whom every sensible young man dreams of one day winning for life. Her simple beauty had the charm of angelic modesty, and the imperceptible smile which constantly hovered about her lips seemed to be the reflection of a pure and lovely soul. Her praises resounded on every side. People were never tired of saying: "Happy the man who wins her love! He could not find a better wife."

Now M. Lantin enjoyed a snug little income of $700, and, thinking he could safely assume the responsibilities of matrimony, proposed to this model young girl, and was accepted.

He was unspeakably happy with her; she governed his household so cleverly and economically that they seemed to live in luxury. She lavished the most delicate attentions on her husband, coaxed and fondled him, and the charm of her presence was so great that six years after their marriage M. Lantin discovered that he loved his wife even more than during the first days of their honeymoon.

He only felt inclined to blame her for two things: her love of the theater, and a taste for false jewelry. Her friends (she was acquainted with some officers' wives) frequently procured for her a box at the theater, often for the first representations of the new plays; and her husband was obliged to accompany her, whether he willed or not, to these amusements, though they bored him excessively after a day's labor at the office.

After a time, M. Lantin begged his wife to get some lady of her acquaintance to accompany her. She was at first opposed to such an arrangement; but, after much persuasion on his part, she finally consented—to the infinite delight of her husband.

Now, with her love for the theater came also the desire to adorn her person. True, her costumes remained as before, simple, and in the most correct taste; but she soon began to ornament her ears with huge rhinestones which glittered and sparkled like real diamonds. Around her neck she wore strings of false pearls, and on her arms bracelets of imitation gold.

Her husband frequently remonstrated with her, saying:

"My dear, as you cannnot afford to buy real diamonds, you ought to appear adorned with your beauty and modesty alone, which are the rarest ornaments of your sex."

But she would smile sweetly, and say:

"What can I do? I am so fond of jewelry. It is my only weakness. We cannnot change our natures."

Then she would roll the pearl necklaces around her fingers, and hold up the bright gems for her husband's admiration, gently coaxing him:

"Look! are they not lovely? One would swear they were real."

M. Lantin would then answer,, smilingly:

"You have Bohemian tastes, my dear."

Often of an evening, when they were enjoying a tête-à-tête by the fireside, she would place on the tea table the leather box containing the "trash," as M. Lantin called it. She would examine the false gems with a passionate attention as though they were in some way connected with a deep and secret joy; and she often insisted on passing a necklace around her husband's neck, and laughing heartily would exclaim: "How droll you look!" Then she would throw herself into his arms and kiss him affectionately.

One evening in winter she attended the opera, and on her return was chilled through and through. The next morning she coughed, and eight days later she died of inflammation of the lungs.

M. Lantin's despair was so great that his hair became white in one month. He wept unceasingly; his heart was torn

with grief, and his mind was haunted by the remembrance, the smile, the voice— by every charm of his beautiful, dead wife.

Time, the healer, did not assuage his grief. Often during office hours, while his colleagues were discussing the topics of the day, his eyes would suddenly fill with tears, and he would give vent to his grief in heartrending sobs. Everything in his wife's room remained as before her decease; and here he was wont to seclude himself daily and think of her who had been his treasure—the joy of his existence.

But life soon became a struggle. His income, which in the hands of his wife had covered all household expenses, was now no longer sufficient for his own immediate wants; and he wondered how she could have managed to buy such excellent wines, and such rare delicacies, things which he could no longer procure with his modest resources.

He incurred some debts and was soon reduced to absolute poverty. One morning, finding himself without a cent in his pocket, he resolved to sell something, and, immediately, the thought occurred to him of disposing of his wife's paste jewels. He cherished in his heart a sort of rancor against the false gems. They had always irritated him in the past, and the very sight of them spoiled somewhat the memory of his lost darling.

To the last days of her life, she had continued to make purchases; bringing home new gems almost every evening. He decided to sell the heavy necklace which she seemed to prefer, and which, he thought, ought to be worth about six or seven francs; for although paste it was nevertheless, of very fine workmanship.

He put it in his pocket and started out in search of a jeweler's shop. He entered the first one he saw; feeling a little ashamed to expose his misery, and also to offer such a worthless article for sale.

"Sir," said he to the merchant, "I would like to know what this is worth."

The man took his necklace, examined it, called his clerk and made some remarks in an undertone; then he put the ornament back on the counter, and looked at it from a distance to judge of the effect.

M. Lantin was annoyed by all this detail and was on the point of saying: "Oh! I know well enough it is not worth anything," when the jeweler said: "Sir, that necklace is worth from twelve to fifteen thousand francs; but I could not buy it unless you tell me now whence it comes."

The widower opened his eyes wide and remained gaping, not comprehending the merchant's meaning. Finally he stammered: "You say—are you sure?" The other replied dryly: "You can search elsewhere and see if anyone will offer you more. I consider it worth fifteen thousand at the most. Come back here if you cannot do better."

M. Lantin, beside himself with astonishment, took up the necklace and left the store. He wished time for reflection.

Once outside, he felt inclined to laugh, and said to himself: "The fool! Had I only taken him at his word! That jeweler cannot distinguish real diamonds from paste."

A few minutes after, he entered another store in the Rue de la Paix. As soon as the proprietor glanced at the necklace, he cried out:

"Ah, *parbleu!* I know it well; it was bought here."

M. Lantin was disturbed, and asked:

"How much is it worth?"

"Well, I sold it for twenty thousand francs. I am willing to take it back for eighteen thousand when you inform me, according to our legal formality, how it comes to be in your possession."

This time M. Lantin was dumfounded. He replied:

"But—but—examine it well. Until this moment I was under the impression that it was paste."

Said the jeweler:

"What is your name, sir?"

"Lantin—I am in the employ of the Minister of the Interior. I live at No. 16 Rue des Martyrs."

The merchant looked through his books, found the entry, and said: "That necklace was sent to Mme. Lantin's address, 16 Rue des Martyrs, July 20, 1876."

The two men looked into each other's eyes—the widower speechless with astonishment, the jeweler scenting a thief. The latter broke the silence by saying:

"Will you leave this necklace here for twenty-four hours? I will give you a receipt."

"Certainly," answered M. Lantin, hastily. Then, putting the ticket in his pocket, he left the store.

He wandered aimlessly through the streets, his mind in a state of dreadful confusion. He tried to reason, to understand. He could not afford to purchase such a costly ornament. Certainly not. But, then, it must have been a present!—a present!—a present from whom? Why was it given her?

He stopped and remained standing in the middle of the street. A horrible doubt entered his mind—she? Then all the other gems must have been presents, too! The earth seemed to tremble beneath him,—the tree before him was falling—throwing up his arms, he fell to the ground, unconscious. He recovered his senses in a pharmacy into which the passers-by had taken him, and was then taken to his home. When he arrived he shut himself up in his room and wept until nightfall. Finally, overcome with fatigue, he threw himself on the bed, where he passed an uneasy, restless night.

The following morning he arose and prepared to go to the office. It was hard to work after such a shock. He sent a letter to his employer requesting to be excused. Then he remembered that he had to return to the jeweler's. He did not like the idea; but he could not leave the necklace with that man. So he dressed and went out.

It was a lovely day; a clear blue sky smiled on the busy city below, and men of leisure were strolling about with their hands in their pockets.

Observing them, M. Lantin said to himself: "The rich, indeed, are happy. With money it is possible to forget even the deepest sorrow. One can go where one pleases, and in travel find that distraction which is the surest cure for grief. Oh! if I were only rich!"

He began to feel hungry, but his pocket was empty. He again remembered the necklace. Eighteen thousand francs! Eighteen thousand francs! What a sum!

He soon arrived in the Rue de la Paix, opposite the jeweler's. Eighteen thousand francs! Twenty times he resolved to go in, but shame kept him back. He was hungry, however,—very hungry, and had not a cent in his pocket. He decided quickly, ran across the street in order not to have time for reflection, and entered the store.

The proprietor immediately came forward, and politely offered him a chair; the clerks glanced at him knowingly.

"I have made inquiries, M. Lantin," said the jeweler, "and if you are still resolved to dispose of the gems, I am ready to pay you the price I offered."

"Certainly, sir," stammered M. Lantin.

Whereupon the proprietor took from a drawer eighteen large bills, counted and handed them to M. Lantin, who signed a receipt and with a trembling hand put the money into his pocket.

As he was about to leave the store, he turned toward the merchant, who still wore the same knowing smile, and lowering his eyes, said:

"I have—I have other gems which I have received from the same source. Will you buy them also?"

The merchant bowed: "Certainly, sir."

M. Lantin said gravely: "I will bring them to you." An hour later he returned with the gems.

The large diamond earrings were worth twenty thousand francs; the bracelets thirty-five thousand; the rings, sixteen thousand; a set of emeralds and sapphires, fourteen thousand; a gold chain with solitaire pendant, forty thousand—making the sum of one hundred and forty-three thousand francs.

The jeweler remarked, jokingly:

"There was a person who invested all her earnings in precious stones."

M. Lantin replied, seriously:

"It is only another way of investing one's money."

That day he lunched at Voisin's and drank wine worth twenty francs a bottle. Then he hired a carriage and made a tour of the Bois, and as he scanned the various turn-outs with a contemptuous air he could hardly refrain from crying out to the occupants:

"I, too, am rich!—I am worth two hundred thousand francs."

Suddenly he thought of his employer. He drove up to the office, and entered gaily, saying:

"Sir, I have come to resign my position. I have just inherited three hundred thousand francs."

He shook hands with his former colleagues and confided to them some of his projects for the future; then he went off to dine at the Café Anglais.

He seated himself beside a gentleman of aristocratic bearing, and during the meal informed the latter confidentially that he had just inherited a fortune of four hundred thousand francs.

For the first time in his life he was not bored at the theater, and spent the remainder of the night in a gay frolic.

Six months afterward he married again. His second wife was a very virtuous woman, with a violent temper. She caused him much sorrow,

---

Countess Satan

I.

THEY were discussing dynamite, the social revolution, Nihilism, and even those who cared least about politics had something to say. Some were alarmed, others philosophized, and others again tried to smile.

"Bah!" N—— said, "when we are all blown up, we shall see what it is like. Perhaps, after all, it may be an amusing sensation, provided one goes high enough."

"But we shall not be blown up at all," G——, the optimist, said, interrupting him. "It is all a romance."

"You are mistaken, my dear fellow," Jules de C—— replied. "It is like a romance, but with this confounded Nihilism, everything is the same; it would be a mistake to trust to it. For instance, the manner in which I made Bakounine's acquaintance—"

They knew that he was a good narrator, and it was no secret that his life had been an adventurous one, so they drew closer to him, and listened intently. This is what he told them:

II.

"I met Countess Nisoka W——, that strange woman who was usually called Countess Satan, in Naples. I immediately attached myself to her out of curiosity, and soon fell in love with her.

Not that she was beautiful, for she was a Russian with the bad characteristics of the Russian type. She was thin and squat at the same time, while her face was sallow and puffy, with high cheekbones and a Cossack's nose. But her conversation bewitched everyone.

"She was many-sided, learned, a philosopher, scientifically depraved, satanic. Perhaps the word is rather pretentious, but it exactly expresses what I want to say, for in other words she loved evil for the sake of evil. She rejoiced in other people's vices; she liked to sow the seed of evil, in order to see it flourish. And that, too, by fraud on an enormous scale. It was not enough for her to corrupt individuals, she only did that to keep her hand in; what she wished to do was to corrupt the masses. By slightly altering it after her own fashion, she might have used Caligula's famous wish. She also might have wished that the whole human race had but one head; not in order that she might cut it off, but that she might make the philosophy of Nihilism flourish there.

"What a temptation to become the lord and master of such a monster! I allowed myself to be tempted, and undertook the adventure. The means came unsought for by me, and the only thing that I had to do was to show myself more perverted and satanic than she was herself. And so I played the devil.

" 'Yes,' I said, 'we writers are the best workmen for doing evil, as our books may be bottles of poison. The so-called men of action only turn the handle of the *miltrailleuse* which we have loaded. Formulas will destroy the world, and it is we who invent them.'

" 'That is true,' said she, 'and that is what is wanting in Bakounine, I am sorry to say.'

"That name was constantly in her mouth. So I asked her for details, which she gave me, as she knew the man intimately.

" 'After all,' she said, with a contemptuous grimace, 'he is only a kind of Garibaldi.'

"She told me, although she made fun of him as she did so, about that 'Odyssey' of the barricades and of the hulks which made up Bakounine's history, and which is, nevertheless, the exact truth; about his adventures as chief of the insurgents at Prague and then at Dresden; of his first death sentence; about his imprisonment at Olmütz, in the casemates of the fortress of St. Peter and St. Paul, and in a subterranean dungeon at Schüsselburg; about his exile to Siberia and his wonderful escape down the river harbour, on a Japanese coasting-vessel, and about his final arrival, by way of Yokohama and San Francisco, in London, whence he was directing all the operations of Nihilism.

" 'You see,' she said, 'he is a thorough adventurer, and now all his adventures are over. He got married at Tobolsk and became a mere respectable, middle-class man. And then he has no individual ideas. Herzen, the pamphleteer of "Kolokol," inspired him with the only fertile phrase that he ever uttered: "Land and Liberty!" But that is not yet the definite formula, the general formula—what I may call the dynamite formula. At best, Bakounine would only become an incendiary, and burn down cities. And what is that, I ask you? Bah! A second-hand Rostopt-chin! He wants a prompter, and I offered to become his, but he did not take me seriously.'

* * * * * * *

"It would be useless to enter into all the psychological details which marked the course of my passion for the Countess, and to explain to you more fully the curious and daily growing attraction which she had for me. It was getting exasperating, and the more so as she resisted me as stoutly as the shyest of innocents could have done. At the end of a month of mad Satanism, I saw what her game was. Do you know what she intended? She meant to make me Bakounine's prompter, or, at any rate, that is what she said. But no doubt she reserved the right to herself—at least that is how I understood her—to prompt the prompter, and my passion for her, which she purposely left unsatisfied, assured her that absolute power over me.

"All this may appear madness to you, but it is, nevertheless, the exact truth. In short, one morning she bluntly made the offer:

" 'Become Bakounine's soul, and you shall possess me.'

"Of course I accepted, for it was too fantastically strange to refuse. Don't you think so? What an adventure! What luck! A number of letters between the Countess and Bakounine prepared the way; I was introduced to him at his house, and they discussed me there. I became a sort of Western prophet, a mystic charmer who was ready to nihilize the Latin races, the Saint Paul of the new religion of nothingness, and at last a day was fixed for

us to meet in London. He lived in a small, one-storied house in Pimlico, with a tiny garden in front, and nothing noticeable about it.

"We were first of all shown into the commonplace parlor of all English homes, and then upstairs. The room where the Countess and I were left was small, and very badly furnished. It had a square table with writing materials on it, in the center of the room. This was his sanctuary. The deity soon appeared, and I saw him in flesh and bone—especially in flesh, for he was enormously stout. His broad face, with prominent cheek-bones, in spite of fat; a nose like a double funnel; and small, sharp eyes, which had a magnetic look, proclaimed the Tartar, the old Turanian blood which produced the Attilas, the Genghis-Khans, the Tamerlanes. The obesity which is characteristic of nomad races, who are always on horseback or driving, added to his Asiatic look. The man was certainly not a European, a slave, a descendant of the diestic Aryans, but a scion of the atheistic hordes who had several times already overrun Europe, and who, instead of ideas of progress, have Nihilism buried in their hearts.

"I was astonished, for I had not expected that the majesty of a whole race could be thus revived in a man, and my stupefaction increased after an hour's conversation. I could quite understand why such a Colossus had not wished for the Countess as his Egeria; she was a silly child to have dreamed of acting such a part to such a thinker. She had not felt the profoundness of that horrible philosophy which was hidden under his material activity, nor had she seen the prophet under this hero of the barricades. Perhaps he had not thought it advisable to reveal himself to her; but he revealed himself to me, and inspired me with terror.

"A prophet? Oh! yes. He thought himself an Attila, and foresaw the consequences of his revolution; it was not only from instinct but also from theory that he urged a nation on to Nihilism. The phrase is not his, but Turgenieff's, I believe, but the idea certainly belonged to him. He got his programme of agricultural communism from Herzen, and his destructive radicalism from Pougatcheff, but he did not stop there. I mean that he went on to evil for the sake of evil. Herzen wished for the happiness of the Slav peasant; Pougatcheff wanted to be elected Emperor, but all that Bakounine wanted was to overthrow the actual order of things, no matter by what means, and to replace social concentration by a universal upheaval.

"It was the dream of a Tartar; it was true Nihilism pushed to extreme and practical conclusions. It was, in a word, the applied philosophy of chance, the indeterminate end of anarchy. Monstrous it may be, but grand in its monstrosity!

"And you must note that the typical man of action so despised by the Countess was, in Bakounine, the gigantic dreamer whom I have just shown to you. His dream did not remain a dream, but began to be realized. It was by the care of Bakounine that the Nihilistic party became an entity; a party in which there is a little of everything, you know, but on the whole, a formidable party, the advanced guard of which is true Nihilism, whose object is nothing less than to destroy the Western world, to see it blossom from under the ruins of a general dispersion, the last conception of modern Tartarism.

"I never saw Bakounine again, for the Countess's conquest would have been too dearly bought by any attempt to act a comedy with this 'Old-Man-of-the-Mountain.' And besides that, after this visit, poor Countess Satan appeared to me quite silly. Her famous Satanism was nothing but the flicker of a spirit-lamp, after the general conflagration of which the other had dreamed. She had certainly shown herself very silly, when she could not understand that prodigious monster. And as she had seduced me only by her intellect and her perversity, I was disgusted as soon as she laid aside that mask. I left her without telling her of my intention, and never saw her again, either.

"No doubt they both took me for a spy from the 'Third Section of the Imperial Chancellery.' In that case, they must have thought me very clever to have escaped discovery, and all I have to do is to look out, lest any affiliated members of their society recognize me!"

Then he smiled and, turning to the waiter who had just come in, said: "Open another bottle of champagne, and make the cork pop! It will, at any rate, remind us of the day when we ourselves shall be blown up with dynamite."

A Useful House

ROYAUMONT'S fat sides shook with laughter at the mere recollection of the funny story that he had promised to his friends, and throwing himself back in the great armchair, which he completely filled, that confirmed gossip and busybody, as they called him at the club, at last said:

"It is perfectly true. Bordenave does not owe anyone a penny and can go through any street he likes, and publish those famous memoirs of sheriff's officers, which he has been writing for the last ten years, when he did not dare to go out, and in which he carefully brought out the characters and peculiarities of all those generous distributors of stamped paper with whom he had had dealings—their tricks and wiles, their weaknesses, their jokes, their manner of performing their duties, sometimes with brutal rudeness and at others with cunning good nature, now embarrassed and almost ashamed of their work, and again ironically jovial; as well as the artifices of clerks to get a few crumbs from their employer's cake. The book will soon be published, and Machin, the 'Vaudeville' writer, has promised him a preface, so that it will be a most amusing work. You are surprised, eh? Confess that you are absolutely surprised, and I will lay you any bet you like that you will not guess how our excellent friend, whose existence is an inexplicable problem, has been able to settle with his creditors, and suddenly produce the requisite amount."

"Do get to the facts, confound it," Captain Hardeur said, who was growing tired of all this verbiage.

"All right, I will get to them as quick-ly as possible," Royaumont replied, throwing the stump of his cigar into the fire. " I will clear my throat and begin. I suppose you all of you know that two better friends than Bordenave and Quillanet do not exist; neither of them could do without the other, and they have ended by dressing alike, by having the same gestures, the same laugh, the same walk, and the same inflections of voice, so that one would think that some close bond united them, and that they had been brought up together from childhood.

"There is, however, this difference between them, that Bordenave is completely ruined and that all that he possesses are bundles of mortgages, laughable parchments which attest his ancient race, and chimerical hopes of inheriting money some day, though these expectations are already heavily hypothecated. Consequently he is always on the lookout for some fresh expedient for raising money, though he is superbly indifferent about everything; while Sebastien Quillanet, of the banking house of Quillanet Brothers, must have an income of eight hundred thousand francs a year, but is descended from an obscure laborer who managed to secure some of the national property. Then he becomes an army contractor, speculated on defeat as well as on victory, and does not know now what to do with his money.

"But as the millionaire is timid, dull, and always bored, the spendthrft amuses him by his impertinent ways and jokes; he prompts him when he is at a loss for an answer, extricates him out of his difficulties, serves as his guide in the great forests of Paris which are strewn

531

with so many pitfalls, and helps him to avoid those vulgar adventures which socially ruin a man, no matter how well ballasted he may be. Then he points out to him what women would make suitable mistresses for him, who make a man noted and give·the effect of some rare and beautiful flower pinned into his buttonhole. He is the confidant of his intrigues, his· guest when he gives small, special entertainments, his daily, familiar table companion, and the buffoon whose sly humor stimulates one, and whose witticisms you tolerate."

"Really, really," the captain interrupted him, "you have been going on for more than a quarter of an hour without saying anything."

But Royaumont shrugged his shoulders and continued:

"Oh! you·can be very tiresome when you please, my dear fellow! Last year, when he was at daggers drawn with his people, who were deafening him with recriminations, were· worrying him and threatening him with a lot of annoyance, Quillanet got married. It was a marriage of reason, which apparently changed his habits and his tastes, more especially as the ·banker was at that time keeping a perfect little marvel of a woman, a Parisian jewel of unspeakable attraction and of bewitching· delicacy, that adorable Suzette Marly, who is just like a pocket Venus, and who in some prior stage of existence must have been Phryne or Lesbia. Of course he did not get rid of her, but as he was bound to take some judicious precautions, which are necessary for a man who is deceiving his wife, he rented and furnished a house, with a courtyard in front, and a garden at the back, which

one might think had been built to shelter some amorous folly. It was the ideal that he had dreamed of, warm, snug, elegant, the walls covered with silk hangings of subdued tints, large pier-glasses, allegorical pictures, and filled with luxurious, low·furniture that seemed to invite caresses and embraces.

"Bordenave occupied the ground floor, and ·the next floor· served as a shrine for the banker and his mistress. Well, just a week ago, in order to hide the situation better. Bordenave asked Quillanet and some other friends to one of those luncheons which he understands so well how to order, ·such a delicious luncheon, that before it was quite over, every man had a woman on his lap, and was asking himself whether a kiss from coaxing and naughty lips was not a thousand times more intoxicating than the finest old brandy or the choicest vintage wines, when the butler came in with an embarrassed look, and whispered something to him.

" 'Tell the gentleman· that he has made a mistake, and ask him to leave me in peace.' Bordenave replied to him in an angry voice. The servant went out and returned immediately to say that the intruder was using threats, that he refused to leave the house, and even· spoke of having recourse to the commissary of police. Bordenave frowned, threw his napkin down, upset two glasses, and swaggered out with a red face, swearing and ejaculating:

" 'This is rather too much, and the fellow shall find out what going out of the window means, if he will not leave by the door.' But in the anteroom he found himself face to face with a very cool, polite, impassive gentleman, who said very quietly to him:

" 'You are Count Robert de Borde-nave, I believe, Monsieur?'

" 'Yes, Monsieur.'

" 'And the lease that you signed at the lawyer's, Monsieur Albin Calvert, in the Rue du Frabourg-Poissonnière, is in your name, I believe?'

" 'Certainly, Monsieur.'

" 'Then I regret extremely to have to tell you that if you are not in a position to pay the various accounts which different people have intrusted to me for collection here, I shall be obliged to seize all the furniture, pictures, plate, clothes, etc., which are here in the presence of two witnesses who are waiting for me downstairs in the street.'

" 'I suppose this is some joke, Monsieur?'

" 'It would be a very poor joke, Monsieur le Comte, and one which I should certainly not allow myself toward you!'

"The situation was absolutely critical and ridiculous, the more so, that in the dining-room the women, who were slightly tipsy, were tapping the wine-glasses with their spoons, and calling for him. What could he do except explain his misadventure to Quillanet, who became sobered immediately, and rather than see his shrine of love violated, his secret sin disclosed, and his pictures, ornaments, and furniture sold, gave a check in due form for the claim there and then, though with a very wry face. And in spite of this, some people will deny that men who are utterly broke often have a stroke of luck!"

The Colonel's Ideas

"Upon my word," said Colonel Laporte, "I am old and gouty, my legs are as stiff as two sticks, and yet if a pretty woman were to tell me to go through the eye of a needle, I believe I should take a jump at it, like a clown through a hoop. I shall die like that; it is in the blood. I am an old beau, one of the old *régime,* and the sight of a woman, a pretty woman, stirs me to the tips of my toes. There!

"And then we are all very much alike in France; we remain cavaliers, cavaliers of love and fortune, since God has been abolished, whose bodyguard we really were. But nobody will ever get

the woman out of our hearts; there she is, and there she will remain; we love her, and shall continue to love her, and to commit all kinds of frolics on her account, so long as there is a France on the map of Europe. And even if France were to be wiped off the map, there would always be Frenchmen left.

"When I am in the presence of a woman, of a pretty woman, I feel capable of anything. By Jove, when I feel her looks penetrating me, those confounded looks which set your blood on fire, I could do anything: fight a duel, have a row, smash the furniture, anything just to show that I am the strongest, the bravest, the most daring, and the most devoted of men.

"But I am not the only one—certainly not; the whole French army is like me, that I will swear to. From the common soldier to the general, we all go forward, and to the very end, mark you, when there is a woman in the case, a pretty woman. Remember what Joan of Arc made us do formerly! Come, I'd make a bet that if a pretty woman had taken command of the army on the eve of Sedan, when Marshal MacMahon was wounded, we should have broken through the Prussian lines, by Jove! and have had a drink out of their guns.

"It was not Trochu, but Saint-Geneviève, who was required in Paris, and I remember a little anecdote of the war which proves that we are capable of everything in the presence of a woman.

"I was a captain, a simple captain, at the time, and was in command of a detachment of scouts who were retreating through a district swarming with Prussians. We were surrounded, pursued, tired out, and half dead with fatigue and hunger, and by the next day we had to reach Bar-sur-Tain; otherwise we should be done for, cut off from the main body and killed. I do not know how we managed to escape so far. However, we had ten leagues to go during the night, ten leagues through the snow, and upon empty stomachs. I thought to myself:

" 'It is all over; my poor fellows will never be able to do it.'

"We had eaten nothing since the day before, and the whole day long we remained hidden in a barn, huddled close together, so as not to feel the cold much; we did not venture to speak or even move, and we slept by fits and starts, like you sleep when you are worn out with fatigue.

"It was dark by five o'clock, that wan darkness caused by the snow, and I shook up my men. Some of them would not get up; they were almost incapable of moving or of standing upright, and their joints were stiff from the cold and want of motion.

"In front of us there was a large expanse of flat, bare country; the snow was still falling like a curtain, in large, white flakes, which concealed everything under a heavy, thick, frozen mantle, a mattress of ice. You would have thought that it was the end of things.

" 'Come, my lads, let us start.'

"They looked at the thick, white dust which was coming down, and seemed to think: 'We have had enough of this; we may just as well die here!' Then I took out my revolver, and said:

" 'I will shoot the first man who flinches.' And so they set off, but very slowly, like men whose legs were of very little use to them. I sent four of them three hundred yards ahead, to scout, and the others followed pellmell, walking at random and without any order. I put the strongest in the rear, with orders to quicken the pace of the sluggards with the points of their bayonets in the back.

"The snow seemed as if it were going to bury us alive; it powdered our *képis*** and cloaks without melting, and made phantoms of us, ghosts of wornout soldiers who were very tired, and I said to myself: 'We shall never get out of this, except by a miracle.'

*Forage-caps.

"Sometimes we had to stop for a few minutes, on account of those who could not follow us, hearing nothing but the falling snow, that vague, almost indiscernible sound which the flakes make, as they come down together. Some of the men shook themselves, but others did not move, and so I gave the order to set off again; they shouldered their rifles, and with weary feet we set out again, when suddenly the scouts fell back. Something had alarmed them; they had heard voices in front of them, and so I sent six men and a sergeant on ahead, and waited.

"All at once a shrill cry, a woman's cry, pierced through the heavy silence of the snow, and in a few minutes they brought back two prisoners, an old man and a girl, whom I questioned in a low voice. They were escaping from the Prussians, who had occupied their house during the evening, and who had got drunk. The father had become alarmed on his daughter's account, and, without even telling their servants, they had made their escape into the darkness. I saw immediately that they belonged to the upper classes, and, as I should have done in any case, I invited them to come with us. So we started off together, and as the old man knew the road, he acted as our guide.

"It had ceased snowing; the stars appeared, and the cold became intense. The girl, who was leaning on her father's arm, walked wearily and with jerks, and several times she murmured:

"'I have no feeling at all in my feet.' I suffered more than she did, I believe, to see that poor little woman dragging herself like that through the snow. But suddenly she stopped, and said:

"'Father, I am so tired that I cannot go any further.'

"The old man wanted to carry her, but he could not even lift her up, and she fell on the ground with a deep sigh. We all came round her, and as for me, I stamped on the ground, not knowing what to do, quite unable to make up my mind to abandon that man and girl like that. Suddenly one of the soldiers, a Parisian, whom they had nicknamed 'Pratique,' said:

"'Come, comrades, we must carry the young lady, otherwise we shall not show ourselves Frenchmen, confound it!'

"I really believe that I swore with pleasure, and said: 'That is very good of you, my children; I will take my share of the burden.'

"We could indistinctly see the trees of a little wood on the left, through the darkness. Several men went into it, and soon came back with a bundle of branches twisted into a litter.

"'Who will lend us his cloak? It is for a pretty girl, comrades,' Pratique said, and ten cloaks were thrown to him. In a moment, the girl was lying, warm and comfortable, among them, and was raised upon six shoulders. I placed myself at their head, on the right, and very pleased I was with my charge.

"We started off much more briskly, as if we had been having a drink of wine, and I even heard a few jokes. A woman is quite enough to electrify Frenchmen, you see. The soldiers, who were reanimated and warm, had almost reformed their ranks, and an old *franc-tireur** who was following the litter,

---

*Volunteers, in the Franco-German war of 1870-1871, of whom the Germans often made short work when caught.

waiting for his turn to replace the first of his comrades who might give in, said to one of his neighbors, loud enough for me to hear:

" 'I am not a young man, now; but by Jove, there is nothing like a woman to make you feel queer from head to foot!'

"We went on, almost without stopping, until three o'clock in the morning, when suddenly our scouts fell back again. Soon the whole detachment showed nothing but a vague shadow on the ground, as the men lay on the snow, and I gave my orders in a low voice, and heard the harsh, metallic sound of the cocking of rifles. There, in the middle of the plain, some strange object was moving about. It might have been taken for some enormous animal running about, which uncoiled itself like a serpent, or came together into a coil, then suddenly went quickly to the right or left, stopped, and then went on again. But presently the wandering shape came near, and I saw a dozen lancers, one behind the other, who were trying to find their way, which they had lost.

"By this time they were so near that I could hear the panting of the horses, the clink of the swords, and the creaking of the saddles, and so cried: 'Fire!'

"Fifty rifle-shots broke the stillness of the night; then there were four or five reports, and at last one single shot was heard. When the smoke had cleared away we saw that the twelve men and nine horses had fallen. Three of the animals were galloping away at a furious pace. One of them was dragging the body of its rider behind it. His foot had caught in the stirrup, and his body rebounded from the ground in a horrible way.

"One of the soldiers behind me gave a harsh laugh, and said: 'There are a few more widows now!'

"Perhaps he was married.   And another added: 'It did not take long!'

"A head was put out of the litter:

" 'What is the matter?' she asked; 'you are fighting?'

" 'It is nothing, Mademoiselle,' I replied; 'we have got rid of a dozen Prussians!'

" 'Poor fellows!' she said. But as she was cold, she quickly disappeared beneath the cloaks again, and we started off once more. We marched on for a long time, and at last the sky began to grow pale. The snow became quite clear, luminous, and bright, and a rosy tint appeared in the east. Suddenly a voice in the distance cried:

" 'Who goes there?'

"The whole detachment halted, and I advanced to say who we were. We had reached the French lines, and as my men defiled before the outpost, a commandant on horseback, whom I had informed of what had taken place, asked in a sonorous voice, as he saw the litter pass him:

" 'What have you there?'

"And immediately a small head, covered with light hair, appeared, disheveled and smiling, and replied:

" 'It is I, Monsieur.'

"At this, the men raised a hearty laugh, and we felt quite light-hearted, while Pratique, who was walking by the side of the litter, waved his *képi,* and shouted:

" *'Vive la France!'* And I felt really moved. I do not know why, except that I thought it a pretty and gallant thing to say.

"It seemed to me as if we had just saved the whole of France, and had done something that other men could not have done, something simple, and really patriotic. I shall never forget that little face, you may be sure, and if I had to give my opinion about abolishing drums, trumpets, and bugles, I should propose to replace them in every regiment by a pretty girl, and that would be even better than playing the 'Marseillaise.' By Jove! it would put some spirit into a trooper to have a Madonna like that, a living Madonna, by the colonel's side."

He was silent for a few moments, and then with an air of conviction, and jerking his head, continued:

"You see, we are very fond of women, we Frenchmen!"

Two Little Soldiers

Every Sunday, the moment they were dismissed, the two little soldiers made off. Once outside the barracks, they struck out to the right through Courbevoie, walking with long rapid strides, as though they were on a march.

When they were beyond the last of the houses, they slackened pace along the bare, dusty roadway which goes toward Bézons.

They were both small and thin, and looked quite lost in their coats, which were too big and too long. Their sleeves hung down over their hands, and they found their enormous red breeches, which compelled them to waddle, very much in the way. Under their stiff, high helmets their faces had little character—two poor, sallow Breton faces, simple with an almost animal simplicity, and with gentle and quiet blue eyes.

They never conversed during these walks, but went straight on, each with the same thoughts in his head. This thought atoned for the lack of conversation; it was this that just inside the little wood near Les Champioux they had found a place which reminded them of their own country, where they could feel happy again.

When they arrived under the trees where the roads, from Colombes and from Chatou cross, they would take off their heavy helmets and wipe their foreheads. They always halted on the Bézons bridge to look at the Seine, and would remain there two or three minutes, bent double, leaning on the parapet.

Sometimes they would gaze out over the great basin of Argenteuil, where the skiffs might be seen scudding, with their white, careening sails, recalling perhaps the look of the Breton waters, the harbor of Vanne, near which they lived, and the fishing-boats standing out across the Morbihan to the open sea.

Just beyond the Seine they bought their provisions from a sausage merchant, a baker, and a wine-seller. A piece of blood-pudding, four sous' worth of bread, and a liter of "petit bleu" constituted the provisions, which they carried off in their handkerchiefs. After they had left Bézons they traveled slowly and began to talk.

In front of them a barren plain studded with clumps of trees led to the wood, to the little wood which had seemed to them to resemble the one at Kermarivan. Grainfields and hayfields bordered the narrow path, which lost itself in the young greenness of the crops, and Jean Kerderen would always say to Luc le Ganidec:

"It looks like it does near Plounivon."

"Yes; exactly."

Side by side they strolled, their souls filled with vague memories of their own country, with awakened images as naïve as the pictures on the colored broadsheets which you buy for a penny. They kept on recognizing, as it were, now a corner of a field, a hedge, a bit of moorland, now a crossroad, now a granite cross. Then, too, they would always stop beside a certain landmark, a great stone, because it looked something like the cromlech at Locneuven.

Every Sunday on arriving at the first clump of trees Luc le Ganidec would cut a switch, a hazel switch, and begin gently to peel off the bark, thinking meanwhile of the folk at home. Jean Kerderen carried the provisions.

From time to time Luc would mention a name, or recall some deed of their childhood in a few brief words, which caused long thoughts. And their own country, their dear, distant country, recaptured them little by little, seizing on their imaginations, and sending to them from afar her shapes, her sounds, her well-known prospects, her odors—odors of the green lands where the salt sea-air was blowing.

No longer conscious of the exhala-

tions of the Parisian stables, on which the earth of the *banlieue* fattens, they scented the perfume of the flowering broom, which the salt breeze of the open sea plucks and bears away. And the sails of the boats from the river banks seemed like the white wings of the coasting vessels seen beyond the great plain which extended from their homes to the very margin of the sea.

They walked with short steps, Luc le Ganidec and Jean Kerderen, content and sad, haunted by a sweet melancholy, by the lingering, ever-present sorrow of a caged animal who remembers his liberty.

By the time that Luc had stripped the slender wand of its bark they reached the corner of the wood where every Sunday they took breakfast. They found the two bricks which they kept hidden in the thicket, and kindled a little fire of twigs, over which to roast the blood-pudding at the end of a bayonet.

When they had breakfasted, eaten their bread to the last crumb, and drunk their wine to the last drop, they remained seated side by side upon the grass, saying nothing, their eyes on the distance, their eyelids drooping, their fingers crossed as at mass, their red legs stretched out beside the poppies of the field. And the leather of their helmets and the brass of their buttons glittered in the ardent sun, making the larks, which sang and hovered above their heads, cease in mid-song.

Toward noon they began to turn their eyes from time to time in the direction of the village of Bézons, because the girl with the cow was coming. She passed by them every Sunday on her way to milk and change the pasture of her cow —the only cow in this district which ever went out of the stable to grass. It was pastured in a narrow field along the edge of the wood a little farther on.

They soon perceived the girl, the only human being within vision, and were gladdened by the brilliant reflections thrown off by the tin milk-pail under the rays of the sun. They never talked about her. They were simply glad to see her, without understanding why.

She was a big strong wench with red hair, burned by the heat of sunny days, a sturdy product of the environs of Paris.

Once, finding them seated in the same place, she said:

"Good morning. You two are always here, aren't you?"

Luc le Ganidec, the bolder, stammered:

"Yes, we come to rest."

That was all. But the next Sunday she laughed on seeing them, laughed with a protecting benevolence and a feminine keenness which knew well enough that they were bashful. And she asked:

"What are you doing there? Are you trying to see the grass grow?"

Luc was cheered up by this, and smiled likewise: "Maybe we are."

"That's pretty slow work," said she.

He answered, still laughing: "Well, yes, it is."

She went on. But coming back with a milk-pail full of milk, she stopped again before them, and said:

"Would you like a little? It will taste like home."

With the instinctive feeling that they were of the same peasant race as she,

being herself perhaps also far away from home, she had divined and touched the spot.

They were both touched. Then with some difficulty, she managed to make a little milk run into the neck of the glass bottle in which they carried their wine. And Luc drank first, with little swallows, stopping every minute to see whether he had drunk more than his half. Then he handed the bottle to Jean.

She stood upright before them, her hands on her hips, her pail on the ground at her feet, glad at the pleasure which she had given.

Then she departed, shouting: *"Allons, adieu!* Till next Sunday!"

And as long as they could see her at all, they followed with their eyes her tall silhouette, which faded, growing smaller and smaller, seeming to sink into the verdure of the fields.

When they were leaving the barracks the week after, Jean said to Luc:

"Oughtn't we to buy her something good?"

They were in great embarrassment before the problem of the choice of a delicacy for the girl with the cow. Luc was of the opinion that a little tripe would be the best, but Jean preferred some *berlingots* because he was fond of sweets. His choice fairly made him enthusiastic, and they bought at a grocer's two sous' worth of white and red candies.

They ate their breakfast more rapidly than usual, being nervous with expectation.

Jean saw her first. "There she is!" he cried. Luc added: "Yes, there she is."

While yet some distance off she laughed at seeing them. Then she cried:

"Is everything going as you like it?"

And in unison they asked:

"Are you getting on all right?"

Then she conversed, talked to them of simple things in which they felt an interest—of the weather, of the crops, and of her master.

They were afraid to offer her the candies, which were slowly melting away in Jean's pocket.

At last Luc grew bold, and murmured:

"We have brought you something."

She demanded, "What is it? Tell me!"

Then Jean, blushing up to his ears, managed to get at the little paper cornucopia, and held it out.

She began to eat the little bonbons, rolling them from one cheek to the other where they made little round lumps. The two soldiers, seated before her, gazed at her with emotion and delight.

Then she went to milk her cow, and once more gave them some milk on coming back.

They thought of her all the week; several times they even spoke of her. The next Sunday she sat down with them for a little longer talk; and all three, seated side by side, their eyes lost in the distance, clasping their knees with their hands, told the small doings, the minute details of life in the villages where they had been born, while over there the cow, seeing that the milkmaid had stopped on her way, stretched out toward her its heavy head with its dripping nostrils, and gave a long low to call her.

Soon the girl consented to eat a bit of bread with them and drink a mouthful of wine. She often brought them plums in her pocket, for the season of plums had come. Her presence sharpened the wits of the two little Breton soldiers, and they chattered like two birds.

But, one Tuesday, Luc le Ganidec asked for leave—a thing which had never happened before—and he did not return until ten o'clock at night. Jean racked his brains uneasily for a reason for his comrade's going out in this way.

The next Thursday Luc, having borrowed ten sous from his bedfellow, again asked and obtained permission to leave the barracks for several hours. When he set off with Jean on their Sunday walk his manner was very queer, quite restless, and quite changed. Kerderen did not understand, but he vaguely suspected something without divining what it could be.

They dd not say a word to one another until they reached their usual halting-place, where, from their constant sitting in the same spot the grass was quite worn away. They ate their breakfast slowly. Neither of them felt hungry.

Before long the girl appeared. As on every Sunday, they watched her coming. When she was quite near, Luc rose and made two steps forward. She put her milk-pail on the ground and kissed him. She kissed him passionately, throwing her arms about his neck, without noticing Jean, without remembering that he was there, without even seeing him.

And he sat there desperate, poor Jean, so desperate that he did not understand, his soul quite overwhelmed, his heart bursting, but not yet understanding himself. Then the girl seated herself beside Luc, and they began to chatter.

Jean did not look at them. He now divined why his comrade had gone out twice during the week, and he felt within him a burning grief, a kind of wound, that sense of rending which is caused by treason.

Luc and the girl went off together to change the position of the cow. Jean followed them with his eyes. He saw them departing side by side. The red breeches of his comrade made a bright spot on the road. It was Luc who picked up the mallet and hammered down the stake to which they tied the beast.

The girl stooped to milk her, while he stroked the cow's sharp spine with a careless hand. Then they left the milk-pail on the grass, and went deep into the wood.

Jean saw nothing but the wall of leaves where they had entered; and he felt himself so troubled that if he had tried to rise he would certainly have fallen. He sat motionless, stupefied by astonishment and suffering, with an agony which was simple but deep. He wanted to cry, to run away, to hide himself, never to see anybody any more.

Soon he saw them issuing from the thicket. They returned slowly, holding each other's hands as in the villages do those who are promised. It was Luc who carried the pail.

They kissed one another again before they separated, and the girl went off after having thrown Jean a friendly "Good evening" and a smile which was full of meaning. To-day she no longer thought of offering him any milk.

The two little soldiers sat side by side, motionless as usual, silent and calm, their placid faces betraying nothing of all which troubled their hearts. The sun fell on them. Sometimes the cow lowed, looking at them from afar.

At their usual hour they rose to go back. Luc cut a switch. Jean carried the empty bottle to return it to the wine-seller at Bézons. Then they sallied out upon the bridge, and, as they did every Sunday, stopped several minutes in the middle to watch the water flowing.

Jean leaned, leaned more and more, over the iron railing, as though he saw in the current something which attracted him. Luc said: "Are you trying to drink?" Just as he uttered the last word Jean's head overbalanced his body, his legs described a circle in the air, and the little blue and red soldier fell in a heap, struck the water, and disappeared.

Luc, his tongue paralyzed with anguish, tried in vain to shout. Farther down he saw something stir; then the head of his comrade rose to the surface of the river and sank immediately. Farther still he again perceived a hand, a single hand, which issued from the stream and then disappear. That was all.

The bargemen who dragged the river did not find the body that day.

Luc set out alone for the barracks going at a run, his soul filled with despair. He told of the accident, with tears in his eyes, and a husky voice, blowing his nose again and again: "He leaned over —he—he leaned over—so far—so far that his head turned a somersault; and —and—so he fell—he fell—"

Choked with emotion, he could say no more. If he had only known!

Ghosts

Just at the time when the Concordat was in its most flourishing condition, a young man belonging to a wealthy and highly respectable middle-class family went to the office of the head of the police at P——, and begged for his help and advice, which was immediately promised him.

"My father threatens to disinherit me," the young man began, "although I have never offended against the laws of the State, of morality, or against his paternal authority, merely because I do not share his blind reverence for the Catholic Church and her clergy. On that account he looks upon me, not merely as Latitudinarian but as a perfect Atheist, and a faithful old manservant of ours, who is much attached to me, and who accidentally saw my father's will, told me in confidence that he had left all his property to the Jesuits. I think this is highly suspicious, and I fear that the priests have been maligning me to my father. Until less than a year ago, we used to live very quietly and happily together, but ever since he has had so much to do with the clergy, our domestic peace and happiness are at an end."

"What you have told me," replied the official, "is as likely as it is regrettable, but I fail to see how I can interfere in the matter. Your father is in full possession of all his mental faculties, and can dispose of all his property exactly as he pleases. I think that your protest is premature; you must wait until his will can legally take effect, and then you can invoke the aid of justice. I am sorry to say that just now I can do nothing for you."

"I think you will be able to," the young man replied; "for I believe that a very clever piece of deceit is being carried on."

"How? Please explain yourself more clearly."

"When I remonstrated with him, yesterday evening, he referred to my dead mother, and at last assured me, in a voice of the deepest conviction, that she had frequently appeared to him, had threatened him with all the torments of the damned, if he did not disinherit his son, who had fallen away from God, and leave all his property to the Church. Now I do not believe in ghosts."

"Neither do I," the police director replied, "but I cannot well do anything on such grounds, having nothing but superstitions to go upon. You know how the Church rules all our affairs since the Concordat with Rome, and if I investigate this matter and obtain no results, I am risking my post. It would be very different if you could adduce any proofs for your suspicions. I do not deny that I should like to see the clerical party, which will, I fear, be the ruin of Austria, receive a staggering blow; try, therefore, to get to the bottom of this business, and then we will talk it over again."

About a month passed, without the young Latitudinarian being heard of. Suddenly, he came one evening, in a great state of excitement, and told the Inspector that he was in a position to expose the priestly deceit which he had mentioned, if the authorities would assist him. The police director asked for further information.

"I have obtained a number of important clues," said the young man. "In the first place, my father confessed to me that my mother did not appear to him in our house, but in the churchyard where she is buried. My mother was consumptive for many years, and a few weeks before her death she went to the village of S——, where she died and was buried. In addition to this, I found out from our footman that my father has already left the house twice, late at night, in company of X——, the Jesuit priest, and that on both occasions he did not return till morning. Each time he was remarkably uneasy and low-spirited after his return, and had three masses said for my dead mother. He also told me just now that he has to leave home this evening on business, but, immediately after he told me that, our footman saw the Jesuit go out of the house. We may, therefore, assume that he intends this evening to consult the spirit of my dead mother again, and this would be an excellent opportunity to solve the matter, if you do not object to opposing the most powerful force in the Empire for the sake of such an insignificant individual as myself."

"Every citizen has an equal right to the protection of the State," the police director replied; "and I think that I have shown often enough that I am not wanting in courage to perform my duty, no matter how serious the consequences may be. But only very young men act without any prospects of success, because they are carried away by their feelings. When you came to me the first time, I was obliged to refuse your request for assistance, but to-day your request is just and reasonable. It is now eight o'clock; I shall expect you in two hours' time, here in my office. At present, all you have to do is to hold your tongue; everything else is my affair."

As soon as it was dark, four men got into a closed carriage in the yard of the police-office, and were driven in the direction of the village of S——. Their carriage, however, did not enter the village, but stopped at the edge of a small wood in the immediate neighborhood. Here all four alighted: the police director, accompanied by the young Latitudinarian, a police sergeant, and an ordinary policeman, the latter however, dressed in plain clothes.

"The first thing for us to do is to examine the locality carefully," said the police director. "It is eleven o'clock and the exorcisers of ghosts will not arrive before midnight, so we have time to look round us, and to lay our plans."

The four men went to the churchyard, which lay at the end of the village, near the little wood. Everything was as still as death, and not a soul was to be seen. The sexton was evidently sitting in the public house, for they found the door of his cottage locked, as well as the door of the little chapel that stood in the middle of the churchyard.

"Where is your mother's grave?" the police director asked. As there were only a few stars visible, it was not easy to find it, but at last they managed it, and the police director surveyed the neighborhood of it.

"The position is not a very favorable one for us," he said at last; "there is nothing here, not even a shrub, behind which we could hide."

But just then, the policeman reported

that he had tried to get into the sexton's hut through the door or a window, and that at last he had succeeded in doing so by breaking open a square in a window which had been mended with paper, that he had opened it and obtained possession of the key, which he brought to the police director.

The plans were very quickly settled. The police director had the chapel opened and went in with the young Latitudinarian; then he told the police sergeant to lock the door behind him and to put the key back where he had found it, and to shut the window of the sexton's cottage carefully. Lastly, he made arrangements as to what they were to do, in case anything unforeseen should occur, whereupon the sergeant and the constable left the churchyard, and lay down in a ditch at some distance from the gate, but opposite to it.

Almost as soon as the clock struck half past eleven, they heard steps near the chapel, whereupon the police director and the young Latitudinarian went to the window in order to watch the beginning of the exorcism, and as the chapel was in total darkness, they thought that they should be able to see without being seen; but matters turned out differently from what they expected.

Suddenly, the key turned in the lock. They barely had time to conceal themselves behind the altar, before two men came in, one of whom was carrying a dark lantern. One was the young man's father, an elderly man of the middle class, who seemed very unhappy, and depressed, the other the Jesuit father X——, a tall, lean, big-boned man, with a thin, bilious face, in which two large gray eyes shone restlessly under bushy,

black eyebrows. He lit the tapers, which were standing on the altar, and began to say a "Requiem Mass;" while the old man kneeled on the altar steps and served him.

When it was over, the Jesuit took the book of the Gospels and the holy-water sprinkler, and went slowly out of the chapel, the old man following him with the holy-water basin in one hand, and a taper in the other. Then the police director left his hiding place, and stooping down, so as not to be seen, crept to the chapel window, where he cowered down carefully; the young man followed his example. They were now looking straight at his mother's grave.

The Jesuit, followed by the superstitious old man, walked three times round the grave; then he remained standing before it, and by the light of the taper read a few passages from the Gospel. Then he dipped the holy-water sprinkler three times into the holy-water basin, and sprinkled the grave three times. Then both returned to the chapel, kneeled down outside it with their faces toward the grave, and began to pray aloud, until at last the Jesuit sprang up, in a species of wild ecstasy, and cried out three times in a shrill voice:

*"Exsurge! Exsurge! Exsurge!"**

Scarcely had the last words of the exorcism died away, when thick, blue smoke rose out of the grave, rapidly grew into a cloud, and began to assume the outlines of a human body, until at last a tall, white figure stood behind the grave, and beckoned with its hand.

"Who art thou?" the Jesuit asked sol-

*Arise.

emnly, while the old man began to cry.

"When I was alive, I was called Anna Maria B——," replied the ghost in a hollow voice.

"Will you answer all my questions?" the priest continued.

"As far as I can."

"Have you then yet been delivered from purgatory by our prayers, and by all the Masses for your soul, which we have said for you?"

"Not yet, but soon, soon I shall be."

"When?"

"As soon as that blasphemer, my son, has been punished."

"Has that not already happened? Has not your husband disinherited his lost son, and in his place made the Church his heir?"

"That is not enough."

"What must he do besides?"

"He must deposit his will with the Judicial Authorities, as his last will and testament, and drive the reprobate out of his house."

"Consider well what you are saying; must this really be?"

"It must, or otherwise I shall have to languish in purgatory much longer," the sepulchral voice replied with a deep sigh; but the next moment the ghost yelled out in terror: "Oh! Good Lord!" and began to run away as fast as it could. A shrill whistle was heard, and then another, and the police director laid his hand on the shoulder of the exorciser with the remark:

"You are in custody."

Meanwhile, the police sergeant and the policeman, who had come into the churchyard, had caught the ghost, and dragged it forward. It was the sexton, who had put on a flowing, white dress, and wore a wax mask, which bore a striking resemblance to his mother, so the son declared.

When the case was heard, it was proved that the mask had been very skillfully made from a portrait of the deceased woman. The government gave orders that the matter should be investigated as secretly as possible, and left the punishment of Father X—— to the spiritual authorities, which was a matter of necessity, at a time when priests were outside of the jurisdiction of the civil authorities. It is needless to say that Father X—— was very comfortable during his imprisonment in a monastery, in a part of the country which abounded with game and trout.

The only valuable result of the amusing ghost story was that it brought about a reconciliation between father and son; the former, as a matter of fact, felt such deep respect for priests and their ghosts in consequence of the apparition, that a short time after his wife had left purgatory for the last time in order to talk with him, he turned Protestant.

Was It a Dream?

"I HAD loved her madly!

"Why does one love? Why does one love? How queer it is to see only one being in the world, to have only one thought in one's mind, only one desire in the heart, and only one name on the lips—a name which comes up continually, rising, like the water in a spring, from the depths of the soul to the lips, a name which one repeats over and over again, which one whispers ceaselessly, everywhere, like a prayer.

"I am going to tell you our story, for love only has one, which is always the same. I met her and lived on her tenderness, on her caresses, in her arms, in her dresses, on her words, so completely wrapped up, bound, and aborbed in everything which came from her, that I no longer cared whether it was day or night, or whether I was dead or alive, on this old earth of ours.

"And then she died. How? I do not know; I no longer know anything. But one evening she came home wet, for it was raining heavily, and the next day she coughed, and she coughed for about a week, and took to her bed. What happened I do not remember now, but doctors came, wrote, and went away. Medicines were brought, and some women made her drink them. Her hands were hot, her forehead was burning, and her eyes bright and sad. When I spoke to her, she answered me, but I do not remember what we said. I have forgotten everything, everything, everything! She died, and I very well remember her slight, feeble sigh. The nurse said: 'Ah!' and I understood, I understood!

"I knew nothing more, nothing. I saw a priest, who said: 'Your mistress?' and it seemed to me as if he were insulting her. As she was dead, nobody had the right to say that any longer, and I turned him out. Another came who was very kind and tender, and I shed tears when he spoke to me about her.

"They consulted me about the funeral, but I do not remember anything that they said, though I recollected the coffin, and the sound of the hammer when they nailed her down in it. Oh! God, God!

"She was buried! Buried! She! In that hole! Some people came—female friends. I made my escape and ran away. I ran, and then walked through the streets, went home, and the next day started on a journey.

* * * * * * *

"Yesterday I returned to Paris, and when I saw my room again—our room, our bed, our furniture, everything that remains of the life of a human being after death—I was seized by such a violent attack of fresh grief, that I felt like opening the window and throwing myself out into the street. I could not remain any longer among these things, between these walls which had inclosed and sheltered her, which retained a thousand atoms of her, of her skin and of her breath, in their imperceptible crevices. I took up my hat to make my escape, and just as I reached the door, I passed the large glass in the hall, which she had put there so that she might look at herself every day from head to foot as she went out, to see if her toilette looked well and was correct and pretty from her little boots to her bonnet.

"I stopped short in front of that looking-glass in which she had so often been reflected—so often, so often, that it must have retained her reflection. I was standing there trembling with my eyes fixed on the glass—on that flat, profound, empty glass—which had contained her entirely, and had possessed her as much as I, as my passionate looks had. I felt as if I loved that glass. I touched it; it was cold. Oh! the recollection! sorrowful mirror, burning mirror, horrible mirror, to make men suffer such torments! Happy is the man whose heart forgets everything that it has contained, everything that has passed before it, everything that has looked at itself in it, or has been reflected in its affection, in its love! How I suffer!

"I went out without knowing its, without wishing it, and toward the cemetery. I found her simple grave, a white marble cross, with these few words:

" 'She loved, was loved, and died.'

"She is there below, decayed! How horrible! I sobbed with my forehead on the ground, and I stopped there for a long time, a long time. Then I saw that it was getting dark and a strange, mad wish, the wish of a despairing lover, seized me. I wished to pass the night, the last night in weeping on her grave. But I should be seen and driven out. How was I to manage? I was cunning and got up and began to roam about in that city of the dead. I walked and walked. How small this city is, in comparison with the other, the city in which we live. And yet, how much more numerous the dead are than the living. We want high houses, wide streets, and much room for the four generations who see the daylight at the same time, drink water from the spring, and wine from the vines, and eat bread from the plains.

"And for all the generations of the dead, for all that ladder of humanity that has descended down to us, there is scarcely anything, scarcely anything! The earth takes them back, and oblivion effaces them. Adieu!

"At the end of the cemetery, I suddenly perceived that I was in its oldest part, where those who had been dead a long time are mingling with the soil, where the crosses themselves are decayed, where possibly newcomers will be put to-morrow. It is full of untended roses, of strong and dark cypress-trees, a sad and beautiful garden, nourished on human flesh.

"I was alone, perfectly alone. So I crouched in a green tree and hid myself there completely amid the thick and somber branches. I waited, clinging to the stem, like a shipwrecked man does to a plank.

"When it was quite dark, I left my refuge and began to walk softly, slowly, inaudibly through that ground full of dead people. I wandered about for a long time, but could not find her tomb again. I went on with extended arms, knocking against the tombs with my hands, my feet, my knees, my chest, even with my head, without being able to find her. I groped about like a blind man finding his way, I felt the stones, the crosses, the iron railings, the metal wreaths, and the wreaths of faded flowers! I read the names with my fingers, by passing them over the letters. What a night! What a night! I could not find her again!

"There was no moon. What a night! I was frightened, horribly frightened in these narrow paths, between two rows of graves. Graves! graves! graves! nothing but graves! On my right, on my left, in front of me, around me, everywhere there were graves! I sat down on one of them, for I could not walk any longer, my knees were so weak. I could hear my heart beat! And I heard something else as well. What? A confused, nameless noise. Was the noise in my head, in the impenetrable night, or beneath the mysterious earth, the earth sown with human corpses? I looked all around me, but I cannot say how long I remained there; I was paralyzed with terror, cold with fright, ready to shout out, ready to die.

"Suddenly, it seemed to me that the slab of marble on which I was sitting, was moving. Certainly it was moving, as if it were being raised. With a bound, I sprang on to the neighboring tomb, and I saw, yes, I distinctly saw the stone which I had just quitted rise upright. Then the dead person appeared, a naked skeleton, pushing the stone back with its bent back. I saw it quite clearly, although the night was so dark. On the cross I could read:

"'Here lies Jacques Olivant, who died at the age of fifty-one. He loved his family, was kind and honorable, and died in the grace of the Lord.'

"The dead man also read what was inscribed on his tombstone; then he picked up a stone off the path, a little, pointed stone, and began to scrape the letters carefully. He slowly effaced them, and with the hollows of his eyes he looked at the places where they had been engraved. Then with the tip of the bone that had been his forefinger, he wrote in luminous letters, like those lines which boys trace on walls with the tip of a lucifer match:

"'Here reposes Jacques Olivant, who died at the age of fifty-one. He hastened his father's death by his unkindness, as he wished to inherit his fortune, he tortured his wife, tormented his children, deceived his neighbors, robbed everyone he could, and died wretched.'

"When he had finished writing, the dead man stood motionless, looking at his work. On turning round I saw that all the graves were open, that all the dead bodies had emerged from them, and that all had effaced the lines inscribed on the gravestones by their relations, substituting the truth instead. And I saw that all had been the tormentors of their neighbors—malicious, dishonest, hypocrites, liars, rogues, calumniators, envious; that they had stolen, deceived, performed every disgraceful, every abominable action, these good fathers, these faithful wives, these devoted sons, these chaste daughters, these honest tradesmen, these men and women who were called irreproachable. They were all writing at the same time, on the threshold of their eternal abode, the truth, the terrible and the holy truth of which everybody was ignorant, or pretended to be ignorant, while they were alive.

"I thought that *she* also must have written something on her tombstone, and now running without any fear among the half-open coffins, among the corpses and skeletons, I went toward her, sure that I should find her immediately. I recognized her at once, without seeing her face, which was covered by the winding-sheet, and on the marble cross, where shortly before I had read:

"'She loved, was loved, and died.'

I now saw:

" 'Having gone out in the rain one day, in order to deceive her lover, she caught cold and died.'

*   *   *   *   *   *

"It appears that they found me at daybreak, lying on the grave unconscious."

The New Sensation

LITTLE Madame d'Ormonde certainly had the devil in her. She rejoiced in a fantastic, baffling brain, through which the most unheard-of caprices passed, in which ideas danced and jostled each other, like those pieces of differently colored glass in a kaleidoscope, which form such strange figures when they have been shaken. In her *Parisine* was fermenting to such an extent—you know the analysis of *Parisine,* which Roqueplan lately gave—that the most learned member of The Institute would have wasted his science and his wisdom if he had tried to follow her slips and her subterfuges.

That was, very likely, the reason why she attracted, retained, and infatuated even those who had paid their debt to implacable love—men who thought they were strong, free from those passions under the influence of which men lose their heads, and beyond the reach of woman's perfidious snares. Perhaps, it was her small, soft, delicate, white hands, which always smelled of some subtle, delicious perfume, and those small fingers which men kissed almost with devotion, and with absolute pleasure. Or, perhaps, it was her silky, golden hair, or her large, blue eyes, full of enigma, of curiosity, of desire, or her changeable mouth, small and infantine at one moment, when she was pouting, and smiling and as open as a rose that is unfolding in the sun when she opened it in a laugh and showed her pearly teeth, so that it became a target for kisses. Who will ever be able to explain the magic and sorcery which some Chosen Women exercise over all men, the despotic authority against which nobody would think of rebelling?

Among the numerous men who had wooed her, who were anxiously waiting for that wonderful moment when her heart would beat, when this mocking companion would grow tired and abandon herself to the pleasure of loving and of being loved, would become intoxicated with the honey of caresses, and would not longer refuse her lips to kisses, like some restive animal that fears to joke, none had so made up his mind to win the game, and pursue this deceptive siege, as Xavier de Fontrailles. He labored for his object with a patient energy and a strength of will which no snubs could weaken—with the ardent fervor of a believer who has started on a long pilgrimage, and who supports all the suffering of the long journey with the fixed and consoling idea that one day he will be able to throw himself on his knees at the shrine where he would worship, and to listen to the divine words which will mean Paradise to him.

He gave way to Madame d'Ormonde's slightest whims, did all he could to amuse her, never hurt her feelings, strove to become a friend whom she could not do without, *the* friend of whom, in the end, a woman grows more jealous than she does of her husband, and to whom she confesses everything, her daily worries and her dreams of the future.

She would very likely have suffered and wept, have felt a void in her existence, if they had separated forever, if he had disappeared. She would not have hesitated to defend him, even at the risk of compromising herself and of passing as his mistress, if any one had attacked him in her presence, and sometimes she would say, with a sudden, laughing sadness in her voice:

"If I were really capable of loving for five minutes consecutively, I should love you."

When they were walking in the Boise de Boulogne, while the victoria was waiting near Armenonville, during afternoon talks when, as he used to say, they were hanging over the abyss until they both grew giddy, and spoke of love madly and ceaselessly,—returning to the subject constantly, and steeping themselves with it,—Madame d'Ormonde would occasionally propound one of her favorite theories. Yes, she certainly understood what possession of a beloved object was, that touch of madness which seizes you from head to foot, which fires your blood, making you forget everything else in a man's embraces, in that supreme pleasure which overwhelms you, and which rivets two beings together forever, in heart and in brain. But she cared for it only at some un-expected moment, in a strange place, with a touch of something novel about it, which one would remember all one's life, of something amusing and almost maddening, which one had been in search of for a long time, and which imparted a breath of romance, as it were, into the commonplace details of ordinary love.

And Xavier de Fontrailles did all he could to discover such a place, but failed. He tried a bachelor's lodgings with silk tapestry, like a boudoir of the seventeenth century, a villa hidden like a nest among trees and rosebushes, a Japanese house furnished in extraordinary fashion and very expensively, with latticed windows from which one could see the sea, an old melancholy palace, from which one could see the Grand Canal, rooms, hotels, queer quarters, private rooms in restaurants, and small country houses in the recesses of woods.

Madame d'Ormonde went on her way without turning her head, but Xavier, alas! became more and more smitten; as amorous as an overgrown schoolboy who has never hitherto had any converse with a woman, and who is foolish enough to pick up the flowers that fall from her bodice, and to be lost and unhappy when he does not see her, or hear her soft, cooing voice, or see her smile.

One evening, however, he had gone with her to the fair at Saint-Cloud. They went into three shows, deafened by the noise of the organs, the whistling of the machinery of the roundabouts, and the hubbub of the crowd that flowed among the booths illuminated by paraffin lamps. As they were passing in front of a fortune-teller's van, Monsieur de Fontrailles stopped and said to Madame d'Ormonde:

"Would you like to have your fortune told?"

The van was a very fine specimen of its kind, and had, no doubt, traveled far and wide. Placards and portraits, bordered by advertisements, hung above the shaky steps, and the small windows with their closed shutters were almost hidden by boxes of sweet basil and mignonette, while an old, bald parrot, with her feathers all ruffled, was asleep just outside.

The fortune-teller was sitting on a chair, quietly knitting a stocking. On their approach she got up, went up to Madame d'Ormonde and said in an unctuous voice:

"I reveal the present, the past, and the future, and even the name of the future husband or wife, and of deceased relations, as well as my client's present and future circumstances. I have performed before crowned heads. The Emperor of Brazil came to me, with the illustrious poet, Victor Hugo. My charge is five francs for telling your fortune from the cards or by your hand, and twenty francs for the whole lot. Would you like the lot, Madame?"

Madame d'Ormonde gave vent to a burst of sonorous laughter, like a street girl who is amusing herself. But they went in and Monsieur de Fontrailles opened the glass door, which was covered by a heavy red curtain. When they entered, the young woman uttered an exclamation of surprise. The interior of the van was full of roses, arranged in the most charming manner, as if for a lovers' meeting. On a table covered with a damask cloth, surrounded by piles of cushions, a supper was waiting for chance comers, and at the other end, concealed by heavy hangings, one could see a large, wide bed, one of those beds which give rise to suggestion!

Xavier had shut the door again, and Madame d'Ormonde looked at him in a strange manner, with rather flushed cheeks, with palpitating nostrils, and with a look in her eyes such as he had never seen in them before. In a very low voice, while his heart beat violently, he whispered into her ear:

"Well, does the decoration please you this time?"

She replied by holding up her lips to him, and then filled two glasses with extra dry champagne, which was as pale as the skin of a fair woman. Then she said, almost as if already rather drunk:

"I am decidedly worth a big stake!"

It was in this fashion that Madame d'Ormonde, for the first and last time, deceived her husband; and it was at the fair at Saint-Cloud, in a fortune-teller's van.

Virtue!

EVERY Friday, regularly, about eleven o'clock in the morning, he came into the courtyard, put down his soft hat at his feet, struck a few chords on his guitar and began a ballad in a full, rich voice. And soon at every window in the four sides of that dull, barracklike building appeared some girls, one in an elegant dressing-gown, another in a little jacket, most of them with their bosoms and arms bare, all of them just out of bed, with their hair hastily twisted up, their eyes blinking in the sudden blaze of sunlight, their complexions dull, and their eyes still heavy with sleep.

They swayed in time to his slow melody, and gave themselves up to the enjoyment of it. Pennies, and even silver poured into the handsome singer's hat, and more than one of them would have liked to follow the penny which she threw to him, and go with this singer who had the voice of a siren. For he seemed to say to all these amorous girls: "Come, come to my retreat, for there you will find a palace of crystal and gold, wreaths which are always fresh, and happiness and love which never die."

That was what they seemed to hear, these unhappy girls, when they heard him sing the old legends which in childhood they had believed. That was what they understood by the simple words of the ballad—that and nothing else. How could anyone doubt it, seeing the fresh roses on their cheeks, and the tender lights which flickered like mystic fires in their eyes, now for the moment, once more the eyes of innocent young girls? But, alas! of young girls who had grown up too quickly, who were too precocious, and who had too soon become what they were, poor vendors of love, always in search of that love for which they were paid.

That was why, when he had finished his second ballad, and sometimes sooner, concupiscent looks appeared in their eyes. The boatman of their dreams, the water-sprite of the fairy tales, vanished in the mist of childish recollections, and the singer reassumed his real shape, that of a wandering minstrel and strolling player, whom they wished to requite with love. And the coppers and small silver were showered on him again, with engaging smiles, with the leers of amorous women, even with a *"P'st, P'st,"* which soon transformed the barracklike courtyard into an enormous cage full of twittering birds. Several of them could not restrain themselves, but ejaculated, their eyes filled with desire: "How handsome—good heavens, *how* handsome he is!"

He was really handsome — nobody could deny it, even too handsome, with that regular beauty which almost palls on you. He had large, gentle, almond-shaped eyes, a Grecian nose, a bow-shaped mouth hidden by a heavy mustache, and long, black, curly hair; in short, a head fit to be put into a hairdresser's window, or, better still, perhaps, on to the front page of the ballads he was singing. What made him still handsomer was that his self-conceit wore a cloak of sovereign indifference, for not only was he blind to the ogling and deaf to the *"P'st, P'st,"* but when he had finished he shrugged his shoulders, winked mischievously, and curled his lips contemptuously, as if to say: "The stove is not being heated for you, my little kittens!'

You would have thought that he wished to show his contempt, make himself commonplace in the eyes of these amorous girls, and to dampen their ardor, for he cleared his throat ostentatiously and offensively, far more than was necessary, after singing, as if he would have liked to spit at them. But even this did not make him unpoetical in their eyes, and most of them, absolutely mad over him, went so far as to say that he did it "like a swell!"

The girl who in her enthusiasm had been the first to utter an exclamation of intense passion, after tossing him small silver, had thrown him a twenty-franc gold-piece, and made up her mind to have an answer. This morning instead of a *"P'st, P'st"* she spoke out boldly despite the presence and silence of the others.

At first they were dumfounded at her audacity, and then all their cheeks flushed with jealousy, and the flame of desire shot from their eyes. Then from every window there came a perfect torrent of:

"Yes, come up, come up." "Don't go there! Come here."

Meanwhile, there was a shower of half-pence, of francs, of gold coins, of cigars and oranges, while lace pocket handkerchiefs, silk neckties, and scarfs fluttered in the air and fell round the singer, like a flight of many-colored butterflies.

The minstrel picked up the spoil calmly, almost carelessly, stuffed the money into his pocket, made a bundle of the furbelows, which he tied up as if they had been soiled linen, and then rising up, he put his felt hat on his head and said:

"Thank you, ladies, but indeed I cannot."

They thought that he was embarrassed by so many simultaneous demands, and one of them said: "Let him choose."

"Yes, yes, that is it!" they exclaimed in unison.

But he repeated: "I tell you I cannot."

They put his refusal down to his gallantry, and several of them exclaimed, almost with tears of emotion: "He is all heart!" And the same voice that had spoken before (it was the one who wished to settle the matter amicably) said: "We must draw lots."

"Yes, yes, we will," they all cried. And again there was a deeper silence than before, for it was caused by anxiety, their hearts beating almost audibly.

The singer profited by it to say slowly: "I cannot allow that either; I neither desire all of you at once, nor one after the other—at any time! I tell you once for all."

"Why? Why?" Now they were almost screaming, angry, and sorry at the same time. Their cheeks had turned from scarlet to livid, their eyes flashed fire, and some shook their fists menacingly.

"Silence!" cried the girl, who had spoken first. "Be quiet, you pack of hussies! Let him explain himself, and tell us why!"

"Yes, yes, be quiet! Make him explain himself, in God's name!"

Then, in the expectant silence that ensued, the singer said, opening his arms wide, with a gesture of despairing inabilty to do what they wanted:

"Why do you want me? It is very flattering, but I cannot gratify you, for I have two girls of my own at home."

The Thief

"CERTAINLY," exclaimed Dr. Sorbier, who, while appearing to be thinking of something else, had been listening quietly to those surprising accounts of burglaries and of daring acts which might have been borrowed from the trial of Cartouche. "Certainly, I do not know any viler fault, nor any meaner action than to attack a girl's innocence, to corrupt her, to profit by a moment of unconscious weakness and of madness, when her heart is beating like that of a frightened fawn, when her body, which has been unpolluted up till then, is palpitating with desire and her pure lips seek those of her seducer—when her whole being is feverish and vanquished, and she abandons herself without thinking of the irremediable stain, nor of her fall, nor of the painful awakening on the morrow.

"The man who has brought this about slowly, viciously, and none can tell with what science of evil, and who, in such a case, has not steadiness and self-restraint enough to quench that flame by some icy words, who has not sense enough for two, who cannot recover his self-possession and master the runaway brute within him, who loses his head on the edge of the precipice over which the girl is going to fall, is as contemptible as any man who breaks open a lock, or as any rascal on the lookout for a house left defenseless and without protection, or as any adventurer looking for some easy and profitable stroke of business, or as that thief whose various exploits you have just related to us.

"I, for my part, utterly refuse to absolve him even when extenuating circumstances plead in his favor, even when he is carrying on a dangerous flirtation, in which a man tries in vain to keep his balance and not to exceed the limits of the game any more than at lawn tennis, even when the parts are reversed and a man's adversary is some precocious, curious, seductive girl, who shows you immediately that she has nothing to learn and nothing to experience, except the last chapter of love—one of those girls from whom may fate always preserve our sons, and whom a psychological novel writer has christened 'Demi-Virgins.'

"It is of course difficult and painful for that coarse and unfathomable vanity which is characteristic of every man, and which might be called malism, not to stir such a charming fire, to act the Joseph and the fool, to turn away his eyes, and, as it were, to put wax into his ears, as did the companions of Ulysses when attracted by the divine, seductive songs of the Sirens. It is hard not to touch that pretty table, covered with a perfectly new cloth, at which you are invited to take a seat before anyone else, in such a suggestive voice, and are requested to quench your thirst and to taste that new wine whose fresh and strange flavor you will never forget. But who would hesitate to exercise such self-restraint if, when he rapidly examines his conscience in one of those instinctive moments of reason in which a man thinks clearly and recovers his head—if he were to measure the gravity of the fault, think of the error, think of its consequences, of the reprisals, of the uneasiness which he would always feel in the future, and which would destroy the repose and the happiness of his life?

"You may guess that behind all these moral reflections, such as a gray-beard like myself may indulge in, there is a story hidden, and sad as it is, I am sure it will interest you on account of the strange heroism that it shows."

He was silent for a few moments as if to classify his recollections, and with elbows resting on the arms of his easy-chair, and eyes looking into space, he continued in the slow voice of a hospital professor, who is explaining a case to his class of students, at a bedside:

"He was one of those men who as our grandfathers used to say, never met with a cruel woman, the type of an adventurous knight who was always foraging, who had something of the scamp about him, but who despised danger and was bold even to rashness. He was ardent in the pursuit of pleasure, had an irresistible charm about him, and was one of those men in whom we excuse the greatest excesses as the most natural things in the world. He had run through all his money through gambling and with pretty girls, and so became, as it were, a soldier of fortune, who amused himself whenever and however he could, and was at that time quartered at Versailles.

"I knew him to the very depths of his childish heart, which was only too easily penetrated and sounded. I loved him like some old bachelor uncle loves a nephew who plays him tricks, but who knows how to make him indulgent, and how to wheedle him. He had made me his confidant far more than his adviser, kept me informed of his slightest tricks, though he always pretended to be speaking about one of his friends, and not about himself, and I must confess that

his youthful impetuosity, his careless gaiety, and his amorous ardor sometimes distracted my thoughts and made me envy the handsome, vigorous young fellow who was so happy in being alive. I had not the courage to check him, to show him his right road, and to call out to him 'Take care!' as children do at blindman's bluff.

"And one day, after one of those interminable cotillons, where the couples do not leave each other for hours, but have a loose rein and can disappear together without anybody noticing it, the poor fellow at last discovered what love was, that real love which takes up its abode in the very center of the heart and in the brain, and is proud of being there, which rules like a sovereign and a tyrannous master. He grew desperately enamored of a pretty, but badly brought up girl, who was as disquieting and as wayward as she was pretty.

"She loved him, however, or rather she idolized him despotically, madly, with all her enraptured soul, and all her excited person. Left to do as she pleased by imprudent and frivolous parents, suffering from neurosis, in consequence of the unwholesome friendships contracted at the convent-school, instructed by what she saw and heard and knew was going on around her, in spite of her deceitful and artificial conduct, knowing that neither her father nor her mother, who were very proud of their race as well as avaricious, would ever agree to let her marry the man whom she had taken a liking to,—that handsome fellow who had little besides visionary ideas and debts, and who belonged to the middle classes,—she laid aside all scruples, thought of nothing but of belonging to him altogether, of taking him for her lover, and of triumphing over his desperate resistance as an honorable man.

"By degrees, the unfortunate man's strength gave way, his heart grew softened, his nerves became excited, and he allowed himself to be carried away by the current which buffeted him, surrounded him, and left him on the shore like a waif and a stray.

"They wrote letters full of temptation and of madness to each other, and not a day passed without their meeting, either accidentally, as it seemed, or at parties and balls. She had given him her lips in long, ardent caresses, and she had sealed their compact of mutual passion with kisses of desire and of hope. And at last she brought him to her room, almost in spite of himself."

The doctor stopped, and his eyes suddenly filled with tears, as these former troubles came back to his mind. Then in a hoarse voice, he went on, full of the horror of what he was going to relate:

"Each night, for months, he scaled the garden wall, and holding his breath and listening for the slightest noise, like a burglar who is going to break into a house, he entered by the servants' door, which she had left open, went barefoot down a long passage and up the broad staircase, which creaked occasionally, to the second story, where his mistress's room was, and stopped there nearly the whole night.

"One night, when it was darker than usual, and he was hurrying lest he should be later than the time agreed on, the officer knocked up against a piece of furniture in the anteroom and upset it. It so happened that the girl's mother

had not gone to sleep yet, either because she had a sick headache, or else because she had sat up late over some novel. Frightened at the unusual noise, which disturbed the silence of the house, she jumped out of bed, opened the door, saw some one indistinctly running away and keeping close to the wall, and, immediately thinking that there were burglars in the house, she aroused her husband and the servants by her frantic screams. The unfortunate man knew what he was about, and seeing his dilemma he determined to be taken for a common thief rather than dishonor his adored mistress and betray the secret of their guilty love. So he ran into the drawing-room, felt on the tables and whatnots, filled his pockets at random with valuable knickknacks, and then cowered down behind the grand piano, which barred up a corner of a large room.

"The servants, who had run in with lighted candles, found him, and overwhelming him with abuse, seized him by the collar and dragged him, panting and half dead with shame and terror, to the nearest police station. He defended himself with intentional awkwardness when he was brought up for trial, kept up his part with the most perfect self-possession, and without any signs of the despair and anguish that he felt in his heart. Condemned and degraded and made to suffer martyrdom in his honor as a man and as a soldier, he did not protest, but went to prison as one of those criminals whom society destroys like noxious vermin.

"He died there of misery and of bitterness of spirit, with the name of the fair-haired idol for whom he had sacrificed himself on his lips, as if it had been an ecstatic prayer. He intrusted his will to the priest who administered extreme unction to him, and requested him to give it to me. In it, without mentioning anybody, and without in the least lifting the veil, he at last explained the enigma, and cleared himself of those accusations, the terrible burden of which he had borne until his last breath.

"I have always thought myself, though I do not know why, that the girl married and had several charming children, whom she brought up with austere strictness, and in the serious piety of former days!"

The Diary of a Madman

He was dead—the head of a high tribunal, the upright magistrate, whose irreproachable life was a proverb in all the courts of France. Advocates, young counselors, judges had saluted, bowing low in token of profound respect, remembering that grand face, pale and thin, illumined by two bright, deep-set eyes.

He had passed his life in pursuing crime and in protecting the weak. Swindlers and murderers had no more redoubtable enemy, for he seemed to read in the recesses of their souls their most secret thoughts.

He was dead, now, at the age of eighty-two, honored by the homage and followed by the regrets of a whole people. Soldiers in red breeches had escorted him to the tomb, and men in white cravats had shed on his grave tears that seemed to be real.

But listen to the strange paper found by the dismayed notary in the desk where the judge had kept filed the records of great criminals! It was entitled:

WHY?

June 20, 1851. I have just left court. I have condemned Blonde to death! Now, why did this man kill his five children? Frequently one meets with people to whom killing is a pleasure. Yes, yes, it should be a pleasure—the greatest of all, perhaps, for is not killing most like eating? To make and to destroy! These two words contain the history of the universe, the history of all worlds, all that is, all! Why is it not intoxicating to kill?

June 25. To think that there is a being who lives, who walks, who runs. A being? What is a being? An animated thing which bears in it the principle of motion, and a will ruling that principle. It clings to nothing, this thing. Its feet are independent of the ground. It is a grain of life that moves on the earth, and this grain of life, coming I know not whence, one can destroy at one's will. Then nothing—nothing more. It perishes; it is finished.

June 26. Why, then, is it a crime to kill? Yes, why? On the contrary, it is the law of nature. Every being has the mission to kill; he kills to live, and he lives to kill. The beast kills without ceasing, all day, every instant of its existence. Man kills without ceasing, to nourish himself; but since in addition he needs to kill for pleasure, he has invented the chase! The child kills the insects he finds, the little birds, all the little animals that come in his way. But this does not suffice for the irresistible need of massacre that is in us. It is not enough to kill beasts; we must kill man too. Long ago this need was satisfied by human sacrifice. Now, the necessity of living in society has made murder a crime. We condemn and punish the assassin! But as we cannot live without yielding to this natural and imperious instinct of death, we relieve ourselves, from time to time, by wars. Then a whole nation slaughters another nation. It is a feast of blood, a feast that maddens armies and intoxicates the civilians, women and children, who read, by lamplight at night, the feverish story of massacre.

And do we despise those picked out to accomplish these butcheries of men? No, they are loaded with honors. They are clad in gold and in resplendent stuffs; they wear plumes on their heads and ornaments on their breasts; and they are given crosses, rewards, titles of every kind. They are proud, respected, loved by women, cheered by the crowd, solely because their mission is to shed human blood! They drag through the streets their instruments of death, and the passer-by, clad in black, looks on with envy. For to kill is the great law put by nature in the heart of existence! There is nothing more beautiful and honorable than killing!

June 30. To kill is the law, because Nature loves eternal youth. She seems to cry in all her unconscious acts: "Quick! quick! quick!" The more she destroys, the more she renews herself.

July 3. It must be a pleasure, unique and full of zest, to kill: to place before you a living, thinking being; to make therein a little hole, nothing but a little hole, and to see that red liquid flow which is the blood, which is the life; and then to have before you only a heap of limp flesh, cold, void of thought!

August 5. I, who have passed my life in judgment, condemning, killing by words pronounced, killing by the guillotine those who had killed by the knife, if I should do as all the assassins whom I have smitten have done, I, I—who would know it?

August 10. Who would ever know? Who would ever suspect me, especially if I should choose a being I had no interest in doing away with? ?

August 22. I could resist no longer. I have killed a little creature as an experiment, as a beginning. Jean, my servant, had a goldfinch in a cage hung in the office window. I sent him on an errand, and I took the little bird in my hand, in my hand where I felt its heart beat. It was warm. I went up to my room. From time to time I squeezed it tighter; its heart beat faster; it was atrocious and delicious. I was nearly choking it. But I could not see the blood.

Then I took scissors, short nail scissors, and I cut its throat in three strokes, quite gently. It opened it bill, it struggled to escape me, but I held it, oh! I held it—I could have held a mad dog —and I saw the blood trickle.

And then I did as assassins do—real ones. I washed the scissor and washed my hands. I sprinkled water, and took the body, the corpse, to the garden to hide it. I buried it under a strawberry-plant. It will never be found. Every day I can eat a strawberry from that plant. How one can enjoy life, when one knows how!

My servant cried; he thought his bird flown. How could he suspect me? Ah!

August 25. I must kill a man! I must!

August 30. It is done. But what a little thing! I had gone for a walk in the forest of Vernes. I was thinking of nothing, literally nothing. See! a child on the road, a little child eating a slice of bread and butter. He stops to see me pass and says, "Good day, Mr. President."

And the thought enters my head: "Shall I kill him?"

I answer: "You are alone, my boy?"

"Yes, sir."

"All alone in the wood?"

"Yes, sir."

The wish to kill him intoxicated me like wine. I approached him quite softly, persuaded that he was going to run away. And suddenly I seized him by the throat. He held my wrists in his little hands, and his body writhed like a feather on the fire. Then he moved no more. I threw the body in the ditch, then some weeds on top of it. I returned home and dined well. What a little thing it was! In the evening I was very gay, light, rejuvenated, and passed the evening at the Prefect's. They found me witty. But I have not seen blood! I am not tranquil.

August 31. The body has been discovered. They are hunting for the assassin. Ah!

September 1. Two tramps have been arrested. Proofs are lacking.

September 2. The parents have been to see me. They wept! Ah!

October 6. Nothing has been discovered. Some strolling vagabond must have done the deed. Ah! If I had seen the blood flow it seems to me I should be tranquil now!

October 10. Yet another. I was walking by the river, after breakfast. And I saw, under a willow, a fisherman asleep. It was noon. A spade, as if expressly put there for me, was standing in a potato-field near by.

I took it. I returned; I raised it like a club, and with one blow of the edge I cleft the fisherman's head. Oh! he bled, this one!—rose-colored blood. It flowed into the water quite gently. And I went away with a grave step. If I had been seen! Ah! I should have made an excellent assassin.

October 25. The affair of the fisherman makes a great noise. His nephew, who fished with him, is charged with the murder.

October 26. The examining magistrate affirms that the nephew is guilty. Everybody in town believes it. Ah! ah!

October 27. The nephew defends himself badly. He had gone to the village to buy bread and cheese, he declares. He swears that his uncle had been killed in his absence! Who would believe him?

October 28. The nephew has all but confessed, so much have they made him lose his head! Ah! Justice!

November 15. There are overwhelming proofs against the nephew, who was his uncle's heir. I shall preside at the sessions.

January 25, 1852. To death! to death! to death! I have had him con-

demned to death! The advocate-gen-
eral spoke like an angel! Ah! Yet
another! I shall go to see him executed!

March 10. It is done. They guillotined him this morning. He died very
well! very well! That gave me pleasure! How fine it is to see a man's head
cut off!

Now, I shall wait, I can wait. It

would take such a little thing to let myself be caught.

* * * * * *

The manuscript contained more pages,
but told of no new crime.

Alienist physicians to whom the awful story has been submitted declare
that there are in the world many unknown madmen, as adroit and as terrible
as this monstrous lunatic.

On Perfumes

THREE ladies belonging to that class
of society which has nothing useful to
do, and therefore cannot employ its time
sensibly, were sitting on a bench in the
shade of some pine-trees at Ischl, and
talking incidentally on the subject of
perfumes.

One of the ladies, Princess F——, a
slim, handsome brunette, declared there
was nothing like the smell of Russia
leather; she wore dull brown Russia
leather boots, a Russia leather dress sus-
pender, to keep her petticoats out of
the dirt and dust, a Russia leather belt
which spanned her wasplike waist, and
carried a Russia leather purse. She
even wore a brooch and bracelet of gilt
Russia leather; people declared that her
bedroom was papered with Russia
leather, and that her *cicisbeo* was
obliged to wear high Russia leather
boots and tight breeches, but that, on the
other hand, her husband was excused
from wearing anything at all in Russia
leather.

Countess H——, a very stout lady,
who had formerly been very beautiful

and of a very loving nature, but loving,
after the fashion of her time, *à la*
Parthenia and Griselda, could not get
over the vulgar taste of the young
Princess. All she cared for was the
smell of hay, and she it was who brought
the perfume New Mown Hay into fashion. Her ideal was a freshly mown
field in the moonlight, and when she
rolled slowly along, she looked like a
moving haystack, and exhaled an odor
of hay around her.

The third lady's taste was even more
peculiar than Countess H——'s, and
more vulgar than the Princess's, for the
small, delicate, light-haired Countess
W—— lived only for—the smell of
stables. Her friends could not understand this at all; the Princess raised her
beautiful, full arm with its broad bracelet to her Grecian nose and inhaled the
sweet smell of the Russia leather, while
the sentimental hayrick exclaimed over
and over again:

"How dreadful! What dost thou say
to it, chaste moon?"

The delicate little Countess seemed

very much embarrassed at the effect made by her confession, and tried to justify her taste.

"Prince T—— told me that that smell had quite bewitched him once," she said. "It was in a Jewish town in Galicia, where he was quartered once with his hussar regiment, and a number of poor, ragged circus riders, with half-starved horses, came from Russia and put up a circus with a few poles and some rags of canvas. The Prince went to see them, and found a woman among them, who was neither young nor beautiful, but bold and impudent. She wore a faded, bright red jacket trimmed with old, shabby imitation ermine, which reeked of the stable, as the Prince expressed it. But she bewitched him with the odor, so that every time that the shameless wretch visited him, smelling abominably of the stable, he felt as if he were mesmerized."

"How disgusting!" both the other ladies said, and involuntarily held their noses.

"What dost thou say to it, chaste moon?" the haystack said with a sigh, and the little light-haired Countess was abashed, and held her tongue.

At the beginning of the winter season the three friends were together again in the gay, imperial city on the blue Danube. One morning the Princess accidentally met the enthusiast for hay at the house of the little, light-haired Countess, and was obliged to follow the latter to her private riding-school, where she was taking her daily lesson. As soon as she saw them, she came up, and beckoned her riding-master to her, to help her out of the saddle. He was a young man of extremely good and

athletic build, which was set off by tight breeches and a short, velvet coat. He ran up and took his lovely burden into his arms with visible pleasure, to help her off the quiet, perfectly broken horse.

When the ladies saw the handsome, vigorous man, it was quite enough to explain their little friend's predilection for the smell of a stable. When the latter saw their looks, she blushed up to the roots of her hair, and thought her only way out of the difficulty was to order the riding-master, in a very authoritative manner, to take the horse back to the stable. He merely bowed, with an indescribable smile, and obeyed her.

A few months afterward, Viennese society was alarmed at the news that Countess W—— had been divorced from her husband. The event was unexpected, as they had apparently always lived very happily together, and gossip was unable to mention any man on whom she had bestowed even the most passing attention, beyond the requirements of politeness.

Long afterward, however, a strange report became current. A chattering lady's maid declared that the handsome riding-master had once so far forgotten himself as to strike the Countess with his riding-whip. A groom had told the Count of the occurrence, and when the latter called the insolent fellow to account for it, the Countess covered him with her own body, and thus gave occasion for the divorce.

Years had passed since then and the Countess H—— had grown stouter and more sentimental. Ischl and hayricks were not enough for her any longer;

she spent the winter on lovely Lago Maggiore, where she walked among laurel bushes and cypress-trees, and was rowed about on the warm, moonlight nights.

One evening she was returning home from Isola Bella, in the company of an English lady who was also a great lover of nature, when they met a beautiful private boat in which a very unusual couple were sitting—a small, delicate, light-haired woman, wrapped in a white burnoose, and a handsome, athletic man, in tight, white breeches, a short, black velvet coat trimmed with sable, a red fez on his head, and a riding-whip in his hand.

Countess H—— involuntarily uttered a loud exclamation.

"What is the matter with you?" the English lady asked. "Do you know those people?"

"Certainly! She is a Viennese lady," Countess H—— whispered; "Countess W——."

"Oh! Indeed you are quite mistaken; it is a Count Savelli and his wife. They are a handsome couple, don't you think so?"

When the boat came nearer, Countess H—— saw that it was little Countess W——, and that the handsome man was her former riding-master, whom she had married, and for whom she had bought a title from the Pope*; and as the two boats passed each other, the short sable cloak, which was thrown carelessly over his shoulders, exhaled, like the old cat's skin jacket of the female circus rider, a strong stable perfume.

*Frequently done formerly, and not unknown even now.

The Will

I KNEW that tall young fellow, René de Bourneval. He was an agreeable man, though of a rather melancholy turn of mind, and prejudiced against everything, very skeptical, and fond of tearing worldly hypocrisies to pieces. He often used to say:

"There are no honorable men, or, at any rate, they only appear so when compared to low people."

He had two brothers, whom he shunned, the Messieurs de Courcils. I thought they were by another father, on account of the difference in the name. I had frequently heard that something

strange had happened in the family, but I did not know the details.

As I took a great liking to him, we soon became intimate, and one evening, when I had been dining with him alone, I asked him by chance: "Are you by your mother's first or second marriage?" He grew rather pale; then he flushed, and did not speak for a few moments, he was visibly embarrassed. Then he smiled in that melancholy and gentle manner peculiar to him, and said:

"My dear friend, if it will not weary you, I can give you some very strange particulars about my life. I know you to be a sensible man, so I do not fear that our friendship will suffer by my revelations, and should it suffer, I should not care about having you for my friend any longer.

"My mother, Madame de Courcils, was a poor, little, timid woman, whom her husband had married for the sake of her fortune. Her whole life was a continual martyrdom. Of a loving, delicate mind, she was constantly ill-treated by the man who ought to have been my father, one of those boors called country gentlemen. A month after their marriage he was living with a servant, and besides that, the wives and daughters of his tenants were his mistresses, which did not prevent him from having three children by his wife, that is, if you count me in. My mother said nothing, and lived in that noisy house like a little mouse. Set aside, disparaged, nervous, she looked at people with bright, uneasy, restless eyes, the eyes of some terrified creature which can never shake off its fear. And yet she was pretty, very pretty and fair, a gray blonde, as if her hair had lost its color through her constant fears.

"Among Monsieur de Courcils's friends who constantly came to the château there was an ex-cavalry officer, a widower, a man to be feared, a man at the same time tender and violent, and capable of the most energetic resolution, Monsieur de Bourneval, whose name I bear. He was a tall, thin man, with a heavy black mustache, and I am very like him. He was a man who had read a great deal, and whose ideas were not like those of most of his class. His greatgrandmother had been a friend of J. J. Rousseau, and you might have said that he had inherited something of this ancestral connection. He knew the "Contrat Social" and the "Nouvelle Héloïse" by heart, and, indeed, all those philosophical books which led the way to the overthrow of our old usages, prejudices, superannuated laws, and imbecile morality.

"It seems that he loved my mother, and she loved him, but their intrigue was carried on so secretly that no one guessed it. The poor, neglected, unhappy woman must have clung to him in a despairing manner, and in her intimacy with him must have imbibed all his ways of thinking, theories of free thought, audacious ideas of independent love. But as she was so timid that she never ventured to speak aloud, it was all driven back, condensed, and expressed in her heart, which never opened itself.

"My two brothers were very cruel to her, like their father, and never gave her a caress. Used to seeing her count for nothing in the house, they treated her rather like a servant, and so I was the only one of her sons who really loved her, and whom she loved.

"When she died I was seventeen, and I must add, in order that you may understand what follows, that there had been a lawsuit between my father and my mother. Their property had been separated, to my mother's advantage, as, thanks to the workings of the law and the intelligent devotion of a lawyer to her interests, she had preserved the right to make her will in favor of anyone she pleased.

"We were told that there was a will lying at the lawyer's, and were invited to be present at the reading of it. I can member it, as if it were yesterday. It was a grand, dramatic, yet burlesque and surprising scene, brought about by the posthumous revolt of a dead woman, by a cry for liberty from the depths of her tomb, on the part of a martyred woman who had been crushed by a man's habits during her life, and, who, from her grave, uttered a despairing appeal for independence.

"The man who thought that he was my father, a stout, ruddy-faced man, who gave you the idea of a butcher, and my brothers, two great fellows of twenty and twenty-two, were waiting quietly in their chairs. Monsieur de Bourneval, who had been invited to be present, came in and stood behind me. He was very pale, and bit his mustache, which was turning gray. No doubt he was prepared for what was going to happen. The lawyer, after opening the envelope in our presence, double-locked the door and began to read the will, which was sealed with red wax, and the contents of which he knew not."

. My friend stopped suddenly and got up, and from his writing-table took an old paper, unfolded it, kissed it and then continued:

"This is the will of my beloved mother:

"I, the undersigned, Anne-Catherine-Geneviève-Mathilde de Croixluce, the legitimate wife of Léopold-Joseph Gontran de Courcils, sound in body and mind, here express my last wishes:

"I first of all ask God, and then my dear son René, to pardon me for the act I am about to commit. I believe that my child's heart is great enough to understand me, and to forgive me. I have suffered my whole life long. I was married out of calculation, then despised, misunderstood, oppressed, and constantly deceived by my husband.

"I forgive him, but I owe him nothing.

"My eldest sons never loved me, never caressed me, scarcely treated me as a mother, but during my whole life I was everything that I ought to have been, and I owe them nothing more after my death. The ties of blood cannot exist without daily and constant affection. An ungrateful son is less than a stranger; he is a culprit, for he has no right to be indifferent toward his mother.

"I have always trembled before men, before their unjust laws, their inhuman customs, their shameful prejudices. Before God, I have no longer any fear. Dead, I fling aside disgraceful hypocrisy; I dare to speak my thoughts, and to avow and to sign the secret of my heart.

"I therefore leave that part of my fortune of which the law allows me to dispose, as a deposit with my dear lover Pierre-Gennes-Simon de Bourneval, to revert afterward to our dear son René.

"(This wish is, moreover, formulated more precisely in a notarial deed.)

"And I declare before the Supreme Judge who hears me, that I should have cursed Heaven and my own existence, if I had not met my lover's deep, devoted, tender, unshaken affection, if I had not felt in his arms that the Creator made His creatures to love, sustain, and console each other, and to weep together in the hours of sadness.

"Monsieur de Courcils is the father of my two eldest sons; René alone owes his life to Monsieur de Bourneval. I pray to the Master of men and of their destinies to place father and son above social prejudices, to make them love each other until they die, and to love me also in my coffin.

"These are my last thoughts, and my last wish.

"MATHILDE DE CROIXLUCE.

"Monsieur de Courcils had risen, and he cried:

"'It is the will of a mad woman.'

"Then Monsieur de Bourneval stepped forward and said in a loud and penetrating voice: 'I, Simon de Bourneval, solemnly declare that this writing contains nothing but the strict truth, and I am ready to prove it by letters which I possess.'

"On hearing that, Monsieur de Courcils went up to him, and I thought that they were going to collar each other. There they stood, both of them, tall, one stout and the other thin, both trembling. My mother's husband stammered out:

"'You are a worthless wretch!'

"And the other replied in a loud, dry voice:

"'We will meet somewhere else, Monsieur. I should have already slapped your ugly face, and challenged you a long time ago, if I had not, before all else, thought of the peace of mind of that poor woman whom you made to suffer so much during her lifetime.'

"Then, turning to me, he said:

"'You are my son; will you come with me? I have no right to take you away, but I shall assume it, if you will allow me.' I shook his hand without replying, and we went out together; I was certainly three parts mad.

"Two days later Monsieur de Bourneval killed Monsieur de Courcils in a duel. My brothers, fearing some terrible scandal, held their tongues. I offered them, and they accepted, half the fortune which my mother had left me. I took my real father's name, renouncing that which the law gave me, but which was not really mine. Monsieur de Bourneval died three years afterward, and I have not consoled myself yet."

He rose from his chair, walked up and down the room, and, standing in front of me, said:

"I maintain that my mother's will was one of the most beautiful and loyal, as well as one of the grandest, acts that a woman could perform. Do you not think so?"

I gave him both my hands:

"Most certainly I do, my friend."

In His Sweetheart's Livery

At present she is a great lady, an elegant, intellectual woman, and a celebrated actress. But in the year 1847, when our story begins, she was a beautiful, but not very moral girl, and then it was that the young, talented Hungarian poet who was the first to discover her gifts for the stage made her acquaintance.

The slim, ardent girl, with her bright brown hair and her large blue eyes, attracted the careless poet. He loved her, and all that was good and noble in her nature put forth fresh buds and blossoms in the sunshine of his poetic love.

They lived in an attic in the old imperial city on the Danube; she shared his poverty, his triumphs, and his pleasures, and would have become his true and faithful wife, if the Hungarian revolution had not torn him from her arms.

The poet became the soldier of freedom. He followed the Magyar tricolor, and the Honved drums, while she was carried away by the current of the movement in the capital, and might have been seen discharging her musket, like a brave Amazon, at the Croats who were defending the town against Görgey's assaulting battalions.

But at last Hungary was subdued, and was governed as if it had been a conquered country.

It was said that the young poet had fallen at Temesvar. His mistress wept for him, and married another man, which was nothing either new or extraordinary. Her name was now Frau von Kubinyi, but her married life was not happy. One day she remembered that her lover had told her that she had talent for the stage, and as whatever he said had always proved correct, she separated from her husband, studied a few parts, appeared on the stage, and lo! the public, the critics, actors, and writers were lying at her feet.

She obtained a very profitable engagement, and her reputation increased with every part she played. Before the end of a year after her first appearance, she was the lioness of society. Everybody paid homage to her, and the wealthiest men tried to obtain her favors. But she remained cold and reserved, until the General commanding the district, who was a handsome man, of noble bearing, and a gentleman in the highest sense of the word, approached her.

Whether she was flattered at seeing that powerful man—before whom millions trembled, who had power over the life and death, the honor and happiness of so many thousands—fettered by her soft curls, or whether her enigmatical heart for once really felt what true love was, suffice it to say that in a short time she was his acknowledged mistress, and her princely lover surrounded her with the luxury of an Eastern queen.

But just then a miracle occurred— the resurrection of a dead man. Frau von Kubinyi was driving through the Corso in the General's carriage; she was lying back negligently in the soft cushions, and looking carelessly at the crowd on the pavement. Then—she caught sight of a common Austrian soldier and screamed aloud.

Nobody heard that cry, which came from the depths of a woman's heart, nobody saw how pale and how excited that woman was, who usually seemed made of marble, not even the soldier who was the cause of it. He was a Hungarian poet, who, like so many other Honveds,* now wore the uniform of an Austrian soldier.

Two days later, to the poet's no small surprise, he was told to go to the General in command as orderly. When he reported himself to the adjutant, he told him to go to Frau von Kubinyi's, and to await her orders.

Our poet only knew her by report, but he hated and despised intensely the beautiful woman who had sold herself to the enemy of his country; he had no choice, however, but to obey.

When he arrived at her house, he seemed to be expected, for the porter knew his name, took him into his lodge,

---

*A Hungarian word meaning Defender of the Fatherland. The term *Honved* is applied to the Hungarian *Landwehr,* or militia.

and without any further explanation, told him immediately to put on the livery of his mistress, which was lying there ready for him. He ground his teeth, but resigned himself without a word to his wretched though laughable fate; it was quite clear that the actress had some purpose in making the poet wear her livery. He tried to remember whether he could formerly have offended her by his notices as a theatrical critic, but before he could arrive at any conclusion, he was told to present himself to Frau von Kubinyi. She evidently wished to enjoy his humiliation.

He was shown into a small drawing-room, which was furnished with an amount of taste and magnificence such as he had never seen before, and was told to wait. But he had not been alone many minutes, before the door-curtains were parted and Frau von Kubinyi came in, calm but deadly pale, in a splendid dressing-gown of some Turkish material, and he recognized his former mistress.

"Irma!" he exclaimed.

The cry came from his heart, and affected the heart of this pleasure-surfeited woman so greatly that the next moment she was lying on the breast of the man whom she had believed to be dead, but only for a moment, for he freed himself from her.

"We are fated to meet again thus!" she began.

"Not through any fault of mine," he replied bitterly.

"And not through mine either," she said quickly; "everybody thought that you were dead, and I wept for you; that is my justification."

"You are really too kind," he replied sarcastically. "How can you condescend to make any excuses to me? I wear your livery; you have to order, and I have to obey; our relative positions are clear enough."

Frau von Kubinyi turned away to hide her tears.

"I did not intend to hurt your feelings," he continued; "but I must confess that it would have been better for both of us, if we had not met again. But what do you mean by making me wear your livery? Is it not enough that I have been robbed of my happiness? Does it afford you any pleasure to humiliate me as well?"

"How can you think that?" the actress exclaimed. "Ever since I discovered your unhappy lot, I have thought of nothing but the means of delivering you from it, and until I succeed in doing this, however, I can at least make it more bearable for you."

"I understand," the unhappy poet said with a sneer. "And in order to do this, you have begged your present worshiper to turn your former lover into a footman."

"What a thing to say to me!"

"Can you find any other pleasure for it? You wish to punish me for having loved you, idolized you, I suppose?" the poet continued. "So exactly like a woman! But I can perfectly well understand that the situation promises to have a fresh charm for you."

Before he could finish what he was saying, the actress quickly left the room; he could hear her sobbing, but he did not regret his words, and his contempt and hatred for her only increased when he saw the extravagance and the princely luxury with which she was surrounded. But what was the use of his indignation? He was wearing her livery, he was obliged to wait upon her and to obey her, for she had the corporal's cane at her command. It really seemed as if he incurred the vengeance of the offended woman; as if the General's insolent mistress wished to make him feel her whole power; as if he were not to be spared the deepest humiliation.

The General and two of Frau von Kubinyi's friends, who were also servants of the Muses, for one was a ballet dancer and the other an actress, had come to tea, and he was to wait on them.

While it was being made, he heard them laughing in the next room. The blood flew to his head when the butler opened the door and Frau von Kubinyi appeared on the General's arm. She did not, however, look at her new footman, her former lover, triumphantly or contemptuously, but gave him a glance of the deepest commiseration.

Could he, after all, have wronged her?

Hatred and love, contempt and jealousy were struggling in his breast, and when he had to fill the glasses, the bottle shook in his hand.

"Is this the man?" the General said, looking at him closely.

Frau von Kubinyi nodded.

"He was evidently not born for a footman," the General added.

"And still less for a soldier," the actress observed.

These words fell heavily on the unfortunate poet's heart, but she was evidently taking his part, and trying to rescue him from his terrible position.

Suspicion, however, once more gained the day.

"She is tired of all pleasures, and satiated with enjoyment," he said to himself; "she requires excitement and it amuses her to see the man whom she formerly loved, and who, as she knows, still loves her, tremble before her. And when she pleases, she can see me tremble; not for my life, but for fear of the disgrace which she can inflict upon me, at any moment, if it should give her any pleasure."

But suddenly the actress gave him a look, which was so sad and so imploring, that he looked down in confusion.

From that time he remained in her house without performing any duties, and without receiving any orders from her; in fact he never saw her, and did not venture to ask after her. Two months had passed in this way, when the General unexpectedly sent for him. He waited, with many others, in the anteroom. The General came back from parade, saw him, and beckoned him to follow him, and as soon as they were alone, said:

"You are free, as you have been allowed to purchase your discharge."

"Good heavens!" the poet stammered, "how am I to—"

"That is already done," the General replied. "You are free."

"How is it possible? How can I thank your Excellency!"

"You owe me no thanks," he replied; "Frau von Kubinyi bought you out."

The poor poet's heart seemed to stop; he could not speak, nor even stammer a word; but with a low bow, he rushed out and tore wildly through the streets, until he reached the mansion of the woman whom he had so misunderstood, quite out of breath; he must see her again, and throw himself at her feet.

"Where are you going to?" the porter asked him.

"To Frau von Kubinyi's."

"She is not here.

"Not here?"

"She has gone away."

"Gone away? Where to?"

"She started for Paris two hours ago."

An Unfortunate Likeness

IT WAS during one of those sudden changes of the electric light, which at one time throws rays of exquisite pale pink, of a liquid gold filtered through the light hair of a woman, and at another, rays of bluish hue with strange tints, such as the sky assumes at twilight, in which the women with their bare shoulders looked like living flowers—it was, I say, on the night of the first of January at Montonirail's, the dainty painter of tall, undulating figures, of bright dresses of Parisian prettiness —that tall Pescarelle, whom some called "Pussy," though I do not know why, suddenly said in a low voice:

"Well, people were not altogether mistaken, in fact, were only half wrong when they coupled my name with that of pretty Lucy Ponelle. She had caught me, just as a birdcatcher on a frosty morning catches an imprudent wren on a limed twig—in fact, she might have done whatever she liked with me.

"I was under the charm of her enigmatical and mocking smile, that smile in which her teeth gleamed cruelly between her red lips, and glistened as if they were ready to bite and to heighten the pleasure of the most delightful, the ... , kiss by pain.

"I loved everything in her—her feline suppleness, her languid looks which emerged from her half-closed lids, full of promises and temptation, her somewhat extreme elegance, and her hands, those long, delicate white hands, with blue veins, like the bloodless hands of a female saint in a stained glass window, and her slender fingers, on which only the large blooddrop of a ruby glittered.

"I would have given her all my remaining youth and vigor to have laid my burning hands upon the back of her cool, round neck, and to feel that bright, silk, golden mane enveloping me and caressing my skin. I was never tired of hearing her disdainful, petulant voice, those vibrations which sounded as if they proceeded from clear glass, whose music, at times, became hoarse, harsh, and fierce, like the loud, sonorous calls of the Valkyries.

"Good heavens! to be her lover, to be her chattel, to belong to her, to devote one's whole existence to her, to spend one's last half-penny and to sink in misery, only to have the glory and the happiness of possessing her splendid beauty, the sweetness of her kisses, the pink and the white of her demonlike soul all to myself, if only for a few months!

"It makes you laugh, I know,. to think that I should have been caught like that—I who give such good, prudent advice to my friends—I who fear love as I do those quicksands and shoals which appear at low tide and in which one may be swallowed up and disappear!

"But who can answer for himself, who can defend himself against such a danger, as the magnetic attraction that inheres in such a woman? Nevertheless, I got cured and perfectly cured, and that quite accidentally. This is how the enchantment, which was apparently so infrangible, was broken.

"On the first night of a play, I was sitting in the stalls close to Lucy, whose mother had accompanied her, as usual. They occupied the front of a box, side by side. From some unsurmountable attraction, I never ceased looking at the woman whom I loved with all the force of my being. I feasted my eyes on her beauty, I saw nobody except her in the theater, and did not listen to the piece that was being performed on the stage.

"Suddenly, however, I felt as if I had received a blow from a dagger in my heart, and I had an insane hallucination. Lucy had moved, and her pretty head was in profile, in the same attitude and with the same lines as her mother. I do not know what shadow or what play of light had hardened and altered the color of her delicate features, effacing their ideal prettiness, but the more I looked at them both, at the one who was young and the one who was old, the greater the distressing resemblance became.

"I saw Lucy growing older and older, striving against those accumulating years which bring wrinkles in the face, produce a double chin and crow's-feet, and spoil the mouth. *They almost looked like twins.*

"I suffered so, that I thought I should go mad. Yet in spite of myself, instead of shaking off this feeling and making my escape out of the theater, far away into the noise and life of the boulevards, I persisted in looking at the other, at the old one, in examining her, in judging her, in dissecting her with my eyes. I got excited over her flabby cheeks, over those ridiculous dimples, that were half filled up, over that treble chin, that dyed hair, those lusterless eyes, and that nose, which was a caricature of Lucy's beautiful, attractive little nose.

"I had a prescience of the future. I loved her, and I should love her more and more every day, that little sorceress who had so despotically and so quickly conquered me. I should not allow any participation or any intrigue from the day she gave herself to me, and once intimately connected, who could tell whether, just as I was defending myself against it most, the legitimate termination—marriage—might not come?

"Why not give one's name to a woman whom one loves, and whom one trusts? The reason was that I should be tied to a disfigured, ugly creature, with whom I should not venture to be seen in public. My friends would leer at her with laughter in their eyes, and with pity in their hearts for the man who was accompanying those rema...

"And so, as soon as the...

fallen, without saying good day or good evening, I had myself driven to the Moulin Rouge.

*   *   *   *   *   *   *

"Well," Florise d'Anglet exclaimed, "I shall never take mamma to the theater with me again, for the men are really going crazy!"

A Night in Whitechapel

MY FRIEND Ledantec and I were each twenty-five, and we were visiting London for the first time in our lives. It was a Saturday evening in December, cold and foggy, and I think that this combination is more than enough to explain why my friend Ledantec and I managed to get abominably drunk, though, to tell the truth, we were not experiencing any discomfort from it. On the contrary, we were floating in an atmosphere of perfect bliss. We did not speak, certainly, for we were incapable of doing so, but then we had no inclination for conversation. What would be the good of it? We could easily read all our thoughts in each other's eyes, the more so because we knew that we were thinking about nothing whatever.

It was not, however, in order to arrive at that state of delicious, intellectual nullity, that we had gone to mysterious Whitechapel. We had gone into the first public-house we saw, with the firm intention of studying manners and customs there,—not to mention morals, —as spectators, artists, and philosophers, but in the second public-house we entered, we ourselves began to resemble the objects of our investigations, that is to say, sponges soaked in alcohol. Between one public-house and the other, the outer air seemed to squeeze those

sponges dry, and thus we rolled from public-house to public-house, till at last the sponges could hold no more.

Consequently, we had for some time bidden farewell to our studies in morals; they were now limited to two impressions: zigzags through the darkness outside, and a gleam of light outside the public houses. As to the imbibition of brandy, whisky, and gin, that was done mechanically, and our stomachs scarcely noticed it.

But what strange beings we had elbowed with during our long stoppages! What a number of faces to be remembered; what clothes, what attitudes, what talk, and what squalor!

At first we tried to note these things exactly in our memory, but there were so many of them, and our brains got muddled so quickly, that just then we had no very clear recollection of anything or anybody. Even objects immediately before us passed by in vague, dusky phantasmagoria, confounded with things farther away in an inextricable manner. The world became a sort of kaleidoscope to us, seen in a dream through the penumbra of an aquarium.

Suddenly we were roused from this state of somnolence, awakened as if by a blow on the chest, forced to fix our attention on what we saw, for, amid this whirl of strange sights, one stranger than all attracted our eyes, and seemed to say: "Look at me."

It was at the open door of a public house. A ray of light streamed into the street through the half-open door, and the revealing ray fell right on to the specter that had just risen up there, dumb and motionless.

It was indeed a pitiful and terrible specter, and, above all, most real, as it stood out boldly against the dark background of the street, which it made darker still!

Young? yes, the woman was certainly young. There could be no doubt about that, when one looked at her smooth skin, her smiling mouth showing white teeth, and the firm bust which could be plainly noted under her thin dress.

But then, how explain her perfectly white hair, not gray or growing gray, but absolutely white, as white as any octogenarian's?

And then her eyes, those eyes beneath a smooth brow, were surely the eyes of an old woman? Certainly they were, and of how old a woman you could not tell, for it must have taken years of trouble and sorrow, of tears and of sleepless nights, and a long existence, thus to dull, wear out and roughen those vitreous pupils.

Vitreous? Not exactly that. For roughened glass still retains a dull and milky brightness, a recollection, as it were, of its former transparency. But these eyes seemed rather to be of metal which had turned rusty, and really, if pewter could rust, I should have compared them to pewter covered with rust. They had the dead color of pewter, and

at the same time emitted a glance which was the color of reddish water.

But it was not until some time later that I tried to define them approximately by retrospective analysis. At that moment, being altogether incapable of such effort, I could only realize in my own mind the idea of extreme decrepitude and horrible old age which they produced in my imagination.

Have I had said that they were set in very puffy eyelids, which had no lashes whatever, and that on her unwrinkled forehead there was not a vestige of eyebrow? When I tell you this, and emphasize the dullness of their look beneath the hair of an octogenarian, it is not surprising that Ledantec and I said in a low voice at the sight of this woman, who from her physique must have been young:

"Oh! poor, poor old woman!"

Her age was further accentuated by the terrible poverty revealed by her dress. If she had been better dressed, her youthful looks would, perhaps, have struck us more; but her thin shawl, which was all that she had over her chemise, her single petticoat which was full of holes and almost in rags, not nearly reaching to her bare feet, her straw hat with ragged feathers and with ribbons of no particular color through age, seemed altogether so ancient, so prodigiously antique that we were deceived.

From what remote, superannuated, and obsolete period did they all spring? You could not guess, and by a perfectly natural association of ideas, you would infer that the unfortunate creature was as old as her clothes were. Now, by "you" I mean by Ledantec and myself, that is to say, by two men who were abominably drunk and who were arguing with the peculiar logic of intoxication.

Under the softening influence of alcohol we looked at the vague smile on those lips hiding the teeth of a child, without considering the youthful beauty of the latter. We saw nothing but her fixed and almost idiotic smile, which no longer contrasted with the dull expression of her face, but, on the contrary, strengthened it. For in spite of her teeth, to us it was the smile of an old woman, and as for myself, I was really pleased at my acuteness when I inferred that this grandmother with such pale lips had the teeth of a young girl. Still, thanks to the softening influence of alcohol, I was not angry with her for this artifice. I even thought it particularly praiseworthy, since, after all, the poor creature thus conscientiously pursued her calling, which was to seduce men. For there was no possible doubt that this grandmother was nothing more nor less than a prostitute.

And then, drunk! Horribly drunk, much more drunk than Ledantec and I were, for we really could manage to say: "Oh! Pity the poor, poor old woman!" while she was incapable of articulating a single syllable, of making a gesture, or even of imparting a gleam of promise, a furtive flash of allurement to her eyes. With her hands crossed on her stomach, and leaning against the front of the public house, her whole body as stiff as if in a fit of catalepsy, she had nothing alluring about her, save her sad smile. This inspired us with all the more pity because she was even more tipsy than we were, and so, by an identical, spontaneous movement, we each

seized her by an arm to take her into the public-house with us.

To our great astonishment she resisted, and sprang back into the shadow again, out of the ray of light which came through the door. At the same time, she started off through the darkness dragging us with her, for she was clinging to our arms. We went along with her without speaking, not knowing where we were going, but without the least uneasiness on that score. Only, when she suddenly burst into violent sobs as she walked, Ledantec and I began to sob in unison.

The cold and the fog had suddenly congested our brains again, and we had again lost all precise consciousness of our acts, our thoughts, and our sensations. Our sobs had nothing of grief in them; we were floating in an atmosphere of perfect bliss, and I can remember that at that moment it was no longer the exterior world at which I seemed to be looking as through the penumbra of an aquarium; it was myself, a self composed of three, which was changing into something that was floating adrift in something, though what it was I did not know, composed as it was of impalpable fog and intangible water. But it was exquisitely delightful.

From that moment I remember nothing more until something happened which had the effect of a clap of thunder on me, and made me sober in an instant.

Ledantec was standing in front of me, his face convulsed with horror, his hair standing on end, and his eyes staring out of his head. He shouted to me:

"Let us escape! Let us escape!" Whereupon I opened my eyes wide, and found myself lying on the floor, in a room into which daylight was shining. I saw some rags hanging against the wall, two chairs, a broken jug lying on the floor by my side, and in a corner a wretched bed on which a woman was lying, who was no doubt dead, for her head was hanging over the side, and her long white hair reached almost to my feet.

With a bound I was up, like Ledantec. "What!" I said to him, while my teeth chattered: "Did you kill her?"

"No, no," he replied. "But that makes no difference; let us be off."

I felt completely sober by that time, but I did think that he was still suffering somewhat from the effects of last night's drinking; otherwise, why should he wish to escape? Pity for the unfortunate woman forced me to say:

"What is the matter with her? If she is ill, we must look after her."

I went over to the wretched bed, in order to put her head back on the pillow, and discovered that she was neither dead nor ill, but only sound asleep. I also noticed that she was quite young. She still wore that idiotic smile, but her teeth were her own and those of a girl. Her smooth skin and firm bust showed that she was not more than sixteen; perhaps not so much.

"There! You see it, you can see it!" said Ledantec. "Let us be off."

He tried to drag me out. He was still drunk; I could see it by his feverish movements, his trembling hands, and his nervous looks. Then he said:

"I slept beside the old woman; but she is not old. Look at her; look at her; yes, she is old after all!"

And he lifted up her long hair by handfuls; it was like handfuls of white silk, and then he added, evidently in a sort of frenzy, which made me fear an attack of delirium tremens: "To think that I have begotten children, three, four children—who knows how many children, all in one night! And they were born immediately, and have grown up already! Let us be off."

Decidedly it was an attack of madness. Poor Ledantec! What could I do for him? I took his arm and tried to calm him, but he thought that I was going to try and make him go over to her again, and he pushed me away and exclaimed with tears in his voice: "If you do not believe me, look under the bed; the children are there; they are are there, I tell you. Look here, just look here."

He threw himself down flat on his stomach, and actually pulled out one, two, three, four children, who had hidden under the bed. I do not exactly know whether they were boys or girls, but all, like the sleeping woman, had white hair, the hair of octogenarians.

Was I still drunk, like Ledantec, or was I mad? What was the meaning of this strange hallucination? I hesitated for a moment, and shook myself to be sure that I was awake.

No, no, I had all my wits about me, and in reality saw that horrible lot of little brats. They all had their faces in their hands, and were crying and squalling; then one of them suddenly jumped on to the bed; all the others followed his example, and the woman woke up.

And there we stood, while those five pairs of eyes, without eyebrows or eyelashes, eyes of the color of dull pewter, with pupils the color of red water, were steadily fixed on us.

"Let us be off! let us be off!" Ledantec repeated, loosing his hold of me. This time I paid attention to what he said, and after throwing some small change on to the floor, I followed him, to make him understand, when he became quite sober, that he saw before him a poor Albino unfortunate, who had several brothers and sisters.

Lost!

LOVE is stronger than death, and consequently, also, than the greatest disaster.

A young and by no means bad-looking son of Palestine, one of the barons of the Almanac of the *Ghetto*,* who had left the field covered with wounds in the last general engagement on the Stock Exchange, used very frequently to visit the Universal Exhibition in Vienna in 1873, in order to divert his thoughts, and to console himself amid the varied scenes and the numerous objects of attraction there. One day, in the Russian section, he met a newly-married couple, who had a very old coat of arms, but on the other hand, a very modest income.

This latter circumstance frequently emboldened the stockbroker to make secret overtures to the delightful little lady; overtures which might have fascinated certain Viennese actresses, but were an insult to a respectable woman. The Baroness, whose name appeared in the "Almanach de Gotha,"† felt something very like hatred for the man from the *Ghetto*, and for a long time her pretty little head had been full of various plans of revenge.

The stockbroker, who was really and even passionately in love with her, got close to her one day in the Exhibition buildings. He did this the more easily through the flight of the little woman's husband who had scented extravagance as soon as she went up to the show-case of a Russian fur-dealer, before which she remained standing in rapture.

"Do look at that lovely fur," the Baroness said, while her dark eyes expressed her pleasure; "I must have it."

But she looked at the white ticket on which the price was marked.

"Four thousand rubles," she said in despair; "that is about six thousand florins."‡

"Certainly," he replied, "but what of that? It is a sum not worth mentioning in the presence of such a charming lady."

"But my husband is not in a position—"

"Be less cruel than usual for once," the man from the *Ghetto* said to the young woman in a low voice, "and allow me to lay this sable skin at your feet."

*The Jews' quarter in some towns.

†An Almanac published early in Gotha, which contains a full account and genealogies of reigning families, mediatized princes, princely, non-reigning families, etc., etc.

‡$3,000.

"I presume that you are joking.".

"Not I!"

"I think you must be joking, as I cannot think that you intend to insult me."

"But, Baroness, I love you."

"That is one reason more why you should not make me angry."

"But—"

"This is outrageous," cried the energetic little woman; "I could flog you like 'Venus in the Fur'* did her slave."

"Let me be your slave," the Stock Exchange baron replied ardently, "and I will gladly put up with everything from you. Really, in this sable cloak, and with a whip in your hand, you would make a most lovely picture of the heroine of that story."

The Baroness looked at the man for a moment with a peculiar smile.

"Then if I were to listen to you favorably, you would let me flog you?" said she after a pause.

"With pleasure."

"Very well," she replied quickly. "You will let me give you twenty-five cuts with a whip, and I will be yours after the twenty-fifth blow."

"Are you in earnest?"

"Fully."

The man from the *Ghetto* took her hand, and pressed it ardently to his lips.

"When may I come?"

"To-morrow evening at eight o'clock."

"And I may bring the sable cloak and the whip with me?"

"No, I will see about that myself."

Next evening the enamored stockbroker came to the abode of the charming little Baroness, and found her alone, lying on a couch, wrapped in dark fur

and holding a dog whip in her small hand, which the man from the *Ghetto* kissed.

"You know our agreement," she began.

"Of course I do," the Stock Exchange baron replied. "I am to allow you to give me twenty-five cuts with the whip, and after the twenty-fifth you will listen to me."

"Yes, but I am going to tie your hands first of all."

The amorous baron quietly allowed this new Delila to tie his hands behind him, and then at her bidding, he knelt down before her, and she raised her whip and hit him hard.

"Oh! That hurts most confoundedly," he exclaimed.

"I mean it to hurt you," she said with a mocking laugh, and went on thrashing him without mercy. At last the poor fool groaned with pain, but he consoled himself with the thought that each blow brought him nearer to his happiness.

At the twenty-fourth cut, she threw the whip down.

"That only makes twenty-four," the beaten and would-be Don Juan remarked.

"I will make you a present of the twenty-fifth," she said with a laugh.

"And now you are mine, altogether mine," he exclaimed ardently.

"What are you thinking of?"

"Have I not let you beat me?"

"Certainly; but I promised you to grant your wish after the twenty-fifth blow, and you have only received twenty-four," the cruel little atom of

---

*One of Sacher-Masoch's novels.

virtue cried, "and I have witnesses to prove it."

With these words she drew back the curtains over the door, and her husband, followed by two other gentlemen came out of the next room, smiling. For a moment the stockbroker remained speechless on his knees before his Delila; then he gave a deep sigh, and sadly uttered that one, most significant word:

"Lost!"

A Country Excursion

For five months they had been talking of going to lunch at some country restaurant in the neighborhood of Paris, on Madame Dufour's birthday, and as they were looking forward very impatiently to the outing, they had risen very early that morning. Monsieur Dufour had borrowed the milkman's tilted cart, and drove himself. It was a very neat, two-wheeled conveyance, with a hood, and in it Madame Dufour, resplendent in a wonderful, sherry-colored silk dress, sat by the side of her husband.

The old grandmother and the daughter were accommodated with two chairs, and a yellow-haired youth, of whom, however, nothing was to be seen except his head, lay at the bottom of the trap.

When they got to the bridge of Neuilly, Monsieur Dufour said: "Here we are in the country at last!" At that warning, his wife grew sentimental about the beauties of nature. When they got to the crossroads at Courbevoie, they were seized with admiration for the tremendous view down there: on the right was the spire of Argenteuil church, above it rose the hills of Sannois and the mill of Orgemont, while on the left, the aqueduct of Marly stood out against the clear morning sky. In the distance they could see the terrace of Saint-Germain, and opposite to them, at the end of a low chain of hills, the new fort of Cormeilles. Afar—a very long way off, beyond the plains and villages —one could see the somber green of the forests.

The sun was beginning to shine in their faces, the dust got into their eyes, and on either side of the road there stretched an interminable tract of bare, ugly country, which smelled unpleasantly. You would have thought that it had been ravaged by a pestilence which had even attacked the buildings, for skeletons of dilapidated and deserted houses, or small cottages left in an unfinished state, as if the contractors had not been paid, reared their four roofless walls on each side.

Here and there tall factory-chimneys rose up from the barren soil, the only vegetation on that putrid land, where the spring breezes wafted an odor of petroleum and soot, mingled with another smell that was even still less agreeable. At last, however, they crossed the Seine a second time. It was delightful on the bridge; the river sparkled in the sun, and they had a feeling of quiet satisfaction and enjoyment in drinking in purer air, not impregnated by the black smoke of factories, nor by the miasma from the deposits of night-soil. A man whom they met told them that the name of the place was Bézons; so Monsieur Dufour pulled up, and read the attractive announcement outside an eating-house:

"Restaurant Poulin, stews and fried fish, private rooms, arbors, and swings."

"Well! Madame Dufour, will this suit you? Will you make up your mind at last?"

She read the announcement in her turn, and then looked at the house for a time.

It was a white country inn, built by the roadside, and through the open door she could see the bright zinc of the counter, at which two workmen out for the day were sitting. At last she made up her mind, and said:

"Yes, this will do; and, besides, there is a view."

So they drove into a large yard studded with trees, behind the inn, which was only separated from the river by the towing-path, and got out. The husband sprang out first, and held out his arms for his wife. As the step was very high, Madame Dufour, in order to reach him, had to show the lower part of her limbs, whose former slenderness had disappeared in fat. Monsieur Dufour, who was already getting excited by the country air, pinched her calf, and then, taking her in his arms, set her on to the ground, as if she had been some enormous bundle. She shook the dust out of the silk dress, and then looked round, to see in what sort of a place she was.

She was a stout woman, of about thirty-six full-blown and delightful to look at. She could hardly breathe, as she was laced too tightly, which forced the heaving mass of her superabundant bosom up to her double chin. Next, the girl put her hand on to her father's shoulder, and jumped lightly down. The youth with the yellow hair had got down by stepping on the wheel, and he helped Monsieur Dufour to get the grandmother out. Then they unharnessed the horse, which they tied up to a tree, and the carriage fell back, with both shafts in the air. The man and boy took off their coats, washed their hands in a pail of water, and then joined the ladies, who had already taken possession of the swings.

Mademoiselle Dufour was trying to swing herself standing up, but she could not succeed in getting a start. She was a pretty girl of about eighteen; one of those women who suddenly excite your desire when you meet them in the street, and who leave you with a vague feeling of uneasiness and of excited senses. She was tall, had a small waist and large hips, with a dark skin, very large eyes, and very black hair. Her dress clearly marked the outlines of her firm, full figure, which was accentuated by the motion of her hips as she tried to swing herself higher. Her arms were stretched over her head to hold the rope, so that her bosom rose at every movement she made. Her hat, which a gust of wind had blown off, was hanging behind her, and as the swing gradually rose higher and higher, she showed her delicate limbs up to the knees each time, and the wind from the perfumed petticoats, more heady than the fumes of wine, blew into the faces of her father and friend, who were looking at her in admiration.

Sitting in the other swing, Madame Dufour kept saying in a monotonous voice:

"Cyprian, come and swing me; do come and swing me, Cyprian!"

At last he complied, and turning up his shirt-sleeves, as if he intended to work very hard, with much difficulty he set his wife in motion. She clutched the two ropes, and held her legs out straight, so as not to touch the ground. She enjoyed feeling giddy from the motion of the swing, and her whole figure shook like a jelly on a dish, but as she went higher and higher, she grew too giddy and got frightened. Every time she was coming back, she uttered a shriek, which made all the little urchins come round, and, down below, beneath the garden hedge, she vaguely saw a row of mischievous heads, making various grimaces as they laughed.

When a servant girl came out, they ordered lunch.

"Some fried fish, a stewed rabbit, salad, and dessert," Madame Dufour said, with an important air.

"Bring two quarts of beer and a bottle of claret," her husband said.

"We will have lunch on the grass," the girl added.

The grandmother, who had an affection for cats, had been petting one that belonged to the house, and had been bestowing the most affectionate words on it, for the last ten minutes. The animal, no doubt secretly pleased by her attentions, kept close to the good woman, but just out of reach of her hand, and quietly walked round the trees, against which she rubbed herself, with her tail up, purring with pleasure.

"Hallo!" exclaimed the youth with the yellow hair, who was ferreting about, "here are two swell boats!" They all went to look at them, and saw two beautiful skiffs in a wooden boathouse, which were as beautifully finished as if they had been objects of luxury. They were moored side by side, like two tall, slender girls, in their narrow shining length, and aroused in one a wish to float in them on warm summer mornings and evenings, along flower-covered banks of the river, where the trees dip their branches into the water, where the rushes are continually rustling in the breeze, and where the swift kingfishers dart about like flashes of blue lightning.

The whole family looked at them with great respect.

"They are indeed two swell boats," Monsieur Dufour repeated gravely, and he examined them closely, commenting on them like a connoisseur. He had been in the habit of rowing in his younger days, he said, and when he had that in his hands—and he went through the action of pulling the oars—he did not care a fig for anybody. He had beaten more than one Englishman formerly at the Joinville regattas. He grew quite excited at last, and offered to make a bet that in a boat like that he could row six miles an hour, without exerting himself.

"Lunch is ready," said the waitress, appearing at the entrance to the boathouse. They all hurried off, but two young men were already lunching at the best place, which Madame Dufour had chosen in her mind as her seat. No doubt they were the owners of the skiffs, for they were dressed in boating costume. They were stretched out, almost lying on chairs, and were sunburned, and had on flannel trousers and thin cotton jerseys, with short sleeves, which showed their bars arms, which were as strong as blacksmiths'. They were two strong young fellows, who thought a great deal of their vigor, and who showed in all their movements that elasticity and grace of limb which can only be acquired by exercise, and which is so different to the awkwardness with which the same continual work stamps the mechanic.

They exchanged a rapid smile when they saw the mother, and then a look on seeing the daughter.

"Let us give up our place," one of them said; "it will make us acquainted with them."

The other got up immediately, and holding his black and red boating-cap in his hand, he politely offered the ladies the only shady place in the garden. With many excuses they accepted, and so that it might be more rural, they sat on the grass, without either tables or chairs.

The two young men took their plates, knives, forks, etc., to a table a little way off, and began to eat again. Their bare arms, which they showed continually, rather embarrassed the young girl, who even pretended to turn her head aside, and not to see them. But Madame Dufour, who was rather bolder, tempted by feminine curiosity, looked at them every moment, and no doubt compared them with the secret unsightliness of her husband. She had squatted herself on the ground with her legs tucked under her, after the manner of tailors, and kept wriggling about continually,

under the pretext that ants were crawling about her somewhere. Monsieur Dufour, whom the politeness of the strangers had put into rather a bad temper, was trying to find a comfortable position, which he did not, however, succeed in doing, while the youth with the yellow hair was eating as silently as an ogre.

"It is lovely weather, Monsieur," the stout lady said to one of the boatingmen. She wished to be friendly, because they had given up their place.

"It is, indeed, Madame," he replied; "do you often go into the country?"

"Oh! Only once or twice a year, to get a little fresh air; and you, Monsieur?"

"I come and sleep here every night."

"Oh! That must be very nice?"

"Certainly it is, Madame." And he gave them such a practical account of his daily life, that in the hearts of these shopkeepers, who were deprived of the meadows, and who longed for country walks, it roused that innate love of nature, which they all felt so strongly the whole year round, behind the counter in their shop.

The girl raised her eyes and looked at the oarsman with emotion, and Monsieur Dufour spoke for the first time.

"It is indeed a happy life," he said. And then he added: "A little more rabbit, my dear?"

"No, thank you," she replied, and turning to the young men again, and pointing to their arms, asked: "Do you never feel cold like that?"

They both laughed, and amazed the family by telling of the enormous fatigue they could endure, of bathing while in a state of tremendous perspiration, of rowing in the fog at night, and they struck their chests violently, to show how they sounded.

"Ah! You look very strong," the husband said, and he did not talk any more of the time when he used to beat the English. The girl was looking at them askance now, and the young fellow with the yellow hair, as he had swallowed some wine the wrong way, and was coughing violently, bespattered Madame Dufour's sherry-colored silk dress. Madame got angry, and sent for some water to wash the spots.

Meanwhile it had grown unbearably hot, the sparkling river looked like a blaze of fire and the fumes of the wine were getting into their heads. Monsieur Dufour, who had a violent hiccough, had unbuttoned his waistcoat and the top of his trousers, while his wife, who felt choking, was gradually unfastening her dress. The youth was shaking his yellow wig in a happy frame of mind, and kept helping himself to wine, and as the old grandmother felt drunk, she endeavored to be very stiff and dignified. As for the girl, she showed nothing except a peculiar brightness in her eyes, while the brown skin on the cheeks became more rosy.

The coffee finished them off; they spoke of singing, and each of them sang, or repeated a couplet, which the others repeated enthusiastically. Then they got up with some difficulty, and while the two women, who were rather dizzy, were getting some fresh air, the two males, who were altogether drunk, were performing gymnastic tricks. Heavy, limp, and with scarlet faces, they hung awkwardly on to the iron rings, without being able to raise themselves, while

their shirts were continually threatening to part company with their trousers, and to flap in the wind like flags.

Meanwhile, the two boating-men had got their skiffs into the water. They came back, and politely asked the ladies whether they would like a row.

"Would you like one, Monsieur Dufour?" his wife exclaimed. "Please come!"

He merely gave her a drunken look, without understanding what she said. Then one of the rowers came up, with two fishing-rods in his hand; and the hope of catching a gudgeon, that great aim of the Parisian shopkeeper, made Dufour's dull eyes gleam. He politely allowed them to do whatever they liked, while he sat in the shade, under the bridge, with his feet dangling over the river, by the side of the young man with the yellow hair, who was sleeping soundly close to him.

One of the boating-men made a martyr of himself, and took the mother.

"Let us go to the little wood on the Ile aux Anglais!" he called out, as he rowed off. The other skiff went slower, for the rower was looking at his companion so intently, that he thought of nothing else. His emotion paralyzed his strength, while the girl, who was sitting on the steerer's seat, gave herself up to the enjoyment of being on the water. She felt disinclined to think, felt a lassitude in her limbs, a complete self-relaxation, as if she were intoxicated. She had become very flushed, and breathed pantingly. The effect of the wine, increased by the extreme heat, made all the trees on the bank seem to bow, as she passed. A vague wish for enjoyment, a fermentation of her blood, seemed to pervade her whole body, and she was also a little agitated by this *tête-à-tête* on the water, in a place which seemed depopulated by the heat, with this young man, who thought her so pretty, whose looks seemed to caress her skin, and whose eyes were as penetrating and exciting as the sun's rays.

Their inability to speak increased their emotion, and they looked about them. At last he made an effort and asked her name.

"Henriette," she said.

"Why! My name is Henri," he replied. The sound of their voices calmed them, and they looked at the banks. The other skiff had gone ahead of them, and seemed to be waiting for them. The rower called out:

"We will meet you in the wood; we are going as far as Robinson's,* because Madame Dufour is thirsty." Then he bent over his oars again and rowed off so quickly that he was soon out of sight.

Meanwhile, a continual roar, which they had heard for some time, came nearer, and the river itself seemed to shiver, as if the dull noise were rising from its depths.

"What is that noise?" she asked. It was the noise of the weir, which cut the river in two, at the island. He was explaining it to her, when above the noise of the waterfall they heard the song of a bird, which seemed a long way off.

"Listen!" he said; "the nightingales are singing during the day, so the females must be sitting."

A nightingale! She had never heard one before, and the idea of listening to one roused visions of poetic tenderness in her heart. A nightingale! That is to say, the invisible witness of the lover's interview which Juliette invoked on her balcony†; that celestial music which is attuned to human kisses; that eternal inspirer of all those languorous romances which open idealized visions to the poor, tender, little hearts of sensitive girls!

She wanted to hear a nightingale.

"We must not make a noise," her companion said, "and then we can go into the wood, and sit down close to it."

The skiff seemed to glide. They saw the trees on the island, the banks of which were so low that they could look into the depths of the thickets. They stopped, he made the boat fast, Henriette took hold of Henri's arm, and they went beneath the trees.

"Stoop," he said, so she bent down, and they went into an inextricable thicket of creepers, leaves, and reed-grass, which formed an impenetrable retreat, and which the young man laughingly called "his private room."

Just above their heads, perched in one of the trees which hid them, the bird was still singing. He uttered shakes and *roulades*, and then long, vibrating sounds that filled the air and seemed to lose themselves in the distance, across the level country, through that burning silence which hung low upon the whole country round. They did not speak for fear of frightening the bird away. They were sitting close together, and slowly Henri's arm stole round the girl's waist

*A well-known restaurant on the banks of the Seine, much frequented by the bourgeoisie.

†"Romeo and Juliet," Act III., Scene V.

and squeezed it gently. She took that daring hand, but without anger, and kept removing it whenever he put it round her; not, however, feeling at all embarrassed by this caress, just as if it had been something quite natural which she was resisting just as naturally.

She was listening to the bird in ecstasy. She felt an infinite longing for happiness, for some sudden demonstration of tenderness, for a revelation of divine poesy. She felt such a softening at her heart, and such a relaxation of her nerves, that she began to cry, without knowing why. The young man was now straining her close to him, and she did not remove his arm; she did not think of it. Suddenly the nightingale stopped, and a voice called out in the distance:

"Henriette!"

"Do not reply," he said in a low voice, "you will drive the bird away."

But she had no idea of doing so, and they remained in the same position for some time. Madame Dufour had sat down somewhere or other, for from time to time they heard the stout lady break out into little bursts of laughter.

The girl was still crying; she was filled with strange sensations. Henri's head was on her shoulder, and suddenly he kissed her on the lips. She was surprised and angry, and, to avoid him, she stood up.

They were both very pale when they quitted their grassy retreat. The blue sky looked dull to them, the ardent sun was clouded over to their eyes, they perceived not the solitude and the silence. They walked quickly side by side, without speaking or touching each other, appearing to be irreconcilable enemies,

as if disgust had sprung up between them, and hatred between their souls. From time to time Henriette called out: "Mamma!"

By and by they heard a noise in a thicket, and Madame Dufour appeared, looking rather confused, and her companion's face was wrinkled with smiles that he could not check.

Madame Dufour took his arm, and they returned to the boats. Henri went on first, still without speaking, by the girl's side, and at last they got back to Bêzons. Monsieur Dufour, who had sobered up, was waiting for them very impatiently, while the youth with the yellow hair was having a mouthful of something to eat before leaving the inn. The carriage was in the yard, with the horse in, and the grandmother, who had already got in, was frightened at the thought of being overtaken by night, before they got back to Paris, the outskirts not being safe.

The young men shook hands with them, and the Dufour family drove off.

"Good-bye, until we meet again!" the oarsmen cried, and the answers they got were a sigh and a tear.

*   *   *   *   *   *

Two months later, as Henri was going along the Rue des Martyrs, he saw "Dufour, Ironmonger," over a door. So he went in, and saw the stout lady sitting at the counter. They recognized each other immediately, and after an interchange of polite greetings, he inquired after them all.

"And how is Mademoiselle Henriette?" he inquired, specially.

"Very well, thank you; she is married."

"Ah!" Mastering his feelings, he added: "To whom was she married?"

"To that young man who went with us, you know; he has joined us in business."

"I remember him, perfectly."

He was going out, feeling unhappy, though scarcely knowing why, when Madame called him back.

"And how is your friend?" she asked, rather shyly.

"He is very well, thank you."

The Relics

THEY had given him a grand public funeral, like they do to victorious soldiers who have added some dazzling pages to the glorious annals of their country, who have restored courage to desponding hearts and cast over other nations the proud shadow of their country's flag, like a yoke under which those go who are no longer to have a country, or liberty.

During a whole bright, calm night, when falling stars made people think of unknown metamorphoses and the transmigration of souls, tall cavalry soldiers in their cuirasses, sitting as motionless as statues on their horses, had watched by the dead man's coffin, which was resting, covered with wreaths, under the porch of the heroes, every stone of which is engraved with the name of a brave man and of a battle.

The whole town was in mourning, as if it had lost the only object that had possession of its heart and love. The crowd went silently and thoughtfully down the avenue of the Champs-Elysées, and almost fought for the commemorative medals and the common portraits which hawkers were selling, or climbed upon the stands which street boys had erected here and there, from

which they could see over the heads of the crowd.

The Place de la Concorde had something solemn about it, with its circle of statues hung from head to foot with long crape coverings, which looked in the distance like widows, weeping and praying.

According to his last wish, Jean Ramel had been conveyed to the Panthéon in the wretched paupers' hearse, which takes them to the common grave, behind the shambling trot of some thin and broken-winded horse.

That dreadful, black conveyance without any drapery, without plumes and without flowers, followed by Ministers and deputies, by several regiments with their bands, with their flags flying above the helmets and the sabers, by children from the national schools, by delegates from the provinces and by an innumerable crowd of men in blouses, of women, of shopkeepers from every quarter, had a most theatrical effect. Standing on the steps of the Panthéon, at the foot of the massive columns of the portico, the orators successively descanted on Ramel's apotheosis, tried to make their voices dominate over the noise, emphasized their pompous periods, and finished the performance by a poor third act, making people yawn and gradually dispersing the audience. People remembered who that man had been on whom such posthumous honors were being bestowed, and who was having such a funeral: it was Jean Ramel.

Those three sonorous syllables called up a leonine head, with white hair thrown back in disorder like a mane, with features that looked as if they had been cut out with a bill-hook, but which were so powerful, and in which there flamed such life, as to make one forget their vulgarity and ugliness,—with black eyes under bushy eyebrows, eyes which dilated and flashed like lightning, now veiled as if in tears and then filled with serene mildness,—a voice which now growled so as almost to terrify its hearers, and would have filled the hall of some working-man's club, full of the thick smoke from strong pipes, without being affected by it, and then would be soft, coaxing, persuasive, and unctuous as that of a priest who is holding out promises of Paradise, or giving absolution for our sins.

He had had the good luck to be persecuted, to be in the eyes of the people the incarnation of that lying formula which appears on every public edifice, those three words of the Golden Age, which make those who think, those who suffer, and those who govern, smile somewhat sadly—"Liberty, Fraternity, Equality." Luck had been kind to him, had sustained, had pushed him on by the shoulders, and had set him up on his pedestal again when he had fallen as all idols do.

He spoke and he wrote, and always in order to announce the good news to all the multitudes who suffered,—no matter to what grade of society they might belong,—to hold out his hand to them and to defend them, to attack the abuses of the "Code,"—that book of injustice and severity,—to speak the truth boldly, even when it lashed his enemies as if it had been a whip.

His books were like Gospels which are read, chapter by chapter, and warmed the most despairing and the most sorrowing hearts, bringing comfort, hope, and dreams to each.

He had lived very modestly until the end, and appeared to spend nothing, and had only kept one old servant, who spoke to him in the Basque dialect.

That chaste philosopher, who had all his life long feared women's snares and wiles, who had looked upon love as a luxury made only for the rich and idle, which unsettles the brain and interferes with acuteness of thought, had allowed himself to be caught like an ordinary man—late in life—when his hair was white and his forehead deeply wrinkled.

It was not, however, as happens in the visions of solitary ascetics, some strange queen or female magician, with stars in her eyes and witchery in her voice, or some loose woman who holds up the symbolical lamp immodestly, to light up her radiant nudity and the pink and white bouquet of her sweet smelling skin, or some woman in search of voluptuous pleasures, whose lascivious appeals it is impossible for any man to listen to without being excited to the very depths of his being. Neither a Princess out of some fairy tale, nor a frail beauty who was expert in reviving the ardor of old men, and of leading them astray, nor a woman disgusted with her ideals, finding them all alike, who dreams of awakening the heart of one of those men who suffer, who afford so much alleviation to human misery, who seem to be surrounded by a halo, and who never know anything but the true, the beautiful, and the good.

It was only a little girl of twenty, who was as pretty as a wild flower, had a ringing laugh, white teeth, and a mind that was as spotless as a new mirror, in which no figure has been reflected as yet.

He was an exile at the time for having given public expression to what he thought, and was living in an Italian village which was buried in chestnut-trees and situated on the shores of a lake so narrow and so transparent that it might have been taken for some nobleman's fish-pond, an emerald in a large park. It consisted of about twenty red-tiled houses; steep paths paved with flint led up the side of the hills among the vines, where the Madonna, full of grace and goodness, extended her indulgences from shrines which contained dusty, tinsel nosegays.

For the first time in his life Ramel remarked that there were some lips that were more desirable, more smiling than others, that there was hair in which it must be delicious to bury the fingers as in fine silk, and which it must be delightful to kiss, and that there were eyes which contained an infinitude of caresses. He wandered right through the eclogue, which at length revealed true happiness to him, and he had a child, a son. by her.

This was the only secret that Ramel jealously concealed, and of which no more than two or three of his oldest

friends knew aught. While he hesitated about spending twopence on himself, and went to the Institute and to the Chamber of Deputies outside an omnibus, Pepa led the happy life of a millionaire who is not frightened of the to-morrow, and brought up her son like a little prince, with a tutor and three servants, who had nothing to do but to look after him.

All that Ramel made went into his mistress's hands, and when he felt that his last hour was approaching, and that there was no hope of his recovery—in full possession of his faculties and with joy in his dull eyes, he gave his name to Pepa, and made her his lawful widow, in the presence of all his friends. She inherited everything that her former lover left behind, a considerable income from the royalties on his books, and also his pension, which the State continued to pay to her.

Little Ramel throve wonderfully amid all this luxury, and gave free scope to his instincts and his caprices, without his mother ever having the courage to reprove him in the least, and he did not bear the slightest resemblance to Jean Ramel.

Full of pranks, effeminate, a superfine dandy, and precociously vicious, he suggested the idea of those pages at the Court of Florence, whom we meet with in the "Decameron," and who were the playthings for the idle hands of patrician ladies.

He was very ignorant, lived at a great rate, bet on races, and played cards for heavy stakes with seasoned gamblers, old enough to be his father. It was distressing to hear this lad joke about the memory of him whom he called *the old man,* and persecute his mother because of the worship and adoration which she felt for Jean Ramel, whom she spoke of as if he had become a demigod, when he died, as in the Roman theogony.

He would have liked altogether to have altered the arrangement of that sanctuary, the drawing-room, where Pepa kept some of her husband's manuscripts, the furniture that he had most frequently used, the bed on which he had died, his pens, his clothes, and his weapons. And one evening, not knowing how to dress himself up more originally than the rest for a masked ball that stout Toinette Danicheff was going to give as a housewarming, without saying a word to his mother, he took down the Academician's dress, the sword and cocked hat that had belonged to Jean Ramel, and put it on as if it had been a disguise on Shrove Tuesday.

Slightly built and with thin arms and legs, the wide clothes hung on him. He was a comical sight with the embroidered skirt of his coat sweeping the carpet, and his sword knocking against his heels. The elbows and the collar were shiny and greasy from wear, for the Master had worn it until it was threadbare, to avoid having to buy another, and had never thought of replacing it.

He made a tremendous hit, and fair Liline Ablette laughed so at his grimaces and his disguise, that that night she threw over Prince Noureddin for him, although he had paid for her house, her horses, and everything else, and allowed her six thousand francs a month for extras and pocket money,

---

A Rupture

"It is just as I tell you, my dear fellow. Those two poor things whom we all of us envied, who looked like a couple of doves when they are billing and cooing, and were always *spooning,* until they made themselves ridiculous, now hate each other just as much as they used to adore each other. It is a complete break, and one of those which cannot be mended like an old plate! And all for a bit of nonsense, for something so funny that it ought to have brought them closer together and have amused them immensely.

"But how can a man explain himself when he is dying of jealousy and keeps repeating to his terrified mistress: 'You are lying! you are lying!' When he shakes her, interrupts her while she is speaking, and says such hard things to her that at last she flies into a rage, and thinks of nothing but of giving him *tit for tat* and of paying him out in his own coin, does not care a straw about destroying his happiness, consigns everything to the devil, and talks a lot of bosh which she certainly does not believe—can you blame her? And then, because there is nothing so stupid and so obstinate in the whole world as a lover, neither he nor she will take the first step, and own to having been in the wrong, and apologize for having gone too far. Both wait and watch and do not even write a few lines about nothing, a subterfuge which would restore peace. No, they let day succeed day, and there are feverish and sleepless nights when the bed seems so hard, so cheerless, and so large, and habits get weakened and the fire of love that was still smoldering at the bottom of each heart dies in smoke. By degrees both find some reason for what they wish to do, think themselves idiots to lose the time which will never return, in that fashion, and so *good-bye,* and there you are! That is how Josine Cadenette and that great idiot Servance separated."

Lalie Spring had lighted a cigarette, and the blue smoke played about her fine, fair hair, making one think of those last rays of the setting sun which pierce through the clouds at sunset. Resting her elbows on his knees, and with her chin in her hand in a dreamy attitude, she murmured:

"Sad, isn't it?"

"Bah!" I replied, "at their age people easily console themselves, and everything begins over again, even love!"

"Well, Josine has already found somebody else—"

"And did she tell you her story?"

"Of course she did, and it is such a joke! You know that Servance is one of those fellows you would wish to have when you have time to amuse yourself, so self-possessed that he would be capable of ruining all the older ones in a girls' school, and given to trifling as much as most men, so that Josine calls him 'perpetual motion.' He would have liked to prolong his fun until the Day of Judgment, and seemed to fancy that

beds were not made to sleep in at all. But she could not get used to being deprived of nearly all her rest, and it really made her ill. But as she wished to be as conciliatory as possible, to love and to be loved as ardently as in the past, and also to sleep off the effects of her happiness peacefully, she rented a small room in a distant quarter, in a quiet shady street, giving out that she had just come from the country, and put hardly any furniture into it except a good bed and a dressing-table.

"Then she invented an old aunt, who was ill and always grumbling, who suffered from heart disease and lived in one of the suburbs, and so, several times a week, Josine took refuge in her sleeping place, and used to sleep late there as if it had been some delicious abode, where one forgets the whole world. Once they forgot to call her at the proper time; she got back late, tired, with red and swollen eyelids, involved herself in lies, contradicted herself, and looked so much as if she had just come from the confessional, feeling horribly ashamed of herself, or, as if she had hurried home from some assignation, that Servance worried himself about it, thought that he was being made a fool of, as so many of his comrades were, got into a rage and made up his mind to set the matter straight, and to discover who this aunt was who had so suddenly fallen from the skies.

"He applied to an obliging agency, where they excited his jealousy, exasperated him day after day by making him believe that Josine Cadenette was making an absolute fool of him, had no more a sick aunt than she had any virtue, but that during the day she continued the little debaucheries which she committed with him at night, and that she shamelessly frequented some discreet bachelor's lodgings, where probably more than one of his best friends was amusing himself at his expense, and having his share of the cake.

"He was fool enough to believe these fellows, instead of going and watching Josine himself, putting his nose into the business, and finding and knocking at the door of her room. He wanted to hear no more, and would not listen to her. For a trifle, in spite of her tears, he would have turned the poor thing into the streets, as if she had been a bundle of dirty linen. You may guess how she flew out at him and told him all sorts of things to annoy him; she let him believe he was not mistaken, that she had had enough of his affection, and that she was madly in love with another man. He grew very pale when she said that, looked at her furiously, clenched his teeth, and said in a hoarse voice:

"'Tell me his name, tell me his name!'

"'Oh!' she said, chaffingly, 'you know him very well!' and if I had not happened to have gone in I think there would have been a tragedy. How stupid they are: they were so happy and loved each other so. And now Josine is living with fat Schweinssohn, a low scoundrel who will live upon her, and Servance has taken up with Sophie Labisque, who might easily be his mother. You know her, that bundle of red and yellow, who has been at that kind of thing for eighteen years, and whom Laglandée has christened 'Saecula saeculorum!'"

"By Jove! I should rather think I did!"

Margot's Tapers

I.

On the evening of Midsummer day, Margot Fresquyl had allowed herself to taste for the first time the delicious intoxication of the mortal sin of loving.

While most of the young people were holding one another's hands and dancing in a circle round the burning logs, the girl had shyly taken the deserted road which lead to the wood, leaning on the arm of her partner, a tall, vigorous farm-servant, whose Christian name was Tiennou, which, by the way, was the only name he had borne from his birth.

For he was entered on the register of births with this curt note, "Father and mother unknown," having been found on St. Stephen's Day under a shed on a farm, where some poor, despairing wretch had abandoned him, perhaps even without turning her head to look at him.

For months Tiennou had madly worshiped the pretty blond girl, who was now trembling as he clasped in his arms, under the sweet coolness of the leaves. He well remembered how she had dazzled him—like some ecstatic and ineffaceable vision,—the first time that he saw her in her father's mill, where he had gone to ask for work. She stood out all rosy from the warmth of the day, amid the impalpable clouds of flour, which diffused a misty whiteness through the air. With her hair hanging about her in untidy curls, as if she had just awakened from a profound sleep, she stretched herself lazily, her bare arms clasped behind her head, yawning so as to show her white teeth, which glistened like those of a young wolf, and from beneath her unbuttoned bodice her maiden bosom appeared with innocent immodesty. He told her that he thought her adorable, so stupidly that she made fun of him and scourged him with her cruel laughter. From that day, he spent his life in Margot's shadow. He might have been taken for one of those wild beasts ardent with desire, which ceaselessly utter maddened cries to the stars on nights when the constellations bathe the dark coverts in warm light. Margot met him wherever she went, and seized with pity, and by degrees attracted by his ardor, by his dumb entreaties, by the burning looks which flashed from his large eyes, she had returned his love. She had dreamed restlessly that during a whole night she had been in his vigorous arms, which pressed her like corn that is being crushed in the mill; that she was obeying a man who had subdued her, and was learning strange things which other girls talked about in a low voice when drawing water at the well.

She had, however, been obliged to wait until Midsummer day, for the miller watched over his heiress very carefully.

The two lovers told each other all this as they were going along the dark road, innocently giving utterance to words of happiness which rose to their lips like the refrain of a forgotten song. At times they were silent, not knowing what more to say and not daring to embrace each other any more. The night was soft and warm, the warmth of a half-closed alcove in a bedroom, and had the effect of a tumbler of new wine.

The leaves were sleeping motionless and in supreme peace, and in the distance they could hear the monotonous trill of the brooks as they flowed over the stones. Amid the faint noise of the insects, the nightingales were answering each other from tree to tree. Everything seemed alive with hidden life, the sky was bright, and the falling stars might have been taken for white forms wandering among the dark trunks of the trees.

"Why have we come?" Margot asked, in a panting voice. "Do you not want me any more, Tiennou?"

"Alas! I dare not," he replied. "Listen: you know that I was picked up on the highroad, that I have nothing in the world except my two arms, and that miller Fresquyl will never let his daughter marry a poor devil like me."

She interrupted him with a painful gesture, and putting her lips to his, she said:

"What does that matter? I love you, and I want you. Take me."

And thus it was, on St. John's eve, that Margot Fresquyl for the first time yielded to the mortal sin of love.

II.

Did the miller guess his daughter's secret when he heard her singing merrily from dawn till dusk and saw her sitting dreaming at her window instead of sewing as she was in the habit of doing?

Did he see it when she threw ardent kisses from the tips of her fingers to her lover at a distance?

Whether he did or not, he shut up poor Margot in the mill as if it had been a prison. No more love or pleasure, no more meetings at night on the verge of the wood. When she chatted with the passers-by, or tried furtively to open the gate of the inclosure to make her escape, her father beat her as if she had been some disobedient animal, beat her until she would fall on her knees, on the floor with clasped hands, scarcely able to move, her whole body covered with purple bruises.

She pretended to obey him, but she revolted in her whole being, and the string of bitter insults which he heaped upon her rang in her head. With clenched hands, and a gesture of terrible hatred, she cursed him for standing in the way of her love. At night, she rolled about on her bed, bit the sheets, moaned, stretched herself out for imaginary embraces, maddened by the longing with which her body was still palpitating. She called out Tiennou's name aloud, she broke the peaceful stillness of the sleeping house with her heartrending sobs, and her weeping drowned the monotonous sound of the water dripping under the arch of the mill, between the immovable paddles of the wheel.

III.

Then came that terrible week in October when the unfortunate young fellows who had drawn bad numbers had to join their regiments.* Tiennou was one of them. Margot was desperate at the thought of not seeing him for five interminable years, and grieving that they could not even, at that hour of sad farewell, be alone and exchange those consoling words which afterward soften the pang of absence.

Tiennou prowled about the house, like a starving beggar, and one morning, while the miller was mending the wheel, he managed to see Margot.

"I will wait for you in the old place to-night," he whispered, in terrible grief. "I know it is the last time. I shall throw myself into some deep hole in the river if you do not come!"

"I will be there, Tiennou," she replied, in a bewildered manner. "I swear I will be there, even if I have to do something terrible to enable me to come!"

*　　*　　*　　*　　*　　*　　*

The village was on fire, illumining the dark night, and the flames, fanned by the wind, rose up like evil torches. The thatched roofs, the ricks of corn, the haystacks, and the barns fell in and crackled like rockets, while the sky looked as if it was illuminated by an aurora borealis. Fresquyl's mill was smoking, and its calcined ruins were reflected on the deep water. The sheep and cows were running about the fields in terror, the dogs were howling, and the women were sitting on the broken furniture, crying and wringing their hands. At this time Margot was abandoning herself to her lover's ardent

---

*Written before universal service was obligatory, and when soldiers were selected by conscription, a certain proportion of those who drew high numbers being exempt from service.

caresses, and with her arms round his neck she said to him, tenderly:

"You see that I have kept my promise. I set fire to the mill so that I might be able to get out. So much the worse if all have suffered. But I do not care as long as you love me, are happy with me!"

And pointing to the fire, which was still burning fiercely in the distance, she added with a burst of savage laughter:

"Tiennou, we shall not have such beautiful tapers at our wedding Mass when you come back from your regiment!"

And thus it was that for the second time Margot Fresquyl yielded to the mortal sin of love.

The Accent

It was a large sheltered house, with long white terraces shaded by vines, from which one could see the sea. Large pines stretched a dark arch over the ruined *façade,* and there was a look of neglect, of want, and wretchedness about the place, such as irreparable losses, departure to other countries, and death leave behind them.

The interior wore a strange look, with half unpacked trunks serving for wardrobes, with piles of bandboxes, and for seats an array of worm-eaten armchairs, into which bits of velvet and silk, cut from old dresses, had been patched at random. Along the walls there were rows of rusty nails which made one think of old portraits and of pictures full of family history, which had one by one been sold for a song to some second-hand furniture broker.

The rooms were in disorder and furnished at random, while velvets hanging from the ceilings and in the corners seemed to show that as the servants were no longer paid except by promises, they no longer did more than occasionally give them an accidental, careless touch with the duster. The drawing-room, which was extremely large, was full of useless knickknacks, the sort of rubbish which is put up for sale at stalls at watering-places, daubs—they could not be called paintings—of portraits and of flowers, and an old piano with yellow keys.

Such is the home where she who had been called the handsome Madame de Maurillac was spending her monotonous existence, like some unfortunate doll which inconstant, childish hands have thrown into a corner in a loft—she who had almost passed for a professional seductress, and whose coquetries, at least so the faithful ones of the Party said, had been able to excite a passing and last spark of desire in the dull eyes of the Emperor.

Like many others, she and her husband had waited for his return from Elba, had discounted a fresh, immediate chance, had kept up boldly and spent the remains of fortune in the game of luxury.

On the day when the illusion vanished, and he was forced to awake from his dream, Monsieur de Maurillac, without considering that he was leaving his wife and daughter behind him almost penniless, and not strong enough morally to make up his mind to come down in the world, to vegetate, to fight creditors, to accept some sinecure, poisoned himself, like a shopgirl forsaken by her lover.

Madame de Maurillac did not mourn for him. As this lamentable event had made her interesting, and as she was assisted and supported by unexpected acts of kindness, and had a good adviser in one of those old Parisian lawyers who can extricate you out of the worst difficulties, she managed to save something from the wreck, and to keep a small income. Then reassured and emboldened, and resting her ultimate illusions and her frail hopes on her daughter's radiant beauty, she prepared for that last game in which they would risk everything, and hoping also that she might herself marry again, the ancient flirt arranged a double existence.

For months and months she would disappear from the world, and, as a pretext for her isolation and for hiding herself in the country, alleged her daughter's delicate health, and the important interests she had to look after in the South of France.

Her frivolous friends looked upon this as a great act of heroism, as something almost superhuman, and so courageous, that they tried to distract her by their incessant letters, and religiously informed her of all the scandals and love adventures that came to light in the suburbs as well as in the apotheosis of the capital.

The difficult struggle which Madame de Maurillac had to keep up in order to maintain her rank was really as fine as any campaign in the twilight of defeat, a slow retreat where men only give way inch by inch, fighting until the last cartridge is expended or fresh troops arrive, to bar the way to the enemy, and save the threatened flag.

Broken in by the same discipline, and haunted by the same dream, mother and daughter lived on almost nothing in the dull, dilapidated house which the peasants called the château, and economized like poor people who only have a few hundred francs a year to live on. But Fabienne de Maurillac developed well in spite of everything, and grew up into a woman—like some rare flower preserved from all contact with the outer air and reared in a hothouse.

In order that she might not lose her Parisian accent by speaking too much with the servants, who had remained peasants though in livery, Madame de Maurillac, who had not been able to bring a lady's maid with her, on account of the extra cost which traveling expenses and wages would have entailed, and who, moreover, was afraid that some indiscretion might betray her maneuver and cover her with ridicule, made up her mind to wait on her daughter herself. And Fabienne talked with nobody but her, saw nobody but her, and was like a little novice in a convent. Nobody was allowed to speak to her, or to interfere with her walks in the large garden, or on the white terraces that were reflected in the blue water.

As soon, however, as the season for the country and the seaside came, they packed up their trunks, and locked the doors of their house of exile. As they were not known, and took those terrible trains which stop at every station, by which you arrive at your destination in the middle of the night, with the certainty that nobody will be waiting for you and see you get out of the carriage, they traveled third class, so that they might have a few bank notes the more with which to make a show.

A fortnight in Paris in the family house at Auteuil, a fortnight in which to try on dresses and bonnets and to show themselves, and then Trouville, Aix, or Biarritz, the whole show complete, with parties succeeding parties, money spent as if they did not know its value, balls at the Casinos, constant flirtations, compromising intimacies with that kind of admirers who immediately surround two pretty women, one in the radiant beauty of her eighteen years, and the other in the brightness of that maturity which the beautiful September days bring with them.

Unfortunately, however, they had to do the same thing over again every year, and as if bad luck were continuing to follow them implacably, Madame de Maurillac and her daughter did not succeed in their endeavors, did not manage during the usual absence from home to make some eligible bachelor fall in love immediately, and ask for Fabienne's hand. Consequently, they were very unhappy. Their energies flagged, and their courage left them, like water that escapes, drop by drop, through a crack in a jug. They grew low-spirited, and no longer dared to be open toward each other and to exchange confidences and projects.

Fabienne, with her pale cheeks, her large eyes with blue circles round them, and her closed lips, looked like a captive princess tormented by constant *ennui*, who is troubled by evil suggestions, and dreams of flight and of escape from the prison where Fate holds her captive.

One night, when the sky was covered with heavy thunderclouds and the heat was most oppressive, Madame de Maurillac called to her daughter, whose room was next to hers. After calling her loudly for some time in vain, she sprang out of bed in fright and almost broke open the door with her trembling hands. The room was empty, and the pillows untouched.

Then, half mad and foreseeing some irreparable misfortune, the poor woman ran all over the large house, and rushed out into the garden, where the air was heavy with the scent of flowers. She acted like some wild animal that is pursued by a pack of hounds, trying to penetrate the darkness with her anxious looks, and gasping as if some one were holding her by the throat. Suddenly she staggered, uttered a painful cry, and fell down in a fit.

There, before her in the shadow of the myrtle-trees, Fabienne was sitting on the knees of a man—of the gardener—with both her arms round his neck, kissing him ardently. As if to defy her, and to show her how vain all her precautions and her vigilance had been, the girl was telling her lover, *in the country dialect,* and in a cooing and delightful voice, how she adored him and belonged to him.

Madame de Maurillac is in a lunatic asylum, and Fabienne has married the gardener.

Could she have done better?

Profitable Business

HE CERTAINLY did not think himself a saint, nor did he put forth any hypocritical pretensions to virtue. Nevertheless, he thought as highly of himself as he did of anybody else, perhaps, even a trifle more highly. And that, quite impartially, without any more self-love than was necessary, and without having to accuse himself of being self-conceited. He did himself justice, that was all. He had good moral principles, and applied them, if the truth must be told, not only to judging the conduct of others, but also to the regulation of his own conduct, as he would have been very vexed if he had not been able to think of himself:

"On the whole, I am what people call a perfectly honorable man."

Luckily, he had never (oh! never) been obliged to doubt the excellent opinion he had of himself, an opinion which he liked to express thus, in moments of rhetorical expansion:

"My whole life gives me the right to shake hands with myself."

A subtle psychologist would perhaps have found some flaws in his mailed self-righteousness, sanctimoniously satisfied with itself. For example, it was quite certain that our friend had no scruples in making profit out of the vices or misfortunes of his neighbors, provided that he was not, in his own opinion, the person who was solely or chiefly responsible for them. But on the whole this was only one way of looking at it, and there was plenty of material for casuistic argument on the point. This sort of discussion is particularly unpleasant to such simple natures as this worthy fellow's. He would

probably have said to the psychologist:
"Why go on a wild-goose chase? You can see that I am perfectly sincere."

Do not believe, however, that this perfect sincerity prevented him from having elevated views. He prided himself on having a weakness for imagination and the unforeseen, and though he would have been offended at being called a dishonorable man, he would, perhaps, have been still more hurt of anybody had accused him of middle-class tastes.

As to affairs of the heart he expressed a most virtuous horror of adultery, for if guilty of that he would not have been able to bear that testimony to himself, which was so sweet to his conscience:

"Ah! I rejoice to say that I never wronged anybody!"

On the other hand, he was not satisfied with pleasures which are paid for by the hour, and which debase *the noblest desires of the heart* to the vulgar satisfaction of a physical requirement. What he required, he used to say, while lifting his eyes up to heaven, was:

"I crave for something more ideal than that!"

The search after the ideal did not, indeed, cost him any great effort. It was limited to shunning licensed houses of ill-fame, and to avoiding street-walkers.

It consisted chiefly in trying to be gallant with women, in trying to persuade himself that they liked him for his own sake, and in preferring those whose manner, dress, and looks allowed room for suppositions and romantic illusions, such as:

"She might be taken for a little work-girl, who is still virtuous." "No, I rather think she is a widow, who has met with misfortune." "What if she be a fashionable lady in disguise!" And other silly sayings, which he knew were nonsense, when he uttered them, but the imaginary flavor of which was very pleasant to him all the same.

With such tastes, it was only natural that this epicure should follow and jostle women in the large shops, and wherever there was a crowd, and that he should especially look out for ladies of easy virtue, for nothing is more exciting than half-closed shutters, behind which a face is indistinctly seen, and from which one hears a furtive call.

He would say to himself: "Who is she? Is she young and pretty? Is she some old woman, who is skillful at her business, but who does not venture to show herself any longer? Or is she some beginner, who has not yet acquired the boldness of an old hand? In any case, it is the unknown; perhaps, my ideal—at least during the time it takes me to find my way upstairs." And as he went up, his heart always beat as it does at a first meeting with a woman beloved.

But he had never felt such a delicious shiver as he did on the day on which he penetrated into that old house in the blind alley in Ménilmontant. He did not know why, for he had often gone after so-called love in much stranger places; but now, without any reason, he had the presentiment that he was about to meet with an adventure, and that gave him a delightful sensation.

The woman who had beckoned to him lived on the third floor. All the way upstairs his excitement increased, and his heart was beating violently when he reached the landing. As he was going up, he smelled a peculiar odor, which grew stronger and stronger, and though he tried to analyze it, all he could decide was that it smelled like a chemist's shop.

The door on the right, at the end of the passage, was opened as soon as he put his foot on the landing, and the woman said, in a low voice:

"Come in, my dear."

A very strong smell met his nostrils through the open door, and he exclaimed:

"How stupid I was! I know what it is now; carbolic acid, is it not?"

"Yes," the woman replied. "Don't you like it, my dear? It is very wholesome, you know."

The woman was not ugly, although not young; she had very good eyes, although these were sad and sunken in her head. Evidently she had been crying very much quite recently, and that imparted a special spice to the vague smile she put on, so as to appear more amiable.

Seized by his romantic ideas, and under the influence of the presentiment which he had had just before, he thought —and the idea filled him with pleasure—

"She is some widow, whom poverty has forced to sell herself."

The room was small, but very clean and tidy, which confirmed him in his conjecture, and as he was curious to verify it, he went into the three rooms, which opened into one another. The bedroom came first; next came a sort of drawing-room, and then a dining-room which evidently served as a kitchen, for a Dutch tiled stove stood in the middle of it, on which a stew was sim-.

mering. The smell of carbolic acid was even stronger in that room. He remarked it, and added with a laugh:

"Do you put it in your soup?"

And as he said this, he grasped the handle of the door which led into the next room, for he wanted to see everything, even that nook, which was apparently a store cupboard. But the woman seized him by the arm, and pulled him violently back.

"No, no," she said, almost in a whisper, and in a hoarse and suppliant voice; "no, dear, not there, not there, you must not go in there."

"Why?" said he, for his wish to go in was now stronger.

"Because if you go in there, you will have no inclination to remain with me, and I want you to stay. If you only knew!"

"Well, what?" And with a violent movement he opened the glazed door. The smell of carbolic acid seemed almost to strike him in the face, and what he saw made him recoil still more, for on a small iron bedstead lay the dead body of a woman fantastically illumined by a single wax candle. In horror he turned to escape.

"Stop, my dear," the woman sobbed; and clinging to him she told him amid a flood of tears that her friend had died two days previously, and that there was no money to bury her. Said she, "You can understand that I want it to be a respectable funeral, we were so very fond of each other! Stop here,

my dear, do stop. I only want ten francs more. Don't go away."

They had gone back into the bedroom, and she was trying to detain him:

"No," he said, "let me go. I will give you the ten francs, but I will not stay here; I cannot."

He took his purse out of his pocket, extracted a ten-franc piece, put it on the table, and then went to the door. When he had reached it, a thought suddenly struck him, as if somebody were reasoning with him, without his knowledge.

"Why lose these ten francs? Why not profit by this woman's good intentions. She certainly behaved pluckily, and if I had not known about the matter, I should certainly not have gone away for some time. Well then?"

Then other and obscurer suggestions whispered to him:

"She was her friend! They were so fond of each other! Was it friendship or love? Oh! love apparently. Well, it would really be avenging morality, if this woman were forced to be faithless to that monstrous love." Then he turned round to her and said in a low and trembling voice: "Look here! If I give you twenty francs instead of ten, I suppose you could buy some flowers for her, as well?"

The unhappy woman's face brightened with pleasure and gratitude.

"Will you really give me twenty?"

"Yes," he replied, "and more perhaps. It quite depends upon yourself."

Bertha

My OLD friend—one has friends occasionally who are much older than oneself—my old friend Doctor Bonnet had often invited me to spend some time with him at Riom, and as I did not know Auvergne, I made up my mind to go there in the summer of 1876.

I got there by the morning train, and the first person I saw on the platform was the doctor. He was dressed in a gray suit, and wore a soft, black, wide-brimmed, high-crowned felt hat, which was narrow at the top like a chimney pot, a hat which hardly anyone except an Auvergnant would wear, and which smacked of the charcoal-burner. Dressed like that, the doctor had the appearance of an old young man, with a spare body under a thin coat, and a large head covered with white hair.

He embraced me with the evident pleasure which country people feel when they meet long expected friends, and stretching out his arm said proudly: "This is Auvergne!"

I saw nothing before me, except a range of mountains, whose summits, which resembled truncated cones, must have been extinct volcanoes.

Then, pointing to the name of the station, he said:

"*Riom,* the fatherland of magistrates, the pride of the magistracy, ought rather to be the fatherland of doctors."

"Why?" I asked.

"Why?" he replied with a laugh. "If you transpose the letters, you have the Latin word *mori,* to die. That is the reason why I settled here, my young friend."

And delighted at his own joke, he carried me off, rubbing his hands.

As soon as I had swallowed a cup of coffee, he made me go and see the town. I admired the chemist's house, and the other celebrated houses, which were all black, but as pretty as knickknacks, with their *façades* of sculptured stone. I admired the statue of the Virgin, the patroness of butchers, and he told me an amusing story about this, which I will relate some other time. Then Doctor Bonnet said to me:

"I must beg you to excuse me for a few minutes while I go and see a patient, and then I will take you to Chatel-Guyon, so as to show you the general aspect of the town, and all the mountain chain of the Puy-de-Dôme, before lunch. You can wait for me outside; I shall only go upstairs and come down immediately."

He left me outside one of those old, gloomy, silent, melancholy houses which one sees in the provinces. This one appeared to look particularly sinister, and I soon discovered the reason. All the large windows on the first floor were half boarded up with wooden shutters. The upper part of them alone could be opened, as if one had wished to prevent the people who were locked up in that huge stone trunk from looking into the street.

When the doctor came down again, I told him how it had struck me, and he replied:

"You are quite right; the poor creature who is living there must never see what is going on outside. She is a madwoman, or rather an idiot, what you Normans would call a *Niente.** It is

---

*A *Nothing, i. e.,* an idiot.

a miserable story, but a very singular pathological case at the same time. Shall I tell you of it?"

I begged him to do so, and he continued:

"Twenty years ago, the owners of this house, who were my patients, had a daughter who was seemingly like all other girls. But I soon discovered that while her body became admirably developed, her intellect remained stationary.

"She began to walk very early, but could not talk. At first I thought she was deaf, but discovered that although she heard perfectly, she did not understand anything that was said to her. Violent noises made her start and frightened her, without her understanding how they were caused.

"She grew up into a superb woman, but she was dumb, from an absolute want of intellect. I tried all means to introduce a gleam of sense into her head, but nothing succeeded. I thought that I noticed that she knew her nurse, though as soon as she was weaned, she failed to recognize her mother. She could never pronounce that word, which is the first that children utter, and the last which men murmur when dying on the field of battle. She sometimes tried to talk, but produced nothing but incoherent sounds.

"When the weather was fine, she laughed continually, emitting low cries which might be compared to the twittering of birds. When it rained she cried and moaned in a mournful, terrifying manner, like the howling of a dog when death occurs in a house.

"She was fond of rolling on the grass, like young animals do, and of running about madly. She used to clap her hands every morning when the sun shone into her room, and would jump out of bed and insist, by signs, on being dressed as quickly as possible, so that she might get out.

"She did not appear to distinguish between people, between her mother and her nurse, or between her father and me, or between the coachman and the cook. I liked her parents, who were very unhappy on her account, very much, and went to see them nearly every day. I dined with them tolerably frequently, which enabled me to remark that Bertha (they had called her Bertha) seemed to recognize the various dishes, and to prefer some to others. At that time she was twelve years old, but as fully formed in figure as a girl of eighteen, and taller than I was. Then, the idea struck me of developing her greediness, and by such means to try and produce some slight power of discernment into her mind—to force her, by the diversity of flavors, if not by reason, to arrive at instinctive distinctions, which would of themselves constitute a species of analysis akin to thought. Later on, by appealing to her senses, and by carefully making use of those which could serve us, we might hope to obtain a kind of reaction on her intellect, and by degrees increase the involuntary action of her brain.

"One day I put two plates before her, one of soup, and the other of very sweet vanilla cream. I made her taste each of them successively, then I let her choose for herself, and she ate the plate of cream. In a short time I made her very greedy, so greedy that it appeared as if the only idea she had in her head was the desire for eating. She recognized the various dishes perfectly, stretched out her hands toward those that she liked, and took hold of them eagerly, crying when they were taken from her. Then I thought I would try and teach her to come to the dining-room, when the dinner bell rang. It took a long time, but I succeeded in the end. In her vacant intellect, there was a fixed correlation between the sound and her taste, a correspondence between two senses, an appeal from one to the other, and consequently a sort of connection of ideas,—if one can term an instinctive hyphen between two organic functions an idea, — and so I carried my experiments further, and taught her, with much difficulty, to recognize meal-times on the face of the clock.

"It was impossible for me for a long time to attract her attention to the hands, but I succeeded in making her remark the clockwork and the striking apparatus. The means I employed were very simple. I asked them not to have the bell rung for lunch, but that everybody should get up and go into the dining-room when the little brass hammer struck twelve o'clock; but I found great difficulty in making her learn to count the strokes. She ran to the door each time she heard the clock strike, but by degrees she learned that all the strokes had not the same value as regarded meals, and she frequently fixed her eyes, guided by her ears, on the dial of the clock.

"When I noticed that, I took care, every day at twelve and at six o'clock, to place my fingers on the figures twelve and six, as soon as the moment she was

waiting for, had arrived. I soon noticed that she attentively followed the motion of the small brass hands, which I had often turned in her presence.

"She had understood! Perhaps I should rather say that she had seized the idea. I had succeeded in getting the knowledge, or rather the sensation of the time into her, just as is the case with carp, who certainly have no clocks, but know that they are fed every day at a certain time.

"When once I had obtained that result, all the clocks and watches in the house occupied her attention almost exclusively. She spent her time in looking at them, in listening to them, and in waiting for meal-times, and once something very funny happened. The striking apparatus of a pretty little Louis XVI. clock that hung at the head of her bed had got out of order, and she noticed it. She sat for twenty minutes, with her eyes on the hands, waiting for it to strike ten, but when the hand passed the figure, she was astonished at not hearing anything. So stupefied was she, indeed, that she sat down, no doubt overwhelmed by a feeling of violent emotion, such as attacks us in the face of some terrible catastrophe. She had the wonderful patience to wait until eleven o'clock, in order to see what would happen, but, as she naturally heard nothing, she was suddenly either seized with a wild fit of rage at having been deceived and imposed upon by appearances, or else was overcome by the fear which a frightened creature feels at some terrible mystery, or by the furious impatience of a passionate individual who meets with some obstacle. She took up the tongs from the fireplace, and struck the clock so violently that she broke it to pieces in a moment.

"It was evident, therefore, that her brain did act and calculate, obscurely it is true, and within very restricted limits, for I could never succeed in making her distinguish persons as she distinguished the time. To stir her intellect, it was necessary to appeal to her passions, in the material sense of the word, and we soon had another, and alas! a very terrible proof of this!

*   *   *   *   *   *

"She had grown up into a splendid girl; a perfect type of a race, a sort of lovely and stupid Venus. She was sixteen, and I have rarely seen such perfection of form, such suppleness, and such regular features. I said she was a Venus; yes, a fair, stout, vigorous Venus, with large, bright, vacant eyes, blue as the flowers of the flax plant. She had a large mouth with full lips, the mouth of a glutton, of a sensualist, a mouth made for kisses. Well, one morning her father came into my consulting-room, with a strange look on his face, and sitting down, without even replying to my greeting, he said:

" 'I want to speak to you about a very serious matter. Would it be possible—would it be possible for Bertha to marry?'

" 'Bertha to marry! Why, it is quite impossible!'

" 'Yes, I know, I know,' he replied. 'But reflect, doctor—don't you think—perhaps—we hoped—if she had children —it would be a great shock to her, but a great happiness, and who knows whether maternity might not rouse her intellect?'

"I was in a state of great perplexity.

He was right, and it was possible that such a new situation, and that wonderful instinct of maternity which beats in the hearts of the lower animals as it does in the heart of a woman, which makes a hen fly at a dog's jaws to defend her chickens, might bring about a revolution, an utter change in her vacant mind, and set the motionless mechanism of her thoughts into movement. And then, moreover, I immediately remembered a personal instance. Some years previously I had possessed a spaniel bitch which was so stupid that I could do nothing with her, but when she had had pups she became, if not exactly clever, yet as intelligent as many other dogs who have not been thoroughly broken.

"As soon as I foresaw the possibility of this, the wish to get Bertha married grew on me, not so much out of friendship for her and her poor parents, as from scientific curiosity. What would happen? It was a singular problem, and I said to her father:

" 'Perhaps you are right. You might make the attempt—but—but you will never find a man to consent to marry her.'

" 'I have found somebody,' he said in a low voice.

"I was dumfounded, and said: 'Somebody really suitable? Some one of your own rank and position in society?'

" 'Decidedly,' he replied.

" 'Oh! And may I ask his name?'

" 'I came on purpose to tell you and to consult you. It is Monsieur Gaston du Boys de Lucelles.'

"I felt inclined to exclaim: 'What a wretch,' but I held my tongue, and after

a few moments' silence, I said:
"'Oh! Very good. I see nothing against it.'"

"The poor man shook me heartily by the hand, and said:

"'She is to be married next month.'"

*   *   *   *   *   *   *

"Monsieur Gaston du Boys de Lucelles was a scapegrace of good family, who, after having spent all that he had inherited from his father, and having incurred debts by all kinds of doubtful means, had been trying to discover some other way of obtaining money. Hence this method. He was a good-looking young fellow, and in capital health, but fast—one of that odious tribe of provincial fast men—and appeared to me to be the sort of a husband who could be got rid of later, by making him an allowance. He came to the house to pay his addresses, and to strut about before the idiot girl, who, however, seemed to please him. He brought her flowers, kissed her hands, sat at her feet, and looked at her with affectionate eyes; but she took no notice of any of his attentions, and made no distinction between him and the other persons about her.

"However, the marriage took place, and you may guess how excited my curiosity was. I went to see Bertha the next day, to try and discover from her looks whether any feeling had been roused in her, but I found her just the same as she was every day, wholly taken up with the clock and dinner, while he, on the contrary, appeared really in love, and tried to rouse his wife's spirits and affection by little endearments and such caresses as one bestows on a kitten. He could think of nothing better.

"I called upon the married couple pretty frequently, and I soon perceived that the young woman knew her husband, and gave him those eager looks which she had hitherto only bestowed on sweet dishes.

"She followed his movements, knew his step on the stairs or in the neighboring rooms and clapped her hands when he came in. Her face was changed and brightened by the flames of profound happiness and of desire. She loved him with her whole body and with all her being, to the very depths of her poor, weak soul, and with all her heart, the poor heart of some grateful animal. It was really a delightful and innocent picture of simple passion, of carnal yet modest passion, such as nature planted in mankind, before man complicated and disfigured it by all the various shades of sentiment. But he soon grew tired of this ardent, beautiful, dumb creature, and did not spend more than an hour a day with her, thinking it sufficient to devote his nights to her, and she began to suffer in consequence. She used to wait for him from morning till night, with her eyes on the clock. She did not even look after the meals now, for he took all his away from home, Clermont Chatel-Guyon, Royat, no matter where, as long as he was not obliged to come home.

"She began to grow thin; every other thought every other wish, every other expectation, and every other confused hope disappeared from her mind, and the hours during which she did not see him became hours of terrible suffering to her. Soon he used frequently not to come home at night; he spent them with women at the Casino at Royat, and did not come home until daybreak. But she never went to bed before he returned. She would remain sitting motionless in an easy-chair, with her eyes fixed on the clock, which turned so slowly and regularly round the china face on which the hours were painted.

"When she heard the trot of his horse in the distance, she would sit up with a start. When he came into the room, she would get up with the movements of a phantom, and point to the clock, as if to say to him: 'Look how late it is!'

"He began to be afraid of this amorous and jealous, half-witted woman, and flew into a rage, like brutes do; and one night he even went so far as to strike her, so they sent for me. When I arrived she was writhing and screaming in a terrible crisis of pain, anger, passion, how do I know what? Can anyone tell what goes on in such undeveloped brains?

"I calmed her by subcutaneous injections of morphine, and forbade her to see that man again, for I saw clearly that marriage would infallibly kill her, by degrees.

*   *   *   *   *   *   *

"Then she went mad! Yes, my dear friend, that idiot has gone mad. She is always thinking of him and waiting for him; she waits for him all day and night, awake or asleep, at this very moment, ceaselessly. When I saw her getting thinner and thinner, never taking her eyes off the clocks, I had them removed from the house. I thus make it impossible for her to count the hours, or to remember, from her indistinct reminiscences, at what time he used to come home. I hope to destroy the recollection of it in time, and to extinguish

that ray of thought which I had kindled with so much difficulty.

"The other day I tried an experiment. I offered her my watch. She took it and looked at it for some time; then she began to scream terribly, as if the sight of that little object had suddenly aroused her recollection, which was beginning to grow indistinct. She is pitiably thin now, with hollow and brilliant eyes, and she walks up and down ceaselessly, like a wild beast does in its cage. I have had bars put to the windows, and have had the seats fixed to the floor, so as to prevent her from looking to see whether he is coming.

"Oh! her poor parents! What a life they must lead!"

We had got to the top of the hill, and the doctor turned round and said to me:

"Look at Riom from here."

The gloomy town looked like some ancient city. Behind it, a green, wooded plain studded with towns and villages, and bathed in a soft blue haze, extended until it was lost in the distance. Far away on my right, there was a range of lofty mountains with round summits, or truncated cones, and the doctor began to enumerate the villages, towns, and hills and to give me the history of all of them. But I did not listen to him; I was thinking of nothing but the mad woman, and only saw her. She seemed to be hovering over that vast extent of country like a mournful ghost, and I asked him abruptly:

"What has become of the husband?"

My friend seemed rather surprised, but after a few moments' hesitation, he replied:

"He is living at Royat, on an allowance that they make him, and is quite happy; he leads a very fast life."

As we were going slowly back, both of us silent and rather low-spirited, an English dogcart, drawn by a thoroughbred horse, came up behind us and passed us rapidly. The doctor took me by the arm:

"There he is," he said.

I saw nothing except a gray felt hat, cocked over one ear, above a pair of broad shoulders, driving off in a cloud of dust.

The Last Step

MONSIEUR DE SAINT-JUÉRY would not have deceived his old mistress for anything in the world. Perhaps it was from an instinctive fear, for he had heard of adventures that turn out badly, make a scandal, and bring about hateful family quarrels, crises from which one emerges enervated and exasperated with destiny, and, as it were, with the weight of a cannon-ball on one's feet. Perhaps also from his need for a calm, sheep-like existence, undisturbed by any shock; perhaps from the remnants of the love which had made him, during the first years of their connection, the slave of the proud dominating beauty, and of her enthralling charms.

He kept out of the way of temptation almost timidly, was faithful to her, and was as submissive as a spaniel. He paid her every attention, did not appear to notice that the outlines of her figure, which had formerly been so harmonious and supple, were getting too full and puffy, that her face, which used to remind him of a blush rose, was getting wrinkled, and that her eyes were getting dull. He admired her in spite of everything, almost blindly, and clothed her with imaginary charms, with an autumnal beauty, with the majestic and serene softness of an October twilight, and with the last blossoms which fall to the walks strewn with dead leaves.

But although their connection had lasted for many years, though they were as closely bound to each other as if they had been married, and although Charlotte Guindal pestered him with entreaties, and upset him with continual quarrels on the subject, despite also the fact that he believed her to be absolutely faithful to him and worthy of his most prefect confidence and love, Monsieur de Saint-Juéry had never been able to make up his mind to give her his name, and to put their connection on a legal footing.

He really suffered from this, but remained firm and defended his position, quibbled, sought for subterfuges, and replied by the eternal and vague: "What would be the good of it?" This made Charlotte furious and caused her to say angry and ill-tempered things. But he remained passive and listless, with his back bent like a restive horse under the whip.

He asked her whether it was really

necessary to their happiness, as they had no children. Did not everybody think that they were married? Was not she everywhere called Madame de Saint-Juéry and had their servants any doubt that they were in the service of respectable, married people? Was not the name which had been transmitted to a man from father to son, unstained, honored, and often with a halo of glory round it, a sacred trust, which no one had a right to touch? What would she gain if she bore it legitimately? Did she for a moment suppose that she would rise higher in people's estimation and be admitted into society, or that people would forget that she had been his regular mistress before becoming his wife? Did not everybody know that formerly, before he rescued her from that Bohemian life in which she had been vainly waiting for a chance, and was losing her good looks, Charlotte Guindal frequented all the public balls, and showed her legs liberally at the Moulin-Rouge?*

Charlotte knew his crabbed though kindly character—a character at the same time logical and obstinate — too well to hope that she would ever be able to overcome his opposition and scruples, except by some clever, feminine trick, some piece of comedy. So she appeared to be satisfied with his reasons and to renounce her desire. Outwardly she showed an equable and conciliatory temper, and no longer worried Monsieur de Saint-Juéry with her recriminations. Thus time went by in calm monotony, without fruitless battles or fierce disputes.

Charlotte Guindal's medical man was Doctor Rabatel, one of those clever men who appear to know everything, but whom a country surgeon would shame by a few questions. He was one of those men who wish to impress everybody with their apparent value, and who make use of their medical knowledge as if it were some productive commercial house, which carried on a suspicious business; who can scent out persons whom they can manage as they please, as if they were a piece of wax, keeping them in a state of continual terror by holding the idea of death constantly before their eyes.

Having obtained this mastery they scrutinize their patients' consciences as well as the cleverest priest could do, make sure of being well paid for their complicity as soon as they have obtained a footing anywhere, and find out the family secrets in order to use them as a weapon for extorting money on occasions.

Dr. Rabatel felt sure immediately that this middle-aged lady wanted something of him. By some extraordinary perversion of taste, he was rather fond of the remains of a good-looking woman, if they were well got up, and offered to him. He liked that high flavor which arises from soft lips made tender through years of love, from gray hair powered with gold, from a body engaged in its last struggle, which dreams of one more victory before abdicating power altogether. So he did not hesitate to become his new patient's lover.

When winter came, however, a thorough change took place in Charlotte's health, which had hitherto been so good.

*A *café chantant* and casino.

She had no strength left, she felt ill after the slightest exertion, complained of internal pains, and spent whole days lying on the couch, with set eyes and without uttering a word, so that everybody thought that she was dying of one of those mysterious maladies which cannot be coped with, but by degrees undermine the whole human system. It was sad to see her sinking, lying motionless on her pillows. A mist seemed to have come over her eyes, her hands lay helplessly on the bed, and her mouth seemed sealed by some invisible finger. Monsieur de Saint-Juéry was in despair; he cried like a child, and he winced as if somebody had plunged a knife into him when the doctor said to him in his unctuous voice:

"I know that you are a brave man, my dear sir, and I may venture to tell you the whole truth. Madame de Saint-Juéry is doomed, irrevocably doomed. Nothing but a miracle can save her, and alas! there are no miracles in these days. The end is only a question of a few hours, and may come quite suddenly."

Monsieur de Saint-Juéry had thrown himself into a chair, and was sobbing bitterly, covering his face with his hands.

"My poor dear, my poor darling," he said, through his tears.

"Pray compose yourself, and be brave," the doctor continued, sitting down by his side, "for I have something serious to say to you, and to convey to you our poor patient's last wishes. A few minutes ago, she told me the secret of your double life, and of your connection with her. In view of death, which she feels approaching rapidly, for she is under no delusion, the unhappy woman wishes to die at peace with Heaven, with the consolation of having corrected her equivocal position and of having become your wife."

Monsieur de Saint-Juéry sat upright, with a bewildered look, while he moved his hands nervously; in his grief he was incapable of manifesting any will of his own, or of opposing this unexpected attack.

"Oh! anything that Charlotte wishes, doctor; anything, and I will myself go and tell her so, on my knees!"

*　　*　　*　　*　　*　　*　　*

The wedding took place discreetly, with something funereal about it, in the darkened room, where the words which were spoken had a strange sound, almost of anguish. Charlotte, who was lying in bed, her eyes dilated through happiness, had put both trembling hands into those of Monsieur de Saint-Juéry, and she seemed to expire with the word "Yes" on her lips. The doctor looked at the moving scene, grave and impassive, his chin buried in his white cravat, and his two arms resting on the mantelpiece, while his eyes twinkled behind his glasses.

The next week, Madame de Saint-Juéry began to get better, and that wonderful recovery, about which Monsieur Saint-Juéry with effusive gratitude tells everybody who will listen to him, has so increased Doctor Rabatel's reputation that at the next election he will be made a member of the Academy of Medicine.

VOLUME VI

A Mésalliance

It is a generally acknowledged truth that the prerogatives of the nobility are only maintained at the present time through the weakness of the middle classes. Many of these, who have established themselves and their families by their intellect, industry, and struggles, fall into a state of bliss, which reminds those who see it of intoxication, as soon as they are permitted to enter aristocratic circles, or can be seen in public with barons and counts, and above all, when these treat them in a friendly manner, no matter from what motive, or when they see a prospect of a daughter of theirs driving in a carriage with armorial bearings on the panels.

Many women and girls of the citizen class would not hesitate for a moment to refuse an honorable, good-looking man of their own class, in order to go to the altar with the oldest, ugliest, stupidest dotard among the aristocracy.

I shall never forget saying in joke, shortly before her marriage, to a young, well-educated girl of a wealthy, middle-class family, who had the figure and the bearing of a queen, not to forget an ermine cloak in her trousseau.

"I know it would suit me capitally," she replied in all seriousness, "and I should certainly have worn one if I had married Baron R——, which I was nearly doing, as you know, but it is not suitable for the wife of a government official."

When a girl of the middle classes wanders from the paths of virtue, her fall may, as a rule, be rightly ascribed to her hankering after the nobility.

In a small German town there lived, some years ago, a tailor whom we will call Löwenfuss, a man who, like all knights of the shears, was equally full of aspirations after culture and liberty. After working for one master for some time as a poor journeyman, he married his daughter, and after his father-in-law's death succeeded to the business. As he was industrious, lucky, and managed it well, he soon grew very well off, and was in a position to give his daughters an education which many a nobleman's children might have envied. They learned not only French and music, but also acquired many more solid branches of knowledge, and as they were both pretty and charming girls, they soon became much thought of and sought after.

Fanny, the elder, was especially her father's pride and a favorite in society. She was of middle height, slim, with a thoroughly maidenly figure, and with an almost Italian face, in which two large, dark eyes seemed to ask for love and submission at the same time. Yet this girl with her plentiful, black hair was not in the least intended to command, for she was one of those romantic women who will give themselves, or even throw themselves, away, but who can never be subjugated. A young physician fell in love with her, and wished to marry her; Fanny returned his love, and her parents gladly accepted him as a son-in-law. But she made it a condition that he should visit her freely and frequently for two years, before she would consent to become his wife, and she declared that she would not go to the altar with him until she was convinced that not only their hearts but also that their characters harmonized. He agreed to her wish, and became a regular visitor at the house of the educated tailor; they were happy hours for the lovers; they played, sang, and read together, and he told the girl some of his medical experiences which excited and moved her.

Just then, an officer went one day to the tailor's shop to order some civilian's clothes. This was not an unusual event in itself, but it was soon to be the cause of one; for accidentally the daughter of *the artist in clothes* came into the shop, just as the officer was leaving it. On seeing her, he paused and asked the tailor who the young lady was.

"My daughter," the tailor said, proudly.

"May I beg you to introduce me to the young lady, Herr Löwenfuss?" said the hussar.

"I feel flattered at the honor you are doing me," the tailor replied, with evident pleasure.

"Fanny, the captain wishes to make your acquaintance; this is my daughter Fanny, Captain—"

"Captain Count Kasimir W——," the hussar interrupted him, as he went up to the pretty girl, and paid her a compliment or two. They were very commonplace, stale, everyday phrases, but in spite of this they pleased the girl, intelligent as she was, because it was a cavalry officer and a Count to boot who addressed them to her. And when at last the captain in the most friendly manner, asked the tailor's permission to be allowed to visit at his house, both father and daughter granted it to him most readily.

The very next day Count W——paid his visit, in full-dress uniform, and when Frau Löwenfuss made some observations about it, how handsome it was, and how well it became him, he told them that he should not wear it much longer, as he intended to quit the service soon, and to look for a wife in whom birth and wealth were matters of secondary consideration, while a good education and a knowledge of domestic matters were of paramount importance; adding that as soon as he had found one, he meant to retire to his estates.

From that moment, papa and mamma Löwenfuss looked upon the Count as their daughter's suitor. It is certain that he was madly in love with Fanny; he used to go to their house every evening, and made himself so looked for by all of them that the young doctor soon felt himself to be superfluous, and so his visits became rarer and rarer. The Count confessed his love to Fanny on a moonlight night, while they were sitting in an arbor covered with honeysuckle, which formed nearly the whole of Herr Löwenfuss's garden. He swore that he loved, that he adored her, and when at last she lay trembling in his arms he tried to take her by storm. But that bold cavalry exploit did not succeed, and the good-looking hussar found out for the first time in his life that a woman can at the same time be romantic, passionately in love, and virtuous.

The next morning the tailor called on the Count, and begged him very humbly to state what his intentions with regard to Fanny were. The enamored hussar declared that he was determined to make the tailor's little daughter Countess W——. Herr Löwenfuss was so much overcome by his feelings, that he showed great inclination to embrace his future son-in-law. The Count, however, laid down certain conditions. The whole matter must be kept a profound secret, for he had every prospect of inheriting half-a-million of florins,* on the death of an aunt who was already eighty years old, which he should risk by a *mésalliance*.

When they heard this, the girl's parents certainly hesitated for a time to give their consent to the marriage, but the handsome hussar, whose ardent passion carried Fanny away, at last gained the victory. The doctor received a pretty little note from the tailor's daughter, in which she told him that she gave him back his promise, as she had not found her ideal in him. Fanny then signed a deed, by which she formally renounced all claims to her father's property, in favor of her sister, and left her home and her father's house with the Count under cover of the night, in order to accompany him to Poland, where the marriage was to take place in his castle.

Of course malicious tongues declared that the hussar had abducted Fanny. But her parents smiled at such reports, for they knew better, and the moment when their daughter would return as Countess W—— would amply recompense them for everything.

Meanwhile the Polish Count and the romantic German girl were being carried by the train through the dreary plains of Masovia.† They stopped in a large town to make some purchases, and the Count, who was very wealthy

and liberal, provided his future wife with everything that befitted a Countess and a girl could fancy, and then they continued their journey. The country grew more picturesque but more melancholy as they went further east; the somber Carpathians rose from the snow-covered plains, and villages, surrounded by white glistening walls, and stunted willows stood by the side of the roads, ravens sailed through the white sky, and here and there a small peasants' sledge shot by, drawn by two thin horses.

At last they reached the station. There the Count's steward was waiting for them with a carriage and four, which brought them to their destination almost as swiftly as the iron steed.

The numerous servants were drawn up in the yard of the ancient castle to receive their master and mistress, and gave loud cheers for her, for which she thanked them smilingly. When she went into the dim, arched passages, and the large rooms, for a moment she felt a strange feeling of fear, but she quickly checked it, for was not her most ardent wish to be fulfilled in a couple of hours?

She put on her bridal attire, in which a half-comical, half-sinister looking old woman with a toothless mouth and a nose like an owl's assisted her. Just as she was fixing the myrtle wreath on to her dark curls, the bell began to ring, which summoned her to her wedding. The Count himself, in full uniform, led her to the chapel of the castle, where the priest, with the steward and the castellan as witnesses, and the footmen

---

*About $250,000.

†A division of Poland, of which Warsaw is the capital.

in grand liveries, were awaiting the handsome young couple.

After the wedding, the marriage certificate was signed in the vestry, and a groom was sent to the station, where he dispatched a telegram to her parents, to the effect that the hussar had kept his word, and that Fanny Löwenfuss had become Countess Faniska W ——.

Then the newly-married couple sat down to a beautiful little dinner in company with the chaplain, the steward, and the castellan. The champagne made them all very cheerful, and at last the Count knelt down before his young and beautiful wife, boldly took her white satin slipper off her foot, filled it with wine, and emptied it to her health.

At length night came, a thorough, Polish wedding-night, and Faniska, who had just assumed a demi-toilette, was looking at herself with proud satisfaction in the great mirror that was fastened into the wall, from top to bottom. A white satin train flowed down behind her like rays from the moon, a half-open jacket of bright green velvet, trimmed with valuable ermine, covered her voluptuous, virgin bust and her classic arms, only to show them all the more seductively at the slightest motion, while the wealth of her dark hair, in which diamonds hung here and there like glittering dewdrops, fell down her neck and mingled with the white fur. The Count entered in a red velvet dressing-gown trimmed with sable; at a sign from him, the old woman who was waiting on his divinity left the room, and the next moment he was lying like a slave at the feet of his lovely young wife, who raised him up and was pressing him to her heaving bosom, when a noise which she had never heard before, a wild howling, startled the loving woman in the midst of her bliss.

"What was that?" she asked, trembling.

The Count went to the window without speaking, and she with him, her arms round him. She looked half timidly, half curiously out into the darkness, where large bright spots were moving about in pairs, in the park at her feet.

"Are they will-o'-the-wisps?" she whispered.

"No, my child, they are wolves," the Count replied, fetching his double-barreled gun, which he loaded. Then he went out on the snow-covered balcony, while she drew the fur more closely over her bosom, and followed him.

"Will you shoot?" the Count asked her in a whisper, and when she nodded, he said: "Aim straight at the first pair of bright spots that you see; they are the eyes of those amiable brutes."

Then he handed her the gun and pointed it for her.

"That is the way—are you pointing straight?"

"Yes."

"Then fire."

A flash, a report, which the echo from the hills repeated four times, and two of the unpleasant looking lights had vanished.

Then the Count fired, and by that time their people were all awake; they drove away the wolves with torches and laid the two large animals, the spoils of a Polish wedding-night, at the feet of their young mistress.

The days that followed resembled that

night. The Count showed himself a most attentive husband, his wife's knight and slave, and she felt quite at home in that dull castle. She rode, drove, smoked, read French novels, and beat her servants as well as any Polish Countess could have done. In the course of a few years, she presented the Count with two children, and although he appeared very happy at that, yet, like most husbands, he grew continually cooler, more indolent, and neglectful of her. From time to time he left the castle to see after his affairs in the capital, and the intervals between these journeys became continually shorter. Faniska felt that her husband was tired of her, and much as it grieved her, she did not let him notice it; she was always the same.

But at last the Count remained away altogther. At first he used to write, but at last the poor, weeping woman did not even receive letters to comfort her in her unhappy solitude, and his lawyer sent the money that she and the children required.

She conjectured, hoped, doubted, suffered, and wept for more than a year; then she suddenly went to the capital and appeared unexpectedly in his apartments. Painful explanations followed, until at last the Count told her that he no longer loved her, and would not live with her for the future. When she wished to make him do so by legal means, and intrusted her case to a celebrated lawyer, *the Count denied that she was his wife*. She produced her marriage certificate, and lo! the most infamous fraud came to light. A confidential servant of the Count had acted the part of the priest, so that the tailor's beautiful daughter had, as a matter of fact, merely been the Count's mistress, and her children therefore were bastards.

The virtuous woman then saw, when it was too late, that it was *she* who had formed a *mésalliance*. Her parents would have nothing to do with her, and at last it came out that the Count was married long before he knew her, but that he did not live with his wife.

Then Fanny applied to the police magistrates; she wanted to appeal to justice; but was dissuaded from taking criminal proceedings; for although they would certainly lead to the punishment of her daring seducer, they would also bring about her own ruin.

At last, however, her lawyer effected a settlement between them, which was favorable to Fanny, and which she accepted for the sake of her children. The Count paid her a considerable sum down, and gave her the gloomy castle to live in. Thither she returned with a broken heart, and from that time lived alone, a sullen misanthrope, a fierce despot.

From time to time, you may meet wandering through the Carpathians a pale woman of almost unearthly beauty, wearing a magnificent sable-skin jacket and carrying a gun over her shoulder, in the forest, or in the winter in a sledge, driving her foaming horses until they nearly drop from fatigue, while the harness bells utter a melancholy sound, and at last die away in the distance, like the weeping of a solitary, deserted human heart.

An Honest Deal

AMONG my numerous friends in Vienna there is an author who has always amused me by his childish idealism.

Not by his idealism from an abstract point of view, for in spite of my pessimism I am an absurd idealist, and because I am perfectly well aware of this, I never, as a rule, laugh at other people's idealism. But his brand was really too funny.

He was a serious man of great capabilities who only just fell short of being learned. He had a clear, critical intellect; was a man without any illusions about society, the state, literature, or anything else, and especially about women; but he was the craziest optimist as soon as he got upon the subject of actresses, theatrical princesses, and heroines. He was one of those men who, like Hackländer, cannot discover the Ideal of Virtue anywhere but in a ballet girl.

My friend was always in love with some actress or other—of course only platonically—and by preference with some girl of rising talent, whose literary knight he constituted himself, until the time came when her admirers laid something much more substantial than laurel wreaths at her feet. Then he withdrew and sought for fresh talent which would allow itself to be patronized by him.

He was never without a photograph of his ideal in his breast pocket, and when he was in a good temper, he used to show me one or other of them— whom I had of course never seen—with a knowing smile. Once, when we were sitting in a *café* in the Prater, he took out a portrait without saying a word, and laid it on the table before me.

It was the portrait of a beautiful woman, but what struck me in it first of all, was not the almost classic cut of her features, but her white eyes.

"If she had not the black hair of a living woman, I should take her for a statue," I said.

"Certainly," my friend replied; "for a statue of Venus, perhaps for the Venus of Milo herself."

"Who is she?"

"A young actress."

"That is a matter of course in your case; what I meant was, what is her name?"

My friend told me. It was a name which is at present one of the best known on the German stage, a name with which a number of earthly adventures are connected, as every Viennese knows. Compared with hers those of Venus herself were but innocent toying, but I then heard of her for the first time.

My idealist described her as a woman of the highest talent—which I believed, and as an angel of purity—which I did not believe; on that particular occasion, however, I at any rate did not believe the contrary.

A few days later, I was accidentally turning over the leaves of the portrait album of another intimate friend of mine, who was a thoroughly careless, somewhat dissolute Viennese, and I came across that strange, female face with the dead eyes again.

"How did you come by the picture of this Venus?" I asked him.

"Well, she certainly is a Venus," he replied, "but one of that cheap kind whc are to be met with in the Graben,* which is their ideal grove."

"Impossible!"

"I give you my word of honor it is so."

I could say nothing more after that. So my intellectual friend's new ideal, that woman of the highest dramatic talent, that wonderful woman with the white eyes, was a street Venus!

But my friend was right in one respect. He had not deceived himself with regard to her wonderful dramatic gifts, and she very soon made a career for herself. From being a mute character on some suburban stage, she rose in two years to be the leading actress at one of the principal theaters.

My friend interested himself in her behalf with the manager of it, who was not blinded by any prejudices. She acted in a rehearsal, and pleased him; whereupon he sent her to star in the provinces. My friend accompanied her, and took care she was well puffed.

She went on the boards as Schiller's "Marie Stuart," and achieved the most brilliant success. Before she had finished her starring tour, she obtained an engagement at a large theater in a northern town, where her appearance was the signal for a triumphant success.

Her reputation, that is her reputation as a most gifted actress, grew very high in less than a year, and the manager of the Court theater invited her to star there.

She was received with some doubt at first, but she soon overcame all prejudices and uncertainty; the applause grew more and more vehement at every performance, and at the close of the season her future was decided. She ob-

tained a splendid engagement, and soon afterward became a leader at the Court theater.

A well-known author wrote a racy novel, of which she was the heroine; one of the leading bankers and financiers was at her feet; she was a most popular personage, and the lioness of the capital; she had splendid apartments, and all her surroundings were of the most luxurious character. She had reached that stage in her career at which my idealistic friend, who had constituted himself her literary knight, quietly took his leave of her, and went in search of fresh talent.

But the beautiful woman with the dead eyes and the dead heart seemed destined to be the scourge of the idealists, quite against her will. Scarcely had one spread his wings and flown away from her, than another fell out of the nest into her net.

A very young student, who was neither handsome nor of good family, and certainly not rich or even well off, but who was enthusiastic, intellectual, and impressionable, saw her as "Marie Stuart," as "The Maid of Orléans," "The Lady with the Camelias," and in most of the plays of the best French dramatists, for the manager was making experiments with her, and she was doing the same with her talents.

The poor student was enraptured with the celebrated actress, and at the same time conceived a passion for the woman which bordered on madness.

He saved up penny by penny, he nearly starved himself, in order that he might be able to pay for a seat in the

*The street where most of the best shops are to be found, and much frequented by venal beauties.

gallery whenever she acted, and be able to devour her with his eyes. He always got a seat in the front row, for he was always outside three hours before the doors opened, so as to be one of the first to gain his Olympus, the seat of the theatrical enthusiasts. He grew pale, and his heart beat violently when she appeared; he laughed when she wept, applauded her, as if he had been paid to do it by the highest favors that a woman can bestow, and yet she did not know him, and was ignorant of his very existence.

The regular frequenters of the Court theater noticed him at last, and spoke about his infatuation for her, until at last she heard about him. Still she did not know him, and although he could not send her any costly jewelry, not even a bouquet, he at last succeeded in attracting her attention.

When she had finished acting and the audience had gone home, she would leave the theater wrapped in valuable furs and get into the carriage of her banker, which was waiting for her at the stage door. He always stood there, often up to his ankles in snow, or in the pouring rain.

At first she did not notice him, but when her maid said something to her in a whisper on one occasion, she looked round in surprise, and he got a look from those large eyes, which were not dead then, but dark and bright—a look which recompensed him for all his sufferings and filled him with a proud hope, which constantly gained more power over the young idealist, usually so modest.

At last there was a thorough, silent understanding between the theatrical

princess and her dumb adorer. When she put her foot on the carriage step, she looked round at him, and every time he stood there, devouring her with his eyes; she saw it and got contentedly into her carriage, but she did not see how he ran after her carriage, or how he reached her house, panting for breath, when she did, or how he lay down outside after the door had closed behind her.

One stormy summer night, when the wind was howling in the chimneys, and the rain was beating against the windows and on the pavement, the poor student was again lying on the stone steps outside her house. The front door was opened very cautiously and quietly; for it was not the economical banker who was leaving the house, but a wealthy young officer whom the maid was letting out; he kissed the pretty little Cerberus as he put a gold coin into her hand, and then accidentally trod on the idealist, who was lying outside.

They all three simultaneously uttered a cry; the girl blew out the candle, the officer instinctively half drew his sword, and the student ran away.

Ever since that night, the poor, crazy fellow went about with a dagger, which he concealed in his belt. It was his constant companion to the theater and the stage door, where the actress's carriage used to wait for her, and to her house, where he nightly kept his painful watch.

His first idea was to kill his fortunate rival, then himself, then the theatrical princess, but at last he lay down again outside her door, or stood on the pavement and watched the shadows that flitted hither and thither on her window, his head turned by the magic spell of the woman.

And then, the most incredible thing happened, something which he could never have hoped for, and which he scarcely believed when it did occur.

One evening, when she had been playing a very important part, she kept her carriage waiting much longer than usual. At last she appeared, and got into it; she did not shut the door, however, but beckoned to the young idealist to follow her.

He was almost delirious with joy, just as a moment before he had been almost mad from despair. He obeyed her immediately, and during the drive he lay at her feet and covered her hands with kisses. She allowed it quietly and even merrily, and when the carriage stopped at her door, she let him lift her out of the carriage, and went upstairs leaning on his arm.

There, the lady's maid showed him into a luxuriously furnished drawing-room, while the actress changed her dress.

Presently she appeared in her *peignoir*, sat down carelessly in an easy chair, and asked him to sit down beside her.

"You take a great interest in me?" she said.

"You are my ideal!" the student cried enthusiastically.

The theatrical princess smiled, and said:

"Well, I will at any rate be an honest ideal; I will not deceive you, and you shall not be able to say that I have misused your youthful enthusiasm. I will give myself to you."

"Oh! Heavens!" the poor idealist exclaimed, throwing himself at her feet.

"Wait a moment! Wait a moment!" Wait a moment!" she said, with a smile, I have not finished yet. I can only love a man who is in a position to provide me with all those luxuries which an actress or, if you like, which I, cannot do without. As far as I know you are poor, but I will belong to you—only for to-night, however—and in return you must promise me not to rave about me, or to follow me, from to-night. Will you do this?"

The wretched idealist was kneeling before her; he was having a terrible mental struggle.

"Will you promise me to do this?" she said again.

"Yes," he said, almost groaning.

The next morning a man who had buried his ideal tottered downstairs. He was pale enough; almost as pale as a corpse; but in spite of this, he is still alive, and if he has any ideal at all at present, it is certainly not a theatrical princess.

The Log

It was a small drawing-room, with thick hangings, and with a faint aromatic smell of flowers and scent in the air. A large fire was burning in the grate, and one lamp, covered with a shade of old lace, on the corner of the mantel piece threw a soft light on to the two persons who were talking.

She, the mistress of the house, was an old lady with white hair, one of those adorable old ladies whose unwrinkled skin is as smooth as the finest paper, and is scented, impregnated with perfume, the delicate essences used in the bath for so many years having penetrated through the epidermis.

He was a very old friend, who had never married, a constant friend, a companion in the journey of life, but nothing else.

They had not spoken for about a minute, and were both looking at the fire, dreaming of nothing in particular. It was one of those moments of sympathetic silence between people who have no need to be constantly talking in order to be happy together. Suddenly a large log, a stump covered with burning roots, fell out. It fell over the firedogs on to the drawing-room floor, scattering great sparks all round. The old lady sprang up with a scream, as if to run away, but he kicked the log back on to the hearth and trod out the burning sparks with his boots.

When the disaster was repaired, there was a strong smell of burning. Sitting down opposite to his friend, the man looked at her with a smile, and said, as he pointed to the log:

"That accident recalls the reason I never married."

She looked at him in astonishment, with the inquisitive gaze of women who wish to know everything, eying him as women do who are no longer young, with intense and malicious curiosity. Then she asked:

"How so?"

"Oh! it is a long story," he replied; "a rather sad and unpleasant story.

"My old friends were often surprised at the coldness which suddenly sprang up between one of my best friends, whose Christian name was Julien, and myself. They could not understand how two such intimate and inseparable friends as we had been could suddenly become almost strangers to one another. I will tell you the reason of it.

"He and I used to live together at one time. We were never apart, and the friendship that united us seemed so strong that nothing could break it.

"One evening when he came home, he told me that he was going to be married, and it gave me a shock just as if he had robbed me or betrayed me. When a man's friend marries, all is over between them. The jealous affection of a woman, a suspicious, uneasy, and carnal affection, will not tolerate that sturdy and frank attachment, that attachment of the mind and of the heart, and the mutual confidence which exists between two men.

"However great the love may be that unites them, a man and a woman are always strangers in mind and intellect; they remain belligerents, they belong to different races. There must always be a conqueror and a conquered, a master and a slave; now the one, now the other—they are never equal. They press each other's hands, hands trembling with amorous passion; but they never press them with a long, strong, loyal pressure, a pressure which seems to open hearts and to lay them bare in a burst of sincere, strong, manly affection. Ancient philosophers, as a consolation for old age, sought for a good reliable friend, and grew old with him in that communion of thought which exists between men. They did not marry and procreate children who would, when grown, abandon them.

"Well, my friend Julien married. His wife was pretty, charming, a light, curly-haired, plump, bright little woman, who seemed to worship him. At first I went but rarely to their house, as I was afraid of interfering with their affection, and averse to being in their way. But somehow they attracted me to their house; they were constantly inviting me, and seemed very fond of me. Consequently, by degrees I allowed myself to be allured by the charm of their life. I often dined with them, and frequently, when I returned home at night, thought that I would do as he had done, and get married, as I found my empty house very dull. They seemed very much in love with one another, and were never apart.

"Well, one evening, Julien wrote and asked me to go to dinner, and naturally I went.

" 'My dear fellow,' he said, 'I must go out directly afterward on business, and I shall not be back until eleven o'clock, but I shall not be later. Can I depend on you to keep Bertha company?'

"The young woman smiled.

" 'It was my idea,' she said, 'to send for you.'

"I held out my hand to her.

" 'You are as nice as ever,' I said, and I felt a long, friendly pressure of my fingers, but I paid no attention to it. We sat down to dinner, and at eight o'clock Julien went out.

"As soon as he had gone, a kind of strange embarrassment immediately seemed to come over his wife and me. We had never been alone together yet, and in spite of our daily increasing intimacy this *tête-à-tête* placed us in a new position. At first I spoke vaguely of those indifferent matters with which one fills up an embarrassing silence, but she did not reply, and remained opposite to me looking down in an undecided manner, as if thinking over some difficult subject. As I was at a loss for commonplace ideas, I held my tongue. It is surprising how hard it is at times to find anything to say.

"And then, again, I felt in the air, in my bones, so to speak, something which it is impossible for me to express, that mysterious premonition which tells you beforehand of the secret intentions, be they good or evil, of another person with respect to yourself.

"The painful silence lasted some time, and then Bertha said to me:

" 'Will you kindly put a log on the fire, for it is going out.'

"So I opened the box where the wood was kept, which was placed just where yours is, took out the largest log, and put it on top of the others, which were three-parts burned, and then silence reigned in the room again.

"In a few minutes the log was burning so brightly that it scorched our faces, and the young woman raised her eyes to me—eyes that had a strange look to me.

" 'It is too hot now,' she said; 'let us go and sit on the sofa over there.'

"So we went and sat on the sofa,

and then she said suddenly, looking me full in the face:

" 'What should you do if a woman were to tell you that she was in love with you?'

" 'Upon my word,' I replied, very much at a loss for an answer, I cannot imagine such a case; but it would very much depend upon the woman.'

"She gave a hard, nervous, vibrating laugh; one of those false laughs which seem as if they would break thin glasses, and then she added: 'Men are never venturesome or acute.' And after a moment's silence, she continued: 'Have you ever been in love, Monsieur Paul?' I was obliged to acknowledge that I certainly had been, and she asked me to tell her all about it, whereupon I made up some story or other. She listened to me attentively with frequent signs of approbation or contempt, and then suddenly she said:

" 'No, you understand nothing about the subject. It seems to me that real love must unsettle the mind, upset the nerves, and distract the head; that it must—how shall I express it?—be dangerous, even terrible, almost criminal and sacrilegious; that it must be a kind of treason; I mean to say that it is almost bound to break laws, fraternal bonds, sacred obstacles; when love is tranquil, easy, lawful, and without danger, is it really love?'

"I did not know what answer to give her, and this philosophical reflection occurred to me: 'Oh! female brain, here indeed you show yourself!'

"While speaking, she had assumed a demure, saintly air; and resting on the cushions, she stretched herself out at full length, with her head on my shoulders and her dress pulled up a little, so as to show her red silk stockings, which looked still brighter in the firelight. In a minute or two she continued:

" 'I suppose I have frightened you?' I protested against such a notion, and she leaned against my breast altogether, and without looking at me she said: 'If I were to tell you that I love you, what would you do?'

"And before I could think of an answer, she had thrown her arms round my neck, had quickly drawn my head down and put her lips to mine.

"My dear friend, I can tell you that I did not feel at all happy! What! deceive Julien?—become the lover of this little, silly, wrong-headed, cunning woman, who was no doubt terribly sensual, and for whom her husband was already not sufficient! To betray him continually, to deceive him, to play at being in love merely because I was attracted by forbidden fruit, danger incurred and friendship betrayed! No, that did not suit me, but what was I to do? To imitate Joseph would be acting a very stupid and, moreover, difficult part, for this woman was maddening in her perfidy, inflamed by audacity, palpitating, and excited. Let the man who has never felt on his lips the warm kiss of a woman who is ready to give herself to him throw the first stone at me!

"Well, a minute more—you understand what I mean? A minute more and —I should have been—no, she would would have been—when a loud noise made us both jump up. The log had fallen into the room, knocking over the fire-irons and the fender, and was scorching the carpet, having rolled under an armchair.

"I jumped up like a madman, and as I was replacing the log on the fire, the door opened hastily, and Julien came in.

"'I have done,' he said, in evident pleasure. "The business was over two hours sooner than I expected!'

"Yes, my dear friend, without that log, I should have been caught in the very act, and you know what the consequences would have been!

"You may be sure that I took good care never to be overtaken in a similar situation again; never, never. Soon afterward I saw Julien was giving me the 'cold shoulder,' as they say. His wife was evidently undermining our friendship; by degrees he got rid of me, and we have altogether ceased to meet.

"That is why I have not got married; it ought not to surprise you, I think."

Delila

In a former reminiscence, we made the acquaintance of a lady who had done the police many services in former years, and whom we called Wanda von Chabert. It is no exaggeration, if we say that she was at the same time the cleverest, the most charming, and the most selfish woman one could possibly meet. She was certainly not exactly what is called beautiful, for neither her face nor her figure were symmetrical enough for that, but if her head was not beautiful in the style of the antique, neither like the "Venus" of Milo nor Ludovisi's "Juno," it was, on the other hand, in the highest sense delightful, like the ladies whom Watteau and Mignard painted. Everything in her little face, framed by soft brown hair, was attractive and seductive; her low, Grecian forehead, her bright, almond-shaped eyes, her small nose, her full voluptuous lips, her middling height, and her small waist with its, perhaps, almost too full bust, and above

all her walk, that half indolent, half coquettish swaying of her hips, were all maddeningly alluring.

And this woman, who was born for love, was as eager for pleasure and as amorous as few other women have ever been. For that very reason she never ran any danger of allowing her victims to escape from her pity. On the contrary, she soon grew tired of each of her favorites, and her connection with the police was then extremely useful to her, in getting rid of an inconvenient or jealous lover.

Before the war between Austria and Italy in 1859, Frau von Chabert was in London, where she lived alone in a small, one-storied house with her servants, in constant communication with emigrants from all countries.

She herself was thought to be a Polish refugee, and the luxury by which she was surrounded, and her fondness for sport, and above all for horses, which was remarkable even in England, made people give her the title of Countess. At that period Count T—— was one of the most prominent members of the Hungarian propaganda, and Frau von Chabert was commissioned to pay particular attention to all he said and did. But in spite of all the trouble she took, she had not hitherto even succeeded in making his acquaintance. He lived the life of a misanthrope, quite apart from the great social stream of London, and he was not believed to be either gallant, or ardent in love. Fellow-countrymen of his, who had known him during the Magyar revolution, described him as very cautious, cold, and silent, so that if any man possessed a charm against the toils which she set for him, it was he.

Just then it happened that as Wanda was riding in Hyde Park quite early one morning before there were many people about, her thoroughbred English mare took fright, and threatened to throw the plucky rider, who did not for a moment lose her presence of mind, from the saddle. Before her groom had time to come to her assistance, a man in a Hungarian braided coat rushed from the path, and caught hold of the animal's reins. When the mare had grown quite quiet, he was about to go away with a slight bow, but Frau von Chabert detained him, so that she might thank him and so have the leisure to examine him more closely. He was neither young nor handsome, but was well made like all Hungarians are, with an interesting and very expressive face. He had a sallow complexion, set off by a short, black full beard, and he looked as if he were

suffering. He fixed two, great, black fanatical eyes on the beautiful young woman who was smiling at him so amiably, and it aroused in the soul of the excitable woman that violent but passing feeling which she called love. She turned her horse and accompanied the stranger at a walk, and he seemed to be even more charmed by her chatter than by her appearance, for his grave face grew more and more animated, and at last he himself became quite friendly and talkative. When he took leave of her, Wanda gave him her card, on the back of which her address was written, and he immediately gave her his in return.

She thanked him and rode off, looking at his name as she did so; it was Count T——.

She felt inclined to give a shout of pleasure when she found that the noble quarry she had been hunting so long had at last come into her toils. But she did not even turn her head round to look at him, such was the command which that woman had over herself and her movements.

Count T—— called upon her the very next day; soon he came every day, and in less than a month after that innocent adventure in Hyde Park, he was at her feet; for when Frau von Chabert made up her mind to be loved, nobody was able to withstand her. She became the Count's confidant almost as speedily as she had become his mistress, and every day and almost every hour she, with the most delicate coquetry, laid fresh fetters on the Hungarian Samson. Did she love him?

Certainly she did, after her own fashion, and at first she had not the remotest idea of betraying him; she even succeeded in completely concealing her connection with him, not only in London but also in Vienna.

Then the war of 1859 broke out, and like most Hungarian and Polish refugees, Count T—— hurried off to Italy, in order to place himself at the disposal of that great and patriotic Piedmontese statesman, Cavour.

Wanda went with him, and took the greatest interest in his revolutionary intrigues in Turin; for some time she seemed to be his right hand, and it looked as if she had become unfaithful to her present patrons. Through his means, she soon became on intimate terms with the Piedmontese government circles, and that was his destruction.

A young Italian diplomatist, who frequently negotiated with Count T——, or in his absence, with Wanda, fell madly in love with the charming Polish woman. Wanda, who was never cruel, more especially when she herself had caught fire, allowed herself to be conquered by the handsome, intellectual, daring man. In measure as her passion for the Italian increased, so her feeling for Count T—— declined, till at last she felt that her connection with him was nothing but a hindrance and a burden. As soon as Wanda had reached that point, her adored was as good as lost.

Count T—— was not a man whom she could just cooly dismiss, or with whom she might venture to trifle, and this she knew perfectly well. So in order to avoid a catastrophe, the consequences of which might be incalculable for her, she did not let him notice

the change in her feelings toward him at first, and kept the Italian, who belonged to her, at proper distance.

When peace had been concluded, and the great, peaceful revolution which found its provisional settlement in the Constitution of February, and in the Hungarian agreement, began in Austria, the Hungarian refugees determined to send Count T—— to Hungary, that he might assume the direction of affairs there. But as he was still an outlaw, and as the death sentence of Arad hung over his head like the sword of Damocles, he consulted with Wanda about the ways and means of reaching his fatherland unharmed and of remaining there undiscovered. Although that clever woman thought of a plan immediately, yet she told Count T—— that she would think the matter over. She did not bring forward her proposition for a few days, but when she did, it was received by the Count and his friends with the highest approval, and was immediately carried into execution. Frau von Chabert went to Vienna as Marchioness Spinola, and Count T—— accompanied her as her footman; he had cut his hair short and shaved off his beard, so that in his livery, he was quite unrecognizable. They passed the frontier in safety, and reached Vienna without any interference from the authorities. There they first of all went to a small hotel, but soon took a small handsome flat in the center of the town. Count T—— immediately hunted up some members of his party, who had been in constant communication with the emigrants since Világos, and the conspiracy was soon in excellent train. Wanda spent her time with a hussar officer, without, however, losing sight of her lover and his dangerous activity for a moment, on that account.

And at last, when the fruit was ripe for falling into her lap, she was sitting in the private room of the Minister of Police, opposite to the man with whom she was going to make the evil compact.

"The emigrants must be very uneasy and disheartened at an agreement with, and reconciliation to, Hungary," he began.

"Do not deceive yourself," Frau von Chabert replied; "nothing is more dangerous in politics than optimism, and the influence of the revolutionary propaganda was never greater than it is at present. Do not hope to conciliate the Magyars by half concessions, and above all things, do not underestimate the movement which is being organized openly, in broad daylight."

"You are afraid of a revolution?"

"I know that they are preparing for one, and that they expect everything from that alone."

The skeptical man smiled.

"Give me something besides views and opinions, and then I will believe."

"I will give you the proof," Wanda said, "but before I do you the greatest service that lies in my power, I must be sure that I shall be rewarded for all my skill and trouble."

"Can you doubt it?"

"I will be open with you," Wanda continued. "During the insurrectionary war in Transylvania, Urban had excellent spies, but they have not been paid to this day. I want money."

"How much?"

With inimitable ease, the beautiful woman mentioned a considerable sum. The skeptical man got up to give a few orders, and a short time afterward the money was in Wanda's hands.

"Well?"

"The emigrants have sent one of their most influential and talented members to organize the revolution in Hungary."

"Have they sent him already?"

"More than that: Count T—— is in Vienna at this moment."

"Do you know where he is hiding?"

"Yes."

"And you are sure that you are not mistaken?"

"I am most assuredly not mistaken," she replied with a frivolous laugh; "Count T——, who was my admirer in London and Turin, is here in my house, as my footman."

An hour later, the Count was arrested. But Wanda only wished to get rid of her tiresome adorer, and not to destroy him. She had been on the most intimate terms with him, and had taken part in his political plans and intrigues long enough to be able to give the most reliable information about him personally, as well as about his intentions. That information was of such kind that, in spite of the past, and of the Count's revolutionary standpoint, they thought they had in him the man who was capable of bringing about a real reconciliation between the monarch and his people. In consequence of this, Count T——, who thought that he had incurred the gallows, stood in the Emperor's presence, and the manner in which the latter expressed his generous intentions with regard to Hungary carried the old rebel away, and he gave him his word of honor that he would bring the nation back to him, reconciled. And he kept his word, although, perhaps, not exactly in the sense in which he gave it.

He was allowed full liberty in going to Hungary, and Wanda accompanied him. He had no suspicion that even in his mistress's arms he was under police supervision, and from the moment when he made his appearance in his native land officially, as the intermediary between the crown and the people, she had a fresh interest in binding a man of such importance, whom everybody regarded as Hungary's future Minister-President, to herself.

He began to negotiate, and at first everything went well. But soon the yielding temper of the government gave rise continually to fresh demands. Before long, what one side offered and what the other side demanded were so far apart that no immediate agree-ment could be thought of. The Count's position grew more painful every day; he had pledged himself too deeply to both sides, and in vain he sought for a way out of the difficulty.

Then one day the Minister of Police unexpectedly received a letter from Wanda, in which she told him that Count T——, urged on by his fellow-countrymen, and branded as a traitor by the emigrants, was on the point of heading a fresh conspiracy.

Thereupon, the government energetically reminded that thoroughly honest and noble man of his word of honor, and Count T——, who saw that he was unable to keep it, ended his life by a pistol bullet.

Frau von Chabert left Hungary immediately after the sad catastrophe, and went to Turin, where new lovers, new splendors, and new laurels awaited her.

We may, perhaps, hear more of her.

The Ill-omened Groom ✕

AN impudent theft, to a very large amount, had been committed in the Capital. Jewels, a valuable watch set with diamonds, a miniature in a frame studded with brilliants, and a considerable sum in money, the whole amounting in value to a hundred and fifteen thousand florins,* had been stolen. The banker himself went to the Director of Police,† to give notice of the robberies, but at the same time begged as a special favor, that the investigation might be carried on as quietly and considerately as possible, as he declared that he had not the slightest ground for suspecting anybody in particular, and did not wish any innocent person to be accused.

'First of all, give me the names of all the persons who regularly go into your bedroom," the Police-director said.

---

*About $57,500.

†Head of the **Criminal Investigation** Department.—EDITOR.

"Nobody, except my wife, my children, and Joseph, my valet; a man for whom I would answer, as I would for myself."

"Then you think him absolutely incapable of committing such a deed?"

"Most decidedly I do," the banker replied.

"Very well, then. Now, can you remember whether on the day on which you first missed the articles that have been stolen, or an any day immediately preceding it, anybody who was not a member of your household happened by chance to go to your bedroom?"

The banker thought for a moment, and then said with some hesitation:

"Nobody, absolutely nobody."

The experienced official, however, was struck by the banker's slight embarrassment and momentary blush. So he took his hand, and looking him straight in the face, he said:

"You are not quite candid with me; somebody was with you, and you wish to conceal the fact from me. You must tell me everything."

"No, no; indeed there was nobody here."

"Then at present there is only one person on whom any suspicion can rest—and that is your valet."

"I will vouch for his honesty," the banker replied immediately.

"You may be mistaken, and I shall be obliged to question the man."

"May I beg you to do it with every possible consideration?"

"You may rely upon me for that."

An hour later, the banker's valet was in the Police-director's private room. The latter first of all looked at his man very closely, and then came to the conclusion that such an honest, unembarrassed face and such quiet, steady eyes could not possibly belong to a criminal.

"Do you know why I have sent for you?"

"No, your Honor."

"A large theft has been committed in your master's house," the Police-director continued, "from his bedroom. Do you suspect anybody? Who has been into the room within the last few days?"

"Nobody but myself, except my master's family."

"Do you not see, my good fellow, that by saying that, you throw suspicion on yourself?"

"Surely, sir," the valet exclaimed, "you do not believe—"

"I must not believe anything; my duty is merely to investigate and to follow up any traces that I may discover," was the reply. "If you have been the only person to go into the room within the last few days, I must hold you responsible."

"My master knows me—"

The Police-director shrugged his shoulders. "Your master has vouched for your honesty, but that is not enough for me. You are the only person on whom, at present, any suspicion rests, and therefore I must—sorry as I am to do so—have you arrested."

"If that is so," the man said, after some hesitation, "I prefer to speak the truth, for my good name is more to me than my situation. Somebody was in my master's apartments yesterday."

"And this somebody was—?"

"A lady."

"A lady of his acquaintance?"

The valet did not reply for some time.

"It must come out," he said at length. "My master has a mistress—you understand, sir, a blond, beautiful woman. He has furnished a house for her and goes to see her, but secretly of course, for if my mistress were to find it out, there would be a terrible scene. This person was with him yesterday."

"Were they alone?"

"I showed her in, and she was in his bedroom with him; but I had to call him out after a short time, as his confidential clerk wanted to speak to him, and so she was in the room alone for about a quarter of an hour."

"What is her name?"

"Cæcilia K——, she is a Hungarian." At the same time, the valet gave him her address.

Then the Director of Police sent for the banker, who, on being brought face to face with his valet, was obliged to acknowledge the truth of the facts which the latter had alleged, painful as it was for him to do so; whereupon orders were given to take Cæcilia K—— into custody.

In less than half an hour, however, the police officer who had been dispatched for that purpose returned and said that she had left her apartments, and most likely the Capital also, the previous evening. The unfortunate banker was almost in despair. Not only had he been robbed of a hundred and fifteen thousand florins, but at the same time he had lost the beautiful woman whom he loved with all the passion of which he was capable. He could not grasp the idea that a woman whom he had surrounded with Asiatic luxury, whose strangest whims he had gratified, and whose tyranny he had borne so patiently, could have deceived him so shamefully. And now he had a quarrel with his wife, and an end of all domestic peace, into the bargain.

The only thing the police could do was to raise a hue and cry after the lady, who had denounced herself by her flight, but it was all of no use. In vain did the banker, in whose heart hatred and thirst for revenge had taken the place of love, implore the Director of Police to employ every means to bring the beautiful criminal to justice, and in vain did he undertake to be responsible for all the costs of her prosecution, no matter how heavy they might be. Special police officers were told off to try and discover her, but Cæcilia K—— was so rude as not to allow herself to be caught.

Three years had passed, and the unpleasant story appeared to have been forgotten. The banker had obtained his wife's pardon and—what he cared about a good deal more—had found another charming mistress, and the police did not appear to trouble themselves about the beautiful Hungarian any more.

We must now change the scene to London. A wealthy lady who created much sensation in society, and who made many conquests both by her beauty and her free behavior, was in want of a groom. Among the many applicants for the situation there was a young man, whose good looks and manners gave people the impression that he must have been very well educated. This was a recommendation in the eyes of the lady's maid, and she took him immediately to her mistress's boudoir. When he entered he saw a beautiful, voluptuous looking woman of at most, twenty-five years of age, with large, bright eyes, and with blue-black hair which seemed to increase the brilliancy of her fair complexion, lying on a sofa. She looked at the young man, who also had thick, black hair. He turned his glowing black eyes to the floor, beneath her searching gaze, with evident satisfaction, and she seemed particularly taken with his slender, athletic build. Then she said half lazily and half proudly:

"What is your name?"

"Lajos Mariassi."

"A Hungarian?"

And there was a strange look in her eyes.

"Yes."

"How did you come here?"

"I am one of the many emigrants who have forfeited their country and their life. I, who come of a good family, and who was an officer of the Honveds, must now go into service, and thank God if I find a mistress who is at the same time beautiful and an aristocrat, as you are."

Miss Zoë—that was the lovely woman's name—smiled, and at the same time showed two rows of pearly teeth.

"I like your looks," she said, "and I feel inclined to take you into my service if you are satisfied with my terms."

"A lady's whim," said the maid to herself, when she noticed the ardent looks which Miss Zoë gave her manservant; "it will soon pass away." But that experienced female was mistaken that time.

Zoë was really in love, and the respect with which Lajos treated her put her into a very bad temper. One evening, when she intended to go to the Italian Opera, she countermanded her carriage, refused to see the noble adorer who wished to throw himself at her feet, and ordered her groom to be sent up to her boudoir.

"Lajos," she began, "I am not at all satisfied with you."

"Why, Madame?"

"I do not wish to have you about me any longer; here are your wages for three months. Leave the house immediately." And she began to walk up and down the room impatiently.

"I will obey you, Madame," the groom replied, "but I shall not take my wages."

"Why not?" she asked hastily.

"Because then I should be under your authority for three months," Lajos said, "and I intend to be free, this very moment, so that I may be able to tell you that I entered your service, not for the sake of your money, but because I love and adore you as a beautiful woman."

"You love me!" Zoë exclaimed. "Why did you not tell me sooner? I merely wished to banish you from my presence, because I love you, and did not think that you loved me. But you shall smart for having tormented me so. Come to my feet immediately."

The groom kneeled before the lovely creature, whose moist lips sought his at the same instant.

From that moment Lajos became her favorite. Of course he was not allowed to be jealous, as a young lord was still her official lover, and had the pleasure of paying for everything. Besides, there was a whole army of so-called "good friends," who were fortunate enough to obtain a smile now and then, and occasionally something more, and who, in return, had permission to present her with rare flowers or diamonds.

The more intimate Zoë became with Lajos, the more uncomfortable she felt when he looked at her, as he frequently did, with undisguised contempt. She was wholly under his influence and was afraid of him, and one day, when he was playing with her dark curls, he said jerringly:

"It is said that contrasts usually attract each other, and yet you are as dark as I am."

She smiled, then tore off her black curls, and immediately the most charming, fair-haired woman was sitting by the side of Lajos, who looked at her attentively, but without any surprise.

He left his mistress at about midnight, in order to look after the horses, as he said, and she put on a very pretty nightdress and went to bed. She remained awake for fully an hour, expecting her lover, and then she went to sleep. But in two hours' time she was roused from her slumbers, and saw a Police Inspector and two constables by the side of her magnificent bed.

"Whom do you want?" she cried.

"Cæcila K——."

"I am Miss Zoë."

"Oh! I know you," the Inspector said with a smile; "be kind enough to take off your dark locks, and you will be Cæcilia K——. I arrest you, in the name of the law."

"Good heavens!" she stammered, "Lajos has betrayed me."

"You are mistaken, Madame," the Inspector replied; "he has merely done his duty."

"What? Lajos—my lover?"

"No, Lajos, the detective."

Cæcilia got out of bed, and the next moment sank fainting on to the floor.

The Odalisque of Senichou

IN SENICHOU, which is a suburb of Prague, there lived about twenty years ago two poor but honest people, who earned their bread by the sweat of their brow. The man worked in a large printing establishment, and his wife employed her spare time as a laundress. Their pride and their only pleasure was their daughter Viteska, a vigorous, voluptuous, handsome girl of eighteen, whom they brought up very well and carefully. She worked as a dressmaker, and was thus able to help her parents a little. She made use of her leisure moments to improve her education, and especially her music, was a general favorite in the neighborhood on account of her quiet and modest demeanor, and was looked upon as a model by the whole suburb.

When she went to work in town, the tall girl, with her magnificent head—which resembled that of an ancient Amazon in its wealth of black hair—and dark, sparkling yet liquid eyes, attracted the looks of passers-by, in spite of her shabby dress, much more than the graceful, well-dressed ladies of the aristocracy. Frequently some wealthy young lounger would follow her home; and even try to get into conversation with her, but she always managed to get rid of them and their importunities. She did not require any protector, for she was quite capable of protecting herself from any insults.

One evening, however, she met a man on the suspension bridge whose strange appearance drew from her a look which evinced some interest, but perhaps even more surprise. He was a tall, handsome man with bright eyes and a black beard, was very sunburned, and in his long coat—which was like a caftan—with a red fez on his head, he gave those who saw him the impression of an Oriental. He had noticed her look all the more as he himself had been struck by her poor, and at the same time regal, appearance. He remained standing and looking at her in such a way that he seemed to be devouring her with his eyes, and Viteska, who was usually so fearless, looked down. She hurried on and he followed her; the quicker she walked, the more rapidly he followed her, and, at last, when they were in a narrow, dark street in the suburb, he suddenly said in an insinuating voice:

"May I offer you my arm, my pretty girl?"

"You can see that I am old enough to look after myself," Viteska replied hastily; "I am much obliged to you, and must beg you not to follow me any more; I am known in this neighborhood, and it might damage my reputation."

"Oh! You are very much mistaken if you think you will get rid of me so easily," he replied. "I have just come from the East and am returning there soon. Come with me, and as I fancy that you are as sensible as you are beautiful, you will certainly make your fortune there. I will bet that before the end of a year, you will be covered with diamonds and be waited on by eunuchs and female slaves."

"I am a respectable girl, sir," she replied proudly, and tried to go on in front, but the stranger was immediately at her side again

"You were born to rule," he whispered to her. "Believe me, and I understand the matter, that you will live to be a Sultaness, if you have any luck."

The girl did not give him any answer, but walked on.

"But, at any rate, listen to me," the tempter continued.

"I will not listen to anything; because I am poor, you think it will be easy for you to seduce me," Viteska exclaimed; "but I am as virtuous as I am poor, and I should despise any position which I had to buy with my shame."

They had reached the little house where her parents lived, and she ran in quickly and slammed the door behind her.

When she went into the town the next morning, the stranger was waiting at the corner of the street where she lived, and bowed to her very respectfully.

"Allow me to speak a few words with you," he began. "I feel that I ought to beg your pardon for my behavior yesterday."

"Please let me go on my way quietly,"

the girl replied. "What will the neighbors think of me?"

"I did not know you," he went on, without paying any attention to her angry looks, "but your extraordinary beauty attracted me. Now that I know that you are as virtuous as you are charming, I wish very much to become better acquainted with you. Believe me, I have the most honorable intentions."

Unfortunately, the bold stranger had taken the girl's fancy, and she could not find it in her heart to refuse him.

"If you are really in earnest," she stammered in charming confusion, "do not follow me about in the public streets, but come to my parents' house like a man of honor, and state your intentions there."

"I will certainly do so, and immediately, if you like," the stranger replied, eagerly.

"No, no," Viteska said; "but come this evening if you like."

The stranger bowed and left her, and really called on her parents in the evening. He introduced himself as Ireneus Krisapolis, a merchant from Smyrna, spoke of his brilliant cricumstances, and finally declared that he loved Viteska passionately.

"That is all very nice and right," the cautious father replied, "but what will it all lead to? Under no circumstances can I allow you to visit my daughter. Such a passion as yours often dies out as quickly as it arises, and a respectable girl is easily robbed of her virtue."

"And suppose I make up my mind to marry your daughter?" the stranger asked, after a moment's hesitation.

"Then I shall refer you to my child, for I shall never force Viteska to marry against her will," her father said.

The stranger seized the pretty girl's hand, and spoke in glowing terms of his love for her, of the luxury with which she would be surrounded in his house, of the wonders of the East, to which he hoped to take her, and at last Viteska consented to become his wife. Thereupon the stranger hurried on the arrangements for the wedding in a manner that made the most favorable impression on them all, and during the time before their marriage, he virtually lay at her feet like a humble slave.

As soon as they were married, the newly-married couple set off on their journey to Smyrna and promised to write as soon as they got there. But a month, then two and three, passed without the parents—whose anxiety increased every day—receiving a line from them until at last the father in terror applied to the police.

The first thing was to write to the Consul at Smyrna for information: his reply was to the effect that no merchant of the name of Ireneus Krisapolis was known in Smyrna, and that he had never been there. The police, at the entreaties of the frantic parents, continued their investigations, but for a long time without any result. At last, however, they obtained a little light on the subject, but it was not at all satisfactory. The police at Pesth said that a man whose personal appearance exactly agreed with the description of Viteska's husband had a short time before carried off two girls from the Hungarian capital to Turkey, evidently intending to trade in that coveted, valuable commodity there, but that when he found that the authorities were on his track he had escaped from justice by sudden flight.

*   *   *   *   *   *

Four years after Viteska's mysterious disappearance, two persons, a man and a woman, met in a narrow street in Damascus, in a manner scarcely less strange than that in which the Greek merchant met Viteska on the suspension bridge in Prague. The man with the black beard, the red fez, and the long, green caftan, was no one else than Ireneus Krisapolis; matters appeared to be going well with him; he had his hands comfortably thrust into the red shawl which he had round his waist, and a negro was walking behind him with a large parasol, while another carried his *chibouque* after him. A noble Turkish lady met him in a litter borne by four slaves; she was wrapped like a ghost in a white veil, only that a pair of large, dark, threatening eyes flashed at the merchant.

He smiled, for he thought that he had found favor in the eyes of an Eastern houri, and that flattered him. But he soon lost sight of her in the crowd, and forgot her almost immediately. The next morning, however, a eunuch of the Pasha's came to him, to his no small astonishment, and told him to come with him. He took him to the Sultan's most powerful deputy, who ruled as an absolute despot in Damascus. They went through dark, narrow passages, and curtains were pushed aside, which rustled behind them again. At last they reached a large rotunda, the center of which was occupied by a beautiful fountain, while scarlet divans ran all around it. Here the eunuch told the merchant

to wait, and left him. He was puzzling his brains as to the meaning of it all, when suddenly a tall, commanding woman came into the apartment. Again a pair of large, threatening eyes looked at him through the veil, while he knew from her green, gold-embroidered caftan, that if it was not the Pasha's wife, it was at least one of his favorites who was before him. So he hurriedly knelt down, and crossing his hands on his breast, he put his head on the ground before her. But a clear, diabolical laugh made him look up, and when the beautiful *odalisque* threw back her veil, he uttered a cry of terror, for his wife, his deceived wife, whom he had sold, was standing before him.

"Do you know me?" she asked with quiet dignity.

"Viteska!"

"Yes, that was my name when I was your wife," she replied quickly, in a contemptuous voice; "but now that I am the Pasha's wife, my name is Sarema. I do not suppose you ever expected to find me again, you wretch, when you sold me in Varna to an old Jewish profligate, who was only half alive. You see I have got into better hands, and I have made my fortune, as you said I should do. Well? What do you expect of me; what thanks, what reward?"

The wretched man was lying overwhelmed at the feet of the woman whom he had so shamefully deceived, and could not find a word to say. He felt that he was lost, and had not even got the courage to beg for mercy.

"You deserve death, you miscreant," Sarema continued. "You are in my hands, and I can do whatever I please with you, for the Pasha has left you punishment to me alone. I ought to have you impaled, and to feast my eyes on your death agonies. That would be the smallest compensation for all the years of degradation that I have been through, and which I owe to you."

"Mercy, Viteska! Mercy!" the wretched man cried, trembling all over, and raising his hands to her in supplication.

The *odalisque's* only reply was a laugh, in which rang all the cruelty of an insulted woman's deceived heart. It seemed to give her pleasure to see the man whom she had loved, and who had so shamefully trafficked in her beauty, in mortal agony, cringing before her, whining for his life, as he grovelled on his knees. At last she seemed to relent somewhat.

"I will give you your life, you miserable wretch," she said, "but you shall not go unpunished." So saying, she clapped her hands, and four black eunuchs came in. They seized the favorite's unfortunate husband and in a moment bound his hands and feet.

"I have altered my mind, and he shall not be put to death," Sarema said, with a smile that made the traitor's blood run cold in his veins. "But give him a hundred blows with the bastinado, and I will stand by and count them."

"For God's sake," the merchant screamed, "I can never endure it."

"We will see about that," the favorite said, coldly; "if you die under it, it was allotted you by fate; I am not going to retract my orders."

She threw herself down on the cushions, and began to smoke a long pipe, which a female slave handed to her on her knees. At a sign from her the eunuchs tied the wretched man's feet to the pole, by which the soles of the culprit were raised, and began the terrible punishment. Already at the tenth blow the merchant began to roar like a wild animal, but the wife whom he had betrayed remained unmoved, carelessly blowing the blue wreaths of smoke into the air. Resting on her lovely arm, she watched his features, which were distorted by pain, with merciless enjoyment.

During the last blows he only groaned gently, and then he fainted.

*   *   *   *   *   *

A year later the dealer was caught with his female merchandise by the police in an Austrian town and handed over to justice, when he made a full confession. By that means the parents of the "Odalisque of Senichou" heard of their daughter's position. As they knew that she was happy and surrounded by luxury, they made no attempt to get her out of the Pasha's hands, who, like a thorough Mussulman, had become the slave of his slave.

The unfortunate husband was sent over to the frontier when he was released from prison. His shameful traffic, however, flourishes still, in spite of all the precautions of the police and of the consuls. Every year he provides the harems of the East with those voluptuous *Boxclanas*, especially from Bohemia and Hungary, who, in the eyes of a Mussulman, vie with the slender Circassian women for the prize of beauty.

Bric-à-Brac

"IF YOU would like to see the interesting bric-à-brac there, come with me," said my friend, Boisrené.

He then led me to the first story of a beautiful house, in a great street in Paris. We were received by a very strong man, of perfect manners, who took us from piece to piece showing us rare objects of which he mentioned the price carelessly. Great sums, ten, twenty, thirty, fifty thousand francs, came from his lips with so much grace and facility that one could not doubt that millions were shut up in the strong boxes of this merchant man of the world.

I had known him by name for a long time. Very clever, very tactful, very intelligent, he served as intermediary for all sorts of transactions. In touch with all the richest amateurs of Paris, and even of Europe and America, knowing their tastes, their preferences for the moment, he brought them by a word or a dispatch, if they lived in some far-off town, when he knew that some object was to be sold that would please them.

Men in the best of society had had recourse to him in times of embarrassment, perhaps to get money for play, perhaps to pay a debt, perhaps to sell a picture, a family jewel, or a tapestry, or even to sell a horse, where the owner was in close straits.

It was said that he never refused his services when he could foresee any chance of gain.

Boisrené seemed intimate with this curiosity merchant. They had managed more than one affair together. I myself looked at the man with much interest.

He was tall, thin, bald, and very elegant. His sweet, insinuating voice, had a particular charm, a tentative charm, which gives to things a special value. When he held an article in his fingers, he turned it, re-turned it, and looked at it with so much directness, tactfulness, elegance, and sympathy that the object was at once embellished, transformed by his touch and his look. And one would immediately estimate it at a higher cost than before it passed from the show-case to his hand.

"And your Christ, the beautiful Christ of the Renaissance," said Boisrené, "that you showed me last year?"

The man smiled and replied:

"It is sold, and in rather a strange fashion. In fact, the whole story of a Parisian woman is in the sale. Would you like me to tell it to you?"

"Yes, indeed."

"Do you know the Baroness Samoris?"

"Yes and no. I have only seen her once, but I know who she is!"

"You know fully?"

"Yes."

"Are you willing to tell me, that I may see whether you are deceived or not?"

"Very willing. Madame Samoris is a woman of the world who has a daughter without ever having had a husband, as the saying goes. But, if she has not had a husband, she has lovers, after a discreet fashion, so that they are received into certain society which is tolerant or blind. She is constant at Church, receives the sacrament with reflection, after the fashion of one who knows, and never will compromise herself. She hopes her daughter will make a good marriage. Is it not so?"

"Yes, but I will complete your information; she is a kept woman who makes herself respected by her lovers more than if she did not live with them. That is rare merit; for in this way one obtains whatever is desired of a man. The one whom she chooses, without which a man would have doubts, pays court a long time, desires her with fear, solicits with shame, obtains with astonishment, and possesses with consideration. He does not perceive that he pays, so much tact does she use in taking; and she maintains their relation with such a tone of reserve, of dignity, of propriety, that in going away from her he would slap the face of a man capable of suspecting the virtue of his mistress. And that with the best faith in the world.

"I have rendered some services to this woman in many of her undertakings. She has no secrets from me.

"Somewhere in the first days of January, she came to me to borrow thirty thousand francs. I had not the amount at hand, you understand, but as I desired to oblige her, I begged her to tell me her situation fully, that I might see if there was anything I could do for her.

"She told me things in such precautionary language as she might use in relating a most delicate story for her daughter's first communion. I finally understood that times were hard and that she found herself without a sou. The commercial crisis, political disturbances which the government actually seemed to entertain with pleasure, rumors of war, and the general constraint had made money hesitate, even in the hands of lovers. And then, she could not, this honest woman, give herself to the first comer.

"A man of the world, of the best world, was necessary for her, one who would preserve her reputation while furnishing the daily needs. A rake would compromise her forever, even though he were very rich, and make the marriage of her daughter problematical. She could not think of business arrangements, of dishonoring intermediaries who might be able to relieve her of her embarrassment for a time. She must maintain the standard of her house, continue to receive with open doors, in order not to lose the hope of finding, among her visitors, the discreet and distinguished friend whom she was waiting to choose.

"For my part, I observed to her that there seemed little chance of my thirty thousand francs returning to me, since, when they were eaten up, she would have to obtain sixty thousand at a single blow in order to give me half.

"She was disconsolate while listening to me, and I could think of nothing to be done, when an idea, a truly genial idea, crossed my mind. I had just bought the Christ of the Renaissance which I showed you, an admirable piece, the most beautiful in that style that I have ever seen.

" 'My dear friend,' said I to her, 'I am going to make you take this little ivory home with you. You can invent an ingenious story, touching, poetic, whatever you wish, which will explain your desire of parting with it. It can be understood that it is an heirloom of the family, inherited from your father.

" 'I will see some amateurs for you and take them there myself. The rest you will attend to. I will let you understand their situation by a word, a watchword. This piece is worth fifty thousand francs, but I let you have it for thirty thousand. The difference will be yours."

"She reflected some moments with a profound air and then replied:

" 'Yes, perhaps it is a good idea. I thank you very much.'

"The next day I sent the Christ of the Renaissance to her house, and that evening I sent to her the Baron Saint-Hospital. For three months I addressed clients to her, clients of the best, who were confident of my judgment in business. But I heard no one speak to her.

"Then, having received a foreign customer who spoke very bad French, I decided to present him myself at the house of Madame Samoris, in order to let him see the piece.

"A footman all in black received us and showed us into a pretty drawing-room, furnished with taste, where we waited some minutes. She appeared, charming, extending her hand to me, making us be seated. When I explained the motive of my visit, she rang.

"The footman reappeared.

" 'See if Miss Isabelle can let us enter her chapel,' she said to him.

"The young girl herself brought the response. She was about fifteen, with a good, modest appearance, and all the freshness of youth. She wished to guide us herself into her chapel.

"It was a sort of pious boudoir, where a silver lamp was burning before the Christ of the Renaissance, my property, couched on a bed of black velvet. The setting of the scene was charming and very clever. The child made the sign of the cross, and then said: 'Look, gentlemen, is it not beautiful?'

"I took the object, examined it, and declared it remarkable. The stranger, also, considered it, but he seemed much more occupied with the women than with the Christ.

"One felt good in their home, felt the incense, the flowers, the perfume. One found complete repose there. It was truly a comfortable dwelling, inviting to rest.

"When we had re-entered the drawing-room, I broached, with reserve and delicacy, the question of price. Madame Samoris asked, lowering her eyes, fifty thousand francs. Then she added:

" 'If you wish to see it again, sir, I scarcely ever go out before three o'clock, and you will find me here any day.'

"In the street, the stranger asked me some details about the Baroness, whom he found charming. But I did not undertake to say much for her, nor of her.

"Three months more passed.

"One morning, not more than five days ago, she came to my house at the breakfast hour and, placing a pocket-book in my hand, said: 'My dear, you are an angel. Here are fifty thousand francs! *I* have bought your Christ of the Renaissance, and I pay twenty thousand francs more than the price agreed upon, on the condition that you will always—always send me clients—because the piece is still for sale.' "

The Artist's Wife

CURVED like a crescent moon, the little town of Étretat, with its white cliffs and its blue sea, is reposing under the sun of a grand July day. At the two points of the crescent are the two gates, the little one at the right, and the large one at the left, as if it were gradually advancing to the water—on one side a dwarfed foot, on the other, a leg of giant proportions; and the spire, nearly as high as the cliff, large at the base and fine at the summit, points its slim head toward the heavens.

Along the beach, upon the float, a crowd is seated watching the bathers. Upon the terrace of the Casino, another crowd, seated or walking, parades under the full light of day, a garden of pretty costumes, shaded by red and blue umbrellas embroidered in great flowers of silk. At the end of the promenade, on the terrace, there are other people, calm, quiet, walking slowly along up and down, as far as possible from the elegant multitude.

A young man, well-known, and celebrated as a painter, John Summer, was walking along with a listless air beside an invalid chair in which reposed a young woman, his wife. A domestic rolled the little carriage along, gently, while the crippled woman looked with sad eyes upon the joy of the heavens, the joy of the day, and the joy of other people.

They were not talking, they were not looking at each other. The woman said: "Let us stop a little."

They stopped, and the painter seated himself upon a folding chair arranged for him by the valet. Those who passed behind the couple, sitting there mute and motionless, regarded him with pitying looks. A complete legend of devotion had found its way about. He had married her in spite of her infirmity, moved by his love, they said.

Not far from there, two young men were seated on a capstan, chatting and looking off toward the horizon.

"So, it is not true," said one of them, "I tell you I know much of John Summer's life."

"Then why did he marry her? For she was really an invalid at the time, was she not?"

"Just as you see her now. He married her—he married her—as one marries—well, because he was a fool!"

"How is that?"

"How is that? That is how, my friend. That is the whole of it. One is a goose because he is a goose. And then you know, painters make a specialty of ridiculous marriages; they nearly always marry their models, or some old mistress, or some one of the women among the varied assortment they run up against. Why is it? Does anyone know? It would seem, on the contrary, that constant association with this race that we call models would be enough to disgust them forever with that kind of female. Not at all. After having made them pose, they marry them. Read that little book of Alphonse Daudet, 'Artists' Wives,' so true, so cruel, and so beautiful.

"As for the couple you see there, the accident that brought about that marriage was of a unique and terrible kind. The little woman played a comedy, or rather a frightful drama. In fact, she risked all for all. Was she sincere? Does she really love John? Can one ever know that? Who can determine, with any precision, the real from the make-believe, in the acts of women? They are always sincere in an eternal change of impressions. They are passionate, criminal, devoted, admirable, and ignoble, ready to obey unseizable emotions. They lie without ceasing, without wishing to, without knowing it, without comprehension, and they have with this, in spite of this, an absolute freedom from sensation and sentiment, which they evince in violent resolutions, unexpected, incomprehensible folly, putting to rout all our reason, all our custom of deliberation, and all our combination of egotism. The unforeseen bluntness of their determination makes them, to us, indecipherable enigmas. We are always asking: 'Are they sincere? Are they false?'

"But, my friend, they are sincere and false at the same time, because it is in their nature to be the two extremes and neither the one nor the other. Look at the means the most honest employ for obtaining what they wish. They are both complicated and simple, these means are. So complicated that we never guess them in advance, so simple that after we have been the victims of them, we cannot help being astonished and saying to ourselves: 'My! Did she play me as easily as that?' And they succeed always, my good friend, especially when it is a question of making us marry them.

"But here is John Summer's story:

"The little wife was a model, as the term is usually understood. She posed for him. She was pretty, particularly elegant, and possessed, it appears, a divine figure. He became her lover, as one becomes the lover of any seductive woman he sees often. He imagines he loves her with his whole soul. It is a singular phenomenon. As soon as one desires a woman, he believes sincerely that he can no longer live without her. They know very well that their time has arrived. They know that disgust always follows possession; that, in order to pass one's existence by the side of another being, not brutal, physical appetite, so quickly extinguished, is the need, but an accordance of soul, of temperament, of humor. In a seduction that one undertakes, in bodily form, it is necessary to mingle a certain sensual intoxication with a charming depth of mind.

"Well, he believed that he loved her; he made her a heap of promises of fidelity and lived completely with her. She was gentle and endowed with that undeniable elegance which the Parisian woman acquires so easily. She tippled and babbled and said silly things, which seemed *spirituelle*, from the droll way in which she put them. She had each moment some little trick or pretty gesture to charm the eye of the painter. When she raised an arm, or stooped down, her movements were always perfect, exactly as they should be.

"For three months John did not perceive that, in reality, she was like all models. They rented for the summer a little house at Andressy. I was there one evening, when the first disquiet germinated in the mind of my friend.

"As the night was radiant, we wished to take a turn along the bank of the river. The moon threw in the water a glittering shower of light, crumbling its yellow reflections in the eddy, in the current, in the whole of the large river, flowing slowly along.

"We were going along the bank, a little quiet from the vague exaltation which the dreaminess of the evening threw about us. We were wishing we might accomplish superhuman things, might love some unknown beings, deliciously poetic. Strange ecstasies, desires, and aspirations were trembling in us.

"And we kept silent, penetrated by the serene and living freshness of the charming night, by that freshness of the moon which seems to go through the body, penetrate it, bathe the mind, perfume it and steep in it happiness.

"Suddenly Josephine (she called herself Josephine) cried out:

" 'Oh! did you see the great fish that jumped down there?'

"He replied, without looking or knowing: 'Yes, dearie.'

"She was angry. 'No, you have not seen it since your back was turned to it.'

"He laughed. 'Yes, it is true. It is so fine here that I was thinking of nothing.'

"She was silent; but at the end of a minute, the need of speaking seized her, and she asked:

" 'Are you going to Paris to-morrow?'

"He answered: 'I don't know.'

"Again she was irritated:

" 'Perhaps you think it is amusing to walk out without saying anything,' she said; 'one usually talks if he is not too stupid.'

"He said nothing. Then, knowing well, thanks to her wicked, womanly in-

stinct, that he would be exasperated, she began to sing that irritating air with which our ears and minds had been wearied for the past two years:

" 'I was looking in the air.'

"He murmured: 'I beg you be quiet.'

"She answered furiously: 'Why should I keep quiet?'

"He replied: 'You will arouse the neighborhood.'

"Then the scene took place, the odious scene, with unexpected reproaches, tempestuous recriminations, then tears. All was over. They went back to the house. He allowed her to go on without reply, calmed by the divine evening and overwhelmed by the whirlwind of foolishness.

"Three months later, he was struggling desperately in the invincible, invisible bonds with which habit enlaces our life. She held him, oppressed him, martyrized him. They quarreled from morning until evening, insulting and combating each other.

"Finally, he wished to end it, to break, at any price. He sold all his work, realizing some twenty thousand francs (he was then little known) and, borrowing some money from friends, he left it all on the chimney-piece with a letter of adieu.

"He came to my house as a refuge. Toward three o'clock in the afternoon, the bell rang. I opened the door. A woman jumped into my face, brushed me aside, and rushed into my studio; it was she.

"He stood up on seeing her enter. She threw at his feet the envelope containing the bank-notes, with a truly noble gesture and said, with short breath:

" 'Here is your money. I do not care for it.'

"She was very pale and trembling, ready, apparently for any folly. He, too, grew pale, pale from anger and vexation, ready, perhaps, for any violence.

"He asked: 'What do you want, then?'

"She replied: 'I do not wish to be treated like a child. You have implored me and taken me. I ask you for nothing —only protect me.'

"He stamped his foot, saying: 'No, it is too much! And if you believe that you are going—'

"I took hold of his arm. 'Wait, John,' said I, 'let me attend to it.'

"I went toward her, and gently, little by little, I reasoned with her, emptying the sack of arguments that are usually employed in such cases. She listened to me motionless, with eyes fixed, obstinate and dumb. Finally, thinking of nothing more to say, and seeing that the affair would not end pleasantly, I struck one more last note. I said:

" 'He will always love you, little one, but his family wishes him to marry, and you know—'

"This was a surprise for her! 'Ah!— Ah!—now I comprehend—' she began.

"And turning toward him she continued: 'And so—you are going to marry!'

"He answered carelessly: 'Yes.'

"Then she took a step forward: 'If you marry, I will kill myself—you understand.'

" 'Well, then, kill yourself,' he hissed over his shoulder.

"She choked two or three times, her throat seeming bound by a frightful anguish. 'You say—you say— Repeat it!'

"He repeated: 'Well, kill yourself, if that pleases you!'

"She replied, very pale with fright: 'It is not necessary to dare me. I will throw myself from that window.'

"He began to laugh, advanced to the window, opened it, bowed like a person allowing some one to precede him, saying:

" 'Here is the way; after you!'

"She looked at him a second with fixed eyes, terribly excited; then, taking a leap, as one does in jumping a hedge in the field, she passed before him, before me, leaped over the sill and disappeared.

"I shall never forget the effect that this open window made upon me, after having seen it traversed by that falling body; it appeared to me in a second, great as the sky and as empty as space. And I recoiled instinctively, not daring to look, as if I had fallen myself.

"John, dismayed, made no motion.

"They took up the poor girl with both legs broken. She could never walk again.

"Her lover, foolish with remorse; and perhaps touched by remembrance, took her and married her. There you have it, my dear."

The evening was come. The young woman, being cold, wished to go in; and the domestic began to roll the invalid's little carriage toward the village. The painter walked along beside his wife, without having exchanged a word with her for an hour.

In the Spring

WHEN the first fine spring days come, and the earth awakes and assumes its garment of verdure, when the perfumed warmth of the air caresses your face and fills your lungs, and even seems to reach your heart, you feel vague longings for an undefined happiness, a wish to run, to walk anywhere and everywhere, to inhale the soul of the spring. As the winter had been very severe the year before, this longing assumed an intoxicating feeling in May; it was like a superabundance of sap.

Well, one morning on waking, I saw from my window the blue sky glowing in the sun above the neighboring houses. The canaries hanging in the windows were singing loudly, and so were the servants on every floor; a cheerful noise rose up from the streets, and I went out, with my spirits as bright as the day, to go—I did not exactly know where. Everybody I met seemed to be smiling; an air of happiness appeared to pervade everything in the warm light of returning spring. One might almost have said that a breeze of love was blowing through the city, and the young women whom I saw in the streets in morning toilettes, in the depths of whose eyes there lurked a hidden tenderness, and who walked with languid grace, filled my heart with agitation.

Without knowing how or why, I found myself on the banks of the Seine. Steamboats were starting for Suresnes, and suddenly I was seized by an unconquerable wish for a walk through the wood. The deck of the *mouche** was crowded with passengers, for the sun in early spring draws you out of the house, in spite of yourself, and everyone is active, visiting and gossiping with the people sitting near.

I had a female neighbor; a little workgirl, no doubt, who possessed the true Parisian charm. Her little head had light curly hair like frizzed light, which came down to her ears and to the nape of her neck, danced in the wind, and then became such fine, such light-colored down, that you could scarcely see it, but on which you felt an irresistible desire to impress a shower of kisses.

Under the magnetism of my looks, she turned her head toward me, and then immediately looked down, while a slight dimpling of the flesh, the forerunner of a smile, also showed that fine, pale down which the sun was gilding a little.

The calm river grew wider; the atmosphere was warm and perfectly still, but a murmur of life seemed to fill all space.

My neighbor raised her eyes again, and, this time, as I was still looking at her, she smiled, decidedly. She was charming, and in her passing glance I saw a thousand things of which I had hitherto been ignorant. I saw in it unknown depths, all the charm of tenderness, all the poetry which we dream of, all the happiness which we are continually in search of. I felt an insane longing to open my arms and to carry her off somewhere, so as to whisper the sweet music of words of love into her ears.

I was just going to speak to her when

*Fly. A name given to the small steamboats on the Seine.

639

somebody touched me on the shoulder. Turning round in some surprise, I saw an ordinary looking man, who was neither young nor old, and who gazed at me sadly:

"I should like to speak to you," he said.

I made a grimace, which he no doubt saw, for he added:

"It is a matter of importance."

I got up, therefore, and followed him to the other end of the boat, and then he said:

"Monsieur, when winter comes, with its cold, wet, and snowy weather, your doctor says to you constantly: 'Keep your feet warm, guard against chills, colds, bronchitis, rheumatism, and pleurisy.'

"Then you are very careful, you wear flannel, a heavy great-coat, and thick shoes, but all this does not prevent you from passing two months in bed. But when spring returns, with its leaves and flowers, its warm, soft breezes, and its smell of the fields, causing you vague disquiet and causeless emotion, nobody says to you:

" 'Monsieur, beware of love! It is lying in ambush everywhere; it is watching for you at every corner; all its snares are laid, all its weapons are sharpened, all its guiles are prepared! Beware of love. Beware of love. It is more dangerous than brandy, bronchitis, or pleurisy! It never forgives, and makes everybody commit irreparable follies.'

"Yes, Monsieur, I say that the French government ought to put large public notices on the walls, with these words: 'Return of spring. French citizens, beware of love'; just as they put: 'Beware of paint.'

"However, as the government will not do this, I must supply its place, and I say to you: 'Beware of love,' for it is just going to seize you, and it is my duty to inform you of it, just as in Russia they inform anyone that his nose is frozen."

I was much astonished at this individual, and assuming a dignified manner, I said:

"Really, Monsieur, you appear to me to be interfering in a matter which is no business of yours."

He made an abrupt movement, and replied:

"Ah, Monsieur, Monsieur! If I see that a man is in danger of being drowned at a dangerous spot, ought I to let him perish? So just listen to my story, and you will see why I ventured to speak to you like this.

"It was about this time last year that it occurred. But, first of all, I must tell you that I am a clerk in the Admiralty, where our chiefs, the commissioners, take their gold lace as quill-driving officers seriously, and treat us like foretop men on board a ship. Well, from my office I could see a small bit of blue sky and the swallows, and I felt inclined to dance among my portfolios.

"My yearning for freedom grew so intense, that, in spite of my repugnance, I went to see my chief, who was a short, bad-tempered man, who was always cross. When I told him that I was not well, he looked at me, and said: 'I do not believe it, Monsieur, but be off with you! Do you think that any office can go on with clerks like you?' I started at once, and went down the Seine. It was a day like this, and I took the *mouche* to go as far as Saint-Cloud. Ah! What a good thing it would have been if my chief had refused me permission to leave the office for the day!

"I seemed to expand in the sun. I loved it all; the steamer, the river, the trees, the houses, my fellow-passengers, everything. I felt inclined to kiss something, no matter what; it was love laying its snare. Presently, at the Trocadéro, a girl, with a small parcel in her hand, came on board and sat down opposite to me. She was certainly pretty; but it is surprising, Monsieur, how much prettier women seem to us when it is fine, at the beginning of the spring. Then they have an intoxicating charm, something quite peculiar about them. It is just like drinking wine after the cheese.

"I looked at her, and she also looked at me, but only occasionally, like that girl did at you, just now; but at last, by dint of looking at each other constantly, it seemed to me that we knew each other well enough to enter into conversation, and I spoke to her, and she replied. She was decidedly pretty and nice, and she intoxicated me, Monsieur!

"She got out at Saint-Cloud, and I followed her. She went and delivered her parcel, but when she returned, the boat had just started. I walked by her side, and the warmth of the air made us both sigh.

" 'It would be very nice in the wood,' I said.

" 'Indeed, it would!' she replied.

" 'Shall we go there for a walk, Mademoiselle?'

"She gave me a quick, upward look, as if to see exactly what I was like, and then, after a little hesitation, she accepted my proposal, and soon we were there, walking side by side. Under the foliage, which was still rather thin, the tall, thick, bright, green grass was inundated by the sun and full of small insects making love to one another, and birds were singing in all directions. My companion began to jump and to run, intoxicated by the air and the smell of the country, and I ran and jumped behind her. How stupid we are at times, Monsieur!

"Then she wildly sang a thousand things; opera airs and the song of *Musette!* The song of *Musette!* How poetical it seemed to me, then! I almost cried over it. Ah! Those silly songs make us lose our heads; take my advice, never marry a woman who sings in the country, especially if she sings the song of *Musette!*

"She soon grew tired, and sat down on a grassy slope, and I sat down at her feet. I took her hands, her little hands, so marked with the needle, and they moved me. I said to myself: 'These are the sacred marks of toil.' Oh, Monsieur! do you know what those sacred marks of labor mean? They mean all the gossip of the workroom, the whispered blackguardism, the mind soiled by all the filth that is talked; they mean lost chastity, foolish chatter, all the wretchedness of daily bad habits, all the narrowness of ideas which belongs to women of the lower orders, united in the girl whose sacred fingers bear *the sacred marks of toil.*

"Then we looked into each other's eyes for a long while. What power a woman's eye has! How it agitates us, how it invades our very being, takes possession of us, and dominates us. How profound it seems, how full of infinite promise! People call that looking into each other's souls! Oh! Monsieur, what humbug! If we could see into each other's souls, we should be more careful of what we did. However, I was caught, and crazy after her, and tried to take her into my arms, but she said: 'Hands off!' Then I threw myself down, and opened my heart to her, and poured out all the affection that was suffocating me, my head on her knees. She seemed surprised at my manner, and gave me a sidelong glance, as if to say: 'Ah! So that is the way women make a fool of you, old fellow! Very well, we will see.' In love, Monsieur, men are the artists, and women are the dealers.

"No doubt I could have won her, and I saw my own stupidity later, but what I wanted was not a woman's person, it was love, it was the ideal. I was sentimental, when I ought to have been using my time to a better purpose.

"As soon as she had had enough of my declarations of affection, she got up, and we returned to Saint-Cloud, but I did not leave her until we got to Paris. But she looked so sad as we were returning, that at last I asked her what was the matter.

"'I am thinking,' she replied, 'that this has been one of those days of which we have but few in life.'

"And my heart beat as if it would break my ribs.

"I saw her on the following Sunday, and the next Sunday, and every Sunday. I took her to Bougival, Saint-Germain, Maison-Lafitte, Poissy; to every suburban resort of lovers.

"The little jade, in turn, pretended to love me, until, at last, I altogether lost my head, and three months later I married her.

"What can you expect, Monsieur, when a man is a clerk, living alone, without any relations, or anyone to advise him? You say to yourself: 'How sweet life would be with a wife!'

"And so you get married, and she calls you names from morning till night, understands nothing, knows nothing, chatters continually, sings the song of *Musette* at the top of her voice (oh! that song of *Musette,* how tired one gets of it!); quarrels with the charcoal dealer, tells the porter all her domestic details, confides all the secrets of her bedroom to the neighbor's servant, discusses her husband with the tradespeople, and has her head so stuffed with stupid stories, with idiotic superstitions, with extraordinary ideas, and monstrous prejudices, that I—for what I have said, applies particularly to myself — shed tears of discouragement every time I talk to her."

He stopped, as he was rather out of breath, and very much moved. I looked at him, for I felt pity for this poor, artless devil, and I was just going to give him some sort of answer, when the boat stopped. We were at Saint-Cloud.

The little woman who had so taken my fancy got up in order to land. She passed close to me, and gave me a side glance and a furtive smile — one of those smiles that drive you wild; then she jumped on the landing-stage. I sprang forward to follow her, but my neighbor laid hold of my arm. I shook myself loose, however, whereupon he seized the skirt of my coat, and pulled me back, exclaiming:

"You shall not go! You shall not go!" in such a loud voice, that everybody turned round and laughed. I remained standing motionless and furious, but without venturing to face scandal and ridicule, and the steamboat started.

The little woman on the landing-stage looked at me as I went off with an air of disappointment, while my persecutor rubbed his hands and whispered to me:

"You must admit that I have done you a great service."

The Real One and the Other

"WELL, really," said Chasseval, standing with his back to the fire, "could any of those respectable shopkeepers and wine-growers have possibly believed that that pretty little Parisian woman, with soft innocent eyes, like those of a Madonna, with smiling lips and golden hair, who always dressed so simply, was their candidate's mistress?"

She was a wonderful help to him, and accompanied him even to the most outlying farms; went to the meetings in the small village *cafés*, had a pleasant and suitable word for everyone, did not recoil at a glass of mulled wine or a grip of the hand, and was always ready to join the *farandole*.* She seemed to be so in love with Eliéane Rulhière, to trust him so entirely, to be so proud of forming half of his life, and of belonging to him, giving him such looks full of pleasure and of hope, and listening to all he said so intently, that voters who might have hesitated allowed themselves by degrees to be talked over and persuaded, and promised their votes to the young doctor whose name they never heard mentioned in the district before.

That electoral campaign had been like a truant's escapade for Jane Dardenne; it was a delightful and unexpected holiday, and as she was an actress at heart, she played her part seriously, and threw herself into her character, enjoying herself more than she had ever enjoyed herself in her most adventurous outings.

And then there came in the pleasure of being taken for a woman of the world, of being flattered, respected, and envied, of getting out of the usual groove for a time, and also the dream that this journey of a few weeks would have this result, that her lover would not separate from her on their return, but would sacrifice the woman whom he no longer loved, and whom he ironically used to call his "Cinderella," to her.

At night, when they had laid aside all pretense, and were alone in their room in the hotel, she coaxed him and flattered him, spurred his ambition on, threw her quivering arms around him,

---

*A dance in Provence in which the dancers form a chain, and the movements are directed by the leader.

and amid her kisses, whispered those words to him which make a man proud, warm his heart, and give him strength, like a dram of alcohol.

The two between them captured the district, and won the election easily, for in spite of his youth, Eliéane Rulhière was elected by a majority of five thousand. Then, of course, there were more *fêtes* and banquets, at which Jane was present, and where she was received with enthusiastic shouts; there were fireworks, where she was obliged to set light to the first rocket, and balls at which she astonished these worthy people by her affability. And when they left, three little girls dressed in white, as if they were going to be confirmed, came on to the platform and recited some verses complimentary to her, while the band played the "Marseillaise," the women waved their pocket handkerchiefs, and the men their hats; and leaning out of the carriage window, looking charming in her traveling costume, with a smile on her lips and moist eyes, as was fitting at such a pathetic leave-taking, actress as she was, with a sudden and childlike gesture she blew kisses to them from the tips of her fingers, and said:

"Good-bye, my friends, good-bye, only for the present; I shall never forget you!"

The deputy, who was also very effusive, had invited his principal supporters to come and see him in Paris, as there were plenty of excursion trains. They all took him at his word, and Rulhière was obliged to invite them all to dinner.

In order to avoid any possible mishaps, he gave his wife a foretaste of their guests. He told her that they were rather noisy, talkative, and un-polished, and that they would, no doubt, astonish her by their manners and their accent, but that, as they had great influence, and were excellent men, they deserved a good reception. It was a very useful precaution, for when they came into the drawing-room in their new clothes, beaming with pleasure, and with hair pomatumed as if they had been going to a country wedding, they felt inclined to fall down before the new Madame Rulhière to whom the deputy introduced them, and who seemed to be perfectly at home there.

At first they were embarrassed, felt uncomfortable, and out of place, did not know what to say, and had to seek their words. They buttoned and unbuttoned their gloves, answered her questions at random, and racked their brains to discover the solution of the enigma. Captain Mouredus looked at the fire, with the fixed gaze of a somnambulist; Marius Barbaste scratched his fingers mechanically; while the three others, the factory manager, Casemajel, Roquetton, the lawyer, and Dustugue, the hotel proprietor, looked at Rulhière anxiously.

The lawyer was the first to recover himself. He got up from his armchair laughing heartily, dug the deputy in the ribs with his elbow, and said:

"I understand it all, I understand it; you thought that people do not come to Paris to be bored, eh? Madame is delightful, and I congratulate you, Monsieur."

He gave a wink, and made signs behind his back to his friends, and then the captain had his turn.

"We are not boobies, and that fellow Roquetton is the most knowing of the lot of us. Ah! Monsieur Rulhière, without any exaggeration, you are the cream of good fellows."

And with a flushed face, and expanding his chest, he said sonorously:

"They certainly turn them out very pretty in your part of the country, my little lady!"

Madame Rulhière, who did not know what to say, had gone to her husband for protection; but she felt much inclined to go to her own room under some pretext or other, in order to escape from her intolerable task. She kept her ground, however, during the whole of dinner, which was a noisy, jovial meal, during which the five electors, with their elbows on the table, and their waistcoats unbuttoned, and half drunk, told coarse stories and swore like troopers. But as the coffee and the liqueurs were served in the smoking-room she took leave of her guests in an inpatient voice, and went to her own room with the hasty step of an escaped prisoner, who is afraid of being retaken.

The electors sat staring after her with gaping mouths, and Mourédus lit a cigar, and said:

"Just listen to me, Monsieur Rulhière; it was very kind of you to invite us here, to your little quiet establishment, but to speak to you frankly, I should not in your place wrong my lawful wife for such a stuck-up piece of goods as this one is."

"The captain is quite right," Roquetton the notary opined; "Madame Rulhière, the lawful Madame Rulhière, is much more amiable and altogether nicer. You are a scoundrel to deceive her: but when may we hope to see her?"

And with a paternal grimace, he added:

"But do not be uneasy, we will all hold our tongues; it would be too sad if she were to find it out."

The Carter's Wench

THE driver, who had jumped from his box, was now walking slowly by the side of his thin horses, waking them up every moment by a cut of the whip or a coarse oath. He pointed to the top of the hill, where the windows of a solitary house, although it was very late and quite dark, were shining like yellow lamps, and said to me:

"One gets good liquor there, Monsieur, and well served, by George!"

His eyes flashed in his thin, sunburned face, which was a deep brickdust color, and he smacked his lips like a drunkard, at the remembrance of a bottle of prime liquor that he had lately imbibed. Then drawing himself up in his blouse he shivered like an ox, when it is sharply pricked with the goad.

"Yes—well served by a wench who will turn your head for you before you have tilted your elbow and drunk a glass!"

The moon was rising behind the snow-covered mountain peaks, reddening them to blood with its rays, and tingeing the dark, broken clouds, which whirled and floated about the summits, reminding the traveler of some terrible Medusa's head. The gloomy plains of Capsir, which are traversed by torrents, extensive meadows in which undefined forms were moving about, fields of rye like huge golden tablecovers, and here and there wretched villages and broad sheets of water, into which the stars gazed in melancholy manner, opened out to the view. Damp gusts of wind swept along the road, bringing a strong smell of hay, of resin, and of unknown flowers with them, and erratic masses of rock, which were scattered on the surface like huge boundary stones, presented spectral outlines.

The driver pulled his broad-brimmed felt hat over his eyes, twirled his large mustache, and said in an obsequious voice:

"Does Monsieur wish to stop here? This is the place!"

It was a wretched, wayside public-house, with a reddish slate roof, that looked as if it were suffering from leprosy. Before the door there stood three wagons drawn by mules and loaded with huge stems of trees, which took up nearly the whole of the road. The animals, who were used to halting there, were dozing, and their heavy loads exhaled the smell of a pillaged forest.

Inside, three wagoners, one of whom was an old man, while the other two were young, were sitting in front of the fire, which crackled loudly. There were bottles and glasses on a large round table by their side, and they were singing and laughing boisterously. A woman with large round hips, and with a lace cap pinned on to her hair, in the Catalan fashion, who looked strong and bold, had a certain amount of gracefulness about her, and a pretty, but untidy head, was urging them to undo the strings of their great leather purses. She replied to their somewhat indelicate jokes in a shrill voice, as she sat on the knee of the youngest and allowed him to kiss her and caress her without any signs of shame.

The coachman pushed open the door like a man who knows that he is at home.

"Good evening, Glaizette, and everybody; there is room for two more, I suppose?"

The wagoners did not speak, but looked at us furtively and angrily, like dogs whose food has been taken from them, and who show their teeth, ready to bite. The girl shrugged her shoulders, and looked into their eyes like some female wild-beast tamer; then she asked us with a strange smile:

"What am I to get you?"

"Two glasses of cognac and the best you have in the cupboard, Glaizette," the coachman replied, rolling a cigarette.

While she was uncorking the bottle I noticed how green her eyeballs were; it was a fascinating, tempting green, like the hue of the great green grasshopper. I saw, too, how small her hands were, which showed that she did not use them much. Her teeth were very white, and her voice, which was rather rough, though cooing, had a cruel, and at the same time a coaxing, sound. I fancied I saw her, as in a vision, reclining triumphantly on a couch, indifferent to the fights which were going on about her, always waiting, longing for him who would prove himself the stronger and come out victorious. She was, in short, a hospitable dispenser of love, by the side of that difficult, stony road, who opened her arms to poor men, and made them forget everything in the profusion of her kisses. She probably knew secrets which nobody in the world besides herself should know, secrets which her sealed lips would carry away inviolate to the other world. She could never yet have loved, and would never really love, because she was vowed to passing kisses, which are so soon forgotten.

I was anxious to escape from her as soon as possible; to fly from the spell of her pale, green eyes, and her mouth that bestowed caresses from pure charity, to feel her beautiful white hands no longer so near me. So I threw her a piece of gold and made my escape without saying a word, without waiting for any change, and without even wishing her good night, for I felt the caress of her smile, and the disdainful restlessness of her looks.

The carriage started off at a gallop to Formiguères, amid a furious jingling of bells. I could not sleep any more; I wanted to know where that woman came from, but I was ashamed to ask the driver, or to show any interest in such a creature. But when he began to talk, as we were going up another hill, divining my sweet thoughts, he told me all he knew about Glaizette. I listened to him with the attention of a child, to whom somebody is telling some wonderful fairy tale.

She came from Fontpédrouze, a muleteers' village, where the men spend their time in drinking and gambling at the inn, when they are not traveling on the highroads with their mules. The women do all the field work, carry the heaviest loads on their back, and lead a life of pain and misery.

Her father kept an inn, and the girl grew up very happily. She was courted before she was fifteen, and was so coquettish that she was generally found in front of her looking-glass, smiling at her own beauty, arranging her hair, and trying to make herself like a young lady on the *prado*. Now as none of the family knew how to keep a half-penny, but spent more than they earned, resembling cracked jugs, from which the water escapes drop by drop, they found themselves ruined one fine day, just as if they had been at the bottom of a blind alley. So on the Feast of our Lady of Succor, when people go on a pilgrimage to Font Romea, and the villages are consequently deserted, the innkeeper set fire to the house. The crime was discovered through La Glaizette, who could not make up her mind to leave the looking-glass with which her room was adorned behind her, and so had carried it off under her petticoat.

The parents were sentenced to many years' imprisonment. Compelled to live the best way she could, the girl became a servant, passed from hand to hand, inherited some property from an old farmer whom she had caught as you catch a thrush on a twig covered with bird-lime, and with the money had built this public-house on the new road which was being built across the Capsir.

"A regular bad one, Monsieur," said the coachman in conclusion, "a vixen such as one does not see now in the worst garrison towns, one who would open the door to the whole confraternity, yet not at all avaricious, and thoroughly honest."

I interrupted him in spite of myself, as if his words had pained me. I thought of those pale green eyes, those magic eyes, eyes to be dreamed about, which were the color of grasshoppers. I looked for them, and saw them in the darkness; they danced before me like phosphorescent lights, and I would have given the whole contents of my purse to that man if he would only have been silent and have urged his horses on to full speed, so that their mad gallop might carry me off quickly, quickly and further, continually further from that girl.

The Rendezvous

ALTHOUGH she had her bonnet and jacket on, with a black veil over her face, and another in her pocket, which would be put on over the other as soon as she had got into a cab, she was tapping the top of her little boot with the point of her parasol, and remained sitting in her room, unable to make up her mind to keep this appointment.

And yet how many times within the last two years had she dressed herself thus, when she knew that her husband would be on the Stock Exchange, in order to go to the bachelor chambers of handsome Viscount de Martelet.

The clock behind her was ticking loudly, a book which she had half read was lying open on a little rosewood writing-table, between the windows, and a strong sweet smell of violets from two bunches in Dresden china vases mingled with a vague smell of verbena which came through the half-open door of her dressing-room.

The clock struck three, she rose up from her chair, turned round to look at herself in the glass and smiled. "He is already waiting for me, and will be getting tired."

Then she left the room, told her footman that she would be back in an hour, at the latest—which was a lie—went downstairs, and ventured into the street on foot.

It was toward the end of May, that delightful time of the year when spring seems to be besieging Paris, flowing over its roofs, invading its houses through their walls, and making the city look gay, shedding brightness over its granite *façades*, the asphalt of its pavements, the stones on its streets, bathing and intoxicating it with new life, like a forest putting on its spring vesture.

Madame Haggan went a few steps to the right, intending, as usual, to go along the Parade Provence, where she would hail a cab. But the soft air, that feeling of summer which penetrates our breasts on some days, now took possession of her so suddenly that she changed her mind and went down the Rue de la Chaussée d'Antin, without knowing why, but vaguely attracted by a desire to see the trees in the Place da la Trinité.

"He may just wait ten minutes longer for me," she said to herself. And the idea pleased her as she walked slowly through the crowd. She fancied that she saw him growing impatient, looking at the clock, opening the window, listening at the door, sitting down for a few moments, getting up again, not daring to smoke, as she had forbidden him to do so when she was coming to him, and throwing despairing looks at his box of cigarettes.

She walked slowly, interested in what she saw, the shops and the people she met, walking slower and slower, and so little eager to get to her destination, that she only sought for some pretext for stopping. At the end of the street, in the little square, the green lawns attracted her so much that she went in, took a chair, and, sitting down, watched the hands of the clock as they moved.

Just then, the half hour struck, and her heart beat with pleasure when she heard the chimes. She had gained half-an-hour, then it would take her a quarter of an hour to reach the Rue de Miromesnil, and a few minutes more in strolling along—an hour! a whole hour saved from her rendezvous! She would not stop three-quarters of an hour, and that business would be finished once more.

She disliked going there as a patient dislikes going to the dentist. She had an intolerable recollection of all their past meetings, one a week on an average, for the last two years; and the thought that another was to take place immediately made her shiver with misery from head to foot. Not that it was exactly painful, like a visit to the dentist, but it was wearisome, so weari-some, so complicated, so long, so unpleasant, that anything, even a visit to the dentist, would have seemed preferable to her.

She went on, however, but very slowly, stopping, sitting down, going hither and thither, but she went. Oh! how she would have liked to miss this meeting, but she had left the unhappy Viscount in the lurch, twice running, during the last month, and she did not dare to do it again so soon. Why did she go to see him? Oh! why? Because she had acquired the habit of doing it, and had no reason to give poor Martelet when he wanted to know *the why!* Why had she begun it? Why? She did not know herself, any longer. Had she been in love with him? Very possibly! Not very much, but a little, a long time ago! He was very nice, much sought after, perfectly dressed, most courteous, and after the first glance, he was a perfect lover for a fashionable woman.

He had courted her for three months —the normal period, an honorable strife and sufficient resistance—and then she had consented. What emotion, what nervousness, what terrible, delightful fear, attended that first meeting in his small, ground-floor bachelor rooms, in the Rue de Miromesnil. Her heart? What did her little heart of a woman who had been seduced, vanquished, conquered, feel when she for the first time entered the door of the house which was her nightmare? She really did not know! She had quite forgotten. One remembers a fact, a date, a thing, but one hardly remembers, after the lapse of two years, what an emotion, which soon vanished because it was very slight, was like. But she had certainly not forgotten the others, that rosary of meetings, that road to the cross of love and its stations, which were so monotonous, so fatiguing, so similar to each other, that she felt nauseated.

The very cabs were not like the other cabs which you use for ordinary purposes! Certainly, the cabmen guessed. She felt sure of it, by the very way they looked at her, and the eyes of these Paris cabmen are terrible! When you realize that these jehus constantly identify in the Courts of Justice, after a lapse of several years, the faces of criminals whom they have only driven once, in the middle of the night, from some street or other to a railway station, and that they carry daily almost as many passengers as there are hours in the day, and that their memory is good enough for them to declare: "That is the man whom I took up in the Rue des Martyrs, and put down at the Lyons Railways Station, at 12 o'clock at night, on July 10, last year!" Is it not terrible to risk what a young woman risks when she is going to meet her lover, and has to trust her reputation to the first cabman she meets? In two years she had employed at least one hundred or more of them in that drive to the Rue de Miromesnil, reckoning only one a week. They were so many witnesses, who might appear against her at a critical moment.

As soon as she was in the cab, she took another veil, as thick and dark as a domino mask, out of her pocket, and put it on. That hid her face, but what about the rest, her dress, her bonnet, and her parasol? They might be remarked—they might, in fact, have been seen already. Oh! What misery she endured in this Rue de Miromesnil! She thought she recognized the foot-passengers, the servants, everybody, and almost before the cab had stopped, she jumped out and ran past the porter who was standing outside his lodge. He must know everything, everything!—her address, her name, her husband's profession,—everything, for those porters are the most cunning of policemen! For two years she had intended to bribe him, to give him (to throw at him one day as she passed him) a hundred franc banknote, but she had never dared to do it. She was frightened. What of? She did not know! Of his calling her back, if he did not understand? Of a scandal? Of a crowd on the stairs? Of being arrested, perhaps? To reach the Viscount's door, she had only to ascend half a flight of stairs, but it seemed to her as high as the tower of Saint Jacques's Church.

As soon as she had reached the vestibule, she felt as if she were caught in a trap. The slightest noise before or behind her nearly made her faint. It was impossible for her to go back, because of that porter who barred her retreat; and if anyone came down at that moment she would not dare to ring at Martelet's door, but would pass it as if she had been going elsewhere! She would have gone up, and up, and up! She would have mounted forty flights of stairs! Then, when everything seemed quiet again down below, she would run down feeling terribly frightened, lest she should not recognize the apartment.

He would be there in a velvet coat lined with silk, very stylish, but rather ridiculous, and for two years he had never altered his manner of receiving her, not in a single movement! As soon as he had shut the door he used to say: "Let me kiss your hands, my dear, dear friend!" Then he would follow her into the room, where with closed shutters and lighted candles, out of refinement, no doubt, he would kneel down before her and look at her from head to foot with an air of adoration. On the first occasion that had been very nice and very successful; but now it seemed to her as if she saw Monsieur Delaunay acting the last scene of a successful piece for the hundred and twentieth time. He might really change his manner of acting. But no, he never altered his manner of acting, poor fellow. What a good fellow he was, but so commonplace!

And how difficult it was to undress and dress without a lady's maid! Perhaps that was the moment when she began to take a dislike to him. When he said: "Do you want me to help you?" she could have killed him. Certainly there were not many men as awkward as he was, or as uninteresting. Certainly little Baron de Isombal would never have asked her in such a manner: "Do you want me to help you?" He would have helped her, he was so witty, so funny, so active. But there! He was a diplomatist, he had been about in the world, and had roamed everywhere, and, no doubt, had dressed and undressed women arrayed in every possible fashion!

The church clock struck the three-quarters. She looked at the dial, and said: "Oh, how anxious he will be!" and then she quickly left the square. But she had not taken a dozen steps outside, when she found herself face to face with a gentleman who bowed profoundly to her.

"Why! Is that you, Baron?" she said, in surprise. She had just been thinking of him.

"Yes, madame. And then, after asking how she was, he continued: "Do you know that you are the only one —you will allow me to say of my lady friends, I hope—who has not yet seen my Japanese collection?"

"But, my dear Baron, a lady cannot go to a bachelor's room like this."

"What do you mean? That is a great mistake, when it is a question of seeing a rare collection!"

"At any rate, she cannot go alone."

"And why not? I have received a number of ladies alone, only for the sake of seeing my collection! They come every day. Shall I tell you their names? No—I will not do that, one must be discreet, even when one is not guilty. As a matter of fact, there is nothing improper in going to the house of a well-known seriously minded man who holds a certain position, unless one goes for an improper reason!"

"Well, what you have said is certainly correct, at bottom."

"So you will come and see my collection?"

"When?"

"Well, now, immediately."

"Impossible, I am in a hurry."

"Nonsense, you have been sitting in the square for this last half hour."

"You were watching me?"

"I was looking at you."

"But I am sadly in a hurry."

"I am sure you are not. Confess that you are in no particular hurry."

Madame Haggan began to laugh, and said: "Well, no—not very."

A cab passed close by them, and the little Baron called out: "Cabman!" The vehicle stopped, and opening the door, he said: "Get in, madame."

"But, Baron! No, it is impossible to-day; I really cannot."

"Madame, you are acting very imprudently. Get in! People are beginning to look at us, and you will collect a crowd; they will think I am trying to carry you off, and we shall both be arrested; please get in!"

She got in, frightened and bewildered, and he sat down by her side, saying to the cabman: "Rue de Provence."

But suddenly she exclaimed: "Good heavens! I have forgotten a very important telegram; please drive to the nearest telegraph office first of all."

The cab stopped a little farther on, in the Rue de Châteaudun, and she said to the Baron: "Would you kindly get me a fifty-centimes telegraph form? I promised my husband to invite Martelet to dinner to-morrow, and had quite forgotten it."

When the Baron returned and gave her the blue telegraph form, she wrote in a pencil:

"My dear friend, I am not at all well. I am suffering terribly from neuralgia, which keeps me in bed. Impossible to go out. Come and dine to-morrow night, so that I may obtain my pardon.
"JEANNE."

She wetted the gum, fastened it carefully, and addressed it to "Viscount de Martelet, 240 Rue de Miromesnil," and then, giving it back to the Baron, she said: "Now, will you be kind enough to throw this in the telegram box?"

Solitude

WE had been dining at the house of a friend, and the dinner had been very gay. After it broke up, one of the party, an old friend, said to me:

"Let us take a stroll in the Champs-Elysées."

I agreed, and we went out, slowly walking up the long promenade, under trees hardly yet covered with leaves. There was hardly a sound, save that confused and constant murmur which Paris makes. A fresh breeze fanned our faces, and a legion of stars were scattered over the black sky like a golden powder.

My companion said to me:

"I do not know why, but I breathe better here at night than anywhere else. It seems to me that my thoughts are enlarged. I have at times, a sort of glimmering in my soul, that makes me believe, for a second, that the divine secret of things is about to be discovered. Then the window is closed, and my vision is ended."

From time to time we saw two shadows glide along the length of the thickets; then we passed a bench, where two people, seated side by side, made but one black spot.

My friend murmured:

"Poor things! They do not inspire me with disgust, but with an immense pity. Among all the mysteries of human life there is one which I have penetrated; our great torment in this existence comes from the fact that we are eternally alone—all our efforts and all our actions are directed toward escaping this solitude. Those two lovers there on the benches in the open air are seeking, as we—as all creatures are seeking, to make their isolation cease, if only for a minute or less. They are living and always will live alone; and we also.

"This is more or less apparent to all of us. For some time I have endured this abominable pain of having understood, of having discovered the frightful solitude in which I live, and I know that nothing can make it cease—nothing. Do you hear? Whatever we may attempt, whatever we may do, whatever may be the misery of our hearts, the appeal of our lips, the clasp of our arms, we are always alone. I have asked you to walk to-night, so that I shall not have to enter my own house, because now I suffer horribly from the solitude of my home. What good does it do me? I speak to you, you listen to me, yet we are both alone, side by side but alone. You understand?

" 'Blessed are the poor in spirit,' say the Scriptures. They have the illusion of happiness. They do not feel our solitary misery, they do not wander, as I do, through life, without contact save of elbows, without joy save the egotistic satisfaction of understanding, of seeing, of divining, and of suffering eternally from the knowledge of our never-ending isolation.

"You think me slightly deranged—do you not? Listen to me. Since I have felt the solitude of my being, it seems to me that I am daily sinking more deeply into a dark vault, whose sides I cannot find, whose end I do not know, and which, perhaps, has no end. I sink without anyone with me, or around me, without any living person making this same gloomy journey. This vault is life. Sometimes I hear noises, voices, cries. I timidly advance toward these confused sounds. But I never know exactly from whom they come; I never meet anybody, I never find another hand in this darkness that surrounds me. Do you understand?

"Some men have occasionally divined this frightful suffering. De Musset has written:

" 'Who comes? Who calls me? No one.
I am alone. One o'clock strikes.
O Solitude! O Misery!'

But with him there is only a passing doubt, and not a definite certainty as with me. He was a poet; he peopled life with fantasies, with dreams. He was never really alone. I—I am alone.

"Gustave Flaubert, one of the great unfortunates of this world, because he was one of the great lights, wrote to a friend this despairing phrase: 'We are all in a desert. Nobody understands anybody.'

"No, nobody understands anybody—whatever one thinks, whatever one says, whatever one attempts. Does the earth know what passes in those stars that are hurled like a spark of fire across the firmament—so far that we perceive only the splendor of some? Think of the innumerable army of others lost in infinitude—so near to each other that they form perhaps a whole, as the molecules of a body!

"Well, man does not know what passes in another man any more. We are farther from one another than the stars, and far more isolated, because thought is unfathomable.

"Do you know anything more frightful than this constant contact with beings that we cannot penetrate? We love one another as if we were fettered, very close, with extended arms, without succeeding in reaching one another. A torturing need of union hampers us, but all our efforts remain barren, our abandonment useless, our confidences unfruitful, our embraces powerless, our caresses vain. When we wish to join each other, our sudden emotions make us only clash against each other.

"I never feel myself more alone than when I open my heart to some friend, because I then better understand the insuperable obstacle. He is there, my friend; I see his clear eyes above me, but the soul behind them I do not see. He listens to me. What is he thinking? Yes, what *is* he thinking? You do not understand this torment! He hates me, perhaps,—or scorns me,—or mocks me! He reflects upon what I have said; he judges me, he rails at me, he condemns me, and considers me either very mediocre or a fool.

"How am I to know what he thinks? How am I to know whether he loves me as I love him, and what is at work in that little round head? What a mystery is the unknown thought of a being, the hidden and independent

thought, that we can neither know nor control, neither command nor conquer!

"And I! I have wished in vain to give myself up entirely; to open all the doors of my soul, and I do not succeed in giving myself up. I still remain in the depth, the very depth, the secret abode of me, where no one can penetrate. No one can discover it, or enter there, because no one resembles me, because no one understands anyone.

"You, at least, understand me at this moment; no: you think I am mad! You examine me; you shrink from me! You ask yourself: 'What's the matter with him to-night?' But if you succeed in seizing, in divining, one day, my horrible and subtle suffering, come to me and say only: 'I have understood you!' and you will make me happy, for a second, perhaps.

"Women make me still more conscious of my solitude. Misery! Misery! How I have suffered through women; because they, more than men, have often given me the illusion of not being alone!

"When one falls in love it seems as though one expands. A superhuman felicity envelops you! Do you know why? Do you know why you feel then this sensation of exceeding happiness? It is simply because one imagines himself no longer alone. Isolation, the abandonment of the human being seems to cease. What an error!

"More tormented even than we, by this eternal need of love which gnaws at our solitary heart, are women, the great delusion and the dream.

"You know those delicious hours passed face to face with a being with long hair, charming features, and a look that excited us to love. What delirium misleads our mind! What illusion carries us away! Does it not seem that presently our souls shall form but one? But this 'presently' never comes; and, after weeks of waiting, of hope, and of deceptive joy, you find yourself again, one day, more alone than you have ever been before.

"After each kiss, after each embrace, the isolation is increased. And how frightfully one suffers!

"Has not Sully Prudhomme written:

" 'Caresses are only restless transports,
   Fruitless attempts of poor love which essay
   The impossible union of souls by the bodies.'

"And then—good-bye. It is over. One hardly recognizes the woman who has been everything to us for a moment of life, and whose thoughts, intimate and commonplace, undoubtedly, we have never known.

"At the very hour when it would seem, in that mysterious accord of beings, in the complete intermingling of ideas and of aspirations, that you were sounding the very depth of her soul, one word—one word only, sometimes—will reveal your error, will show you, like a flash of lightning in the night, the black abyss between you.

"And still, that which is best in the world is to pass a night near a woman you love, without speaking, completely happy in the sole sensation of her presence. Ask no more, for two beings have never yet been united.

"As to myself, now, I have closed my soul. I tell no more to anybody what I believe, what I think, or what I love. Knowing myself condemned to this horrible solitude, I look upon things without expressing my opinion. What matter to me opinions, quarrels, pleasures, or beliefs! Being unable to participate with anyone, I have withdrawn myself from all. My invisible self lives unexplored. I have common phrases for answers to the questions of each day, and a smile which says 'Yes,' when I do not even wish to take the trouble of speaking. Do you understand?"

We had traversed the long avenue to the Arc de Triomphe, and had then walked back to the Place de la Concorde, for he had said all this slowly, adding many other things which I no longer remember.

He stopped, and stretching his arm toward the great granite obelisk standing on the pavement of Paris, losing its long Egyptian profile in the night of the stars—an exiled monument, bearing on its side the history of its country written in strange signs—said brusquely: "Look—we are all like that stone."

Then he left me without adding a word. Was he intoxicated? Was he mad? Was he wise? I do not yet know. Sometimes it seems to me that he was right; sometimes it seems to me that he had lost his mind.

The Man with the Blue Eyes

MONSIEUR PIERRE AGÉNOR DE VARG-NES, the Examining Magistrate, was the exact opposite of a practical joker. He was dignity, staidness, correctness personified. As a sedate man, he was quite incapable of being guilty, even in his dreams, of anything resembling a practical joke, however remotely. I know nobody to whom he could be compared, unless it be the present president* of the French Republic. I think it is useless to carry the analogy any further, and having said thus much, it will be easily understood that a cold shiver passed through me when I heard the following:

At about eight o'clock, one morning last winter, as he was leaving the house to go to the Palais de Justice, his footman handed him a card, on which was printed:

DOCTOR JAMES FERDINAND,
Member of the Academy of Medicine,
PORT-AU-PRINCE,
Chevalier of the Legion of Honor.

At the bottom of the card, there was written in pencil: "From Lady Frogère."

Monsieur de Vargnes knew the lady very well. She was a very agreeable Creole from Haïti, whom he had met in many drawing-rooms, and, on the other hand, though the doctor's name did not awaken any recollections in him, his quality and titles alone demanded the courtesy of an interview, however short it might be. Therefore, although he was in a hurry to get out, Monsieur de Vargnes told the footman to show in his early visitor, but to tell him beforehand that his master was much pressed for time, as he had to go to the Law Courts.

When the doctor came in, in spite of his usual imperturbability, the magistrate could not restrain a movement of surprise, for the doctor presented the strange anomaly of being a negro of the purest, blackest type, with the eyes of a white man—of a man from the North—pale, cold, clear, blue eyes. His surprise increased, when, after a few words of excuse for an untimely visit, the doctor added, with an enigmatical smile:

"My eyes surprise you, do they not? I was sure that they would, and, to tell you the truth, I came here in order that you might look at them well, and never forget them."

His smile, and his words, even more than his smile, seemed to be those of a madman. He spoke very softly, with that childish, lisping voice which is peculiar to negroes, and his mysterious, almost menacing, words consequently sounded all the more as if they were uttered at random by a man bereft of reason. But the doctor's looks, the looks of those pale, cold, clear, blue eyes, were certainly not those of a madman. They clearly expressed menace, yes, menace, as well as irony, and above all, implacable ferocity, and their glance was like a flash of lightning, which one could never forget.

"I have seen," Monsieur de Vargnes used to say, when speaking about it, "the looks of many murderers, but in none of them have I ever observed

*Jules Grévy.

656

such a depth of crime, and of impudent security in crime."

And this impression was so strong that Monsieur de Vargnes thought he was the victim of some hallucination, especially as when he spoke about his eyes, the doctor continued with a smile, and in his most childish accents:

"Of course, Monsieur, you cannot understand what I am saying to you, and I must beg your pardon for it. To-morrow you will receive a letter which will explain it all to you, but, first of all, it was necessary that I should let you have a good, a careful look at my eyes, my eyes, which are myself, my only and true self, as you will see."

With these words, and with a polite bow, the doctor went out, leaving Monsieur de Vargnes extremely surprised, and a prey to doubt. He said to himself: "Is he merely a madman? The fierce expression and the criminal depths of his looks are perhaps caused merely by the extraordinary contrast between his fierce looks and his pale eyes."

And absorbed in these thoughts, Monsieur de Vargnes unfortunately allowed several minutes to elapse. Then he thought to himself suddenly:

"No, I am not the sport of any hallucination, and this is no case of an optical phenomenon. This man is evidently some terrible criminal, and I have altogether failed in my duty in not arresting him myself at once, illegally, even at the risk of my life."

The judge ran downstairs in pursuit of the doctor, but it was too late; he had disappeared. In the afternoon, he called on Madame de Frogère, to ask her whether she could tell him anything about the matter. She, however, did not know the negro doctor in the least, and was even able to assure him that he was a fictitious personage, for, as she was well acquainted with the upper classes in Haïti, she knew that the Academy of Medicine at Port-au-Prince had no doctor of that name among its members. As Monsieur de Vargnes persisted, and gave descriptions of the doctor, especially mentioning his extraordinary eyes Madame de Frogère began to laugh, and said:

"You have certainly had to do with a hoaxer, my dear Monsieur. The eyes which you have described are certainly those of a white man, and the individual must have been painted."

On thinking it over, Monsieur de Vargnes remembered that the doctor had nothing of the negro about him but his black skin, his woolly hair and beard, and his way of speaking, which was easily imitated. He had not the characteristic, undulating walk. Perhaps, after all, he was only a practical joker, and during the whole day, Monsieur de Vargnes took refuge in that view, which rather wounded his dignity as a man of consequence, but appeased his scruples as a magistrate.

The next day, he received the promised letter, which was written, as well as addressed, in characters cut out of the newspapers. It was as follows:

"MONSIEUR:

"Doctor James Ferdinand does not exist, but the man whose eyes you saw does, and you will certainly recognize his eyes. This man has committed two crimes, for which he does not feel any remorse, but, as he is a psychologist, he is afraid of some day yielding to the irresistible temptation of confessing his crimes. You know better than anyone (and that is your most powerful aid), with what imperious force criminals, especially intellectual ones, feel this temptation. That great poet, Edgar Allan Poe, has written masterpieces on this subject, which express the truth exactly, but he has omitted to mention the last phenomenon, which I will tell you. Yes, I, a criminal, feel a terrible wish for somebody to know of my crimes, and when this requirement is satisfied, when my secret has been revealed to a confidant, I shall be tranquil for the future, and be freed from this demon of perversity, which only tempts us once. Well! Now that is accomplished. You shall have my secret: from the day that you recognize me by my eyes, you will try and find out what I am guilty of, and how I was guilty, and you will discover it, being a master of your profession, which, by-the-bye, has procured you the honor of having been chosen by me to bear the weight of this secret, which now is shared by us, and by us two alone. I say, advisedly, *by us two alone.* You could not, as a matter of fact, prove the reality of this secret to anyone, unless I were to confess it, and I defy you to obtain my public confession, as I have confessed it to you, *and without danger to myself."*

Three months later, Monsieur de Vargnes met Monsieur X —— at an evening party, and at first sight, and without the slightest hesitation, he recognized in him those very pale, very cold, and very clear blue eyes, eyes which it was impossible to forget.

The man himself remained perfectly impassive, so that Monsieur de Vargnes was forced to say to himself:

"Probably I am the sport of an hallucination at this moment, or else there are two pairs of eyes that are perfectly similar, in the world. And what eyes! Can it be possible?"

The magistrate instituted inquiries

into his life, and he discovered this, which removed all his doubts.

Five years previously, Monsieur X—— had been a very poor but very brilliant medical student, who although he never took his doctor's degree, had already made himself remarkable by his microbiological researches.

A young and very rich widow had fallen in love with him and married him. She had one child by her first marriage, and in the space of six months, first the child and then the mother died of typhoid fever. Thus Monsieur X—— had inherited a large fortune, in due form, and without any possible dispute. Everybody said that he had attended to the two patients with the utmost devotion. Now, were these two deaths the two crimes mentioned in his letter?

But then, Monsieur X—— must have poisoned his two victims with the microbes of typhoid fever, which he had skillfully cultivated in them, so as to make the disease incurable, even by the most devoted care and attention. Why not?

"Do you really believe it?" I asked Monsieur de Vargnes.

"Absolutely," he replied. "And the most terrible thing about it is that the villain is right when he defies me to force him to confess his crime publicly, for I see no means of obtaining a confession, none whatever. For a moment I thought of magnetism, but who could magnetize that man with those pale, cold, bright eyes? With such eyes, he would force the magnetizer to denounce himself as the culprit."

And then he said, with a deep sigh:

"Ah! Formerly there was something good about justice!"

When he saw my inquiring looks, he added in a firm and perfectly convinced voice:

"Formerly, justice had torture at its command."

"Upon my word," I replied, with all an author's unconscious and simple egotism, "it is quite certain that without the torture, this strange tale will have no conclusion, and that is very unfortunate, so far as regards the story I intended to make out of it."

An Artifice

THE old doctor and his young patient were talking by the side of the fire. There was nothing really the matter with her, except that she had one of those little feminine ailments from which pretty women frequently suffer—slight *anaemia,* nervous attack, and a suspicion of fatigue, probably of that fatigue from which newly-married people often suffer at the end of the first month of their married life, when they have made a love match.

She was lying on the couch and talking, "No, doctor," she said; "I shall never be able to understand a woman deceiving her husband. Even allowing that she does not love him, that she pays no heed to her vows and promises, how can she give herself to another man? How can she conceal the intrigue from other people's eyes? How can it be possible to love amid lies and treason?"

The doctor smiled, and replied: "It is perfectly easy, and I can assure you that a woman does not think of all those little subtle details, when she has made up her mind to go astray. I even feel certain that no woman is ripe for true love until she has passed through all the promiscuousness and all the irksome-ness of married life, which, according to an illustrious man, is nothing but an exchange of ill-tempered words by day and perfunctory caresses at night. Nothing is more true, for no woman can love passionately until after she has married.

"As for dissimulation, all women have plenty of it on hand on such occasions. The simplest of them are wonderful tacticians, and extricate themselves from the greatest dilemmas in an extraordinary way."

The young woman, however, seemed incredulous. "No, doctor," she said; "one never thinks, until after it has happened, of what one ought to have done in a dangerous affair, and women are certainly more liable than men to lose their head on such occasions."

The doctor raised his hands: "After it has happened, you say! Now I will tell you something that happened to one of my female patients, whom I always considered an immaculate woman.

"It happened in a provincial town. One night when I was sleeping profoundly, in that deep, first sleep from which it is so difficult to rouse yourself, it seemed to me in my dreams as if the bells in the town were sounding a fire alarm and I woke up with a start. It was my own bell which was ringing wildly, and as my footman did not seem to be answering the door, I in turn pulled the bell at the head of my bed. Soon I heard banging and steps in the silent house, and then Jean came into my room and handed me a letter which said: 'Madame Lelièvre begs Dr. Siméon to come to her immediately.'

"I thought for a few moments, and then I said to myself: 'A nervous attack, vapors, nonsense; I am too tired.' And so I replied: 'As Doctor Siméon is not at all well, he must beg Madame Lelièvre to be kind enough to call in his colleague, Monsieur Bonnet.'

"I put the note into an envelope, and went to sleep again, but about half an hour later, the street bell rang again, and Jean came to me and said: 'There is somebody downstairs—I do not quite know whether it is a man or a woman, as the individual is so wrapped up—who wishes to speak to you immediately. He says it is a matter of life and death for two people. Whereupon, I sat up in bed and told him to show the person in.

"A kind of black phantom appeared, who raised her veil as soon as Jean had left the room. It was Madame Bertha Lelièvre, quite a young woman, who had been married for three years to a large shopkeeper in the town, and was said to have been the prettiest girl in the neighborhood.

"She was terribly pale, her face was contracted like the faces of mad people are, occasionally, and her hands trembled violently. Twice she tried to speak without being able to utter a sound, but at last she stammered out:

" 'Come — quick — quick, doctor— Come—my—my lover has just died in my bedroom.' She stopped, half suffocated with emotion, and then went on: 'My husband will—be coming home from the club very soon.'

"I jumped out of bed, without even considering that I was only in my nightshirt, and dressed myself in a few moments. Then I said: 'Did you come a short time ago?'

" 'No,' she said, standing like a statue petrified with horror. 'It was my servant—she knows.' And then, after a short silence, she went on: 'I was there —by his side.' And she uttered a sort of cry of horror, and after a fit of choking, which made her gasp, she wept violently, shaking with spasmodic sobs for a minute or two. Then her tears suddenly ceased, as if dried by an internal fire, and with an air of tragic calmness, she said: 'Let us make haste.'

"I was ready, but I exclaimed: 'I quite forgot to order my carriage.'

" 'I have one,' she said; 'it is his, which was waiting for him!' She wrapped herself up, so as to completely conceal her face, and we started.

"When she was by my side in the darkness of the carriage, she suddenly seized my hand, and crushing it in her delicate fingers she said, with a shaking voice, that proceeded from a distracted heart: 'Oh! If you only knew, if you only knew what I am suffering! I loved him, I have loved him distractedly, like a mad woman, for the last six months.'

" 'Is anyone up in your house?' I asked.

" 'No, nobody except Rose, who knows everything.'

"We stopped at the door. Evidently everybody was asleep, and we went in without making any noise, by means of her latchkey, and walked upstairs on tiptoe. The frightened servant was sitting on the top of the stairs, with a lighted candle by her side, as she was afraid to stop by the dead man. I went into the room, which was turned upside down, as if there had been a struggle in it. The bed, which was tumbled and open, seemed to be waiting for somebody; one of the sheets was thrown on to the floor, and wet napkins, with which they had bathed the young man's temples, were lying by the side of a wash-hand basin and a glass, while a strong smell of vinegar pervaded the room.

"The dead man's body was lying at full length in the middle of the room, and I went up to it, looked at it, and touched it. I opened the eyes, and felt the hands, and then, turning to the two women, who were shaking as if they were frozen, I said to them: 'Help me to lift him on to the bed.' When we had laid him gently on to it, I listened to his heart, put a looking-glass to his lips, and then said: 'It is all over; let us make haste and dress him.' It was a terrible sight!

"I took his limbs one by one, as if they had belonged to some enormous doll, and held them out to the clothes which the women brought, and they put on his socks, drawers, trousers, waistcoat, and lastly the coat; but it was a difficult matter to get the arms into the sleeves.

"When it came to buttoning his boots, the two women kneeled down, while I held the light. As his feet were rather swollen, it was very difficult, and as they could not find a button hook, they had to use their hairpins. When the terrible toilette was over, I looked at our work and said: 'You ought to arrange his hair a little.' The girl went and brought her mistress's large-toothed comb and brush, but as she was trembling, and pulling out his long, tangled hair in doing it, Madame Lelièvre took the comb out of her hand, and arranged his hair as if she were caressing him. She parted it, brushed his beard, rolled his mustaches gently round her fingers, as she had no doubt been in the habit of doing, in the familiarities of their intrigue.

"Suddenly, however, letting go of his hair, she took her dead lover's inert head in her hands, and looked for a long time in despair at the dead face, which no longer could smile at her. Then, throwing herself on to him, she took him into her arms and kissed him ardently. Her kisses fell like blows on to his closed mouth and eyes, on to his forehead and temples, and then, putting her lips to his ear, as if he could still hear her, and as if she were about to whisper something to him, to make their embraces still more ardent, she said several times, in a heartrending voice: 'Adieu, my darling!'

"Just then the clock struck twelve, and I started up. 'Twelve o'clock!' I exclaimed. 'That is the time when the club closes. Come, Madame, we have not a moment to lose!'

"She started up, and I said: 'We must carry him into the drawing-room.' When we had done this, I placed him on a sofa, and lit the chandeliers, and just then the front door was opened and shut noisily. The husband had come back, and I said: 'Rose, bring me the basin and the towels, and make the room look tidy. Make haste, for heaven's sake! Monsieur Lelièvre is coming in.

"I heard his steps on the stairs, and then his hands feeling along the walls. 'Come here, my dear fellow,' I said; 'we have had an accident.'

"And the astonished husband appeared in the door with a cigar in his mouth, and said: 'What is the matter? What is the meaning of this?'

" 'My dear friend,' I said, going up to him; 'you find us in great embarrassment. I had remained late, chatting with your wife and our friend, who had brought me in his carriage, when he suddenly fainted, and in spite of all we have done, he has remained unconscious for two hours. I did not like to call in strangers, and if you will now help me downstairs with him, I shall be able to attend to him better at his own house.'

"The husband, who was surprised, but quite unsuspicious, took off his hat. Then he took his rival, who would be quite inoffensive for the future, under the arms. I got between his two legs, as if I had been a horse between the shafts, and we went downstairs, while his wife lighted us. When we got outside, I held the body up, so as to deceive the coachman, and said: 'Come,

my friend; it is nothing; you feel better already, I expect. Pluck up your courage, and make an attempt. It will soon be over.' But as I felt that he was slipping out of my hands, I gave him a slap on the shoulder, which sent him forward and made him fall into the carriage; then I got in after him.

"Monsieur Lelièvre, who was rather alarmed, said to me: 'Do you think it is anything serious?' To which I replied, *No*,' with a smile, as I looked at his wife, who had put her arm into that of her legitimate husband, and was trying to see into the carriage.

"I shook hands with them, and told my coachman to start, and during the whole drive the dead man kept falling against me. When we got to his house, I said that he had become unconscious on the way home, and helped to carry him upstairs, where I certified that he was dead, and acted another comedy to his distracted family. At last I got back to bed, not without swearing at lovers."

The doctor ceased, though he was still smiling, and the young woman, who was in a very nervous state, said: "Why have you told me that terrible story."

He gave her a gallant bow, and replied:

"So that I may offer you my services, if necessary."

The Specter

In speaking of a recent lawsuit, our conversation had turned on sequestration, and each of us, thereupon, had a story to tell—a story affirmed to be true. We were a party of intimate friends, who had passed a pleasant evening, now drawing to a close, in an old family residence in the Rue de Grenelle. The aged Marquis de la Tour-Samuel, bowed 'neath the weight of eighty-two winters, at last rose, and leaning on the mantelpiece, said, in somewhat trembling tones:

"I also know something strange, so strange that it has been a haunting memory all my life. It is now fifty-six years since the incident occurred, and yet not a month has passed in which I have not seen it again in a dream, so great was and is the impression of fear it left on my mind. For ten minutes I experienced such horrible fright that, ever since, a sort of constant terror has made me tremble at unexpected noises, and objects half-seen in the gloom of night inspire me with a mad desire to take flight. In short, I am afraid of the dark!

"Ah, no! I would not have avowed that before having reached my present age! Now I can say anything. I have never receded before real danger. So at eighty-two years of age, I do not feel compelled to be brave over an imaginary danger.

"The affair upset me so completely, and caused me such lasting and mysterious uneasiness, that I never spoke of it to anyone. I will now tell it to you exactly as it happened, without any attempt at explanation.

"In July, 1827, I was in garrison at Rouen. One day, as I was walking on the quay, I met a man whom I thought I recognized, without being able to recall exactly who he was. Instinctively, I made a movement to stop; the stranger perceived it and at once extended his hand.

"He was a friend to whom I had been deeply attached as a youth. For five years I had not seen him, and he seemed to have aged half a century. His hair was quite white, and he walked with a stoop as though completely worn out. He apparently comprehended my surprise, for he told me of the misfortune which had shattered his life.

"Having fallen madly in love with a young girl he had married her, but, after a year of more than earthly happiness, she died suddenly of heart failure. He had left his château on the very day of her burial and had come to live at Rouen. There he still dwelt, more dead than alive, desperate and solitary, exhausted by grief, and so miserable that he thought constantly of suicide.

"'Now that I have found you again,' said he, 'I will ask you to render me an important service. It is to go to my old home and get for me, from the desk of my bedroom—our bedroom—some papers which I greatly need. I cannot send a servant or an agent, as discretion and absolute silence are necessary. As for myself, nothing on earth would induce me to re-enter that house. I will give you the key of the room, which I myself locked on leaving, and the key of my desk—also a note to my gardener, telling him to open the château for you. But come and breakfast with me to-morrow, and we will arrange all that.'

"I promised to do him the slight favor he asked. For that matter, it was nothing of a trip, his property being but a few miles distant from Rouen and easily reached in an hour on horseback.

"At ten o'clock the following day I

breakfasted, *tête-à-tête,* with my friend, but he scarcely spoke.

"He begged me to pardon him; the thought of the visit I was about to make to that room, the scene of his dead happiness, overwhelmed him, he said. He, indeed, seemed singularly agitated and preoccupied, as though undergoing some mysterious mental combat.

"At length he explained to me exactly what I had to do. It was very simple. I must take two packages of letters and a roll of papers from the first drawer on the right of the desk of which I had the key. He added, 'I need not beg you to refrain from glancing at them.'

"I was wounded at that remark, and told him so somewhat sharply. He stammered, 'Forgive me, I suffer so,' and tears came to his eyes.

"At about one o'clock I took leave of him to accomplish my mission.

"The weather was glorious, and I cantered over the turf, listening to the songs of the larks and the rhythmical striking of my sword against my boot. Then I entered the forest and walked my horse. Branches of the trees caressed my face as I passed, and, now and then, I caught a leaf with my teeth, from sheer gladness of heart at being alive and strong on such a radiant day.

"As I approached the château, I took from my pocket the letter I had for the gardener, and was astonished at finding it sealed. I was so irritated that I was about to turn back without having fulfilled my promise, but reflected that I should thereby display undue susceptibility. My friend's state of mind might easily have caused him to close the envelope without noticing that he did so.

"The manor seemed to have been abandoned for twenty years. The open gate was dropping from its hinges; the walks were overgrown with grass, and the flower-beds were no longer distinguishable.

"The noise I made by tapping loudly on a shutter brought an old man from out a door near by, who seemed stunned with astonishment at seeing me. On receiving my letter, he read it, reread it, turned it over and over, looked me up and down, put the paper in his pocket, and finally asked:

"'Well! what is it you wish?'

"I replied shortly: 'You ought to know, since you have just read your master's orders. I wish to enter the château.'

"He seemed overcome. 'Then you are going in—in her room?'

"I began to lose patience and said sharply: 'Of course; but is that your affair?'

"He stammered in confusion: 'No—sir—but it is because—that is, it has not been opened since—since the—death. If you will be kind enough to wait five minutes, I will go to—to see if—'

"I interrupted him, angrily: 'Look here, what do you mean with your tricks? You know very well you cannot enter the room, since I have the key!'

"He no longer objected. 'Then, sir, I will show you the way.'

"'Show me the staircase and leave me. I'll find my way without you.'

"'But—sir—indeed—'

"This time I silenced him effectually, pushed him aside, and went into the house.

"I first traversed the kitchen; then two rooms occupied by the servant and his wife; next, by a wide hall, I reached the stairs, which I mounted, and recognized the door indicated by my friend.

"I easily opened it and entered. The apartment was so dark that, at first, I could distinguish nothing. I stopped short, my nostrils penetrated by the disagreeable, moldy odor of long-unoccupied rooms. Then, as my eyes slowly became accustomed to the darkness, I saw plainly enough, a large and disordered bedroom, the bed without sheets, but still retaining its mattresses and pillows, on one of which was a deep impression, as though an elbow or a head had recently rested there.

"The chairs all seemed out of place. I noticed that a door, doubtless that of a closet, had remained half open.

"I first went to the window, which I opened to let in the light; but the fastenings of the shutters had grown so rusty that I could not move them. I even tried to break them with my sword, but without success. As I was growing irritated over my useless efforts, and could now see fairly well in the semi-obscurity, I renounced the idea of getting more light and went over to the writing-table.

"Seating myself in an armchair and letting down the lid of the desk, I opened the designated drawer. It was full to the top. I needed but three packages, which I knew how to recognize, and began searching for them.

"I was straining my eyes in the effort to read the superscriptions, when I seemed to hear, or rather feel, something rustle back of me. I paid no attention, believing that a draught from

the window was moving some drapery. But, in a minute or so, another movement, almost imperceptible, sent a strangely disagreeable little shiver over my skin. It was so stupid to be affected, even slightly, that self-respect prevented my turning around. I had then found the second packet I needed and was about to lay my hand on the third when a long and painful sigh, uttered just over my shoulder, made me bound like a madman from my seat and land several feet away. As I jumped I had turned about, my hand on the hilt of my sword, and, truly, had I not felt it at my side, I should have taken to my heels like a coward.

"A tall woman, dressed in white, stood gazing at me from the back of the chair where I had been sitting an instant before.

"Such a shudder ran through all my limbs that I nearly fell backward. No one can understand unless he has felt it, that frightful, unreasoning terror! The mind becomes vague; the heart ceases to beat; the entire body grows as limp as a sponge.

"I do not believe in ghosts, nevertheless I completely gave way to a hideous fear of the dead; and I suffered more in those few moments than in all the rest of my life, from the irresistible anguish of supernatural fright. If she had not spoken, I should have died, perhaps! But she spoke, she spoke in a sweet, sad voice, that set my nerves vibrating. I dare not say that I became master of myself and recovered my reason. No! I was so frightened that I scarcely knew what I was doing; but a certain innate pride, a remnant of soldierly instinct, made me, almost in spite of myself, maintain a creditable countenance.

"She said: 'Oh! sir, you can render me a great service.'

"I wanted to reply, but it was impossible for me to pronounce a word. Only a vague sound came from my throat.

"She continued: 'Will you? You can save me, cure me. I suffer frightfully. I suffer, oh! how I suffer!' and she slowly seated herself in the armchair, still looking at me.

" 'Will you?' she said.

"I replied 'Yes' by a nod, my voice still being paralyzed.

"Then she held out to me a tortoise-shell comb, and murmured:

" 'Comb my hair, oh! comb my hair; that will cure me; it must be combed. Look at my head—how I suffer; and my hair pulls so!'

"Her hair, unbound, very long and very black, it seemed to me, hung over the back of the chair and touched the floor.

"Why did I receive that comb with a shudder, and why did I take in my hands the long, black hair which gave to my skin a gruesomely cold sensation, as though I were handling snakes? I cannot tell.

"That sensation has remained in my fingers and I still tremble when I think of it.

"I combed her hair. I handled, I know not how, those icy locks. I twisted, knotted, and plaited, and braided them. She sighed and bowed her head, seeming to be happy. Suddenly she said: 'Thank you!' snatched the comb from my hands, and fled by the door that I had noticed ajar.

"Left alone, I experienced for several seconds the horrible agitation of one who awakens from a nightmare. At length I regained my full senses; I ran to the window, and with a mighty effort burst open the shutters, letting a flood of light into the room. Immediately I sprang to the door by which she had departed. I found it closed and immovable!

"Then a mad desire to flee came on me like a panic, the panic which soldiers know in battle. I seized the three packets of letters on the open secretary; ran from the room, dashed down the stairs, found myself outside, I know not how, and seeing my horse a few steps off, leaped into the saddle and galloped away.

"I stopped only when I reached Rouen and my lodgings. There I shut myself into my room to reflect. For an hour I anxiously strove to convince myself that I had been the victim of a hallucination. I was about ready to believe that all I had seen was a vision, an error of my senses, when, as I approached the window, my eyes fell, by chance, upon my chest. Around the buttons of my uniform were entwined a quantity of long, black hairs! One by one, with trembling fingers, I plucked them off and threw them away.

"I then called my orderly, feeling unable to see my friend that day; wishing, also, to reflect more fully upon what I ought to tell him. I had his letters carried to him, for which he gave the messenger a receipt. He asked after me most particularly, and, on being told I was ill—had had a sunstroke—appeared exceedingly anxious. Next morning I went to him, determined to tell him the truth. He had gone out the evening before and not yet returned. I called again during the day; my friend was still absent. After waiting a week longer without news of him, I advised the authorities, and a judicial search was instituted. Not the slightest trace of his whereabouts or manner of disappearance was discovered.

"A minute inspection of the abandoned château revealed nothing of a suspicious character. There was no indication that a woman had been concealed there.

"After these fruitless researches all further efforts were abandoned, and in the fifty-six years that have elapsed since then I have heard nothing more."

The Relic

"To the Abbé Louis d'Ennemare, at Soissons:

"MY DEAR ABBÉ,—

"My marriage with your cousin is broken off in the stupidest manner, on account of a foolish trick which I involuntarily played my intended, in a fit of embarrassment, and I turn to you, my old school-fellow to help me out of the difficulty. If you can, I shall be grateful to you until I die.

"You know Gilberte, or rather you think you know her, for do we ever understand women? All their opinions, their ideas, their creeds, are a surprise to us. They are all full of twists and turns, of the unforeseen, or unintelligible arguments, of defective logic, and of obstinate ideas, which seem final, but which they alter because a little bird comes and perches on the window ledge.

"I need not tell you that your cousin is very religious, as she was brought up by the *White* (or was it the *Black?*) *Ladies* at Nancy. You know that better than I do, but what you perhaps do not know is that she is just as excitable about other matters as she is about religion. She is as unstable as a leaf whirled away by the wind; and she is more of a girl than a woman, for she is moved or irritated in a moment, loves in a moment, hates in a moment, and changes in a moment. She is pretty, as you know, and more charming than I can say or you can guess.

"Well, we became engaged, and I adored her, as I adore her still, and she appeared to love me.

"One evening, I received a telegram summoning me to Cologne for a consultation, which might be followed by a serious and difficult operation. As I had to start the next morning, I went to wish Gilberte good-bye, and tell her that I should not dine with them on Wednesday, but on Friday, the day of my return. Ah! Take care of Fridays, for I assure you they are unlucky!

"When I told her that I had to go to Germany, I saw that her eyes filled with tears, but when I said I should be back very soon, she clapped her hands, and said:

" 'I am very glad you are going, then!

You must bring me back something; a mere trifle, just a souvenir, but a souvenir that you have chosen for me. You must find out what I should like best, do you hear? And then I shall see whether you have any imagination.'

"She thought for a few moments and then added:

" 'I forbid you to spend more than twenty francs on it. I want it for the intention and for the remembrance of your penetration, and not for its intrinsic value.'

"And then, after another moment's silence, she said, in a low voice, and with downcast eyes:

" 'If it costs you nothing in money, and if it is something very ingenious and pretty, I will—I will kiss you.'

"The next day, I was in Cologne. It was a case of a terrible accident, which had thrown a whole family into despair, and a difficult amputation was necessary. They put me up—I might almost say, they locked me up, and I saw nobody but people in tears, who almost deafened me with their lamentations. I operated on a man who appeared to be in a moribund state, and nearly died under my hands. I remained with him two nights, and then, when I saw that there was a chance of his recovery, I drove to the station. I had, however, made a mistake in the trains, and had an hour to wait, and so I wandered about the streets, still thinking of my poor patient, when a man accosted me. I do not know German, and he was totally ignorant of French, but at last I made out that he was offering me some reliques. I thought of Gilberte, for I knew her fanatical devotion, and here was my present ready

to hand, so I followed the man into a shop where religious objects were for sale, and I bought *a small piece of a bone of one of the Eleven Thousand Virgins*.

"The pretended relic was inclosed in a charming old silver box, and that determined my choice. Putting my purchase into my pocket, I went to the railway station, and so to Paris.

"As soon as I got home, I wished to examine my purchase again, and on taking hold of it, I found that the box was open and the relic lost! It was no good to hunt in my pocket, and to turn it inside out; the small bit of bone, which was no bigger than half a pin, had disappeared.

"You know my dear little Abbé, that my faith is not very great, but, as my friend you are magnanimous enough to put up with my coldness, to leave me alone, and wait for the future, as you say. But I absolutely disbelieve in the relics of second-hand dealers in piety, and you share my doubts in that respect. Therefore, the loss of that bit of sheep's carcass did not grieve me, and I easily procured a similar fragment, which I carefully fastened inside my casket and then I went to see my intended.

"As soon as she saw me, she ran up to me, smiling and anxious, and said to me:

" 'What have you brought?'

"I pretended to have forgotten, but she did not believe me, and I made her beg me, and beseech me, even. But when I saw that she was devoured by curiosity, I gave her the sacred silver box. She appeared overjoyed.

" 'A relic! Oh! A relic!'

"And she kissed the box passionately,

so that I was ashamed of my deception. She was not quite satisfied, however, and her uneasiness soon turned to terrible fear, and looking straight into my eyes, she said:

" 'Are you sure that it is authentic?'

" 'Absolutely certain.'

" 'How can you be so certain?'

"I was caught, for to say that I had bought it through a man in the streets would be my destruction. What was I to say? A wild idea struck me, and I said, in a low, mysterious voice:

" 'I stole it for you.'

"She looked at me with astonishment and delight in her large eyes.

" 'Oh! You stole it? Where?'

" 'In the cathedral; in the very shrine of the Eleven Thousand Virgins.'

"Her heart beat with pleasure, and she murmured:

" 'Oh! Did you really do that for me? Tell me all about it!'

"There was an end of it, and I could not go back. I made up a fanciful story, with precise details. I had given the custodian of the building a hundred francs to be allowed to go about the building by myself; the shrine was being repaired, but I happened to be there at the breakfast time of the workmen and clergy; by removing a small panel, I had been enabled to seize a small piece of bone (oh! so small), among a quantity of others (I said a quantity, as I thought of the amount that the remains of the skeletons of eleven thousand virgins must produce). Then I went to a goldsmith's and bought a casket worthy of the relic; and I was not sorry to let her know that the silver box cost me five hundred francs.

"But she did not think of that; she listened to me, trembling, in an ecstasy, and whispering: 'How I love you!' she threw herself into my arms.

"Just note this: I had committed sacrilege for her sake; I had committed a theft; I had violated a shrine; violated and stolen holy relics, and for that she adored me, thought me loving, tender, divine. Such is woman, my dear Abbé, every woman.

"For two months I was the best of lovers. In her room she had made a kind of magnificent chapel in which to keep this bit of mutton chop which, as she thought, had made me commit that love-crime, and she worked up her religious enthusiasm in front of it every morning and evening. I had asked her to keep the matter secret, for fear, as I said, that I might be arrested, condemned, and given over to Germany, and she kept her promise.

"Well, at the beginning of the summer she was seized by an irresistible wish to see the scene of my exploit, and she begged her father so persistently (without telling him her secret reason), that he took her to Cologne, but without telling me of their trip, according to his daughter's wish.

"I need not tell you that I had not seen the interior of the cathedral. I do not know where the tomb (if there be a tomb) of the Eleven Thousand Virgins is, and then, it appears that it is unapproachable, alas!

"A week afterward I received ten lines, breaking off our engagement, and then an explanatory letter from her father, whom she had, somewhat late, taken into her confidence.

"At the sight of the shrine, she had suddenly seen through my trickery and my lie, and had also found out that I was innocent of any other crime. Having asked the keeper of the relics whether any robbery had been committed, the man began to laugh, and pointed out to them how impossible such a crime was, but from the moment I had plunged my profane hand into venerable relics, I was no longer worthy of my fair-haired and delicate betrothal.

"I was forbidden the house! I begged and prayed in vain, nothing could move the fair devotee, and I grew ill from grief. Well, last week, her cousin, Madame d'Arville, who is also your relative, sent word that she should like to see me, and when I called, she told me on what conditions I might obtain my pardon, and here they are. I must bring Gilberte a relic, a real, authentic relic, certified to be such by our Holy Father, the Pope, of some virgin and martyr, and I am going mad from embarrassment and anxiety.

"I will go to Rome, if needful, but I cannot call on the Pope unexpectedly and tell him my stupid adventure; and, besides, I doubt whether they let private individuals have relics. Could not you give me an introduction to some cardinal, or only to some French prelate, who possesses some remains of a female saint? Or perhaps you may have the precious object she wants in your collection?

"Help me out of my difficulty, my dear Abbé, and I promise you that I will be converted ten years sooner than I otherwise should be!

"Madame d'Arville, who takes the matter seriously, said to me the other day:

" 'Poor Gilberte will never marry.'

"My dear old schoolfellow, will you allow your cousin to die the victim of a stupid piece of business on my part? Pray prevent her from being the eleventh thousand and one virgin.

"Pardon me, I am unworthy, but I embrace you, and love you with all my heart.

"Your old friend,
"HENRI FONTAL."

The Marquis

It was quite useless to expostulate when obstinate little Sonia, with a Russian name and Russian caprices, had said: "I choose to do it." She was so delicate and pretty, with her slightly turned-up nose and her rosy and childish cheeks. Every female perversity was reflected in the depths of her strange eyes, which were the color of the sea on a stormy evening. Yes, she was very charming, very fantastic, and above all, so Russian, so deliciously and imperiously Russian, the more so as she came from Montmartre. In spite of this, not one of the seven lovers who composed her usual court had laughed when their enslaver said one day:

"You know my feudal castle at Pludun-Herlouët, near Saint Jacut-de-la-Mer, which I bought two years ago, and in which I have not yet set foot? Very well, then! The day after to-morrow, which is the first of May, we will have a housewarming there."

The seven had not asked for any further explanation, but had accompanied little Sonia, and were now ready to sit down to dinner under her presidency in the dining-room of the old castle, which was about ten hours' distant from Paris. They had arrived there that morning; they were going to have dinner and supper together, and were to start off again at daybreak next morning; such were Sonia's orders, and nobody had made the slightest objection.

Two of her admirers, however, who were not yet used to her sudden whims, had felt some surprise. But this was quickly checked by expressions of enthusiastic pleasure on the part of the others.

"What a delightfully original idea! Nobody else would have thought of such a thing! Positively, nobody else. Oh! these Russians!" But those who had known her for some time, and who had been consequently educated not to be surprised at anything, found it all quite natural.

It was half past six in the evening, and the gentlemen were going to dress. Sonia had made up her mind to keep on her morning-gown, or if she dressed, she would do so later. Just then, she was not inclined to move out of her great rocking-chair from which she could see the sun setting over the sea. The sight always delighted her very much. It might have been taken for a large, red billiard ball, rebounding from the green cloth. How funny it was! And how lucky that she was all alone to

look at it, for those seven would not have understood it at all! Men never have any soul, have they?

The sunset was novel at first, but at length it made her sad, and Sonia's heart felt almost heavy, though the very sadness was sweet. She was congratulating herself more than ever on being alone, so as to enjoy that languor which was like a gentle dream when, in perfect harmony with that melancholy and sweet sensation, a voice rose from the road beneath the terrace, a tremulous, but fresh and pure voice, and sang the following words to a slow melody:

> "Walking in Paris,
> Having a drink,
> A friend of mine whispered;
> *What do you think?*
> *If love makes you thirsty,*
> *Then wine makes you lusty."*

The sound died away, as the singer continued on his way, and Sonia was afraid that she should not hear the rest. That would have been terrible; so she jumped out of the rocking-chair, ran to the balustrade of the terrace, and leaning over it, she called out: "Sing it again! I insist on it. The song, the whole song!"

On hearing this, the singer looked round and then came back — without hurrying, however, and as if prompted by curiosity rather than by any desire to comply with her order. Holding his hand over his eyes, he looked at Sonia attentively, and she, on her part, had plenty of time to look closely at him.

He was an old man of about sixty-five, and his rags and the wallet over his shoulder denoted a beggar, but Sonia immediately noticed that there was a certain amount of affectation in his wretchedness. His hair and beard were not matted and ragged, as is usual with beggars, and evidently he had them cut occasionally. Besides he had a fine, and even distinguished face, as Sonia said to herself. But she did not pay much attention to that, as for some time she had noticed that old men at the seaside nearly all looked like gentlemen.

When he got to the foot of the terrace the beggar stopped, wagged his head and said: "Pretty! The little woman is very pretty!" But he did not obey Sonia's order, and she repeated it, almost angrily this time, beating a violent tattoo on the stonework: "The song, the whole song!"

He did not seem to hear, but stood there gaping, with a vacant smile on his face, and as his head was inclined toward his left shoulder, a thin stream of saliva trickled from his lips on to his beard. His looks became more and more ardent. "How stupid I am!" thought Sonia suddenly. "Of course he is waiting for something." She felt in her pocket, in which she always carried some gold by way of half-pence, took out a twenty-franc piece and threw it down to the old man. He, however, did not take any notice of it, but continued looking at her ecstatically. He was only roused from his state of bliss by receiving a handful of gravel which she threw at him, right in his face.

"Do sing!" she exclaimed. "You must; I will have it; I have paid you."

Still smiling, he picked up the napoleon and threw it back on to the terrace, and then said proudly, though in a very gentle voice: "I do not ask for charity, little lady; but if it give you

pleasure, I will sing you the whole song, the whole of it, as often as you please." And he began the song again, in his tremulous voice, which was more tremulous than it had been before, as if he were much touched.

Sonia was overcome and unconsciously moved to tears; delighted because the man had spoken to her so familiarly, and rather ashamed at having treated him as a beggar. Her whole being was carried away by the slow rhythm of the melody, which related an old love story, and when he had ended he again looked at her with a smile. As she was crying he said to her:

"I daresay you have a beautiful horse, or a little dog that you are very fond of, which is ill? Take me to it, and I will cure it: I understand it thoroughly. I will do it *gratis,* because you are so pretty."

She could not help laughing:

"You must not laugh," he said. "What are you laughing at? Because I am poor? But I am not, for I had work yesterday, and again to-day. I have a bag full. See, look here!" And from his belt he drew a leather purse in which coppers rattled. He poured them out into the palm of his hand, and said merrily: "You see, little one, I have a purse. Forty-seven sous; forty-seven!"*

"So you will not take my napoleon?" Sonia said:

"Certainly not," he replied. "I do not want it; and then, I tell you again, I will not accept alms. So you do not know me?"

"No, I do not."

———

*About 47 cents.

"Very well, ask anyone in the neighborhood. Everybody will tell you that the Marquis does not live on charity."

The Marquis! At that name she suddenly remembered that two years ago she had heard his story. It was at the time that she bought the property, and the vendor had mentioned the Marquis as one of the curiosities of the soil. He was said to be half silly, at any rate an original, almost in his dotage, living by any lucky bits that he could make as horse-coper and veterinary. The peasants gave him a little work, as they feared that he might throw spells over anyone who refused to employ him. They also respected him on account of his former wealth and of his title, for he had been very rich, and really was a marquis. It was said that he had ruined himself in Paris by speculating. The reason, of course, was *women!*

At that moment the dinner bell began to ring, and a wild idea entered Sonia's head. She ran to the little door that opened on to the terrace, overtook the musician, and with a ceremonious bow she said to him: "Will you give me the pleasure and the honor of dining with me, Marquis?"

The old man left off smiling and grew serious: he put his hand to his forehead, as if to bring old recollections back, and then with a very formal, old-fashioned bow, he said: "With pleasure, my dear." And letting his wallet drop, he offered Sonia his arm.

When she introduced this new guest to them, all the seven, even to the best drilled, started. "I see what disturbs you," she said. "It is his dress. Well! It really leaves much to be desired.

But wait a moment, that can soon be arranged."

She rang for her lady's maid and whispered something to her. Then she said: "Marquis, your bath is ready in your dressing-room. If you will follow Sabina she will show you to it. These gentlemen and I will wait dinner for you." And as soon as he had gone out she said to the youngest there: "And now, Ernest, go upstairs and undress; I will allow you to dine in your morning coat, and you will give your dress coat and the rest to Sabina, for the Marquis."

Ernest was delighted at having to play a part in the piece, and the six others applauded. "Nobody else could think of such things; nobody, nobody!"

Half an hour later they were sitting at dinner, the Marquis in a dress coat on Sonia's left. It was a great disappointment for the seven. They had reckoned on having some fun with him, and especially Ernest, who being a wit, had intended to *draw him*. But at the first attempt of this sort, Sonia had given him a look which they all understood. Dinner began very ceremoniously for the seven, but merrily and without restraint between Sonia and the old man.

They cut very long faces, did the seven, but inwardly, if one may say so, for of course they could not dream of showing how put out they were. But the inward long faces grew longer still, when Sonia said to the old fellow, quite suddenly: "How stupid these gentlemen are! Suppose we leave them to themselves?"

The Marquis rose, offered her his arm again and said: "Where shall we go to?"—But Sonia's only reply was to sing the couplet of that song, which she had remembered:

"For three years I passed
The nights with my love,
On a beautiful couch
In a splendid alcove.
Though wine makes me sleepy,
Yet love keeps me frisky."

The seven, who were altogether exasperated this time, and could not conceal their vexation, saw the couple disappear through the door which led to Sonia's apartments.

"Hum!" Ernest ventured to say, "this is really rather strong!"

"Yes," the eldest of the menagerie replied. "It certainly is rather strong, but it will do! You know there is nobody like her for thinking of such things!"

The next morning, the château bell woke them up at six o'clock, the hour they had agreed on to return to Paris. The seven men asked each other whether they should go and wish Sonia good morning, as usual, before she was out of her room. Ernest hesitated more than any of them about it, and it was not until Sabina, her maid, came and told them that her mistress insisted upon it, that they could make up their minds to do so. They were surprised to find Sonia in bed by herself.

"Well!" Ernest asked boldly, "and what about the Marquis?"

"He left very early," Sonia replied.

"A queer sort of Marquis, I must say!" Ernest observed, contemptuously, and growing bolder: "Why, I should like to know?"

Sonia replied, drawing herself up. "The man has his own habits, I suppose!"

"Do you know, Madame," Sabina observed, "that he came back half an hour after he left?"

"Ah!" said Sonia, getting up and walking about the room. "He came back? What did he want, I wonder?"

"He did not say, Madame. He merely went upstairs to see you. He was dressed in his old clothes again."

Suddenly Sonia uttered a loud cry, and clapped her hands, and the seven came round to see what had caused her emotion.

"Look here! Just look here!" she cried. "Do look on the mantelpiece! It is really charming! Do look!"

And with a smiling, yet somewhat melancholy expression in her eyes, with a tender look which they could not understand, she showed them a small bunch of wild flowers, by the side of a heap of half-pennies. Mechanically she took them up and counted them, and then began to cry.

There were forty-seven of them.

A Deer Park in the Provinces

IT is not very long ago that an Hungarian Prince, who was an officer in the Austrian cavalry regiment, was quartered in a wealthy Austrian garrison town. The ladies of the local aristocracy naturally did everything they could to allure the new-comer, who was young, good-looking, animated, and amusing, into their nets, and at last one of these ripe beauties, who was now resting on her amorous laurels, after innumerable victories on the hot floors of Viennese society, succeeded in taking him in her toils. But only for a short time, for she had very nearly reached that limit in age where, on the man's side, love ceases and esteem begins. She had more sense, however, than most women, and she recognized the fact in good time. As she did not wish to give up the leading part which she played in society there so easily she reflected as to what means she could employ to bind him to her in another manner. It is well known that the notorious Madame de Pompadour, who was one of the mistresses of Louis XV. of France, when her own charms did not suffice to fetter that changeable monarch, conceived the idea of securing the chief power in the State and in society for herself, by having a pavilion in the deer park—which belonged to her, and where Louis XV. was in the habit of hunting—fitted up with every accommodation of a harem, where she brought beautiful women and girls of all ranks of life to the arms of her royal lover.

Inspired by such an historical example, the Baroness began to arrange evening parties, balls, and private theatricals in the winter, and, in the summer excursions into the country. Thus she gave the Prince, who at that time was still, so to say, at her feet, the opportunity of plucking fresh flowers. But even this clever expedient did not avail in the long run, for beautiful women were scarce in that provincial town, and the few which the local aristocracy could produce were not able to offer the Prince any fresh attraction, when he had made their closer acquaintance. At last, therefore, he turned his back on these highly-born Messalinas, and began to bestow marked attention on the pretty women and girls of the middle classes, either in the streets or when he was in his box at the theater.

There was one girl in particular, the daughter of a well-to-do merchant, who was supposed to be the most beautiful girl in the capital. On her his opera glass was constantly leveled, and he even followed her occasionally without being noticed. But this modern Pompadour soon got wind of his unprincely taste, and determined to do everything in her power to keep her lover and the whole nobility, which was also threatened, from such an unheard-of disgrace as the intrigue of a prince with a girl of the middle classes.

"It is really sad," the outraged Baroness once said to me, "that in these days princes and monarchs choose their mistresses only from the stage, or from the scum of the people. But it is the fault of our ladies themselves. They mistake their vocation! Ah! Where are those delightful times when the daughters of the first families looked upon it as an honor to become their prince's mistress?"

Consequently, the horror of the blue-blooded, aristocratic lady was intense when the Prince, in his usual, amiable, careless manner, suggested to her to people her deer park with girls of the lower orders.

"It is a ridiculous prejudice," the Prince said on that occasion, "which obliges us to shut ourselves off from the other ranks, and to confine ourselves altogether to our own circle, for monotony and boredom are the inevitable consequences of it. How many honorable men of sense and education, and especially how many charming women and girls there are, not of the aristocracy, who would infuse fresh life and a new charm into our dull, listless society! I very much wish that a lady like you would make a beginning, would give up an exclusiveness which cannot be maintained in these days, and would enrich our circle with the charming daughters of middle-class families."

A wish of the Prince's was as good as a command; so the Baroness made a wry face, but accommodated herself to circumstances, and promised to invite some of the prettiest girls of the plebes to a ball in a few days. She really issued a number of invitations, and even condescended to drive to the house of each of them in person.

"But I must ask one thing of you," she said to each of the pretty girls, "and that is to come dressed as simply as possible; washing muslins will be best. The Prince dislikes all finery and ostentation, and he would be very vexed with me if I were the cause of any extravagance on your part."

The great day arrived. It was quite an event for the little town, and all classes of society were in a state of the greatest excitement. The pretty, plebeian girls, with the one whom the Prince had first noticed at their head, appeared in all their innocence, in plain, washing dresses, according to the Prince's orders, with their hair plainly dressed, and without any ornament except their own fresh charms. They were all captives in the den of the proud, aristocratic Baroness, and the poor little mice were very much terrified when suddenly the aristocratic ladies came into the ball-room, rustling in whole oceans of silks and lace, with their haughty heads changed into so many hanging gardens of Semiramis, loaded with all the treasures of the Indies, and radiant as the sun.

At first the poor girls looked down in shame and confusion, and the Baroness's eyes glistened with all the joy of triumph. But her ill-natured pleasure did not last long, for the intrigue on which the Prince's ignoble passions were to make shipwreck recoiled on the highly-born lady patroness of the deer park.

No, the aristocratic ladies in their magnificent toilettes did not throw the girls from the middle classes into the shade. On the contrary, these pretty girls in their washing dresses, and with the plain but splendid ornament of their abundant hair, looked more charming than they would have looked in silk dresses and long trains, with flowers in their hair; and the novelty and unwontedness of their appearance there allured not only the Prince, but all the other gentlemen and officers, so that the proud granddaughters of heraldic lions, griffins, and eagles were quite neglected by the gentlemen, who danced almost exclusively with the pretty girls of the middle class.

The faded lips of the Baroness and Countesses uttered many a "For shame!" but all in vain. Neither was it any good for the Baroness to make up her mind that she would never again put a social medley before the Prince in her drawing-room, for he had seen through her intrigue, and gave her up altogether, *Sic transit gloria mundi!*

The Baroness, however, consoled herself as best she could.

An Adventure

"COME! Come!" said Pierre Dufaille, shrugging his shoulders. "Do you know what you are talking about, when you say that there are no more adventures? Say that there are no more adventurous men and you will be right! Yes, nobody takes a chance, in these days, for as soon as there is any slight mystery, or a spice of danger, they draw back. If, however, a man is willing to go into anything blindly and to run the risk of anything that may happen he can still meet with adventures. Even I, who never look for them, met with one in my life, and a very startling one. Let me tell you of it.

"I was staying in Florence, and was living very quietly. All I indulged in, in the way of adventures, was to listen occasionally to the immoral proposals with which every stranger is beset at night on the Piazza della Signora, by some worthy Pandarus or other, with a head like that of a venerable priest. These excellent fellows generally introduce you to their families, where debauchery is carried on in a very simple and almost patriarchal fashion, and where one does not run the slightest risk.

"One day as I was admiring Benvenuto Cellini's wonderful Perseus, in front of the Loggia dei Lanzi, I suddenly felt my sleeve pulled somewhat roughly. On turning round, I found myself face to face with a woman of about fifty who said to me with a strong German accent: 'You are French, Monsieur, are you not?'

" 'Certainly, I am,' I replied.

" 'And would you like to go home with a very pretty woman?'

" 'Most certainly I should," I replied, with a laugh.

"Nothing could have been funnier than the looks and serious air of the procuress, save the strangeness of the proposal, made in broad daylight, and in very bad French. It was even worse when she added: 'Do you know everything they do in Paris?'

" 'What do you mean, my good woman?' I asked her, rather startled. 'What is done in Paris that is not done everywhere else?'

"However, when she explained her meaning, I replied that I certainly did not, and as I was not quite so immodest as the lady, I blushed a little. But not for long, for almost immediately afterward I grew pale, when she said: 'I want to assure myself of it personally.' And she said this in the same phlegmatic manner, which did not seem so funny to me now, but, on the contrary, rather frightened me.

. " 'What!' I said. 'Personally! You! Explain yourself!'

"If I had been rather surprised before, I was now altogether astonished at her explanation. It was indeed an adventure — almost like a romance. I could scarcely believe my ears, but this is what she told me.

"She was the confidential attendant on a lady moving in high society, who wished to be initiated into the most secret refinements of Parisian high life, and had done me the honor of choosing me for her companion. But then, this preliminary test!

" 'By Jove!' I said to myself, 'this old German hag is not so stupid as she looks!' And I laughed in my sleeve, as I listened inattentively to what she was saying to presuade me.

" 'My mistress is the prettiest woman you can dream of; a real beauty; springtime! A flower!'

" 'You must excuse me, but if your mistress is really like springtime and a flower, you (pray excuse me for being so blunt) are not exactly that, and perhaps I should not exactly be in a mood to humor you, my dear lady, in the same way that I might her.'

"She jumped back, astonished in turn: 'Why, I only want to satisfy myself with my own eyes; not by injuring you.' And she finished her explanation, which had been incomplete before. All she had to do was to go with me to 'Mother Patata's well-known establishment, and there to be present while I conversed with one of its fair and frail inhabitants.

" 'Oh!' I said to myself, 'I was mistaken in her tastes. She is of course an old, shriveled-up woman, as I guessed,

but she is a specialist. This is interesting; upon my word! I never met with such a one before!'

"Here, gentlemen, I must beg you to allow me to hide my face for a moment. What I said was evidently not strictly correct, and I am rather ashamed of it; my excuse must be, that I was young, that Patata's was a celebrated place, of which I had heard wonderful things said, but the entry to which was barred me, on account of my small means. Five napoleons was the price! Fancy! I could not treat myself to it, and so I accepted the good lady's offer. I do not say that it was not disagreeable, but what was I to do? And then, the old woman was a German, and so her five napoleons were a slight return for our five milliards, which we paid them as our war indemnity.

"Well, Patata's boarder was charming, the old woman was not too troublesome, and your humble servant did his best to sustain the ancient glory of Frenchmen.

"Let me drink my disgrace to the dregs! On the next day but one after, I was waiting at the statue of Perseus. It was shameful, I confess, but I enjoyed the partial restitution of the five milliards, and it is surprising how a Frenchman loses his dignity when he is traveling.

"The good lady made her appearance at the appointed time. It was quite dark and I followed her without a word, for, after all, I was not very proud of the part I was playing. But if you only knew how fair that little girl at Patata's was. As I went along, I thought only of her, and did not pay any attention to where we were going. I was only roused from my reverie by hearing the old woman say: 'Here we are. Try and be as entertaining as you were the day before yesterday.'

"We were not outside Patata's house, but in a narrow street running by the side of a palace with high walls, and in front of us was a small door, which the old woman opened gently.

"For a moment I felt inclined to draw back. Apparently the old hag was also ardent on her own account! She had me in a trap! No doubt she wanted in her turn to make use of my small talents! But, no! That was impossible!

"'Go in! Go in!' she said. 'What are you afraid of? My mistress is so pretty, so pretty, much prettier than the little girl of the other day.'

"So it was really true, this story out of 'The Arabian Nights?' Why not? And after all, what was I risking? The good woman would certainly not injure me, and so I went in, though somewhat nervously.

"My friend, what an hour I spent there! Paradise! It would be useless, impossible to describe it to you. Apartments fit for a princess, and one of those princesses out of fairy tales, a fairy herself. An exquisite German woman, exquisite as German women can be, when they try. An Undine of Heinrich Heine's, with hair like the Virgin Mary's, innocent blue eyes, and a skin like strawberries and cream.

"Suddenly, however, my Undine got up, and her face convulsed with fury and pride. Then, she rushed behind some hangings, where she began to give vent to a flood of German words, which I did not understand, while I remained standing, dumfounded. But just then the old woman came in, and said, shaking with fear: 'Quick, quick; dress yourself and go, if you do not wish to be killed.'

"I asked no questions, for what was the good of trying to understand? Besides, the old woman, who grew more and more terrified, could not find any French words, and chattered wildly. I jumped up and got into my shoes and overcoat and ran down the stairs and into the street.

"Ten minutes later, I recovered my breath and my senses, without knowing what streets I had been through, nor where I had come from, and I stole furtively into my hotel, as if I had been a malefactor.

"In the *cafés* the next morning, nothing was talked of except a crime that had been committed during the night. A German Baron had killed his wife with a revolver, but had been liberated on bail, as he had appealed to his counsel, to whom he had given the following explanation, to the truth of which the lady companion of the Baroness had certified.

"She had been married to her husband almost by force; she detested him, and had some particular reasons (which were not specified) for her hatred of him. In order in have her revenge on him, she had had him seized, bound, and gagged by four hired ruffians, who had been caught, and who had confessed everything. Thus, reduced to immobility, and unable to help himself, the Baron had been obliged to witness a degrading scene, in which his wife caressed a Frenchman, and thus outraged conjugal fidelity and German honor at the same time. As soon as he was set at liberty, the Baron had punished his faithless wife, and was now seeking her accomplice."

"And what did you do?" some one asked Pierre Dufaille.

"The only thing I could do, by George!" he replied. "I put myself at the poor devil's disposal; it was his right, and so we fought a duel. Alas! It was with swords, and he ran me right through the body. That was also his right, but he exceeded his right when he called me her *ponce*. Then I gave him his change, and as I fell, I called out with all the strength that remained to me: 'A Frenchman! A Frenchman! Long live France!'"

The Bed 9

On a hot afternoon during last summer, the large auction rooms seemed asleep, and the auctioneers were knocking down the various lots in a listless manner. In a back room, on the first floor, two or three lots of old silk ecclesiastical vestments were lying in a corner.

They were copes for solemn occasions, and graceful chasubles on which embroidered flowers surrounded symbolic letters on a yellowish ground, which had originally been white. Some secondhand dealers were there, two or three men with dirty beards, and a fat woman with a big stomach, one of those women who deal in secondhand finery and manage illicit love affairs, women who are brokers in old and young human flesh, just as much as they are in new and old clothes.

Presently, a beautiful Louis XV. chasuble was put up for sale, which was as pretty as the dress of a marchioness of that period. It had retained all its colors, and was embroidered with lilies of the valley round the cross, and long blue irises, which came up to the foot of the sacred emblem, and with wreaths of roses in the corners. When I had bought it, I noticed that there was a faint scent about it, as if it were permeated with the remains of incense, or still pervaded by delicate, sweet scents of bygone years, by the memory of a perfume, the soul of an evaporated essence.

When I got home, I wished to have a small chair of the same period covered with it; and as I was handling it in order to take the necessary measures, I felt some paper beneath my fingers. When I cut the lining, some letters fell at my feet. They were yellow with age, and the faint ink was the color of rust; outside the sheets, which were folded in the fashion of years long past, it was addressed in a delicate hand "To Monsieur l'Abbé d'Argence."

The first three letters merely settled places of meeting, but here is the third:

"MY FRIEND,—I am very unwell, ill in fact, and I cannot leave my bed. The rain is beating against my windows, and I lie dreaming comfortably and warmly

uries since they were first put up?.
"Here is a young woman lying in
his bed.

"From time to time she sighs, and
hen she groans, and cries out; her
¹other is with her, and presently a little
reature that makes a noise like a cat
¹ewing, and which is all shiveled and
wrinkled, appears. It is a male child to
·hich she has given birth, and the young
¹other feels happy in spite of her pain;
¹he is nearly suffocated with joy at that
rst cry, and stretches out her arms,
¹nd those around her shed tears of
leasure. For that little morsel of hu·
¹anity which has come from her means
·erpetuation of the blood, of the heart,
¹nd of the soul of the old people, who
·re looking on, trembling with excite-
¹ent.

"And then, here are two lovers, who
¹r the first time are together in that
·bernacle of life. They tremble; but
·ansported with delight, they have the
·licious sensation of being close to·
·ther, and by degrees their lips meet.
¹hat divine kiss makes them one, that
·ss which is the gate of a terrestrial
·aven, that kiss which speaks of hu·
·an delights, which continually prom-
·s them, announces them, and pre-
·des them. And their bed is agitated
·e the tempestuous sea, it bends and
·urmurs, and itself seems to become
·imated and joyous, for the maddening
·ystery of love is being accomplished
· it. What is there sweeter, what more
·rfect in this world than those em-
·aces which make one single being out
· two, and which give to both of them
· the same moment the same thought,
·· same expectation, and the same
·ddening pleasure, a joy which de-

scends upon them like a celestial and
devouring fire?

"Do you remember those lines from
some old poet, which you read to me
last year? I should like to have them
embroidered on the top of my bed,
where Pyramus and Thisbe are continu
ally looking at me out of their tapes
tried eyes.

"And think of death, my friend, o
all those who have breathed out thei
last sigh to God in this bed. For it i
also the tomb of hopes ended, the doo
which closes everything, after havin
been the entrance to the world. Wha
cries, what anguish, what sufferings
what groans; how many arms stretche
out toward the past; what appeals t
a happiness that has vanished foreve
what convulsions, what death-rattle
what gaping lips and distorted eye
have there not been in this bed fro
which I am writing to you, during th
three centuries that it has sheltered h
man beings!

———

Under

As he was a man of quiet and regul
habits, of a simple and affectionate d
position, and had nothing to disturb t
even tenor of his life, Monsieur
Loubancourt suffered from widow
hood more than most men do. He
gretted his lost happiness, was ang
with the fate which separated a unit
couple so brutally, the fate which b
pitched upon a tranquil existence, wh
sleepy quietude had not been troubled

under my eider-down coverlet. I have a book of which I am very fond, and which seems as if it really applied to me. Shall I tell you what it is? No, for you would only scold me. Then, when I have read a little, I think, and will tell you what about.

"Having been in bed for three days, I think about my bed, and even in my sleep I meditate on it still. I have come to the conclusion that the bed comprehends our whole life; for we were born in it, we live in it, and we shall die in it. If, therefore, I had Monsieur de Crébillon's pen, I should write the history of a bed, and what exciting and terrible, as well as delightful and moving, occurrences would not such a book contain! What lessons and what subjects for moralizing could one not draw from it, for everyone?

"You know my bed, my friend, but you will never guess how many things I have discovered in it within the last three days, and how much more I love it, in consequence. It seems to me to be inhabited, haunted, if I may say so, by a number of people I never thought of who, nevertheless, have left something of themselves in that couch.

"Ah! I cannot understand people who buy new beds, beds to which no memories or cares are attached. Mine, ours, which is so shabby, and so spacious, must have held many existences in it, from birth to the grave. Think of that, my friend; think of it all; review all those lives, a great part of which was spent between these four posts, surrounded by these hangings embroidered by human figures, which have seen so many things. What have they seen during the three cen-

"The bed, you must remember. is the symbol of life; I have discovered this within the last three days. There is nothing good except the bed, and are not some of our best moments spent in sleep?

"But then, again, we suffer in bed! It is the refuge of those who are ill and suffering; a place of repose and comfort for worn-out bodies, in one word, a part and parcel of humanity.

"Many other thoughts have struck me, but I have no time to note them down for you, and then, should I remember them all? Besides that I am so tired that I mean to shake up my pillows, stretch myself out at full length, and sleep a little. But be sure and come to see me at three o'clock to-morrow; perhaps I may be better, and able to prove it to you.

"Good-bye, my friend; here are my hands for you to kiss, and I also offer you my lips."

---

the Yoke

any cares or chimeras, in order to rob it of happiness.

Had he been younger, he might, perhaps, have been tempted to form a new line, to fill up the vacant place, and to marry again. But when a man is nearly sixty such ideas make people laugh, for they have something ridiculous and insane about them. So he dragged on his dull and weary existence, shunned all those familiar objects which constantly recalled the past to him and flitted from hotel to hotel without taking interest in anything, or becoming intimate with anyone, even temporarily; inconsolable, silent, enigmatic, and funereal in his eternal black clothes.

He was generally alone—though on rare occasions he was accompanied by his only son who used to yawn by stealth, and seemed to be mentally counting the hours as if he were performing some hateful, enforced duty in spite of himself.

Two years of this crystallization slipped by and one was as monotonous and as void of incident as the other.

One evening, however, in a boarding-house at Cannes, where he was staying on his wanderings, a young woman dressed in mourning, a new arrival, sat next to him at dinner. She had a sad, pale face that told of suffering, a beautiful figure, and large, blue eyes with deep rings round them, which, nevertheless, were like stars in the twilight.

All remarked her and although Loubancourt usually took no notice of women, no matter who they were, ugly or pretty, he looked at her and listened to her. He felt less lonely by her side, though he did not know why. He trembled with instinctive and confused happiness, just as if in some distant country he had found some female friend or relative, who at last would understand him, tell him some news, and talk to him in his dear native language about everything that a man leaves behind him when he exiles himself from home.

What strange affinity had thus thrown them together? What secret forces had brought their grief in contact? What made him so sanquine and so calm, and incited him to take her suddenly into his confidence, and urged him on to resistless curiosity?

She was an experienced traveler, who had no illusions, and was in search of adventure; one of those women who frequently change their name, and who, as they have made up their mind to swindle if luck is not on their side, play the continuous rôle of adventuress; one who could put on every accent; who for the sake of her purse could transform herself into a Slav, or into an American, or simply into a provincial; who was ready to take part in any comedy in order to make money, and not be obliged to waste strength and brains on fruitless struggles or on wretched expedients. Thus she immediately guessed the state of this melancholy sexagenarian's mind, and the illusion which attracted him to her. She scented the spoils which offered themselves to her without struggle, and divined under what guise she could make herself accepted and loved.

She initiated him into depths of griefs which were unknown to him, by phrases which were cut short by sighs, by fragments of her story, which she finished by a disgusted shrug of the shoulders and a heartrending smile, and by insensibly exciting his feelings. In a word, she triumphed over the last remaining doubts which might still have mingled with the affectionate pity with which that poor, solitary heart, so full of bitterness, overflowed.

And so, for the first time since he had become a widower, the old man confided in another person, poured out his old heart into the soul which seemed to be so like his own, which seemed to offer him a haven of cheer where the wounds of his heart could be healed. He longed to throw himself into those sisterly arms, to dry his tears, and to still his grief there.

*   *   *   *   *   *

Monsieur de Loubancourt, who had married at twenty-five, as much from love as from judgment, had lived quietly and peacefully in the country, rarely visiting Paris. He was ignorant of female wiles and of the temptations offered by creatures like Wanda Pulska, who are made up of lies, and only care for pleasure, a virgin soil on which any evil will grow.

She attached herself to him, became his shadow, and by degrees, part of his life. She showed herself to be a charitable woman who devoted herself to an unhappy man, endeavored to console him, and in spite of her youth was willing to be his inseparable companion in his slow, daily walks. She never appeared to tire of his anecdotes and reminiscences, and she played cards with him. She waited on him carefully when he was confined to his bed, appeared to have no sex, in fact, transformed herself; and though she handled him skillfully, she seemed ingenuous and ignorant of evil. She acted like an innocent young girl, who has just been confirmed; but for all that, she chose dangerous hours and certain spots in which to be sentimental and to ask questions which agitated and disconcerted him, abandoning her slender fingers to his feverish hands, which pressed and held them in a tender clasp.

And then, there were wild declarations of love, prayers and sobs which frightened her; wild adieus, which were not followed by his departure, but which brought about a touching reconciliation and the first kiss; and then, one night, while they were traveling together, he opened the door of her bedroom at the hotel, which she had not locked, and came in like a madman. There was the phantom of resistance, and the fallacious submission of a woman who was overcome by so much tenderness, who rebelled no longer, but who accepted the yoke of her master and lover. And then, the conquest of the body after the conquest of the heart, while she forged his chains link by link, with pleasures which besot and corrupt old men, and dry up their brains, until at last he allowed himself to be induced, almost unconsciously, to make an odious and stupid will.

Informed, perhaps, by anonymous letters, or astonished because his father kept him altogether at a distance from him and gave no signs of life, Monsieur de Loubancourt's son joined them in Provence. But Wanda Pulska, who had been preparing for that attack for a long time, waited for it fearlessly.

She did not seem discomposed at that sudden visit, but was very charming and affable toward the newcomer, reassured him by the careless airs of a girl, who took life as it came, who was suffering from the consequences of a fault, and did not trouble her head about the future.

He envied his father and grudged him such a treasure. Although he had come to combat her dangerous influence, and to treat the woman who had assumed the place made vacant by death

—who governed her lover as his sovereign mistress—as an enemy, he shrank from his task, panted with desire, lost his head, and thought of nothing but treason and of an odious partnership.

She managed him even more easily than she had managed Monsieur de Loubancourt, molded him just as she chose, made him her tool, without even giving him the tips of her fingers, or granting him the slightest favor, induced him to be so imprudent that the old man grew jealous, watched them, discovered the intrigue, and found mad letters in which his son stormed, begged, threatened, and implored.

One evening, when she knew that her lover had come in, and was hiding in a dark cupboard in order to watch them, Wanda happened to be alone in the drawing-room, which was full of light and of beautiful flowers, with this young fellow of five-and-twenty. He threw himself at her feet and declared his love, and besought her to run away with him. When she tried to bring him to reason and repulsed him, and told him in a loud and distinct voice how she loved Monsieur de Loubancourt, he seized her wrists with brutal violence, and, maddened with passion, stammered out words of love and lust.

"Let me go," she cried, "let me go immediately. You are a brute to take advantage of a woman like that. Please let me go, or I shall call the servants to my assistance."

The next moment the old man, terrible in his rage, rushed out of his hiding place with clenched fists and a slobbering mouth, threw himself on the startled son, and pointing to the door with a superb gesture, said:

"You are a dirty scoundrel, sir. Get out of my house immediately, and never let me see you again!"

*   *   *   *   *   *

The comedy was over. Grateful for such fidelity and real affection, Monsieur de Loubancourt married Wanda Pulska, whose name appeared on the civil register—a detail of no importance to a man who was in love—as Frida Krubstein; she came from Saxony, and had been a servant at an inn. Then he disinherited his son, as far as he could.*

And now that she is a respectable and respected widow, Madame de Loubancourt is received everywhere by society in those places of winter resort where people's antecedents are rarely gone into, and where women of noble name, who are pretty and can waltz—like the Germans can—are always well received.

*According to French law, nobody can altogether disinherit a child, and no son or daughter can be "cut off" with the proverbial "shilling."

A Fashionable Woman

It can easily be proved that Austria is far richer in talented men, in every domain, than North Germany, but while men are systematically drilled there for the vocation which they choose, just as Prussian soldiers are, with us they lack the necessary training, especially technical training, and consequently very few of them get beyond mere dilettantism. Leo Wolfram was one of these intellectual dilettantes, and the more pleasure one took in his materials and characters, which were usually taken boldly from real life, and woven into a certain political, and what is still more, a plastic plot, the more one was obliged to regret that Wolfram had never learned to compose or to mold his characters or to write—in one word, that he had never become a literary artist. But how greatly he had in himself the materials for a master of narration, his "Dissolving Views," and still more his "Goldkind,"* prove.

"Goldkind" is a striking type of our modern society, and contains all the elements of a classic novel, although of course in a crude, unfinished state. What an exact reflection of our social circumstances Leo Wolfram gave in that story will be shown by our present reminiscences, in which a lady of that race plays the principal part.

Some ten years ago, four very stylishly dressed persons used to dine every day in a corner of the small dining-room of one of the best hotels in Vienna, and both there and elsewhere gave occasion for a great amount of talk. They were an Austrian landowner, his charming wife, and two young diplomatists, one of whom came from the North, while the other was a pure son of the South. There was no doubt that the lady came in for the greatest share of the general interest in every respect.

The practiced observer and discerner of human nature easily recognized in her one of those characters which Goethe has so aptly named "problematical." She was one of those individuals who are always dissatisfied and at variance with themselves and with the world, who are a riddle to themselves, and can never be relied on. With the interesting and captivating, though unfortunate contradictions of her nature, she made a strong impression on everybody, as well as by her mere outward appearance. She was one of those women who are called beautiful, without their being really so. Her face, as well as her figure, lacked æsthetic lines, but there was no doubt, that, in spite of that, or perhaps on that very account, she was the most dangerously fascinating woman that one could imagine.

She was tall and thin, and there was a certain hardness about her figure which became a charm through the vivacity and grace of her movements. Her features harmonized with her figure, for she had a high, clever, cold forehead, a strong mouth with sensual lips, and an angular, sharp chin, the effect of which, however, was diminished by her small slightly turned-up nose, her beautifully arched eye-brows, and her large, animated, swimming blue eyes.

In her face, which was almost too full of expression for a woman, there was as much feeling, kindness, and candor as there was calculation, coolness, and deceit, and when she was angry and curled her upper lip, so as to show her dazzlingly white teeth, it had a devilish look of wickedness and cruelty. At

---

*Golden Child.

that time, when women still wore their own hair, the beauty of her long, chestnut plaits, which she coiled on the top of her head like a crown, was very striking. Besides this, she was remarkable for her elegant and tasteful dresses, and for a bearing which blended with the dignity of a lady of rank, that indefinable something which makes actresses and women who belong to the higher classes of the *demi-monde* so interesting to us.

In Paris she would have been taken for a *demi-mondaine,* but in Vienna the best drawing-rooms were open to her, and she was not looked upon as more respectable or less respectable than any other aristocratic beauties.

Her husband belonged to that class of men whom the witty Balzac so delightfully calls *les hommes prédestinés* in his "Physiologie du Mariage." Without doubt, he was a very good-looking man, but he bore that stamp of insignificance which often conceals coarseness and vulgarity, and was one of those men who, in the long run, become unendurable to a woman of refined tastes. He had a good private income, but his wife understood the art of enjoying life, and so a deficit in the yearly accounts of the young couple became the rule, without causing the lively lady to check her noble passions in the least on that account. She kept horses and carriages, rode with the greatest boldness, had her box at the opera, and gave beautiful little suppers, which at that time was the fad among Viennese women of her class.

One of the two young diplomats who accompanied her, a young Count, belonging to a well-known family in North

Germany, a perfect gentleman in the highest sense of the word, was looked upon as her adorer, while the other, the Count's most intimate friend, in spite of his ancient name and his position as *attaché* to a foreign legation, gave people a distinct impression that he was an adventurer of the sort the police watch closely. He had the reputation of being an unscrupulous and dangerous duelist. Short, thin, with a yellow complexion, with strongly-marked but engaging features, an aquiline nose, and bright, dark eyes, he was the typical picture of a man who seduces women and kills men.

The lady appeared to be in love with the Count and to take an interest in his friend. At least, that was the construction that the others in the dining-room put upon the situation, so far as it could be made out from the behavior and looks of the people concerned,—especially from their looks, for it was strange how devotedly and ardently the beautiful woman's blue eyes would rest on the Count, and with what wild, diabolical intensity she would gaze at the Italian from time to time. It was hard to guess whether there was more love or more hatred in that glance. None of the four, however, who were then dining and chatting so gaily together, had any presentiment that they were amusing themselves over a mine, which might explode at any moment, and bury them all.

It was the husband who provided the tinder. One day he told her that she must make up her mind to the most rigid retrenchment, must give up her box at the opera and sell her carriage and horses, if she did not wish to risk her whole position in society. His creditors had lost all patience, and were threatening to distrain on his property, and even to put him in prison. She made no reply to this revelation, but during dinner she said to the Count, in a whisper, that she must speak to him later, and would, therefore, come to see him at his house. When it was dark she came thickly veiled and after she had responded to his demonstrations of affection for some time, with more patience than amiableness, she began (their conversation is extracted from his diary):

"You are so unconcerned and happy, while misery and disgrace are threatening me!"

"Please explain what you mean!"

"I have incurred some debts."

"Again?" he said reproachfully; then he added: "Why do you not come to me at once, for you must do it in the end, and then at least you would avoid any exposure?"

"Please do not take me to task," she replied; "you know it only makes me angry. I want some money; can you give me some?"

"How much do you want?"

She hesitated, for she had not the courage to name the real amount, but at last she said, in a low voice:

"Five thousand florins.*"

It was evidently only a small portion of what she really required, so he replied:

"I am sure you want more than that!"

"No."

"Really not?"

"Do not make me angry."

He shrugged his shoulders, went to his strong box, and gave her the money,

whereupon she nodded, and giving him her hand, she said: "You are always kind, and as long as I have you, I am not afraid; but if I were to lose you, I should be the most unhappy woman in the world."

"You always have the same fears; but I shall never leave you; it would be impossible for me to separate from you," the Count exclaimed.

"And if you die?" she interrupted him hastily.

"If I die?" the Count said with a peculiar smile. "I have provided for you in that eventuality also."

"Do you mean to say," she stammered, flushing, and her large, lovely eyes rested on her lover with an indescribable expression in them. He, however, opened a drawer in his writing-table and took out a document, which he gave her. It was his will. She opened it with almost indecent haste, and when she saw the amount—thirty thousand florins—she grew pale to her very lips.

That moment the germs of a crime were sown in her breast, but one of those crimes which cannot be touched by the Criminal Code. A few days after she paid her visit to the Count, she herself received one from the Italian. In the course of conversation he took a jewel case out of his breast pocket, asked her opinion of the ornaments, as she was well known for her taste in such matters, and told her at the same time that it was intended as a present for an actress, with whom he was on intimate terms.

"It is a magnificent set!" she said, as

---

*About $2500, nominally.

she looked at it. "You have made an excellent selection." Then she suddenly became absorbed in thought, while her nostrils began to quiver, and that touch of cold cruelty played on her lips.

"Do you think that the lady for whom this ornament is intended will be pleased with it?" asked the Italian.

"Certainly," she replied; "I myself would give a great deal to have it."

"Then may I venture to offer it to you?" the Italian said.

She blushed, but did not refuse it. The same evening she rushed into her lover's room in a state of the greatest excitement.

"I am beside myself," she stammered; "I have been most deeply insulted."

"By whom?" the Count asked, excitedly.

"By your friend, who has dared to send me some jewelry to-day. I suppose he looks upon me as a lost woman; perhaps I am already looked upon as belonging to the *demi-monde,* and this I owe to you, to you alone, and to my mad love for you, to which I have sacrificed my honor and everything — everything!"

She threw herself down and sobbed, and would not be pacified until the Count gave her his word of honor that he would set aside every consideration for his friend, and obtain satisfaction for her at any price. He met the Italian the same evening at a card party and questioned him.

"I did not, in the first place, send the lady the jewelry, but gave it to her myself — not, however, until she had asked me to do so."

"That is a shameful lie!" the Count shouted, furiously. Unfortunately, there were others present, and his friend took the matter seriously, so the next morning he sent his seconds to the Count.

Some of their real friends tried to settle the matter in another way, but his bad angel, his mistress, who required thirty thousand florins, drove the Count to his death. He was found in the Prater with his friend's bullet in his chest. A letter in his pocket spoke of suicide, but the police did not doubt for a moment that a duel had taken place. Suspicion soon fell on the Italian, but when they went to arrest him, he had already made his escape.

The husband of the beautiful, problematical woman called on the dead man's broken-hearted father, who had hastened to Vienna on receipt of a telegraphic message, a few hours after his arrival, and demanded the money.

"My wife was your son's most intimate friend," he stammered, in embarrassment, in order to justify his action as well as he could.

"Oh! I know that," the old Count replied, "and female friends of that kind want to be paid immediately, and in full. Here are the thirty thousand florins."

And our "Goldkind?" She paid her debts, and then withdrew from the scene for a while. She had been compromised, certainly—but then, she had risen in value in the eyes of those numerous men who can only adore and sacrifice themselves for a woman when her foot is on the threshold of vice and crime.

I saw her last during the Franco-German war, in the beautiful Mirabellgarden at Salzberg. She did not seem to feel any qualms of conscience, for she had become considerably stouter, which made her more attractive, more beautiful, and consequently, more dangerous, than before.

Words of Love

"SUNDAY,———

"YOU do not write to me, I never see you, you never come, so I must suppose that you have ceased to love me. But why? What have I done? Pray tell me, my own dear love. I love you so much, so dearly! I should like always to have you near me, to kiss you all day while I call you every tender name that I could think of. I adore you, I adore you, I adore you, my beautiful cock. Your affectionate hen.

"SOPHIE."

"MONDAY,———

"MY DEAR FRIEND:

"You will understand absolutely nothing of what I am going to say to you, but that does not matter, and if my letter happens to be read by another woman, it may be profitable to her.

"Hod you been deaf and dumb, I should no doubt have loved you for a very long time, and the cause of what has happened is that you can talk; that is all.

"In love, you see, dreams are always made to sing, but in order that they may do so, they must not be interrupted, and when one talks between two kisses, one always interrupts that frenzied dream which our souls indulge in, that is, unless they utter sublime words; and sublime words do not come out of the little mouths of pretty girls.

"You do not understand me at all, do you? So much the better; I will go on. You are certainly one of the most charming and adorable women I have ever seen.

"Are there any eyes on earth that contain more dreams than yours, more unknown promises, greater depths of love? I do not think so. And when that mouth of yours, with its curved lips, smiles and shows the ivory gates within, one is tempted to say that from this ravishing mouth comes ineffable music, something inexpressibly delicate, a sweetness which extorts sighs.

"It is then that you speak to me, and that is what troubles me, don't you see, troubles me more than tongue can tell. I would prefer never to see you at all.

"You go on pretending not to understand anything, do you not? But I calculated on that.

"Do you remember the first time you came to see me at my residence? How gaily you stepped inside, an odor of violets, which clung to your skirts, heralding your entrance; how we looked at each other, for ever so long, without uttering a word, after which we embraced like two fools. Then from that time to the end we never exchanged a word. .

"But when we separated, did not our trembling hands and our eyes say many things, things which cannot be expressed in any language. At least, I thought so; and when you went away, you murmured:

" 'We shall meet again soon!'

"That was all you said, and you will never guess what delightful dreams you left me, all that I, as it were, caught a glimpse of, all that I fancied I could guess in your thoughts.

"You see, my poor child, for men who are not stupid, who are rather refined and somewhat superior, love is such a complicated instrument that the merest trifle puts it out of order. You women never perceive the ridiculous side of certain things when you love, and you fail to see the grotesqueness of some expressions.

"Why does a word which sounds quite right in the mouth of a small, dark woman seem quite wrong and funny in the mouth of a fat, light-haired woman? Why are the wheedling ways of the one altogether out of place in the other?

"Why is it that certain caresses which are delightful from the one should be wearisome from the other? Why? Because in everything, and especially in love, perfect harmony—absolute agreement in motion, voice, words, and in demonstrations of tenderness, is necessary in the person who moves, speaks, and manifests affection; harmony is necessary in age, in height, in the color of the hair, and in the style of beauty.

"If a woman of thirty-five, who has arrived at the age of violent tempestuous passion, were to preserve the slightest traces of the caressing archness of her love affairs at twenty, were not to understand that she ought to express herself differently, look at her lover differently and kiss him differently, were not to see that she ought to be a Dido and not a Juliette, she would infallibly disgust nine lovers out of ten, even if they could not account to themselves for their estrangement. Do you understand me? No? I hoped so.

"From the time that you gave rein to your tenderness, it was all over for me, my dear friend. Sometimes we would embrace for five minutes, in one interminable kiss, one of those kisses which makes lovers close their eyes, lest part of it should escape through their clouded soul which it is ravaging. And then, when our lips separated, you would say to me:

" 'That was nice, you fat old dog.'

"At such moments, I could have beaten you; for you gave me successively all the names of animals and vegetables which you doubtless found in some cookery book, or gardener's manual. But that is nothing.

"The caresses of love are brutal, bestial, and if one comes to think of it, grotesque! Oh! My poor child, what joking elf, what perverse sprite could have prompted the concluding words of your letter to me? I have made a collection of them, but out of love for you, I will not show them to you.

"And sometimes you really said things which were quite inopportune. For instance you managed now and then to let out an exalted *I love you!* on such singular occasions that I was obliged to restrain a strong desire to laugh. There are times when the words *I love you!* are so out of place that they become indecorous; let me tell you that.

"But you do not understand me, and many other women also will not understand me, but think me stupid, though that matters very little to me. Hungry men eat like gluttons, but people of refinement are disgusted at it and often feel an invincible dislike for a dish, on account of a mere trifle. It is the same with love, as with cookery.

"What I cannot comprehend for example is that certain women who fully understand the irresistible attraction of fine, embroidered stockings, the exquisite charm of shades, the witchery of valuable lace concealed in the depths of their underclothing, the exciting zest of hidden luxury, and all the subtle delicacies of female elegance, never understands the invincible disgust with which words that are out of place or foolishly tender, inspire us.

"At times coarse and brutal expressions work wonders, as they excite the senses and make the heart beat, and they are allowable at the hours of combat. Is not that sentence of Cambronne's sublime?*

"Nothing shocks us that comes at the right time; but then, we must also know when to hold our tongue, and to avoid phrases à la Paul de Kock, at certain moments.

"And I embrace you passionately, on the condition that you say nothing.

"RENÉ."

---

*At Waterloo, General Cambronne is reported to have said, when called on to surrender: "The Guard dies, but does not surrender." But according to Victor Hugo, in "Les Misérables," he used the expression *"Merde!"* which cannot be put into English fit for ears polite.

The Upstart

You know good-natured, stout Dupontel, who looks like the type of a happy man, with fat cheeks the color of ripe apples, a small, reddish mustache, turned up over his thick lips, prominent eyes, which never know any emotion or sorrow, and remind one of the calm eyes of cows and oxen, and a long back fixed on to two wriggling crooked legs, which have obtained for him the nickname of "corkscrew" from some nymph of the ballet.

Dupontel, who had taken the trouble to be born, but not like the grand seigneurs whom Beaumarchais made fun of once upon a time, was ballasted with a respectable number of millions, as be-

fitted the sole heir of a house that had sold household utensils and appliances for over a century.

Naturally, like every other upstart who respects himself, he wished to appear to be something, to be known as a clubman, and to play to the gallery, because he had been educated at Vaugirard and knew a little English, had gone through his voluntary service in the army for twelve months* at Rouen;

---

*Although, in France, as in Germany, military service is compulsory, men are allowed to serve in both countries as *one-year volunteers;* they enjoy certain privileges, find their own uniform, etc., which entails, of course, considerable expense.

was a tolerable singer, could drive four-in-hand, and play lawn-tennis.

Always studiously well-dressed, correct in every way, he copied his way of from the three or four snobs who set the fashion, reproduced other people's witticisms, learned anecdotes and jokes by heart, like a lesson, to use them again at small parties, constantly laughed, without knowing why his friends burst into roars of merriment, and was in the habit of keeping pretty girls for the pleasure of his best friends. Of course, he was a perfect fool, but after all, was a capital fellow, to whom it was only right to extend a good deal of indulgence.

When he had taken his thirty-first mistress, and had made the discovery that in love money does not create happiness two-thirds of the time, that they had all deceived him, and made him perfectly ridiculous at the end of a week, Charles Dupontel made up his mind to settle down as a respectable married man, and to marry not from calculation or from reason, but for love.

One autumn afternoon, at Auteuil, he noticed in front of the club stand among a number of pretty women who were standing round the braziers, a girl with such a lovely, delicate complexion that it looked like apple blossoms. Her hair was like threads of gold, and she was so slight and supple that she reminded him of those outlines of saints which one sees in old stained glass church windows. There was also something enigmatical about her, for she had the delightfully ingenuous look of a school-girl during the holidays, combined with the *savoir faire* of some enlightened young lady, who already knows the how

and the why of everything, who is exuberant with youth and life, and who is eagerly waiting for the moment when her marriage will at length allow her to say and to do everything that comes into her head to amuse herself to satiety.

Then she had such small feet that they would have gone into a woman's hand, a waist that could have been clasped by a bracelet, turned-up eyelashes, which fluttered like the wings of a butterfly, an impudent and saucy nose, and a vague mocking smile that made folds in her lips, like the petals of a rose.

Her father was a member of the Jockey Club. He was generally "cleaned," as they call it, in great races, but managed by his coolness and wit to keep himself afloat. He belonged to a race which could prove that his ancestors had been at the Court of Charlemagne, and not as musicians or cooks, as some people declared.

Her youth and beauty, and her father's pedigree, dazzled Dupontel, upset his brain, and altogether turned him upside down. The combination seemed to him to be a mirage of happiness and of pride of family.

He got introduced to her father at the end of a game of a *baccarat*, invited him to shoot with him, and a month later, as if it were an affair to be hurried over, he asked for and obtained the hand of Mademoiselle Thérèse de Montsaigne. Then he felt as happy as a miner who has discovered a vein of precious metal.

The young woman did not require more than twenty-four hours to discover that her husband was nothing but a ridiculous puppet, and immediately set about to consider how she might best escape from her cage, and befool the poor fellow, who loved her with all his heart.

She deceived him without the least pity or the slightest scruple; she did it as from instinctive hatred, as if it were necessary for her not only to make him ridiculous, but also to forget that she ought to sacrifice her virgin dreams to him, to belong to him, and to submit to his hateful caresses without being able to repel him.

She was cruel, like all women are when they do not love, and delighted in doing audacious and absurd things, in visiting everything, and in braving danger. She seemed like a young colt intoxicated with the sun, the air, and its liberty, which gallops wildly across the meadows, jumps hedges and ditches, kicks, and whinnies joyously, and rolls about in the long, sweet grass.

But Dupontel remained quite imperturbable; he had not the slightest suspicion, and was the first to laugh when anybody told him some good story of a husband who had been cuckolded, although his wife repelled him, quarreled with him, and constantly pretended to be out of sorts or tired out, in order to escape from him. She seemed to take a malicious pleasure in checkmating him by her personal remarks, her disenchanting answers, and her apparent listlessness.

They saw a great deal of company, and he called himself Du Pontel now, even entertaining thoughts of buying a title from the Pope. He only read certain newspapers, kept up a regular correspondence with the Orléans Princes, was thinking of starting a racing stable, and finished up by believing that he really was a fashionable man. He strutted about and was puffed out with conceit, having probably never read La Fontaine's fable of the ass that is laden with relics which people salute, and takes the bow himself.

Suddenly, however, anonymous letters disturbed his quietude, and tore the bandage from his eyes.

At first he tore them up without reading them, and shrugged his shoulders disdainfully; but he received so many of them, and the writers seemed so determined to dot his i's and cross his t's and to clear his brain for him, that the unhappy man began to grow disturbed, and to watch and to ferret about. He instituted minute inquiries, and arrived at the conclusion that he no longer had the right to make fun of other husbands—that he was the perfect counterpart of *Sganarelle*.*

Furious at having been duped, he set a whole private inquiry agency to work, continually acted a part, and one evening appeared unexpectedly with a commissary of police in the snug little bachelor's quarters which concealed his wife's escapades.

Thérèse, pale with terror and terribly frightened, at her wits' end at being thus surprised in all the disorder of her lover's apartments, hid herself behind the bed curtains, while he, who was an officer of dragoons, very much vexed at being mixed up in such a pinchbeck

*The *Cocu Imaginaire* (The Imaginary Cuckold), in Molière's play of that name.

scandal, and at being caught in a silk shirt by men who were so correctly dressed in frock coats, frowned angrily, and had to restrain himself from throwing his victim out of the window.

The police commissioner, who was calmly looking at this little scene with the coolness of experience, prepared to verify the fact that they were caught *in flagrante delictu,* and in an ironical voice said to the husband, who had claimed his services:

"I must ask for you name in full, Monsieur?"

"Charles Joseph Edward Dupontel," was the answer. And as the commissary was writing it down from his dictation, he added suddenly: "Du Pontel in two words, if you please, Monsieur le Commissionnaire!"

Happiness

THE sky was blue, with light clouds that looked like swans slowly sailing on the waters of a lake, and the atmosphere was so warm, so saturated with the subtle odors of the mimosas, that Madame de Viellemont ordered coffee to be served on the terrace which overlooked the sea.

As the steam rose from the delicate china cups, one felt an almost inexpressible pleasure in watching the sails as they gradually disappeared in the mysterious distance. The almost motionless sea had the sheen of jewels and attracted the eyes like the looks of a dreamy woman.

Monsieur de Pardeillac, who had just arrived from Paris, fresh from the remembrance of the last election there, from that carnival of variegated posters which for weeks had imparted the strange aspect of an Oriental bazaar to the whole city, had just been relating the victory of "The General," and went on to say that those who had thought that the game was lost were beginning to hope again.

After listening to him, old Count de Lancolme, who had spent his whole life in rummaging libraries, and who had certainly annotated more manuscripts than any Benedictine friar, shook his bald head and exclaimed in his shrill, rather mocking voice:

"Will you allow me to tell you a very old story, which came into my head while you were speaking, my dear friend? I read it formerly in an old Italian city, though I forget at this moment where.

"It happened in the fifteenth century, which is far removed from our epoch, but you shall judge for yourselves whether it might not have happened yesterday.

"Since the day, when mad with rage and rebellion, the town had made a bonfire of the Ducal palace, and had ignominiously expelled the patrician who had been their *podestat** as if he had been some vicious scoundrel, had thrust his lovely daughter into a con-

---

*A Venetian or Genoese magistrate.

vent and had forced his sons, who might have claimed their parental heritage and have again imposed the abhorred yoke upon them, into a monastery, the town had never known any prosperous times. One after another, the shops closed, and money became as scarce as if some invasion of barbarian hordes had emptied the State Treasury and stolen the last gold coin.

"The poor people were in abject misery, and in vain held out their hands to passers-by under the church porches and in the squares. Only the watchmen disturbed the silence of the starlit nights, by the monotonous and melancholy call which announced the flight of the hours as they passed.

"There were no more serenades; no longer did viol and flute trouble the slumbers of the lover's choice; no longer were amorous arms thrown round women's supple waists, or bottles of red wine put to cool in the fountains under the trees. There were no more love adventures, to the rhythm of laughter and of kisses; nothing but heavy, monotonous weariness, and anxiety as to what the next day might bring forth, and ceaseless, unbridled ambitions and lusts.

"The palaces were deserted, one by one, as if the plague were raging, and the nobility had fled to Florence and to Rome. In the beginning, the common people, artisans and shopkeepers, had installed themselves in power, as in a conquered city, had seized posts of honor and well-paid offices, and had sacked the Treasury with their greedy and eager hands. After them came the middle classes, and these solemn upstarts and hypocrites, like leather bottles blown out with wind, acting like tyrants and lying without the least shame, disowned their former promises, and would soon have given the finishing stroke to the unfortunate city, which was already on its last legs.

"Discontent was increasing, and the *sbirri** could scarcely find time to tear the seditious placards, posted up by unknown hands, from the walls.

"But now that the old *podestat* had died in exile, worn out with grief, and his children, brought up under monastic rule, were accustomed to nothing but prayer, and thought only of their own salvation, there was nobody to take his place.

"And so these kinglets profited by the occasion to strut about at their ease like nobles, to stuff themselves with luxurious meals, to increase their property by degrees, to put everything up for sale, and to get rid of those who, later on, would have called for accountings, and have nailed them to the pillory by their ears.

"Their arrogance knew no bounds, and when they were questioned about their acts, they only replied by menaces or raillery. This state of affairs lasted for twenty years, when, as war was imminent with Lucca, the Council raised troops and enrolled mercenaries. Several battles were fought, in which the enemy was beaten and was obliged to flee, abandoning their colors, their arms, prisoners, and all the booty in their camp.

"The man who led the soldiers to victory, whom they had acclaimed as a triumphant and laurel-crowned Caesar

*Italian police officers.

around their camp-fires, was a poor *condottiere*,* who possessed nothing in the world except his clothes, his buff jerkin, and his heavy sword.

"They called him 'Hercules,' on account of his strong muscles, his imposing build, and his large head, and also 'Malavista' because in battle he had no pity, no weakness, but seemed, with his great murderous arms, as if he had the long reach of death itself. He had neither title-deeds, fortune, nor relatives, for he had been born one night in the tent of a female camp follower. For a long time, an old broken drum had been his cradle, and he had grown up without knowing those maternal kisses and endearments that warm the heart, or the pleasure of sleeping on a soft bed, or of eating decent beef. He had known what it was to tighten his sword belt when luck had turned—like a weathercock when the wind shifts, and sometimes would gladly have given his share of the next booty for a mouldy crust of bread and a glass of water.

"He was a simple and brave man, whose heart was as virgin as some shore on which no human has ever yet left its imprint.

"The Chiefs of the Council were imprudent enough to summon Hercules Malavista within the walls of the town, and to celebrate his arrival with almost imperial splendor—more, however, to deceive the people and to regain their waning popularity by means of a ceremony copied from pagan Rome, than to honor and recompense the services of a soldier whom they despised at the bottom of their hearts.

"The bells rang a full peal, and the archbishop and clergy and choir boys went to meet the Captain, singing psalms and hymns of joy, as if it were Easter. The streets and squares were strewn with branches of box, roses, and marjoram, while the meanest homes were decorated with flags and hung with drapery and rich stuffs.

"The conqueror came in through Trajan's gate, bare-headed, and with the symbolical golden laurel wreath on his head. Sitting on his horse, which was as black as a starless night, he appeared even taller, more vigorous and more masculine than he really was. He had a joyous and tranquil smile on his lips, and a hidden fire burning in his eyes. His soldiers bore flags and the trophies that he had gained before him, and behind him there was a noise of clashing partisans and crossbows, and of loud voices shouting *vivats* in his honor.

"In this fashion, he traversed all the quarters of the town, and even the suburbs. The women thought him handsome and proud, blew kisses to him, and held up their children so that they might see him, and he might touch them. The men cheered him, and looked at him with emotion, and many of them reflected and dreamed about this bright, unknown man, who appeared to be surrounded by a halo of glory.

"The members of the Council began to perceive the extent of the almost irreparable fault they had committed. They did not know what to do in order to ward off the danger by which they were menaced, and to rid

*An Italian mercenary or free-lance, in the Middle Ages.

themselves of a guest who was quite ready to become their master. They saw clearly that their hours were numbered, that they were approaching the fatal period at which rioting becomes imminent, and leaders are carried away like pieces of straw in a swift current.

"Hercules could not show himself in public without being received with shouts of acclamation and noisy greetings, and deputations from the nobility, as well as from the people, came repeatedly and told him that he had only to make a sign and to say a word, for his name to be in every mouth, and for his authority to be accepted. They begged him on their knees to accept the supreme authority, as though he would be conferring a favor on them, but the free-lance did not seem to understand them, and repelled their offers with the superb indifference of a soldier who has nothing to do with the people or a crown.

"At length, however, his resistance grew weaker; he felt the intoxication of power and grew accustomed to the idea of holding the lives of thousands in his hands, of having a palace, arsenals full of arms, chests full of gold, ships which he could send on adventurous cruises wherever he pleased, of governing that city, with all its houses and all its churches, and of being a leading figure at all grand functions in the cathedral.

"The shopkeepers and merchants were overcome by terror at the idea, and bowed before th shadow of the sword, which might sweep them all away and upset their false weights and scales. So they assembled secretly in a monastery of the Carmelite friars out-

side the gates of the city and a short time afterward the weaver Marconelli and the money changer Rippone brought Giaconda, who was one of the most beautiful courtesans in Venice, who knew every secret in the Art of Love, and whose kisses were a foretaste of Paradise, back with them from that city. She soon managed to touch the soldier with her delicate, fair skin, to make him inhale its bewitching odor in close embrace, to dazzle him with her large, dark eyes, in which the reflection of stars seemed to shine, and when he had once tasted that feast of love, and drunk the heavy wine of kisses, when he had clasped that pink and white body in his arms, and had listened to a voice which sounded as soft as music and promised him eternities of joy and eternities of pleasures, Hercules lost his head, and forgot his dreams and his oaths.

"Why lose precious hours in conspiring, in deluding himself with chimeras; why risk his life when he loved and was loved—when the minutes were all too short to detach his lips from those of the woman he loved?

"And so he did whatever Giaconda demanded.

"They fled from the city, without even telling the sentinels who were on guard before his palace. They went far, far away as they could not find any retreat that was sufficiently unknown and hidden. At last they stopped at a small quiet fishing village, where there were gardens full of lemon trees, where the deserted beach looked as if it were covered with gold, and where the sea was a deep blue until it was lost in the distance. And while the Captain and the courtesan loved each other and wore themselves out with pleasure—with the enchantment of the sea close to them—the irritated citizens whom he had left were clamoring for their idol, were indignant at his desertion, and tore up the paving stones in the streets to hurl at the man who had betrayed their confidence and worship.

"So they pulled his statue down from its pedestal, amid spiteful songs and jokes, and the members of the Council breathed again, no longer afraid of Malavista's great sword."

Christmas Eve

THE Christmas-eve supper!* Oh! no, I shall never go in for that again!" Stout Henri Templier said that in a furious voice, as if some one had proposed some crime to him, while the others laughed and said:

"What are you flying into a rage about?"

"Because a Christmas-eve supper played me the dirtiest trick in the world, and ever since I have felt an insurmountable horror for that night of imbecile gaiety."

"Tell us about it."

"You want to know what it was? Very well then, just listen.

"You remember how cold it was two years ago at Christmas; cold enough to kill poor people in the streets. The Seine was covered with ice; the pavements froze one's feet through the soles of one's boots, and the whole world seemed to be at the point of congealing.

"I had a big piece of work on, and refused every invitation to supper, as I preferred to spend the night at my writing table. I dined alone and then began to work. But about ten o'clock I grew restless at the thought of the gay and busy life all over Paris, at the noise in the streets which reached me in spite of everything, at my neighbors' preparations for supper, which I heard through the walls. I hardly new any longer what I was doing; I wrote nonsense, and at last I came to the conclusion that I had better give up all hope of producing any good work that night.

"I walked up and down my room; I sat down and got up again. I was certainly under the mysterious influence of the enjoyment outside, and I resigned myself to it. So I rang for my servant, and said to her:

"'Angela, go and get a good supper for two; some oysters, a cold partridge, some crayfish, ham, and some cakes. Put out two bottles of champagne, lay the cloth and go to bed.'

"She obeyed in some surprise, and when all was ready, I put on my greatcoat and went out. The great question remained: 'Whom was I going to bring in to supper?' My female friends had

*A great institution in France, and especially in Paris, at which black puddings are an indispensable dish.

all been invited elsewhere, and if I had wished to have one, I ought to have seen about it beforehand. So I thought that I would do a good action at the same time, and said to myself:

" 'Paris is full of poor and pretty girls who will have nothing on the table to-night, and who are on the lookout for some generous fellow. I will act the part of Providence to one of them this evening; and I will find one if I have to go to every pleasure resort and I will hunt till I find one to my choice. So I started off on my search.

"I certainly found many poor girls who were on the lookout for some adventure, but they were ugly enough to give a man a fit of indigestion, or thin enough to freeze in their tracks if they stopped, and you all know that I have a weakness for stout women. The more flesh they have, the better I like them, and a female colossus would be my ideal.

"Suddenly, opposite the 'Théâtre des Variétés,' I saw a figure to my liking. I trembled with pleasure, and said:

" 'By jove! What a fine girl!'

"It only remained for me to see her face, for a woman's face is the dessert.

"I hastened on, overtook her, and turned round suddenly under a gas lamp. She was charming, quite young, dark, with large, black eyes, and I immediately made my proposition which she accepted without any hesitation, and a quarter of an hour later we were sitting at supper in my lodgings. 'Oh! how comfortable it is here,' she said as she came in, and looked about her with evident satisfaction at having found a supper and a bed on that bitter night.

She was superb; so beautiful that she astonished me, and so stout that she fairly captivated me.

"She took off her cloak and hat, sat down and began to eat; but she seemed in low spirits, and sometimes her pale face twitched as if she were suffering from hidden sorrow.

" 'Have you anything troubling you!' I asked her.

" 'Bah! Don't let us think of troubles!'

"And she began to drink. She emptied her champagne glass at a draught, filled it again, and emptied it again, without stopping, and soon a little color came into her cheeks and she began to laugh.

"I adored her already, kissed her continually, and discovered that she was neither stupid, nor common, nor coarse as ordinary street-walkers are. I asked her for some details about her life, but she replied:

" 'My little fellow, that is no business of yours!' Alas! an hour later!

"At last it was time to retire, and while I was clearing the table, which had been laid in front of the fire, she undressed herself quickly, and got in. My neighbors were making a terrible din, singing and laughing like lunatics, and so I said to myself:

" 'I was quite right to go out and bring in this girl; I should never have been able to do any work.'

"At this moment, however, a deep groan made me look around, and I said:

" 'What is the matter with you, my dear?'

"She did not reply, but continued to utter painful sighs, as if she were suffering horribly, and I continued:

" 'Do you feel ill?' And suddenly she uttered a cry, a heartrending cry, and I rushed up to the bed, with a candle in my hand.

"Her face was distorted with pain, and she was wringing her hands, panting and uttering long, deep groans, which sounded like a rattle in the throat, and were painful to hear. I asked her in consternation:

" 'What is the matter with you? Do tell me what is the matter.'

" 'Oh! the pain! the pain!' she said. I pulled up the bedclothes, and I saw, my friends, that she was in labor.

"Then I lost my head, and ran and knocked at the wall with my fists, shouting: 'Help! help!'

"My door was opened almost immediately, and a crowd of people came in, men in evening clothes, women in full dress, harlequins, Turks, musketeers, and the inroad startled me so, that I could not explain myself, while they who had thought that some accident had happened or that a crime had been committed, could not understand what was the matter. At last, however, I managed to say:

" 'This—this—woman—is being confined.'

"Then they looked at her, and gave their opinion. A frair, especially, declared that he knew all about it, and wished to assist nature, but as they were all as drunk as pigs I was afraid that they would kill her. So I rushed downstairs without my hat, to fetch an old doctor, who lived in the next street. When I came back with him, the whole house was up; the gas on the stairs had been relighted, the lodgers from every floor were in my room, while four boatmen were finishing my champagne and cray-fish.

"As soon as they saw me they raised a loud shout. A milkmaid presented me with a horrible little wrinkled specimen of humanity, that was mewing like a cat, and said to me:

" 'It is a girl.'

"The doctor examined the woman, declared that she was in a dangerous state, as the event had occurred immediately after supper, and took his leave, saying he would immediately send a sick nurse and a wet nurse. An hour later, the two women came, bringing all that was requisite with them.

"I spent the night in my armchair, too distracted to be able to think of the consequences, and almost as soon as it was light the doctor came again. He found his patient very ill, and said to me:

" 'Your wife, Monsieur—'

" 'She is not my wife,' I interrupted him.

" 'Very well then, your mistress; it does not matter to me.'

"He told me what must be done for her, what her diet must be, and then wrote a prescription.

"What was I to do? Could I send the poor creature to the hospital? I should have been looked upon as a brute in the house and in all the neighborhood. So I kept her in my rooms, and she had my bed for six weeks.

"I sent the child to some peasants at Poissy to be taken care of, and she still costs me fifty francs* a month, for as I had paid at first, I shall be

_____

*$10.

obliged to go on paying as long as I live. Later on, she will believe that I am her father. But to crown my misfortunes, when the girl had recovered, I found that she was in love with me, madly in love with me, the baggage!"

"Well?"

"Well, she had grown as thin as a homeless cat, and I turned the skeleton out of doors. But she watches for me in the streets, hides herself, so that she may see me pass, stops me in the evening when I go out, in order to kiss my hand, and, in fact, worries me enough to drive me mad. That is why I never keep Christmas eve now."

The Awakening

DURING the three years that she had been married, she had not left the Val de Ciré, where her husband possessed two cotton-mills. She led a quiet life, and, although without children, she was quite happy in her house among the trees, which the work-people called the "château."

Although Monsieur Vasseur was considerably older than she was, he was very kind. She loved him, and no guilty thought had ever entered her mind.

Her mother came and spent every summer at Ciré, and then returned to Paris for the winter, as soon as the leaves began to fall.

Jeanne coughed a little every autumn, for the narrow valley through which the river wound was very foggy for five months in the year. First of all, slight mists hung over the meadows, making all the low-lying ground look like a large pond, out of which the roofs of the houses rose. Then a white vapor, which rose like a tide, enveloped everything, turning the valley into a phantom land, through which men moved like ghosts, without recognizing each other ten yards off, and the trees,

wreathed in mist and dripping with moisture, rose up through it.

But the people who went along the neighboring hills, and looked down upon the deep, white depression of the valley, saw the two huge chimneys of Monsieur Vasseur's factories rising above the mist below. Day and night they vomited forth two long trails of black smoke, the sole indication that people were living in the hollow, which looked as if it were filled with a cloud of cotton.

That year, when October came, the medical men advised the young woman to go and spend the winter in Paris with her mother, as the air of the valley was dangerous for her weak chest, and she went. For a month or so, she thought continually of the house which she had left, the home to which she seemed rooted, the well-known furniture and quiet ways of which she loved so much. But by degrees she grew accustomed to her new life, and got to like entertainments, dinner and evening parties, and balls.

Till then she had retained her girlish

manners, had been undecided and rather sluggish, walked languidly, and had a tired smile, but now she became animated and merry, and was always ready for pleasure. Men paid her marked attentions, and she was amused at their talk and made fun of their gallantries, as she felt sure that she could resist them, for she was rather disgusted with love from what she had learned of it in marriage.

The idea of giving up her body to the coarse caresses of such bearded creatures made her laugh with pity and shudder a little with ignorance.

She asked herself how women could consent to degrading contacts with strangers, the more so as they were already obliged to endure them with their legitimate husbands. She would have loved her husband much more if they had lived together like two friends, and had restricted themselves to chaste kisses, which are the caresses of the soul.

But she was much amused by their compliments, by the desire which showed itself in their eyes, a desire she did not share, by declarations of love whispered into her ear as they were returning to the drawing-room after some grand dinner, by words murmured so low that she almost had to guess them, words which left her blood quite cool, and her heart untouched, while gratifying her unconscious coquetry, kindling a flame of pleasure within her, making her lips open, her eyes grow bright, and her woman's heart, to which homage was due, quiver with delight.

She was fond of those *tête-à-têtes* in the dusk, when a man grows pressing,

hesitates, trembles and falls on his knees. It was a delicious and new pleasure to her to know that they felt a passion which left her quite unmoved, able to say *no* by a shake of the head and by pursing her lips, able to withdraw her hands, to get up and calmly ring for lights, and to see the man who had been trembling at her feet get up, confused and furious when he heard the footman coming.

She often uttered a hard laugh, which froze the most burning words, and said harsh things, which fell like a jet of icy water on the most ardent protestations, while the intonations of her voice were enough to make any man who really loved her kill himself. There were two especially who made obstinate love to her, although they did not at all resemble one another.

One of them, Paul Péronel, was a tall man of the world, gallant and enterprising, a man who was accustomed to successful love affairs, one who knew how to wait, and when to seize his opportunity.

The other, Monsieur d'Avancelle, quivered when he came near her, scarcely ventured to express his love, but followed her like a shadow, and gave utterance to his hopeless desire by distracted looks, and the assiduity of his attentions to her. She made him a kind of servant and treated him as if he had been her slave.

She would have been much amused if anybody had told her that she would love him, and yet she did love him, after a singular fashion. As she saw him continually, she had grown accustomed to his voice, to his gestures, and to his manner, just as one grows accustomed to those with whom one meets continually. Often his face haunted her in her dreams, and she saw him as he really was; gentle, delicate in all his actions, humble, but passionately in love. She would awake full of these dreams. fancying that she still heard him and felt him near her, until one night (most likely she was feverish) she saw herself alone with him in a small wood, where they were both sitting on the grass. He was saying charming things to her, while he pressed and kissed her hands. She could feel the warmth of his skin and of his breath and she was stroking his hair in a very natural manner.

We are quite different in our dreams to what we are in real life. She felt full of love for him, full of calm and deep love, and was happy in stroking his forehead and in holding him against her. Gradually he put his arms around her, kissed her eyes and her cheeks without her attempting to get away from him; their lips met, and she yielded. When she saw him again, unconscious of the agitation that he had caused her, she felt that she grew red, and while he was telling her of his love, she was continually recalling to mind their previous meeting, without being able to get rid of the recollection.

She loved him, loved him with refined tenderness, chiefly from the remembrance of her dream, although she dreaded the accomplishment of the desires which had arisen in her mind.

At last he perceived it, and then she told him everything, even to the dread of his kisses, and she made him swear that he would respect her, and he did so. They spent long hours of transcendental

love together, during which their souls alone embraced, and when they separated, they were enervated, weak, and feverish.

Sometimes their lips met, and with closed eyes they reveled in that long, yet chaste caress. She felt, however, that he could not resist much longer, and as she did not wish to yield, she wrote and told her husband that she wanted to come to him, and to return to her tranquil, solitary life. But in reply, he wrote her a very kind letter, and strongly advised her not to return in the middle of the winter, and so expose herself to the sudden change of climate, and to the icy mists of the valley, and she was thunderstruck and angry with that confiding man, who did not guess, who did not understand, the struggles of her heart.

February was a warm, bright month, and although she now avoided being alone with Monsieur Avancelle, she sometimes accepted his invitation to drive round the lake in the Bois de Boulogne with him, when it was dusk.

On one of those evenings, it was so warm that it seemed as if the sap in every tree and plant were rising. Their cab was going at a walk; it was growing dusk, and they were sitting close together, holding each other's hands, and she said to herself:

"It is all over, I am lost!" for she felt her desires rising in her again, the imperious demand for that supreme embrace which she had undergone in her dream. Every moment their lips sought each other, clung together, and separated, only to meet again immediately.

He did not venture to go into the

house with her, but left her at her door, more in love with him than ever, and half fainting.

Monsieur Paul Péronel was waiting for her in the little drawing-room, without a light, and when he shook hands with her, he felt how feverish she was. He began to talk in a low, tender voice, lulling her tired mind with the charm of amorous words.

She listened to him without replying, for she was thinking of the other; she thought she was listening to the other, and thought she felt him leaning against her, in a kind of hallucination. She saw only him, and did not remember that any other man existed on earth, and when her ears trembled at those three syllables: "I love you," it was he, the other man, who uttered them, who kissed her hands, who strained her to his breast like the other had done shortly before in the cab. It was he who pressed victorious kisses on her lips, it was he whom she held in her arms and embraced, to whom she was calling, with all the longings of her heart, with all the overwrought ardor of her body.

When she awoke from her dream, she uttered a terrible cry. Paul Péronel was kneeling by her and was thanking her passionately, while he covered her disheveled hair with kisses, and she almost screamed out: "Go away! go away! go away!"

And as he did not understand what she meant, and tried to put his arm round her waist again, she writhed, as she stammered out:

"You are a wretch, and I hate you! Go away! go away!" And he got up in great surprise, took up his hat and went.

The next day she returned to Val de Ciré, and her husband, who had not expected her for some time, blamed her for her freak.

"I could not live away from you any longer," she said.

He found her altered in character and sadder than formerly, but when he said to her: "What is the matter with you? You seem unhappy. What do you want?" she replied:

"Nothing. Happiness exists only in our dreams in this world."

Avancelle came to see her the next summer, and she received him without any emotion and without regret, for she suddenly perceived that she had never loved him, except in a dream, from which Paul Péronel had brutally roused her.

But the young man, who still adored her, thought as he returned to Paris:

"Women are really very strange, complicated, and inexplicable beings."

The White Lady

FORTUNA, goddess of chance and good luck, has always been Cupid's best ally, and Arnold T., who was a lieutenant in a hussar regiment, was evidently a special favorite of both deities.

This good-looking, well-bred young

officer had been an enthusiastic admirer of the two Countesses W., mother and daughter, during a tolerably long leave of absence, which he spent with his relations in Vienna. He had admired them in the Prater, had worshipped them at the opera, but he had never had an opportunity of making their acquaintance, and when he was back at his dull quarters in Galicia, he liked to think about those two aristocratic beauties. Last summer his regiment was transferred to Bohemia, to a wildly romantic district, which has been made illustrious by a talented writer. It abounds in magnificent woods, lofty mountain-forests, and castles, and is a favorite summer resort of the neighboring aristocracy.

Who can describe his joyful surprise when he and his men were quartered in an old, weatherbeaten castle in the middle of a wood, and he learned from the house-steward who received him that the owner of the castle was the husband, and, consequently, also the father of his Viennese ideals. An hour after he had taken possession of his old-fashioned but beautifully furnished room in a side-wing of the castle, he put on his full-dress uniform, and throwing his dolman over his shoulders went to pay his respects to the Count and the ladies.

He was received with the greatest cordiality. The Count was delighted to have a companion when he went out shooting, and the ladies were no less pleased at having some one to accompany them on their walks in the forests, or on their rides, so that he felt only half on the earth and half in the seventh heaven of Mohammedan bliss. Before supper he found time to inspect the house more closely, and even to take a sketch of the large, gloomy building from a favorable point. The ancient seat of the Counts of W. was really very gloomy. The walls, which were crumbling away here and there, were covered with dark ivy; the round towers harbored jackdaws, owls, and hawks; an Æolian harp complained and sighed and wept in the wind; the stones in the castle yard were overgrown with grass; the cloisters re-echoed to every footstep; great ancestral portraits hung on the walls, coated as it were with dark, mysterious veils by the centuries which had passed over them. All this recalled to him the legends and fairy tales of his youth, and he involuntarily thought of the "Sleeping Beauty in the Wood" and of "Blue Beard," of the cruel mistress of the Kynast,* and of that aristocratic tigress of the Carpathians, who obtained the unfading charm of eternal youth by bathing in human blood.

He came in to supper, where he found himself for the first time in the company of all the members of the family, just in the frame of mind that was suitable for ghost stories, and was not a little surprised when his host told him, half smiling and half seriously, that the "White Lady" was disturbing the

*A castle, now a well-preserved ruin, in the Giant Mountains in N. Germany. The legend is that its mistress, Kunigerude, vowed to marry nobody except the Knight who should ride round the parapet of the castle, and many perished in the attempt. At last one of them succeeded in performing the feat, but he merely sternly rebuked her, and took his leave. He was accompanied by his wife, disguised as his page, according to some versions of the legend.

castle again, and that she had latterly been seen very often.

"Yes, indeed," Countess Ida exclaimed, "you must take care, Baron, for she haunts the very wing where your room is."

The hussar was just in the frame of mind to take the matter seriously, but, on the other hand, when he saw the dark, ardent eyes of the Countess, and then the merry blue eyes of her daughter, fixed on him, any real fear of ghosts was quite out of the question with him. For Baron T. feared nothing in this world, but he possessed a very lively imagination, which could conjure up threatening forms from another world so plainly that sometimes he felt very uncomfortable at his own fancies. But on the present occasion the malicious apparition had no power over him; the ladies took care of that, for both of them were beautiful and amiable.

The Countess was a mature Venus of thirty-six, of middle height, with bright eyes, thick dark hair, beautiful white teeth, and with the voluptuous figure of a true Viennese, while her daughter, Ida, who was seventeen, had light hair, the pert little nose of the china figures of shepherdesses in the dress of the period of Louis XIV., and was short, slim, and full of French grace. Besides them and the Count, a son of twelve and his tutor were present at supper. It struck the hussar as strange that the tutor, who was a strongly-built young man, with a winning face and those refined manners which the greatest plebeian quickly acquires when brought into close and constant contact with the aristocracy, was treated with great consideration by all the family except the Countess, who treated him very haughtily. She assumed a particularly imperious manner toward her son's tutor, and she either found fault with, or made fun of, everything that he did, while he put up with it all with smiling humility.

Before supper was over their conversation again turned on the ghost, and Baron T. asked whether they did not possess a picture of the White Lady.

"Of course we have one," they all replied at once; whereupon Baron T. begged to be allowed to see it.

"I will show it to you to-morrow," the Count said.

"No, papa, now, immediately," the younger lady said mockingly; "just before the ghostly hour, such a thing creates a much greater impression."

All who were present, not excepting the boy and his tutor, took a candle. Then they walked, as if in a torchlight procession, to the wing of the house where the hussar's room was. There was a life-size picture of the White Lady hanging in a Gothic passage near his room, among other ancestral portraits, and it by no means made a terrible impression on anyone who looked at it, but rather the contrary. The ghost, dressed in stiff, gold brocade and purple velvet, and with a hawk on her wrist, looked like one of those seductive Amazons of the fifteenth century who knew the art of laying men and game at their feet with equal skill.

"Don't you think that the White Lady is very like mamma?" Countess Ida said, interrupting the Baron's silent contemplation of the picture.

"There is no doubt of it," the hussar replied, while the Countess smiled and the tutor turned red. They were still standing before the picture, when a strong gust of wind suddenly extinguished all the lights, and they all uttered a simultaneous cry.

"The White Lady," the little Count whispered, but she did not come, and as it was luckily a moonlight night, they soon recovered from their momentary shock. The family retired to their apartments, while the hussar and the tutor went to their own rooms, which were situated in the wing of the castle which was haunted by the White Lady; the officer's apartment being scarcely thirty yards from the portrait, while the tutor's was rather further down the corridor.

The hussar went to bed, and was soon fast asleep, and though he had rather uneasy dreams nothing further happened. But while they were at breakfast the next morning, the Count's body-servant told them, with every appearance of real terror, that as he was crossing the courtyard at midnight, he had suddenly heard a noise like bats in the open cloisters, and when he looked he distinctly saw the White Lady gliding slowly through them. But they merely laughed at the poltroon, and though our hussar laughed also, he fully made up his mind, without saying a word about it, to keep a lookout for the ghost that night.

Again they had supper alone, without any company, had some music and pleasant talk, and separated at half past eleven. The hussar, however, only went to his room for form's sake; he loaded his pistols, and when all was quiet in the castle, he crept down into the court-yard and took up his position behind a pillar which was quite hidden in the shade, while the moon, which was nearly at the full, flooded the cloisters with its clear, pale light.

There were no lights to be seen in the castle except from two windows, which were those of the Countess's apartments, and soon they were also extinguished. The clock struck twelve, and the hussar could scarcely breathe from excitement; the next moment, however, he heard the noise which the Count's body-servant had compared to that of bats, and almost at the same instant a white figure glided slowly through the open cloisters and passed so close to him, that it almost made his blood curdle. Then it disappeared in the wing of the castle which he and the tutor occupied.

The officer, who was usually so brave, stood as though he was paralyzed for a few moments. But then he took heart, and feeling determined to make the nearer acquaintance of the spectral beauty, he crept softly up the broad staircase and took up his position in a deep recess in the cloisters, where nobody could see him.

He waited for a long time; he heard every quarter strike, and at last, just before the close of the "witching hour," he heard the same noise like the rustling of bats, and then she came. He felt the flutter of her white dress, and she stood before him—it was indeed the Countess.

He presented his pistol at her as he challenged her, but she raised her hand menacingly.

"Who are you?" he exclaimed. "If you are really a ghost, prove it, for I am going to fire."

"For heaven's sake!" the White Lady whispered, and at the same instant two white arms were thrown round him, and he felt a full, warm bosom heaving against his own.

After that night the ghost appeared more frequently still. Not only did the White Lady make her appearance every night in the cloisters, only to disappear in the proximity of the hussar's rooms as long as the family remained at the castle, but she even followed them to Vienna.

Baron T., who went to that capital on leave of absence during the following winter, and who was the Count's guest at the express wish of his wife, was frequently told by the footman that although hitherto she had seemed to be confined to the old castle in Bohemia, she had shown herself now here, now there, in the mansion in Vienna, in a white dress making a noise like the wings of a bat, and bearing a striking resemblance to the beautiful Countess.

Madame Baptiste

WHEN I went into the waiting-room at the station at Loubain, the first thing I did was to look at the clock, and I found that I had two hours and ten minutes to wait for the Paris express.

I felt suddenly tired, as if I had walked twenty miles. Then I looked about me, as if I could find some means of killing the time on the station walls. At last I went out again, and halted outside the gates of the station, racking my brains to find something to do. The street, which was a kind of boulevard planted with acacias, between two rows of houses of unequal shape and different styles of architecture, houses such as one only sees in a small town, ascended a slight hill, and at the extreme end of it there were some trees, as if it ended in a park.

From time to time a cat crossed the street, and jumped over the gutters, carefully. A cur sniffed at every tree, and hunted for fragments from the kitchens, but I did not see a single human being. I felt listless and disheartened. What could I do with myself? I was already thinking of the inevitable and interminable visit to the small *café* at the railway station, where I should have to sit over a glass of undrinkable beer, and an illegible newspaper, when I saw a funeral procession coming out of a side street into the one in which I was, and the sight of the hearse was a relief to me. It would, at any rate, give me something to do for ten minutes.

Suddenly, however, my curiosity was aroused. The corpse was followed by eight gentlemen, one of whom was weeping, while the others were chatting together. But there was no priest, and I thought to myself: "This is a non-religious funeral," but then I reflected that a town like Loubain must contain at least a hundred freethinkers, who would have made a point of making a manifestation. What could it be then? The rapid pace of the procession clearly proved that the body was to be buried without ceremony, and, consequently, without the intervention of religion.

My idle curiosity framed the most complicated suppositions, and as the hearse passed a strange idea struck me, which was to follow it with the eight gentlemen. That would take up my time for an hour, at least, and I, accordingly, walked with the others, with a sad look on my face, and on seeing this, the two last turned round in surprise, and then spoke to each other in a low voice.

No doubt, they were asking each other whether I belonged to the town, and then they consulted the two in front of them, who stared at me in turn. The close attention they paid me annoyed me, and to put an end to it, I went up to them, and after bowing, said:

"I beg your pardon, gentlemen, for interrupting your conversation, but seeing a civil funeral, I have followed it, although I did not know the deceased gentleman whom you are accompanying."

"It is a woman," one of them said.

I was much surprised at hearing this, and asked:

"But it is a civil funeral, is it not?"

The other gentleman, who evidently wished to tell me all about it, then said: "Yes and no. The clergy have refused to allow us the use of the church."

On hearing that, I uttered a prolonged A—h! of astonishment. I could not understand it at all, but my obliging neighbor continued:

"It is rather a long story. This young woman committed suicide, and that is the reason why she cannot be buried with any religious ceremony. The gentleman who is walking first, and who is crying, is her husband."

I replied, with some hesitation:

"You surprise and interest me very much, Monsieur. Shall I be indiscreet if I ask you to tell me the facts of the case? If I am troubling you, think that I have said nothing about the matter."

The gentleman took my arm familiarly.

"Not at all, not at all. Let us stop a little behind the others, and I will tell it to you, although it is a very sad story. We have plenty of time before getting to the cemetery, whose trees you see up yonder, for it is a stiff pull up this hill."

And he began:

"This young woman, Madame Paul Hamot, was the daughter of a wealthy merchant in the neighborhood, Monsieur Fontanelle. When she was a mere child of eleven. she had a terrible adventure; a footman violated her. She nearly died, in consequence, and the wretch's brutality betrayed him. A terrible criminal case was the result, and as it was proved that for three months the poor young martyr had been the victim of that brute's disgraceful practices, he was sentenced to penal servitude for life.

"The little girl grew up, stigmatized by her disgrace, isolated, without any companions, and grownup people would scarcely kiss her, for they thought they would soil their lips if they touched her forehead. She became a sort of monster, a phenomenon to all the town.

People said to each other in a whisper: "You know little Fontanelle," and everybody turned away in the streets when she passed. Her parents could not even get a nurse to take her out for a walk, and the other servants held aloof from her, as if contact with her would poison everybody who came near her.

"It was pitiable to see the poor child when the brats played every afternoon. She remained quite by herself, standing by her maid, and looking at the other children amusing themselves. Sometimes, yielding to an irresistible desire to mix with the other children, she advanced, timidly, with nervous gestures, and mingled with a group, with furtive steps, as if conscious of her own infamy. And immediately the mothers, aunts, and nurses used to come running from every seat, taking the children intrusted to their care by the hand and dragging them brutally away.

"Little Fontanelle would remain isolated, wretched, without understanding what it meant, and then would begin to cry, heartbroken with grief, and to run and hide her head in her nurse's lap, sobbing.

"As she grew up, it was worse still. They kept the girls from her, as if she were stricken with the plague. Remember that she had nothing to learn, nothing; that she no longer had the right to the symbolical wreath of orange-flowers; that almost before she could read, she had penetrated that redoubtable mystery which mothers scarcely allow their daughters to guess, trembling as they enlighten them on the night of their marriage.

"When she went through the streets, always accompanied by a governess—as if her parents feared some fresh, terrible adventure—with her eyes cast down under the load of that mysterious disgrace which she felt was always weighing upon her, the other girls, who were not nearly so innocent as people thought, whispered and giggled as they looked at her knowingly, and immediately turned their heads absently if she happened to look at them. People scarcely greeted her; only a few men bowed to her, and the mothers pretended not to see her, while some young blackguards called her "Madame Baptiste," after the name of the footman who had outraged and ruined her.

"Nobody knew the secret torture of her mind for she hardly ever spoke and never laughed; her parents themselves appeared uncomfortable in her presence, as if they bore her a constant grudge for some irreparable fault.

"An honest man would not willingly give his hand to a liberated convict, would he, even if that convict were his own son? And Monsieur and Madame Fontanelle looked on their daughter as they would have done on a son who had just been released from the hulks. She was pretty and pale, tall, slender, distinguished-looking, and she would have pleased me very much, Monsieur, but for that unfortunate affair.

"Well, when a new sub-prefect was appointed here eighteen months ago, he brought his private secretary with him. He was a queer sort of fellow, who had lived in the Latin Quarter,* it appears. He saw Mademoiselle Fontanelle, and fell in love with her, and when told of

*The students' quarter in Paris, where many of them lead fast lives.

what occurred, he merely said: 'Bah! That is just a guarantee for the future, and I would rather it should have happened before I married her, than afterward. I shall sleep tranquilly with that woman.'

"He paid his addresses to her, asked for her hand, and married her, and then, not being deficient in boldness, he paid wedding-calls,* as if nothing had happened. Some people returned them, others did not, but at last the affair began to be forgotten and she took her proper place in society.

"She adored her husband as if he had been a god, for you must remember that he had restored her to honor and to social life, that he had braved public opinion, faced insults, and, in a word, performed a courageous act, such as few men would accomplish, and she felt the most exalted and unceasing love for him.

"When she became pregnant, and it was known, the most particular people and the greatest sticklers opened their doors to her, as if she had been definitely purified by maternity.

"It is funny, but true, and thus everything was going on as well as possible, when, the other day, occurred the feast of the patron saint of our town. The prefect, surrounded by his staff and the authorities, presided at the musical competition, and when he had finished his speech, the distribution of medals began, which Paul Hamot, his private secretary, handed to those who were entitled to them.

"'As you know, there are always jealousies and rivalries, which make people

*In France and Germany, the newly-married couple pay the wedding-calls, which is the reverse of our custom.

forget all propriety. All the ladies of the town were there on the platform, and, in his proper turn, the bandmaster from the village of Mourmillon came up. This band was only to receive a second-class madel, for you cannot give first-class medals to everybody, can you? But when the private secretary handed him his badge, the man threw it in his face and exclaimed:

"'You may keep your medal for Baptiste. You owe him a first-class one, also, just as you do me.'

"There were a number of people there who began to laugh. The common herd are neither charitable nor refined, and every eye was turned toward that poor lady. Have you ever seen a woman going mad, Monsieur? Well, we were present at the sight! She got up, and fell back on her chair three times in succession, as if she wished to make her escape, but saw that she could not make her way through the crowd. Then another voice in the crowd exclaimed:

"'Oh! Oh! Madame Baptiste!'

"And a great uproar, partly laughter and partly indignation, arose. The word was repeated over and over again; people stood on tiptoe to see the unhappy woman's face; husbands lifted their wives up in their arms so that they might see her, and people asked.

"'Which is she? The one in blue?'

"The boys crowed like cocks and laughter was heard all over the place.

"She did not move now on her state chair, just as if she had been put there for the crowd to look at. She could not move, nor disappear, nor hide her face. Her eyelids blinked quickly, as if a vivid light were shining in her face,

REVENGE 713

and she panted like a horse that is going up a steep hill, so that it almost broke one's heart to see it. Meanwhile, however, Monsieur Hamot had seized the ruffian by the throat, and they were rolling on the ground together, amid a scene of indescribable confusion, and the ceremony was interrupted.

"An hour later, as the Hamots were returning home, the young woman, who had not uttered a word since the insult, but who was trembling as if all her nerves had been set in motion by springs, suddenly sprang on the parapet of the bridge, and threw herself into the river, before her husband could prevent it. The water is very deep under the arches, and it was two hours before her body was recovered. Of course, she was dead."

The narrator stopped, and then added:

"It was, perhaps, the best thing she could do in her position. There are some things which cannot be wiped out, and now you understand why the clergy refused to have her taken into church. Ah! If it had been a religious funeral, the whole town would have been present, but you can understand that her suicide, added to the other affair, made families abstain from attending her funeral. And then, it is not an easy matter, here, to attend a funeral which is performed without religious rites."

We passed through the cemetery gates, and I waited, much moved by what I had heard, until the coffin had been lowered into the grave before I went up to the poor husband, who was sobbing violently, to press his hand vigorously. He looked at me in surprise through his tears, and said:

"Thank you, Monsieur."

I was not sorry that I had followed the funeral.

Revenge

As they were still speaking of Pranzini, M. Maloureau, who had been Attorney-General under the Empire, said:

"I knew another case like that, a very curious affair, curious from many points, as you shall see.

"I was at that time Imperial attorney in the province, and stood very well at Court, thanks to my father, who was first President at Paris. I had charge of a still celebrated case, called 'The Affair of Schoolmaster Moiron.'

"M. Moiron, a schoolmaster in the north of France, bore an excellent reputation in all the country thereabout. He was an intelligent, reflective, very religious man, and had married in the district of Boislinot, where he practiced his profession. He had had three children, who all died in succession from weak lungs. After the loss of his own little ones, he seemed to lavish upon the urchins confided to his care all the tenderness concealed in his heart. He bought, with his own pennies, playthings for his best pupils, the diligent and good. He allowed them to have play dinners, and gorged them with dainties of candies and cakes. Everybody loved and praised this brave man, this brave heart, and it was like a blow when five of his pupils died of the same disease that had carried off his children. It was believed that an epidemic prevailed, caused by the water being made impure from drought. They looked for the cause, without discovering it, more than they did at the symptoms, which were very strange. The children appeared to be taken with a languor, could eat nothing, complained of pains in the stomach, and finally died in most terrible agony.

"An autopsy was made of the last to die, but nothing was discovered. The entrails were sent to Paris and analyzed, but showed no sign of any toxic substance.

"For one year no further deaths occurred; then two little boys, the best pupils in the class, favorites of father Moiron, expired in four days' time. An examination was ordered, and in each body fragments of pounded glass were found imbedded in the organs. They concluded that the two children had eaten imprudently of something carelessly prepared. Sufficient broken glass remained in the bottom of a bowl of milk to have caused this frightful accident, and the matter would have rested there had not Moiron's servant been taken ill in the interval. The physician found the same morbid signs that he observed in the preceding attacks of the children, and, upon questioning her, finally obtained the confession that she had stolen and eaten some bonbons, bought by the master for his pupils.

"Upon order of the court, the schoolhouse was searched and a closet was found, full of sweetmeats and dainties for the children. Nearly all these edibles contained fragments of glass or broken needles.

"Moiron was immediately arrested. He was so indignant and stupefied at the weight of suspicion upon him that he was nearly overcome. Nevertheless, the indications of his guilt were so apparent that they fought hard in my mind against my first conviction, which was based upon his good reputation, his entire life of truthfulness, and the absolute absence of any motive for such a crime.

"Why should this good, simple religious man kill children, and the children whom he seemed to love best? Why should he select those he had feasted with dainties, for whom he had spent in playthings and bonbons half his stipend?

"To admit this, it must be concluded that he was insane. But Moiron seemed so reasonable, so calm, so full of judgment and good sense! It was impossible to prove insanity in him.

"Proofs accumulated, nevertheless! Bonbons, cakes, *pâtés* of marshmallow, and other things seized at the shops where the schoolmaster got his supplies, were found to contain no suspected fragment.

"He pretended that some unknown enemy had opened his closet with a false key and placed the glass and needles in the eatables. And he implied a story of heritage dependent on the death of a child, sought out and discovered by a peasant, and so worked up as to make the suspicion fall upon the schoolmaster. This brute, he said, was not interested in the other poor children who had to die also.

"This theory was plausible. The man appeared so sure of himself and so pitiful, that we should have acquitted him without doubt, if two overwhelming discoveries had not been made at one blow. The first was a snuffbox full of ground glass! It was his own snuffbox, in a secret drawer of his secretary, where he kept his money.

"He explained this in a manner not acceptable, by saying that it was the last ruse of an unknown guilty one. But a merchant of Saint-Marlouf presented himself at the house of the judge, telling him that Moiron had bought needles of him many times, the finest needles he could find, breaking them to see whether they suited him.

"The merchant brought as witnesses a dozen persons who recognized Moiron at first glance. And the inquest revealed the fact that the schoolmaster was at Saint-Marlouf on the days designated by the merchant.

"I pass over the terrible depositions of the children upon the master's choice of dainties, and his care in making the little ones eat in his presence and destroying all traces of the feast.

"Public opinion, exasperated, recalled capital punishment, and took on a new force from terror which permitted no delays or resistance.

"Moiron was condemned to death. His appeal was rejected. No recourse remained to him for pardon. I knew from my father that the Emperor would not grant it.

"One morning, as I was at work in my office, the chaplain of the prison was announced. He was an old priest who had a great knowledge of men and a large acquaintance among criminals. He appeared troubled and constrained. After talking a few moments of other things, he said abruptly, on rising:

"'If Moiron is decapitated, Monsieur Attorney-General, you will have allowed the execution of an innocent man.'

"Then, without bowing, he went on, leaving me under the profound effect of his words. He had pronounced them in a solemn, affecting fashion, opening lips, closed and sealed by confession, in order to save a life.

"An hour later I was on my way to Paris, and my father, at my request, asked an immediate audience with the Emperor.

"I was received the next day. Napoleon III. was at work in a little room when we were introduced. I exposed the whole affair, even to the visit of the priest, and, in the midst of the story, the door opened behind the chair of the Emperor, and the Empress, who believed him alone, entered. His Majesty consulted her. When she had run over the facts, she explained:

"'This man must be pardoned! He must, because he is innocent.'

"Why should this sudden conviction of a woman so pious throw into my mind a terrible doubt?

"Up to that time I had ardently desired a commutation of the sentence. And now I felt myself the puppet, the dupe of a criminal ruse, which had employed the priest and the confession as a means of defense.

"I showed some hesitation to their Majesties. The Emperor remained undecided, solicited on one hand by his natural goodness, and on the other held back by the fear of allowing himself to play a miserable part; but the Empress, convinced that the priest had obeyed a divine call, repeated: 'What does it matter? It is better to spare a guilty man than to kill an innocent one.' Her advice prevailed. The penalty of death was commuted, and that of hard labor was substituted.

"Some years after I heard that Moiron, whose exemplary conduct at Toulon had been made known again to the Emperor, was employed as a domestic by the director of the penitentiary. And then I heard no word of this man for a long time.

"About two years after this, when I was passing the summer at the house of my cousin, De Larielle, a young priest came to me one evening, as we were sitting down to dinner, and wished to speak to me.

"I told them to let him come in, and he begged me to go with him to a dying man, who desired, before all else, to see me. This had happened often, during my long career as judge, and, although I had been put aside by the Republic, I was still called upon from time to time in like circumstances.

"I followed the ecclesiastic, who made me mount into a little miserable lodging, under the roof of a high house. There, upon a pallet of straw, I found a dying man, seated with his back against the wall, in order to breathe. He was a sort of grimacing skeleton, with deep, shining eyes.

"When he saw me he murmured: 'You do not know me?'

" 'No.'

" 'I am Moiron.'

"I shivered, but said: 'The schoolmaster?'

" 'Yes.'

" 'How is it you are here?'

" 'That would be too long—I haven't time—I am going to die—They brought me this curate—and as I knew you were here, I sent him for you—It is to you that I wish to confess—since you saved my life before—the other time—'

"He seized with his dry hands the straw of his bed, and continued, in a rasping, bass voice:

" 'Here it is—I owe you the truth—to you, because it is necessary to tell it to some one before leaving the earth.

" 'It was I who killed the children—all—it was I—for vengeance!

" 'Listen. I was an honest man, very honest—very honest—very pure—adoring God—the good God—the God that they teach us to love, and not the false God, the executioner, the robber, the murderer who governs the earth— I had never done wrong, never committed a villainous act. I was pure as one unborn.

" 'After I was married I had some children, and I began to love them as never father or mother loved their own. I lived only for them. I was foolish. They died, all three of them! Why? Why? What had I done? I? I had a change of heart, a furious change. Suddenly I opened my eyes as of one awakening; and I learned that God is wicked. Why had He killed my children? I opened my eyes and I saw that He loved to kill. He loves only that, Monsieur. He exists only to destroy! God is a murderer! Some death is necessary to Him every day. He causes them in all fashions, the better to amuse Himself. He has invented sickness and accident in order to divert Himself through all the long months and years. And, when He is weary, He has epidemics, pests, the cholera, quinsy, smallpox.

" 'How do I know all that this monster has imagined? All these evils are not enough to suffice. From time to time He sends war, in order to see two hundred thousand soldiers laid low, bruised in blood and mire, with arms and legs torn off, heads broken by bullets, like eggs that fall along the road.

" 'That is not all. He has made men who eat one another. And then, as men become better than He, He has made beasts to see the men chase them, slaughter, and nourish themselves with them. That is not all. He has made all the little animals that live for a day, flies which increase by myriads in an hour, ants, that one crushes, and others, many, so many that we cannot even imagine them. And all kill one another, chase one another, devour one another, murdering without ceasing. And the good God looks on and is amused, because He sees all for Himself, the largest as well as the smallest, those which are in drops of water, as well as those in the stars. He looks at them all and is amused! Ugh! Beast!

" 'So I, Monsieur, I also have killed some children. I acted the part for Him. It was not He who had them. It was not He, it was I. And I would have killed still more, but you took me away. That's all!'

" 'I was going to die, guillotined. I! How He would have laughed, the reptile! Then I asked for a priest, and lied to him. I confessed. I lied, and I lived.

" 'Now it is finished. I can no longer escape Him. But I have no fear of Him, Monsieur, I understand Him too well.'

"It was frightful to see this miserable creature, hardly able to breathe, talking in hiccoughs, opening an enormous mouth to eject some words scarcely heard, pulling up the cloth of his straw bed, and, under a cover nearly black, moving his meager limbs as if to save himself.

"Oh! frightful being and frightful remembrance!

I asked him: 'You have nothing more to say?'

" 'No, Monsieur.'

" 'Then, farewell.'

" 'Farewell, sir, one day or the other.'

"I turned toward the priest whose somber silhouette was on the wall.

" 'You will remain, M. Abbé?'

" 'I will remain.'

"Then the dying man sneered: 'Yes, yes, he sends crows to dead bodies.'

"As for me, I had seen enough. I opened the door and went away in self-protection."

An Old Maid

In Argenteuil they called her Queen Hortense. No one ever knew the reason why. Perhaps because she spoke firmly, like an officer in command. Perhaps because she was large, bony, and imperious. Perhaps because she governed a multitude of domestic animals, hens, dogs, cats, canaries, and parrots,—those animals so dear to old maids. But she gave these familiar subjects neither dainties, nor pretty words, nor those tender puerilities which seem to slip from the lips of a woman to the velvety coat of the cat she is fondling. She governed her beasts with authority. She ruled.

She was an old maid, one of those old maids with cracked voice, and awkward gesture, whose soul seems hard. She never allowed contradiction from any person, nor argument, nor would she tolerate hesitation, or indifference, or idleness, or fatigue. No one ever heard her complain, or regret what was, or desire what was not. "Each to his part," she said, with the conviction of a fatalist. She never went to church, cared nothing for the priests, scarcely believed in God, and called all religious things "mourning merchandise."

For thirty years she had lived in her little house, with its tiny garden in front, extending along the street, never modifying her garments, changing only maids, and that mercilessly, when they became twenty-one years old.

She replaced, without tears and without regrets, her dogs or cats or birds, when they died of old age, or by accident, and she buried trespassing animals in a flower-bed, heaping the earth above them and treading it down with perfect indifference.

She had in the town some acquaintances, the families of employers, whose men went to Paris every day. Sometimes they would invite her to go to the theater with them. She inevitably fell asleep on these occasions, and they were obliged to wake her when it was time to go home. She never allowed anyone

to accompany her; having no fear by night or day. She seemed to have no love for children.

She occupied her time with a thousand masculine cares, carpentry, gardening, cutting or sawing wood, repairing her old house, even doing mason's work when it was necessary.

She had some relatives who came to see her twice a year. Her two sisters, Madame Cimme and Madame Columbel, were married, one to a florist, the other to a small householder. Madame Cimme had no children; Madame Columbel had three. Henry, Pauline, and Joseph. Henry was twenty-one, Pauline and Joseph were three, having come when one would have thought the mother past the age. No tenderness united this old maid to her kinsfolk.

In the spring of 1882, Queen Hortense became suddenly ill. The neighbors went for a physician, whom she drove away. When the priest presented himself she got out of bed, half naked, and put him out of doors. The little maid, weeping, made gruel for her.

After three days in bed, the situation became so grave that the carpenter living next door, after counsel with the physician (now reinstated with authority), took it upon himself to summon the two families.

They arrived by the same train, about ten o'clock in the morning; the Columbels having brought their little Joseph.

When they approached the gate, they saw the maid seated in a chair against the wall, weeping. The dog lay asleep on the mat before the door, under a broiling sun; two cats, that looked as if dead, lay stretched out on the window-sills, with eyes closed and paws and tails extended at full length. A great glossy hen was promenading before the door, at the head of a flock of chickens, covered with yellow down, and in a large cage hung against the wall, covered with chickweed, were several birds, singing themselves hoarse in the light of this hot spring morning.

Two others, inseparable, in a little cage in the form of a cottage, remained quiet, side by side on their porch.

M. Cimme, a large, wheezy personage, who always entered a room first, putting aside men and women when it was necessary, remarked to the maid: "Eh, Celeste! Is it so bad as that?"

The little maid sobbed through her tears:

"She doesn't know me any more. The doctor says it is the end."

They all looked at one another.

Madame Cimme and Madame Columbel embraced each other instantly, not saying a word.

They resembled each other much, always wearing braids of hair and shawls of red cashmere, as bright as hot coals.

Cimme turned toward his brother-in-law, a pale man, yellow and thin, tormented by indigestion, who limped badly, and said to him in a serious tone:

"Gad! It was time!"

But no one dared to go into the room of the dying woman situated on the ground floor. Cimme himself stopped at that step. Columbel was the first to decide upon it; he entered, balancing himself like the mast of a ship, making a noise on the floor with the iron of his cane.

The two women ventured to follow, and M. Cimme brought up the line.

Little Joseph remained outside, playing with the dog.

A ray of sunlight fell on the bed, lighting up the hands which moved nervously, opening and shutting without ceasing. The fingers moved as if a thought animated them, as if they would signify something, indicate some idea, obey some intelligence. The rest of the body remained motionless under the covers. The angular figure gave no start. The eyes remained closed.

The relatives arranged themselves in a semicircle and, without saying a word, regarded the heaving breast and the short breathing. The little maid had followed them, still shedding tears.

Finally, Cimme asked: "What was it the doctor said?"

The servant whispered: "He said we should leave her quiet, that nothing more could be done."

Suddenly the lips of the old maid began to move. She seemed to pronounce some silent words, concealed in her dying brain, and her hands quickened their singular movement.

Then she spoke in a little, thin voice, quite unlike her own, an utterance that seemed to come from far off, perhaps from the bottom of that heart always closed.

Cimme walked upon tiptoe, finding this spectacle painful. Columbel, whose lame leg wearied him, sat down.

The two women remained standing.

Queen Hortense muttered something quickly, which they were unable to understand. She pronounced some names, called tenderly some imaginary persons:

"Come here, my little Philip, kiss your mother. You love mamma, don't you, my child? You, Rose, you will watch your little sister while I am out. Especially, don't leave her alone, do you hear? And I forbid you to touch matches."

She was silent some seconds; then, in a loud tone, as if she would call, she said: "Henrietta!" She waited a little and continued: "Tell your father to come and speak to me before going to his office." Then suddenly: "I am suffering a little to-day, dear; promise me you will not return late; you will tell your chief that I am ill. You know it is dangerous to leave the children alone when I am in bed. I am going to make you a dish of rice and sugar for dinner. The little ones like it so much. Claire will be the happy one!"

She began to laugh, a young and noisy laugh, as she had never laughed before. "Look, John," she said, "what a droll head he has. He has smeared himself with the sugarplums, the dirty thing! Look! my dear, how funny he looks!"

Columbel, who changed the position of his lame leg every moment, murmured: "She is dreaming that she has children and a husband; the end is near."

The two sisters did not move, but seemed surprised and stupid.

The little maid said: "Will you take off your hats, and your shawls, and go into the other room?"

They went out without having said a word. And Columbel followed them limping, leaving the dying woman alone again.

When they were relieved of their outer garments, the women seated themselves. Then one of the cats left the window, stretched herself, jumped into the room, then upon the knees of Ma-

dame Cimme, who began to caress her.

They heard from the next room the voice of agony, living, without doubt, in this last hour, the life she had expected, living her dreams at the very moment when all would be finished for her.

Cimme, in the garden, played with the little Joseph and the dog, amusing himself much, with the gaiety of a great man in the country, without thought of the dying woman.

But suddenly he entered, addressing the maid: "Say, then, my girl, are you going to give us some luncheon? What are you going to eat, ladies?"

They decided upon an omelet of fine herbs, a piece of fillet with new potatoes, a cheese, and a cup of coffee.

And as Madame Columbel was fumbling in her pocket for her purse, Cimme stopped her, and turning to the maid said, "You need money?" and she answered: "Yes, sir."

"How much?"

"Fifteen francs."

"Very well. Make haste, now, my girl, because I am getting hungry."

Madame Cimme, looking out at the climbing flowers bathed in the sunlight, and at two pigeons making love on the roof opposite, said, with a wounded air: "It is unfortunate to have come for so sad an event. It would be nice in the country, to-day."

Her sister sighed without response, and Columbel murmured, moved perhaps by the thought of a walk:

"My leg plagues me awfully."

Little Joseph and the dog made a terrible noise, one shouting with joy and the other barking violently. They played at hide-and-seek around the three flower-beds, running after each other like mad.

The dying woman continued to call her children, chatting with each, imagining that she was dressing them, that she caressed them, that she was teaching them to read: "Come, Simon, repeat, A, B, C, D. You do not say it well; see, D, D, D, do you hear? Repeat, then—"

Cimme declared: "It is curious what she talks about at this time."

Then said Madame Columbel: "It would be better, perhaps, to go in there."

But Cimme dissuaded her from it:

"Why go in, since we are not able to do anything for her? Besides we are as well off here."

No one insisted. Madame observed the two green birds called inseparable. She remarked pleasantly upon this singular fidelity, and blamed men for not imitating these little creatures. Cimme looked at his wife and laughed, singing with a bantering air, "Tra-la-la, Tra-la-la," as if to say he could tell some things about her fidelity to him.

Columbel, taken with cramps in his stomach, struck the floor with his cane. The other cat entered, tail in the air. They did not sit down at table until one o'clock.

When he had tasted the wine, Columbel, whom some one had recommended to drink only choice Bordeaux, called the servant:

"Say, is there nothing better than this in the cellar?"

"Yes, sir! there is some of the wine that was served to you when you were here before."

"Oh, well, go and bring three bottles."

They tasted this wine, which seemed excellent. Not that it proved to be remarkable, but it had been fifteen years in the cellar. Cimme declared it was just the wine for sickness.

Columbel, seized with a desire of possessing some of it, asked of the maid: "How much is left of it, my girl?"

"Oh, nearly all, sir; Miss never drinks any of it. It is the heap at the bottom."

Then Columbel turned toward his brother-in-law: "If you wish, Cimme, I will take this wine instead of anything else; it agrees with my stomach wonderfully."

The hen, in her turn, had entered with her troop of chickens; the two women amused themselves by throwing crumbs to them. Joseph and the dog, who had eaten enough, returned to the garden.

Queen Hortense spoke continually, but the voice was lower now, so that it was no longer possible to distinguish the words.

When they had finished the coffee, they all went in to learn the condition of the sick one. She seemed calm.

They went out and seated themselves in a circle in the garden, to aid digestion.

Presently the dog began to run around the chairs with all speed, carrying something in his mouth. The child ran after him violently. Both disappeared into the house. Cimme fell asleep, with his stomach in the sun.

The dying one began to speak loud again. Then suddenly she shouted.

The two women and Columbel hastened in to see what had happened. Cimme awakened but did not move, liking better things as they were.

The dying woman was sitting up,

staring with haggard eyes. Her dog, to escape the pursuit of little Joseph, had jumped upon the bed, startling her from the death agony. The dog was in-trenched behind the pillow, peeping at his comrade with eyes glistening, ready to jump again at the least movement. He held in his mouth one of the slippers of his mistress, shorn of its heel in the hour he had played with it.

The child, intimidated by the woman rising so suddenly before him, remained motionless before the bed.

The hen, having just entered, had jumped upon a chair, frightened by the noise. She called desperately to her chickens, which peeped, frightened, from under the four legs of the seat.

Queen Hortense cried out with a piercing tone: "No, no, I do not wish to die! I am not willing! Who will bring up my children? Who will care for them? Who will love them? No, I am not willing! I am not—"

She turned on her back. All was over.

The dog, much excited, jumped into the room and skipped about.

Columbel ran to the window and called his brother-in-law: "Come quickly! come quickly! I believe she is gone."

Then Cimme got up and resolutely went into the room, muttering: "It was not as long as I should have believed."

Complication

AFTER swearing for a long time that he would never marry, Jack Boudillère suddenly changed his mind. It happened one summer at the seashore, quite un-expectedly.

One morning, as he was extended on the sand, watching the women come out of the water, a little foot caught his at-tention, because of its slimness and deli-cacy. Raising his eyes higher, the entire person seemed attractive. Of this entire person he had, however, seen only the ankles and the head, emerging from a white flannel bathing suit, fastened with care. He may be called sensuous and impressionable, but it was by grace of form alone that he was captured. Af-terward, he was held by the charm and sweet spirit of the young girl, who was simple and good and fresh, like her cheeks and her lips.

Presented to the family, he was pleased, and straightway became love-mad. When he saw Bertha Lannis at a distance, on the long stretch of yellow sand, he trembled from head to foot. Near her he was dumb, incapable of say-ing anything or even of thinking, with a kind of bubbling in his heart, a hum-ming in his ears, and a frightened feel-ing in his mind. Was this love?

He did not know, he understood noth-ing of it, but the fact remained that he was fully decided to make this child his wife.

Her parents hesitated a long time, de-terred by the bad reputation of the young man. He had a mistress, it was said,—an old mistress, an old and strong entanglement, one of those chains that is believed to be broken, but which con-tinues to hold, nevertheless. Beyond this, he had loved, for a longer or shorter period, every woman who had come within reach of his lips.

But he withdrew from the woman with whom he had lived, not even consenting to see her again. A friend arranged her pension, assuring her a subsistence. Jack paid, but he did not wish to speak to her, pretending henceforth that he did not know her name. She wrote letters which he would not open. Each week brought him a new disguise in the handwriting of the abandoned one. Each week a greater anger developed in him against her, and he would tear the envelope in two, without opening it, without reading a line, knowing beforehand the reproaches and complaints of the contents.

One could scarcely credit her perseverance, which lasted the whole winter long, and it was not until spring that her demand was satisfied.

The marriage took place in Paris during the early part of May. It was decided that they should not take the regular wedding journey. After a little ball, composed of a company of young cousins who would not stay past eleven o'clock, and would not prolong forever the care of the day of ceremony, the young couple intended to pass their first night at the family home and to set out the next morning for the seaside, where they had met and loved.

The night came, and they were dancing, in the great drawing-room. The newly-married pair had withdrawn from the rest into a little Japanese boudoir shut off by silk hangings, and scarcely lighted this evening except by the dim rays from a colored lantern in the shape of an enormous egg, which hung from the ceiling. The long window was open, allowing at times a fresh breath of air from without to blow upon their faces, for the evening was soft and warm, full of the odor of springtime.

They said nothing, but held each other's hands, pressing them from time to time with all their force. She was a little dismayed by this great change in her life, but smiling, emotional, ready to weep, often ready to swoon from joy, believing the entire world changed because of what had come to her, a little disturbed without knowing the reason why, and feeling all her body, all her soul, enveloped in an indefinable, delicious lassitude.

Her husband she watched persistently, smiling at him with a fixed smile. He wished to talk but found nothing to say, and remained quiet, putting all his ardor into the pressure of the hand. From time to time he murmured "Bertha!" and each time she raised her eyes to his with a sweet and tender look. They would look at each other a moment, then his eyes, fascinated by hers, would fall.

They discovered no thought to exchange. But they were alone, except as a dancing couple would sometimes cast a glance at them in passing, a furtive glance, as if it were the discreet and confidential witness of a mystery.

A door at the side opened, a domestic entered, bearing upon a tray an urgent letter which a messenger had brought. Jack trembled as he took it, seized with a vague and sudden fear, the mysterious, abrupt fear of misfortune.

He looked long at the envelope, not knowing the handwriting, not daring to open it, wishing not to read, not to know the contents, desiring to put it in his pocket and to say to himself: "To-morrow, to-morrow, I shall be far away and it will not matter!" But upon the corner were two words underlined: *very urgent,* which frightened him. "You will permit me, my dear," said he, and he tore off the wrapper. He read the letter, growing frightfully pale, running over it at a glance, and then seeming to spell it out.

When he raised his head his whole countenance was changed. He stammered: "My dear little one, a great misfortune has happened to my best friend. He needs me immediately, in a matter of—of life and death. Allow me to go for twenty minutes. I will return immediately."

She, trembling and affrighted, murmured: "Go, my friend!" not yet being enough of a wife to dare to ask or demand to know anything. And he disappeared. She remained alone, listening to the dance music in the next room.

He had taken a hat, the first he could find, and descended the staircase upon the run. As soon as he was mingled with the people on the street, he stopped under a gaslight in a vestibule and re-read the letter. It said:

"SIR: The Ravet girl, your old mistress, has given birth to a child which she asserts is yours. The mother is dying and implores you to visit her. I take the liberty of writing to you to ask whether you will grant the last wish of this woman, who seems to be very unhappy and worthy of pity.

      "Your servant,
        D. BONNARD."

When he entered the chamber of death, she was already in the last agony.

He would not have known her. The physician and the two nurses were caring for her, dragging across the room some buckets full of ice and linen.

Water covered the floor, two tapers were burning on a table; behind the bed, in a little wicker cradle, a child was crying, and, with each of its cries, the mother would try to move, shivering under the icy compresses.

She was bleeding, wounded to death, killed by this birth. Her life was slipping away; and, in spite of the ice, in spite of all care, the hemorrhage continued, hastening her last hour.

She recognized Jack, and tried to raise her hand. She was too weak for that, but the warm tears began to glide down her cheeks.

He fell on his knees beside the bed, seized one of her hands and kissed it frantically; then, little by little, he approached nearer to the wan face which strained to meet him. One of the nurses, standing with a taper in her hand, observed them, and the doctor looked at them from the remote corner of the room.

With a far-off voice, breathing hard, she said: "I am going to die, my dear; promise me you will remain till the end. Oh! do not leave me now, not at the last moment!"

He kissed her brow, her hair with a groan. "Be tranquil!" he murmured, "I will stay."

It was some minutes before she was able to speak again, she was so weak and overcome. Then she continued: "It is yours, the little one. I swear it before God, I swear it to you upon my soul, I swear it at the moment of death. I have never loved any man but you—

promise me not to abandon it—" He tried to take in his arms the poor, weak body, emptied of its life blood. He stammered, excited by remorse and chagrin: "I swear to you I will bring it up and love it. It shall never be separated from me." Then she held Jack in an embrace. Powerless to raise her head, she held up her blanched lips in an appeal for a kiss. He bent his mouth to receive this poor, suppliant caress.

Calmed a little, she murmured in a low tone: "Take it, that I may see that you love it."

He placed it gently on the bed between them. The little creature ceased to cry. She whispered: "Do not stir!" And he remained motionless. There he stayed, holding in his burning palms a hand that shook with the shiver of death, as he had held, an hour before, another hand that had trembled with the shiver of love. From time to time he looked at the hour, with a furtive glance of the eye, watching the hand as it passed midnight, then one o'clock, then two.

The doctor retired. The two nurses, after roaming around for some time with light step, slept now in their chairs. The child slept, and the mother, whose eyes were closed, seemed to be resting also.

Suddenly, as the pale daylight began to filter through the torn curtains, she extended her arms with so startling and violent a motion that she almost threw the child upon the floor. There was a rattling in her throat; then she turned over motionless, dead.

The nurses hastened to her side, declaring: "It is over."

He looked once at this woman he had loved, then at the hand that marked four o'clock, and, forgetting his overcoat, fled in his evening clothes with the child in his arms.

After she had been left alone, his young bride had waited calmly at first, in the Japanese boudoir. Then, seeing that he did not return, she went back to the drawing-room, indifferent and tranquil in appearance, but frightfully disturbed. Her mother, perceiving her alone, asked where her husband was. She replied: "In his room; he will return presently."

At the end of an hour, as everybody asked about him, she told of the letter, of the change in Jack's face, and her fears of some misfortune.

They still waited. The guests had gone; only the parents and ner relatives remained. At midnight, they put the bride in her bed, shaking with sobs. Her mother and two aunts were seated on the bed listening to her weeping. Her father had gone to the police headquarters to make inquiries. At five o'clock a light sound was heard in the corridor. The door opened and closed softly. Then suddenly a cry, like the mewing of a cat, went through the house, breaking the silence.

All the women of the house were out with one bound, and Bertha was the first to spring forward, in spite of her mother and her aunt, clothed only in her night-robe.

Jack, standing in the middle of the room, livid, breathing hard, held the child in his arms.

The four women looked at him frightened; but Bertha suddenly became rash, her heart wrung with anguish, and ran to him saying: "What is it? What have you there?"

He had a foolish air, and answered in a husky voice: "It is—it is—I have here a child, whose mother has just died." And he put into her arms the howling little marmot.

Bertha, without saying a word, seized the child and embraced it, straining it to her heart. Then, turning toward her husband with her eyes full of tears, she said: "The mother is dead, you say?" He answered: "Yes, just died—in my arms—I had broken with her since last summer — I knew nothing about it—only the doctor sent for me and—"

Then Bertha murmured: "Well, we will bring up this little one."

Forgiveness

SHE had been brought up in one of those families who live shut up within themselves, entirely apart from the rest of the world. They pay no attention to political events, except to chat about them at the table, and changes in government seem so far, so very far away that they are spoken of only as a matter of history—like the death of Louis XVI., or the advent of Napoleon.

Customs change, fashions succeed each other, but changes are never perceptible in this family, where old traditions are always followed. And if some impossible story arises in the neighborhood, the scandal of it dies at, the threshold of this house.

The father and mother, alone in the evening, sometimes exchange a few words on such a subject, but in an undertone, as if the walls had ears.

With great discretion, the father says: "Do you know about this terrible affair in the Rivoil family?"

And the mother replies: "Who would have believed it? It is frightful!"

The children doubt nothing, but come to the age of living, in their turn, with a bandage over their eyes and minds, without knowing that one does not always think as he speaks, nor speaks as he acts, without knowing that it is necessary to live at war with the world, or at least, in armed peace, without surmising that the ingenuous are frequently deceived, the sincere trifled with, and the good wronged.

Some live until death in this blindness of probity, loyalty, and honor; so upright that nothing can open their eyes. Others, undeceived, without knowing much, are weighed down with despair, and die believing that they are the puppets of an exceptional fatality the miserable victims of unlucky circumstances or particularly bad men.

The Savignols arranged a marriage for their daughter when she was eighteen. She married a young man from Paris, George Barton, whose business was on the Exchange. He was an attractive youth, with a smooth tongue, and he observed all the outward proprieties necessary. But at the bottom of his heart he sneered a little at his guileless parents-in-law, calling them, among his friends, "My dear fossils." He belonged to a good family, and the young girl was rich. He took her to live in Paris.

She became one of the provincials of Paris, of whom there are many. She remained ignorant of the great city, of its elegant people, of its pleasures and its customs, as she had always been ignorant of the perfidy and mystery of life.

Shut up in her own household, she scarcely knew the street she lived in, and when she ventured into another quarter, it seemed to her that she had journeyed far, into an unknown, strange city. She would say in the evening:

"I crossed the boulevards to-day."

Two or three times a year, her husband took her to the theater. These were feast-days not to be forgotten, which she recalled continually.

Sometimes at table, three months afterward, she would suddenly burst out laughing and exclaim:

"Do you remember that ridiculous actor who imitated the cock's crowing?"

All her interests were within the boundaries of the two allied families, who represented the whole of humanity to her. She designated them by the distinguishing prefix "the," calling them respectively "the Martinets," or "the Michelins."

Her husband lived according to his fancy, returning whenever he wished, sometimes at daybreak, pretending business, and feeling in no way constrained, so sure was he that no suspicion would ruffle this candid soul.

But one morning she received an anonymous letter. She was too much astonished and dismayed to scorn this letter, whose author declared himself to be moved by interest in her happiness, by hatred of all evil and love of truth. Her heart was too pure to understand fully the meaning of the accusations.

But it revealed to her that her husband had had a mistress for two years, a young widow, Mrs. Rosset, at whose house he passed his evenings.

She knew neither how to pretend, nor to spy, nor to plan any sort of ruse. When he returned for luncheon, she threw him the letter, sobbing, and then fled to her room.

He had time to comprehend the matter and prepare his response before he rapped at his wife's door. She opened it immediately, without looking at him. He smiled, sat down, and drew her to his knee. In a sweet voice, and a little jocosely, he said:

"My dear little one, Mrs. Rosset is a friend of mine. I have known her for ten years and like her very much. I may add that I know twenty other families of whom I have not spoken to you, knowing that you care nothing for the world or for forming new friendships. But in order to finish, once for all, these infamous lies, I will ask you to dress yourself, after luncheon, and we will go to pay a visit to this young lady, who will become your friend at once, I am sure." She embraced her husband eagerly; and, from feminine curiosity, which no sooner sleeps than wakes again, she did not refuse to go to see this unknown woman, of whom, in spite of all, she was still suspicious. She felt by instinct that a known danger is sooner overcome.

They were ushered into a little apartment on the fourth floor of a handsome house. It was a coquettish little place, full of bric-à-brac and ornamented with works of art. After about five minutes' waiting, in a drawing-room where the light was dimmed by its generous window draperies and portières, a door opened and a young woman appeared. She was very dark, small, rather plump, and looked astonished, although she smiled. George presented them. "My wife, Madame Julie Rosset."

The young widow uttered a little cry of astonishment and joy, and came forward with both hands extended. She had not hoped for this happiness, she said, knowing that Madame Barton saw no one. But she was so happy! She was so fond of George! (She said George quite naturally, with sisterly familiarity.) And she had had great desire to know his young wife, and to love her, too.

At the end of a month these two friends were never apart from each other. They met every day, often twice a day, and nearly always dined together, either at one house or at the other. George scarcely even went out now, no longer pretended delay on account of business, but said he loved his own chimney corner.

Finally, an apartment was left vacant in the house where Madame Rosset resided. Madame Barton hastened to take it in order to be nearer her new friend.

During two whole years there was a friendship between them without a cloud, a friendship of heart and soul, tender, devoted, and delightful. Bertha could not speak without mentioning Julie's name, for to her Julie represented perfection. She was happy with a perfect happiness, calm and secure.

But Madame Rosset fell ill. Bertha never left her. She passed nights of despair; her husband, too, was brokenhearted.

One morning, in going out from his visit the doctor took George and his wife aside, and announced that he found the condition of their friend very grave.

When he had gone out, the young people, stricken down, looked at each other and then began to weep.

They both watched that night near the bed. Bertha would embrace the sick one tenderly, while George, standing silently at the foot of her couch, would look at them with dogged persistence. The next day she was worse.

Finally, toward evening, she declared herself better, and persuaded her friends to go home to dinner.

They were sitting sadly at table, scarcely eating anything, when the maid brought George an envelope. He opened it, turned pale, and rising, said to his wife, in a constrained way: "Excuse me, I must leave you for a moment. I will return in ten minutes. Please don't go out." And he ran into his room for his hat.

Bertha waited, tortured by a new fear. But, yielding in all things, she would not go up to her friend's room again until he had returned.

As he did not re-appear, the thought came to her to look in his room to see whether he had taken his gloves, which would show whether he had really gone somewhere.

She saw them there, at first glance. Near them lay a rumpled paper.

She recognized it immediately; it was the one that had called George away.

And a burning temptation took possession of her, the first of her life, to read—to know. Her conscience struggled in revolt, but curiosity lashed her on and grief directed her hand. She seized the paper, opened it, recognized the trembling handwriting as that of Julie, and read:

"Come alone and embrace me, my poor friend; I am going to die."

She could not understand it all at once, but stood stupefied, struck especially by the thought of death. Then, suddenly, the familiarity of it seized upon her mind. This came like a great light, illuminating her whole life, showing her the infamous truth, all their treachery, all their perfidy. She saw now their cunning, their sly looks, her good faith played with, her confidence turned to account. She saw them looking into each other's faces, under the shade of her lamp at evening, reading from the same book, exchanging glances at the end of certain pages.

And her heart, stirred with indignation, bruised with suffering, sunk into an abyss of despair that had no boundaries.

When she heard steps, she fled and shut herself in her room.

Her husband called her: "Come quickly, Madame Rosset is dying!"

Bertha appeared at her door and said with trembling lip:

"Go alone to her; she has no need of me."

He looked at her sheepishly, careless from anger, and repeated:

"Quick, quick! She is dying!"

Bertha answered: "You would prefer it to be I."

Then he understood, probably, and left her to herself, going up again to the dying one.

There he wept without fear, or shame, indifferent to the grief of his wife, who would no longer speak to him, nor look at him, but who lived shut in with her disgust and angry revolt, praying to God morning and evening.

They lived together, nevertheless, eating together face to face, mute and hopeless.

After a time, he tried to appease her a little. But she would not forget. And so the life continued, hard for them both.

For a whole year they lived thus, strangers one to the other. Bertha almost became mad.

Then one morning, having set out at dawn, she returned toward eight o'clock carrying in both hands an enormous bouquet of roses, of white roses, all white.

She sent word to her husband that she would like to speak to him. He came in disturbed, troubled.

"Let us go out together," she said to him. "Take these flowers, they are too heavy for me."

He took the bouquet and followed his wife. A carriage awaited them, which started as soon as they were seated.

It stopped before the gate of a cemetery. Then Bertha, her eyes full of tears, said to George: "Take me to her grave."

He trembled, without knowing why, but walked on before, holding the flowers in his arms. Finally he stopped before a shaft of white marble and pointed to it without a word.

She took the bouquet from him, and, kneeling, placed it at the foot of the grave. Then her heart was raised in suppliant, silent prayer.

Her husband stood behind her, weeping, haunted by memories.

She arose and put out her hands to him.

"If you wish, we will be friends," she said.

The White Wolf

THIS is the story the old Marquis d'Arville told us after a dinner in honor of Saint-Hubert, at the house of Baron des Ravels. They had run down a stag that day. The Marquis was the only one of the guests who had not taken part in the chase. He never hunted.

During the whole of the long repast, they had talked of scarcely anything but the massacre of animals. Even the ladies interested themselves in the sanguinary and often unlikely stories, while the orators mimicked the attacks and combats between man and beast, raising their arms and speaking in thunderous tones.

M. d'Arville talked much, with a certain poesy, a little flourish, but full of effect. He must have repeated this story often, it ran so smoothly, never halting at a choice of words in which to clothe an image.

"Gentlemen, I never hunt, nor did my father, nor my grandfather, nor my great-great-grandfather. The last named was the son of a man who hunted more than all of you. He died in 1764. I will tell you how. He was named John, and was married, and became the father of the man who was my great-great-grandfather. He lived with his younger brother, Francis d'Arville, in our castle, in the midst of a deep forest in Lorraine.

"Francis d'Arville always remained a boy through his love for hunting. They both hunted from one end of the year to the other without cessation or weariness. They loved nothing else, understood nothing else, talked only of this, and lived for this alone.

"They were possessed by this terrible, inexorable passion. It consumed them, having taken entire control of them, leaving no place for anything else. They had agreed not to put off the chase for any reason whatsoever. My great-great-grandfather was born while his father was following a fox, but John d'Arville did not interrupt his sport, and swore that the little beggar might have waited until after the death-cry! His brother Francis showed himself still more hot-headed than he. The first thing on rising, he would go to see the dogs, then the horses; then he would shoot some birds about the place, even when about to set out hunting big game.

"They were called in the country Monsieur the Marquis and Monsieur the Cadet, noblemen then not acting as do those of our time, who wish to establish in their titles a descending scale of rank, for the son of a marquis is no more a count, or the son of a viscount a baron, than the son of a general is a colonel by birth. But the niggardly vanity of the day finds profit in this arrangement. To return to my ancestors:

"They were, it appears, immoderately large, bony, hairy, violent, and vigorous. The younger one was taller than the elder, and had such a voice that, according to a legend he was very proud of, all the leaves of the forest moved when he shouted.

"And when mounted, ready for the chase, it must have been a superb sight to see these two giants astride their great horses.

"Toward the middle of the winter of that year, 1764, the cold was excessive and the wolves became ferocious.

"They even attacked belated peasants, roamed around houses at night, howled from sunset to sunrise, and ravaged the stables.

"At one time a rumor was circulated. It was said that a colossal wolf, of grayish-white color, which had eaten two children, devoured the arm of a woman, strangled all the watchdogs of the country, was now coming without fear into the house inclosures and smelling around the doors. Many inhabitants affirmed that they had felt his breath, which made the lights flicker. Shortly a panic ran through all the province. No one dared to go out after nightfall. The very shadows seemed haunted by the image of this beast.

"The brothers D'Arville resolved to find and slay him. So they called together for a grand chase all the gentlemen of the country.

"It was in vain. They had beaten the forests and scoured the thickets, but had seen nothing of him. They killed wolves, but not that one. And each night after such a chase, the beast, as if to avenge himself, attacked some traveler, or devoured some cattle, always far from the place where they had sought him.

"Finally, one night he found a way into the swine-house of the castle D'Arville and ate two beauties of the best breed.

"The two brothers were furious, interpreting the attack as one of bravado on the part of the monster—a direct injury, a defiance. Therefore, taking all their best-trained hounds, they set out to run down the beast, with courage excited by anger.

"From dawn until the sun descended behind the great nut-trees, they beat about forests with no result.

"At last, both of them, angry and disheartened, turned their horses' steps into a by-path bordered by rushwood. They were marveling at the baffling power of this wolf, when suddenly they were seized with a mysterious fear.

"The elder said:

"'This can be no ordinary beast. One might say he can think like a man.'

"The younger replied:

"'Perhaps we should get our cousin, the Bishop, to bless a bullet for him, or ask a priest to pronounce some words to help us.'

"Then they were silent.

"John continued: 'Look at the sun, how red it is. The great wolf will do mischief to-night.'

"He had scarcely finished speaking when his horse reared. Francis's horse started to run at the same time. A large bush covered with dead leaves rose before them, and a colossal beast, grayish white, sprang out, scampering away through the wood.

"Both gave a grunt of satisfaction, and bending to the necks of their heavy horses, they urged them on with the weight of their bodies, exciting them, hastening with voice and spur, until these strong riders seemed to carry the weight of their beasts between their knees, carrying them by force as if they were flying.

"Thus they rode, crashing through forests, crossing ravines, climbing up the sides of steep gorges, and sounding the horn, at frequent intervals, to arouse the people and the dogs of the neighborhood.

"But suddenly, in the course of this breakneck ride, my ancestor struck his forehead against a large branch and fractured his skull. He fell to the ground as if dead, while his frightened horse disappeared in the surrounding thicket.

"The younger D'Arville stopped short, sprang to the ground, seized his brother in his arms, and saw that he had lost consciousness.

"He sat down beside him, took his disfigured head upon his knees, looking earnestly at the lifeless face. Little by little a fear crept over him, a strange fear that he had never before felt, fear of the shadows, of the solitude, of the lonely woods, and also of the chimerical wolf, which had now come to be the death of his brother.

"The shadows deepened, the branches of the trees crackled in the sharp cold. Francis arose shivering, incapable of re-

maining there longer, and already feeling his strength fail. There was nothing to be heard, neither the voice of dogs nor the sound of a horn; all within this invisible horizon was mute. And in this gloomy silence and the chill of evening there was something strange and frightful.

"With his powerful hands he seized John's body and laid it across the saddle to take it home; then mounted gently behind it, his mind troubled by horrible, supernatural images, as if he were possessed.

"Suddenly, in the midst of these fears, a great form passed. It was the wolf. A violent fit of terror seized upon the hunter; something cold, like a stream of ice-water seemed to glide through his veins, and he made the sign of the cross, like a monk haunted with devils, so dismayed was he by the reappearance of the frightful wanderer. Then, his eyes falling upon the inert body before him, his fear was quickly changed to anger, and he trembled with inordinate rage.

"He pricked his horse and darted after him.

"He followed him through copses, over ravines, and around great forest trees, traversing woods that he no longer recognized, his eye fixed upon a white spot, which was ever flying from him as night covered the earth.

"His horse also seemed moved by an unknown force. He galloped on with neck extended, crashing over small trees and rocks, with the body of the dead stretched across him on the saddle. Brambles caught in his mane; his head, where it had struck the trunks of trees, was spattered with blood; the marks of the spurs were over his flanks.

"Suddenly the animal and its rider came out of the forest, rushing through a valley as the moon appeared above the hills. This valley was stony and shut in by enormous rocks, over which it was impossible to pass; there was no other way for the wolf but to turn on his steps.

"Francis gave such a shout of joy and revenge that the echo of it was like the roll of thunder. He leaped from his horse, knife in hand.

"The bristling beast, with rounded back, was awaiting him; his eyes shining like two stars. But before joining in battle, the strong hunter, grasping his brother, seated him upon a rock, supporting his head, which was now but a mass of blood, with stones, and cried aloud to him, as to one deaf: 'Look, John! Look here!'

"Then he threw himself upon the monster. He felt himself strong enough to overthrow a mountain, to crush the very rocks in his hands. The beast meant to kill him by sinking his claws in his vitals; but the man had seized him by the throat, without even making use of his weapon, and strangled him gently, waiting until his breath stopped and he could hear the death-rattle at his heart. And he laughed, with the joy of dismay, clutching more and more with a terrible hold, and crying out in his delirium:

'Look, John! Look!' All resistance ceased. The body of the wolf was limp. He was dead.

"Then Francis, taking him in his arms, threw him down at the feet of his elder brother, crying out in expectant voice: 'Here, here, my little John, here he is!'

"Then he placed upon the saddle the two bodies, the one above the other, and started on his way.

"He returned to the castle laughing and weeping, like Gargantua at the birth of Pantagruel, shouting in triumph and stamping with delight in relating the death of the beast, and moaning and tearing at his beard in calling the name of his brother.

"Often, later, when he recalled this day, he would declare, with tears in his eyes: 'If only poor John had seen me strangle the beast, he would have died content, I am sure!'

"The widow of my ancestor inspired in her son a horror of the chase, which was transmitted from father to son down to myself."

The Marquis d'Arville was silent. Some one asked: "Is the story a legend or not?"

And the narrator replied:

"I swear to you it is true from beginning to end."

Then a lady, in a sweet little voice, declared:

"It is beautiful to have passions like that."

Toine

EVERYBODY for ten leagues round knew Toine, fat Toine, "Toine-my-Fine," Antoine Mâcheblé, the landlord of Tournevent.

He had made famous this village, buried in the depths of the valley which descended to the sea. It was a poor peasant hamlet, composed of a dozen Norman houses surrounded by ditches and encircled by trees. The houses were huddled together in this shrub-covered ravine, behind the curve of the hill, which had caused the village to be called Tournevent. As birds conceal themselves in the furrows during a storm, they seemed to have sought a shelter in this hollow, a shelter against the fierce salt winds of the sea, which gnawed and burned like fire and withered and destroyed like the blasts of winter.

The whole hamlet seemed to be the property of Antoine Mâcheblé, who was besides often called Toine, and Toine-my-Fine, on account of a manner of speech of which he constantly availed himself. "My Fine is the best in France," he would say. His *fine* was his cognac, be it understood. For twenty years he had watered the country with his cognac, and in serving his customers he was in the habit of saying: "It warms the stomach and clears the head; there is nothing better for your health, my son." He called everybody "my son," although he had never had a son of his own.

Ah, yes, everyone knew old Toine, the biggest man in the canton, or even in the *arrondissement*. His little house seemed too ridiculously small to contain him, and when he was seen standing in his doorway, where he spent the greater part of every day, one wondered how he could enter his dwelling. But he did enter each time a customer presented himself, for Toine-my-Fine was invited by right to levy a little glass on all who drank in his house.

His *café* bore on its sign the legend "The Rendezvous of Friends," and old Toine was truly the friend of all the country round. People came from Fécamp and Montivilliers to see him and tipple with him and to hear his stories— for this great, good-natured man could make a tombstone laugh. He could joke without giving offense, wink an eye to express what he dare not utter, and punch one's ribs in a fit of gaiety, so as to force a laugh in spite of oneself. And then it was a curiosity just to see him drink. He drank all that was offered him by everybody, with a joy in his wicked eye, a joy which came from a double pleasure: the pleasure of regaling himself first, and the pleasure of heaping up money at the expense of his friends afterward. The blackguards of the community wondered why Toine had no children, and one day asked him as much. With a wicked wink he replied: "My wife is not attractive enough for such a fine fellow as I am."

The quarrels of Toine and his homely wife were as much enjoyed by the tipplers as was their favorite cognac, for they had squabbled through the whole thirty years of their married life. Only Toine was good-natured over it, while his wife was furious. She was a tall peasant woman who walked with long stilt-like strides and carried on her thin, flat body the head of an ugly screech owl. She spent her whole time in rearing poultry in the little yard behind the public-house, and was renowned for the success with which she fattened her fowls.

When any of the great ladies of Fécamp gave a feast to the people of quality, it was necessary to the success of the repast that it should be garnished with the celebrated fowls from mother Toine's poultry-yard.

But she was born with a vile temper and had continued to be dissatisfied with everything. Angry with everybody, she was particularly so with her husband. She jeered at his gaiety, his popularity, his good health, and his *embonpoint;* she treated him with the utmost contempt because he got his money without working for it, and because, as she said, he ate and drank as much as ten ordinary men. She declared every day that he was only fit to be littered in the stable with the naked swine, whom he resembled, and that he was only a mass of fat that made her sick at her stomach. "Wait a little, wait a little," she would shriek in his face, "we shall soon see what is going to happen! This great wind-bag will burst like a sack of grain!"

Toine laughed till he shook like a bowl of jelly and, tapping his enormous belly, replied: "Ah, my old hen, let us see you try to make your chickens as fat as this."

And rolling up his sleeve he showed his brawny arm. "Do you not see the feathers growing already?" he cried. And the customers would strike their fists on the table and fairly writhe with joy, and would stamp their feet and spit upon the floor in a delirium of delight.

The old woman grew more furious than ever, and shouted at the top of her lungs: "Just wait a bit, we shall see what will happen. Your Toine-my-Fine will burst like a sack of grain."

And she rushed out, maddened with rage at the laughter of the crowd of drinkers.

Toine, in fact, was a wonder to see, so fat and red and short of breath had he grown. He was one of those enormous creatures with whom Death seems to amuse himself by tricks, gaieties, and fatal, buffooneries, making irresistibly comic the slow work of destruction. Instead of showing himself, as toward others, in white hairs, shrunken limbs, wrinkles, and general feebleness which made one say with a shiver: "Heavens, how he has changed!" he took pleasure in fattening Toine; in making a droll monster of him, in reddening his face and giving him the appearance of superhuman health; and the deformities which he inflicted on other beings became in Toine's case laughable and diverting instead of sinister and pitiable.

"Wait a little, wait a little," muttered mother Toine, as she scattered the grain about her poultry-yard, "we are going to see what will happen!"

II.

It happened that Toine had a seizure, and fell smitten with a paralytic stroke. They carried the giant to the little chamber partitioned off at the rear of the *café* in order that he might hear what was going on on the other side of the wall, and converse with his friends, for his brain remained clear while his enormous body was prone and helpless. They hoped for a time that his mighty limbs would recover some of their energy, but this hope disappeared very soon, and Toine-my-Fine was forced to pass his days and nights in his bed, which was made up but once a week, with the help of four friends who lifted him by his four limbs while his mattress was turned. He continued cheerful, but with a different kind of gaiety; more timid, more humble, and with the pathetic fear of a little child in the presence of his wife, who scolded and raged all the day long. "There he lies, the great glutton, the good-for-nothing idler, the nasty thing!" she cried. Toine replied nothing, only winking his eye behind the old woman's back, and turned over in the bed, the only movement he was able to make. He called this change "making a move to the north, or a move to the south." His only entertainment now was to listen to the conversation in the *café* and to join in the talk across the wall, and when he recognized the voice of a friend he would cry: "Hello, my son; is it thou, Célestin?"

And Célestin Maloisel would reply: "It is me, father Toine. How do you gallop to-day, my great rabbit?"

"I cannot gallop yet, Célestin," Toine would answer, "but I am not growing thin, either. The shell is good." Soon he invited his intimates into his chamber for company, because it pained him to see them drinking without him. He told them it grieved him not to be able to take his cognac with them. "I can stand everything else," he said; "but not to drink with you makes me sad, my sons."

Then the screech-owl's head of mother Toine would appear at the window, and she would say: "Look, look at him! this great hulking idler, who must be fed and washed and scoured like a pig!"

And when she disappeared a red-plumaged rooster sometimes perched on the window-sill, and, looking about with his round and curious eye, gave forth a shrill crow. And sometimes two or three hens flew in and scratched and pecked about the floor, attracted by the crumbs, which fell from father Toine's plate.

The friends of Toine-my-Fine very soon deserted the *café* for his chamber, and every afternoon they gossiped around the bed of the big man. Bedridden as he was, this rascal of a Toine still amused them; he would have made the devil himself laugh, the jolly fellow! There were three friends who came every day: Célestin Maloisel, a tall, spare man with a body twisted like the trunk of an apple-tree; Prosper Horslaville, a little dried-up old man with a nose like a ferret, malicious and sly as a fox; and Césaire Paumelle, who never uttered a word, but who enjoyed himself all the same. These men brought in a board from the yard which they placed across the bed and on which they played dominoes from two o'clock in the afternoon until six. But mother Toine soon interfered: she could not endure that her husband should amuse himself by playing dominoes in his bed, and, each time she saw the play, she bounded into the room in a rage, overturned the board, seized the dominoes, and carried them into the *café*, declaring that it was enough to feed this great lump of tallow without seeing him divert himself at the expense of hard-wording people. Célestin Maloisel bent his head before the storm, but Prosper Horslaville tried to further excite the old woman, whose rages amused him. Seeing her one day more exasperated than usual, he said: "Hello, mother Toine! Do you know what I would do if I were in your place?"

She waited for an explanation, fixing her owl-like eyes upon him. He continued:

"Your husband, who never leaves his bed, is as hot as an oven. I should set him to hatching out eggs."

She remained stupefied, thinking he was jesting, watching the meager and sly face of the peasant, who continued: "I would put five eggs under each arm the same day that I set the yellow hen; they would all hatch out at the same time; and when they were out of their shells, I would put your husband's chicks under the hen for her to bring up. That would bring you some poultry, mother Toine."

The old woman was amazed. "Can that be?" she asked.

Prosper continued: "Why can't it? Since they put eggs in a warm box to hatch, one might as well put them in a warm bed."

She was greatly impressed with this reasoning, and went out composed and thoughtful.

Eight days later she came into Toine's chamber with her apron full of eggs, and said: "I have just put the yellow hen to set with ten eggs under her; here are ten for you! Be careful not to break them!"

Toine was astonished. "What do you mean?" he cried.

"I mean that you shall hatch them, good-for-nothing."

Toine laughed at first, then as she in-sisted he grew angry, he resisted and obstinately refused to allow her to put the eggs under his great arms, that his warmth might hatch them. But the baffled old woman grew furious and declared: "You shall have not a bite to eat so long as you refuse to take them— there, we'll see what will happen!"

Toine was uneasy, but he said nothing till he heard the clock strike twelve; then he called to his wife, who bawled from the kitchen: "There is no dinner for you to-day, you great idler!"

He thought at first she was joking, but when he found she was in earnest he begged and prayed and swore by fits; turned himself to the north and the south, and, growing desperate under the pangs of hunger and the smell of the viands, he pounded on the wall with his great fists, until at last worn out and almost famished, he allowed his wife to introduce the eggs into his bed and place them under his arms. After that he had his soup.

When his friends arrived as usual, they believed Toine to be very ill; he seemed constrained and in pain.

Then they began to play dominoes as formerly, but Toine appeared to take no pleasure in the game, and put forth his hand so gingerly and with such evident precaution that they suspected at once something was wrong.

"Hast thou thy arm tied?" demanded Horslaville.

Toine feebly responded: "I have a feeling of heaviness in my shoulder."

Suddenly some one entered the *café*, and the players paused to listen. It was the mayor and his assistant, who called for two glasses of cognac and then began to talk of the affairs of the country.

As they spoke in low tones, Toine tried to press his ear against the wall; and forgetting his eggs, he gave a sudden lunge "to the north," which made an omelet of them in short order. At the oath he uttered, mother Toine came running in, and divining the disaster she uncovered him with a jerk. She stood a moment too enraged and breathless to speak. at the sight of the yellow poultice pasted on the flank of her husband. Then, trembling with fury, she flung herself on the paralytic and began to pound him with great force on the body, as though she were pounding her dirty linen on the banks of the river. She showered her blows upon him with the force and rapidity of a drummer beating his drum.

The friends of Toine were choking with laughter, coughing, sneezing, uttering exclamations, while the frightened man parried the attacks of his wife with due precaution in order not to break the five eggs he still had on the other side.

III.

TOINE was conquered. He was compelled to hatch eggs. He had to renounce the innocent pleasure of dominoes, to give up any effort to move to the north or south, for his wife deprived him of all nourishment every time he broke an egg. He lay on his back, with his eyes fixed on the ceiling, his arms extended like wings, warming against his immense body the incipient chicks in their white shells. He spoke only in low tones as if he feared a noise as much as a movement, and he asked often about the yellow hen in the poultry-yard, who was engaged in the same task as himself. The old woman went from the hen to her husband, and from her husband to the hen, possessed and preoccupied with the little broods which were maturing in the bed and in the nest. The country people, who soon learned the story, came in, curious and serious to get the news of Toine. They entered on tiptoe as one enters a sick-chamber and inquired with concern:

"How goes it, Toine?"

"It has to go," he answered; "but it is so long, I am tired of waiting. I get excited and feel cold shivers galloping all over my skin."

One morning his wife came in very much elated and exclaimed: "The yellow hen has hatched seven chicks; there were but three bad eggs!"

Toine felt his heart beat. How many would he have?

"Will it be soon?" he asked, with the anguish of a woman who is about to become a mother.

The old woman, who was tortured by the fear of failure, answered angrily:

"It is to be hoped so!"

They waited.

The friends, seeing that Toine's time was approaching, became very uneasy themselves. They gossiped about it in the house, and kept all the neighbors informed of the progress of affairs. Toward three o'clock Toine grew drowsy. He slept now half the time. He was suddenly awakened by an unusual tickling under his left arm. He put his hand carefully to the place and seized a little beast covered with yellow down, which struggled between his fingers. His emotion was so great that he cried out and let go the chick, which ran across his breast. The *café* was full of people. The customers rushed into the room and circled around the bed, while mother Toine, who had arrived at the first sound, carefully caught the fledgeling as it nestled in her husband's beard. No one uttered a word. It was a warm April day; one could hear through the open window the clucking of the yellow hen calling to her new born. Toine, who perspired with emotion and agony, murmured: "I feel another one under my left arm."

His wife plunged her great, gaunt hand under the bedclothes and drew forth a second chick with all the precautions of a midwife.

The neighbors wished to see it and passed it from hand to hand, regarding it with awe as though it were a phenomenon. For the space of twenty minutes no more were hatched, then four chicks came out of their shells at the same time. This caused a great excitement among the watchers.

Toine smiled, happy at his success, and began to feel proud of this singular paternity. Such a sight had never been seen before. This was a droll man, truly! "That makes six," cried Toine. *"Sacre bleu,* what a christening there will be!" and a great laugh rang out from the public. Other people now crowded into the *café* and filled the doorway, with outstretched necks and curious eyes.

"How many has he?" they inquired. "There are six."

Mother Toine ran with the new fledgelings to the hen, who, clucking distractedly, erected her feathers and spread wide her wings to shelter her increasing flock of little ones.

"Here comes another one!" cried Toine. He was mistaken—there were three of them. This was a triumph! The last one chipped its shell at seven o'clock in the evening. All Toine's eggs were good! He was delivered, and delirious with joy, he seized and kissed the frail little creature on the back. He could have smothered it with caresses. He wished to keep this little one in his bed until the next day, moved by the tenderness of a mother for this being to whom he had given life; but the old woman carried it away, as she had done the others, without listening to the supplications of her husband.

The friends of Toine went home delighted, conversing of the event by the way.

Horslaville remained after the others had gone, and approaching the ear of Toine whispered: "You will invite me to the first fricassee, will you not?"

At the idea of a fricassee, the visage of Toine brightened and he answered:

"Certainly I will invite thee, my son."

An Enthusiast

WE WERE just passing through Gisors, when I was awakened by hearing a trainman call the name of the town. I was falling off to sleep again when a frightful jolt threw me across to a large lady opposite me.

A wheel had broken on the locomotive, which was now lying across the track. The tender and baggage-car were also derailed and were lodged by the side of the great, dying machine, which moaned and groaned and sputtered and puffed, like a fallen horse in the street, whose breast heaves and nostrils smoke, wheezing and shivering in its whole body, yet incapable of any effort toward getting up and continuing on the way.

Our engine proved to be neither dead nor wounded; there was only some derangement, but the train could not go on; and we stood looking at the maimed iron beast that could no longer draw us, but lay, barring the track. It would be necessary, without doubt, to have a relief train sent out from Paris.

It was ten o'clock in the morning, and I decided immediately to go back to Gisors for breakfast. In walking along upon the track, I said to myself: "Gisors, Gisors, I certainly know some one here. Who is it? Gisors? Let me see. I have some friend in this town." The name immediately sprang into my mind: "Albert Marambot."

He was an old comrade in college, whom I had not seen for a dozen years or so, and who was a practitioner of the medical profession at Gisors. Often he had written inviting me to visit him; I had always promised to go but had never gone. Now I would certainly take advantage of the opportunity.

I asked the first passer-by if he knew where Dr. Marambot lived? He replied without hesitation, with the drawling accent of the Norman:

"Dauphine Street."

Soon I found on the door of the house indicated a large copper plate on which was engraved the name of my old comrade. I rang; the servant who opened the door, a girl with yellow hair and slow motion, kept repeating in a stupid fashion: "He's gone out, he's gone out."

I heard a sound of forks and glasses inside, and called out: "Hey, there! Marambot!" A door opened and a large, well-favored man appeared, looking disturbed, and holding a napkin in his hand.

I never should have known him. One would say he was forty-five, at least; and in a second his whole provincial life appeared before me, dulling, stupefying, and aging him. In a single bound of thought, more rapid than the gesture of extending my hand to him, I knew his whole existence, his manner of life, his bent of mind, and his theories of living. I suspected the long repasts which had rounded his body, the little naps after dinner, in the torpor of a heavy digestion sprinkled with brandy, and the vague contemplation of the sick, with thoughts of roast fowl waiting before the fire. His conversation on cooking, cider, brandy, and wine, upon certain dishes and well-made sauces appropriate for them, revealed to me nothing more than I perceived in the red puffiness of his cheeks, the heaviness of his lips, and the dullness of his eyes.

I said to him: "You do not know me. I am Raoul Aubertin."

He opened his arms and almost stifled me. His first word was:

"You certainly haven't breakfasted?"

"No."

"What luck! I am just sitting down at the table, and I have an excellent trout."

Five minutes later, I was seated at

the table opposite him. I said to him: "You are still a bachelor?"

"Surely!" he answered.

"And you manage to amuse yourself here?"

"I never find it tedious; I am too much occupied. I have my patients and my friends, eat well, sleep well, and love to laugh and to hunt. That is the way it goes."

"Then life does not get monotonous in this little town?"

"No, my dear fellow, not when one is busy. A little town, when you come to sum it up, is like a large one. Events and pleasures are less varied, but they take on more importance. Relatives and friends are less numerous, but we meet them oftener. When we know every window in sight, each one interests us, and we are more curious about them than we should be about a whole street in Paris. It is very amusing, a little town, you know, very amusing, very amusing. Now, this Gisors; I have it on the end of my fingers from its origin up to to-day. You have no idea how comical its history it."

"You are a native of Gisors?"

"I? No, I come from Gournay, its neighbor and rival. Gournay is to Gisors what Lucullus was to Cicero. Here, all is for glory; they are called 'the proud people of Gisors.' At Gournay, all is for the stomach; they are spoken of as 'the eaters of Gournay.' It is very funny, this country is."

I noticed that I was eating something truly exquisite, some fish roe enveloped in a case of jelly, the viand aromatic with herbs, and the jelly delicately seasoned.

Smacking my lips, for the sake of flattering Marambot, I said: "This is good!"

He smiled. "Two things are necessary for this," said he, "and difficult to obtain, good jelly and good eggs. Oh! good eggs, how rare they are! with the yellow of a reddish tinge, and well flavored! I myself have a preference for two things, eggs and poultry. I keep my egg-layers in a special way. I have my own ideas. In the egg, as in the flesh of the chicken, or of mutton, or beef, we find, and ought to taste, the substance, the quintessence of the nourishment of the animal. How much better one can eat if he pays attention to these things."

I laughed. "You are an epicure, then?"

"Surely! It is only imbeciles who are not epicures. One is an epicure as he is artistic, as he is well-informed, as he is poetical. Taste is a delicate organ, as respectable and as capable of being perfected as the eye or the ear. To lack taste is to be deprived of an exquisite faculty,—that of discerning the quality of food, as one discerns the qualities of a book or a work of art; it is to be deprived of an essential sense, of an attribute of human superiority; it is to belong to one of the innumerable classes of the infirm, or disgraced, or simpletons that compose our race; it is to have the mouth of a beast, and, in a word, the mind of a beast. A man who cannot distinguish between a crayfish and a lobster, a herring and this admirable fish that carries in it all the savors and aromas of the sea, between a mackerel and a white-fish, a winter pear and a Duchesse, is capable of confounding Balzac with Eugene Sué, a symphony of

Beethoven with a military march by the leader of a regiment band, and the Apollo Belvedere with the statue of General Blanmont!"

"Who is this General Blanmont?" I asked.

"Ah! it is true, you do not know him! That shows, indeed, that you do not know Gisors! My dear friend, I said a moment ago, that we call the people of this town 'the proud people of Gisors.' Never was epithet more merited. But —we will breakfast first, and then I shall tell you about our town, and take you around to visit it." ·

He ceased speaking from time to time to drink slowly a little glass of wine which he looked at tenderly before setting on the table. With napkin fastened about his neck, with cheek-bones reddening, and whiskers blossoming about his mouth as if worked, he was amusing to look at.

He made me eat to suffocation. Then, when I wished to go back to the railway station, he seized me in his arms and drew me away in another street. The town, of a pretty, provincial character, was overlooked by its fortress, the most curious monument of military architecture of the eighth century that there is in France. The rear of the fortress overlooked, in its turn, a long, green valley, where the heavy cows of Normandy browsed and chewed their cuds in the pastures.

The doctor said to me: "Gisors, town of four thousand inhabitants, on the borders of the Eure, was mentioned in the 'Commentaries' of Cæsar: Cæsaris ostium, then, Cæsartium, Cæsortium, Gisortium, Gisors. I could take you to the encampment of the Roman army,

of which there are traces quite visible still."

I laughed and replied: "My dear friend, it seems to me that you are threatened with a special malady that you ought to study—you, a medical man —something that might be called the spirit of rivalry."

He stopped short. "The spirit of rivalry, my friend," said he, "is nothing else than natural patriotism. I love my house, my town, and my province throughout its whole extent, because I find there the customs of my village; but, if I love the frontier, if I defend it, if I am angry when the stranger sets his foot there, it is because I already feel my own house menaced; because the frontier, which I do not know, is the road to my province. Thus I am a Norman, a true Norman; and in spite of my rancor against Germany and my desire for vengeance, I do not detest it, I do not hate it by instinct as I hate the English, the veritable enemy, the hereditary enemy, the natural enemy of the Norman, because the English have passed over the soil settled by my ancestors, and pillaged and ravaged it twenty times, and the aversion to this perfidious people has been transmitted to me with life itself, from my father— Wait, here is the statue of the general."

"What general?"

"General Blanmont. We thought we ought to have a statue. We are not 'the proud people of Gisors' for nothing! Then, we discovered General Blanmont. Just look through the glass door in this library."

I turned toward the front of a bookcase where a small collection of volumes, yellow, red, and blue, met my eye. In reading the titles, a desire to laugh seized me; they were: "Gisors, Its Origin and Future, By M. X—— Member of Many Learned Societies"; "History of Gisors, By Abbé——"; "Gisors, from Cæsar to Our Time, by Dr. C. D.——"; "The Glories of Gisors, by an Inquirer."

"My dear boy," began Marambot, "not a year passes, not one year, you understand, without at least one new history of Gisors appearing. We have twenty-three of them."

"And who are the celebrities of Gisors?" I asked.

"Oh! I cannot tell you all of them; I shall only tell you the principal ones: First, we have General Blanmont, then Baron Davillier, the celebrated ceramist who explored Spain and the Balearic Islands, and revealed to collectors some admirable Spanish-Arabian porcelains. In letters, we have a journalist of great merit, now dead, Charles Brainne, and among the living, the very eminent director of the 'Rouen Gazetteer,' Charles Lapierre, and many more, still many more."

We were going along rapidly through a steep street beaten upon by a June sun so hot that it had driven the inhabitants within doors. Suddenly, at the other end of this road, a man appeared —a drunken man, reeling. He came on, with head down, arms hanging at his sides, and tottering limbs, at a jerky gait of six or eight rapid steps, followed by a rest. Then an energetic bound would take him to the middle of the street, where he would stop short and balance himself upon his feet, hesitating between a fall and a new attack of energy. Then he would repeat the operation in another direction. Finally he ran against a house, where he seemed to stick fast, as if he would enter it through the wall. Then he turned and looked before him, his mouth open, his eyes blinking in the sun; and with a wrench of his back, he detached himself from the wall and started again.

A little yellow dog, a famished cur, followed him barking, stopping when he stopped and starting when he started.

"Wait," said Marambot, "there is one of Madame Huisson's rose-winners."

I was much astonished, and replied: "Madame Huisson's rose-winners—what do you mean?"

The doctor laughed. "Oh! It is a way we have here of calling a man a drunkard. It comes from an old story now passed into legend, which was true nevertheless, in all points."

"Is it amusing, this story?"

"Very amusing."

"Then tell it, will you?"

"Very willingly. There was once in this town an old lady, very virtuous herself and the protector of virtue, who was called Madame Huisson. And you must know I am telling you true names and not fictitious ones. Madame Huisson occupied herself with good works, helping the poor and encouraging those that merited it. She was little, walking with quick, short steps, and wore a black silk wig. She was very polite and ceremonious, on excellent terms with the good God, as represented by Abbé Malou, and she had a profound, inborn horror of the vice the Church calls luxury. Pregnancies before marriage made her lose her temper, exasperating her to the point of making her beside herself.

"It was the epoch when they were crowning virtue with roses in the suburbs of Paris, and the idea came to Madame Huisson to have the same kind of festival in Gisors. She discussed it with Abbé Malou, who immediately made out a list of candidates for her.

"But Madame Huisson had in her service as maid an old woman named Frances, as strict as her mistress. When the priest had gone, the mistress called her servant and said to her: 'Frances, here are the names of some girls that the curate proposes for the prize of virtue; make it your business to find out what people think of them around here.'

"And Frances began to go about the country. She culled all the deceptions, stories, suspicions, and tattle, and, for fear of forgetting some of the details, she wrote them down with her expenses in her kitchen-book, and every morning she took the book to Madame Huisson who read it carefully, after adjusting her spectacles over her thin nose:

" 'Bread, four sous. Milk, two sous. Butter, eight sous.
" 'Malvina Levesque went wild last year with Matthew Poilu. One leg of mutton, twenty-five sous. Salt, one sou.
" 'Rosalie Vatinel was met in the wood with Cæsar Pienoir, at dusk, by Mrs. Onesime, ironer, the twentieth of July. Radishes, one sou. Vinegar, two sous. Sorrel, two sous. Josephine Durdent, that nobody had believed had any fault, is found to have a correspondence with the son of Oportun, who is in service at Rouen, and who sent her a bonnet by the diligence for a present.'

"Not a girl escaped intact in this scrupulous inquisition. Frances asked questions of everybody,—the neighbors, the traders, the schoolmaster, the sisters of the school,—and summed up the reports.

"As there is not a girl in the universe upon whom comments have not been passed, at one time or another, not a single young woman beyond slander was found in the whole countryside.

"Now, Madame Huisson wished her rose-winner to be like Cæsar's wife, above suspicion, and she stood amazed, desolate, and in despair before the kitchen-book of her maidservant.

"They enlarged the circle of inquiry even to the neighboring villages, but found no favorable result. The mayor was consulted. All his protégées were judged unsatisfactory. Those of Dr. Barbesol had no greater success, in spite of the precision of scientific guaranties.

"One morning Frances came in from one of her tours, and said to her mistress:

" 'It seems, Madame, that if you wish to crown somebody, there is nobody but Isidore in all the vicinity that is worthy of it.'

Madame Huisson remained quiet and thoughtful.

"She knew Isidore well, the son of Virginia, the fruit-seller. His proverbial chastity had been the delight of Gisors for many years, serving as a pleasant theme of conversation and amusement for the girls, who made themselves very merry at his expense. Over twenty-one in age, large, awkward, slow, and timid, he helped his mother at her trade, passing his days in picking over fruits and vegetables, seated on a chair before the door.

"He had an abnormal fear of petticoats that caused him to lower his eyes when a fair customer looked at him and smiled; and this timidity, being well known, rendered him the sport of all the wags of the place. Bold words, impure allusions, expressions of doubtful meaning, made him blush so quickly that Dr. Barbesol nicknamed him the thermometer of modesty. Did he know anything or did he not? his rogues of neighbors would ask one another. Was it simply a presentiment of unknown mysteries, or honest indignation for vile relations intended for love alone, which seemed to move so strongly the son of Virginia, the fruit-seller? The imps of the neighborhood would run up before his shop and throw pieces of filth in his face, just to see him lower his eyes. The girls amused themselves passing and repassing his door, calling out bewitchingly to him, until he would go into the house. Some of the boldest would provoke him openly, for the sake of laughing at him, asking him to meet them, and proposing abominable things.

"And so Madame Huisson kept thinking.

"Certainly, Isidore was a case of exceptional virtue, notorious and unassailable. No one, even the most sceptical, the most incredulous, could or would have dared to have a suspicion that Isidore was guilty of the slightest infraction of the moral law. No one had ever seen him in a *café*, or met him in the streets in the evening. He went to bed at eight o'clock and arose at four. He was perfection; a pearl.

"Nevertheless, Madame Huisson hesitated. The idea of substituting a masculine rose-winner for a feminine troubled her, disturbing her not a little, and she resolved to consult Abbé Malou.

"The abbé replied: 'What do you wish to recompense, Madame? It is virtue, is it not, and nothing but virtue? What matters it, then, whether it be male or female? Virtue is eternal; it has neither country nor sex; it is simply virtue!'

"Thus encouraged, Madame Huisson went to find the mayor. He approved of it at once. 'Let us make it a beautiful ceremony,' said he; 'and in one year, if we find a young woman as worthy as Isidore, we will then crown her. In this way we shall set a beautiful example to Nantes. Let us not be exclusive, but welcome merit wherever we find it.'

"Isidore, engaged for the occasion, blushed very red, but seemed content. The ceremony was fixed for the fifteenth of August, the feast-day of the Virgin Mary, and also that of the Emperor Napoleon.

"The municipality decided to give a grand demonstration in honor of this solemnity and ordered as a stage for the crowners an enlargement of the charming ramparts of the old fortress, which I shall soon take you to see.

"By a natural revolution of public spirit, Isidore's virtue, scoffed at until that day, had suddenly become respectable, since it would bring him five hundred francs, besides a little expense-book, which was a mountain of consideration and glory to spare. The girls now regretted their frivolity, their laughter, and their freedom of manner; and Isidore, although as modest and timid as ever, had taken on a little air of satisfaction which bespoke an inward joy.

"On the eve of the fifteenth of August, the whole of Dauphine Street was hung with draperies. Ah! I have forgotten to tell you from what event the street received its name. It appears that, years ago, the princess—some princess, I don't know her name—had been detained so long by the authorities in some public demonstration, that, in the midst of a triumphal march across the town, she stopped the procession before one of the houses of this street and exclaimed: 'Oh! what a pretty house! How I wish I might visit it! To whom does it belong?' They gave her the name of the owner, who was sought out and led, proud but confused, before the princess. She got out of her carriage, entered the house, inspected it from top to bottom, even remaining in one particular room for some minutes. When she had gone, the people, flattered by the honor received by a citizen of Gisors, cried: 'Long live the Princess!' But a little song was composed by a joker, and the street received a royal name, because of the lines, which ran thus:

> " 'The Princess, in a hurry,
> Without priest, as she ought to,
> Had, with a little water,
> Baptized it.'

"But to return to Isidore. They threw flowers all along the course of the procession, as they do for processions on the church feast-days. The National Guard was on foot under orders from its chief, Commander Desbarres, an old soldier of the Grand Army, who displayed with pride the cross of honor given to him by Napoleon himself, for the beard of a Cossack culled with a single blow of the saber by the commander from the chin of its owner in the retreat from Russia.

"The company he commanded, besides being a corps composed of the *élite*, celebrated in all the province, was the company of Gisors grenadiers, who were in demand at every celebration of note within a radius of fifteen or twenty miles. They tell how King Louis-Philippe, passing in review the militia of Eure, once stopped in astonishment before the Gisors company and exclaimed: 'Oh! who are these handsome grenadiers?'

" 'From Gisors,' replied the general.

" 'I can scarcely believe it,' murmured the king.

"Now, Commander Desbarres came with these men, music at the head, to take Isidore from his mother's shop. After a little air had been played under his windows, the rose-winner himself appeared on the threshold. He was clothed in white duck from head to foot, and wore on his head a straw cap which had on it, like a cockade, a bouquet of orange-flowers.

"This question of costume had much disturbed Madame Huisson, who hesitated a long time between the black coat of the first communicant and the complete suit of white. But Frances, her counselor, decided in favor of the white, as it would tend to give the rose-winner the air of a great poet.

"Behind him appeared his protector, his god-mother, Madame Huisson, triumphant. She took his arm upon going out, and the mayor walked at the other side of the hero. The drums beat. Commander Desbarres shouted: 'Present arms!' And the procession started on its march to the church, amid a large concourse of people assembled from all the neighboring towns and villages.

"After a short mass and a touching address by Abbé Malou, they repaired to the coronation grounds, where the banquet was served under a tent. Before sitting down at the table, the mayor had a word to say. Here is his discourse *verbatim*. I learned it by heart because it was so beautiful:

" 'Young man, a good woman, loved by the poor and respected by the rich, Madame Huisson, whom the entire country thanks here through my voice, had the thought, the happy, beneficent thought, of founding in this town a prize of virtue, which would be a precious encouragement offered to the inhabitants of this beautiful country.

" 'You, young man, are the first one crowned in the dynasty of chastity, and of this wise woman. Your name will remain at the head of this list of the deserving ones; and it will be necessary that your life, you understand, your whole life shall be in accord with this beginning. To-day, face to face with this noble woman who recompenses your virtuous conduct, face to face with these soldier-citizens who have taken up arms in your honor, and with these sympathetic people, reunited to cheer you, or rather to cheer in your virtue, may you contract the solemn engagement toward this town, toward all of us to set, until the day of your death, the excellent example of your youth. Do not forget, young man, that you are the first grain sown in the field of hope; give us the fruits that we expect from you.'

"The mayor took three steps, opened his arms, and pressed the sobbing Isidore to his heart.

"The rose-winner was sobbing, but without knowing why, from a confusion of emotion, pride and a tenderness, vague and joyous.

Then the mayor put in his hand a silk purse which rung with gold, five hundred francs in gold! And in the other hand he put the little expense-book. Then, in a solemn voice, he pronounced these words; 'Homage, Glory, and Riches, to Virtue!'

"Commander Desbarres shouted: 'Bravo!' The grenadiers followed his example, and the people applauded. Madame Huisson was drying her eyes.

"Then they took their places around the table where the banquet was served. It was magnificent and prolonged. Dish followed dish; yellow cider and red wine fraternized in neighboring glasses and mingled in the same stomachs. The rattle of dishes and of voices and the music, which played softly, made a continuous, profound rumble that lost itself in the clear sky where the swallows were flying. Madame Huisson readjusted her black silk wig from time to time, as it became tipped over one ear in her chat with Abbé Malou. The mayor, excited, talked politics with Commander Desbarres, and Isidore ate, Isidore drank, as he never had eaten or drunk before! He took and retook of everything, perceiving for the first time that it was sweet to feel himself filled with good things, which first gave pleasure to his palate. He had adroitly loosened the buckle of his trousers, which bound him under the pressure of growing corpulence, and silent, a little disturbed by the knowledge that a drop of wine had fallen on his white coat, he ceased to eat in order to carry his glass to his mouth and keep it there as long as possible, that he might taste the wine slowly.

"The hour of the toasts struck. They were numerous and well applauded. The evening came; they had been at the table since midday. Already vapors soft and milky-white were floating in the valley, clothing lightly with the shadow of night the brooks and the fields; the sun touched the horizon; the cows bellowed from afar in the brown haze of the pastures. The feast was ended. They were going back to Gisors. The procession, broken now, was marching helter-skelter. Madame Huisson had taken Isidore's arm and was giving him numerous injunctions, hurried but excellent.

"They arrived at the door of the fruit-seller, and the rose-winner was left at his mother's house. She had not yet returned. Invited by her family to celebrate the triumph of her son, she had taken luncheon with her sister, after following the procession as far as the banquet tent. So Isidore was alone in the shop, which was almost dark.

"He seated himself upon a chair, agitated by wine and by pride, and looked about him. Carrots, cabbages, and onions diffused through the closed room the strong odor of vegetables, mingling their rude garden aroma with a sweet, penetrating fragrance, the fresh and light perfume escaping from a basket of peaches.

"The rose-winner took a peach and ate it, although he was already as round as a pumpkin. Then, suddenly excited with joy, he began to dance, and something rattled in his coat. He was surprised, thrust his hand in his pocket and brought out the purse with the fire hundred francs which he had forgotten in his drunkenness. Five hundred francs! What a fortune! He turned the money out upon the counter and dropped it slowly through his fingers, so as to see them all at the same time. There were twenty-five of them, twenty-five round pieces of gold! All gold! They shone upon the wood in the thick shadows, and he counted them and recounted them, placing his finger upon each one, murmuring: 'One, two, three, four, five, —one hundred; six, seven, eight, nine, ten,—two hundred.' Then he put them in his purse again and concealed it in his pocket.

"Who can know and who can say what sort of combat took place in the soul of this rose-winner between the evil and the good, the tumultuous attack of Satan, his snares and deceits, the temptations that he threw into this timid, virgin heart? What suggestions, what images, what covetous desires had the Rogue of all rogues invented for moving and ruining this chosen soul? He seized his cap, chosen by Madame Huisson, his cap which still bore the bouquet of orange-flowers, and, going out by the street back of the house, he disappeared into the night.

*   *   *   *   *   *

"Virginia, the fruit-seller, having been told that her son had returned, came back almost immediately and found the house empty. She waited without being astonished at first; then, at the end of a quarter of an hour, she began to inquire. The neighbors in Dauphine Street had seen Isidore enter the house and had not seen him go out again. Then they searched for him, but could not find him. The fruit-seller, much disturbed, ran to the mayor. The mayor knew nothing about the youth, except that he had left him at his mother's door. Madame Huisson left her bed, when she heard that her protégé had disappeared. She immediately put on her wig, and went to Virginia's house. Virginia, who had a soul easily moved, wept tears among her cabbages, carrots and onions.

"They feared some accident. What? Commander Desbarres called out the mounted police, who made a tour around the whole town; he found, on the road from Pontoise, the little bouquet of orange-flowers. It was placed upon a table around which the authorities sat in deliberation. The rose-winner had been the victim of some stratagem on account of jealousy; but how? What means had they employed to carry off this innocent one, and to what end?

"Weary of searching without finding, the authorities retired. Virginia, alone, watched in her tears.

"The next evening, when the diligence from Paris was passing through the village on its return, the people of Gisors learned with surprise that their rose-winner had stopped the coach two hundred meters from their town, had mounted, paid for his place with a louis of the money they had given him, and that he had alighted calmly in the heart of the great city.

"The excitement in the country was considerable. Letters were exchanged between the mayor and the chief of police at Paris, but they led to no discovery. Day followed day, until a week had passed.

"Then one morning Dr. Barbesol, going out at an early hour, saw a man sitting in a doorway, clothed in grimy white, sleeping with his head against the wall. He approached him and recognized Isidore. Trying to awaken him, he found it impossible. The ex-rose-winner slept with a sleep so profound, unconquerable, and unusual, that the doctor, much surprised, sought aid in carrying the young man to Boncheval's pharmacy. When they lifted him, a bottle, apparently empty, was lying under him, and, having smelled of it, the doctor declared it had contained brandy. It was an indication that served their purpose. They understood. Isidore was drunk; had been drunk and besotted for eight days, and was too disgusting to be touched by a ragpicker. His beautiful costume of white duck had become a grimy rag, yellow, greasy, muddy, slashed, and wholly debased; and his person exhaled all sorts of nauseating odors from the brook of vice.

"He was washed, preached to, shut up, and for four days did not go out. He seemed honest and repentant. They had not found upon him either the purse with the five hundred francs, or the expense-book, or his gold watch, a sacred inheritance from his father, the fruiterer.

"On the fifth day, he risked himself in Dauphine Street. Curious looks followed him, and he went along by the houses with lowered head and shifty eyes. They lost sight of him on the way from the town through the valley. But two hours later he reappeared, giggling, and hitting himself against walls. He was drunk again, hopelessly drunk.

"Nothing could cure him. Driven out by his mother, he became a driver of coal wagons for the business house of Pougrisel, which exists to-day. His reputation as a drunkard became so great, and extended so far, that even at Evreux they spoke of the rose-winner of Madame Huisson, and the legends of the country have preserved this nickname.

"A good deed is never lost."

*   *   *   *   *   *

Dr. Marambot rubbed his hands in finishing his history.

"Did you know this rose-winner yourself?" I inquired.

"Yes," said he, "I had the honor of shutting his eyes."

"How did he die?"

"In a crisis of delirium tremens, naturally."

We had come to the old fortress, heaped with ruined walls overlooking the tower of St. Thomas of Canterbury, and the tower called the Prisoner. Marambot told me the history of this prisoner, who, with the end of a nail, covered the walls of his dungeon with sculpture, following the movements of the sun across the narrow slit in a murderer's cell.

Then I learned that Clotaire II. had given Gisors to his cousin Saint Romain, Bishop of Rouen; that Gisors ceased to be the capital of Vexin after the treaty of St. Clair on the Epte; that the town is the first strategic point of that part of France; and that it has been, on account of this advantage, taken and retaken an infinite number of times. Upon the order of William the Red, the celebrated engineer, Robert de Bellesme, constructed there a powerful fortress, attacked later by Louis the Great, then by the Norman barons; it was defended by Robert de Candos, ceded finally by Louis the Great to Goeffrey Plantagenet, and was retaken from the English, following the treaty of the Templars. It was disputed between Philip Augustus and Richard the Lion-Hearted; burned by Edward III. of England, who could not take the castle; rebuilt by the English again in 1419; surrendered later to Charles VII. by Richard de Marbury; taken by the Duke of Calabre, occupied by the League, inhabited by Henry IV., etc.

And Marambot, convinced, almost eloquent, repeated: "What scoundrels those English are! And what drinkers, my dear friend, and all rose-winners, are those hypocrites, every one of them!"

After that there was a silence, and he held out his arms to the thin little river that glistened through the level fields. Then he said:

"You know that Henry Monnier was one of the most assiduous of fishermen on the banks of the Epte?"

"No, I did not know it."

"And Bouffé, my dear fellow, Bouffé was here as painter and glazier."

"Oh! come, now!"

"Yes, truly. How can you be so ignorant of these things?"

The Traveler's Story

WE went up on the bridge again after dinner. The Mediterranean before us had not a ripple on its whole surface, in which a great, calm moon was reflected. The huge steamer sped along, throwing to the heavens sown with stars a great serpent of black smoke. And behind us the whitened water, agitated by the rapid passing of the heavy ship, seemed to be in torture, beaten into froth by the screw, and changed from its smooth splendor where it lay quiet under the rays of the brilliant moon.

We were there, several of us, silent, admiring, our eyes turned toward Africa, whither we were bound. The commander, smoking a cigar as he stood among us, suddenly took up the conversation of the dinner-table:

"Yes, I did have some fears that day. My ship had been six hours with that rocking in the hold, beaten by the sea. Happily, we were picked up toward evening, by an English collier that had spied us."

Then a great man of burly figure and grave aspect, one of those men who seem to have come from some unknown and distant country, from the midst of incessant dangers, whose tranquil eye, in its profundity, appears to hold in some way the foreign landscapes he has seen, —one of those men who give the impression of possessing great courage, spoke for the first time:

"You say, commander, that you were afraid. I cannot believe that. You deceive yourself in the word, and in the sensation you experienced. An energetic man is never afraid in the face of pressing danger. He is moved, excited, anxious, but fear is another thing."

The commander, laughing, replied: "Nonsense! I tell you frankly that I was afraid."

Then the man with the bronze tint said in a slow manner:

"Allow me to explain myself! Fear (and the hardiest men can experience fear) is something frightful, an atrocious sensation, like the decomposition of the soul, a frightful spasm of thought and of the heart, of which the mere remembrance sends a shiver of agony through the frame. But this is not felt when one is brave, nor before an attack, nor before inevitable death, nor before any of all the known forms of peril; it is felt in abnormal circumstances, under certain mysterious influences, in the face of vague dangers. True fear is something like a reminiscence of fantastic terrors of other times. A man who believes in spirits, and who imagines that he sees a specter in the night, should understand fear in all its horror.

"As for me, I have understood what fear is, in broad day. It was about ten years ago. I also felt it again last winter, one night in December.

"Yet I have taken many chances, had many adventures that seemed mortal. I have often fought. I have been left for dead by robbers. I have been condemned as an insurgent, in America, doomed to be hanged, and thrown into the sea from the bridge of a ship in China. Each time I believed myself lost, but undertook to make the best of it immediately, without grief or even regret.

"But fear—that is something else.

"I had a presentiment in Africa—although presentiment in a daughter of the north—the sun dissipates it like a fog. Notice that well, gentlemen. Among the Orientals, life counts for nothing. They are always resigned to meet death. Nights are clear and free from the disquieting shadows which haunt the brains of the people of cold countries. In the Orient they understand panic, but they are ignorant of fear.

"Well! Here is what happened to me on African soil:

"I had crossed the great dunes in the

south of Ouargla. That is one of the strangest countries in the world. You are familiar with level sand, the true sand of the interminable shore of the sea. Well, figure to yourselves the ocean itself sand, and in the midst of a hurricane; imagine a silent tempest of motionless waves in yellow dust. They are as high as mountains, these unequal waves, differing from each other, and raised suddenly, like unchained billows, but greater still, and streaked like water waves. Upon this furious sea, mute, immovable, the sun of the south turns its implacable and direct flame, devouring it. It is necessary to climb these waves of golden ashes, to redescend, to climb again, to climb incessantly, without repose and without shade. Horses puff, sinking to their knees, and slipping in, they go down the other side of these surprising little hills.

"We were two friends, followed by eight *spahis* and four camels with their drivers. We could no longer speak, as we were suffocated with heat and fatigue and parched with thirst, like this burning desert. Suddenly one of our men uttered a kind of cry. All stopped, and we remained motionless, surprised by an inexplicable phenomenon, known only to travelers in these lost countries.

"Somewhere, near us, in an indeterminate direction, a drum was beating, the mysterious drum of the dunes. It was heard distinctly, at first vibrating loudly, then more feebly, stopping, then taking up its fantastic rolling again.

"The Arabs, much frightened, looked at one another, and one said in his own language: 'Death is upon us.'

"Just then, suddenly, my companion, my friend, almost my brother, fell on his head from his horse, overcome with sunstroke. And for the next two hours, during which I tried in vain to save him, that unseizable drum filled my ears with its monotonous noise, intermittent and incomprehensible.

"I felt slipping into my bones a fear, true fear, hideous fear, in the face of my dead friend, well-beloved, in this hole, burning up in the sun, between four mountains of sand, where an unknown echo brought to us the rapid beating of a drum, two hundred miles from any French village.

"That day, I understood what it was to have fear; and I understood it still better on one other occasion."

The commander interrupted the speaker: "Pardon, sir, but this drum? What was it?"

The traveler answered: "That I do not know. No one knew. The officers, often surprised by this singular noise, attributed it generally to a great echo, multiplied, swelled immeasurably by the little valleys of the dunes, caused by particles of sand being carried in the wind and hurled against a bunch of dried herbs; because they always noticed that the phenomenon was produced in the neighborhood of plants dried in the sun, and hard as parchment. This drum, then, was a kind of mirage of sound. That is all. But I learned that later.

"Now I come to my second emotion.

"This came to me last winter, in a forest in the northeast of France. The night fell two hours earlier than usual, the sky was so cloudy. I had for a guide a peasant, who walked at my side through a little road, under an arch of pines, through which the unchained wind howled dismally. Between the hilltops

I could see clouds scurrying away in line, lost clouds, which seemed to be fleeing before some fright. Sometimes, under a powerful whirlwind, the whole forest bowed in the same breath with a groan of suffering. And the cold took me by force, in spite of my rapid walk and heavy clothing.

"We were going to take supper and sleep at the house of a forest guide whose house was not far from the place where we were. I was going there to hunt.

"My guide would sometimes raise his eyes and mutter: 'Bad weather!' Then he spoke of the people to whose house we were going. The father had killed a poacher, two years before, and since then he had seemed somber, as if haunted by a memory. His two sons were married and lived with him.

"The shadows were profound. I could see nothing before me, nor about me; and the branches of the trees, clashing against each other, filled the night with confusion. Finally I perceived a light, and soon my companion knocked on a door. The sharp cries of women responded. Then the voice of a man, a strangled voice, asked: 'Who is there?' My guide gave our names. We entered. It was a picture never to be forgotten.

"An old man with white hair and a mad expression of the eye, awaited us in the middle of the kitchen with a loaded gun in his hand, while two great fellows, armed with hatchets, guarded the door. I distinguished in the dark corner two women on their knees, their faces turned against the wall.

"They explained it. The old man put up his gun and ordered them to prepare my room; then, as the women did not budge, he said brusquely:

" 'You see, sir, I killed a man here, two years ago to-night. Last year he came back to me. I am expecting him this evening.'

"Then he added, in a tone that made me laugh.

" 'So, we are not quite easy.'

"I reassured him as best I could, happy to have come just at this time to assist at the spectacle of this superstitious terror. I told stories, and succeeded in calming them all somewhat.

"Near the entrance was an old dog, whiskered and nearly blind, one of those dogs that resemble people we know, asleep, with his nose in his paws.

"Outside, the raging tempest was beating against the little house, and through a small hole, a kind of Judas-place, near the door, I suddenly saw, by a sharp flash of lightning, a clump of great trees over-turned by the wind.

"In spite of my efforts, I felt sure that a profound terror held these people, and each time that I ceased to speak, all ears seemed to be listening to something in the distance. Weary of trying to dispel these imbecile fears, I asked permission to go to bed, when the old guard suddenly made a bound from his chair, seized his gun again, and stuttered, in a far-away voice:

" 'Here he is! Here he is! I'm waiting for him!'

"The two women fell upon their knees in their corners, concealing their faces, and the sons took up their hatchets. I was trying to appease them again when the sleeping dog awoke suddenly, and, raising his head, stretching his neck, and looking toward the fire with eyes almost closed, began to utter the most lugubrious howls, of the sort that gave a start to travelers in the country at night. All eyes were turned toward him; he remained motionless, resting upon his paws, as if haunted by a vision.

"He was howling at something invisible, unknown, frightful, no doubt, because his hair was bristling. The guide, now livid, cried out:

"'He feels him! He feels him! He was there when I killed him!'

"And the two excited women began to howl with the dog.

"In spite of myself a great shiver ran down between my shoulders. The sight of the terrified animal in that place, at that hour, in the midst of those benighted people, was frightful.

"For an hour, the dog howled without ceasing; his wails sounded as if he were in agony from a dream. And fear, ungovernable fear, entered my being. Fear of what? Did I know what? It was fear, and that was all.

"We remained motionless, livid, in expectation of some frightful event, with listening ear and beating heart, starting at the least noise. And the dog began to go about the room, touching the walls, and growling. That beast nearly made us mad!

"The peasant who had brought me threw himself upon the animal, in a kind of paroxysm of furious terror, and opening the door, with a little push threw it outside.

"He was then silent, and all of us remained plunged in a silence more terrifying still. Suddenly we all started with surprise. A form glittered on the wall,

the outside wall toward the forest; then it passed against the door, which it seemed to touch with hesitating hand; then we heard nothing for two minutes, which almost drove us out of our senses; then it returned, always rubbing against the wall; and it scratched lightly, as a child does with his nail; then suddenly a head appeared against the glass, a white head, with luminous eyes like those of a deer. And there came from his mouth an indistinct sound, a plaintive murmur.

"Then a fearful noise resounded through the kitchen. The old guide had shot. And immediately the sons hurried to block up the door, putting against it the great table and bringing the side-table to its assistance.

"And I swear to you that from the fracas of that gunshot, which I had not expected, I had such an agony of heart and soul and body that I felt myself swooning, ready to die of fear.

"We remained there until light, incapable of moving, not saying a word, stiff with indescribable fright.

"They did not dare take down the barricade until, through a crevice in the door, they saw a ray of daylight.

"At the foot of the wall, opposite the door, the old dog lay, his mouth pierced with a ball.

"He had gone out of the yard, crossing through a hole under the fence."

The man with the bronzed visage was silent; but he added soon:

"That night I ran into no danger; but I would rather encounter all the hours that have brought me the greatest peril than that one minute of the shooting at the shaggy head of the old dog."

VOLUME VII

A Jolly Fellow

THEY called him Saint Anthony, because his name was Anthony, and also, perhaps because he was a joyous good lover, fond of joking, powerful at eating and drinking, and had a vigorous hand with servants, although he was more than sixty years old. He was a tall peasant of the country of Caux, of high color, great in chest and girth, and was perched upon long legs that seemed too thin for the weight of his body

A widower, he lived alone with his maid and his two menservants on his farm, which he directed in sly, jovial fashion, careful of his interests, attending to business affairs, the breeding of the cattle, and the cultivation of the land. His two sons and three daughters, married to advantage, lived in the neighborhood, and came, once a month, to dine with their father. His vigor was known in all the country about; people said, as if it were a proverb: "He is as strong as Saint Anthony."

When the Prussian invasion occurred, Saint Anthony, at the inn, promised to eat an army, for, like a true Norman, he was a romancer, and a little of a coward and a blusterer. He brought his heavy fist down on the wooden table, making it jump, while the cups and glasses danced, and he cried out, with red face and cunning eye, in the false anger of the jovial fellow: "In Heaven's name! Will it be necessary to eat some of them?" He counted on the Prussians not coming any farther than Tanneville; but when he learned that they were at Rautot, he would not go out of his house, and he watched without ceasing through the little window of his kitchen, expecting every moment to see the glint of bayonets.

One morning, as he was eating soup with his servants, the door opened and the mayor of the commune, Master Chicot, appeared, followed by a soldier, wearing on his head a black cap set off with a point of copper. Saint Anthony arose with a bound; everybody looked at him, expecting to see him cut the Prussian in pieces; but he contented himself with shaking hands with the mayor, who said to him: "Here's one of 'em for you to take care of, Saint Anthony. They came in the night. I haven't been surly with them, seeing they talk of shooting and burning if the least thing happens. You are warned. Give him something to eat. He seems a good lad. I am going to the other houses to seek quarters for the rest of them. There is enough for everybody." And he went out.

Father Anthony looked at his Prussian and grew pale. He was a great boy, fat and white, with blue eyes and blond hair, bearded up to the cheek-bones, and he seemed stupid and timid, like a good child. The Norman rogue comprehended him immediately, as he thought, and, reassured, made him a sign to sit down. Then he asked: "Will you have some soup?"

The stranger did not understand. Anthony then made an audacious move, and, pushing a full plate under the nose of his unexpected guest, he said: 'There, eat that, you big pig!"

The soldier responded: "*Ja,*" and began to eat ravenously, while the farmer, triumphant, feeling his power recognized, winked his eye at his servants, who

755

made strange faces and had a great desire to laugh but were restrained by fear.

When the Prussian had cleared his plate, Saint Anthony served him another, the contents of which disappeared like the first, but he recoiled before the third helping, which the farmer tried by force to make him eat, repeating: "Come, now, put that inside of you. You shall grow fat, or I'll know the reason why, my pig!"

And the soldier, comprehending nothing except that he was urged to eat all he wanted, laughed with a contented air, making a sign that he was full.

Then Saint Anthony, suddenly becoming familiar, tapped him on the front, saying: "He has enough in his paunch, has my pig!" But upon this he doubled himself with laughter, growing red enough for an attack of apoplexy, and was unable to speak for a moment. An idea had seized him which suffocated him with laughter: "That's it! That's it!" he cried, "Saint Anthony and his pig! I am Saint Anthony and this is my pig!" And the three servants laughed loudly in their turn.

The old man was so pleased with his jest that he ordered the maid to bring some brandy, of the ten-year-old brand, with which he regaled everybody. They drank with the Prussian, who smacked his lips as a bit of delicate flattery, in order to indicate that he found it delicious. And Saint Anthony cried out in his face: "Yes! This is something fine! You don't find anything like it at home, my pig!"

After this, father Anthony never went out without his Prussian. He had found his opportunity. It was vengeance to

him, the vengeance of a great rogue. And all the people of the countryside, who were trembling with fear, laughed until in torture, behind the backs of their conquerors, at the farce of Saint Anthony and his pig. Indeed, as a joke, they thought it had not its equal. He had only to say a few things like this: "Go along, pig! Go!" in order to provoke convulsions of merriment.

He would go among his neighbors every afternoon with his German, their arms around each other, and would present him with a gay air, tapping him on the shoulder and saying: "See! Here is my pig! Look at him and tell me if you think he is getting fat, this here animal!"

And the peasants fairly bubbled with laughter—he was such a wag, this rogue of an Anthony!

"I'll sell him to you, Cæsar," he would say, "for three pistoles."

"I take him, Anthony, and invite you to come and have some of the pudding."

"Me," said Anthony, "what I want is some of the feet."

"Punch his body and see how fat he is!" said Cæsar.

And everybody would wink slyly, not laughing too much, however, for fear the Prussian might surmise finally that they were mocking him. Anthony alone, growing bolder every day, would pinch the calves of his legs, crying out: "Nothing but fat!" or strike him on the back and shout: "There's some good bacon!" Then the old man, capable of lifting an anvil, would seize him in his arms and raise him up in the air, declaring: "He weighs six hundred and not a bit of waste!"

He got into the habit of offering his

pig something to eat wherever they went. It was the great pleasure, the great diversion of every day. "Give him whatever you like," he would say, "he will swallow it." And when they would inquire if the man wished some bread and butter, potatoes, cold mutton, or venison, Anthony would say to him: "Here you are now, it's your choice!"

The soldier, stupid and gentle, ate for politeness, enchanted with so much attention; he would make himself sick rather than refuse; and he was growing fat truly, too stout for his uniform, which fairly delighted Saint Anthony, who kept telling him: "You know, my pig, it's pretty soon going to be necessary for you to have a new cage."

They became apparently the best friends in the world. And when the old man went on business into the surrounding country, the Prussian accompanied him of his own accord, for the sole pleasure of being with him.

The weather was very rigorous; it had frozen hard; the terrible winter of 1870 seemed to throw all plagues together upon France.

Father Anthony, who looked out for things ahead and took advantage of opportunities, foreseeing that he would need manure for his spring work, bought some of a neighbor who found himself in straits; he arranged to go each evening with his cart and bring it home, a load at a time. And so, toward evening of each day, he was to be seen on the way to Haules's farm, half a mile distant, always accompanied by his pig. And everybody ran along with them, as they go on Sunday to a grand mass, for each day was a feast-day for feeding the animal.

But the time came when the soldier began to be suspicious. And, when they laughed too much he rolled his eyes as if disturbed, and sometimes they sent forth a spark of anger.

One evening, when he had eaten to the extent of his capacity, he refused to swallow another morsel, and undertook to start up and go away. But Saint Anthony stopped him with a blow on the wrist and, placing his two hands on the Prussian's shoulders, he sat him down again so hard that the chair cracked under him.

A perfect tempest of gaiety followed; and Anthony, radiant, picked up his pig, rubbing the wounded spot, with the semblance of healing it. Then he declared: "Since you won't eat, you shall drink, by jiminy!" And somebody went to the alehouse for brandy.

The soldier rolled his eyes in wicked fashion; but he drank, nevertheless, as much as they wished; and Saint Anthony held his head; to the great amusement of his assistants.

The Norman, red as a tomato, with fiery eye, filled the glasses, drinking and guying him with: "To your sweetheart!" And the Prussian, without a word, encompassed glass after glass of these bumpers of cognac.

It was a struggle, a battle, a defense! In Heaven's name! who could drink the most? They could take no more, either of them, when the bottle was drained, but neither was conquered. They were neck and neck, and that was all. It would be necessary to start over the next day.

They went out stumbling, and started homeward beside the cart filled with manure, which two horses dragged slowly along. The snow began to fall, and the night, without a moon, seemed to shed a sad light over this death of the plains. The cold took hold of the two men, increasing their drunkenness, and Saint Anthony, discontented at not having triumphed, amused himself with pushing his pig by the shoulder, trying to make him fall over into the ditch. The man evaded the attacks by retreat; and each time he would mutter some German words in an irritated tone, which made the farmer laugh heartily. Finally, the Prussian became angry; and just at the moment when Anthony gave him another push, he responded with a terrible blow of the fist which made the old colossus totter.

Then, inflamed with brandy, the old fellow seized the man by the arms and shook him for some seconds, as if he had been a child, and then threw him with all his might to the other side of the road. Content with his execution, he folded his arms and laughed in good earnest.

But the soldier got up quickly, bareheaded, his cap having rolled off, and, drawing his sword, made a plunge for father Anthony. When the farmer saw this he seized his great fork of yellow holly, strong and supple as a beef tendon.

The Prussian came on with his head lowered, weapon in front of him, sure of killing his foe. But the old man, grasping with firm hand the blade whose point was aimed to pierce his body, turned it aside, and struck his enemy such a sharp blow upon the temple, with the point of the fork, that he fell at his feet. Then the peasant looked at his fallen foe frightened, stupefied with astonishment, seeing the body shaken with spasms at first, and then lying motionless upon its face. He stooped, turned him over and looked at him a long time. The man's eyes were closed, and a little stream of blood was running from a hole in the forehead. In spite of the darkness, father Anthony could distinguish the brown spot of blood on the snow.

He remained there, bewildered, while his cart went on at the horses' regular step. What was to be done? He would shoot him! Then the Prussians would burn his place and work ruin throughout the country! But what should he do? What should he do? How conceal the body, conceal the death, deceive the Prussians? He could hear voices in the distance, in the silence of the snowstorm. Then he became excited, and, seizing the cap, he put it on the man's head again; and, taking him by the back, he raised him up, ran, overtook his team, and threw the body on the manure. Once at home, he could think what to do.

He went along with short steps, racking his brain but unable to decide anything. He understood the matter and felt sure that he was lost. Finally he came to his house. A bright light shone through a dormer window; his servant was not yet asleep. Then he made his wagon back quickly to the edge of a hole in the field. He thought by overturning the load the body would fall underneath, in the ditch; and he tipped the cart over. As he had thought, the man was buried under the manure. Anthony evened off the heap with his fork, and stuck it in the ground at the side. He called his manservant, ordered him to put the horses in the stable, and went to his chamber.

He went to bed, reflecting continually upon what he had done, but no helpful idea came to him, and his fear increased when he was quiet in bed. The Prussians would shoot him! The sweat of fear started out upon him; his teeth chattered; he got up, shivering so that he could scarcely hold his clothes to get into them. He went down into the kitchen, took a bottle of liquor from the sideboard, and went back to his chamber. He drank two large glasses of liquor in succession, adding a new drunkenness to the old one, without calming the agony of his soul. He felt that he had made a pretty mess of it this time!

He walked the floor to and fro, seeking a ruse or explanation for his wickedness. And from time to time he would rinse his mouth with a draught of the ten-year-old cognac to put some heart into his body. But he could think of nothing, nothing. Toward midnight, his watchdog, a kind of half wolf, which he called "Devour," began the howl of death. Father Anthony trembled to the marrow. And each time that the beast began his long, mournful wail again, a shiver of fear would run along the skin of the old man.

He had fallen upon a chair, with weak knees; he was besotted; unable to do more, expecting that Devour would continue his wailing, and his nerves were played upon by every form of fear that could set them vibrating. The clock downstairs struck five. The dog was still howling, and the farmer was becoming mad. He got up and started to unchain the animal, so that he might no longer listen to it. He went downstairs, opened the door, and went out into the night.

The snow was falling still. All was white. The farm buildings were great, black spots. As he approached the kennel, the dog pulled on his chain. He loosed him. Then, Devour made a bound, stopped short, with hair bristling, paws trembling, smelling the air, his nose turned toward the manure heap.

Saint Anthony trembled from head to foot, muttering: "What's the matter with you, dirty beast?" And he advanced some steps, casting a penetrating eye through the uncertain shadows, the undefined shadows of the courtyard. Then he saw the form of a man seated on his manure-heap!

He looked at the figure, and gasped with horror, motionless. But suddenly he perceived near him the handle of his fork stuck in the earth. He pulled it from the soil, and, in one of those transports of fear which make cowardly men more bold, he rushed on with it, to see who the man was.

It was he, the Prussian, soiled from his bed of manure, the warmth of which had revived him and partly brought him back to his senses. He had seated himself mechanically, and was resting there upon the snow which had powdered him well, over the filth and blood, still besotted by drunkenness, stunned by the blow, and exhausted from his wounds.

He perceived Anthony and, too much stupefied to understand anything, he made a movement as if to rise. The old man, as soon as he recognized him, fumed like a wild beast. He sputtered: "Ah! pig! pig! you are not dead! you have come to denounce me right away—

Wait—wait!" And throwing himself upon the German, he raised his four-pointed fork like a lance and brought it down, with all the force of his two arms, in the man's breast, even to the handle. The soldier turned over on his back with a long death-sigh, while the old farmer drew the weapon from the wound and replunged it in the body, blow upon blow, striking like a madman, stamping with his feet upon the head and the rest of the body, which was still palpitating, and from which the blood spouted in great jets.

Then he stopped, overcome with the violence of his effort, breathing the air in great draughts, appeased by the accomplishment of his deed.

As the cocks began to crow in the poultry-yard, and the day was dawning, he set himself to work to bury the man. He dug into the manure-heap, until he came to earth, then dug still deeper, working in a disorderly fashion, with furious force in his arms and his whole body. When the trench was long enough, he rolled the dead body into it with the fork, replaced the earth, kicking it about until it was level, put the manure over it again, and smiled to see the snow thicken and complete his work, wholly covering all traces with its white veil.

Then he stuck his fork into the manure and returned to the house. His bottle was still half full upon the table. He emptied it with a gulp, threw himself upon the bed, and slept profoundly.

He awoke sobered, his mind calm and active, capable of judging the case and foreseeing results. At the end of an hour, he was scouring the country asking everybody the whereabouts of the soldier. He went to the officers, to find out, he said, why they had taken his man away.

As the Prussians knew nothing of the peculiar situation between the two men, they were not suspicious; and Anthony even directed the search, affirming that the Prussian had gone running after some petticoat nearly every evening.

An old refugee policeman, who kept an inn in a neighboring village, and who had a pretty daughter, was arrested on suspicion of being the murderer, and was shot.

A Lively Friend

THEY had been constantly in each other's society for a whole winter in Paris. After having lost sight of each other, as generally happens in such cases, after leaving college, the two friends met again one night, long years after, already old and white-haired, the one a bachelor, the other married.

M. de Meroul lived six months in Paris and six months in his little château at Tourbeville. Having married the daughter of a gentleman in the district, he had lived a peaceful, happy life with the indolence of a man who has nothing to do. With a calm temperament and a sedate mind, without any intellectual audacity or tendency toward revolutionary independence of thought, he passed his time in mildly regretting the past, in deploring the morals and the institutions of to-day, and in repeating every moment to his wife, who raised her eyes to heaven, and sometimes her hands also, in token of energetic assent:

"Under what a government do we live, great God!"

Madame de Meroul mentally resembled her husband, just as if they had been brother and sister. She knew by tradition that one ought, first of all, to reverence the Pope and the King!

And she loved them and respected them from the bottom of her heart, without knowing them, with a poetic exaltation, with a hereditary devotion, with all the sensibility of a well-born woman. She was kindly in every feeling of her soul. She had no child, and was incessantly regretting it.

When M. de Meroul came across his old school-fellow Joseph Mouradour at a ball, he experienced from this meeting a profound and genuine delight, for they had been very fond of one another in their youth.

After exclamations of astonishment over the changes caused by age in their bodies and their faces, they had asked one another a number of questions as to their respective careers.

Joseph Mouradour, a native of the south of France, had become a councillor-general in his own neighborhood. Frank in his manners, he spoke briskly and without any circumspection, telling all his thoughts with sheer indifference to prudential considerations. He was a Republican, of that race of good-natured Republicans who make their own ease the law of their existence, and who carry freedom of speech to the verge of brutality.

He called at his friend's address in Paris, and was immediately a favorite, on account of his easy cordiality, in spite of his advanced opinions. Madame de Meroul exclaimed:

"What a pity! such a charming man!"

M. de Meroul said to his friend, in a sincere and confidential tone: "You cannot imagine what a wrong you do to our country." He was attached to his friend nevertheless, for no bonds are more solid than those of childhood renewed in later life. Joseph Mouradour chaffed the husband and wife, called them "my loving turtles," and occasionally gave vent to loud declarations against people who were behind the age, against all sorts of prejudices and traditions.

When he thus directed the flood of his democratic eloquence, the married pair, feeling ill at ease, kept silent through a sense of propriety and good-breeding; then the husband tried to turn off the conversation in order to avoid any friction. Joseph Mouradour did not want to know anyone unless he was free to say what he liked.

Summer came round. The Merouls knew no greater pleasure than to receive their old friends in their country house at Tourbeville. It was an intimate and healthy pleasure, the pleasure of homely gentlefolk who had spent most of their lives in the country. They used to go to the nearest railway station to meet some of their guests, and drove them to the house in their carriage, watching for compliments on their district, on the rapid vegetation, on the condition of the roads in the department, on the cleanliness of the peasant's houses, on the bigness of the cattle they saw in the fields, on everything that met the eye as far as the edge of the horizon.

They liked to have it noticed that their horses trotted in a wonderful manner for an animal employed a part of the year in field-work; and they awaited with anxety the newcomer's opinion on their family estate, sensitive to the slightest word, grateful for the slightest gracious attention.

Joseph Mouradour was invited, and he announced his arrival. The wife and the husband came to meet the train, delighted to have the opportunity of doing the honors of their house.

As soon as he perceived them, Joseph Mouradour jumped out of his carriage with a vivacity which increased their satisfaction. He grasped their hands warmly, congratulated them, and intoxicated them with compliments.

He was quite charming in his manner as they drove along the road to the house; he expressed astonishment at the height of the trees, the excellence of the crops, and the quickness of the horse.

When he placed his foot on the steps in front of the château, M. de Meroul said to him with a certain friendly solemnity:

"Now you are at home."

Joseph Mouradour answered: "Thanks, old fellow; I counted on that. For my part, besides, I never put myself out with my friends. That's the only hospitality I understand."

Then he went up to his own room, where he put on the costume of a peasant, as he was pleased to describe it, and he came down again not very

long after, attired in blue linen, with yellow boots, in the careless rig-out of a Parisian out for a holiday. He seemed, too, to have become more common, more jolly, more familiar, having assumed along with his would-be rustic garb a free and easy swagger which he thought suited the style of dress. His new apparel somewhat shocked M. and Madame de Meroul, who even at home on their estate always remained serious and respectable, as the particle "de" before their name exacted a certain amount of ceremonial even with their intimate friends.

After lunch they went to visit the farms; and the Parisian stupefied the respectable peasant by talking to them as if he were a comrade of theirs.

In the evening, the curé dined at the house— a fat old priest, wearing his Sunday suit, who had been specially asked that day in order to meet the newcomer.

When Joseph saw him he made a grimace, then he stared at the priest in astonishment as if he belonged to some peculiar race of beings, the like of which he had never seen before at such close quarters. He told a few stories allowable enough with a friend after dinner, but apparently somewhat out of place in the presence of an ecclesiastic. He did not say, "Monsieur l'Abbé," but merely "Monsieur"; and he embarrassed the priest with philosophical views as to the various superstitions that prevailed on the surface of the globe.

He remarked:

"Your God, Monsieur, is one of those persons whom we must respect, but also one of those who must be discussed. Mine is called Reason; he has from time immemorial been the enemy of yours."

The Merouls, greatly put out, attempted to divert his thoughts. The curé left very early.

Then the husband gently remarked:

"You went a little too far with that priest."

But Joseph immediately replied:

"That's a very good joke, too! Am I to bother my brains about a devil-dodger? At any rate, do me the favor of not ever again having such an old fogy to dinner. Confound his impudence!"

"But, my friend, remember his sacred character."

Joseph Mouradour interrupted him:

"Yes, I know. We must treat them like girls who get roses for being well behaved! That's all right, my boy! When these people respect my convictions, I will respect theirs!"

This was all that happened that day.

Next morning Madame de Meroul, on entering her drawing-room, saw lying on the table three newspapers which made her draw back in horror, "Le Voltaire," "La République Française," and "La Justice."

Presently Joseph Mouradour, still in his blue blouse, appeared on the threshold, reading "L'Intransigéant" attentively. He exclaimed:

"Here is a splendid article by Rochefort. That fellow is marvelous."

He read the article in a loud voice, laying so much stress on its most striking passages that he did not notice the entrance of his friend.

M. de Meroul had a paper in each hand: "Le Gaulois" for himself and "Le Clarion" for his wife.

The ardent prose of the master-writer who overthrew the empire, violently declaimed, recited in the accent of the south, rang through the peaceful drawing-room, shook the old curtains with their rigid folds, seemed to splash the walls, the large upholstered chairs, the solemn furniture fixed in the same position for the past century, with a hail of words, rebounding, impudent, ironical, and crushing.

The husband and the wife, the one standing, the other seated, listened in a state of stupor, so scandalized that they no longer even ventured to make a gesture. Mouradour flung out the concluding passage in the article as one sets off a stream of fireworks; then in an emphatic tone he remarked:

"Thats a stinger, eh?"

But suddenly he perceived the two prints belonging to his friend, and he seemed himself for a moment overcome with astonishment. Then he came across to his host with great strides, demanding in an angry tone:

"What do you want to do with these papers?"

M. de Meroul replied in a hesitating voice:

"Why, these—these are my—my newspapers."

"Your newspapers! Look here, now, you are only laughing at me! You will do me the favor to read mine, to stir you up with a few new ideas, and, as for yours—this is what I do with them—"

And before his host, filled with confusion, could prevent him, he seized the two newspapers and flung them out through the window. Then he grave' placed "La Justice" in the hand'

Madame de Meroul and "Le Voltaire" in those of her husband, himself sinking into an armchair to finish "L'Intransigéant."

The husband and the wife, through feelings of delicacy, made a show of reading a little, then they handed back the Republican newspapers which they touched with their finger-tips as if they had been poisoned.

Then Mouradour burst out laughing and said:

"A week of this sort of nourishment, and I'll have you converted to my ideas."

At the end of a week, in fact, he ruled the house. He had shut the door on the curé, whom Madame de Meroul went to see in secret. He gave orders that neither the "Gaulois" nor the "Clarion" were to be admitted into the house, which a manserveant went to get in a mysterious fashion at the post-office, and which, on his entrance, were hidden away under the sofa cushions. He regulated everything just as he liked, always charming, always good-natured, a jovial and all-powerful tyrant.

Other friends were about to come on a visit, religious people with Legitimist opinions. The master and mistress of the château considered it would be impossible to let them meet their lively guest, and not knowing what to do, announced to Joseph Mouradour one evening that they were obliged to go away from home for a few days about a little matter of business, and they begged of him to remain in the house alone.

He showed no trace of emotion, and replied:

"Very well: tis all the same to me; I'll wait here for you as long as you like. What I say is this—there need be no ceremony between friends. You're quite right to look after your own affairs— why the devil shouldn't you? I'll not take offense at your doing that, quite the contrary. It only makes me feel quite at my ease with you. Go, my friends—I'll wait for you."

M. and Madame de Meroul started next morning.

He is waiting for them.

The Blind Man

How is it that the sunlight gives us such joy? Why does this radiance when it falls on the earth fill us so much with the delight of living? The sky is all blue, the fields are all green, the houses all white; and our ravished eyes drink in those bright colors which bring mirthfulness to our souls. And then there springs up in our hearts a desire to dance, a desire to run, a desire to sing, a happy lightness of thought, a sort of enlarged tenderness; we feel a longing to embrace the sun.

The blind, as they sit in the doorways, impassive in their eternal darkness remain as calm as ever in the midst of this fresh gaiety, and, not comprehending what is taking place around them, they continue every moment to stop their dogs from gamboling.

When, at the close of the day, they are returning home on the arm of a young brother or a little sister, if the child says: "It was a very fine day!" the other answers; "I could notice that 'twas fine. Lulu wouldn't keep quiet."

I have known one of these men whose life was one of the most cruel martyrdoms that could possibly be conceived.

He was a peasant, the son of a Norman farmer. As long as his father and mother lived, he was more or less taken care of; he suffered little save from his horrible infirmity; but as soon as the old people were gone, a life of atrocious misery commenced for him. A dependent on a sister of his, everybody in the farmhouse treated him as a beggar who is eating the bread of others. At every meal the very food he swallowed was made a subject of reproach against him; he was called a drone, a clown; and although his brother-in-law had taken possession of his portion of the inheritance, the soup was given to him grudgingly—just enough to save him from dying.

His face was very pale and his two big white eyes were like wafers. He remained unmoved in spite of the insults inflicted upon him, so shut up in himself that one could not tell whether he felt them at all.

Moreover, he had never known any tenderness, his mother had always treated him very unkindly, caring scarcely at all for him; for in country places the useless are obnoxious, and the peasants would be glad, like hens, to kill the infirm of their species.

As soon as the soup had been gulped down, he went to the door in summer time and sat down, to the chimney-corner in winter time, and, after that, never stirred till night. He made no gesture, no movement; only his eyelids, quivering from some nervous affection, fell down sometimes over his white sightless orbs. Had he any intellect, any thinking faculty, any consciousness of his own existence? Nobody cared to inquire as to whether he had or no.

For some years things went on in this fashion. But his incapacity for doing anything as well as his impassiveness eventually exasperated his relatives, and he became a laughing-stock, a sort of martyred buffoon, a prey given over to native ferocity, to the savage gaiety of the brutes who surrounded him.

It is easy to imagine all the cruel practical jokes inspired by his blindness. And, in order to have some fun in return for feeding him, they now converted his meals into hours of pleasure for the neighbors and of punishment for the helpless creature himself.

The peasants from the nearest houses came to this entertainment; it was talked about from door to door, and every day the kitchen of the farmhouse was full of people. For instance, they put on the table in front of his plate, when he was beginning to take the soup, a cat or a dog. The animal instinctively scented out the man's infirmity, and, softly approaching, commenced eating noiselessly, lapping up the soup daintily; and when a rather loud licking of the tongue awakened the poor fellow's attention, it would prudently scamper away to avoid the blow of the spoon directed at it by the blind man at random!

Then the spectators, huddled against the walls, burst out laughing, nudged each other, and stamped their feet on the floor. And he, without ever uttering a word, would continue eating with the aid of his right hand, while stretching out his left to protect and defend his plate.

At another time they made him chew corks, bits of wood, leaves, or even filth, which he was unable to distinguish.

After this, they got tired even of these practical jokes; and the brother-in-law, mad at having to support him always, struck him, cuffed him incessantly, laughing at the useless efforts of the other to ward off or return the blows. Then came a new pleasure—the pleasure of smacking his face. And the plowmen, the servant-girls, and even every passing vagabond were every moment giving him cuffs, which caused his eyelashes to twitch spasmodically. He did not know where to hide himself and remained with his arms always held out to guard against people coming too close to him.

At last he was forced to beg.

He was placed somewhere on the highroad on market-days, and, as soon as he heard the sound of footsteps or the rolling of a vehicle, he reached out his hat, stammering:

"Charity, if you please!"

But the peasant is not lavish, and, for whole weeks, he did not bring back a sou.

Then he became the victim of furious, pitiless hatred. And this is how he died.

One winter, the ground was covered with snow, and it froze horribly. Now his brother-in-law led him one morning at this season a great distance along the highroad in order that he might solicit alms. The blind man was left there all day, and, when night came on, the brother-in-law told the people of his house that he could find no trace of the mendicant. Then he added:

"Pooh! best not bother about him! He was cold, and got some one to take him away. Never fear! he's not lost. He'll turn up soon enough to-morrow to eat the soup."

Next day he did not come back.

After long hours of waiting, stiffened with the cold, feeling that he was dying, the blind man began to walk. Being unable to find his way along the road, owing to its thick coating of ice, he went on at random, falling into dikes, getting up again, without uttering a sound, his sole object being to find some house where he could take shelter.

But by degrees the descending snow made a numbness steal over him, and his feeble limbs being incapable of carrying him farther, he had to sit down in the middle of an open field. He did not get up again.

The white flakes which kept continually falling buried him, so that his body, quite stiff and stark, disappeared under the incessant accumulation of their rapidly thickening mass; and nothing any longer indicated the place where the corpse was lying.

His relatives made pretense of inquiring about him and searching for him for about a week. They even made a show of weeping.

The winter was severe, and the thaw did not set in quickly. Now, one Sunday, on their way to mass, the farmers noticed a great flight of crows, who were whirling endlessly above the open field, and then, like a shower of black rain, descended in a heap at the same spot, ever going and coming.

The following week these gloomy birds were still there. There was a crowd of them up in the air, as if they had gathered from all corners of the horizon; and they swooped down with a great cawing into the shining snow, which they filled curiously with patches of black, and in which they kept rummaging obstinately. A young fellow went to see what they were doing, and discovered the body of the blind man, already half devoured, mangled. His wan eyes had disappeared, pecked out by the long voracious beaks.

And I can never feel the glad radiance of sunlit days without sadly remembering and gloomily pondering over the fate of the beggar so deprived of joy in life that his horrible death was a relief for all those who had known him.

The Impolite Sex

MADAME DE X. TO MADAME DE L.

ETRETAT, Friday.

MY DEAR AUNT,—I am going to pay you a visit without making much fuss about it. I shall be at Les Fresnes on the second of September, the day before the hunting season opens; I do not want to miss it, so that I may tease these gentlemen. You are very obliging, Aunt, and I would like you to allow them to dine with you, as you usually do when there are no strange guests, without dressing or shaving for the occasion, on the ground that they are fatigued.

They are delighted, of course, when I am not present. But I shall be there, and I shall hold a review, like a general, at the dinner-hour; and, if I find a single one of them at all careless in dress, no matter how little, I mean to send him down to the kitchen to the servant-maids.

The men of to-day have so little consideration for others and so little good manners that one must be always severe with them. We live indeed in an age of vulgarity. When they quarrel with one another, they attack one another with insults worthy of street porters, and, in our presence, they do not conduct themselves even as well as our servants. It is at the seaside that you see this most clearly. They are to be found there in battalion, and you can judge them in the lump. Oh, what coarse beings they are!

Just imagine, in a train, one of them, a gentleman who looked well as I thought, at first sight, thanks to his tailor, was dainty enough to take off his boots in order to put on a pair of old shoes! Another, an old man, who was probably some wealthy upstart (these are the most ill-bred), while sitting opposite to me, had the delicacy to place his two feet on the seat quite close to me. This is a positive fact.

At the watering-places, there is an unrestrained outpouring of unmannerliness. I must here make one admission—that my indignation is perhaps due to the fact that I am not accustomed to associate as a rule with the sort of people one comes across here, for I should be less shocked by their manners if I had the opportunity of observing them oftener. In the inquiry-office of the hotel I was nearly thrown down by a young man, who snatched the key over my head. Another knocked against me so violently without begging my pardon or lifting his hat, coming away from a ball at the Casino, that he gave me a pain in the chest. It is the same way with all of them. Watch them addressing ladies on the terrace: they scarcely ever bow. They merely raise their hands to their headgear. But indeed, as they are all more or less bald, it is the best plan.

But what exasperates and disgusts me especially is the liberty they take of talking publicly, without any precaution whatsoever, about the most revolting adventures. When two men are together, they relate to each other, in the broadest language and with the most abominable comments, really horrible stories, without caring in the slightest degree whether a woman's ear is within reach of their voices. Yesterday, on the beach, I was forced to go away from the place where I sat in order not to be any longer the involuntary confidant of an obscene anecdote, told in such immodest language that I felt as much humiliated as I was indignant at having heard it. Would not the most elementary good-breeding have taught them to speak in a lower tone about such matters when we are near at hand? Etretat is, moreover, the country of gossip and scandal. From five to seven o'clock you can see people wandering about in quest of nasty stories about others, which they retail from group to group. As you remarked to me, my dear Aunt, tittle-tattle is the mark of petty individuals and petty minds. It is also the consolation of women who are no longer loved or sought after. It is enough for me to observe the women who are fondest of gossiping to be persuaded that you are quite right.

The other day I was present at a musical evening at the Casino, given by a remarkable artist, Madame Masson, who sings in a truly delightful manner. I took the opportunity of applauding the admirable Coquelin, as well as two charming boarders of the Vaudeville, M—— and Meillet. I was able, on the occasion, to see all the bathers collected together this year on the beach. There were not many persons of distinction among them.

One day I went to lunch at Yport. I noticed a tall man with a beard who was coming out of a large house like a castle. It was the painter, Jean Paul Laurens. He is not satisfied apparently with imprisoning the subjects of his pictures; he insists on imprisoning himself.

Then I found myself seated on the shingle close to a man still young, of gentle and refined appearance, who was reading some verses. But he read them with such concentration, with such passion, I may say, that he did not even raise his eyes toward me. I was somewhat astonished, and I asked the conductor of the baths, without appearing to be much concerned, the name of this gentleman. I laughed inwardly a little at this reader of rhymes: he seemed behind the age, for a man. This person, I thought, must be a simpleton. Well, Aunt, I am now infatuated about this stranger. Just fancy, his name is Sully Prudhomme! I turned round to look at him at my ease, just where I sat. His face possesses the two qualities of calmness and elegance. As somebody came to look for him, I was able to hear his voice, which is sweet and almost timid. He would certainly not tell obscene stories aloud in public, or knock against ladies without apologizing. He is sure to be a man of refinement, but his refinement is of an almost morbid, vibrating character. I will try this winter to get an introduction to him.

I have no more news to tell you, my dear Aunt, and I must interrupt this letter in haste, as the post-hour is near. I kiss your hands and your cheeks.

Your devoted niece,

BERTHE DE X.

P.S.—I should add, however, by way of justification of French politeness, that our fellow-countrymen are, when traveling, models of good manners in comparison with the abominable English, who seem to have been brought up by stableboys, so much do they take care not to incommode themselves in any way, while they always incommode their neighbors.

MADAME DE L. TO MADAME DE X.

LES FRESNES, Saturday.

MY DEAR CHILD,—Many of the things you have said to me are very reasonable, but that does not prevent you from being wrong. Like you, I used formerly to feel very indignant at the impoliteness of men, who, as I supposed, constantly treated me with neglect; but as I grew older and reflected on everything, putting aside coquetry and observing things without taking any part in them myself, I perceived this much—that if men are not always po-

lite, women are always indescribably rude.

We imagine that we should be permitted to do anything, my darling, and at the same time we consider that we have a right to the utmost respect, and in the most flagrant manner we commit actions devoid of that elementary goodbreeding of which you speak with passion.

I find, on the contrary, that men have, for us, much consideration, as compared with our bearing toward them. Besides, darling, men must needs be, and are, what we make them. In a state of society where women are all true gentlewomen all men would become gentlemen.

Mark my words; just observe and reflect.

Look at two women meeting in the street. What an attitude each assumes toward the other! What disparaging looks! What contempt they throw into each glance! How they toss their heads while they inspect each other to find something to condemn! And, if the footpath is narrow, do you think one woman will make room for another, or will beg pardon as she sweeps by? When two men jostle each other by accident in some narrow lane, each of them bows and at the same time gets out of the other's way, while we women press against each other, stomach to stomach, face to face, insolently staring each other out of countenance.

Look at two women who are acquaintances meeting on a staircase before the drawing-room door of a friend of theirs to whom one has just paid a visit, and to whom the other is about to pay a visit. They begin to talk to each other, and block up the passage. If anyone happens to be coming up behind them, man or woman, do you imagine that they will put themselves half an inch out of their way? Never! never!

I was waiting myself, with my watch in my hands, one day last winter, at a certain drawing-room door. Behind me two gentlemen were also waiting without showing any readiness to lose their temper, like me. The reason was that they had long grown accustomed to our unconscionable insolence.

The other day, before leaving Paris, I went to dine with no less a person than your husband in the Champs-Elysées, in order to enjoy the open air. Every table was occupied. The waiter asked us not to go, and there would soon be a vacant table.

At that moment, I noticed an elderly lady of noble figure, who, having paid the amount of her check, seemed on the point of going away. She saw me, scanned me from head to foot, and did not budge. For more than a full quarter of an hour she sat there, immovable, putting on her gloves, and calmly staring at·those who were waiting like myself. Now, two young men who were just finishing their dinner, having seen me in their turn, quickly summoned the waiter in order to pay whatever they owed, and at once offered me their seats, even insisting on standing while waiting for their change. And, bear in mind, my fair niece, that I am no longer pretty, like you, but old and white-haired.

It is we (do you see?) who should be taught politeness; and the task would-be such a difficult one that Hercules himself would not be equal to it. You speak to me about Etretat, and about the people who indulge in "tittle-tattle" along the beach of that delightful watering-place. It is a spot now lost to me, a thing of the past, but I found much amusement there in days gone by.

There were only a few of us, people in good society, really good society, and a few artists, and we all fraternized. We paid little attention to gossip in those days.

Well, as we had no insipid Casino, where people only gather for show, where they talk in whispers, where they dance stupidly, where they succeed in thoroughly boring one another, we sought some other way of passing our evenings pleasantly. Now, just guess what came into the head of one of our husbandry? Nothing else than to go and dance each night in one of the farmhouses in the neighborhood.

We started out in a group with a street-organ, generally played by Le Poittevin, the painter, with a cotton nightcap on his head. Two men carried lanterns. We followed in procession, laughing and chattering like a pack of fools.

We woke up the farmer and his servant-maids and laboring men. We got them to make onion-soup (horror), and we danced under the apple-trees, to the sound of the barrel-organ. The cocks waking up began to crow in the darkness of the outhouses; the horses began prancing on the straw of their stables. The cool air of the country caressed our cheeks with the smell of grass and of new-mown hay.

How long ago it is! How long ago it is. It is thirty years since then!

I do not want you, my darling, to

come for the opening of the hunting season. Why spoil the pleasure of our friends by inflicting on them fashionable toilettes after a day of vigorous exercise in the country? This is the way, child, that men are spoiled. I embrace you.

Your old aunt, GENEVIEVE DE L.

The Corsican Bandit

THE road, with a gentle winding, reached the middle of the forest. The huge pine-trees spread above our heads a mournful-looking vault, and gave forth a kind of long, sad wail, while at either side their straight, slender trunks formed, as it were, an army of organ-pipes, from which seemed to issue the low, monotonous music of the wind through the tree-tops.

After three hours' walking there was an opening in this row of tangled branches. Here and there an enormous pine-parasol, separated from the others, opening like an immense umbrella, displayed its dome of dark green; then, all of a sudden, we gained the boundary of the forest, some hundreds of meters below the defile which leads into the wild valley of Niolo.

On the two projecting heights which commanded a view of this pass, some old trees, grotesquely twisted, seemed to have mounted with painful efforts, like scouts who had started in advance of the multitude heaped together in the rear. When we turned round we saw the entire forest stretched beneath our feet, like a gigantic basin of verdure, whose edges, which seemed to reach the sky, were composed of bare racks shutting in on every side.

We resumed our walk, and, ten minutes later, we found ourselves in the defile.

Then I beheld an astonishing landscape. Beyond another forest, a valley, but a valley such as I had never seen before, a solitude of stone ten leagues long, hollowed out between two high mountains, without a field or a tree to be seen. This was the Niolo valley, the fatherland of Corsican liberty, the inaccessible citadel, from which the invaders had never been able to drive out the mountaineers.

My companion said to me: "It is here, that all our bandits have taken refuge."

Ere long we were at the further end of this chasm, so wild, so inconceivably beautiful.

Not a blade of grass, not a plant—nothing but granite. As far as our eyes could reach we saw in front of us a desert of glittering stone, heated like an oven by a burning sun which seemed to hang for that very purpose right above the gorge. When we raised our eyes toward the crests we stood dazzled and stupefied by what we saw. They looked red and notched like festoons of coral, for all the summits are made of porphyry; and the sky overhead seemed violet, lilac, discolored by the vicinity of these strange mountains. Lower down the granite was of scintillating gray, and under our feet it seemed rasped, pounded; we were walking over shining powder. At our right, along a long and irregular course, a tumultuous torrent ran with a continuous roar. And we staggered along under this heat, in this light, in this burning, arid, desolate valley cut by this ravine of turbulent water which seemed to be ever hurrying onward, without being able to fertilize these rocks, lost in this furnace which greedily drank it up without being penetrated or refreshed by it.

But suddenly there was visible at our right a little wooden cross sunk in a little heap of stones. A man had been killed there; and I said to my companion:

"Tell me about your bandits."

He replied:

"I knew the most celebrated of them, the terrible St. Lucia. I will tell you his history.

"His father was killed in a quarrel by a young man of the same district, it is said; and St. Lucia was left alone with his sister. He was a weak and timid youth, small, often ill, without any energy. He did not proclaim the *vendetta* against the assassin of his father. All his relatives came to see him, and implored of him to take vengeance; he remained deaf to their menaces and their supplications.

"Then, following the old Corsican custom, his sister, in her indignation, carried away his black clothes, in order that he might not wear mourning for a dead man who had not been avenged. He was insensible to even this outrage, and rather than take down from the rack his father's gun, which was still loaded,

he shut himself up, not daring to brave the looks of the young men of the district.

"He seemed to have even forgotten the crime, and he lived with his sister in the obscurity of their dwelling.

"But, one day, the man who was suspected of having committed the murder was about to get married. St. Lucia did not appear to be moved by this news; but, no doubt out of sheer bravado, the bridegroom, on his way to the church, passed before the two orphans' house.

"The brother and the sister, at their window, were eating little fried cakes when the young man saw the bridal procession moving past the house. Suddenly he began to tremble, rose up without uttering a word, made the sign of the cross, took the gun which was hanging over the fireplace, and went out.

"When he spoke of this later on, he said: 'I don't know what was the matter with me; it was like fire in my blood; I felt that I should do it, that in spite of everything, I could not resist, I concealed the gun in a cave on the road to Corte.'

"An hour later, he came back, with nothing in his hand, and with his habitual sad air of weariness. His sister believed that there was nothing further in his thoughts.

"But when night fell he disappeared.

"His enemy had, the same evening, to repair to Corte on foot, accompanied by his two bridesmen.

"He was pursuing his way, singing as he went, when St. Lucia stood before him, and looking straight in the murderer's face, exclaimed: 'Now is the time!' and shot him point-blank in the chest.

"One of the bridesmen fled; the other stared at the young man, saying:

" 'What have you done, St. Lucia?'

"Then he was going to hasten to Corte for help, but St. Lucia said in a stern tone:

" 'If you move another step, I'll shoot you through the legs.'

"The other, aware that till now he had always appeared timid, said to him: 'You would not dare to do it!' and he was hurrying off when he fell, instaneously, his thigh shattered by a bullet.

"And St. Lucia, coming over to where he lay, said:

" 'I am going to look at your wound; if it is not serious, I'll leave you there; if it is mortal, I'll finish you off.'

"He inspected the wound, considered it mortal, and slowly re-loading his gun, told the wounded man to say a prayer, and shot him through the head.

"Next day he was in the mountains.

"And do you know what this St. Lucia did after this?

"All his family were arrested by the gendarmes. His uncle, the curé, who was suspected of having incited him to this deed of vengeance, was himself put into prison, and accused by the dead man's relatives. But he escaped, took a gun in his turn, and went to join his nephew in the cave.

"Next, St. Lucia killed, one after the other, his uncle's accusers, and tore out their eyes to teach the others never to state what they had seen with their eyes.

"He killed all the relatives, all the connections of his enemy's family. He massacred during his life fourteen gendarmes, burned down the houses of his adversaries, and was up to the day of his death the most terrible of the bandits, whose memory we have preserved."

* * * * * *

The sun disappeared behind Monte Cinto and the tall shadow of the granite mountain went to sleep on the granite of the valley. We quickened our pace in order to reach before night the little village of Albertaccio, nothing better than a heap of stones welded beside the stone flanks of a wild gorge. And I said as I thought of the bandit:

"What a terrible custom your *vendetta* is!"

My companion answered with an air of resignation:

"What would you have? A man must do his duty!"

The Duel

IN SOCIETY, they called him "The handsome Signoles." He called himself Viscount Gontram Joseph de Signoles.

An orphan and master of a sufficient fortune, he cut something of a figure, as the saying is. He had an attractive form, enough readiness of speech to make some attempt at wit, a certain natural grace of manner, an air of nobility and pride, and a mustache which was both formidable and pleasant to the eye—a thing that pleases the ladies.

He was in demand in drawing-rooms, sought for by waltzers, and he inspired in men that smiling enmity which one has for people of energetic physique. He was suspected of some love affairs which showed him capable of much discretion, for a young man. He lived happily, tranquil, in a state of moral well-being most complete. It was well known that he was good at handling a sword, and still better with a pistol.

"If I were to fight," he said, "I should choose a pistol. With that weapon, I am sure of killing my man."

Now, one evening, having escorted two young women, friends of his, to the theater, being also accompanied by their husbands, he offered them, after the play, an ice at Tortoni's. They had been there about ten minutes, when he perceived that a gentleman, seated at a neighboring table, gazed persistently at one of the ladies of his party. She seemed troubled and disturbed, lowering her eyes. Finally, she said to her husband:

"That man is staring me out of countenance. I do not know him; do you?"

The husband, who had seen nothing, raised his eyes but declared:

"No, not at all."

The young woman replied, half laughing, half angry: "It is very annoying; that individual is spoiling my ice."

The husband shrugged his shoulders, replying:

"Pshaw! Pay no attention to him. If we were to notice all the insolent people we meet, there would be no end to it."

But the Viscount arose brusquely. He could not allow this unknown man to spoil an ice he had offered. It was to him that the injury was addressed, as it was through him and for him that his friends had entered this *café*. The affair, then, concerned him only. He advanced toward the man and said to him:

"You have, sir, a manner of looking at these ladies that is not to be tolerated. I beg to ask you to cease this attention."

The other replied: "So you command me to keep the peace, do you?"

With set teeth, the Viscount answered: "Take care, sir, or you will force me to forget myself!"

The gentleman replied with a single word, an obscene word which resounded from one end of the *café* to the other, and made each guest start with a sudden movement as if they were all on springs. Those that were in front turned around; all the others raised their heads; three waiters turned about on their heels as if on pivots; the two ladies at the counter bounded forward, then entirely turned their backs upon the scene, as if they had been two automatons obeying the same manipulation.

There was a great silence. Then, suddenly, a sharp noise rent the air. The Viscount had struck his adversary. Everybody got up to interpose. Cards were exchanged.

After the Viscount had returned home, he walked up and down his room at a lively pace for some minutes. He was too much agitated to reflect upon anything. One idea only hovered over his mind: "a duel"; and yet this idea awoke in him as yet, no emotion whatever. He had done what he ought to do; he had shown himself what he ought to be. People would talk of it, approve of it, and congratulate him. He said aloud, in a high voice, as one speaks when he is much troubled in thought:

"What a beast that man is."

Then he sat down and began to reflect. He would have to find some seconds in the morning. Whom should he choose? He thought over the people of his acquaintance who were the most celebrated and in the best positions. He took finally, Marquis de la Tour-Noire and Colonel Bourdin, a great lord and a soldier who was very strong. Their names would carry in the journals. He perceived that he was thirsty and he drank, one after the other, three glasses of water; then he began to walk again. He felt himself full of energy. By showing himself hot-brained, resolute in all things, by exacting rigorous, dangerous conditions, and by claiming a serious duel, a very serious one, his adversary would doubtless withdraw and make some excuses.

He took up the card which he had drawn from his pocket and thrown upon the table and re-read it as he had in the *café*, by a glance of the eye, and again in the cab, on returning home, by the light of a gas jet: "George Lamil, 51 Moncey street." That was all.

He examined these assembled letters which appeared so mysterious to him, his senses all confused: George Lamil? Who was this man? What had he done? Why had he looked at that woman in such a way? Was it not revolting that a stranger, an unknown should come to trouble his life thus, at a blow, because he had been pleased to fix his insolent gaze upon a woman? And the Viscount repeated again, in a loud voice:

"What a brute."

Then he remained motionless, standing, thinking, his look ever fixed upon the card. A certain anger against this piece of paper was awakened in him, a hateful anger which was mingled with a strange sentiment of malice. It was stupid, this whole story! He took a penknife which lay open at his hand, and pricked the card through the middle of the printed name, as if he were using a poignard upon some one.

So he must fight! Should he choose the sword or pistol, for he considered himself the insulted one. With the sword he risked less; but with the pistol, there was a chance of his adversary withdrawing. It is rarely that a duel with the sword is mortal, a reciprocal prudence hindering the combatants from keeping near enough to each other for the point to strike very deep; with the pistol he risked his life very seriously; but he could also meet the affair with all the honors of the situation and without arriving at a meeting. He said aloud:

"It is necessary to be firm. He will be afraid."

The sound of his own voice made him tremble and he began to look about him. He felt very nervous. He drank still another glass of water, then commenced to undress, preparatory to retiring.

When he was ready, he put out his light and closed his eyes. Then he thought:

"I have all day to-morrow to busy myself with my affairs. I must sleep first, in order to be calm."

He was very warm under the clothes, but he could not succeed in falling asleep. He turned and turned again, remained for five minutes upon his back, then placed himself upon his left side, then rolled over to the right.

He was still thirsty. He got up and drank. Then a kind of disquiet seized him:

"Can it be that I am afraid?" said he.

Why should his heart begin to beat so foolishly at each of the customary noises about his room?—when the clock was going to strike and the spring made that little grinding noise as it raised itself to make the turn? And he found it was necessary for him to open his mouth in order to breathe for some seconds following this start, so great was his feeling of oppression. He began to reason with himself upon the possibilities of the thing:

"What have I to fear?"

No, certainly, he should not fear, since he was resolved to follow it out to the end and since he had fully made up his mind to fight without a qualm. But he felt himself so profoundly troubled that he asked himself:

"Can it be that I am afraid in spite of myself?"

And this doubt invaded him, this disquiet, this fear; if a force more powerful than his will, dominating, irresistible, should conquer him, what would happen to him? Yes, what would happen? Certainly he could walk upon the earth, if he wished to go there. But if he should tremble? And if he should lose consciousness? And he thought of his situation, of his reputation, of his name.

And a singular desire took possession of him to get up and look at himself in the glass. He relighted his candle. When he perceived his face reflected in the polished glass, he scarcely knew himself, and it seemed to him that he had never seen himself before. His eyes appeared enormous; he was pale, certainly; he was pale, very pale.

He remained standing there before the mirror. He put out his tongue as if to examine the state of his health, and suddenly this thought entered his brain after the fashion of a bullet:

"After to-morrow at this time, I shall perhaps be dead."

And his heart began to beat furiously.

"After to-morrow at this time, I shall perhaps be dead. This person opposite me, this being I have so often seen in this glass, will be no more. How can it be! I am here, I see myself, I feel that I am alive, and in twenty-four hours I shall be stretched upon that bed, dead, my eyes closed, cold, inanimate, departed."

He turned around to the bed and distinctly saw himself stretched on his back in the same clothes he had worn on going out. In his face were the lines of death, and a rigidity in the hands that would never stir again.

Then a fear of his bed came over him, and in order to see it no more he passed into his smoking-room. Mechanically he took a cigar, lighted it, and began to walk about. He was cold. He went toward the bell to waken his valet; but he stopped with his hand on the cord:

"This man would perceive at once that I am afraid."

He did not ring, but made a fire. His hands trembled a little from a nervous shiver when they came in contact with any object. His mind wandered; his thoughts from trouble became frightened, hasty, and sorrowful; an intoxication seemed to invade his mind as if he were drunk. And without ceasing he asked:

"What am I going to do? What is going to become of me?"

His whole body was vibrating, traversed by a jerking and a trembling; he got up and approached the window, opening the curtains.

The day had dawned, a summer day. A rose-colored sky made the city rosy on roof and wall. A great fall of spread out light, like a caress from the rising sun, enveloped the waking world; and, with this light, a gay, rapid, brutal hope invaded the heart of the Viscount! He was a fool to allow himself to be thus cast down by fear, even before anything was decided, before his witnesses had seen those of this George Lamil, before he yet knew whether he were going to fight a duel.

He made his toilette, dressed himself, and walked out with firm step.

He repeated constantly, in walking: "It will be necessary for me to be energetic, very energetic. I must prove that I am not afraid."

His witnesses, the Marquis and the Colonel, placed themselves at his disposal and, after having shaken hands with him energetically, discussed the conditions. The Colonel asked:

"Do you wish it to be a serious duel?"

The Viscount responded: "Very serious."

The Marquis continued: "Will you use a pistol?"

"Yes."

"We leave you free to regulate the rest."

The Viscount enunciated, in a dry, jerky voice:

"Twenty steps at the order, and on raising the arm instead of lowering it. Exchange of bullets until one is grievously wounded."

The Colonel declared, in a satisfied tone:

"These are excellent conditions. You shoot well, all the chances are in your favor."

They separated. The Viscount returned home to wait for them. His agitation, appeased for a moment, grew now from minute to minute. He felt along his arms, his legs, and in his breast a kind of trembling, of continued vibration; he could not keep still, either sitting or standing. There was no longer an appearance of saliva in his mouth, and each instant he made a noisy movement with his tongue, as if to unglue it from the roof of his mouth.

He wished to breakfast but he could not eat. Then the idea came to him of drinking to give himself courage and he brought out a small bottle of rum, which he swallowed in six glasses, one after the other.

A heat, like that of a burning fire, invaded him, followed almost immediately by a numbness of the soul. He thought:

"I have found the remedy. Now all goes well."

But at the end of an hour, he had emptied the bottle and his state of agitation became intolerable. He felt a foolish impulse to roll on the ground, to cry out and bite. Then night fell.

A stroke of the bell gave him such a shock that he had not sufficient strength left to rise and receive his witnesses. He dared not even speak to them to say "Good evening," to pronounce a single word, for fear that they would discover a change in his voice.

The Colonel announced:

"All is arranged according to the conditions that you have fixed upon. Your adversary claimed the privileges of the offended, but he soon yielded and accepted all. His witnesses are two military men."

The Viscount pronounced the word: "Thanks."

The Marquis continued:

"Excuse us if we only come in and go out, for we have still a thousand things to occupy our attention. A good doctor will be necessary, since the combat is only to cease after a severe wound, and you know that bullets are no trifles. Then, a place must be found, in some proximity to a house, where we may carry the wounded, if necessary, etc., etc.; finally we have but two or three hours for it."

The Viscount, for the second time, articulated:

"Thanks."

The Colonel asked:

"How is it with you? Are you calm?"

"Yes, very calm, thank you."

The two men then retired.

When he again found himself alone, it seemed to him that he was mad. His domestic having lighted the lamps, he seated himself before his table to write some letters. After having traced, at the top of a page: "This is my testament—" he arose with a shake and put it away from him, feeling himself incapable of forming two ideas, or of sufficient resolution to decide what was to be done.

So he was going to fight a duel! There was no way to avoid it. How could he ever go through it? He wished to fight, it was his intention and firm resolution so to do; and yet, he felt, that in spite of all his effort of mind and all the tension of his will, he would not be able to preserve even the necessary force to go to the place of meeting. He tried to imagine the combat, his own attitude, and the position of his adversary.

From time to time, his teeth chattered in his mouth with a little hard noise. He tried to read, and took down the Chateauvillard code of dueling. Then he asked himself:

"Has my opponent frequently fought? Is he known? Is he classed? How am I to know?"

He remembered Baron de Vaux's book up experts with the pistol, and he ran through it from one end to the other. George Lamil was not mentioned. Nevertheless, if this man were not an expert, he would not so readily have accepted this dangerous weapon and these mortal conditions.

He opened, in passing, a box of Gastinne Renettes which stood on a little stand, took out one of the pistols, held it in a position to fire, and raised his arm. But he trembled from head to foot and the gun worked upon all his senses.

Then he said: "It is impossible. I cannot fight in this condition."

He looked at the end of the barrel, at that little black, deep hole that spits out death, he thought of the dishonor, of the whisperings in his circle, of the laughs in the drawing-rooms, of the scorn of the ladies, of the allusions of the journals, of all the insults that cowards would throw at him.

He continued to examine the weapon, and, raising the cock, he suddenly saw a priming glittering underneath like a little red flame. The pistol was loaded then, through a chance forgetfulness. And he found in this discovery a confused, inexplicable joy.

If in the presence of the other man he did not have that calm, noble bearing that he should have, he would be lost forever. He would be spotted, branded with the sign of infamy, hunted from the world! And this calm, heroic bear-

ing he would not have, he knew it, he felt it. However, he was brave, since he did wish to fight! He was brave, since. . . . The thought that budded never took form, even in his own mind; for, opening his mouth wide he brusquely thrust the barrel of his pistol into his throat, and pulled the trigger. . . .

When his valet, hearing the report, hastened to him, he found him dead upon his back. A jet of blood had splashed upon the white paper on the table and made a great red spot upon these four words:

"This is my testament."

The Love of Long Ago

THE old-fashioned château was built on a wooded height. Tall trees surrounded it with dark greenery; and the vast park extended its vistas here over a deep forest and there over an open plain. Some little distance from the front of the mansion stood a huge stone basin in which marble nymphs were bathing. Other basins arranged in order succeeded each other down as far as the foot of the slope, and a hidden fountain sent cascades dancing from one to the other.

From the manor-house, which preserved the grace of a superannuated coquette, down to the grottos incrusted with shellwork, where slumbered the loves of a bygone age, everything in this antique demesne had retained the physiognomy of former days. Everything seemed to speak still of ancient customs, of the manners of long ago, of faded

gallantries, and of the elegant trivialities so dear to our grandmothers.

In a parlor in the style of Louis XV., the walls of which were covered with shepherds courting shepherdesses, beautiful ladies in hoop petticoats, and gallant gentlemen in wigs, a very old woman, who seemed dead as soon as she ceased to move, was almost lying down in a large easy-chair while her thin, mummy-like hands hung down, one at each side of her.

Her eyes were gazing languidly toward the distant horizon as if they sought to follow the park visions of her youth. Through the open window every now and then came a breath of air laden with the scent of grass and the perfume of flowers. It made her white locks flutter around her wrinkled forehead and old memories sweep through her brain.

Beside her on a tapestried stool, a

young girl, with long, fair hair hanging in plaits over her neck, was embroidering an altar-cloth. There was a pensive expression in her eyes, and it was easy to see that, while her agile fingers worked, her brain was busy with thoughts.

But the old lady suddenly turned her head.

"Berthe," she said, "read something out of the newspapers for me, so that I may still know sometimes what is happening in the world."

The young girl took up the newspaper, and cast a rapid glance over it.

"There is a great deal about politics, grandmamma; am I to pass it by?"

"Yes, yes, darling. Are there no accounts of love affairs? Is gallantry, then, dead in France that they no longer talk about abductions or adventures as they did formerly?"

The girl made a long search through the columns of the newspaper.

"Here is one," she said. "It is entitled, 'A Love-Drama.'"

The old woman smiled through her wrinkles. "Read that for me," she said.

And Berthe commenced. It was a case of vitriol-throwing. A wife, in order to avenge herself on her husband's mistress, had burned her face and eyes. She had left the Assize-Court acquitted, declared to be innocent, amid the applause of the crowd.

The grandmother moved about excitedly in her chair, and exclaimed:

"This is horrible—why, it is perfectly horrible! See whether you can find anything else to read for me, darling."

Berthe again made a search; and further down in the reports of criminal cases at which her attention was still directed. She read:

"'Gloomy Drama.—A shopgirl, no longer young, allowed herself to yield to the embraces of a young man. Then, to avenge herself on her lover, whose heart proved fickle, she shot him with a revolver. The unhappy man is maimed for life. The jury consisted of men of moral character, and took the part of the murderess—regarding her as the victim of illicit love. They honorably acquitted her.'"

This time, the old grandmother appeared quite shocked, and, in a trembling voice, said:

"Why, you are mad, then, nowadays. You are mad! The good God has given you love, the only allurement in life. Man has added to this gallantry, the only distraction of our dull hours, and here are you mixing up with vitriol and revolvers, as if one were to put mud into a flagon of Spanish wine."

Berthe did not seem to understand her grandmother's indignation.

"But, grandmamma, this woman avenged herself. Remember, she was married, and her husband deceived her."

The grandmother gave a start.

"What ideas have they been putting into the heads of you young girls of to-day?"

Berthe replied:

"But marriage is sacred, grandmamma."

The grandmother's heart, which had its birth in the great age of gallantry, gave a sudden leap.

"It is love that is sacred," she said. "Listen, child, to an old woman who has seen three generations and who has had a long, long experience of men and women. Marriage and love have nothing in common. We marry to found a family, and we cannot dispense with marriage. If society is a chain, each family is a link in that chain. In order to weld those links, we always seek for metals of the same kind. When we marry, we must bring together suitable conditions; we must combine fortunes, unite similar races, and aim at the common interests, which are riches and children. We marry only once, my child, because the world requires us to do so, but we may love twenty times in one lifetime because nature has made us able to do this. Marriage, you see, is law, and love is an instinct, which impels us sometimes along a straight and sometimes along a crooked path. The world has made laws to combat our instincts—it was necessary to make them; but our instincts are always stronger, and we ought not to resist them too much, because they come from God, while the laws only come from men. If we did not perfume life with love, as much love as possible, darling, as we put sugar into drugs for children, nobody would care to take it just as it is."

Berthe opened her eyes widely in astonishment. She murmured:

"Oh! grandmamma, we can only love once."

The grandmother raised her trembling hands toward Heaven, as if again to invoke the defunct god of gallantries. She exclaimed indignantly:

"You have become a race of serfs, a race of common people. Since the Revolution, it is impossible any longer to recognize society. You have attached big words to every action, and wearisome duties to every corner of existence; you believe in equality and eternal passion. People have written verses telling you that people have died of love. In my time, verses were written to teach men to love every woman. And we!—when we liked a gentleman, my child, we sent him a page. And when a fresh caprice came into our hearts, we were not slow in getting rid of the last lover—unless we kept both of them."

The old woman smiled with a keen smile, and a gleam of roguery twinkled in her gray eye, the sprightly, sceptical roguery of those people who did not believe that they were made of the same clay as the others, and who lived as rulers for whom common restrictions were not made.

The young girl, turning very pale, faltered out:

"So then, women have no honor."

The grandmother ceased to smile. In she had kept in her soul some of Voltaire's irony, she had also a little of Rousseau's glowing philosophy: "No honor! because we loved, and dared to say so, and even boasted of it? But, my child, if one of us, among the greatest ladies in France, were to live without a lover, she would have the entire court laughing at her. Those who wished to live differently had only to enter a convent. And you imagine perhaps that your husbands will love you alone all their lives. As if, indeed, this could be the case. I tell you that marriage is a thing necessary in order that society should exist. but it is not in the nature of our race, do you understand? There is only one good thing in life, and that is love. And how you misunderstand it! how you spoil it! You treat it as something solemn, like a sacrament, or something to be bought, like a dress."

The young girl caught the old woman's trembling hands in her own.

"Hold your tongue, I beg of you, grandmamma!"

And, on her knees, with tears in her eyes, she prayed to Heaven to bestow on her a great passion, one eternal passion alone, in accordance with the dream of modern poets, while her grandmother, kissing her on the forehead, still penetrated by that charming, healthy logic by which philosophers of gallantry sprinkled salt upon the life of the eighteenth century, murmured:

"Take care, my poor darling! If you believe in such follies as this, you will be very unhappy."

The Farmer's Wife

ONE day Baron René du Treilles said to me:

"Will you come and open the hunting season with me in my farmhouse at Marinville? By doing so, my dear fellow, you will give me the greatest pleasure. Besides, I am all alone. This will be a hard hunting-bout, to start with, and the house where I sleep is so primitive that I can only bring my most intimate friends there."

I accepted his invitation. So on Saturday we started by the railway-line running into Normandy, and alighted at the station of Alvimare. Baron René, pointing out to me a country jaunting-car drawn by a restive horse, driven by a big peasant with white hair, said to me:

"Here is our equipage, my dear boy."

The man extended his hand to his landlord, and the Baron pressed it warmly, asking:

"Well, Maître Lebrument, how are you?"

"Always the same, M'sieu l' Baron."

"We jumped into this hencoop suspended and shaken on two immense wheels. The young horse, after a violent swerve, started into a gallop, flinging us into the air like balls. Every fall backward on to the wooden bench gave me the most dreadful pain.

The peasant kept repeating in his calm, monotonous voice:

"There, there! it's all right, all right, Moutard, all right!"

But Moutard scarcely heard and kept scampering along like a goat.

Our two dogs behind us, in the empty part of the hencoop, stood erect and sniffed the air of the plains as if they could smell the game.

The Baron gazed into the distance, with a sad eye. The vast Norman landscape, undulating and melancholy as an immense English park, with farmyards surrounded by two or four rows of trees and full of dwarfed apple-trees which rendered the houses invisible, gave a vista, as far as the eye could see, of old forest-trees, tufts of wood and hedgerows, which artistic gardeners provide for when they are tracing the lines of princely estates.

And René de Treilles suddenly exclaimed:

"I love this soil; I have my very roots in it."

A pure Norman, tall and strong, with the more or less projecting paunch of the old race of adventurers who went to found kingdoms on the shores of every ocean, he was about fifty years of age, ten years less perhaps than the farmer who was driving us. The latter was a lean peasant, all skin and bone, one of those men who live a hundred years.

After two hours' traveling over stony roads, across that green and monotonous plain, the vehicle entered one of those fruit-gardens which adorn the fronts of farmhouses, and drew up before an old structure falling into decay, where an old maid-servant stood waiting at the side of a young fellow who seized the horse's bridle.

We entered the farmhouse. The smoky kitchen was high and spacious. The copper utensils and the earthenware glistened under the reflection of the big fire. A cat lay asleep under the table. Within, you inhaled the odor of milk, of apples, of smoke, that indescribable smell peculiar to old houses where peasants have lived—the odor of the soil, of the walls, of furniture, of stale soup, of washing, and of the old inhabitants, the smell of animals and human beings intermingled, of things and of persons, the odor of time and of things that have passed away.

I went out to have a look at the farmyard. It was big, full of old apple-trees dwarfed and crooked, and laden with fruit which fell on the grass around them. In this farmyard the smell of apples was as strong as that of the orange-trees which blossom on the banks of southern rivers.

Four rows of beeches surrounded this inclosure. They were so tall that they seemed to touch the clouds, at this hour of nightfall, and their summits, through which the night winds passed, shook and sang a sad, interminable song.

I re-entered the house. The Baron was warming his feet at the fire and was listening to the farmer's talk about country matters. He talked about marriages, births, and deaths, then about the fall in the price of corn and the the latest news about the selling value of cattle. The "Veularde" (as he called a cow that had been bought at the fair of Veules) had calved in the middle of June. The cider had not been first-class last year. The apricot-apples were almost disappearing from the country.

Then we had dinner. It was a good rustic meal, simple and abundant, long and tranquil. And while we were dining, I noticed the special kind of friendly familiarity between the Baron and the peasant which had struck me from the start.

Without, the beeches continued sobbing in the nightwind, and our two dogs shut up in a shed were whining and howling in uncanny fashion. The fire was dying out in the big grate. The maid-servant had gone to bed. Maître Lebrument said in his turn:

"If you don't mind, M'sieu l' Baron, I'm going to bed. I am not used to staying up late."

The Baron extended his hand toward him and said: "Go, my friend." in so cordial a tone that I said, as soon as the man had disappeared:

"He is devoted to you, this farmer?"

"Better than that, my dear fellow! It is a drama, an old drama, simple and very sad, that attaches him to me. Here is the story:

"You know my father was a colonel in a cavalry regiment. His orderly was this young fellow, now an old man, the son of a farmer. Then, when my father retired from the army, he took this retired soldier, then about forty, as his servant. I was at that time about thirty. We lived then in our old château of Valrenne near Caudebec-in-Caux.

"At this period, my mother's chambermaid was one of the prettiest girls you could see, fair-haired, slender, and sprightly in manner, a genuine specimen of the fascinating Abigail, such as we scarcely ever find nowadays. To-day these creatures spring up into hussies before their time. Paris, with the aid of the railways, attracts them, calls them, takes hold of them as soon as they are bursting into womanhood—these little wenches, who, in old times, remained simple maid-servants. Every man passing by, as long ago recruiting sergeants did with conscripts, entices and debauches them—foolish lassies—till now we have only the scum of the female sex for servant-maids, all that is dull, nasty, common, and ill-formed, too ugly even for gallantry.

"Well, this girl was charming, and I often gave her a kiss in dark corners—nothing more, I swear to you! She was virtuous, besides; and I had some respect for my mother's house, which is more than can be said of the blackguards of the present day.

"Now it happened that my father's man-servant, the ex-soldier, the old farmer you have just seen, fell in love with this girl, but in an unusual sort of way. The first thing we noticed was that his memory was affected; he did not pay attention to anything.

"My father was incessantly saying: 'Look here, Jean! What's the matter with you? Are you unwell?'

" 'No, no, M'sieu l' Baron. There's nothing the matter with me.'

"Jean got thin. Then, when serving at table, he broke glasses and let plates fall. We thought he must have been attacked by some nervous malady, and we sent for the doctor, who thought he could detect symptoms of spinal disease. Then my father, full of anxiety about his faithful man-servant, decided to place him in a private hospital. When the poor fellow heard of my father's intentions, he made a clean breast of it.

" 'M'sieu l' Baron—'

" 'Well, my boy?'

" 'You see, the thing I want is not physic.'

" 'Ha! what is it, then?'

" 'It's marriage!'

"My father turned round and stared at him in astonishment.

" 'What's that you say—eh?'

" 'It's marriage.'

" 'Marriage? So then, you donkey, you're in love.'

" 'That's how it is, M'sieu l' Baron.'

"And my father began to laugh in such an immoderate fashion that my mother called through the wall of the next room:

" 'What in the name of goodness is the matter with you, Gontran?'

"My father replied:

" 'Come here, Catherine.'

"And when she came in, he told, with tears in his eyes from sheer laughter, that his idiot of a servant-man was love-sick.

"But my mother, instead of laughing, was deeply affected.

" 'Who is it that you have fallen in love with, my poor fellow?' she asked.

"He answered, without hesitation:

" 'With Louise, Madame la Baronne.'

"My mother said, with the utmost gravity: 'We must try to arrange the matter the best way we can.'

"So Louise was sent for, and questioned by my mother. She said in reply that she knew all about Jean's liking for her, that in fact Jean had spoken to her about it several times, but that she did not want him. She refused to say why.

"And two months elapsed during which my father and mother never ceased to urge this girl to marry Jean. As she declared she was not in love with any other man, she could not give any serious reason for her refusal. My father, at last, overcome her resistance by means of a big present of money, and started the pair of them on a farm on the estate—this very farm. At the end of three years, I learned that Louise had died of consumption. But my father and my mother died, too, in their turn, and it was two years more before I found myself face to face with Jean.

"At last, one autumn day, about the end of October, the idea came into my head to go hunting on this part of my estate, which my tenant had told me was full of game.

"So, one evening, one wet evening, I arrived at this house. I was shocked to find the old soldier who had been my father's servant perfectly white-haired, though he was not more than forty-five or forty-six years of age. I made him dine with me, at the very table where we're now sitting. It was raining hard. We could hear the rain battering at the roof, the walls, and the windows, flowing in a perfect deluge into the farm-yard; and my dog was howling in the shed where the other dogs are howling to-night.

"All of a sudden, when the servant-maid had gone to bed, the man said in a timid voice:

" 'M'sieu l' Baron.'

" 'What is it, my dear Jean?'

" 'I have something to tell you.'

" 'Tell it, my dear Jean.'

' You remember Louise, my wife?'

" 'Certainly, I do remember her.'

" 'Well, she left me a message for you.'

" 'What was it?'

" 'A—a—well, it was what you might call a confession.'

" 'Ha! And what was it about?'

" 'It was—it was—I'd rather, all the same, tell you nothing about it—but I must—I must. Well, it's this—it wasn't consumption she died of at all. It was grief—well, that's the long and the short of it. As soon as she came to live here, after we were married, she grew thin; she changed so that you wouldn't know her at the end of six months—no, you wouldn't know her, M'sieu l' Baron. It was all just as before I married her, but it was different, too, quite another sort of thing.

" 'I sent for the doctor. He said it was her liver that was affected—he said it was what he called a "hepatic" complaint—I don't know these big words M'sieu l' Baron. Then I bought medicine for her, heaps on heaps of bottles, that cost about three hundred francs. But she'd take none of them; she wouldn't have them; she said: "It's no use, my poor Jean; it wouldn't do me any good." I saw well that she had some hidden trouble; and then I found her one time crying and I didn't know what to do—no, I didn't know what to do. I bought caps and dresses and hair-oil and earings for her. No good! And I saw that she was going to die. And so one night in the end of November, one snowy night, after remaining the whole day without stirring out of the bed, she told me to send for the curé. So I went for him. As soon as he had come, she saw him. Then, she asked him to let me come into the room and she said to me: "Jean, I'm going to make a confession to you. I owe it to you, Jean. I have never been false to you, never!—never, before or after you married me. M'sieu le Curé is there, and can tell it is so, and he knows my soul. Well, listen, Jean. If I am dying, it is because I was not able to console myself for leaving the château—because—I was too—too fond of the young Baron, Monsieur René—too fond of him, mind you, Jean,—there was no harm in it! This is the thing that's killing me. When I could see him no more, I felt that I should die. If I could only have seen him, I might have lived; only seen him, nothing more. I wish you'd tell it to him some day, by-and-by, when I am no longer here. You will tell him—swear you will, Jean —swear it in the presence of M'sieu le Curé! It will console me to know that

he will know it one day—that this was the cause of my death! Swear it!"

"'Well, I gave her my promise, M'sieu l' Baron! and, on the faith of an honest man, I have kept my word.'

"And then he ceased speaking, his eyes filling with tears.

*   *   *   *   *   *

"Upon my soul, my dear boy, you can't form any idea of the emotion that filled me when I heard this poor devil, whose wife I had caused the death of without knowing it, telling me this story on that wet night in this very kitchen.

"I exclaimed: "Ah! my poor Jean! my poor Jean!'

"He murmured: 'Well, that's all, M'sieu l' Baron. I could do nothing, one way or another—and now its all over!"

"I caught his hand across the table, and I began to cry.

"He asked: 'Will you come and see her grave?' I nodded by way of assent, for I couldn't speak. He rose up, lighted a lantern, and we walked through the blinding rain which, in the light of the lamp, looked like falling arrows.

"He opened a gate, and I saw some crosses of blackwood.

"Suddenly, he said: 'There it is, in front of a marble slab,' and he flashed the lantern close to it so that I could read the inscription:

"'To LOUISE-HORTENSE MARINET, WIFE of *Jean-François Lebrument, farmer.*
She was a faithful Wife! God rest her Soul!'

"We fell on our knees in the damp grass, he and I, with the lantern between us, and I saw the rain beating on the white marble slab. And I thought of the heart of her sleeping there in her grave. Ah! poor heart! poor heart!

*   *   *   *   *   *

"Since then, I have been coming here every year. And I don't know why, but I feel as if I were guilty of some crime in the presence of this man who always shows that he forgives me!"

Beside a Dead Man

He was slowly dying, as consumptives die. I saw him sitting down every day at two o'clock under the windows of the hotel, facing the tranquil sea, on an open-air bench. He remained for some time without moving, in the heat of the sun, gazing mournfully at the Mediterranean. Every now and then he cast a glance at the lofty mountain with vaporous summits which shuts in Mentone; then, with a very slow movement, he crossed his long legs, so thin that they seemed two bones, around which fluttered the cloth of his trousers, and opened a book, which was always the same. And then he did not stir any more, but read on, read on with his eye and with his mind; all his poor expiring body seemed to read, all his soul plunged, lost itself, disappeared, in this book, up to the hour when the cool air made him cough a little. Then he got up and re-entered the hotel.

He was a tall German, with a fair beard, who breakfasted and dined in his own room, and spoke to nobody.

A vague curiosity attracted me to him. One day I sat down by his side, having taken up a book, too, to keep up appearances, a volume of Musset's poems.

And I began to run through "Rolla."

Suddenly, my neighbor said to me, in good French:

"Do you know German, Monsieur?"

"Not at all, Monsieur."

"I am sorry for that. Since chance has thrown us side by side, I could have lent you, I could have shown you, an inestimable thing—this book which I hold in my hand."

"What is, pray?"

"It is a copy of my master, Schopenhauer, annotated with his own hand. All the margins, as you may see, are covered with his handwriting."

I took the book from him reverently, and I gazed at those forms incomprehensible to me, but which revealed the immortal thoughts of the greatest shatterer of dreams who had ever dwelt on earth.

And Musset's verses arose in my memory:

"Hast thou found out, Voltaire, that it is bliss to die,
Or does thy hideous smile over thy bleached bones fly?"

And involuntarily I compared the childish sarcasm, the religious sarcasm, of Voltaire with the irresistible irony of the German philosopher whose influence is henceforth ineffaceable.

Let us protest and let us be angry, let us be indignant or let us be enthusiastic. Schopenhauer has marked humanity with the seal of his disdain and of his disenchantment. A disabused pleasure-seeker, he overthrew beliefs, hopes, poetic ideals, and chimeras, destroyed the aspirations, ravaged the confidence of souls, killed love, dragged down the chivalrous worship of women, crushed the illusions of hearts, and accomplished the most gigantic task ever attempted by scepticism. He passed over everything with his mocking spirit, and left everything empty. And even to-day those who execrate him seem to carry portions of his thought, in spite of themselves, in their own souls.

"So, then, you were intimately acquainted with Schopenhauer?" I said to the German.

He smiled sadly.

"Up to the time of his death, Monsieur."

And he spoke to me about the philosopher and told me about the almost supernatural impression which this strange being made on all who came near him.

He gave me an account of the interview of the old iconoclast with a French politician, a *doctrinaire* Republican, who wanted to get a glimpse of this man, and found him in a noisy tavern, seated in the midst of his disciples, dry, wrinkled, laughing with an unforgettable laugh, eating and tearing ideas and beliefs with a single word, as a dog tears with one bite of his teeth the tissues with which he plays.

He repeated for me the comment of this Frenchman as he went away, scared and terrified: "I thought that I had spent an hour with the devil."

Then he added:

"He had, indeed, Monsieur, a frightful smile, which terrified us even after his death. I can tell you an anecdote about it not generally known, if it has any interest for you."

And he began, in a tired voice, interrupted by frequent fits of coughing:

"Schopenhauer had just died, and it was arranged that we should watch, in turn, two by two, till morning.

"He was lying in a large apartment, very simple, vast, and gloomy. Two wax-candles were burning on the bedside stand.

"It was midnight when I took up my task of watching along with one of our comrades. The two friends whom we replaced had left the apartment, and we came and sat down at the foot of the bed.

"The face was not changed. It was laughing. That pucker which we knew so well lingered still around the corners of the lips, and it seemed to us that he was about to open his eyes, to move, and to speak. His thought, or rather his thoughts, enveloped us. We felt ourselves more than ever in the atmosphere of his genius, absorbed, possessed by him. His domination seemed to us even more sovereign now that he was dead. A sense of mystery was blended with the power of this incomparable spirit.

"The bodies of these men disappear, but they remain themselves; and in the night which follows the stoppage of their heart's beating, I assure you, Monsieur, they are terrifying.

"And in hushed tones we talked about him, recalling to mind certain sayings, certain formulas of his, those startling maxims which are like jets of flame flung, by means of some words, into the darkness of the Unknown Life.

" 'It seems to me that he is going to speak,' said my comrade. And we stared with uneasiness bordering on fear at the motionless face with its eternal laugh. Gradually, we began to feel ill at ease, oppressed, on the point of fainting. I faltered:

" 'I don't know what is the matter with me, but, I assure you I am not well.'

"And at that moment we noticed that there was an unpleasant odor from the corpse.

"Then, my comrade suggested that we should go into the adjoining room, and leave the door open; and I assented to this proposal.

"I took one of the wax-candles which burned on the bedside stand, and I left the second behind. Then we went and sat down at the other end of the adjoining apartment, so as to be able to see from where we were the bed and the corpse clearly revealed by the light.

"But he still held possession of us. One would have said that his immaterial essence, liberated, free, all-powerful, and dominating, was flitting around us. And sometimes, too, the dreadful smell of the decomposing body came toward us and penetrated us, sickening and indefinable.

"Suddenly a shiver passed through our bones: a sound, a slight sound, came from the death-chamber. Immediately we fixed our glances on him, and we saw, yes, Monsieur, we saw distinctly, both of us, something white flying over

the bed, falling on the carpet, and vanishing under the armchair.

"We were on our feet before we had time to think of anything, distracted by stupefying terror, ready to run away. Then we stared at each other. We were horribly pale. Our hearts throbbed so fiercely that our clothes swelled over our chests. I was the first to speak.

" 'You saw?'

" 'Yes, I saw.'

" 'Can it be that he is not dead?'

" 'Why not, when the body is putrefying?'

" 'What are we to do?'

"My companion said in a hesitating tone:

" 'We must go and look.'

"I took our wax-candle and I entered first, searching with my eye through all the large apartment with its dark corners. There was not the least movement now, and I approached the bed. But I stood transfixed with stupor and fright: Schopenhauer was no longer laughing! He was grinning in a horrible fashion, with his lips pressed together and deep hollows in his cheeks. I stammered out:

" 'He is not dead!'

"But the terrible odor rose up to my nose and stifled me. And I no longer moved, but kept staring fixedly at him, scared as if in the presence of an apparition. Then my companion, having seized the other wax-candle, bent forward. Then, he touched my arm without uttering a word. I followed his glance, and I saw on the floor, under the armchair by the side of the bed, all white on the dark carpet, open as if to bite, Schopenhauer's set of artificial teeth.

"The work of decomposition, loosening the jaws, had made it jump out of the mouth.

— "I was really frightened that day, Monsieur."

And as the sun was sinking toward the glittering sea, the consumptive German rose from his seat, gave me a parting bow, and retired into the hotel.

A Queer Night in Paris

MAITRE SAVAL, notary at Vernon, was passionately fond of music. Still young, though already bald, always carefully shaved, a little corpulent, as was fitting, wearing a gold *pince-nez* instead of old-fashioned spectacles, active, gallant, and joyous, he passed in Vernon for an artist. He thrummed on the piano and played on the violin, and gave musical evenings where interpretations were given of new operas.

He had even what is called a bit of a voice; nothing but a bit, a very little bit of a voice; but he managed it with so much taste that cries of "Bravo!" "Exquisite!" "Surprising!" "Adorable!" issued from every throat as soon as he had murmured the last note.

He was a subscriber to a music publisher in Paris, who sent all new pieces to him. From time to time to the high society of the town he sent little notes something in this style:

"Your are invited to be present on Monday evening at the house of M. Saval, notary, Vernon, at the first production of 'Sais.' "

A few officers, gifted with good voices formed the chorus. Two or three of the vinedressers' families also sang. The notary filled the part of leader of the orchestra with so much skill that the band-master of the 190th regiment of the line said one day, at the Café de l'Europe:

"Oh! M. Saval is a master. It is a great pity that he did not adopt the career of an artist."

When his name was mentioned in a drawing-room, there was always found somebody to declare: "He is not an amateur; he is an artist, a genuine artist." And two or three persons would repeat, in a tone of profound conviction: "Oh! yes, a genuine artist," laying particular stress on the word "genuine."

Every time that a new work was interpreted at a big Parisian theater, M. Saval paid a visit to the capital. Last year, according to his custom, he went to hear "Henry VIII." He then took the express which arrives in Paris at 4:30 P. M., intending to return by the 12:35 A. M. train so as not to have to sleep at a hotel. He had put on evening dress, a black coat and white tie, which he concealed under his overcoat with the collar turned up.

As soon as he had planted his foot on the Rue d'Amsterdam, he felt in quite a jovial mood, and said to himself:

"Decidedly the air of Paris does not

resemble any other air. It has in it something indescribably stimulating, exciting, intoxicating, which fills you with a strange longing to gambol and to do many other things. As soon as I arrive here, it seems to me, all of a sudden, that I have taken a bottle of champagne. What a life one can lead in this city in the midst of artists! Happy are the elect, the great men who enjoy renown in such a city! What an existence is theirs!"

And he made plans; he would have liked to know some of those celebrated men, to talk about them in Vernon, and to spend an evening with them from time to time in Paris.

But suddenly an idea struck him. He had heard allusions to little *cafés* in the outer boulevards at which well-known painters, men of letters, and even musicians gathered, and he proceeded to go toward Montmartre at a slow pace.

He had two hours before him. He wanted to have a look round. He passed in front of taverns frequented by belated Bohemians, gazing at the different faces, seeking to discover the artists. Finally, he came to the sign of "The Dead Rat," and, allured by the name, he entered.

Five or six women with their elbows resting on the marble tables, were talking in low tones about their love affairs, the quarrels of Lucie with Hortense, and the scoundrelism of Octave. They were no longer young, but were fat or thin, tired out, used up. You could see that they were almost bald; and they drank bocks like men.

M. Saval sat down at some distance from them, and waited, for the hour for taking absinthe was at hand.

A tall young man soon came in and took a seat beside him. The landlady called him "M. Romantin." The notary quivered. Was this the Romantin who had taken a medal at the last Salon?

The young man made a sign to the waiter:

"You will bring up my dinner at once, and then carry to my new studio, 15, Boulevard de Clichy, thirty bottles of beer and the ham I ordered this morning. We are going to have a house-warming."

M. Saval immediately ordered dinner. Then he took off his overcoat, so that his dress coat and his white tie could be seen. His neighbor did not seem to notice him. M. Saval glanced sideways at him, burning with the desire to speak to him.

Two young men entered, in red velvet, and peaked beards in the fashion of Henry III. They sat down opposite Romantin.

The first of the pair said:

"It is for this evening?"

Romantin pressed his hand.

"I believe you, old chap, and everyone will be there. I have Bonnat, Guillemet, Gervex, Béraud, Hébert, Duez, Clairin, and Jean-Paul Laurens. It will be a glorious blowout! And women, too! Wait till you see! Every actress without exception—of course I mean, you know all those who have nothing to do this evening."

The landlord of the establishment came across.

"Do you often have this housewarming?"

The painter replied:

"Certainly—every three months, each quarter."

M. Saval could not restrain himself any longer, and in a hesitating voice said:

"I beg your pardon for intruding on you, Monsieur, but I heard your name pronounced, and I would be very glad to know if you really are M. Romantin whose work in the last Salon I have so much admired."

The painter answered:

"I am the person, Monsieur."

The notary then paid the artist a very well-turned compliment, showing that he was a man of culture. The painter, gratified, thanked him politely in reply. Then they chatted. Romantin returned to the subject of his house-warming going into details as to the magnificence of the forthcoming entertainment.

M. Saval questioned him as to all the men he was going to receive, adding:

"It would be an extraordinary piece of good fortune for a stranger, to meet at one time, so many celebrities assembled in the studio of an artist of your rank."

Romantin, overcome, answered: "If it would be agreeable to you, come."

M. Saval accepted the invitation with enthusiasm, reflecting:

"I'll always have time enough to see 'Henry VIII.'"

Both of them had finished their meal. The notary insisted on paying the two bills, wishing to repay his neighbor's civilities. He also paid for the drinks of the young fellows in red velvet; then he left the establishment with the painter.

They stopped in front of a very long house, by no means high, the first story of which had the appearance of an interminable conservatory. Six studios stood in a row with their fronts facing the boulevards.

Romantin was the first to enter. Ascending the stairs, he opened a door, and lighted a match and then a candle.

They found themselves in an immense apartment, the furniture of which consisted of three chairs, two easels, and a few sketches lying on the floor along the walls. M. Saval remained standing at the door in a stupefied state of mind.

The painter remarked:

"Here you are! We've got to the spot; but everything has yet to be done."

Then, examining the high, bare apartment, whose ceiling was veiled in shadows, he said:

"We might make a great deal out of this studio."

He walked around it, surveying it with the utmost attention, then went on:

"I have a mistress who might easily give us a helping hand. Women are incomparable for hanging drapery. But I sent her to the country to-day in order to get her off my hands this evening. It is not that she bores me, but she is too much lacking in the ways of good society. It would be embarrassing to my guests."

He reflected for a few seconds, and then added:

"She is a good girl, but not easy to deal with. If she knew that I was holding a reception, she would tear out my eyes."

M. Saval had not even moved; he did not understand.

. The artist came over to him.

"Since I have invited you, you are going to give me some help."

The notary said emphatically:

"Make any use of me you please. I am at your disposal.

Romantin took off his jacket.

"Well, citizen, to work! We are first going to clean up."

. He went to the back of the easel, on which there was a canvas representing a cat, and seized a very worn-out broom:

· "I say! Just brush up while I look. after the lighting."

M. Saval took the broom, inspected it, and then began to sweep the floor very awkwardly, raising a whirlwind of dust. · .

. Romantin, disgusted, stopped him: "Deuce take it! you don't know how to sweep the floor! Look at me!"

. And he began to roll before him a heap of grayish sweepings, as if he had done nothing else all his life. Then he gave back the broom to the notary, who imitated him.

In five minutes, such a cloud of dust filled the studio that Romantin asked:

"Where are you? I can't see you any longer." ·

M. Saval, who was coughing, came nearer to him. The painter said to him:

"How are you going to manage to get up a chandelier."

The other stunned, asked:

"What chandelier?"

"Why, a chandelier to light—a chandelier with wax-candles."

· The notary did not understand.

. He answered: "I don't know."

The painter began to jump about, cracking his fingers.

"Well, Monseigneur, I have found out a way."

Then he went more calmly:

"Have you got five francs about you?"

M. Saval replied:

"Why, yes."

The artist said:

"Well! you'll go and buy for me five francs' worth of wax-candles while I go and see the cooper."

And he pushed the notary in his evening coat into the street. At the end of five minutes, they had returned, one of them with the wax-candles, and the other with the hoop of a cask. Then Romantin plunged his hand into a cupboard, and drew forth twenty empty bottles, which he fixed in the form of a crown around the hoop. He then came down, and went to borrow a ladder from the doorkeeper, after having explained that he obtained the favors of the old woman by painting the portrait of her cat exhibited on the easel.

When he mounted the ladder, he said to M. Saval:

"Are you active?"

. The other, without understanding answered:

"Why, yes."

"Well, you just climb up there, and fasten this chandelier for me to the ring of the ceiling. Then you must put a wax-candle in each bottle, and light it. I tell you I have a genius for lighting up. But off with your coat, damn it! you are just like a Jeames."

The door was opened violently. A woman appeared, with her eyes flashing, and remained standing on the threshold. Romantin gazed at her with a look of terror. She. waited some seconds, crossed her arms over her breast, and then in a shill, vibrating, exasperated voice said:

"Ha! you villain, is this the way you leave me?"

Romantin made no reply. She went on:

"Ha! you scoundrel! You are again doing the swell, while you pack me off to the country. You'll soon see the way I'll settle your jollification. Yes, I'm going to receive your friends."

She grew warmer:

"I'm going to slap their faces with the bottles and the wax-candles."

Romantin uttered one soft word:

"Mathilde."

But she did not pay any attention to him; she went on:

"Wait a little, my fine fellow! wait a little!"

Romantin went over to her, and tried to take her by the hands:

"Mathilde."

But she was now fairly under way; and on she went, emptying the vials of her wrath with strong words and reproaches. They flowed out of her mouth, like a stream sweeping a heap of filth along with it. The words hurled out seemed struggling for exit. She stuttered, stammered, yelled, suddenly recovering her voice to cast forth an insult or a curse.

He seized her hands without her having even noticed it. She did not seem to see anything, so much occupied was she in holding forth and relieving her heart. And suddenly she began to weep. The tears flowed from her eyes without making her stem the tide of her complaints. But her words had taken a howling, shrieking tone; they were a continuous cry interrupted by sobbings. She commenced afresh twice or three times, till she stopped as if something were choking her, and at last she ceased with a regular flood of tears.

Then he clasped her in his arms and kissed her hair, himself affected.

"Mathilde, my little Mathilde, listen. You must be reasonable. You know, if I give a supper party to my friends, it is to thank these gentlemen for the medal I got at the Salon. I cannot receive women. You ought to understand that. It is not the same with artists as with other people."

She stammered in the midst of her tears:

"Why didn't you tell me this?"

He replied:

"It was in order not to annoy you, not to give you pain. Listen, I'm going to see you home. You will be very sensible, very nice; you will remain quietly waiting for me in bed, and I'll come back as soon as it's over."

She murmured:

"Yes, but you will not begin over again?"

"No, I swear to you!"

He turned toward M. Saval, who had at last hooked on the chandelier:

"My dear friend, I am coming back in five minutes. If anyone arrives in my absence, do the honors for me, will you not?"

And he carried off Mathilde, who kept drying her eyes with her handkerchief as she went along.

Left to himself, M. Saval succeeded in putting everything around him in order. Then he lighted the wax-candles and waited.

He waited for a quarter of an hour, half an hour, an hour. Romantin did not return. Then, suddenly, there was a dreadful noise on the stairs, a song shouted out in chorus by twenty mouths and a regular march like that of a Prussian regiment. The whole house was shaken by the steady tramp of feet. The door flew open, and a motly throng appeared—men and women in a row, holding one another arm in arm, in pairs, and kicking their heels on the floor, in proper time—advancing into the studio like a snake uncoiling itself. They howled:

"Come, let us all be merry,
Pretty maids and soldiers gay!"

M. Saval, thunderstruck, remained standing in evening dress under the chandelier. The procession of revellers caught sight of him, and uttered a shout:

"A Jeames! À Jeames!"

And they began whirling round him, surrounding him with a circle of vociferation. Then they took each other by the hand and went dancing about madly.

He attempted to explain:

"Messieurs — Messieurs — Mesdames —"

But they did not listen to him. They whirled about, they jumped, they brawled.

At last the dancing ceased. M. Saval uttered the word:

"Messieurs—"

A tall, young fellow, fair-haired and bearded to the nose, interrupted him:

"What's your name, my friend?"

The notary, quite scared, said:

"I am M. Saval."

A voice exclaimed:

"You mean Baptiste."

A woman said:

"Let the poor waiter alone! You'll end by making him get angry. He's paid to attend on us, and not to be laughed at by us."

Then, M. Saval noticed that each guest had brought his own provisions. One held a bottle of wine, another a pie. This one had a loaf of bread, that one a ham.

The tall, fair, young fellow placed in his hands an enormous sausage, and gave him orders:

"Go and settle up the sideboard in the corner over there. You are to put the bottles at the left and the provisions at the right."

Saval, getting quite distracted, exclaimed:

"But, Messieurs, I am a notary!"

There was a moment's silence and then a wild outburst of laughter. One suspicious gentleman asked:

"How are you here?"

He explained, telling about his project of going to the opera, his departure from Vernon, his arrival in Paris, and the way in which he had spent the evening.

They sat around him to listen to him; they greeted him with words of applause, and called him Scheherazade.

Romantin did not come back. Other guests arrived. M. Saval was presented to them so that he might begin his story over again. He declined; they forced him to relate it. They fixed him on one of three chairs between two women who kept constantly filling his glass. He drank; he laughed; he talked;

he sang, too. He tried to waltz with his chair, and fell on the floor.

From that moment, he forgot everything. It seemed to him, however, that they undressed him, put him to bed, and that his stomach got sick.

When he awoke, it was broad daylight, and he lay stretched with his feet against a cupboard, in a strange bed.

An old woman with a broom in her hand was glaring angrily at him. At last, she said:

"Clear out, you blackguard! Clear out! What right has anyone to get drunk like this?"

He sat up in his bed, feeling very ill at ease. He asked:

"Where am I?"

"Where are you, you dirty scamp? You are drunk. Take your rotten carcass out of here as quick as you can,—and lose no time about it!"

He wanted to get up. He found that he was naked in the bed. His clothes had disappeared. He blurted out:

"Madame, I—"

Then he remembered. What was he to do? He asked:

"Did Monsieur Romantin come back?"

The doorkeeper shouted:

"Will you take your dirty carcass out of this so that he at any rate may not catch you here?"

M. Saval said, in a state of confusion:

"I haven't got my clothes; they have been taken away from me."

He had to wait, to explain his situation, give notice to his friends, and borrow some money to buy clothes. He did not leave Paris till evening.

And, when people talk about music to him in his beautiful drawing-room in Vernon, he declares with an air of authority that painting is a very inferior art.

A Duel

THE war was over. The Germans occupied France. The country was panting like a wrestler lying under the knee of his successful opponent.

The first trains from Paris, after the city's long agony of famine and despair, were making their way to the new frontiers, slowly passing through the country districts and the villages. The passengers gazed through the windows at the ravaged fields and burned hamlets. Prussian soldiers, in their black hamlets with brass spikes, were smoking their pipes on horseback or sitting on chairs in front of the houses which were still left standing. Others were working or talking just as if they were members of the families. As you passed through the different towns, you saw entire regiments drilling in the squares, and, in spite of the rumble of the carriage-wheels, you could, every moment, hear the hoarse words of command.

M. Dubuis, who during the entire siege had served as one of the National Guard in Paris, was going to join his wife and daughter, whom he had prudently sent away to Switzerland before the invasion.

Famine and hardship had not diminished the big paunch so characteristic of the rich, peace-loving merchant. He had gone through the terrible events of the past year with sorrowful resignation and bitter complaints at the savagery of men. Now that he was journeying to the frontier at the close of the war, he saw the Prussians for the first time, although he had done duty at the ramparts, and staunchly mounted guard on cold nights.

He stared with mingled fear and anger at those bearded armed men installed all over French soil as if in their own homes, and he felt in his soul a kind of fever of impotent patriotism even while he yielded to that other instinct of discretion and self-preservation which never leaves us. In the same compartment, two Englishmen, who had come to the country as sight-seers, were gazing around with looks of stolid curiosity. They were both stout also, and kept chattering in their own language, sometimes referring to their guidebook, and reading in loud tones the names of the places indicated.

Suddenly, the train stopped at a little village station, and a Prussian officer jumped up with a great clatter of his saber on the double footboard of the railway-carriage. He was tall, wore a tight-fitting uniform, and his face had a very shaggy aspect. His red hair seemed to be on fire and his long mustache and beard, of a paler color, was stuck out on both sides of his face, which it seemed to cut in two.

The Englishmen at once began staring at him with smiles of newly-awakened interest, while M. Dubuis made a show of reading a newspaper. He sat crouched in a corner, like a thief in the presence of a gendarme.

The train started again. The Englishmen went on chatting, and looking out for the exact scene of different battles; and, all of a sudden, as one of them stretched out his arm toward the horizon to indicate a village, the Prussian officer remarked in French, extending his long legs and lolling backward:

"We killed a dozen Frenchmen in that village, and took more than a hundred prisoners."

The Englishmen, quite interested, immediately asked:

"Ha! and what is the name of this village?"

The Prussian replied:

"Pharsbourg."

He added: "We caught these French blackguards by the ears."

And he glanced toward M. Dubuis, laughing into his mustache in an insulting fashion.

The train rolled on, always passing through hamlets occupied by the victorious army. German soldiers could be seen along the roads, on the edges of fields, standing in front of gates, or chatting outside *cafés*. They covered the soil like African locusts.

The officer said, with a wave of his hand:

"If I were in command, I'd take Paris, burn everything, and kill everybody. No more France!"

The Englishmen, through politeness, replied simply:

"Ah! yes."

He went on:

"In twenty years, all Europe, all of it, will belong to us. Prussia is more than a match for all of them."

The Englishmen, getting uneasy, said nothing in answer to this. Their faces, which had become impassive, seemed made of wax behind their long whiskers. Then the Prussian officer began to laugh. And then, lolling back, he began to sneer. He sneered at the downfall of France, insulted the prostrate enemy; he sneered at Austria which had been recently conquered; he sneered at the furious but fruitless defense of the departments; he sneered at the Garde Mobile and at the useless artillery. He announced that Bismarck was going to build a city of iron with the captured cannons. And suddenly he pushed his boots against the thigh of M. Dubuis, who turned his eyes away, reddening to the roots of his hair.

The Englishmen seemed to have assumed an air of complete indifference, as if they had found themselves all at once shut up in their own island, far from the din of the world.

The officer took out his pipe, and looking fixedly at the Frenchman, said:

"You haven't got any tobacco—have you?"

M. Dubuis replied:

"No, Monsieur."

The German said:

"You might go and buy some for me when the train stops next."

And he began laughing afresh, as he added:

"I'll let you have the price of a drink."

The train whistled and slackened its pace. They had reached a station which had been burned down and here there was a regular stop.

The German opened the carriage door, and, catching M. Dubuis by the arm, said:

"Go, and do what I told you—quick, quick!"

A Prussian detachment occupied the station. Other soldiers were looking on from behind wooden gratings. The engine was already getting up steam in order to start off again. Then M. Dubuis hurriedly jumped on the platform, and, in spite of the warnings of the station-master, dashed into the adjoining compartment.

    *   *   *   *   *   *

He was alone! He tore open his waistcoat, so rapidly did his heart beat, and, panting for breath, he wiped the perspiration off his forehead.

The train drew up at another station. And suddenly the officer appeared at the carriage door, and jumped in, followed close behind by the two Englishmen, who were impelled by curiosity. The German sat facing the Frenchman, and, laughing still, said:

"You did not want to do what I asked you."

M. Dubuis replied: "No, Monsieur."

The train had just left the station, when the officer said:

"I'll cut off your mustache to fill my pipe with." And he put out his hand toward the Frenchman's face.

The Englishmen kept staring in the same impassive fashion with fixed glances. Already the German had caught hold of the mustache and was tugging at it, when M. Dubuis, with a back-stroke of his hand threw back the officer's arm, and seizing him by the collar, flung him down on the seat. Then, excited to a pitch of fury, with his temples swollen and his eyes glaring he kept throttling the officer with one hand while with the other clenched, he began to strike him violent blows in the face. The Prussian struggled, tried to draw his saber, and to get a grip, while lying back, of his adversary. But M. Dubuis crushed him with the enormous weight of his stomach, and kept hitting him without taking breath or knowing where his blows fell. Blood flowed down the face of the German, who, choking and with a rattling in his throat, spat forth his broken teeth, and vainly strove to shake off this infuriated man who was killing him.

The Englishmen had got on their feet and came closer to see better. They remained standing, full of mirth and curiosity, ready to bet for or against each of the combatants.

And suddenly M. Dubuis, exhausted by his violent efforts, went and resumed his seat without uttering a word.

The Prussian did not attack him, for the savage assault had scared and terrified the officer. When he was able to breathe freely, he said:

"Unless you give me satisfaction with pistols, I will kill you."

M. Dubuis replied:

"Whenever you like. I'm quite ready."

The German said:

"Here is the town of Strasbourg. I'll get two officers to be my seconds, and there will be time before the train leaves the station."

M. Dubuis, who was puffing as much as the engine, said to the Englishmen:

"Will you be my seconds?" They both answered together:

"Oh! yes."

And the train stopped.

In a minute, the Prussian had found two comrades who carried pistols, and they made their way toward the ramparts.

The Englishmen were continually looking at their watches, shuffling their feet, and hurrying on with the preparations, uneasy lest they should be too late for the train.

M. Dubuis had never fired a pistol in his life. They made him stand twenty paces away from his enemy. He was asked:

"Are you ready?"

While he was answering "Yes, Monsieur," he noticed that one of the Englishmen had opened his umbrella in order to keep off the rays of the sun.

A voice gave the word of command.

"Fire!"

M. Dubuis fired at random without minding what he was doing, and he was amazed to see the Prussian staggering in front of him, lifting up his arms, and immediately afterward, falling straight on his face. He had killed the officer.

One of the Englishmen ejaculated "Ah!" quivering with delight, satisfied curiosity, and joyous impatience. The other, who still kept his watch in his hand, hurried him in double-quick time toward the station, his fellow-countryman counting their steps, with his arms pressed close to his sides: "One! two! one! two!"

And all three marching abreast they rapidly made their way to the station like three grotesque figures in a comic newspaper.

The train was on the point of starting. They sprang into their carriage.

Then the Englishmen, taking off their traveling-caps, waved them three times over their heads, exclaiming:

"Hip! hip! hip! hurrah!"

Then gravely, one after the other, they stretched out their right hands to M. Dubuis, and then went back and sat in their own corner.

The Umbrella

MME. OREILLE was a very economical woman; she thoroughly knew the value of a half-penny, and possessed a whole storehouse of strict principles with regard to the multiplication of money, so that her cook found the greatest difficulty in making what the servants call their "market-penny," while her husband was hardly allowed any pocket-money at all. They were, however, very comfortably off, and had no children. It really pained Mme. Oreille to see any money spent; it was like tearing at her heartstrings when she had to take any of those nice crownpieces out of her pocket; and whenever she had to spend anything, no matter how necessary it was, she slept badly the next night.

Oreille was continually saying to his wife:

"You really might be more liberal, as we have no children and never spend our income."

"You don't know what may happen," she used to reply. "It is better to have too much than too little."

She was a little woman of about forty, very active. rather hasty, wrinkled, very neat and tidy, and with a very short temper. Her husband very often used to complain of all the privations she made him endure; some of them were particularly painful to him, as they touched his vanity.

He was one of the upper clerks in the War Office, and only stayed there in obedience to his wife's wish, so as to increase their income, which they did not nearly spend.

For two years he had always come to the office with the same old patched umbrella, to the great amusement of his fellow-clerks. At last he got tired of their jokes, and insisted upon his wife buying him a new one. She bought one for eight francs and a-half, one of those cheap things which large houses sell as an advertisement. When the others in the office saw the article, which was being sold in Paris by the thousand, they began their jokes again, and Oreille had a dreadful time of it with them. They even made a song about it, which he heard from morning till night all over the immense building.

Oreille was very angry, and peremptorily told his wife to get him a new one, a good silk one, for twenty francs, and to bring him the bill, so that he might see that it was all right.

She bought him one for eighteen francs, and said, getting red with anger as she gave it to her husband:

"This will last you for five years at least."

Oreille felt quite triumphant, and obtained a small ovation at the office with his new acquisition. When he went home in the evening, his wife said to him, looking at the umbrella uneasily:

"You should not leave it fastened up with the elastic; it will very likely cut the silk. You must take care of it, for I shall not buy you a new one in a hurry."

She took it, unfastened it, and then remained dumfounded with astonishment and rage. In the middle of the silk there was a hole as big as a sixpenny-piece, as if made with the end of a cigar.

"What is that?" she screamed.

Her husband replied quietly, without looking at it:

"What is it? What do you mean?"

She was choking with rage and could hardly get out a word.

"You—you—have burned—your umbrella! Why—you must be—mad! Do you wish to ruin us outright?"

He turned round hastily, as if frightened.

"What are you talking about?"

"I say that you have burned your umbrella. Just look here—"

And rushing at him, as if she were going to beat him, she violently thrust the little circular burned hole under his nose.

He was so utterly struck dumb at the sight of it that he could only stammer out:

"What—what is it? How should I know? I have done nothing, I will swear. I don't know what is the matter with the umbrella."

"You have been playing tricks with it at the office; you have been playing the fool and opening it, to show it off!" she screamed.

"I only opened it once, to let them see what a nice one it was, that is all, I declare."

But she shook with rage, and got up one of those conjugal scenes which make a peaceable man dread the domestic hearth more than a battlefield where bullets are raining.

She mended it with a piece of silk cut out of the old umbrella, which was of a different color, and the next day Oreille went off very humbly with the mended article in his hand. He put it into a cupboard, and thought no more of it than of some unpleasant recollection.

But he had scarcely got home that evening when his wife took the umbrella from him, opened it, and nearly had a fit when she saw what had befallen it, for the disaster was now irreparable. It was covered with small holes which, evidently, proceeded from burns, just as if some one had emptied the ashes from a lighted pipe on to it. It was done for utterly, irreparably.

She looked at it without a word, in too great a passion to be able to say anything. He also, when he saw the damage, remained almost dumb, in a state of frightened consternation.

They looked at each other; then he looked on to the floor. The next moment she threw the useless article at his head, screaming out in a transport of the most violent rage, for she had now recovered her voice:

"Oh! you brute! you brute! You did it on purpose, but I will pay you out for it. You shall not have another."

And then the scene began again. After the storm had raged for an hour, he, at last, was enabled to explain himself. He declared that he could not understand it at all, and that it could only proceed from malice or from vengeance.

A ring at the bell saved him; it was a friend whom they were expecting to dinner.

Mme. Oreille submitted the case to him. As for buying a new umbrella, that was out of the question; her husband should not have another. The friend very sensibly said that in that case his clothes would be spoiled, and they were certainly worth more than the umbrella. But the little woman, who was still in a rage, replied:

"Very well, then, when it rains he may have the kitchen umbrella, for I will not give him a new silk one."

Oreille utterly rebelled at such an idea.

"All right," he said; "then I shall resign my post. I am not going to the office with the kitchen umbrella."

The friend interposed:

"Have this one recovered; it will not cost much."

But Mme. Oreille, being in the temper that she was, said:

"It will cost at least eight francs to recover it. Eight and eighteen are twenty-six. Just fancy, twenty-six francs for an umbrella! It is utter madness!"

The friend, who was only a poor man of the middle classes, had an inspiration:

"Make your fire insurance pay for it. The companies pay for all articles that are burned, as long as the damage has been done in your own house."

On hearing this advice the little woman calmed down immediately, and then, after a moment's reflection, she said to her husband:

"To-morrow, before going to your office, you will go to the Maternelle Insurance Company, show them the state your umbrella is in, and make them pay for the damage."

M. Oreille fairly jumped, he was so startled at the proposal.

"I would not do it for my life! It is eighteen francs lost, that is all. It will not ruin us."

The next morning he took a walking-stick when he went out, for luckily, it was a fine day.

Left at home alone, Mme. Oreille could not get over the loss of her eighteen francs by any means. She had put the umbrella on the dining-room table, and she looked at it without being able to come to any determination.

Every moment she thought of the insurance company, but she did not dare to encounter the quizzical looks of the gentlemen who might receive her, for she was very timid before people, and grew red at a mere nothing, feeling embarrassed when she had to speak to strangers.

But regret at the loss of the eighteen francs pained her as if she had been wounded. She tried not to think of it any more, and yet every moment the recollection of the loss struck her painfully. What was she to do, however? Time went on, and she could not decide; but suddenly, like all cowards, she made up her mind.

"I will go, and we will see what will happen."

But first of all she was obliged to prepare the umbrella so that the disaster might be complete, and the reason of it quite evident. She took a match from the mantelpiece, and between the ribs she burned a hole as big as the palm of her hand. Then she rolled it up carefully, fastened it with the elastic band, put on her bonnet and shawl, and went quickly toward the Rue de Rivoli, where the insurance office was.

But the nearer she got the slower she walked. What was she going to say, and what reply would she get?

She looked at the numbers of the houses; there were still twenty-eight. That was all right, she had time to consider, and she walked slower and slower. Suddenly she saw a door on which was a large brass plate with "La Maternelle Insurance Office" engraved on it. Already! She waited for a moment, for she felt nervous and almost ashamed; then she went past, came back, went past again, and came back again.

At last she said to herself:

"I must go in, however, so I may as well do it now as later."

She could not help noticing, however, how her heart beat as she entered. She went into an enormous room with grated wicket openings all round, and a man behind each of them, and as a gentleman, carrying a number of papers, passed her, she stopped him and said, timidly:

"I beg your pardon, Monsieur, but can you tell me where I must apply for payment for anything that has been accidentally burned?"

He replied in a sonorous voice:

"The first door on the left; that is the department you want."

This frightened her still more, and she felt inclined to run away, to make no claim, to sacrifice her eighteen francs. But the idea of that sum revived her courage, and she went upstairs, out of breath, stopping at almost every other step.

She knocked at a door which she saw on the first landing, and a clear voice said, in answer:

"Come in!"

She obeyed mechanically, and found herself in a large room where three solemn gentlemen, each with a decoration in his buttonhole, were standing talking.

One of them asked her: "What do you want, Madame?"

She could hardly get out her words, but stammered: "I have come—I have come on account of an accident, something—"

He very politely pointed out a seat to her.

"If you will kindly sit down I will attend to you in a moment."

And, returning to the other two, he went on with the conversation.

"The company, gentlemen, does not consider that it is under any obligation to you for more than four hundred thousand francs, and we can pay no attention to your claim to the further sum of a hundred thousand, which you wish to make us pay. Besides that, the surveyor's valuation—"

One of the others interrupted him:

"That is quite enough, Monsieur; the law courts will decide between us, and we have nothing further to do than to take our leave." And they went out after mutual ceremonious bows.

Oh! if she could only have gone away with them, how gladly she would have done it; she would have run away and given up everything. But it was too late, for the gentleman came back, and said, bowing:

"What can I do for you, Madame?"

She could scarcely speak, but at last she managed to say:

"I have come—for this."

The manager looked at the object which she held out to him in mute astonishment. With trembling fingers she tried to undo the elastic, and succeeded, after several attempts, and hastily opened the damaged remains of the umbrella.

"It looks to me to be in a very bad state of health," he said, compassionately.

"It cost me twenty francs," she said, with some hesitation.

He seemed astonished. "Really! As much as that?"

"Yes, it was a capital article, and I wanted you to see the state it is in."

"Very well, I see; very well. But I really do not understand what it can have to do with me."

She began to feel uncomfortable; perhaps this company did not pay for such small articles, and she said:

"But—it is burned."

He could not deny it.

"I see that very well," he replied.

She remained open-mouthed, not knowing what to say next; then suddenly forgetting that she had left out the main thing, she said hastily:

"I am Mme. Oreille; we are assured in La Maternelle, and I have come to claim the value of this damage. I only wanted you to have it recovered," she added quickly, fearing a positive refusal.

The manager was rather embarrassed, and said:

"But, really, Madame, we do not sell umbrellas; we cannot undertake such kinds of repairs."

The little woman felt her courage reviving; she was not going to give up without a struggle; she was not even afraid now, so she said:

"I only want you to pay me the cost of repairing it; I can quite well get it done myself."

The gentleman seemed rather confused.

"Really, Madame, it is such a very small matter! We are never asked to give compensation for such trivial losses. You must allow that we cannot make good pocket-handkerchiefs, gloves, brooms, slippers, all the small articles which are every day exposed to the chances of being burned."

She got red, and felt inclined to fly into a rage.

"But, Monsieur, last December one of our chimneys caught fire, and caused at least five hundred francs' damage. M. Oreille made no claim on the company, and so it is only just that it should pay for my umbrella now."

The manager, guessing that she was telling a lie, said, with a smile:

"You must acknowledge, Madame, that it is very surprising that M. Oreille should have asked no compensation for damages amounting to five hundred francs, and should now claim five or six francs for mending an umbrella."

She was not the least put out, and replied:

"I beg your pardon, Monsieur, the five hundred francs affected M. Oreille's pocket, whereas this damage, amounting to eighteen francs, concerns Mme.

Oreille's pocket only, which is a totally different matter."

As he saw that he had no chance of getting rid of her, and that he would only be wasting his time, he said, resignedly:

"Will you kindly tell me how the damage was done?"

She felt that she had won the victory, and said:

"This is how it happened, Monsieur: In our hall there is a bronze stick- and umbrella-stand, and the other day, when I came in, I put my umbrella into it. I must tell you that just above there is a shelf for the candlesticks and matches. I put out my hand, took three or four matches, and struck one, but it missed fire, so I struck other, which ignited, but went out immediately, and a third did the same."

The manager interrupted her, to make a joke.

"I suppose they were, Government matches, then?"

She did not understand him, and went on:

"Very likely. At any rate, the fourth caught fire, and I lit my candle, and went into my room to go to bed; but in a quarter-of-an-hour I fancied that I smelled something burning, and I have always been terribly afraid of fire. If ever we have an accident it will not be my fault, I assure you. I am terribly nervous since our chimney was on fire, as I told you; so I got up, and hunted about everywhere, sniffing like a dog after game, and at last I noticed that my umbrella was burning. Most likely a match had fallen between the folds and burned it. You can see how it has damaged it."

The manager had taken his cue, and asked her:

"What do you estimate the damage at?"

She did not know what to say, as she was not certain what amount to put on it, but at last she replied:

"Perhaps you had better get it done yourself. I will leave it to you."

He, however, naturally refused.

"No, Madame, I cannot do that. Tell me the amount of your claim, that is all I want to know."

"Well!—I think that— Look here, Monsieur, I do not want to make any money out of you, so I will tell you what we will do. I will take my umbrella to the maker, who will recover it in good, durable silk, and I will bring the bill to you. Will that suit you, Monsieur?"

"Perfectly, Madame; we will settle it on that basis. Here is a note for the cashier, who will repay you whatever it costs you."

He gave Mme. Oreille a slip of paper. She took it, got up, and went out, thanking him, for she was in a hurry to escape lest he should change his mind.

She went briskly through the streets, looking out for a really good umbrella-maker, and when she found a shop which appeared to be a first-class one, she went in, and said, confidently:

"I want this umbrella recovered in silk, good silk. Use the very best and strongest you have; I don't mind what it costs."

The Question of Latin

THIS question of Latin, with which we were so much bothered some time since, recalls to my mind a story—a story of my youth.

I was finishing my studies with a teacher, in a big central town, at the Institution Robineau, celebrated through the entire province owing to the special attention paid there to Latin studies.

For the past ten years, the Institution Robineau beat at every competitive examination the Imperial "lycée" of the town, and all the colleges of the Subprefecture; and these constant successes were due, they said, to an usher, a simple usher, M. Piquedent, or rather Père Piquedent.

He was one of those middle-aged men, quite gray, whose real age it is impossible to know, and whose history we can guess at first glance. Having entered as an usher at twenty into the first institution that presented itself so that he could proceed to take out his degree of Doctor of Laws, he found himself so much enmeshed in this sinister life that he remained as usher all his life. But his love for Latin did not leave him, but harassed him like an unhealthy passion. He continued to read the poets, the prose-writers, the historians, to interpret them, to study their meaning, to comment on them with a perseverance bordering on madness.

One day, the idea came into his head to force all the students of his class to answer him in Latin only; and he persisted in this resolution until at last they were capable of sustaining an entire conversation with him just as they would in their mother-tongue. He listened to them, as a leader of an orches-tra listens to his musicians rehearsing, and, striking his desk every moment with his ruler, he exclaimed:

"Monsieur Lefrère, Monsieur Lefrère, you are committing a solecism! You are not recalling the rule to mind.

"Monsieur Plantel, your turn of phrase is altogether French and in no way Latin. You must understand the genius of a language. Look here, listen to me."

Now it came to pass that the pupils of the Institution Robineau carried off, at the end of the year, all the prizes for composition, translation, and Latin conversation.

Next year, the principal, a little man, as cunning as an ape, and with the same grinning and grotesque physique, got printed on his programmes, on his advertisements, and painted on the door of his institution:

"Latin Studies a Specialty. Five first prizes carried off in the five classes of the lycée.

"Two prizes of honor at the general Competitive Examinations with all the lycées and colleges of France."

For ten years the Institution Robineau triumphed in the same fashion. Now, my father, allured by these successes, sent my as a day-pupil to Robineau's—or, as we called it, Robinetto or Robinettino—and made me take special private lessons from Père Piquedent at the rate of five francs per hour, out of which the usher got two francs and the principal three francs. I was at the time in my eighteenth year, and was in the philosophy class.

These private lessons were given in a little room looking out on the street.

It so happened that Père Piquedent, instead of talking Latin to me, as he did when teaching publicly in the Institution, kept telling about his troubles in French. Without relations, without friends, the poor man conceived an attachment for me, and poured out into my heart his own misery.

He had never for the last ten or fifteen years chatted confidentially with anyone.

"I am like an oak in a desert," he said—"*sicut quercus in solitudine*."

The other ushers disgusted him. He knew nobody in the town since he had no liberty for the purpose of making acquaintances.

"Not even the nights, my friend, and that is the hardest thing on me. The dream of my life is to have a room of my own with furniture, my own books, little things that belonged to myself and which others could not touch. And I have nothing of my own, nothing except my shirt and my frock-coat, nothing, not even my mattress and my pillow! I have not four walls to shut myself up in, except when I come to give a lesson in this room. Do you see what this means—a man forced to spend his life without ever having the right, without ever finding the time to shut himself up all alone, no matter where, to think, to reflect, to work, to dream? Ah! my dear boy, a key, the key of a door which one can open—this is happiness, mark you, the only happiness!

"Here, all day long, the study with all those dirty brats jumping about in it, and during the night the dormitory with the same dirty brats snoring. And I have to sleep in the public bed at the end of two rows of beds occupied by these brats whom I must look after. I can never be alone, never! If I go out, I find the street full of people, and, when I am tired of walking, I go into some *café* crowded with smokers and billiard players. I tell you that it is a regular prison."

I asked him:

"Why did you not take up some other line, Monsieur Piquedent?"

He exclaimed:

"What, my little friend? I am not a bootmaker or a joiner or a hatter or a baker or a hairdresser. I only know Latin, and I have not the diploma which would enable me to sell my knowledge at a high price. If I were a doctor, I would sell for a hundred francs, what I now sell for a hundred sous; and I would supply it probably of an inferior quality, for my academic rank would be enough to sustain my reputation."

Sometimes, he would say to me:

"I have no rest in life except in the hours spent with you. Don't be afraid! you'll lose nothing by that. I'll make it up to you in the study by teaching you to speak twice as much Latin as the others."

One day, I grew bolder and offered him a cigarette. He stared at me with astonishment at first, then he gave a glance toward the door:

"If anyone were to come in, my dear boy!"

"Well, let us smoke at the window," said I.

And we went and leaned with our elbows on the window-sill facing the street, keeping our hands over the little rolls of tobacco wrapped up in tissue-paper so that they concealed them from view like a shell. Just opposite to us was a laundry. Four women in white bodices were passing over the linen spread out before them the heavy and hot irons, letting a damp fume escape from them.

Suddenly, another, a fifth carrying on her arm a large basket which made her back stoop, came out to bring the customers their shirts and chemises, their handkerchiefs and their sheets. She stopped on the threshold as if she were already fatigued; then, she raised her eyes, smiled when she saw us smoking, flung at us, with her left hand, which was free, the sly kiss characteristic of a free-and-easy workingwoman; and she went away at a slow pace dragging her shoes after her.

She was a damsel of about twenty, small, rather thin, pale, rather pretty, with the manners of a street-wench, and eyes laughing under her-illcombed fair hair.

Père Piquedent, affected, began murmuring:

"What an occupation for a woman. Really a trade only fit for a horse."

And he spoke with emotion about the misery of the people. He had a heart which swelled with lofty democratic sentiment, and he referred to the fatiguing pursuits of the working class with phrases borrowed from Jean-Jacques Rousseau and with sobs in his throat.

Next day, as we wer eresting our elbows at the same wind,w, the same workwoman perceived us, and cried out to us:

"Good day, my scholars!" in a comical sort of tone, while she made a contemptuous gesture with her hands.

I flung her a cigarette, which she immediately began to smoke. And the four

other ironers rushed out to the door with outstretched hands to get cigarettes also.

And, each day, a friendly relationship was being formed between the working-women of the pavement and the idlers of the boarding-school.

Père Piquedent was really a comic sight to look at. He trembled at being noticed, for he might have lost his place; and he made timid and ridiculous gestures, quite a theatrical display of amorousness, to which the women responded with a regular fusillade of kisses.

A perfidious idea sprang up in my head. One day, on entering our room, I said to the old usher in a low tone:

"You would not believe it, Monsieur Piquedent, I met the little washerwoman! You know the one—the woman who had the basket—and I spoke to her!"

He asked, rather excited by the tone I had taken:

"What did she say to you?"

"She said to me—goodness gracious! —she said she thought you were very nice. The fact of the matter is, I believe—that she is a little in love with you." I saw that he was growing pale. He exclaimed:

"She is laughing at me, of course. These things don't happen at my age."

I said gravely:

"How is that? You are very nice."

As I felt that my trick had produced its effect on him, I did not press the matter.

But every day I pretended that I had met the little laundress and that I had spoken to her about him, so that in the end he believed me, and sent her ardent and earnest kisses.

Now, it happened that, one morning, on my way to the boarding-school, I really came across her. I accosted her without hesitation, as if I had known her for the last ten years.

"Good day, Mademoiselle. Are you quite well?"

"Very well, Monsieur, thank you."

"Will you have a cigarette?"

"Oh! not in the street."

"You can smoke it at home."

"In that case, I will."

"Let me tell you, Mademoiselle, there's something you don't know."

"What is that, Monsieur?"

"The old gentleman—my old professor, I mean—"

"Père Piquedent."

"Yes, Père Piquedent. So you know his name?"

"Faith, I do! What of that?"

"Well, he is in love with you!"

She burst out laughing like a crazy woman and exclaimed:

"This is only humbug!"

"Oh! no, 'tis no humbug! He keeps talking of you all the time he is giving lessons. I bet that he'll marry you!"

She ceased laughing. The idea of marriage makes every girl serious. Then, she repeated, with an incredulous air:

"This is humbug!"

"I swear to you 'tis true."

She picked up her basket which she had laid down at her feet.

"Well, we'll see," she said. And she went away.

Presently, when I had reached the boarding-school, I took Père Piquedent aside, and said:

"You must write to her: she is mad about you."

And he wrote a long letter of a soft and affectionate character full of phrases and circumlocutions, metaphors and similes, philosophy and academic gallantry; and I took on myself the responsibility of delivering it to the young woman.

She read it with gravity, with emotion; then, she murmured:

"How well he writes! It is easy to see he has got education! Does he really mean to marry me?"

I replied intrepidly: "Faith, he has lost his head about you!"

"Then he must invite me to dinner on Sunday at the Île des Fleurs."

I promised that she would be invited.

Père Piquedent was much touched by everything I told him about her.

I added:

"She loves you, Monsieur Piquedent, and I believe her to be a decent girl. It is not right to seduce her and then abandon her."

He replied in a firm tone:

"I hope I, too, am a decent man, my friend."

I confess I had at the time no plan. I was playing a practical joke, a schoolboy's practical joke, nothing more. I had been aware of the simplicity of the old usher, his innocence, and his weakness. I amused myself without asking myself how it would turn out. I was eighteen, and had been for a long time looked upon at the lycée as a knowing practical joker.

So, it was agreed that Père Piquedent and I should set out in a hackney-coach for the ferry of Queue de Vache, that we should there pick up Angèle, and

that I should get them to come into my
boat, for at this time I was fond of
boating. I would then bring them to the
Île des Fleurs, where the three of us
would dine. I had made it my business
to be present, in order the better to enjoy my triumph, and the usher, consenting to my arrangement, proved clearly,
in fact, that he had lost his head by thus
risking his post.

When we arrived at the ferry where
my boat had been moored since morning, I saw in the grass, or rather above
the tall weeds of the bank, an enormous
red parasol, resembling a monstrous wild
poppy. Under the parasol waited the little laundress in her Sunday clothes. I
was surprised. She was really nice-
looking, though pale, and graceful,
though with a suburban gracefulness.

Père Piquedent raised his hat and
bowed. She put out her hand toward
him and they stared at one another
without uttering a word. Then they
stepped into my boat and I took the
oars.

They were seated side by side on the
seat near the stern. The usher was
the first to speak:

"This is nice weather for a row in a
boat."

She murmured: "Oh! yes."

She drew her hand through the current, skimming the water with her
fingers, which raised up a thin transparent little stream like a sheet of glass.
It made a light sound, a gentle ripple,
as the boat moved along.

When they were in the restaurant,
she took it on herself to speak and
order dinner—fried fish, a chicken, and
salad; then, she led us on toward the
isle which she knew perfectly.

After this, she was gay, romping,
and even rather mocking.

Up to the dessert, no question of
love arose. I had treated them to
champagne and Père Piquedent was
tipsy. Herself slightly elevated, she
called out to him:

"Monsieur Piquenez."

He said all of a sudden:

"Mademoiselle, Monsieur Raoul has
communicated my sentiments to you."

She became as serious as a judge:

"Yes, Monsieur."

"Are you going to give any answer?"

"We never reply to these questions!"

He panted with emotion, and went
on:

"After all, a day will come when I
may make you like me."

She smiled: "You big fool! You
are very nice."

"In short, Mademoiselle, do you
think that, later on, we might—"

She hesitated a second; then in a
trembling voice she said:

"Is it in order to marry me you say
that? For never otherwise, you know."

"Yes, Mademoiselle!"

"Well, that's all right, Monsieur
Piquedent!"

It is thus that these two silly creatures promised marriage to each other
through the wiles of a reckless schoolboy. But I did not believe that it was
serious, nor indeed did they themselves,
perhaps.

On her part there was a certain feeling of hesitation:

"You know, I have nothing—not four
sous."

He stammered, for he was as drunk
as Silenus:

"I have saved five thousand francs."

She exclaimed triumphantly:

"Then we can set up in business?"

He became restless: "In what business?"

"What do I know about that? We shall see. With five thousand francs, we could do many things. You don't want me to go and live in your boarding school, do you?"

He had not looked forward so far as this, and he stammered in great perplexity:

"What business could we set up in? It is not convenient, for all I know is Latin!"

She reflected in her turn, passing in review all the professions which she had longed for.

"You could not be a doctor?"

"No, I have not the diploma."

"Or a chemist?"

"No more than the other."

She uttered a cry, a cry of joy. She had discovered it.

"Then we'll buy a grocer's shop! Oh! what luck! we'll buy a grocer's shop! Not on a big scale, all the some; with five thousand francs one cannot go far."

He was shocked at the suggestion:

"No, I can't be a grocer. I am— I am—too well known. I only know Latin—that's all I know."

But she poured a glass of champagne down his throat. He drank it and was silent.

We got back into the boat. The night was dark, very dark. I saw clearly, however, that he had caught her by the waist, and that they were hugging each other again and again.

It was a frightful catastrophe. Our escapade was discovered with the result that Père Piquedent was dismissed. And my father, in a fit of anger, sent me to finish my course of philosophy at Ribaudet's School.

Six months later I passed for my degree of Bachelor of Arts. Then I went to study law in Paris, and I did not return to my native town till ten years after.

At the corner of the Rue de Serpent, a shop caught my eye. Over the door were the words: "Colonial products— Piquedent"; then underneath so as to enlighten the most ignorant: "Grocery."

I exclaimed: *"Quantum mutatus ab illo!"*

He raised his head, left his female customer, and rushed toward me with outstretched hands.

"Ah! my young friend, my young friend, here you are! What luck! What luck!"

A beautiful woman, very plump, abruptly left the counter and flung herself on my breast. I had some difficulty in recognizing her, so fat had she grown.

I asked: "So then you're going on well?"

Piquedent had gone back to weigh the groceries:

"Oh! very well, very well, very well. I have made three thousand francs clear this year!"

"And what about the Latin, Monsieur Piquedent?"

"Oh! goodness gracious! the Latin— the Latin—the Latin. Well, you see, it does not keep the pot boiling!"

Mother and Son!!!

We were chatting in the smoking-room after a dinner at which only men were present. We talked about unexpected legacies, strange inheritances. Then M. le Brument, who was sometimes called "the illustrious master" and at other times the "illustrious advocate," came and stood with his back to the fire.

"I have," he said, "just now to search for an heir who disappeared under peculiarly terrible circumstances. It is one of those simple and ferocious dramas of ordinary life, a thing which possibly happens every day, and which is nevertheless one of the most dreadful things I know. Here are the facts:

"Nearly six months ago I got a message to come to the side of a dying woman. She said to me:

"'Monsieur, I want to intrust to you the most delicate, the most difficult, and the most wearisome mission that can be conceived. Be good enough to take cognizance of my will, which is there on the table. A sum of five thousand francs is left to you as a fee if you do not succeed and of a hundred thousand francs if you do succeed. I want to have my son found after my death.'

"She asked me to assist her to sit up in the bed, in order that she might be able to speak with greater ease, for her voice, broken and gasping, was gurgling in her throat.

"I saw that I was in the house of a very rich person. The luxurious apartment with a certain simplicity in its luxury, was upholstered with materials solid as the walls, and their soft surfaces imparted a caressing sensation, so that every word uttered seemed to penetrate their silent depths and to disappear and to die there.

"The dying woman went on:

"'You are the first to hear my horrible story. I will try to have strength enough to go on to the end of it. You must know everything so that you, whom I know to be a kind-hearted man as well as a man of the world should have a sincere desire to aid me with all your power.

"'Listen to me.

"'Before my marriage, I loved a young man, whose suit was rejected by my family because he was not rich enough. Not long afterward, I married a man of great wealth. I married him through ignorance, through obedience, through indifference, as young girls do marry.

"'I had a child, a boy. My husband died in the course of a few years.

"'He whom I had loved had got married, in his turn. When he saw that I was a widow, he was crushed by horrible grief at knowing that he was not free. He came to see me; he wept and sobbed so bitterly before my eyes that it was enough to break my heart. He at first came to see me as a friend. Perhaps I ought not to have seen him. What could I do? I was alone, so sad, so solitary, so hopeless! And I loved him still. What sufferings we women have sometimes to endure!

"'I had only him in the world, my parents also being dead. He came frequently; he spent whole evenings with me. I should not have let him come so often, seeing that he was married. But I had not enough will-power to prevent him from coming.

" 'How am I to tell you what next happened? He became my lover. How did this come about? Can I explain it? Can anyone explain such things? Do you think it could be otherwise when two human beings are drawn toward each other by the irresistible force of a passion by which each of them is possessed? Do you believe, Monsieur, that it is always in our power to resist, that we can keep up the struggle forever, and refuse to yield to the prayers, the supplications, the tears, the frenzied words, the appeals on bended knees, the transports of passion, with which we are pursued by the man we adore, whom we want to gratify in his slightest wishes, whom we desire to crowd with every possible happiness, and whom, if we are to be guided by a worldly code of honor, we must drive to despair. What strength would it not require? What a renunciation of happiness? what self-denial? and even what virtuous selfishness?

" 'In short, Monsieur, I was his mistress; and I was happy. For twelve years, I was happy. I became—and this was my greatest weakness and my greatest piece of cowardice—I became his wife's friend.

" 'We brought up my son together; we made a man of him, a thorough man, intelligent, full of sense and resolution, of large and generous ideas. The boy reached the age of seventeen.

" 'He, the young man, was fond of my—my lover, almost as fond of him as I was myself, for he had been equally cherished and cared for by both of us. He used to call him his "dear friend" and respected him immensely, having never received from him anything but wise counsels and a good example of rectitude, honor, and probity. He looked upon him as an old, loyal, and devoted comrade of his mother, as a sort of moral father, tutor, protector— how am I to describe it?

" 'Perhaps the reason why he never asked any questions was that he had been accustomed from his earliest years to see this man in the house, by his side, and by my side, always concerned about us both.

" 'One evening the three of us were to dine together (these were my principal festive occasions), and I waited for the two of them, asking myself which of them would be the first to arrive. The door opened; it was my old friend. I went toward him with outstretched arms; and he drew his lips toward mine in a long, delicious kiss.

" 'All of a sudden, a sound, a rustling which was barely audible, that mysterious sensation which indicated the presence of another person, made us start and turn round with a quick movement. Jean, my son, stood there, livid, staring at us.

"There was a moment of atrocious confusion. I drew back holding out my hands toward my son as if in supplication; but I could see him no longer. He had gone.

" 'We remained facing each other— my lover and I—crushed, unable to utter a word. I sank down on an armchair, and I felt a desire, a vague, powerful desire to fly, to go out into the night and to disappear forever. Then, convulsive sobs rose up in my throat, and I wept, shaken with spasms, with my heart torn asunder, all my nerves writhing with the horrible sensation of an irremediable misfortune, 'und with that dreadful sense of shame which, in such moments as this, falls on a mother's heart.

" 'He looked at me in a scared fashion, not venturing to approach me or to speak to me or to touch me, for fear of the boy's return. At last he said:

"I am going to follow him— to talk to him—to explain matters to him. In short, I must see him and let him know—"

" 'And he hurried away.

" 'I waited—I waited in a distracted frame of mind, trembling at the least sound, convulsed with terror, and filled with some unutterably strange and intolerable emotion by every slight crackling of the fire in the grate.

" 'I waited for an hour, for two hours, feeling my heart swell with a dread I had never before experienced, with such an anguish as I would not wish the greatest of criminals to experience. Where was my son? What was he doing?

" 'About midnight, a messenger brought me a note from my lover. I still know its contents by heart:

" ' "Has your son returned? I did not find him. I am down here. I do not want to go up at this hour."

" 'I wrote in pencil on the same slip of paper:

" ' "Jean has not returned. You must go and find him."

" 'And I remained all night in the armchair, waiting for him.

" 'I felt as if I were going mad. I longed to run wildly about, to roll myself on the floor. And yet I did not even stir, but kept waiting hour after hour. What was going to happen? I tried to imagine, to guess. But I could form no conception, in spite of my efforts, in spite of the tortures of my soul!

" 'And now my apprehension was lest they might meet. What would they do in that case? What would my son do? My mind was lacerated by fearful doubts, by terrible suppositions.

" 'You understand what I mean, do you not, Monsieur?

" 'My chambermaid, who knew nothing, who understood nothing, was coming in every moment, believing, naturally that I had lost my reason. I had sent her away with a word or a movement of the hand. She went for the doctor, who found me in the throes of a nervous fit.

" 'I was put to bed. Then came an attack of brain-fever. When I regained consciousness, after a long illness, I saw beside my bed my—lover —alone. I exclaimed:

" ' "My son? Where is my son?"

" 'He replied:

" ' "I assure you every effort has been made by me to find him, but I have failed!"

" 'Then, becoming suddenly exasperated and even indignant,—for women are subject to such outbursts of unaccountable and unreasoning anger,—I said:

" ' "I forbid you to come near me or to see me again unless you find him. Go away!"

" 'He did go away.

" 'I have never seen one or the other of them since, Monsieur, and thus I have lived for the last twenty years.

" 'Can you imagine what all this meant to me? Can you understand this monstrous punishment, this slow, perpetual laceration of a mother's heart, this abominable, endless waiting? Endless, did I say? No: it is about to end, for I am dying. I am dying without ever again seeing either of them—either one or the other!

" 'He—the man I loved—has written to me every day for the last twenty years; and I—I have never consented to see him, even for one second; for I had a strange feeling that if he came back here, it would be at that very moment my son would again make his appearance! Ah! my son! my son! Is he dead? Is he living? Where is he hiding? Over there perhaps, at the other side of the ocean, in some country so far away that even its very name is unknown to me! Does he ever think of me? Ah! if he only knew! How cruel children are! Did he understand to what frightful suffering he condemned me, into what depths of despair, into what tortures, he cast me while I was still in the prime of life, leaving me to suffer like this even to this moment when I am going to die—me, his mother, who loved him with all the violence of a mother's love! Oh! isn't it cruel, cruel?

" 'You will tell him all this, Monsieur—will you not? You will repeat for him my last words:

" ' "My child, my dear, dear child, be less harsh toward poor women! Life is already brutal and savage enough in its dealing with them. My dear son, think of what the existence of your poor mother has been ever since the day when you left her. My dear child, forgive her, and love her, now that she is dead, for she has had to endure the most frightful penance ever inflicted on a woman."

"She gasped for breath shuddering, as if she had addressed her last words to her son and as if he stood by her bedside.

"Then she added:

" 'You will tell him also, Monsieur, that I never again saw—the other.'

"Once more she ceased speaking, then, in a broken voice she said:

" 'Leave me now, I beg of you. I want to die all alone, since they are not with me.' "

Maître le Brument added:

"I left the house, Messieurs, crying like a fool, so vehemently, indeed, that my coachman turned round to stare at me.

"And to think that every day heaps of dramas like this are being enacted all around us!

"I have not found the son—that son —well, say what you like about him, but I call him that criminal son!"

He?[*]

My dear friend, you cannot understand it by any possible means, you say, and I perfectly believe you. You think I am going mad? It may be so, but not for the reasons which you suppose.

Yes, I am going to get married, and I will tell you what has led me to take that step.

My ideas and my convictions have not changed at all. I look upon all legalized cohabitation as utterly stupid, for I am certain that nine husbands out of ten are cuckolds; and they get no more than their deserts for having been idiotic enough to fetter their lives and renounce their freedom in love, the only happy and good thing in the world, and for having clipped the wings of fancy which continually drives us on toward all women. You know what I mean. More than ever I feel that I am incapable of loving one woman alone, because I shall always adore all the others too much. I should like to have a thousand arms, a thousand mouths, and a thousand—*temperaments,* to be able to strain an army of these charming creatures in my embrace at the same moment.

And yet I am going to get married!

I may add that I know very little of the girl who is going to become my wife to-morrow; I have only seen her four or five times. I know that there is nothing unpleasant about her, and that is enough for my purpose. She is small, fair, and stout; so of course the day after to-morrow I shall ardently wish for a tall, dark, thin woman.

She is not rich, and belongs to the middle classes. She is a girl such as

you may find by the gross, well adapted for matrimony, without any apparent faults, and with no particularly striking qualities. People say of her: "Mlle. Lajolle is a very nice girl," and to-morrow they will say: "What a very nice woman Madame Raymon is." She belongs, in a word, to that immense number of girls who make very good wives for us till the moment comes when we discover that we happen to prefer all other women to that particular woman we married.

"Well," you will say to me, "what on earth do you get married for?"

I hardly like to tell you the strange and seemingly improbable reason that urged me on to this senseless act; the fact, however, is that I am frightened of being alone!

I don't know how to tell you or to make you understand me; but my state of mind is so wretched that you will pity and despise me.

I do not want to be alone any longer at night; I want to feel that there is some one close to me touching me, a being who can speak and say something, no matter what it be.

I wish to be able to awaken somebody by my side, so that I may be able to ask some sudden question even, if I feel inclined, so that I may hear a human voice, and feel that there is some waking soul close to me, some one whose

[*]It was in this story that the first gleams of De Maupassant's approaching madness became apparent. Thenceforward he began to revel in the strange and terrible, until his malady had seized him wholly. "The Diary of a Madman," is in a similar vein.

816

reason is at work — so that when I hastily light the candle I may see some human face by my side—because—because—I am ashamed to confess it—because I am afraid of being alone.

Oh! you don't understand me yet.

I am not afraid of any danger; if a man were to come into the room I should kill him without trembling. I am not afraid of ghosts, nor do I believe in the supernatural. I am not afraid of dead people, for I believe in the total annihilation of every being that disappears from the face of this earth.

Well,—yes, well, it must be told; I am afraid of myself, afraid of that horrible sensation of incomprehensible fear.

You may laugh, if you like. It is terrible and I cannot get over it. I am afraid of the walls, of the furniture, of the familiar objects, which are animated, as far as I am concerned, by a kind of animal life. Above all, I am afraid of my own dreadful thoughts, of my reason, which seems as if it were about to leave me, driven away by a mysterious and invisible agony.

At first I feel a vague uneasiness in my mind which causes a cold shiver to run all over me. I look round, and of course nothing is to be seen, and I wish there were something there, no matter what, as long as it were something tangible: I am frightened, merely because I cannot understand my own terror.

If I speak, I am afraid of my own voice. If I walk, I am afraid of I know not what, behind the door, behind the curtains, in the cupboard, or under my bed, and yet all the time I know there is nothing anywhere, and I turn round

suddenly because I am afraid of what is behind me, although there is nothing there, and I know it.

I get agitated; I feel that my fear increases, and so I shut myself up in my own room, get into bed, and hide under the clothes, and there, cowering down rolled into a ball, I close my eyes in despair and remain thus for an indefinite time, remembering that my candle is alight on the table by my bedside, and that I ought to put it out, and yet—I dare not do it!

It is very terrible, is it not, to be like that?

Formerly I felt nothing of all that; I came home quite comfortably, and went up and down in my rooms without anything disturbing my calmness of mind. Had anyone told me that I should be attacked by a malady—for I can call it nothing else—of most improbable fear, such a stupid and terrible malady as it is, I should have laughed outright. I was certainly never afraid of opening the door in the dark; I used to go to bed slowly without locking it, and never got up in the middle of the night to make sure that everything was firmly closed.

It began last year in a very strange manner, on a damp autumn evening. When my servant had left the room, after I had dined, I asked myself what I was going to do. I walked up and down my room for some time, feeling tired without any reason for it, unable to work, and without enough energy to read. A fine rain was falling, and I felt unhappy, a prey to one of those fits of casual despondency which make use feel inclined to cry, or to talk, no matter to whom, so as to shake off our depressing thoughts.

I felt that I was alone and that my rooms seemed to me to be more empty than they had ever been before. I was surrounded by a sensation of infinite and overwhelming solitude. What was I to do? I sat down, but then a kind of nervous impatience agitated my legs, so that I got up and began to walk about again. I was feverish, for my hands, which I had clasped behind me, as one often does when walking slowly, almost seemed to burn one another. Then suddenly a cold shiver ran down my back, and I thought the damp air might have penetrated into my room, so I lit the fire for the first time that year, and sat down again and looked at the flames. But soon I felt that I could not possibly remain quiet. So I got up again and determined to go out, to pull myself together, and to seek a friend to bear me company.

I could not find anyone, so I went on to the boulevards to try and meet some acquaintance or other there.

I was wretched everywhere, and the wet pavement glistened in the gaslight, while the oppressive mist of the almost impalpable rain lay heavily over the streets and seemed to obscure the light from the lamps.

I went on slowly, saying to myself, "I shall not find a soul to talk to."

I glanced into several *cafés,* from the Madeleine as far as the Faubourg Poissonière, and saw many unhappy-looking individuals sitting at the tables, who did not seem even to have enough energy left to finish the refreshments they had ordered.

For a long time I wandered aimlessly up and down, and about midnight I started off for home; I was very calm and very tired. My *concierge** opened the door at once, which was quite unusual for him, and I thought that another lodger had no doubt just come in.

When I go out I always double-lock the door of my room. Now I found it merely closed, which surprised me; but I supposed that some letters had been brought up for me in the course of the evening.

I went in, and found my fire still burning so that it lighted up the room a little. In the act of taking up a candle, I noticed somebody sitting in my armchair by the fire, warming his feet, with his neck toward me.

I was not in the slightest degree frightened. I thought very naturally that some friend or other had come to see me. No doubt the porter, whom I had told when I went out, had lent him his own key. In a moment I remembered all the circumstances of my return, how the street door had been opened immediately, and that my own door was only latched, and not locked.

I could see nothing of my friend but his head. He had evidently gone to sleep while waiting for me, so I went up to him to rouse him. I saw him quite clearly; his right arm was hanging down and his legs were crossed, while his head, which was somewhat inclined to the left of the armchair, seemed to indicate that he was asleep. "Who can it be" I asked myself. I could not see clearly, as the room was rather dark, so I put out my hand to

*Hall-porter.

touch him on the shoulder, and it came in contact with the back of the chair. There was nobody there; the seat was empty.

I fairly jumped with fright. For a moment I drew back as if some terrible danger had suddenly appeared in my way; then I turned round again, impelled by some imperious desire to look at the armchair again. I remained standing upright, panting with fear, so upset that I could not collect my thoughts, and ready to drop.

But I am naturally a cool man, and soon recovered myself. I thought: "It is a mere hallucination, that is all," and I immediately began to reflect about this phenomenon. Thoughts fly very quickly at such moments.

I had been suffering from a hallucination, that was an incontestable fact. My mind had been perfectly lucid and had acted regularly and logically, so there was nothing the matter with the brain. It was only my eyes that had been deceived; they had had a vision, one of those visions which lead simple folk to believe in miracles. It was a nervous accident to the optical apparatus, nothing more; the eyes were rather overwrought, perhaps.

I lit my candle, and when I stooped down to the fire in so doing, I noticed that I was trembling, and I raised myself up with a jump, as if somebody had touched me from behind.

I was certainly not by any means reassured.

I walked up and down a little, and hummed a tune or two. Then I double-locked my door, and felt rather reassured; now, at any rate, nobody could come in.

I sat down again, and thought over my adventure for a long time; then I went to bed, and put out my light.

For some minutes all went well; I lay quietly on my back. Then an irresistible desire seized me to look round the room, and I turned on to my side.

My fire was nearly out and the few glowing embers threw a faint light on to the floor by the chair, where I fancied I saw the man sitting again.

I quickly struck a match, but I had been mistaken, for there was nothing there; I got up, however, and hid the chair behind my bed, and tried to get to sleep as the room was now dark. But I had not forgotten myself for more than five minutes when in my dream I saw all the scene which I had witnessed as clearly as if it were reality. I woke up with a start, and, having lit the candle, sat up in bed, without venturing even to try and go to sleep again.

Twice, however, sleep overcame me for a few moments in spite of myself, and twice I saw the same thing again, till I fancied I was going mad. When day broke, however, I thought that I was cured, and slept peacefully till noon.

It was all past and over. I had been feverish, had had the nightmare; I don't know what. I had been ill, in a word, but yet I thought that I was a great fool.

I enjoyed myself thoroughly that evening; I went and dined at a restaurant; afterward I went to the theater, and then started home. But as I got near the house I was seized by a strange feeling of uneasiness once more; I was afraid of *seeing* him again. I was not afraid of him, not afraid of his presence, in which I did not believe; but I was afraid of being deceived again; I was afraid of some fresh hallucination, afraid lest fear should take possession of me.

For more than an hour I wandered up and down the pavement; then I thought that I was really too foolish, and returned home. I panted so that I could scarcely get upstairs, and remained standing outside my door for more than ten minutes; then suddenly I took courage and pulled myself together. I inserted my key into the lock, and went in with a candle in my hand. I kicked open my half-open bedroom door, and gave a frightened look toward the fireplace; there was nothing there. A—h!

What a relief and what a delight! What a deliverance: I walked up and down briskly and boldly, but I was not altogether reassured, and kept turning round with a jump; the very shadows in the corners disquieted me.

I slept badly, and was constantly disturbed by imaginary noises, but I did not see *him;* no, that was all over.

Since that time I have been afraid of being alone at night. I feel that the specter is there, close to me, around me; but it has not appeared to me again. And supposing it did, what would it matter, since I do not believe in it and know that it is nothing?

It still worries me, however, because I am constantly thinking of it: *his right arm hanging down and his head inclined to the left like a man who was asleep—* Enough of that, in Heaven's name! I don't want to think about it!

Why, however, am I so persistently possessed with this idea? His feet were close to the fire!

He haunts me; it is very stupid, but so it is. Who and what is HE? I know that he does not exist except in my cowardly imagination, in my fears, and in my agony! There—enough of that!

Yes, it is all very well for me to reason with myself, *to stiffen myself,* so to say; but I cannot remain at home, because I know he is there. I know I shall not see him again; he will not show himself again; that is all over. But he is there all the same in my thoughts. He remains invisible, but that does not prevent his being there. He is behind the doors, in the closed cupboards, in the wardrobe, under the bed, in every dark corner. If I open the door or the cupboard, if I take the candle to look under the bed and throw a light on to the dark places, he is there no longer, but I feel that he is behind me. I turn round, certain that I shall not see him, that I shall never see him again; but he is, none the less, behind me.

It is very stupid, it is dreadful; but what am I to do? I cannot help it.

But if there were two of us in the place, I feel certain that he would not be there any longer, for he is there just because I am alone, simply and solely because I am alone!

VOLUME VIII

The Avenger

WHEN M. Antoine Leuillet married the Widow Mathilde Souris, he had been in love with her for nearly ten years.

M. Souris had been his friend, his old college chum. Leuillet was very fond of him, but found him rather a muff. He often used to say: "That poor Souris will never set the Seine on fire."

When Souris married Mlle. Mathilde Duval, Leuillet was surprised and somewhat vexed, for he had a slight weakness for her. She was the daughter of a neighbor of his, a retired haberdasher with a good deal of money. She was pretty, well-mannered, and intelligent. She accepted Souris on account of his money.

Then Leuillet cherished hopes of his friend's wife. He was a handsome man, not at all stupid, and also well off. He was confident that he would succeed; he failed. Then he fell in love with her, and he was the sort of lover who is rendered timid, prudent, and embarrassed by intimacy with the husband. Mme. Souris fancied that he no longer meant anything serious by his attentions to her, and she became simply his friend. This state of affairs lasted nine years.

Now, one morning, Leuillet received a startling communication from the poor woman. Souris had died suddenly of aneurism of the heart.

He got a terrible shock, for they were of the same age; but, the very next moment a sensation of profound joy, of infinite relief, of deliverance, penetrated his body and soul. Mme. Souris was free.

He had the tact, however, to make such a display of grief as the occasion required; he waited for the proper time to elapse, and attended to all the conventional usages. At the end of fifteen months, he married the widow.

His conduct was regarded as not only natural but generous. He had acted like a good friend and an honest man. In short, he was happy, quite happy.

They lived on terms of the closest confidence, having from the first understood and appreciated each other. One kept nothing secret from the other, and they told each other their inmost thoughts. Leuillet now loved his wife with a calm, trustful affection; he loved her as a tender, devoted partner, who is an equal and confidant. But there still lingered in his soul a singular and unaccountable grudge against the deceased Souris, who had been the first to possesss this woman, who had even robbed her of her youth and her soul, and who had had even robbed her of her poetic attributes. The memory of the dead husband spoiled the happiness of the living husband; and this posthumous jealousy now began to torment Leuillet's heart day and night.

The result was that he was incessantly talking about Souris, asking a thousand minute and intimate questions about him, and seeking information as to all of his habits and personal characteristics. And he pursued him with railleries even into the depths of the tomb, recalling with self-satisfaction his oddities, emphasizing his absurdities, and pointing out his defects.

Constantly he would call out to his wife from one end to the other of the house:

"Hello, Mathilde!"

"Here I am dear."

"Come and let us have a chat."

She always came over to him, smiling, well aware that Souris was to be the subject of the chat, and anxious to gratify her second husband's harmless fad.

"I say! do you remember how Souris wanted one day to prove to me that small men are always better loved than big men?"

And he launched out into reflections unfavorable to the defunct husband, who was small, and discreetly complimentary to himself as he happened to be tall.

And Mme. Leuillet let him think that he was quite right; and she laughed very heartily, turned the first husband into ridicule in a playful fashion for the amusement of his successor, who always ended by remarking:

"Never mind! Souris was a muff!"

They were happy, quite happy. And Leuillet never ceased to testify his unabated attachment to his wife by all the usual manifestations.

Now, one night, when they happened to both be kept awake by a renewal of youthful ardor, Leuillet who held his wife clasped tightly in his arms and had his lips glued to hers said:

"Tell me this darling."

"What?"

"Souris—'tisn't easy to put the question—was he very—very loving?"

She gave him a warm kiss, as she murmured:

"Not as much as you, my sweet."

His male vanity was flattered and he went on:

"He must have been—rather a flat—eh?"

She did not answer. There was merely a sly little laugh on her face, which she pressed close to her husband's neck.

He persisted in his questions:

"Come now! Don't deny that he was a flat—well, I mean, rather an awkward sort of fellow?"

She nodded slightly.

"Well yes, rather awkward."

He went on:

"I'm sure he used to weary you many a night—isn't that so?"

This time she had an access of frankness, and she replied:

"Oh! yes."

He embraced her once more when she made this acknowledgment, and murmured:

"What an ass he was! You were not happy with him?"

"No. He was not always jolly."

Leuillet felt quite delighted, making a comparison in his own mind between his wife's former situation and her present one.

He remained silent for some time; then, with a fresh outburst of curiosity, he said:

"Tell me this!"

"What?"

"Will you be quite candid—quite candid with me?"

"Certainly, dear."

"Well, look here! Were you ever tempted to—to deceive this imbecile, Souris?"

Mme. Leuillet uttered a little "Oh!" in a shamefaced way and again cuddled her face closer to her husband's chest.. But he could see that she was laughing.

"Come now, confess it! He had a head just suited for a cuckold, this blockhead! It would be so funny! The good Souris! Oh! I say, darling, you might tell it to me—only to me!"

He emphasized the words "to me," feeling certain that if she wanted to show any taste when she deceived her husband, he, Leuillet would have been the man; and he quivered with joy at the expectation of this avowal, sure that if she had not been the virtuous woman she was he could not have won her then.

But she did not reply, laughing incessantly as if at the recollection of something infinitely comic.

Leuillet, in his turn, burst out laughing at the notion that he might have made a cuckold of Souris. What a good joke! What a capital lot of fun to be sure!

He exclaimed in a voice broken by convulsions of laughter:

"Oh! poor Souris! poor Souris! Ah! yes, he had that sort of head—oh, certainly he had!"

And Mme. Leuillet now twisted herself under the sheets laughing till the tears almost came into her eyes.

And Leuillet repeated: "Come, confess it! confess it! Be candid. You must know that it cannot be unpleasant to me to hear such a thing."

Then she stammered, still choking with laughter:

"Yes, yes."

Her husband pressed her for an answer:

"Yes what? Look here! tell me everything."

She was now laughing in a more subdued fashion, and, raising her mouth up to Leuillet's ear, which was held toward her in anticipation of some pleasant piece of confidence she whispered: "Yes—I did deceive him!"

He felt a cold shiver down his back, and utterly dumfounded, he gasped:

"You — you — did — really—deceive him?"

She was still under the impression that he thought the thing infinitely pleasant, and replied:

"Yes—really—really."

He was obliged to sit up in bed so great was the shock he received, holding his breath, just as overwhelmed as if he had just been told that he was a cuckold himself. At first he was unable to articulate properly; then after the lapse of a minute or so, he merely ejaculated:

"Ah!"

She, too, had stopped laughing now, realizing her mistake too late.

Leuillet at length asked:

"And with whom?"

She kept silent, cudgeling her brain to find some excuse.

He repeated his question:

"With whom?"

At last, she said:

"With a young man."

He turned toward her abruptly, and in a dry tone, said:

"Well, I suppose it wasn't with some kitchen-slut. I ask you who was the young man—do you understand?"

She did not answer. He tore away the sheet which she had drawn over her head, and pushed her into the middle of the bed, repeating:

"I want to know with what young man—do you understand?"

Then, she replied, having some difficulty in uttering the words:

"I only wanted to laugh." But he fairly shook with rage:

"What? How is that? You only wanted to laugh? So then you were making game of me? I'm not going to be satisfied with these evasions, let me tell you! I ask you what was the young man's name?"

She did not reply, but lay motionless on her back.

He caught hold of her arm and pressed it tightly:

"Do you hear me, I say? I want you to give me an answer when I speak to you."

Then she said, in nervous tones:

"I think you must be going mad! Let me alone!"

He trembled with fury, so exasperated that he scarcely knew what he was saying, and, shaking her with all his strength, he repeated:

"Do you hear me? do you hear me?"

She wrenched herself out of his grasp with a sudden movement and with the tips of her fingers slapped her husband on the nose. He entirely lost his temper, feeling that he had been struck, and angrily pounced down on her.

He now held her under him, boxing her ears in a most violent manner, and exclaiming:

"Take that—and that—and that— there you are, you trollop, you strumpet —you strumpet!"

Then when he was out of breath, exhausted from beating her, he got up and went over to the bureau to get himself a glass of sugared orange-water, almost ready to feint after his exertion.

And she lay huddled up in bed, crying and heaving great sobs, feeling that there was an end of her happiness, and that it was all her own fault.

Then in the midst of her tears, she faltered:

"Listen, Antoine, come here! I told you a lie—listen! I'll explain it to you."

And now, prepared to defend herself, armed with excuses and subterfuges, she slightly raised her head all disheveled under her crumpled nightcap.

And he turning toward her, drew close to her, ashamed of having whacked her, but feeling still in his heart's core as a husband an inexhaustible hatred against the woman who had deceived his predecessor, Souris.

The Conservatory

MONSIEUR and Mme. Lerebour were about the same age. But Monsieur looked younger, although he was the weaker of the two. They lived near Mantes in a pretty estate which they had bought after having made a fortune by selling printed cottons.

The house was surrounded by a

beautiful garden, containing a poultry yard, Chinese *kiosques,* and a little conservatory at the end of the avenue. M. Lerebour was short, round and jovial, with the joviality of a shopkeeper of epicurean tastes. His wife, lean, self-willed, and always discontented had not succeeded in overcoming her husband's good-humor. She dyed her hair, and sometimes read novels, which made dreams pass through her soul, although she affected to despise writings of this kind. People said she was a woman of strong passions without her having ever done anything to sustain that opinion. But her husband sometimes said: "My wife is a gay woman," with a certain knowing air which awakened suppositions.

For some years past, however, she had shown herself aggressive toward M. Lerebour, always irritated and hard, as if a secret and unavoidable grief tormented her. A sort of misunderstanding was the result. They scarcely spoke to each other, and Madame, whose name was Palmyre, was incessantly heaping unkind compliments, wounding allusions, bitter words, without any apparent reason, on Monsieur, whose name was Gustave.

He bent his back, bored though gay, all the same, endowed with such a fund of contentment that he endured her domestic bickerings. He asked himself, nevertheless, what unknown cause could have thus embittered his spouse, for he had a strong feeling that her irritation had a hidden reason, but so difficult to penetrate that his efforts to do so were in vain.

He often said to her: "Look here my dear, tell me what you have against me. I feel that you are concealing something."

She invariably replied: "But there is nothing the matter with me, absolutely nothing. Besides, if I had some cause for discontent, it would be for you to guess at it. I don't like men who understand nothing, who are so soft and incapable that one must come to their assistance to make them grasp the slightest thing."

He murmured dejectedly: "I see clearly that you don't want to say anything."

And he went away still striving to unravel the mystery.

The nights especially became painful to him, for they always shared the same bed, as one does in good and simple households. It was not, therefore, mere ordinary ill-temper that she displayed toward him. She chose the moment when they were lying side by side to load him with the liveliest raillery. She reproached him principally with his corpulence: "You take up all the room, you are becoming so fat."

And she forced him to get up on the slightest pretext, sending him downstairs to look for a newspaper she had forgotten, or a bottle of orange-water, which he failed to find as she had herself hidden it away. And she exclaimed in a furious and sarcastic tone: "You might, however, know where to find it, you big booby!" When he had been wandering about the sleeping house for a whole hour, and returned to the room empty-handed, the only thanks she gave him was to say: "Come, get back to bed, it will make you thin to take a little walking; you are becoming as flabby as a sponge."

She kept waking him every moment by declaring that she was suffering from cramps in her stomach, and insisting on his rubbing her with flannel soaked in eau de Cologne. He would make efforts to cure her, grieved at seeing her ill, and would propose to go and rouse up Céleste, their maid. Then she would get angry, crying: "You must be a fool. Well! it is over; I am better now, so go back to bed, you big lout."

To his question: "Are you quite sure you have got better?" she would fling this harsh answer in his face:

"Yes, hold your tongue! let me sleep! Don't worry me any more about it! You are incapable of doing anything, even of rubbing a woman."

He got into a state of deep dejection: "But, my darling—"

She became exasperated: "I want no 'buts.' Enough, isn't it? Give me some rest now. And she turned her face to the wall.

Now, one night, she shook him so abruptly that he started up in terror, and found himself in a sitting posture with a rapidity which was not habitual to him. He stammered:

"What? What's the matter?"

She caught him by the arm and pinched him till he cried out. Then she gave him a box on the ear: "I hear some noise in the house."

Accustomed to the frequent alarms of Mme. Lerebour he did not disturb himself very much and quietly asked:

"What sort of noise, my darling?"

She trembled as if she were in a state of terror and replied: "Noise—

why noise—the noise of footsteps. There is some one."

He remained incredulous: "Some one? You think so? But no; you must be mistaken. Besides whom do you think it can be?"

She shuddered:

Who? Who? Why, thieves, of course, you imbecile!"

He plunged softly under the sheets: "Ah! no, my darling! There is nobody. I dare say you dreamed it."

Then, she flung off the coverlet, and, jumping out of bed, in a rage: "Why, then, you are just as cowardly as you are incapable! In any case, I shall not let myself be massacred owing to your pusillanimity." And snatching up the tongs from the fireplace, she placed herself in a fighting attitude in front of the bolted door.

Moved by his wife's display of valor, perhaps ashamed, he rose up in his turn sulkily, and without taking off his nightcap he seized the shovel, and placed himself face to face with his better half.

They waited for twenty minutes in the deepest silence. No fresh noise disturbed the repose of the house. Then, Madame, becoming furious, got back into bed saying: "Nevertheless I'm sure there is some one."

In order to avoid anything like a quarrel he did not make an allusion during the next day to this panic. But, next night, Mme. Lerebour woke up her husband with more violence still than the night before; and, panting, she stammered: "Gustave, Gustave, somebody has just opened the garden-gate!"

Astonished at this persistence, he

fancied that his wife must have had an attack of somnambulism, and was about to make an effort to shake off this dangerous state when he thought he heard, in fact, a slight sound under the walls of the house. He rose up, rushed to the window and he saw—yes, he saw—a white figure quickly passing along one of the garden-walks.

He murmured, as if he were on the point of fainting: "There is some one." Then, he recovered his self-possession, felt more resolute, and suddenly carried away by the formidable anger of a proprietor whose territory has been encroached upon, he said: "Wait! wait, and you shall see!"

He rushed toward the writing-desk, opened it, took out the revolver, and dashed out into the stairs. His wife, filled with consternation, followed him, exclaiming: "Gustave, Gustave, don't abandon me, don't leave me alone! Gustave! Gustave!"

But he scarcely heard her; he had by this time laid his hand on the garden-gate.

Then she went back rapidly and barricaded herself in the conjugal chamber.

*   *   *   *   *   *

She waited five minutes, ten minutes, a quarter of an hour. Wild terror took possession of her. Without doubt, they had killed him; they had seized, garroted, strangled him. She would have preferred to hear the report of the six barrels of the revolver, to know that he was fighting, that he was defending himself. But this great silence, this terrifying silence of the country overwhelmed her.

She rang for Céleste. Céleste did not come in answer to the bell. She rang again, on the point of swooning, of sinking into unconsciousness. The entire house remained without a sound. She pressed her burning forehead to the window, seeking to peer through the darkness without. She distinguished nothing but the blacker shadows of a row of trees beside the gray ruts on the roads.

It struck half past twelve. Her husband had been absent for forty-five minutes. She would never see him again. No! she would never see him again. And she fell on her knees sobbing.

Two light knocks at the door of the apartment called out to her: "Open, pray, Palmyre—'tis I." She rushed forward, opened the door, and standing in front of him, with her arms akimbo and her eyes full of tears, exclaimed: "Where have you been, you dirty brute? Ah! you left me here by myself nearly dead of fright. You care no more about me than if I never existed."

He closed the bedroom door; then he laughed and laughed like a madman, grinning from ear to ear, with his hands on his sides, till the tears came into his eyes.

Mme. Lerebour, stupefied, remained silent.

He stammered: "It was—it was—Céleste, who had an appointment in the conservatory. If you knew what—what I have seen—"

She had turned pale, choking with indignation.

"Eh? Do you tell me so? Céleste? In my house? in—my—house—in my —my—in my conservatory. And you have not killed the man who was her accomplice! You had a revolver and did not kill him? In my house—in my house."

She sat down, not feeling able to do anything.

He danced a caper, snapped his fingers, smacked his tongue, and, still laughing: "If you knew—if you knew—" He suddenly gave her a kiss.

She tore herself away from him and in a voice broken with rage, she said: "I will not let this girl remain one day longer in my house, do you hear? Not one day—not one hour. When she returns to the house, we will throw her out."

M. Lerebour had seized his wife by the waist, and he planted rows of kisses on her neck, loud kisses, as in bygone days. She became silent once more, petrified with astonishment. But he, holding her clasped in his arms, drew her softly toward the bed.

*   *   *   *   *   *

Toward half past nine in the morning, Céleste, astonished at not having yet seen her master and mistress, who always rose early, came and knocked softly at their door.

They were in bed, and were gaily chatting side by side. She stood there astonished, and said: "Madame, it is the coffee."

Mme. Lerebour said in a very soft voice: "Bring it here to me, my girl. We are a little tired; we have slept very badly."

Scarcely had the servant-maid gone than M. Lerebour began to laugh again, tickling his wife under the chin, and repeating: "If you knew. Oh! if you knew."

But she caught his hands: "Look here! keep quiet, my darling, if you laugh like this you will make yourself ill."

And she kissed him softly on the eyes.

*   *   *   *   *   *

Mme. Lerebour has no more fits of sourness. Sometimes on bright nights the husband and wife come, with furtive steps, along the clumps of trees and flower-beds as far as the little conservatory at the end of the garden. And they remain there planted side by side with their faces pressed against the glass as if they were looking at something strange and full of interest going on within.

They have increased Céleste's wages. But M. Lerebour has got thin.

Letter Found on a Corpse

You ask me, Madame, whether I am laughing at you? You cannot believe that a man has never been smitten with love. Well, no, I have never loved, never!

What is the cause of this? I really cannot tell. Never have I been under the influence of that sort of intoxication of the heart which we call love! Never have I lived in that dream, in that exaltation, in that state of madness into which the image of a woman casts us. I have never been pursued, haunted, roused to fever-heat, lifted up to Paradise by the thought of meeting, or by the possession of, a being who had suddenly become for me more desirable than any good fortune, more beautiful than any other creature, more important than the whole world! I have never wept, I have never suffered on account of any of you. I have not passed my nights thinking of one woman without closing my eyes. I have no experience of waking up with the thought and the memory of her shedding her illumination on me. I have never known the wild desperation of hope when she was about to come, or the divine sadness of regret when she parted with me, leaving behind her in the room a delicate odor of violet-powder.

I have never been in love.

I, too, have often asked myself why is this. And truly I can scarcely tell. Nevertheless, I have found some reasons for it; but they are of a metaphysical character, and perhaps you will not be able to appreciate them.

I suppose I sit too much in judgment on women to submit much to their fascination. I ask you to forgive me for this remark. I am going to explain what I mean. In every creature there is a moral being and a physical being. In order to love, it would be necessary for me to find a harmony between these two beings which I have never found. One has always too great a predominance over the other, sometimes the the physical.

The intellect which we have a right to require in a woman, in order to love her, is not the same as virile intellect.

It is more and it is less. A woman must have a mind open, delicate, sensitive, refined, impressionable. She has no need of either power or initiative in thought, but she must have kindness, elegance, tenderness, coquetry, and that faculty of assimilation which, in a little while, raises her to an equality with him who shares her life. Her greatest quality must be tact, that subtle sense which is to the mind what touch is to the body. It reveals to her a thousand little things, contours, angles, and forms in the intellectual life.

Very frequently pretty women have not intellect to correspond with their personal charms. Now the slightest lack of harmony strikes me and pains me at the first glance. In friendship, this is not of importance. Friendship is a compact in which one fairly divides defects and merits. We may judge of friends, whether man or woman, take into account the good they possess, neglect the evil that is in them, appreciate their value exactly, while giving ourselves up to an intimate sympathy of a deep and fascinating character.

In order to love, one must be blind, surrender oneself absolutely, see nothing, reason from nothing, understand nothing. One must adore the weakness as well as the beauty of the beloved object, renounce all judgment, all reflection, all perspicacity.

I am incapable of such blindness, and rebel against a seductiveness not founded on reason. This is not all. I have such a high and subtle idea of harmony that nothing can ever realize my ideal. But you will call me a madman. Listen to me. A woman, in my opinion, may have an exquisite soul and a charming body, without that body and that soul being in perfect accord with one another. I mean that persons who have noses made in certain shape are not to be expected to think in a certain fashion. The fat have no right to make use of the same words and phrases as the thin. You who have blue eyes, Madame, cannot look at life, and judge of things and events as if you had black eyes. The shades of your eyes should correspond, by a sort of fatality, with the shades of your thought. In perceiving these things I have the scent of a bloodhound. Laugh if you like, but it is so.

And yet I imagined that I was in love for an hour, for a day. I had foolishly yielded to the influence of surrounding circumstances. I allowed myself to be beguiled by the mirage of an aurora. Would you like to hear this short history?

*　　*　　*　　*　　*　　*

I met, one evening, a pretty, enthusiastic woman who wanted for the purpose of humoring a poetic fancy, to spend a night with me in a boat on a river. I would have preferred—but, no matter, I consented.

It was in the month of June. My fair companion chose a moonlight night in order to excite her imagination all the better.

We had dined at a riverside inn, and then we set out in the boat about ten o'clock. I thought it a rather foolish kind of adventure; but as my companion pleased me I did not bother myself too much about this. I sat down on the seat facing her, seized the oars, and off we started.

I could not deny that the scene was picturesque. We glided past a wooded isle full of nightingales, and the current carried us rapidly over the river covered with silvery ripples. The grasshoppers uttered their shrill, monotonous cry; the frogs croaked in the grass by the river's bank, and the lapping of the water as it flowed on made around us a kind of confused, almost imperceptible murmur, disquieting, which gave us a vague sensation of mysterious fear.

The sweet charm of warm nights and of streams glittering in the moonlight penetrated us. It seemed bliss to live and to float thus, to dream and to feel by one's side a young woman sympathetic and beautiful.

I was somewhat affected, somewhat agitated, somewhat intoxicated by the pale brightness of the night and the consciousness of my proximity to a lovely woman.

"Come and sit beside me," she said.

I obeyed. She went on:

"Recite some verses for me."

This appeared to me rather too much. I declined; she persisted. She certainly wanted to have the utmost pleasure, the whole orchestra of sentiment, from the moon to the rhymes of poets. In the end, I had to yield, and, as if in mockery, I recited for her a charming little poem by Louis Bouilhet, of which the following are a few strophes:

"I hate the poet who with tearful eye
　　Murmurs some name while gazing
　　　　tow'rds a star,.
　Who sees no magic in the earth or sky,
　　Unless Lizette or Ninon be not far.

The bard who in all Nature nothing sees
    Divine, unless a petticoat he ties
Amorously to the branches of the trees,
    Or nightcap to the grass, is scarcely
      wise.
He has not heard the eternal's thunder-
    tone,
    The voice of Nature in her various
      moods,
He cannot tread the dim ravines alone,
    And of no woman dream 'mid
      whispering woods."

I expected some reproaches. Nothing of the sort. She murmured:

"How true it is!"

I remained stupefied. Had she understood?

Our boat was gradually drawing nearer to the bank, and got entangled under a willow which impeded its progress. I drew my arm around my companion's waist, and very gently moved my lips toward her neck. But she repulsed me with an abrupt, angry movement:

"Have done, pray! You are rude!"

I tried to draw her toward me. She resisted, caught hold of the tree and nearly upset us both into the water. I deemed it the prudent course to cease my importunities.

She went on:

"I would rather have you capsized. I feel so happy. I want to dream—that is so nice." Then, in a slightly malicious tone, she added:

"Have you, then, already forgotton the verses you recited for me just now?"

She was right. I became silent.

She went on:

"Come! row!"

And I plied at the oars once more. I began to find the night long and to see the absurdity of my conduct. My companion said to me:

"Will you make me a promise?"

"Yes. What is it?"

"To remain quiet, well-behaved, and discreet, if I permit you—"

"What? Say what you mean!"

"Here is what I mean! I want to lie down on my back in the bottom of of the boat with you by my side. I forbid you to touch me to embrace me —in short to—caress me."

"If you move, I'll capsize the boat."

And then we lay down side by side, our eyes turned toward the sky, while the boat glided slowly through the water. We were rocked by the gentle movement of the shallop. The light sounds of the night came to us more distinctly in the bottom of the boat, sometimes causing us to start. And I felt springing up within me a strange, poignant emotion, an infinite tenderness something like an irresistible impulse to open my arms in order to embrace, to open my heart in order to love, to give myself, to give my thoughts, my body, my life, my entire being to some one.

My companion murmured like one in a dream:

"Where are we? Where are we going? It seems to me that I am quitting the earth. How sweet it is! Ah! if you loved me—a little!"

My heart began to throb. I had no answer to give. It seemed to me that I loved her. I had not longer any violent desire. I felt happy there by her side and that was enough for me.

And thus we remained for a long, long time without stirring. We caught each other's hands; some delightful force rendered us motionless, an unknown force stronger than ourselves, an alliance, chaste, intimate, absolute, of our persons lying there touching each other. What was this? How do I know? Love perhaps.

Little by little, the dawn appeared. It was three o'clock in the morning. Slowly, a great brightness spread over the sky. The boat knocked against something. I rose up. We had come close to a tiny islet.

But I remained ravished in a state of ecstasy. In front of us stretched the shining firmament, red, rosy, violet, spotted with fiery clouds resembling golden vapors. The river was glowing with purple, and three houses on one side of it seemed to be burning.

I bent toward my companion. I was going to say: "Oh! look!" But I held my tongue, quite dazed, and I could no longer see anything except her. She, too, was rosy, with the rosy flesh tints with which must have mingled a little the hue of the sky. Her tresses were rosy; her eyes were rosy; her teeth were rosy; her dress, her laces, her smile, all were rosy. And in truth I believed, so overpowering was the illusion, that the aurora was there before me.

She rose softly to her feet, holding out her lips to me; and I moved toward her, trembling, delirious, feeling indeed that I was going to kiss Heaven, to kiss happiness, to kiss a dream which had become a woman, to kiss an ideal which had descended into human flesh.

She said to me: "You have a caterpillar in your hair." And suddenly I felt myself becoming as sad as if I had lost all hope in life.

That is all, Madame. It is puerile, stupid. But I am sure that since that day it would be impossible for me to love. And yet—who can tell?

[The young man upon whom this letter was found was yesterday taken out of the Seine between Bougival and Marly. An obliging bargeman, who had searched the pockets in order to ascertain the name of the deceased, brought this paper to the author.]

The Little Cask

JULES CHICOT, the innkeeper, who lived at Épreville, pulled up his tilbury in front of Mother Magloire's farmhouse. He was a tall man of about forty, fat and with a red face and was generally said to be a very knowing customer.

He hitched his horse up to the gatepost and went in. He owned some land adjoining that of the old woman. He had been coveting her plot for a long while, and had tried in vain to buy it a score of times, but she had always obstinately refused to part with it.

"I was born here, and here I mean to die," was all she said.

He found her peeling potatoes outside the farmhouse door. She was a woman of about seventy-two, very thin, shriveled and wrinkled, almost dried-up, in fact, and much bent, but as active and untiring as a girl. Chicot patted her on the back in a very friendly fashion, and then sat down by her on a stool.

"Well, Mother, you are always pretty well and hearty, I am glad to see."

"Nothing to complain of, considering, thank you. And how are you, Monsieur Chicot?"

"Oh! pretty well, thank you, except a few rheumatic pains occasionally; otherwise, I should have nothing to complain of."

"That's all the better!"

And she said no more, while Chicot watched her going on with her work. Her crooked, knotty fingers, hard as a lobster's claws, seized the tubers, which were lying in a pail, as if they had been a pair of pincers, and peeled them rapidly, cutting off long strips of skin with an old knife which she held in the other hand, throwing the potatoes into the water as they were done. Three daring fowls jumped one after another into her lap, seized a bit of peel and then ran away as fast as their legs would carry them with it in their beaks.

Chicot seemed embarrassed, anxious, with something on the tip of his tongue which he could not get out. At last he said hurriedly:

"I say, Mother Magloire—"

"Well, what is it?"

"You are quite sure that you do not want to sell your farm?"

"Certainly not; you may make up your mind to that. What I have said, I have said, so don't refer to it again."

"Very well; only I fancy I have thought of an arrangement that might suit us both very well."

"What is it?"

"Here you are: You shall sell it to me, and keep it all the same. You don't understand? Very well, so just follow me in what I am going to say."

The old woman left off peeling her potatoes and looked at the innkeeper attentively from under her bushy eyebrows, and went on:

"Let me explain myself: Every month I will give you a hundred and fifty francs.* You understand me, I suppose? Every month I will come and bring you thirty crows,† and it will not make the slightest difference in your life—not the very slightest. You will have your own home just as you have now, will not trouble yourself about me, and will owe me nothing; all you will have to do will be to take my money: Will that arrangement suit you?"

He looked at her good-humoredly, one might have said benevolently, and the old woman returned his looks distrustfully, as if she suspected a trap, and said:

"It seems all right, as far as I am concerned, but it will not give you the farm."

"Never mind about that," he said, "you will remain here as long as it pleases God Almighty to let you live; it will be your home. Only you will sign a deed before a lawyer making it over to me after your death. You have no children, only nephews and nieces for whom you don't care a straw. Will

*As near as possible $30.
†The old name, still applied locally to a five-franc piece.

that suit you? You will keep everything during your life, and I will give the thirty crowns a month. It is a pure gain as far as you are concerned."

The old woman was surprised, rather uneasy, but, nevertheless, very much tempted to agree and answered:

"I don't say that I will not agree to it, but I must think about it. Come back in a week and we will talk it over again, and I will then give you my definite answer."

And Chicot went off, as happy as a king who had conquered an empire.

Mother Magloire was thoughtful, and did not sleep at all that night; in fact, for four days she was in a fever of hesitation. She *smelled,* so to say, that there was something underneath the offer which was not to her advantage; but then the thought of thirty crowns a month, of all those coins chinking in her apron, falling to her, as it were, from the skies without her doing anything for it filled her with covetousness.

She went to the notary and told him about it. He advised her to accept Chicot's offer, but said she ought to ask for a monthly payment of fifty crowns instead of thirty, as her farm was worth sixty thousand francs* at the lowest calculation.

"If you live fifteen years longer," he said, "even then he will only have paid forty-five thousand francs† for it."

The old woman trembled with joy at this prospect of getting fifty crowns a month; but she was still suspicious, fearing some trick and she remained a long time with the lawyer asking questions without being able to make up her mind to go. At last she gave

him instructions to draw up the deed, and returned home with her head in a whirl, just as if she had just drunk four jugs of new cider.

When Chicot came again to receive her answer she took a lot of persuading, and declared that she could not make up her mind to agree to his proposal, though she was all the time on tenterhooks lest he should not consent to give the fifty crowns. At last, when he grew urgent, she told him what she expected for her farm.

He looked surprised and disappointed, and refused.

Then, in order to convince him, she began to talk about the probable duration of her life.

"I am certainly not likely to live more than five or six years longer. I am nearly seventy-three, and far from strong, even considering my age. The other evening I though I was going to die, and could hardly manage to crawl into bed."

But Chicot was not going to be taken in.

"Come, come, old lady, you are as strong as the church tower, and will live till you are a hundred at least; you will be sure to see me put underground first."

The whole day was spent in discussing the money, and as the old woman would not give way, the landlord consented to give the fifty crowns, and she insisted upon having ten crowns over and above to strike the bargain.

Three years passed by, and the old dame did not seem to have grown a

*$12000.   †$9000.

day older. Chicot was in despair. It seemed to him as if he had been paying that annuity for fifty years, that he had been taken in, outwitted, and ruined. From time to time he went to see his annuitant, just as one goes in July to see when the harvest is likely to begin. She always met him with a cunning look, and one would have felt inclined to thing that she was congratulating herself on the trick she had played on him. Seeing how well and hearty she seemed, he very soon got into his tilbury again, growling to himself:

"Will you never die, you old brute?"

He did not know what to do, and felt inclined to strangle her when he saw her. He hated her with a ferocious, cunning hatred, the hatred of a peasant who has been robbed, and began to cast about for means of getting rid of her.

One day he came to see her again, rubbing his hands like he did the first time when he proposed the bargain, and, after having chatted for a few minutes, he said:

"Why do you never come and have a bit of dinner at my place when you are in Épreville? The people are talking about it and saying that we are not on friendly terms, and that pains me. You know it will cost you nothing if you come, for I don't look at the price of a dinner. Come whenever you feel inclined; I shall be very glad to see you."

Old Mother Magloire did not need to be told twice, and the next day but one—she was going to the town in any case, it being market-day, in her gig, driven by her man—she, without any demur, put her trap up in Chicot's stable, and went in search of her promised dinner.

The publican was delighted, and treated her like a princess, giving her roast fowl, black pudding, leg of mutton, and bacon and cabbage. But she ate next to nothing. She had always been a small eater and had generally lived on a little soup and a crust of bread-and-butter.

Chicot was disappointed, and pressed her to eat more, but she refused. She would drink next to nothing either, and declined any coffee, so he asked her:

"But surely, you will take a little drop of brandy or liquor?"

"Well, as to that, I don't know that I will refuse." Whereupon he shouted out:

"Rosalie, bring the superfine brandy, —the special,—you know."

The servant appeared, carrying a long bottle ornamented with a paper vine-leaf, and he filled two liquor glasses.

"Just try that; you will find it first-rate."

The good woman drank it slowly in sips, so as to make the pleasure last all the longer, and when she had finished her glass, draining the last drops so as to make sure of all, she said:

"Yes, that is first-rate!"

Almost before she had said it, Chicot had poured her out another glassful. She wished to refuse, but it was too late, and she drank it very slowly, as she had done the first, and he asked her to have a third. She objected, but he persisted.

"It is as mild as milk, you know. I

can drink ten or a dozen without any ill effect; it goes down like sugar, and leaves no headache behind; one would think that it evaporated on the tongue. It is the most wholesome thing you can drink."

She took it, for she really wished to have it, but she left half the glass.

Then Chicot, in an excess of generosity said:

"Look here, as it is so much to your taste, I will give you a small keg of it, just to show that you and I are still excellent friends." Then she took her leave, feeling slightly overcome by the effects of what she had drunk.

The next day the innkeeper drove into her yard, and took a little iron-hooped keg out of his gig. He insisted on her tasting the contents, to make sure it was the same delicious article, and, when they had each of them drunk three more glasses, he said, as he was going away:

"Well, you know, when it is all gone, there is more left; don't be modest for I shall not mind. The sooner it is finished the better pleased I shall be."

Four days later he came again. The old woman was outside her door cutting up the bread for her soup.

He went up to her, and put his face close to hers, so that he might smell her breath; and when he smelled the alcohol he felt pleased.

"I suppose you will give me a glass of *the special?*" he said. And they had three glasses each.

Soon, however, it began to be whispered abroad that Mother Magloire was in the habit of getting drunk all by herself. She was picked up in her kitchen, then in her yard, then in the roads in the neighborhood, and was often brought home like a log.

Chicot did not go near her any more, and when people spoke to him about her, he used to say, putting on a distressed look:

"It is a real pity that she should have taken to drink at her age; but when people get old there is no remedy. It will be the death of her in the long run."

And it certainly was the death of her. She died the next winter. About Christmas time she fell down unconscious in the snow, and was found dead the next morning.

And when Chicot came in for the farm he said:

"It was very stupid of her; if she had not taken to drink she might very well have lived for ten years longer."

Poor Andrew

THE lawyer's house looked on to the Square. Behind it, there was a nice, well-kept garden, with a back entrance into a narrow street which was almost always deserted, and from which it was separated by a wall.

At the bottom of that garden Maître* Moreau's wife had promised, for the first time, to meet Captain

---

*Maître (Master) is the official title of French lawyers.

Sommerive, who had been making love to her for a long time.

Her husband had gone to Paris for a week, so she was quite free for the time being. The Captain had begged so hard, and he loved her so ardently, and she felt so isolated, so misunderstood, so neglected amid all the law business which seemed to be her husband's sole pleasure, that she had given away her heart without even asking herself whether he would give her anything else at some future time.

Then, after some months of Platonic love, of pressing of hands, of kisses rapidly stolen behind a door, the Captain had declared that he would ask permission to exchange, and leave town immediately, if she would not grant him a meeting, a real meeting, during her husband's absence. So at length she yielded to his importunity.

Just then she was waiting, close against the wall, with a beating heart, when at length she heard somebody climbing up the wall, she nearly ran away.

Suppose it were not he, but a thief? But no; some one called out softly, "Matilda!" and when she replied, "Etienne!" a man jumped on to the path with a crash.

It was he,—and what a kiss!

For a long time they remained in each other's arms, with united lips. But suddenly a fine rain began to fall, and the drops from the leaves fell on to her neck and made her start. Whereupon he said:

"Matilda, my adored one, my darling, my angel let us go indoors. It is twelve o'clock, we can have nothing

to fear; please let us go in." "No, dearest; I am too frightened." But he held her in his arms, and whispered in her ear:

"Your servants sleep on the third floor, looking on to the Square, and your room, on the first, looks on to the garden, so nobody can hear us. I love you so that I wish to love you entirely from head to foot." And he embraced her vehemently.

She resisted still, frightened and even ashamed. But he put his arms round her, lifted her up, and carried her off through the rain, which was by this time descending in torrents.

The door was open; they groped their way upstairs; and when they were in the room he bolted the door while she lit a candle.

Then she fell, half fainting, into a chair, while he kneeled down beside her.

At last, she said, panting:

"No! no! Etienne, please let me remain a virtuous woman; I should be too angry with you afterward; and after all, it is so horrid, so common. Cannot we love each other with a spiritual love only? Oh! Etienne!"

But he was inexorable, and then she tried to get up and escape from his attacks. In her fright she ran to the bed in order to hide herself behind the curtains; but it was a dangerous place of refuge, and he followed her. But in haste he took off his sword too quickly, and it fell on to the floor with a crash. And then a prolonged, shrill child's cry came from the next room, the door of which had remained open.

"You have awakened the child," she

whispered, "and perhaps he will not go to sleep again."

He was only fifteen months old and slept in a room adjoining out of hers, so that she might be able to hear him.

The Captain exclaimed ardently:

"What does it matter, Matilda? How I love you; you must come to me, Matilda."

But she struggled and resisted in her fright.

"No! no! Just listen how he is crying; he will wake up the nurse, and what should we do if she were to come? We should be lost. Just listen to me, Etienne. When he screams at night his father always takes him into our bed, and he is quiet immediately; it is the only means of keeping him still. Do let me take him."

The child roared, uttering shrill screams, which pierced the thickest walls and could be heard by passers-by in the streets.

In his consternation the Captain got up, and Matilda jumped out and took the child into her bed, when he was quiet at once.

Etienne sat astride on a chair, and made a cigarette, and in about five minutes Andrew went to sleep again.

"I will take him back," his mother said; and she took him back very carefully to his bed.

When she returned, the Captain was waiting for her with open arms, and put his arms round her in a transport of love, while she, embracing him more closely, said, stammering:

"Oh! Etienne, my darling, if you only knew how I love you; how——"

Andrew began to cry again, and he, in a rage, exclaimed:

"Confound it all, won't the little brute be quiet?"

No, the little brute would not be quiet, but howled all the louder, on the contrary.

She thought she heard a noise downstairs; no doubt the nurse was coming, so she jumped up and took the child into bed, and he grew quiet directly.

Three times she put him back, and three times she had to fetch him again, and an hour before daybreak the Captain had to go, swearing like a proverbial trooper; and, to calm his impatience, Matilda promised to receive him again the next night. Of course he came, more impatient and ardent than ever, excited by the delay.

He took care to put his sword carefully into a corner; he took off his boots like a thief, and spoke so low that Matilda could hardly hear him. At last, he was just going to be really happy when the floor, or some piece of furniture, or perhaps the bed itself, creaked; it sounded as if something had broken; and in a moment a cry, feeble at first, but which grew louder every moment, made itself heard. Andrew was awake again.

He yapped like a fox, and there was not the slightest doubt that if he went on like that the whole house would awake; so his mother, not knowing what to do, got up and brought him. The Captain was more furious than ever, but did not move, and very carefully he put out his hand, took a small piece of the child's skin between his two fingers, no matter where it was, the thighs or elsewhere, and pinched it. The little one struggled and screamed in a deafening manner, but his tormentor pinched everywhere, furiously and more vigorously. He took a morsel of flesh and twisted and turned it, and then let go in order to take hold of another piece, and then another and another.

The child screamed like a chicken having its throat cut, or a dog being mercilessly beaten. His mother caressed him, kissed him, and tried to stifle his cries by her tenderness; but Andrew grew purple, as if he were going into convulsions, and kicked and struggled with his little arms and legs in an alarming manner.

The Captain said, softly:

"Try and take him back to his cradle; perhaps he will be quiet."

And Matilda went into the other room with the child in her arms. As soon as he was out of his mother's bed he cried less loudly, and when he was in his own he was quiet, with the exception of a few broken sobs. The rest of the night was tranquil.

The next night the Captain came again. As he happened to speak rather loudly, Andrew awoke again and began to scream. His mother went and fetched him immediately, but the Captain pinched so hard and long that the child was nearly suffocated by its cries, its eyes turned in its head and it foamed at the mouth. As soon as it was back in its cradle it was quiet, and in four days Andrew did not cry any more to come into his mother's bed.

On Saturday evening the lawyer returned, and took his place again at the domestic hearth and in the conjugal chamber. As he was tired with his journey he went to bed early; but he had not long lain down when he said to his wife:

"Why, how is it that Andrew is not crying? Just go and fetch him, Matilda; I like to feel that he is between us."

She got up and brought the child, but as soon as he saw that he was in that bed, in which he had been so fond of sleeping a few days previous, he wriggled and screamed so violently in his fright that she had to take him back to his cradle.

M. Moreau could not get over his surprise. "What a very funny thing! What is the matter with him this evening? I suppose he is sleepy?"

"He has been like that all the time that you were away; I have never been able to have him in bed with me once."

In the morning the child woke up and began to laugh and play with his toys.

The lawyer, who was an affectionate man, got up, kissed his offspring, and took him into his arms to carry him to their bed. Andrew laughed, with that vacant laugh of little creatures whose ideas are still vague. He suddenly saw the bed and his mother in it, and his happy little face puckered up, till suddenly he began to scream furiously, and struggled as if he were going to be put to the torture.

In his astonishment his father said:

"There must be something the matter with the child," and mechanically he lifted up his little nightshirt.

He uttered a prolonged "O—o—h!" of astonishment. The child's calves, thighs, and buttocks were covered with blue spots as big as half-pennies.

"Just look, Matilda!" the father exclaimed; "this is horrible!" And the mother rushed forward in a fright. It was horrible; no doubt the beginning of some sort of leprosy, of one of those strange affections of the skin which doctors are often at a loss to account for. The parents looked at one another in consternation.

"We must send for the doctor," the father said.

But Matilda, pale as death, was looking at her child, who was spotted like a leopard. Then suddenly uttering a violent cry as if she had seen something that filled her with horror, she exclaimed:

"Oh! the wretch!"

In his astonishment M. Moreau asked: "What are you talking about? What wretch?"

She got red up to the roots of her hair, and stammered:

"Oh, nothing! but I think I can guess —it must be—we ought to send for the doctor. It must be that wretch of a nurse who has been pinching the poor child to make him keep quiet when he cries."

In his rage the lawyer sent for the nurse, and very nearly beat her. She denied it most impudently, but was instantly dismissed, and the Municipality having been informed of her conduct, she will find it a hard matter to get another situation.

A Fishing Excursion

PARIS was blockaded, desolate, famished. The sparrows were few, and anything that was to be had was good to eat.

On a bright morning in January, Mr. Morissot, a watchmaker by trade, but idler through circumstances, was walking along the boulevard, sad, hungry, with his hands in the pockets of his uniform trousers, when he came face to face with a brother-in-arms whom he recognized as an old-time friend.

Before the war, Morissot could be seen at daybreak every Sunday, trudging along with a cane in one hand and a tin box on his back. He would take the train to Colombes and walk from there to the Isle of Marante where he would fish until dark.

It was there he had met Mr. Sauvage who kept a little notion store in the Rue Notre Dame de Lorette, a jovial fellow and passionately fond of fishing like himself. A warm friendship had sprung up between these two and they would fish side by side all day, very often without saying a word. Some days, when everything looked fresh and new and the beautiful spring sun gladdened every heart, Mr. Morissot would exclaim:

"How delightful!" and Mr. Sauvage would answer:

"There is nothing to equal it."

Then again on a fall evening, when the glorious setting sun, spreading its golden mantle on the already tinted leaves, would throw strange shadows around the two friends, Sauvage would say:

"What a grand picture!"

"It beats the boulevard!" would answer Morissot. But they understood each other quite as well without speaking.

The two friends had greeted each other warmly and had resumed their walk side by side, both thinking deeply of the past and present events. They entered a *café,* and when a glass of absinthe had been placed before each Sauvage sighed:

"What terrible events, my friend!"

"And what weather!" said Morissot sadly; "this is the first nice day we have had this year. Do you remember our fishing excursions?"

"Do I! Alas! when shall we go again!"

After a second absinthe they emerged from the *café,* feeling rather dizzy—that light-headed effect which alcohol has on an empty stomach. The balmy air had made Sauvage exuberant and he exclaimed:

"Suppose we go!"

"Where?"

"Fishing."

"Fishing! Where?"

"To our old spot, to Colombes. The French soldiers are stationed near there and I know Colonel Dumoulin will give us a pass."

"It's a go; I am with you."

An hour after, having supplied themselves with their fishing tackle, they arrived at the colonel's villa. He had smiled at their request and had given them a pass in due form.

At about eleven o'clock they reached the advance-guard, and after presenting their pass, walked through Colombes and found themselves very near their destination. Argenteuil, across the way, and

the great plains toward Nanterre were all deserted. Solitary the hill of Orgemont and Sannois rose clearly above the plains; a splendid point of observation.

"See," said Sauvage pointing to the hills, "the Prussians are there."

Prussians! They had never seen one, but they knew that they were all around Paris, invisible and powerful; plundering, devastating, and slaughtering. To their superstitious terror they added a deep hatred for this unknown and victorious people.

"What if we should meet some?" said Morissot.

"We would ask them to join us," said Sauvage in true Parisian style.

Still they hesitated to advance. The silence frightened them. Finally Sauvage picked up courage.

"Come, let us go on cautiously."

They proceeded slowly, hiding behind bushes, looking anxiously on every side, listening to every sound. A bare strip of land had to be crossed before reaching the river. They started to run. At last, they reached the bank and sank into the bushes; breathless, but relieved.

Morissot thought he heard some one walking. He listened attentively, but no, he heard no sound. They were indeed alone! The little island shielded them from view. The house where the restaurant used to be seemed deserted; feeling reassured, they settled themselves for a good day's sport.

Sauvage caught the first fish, Morissot the second; and every minute they would bring one out which they would place in a net at their feet. It was indeed miraculous! They felt that supreme joy which one feels after having been deprived for months of a pleasant pastime. They had forgotton everything; even the war!

Suddenly, they heard a rumbling sound and the earth shook beneath them. It was the cannon on Mont Valérien. Morissot looked up and saw a trail of smoke, which was instantly followed by another explosion. Then they followed in quick succession.

"They are at it again," said Sauvage shrugging his shoulders. Morissot, who was naturally peaceful, felt a sudden, uncontrollable anger.

"Stupid fools! What pleasure can they find in killing each other!"

"They are worse than brutes!"

"It will always be thus as long as we have governments."

"Well, such is life!"

"You mean death!' said Morissot laughing.

They continued to discuss the different political problems, while the cannon on Mont Valérien sent death and desolation among the French.

Suddenly they started. They had heard a step behind them. They turned and beheld four big men in dark uniforms, with guns pointed right at them. Their fishng-lines dropped out of their hands and floated away with the current.

In a few minutes, the Prussian soldiers had bound them, cast them into a boat, and rowed across the river to the island which our friends had thought deserted. They soon found out their mistake when they reached the house, behind which stood a score or more of soldiers. A big burly officer, seated astride a chair, smoking an immense pipe, addressed them in excellent French:

"Well, gentlemen, have you made a good haul?'

Just then, a soldier deposited at his feet the net full of fish which he had taken care to take along with him. The officer smiled and said:

"I see you have done pretty well; but let us change the subject. You are evidently sent to spy upon me. You pretended to fish so as to put me off the scent, but I am not so simple. I have caught you and shall have you shot. I am sorry, but war is war. As you passed the advance-guard you certainly must have the password; give it to me, and I will set you free."

The two friends stood side by side, pale and slightly trembling, but they answered nothing.

"No one will ever know. You will go back home quietly and the secret will disappear with you. If you refuse, it is instant death! Choose!"

They remained motionless; silent. The Prussian officer calmly pointed to the river.

"In five minutes you will be at the bottom of this river! Surely, you have a family, friends waiting for you?"

Still they kept silent. The cannon rumbled incessantly. The officer gave orders in his own tongue, then moved his chair away from the prisoners. A squad of men advanced within twenty feet of them, ready for command.

"I give you one minute; not a second more!"

Suddenly approaching the two Frenchmen, he took Morissot aside and whispered:

"Quick; the password. Your friend

Will not know; he will think I changed my mind." Morissot said nothing.

Then taking Sauvage aside he asked him the same thing, but he also was silent. The officer gave further orders and the men leveled their guns. At that moment, Morissot's eyes rested on the net full of fish lying in the grass a few feet away. The sight made him faint and, though he struggled against it, his eyes filled with tears. Then turning to his friend:

"Farewell! Mr. Sauvage!"

"Farewell! Mr. Morissot."

They stood for a minute, hand in hand, trembling with emotion which they were unable to control.

"Fire!" commanded the officer.

The squad of men fired as one. Sauvage fell straight on his face. Morissot, who was taller, swayed, pivoted and fell across his friend's body his face to the sky; while blood flowed freely from the wound in the breast. The officer gave further orders and his men disappeared. They came back presently with ropes and stones, which they tied to the feet of the two friends, and four of them carried them to the edge of the river. They swung them and threw them in as far as they could. The bodies weighted by stones sank immediately. A splash, a few ripples and the water resumed its usual calmness. The only thing to be seen was a little blood floating on the surface. The officer calmly retraced his steps toward the house muttering:

"The fish will get even now."

He perceived the net full of fish, picked it up, smiled, and called:

"Wilhelm!"

A soldier in a white uniform approached. The officer handed him the fish saying:

"Fry these little things while they are still alive; they will make a delicious meal."

And having resumed his position on the chair, he puffed away at his pipe."

After

"MY DARLINGS," said the Comtesse, "you must go to bed."

The three children, two girls and a boy, rose up to kiss their grandmother.

Then they said "Good night" to M. le Curé, who had dined at the château, as he did every Thursday.

The Abbé Mauduit sat two of the young ones on his knees, passing his long arms clad in black behind the children's necks; and, drawing their heads toward him with a paternal movement, he kissed each of them on the forehead with a long, tender kiss.

Then, he again set them down on the floor, and the little beings went off, the boy in front, and the girls behind.

"You are fond of children, M. le Curé," said the Comtesse.

"Very fond, Madame."

The old woman raised her bright eyes toward the priest.

"And—has your solitude never weighed too heavily on you?"

"Yes, sometimes."

He became silent, hesitated, and then added: "But I was never made for ordinary life."

"What do you know about it?"

"Oh! I know very well. I was made to be a priest; I followed my own path."

The Comtesse kept staring at him: "Look here, M. le Curé, tell me this—tell me how it was that you resolved to renounce forever what makes us love life—the rest of us—all that consoles and sustains us? What is it that drove you, impelled you, to separate yourself from the great natural path of marriage and the family. You are neither an enthusiast nor a fanatic, neither a gloomy person nor a sad person. Was it some strange occurrence, some sorrow, that led you to take lifelong vows?"

The Abbé Mauduit rose up and drew near to the fire, stretching out to the flames the big shoes that country priests generally wear. He seemed still hesitating as to what reply he should make.

He was a tall old man with white hair, and for the last twenty years had been the pastor of the parish of Sainte-Antoine-du-Rocher. The peasants said of him, "There's a good man for you!" And indeed he was a good man, benevolent, friendly to all, gentle, and, to crown all, generous. Like Saint Martin, he had cut his cloak in two. He freely laughed, and wept too, for very little, just like a woman,—a thing that prejudiced him more or less in the hard minds of the country people.

The old Comtesse de Saville living in retirement in her château of Rocher,

in order to bring up her grandchildren, after successive deaths of her son and her daughter-in-law, was very much attached to the curé, and used to say of him. "He has a kind heart!"

The abbé came every Thursday to spend the evening at the château, and they were close friends, with the open and honest friendship of old people.

She persisted:

"Look here M. le Curé! 'tis your turn now to make a confession!"

He repeated: "I was not made for a life like everybody else. I saw it myself, fortunately, in time, and have had many proofs since that I made no mistake on that point.

"My parents, who were mercers in Vedriers, and rather rich, had much ambition on my account. They sent me to a boarding-school while I was very young. You cannot conceive what a boy may suffer at college, by the mere fact of separation, of isolation. This monotonous life without affection is good for some and detestable for others. Young people often have hearts more sensitive than one supposes, and by shutting them up thus too soon, far from those they love, we may develop to an excessive extent a sensibility which is of an overstrung kind, and which becomes sickly and dangerous.

"I scarcely ever played; I never had companions; I passed my hours in looking back to my home with regret; I spent the whole night weeping in my bed. I sought to bring up before my mind recollections of my own home, trifling recollections of little things, little events. I thought incessantly of all I had left behind there. I became almost imperceptibly an oversensitive youth, to whom the slightest annoyances were dreadful griefs.

"Together with this, I remained taciturn, self-absorbed, without expansion, without confidants. This work of mental exaltation was brought about obscurely but surely. The nerves of children are quickly excited; one ought to realize the fact that they live in a state of deep quiescence up to the time of almost complete development. But does anyone reflect that, for certain students, an unjust imposition can be as great a pang as the death of a friend afterward? Does anyone realize the fact that certain young souls have, with very little cause, terrible emotions, and are in a very short time diseased and incurable souls?

"This was my case. This faculty of regret developed itself in me in such a fashion that my existence became a martyrdom.

"I did not speak about it; I said nothing about it; but gradually I acquired a sensibility, or rather a sensitivity, so lively that my soul resembled a living wound. Everything that touched it produced in it twitchings of pain, frightful vibrations, and veritable ravages. Happy are the men whom nature has buttressed with indifference and cased in stoicism.

"I reached my sixteenth year. An excessive timidy had come to me from this aptitude to suffer on account of everything. Feeling myself unprotected against all the attacks of chance or fate, I feared every contact, every approach, every event. I lived on the watch as if under the constant threat of an unknown and always expected misfortune. I was afraid either to speak or to act publicly. I had, indeed, the sensation that life is a battle, a dreadful conflict in which one receives terrible blows, grievous, mortal wounds. In place of cherishing, like all men, the hope of good fortune on the morrow, I only kept a confused fear of it, and I felt in my own mind a desire to conceal myself—to avoid combat in which I should be vanquished and slain.

"As soon as my studies were finished, they gave me six months time to choose a career. Suddenly a very simple event made me see clearly into myself, showed me the diseased condition of my mind, made me understand the danger, and caused me to make up my mind to fly from it.

"Verdiers is a little town surrounded with plains and woods. In the central street stands my parents' house. I now passed my days far from this dwelling which I had so much regretted, so much desired. Dreams were awakened in me, and I walked all alone in the fields in order to let them escape and fly away. My father and my mother quite occupied with business, and anxious about my future, talked to me only about their profits or about my possible plans. They were fond of me in the way that hard-headed, practical people are; they had more reasons than heart in their affection for me. I lived imprisoned in my thoughts, and trembling with eternal uneasiness.

"Now, one evening, after a long walk, as I was making my way home with quick strides so as not to be late, I met a dog trotting toward me. He was a species of red spaniel, very lean, with long curly ears.

"When he was ten paces away from

me, he stopped. I did the same. Then he began wagging his tail, and came over to me with short steps and nervous movements of his whole body, going down on his paws as if appealing to me, and softly shaking his head. He then made a show of crawling with an air so humble, so sad, so suppliant, that I felt the tears coming into my eyes. I came near him; he ran away; then he came back again; and I bent down trying to coax him to approach me with soft words. At last, he was within reach and I gently caressed him with the most careful hands.

"He grew bold, rose up bit by bit, laid his paws on my shoulders, and began to lick my face. He followed me into the house.

"This was really the first being I had passionately loved, because he returned my affection. My attachment to this animal was certainly exaggerated and ridiculous. It seemed to me in a confused sort of way that we were brothers, lost on this earth, and therefore isolated and without defense, one as well as the other. He never quitted my side. He slept at the foot of my bed, ate at my table in spite of the objections of my parents, and followed me in my solitary walks.

"I often stopped at the side of a ditch, and I sat down in the grass. Sam would lie on my knees, and lift up my hand with the end of his nose so that I might caress him.

"One day toward the end of June, as we were on the road from Saint-Pierre-de-Chavrol, I saw the diligence from Pavereau coming along. Its four horses were going at a gallop. It had a yellow box-seat, and imperial crowned with black leather. The coachman cracked his whip; a cloud of dust rose up under the wheels of the heavy vehicle, then floated behind, just as a cloud would do.

"And, all of a sudden, as the vehicle came close to me, Sam, perhaps frightened by the noise and wishing to join me, jumped in front of it. A horse's foot knocked him down. I saw him rolling over, turning round, falling back again on all fours, and then the entire coach gave two big jolts and behind it I saw something quivering in the dust on the road. He was nearly cut in two; all his intestines were hanging through his stomach, which had been ripped open, and spurts of blood fell to the ground. He tried to get up, to walk, but he could only move his two front paws, and scratch the ground with them, as if to make a hole. The two others were already dead. And he howled dreadfully, mad with pain.

"He died in a few minutes. I cannot describe how much I felt and suffered. I was confined to my own room for a month.

"Now, one night my father, enraged at seeing me in such a state for so little, exclaimed:

"'How then will it be when you have real griefs, if you lose your wife or children?'

"And I began to see clearly into myself. I understood why all the small miseries of each day assumed in my eyes the importance of a catastrophe; I saw that I was organized in such a way that I suffered dreadfully from everything, that even painful impression was multiplied by my diseased sensibility, and an atrocious fear of life took possession of me. I was without passions, without ambitions; I resolved to sacrifice possible joys in order to avoid sorrows. Existence is short, but I made up my mind to spend it in the service of others, in relieving their troubles and enjoying their happiness. By having no direct experience of either one or the other, I would only be conscious of passionless emotions.

"And if you only knew how, in spite of this, misery tortures me, ravages me. But what would be for me an intolerable affliction has become commiseration, pity.

"The sorrows which I have every day to concern myself about I could not endure if they fell on my own heart. I could not have seen one of my children die without dying myself. And I have, in spite of everything, preserved such a deep and penetrating fear of circumstances that the sight of the postman entering my house makes a shiver pass every day through my veins, and yet I have nothing to be afraid of now."

The Abbé Mauduit ceased speaking.

He stared into the fire in the huge grate, as if he saw there mysterious things, all the unknown portions of existence which he would have been able to live if he had been more fearless in the face of suffering.

He added, then, in a subdued tone:

"I was right. I was not made for this world."

The Comtesse said nothing at first; but at length, after a long silence, she remarked:

"For my part, if I had not my grandchildren, I believe I would not have the courage to live."

And the Curé rose up without saying another word.

As the servants were asleep in the kitchen, she conducted him herself to the door which looked out on the garden, and she saw his tall shadow, revealed by the reflection of the lamp, disappearing through the gloom of night.

Then she came back, sat down before the fire, and pondered over many things on which we never think when we are young.

The Spasm

THE hotel-guests slowly entered the dining-room, and sat downn in their places. The waiters began to attend on them in a leisurely fashion so as to enable those who were late to arrive, and to avoid bringing back the dishes. The old bathers, the *habitués,* those whose season was advancing, gazed with interest toward the door, whenever it opened, with a desire to see new faces appearing.

This is the principal distraction of health resorts. People look forward to the dinner hour in order to inspect each day's new arrivals, to find out who they are, what they do, and what they think. A vague longing springs up in the mind, a longing for agreeable meetings, for pleasant acquaintances, perhaps for love-adventures. In this life of elbowings, strangers, as well as those with whom we have come into daily contact, assume an extreme importance. Curiosity is aroused, sympathy is ready to exhibit itself, and sociability is the order of the day.

We cherish antipathies for a week and friendships for a month; we see other people with different eyes, when we view them through the medium of the acquaintanceship that is brought about at health-resorts. We discover in men suddenly, after an hour's chat in the evening after dinner, or under the trees in the park where the generous spring bubbles up, a high intelligence and astonishing merits, and, a month afterward, we have completely forgotton these new friends, so fascinating when we first met them.

There also are formed lasting and serious ties more quickly than anywhere else. People see each other every day; they become acquainted very quickly; and with the affection thus originated is mingled something of the sweetness and self-abandonment of long-standing intimacies. We cherish in after years the dear and tender memories of those first hours of friendship, the memory of those first conversations through which we have been able to unveil a soul, of those first glances which interrogate and respond to the questions and secret thoughts which the mouth has not as yet uttered, the memory of that first cordial confidence, the memory of that delightful sensation of opening our hearts to those who are willing to open theirs to us.

And the melancholy of health-resorts, the monotony of days that are alike, help from hour to hour in this rapid development of affection.

*   *   *   *   *   *

Well, this evening, as on every other evening, we awaited the appearance of strange faces.

Only two appeared, but they were very remarkable looking, a man and a woman—father and daughter. They immediately produced the same effect on my mind as some of Edgar Poe's characters; and yet there was about them a charm, the charm associated with misfortune. I looked upon them as the victims of fatality. The man was very tall and thin, rather stooped, with hair perfectly white, too white for his comparatively youthful physiognomy; and there was in his bearing and in his person that austerity peculiar to Protestants. The daughter, who was probably twenty-four or twenty-five, was small in stature, and was also very thin, very pale, and had the air of one worn out with utter lassitude. We meet people like this from time to time, people who seem too weak for the tasks and the needs of daily life, too weak to move about, to walk, to do all that we do every day. This young girl was very pretty, with the diaphanous beauty of a phantom; and she ate with extreme slowness, is if she were almost incapable of moving her arms. It must have been she assuredly who had come to take the waters.

They found themselves facing me at the opposite side of the table; and I at once noticed that the father had a very singular nervous spasm. Every time he wanted to reach an object, his hand made a hook-like movement, a sort of irregular zigzag, before it succeeded in touching what it was in search of; and, after a little while, this action was so wearisome to me that I turned aside my head in order not to see it. I noticed, too, that the young girl, during meals, wore a glove on her left hand.

After dinner I went for a stroll in the park of the thermal establishment. This led toward the little Auvergnese station of Châtel Guyon, hidden in a gorge at the foot of the high mountain, of that mountain from which flow so many boiling springs, rising from the deep bed of extinct volcanoes. Over there, above us, the domes, which had once been craters, raised their mutilated heads on the summit of the long chain. For Châtel Guyon is situated at the spot where the region of domes begins. Beyond it stretches out the region of peaks, and, further on again, the region of precipices.

The Puy de Dôme is the highest of the domes, the Peak of Sancy is the loftiest of the peaks, and Cantal is the most precipitous of these mountain heights.

This evening it was very warm. I walked up and down a shady path, on the side of the mountain overlooking the park, listening to the opening strains of the Casino band. I saw the father and the daughter advancing slowly in my direction. I saluted them, as we are accustomed to salute our hotel-companions at health-resorts; and the man, coming to a sudden halt, said to me:

"Could you not, Monsieur, point out to us a short walk, nice and easy, if that is possible, and excuse my intrusion on you?"

I offered to show them the way toward the valley through which the little river flowed, a deep valley forming a gorge between two tall, craggy, wooded slopes. They gladly accepted my offer, and we talked naturally about the virtues of the waters.

"Oh!" he said, "my daughter has a strange malady, the seat of which is unknown. She suffers from incomprehensible nervous disorders. At one time, the docters think she has an attack of heart disease, at another time, they imagine it is some affection of the liver, and at another time they declare it to be a disease of the spine. To-day, her condition is attributed to the stomach, which is the great caldron and regulator of the body, the Protean source of diseases with a thousand forms and a thousand susceptibilities to attack. This is why we have come here. For my part, I am rather inclined to think it is the nerves, in any case it is very sad."

Immediately the remembrance of the violent spasmodic movement of his hand came back to my mind, and I asked him:

"But is this not the result of heredity? Are not your own nerves somewhat affected?"

"Mine? Oh! no—my nerves have always been very steady."

Then suddenly, after a pause, he went on:

"Ah! You are alluding to the spasm in my hand every time I want to reach for anything? This arises from a terrible experience which I had. Just imagine! this daughter of mine was actually buried alive!"

I could only give utterance to the word "Ah!" so great were my astonishment and emotion.

*   *   *   *   *   *

He continued:

"Here is the story. It is simple. Juliette had been subject for some time to serious attacks of the heart. We believed that she had disease of that organ and we were prepared for the worst.

"One day, she was carried into the house cold, lifeless, dead. She had fallen down unconcsious in the garden. The docter certified that life was extinct. I watched by her side for a day and two nights. I laid her with my own hands in the coffin, which I accompanied to the cemetery where she was deposited in the family vault. It is situated in the very heart of Lorraine.

"I wished to have her interred with her jewels, bracelets, necklaces, rings, all presents which she had got from me and with her first ball-dress on.

"You may easily imagine the state of mind in which I was when I returned home. She was the only companion I had, for my wife has been dead for many years. I found my way to my own apartment in a half-distracted condition, utterly exhausted, and I sank into my easy-chair, without the capacity to think or the strength to move. I was nothing better now than a suffering, vibrating machine, a human being who had, as it were, been flayed alive; my soul was like a living wound.

"My old valet Prosper, who had assisted me in placing Juliette in her coffin, and preparing her for her last

sleep, entered the room noiselessly, and asked:

" 'Does Monsieur want anything?'

"I merely shook my head, by way of answering 'No.'

"He urged: 'Monsieur is wrong. He will bring some illness on himself. Would Monsieur like me to put him to bed?'

"I answered: 'No! let me alone!' And he left the room.

"I know not how many hours slipped away. Oh! what a night, what a night! It was cold. My fire had died out in the huge grate; and the wind, the winter wind, an icy wind, a hurricane accompanied by frost and snow, kept blowing against the window with a sinister and regular noise.

"How many hours slipped away? There I was without sleeping, powerless, crushed, my eyes wide open, my legs stretched out, my body limp, inanimate, and my mind torpid with despair. Suddenly, the great bell of the entrance gate, the bell of the vestibule, rang out.

I got such a shock that my chair cracked under me. The solemn ponderous sound vibrated through the empty château as if through a vault. I turned round to see what the hour was by my clock. It was just two in the morning. Who could be coming at such at hour?

"And abruptly the bell again rang twice. The servants, without doubt, were afraid to get up. I took a wax-candle and descended the stairs. I was on the point of asking: 'Who is there?'

"Then, I felt ashamed of my weakness, and I slowly opened the huge door. My heart was throbbing wildly;

I was frightened; I hurriedly drew back the door, and in the darkness, I distinguished a white figure standing erect, something that resembled an apparition.

. "I recoiled, petrified with horror, faltering:

" 'Who—who—who are you?'

"A voice replied:

" 'It is I, father.'

"It was my daughter. I really thought I must be mad, and I retreated backward before this advancing specter. I kept moving away, making a sign with my hand, as if to drive the phantom away, that gesture which you have noticed,—that gesture of which since then I have never got rid.

"The apparition spoke again:

" 'Do not be afraid, papa; I was not dead. Somebody tried to steal my rings, and cut one of my fingers, the blood began to flow, and this reanimated me.'

And, in fact, I could see that her hand was covered with blood.

"I fell on my knees, choking with sobs and with a rattling in my throat.

"Then, when I had somewhat collected my thoughts, though I was still so much dismayed that I scarcely realized the gruesome good-fortune that had fallen to my lot, I made her go up to my room, and sit down in my easy-chair; then I rang excitedly for Prosper to get him to light up the fire again and to get her some wine and

summon the rest of the servants to her assistance.

"The man entered, stared at my daughter, opened his mouth with a gasp of alarm and stupefaction, and then fell back insensible.

"It was he who had opened the vault, and who had mutilated and then abandoned my daughter, for he could not efface the traces of the theft. He had not even taken the trouble to put back the coffin into its place, feeling sure, besides, that he would not be suspected by me, as I completely trusted him.

"You see, Monsieur, that we are very unhappy people."

* - * * * * *

He stopped.

The night had fallen, casting its shadows over the desolate, mournful vale, and a sort of mysterious fear possessed me at finding myself by the side of those strange beings, of this young girl who had come back from the tomb and this father with his uncanny spasm.

I found it impossible to make any comment on this dreadful story. I only murmured:

"What a horrible thing!"

Then, after a minute's silence, I added:

"Suppose we go back, I think it is getting cold."

And we made our way back to the hotel.

A Meeting

IT WAS all an accident, a pure accident. Tired of standing, Baron d'Etraille went—as all the Princess's rooms were open on that particular evening—into an empty bedroom, which appeared almost dark after coming out of the brilliantly-lighted drawing-rooms.

He looked round for a chair in which to have a doze, as he was sure his wife would not go away before daylight. As soon as he got inside the door he saw the big bed with its azure-and-gold hangings, in the middle of the great room, looking like a catafalque in which love was buried, for the Princess was no longer young. Behind it, a large bright spot looked like a lake seen at a distance from a window. It was a big looking-glass, which, discreetly covered with dark drapery very rarely let down, seemed to look at the bed, which was its accomplice. One might almost fancy that it felt regrets, and that one was going to see in it charming shapes of nude women and the gentle movement of arms about to embrace them.

The Baron stood still for a moment, smiling and rather moved, on the threshold of this chamber dedicated to love. But suddenly something appeared in the looking-glass, as if the phantoms which he had evoked had come up before him. A man and a woman who had been sitting on a low couch hidden in the shade had risen, and the polished surface, reflecting their figures, showed that they were kissing each other before separating.

The Baron recognized his wife and the Marquis de Cervigné. He turned and went away like a man fully master of himself, and waited till it was day before taking away the Baroness. But he had no longer any thoughts of sleeping.

As soon as they were alone, he said:

"Madame, I saw you just now in the Princess de Raynes's room. I need say no more, for I am not fond either of reproaches, acts of violence, or of ridicule. As I wish to avoid all such things, we shall separate without any scandal. Our lawyers will settle your position according to my orders. You will be free to live as you please when you are no longer under my roof; but, as you will continue to bear my name, I must warn you that should any scandal arise, I shall show myself inflexible.

She tried to speak, but he stopped her, bowed, and left the room.

He was more astonished and sad than unhappy. He had loved her dearly during the first period of their married life; but his ardor had cooled, and now he often had a caprice, either in a theater or in society, though he always preserved a certain liking for the Baroness.

She was very young, hardly four-and-twenty, small, slight,—too slight,—and very fair. She was a true Parisian doll: clever, spoiled, elegant, coquettish, witty, with more charm than real beauty. He used to say familiarly to his brother, when speaking of her:

"My wife is charming, attractive, but—there is nothing to lay hold of. She is like a glass of champagne that is all froth—when you have got to the wine it is very good, but there it too little of it, unfortunately."

He walked up and down the room in great agitation, thinking of a thousand things. At one moment he felt in a great rage and felt inclined to give the Marquis a good thrashing, to horsewhip him publicly in the club. But he thought that would not do, it would not be the thing; *he* would be laughed at, and not the other, and he felt that his anger proceeded more from wounded vanity than from a broken heart. So he went to bed, but could not get to sleep.

A few days afterward it was known in Paris that the Baron and Baroness d'Etraille had agreed to an amicable separation on account of incompatibility of temper. Nobody suspected anything, nobody laughed, and nobody was astonished.

The Baron, however, to avoid meeting her, traveled for a year; then he spent the summer at the seaside and the autumn in shooting, returning to Paris for the winter. He did not meet his wife once.

He did not even know what people said about her. At any rate, she took care to save appearances, and that was all he asked for.

He got dreadfully bored, traveled again, restored his old castle of Villebosc—which took him two years; then for over a year he received relays of friends there, till at last, tired of all these commonplace, so-called pleasures, he returned to his mansion in the Rue de Lills, just six years after their separation.

He was then forty-five, with a good crop of gray hair, rather stout, and with that melancholy look of people who have been handsome, sought after, much liked, and are deteriorating daily.

A month after his return to Paris he took cold on coming out of his club, and had a bad cough, so his medical man ordered him to Nice for the rest of the winter.

He started by the express on Monday evening. He was late, got to the station only a very short time before the departure of the train, and had barely time to get into a carriage, with only one other occupant, who was sitting in a corner so wrapped in furs and cloaks that he could not even make out whether it were a man or a woman, as nothing of the figure could be seen. When he perceived that he could not find out, he put on his traveling-cap, rolled himself up in his rugs, and stretched himself out comfortably to sleep.

He did not wake up till the day was breaking, and looked immediately at his fellow-traveler. He had not stirred all night, and seemed still to be sound asleep.

M. d'Etraille made use of the opportunity to brush his hair and his beard, and to try and freshen himself up a little generally, for a night's traveling changes one's looks very much when one has attained a certain age.

A great poet has said:

"When we are young, our mornings are triumphant!"

Then we wake up with a cool skin, a bright eye, and glossy hair. When one grows old one wakes up in a different state. Dull eyes, red, swollen cheeks, dry lips, the hair and beard all disarranged, impart an old, fatigued, worn-out look to the face.

The Baron opened his traveling dressing-case, made himself as tidy as he could, and then waited.

The engine whistled and the train stopped, and his neighbor moved. No doubt he was awake. They started off again, and then an oblique ray of the sun shone into the carriage just on to the sleeper, who moved again, shook himself, and then calmly showed his face.

It was a young, fair, pretty, stout woman, and the Baron looked at her in amazement. He did not know what to believe. He could have sworn that it was his wife—but wonderfully changed for the better: stouter—why, she had grown as stout as he was—only it suited her much better than it did him.

She looked at him quietly, did not seem to recognize him, and then slowly laid aside her wraps. She had that calm assurane of a woman who is sure of herself, the insolent audacity of a first awaking, knowing and feeling that she was in her full beauty and freshness.

The Baron really lost his head. Was it his wife, or somebody else who was as like her as any sister could be? As he had not seen her for six years he might be mistaken.

She yawned, and he knew her by the gesture. She turned and looked at him again, calmly, indifferently, as if she scarcely saw him, and then looked out at the country again.

He was upset and dreadfully per-plexed and waited, looking at her side-ways, steadfastly.

Yes; it was certainly his wife. How could he possibly have doubted? There could certainly not be two noses like that, and a thousand recollections flashed through him, slight details of her body, a beauty-spot on one of her limbs and another on her back. How often he had kissed them! He felt the old feeling of the intoxication of love stealing over him, and he called to mind the sweet odor of her skin, her smile when she put her arms on to his shoulders, the soft intonations of her voice, all her graceful, coaxing ways.

But how she had changed and improved! It was she and yet not she. He thought her riper, more developed, more of a woman, more seductive, more desirable, adorably desirable.

And this strange, unknown woman, whom he had accidently met in a railway-carriage belonged to him; he had only to say to her:

"I insist upon it."

He had formerly slept in her arms, existed only in her love, and now he had found her again certainly, but so changed that he scarcely knew her. It was another, and yet she at the same time. It was another who had been born, formed, and grown since he had left her. It was she, indeed; she whom he had possessed but who was now altered, with a more assured smile and greater self-possession. There were two women in one, mingling a great deal of what was new and unknown with many sweet recollections of the past. There was something singular, disturbing, exciting about it—a kind of mystery of love in which there floated a delicious confusion. It was his wife in a new body and in new flesh which his lips had never pressed.

And he remembered that in six or seven years everything changes in us, only outlines can be recognized, and sometimes even they disappear.

The blood, the hair, the skin, all change and are reconstituted and when people have not seen each other for a long time they find when they meet, another totally different being, although it be the same and bear the same name.

And the heart also can change. Ideas may be modified and renewed, so that in forty years of life we may, by gradual and constant transformations, become four or five totally new and different beings.

He dwelt on this thought till it troubled him; it had first taken possession of him when he surprised her in the Princess's room. He was not the least angry; it was not the same woman that he was looking at—that thin, excitable doll of those days.

What was he to do? How should he address her? and what could he say to her? Had she recognized him?

The train stopped again. He got up, bowed, and said: "Bertha, do you want anything I can bring you?"

She looked at him from head to foot, and answered, without showing the slightest surprise or confusion or anger, but with the most perfect indifference:

"I do not want anything—thank you."

He got out and walked up and down the platform in order to think, and, as it were, to recover his senses after a fall. What should he do now? If he got into another carriage it would look as if he were running away. Should he be polite or importunate? That would look as if he were asking for forgiveness. Should he speak as if he were her master? He would look like a fool, and besides, he really had no right to do so.

He got in again and took his place.

During his absence she had hastily arranged her dress and hair, and was now lying stretched out on the seat, radiant, but without showing any emotion.

He turned to her, and said: "My dear Bertha, since this singular chance has brought us together after a separation of six years—a quite friendly separation—are we to continue to look upon each other as irreconcilable enemies? We are shut up together, *tête-à-tête,* which is so much the better or so much the worse. I am not going to get into another carriage, so don't you think it is preferable to talk as friends till the end of our journey?"

She answered quite calmly again:

"Just as you please."

Then he suddenly stopped, really not knowing what to say; but as he had plenty of assurance, he sat down on the middle seat, and said:

"Well, I see I must pay my court to you; so much the better. It is, however, really a pleasure, for you are charming. You cannot imagine how you have improved in the last six years. I do not know any woman who could give me that delightful sensation which I experienced just now when you emerged from your wraps. I should really have thought such a change impossible."

Without moving her head or looking at him she said: "I cannot say the same with regard to you; you have certainly deteriorated a great deal."

He got red and confused, and then, with a smile of resignation, he said:

"You are rather hard."

"Why?" was her reply. "I am only stating facts. I don't suppose you intend to offer me your love? It must, therefore, be a matter of perfect indifference to you what I think about you. But I see it is a painful subject, so let us talk of something else. What have you been doing since I last saw you?"

He felt rather out of countenance, and stammered:

"I? I have traveled, shot, and grown old, as you see. And you?"

She said, quite calmly: "I have taken care of appearances as you ordered me."

He was very nearly saying something brutal, but he checked himself, and kissed his wife's hand:

"And I thank you," he said.

She was surprised. He was indeed strong and always master of himself.

He went on: "As you have acceded to my first request, shall we now talk without any bitterness?"

She made a little movement of surprise.

"Bitterness! I don't feel any; you are a complete stranger to me; I am only trying to keep up a difficult conversation."

He was still looking at her, carried away in spite of her harshness, and he felt seized with a brutal desire, the desire of the master.

Perceiving that she had hurt his feelings, she said:

"How old are you now? I thought you were younger than you look."

He grew pale:

"I am forty-five;" and then he added: "I forgot to ask after Princess de Raynes. Are you still intimate with her?"

She looked at him as if she hated him:

"Yes, certainly I am. She is very well, thank you."

They remained sitting side by side, agitated and irritated. Suddenly he said:

"My dear Bertha, I have changed my mind. You are my wife, and I expect you to come with me to-day. You have, I think, improved both morally and physically, and I am going to take you back again. I am your husband and it is my right to do so."

She was stupefied, and looked at him, trying to divine his thoughts; but his face was resolute and impenetrable.

"I am very sorry," she said, "but I have made other engagements."

"So much the worse for you," was his reply. "The law gives me the power, and I mean to use it."

They were getting to Marseilles, and the train whistled and slackened speed. The Baroness got up, carefully rolled up her wraps, and then turning to her husband, she said:

"My dear Raymond, do not make a bad use of the *tête-à-tête* which I had carefully prepared. I wished to take precautions, according to your advice, so that I might have nothing to fear from you or from other people, whatever might happen. You are going to Nice, are you not?"

"I shall go wherever you go."

"Not at all; just listen to me, and I am sure that you will leave me in peace. In a few moments, when we get to the station, you will see the Princess de Raynes and Countess Hermit waiting for me with their husbands. I wished them to see us, and to know that we spent the night together in the railway-carriage. Dont be alarmed; they will tell it everywhere as a most surprising fact.

"I told you just now that I had carefully followed your advice and saved appearances. Anything else does not matter, does it? Well, in order to do so, I wished to be seen with you. You told me carefully to avoid any scandal, and I am avoiding it, for, I am afraid —I am afraid—"

She waited till the train had quite stopped, and as her friends ran up to open the carriage door, she said:

"I am afraid that I am *enceinte*."

The Princess stretched out her arms to embrace her, and the Baroness said, pointing to the Baron, who was dumb with astonishment, and trying to get at the truth:

"You do not recognize Raymond? He has certainly changed a good deal and he agreed to come with me so that I might not travel alone. We take little trips like this occasionally, like good friends who cannot live together. We are going to separate here; he has had enough of me already."

She put out her hand, which he took mechanically, and then she jumped out on to the platform among her friends, who were waiting for her.

The Baron hastily shut the carriage door, for he was too much disturbed to say a word or come to any determination. He heard his wife's voice, and their merry laughter as they went away.

He never saw her again, nor did he ever discover whether she had told him a lie or was speaking the truth.

A New Year's Gift

JACQUES DE RANDAL, having dined at home alone, told his valet he might go, and then sat down at a table to write his letters.

He finished out every year by writing and dreaming, making for himself a sort of review of things that had happened since last New Year's Day, things that were now all over and dead; and, in proportion as the faces of his friends rose up before his eyes, he wrote them

a few lines, a cordial "Good morning" on the first of January.

So he sat down, opened a drawer, took out of it a woman's photograph, gazed at it a few moments, and kissed it. Then, having laid it beside a sheet of note-paper, he began:

"MY DEAR IRÈNE: You must have by this time the little souvenir which I sent you. I have shut myself up this evening in order to tell you—"

The pen here ceased to move. Jacques rose up and began walking up and down the room.

For the last six months he had a mistress, not a mistress like the others, a woman with whom one engages in a passing intrigue, of the theatrical world or the *demi-monde,* but a woman whom he loved and won. He was no longer a young man, although still comparatively young, and he looked on life seriously in a positive and practical spirit.

Accordingly, he drew up the balance-sheet of his passion, as he drew up every year the balance-sheet of friendships that were ended or freshly contracted, of circumstances and persons that had entered his life. His first ardor of love having grown calmer, he asked himself, with the precision of a merchant making a calculation, what was the state of his heart with regard to her, and he tried to form an idea of what it would be in the future. He found there a great and deep affection, made up of tenderness, gratitude, and the thousand subtleties which give birth to long and powerful attachments.

A ring of the bell made him start. He hesitated. Should he open? But he deemed it was his duty to open, on this New Year's night, to the Unknown who knocks while passing, no matter whom it may be.

So he took a wax-candle, passed through the ante-chamber, removed the bolts, turned the key, drew the door back, and saw his mistress standing pale as a corpse leaning against the wall.

He stammered: "What is the matter with you?"

She replied: "Are you alone?"

"Yes."

"Without servants?"

"Yes."

"You are not going out?"

"No."

She entered with the air of a woman who knew the house. As soon as she was in the drawing-room, she sank into the sofa, and, covering her face with her hands, began to weep dreadfully.

He kneeled down at her feet, seized hold of her hands to remove them from her eyes, so that he might look at them, and exclaimed:

"Irène, Irène, what is the matter with you? I implore of you to tell me what is the matter with you?"

Then in the midst of her sobs she murmured: "I can no longer live like this."

He did not understand.

"Like this? What do you mean?"

"Yes. I can no longer live like this. I have endured so much. He struck me this afternoon."

"Who—your husband?"

"Yes—my husband."

"Ha!"

He was astonished, having never suspected that her husband could be brutal. He was a man of the world, of the better class, a clubman, a lover of horses, a theater-goer and an expert swordsman; he was known, talked about, appreciated everywhere, having very courteous manners but a very mediocre intellect, an absence of education and of the real culture needed in order to think like all well-bred people, and finally a respect for all conventional prejudices.

He appeared to devote himself to his wife, as a man ought to do in the case of wealthy and well-bred people. He displayed enough anxiety about her wishes, her health, her dresses, and, beyond that, left her perfectly free.

Randal, having become Irène's friend, had a right to the affectionate handclasp which every husband endowed with good manners owes to his wife's intimate acquaintances. Then, when Jacques, after having been for some time the friend, became the lover, his relations with the husband were more cordial.

Jacques had never dreamed that there were storms in this household, and he was scared at this unexpected revelation.

He asked.

"How did it happen? Tell me."

Thereupon she related a long history, the entire history of her life, since the day of her marriage—the first discussion arising out of a mere nothing, then accentuating itself in the estrangement which grows up each day between two opposite types of character.

Then came quarrels, a complete separation, not apparent, but real; next, her husband showed himself aggressive, suspicious, violent. Now, he was jealous, jealous of Jacques, and this day even, after a scene, he had struck her.

She added with decision: "I will not go back to him. Do with me what you like."

Jacques sat down opposite to her, their knees touching each other. He caught hold of her hands:

"My dear love, you are going to commit a gross, an irreparable folly. If you want to quit your husband, put wrongs on one side, so that your situation as a woman of the world may be saved."

She asked, as she cast at him a restless glance:

"Then, what do you advise me?"

"To go back home, and to put up with your life there till the day when you can obtain either a separation or a divorce, with the honors of war."

"Is not this thing which you advise me to do a little cowardly?"

"No; it is wise and reasonable. You have a high position, a reputation to safeguard, friends to preserve, and relations to deal with. You must not lose all these through a mere caprice."

She rose up, and said with violence:

"Well, no! I cannot have any more of it! It is at an end! it is at an end!"

Then, placing her two hands on her lover's shoulders and looking at him straight in the face, she asked:

"Do you love me?"

"Yes."

"Really and truly?"

"Yes."

"Then keep me!"

He exclaimed:

"Keep you? In my own house? Here? Why, you are mad. It would mean losing you forever; losing you beyond hope of recall! You are mad!"

She replied, slowly and seriously, like a woman who feels the weight of her words:

"Listen, Jacques. He has forbidden me to see you again, and I will not play this comedy of coming secretly to your house. You must either lose me or take me."

"My dear Irène, in that case, obtain your divorce, and I will marry you."

"Yes, you will marry me in—two years at the soonest. Yours is a patient love."

"Look here! Reflect! If you remain here, he'll come to-morrow to take you away, seeing that he is your husband, seeing that he has right and law on his side."

"I did not ask you to keep me in your own house, Jacques, but to take me anywhere you like. I thought you loved me enough to do that. I have made a mistake. Good-bye!"

She turned round, and went toward the door so quickly that he was only able to catch hold of her when she was outside the room.

"Listen, Irène."

She struggled, and did not want to listen to him any longer, her eyes full of tears, and with these words only on her lips:

"Let me alone! let me alone! let me alone!"

He made her sit down by force, and falling once more on his knees at her feet, he now brought forward a number of arguments and counsels to make her understand the folly and terrible risk of her project. He omitted nothing which he deemed it necessary to say to convince her, finding in his very affection for her strong motives of persuasion.

As she remained silent and cold, he begged of her, implored of her to listen to him, to trust him, to follow his advice.

When he had finished speaking, she only replied:

"Are you disposed to let me go away now? Take away your hands, so that I may rise up."

"Look here, Irène."

"Will you let go?"

"Irène—is your resolution irrevocable?"

"Do let me go."

"Tell me only whether this resolution, this foolish resolution of yours, which you will bitterly regret, is irrevocable?"

"Yes: let me go!"

"Then stay. You know well that you are at home here. We shall go away to-morrow morning."

She rose up, in spite of him, and said in a hard tone:

"No. It is too late. I do not want sacrifice; I want devotion."

"Stay! I have done what I ought to do; I have said what I ought to say. I have no further responsibility on your behalf. My conscience is at peace. Tell me what you want me to do, and I will obey."

She resumed her seat, looked at him for a long time, and then asked, in a very calm voice:

"Explain, then."

"How is that? What do you wish me to explain?"

"Everything—everything that you have thought about before coming to this resolution. Then I will see what I ought to do."

"But I have thought about nothing at all. I ought to warn you that you are going to accomplish an act of folly. You persist; then I ask to share in this act of folly, and I even insist on it."

"It is not natural to change one's opinion so quickly."

"Listen, my dear love. It is not a question here of sacrifice or devotion. On the day when I realized that I loved you, I said this to myself, which every lover ought to say to himself in the same case: 'The man who loves a woman, who makes an effort to win her, who gets her and who takes her contracts so far as he is himself and so far as she is concerned, a sacred engagement.' It is, mark you, a question of dealing with a woman like you, and not with a woman of an impulsive and yielding disposition.

"Marriage, which has a great social value, a great legal value, possesses in my eyes only a very slight moral value, taking into account the conditions under which it generally takes place.

"Therefore, when a woman, united by this lawful bond, but having no attachment to a husband whom she cannot love, a woman whose heart is free, meets a man for whom she cares, and gives herself to him, when a man who has no other tie takes a woman in this way, I say that they pledge themselves toward each other by this mutual and free agreement much more than by the 'Yes' uttered in the presence of the Mayor.

"I say that, if they are both honorable persons, their union must be more intimate, more real, more healthy than if all the sacraments had consecrated it.

"This woman risks everything. And it is exactly because she knows it, because she gives everything, her heart, her body, her soul, her honor, her life, because she has foreseen all miseries, all dangers, all catastrophes, because she dares to do a bold act, an intrepid act, because she is prepared, determined to brave everything—her husband who might kill her, and society which may cast her out. This is why she is heroic in her conjugal infidelity; this is why her lover in taking her must also have foreseen everything, and preferred her to everything, whatever might happen. I have nothing more to say. I spoke in the beginning like a man of sense whose duty it was to warn you; and now there is left in me only one man—the man who loves you. Say, then, what I am to do!"

Radiant, she closed his mouth with her lips, and said to him in a low tone:

"It is not true, darling! There is nothing the matter! My husband does not suspect anything. But I wanted to see, I wanted to know, what you would do. I wished for a New Year's gift—the gift of your heart—another gift besides the necklace you have just sent me. You have given it to me. Thanks! thanks! God be thanked for the happiness you have given me!"

My Uncle Sosthenes

My uncle Sosthenes was a Freethinker, like many others are, from pure stupidity, people are very often religious in the same way. The mere sight of a priest threw him into a violent rage; he would shake his fist and grimace at him, and touch a piece of iron when the priest's back was turned, forgetting that the latter action showed a belief after all, the belief in the evil eye.

Now when beliefs are unreasonable

one should have all or none at all. I myself am a Freethinker; I revolt at all the dogmas which have invented the fear of death, but I feel no anger toward places of worship, be they Catholic Apostolic, Roman, Protestant, Greek, Russian, Buddhist, Jewish, or Mohammedan. I have a peculiar manner of looking at them and explaining them. A place of worship represents the homage paid by man to "The Unknown." The more extended our thoughts and our views become the more The Unknown diminishes, and the more places of worship will decay. I, however, in the place of church furniture, in the place of pulpits, reading desks, altars, and so on, would fit them up with telescopes, microscopes, and electrical machines; that is all.

My uncle and I differed on nearly every point. He was a patriot, while I was not—for after all patriotism is a kind of religion; it is the egg from which wars are hatched.

My uncle was a Freemason, and I used to declare that they are stupider than old women devotees. That is my opinion, and I maintain it; if we must have any religion at all the old one is good enough for me.

What is their object? Mutual help to be obtained by tickling the palms of each other's hands. I see no harm in it, for they put into practice the Christian precept: "Do unto others as ye would they should do unto you." The only difference consists in the tickling, but it does not seem worth while to make such a fuss about lending a poor devil half-a-crown.

To all my arguments my uncle's reply used to be:

"We are raising up a religion against a religion; Freethought will kill clericalism. Freemasonry is the headquarters of those who are demolishing all deities."

"Very well, my dear uncle," I would reply (in my heart I felt inclined to say, "You old idiot!"); "it is just that which I am blaming you for. Instead of destroying, you are organizing competition; it is only a case of lowering the prices. And then, if you only admitted Freethinkers among you I could understand it, but you admit anybody. You have a number of Catholics among you, even the leaders of the party. Pius IX. is said to have been one of you before he became Pope. If you call a society with such an organization a bulwark against clericalism, I think it is an extremely weak one."

"My dear boy," my uncle would reply, with a wink, "our most formidable actions are political; slowly and surely we are everywhere undermining the monarchical spirit."

Then I broke out: "Yes, you are very clever! If you tell me that Freemasonry is an election-machine, I will grant it you. I will never deny that it is used as a machine to control candidates of all shades; if you say that it is only used to hoodwink people, to drill them to go to the voting-urn as soldiers are sent under fire, I agree with you; if you declare that it is indispensable to all political ambitions because it changes all its members into electoral agents, I should say to you, 'That is as clear as the sun.' But when you tell me that it serves to undermine the monarchical spirit, I can only laugh in your face.

"Just consider that vast and demo-cratic association which had Prince Napoleon for its Grand Master under the Empire; which has the Crown Prince for its Grand Master in Germany, the Czar's brother in Russia, and to which the Prince of Wales and King Humbert and nearly all the royalists of the globe belong."

"You are quite right," my uncle said; "but all these persons are serving our projects without guessing it."

I felt inclined to tell him he was talking a pack of nonsense.

It was, however, indeed a sight to see my uncle when he had a Freemason to dinner.

On meeting they shook hands in a manner that was irresistibly funny; one could see that they were going through a series of secret mysterious pressures. When I wished to put my uncle in a rage, I had only to tell him that dogs also have a manner which savors very much of Freemasonry, when they greet one another on meeting.

Then my uncle would take his friend into a corner to tell him something important, and at dinner they had a peculiar way of looking at each other, and of drinking to each other, in a manner as if to say: "We know all about it, don't we?"

And to think that there are millions on the face of the globe who are amused at such monkey tricks! I would sooner be a Jesuit.

Now in our town there really was an old Jesuit who was my uncle's detesta-tion. Every time he met him, or if he only saw him at a distance, he used to say: "Go on, you toad!" And then, taking my arm, he would whisper to me:

"Look here, that fellow will play me a trick some day or other, I feel sure of it."

My uncle spoke quite truly, and this was how it happened, through my fault also.

It was close on Holy Week, and my uncle made up his mind to give a dinner on Good Friday, a real dinner with his favorite chitterlings and black puddings. I resisted as much as I could, and said:

"I shall eat meat on that day, but at home, quite by myself. Your *manifes-tation,* as you call it, is an idiotic idea. Why should you manifest? What does it matter to you if people do not eat any meat?"

But my uncle would not be persuaded. He asked three of his friends to dine with him at one of the best restaurants in the town, and as he was going to pay the bill, I had certainly, after all, no scruples about *manifesting.*

At four o'clock we took a conspicuous place in the most frequented restaurant in the town, and my uncle ordered dinner in a loud voice, for six o'clock.

We sat down punctually, and at ten o'clock we had not finished. Five of us had drunk eighteen bottles of fine still wines, and four of champagne. Then my uncle proposed what he was in the habit of calling: "The archbishop's feat." Each man put six small glasses in front of him, each of them filled with a different liqueur, and then they had all to be emptied at one gulp, one after another, while one of the waiters counted twenty. It was very stupid, but my uncle thought it was very suit-able to the occasion.

At eleven o'clock he was dead drunk. So we had to take him home in a cab and put him to bed, and one could easily foresee that his anti-clerical demonstration would end in a terrible fit of indigestion.

As·I was going back to my lodgings, being rather drunk myself, with a cheerful Machiavelian drunkenness which quite satisfied all my instincts of scepticism, an idea struck me.

I arranged my necktie, put on a look of great distress, and went and rang loudly at the old Jesuit's door. As he was deaf he made me wait a longish while, but at length he appeared at his window in a cotton nightcap and asked what I wanted.

I shouted out at the top of my voice:

"Make haste, reverend Sir, and open the door; a poor, despairing, sick man is in need of your spiritual ministrations."

The good, kind man put on his trousers as quickly as he could and came down without his cassock. I told him in a breathless voice that my uncle, the Freethinker, had been taken suddenly ill. Fearing it was going to be something serious he had been seized with a sudden fear of death, and wished to see a priest and talk to him; to have his advice and comfort, to make up with the Church, and to confess, so as to be able to cross the dreaded threshold at peace with himself; and I added in a mocking tone:

"At any rate, he wishes it, and if it does him no good it can do him no harm."

The old Jesuit, who was startled, delighted, and almost trembling, said to me:

"Wait a moment, my son, I will come with you."

But I replied: "Pardon me, reverend Father, if I do not go with you; but my convictions will not allow me to do so. I even refused to come and fetch you, so I beg you not to say that you have seen me, but to declare that you had a presentiment—a sort of revelation of his illness."

The priest consented, and went off quickly, knocked at my uncle's door, was soon let in, and I saw the black cassock disappear within that stronghold of Freethought.

I hid under a neighboring gateway to wait for events. Had he been well, my uncle would have half murdered the Jesuit, but I know that he would scarcely be able to move an arm, and I asked myself, gleefully, what sort of a scene would take place between these antagonists—what explanation would be given, and what would be the issue of this situation, which my uncle's indignation would render more tragic still?

I laughed till I had to hold my sides, and said to myself, half aloud: "Oh! what a joke, what a joke!"

Meanwhile it was getting very cold. I noticed that the Jesuit stayed a long time, and thought: "They are having an explanation, I suppose."

One, two, three hours passed, and still the reverend Father did not come out. What had happened? Had my uncle died in a fit when he saw him, or had he killed the cassocked gentleman? Perhaps they had mutually devoured each other? This last supposition appeared very unlikely, for I fancied that my uncle was quite incapable of swallowing a grain more nourishment at that moment.

At last the day broke. I was very

uneasy, and, not venturing to go into the house myself, I went to one of my friends who lived opposite. I roused him, explained matters to him, much to his amusement and astonishment, and took possession of his window.

At nine o'clock he relieved me and I got a little sleep. At two o'clock I, in my turn, replaced him. We were utterly astonished.

At six o'clock the Jesuit left, with a very happy and satisfied look on his face, and we saw him go away with a quiet step.

Then, timid and ashamed, I went and knocked at my uncle's door. When the servant opened it I did not dare to ask her any questions, but went upstairs without saying a word.

My uncle was lying pale, exhausted, with weary, sorrowful eyes and heavy arms, on his bed. A little religious picture was fastened to one of the bed-curtains with a pin.

"Why, uncle," I said, "you in bed still? Are you not well?"

He replied in a feeble voice:

"Oh! my dear boy, I have been very ill; nearly dead."

"How was that, uncle?"

"I don't know; it was most surprising. But what is stranger still is, that the Jesuit priest who has just left—you know, that excellent man whom I have made such fun of—had a divine revelation of my state, and came to see me."

I was seized with an almost uncontrollable desire to laugh, and with difficulty said: "Oh, really!"

"Yes, he came. He heard a Voice telling him to get up and come to me, because I was going to die. It was a revelation."

I pretended to sneeze, so as not to burst out laughing; I felt inclined to roll on the ground with amusement.

In about a minute I managed to say, indignantly: "And you received him, uncle, you? You, a Freethinker, a Freemason? You did not have him thrown out-of-doors?"

He seemed confused, and stammered:

"Listen a moment, it is so astonishing —so astonishing and providential! He also spoke to me about my father; it seems he knew him formerly."

"Your father, uncle? But that is no reason for receiving a Jesuit."

"I know that, but I was very ill, and he looked after me most devotedly all night long. He was perfect; no doubt he saved my life; those men are all more or less doctors."

"Oh! he looked after you all night? But you said just now that he had only been gone a very short time."

"That is quite true; I kept him to breakfast after all his kindness. He had it at a table by my bedside while I drank a cup of tea."

"And he ate meat?"

My uncle looked vexed, as if I had said something very much out of place, and then added:

"Don't joke, Gaston; such things are out of place at times. He has shown me more devotion than many a relation would have done and I expect to have his convictions respected."

This rather upset me, but I answered, nevertheless: "Very well, uncle; and what did you do after breakfast?"

"We played a game of bézique, and then he repeated his breviary while I read a little book which he happened to have in his pocket, and which was not by any means badly written."

"A religious book, uncle?"

"Yes, and no, or rather—no. It is the history of their missions in Central Africa, and is rather a book of travels and adventures. What these men have done is very grand."

I began to feel that matters were going badly, so I got up: "Well, good-bye, uncle," I said, "I see you are going to leave Freemasonry for religion; you are a renegade."

He was still rather confused and stammered:

"Well, but religion is a sort of Free-masonry."

"When is your Jesuit coming back?" I asked.

"I don't—I don't know exactly; to-morrow, perhaps; but it is not certain."

I went out, altogether overwhelmed. My joke turned out very badly for me! My uncle became radically converted, and if that had been all I should not have cared so much. Clerical or Freemason, to me it is all the same; six of one and half-a-dozen of the other; but the worst of it is that he has just made his will—yes, made his will—and has disinherited me in favor of that rascally Jesuit!

All Over ✕

THE Comte de Lormerin had just finished dressing himself. He cast a parting glance at the large glass, which occupied an entire panel of his dressing-room, and smiled.

He was really a fine-looking man still, though he was quite gray. Tall, slight, elegant, with no projecting paunch, with a scanty mustache of doubtful shade on his thin face which seemed fair rather than white, he had presence, that "chic," in short, that indescribable something which establishes between two men more difference than millions of dollars.

He murmured: "Lormerin is still alive!"

And he made his way into the drawing-room, where his correspondence awaited him.

On his table, where everything had its place, the work-table of the gentleman who never works, there were a dozen letters lying beside three newspapers of different opinions. With a single touch of the finger he exposed to view all these letters, like a gambler giving the choice of a card; and he scanned the handwriting—a thing he did each morning before tearing open the envelopes.

It was for him a moment of delightful expectancy, of inquiry, and vague anxiety. What did these sealed mysterious papers bring him? What did they contain of pleasure, of happiness, or of grief? He surveyed them with a rapid sweep of the eye, recognizing in each case the hand that wrote them, selecting them, making two or three lots, according to what he expected from them. Here, friends; there, persons to whom he was indifferent; further on, strangers. The last kind always gave him a little uneasiness. What did they want from him? What hand had traced those curious characters full of thoughts, promises, or threats?

This day, one letter in particular caught his eye. It was simple nevertheless, without seeming to reveal anything; but he regarded it with disquietude, with a sort of internal shiver.

He thought: "From whom can it be? I certainly know this writing, and yet I can't identify it."

He raised it to a level with his face, holding it delicately between two fingers, striving to read through the envelope without making up his mind to open it.

Then he smelled it, and snatched up from the table a little magnifying glass which he used in studying all the niceties of handwriting. He suddenly felt unnerved. "Whom is it from? This hand is familiar to me, very familiar. I must have often read its prosings, yes, very often. But this must have been a long, long time ago. Who the deuce can it be from? Pooh! 'tis only from somebody asking for money."

And he tore open the letter. Then he read:

"MY DEAR FRIEND: You have, without doubt, forgotten me, for it is now twenty-five years since we saw each other. I was young; I am old. When I bade you farewell, I quitted Paris in order to follow into the provinces my husband, my old husband, whom you used to call 'my hospital.' Do you remember him? He died five years ago; and now I am returning to Paris to get my daughter married, for I have a daughter, a beautiful girl of eighteen, whom you have never seen. I informed you about her entrance into the world,

but you certainly did not pay much attention to so trifling an event.

"You, you are always the handsome Lormerin; so I have been told. Well, if you still recollect Lise, whom you used to call 'Lison,' come and dine this evening with her, with the elderly Baronne de Vance, your ever faithful friend, who, with some emotion, stretches out to you, without complaining at her lot, a devoted hand, which you must clasp but no longer kiss, my poor 'Jaquelet.'

"LISE DE VANCE."

Lormerin's heart began to throb. He remained sunk in his armchair, with the letter on his knees, staring straight before him, overcome by poignant feelings that made the tears mount up to his eyes!

If he had ever loved a woman in his life, it was this one, little Lise, Lise de Vance, whom he called "Cinder-Flower" on account of the strange odor of her hair, and the pale gray of her eyes. Oh! what a fine, pretty, charming creature she was, this frail Baronne, the wife of that old, gouty, pimply Baron who had abruptly carried her off to the provinces, shut her up, kept her apart through jealousy, through jealousy of the handsome Lormerin.

Yes, he had loved her, and he believed that he, too, had been truly loved. She gave him the name of Jaquelet, and used to pronounce the word in an exquisite fashion.

A thousand memories that had been effaced came back to him, far off and sweet and melancholy now. One evening, she called on him on her way home from a ball, and they went out for a stroll in the Bois de Boulogne, she in evening dress, he in his dressing-jacket. It was springtime; the weather was beautiful. The odor of her bodice embalmed the warm air,—the odor of her bodice, and also a little, the odor of her skin. What a divine night! When they reached the lake, as the moon's rays fell across the branches into the water, she began to weep. A little surprised, he asked her why.

She replied:

"I don't know. 'Tis the moon and the water that have affected me. Every time I see poetic things they seize hold of my heart and I have to cry."

He smiled, moved himself, considering her feminine emotion charming—the emotion of a poor little woman whom every sensation overwhelms. And he embraced her passionately, stammering:

"My little Lise, you are exquisite."

What a charming love affair, short-lived and dainty it had been, and all over too so quickly, cut short in the midst of its ardor by this old brute of a Baron, who had carried off his wife, and never shown her afterward to anyone!

Lormerin had forgotten, in good sooth, at the end of two or three months. One woman drives out the other so quickly in Paris, when one is a bachelor! No matter! he had kept a little chapel for her in his heart, for he had loved her alone! He assured himself now that this was so.

He rose up, and said aloud: "Certainly, I will go and dine with her this evening!"

And instinctively he turned round toward the glass in order to inspect himself from head to foot. He reflected: "She must have grown old unpleasantly, more than I have!" And he felt gratified at the thought of showing himself to her still handsome, still fresh, of

astonishing her, perhaps of filling her with emotion, and making her regret those bygone days so far, far distant!

He turned his attention to the other letters. They were not of importance.

The whole day, he kept thinking of this phantom. What was she like now? How funny it was to meet in this way after twenty-five years! Would he alone recognize her?

He made his toilette with feminine coquetry, put on a white waistcoat, which suited him better, with the coat, sent for the hairdresser to give him a finishing touch with the curling-iron, for he had preserved his hair, and started very early in order to show his eagerness to see her.

The first thing he saw on entering a pretty drawing-room, freshly furnished, was his own portrait, an old, faded photograph, dating from the days of his good-fortune, hanging on the wall in an antique silk frame.

He sat down, and waited. A door opened behind him. He rose up abruptly, and, turning round, beheld an old woman with white hair who extended both hands toward him.

He seized them, kissed them one after the other with long, long kisses, then, lifting up his head, he gazed at the woman he had loved.

Yes, it was an old lady, an old lady whom he did not recognize. and who, while she smiled, seemed ready to weep.

He could not abstain from murmuring:

"It is you, Lise?"

She replied:

"Yes, it is I; it is I, indeed. You would not have known me, isn't that so? I have had so much sorrow—so much sorrow. Sorrow has consumed my life.

Look at me now—or rather don't look at me! But how handsome you have kept —and young! If I had by chance met you in the street, I would have cried, 'Jaquelet!' Now sit down and let us, first of all, have a chat. And then I'll show you my daughter, my grown-up daughter. You'll see how she resembles me—or rather how I resembled her— no, it is not quite that: she is just like the 'me' of former days—you shall see! But I wanted to be alone with you first. I feared that there would be some emotion on my side, at the first moment. Now it is all over—it is past. Pray be seated, my friend."

He sat down beside her, holding her hand; but he did not know what to say; he did not know this woman—it seemed to him that he had never seen her before. What had he come to do in this house? Of what could he speak? Of the long ago? What was there in common between him and her? He could no longer recall anything to mind in the presence of this grandmotherly face. He could no longer recall to mind all the nice, tender things so sweet, so bitter, that had assailed his heart, some time since, when he thought of the other, of little Lise, of the dainty Cinder-Flower. What then had become of her, the former one, the one he had loved—that woman of far-off dreams, the blonde with gray eyes, the young one who used to call him Jaquelet so prettily?

They remained side by side, motionless, both constrained, troubled, profoundly ill at ease.

As they only talked in commonplace phrases, broken and slow, she rose up and pressed the button of the bell.

"I am going to call Renée," she said.

There was a tap at the door, then the rustle of a dress; next, a young voice exclaimed:

"Here I am, mamma!"

Lormerin remained scared, as if at the sight of an apparition.

He stammered:

"Good day, Mademoiselle."

Then, turning toward the mother:

"Oh! it is you!"

In fact, it was she, she whom he had known in bygone days, the Lise who had vanished and came back! In her he found the woman he had won twenty-five years before. This one was even younger still, fresher, more childlike.

He felt a wild desire to open his arms, to clasp her to his heart again, murmuring in her ear:

"Good day, Lison!"

A man-servant announced: "Dinner is ready, Madame." And they proceeded toward the dining-room.

What passed at this dinner? What did they say to him, and what could he say in reply? He found himself plunged in one of those strange dreams which border on insanity. He gazed at the two women with a fixed idea in his mind, a morbid, self-contradictory idea: "Which is the real one?"

The mother smiled, repeating over and over again: "Do you remember?" And it was in the bright eye of the young girl that he found again his memories of the past. Twenty times, he opened his mouth to say to her: "Do you remember, Lison?—" forgetting this white-haired lady who was regarding him with looks of tenderness.

And yet there were moments when he no longer felt sure, when he lost his head. He could see that the woman of to-day was not exactly the woman of long ago. The other one, the former one, had in her voice, in her glance, in her entire being something which he did not find again in the mother. And he made efforts to recall his ladylove, to seize again what had escaped from her, what this resuscitated one did not possess.

The Baronne said:

"You have lost your old sprightliness, my poor friend."

He murmured: "There are many other things that I have lost!"

But in his heart, touched with emotion, he felt his old love springing to life once more like an awakened wild beast ready to bite him.

The young girl went on chattering, and every now and then some familiar phrase of her mother which she had borrowed, a certain style of speaking and thinking, that resemblance of mind and manner which people acquire by living together, shook Lormerin from head to foot. All these things penetrated him, making the reopened wound of his passion bleed anew.

He got away early, and took a turn along the boulevard. But the image of this young girl pursued him, haunted him, quickened his heart, inflamed his blood. Instead of two women, he now saw only one, a young one, the one of former days returned, and he loved her as he had loved her prototype in bygone years. He loved her with greater ardor, after an interval of twenty-five years.

He went home to reflect on this strange and terrible thing, and to think on what he should do.

But as he was passing, with a wax-candle in his hand before the glass, the large glass in which he had contemplated himself and admired himself before he started, he saw reflected there an elderly, gray-haired man; and suddenly he recollected what he had been in olden days, in the days of little Lise. He saw himself charming and handsome, as he had been when he was loved! Then, drawing the light nearer, he looked at himself more closely, as one inspects a strange thing with a magnifying glass, tracing the wrinkles, discovering those frightful ravages which he had not perceived till now.

And he sat down, crushed at the sight of himself, at the sight of his lamentable image, murmuring:

"All over, Lormerin!"

My Landlady

"AT THAT time," said George Kervelen, "I was living in furnished lodgings in the Rue des Saints-Pères.

"When my father had made up his mind that I should go to Paris to continue my law studies, there had been a long discussion about settling everything. My allowance had been fixed at first at two thousand five hundred francs,* but my poor mother was so anxious, that she

---

*$500 a year.

said to my father that if I spent my money badly I might not take enough to eat, and then my health would suffer, and so it was settled that a comfortable boarding-house should be found for me, and that the amount should be paid to the proprietor himself, or herself, every month.

"Some of our neighbors told us of a certain Mme. Kergaran, a native of Brittany, who took in boarders, and so my father arranged matters by letter with this respectable person, at whose house I and my luggage arrived one evening.

"Mme. Kergaran was a woman of about forty. She was very stout, had a voice like a drill-sergeant, and decided everything in a very abrupt manner. Her house was narrow, with only one window opening on to the street on each story, which rather gave it the appearance of a ladder of windows, or better, perhaps, of a slice of a house sandwiched in between two others.

"The landlady lived on the first floor with her servant, the kitchen and dining-room were on the second, and four boarders from Brittany lived on the third and fourth, and I had two rooms on the fifth.

"A little dark corkscrew staircase led up to these attics. All day long Mme. Kergaran was up and down these stairs like a captain on board ship. Ten times a day she would go into each room, noisily superintending everything, seeing that the beds were properly made, the clothes well brushed, that the attendance was all that it should be; in a word, she looked after her boarders like a mother, and better than a mother.

"I soon made the acquaintance of my four fellow-countrymen. Two were medical and two were law students, but all impartially endured the landlady's despotic yoke. They were as frightened of her as a boy robbing an orchard is of a rural policeman.

"I, however, immediately felt that I wished to be independent; it is my nature to rebel. I declared at once that I meant to come in at whatever time I liked, for Mme. Kergaran had fixed twelve o'clock at night as the limit. On hearing this she looked at me for a few moments, and then said:

"'It is quite impossible; I cannot have Annette called up at any hour of the night. You can have nothing to do out-of-doors at such a time.'

"I replied firmly that, according to the law, she was obliged to open the door for me at any time.

"'If you refuse,' I said, 'I shall get a policeman to witness the fact, and go and get a bed at some hotel, at your expense in which I shall be fully justified. You will, therefore, be obliged either to open the door for me or to get rid of me. Do which you please.'

"I laughed in her face as I told her my conditions. She could not speak for a moment for surprise, then she tried to negotiate, but I was firm, and she was obliged to yield. It was agreed that I should have a latchkey, on my solemn undertaking that no one else should know it.

"My energy made such a wholesome impression on her that from that time she treated me with marked favor; she was most attentive, and even showed me a sort of rough tenderness which was not at all unpleasing. Sometimes when I was in a jovial mood I would kiss her by surprise, if only for the sake of getting the box on the ears which she gave me immediately afterward. When I managed to duck my head quickly enough, her hand would pass over me as swiftly as a ball, and I would run away laughing, while she would call after me:

" 'Uh! you wretch, I will pay you out for that.'

"However, we soon became real friends.

"It was not long before I made the acquaintance of a girl who was employed in a shop, and whom I constantly met. You know what such sort of love affairs are in Paris. One fine day, going to a lecture, you meet a girl going to work arm-in-arm with a friend. You look at her and feel that pleasant little shock which the eyes of some women give you. The next day at the same time, going through the same street, you meet her again, and the next and the succeeding days. At last you speak, and the love affair follows its course just like an illness.

"Well, by the end of three weeks I was on that footing with Emma which precedes intimacy. The fall would indeed have taken place much sooner had I known where to bring it about. The girl lived at home, and utterly refused to go to a hotel. I did not know how to manage, but at last I made the desperate resolve to take her to my room some night at about eleven o'clock, under the pretense of giving her a cup of tea. Mme. Kergaran always went to bed at ten, so that we could get in by means of my latchkey without exciting any attention, and go down again in an hour or two in the same way.

"After a good deal of entreaty on my part, Emma accepted my invitation.

"I did not spend a very pleasant day, for I was by no means easy in my mind. I was afraid of complications, of a catastrophe, of some scandal. At night I went into a *café*, and drank two cups of coffee and three or four glasses of cognac, to give me courage, and when I heard the clock strike half past ten I went slowly to the place of meeting, where she was already waiting for me. She took my arm in a coaxing manner, and we set off slowly toward my lodgings. The nearer we got to the door the more nervous I got, and I thought to myself: 'If only Mme. Kergaran is in bed already.'

"I said to Emma two or three times:

" 'Above all things, don't make any noise on the stairs,' to which she replied, laughing:

" 'Are you afraid of being heard?'

" 'No,' I said, 'but I am afraid of waking the man who sleeps in the room next to me, who is not at all well.'

"When I got near the house I felt as frightened as a man does who is going to the dentist's. All the windows were dark so no doubt everybody was asleep, and I breathed again. I opened the door as carefully as a thief, let my fair companion in, shut it behind me, and went upstairs on tiptoe, holding my breath and striking wax-matches lest the girl should make a false step.

"As we passed the landlady's door I felt my heart beating very quickly. But we reached the second floor then the third, and at last the fifth, and got into my room. Victory!

"However I only dared to speak in a

whisper and took off my boots so as not to make any noise. The tea, which I made over a spirit-lamp, was soon drunk, and then I became pressing, till little by little, as if in play, I, one by one, took off my companion's garments. She yielded while resisting, blushing, confused.

"She had absolutely nothing on except a short white petticoat when my door suddenly opened, and Mme. Kergaran appeared with a candle in her hand, in exactly the same costume as Emma.

"I jumped away from her and remained standing up, looking at the two women, who were looking at each other. What was going to happen?

"My landlady said, in a lofty tone of voice which I had never heard from her before:

" 'Monsieur Kervelen, I will not have prostitutes in my house.'

" 'But, Madame Kergaran,' I stammered, 'the young lady is a friend of mine. She just came in to have a cup of tea.'

" 'People don't take tea in their chemises. You will please make this person go directly.'

"Emma, in a natural state of consternation, began to cry, and hid her face in her petticoat, and I lost my head, not knowing what to do or say. My landlady added with irresistible authority:

" 'Help her to dress, and take her out at once.'

"It was certainly the only thing I could do, so I picked up her dress from the floor, put it over her head, and began to fasten it as best I could. She helped me, crying all the time, hurrying and making all sorts of mistakes and unable to find either buttonholes or laces, while Mme. Kergaran stood by motionless, with the candle in her hand, looking at us with the severity of a judge.

"As soon as Emma was dressed, without even stopping to button her boots, she rushed past the landlady and ran downstairs. I followed her in my slippers and half undressed, and kept repeating: 'Mademoiselle! Mademoiselle!'

"I felt that I ought to say something to her, but I could not find anything. I overtook her just by the street-door, and tried to take her into my arms, but she pushed me violently away, saying in a low, nervous voice:

" 'Leave me alone, leave me alone!' and so ran out into the street, closing the door behind her.

"When I went upstairs again I found that Mme. Kergaran was waiting on the first landing. I went up slowly, expecting, and ready for, anything.

"Her door was open, and she called me in, saying in a severe voice:

" 'I want to speak to you, M. Kervelen.'

"I went in, with my head bent. She put her candle on the mantelpiece, and then, folding her arms over her expansive bosom, which a fine white dressing-jacket hardly covered, she said:

" 'So, Monsieur Kervelen, you think my house is a house of ill-fame?'

"I was not at all proud. I murmured:

" 'Oh dear, no! But Mme. Kergaran, you must not be angry; you know what young men are.'

" 'I know,' was her answer, 'that I will not have such creatures here, so you will understand that. I expect to have my house respected, and I will not have it lose its reputation, you understand me? I know—'

"She went on thus for at least twenty minutes, overwhelming me with the good name of her house, with reasons for her indignation, and loading me with severe reproofs. I went to bed crestfallen, and resolved never again to try such an experiment, so long, at least, as I continued to be a lodger of Mme. Kergaran."

The Horrible

THE shadows of a blamy night were slowly falling. The women remained in the drawing-room of the villa. The men, seated or astride on garden-chairs, were smoking in front of the door, forming a circle round a table laden with cups and wineglasses.

Their cigars shone like eyes in the darkness which, minute by minute, was growing thicker. They had been talking about a frightful accident which had occurred the night before—two men and three women drowned before the eyes of the guests in the river opposite.

General de G—— remarked:

"Yes, these things are affecting, but they are not horrible.

"The horrible, that well-known word, means much more than the terrible. A frightful accident like this moves, upsets, scares; it does not horrify. In order that we should experience horror, something more is needed than the mere excitation of the soul, something more than the spectacle of the dreadful death; there must be a shuddering sense of mystery or a sensation of abnormal terror beyond the limits of nature. A man who dies, even in the most dramatic conditions, does not excite horror; a field of battle is not horrible; blood is not horrible; the vilest crimes are rarely horrible.

"Now, here are two personal examples, which have shown me what is the meaning of horror:

"It was during the war of 1870. We were retreating toward Pont-Audemer, after having passed through Rouen. The army, consisting of about twenty thousand men, twenty thousand men in disorder, disbanded, demoralized, exhausted, was going to reform at Havre.

"The earth was covered with snow. The night was falling. They had not eaten anything since the day before, and were flying rapidly, the Prussians not far off. The Norman country, livid, dotted with the shadows of the trees surrounding the farms, stretched away under a heavy and sinister black sky.

"Nothing else could be heard in the wan twilight save the confused sound, soft and undefined, of a marching throng, an endless tramping, mingled with the vague clink of cant ens or sabers. The men, bent, round-shouldered, dirty, in many cases even in rags, dragged themselves along, hurrying through the snow, with a long broken-backed stride.

"The skin of their hands stuck to the steel of their muskets' butt-ends for it was freezing dreadfully that night. I frequently saw a little soldier take off his shoes in order to walk barefooted, so much did his footgear bruise him; and with every step he left a track of blood. Then, after some time, he sat down in a field for a few minutes' rest, and never got up again. Every man who sat down died.

"Should we have left behind us those poor exhausted soldiers, who fondly counted on being able to start afresh as soon as they had somewhat refreshed their stiffened legs? Now, scarcely had they ceased to move, and to make their almost frozen blood circulate in their veins, than an unconquerable torpor congealed them, nailed them to the ground, closed their eyes, and in one second the overworked human mechanism collapsed. They gradually sank down, their heads falling toward their knees—without, however, quite tumbling over, for their loins and their limbs lost the capacity for moving, and became as hard as wood, impossible to bend or straighten.

"The rest of us, more robust, kept still straggling on, chilled to the marrow of our bones, advancing by dint of forced movement through the night, through that snow, through that cold and deadly country, crushed by pain, by defeat, by despair, above all overcome by the abominable sensation of abandonment, of death, of nothingness.

"I saw two gendarmes holding by the arm a curious-looking little man, old, beardless, of truly surprising aspect.

"They were looking out for an officer, believing that they had caught a spy. The word 'Spy' at once spread through the midst of the stragglers, and they gathered in a group round the prisoner.

A voice exclaimed: 'He must be shot!' And all these soldiers who were falling from utter prostration, only holding themselves on their feet by leaning on their guns, felt of a sudden that thrill of furious and bestial anger which urges on a mob to massacre.

"I wanted to speak! I was at that time in command of a battalion; but they no longer recognized the authority of their commanding officers; they would have shot me.

"One of the gendarmes said: 'He has been following us for the last three days. He has been asking information from everyone about the artillery.'

"I took it on myself to question this person:

" 'What are you doing? What do you want? Why are you accompanying the army?'

"He stammered out some words in some unintelligible dialect. He was, indeed, a strange being, with narrow shoulders, a sly look, and such an agitated air in my presence that I had no longer any real doubt that he was a spy. He seemed very aged and feeble. He kept staring at me from under his eyes with a humble, stupid, and crafty air.

"The men all round us exclaimed:

" 'To the wall! to the wall!'

"I said to the gendarmes:

" 'Do you answer for the prisoner?'

"I had not ceased speaking when a terrible push threw me on my back, and in a second I saw the man seized by the furious soldiers, thrown down, struck, dragged along the side of the road, and flung against a tree. He fell in the snow, nearly dead already.

"And immediately they shot him.

The soldiers fired at him, reloaded their guns, fired again with the desperate energy of brutes. They fought with each other to have a shot at him, filed off in front of the corpse, and kept firing at him, just as people at a funeral keep sprinkling holy water in front of a coffin.

"But suddenly a cry arose of 'The Prussians! the Prussians! and all along the horizon I heard the great noise of this panic-stricken army in full flight.

"The panic, generated by these shots fired at this vagabond, had filled his very executioners with terror; and, without realizing that they were themselves the originators of the scare, they rushed away and disappeared in the darkness.

"I remained alone in front of the corpse with the two gendarmes whom duty had compelled to stay with me.

"They lifted up this riddled piece of flesh, bruised and bleeding.

" 'He must be examined,' said I to them.

"And I handed them a box of vestas which I had in my pocket. One of the soldiers had another box. I was standing between the two.

"The gendarme, who was feeling the body, called out:

" 'Clothed in a blue blouse, trousers, and a pair of shoes.'

"The first match went out; we lighted a second. The man went on, as he turned out the pockets:

" 'A horn knife, check handkerchief, a snuffbox, a bit of pack-thread, a piece of bread.'

"The second match went out; we lighted a third. The gendarme, after having handled the corpse for a long time, said:

" 'That is all.'

"I said:

" 'Strip him. We shall perhaps find something near the skin '

"And, in order that the two soldiers might help each other in this task, I stood between them to give them light. I saw them, by the rapid and speedily extinguished flash of the match, take off the garments one by one, and expose to view that bleeding bundle of flesh still warm, though lifeless.

"And suddenly one of them exclaimed:

" 'Good God, Colonel, it is a woman!'

"I cannot describe to you the strange and poignant sensation of pain that moved my heart. I could not believe it, and I kneeled down in the snow before this shapeless pulp of flesh to see for myself: it was a woman.

"The two gendarmes, speechless and stunned, waited for me to give my opinion on the matter. But I did not know what to think, what theory to adopt.

"Then the brigadier slowly drawled out:

" 'Perhaps she came to look for a son of hers in the artillery, whom she had not heard from.'

"And the other chimed in:

" 'Perhaps indeed that is so.'

"And I, who had seen some terrible things in my time, began to weep. I felt, in the presence of this corpse, in that icy cold night, in the midst of that gloomy plain, at the sight of this mystery, at the sight of this murdered stranger, the meaning of that word 'horror.'

"Now, I had the same sensation last year while interrogating one of the survivors of the Flatters Mission, an Algerian sharpshooter.

"You probably know some of the details of this atrocious drama. It is possible, however, that you are unacquainted with all.

"The Colonel traveled through the desert into the Soudan, and passed through the immense territory of the Touaregs; who are, in that great ocean of sand which stretches from the Atlantic to Egypt and from the Soudan to Algeria, a sort of pirates resembling those who ravaged the seas in former days.

"The guides who accompanied the column belonged to the tribe of Chambaa, of Ouargla.

"One day, they pitched their camp in the middle of the desert, and the Arabs declared that, as the spring was a little farther away, they would go with all their camels to look for water.

"Only one man warned the Colonel that he had been betrayed Flatters did not believe this, and accompanied the convoy with the engineers, the doctors, and nearly all his officers.

"They were massacred round the spring and all the camels captured.

"The Captain of the Arab Intelligence Department at Ouargla, who had remained in the camp, took command of the survivors, spahis and sharpshooters, and commenced the retreat, leaving behind the baggage and the provisions for want of camels to carry them.

"Then they started on their journey through this solitude without shade and without limit, under a devouring sun, which parched them from morning till night.

"One tribe came to tender its sub-mission and brought dates as a tribute. They were poisoned. Nearly all the French died, and among them, the last officer.

"There now only remained a few spahis, with their quartermaster, Pobéguin, and some native sharpshooters of the Chambaa tribe. They had still two camels left. These disappeared one night along with two Arabs.

"Then the survivors feared that they would have to eat each other up. As soon as they discovered the flight of the two men with the two beasts, those who remained separated, and proceeded to march, one by one, through the soft sun, at a distance of more than a gunshot from each other.

"So they went on all day, and, when they reached a spring, each of them came up to drink at it in turn as soon as each solitary marcher had moved forward the number of yards arranged upon. And thus they continued marching the whole day, raising, everywhere they passed in that level burned-up expanse, those little columns of dust which, at a distance, indicate those who are trudging through the desert.

"But, one morning, one of the travelers made a sudden turn, and drew nearer to his neighbor. And they all stopped to look.

"The man toward whom the famished soldier drew near did not fly, but lay flat on the ground, and took aim at the one who was coming on. When he believed he was within gunshot, he fired. The other was not hit, and continued to advance, and cocking his gun in turn, killed his comrade.

"Then from the entire horizon, the others rushed to seek their share. And he who had killed the fallen man, cutting the corpse into pieces, distributed it.

"Then they once more placed themselves at fixed distances, these irreconcilable allies, preparing for the next murder which would bring them together.

"For two days they lived on this human flesh, which they divided among each other. Then, the famine came back, and he who had killed the first man began killing afresh. And again, like a butcher, he cut up the corpse and offered it to his comrades, keeping only his own portion of it. The retreat of cannibals continued. The last Frenchman, Pobéguin, was massacred at the side of a well the very night before the supplies arrived.

"Do you understand now what I mean by the 'horrible?'"

This was the story told us a few nights ago by General de G——.

The First Snowfall ✕

THE long promenade of La Croisette runs in a curve up to the edge of the blue water. Over there, at the right, the Esterel advances far into the sea. It obstructs the view, shutting in the horizon with the pretty southern aspect of its peaked, numerous, and fantastic summits.

At the left, the isles of Sainte-Marguerite and Saint-Honorat, lying in the water, present long aisles of fir-trees.

And all along the great gulf, all along the tall mountains that encircle Cannes, the white villa residences seem to be sleeping in the sunlight. You can see them from a distance, the bright houses, scattered from the top to the bottom of the mountains, dotting the dark greenery with specks of snow.

Those near the water open their gates on the vast promenade which is lashed by the quiet waves. The air is soft and balmy. It is one of those days when in this southern climate the chill of winter is not felt. Above the walls of the gardens may be seen orange-trees and citron-trees full of golden fruit. Ladies advance with slow steps over the sand of the avenue, followed by children rolling hoops or chatting with gentlemen.

*   *   *   *   *   *

A young lady had just passed out through the door of her coquettish little house facing La Croisette. She stops for a moment to gaze at the promenaders, smiles, and, with the gait of one utterly enfeebled, makes her way toward an empty bench right in front of the sea. Fatigued after having gone twenty paces, she sits down out of breath. Her pale face seems that of a dead woman. She coughs, and raises to her lips her transparent fingers as if to stop those shakings that exhaust her.

She gazes at the sky full of sunshine and at the swallows, at the zigzag summits of the Esterel over there, and at the sea, quite close to her, so blue, so calm, so beautiful.

She smiles still, and murmurs:

"Oh! how happy I am!"

She knows, however, that she is going to die, that she will never see the springtime, that in a year, along the same promenade, these same people who pass before her now will come again to breathe the warm air of this charming spot, with their children a little bigger, with their hearts all filled with hopes, with tenderness, with happiness, while at the bottom of an oak coffin the poor flesh which is left to her still to-day will have fallen into a condition of rottenness, leaving only her bones lying in the silk robe which she has selected for a winding-sheet.

She will be no more. Everything in life will go on as before for others. For her life will be over—over forever. She will be no more. She smiles, and inhales as well as she can, with her diseased lungs, the perfumed air of the gardens.

And she sinks into a reverie.

*　　*　　*　　*　　*　　*

She recalls the past. She had been married, four years ago, to a Norman gentleman. He was a strong young man, bearded, healthy looking, with wide shoulders, narrow mind, and joyous disposition.

They had been united through worldly motives which she did not quite understand. She would willingly have said "Yes." She did say "Yes" with a movement of the head in order not to thwart her father and mother. She was a Parisian, gay and full of the joy of living.

Her husband brought her home to his Norman château. It was a huge stone building surrounded by tall trees of great age. A high clump of fir-trees shut out the view in front. On the right an opening in the trees presented a view of the plain which stretched out, quite flat, up to the distant farmsteads. A crossroad passed before the boundary-line leading to the highroad three kilo-meters away.

Oh! she could remember everything—her arrival, her first day in her new abode, and her isolated fate afterward.

When she stepped out of the carriage, she glanced at the old building and laughingly exclaimed:

"It does not look gay!"

Her husband began to laugh in his turn and replied:

"Pooh! we get used to it! You'll see. I never feel bored in it, for my part."

That day they passed their time in embracing each other, and she did not find it too long. This lasted for the best part of three months. The days passed one after the other in insignificant yet absorbing occupations. She learned the value and the importance of the little things of life. She knew that people can interest themselves in the price of eggs which cost a few centimes more or less according to the seasons.

It was summer. She went to the fields to see the harvest cut. The gaiety of the sunshine kept up the gaiety of her heart.

The autumn came. Her husband went hunting. He started in the morning with his two dogs, Medor and Mirza. Then she remained alone, without grieving herself, moreover, at Henry's absence. She was, however, very fond of him, but he was not missed by her. When he returned home, her affection was specially absorbed by the dogs. She took care of them every evening with a mother's affection, caressed them incessantly, gave them a thousand charming little names which she had no idea of applying to her husband.

He invariably told her all about his hunting. He pointed out the places where he found partridges, expressed his astonishment at not having caught any hares in Joseph Ledentu's clover, or else appeared indignant at the conduct of M. Lechapelier, of Havre, who always followed the border of his estates to shoot game that had been started by him, Henry de Parville.

She replied: "Yes, indeed; it is not right," thinking of something else all the while.

The winter came, the Norman winter, cold and rainy. The endless rainstorms came down on the slates of the great many-angled roof, rising like a blade toward the sky. The road seemed like streams of mud, the country a plain of mud, and no noise could be heard save that of water falling; no movement could be seen save the whirling flight of crows rolling themselves out like a cloud, alighting on a field, and then hurrying away again.

About four o'clock, the army of dark, flying creatures came and perched in the tall beeches at the left of the château, emitting deafening cries. During nearly an hour, they fluttered from tree-top to tree-top, seemed to be fighting, croaked, and made the gray branches move with their black wings. She gazed at them, each evening, with a pressure of the heart, so deeply was she penetrated by the lugubrious melancholy of the night falling on the desolate grounds.

Then she rang for the lamp, and she drew near the fire. She burned heaps of wood without succeeding in warming the spacious apartments invaded by the humidity. She felt cold every day, everywhere, in the drawing-room, at meals, in her own apartment. It seemed to her she was cold even in the marrow of her bones. He only came in to dinner, he was always hunting, or else occupied with sowing seed, tilling the soil, and all the work of the country.

He used to come back jolly and covered with mud, rubbing his hands while he exclaimed:

"What wretched weather!" Or else: "It is a good thing to have a fire." Or sometimes: "Well, how are you to-day? Do you feel in good spirits?"

He was happy, in good health, without desires, thinking of nothing else save this simple, sound, and quiet life.

About December, when the snow had come, she suffered so much from the icy-cold air of the château which seemed to have acquired a chill with the centuries it had passed through, as human beings do with years, that she asked her husband one evening:

"Look here, Henry! You ought to have a hot-air plant put into the house; it would dry the walls. I assure you I cannot warm myself from morning till night."

At first he was stunned at this extravagant idea of introducing a hot-air plant into his manor-house. It would have seemed more natural to him to have his dogs fed out of his silver plate. Then, he gave a tremendous laugh which made his chest heave, while he exclaimed:

"A hot-air plant here! A hot-air

plant here! Ha! ha! ha! what a good joke!"

She persisted:

"I assure you, dear, I feel frozen; you don't feel it because you are always moving about; but, all the same, I feel frozen."

He replied, still laughing:

"Pooh! you will get used to it, and besides it is excellent for the health. You will only be all the better for it. We are not Parisians, damn it! to live in hot-houses. And besides the spring is quite near."

*　　*　　*　　*　　*.　*

About the beginning of January, a great misfortune befell her. Her father and her mother died of a carriage-accident. She came to Paris for the funeral. And her mind was entirely plunged in grief on account of it for about six months.

The softness of fine days at length awakened her, and she lived a sad, drifting life of languor until autumn.

When the cold weather came back, she was brought face to face, for the first time, with the gloomy future. What was she to do? Nothing. What was going to happen to her henceforth? Nothing. What expectation, what hope, could revive her heart? None. A doctor who was consulted declared that she would never have children.

Sharper, more penetrating still than the year before, the cold made her suffer continually.

She stretched out her shivering hands to the big flames. The glaring fire burned her face; but icy puffs seemed to slip down her back and to penetrate between the flesh and her underclothing. And she shook from head to foot. Innumerable currents of air appeared to have taken up their abode in the apartment, living, crafty currents of air, as cruel as enemies. She encountered them every moment; they were incessantly buffeting her, sometimes on the face, sometimes on the hands, sometimes on the neck, with their treacherous, frozen breath.

Once more she spoke of a hot-air plant; but her husband heard her request as if she were asking for the moon. The introduction of such an apparatus at Parville appeared to him as impossible as the discovery of the Philosopher's Stone.

Having been at Rouen on business one day he brought back to his wife a dainty foot-warmer made of copper, which he laughingly called a "portable hot-water heater"; and he considered that this would prevent her henceforth from ever being cold.

Toward the end of December she understood that she could not live thus always, and she said timidly one evening at dinner:

"Listen, dear! Are we not going to spend a week or two in Paris before spring?"

He was stupefied:

"In Paris? In Paris? But what are we to do there? No, by Jove! We are better off here. What odd ideas come into your head sometimes."

She faltered:

"It might distract us a little."

He did not understand:

"What is it you want to distract you? Theaters, evening parties, dinners in town? You know, however, well that in coming here you ought not to expect any distractions of that kind!"

She saw a reproach in these words and in the tone in which they were uttered. She relapsed into silence. She was timid and gentle, without resisting power and without strength of will.

In January, the cold weather returned with violence. Then the snow covered the earth.

One evening, as she watched the great whirling cloud of crows winding round the trees, she began to weep, in spite of herself.

Her husband came in. He asked, in great surprise:

"What is the matter with you?"

He was happy, quite happy, never having dreamed of another life or other pleasures. He had been born and had grown up in this melancholy district. He felt well in his own house, at his ease in body and mind.

He did not realize that we may desire events, have a thirst for changing pleasures; he did not understand that it does not seem natural to certain beings to remain in the same places during the four seasons; he seemed not to know that spring, summer, autumn, and winter, have for multitudes of persons, new pleasures in new countries.

She could not say anything in reply, and she quickly dried her eyes. At last she murmured, in a distracted sort of way:

"I am—I—I am a little sad—I am a little bored."

But she was seized with terror for having even said so much, and she added very quickly:

"And besides—I am—I am a little cold."

At this statement he got angry:

"Ah! yes, still your idea of the hot-air plant. But look here, deuce take it! you have only had one cold since you came here."

* * * * * * *

The night came. She went up to her room, for she had insisted on having a separate apartment. She went to bed. Even in the bed, she felt cold. She thought: "Is it to be like this always, always till death?"

And she thought of her husband. How could he have said this:

"You have only had one cold since you came here?"

Then she must get ill; she must cough in order that he might understand what she suffered!

And she was filled with indignation, the angry indignation of a weak, a timid being.

She must cough. Then, without doubt, he would take pity on her. Well, she would cough; he would hear her coughing; the doctor should be called in; he would see that her husband would see.

She got up with her legs and her feet naked, and a childish idea made her smile:

"I want a hot-air plant, and I must have it. I shall cough so much that he'll have to put one into the house."

And she sat down almost naked in a chair. She waited an hour, two hours. She shivered, but she did not catch cold. Then she resolved to make use of a bold expedient.

She noiselessly left her room, descended the stairs, and opened the garden-gate.

The earth, covered with snow, seemed dead. She abruptly thrust forward her naked foot, and plunged it into the light and icy froth. A sensation of cold, painful as a wound, mounted up to her heart. However, she stretched out the other leg and began to descend the steps slowly.

Then she advanced through the grass, saying to herself:

"I'll go as far as the fir-trees."

She walked with quick steps, out of breath, choking every time she drove her foot through the snow.

She touched the first fir-tree with her hand, as if to convince herself that she carried out her plan to the end; then she went back into the house. She believed two or three times that she was going to fall, so torpid and weak did she feel. Before going in, meanwhile, she sat in that icy snow, and she even gathered some in order to rub on her breast.

Then she went in, and got into bed. It seemed to her, at the end of an hour, that she had a swarm of ants in her throat, and that other ants were running all over her limbs. She slept, however.

Next day, she was coughing, and she could not get up.

She got inflammation of the lungs. She became delirious, and in her delirium she asked for a hot-air plant. The doctor insisted on having one put in. Henry yielded, but with an irritated repugnance.

*   *   *   *   *   *   *

She could not be cured. The lungs, severely attacked, made those who attended on her uneasy about her life.

"If she remains here, she will not last as long as the next cold weather," said the doctor.

She was sent to the south. She came to Cannes, recognized the sun, loved the sea, and breathed the air of orange-blossoms. Then in the spring, she returned north. But she lived with the fear of being cured, with the fear of the long winters of Normandy; and as soon as she was better, she opened her window by night while thinking of the sweet banks of the Mediterranean. And now she was going to die. She knew it and yet she was contented.

She unfolds a newspaper which she had not already opened, and reads this heading:

"The First Snow in Paris."

After this, she shivers and yet smiles. She looks across the Esterel which is turning rose-colored under the setting sun. She looks at the vast blue sea, so very blue also, and rises up and returns to the house, with slow steps, only stopping to cough, for she had remained out too long; and she has caught cold, a slight cold.

She finds a letter from her husband. She opens it still smiling, and she reads:

"My dear Love: I hope you are going on well, and that you do not regret too much our beautiful district. We have had for some days past a good frost which announces snow. For my part, I adore this weather, and you understand that I am keeping that cursed hot-air plant of yours going—"

She ceases reading, quite happy at the thought that she has had her hot-air plant. Her right hand, which holds the letter, falls down slowly over her knees, while she raises her left hand to her mouth, as if to calm the obstinate cough which is tearing her chest.

The Wooden Shoes ✕

THE old priest was sputtering out the last words of his sermon over the white caps of the peasant women, and the rough or greasy heads of the men. The large baskets of the farmers' wives who had come from a distance to attend mass were on the ground beside them, and the heavy heat of a July day caused them all to exhale a smell like that of cattle, or of a flock of sheep, and the cocks could be heard crowing through the large west door, which was wide open, as well as the lowing of the cows in a neighboring field.

"As God wishes. Amen!" the priest said. Then he ceased, opened a book, and, as he did every week, began to give notice of all the small parish events for the following week. He was an old man with white hair who had been in the parish for over forty years, and from the pulpit was in the habit of discoursing familiarly to them all; so he went on: "I will recommend Désiré Vallin, who is very ill, to your prayers, and also La Paumelle, who is not recovering from her confinement satisfactorily."

He had forgotten the rest, and so he looked for the slips of paper which were put away in a breviary. At last he found two and continued: "I will not have the lads and girls come into the church-yard in the evening, as they do; otherwise I shall inform the rural policeman. Monsieur Césaire Omont would like to find a respectable girl as servant." He reflected for a few moments, and then added: "That is all, my brethren, and I wish that all of you may find the Divine mercy." And he came down from the pulpit, to finish mass.

When the Malandains had returned to their cottage, which was the last in the village of La Sablière, on the road to Fourville, the father, a thin, wrinkled old peasant, sat down at the table, while his wife took the saucepan off the fire, and Adelaide, the daughter, took the glasses and plates out of the sideboard. Then the father said: "I think that place at Maître Omont's ought to be a good one, as he is a widower and his daughter-in-law does not like him. He is all alone and has money. I think it would be a good thing to send Adelaide there."

His wife put the black saucepan on to the table, took the lid off, and while the steam, which smelled strongly of cabbage, rose into the air she pondered on the suggestion. Presently the old man continued: "He has got some money, that is certain, but any one going there ought to be very sharp, and Adelaide is not that at all."

His wife replied: "I might go and see, all the same," and turning to her daughter, a strapping, silly looking girl with yellow hair and fat, red cheeks like apples, she said: "Do you hear, you great silly? You are to go to Maître Omont's and offer yourself as his servant, and you will do whatever he tells you."

The girl began to laugh in a foolish manner, without replying, and then the three began their dinner. In a few minutes, the father continued: "Listen to me, girl, and try not to make a mistake about what I am going to say to you." And slowly and minutely he laid down for her her line of conduct, anticipating the minutest details, and preparing her for the conquest of an old widower who was on unfriendly terms with his family. The mother ceased eating to listen to him, and she sat there, with her fork in her hand, looking at her husband and her daughter by turns, and following every word with concentrated and silent attention, while Adelaide remained listless, docile, and stupid, with vague and wandering eyes.

As soon as their meal was over, her mother made her put her cap on, and they both started off to see Monsieur Césaire Omont. He lived in a small, brick house adjoining his tenants' cottages, for he had retired, and was living by subdividing and letting his land.

He was about fifty-five years old, and was stout, jovial, and rough-mannered, as rich men often are. He laughed and shouted loud enough to make the walls fall down, drank brandy and cider by the glassful, and was said to be still of an amorous disposition, in spite of his age. He liked to walk about his fields with his hands behind his back, digging his wooden shoes into the fat soil, looking at the sprouting corn or the flowering colza with the eye of a retired farmer, at his ease, who likes to see the crops but does not trouble himself about them any longer. People used to say of him: "There is a Mr. Merry-man, who does not get up in a good temper every day."

He received the two women, as he was finishing his coffee, with his fat stomach against the table, and turning round said: "What do you want?"

The mother was spokeswoman. "This is our girl Adelaide, and I have come to ask you to take her as servant, as Monsieur le Curé told us you wanted one."

Maître Omont looked at the girl, and then he said roughly: "How old is the great she-goat?"

"Twenty last Michaelmas-Day, Monsieur Omont."

"That is settled, she will have fifteen francs a month and her food. I shall expect her to-morrow, to make my soup in the morning." And he dismissed the two women.

The next day Adelaide entered upon her duties, and began to work hard, without saying a word, as she was in the habit of doing at home. About nine o'clock, as she was scrubbing the kitchen floor, Monsieur Omont called her: "Adelaide!"

She came immediately saying: "Here I am, master." As soon as she was opposite him, with her red and neglected hands, and her troubled looks, he said. "Now just listen to me, so that there may be no mistake between us. You are my servant, but nothing else; you understand what I mean. We shall keep our shoes apart."

"Yes, master."

"Each in our own place, my girl, you in your kitchen; I in my dining-room, and with that exception, everything will be for you just as it is for me. Is that settled?"

"Yes, master."

"Very well; that is all right, and now go to your work."

And she went out, to attend to her duties, and at midday she served up her master's dinner in the little drawing-room with the flowered paper on the walls, and then, when the soup was on the table, she went to tell him. "Dinner is ready, master."

He went in and sat down, looked round, unfolded his table napkin, hesitated for a moment and then in a voice of thunder he shouted: "Adelaide!"

She rushed in, terribly frightened, for he had shouted as if he meant to murder her.

"Well, in heaven's name, where is your place?"

"But, master!"

"I do not like to eat alone," he roared; "you will sit there, or go to the devil, if you don't choose to do so. Go and get your plate and glass."

She brought them in, feeling very frightened, and stammered: "Here I am, master," and then sat down opposite to him. He grew jovial; clinked glasses with her, rapped the table, and told her stories to which she listened with downcast eyes, without daring to say a word, and from time to time she got up to fetch some bread, cider, or plates. When she brought in the coffee she only put one cup before him, and then he grew angry again, and growled: "Well, what about yourself?"

"I never take any, master."

"Why not?"

"Because I do not like it."

Then he burst out afresh: "I am not fond of having my coffee by myself, confound it! If you will not take it here, you can go to the devil. Go and get a cup, and make haste about it."

So she went and fetched a cup, sat down again, tasted the black liquor and made faces over it, but swallowed it to the last drop, under her master's furious looks. Then he made her also drink her first glass of brandy as an extra drop, the second as a livener, and the third as a kick behind, and then he told her to go and wash up her plates and dishes, adding, that she was "a good sort of girl."

It was the same at supper, after which she had to play dominoes with him. Then he sent her to bed, saying that he should come upstairs soon. So she went to her room, a garret under the roof, and after saying her prayers, undressed and got into bed. But very soon she sprang up in a fright, for a furious shout had shaken the house. "Adelaide!" She opened her door, and replied from her attic: "Here I am, master."

"Where are you?"

"In bed, of course, master."

Then he roared out: "Will you come downstairs, in heaven's name? I do not like to sleep alone, and, by Jove, if you object, you can just go at once."

Then in her terror she replied from upstairs: "I will come, master." She looked for her candle, and he soon heard her small clogs pattering down the stairs. When she had got to the bottom steps, he seized her by the arm, and as soon as she had left her light wooden shoes by the side of her master's heavy boots, he pushed her into his room, growling out: "Quicker than that, confound it!"

And without knowing what she was saying she answered: "Here I am, here I am, master."

Six months later, when she went to see her parents one Sunday, her father looked at her curiously, and then said: "Are you not *enceinte?*"

She remained thunderstruck, and

looked at her waist, and then said: "No, I do not think so."

Then he asked her, for he wanted to know everything: "Just tell me, didn't you mix your clogs together, one night?"

"Yes, I mixed them the first night, and then every other night."

"Well, then you are *enceinte*, you great fool!"

On hearing that, she began to sob, and stammered: "How could I know? How was I to know?" Old Malandain looked at her knowingly, and appeared very pleased, and then he asked: "What did you not know?" And amid tears she replied: "How was I to know how children were made?" And when her mother came back, the man said, with-out any anger: "There, she is *enceinte,* now."

But the woman was furious, her finer instinct revolted, and she called her daughter, who was in tears, every name she could think of—a "trollop" and a "strumpet." Then, however, the old man made her hold her tongue, and as he took up his cap to go and talk the matter over with Master Césaire Omont, he remarked: "She is actually more stupid than I thought she was; she did not even know what he was doing, the fool!"

On the next Sunday, after the sermon, the old Curé published the banns be-tween Monsieur Onufre-Césaire Omont and Céleste-Adelaide Malandain,

---

Boitelle

PÈRE BOITELLE (Antoine) had the reputation through the whole country of a specialist in dirty jobs. Every time a pit, a dunghill, or a cesspool required to be cleared away, or a dirt-hole to be cleansed out, he was the person employed to do it.

He would come there with his night-man's tools and his wooden shoes covered with dirt, and would set to work, whining incessantly about the nature of his occupation. When people asked him why he did this loathsome work, he would reply resignedly:

"Faith, 'tis for my children whom I must support. This brings in more than anything else."

He had, indeed, fourteen children. If anyone asked him what had become of them, he would say with an air of in-difference:

"There are only eight of them left in the house. One is out at service, and five are married."

When the questioner wanted to know whether they were well married, he replied vivaciously:

"I did not cross them. I crossed them in nothing. They married just as they pleased. We shouldn't go against people's likings—it turns our badly. I am a night-cartman because my parents went against my likings. But for that I would have become a workman like the others."

Here is the way his parents had thwarted him in his likings:

He was at that time a soldier stationed

at Havre, not more stupid than another, or sharper either, a rather simple fellow, in truth. During his hours of freedom his greatest pleasure was to walk along the quay, where the bird-dealers congregate. Sometimes alone, sometimes with a soldier from his own part of the country, he would slowly saunter along by cages where parrots with green backs and yellow heads from the banks of the Amazon, parrots with gray backs and red heads from Senegal, enormous macaws, which looked like birds brought up in conservatories, with their flower-like feathers, plumes, and tufts, paroquets of every shape, painted with minute care by that excellent miniaturist, God Almighty, with the little young birds, hopping about, yellow, blue, and variegated, mingling their cries with the noise of the quay, added to the din caused by the unloading of the vessels, as well as by passengers and vehicles—a violent clamor, loud, shrill, and deafening, as if from some distant, monstrous forest.

Boitelle would stop, with strained eyes, wide-open mouth, laughing and enraptured, showing his teeth to the captive cockatoos, who kept nodding their white or yellow topknots toward the glaring red of his breeches and the copper buckle of his belt. When he found a bird that could talk, he put questions to it, and if it happened at the time to be disposed to reply and to hold a conversation with him, he would remain there till nightfall filled with gaiety and contentment. He also found heaps of fun in looking at the monkeys, and could conceive no greater luxury for a rich man than to possess these animals, just like cats and dogs. This taste for the exotic he had in his blood, as people

have a taste for the chase, or for medicine, or for the priesthood. He could not refrain, every time the gates of the barracks opened, from going back to the quay, as if drawn toward it by an irresistible longing.

Now, on one occasion, having stopped almost in ecstasy before an enormous ararauna, which was swelling out its plumes, bending forward, and bridling up again, as if making the court-courtesies of parrot-land, he saw the door of a little tavern adjoining the bird-dealer's shop opening, and his attention was attracted by a young negress, with a silk kerchief tied round her head, sweeping into the street the rubbish and the sand of the establishment.

Boitelle's attention was soon divided between the bird and the woman, and he really could not tell which of these two beings he contemplated with the greater astonishment and delight.

The negress, having got rid of the sweepings of the tavern, raised her eyes, and, in her turn, was dazzled by the soldier's uniform. There she stood facing him with her broom in her hands as if she were presenting arms for him, while the ararauna continued making courtesies. Now at the end of a few seconds the soldier began to get embarrassed by this attention, and he walked away gingerly so as not to present the appearance of beating a retreat.

But he came back. Almost every day he passed in front of the Colonial tavern, and often he could distinguish through the windowpanes the figure of the little black-skinned maid filling out "bocks" or glasses of brandy for the sailors of the port. Frequently, too, she would come out to the door on seeing him. Soon, without even having exchanged a word, they smiled at one another like old acquaintances; and Boitelle felt his heart moved when he saw suddenly glittering between the dark lips of the girl her shining row of white teeth. At length, he ventured one day to enter, and was quite surprised to find that she could speak French like everyone else. The bottle of lemonade, of which she was good enough to accept a glassful, remained in the solider's recollection memorably delicious; and it became habitual with him to come and absorb in this little tavern on the quay all the agreeable drinks which he could afford.

For him it was a treat, a happiness, on which his thoughts were constantly dwelling, to watch the black hand of the little maid pouring out something into his glass while her teeth, brighter than her eyes, showed themselves as she laughed. When they had kept company in this way for two months, they became fast friends, and Boitelle, after his first astonishment at discovering that this negress was in principle as good as the best girls in the country, that she exhibited a regard for economy, industry, religion, and good conduct, loved her more on that account, and became so much smitten with her that he wanted to marry her.

He told her about his intentions, which made her dance with joy. Besides, she had a little money, left her by a female oyster-dealer, who had picked her up when she had been left on the quay at Havre by an American captain. This captain had found her, when she was only about six years old, lying on bales of cotton in the hold of his ship,

some hours after his departure from New York. On his arrival in Havre, he there abandoned to the care of this compassionate oyster-dealer the little black creature, who had been hidden on board his vessel, he could not tell how or why.

The oyster-woman having died, the young negress became a servant at the Colonial tavern.

Antoine Boitelle added: "This will be all right if my parents don't go against it. I will never go against them, you understand—never! I'm going to say a word or two to them the first time I go back to the country."

On the following week, in fact, having obtained twenty-four hours' leave, he went to see his family, who cultivated a little farm at Tourteville near Yvetot.

He waited till the meal was finished, the hour when the coffee baptized with brandy makes people more open-hearted, before informing his parents that he had found a girl answering so well to his likings in every way that there could not exist any other in all the world so perfectly suited to him.

The old people, at this observation, immediately assumed a circumspect air, and wanted explanations. At first he concealed nothing from them except the color of her skin.

She was a servant, without much means, but strong, thrifty, clean, well-conducted, and sensible. All these were better than money would be in the hands of a bad housewife. Moreover, she had a few sous, left her by a woman who had reared her,—a good number of sous, almost a little dowry,— fifteen hundred francs in the savings' bank. The old people, overcome by his talk, and relying, too, on their own judgment, were gradually giving way, when he came to the delicate point. Laughing in rather a constrained fashion, he said:

"There's only one thing you may not like. She is not white."

They did not understand, and he had to explain at some length and very cautiously, to avoid shocking them, that she belonged to the dusky race of which they had only seen samples among figures exhibited at Epinal. Then, they became restless, perplexed, alarmed, as if he had proposed a union with the Devil.

The mother said: "Black? How much of her is black? Is it the whole of her?"

He replied: "Certainly. Everywhere, just as you are white everywhere."

The father interposed: "Black? Is it as black as the pot?"

The son answered: "Perhaps a little less than that. She is black, but not disgustingly black. The curé's cossack is black; but it is not uglier than a surplice, white is white."

The father said: "Are there more black people besides her in her country?"

And the son, with an air of conviction, exclaimed: "Certainly!"

But the old man shook his head: "This must be disagreeable!"

Said the son: "It isn't more disagreeable than anything else, seeing that you get used to it in no time."

The mother asked: "It doesn't soil linen more than other skins, this black skin?"

"Not more than your own, as it is her proper color."

Then, after many other questions, it was agreed that the parents should see this girl before coming to any decision

and that the young fellow, whose period of service was coming to an end in the course of a month, should bring her to the house in order that they might examine her, and decide by talking the matter over whether or not she was too dark to enter the Boitelle family.

Antoine accordingly announced that on Sunday, the twenty-second of May, the day of his discharge, he would start for Tourteville with his sweetheart.

She had put on, for this journey to the house of her lover's parents, her most beautiful and most gaudy clothes, in which yellow, red, and blue were the prevailing colors, so that she had the appearance of one adorned for a national fête.

At the terminus, as they were leaving Havre, people stared at her very much, and Boitelle was proud of giving his arm to a person who commanded so much attention. Then, in the third-class carriage, in which she took a seat by his side, she excited so much astonishment among the peasants that the people in the adjoining compartments got up on their benches to get a look at her over the wooden partition which divided the different portions of the carriage from one another. A child, at sight of her, began to cry with terror, another concealed his face in his mother's apron. Everything went off well, however, up to their arrival at their destination. But, when the train slackened its rate of motion as they drew near Yvetot, Antoine felt ill at ease, as he would have done at an inspection when he did not know his drill-practice. Then, as he put his head out through the carriage door, he recognized, some distance away, his father, who was holding the bridle of the horse yoked to a carriage, and his mother who had made her way to the railed portion of the platform where a number of spectators had gathered.

He stepped out first, gave his hand to his sweetheart, and holding himself erect, as if he were escorting a general, he advanced toward his family.

The mother, on seeing this black lady, in variegated costume in her son's company, remained so stupefied that she could not open her mouth; and the father found it hard to hold the horse, which the engine or the negress caused to rear for some time without stopping. But Antoine, suddenly seized with the unmingled joy of seeing once more the old people, rushed forward with open arms, embraced his mother, embraced his father, in spite of the nag's fright, and then turning toward his companion, at whom the passengers on the platform stopped to stare with amazement, he proceeded to explain:

"Here she is! I told you that, at first sight, she seems odd; but as soon as you know her, in very truth, there's not a better sort in the whole world. Say good morrow to her without making any bother about it."

Thereupon, Mère Boitelle, herself nearly frightened out of her wits, made a sort of courtesy, while the father took off his cap, murmuring: "I wish you good luck!"

Then, without further delay, they climbed up on the car, the two women at the lower end on seats, which made them jump up and down as the vehicle went jolting along the road, and the two men outside on the front seat.

Nobody spoke. Antoine, ill at ease, whistled a barrack-room air; his father lashed the nag; and his mother, from where she sat in the corner, kept casting sly glances at the negress, whose forehead and cheek-bones shone in the sunlight like well-blacked shoes.

Wishing to break the ice, Antoine turned round.

"Well," said he, "we don't seem inclined to talk."

"We must get time," replied the old woman.

He went on:

"Come! tell us the little story about that hen of yours that laid eight eggs."

It was a funny anecdote of long standing in the family. But, as his mother still remained silent, paralyzed by emotion, he started the talking himself and narrated, with much laughter on his own part, this memorable adventure. The father, who knew it by heart, brightened up at the opening words of the narrative; his wife soon followed his example; and the negress herself, when he had reached the drollest part of it, suddenly gave vent to a laugh so noisy, rolling, and torrentlike that the horse, becoming excited, broke into a gallop for a little while.

This served as the introduction to their acquaintanceship. The company at length began to chat.

On reaching the house they all alighted, and he conducted his sweetheart to a room so that she might take off her dress, to avoid staining it while preparing a good dish intended to win the old people's affections by appealing to their stomachs. Then he drew his parents aside near the door, and with beating heart, asked:

"Well, what do you say now?"

The father said nothing. The mother, less timid, exclaimed:

"She is too black. No, indeed, this is too much for me. It turns my blood."

"That may be, but it is only for the moment."

They then made their way into the interior of the house where the good woman was somewhat affected at the spectacle of the negress engaged in cooking. She at once proceeded to assist her, with petticoats tucked up, active in spite of her age.

The meal was an excellent one—very long, very enjoyable. When they had afterward taken a turn together, Antoine said to his father:

"Well, dad, what do you say to this?"

The peasant took care never to compromise himself.

"I have no opinion about it. Ask your mother."

So Antoine went back to his mother, and, leading her to the end of the room, said:

"Well, mother, what do you think of her?"

"My poor lad, she is really too black. If she were only a little less black, I would not go against you, but this is too much. One would think it was Satan!"

He did not press her, knowing how obstinate the old woman had always been, but he felt a tempest of disappointment sweeping over his heart. He was turning over in his mind what he ought to do, what plan he could devise, surprised, moreover, that she had not conquered them already as she had captivated himself. And they all four set out with slow steps through the corn-fields, having again relapsed into silence. Whenever they passed a fence, they saw a countryman sitting on the stile and a group of brats climbing up to stare at them. People rushed out into the road to see the "black" whom young Boitelle had brought home with him. At a distance they noticed people scampering across the fields as they do when the drum beats to draw public attention to some living phenomenon. Père and Mère Boitelle, scared by this curiosity, which was exhibited everywhere through the country at their approach, quickened their pace, walking side by side, leaving far behind their son, whom his dark companion asked what his parents thought of her.

He hesitatingly replied that they had not yet made up their minds.

But on the village-green, people rushed out of all the houses in a flutter of excitement; and, at the sight of the gathering rabble, old Boitelle took to his heels, and regained his abode, while Antoine, swelling with rage, his sweetheart on his arm, advanced majestically under the battery of staring eyes opened wide in amazement.

He understood that it was at an end, that there was no hope for him, that he could not marry his negress. She also understood it; and as they drew near the farmhouse they both began to weep. As soon as they had got back to the house, she once more took off her dress to aid the mother in her household duties, and followed her everywhere, to the dairy, to the stable, to the henhouse, taking on herself the hardest part of the work, repeating always, "Let me do it, Madame Boitelle," so that, when night came on, the old woman, touched but inexorable, said to her son: "She is a good girl, all the same. 'Tis a pity she is so black; but indeed she is too much so. I couldn't get used to it. She must go back again. She is too black!"

And young Boitelle said to his sweetheart:

"She will not consent. She thinks you are too black. You must go back again. I will go with you to the train. No matter—don't fret. I am going to talk to them after you have started."

He then conducted her to the railway-station, still cheering her up with hope, and, when he had kissed her, he put her into the train, which he watched as it passed out of sight, his eyes swollen with tears. In vain did he appeal to the old people. They would not give their consent.

And when he had told this story, which was known all over the country, Antoine Boitelle would always add:

"From that time forward I have had no heart for anything—for anything at all. No trade suited me any longer, and so I became what I am—a night-cartman."

People would say to him: "Yet you got married."

"Yes, and I can't say that my wife didn't please me, seeing that I've got fourteen children; but she is not the other one, oh! no—certainly not! The other one, mark you, my negress, she had only to give me one glance and I felt as if I were in Heaven!"

Selfishness

WE READ lately in the journals, the following lines:

"BOULOGNE-SUR-MER, January 22.
"A frightful disaster has occurred which throws into consternation our maritime population, so grievously afflicted two years since. The fishing boat, commanded by shipmaster Javel, entering into port, was carried to the west, and broken upon the rocks of the breakwater near the pier. In spite of the efforts of the salvage boat, and of life lines shot out to them, four men and a cabin boy perished. The bad weather continues. We fear new calamities."

Who is this shipmaster Javel? Is he the brother of the one-armed Javel? If this poor man tossed by the waves, and dead perhaps, under the *débris* of his boat cut in pieces, is the one I think he is, he assisted, eighteen years ago, at another drama, terrible and simple as are all the formidable dramas of the billows.

Javel the elder was then master of a smack. The smack is the fishing boat *par excellence*. Solid, fearing no kind of weather, with round body, rolled incessantly by the waves, like a cork, always lashed by the hard, foul winds of the Channel, it travels the sea indefatigably, with sail filled, making in its wake a path which reaches the bottom of the ocean, detaching all the sleeping creatures from the rocks, the flat fishes glued to the sand, the heavy crabs with their hooked claws, and the lobster with his pointed mustaches.

When the breeze is fresh and the waves choppy, the boat puts about to fish. A rope is fastened to the end of a great wooden shank tipped with iron, which is let down by means of two cables slipping over two spools at the extreme end of the craft. And the boat, driving under wind and current, drags after her this apparatus, which ravages and devastates the bottom of the sea.

Javel had on board his younger brother, four men, and a cabin boy. He had set out from Boulogne in fair weather to cast the nets. Then, suddenly, the wind arose and an unlooked-for squall forced the boat along over the waters. It gained the coast of England; but a tremendous sea beat so against the cliffs and the shore that it was impossible to enter port. The little boat put to sea again and returned to the coast of France. The tempest continued to make the piers unapproachable, enveloping them with foam, and shutting off all places of refuge by noise and danger.

The fishing boat set out again, running under the billows, tossed about, shaken up, suffocated in mountains of water, but merry in spite of all, accustomed to heavy weather, which sometimes held it for five or six hours between the two countries, unable to land in the one or the other.

Finally, the hurricane ceased, when they came out into open sea, and although the sea was still high, the commander ordered them to cast the net. Then the great fishing tackle was thrown overboard, and two men at one side and two at the other begin to unwind from rollers the cable which holds it. Sud-

denly it touches the bottom, but a high wave tips the boat. Javel the younger, who is in the prow directing the casting of the net, totters, and finds his arm caught between the cable, stopped an instant by the motion, and the wood on which it slipped. He made a desperate effort with his other hand to lift the cable, but the net already dragged and the rapidly slipping cable would not yield.

Faint from pain, he called. All ran to him. His brother left the helm. They threw their full force upon the rope, forcing it away from the arm it was grinding. It was in vain. "We must cut it," said a sailor, and he drew from his pocket a large knife which could, in two blows, save young Javel's arm. But to cut was to lose the net, and the net meant money, much money—five hundred francs; it belonged to the elder Javel, who held to his property.

With tortured heart he cried out: "No, don't cut; I'll luff the ship." And he ran to the wheel, putting the helm about. The boat scarcely obeyed, paralyzed by the net which counteracted its power, and dragged besides from the force of the leeway and the wind.

Young Javel fell to his knees with set teeth and haggard eyes. He said nothing. His brother returned, fearing the sailor's cutting.

"Wait! wait!" he said, "don't cut, we must cast anchor."

The anchor was thrown overboard, all the chain paid out, and they then tried to take a turn around the capstan with the cables in order to loosen the strain from the weight of the net. They were successful, finally, and released the arm which hung inert under a sleeve of bloody woolen cloth.

Young Javel was nearly beside himself. They removed the covering from his arm, and then saw something horrible; bruised flesh, from which the blood spurted in waves, as if it were forced by a pump. The man himself looked at his arm and murmured: "Fool!"

Then, as the hemorrhage made a river on the deck of the boat, the sailors cried: "He'll lose all his blood. We must bind the vein!"

They then took a rope, a great, black, tarred rope and, twisting it around the member above the wound, bound it with all their strength. Little by little the jets of blood stopped, and finally ceased altogether.

Young Javel arose, his arm hanging by his side. He took it by the other hand, raised it, turned it, shook it. Everything was broken; the bones were crushed completely; only the muscles held it to his body. He looked at it with sad eyes, as if reflecting. Then he seated himself on a folded sail, and his comrades came around him, advising him to soak it continually to prevent its turning black.

They put a bucket near him and, from minute to minute, he would poor water from a glass upon the horrible wound, leaving a thread of color in the clear water.

"You would be better down below," said his brother. He went down, but at the end of an hour came up again, feeling better not to be alone. And then, he preferred the open air. He sat down again upon the sail and continued bathing his arm.

The fishing was good. Large fishes with white bodies were lying beside him, shaken by the spasms of death. He looked at them without ceasing to sprinkle his mangled flesh.

When they started to return to Boulogne, another gale of wind prevented. The little boat began again its mad course, bounding, tumbling, shaking sadly the wounded man.

The night came. The weather was heavy until daybreak. At sunrise, they could see England again, but as the sea was a little less rough, they turned toward France, beating in the wind.

Toward evening, young Javel called his comrades and showed them black traces and a villainous look of decay around that part of his arm which was no longer joined to his body.

The sailors looked at it, giving advice: "That must be gangrene," said one.

"It must have salt water on it," said another.

Then they brought salt water and poured it on the wound. The wounded man became livid, grinding his teeth, and twisting with pain; but he uttered no cry.

When the burning grew less, he said to his brother: "Give me your knife." The brother gave it to him.

"Hold this arm up for me, drawn out straight."

His brother did as he was asked.

Then he began to cut. He cut gently, with caution, severing the last tendons with the sharp blade as one would a thread with a razor. Soon he had only a stump. He fetched a deep sigh and said: "That had to be done. Fool!"

He seemed relieved and breathed with force. He continued to pour water on the part of his arm remaining to him.

The night was still bad and they could not land. When the day appeared, young Javel took his detached arm and examined it carefully. Putrefaction had begun. The comrades came also and examined it, passing it from hand to hand, touching it, turning it over, and smelling it.

His brother said: "It's about time to throw that into the sea."

Young Javel was angry, he replied: "No, oh! no! I will not. It is mine, isn't it? Worse still, it is my arm." He took it and held it between his legs.

"It won't grow any less putrid," said the elder.

Then an idea came to the wounded man. In order to keep the fish which they kept out a long time, they had with them barrels of salt. "Couldn't I put it in there in the brine?" he asked.

"That's so," declared the others.

Then they emptied one of the barrels, already full of fish from the last few days, and, at the bottom, they deposited the arm. Then they turned salt upon it and replaced the fishes, one by one.

One of the sailors made a little joke: "Perhaps I could sell it, if I cried it around town."

And everybody laughed except the Javel brothers.

The wind still blew. They beat about in sight of Boulogne until the next day at ten o'clock. The wounded man still poured water on his arm. From time to time he would get up and walk from one end of the boat to the other. His brother, who was at the wheel, shook his head and followed him with his eye.

Finally, they came into port.

The doctor examined the wound and declared it in good shape. He dressed it perfectly and ordered rest. But Javel could not go to bed without seeing his arm again, and went quickly back to the dock to find the barrel which he had marked with a cross.

They emptied it before him, and he found his arm refreshed, well preserved in the salt. He wrapped it in a napkin brought for this purpose, and took it home.

His wife and children examined carefully this fragment of their father, touching the fingers, taking up the grains of salt that had lodged under the nails. Then they went to the joiner for a little coffin.

The next day a complete procession of the crew of the fishing smack followed the detached arm to its interment. The two brothers, side by side, conducted the ceremony. The parish priest held the coffin under his arm.

Javel the younger gave up going to sea. He obtained a small position in port, and, later, whenever he spoke of the accident, he would say to his auditor, in a low tone: "If my brother had been willing to cut the cable, I should still have my arm, be sure. But he was looking to his own pocket."

VOLUME IX

The Watchdog

MADAME LEFEVRE was a country woman, a widow, one of those half peasants with ribbons and furbelows on her cap, a person who spoke with some care, taking on grandiose airs in public, and concealing a pretentious, brute soul under an exterior comically glossed over, as she concealed her great red hands under gloves of ecru silk.

She had for a servant a simple, rustic, named Rose. The two women lived in a little house with green shutters, on a highway in Normandy, in the center of the country of Caux. As there was a garden spot in front of the house, they cultivated some vegetables.

One night, some one robbed them of a dozen onions. When Rose perceived the larceny, she ran to tell Madame, who came down in a wool petticoat. Here was a sorrow, and a terror, besides! Some one had robbed, robbed Madame Lefevre! And when a robber visits one in the country, he may come again.

And the two frightened women studied the footprints, prattled, and supposed certain things:

"Here," they would say, "they must have passed here. They must have put their foot on the wall and then leaped into the flower bed."

And they trembled for the future. How could they sleep peacefully now?

The news of the robbery spread. The neighbors arrived to prove and discuss the matter, each in his turn. To each newcomer the two women explained their observations and their ideas. A farmer on the other side of them said:

"You ought to keep a dog."

That was true, that was; they ought to keep a dog, even if it were good for nothing but to give an alarm. Not a big dog, Monsieur! What would they do with a big dog? It would ruin them to feed it! But a little dog, a little puppy that could yap.

When everybody was gone, Madame Lefevre discussed this idea of having a dog for a long time. After reflection, she made a thousand objections, terrified at the thought of a bowlful of porridge. Because she was of that race of parsimonious country dames who always carry pennies in their pockets, in order to give alms ostensibly along the street, and to the contributions on Sunday.

Rose, who loved animals, brought forward her reasons and defended them with astuteness. And finally, it was decided that they should have a dog, but a little dog.

They began to look for one, but could only find big ones, swallowers of food enough to make one tremble. The Rolleville grocer had one, very small; but he asked two francs for him, to cover the expense of bringing him up. Madame Lefevre declared that she was willing to feed a dog, but she never would buy one.

Then the baker, who knew the circumstances, brought them, one morning, a little, yellow animal, nearly all paws, with the body of a crocodile, the head of a fox, a tail, trumpet-shaped, a regular plume, large like the rest of his person. Madame Lefevre found this cur that cost nothing very beautiful. Rose embraced it, and then asked its name. The baker said it was, "Pierrot."

He was installed in an old soap box, and he was given first, a drink of water,

He drank. Then they gave him a piece of bread. He ate.

Madame Lefevre, somewhat disturbed, had one idea:

"When he gets accustomed to the house, we can let him run loose. He will find something to eat in roaming around the country."

In fact, they did let him run, but it did not prevent him from being famished. Besides, he only barked to ask for his pittance, in which case, he did indeed bark with fury.

Anybody could enter the garden. Pierrot would go and caress each newcomer, remaining absolutely mute. Nevertheless, Madame Lefevre became accustomed to the beast. She even came to love it, and to give it from her hand, sometimes, pieces of bread dipped in the sauce from her meat.

But she had never dreamed of a tax, and when they came to her for eight francs—eight francs, Madame!—for this little cur of a dog, that would not even bark, she almost fainted from shock. It was immediately decided that they must get rid of Pierrot. No one wanted him. All the inhabitants, for ten miles around, refused him. Then it was resolved that, by some means, they must make him acquainted with the little house. Now, to be acquainted with the little house is to eat of the chalk pit. They make all dogs acquainted with the little house when they wish to get rid of them.

In the midst of a vast plain, there appeared a kind of hut, or rather, the little roof of a cottage, rising above the sod. It is the entrance to the marlpit. One great shaft went down about twenty meters, where it was met by a series of long galleries, penetrating the mine.

Once a year they descended in a sort of carriage and marled the clay. All the rest of the time, the pit serves as a cemetery for condemned dogs; and often, when one passes near the mouth, there comes to his ears plaintive howls, furious barking, and lamentable appeals.

Hunting and shepherd dogs flee with fright at the first sound of these noises; and when one stoops down above this opening, he finds an abominable odor of putrefaction. Frightful dramas have taken place within the bounds of this shadow.

When a beast suffers from hunger at the bottom of the pit for ten or twelve days, nourished only on the remains of his predecessors, sometimes a new animal, larger and more vigorous, is suddenly thrown in. There they are, alone, famished, their eyes glittering. They watch each other, follow each other, hesitate anxiously. But hunger presses; they attack each other, struggling a long time infuriated; and the strong eats the weak, devouring him alive.

When it was decided that they would get rid of Pierrot, they looked about them for an executioner. The laborer who was digging in the road, demanded six sous for the trouble. This appeared exaggerated folly to Madame Lefevre. A neighbor's boy would be content with five sous; that was still too much. Then Rose observed that it would be better for them to take him themselves, because he would not then be tortured on the way and warned of his lot; and so it was decided that they go together at nightfall.

They gave him, this evening, a good soup with a bit of butter in it. He swallowed it to the last drop. And when he wagged his tail with contentment, Rose took him in her apron.

They went at a great pace, like marauders, across the plain. As soon as they reached the pit, Madame Lefevre stooped to listen; she wanted to know if any other beast was howling in there. No, there was no sound. Pierrot would be alone. And Rose, who was weeping, embraced him, then threw him in the hole. And they stooped, both of them, and listened.

They heard first a heavy thud; then the sharp, broken cry of a wounded beast; then a succession of imploring supplications, the head raised to the opening.

He yapped, oh! how he yapped!

They were seized with remorse, with a foolish, inexplicable fear. They jumped up and ran away. And, as Rose ran more quickly, Madame Lefevre would cry: "Wait, Rose, wait for me!"

Their night was filled with frightful nightmares. Madame Lefevre dreamed that she seated herself at the table to eat soup, and when she uncovered the tureen, Pierrot was in it. He darted out and bit her on the nose. She awoke and thought she heard the barking still; she listened; she was deceived. Again she slept, and found herself upon a great road, an interminable road, that she must follow. Suddenly, in the middle of the road, she perceived a basket, a great, farmer's basket, a basket that brought her fear. Nevertheless, she finished by opening it, and Pierrot, hidden within, seized her hand, not loosing it again. And she knew that she was lost, carrying about forever suspended upon her arm, a dog with open mouth.

At the dawn of day, she arose, almost insane, and ran to the pit.

He was barking, barking still; he had barked all night. She began to sob and called him with a thousand caressing names. He responded with all the tender inflections a dog's voice is capable of. Then she wished to see him again, promising herself to make him happy to the day of her death. She ran to the house of the man in charge of the mine, and told him her story. The man listened without laughing. When she had finished, he said: "You want your dog? That will be four francs."

It was a shock. All her grief vanished at a blow.

"Four francs," said she, "Four francs! would you make a murderer of yourself!"

He replied: "You believe that I am going to bring my ropes and tackle and set them up, and go down there with my boy and get bitten, perhaps, by your mad dog, for the pleasure of giving him back to you? You shouldn't have thrown him in there!"

She went away indignant. "Four francs!"

As soon as she entered, she called Rose and told her the demands of the miner. Rose, always resigned, answered: "Four francs! It is considerable money, Madame." Then she added that they might throw the poor dog something to eat, so that it might not die there.

Madame Lefevre approved galdly, and again they set out with a big piece of bread and butter. They broke off morsels, which they threw in one after the other, calling in turn to Pierrot. And as soon as the dog had got one piece, he barked for the next.

They returned that evening, then the next day, every day. But never more than one journey.

One morning, at the moment they dropped the first morsel, they heard suddenly, a formidable barking in the shaft. There were two of them! Another dog had been thrown in, a big dog!

Rose cried: "Pierrot!" And Pierrot answered: "Yap, Yap!" Then they began to feed him, but each time they threw down a bit, they heard a terrible tussle, then the plaintive cries of Pierrot bitten by his companion, who ate all, being the stronger.

Then they specified: "This is for you Pierrot!" Pierrot evidently got nothing.

The two women, amazed, looked at each other. And Madame Lefevre declared in a sharp voice:

"I certainly can't feed all the dogs they throw in there. We must give it up."

Overcome with the idea of all those dogs living at her expense, she went away, carrying even the bread that she had begun to feed to poor Pierrot.

Rose followed, wiping her eyes on the corner of her blue apron.

————●————

The Dancers

"GREAT misfortunes grieve me little," said John Bridelle, an old bachelor who passed for a sceptic. "I have seen war at close range; I could stride over dead bodies pitilessly. The strong brutalities of nature, where we can utter cries of horror or indignation, do not wring our hearts or send the shiver down the back, as do the little wondering sights of life.

"Certainly the most violent grief that one can experience is for a mother the loss of a child, and for a son the loss of a mother. It is violent and terrible, it overturns and lacerates; but one is healed of such catastrophes, as of large, bleeding wounds. But, certain accidents, certain things hinted at, suspected, certain secret griefs, certain perfidy, of the sort that stirs up in us a world of grievous thoughts, which opens before us suddenly the mysterious door of moral suffering, complicated, incurable, so

much the more profound because it seems worthy, so much the more stinging because unseizable, the more tenacious because artificial, these leave upon the soul a train of sadness, a feeling of sorrow, a sensation of disenchantment that we are long in ridding ourselves of.

"I have ever before my eyes two or three things, that possibly had not been noticed by others, but which entered into my sympathies like deep, unhealable stings.

"You will not comprehend, perhaps, the emotion that has relieved me from these rapid impressions. I will tell you only one. It is old, but lives with me as if it occurred yesterday. It may be imagination alone that keeps it fresh in my memory.

"I am fifty years old. I was young then and studious by nature. A little sad, a little dreamy, impregnated with a melancholy philosophy, I never cared much for the brilliant *cafés*, noisy comrades, nor stupid girls. I rose early, and one of my sweetest indulgences was to take a walk alone, about eight o'clock in the morning, in the nursery of the Luxemburg.

"Perhaps you do not know this nursery? It was like a forgotten garden of another century, a pretty garden, like the smile of an old person. Trimmed hedges separated the straight, regular walks, calm walks between two walls of foliage neatly pruned. The great scissors of the gardener clipped without mercy the offshoots of the branches. While here and there were walks bordered with flowers, and clumps of little trees, arranged like collegians promenading, masses of magnificent roses, and regiments of fruit-trees.

"The whole of one corner of this delightful copse was inhabited by bees. Their straw houses, skillfully spaced upon the planks, opened to the sun their great odors, like the opening of a sewing thimble. And all along the path golden flies were buzzing, true mistresses of this peaceful place, ideal inhabitants of these walks and corridors.

"I went there nearly every morning. I would seat myself upon a bench and read. Sometimes, I would allow my book to fall upon my knees, while I dreamed and listened to the living Paris all about me, and enjoyed the infinite repose of these rows of ancient oaks.

"All at once I perceived that I was not alone a frequenter of this spot, reached through an opening in the fence. From time to time I encountered, face to face, an old man in the corner of the thicket. He wore shoes with silver buckles, trousers with a flap, a tobacco-colored coat, lace in place of a cravat, and an unheard-of hat with nap and edges worn, which made one think of the deluge.

"He was thin, very thin, angular, smiling, grimacing. His bright eyes sparkled, agitated by a continual movement of the pupils; and he always carried a superb cane, with a gold head, which must have been a souvenir, and a magnificent one.

"This good man astonished me at first, then interested me beyond measure. And I watched him behind a wall of foliage, and followed him from afar, stopping behind shrubbery, so as not to be seen.

"It happened one morning as he believed himself entirely alone, that he began some singular movements; some little bounds at first, then a bow; then he struck up some capers with his lank legs, then turned cleverly, as if on a pivot, bending and swaying in a droll fashion, smiling as if before the public, making gestures with outstretched arms, twisting his poor body like a jumping-jack, throwing tender, ridiculous salutations to the open air. He was dancing!

"I remained petrified with amazement, asking myself which of the two was mad, he or I. But he stopped suddenly, advanced as actors do upon the stage, bowed, and took a few steps backward, with the gracious smiles and kisses of the comedian, which he threw with trembling hand to the two rows of shapely trees.

"After that, he resumed his walk with gravity.

"From this day, I never lost sight of

him. And each morning he recommenced his peculiar exercise.

"A foolish desire led me to speak to him. I ventured and, having bowed, I said:

" 'It is a fine day, to-day, sir.'

"He bowed. 'Yes, sir, it is like the weather of long ago.'

"A week after this, we were friends, and I knew his history. He had been dancing master at the Opera from the time of Louis XV. His beautiful cane was a gift from Count de Clermont. And when he began to speak of dancing, he never knew when to stop.

"One day he confided in me:

" 'I married La Castris, sir. I will present her to you, if you wish, but she never comes here so early. This garden, you see, is our pleasure and our life. It is all that remains to us of former times. It seems to us that we could not exist if we did not have it. It is old and distinguished, is it not? Here I can seem to breathe air that has not changed since my youth. My wife and I pass every afternoon here. But I, I come again in the morning, because I rise so early.'

"After luncheon, I returned to the Luxemburg, and soon I perceived my friend, who was giving his arm with great ceremony to a little old woman clothed in black, to whom I was presented. It was La Castris, the great dancer, loved of princes, loved of the king, loved of all that gallant century which seems to have left in the world an odor of love.

"We seated ourselves upon a bench. It was in the month of May. A perfume of flowers flitted through all the tidy walks; a pleasant sun glistened between the leaves and spread over us large spots of light. The black robe of La Castris seemed all permeated with brightness.

"The garden was empty. The roll of carriages could be heard in the distance.

" 'Will you explain to me,' said I to the old dancing master, 'what the minuet was?'

"He started. 'The minuet, sir, is the queen of dances and the dance of queens, do you understand? Since there are no more kings, there are no more minuets.'

"And he commenced, in pompous style, a long, dithyrambic eulogy of which I comprehended nothing. I wanted him to describe the step to me, all the movements, the poses. He perplexed and exasperated himself with his lack of strength, and then became nervous and spent. Then, suddenly, turning toward his old companion, always silent and grave, he said:

" 'Elise, will you, I say—will you be so kind as to show this gentleman what the minuet really was?'

"She turned her unquiet eyes in every direction, then rising, without a word, placed herself opposite him.

"Then I saw something never to be forgotten.

"They went forward and back with a child-like apishness, smiling to each other and balancing, bowing and hopping like two old puppets made to dance by some ancient mechanism, a little out of repair, and constructed long ago by some skillful workman following the custom of his day.

"And I looked at them, my heart troubled with extraordinary sensations, my soul moved by an indescribable melancholy. I seemed to see a lamentable, comic apparition, the shadow of a century past and gone. I had a desire to laugh when I felt more like weeping.

"Then they stopped; they had ended the figure of the dance. For some seconds they remained standing before each other, smirking in a most surprising manner; then they embraced each other with a sob.

"I left town three days later for the provinces. I have never seen them again. When I returned to Paris, two years later, they had destroyed the nursery garden. What have the old couple done without the dear garden of other days, with its labyrinths, its odor of long ago, and its walks shaded by graceful elms? Are they dead? Are they wandering through modern streets, like exiles without hope? Are they dancing somewhere, grotesque specters, a fantastic minuet among the cypresses in the cemetery, along the paths beside the tombs, in the moonlight?

"The remembrance haunts me, oppresses and tortures me; it remains with me like a wound. Why? I cannot tell.

"You will find this very ridiculous, without doubt."

Christening

"COME, doctor, a little more cognac." "With pleasure." The old navy doctor watched the golden liquid flow into his glass, held it up to the light, took a sip and kept it in his mouth a long while before swallowing it, and said:

"What a delicious poison! I should say, what a captivating destroyer of humanity! You do not know it as I know it. You may have read that remarkable book called 'L'Assommoir,' but you have not seen a whole tribe of savages exterminated by this same poison. I have seen with my own eyes a strange and terrible drama, which was the result of too much alcohol. It happened not very far from here, in a little village near Pont-l'abbé in Brittany. I was on a vacation and was living in the little country house which my father had left me. You all know that wild country surrounded by the sea—that wicked sea, always lying in wait for some new victim! The poor fishermen go out day and night in their little boats and the wicked sea upsets their boats and swallows them! Fearlessly they go out, yet feeling uneasy as to their safety, but half of the time they are intoxicated. 'When the bottle is full we feel safe, but when it is empty we feel lost'; they say. If you got into their huts, you will never find the father and if you ask the woman what has become of her man, she will answer pointing to the raging sea: 'He stayed there one night, when he had too much drink and my eldest son too.' She has still four strong boys; it will be their turn soon!

"Well, as I have said, I was living at my little country house with one servant, an old sailor, and the Breton family who took care of the place during my absence, which consisted of two sisters and the husband of one of them, who was also my gardener.

"Toward Christmas of that year, the gardener's wife gave birth to a boy and he asked me to be godfather. I could not very well refuse, and on the strength of it he borrowed ten francs from me, 'for the church expenses,' he said.

"The christening was to take place on the second of January. For the past week the ground had been covered with snow and it was bitter cold. At nine o'clock of the morning designated, Kerandec and his sister-in-law arrived in front of my door, with a nurse carrying the baby wrapped up in a blanket, and we started for the church. The cold was terrific and I wondered how the poor little child could stand such cold. These Bretons must be made of iron, I thought, if they can stand going out in such weather at their birth!

"When we arrived at the church the door was closed. The priest had not come yet. The nurse sat on the steps and began to undress the child. I thought at first that she only wanted to arrange his clothes, but to my horror I saw that she was taking every stitch of clothing off his back! I was horrified at such imprudence and I went toward her saying:

" 'What in the world are you doing? Are you crazy? Do you want to kill him?'

" 'Oh, no, master," she answered placidly, 'but he must present himself before God naked.' His father and aunt looked on calmly. It was the custom in Brittany and if they had not done this they said, something would happen to the child.

"I got furiously angry. I called the father all kinds of names; I threatened to leave them and tried to cover the child by force, but in vain. The nurse ran away from me with the poor little naked body, which was fast becoming blue with the biting cold. I had made up my mind to leave these brutes to their ignorance, when I saw the priest coming along followed by the sexton and an altar boy. I ran toward him and told him in a few words what these brutes had done, but he was not a bit surprised; nor did he hurry.

" 'What can I do, my dear sir? It is the custom, they all do it.'

" 'But for goodness sake hurry up,' I cried impatiently.

" 'I cannot go any faster,' he answered, and at last he entered the vestry. We waited outside the church-door and I suffered terribly at hearing that poor little wretch crying with pain. At last the door opened and we went in, but the child had to remain naked during the whole ceremony. It seemed to me as if it would never come to an end. The priest crawled along like a turtle, muttered his Latin words slowly, as if he took pleasure in torturing the poor little baby. At last, the torture came to an end and the nurse wrapped the child in his blanket again. By that time the poor little thing was chilled through and was crying piteously.

" 'Will you come in and sign your name to the register?' asked the priest.

"I turned to the gardener and urged him to go home immediately and warm the child up, so as to avoid pneumonia if there was still time. He promised to follow my advice, and left with his sister-in-law and the nurse. I followed the priest into the vestry, and when I had signed the register, he demanded five francs. As I had given ten francs to the father, I refused. The priest threatened to tear up the certificate and to annul the ceremony, and I, in my turn, threatened to prosecute him. We quarreled for a long time, but at last I paid the five francs.

"As soon as I got home, I ran to Kerandec's house, but neither he, nor his sister-in-law or the nurse had come home. The mother was in bed shivering with cold and she was hungry, not having eaten anything since the day before.

"'Where on earth did they go?' I asked. She did not seem the least bit surprised and answered calmly:

"'They went to have a drink in honor of the christening.' That also was the custom and I thought of my ten francs which I had given the father, and which would pay for the drinks no doubt. I sent some beef-tea to the mother and had a good fire made in her room. I was so angry at those brutes that I made up my mind to discharge them when they came back; but what worried me most was the poor little baby. What would become of him?

"At six o'clock they had not come back. I ordered my servant to wait for them and I went to bed.

"I slept soundly, as a sailor will sleep, until daybreak and did not wake until my servant brought me some hot water. As soon as I opened my eyes I asked him about Kerandec. The old sailor hesitated, then finally answered:

"'He came home past midnight as drunk as a fool; the Kermagan woman and the nurse too. I think they slept in a ditch, and the poor little baby died without their even noticing it.'

"'Dead!' I cried jumping to my feet.

"'Yes, sir, they brought it to the mother, and when she saw it she cried terribly, but they made her drink to forget her sorrow.'

"'What do you mean by "they made her drink?"'

"'This, sir. I only found out this morning. Kerandec had no more liquor and no more money to buy any, so he took the wood alcohol that you gave him for the lamp and they drank that until they had finished the bottle and now the Kerandec woman is very sick.'

"I dressed in haste, seized a cane with the firm intention of chastising those human brutes and ran to the gardener's house. The mother lay helpless, dying from the effects of the alcohol, with the discolored corpse of her baby lying near her, while Kerandec and the Kermagan woman lay snoring on the floor.

"I did everything in my power to save the woman, but she died at noon."

The old doctor having concluded his narrative, took the bottle of cognac, poured out a glass for himself, and having held it up to the light, swallowed the golden liquid and smacked his lips.

A Costly Outing

HECTOR DE GRIBELIN, descendant of an old provincial family, had spent his early years in his ancestral home and had finished his studies under the guidance of an old abbé. The family was far from rich, but they kept up appearances the best way they could. At the age of twenty a position was procured for him at the Navy administration, at one thousand five hundred francs a year, but like a great many, not being prepared for the battle, his first three years of office life had been exceedingly hard.

He had renewed acquaintance with a few old friends of his family, poor like himself, but living in the secluded Faubourg St.-Germain, keeping up appearances at any cost, sacrificing everything in order to hold their rank.

It was there he had met and married a young girl, titled but penniless. Two children had blessed their union. Hector and his wife struggled constantly to make both ends meet and for the past four years they had known no other distractions than a walk on Sunday to the Champs-Elysées, and a few evenings at the theater, a friend giving them tickets.

His chief had just intrusted him with some extra work and he received the extra compensation of three hundred francs. Coming home that night he said to his wife:

"My dear Henriette, we ought to do something with this money; a little outing in the country for the children for instance."

They had a lengthy discussion, and finally decided on a family picnic.

"We have had so very few outings," said Hector, "that we may as well do things right. We will hire a rig for you and the little ones, and I will hire a horse; it will do me good."

They talked of nothing else all week. Each night, he would dance his elder son up and down on his foot and say:

"This is the way papa will ride next Sunday." And the boy would ride chairs all day screaming:

"This is papa on horseback." Even the servant marveled when she heard Hector tell of his feats on horseback when he was home and how he would ride at the side of the carriage.

"When once on a horse I am afraid of nothing," he would say. "If they could give me a frisky animal I would like it all the better. You will see how I ride, and, if you like, we can come back by the Champs-Elysées when everybody is coming home. We shall cut quite a figure, and I should not be sorry to meet some one from the office; there is nothing like it to inspire respect."

At last Sunday came. The carriage and the horse were at the door, and Hector came down immediately, holding a newly-bought riding-whip, to look the horse over. He examined him from head to foot, opened his mouth, told his age, and as the family was coming out at that moment, he discoursed on horses in general and that one in particular, which he declared to be an excellent animal.

When everyone was comfortably placed in the carriage, Hector examined the saddle, and mounting with a spring, dropped on the horse with such force that he immediately set up a dance which almost threw his rider. Hector became flustered and tried to calm him, saying: "Come, old fellow, be quiet." And having succeeded in calming him a little he asked:

"Is everybody ready?"

Everybody said they were and the party proceeded. All eyes were turned on Hector, who affected the English seat and leaped up and down on his saddle in an exaggerated manner. He looked straight before him, contracting his brow and looking very pale. His wife and the servant each held one of the boys on their lap and every minute they would say:

"Look at papa!" And the boys, overcome with joy, uttered piercing screams.

The horse, frightened at so much noise, started off at a gallop and while Hector tried to stop him his hat fell off. The driver had to come down and pick it up, and having recovered it, Hector shouted to his wife:

"Make the children stop screaming, will you? They will make the horse run away."

They arrived at last. The baskets having been opened they lunched on the grass. Although the driver looked after the horses, Hector went every minute to see if his horse wanted anything. He patted him and fed him bread, cake, and sugar.

"He is a great trotter," he said to his wife. "He shook me at first, but you saw how quickly I subdued him. He knows his master now."

They came back by the Champs-Elysées as agreed. The weather being beautiful, the avenue was crowded with carriages and the sidewalks lined with pedestrians. The horse, scenting the stable, suddenly took to his heels. He dashed between carriages like a whirlwind and Hector's efforts to stop him were unavailing. The carriage containing his family was far behind. In front of the Palais de l'Industrie, the horse turned to the right at a gallop. An old woman was at that moment leisurely crossing the street, and Hector, who was unable to stop the horse shouted: "Hey there, hey!" But the old woman was deaf, perhaps, for she slowly kept on until the horse struck her with such force that she turned a triple somersault and landed ten feet away. Several people shouted: "Stop him."

Hector was distracted and held on desperately to the horse's mane, crying: "Help, help!" A terrible shock sent him ovre the horse's head like a bomb, and he landed in the arms of a policeman who was running toward him. An angry crowd gathered. An old gentleman wearing a decoration was especially angry.

"Confound it, sir!" he said, "if you cannot ride a horse why do you not stay at home instead of running over people!"

Four men were carrying the old woman, who to all appearances was dead.

"Take this woman to a drug-store," said the old gentleman, "and let us go to the station-house."

A crowd followed Hector, who walked between two policemen, while a third led his horse. At that moment the carriage appeared, and his wife taking in the situation at a glance, ran toward him; the servant and the children came behind crying. He explained that his horse had knocked a woman down, but it was nothing, he would be home very soon.

Arrived at the station-house, he gave his name, his place of employment, and awaited news of the injured woman. A policeman came back with the information that the woman's name was Mme. Simon, and that she was a charwoman sixty-five years old. She had regained consciousness, but she suffered internally, she claimed. When Hector found that she was not dead, he recovered his spirits and promised to defray the expenses of her illness. He went to the drug-store where they had taken the old woman. An immense crowd blocked the doorway. The old woman was whining and groaning pitifully. Two doctors were examining her.

"There are no bones broken," they said, "but we are afraid she is hurt internally."

"Do you suffer much?" asked Hector.

"Oh, yes."

"Where?"

"I feel as if my inside was on fire."

"Then you are the cause of the accident?" said a doctor approaching.

"Yes, sir," said Hector.

"This woman must go to a sanitarium. I know one where they will take her for six francs a day; shall I fix it for you?"

Hector thanked him gratefully and went home relieved. He found his wife in tears, and he comforted her saying:

"Don't worry, she is much better already. I sent her to a sanitarium, and in three days she will be all right."

After his work the next day he went to see Mme. Simon. She was eating some beef soup which she seemed to relish.

"Well," said Hector, "how do you feel?"

"No better, my poor man," she answered. "I feel as good as dead!"

The doctor advised waiting, complications might arise. He waited three days, then went to see the old woman again. Her skin was clear, her eyes bright, but as soon as she saw Hector she commenced to whine:

"I can't move any more, my poor man; I'll be like this for the rest of my days!"

Hector felt a shiver running up and down his back. He asked for the doctor and inquired about the patient.

"I am puzzled," the doctor said. "Every time we try to lift her up or change her position, she utters heartrending screams; still, I am bound to believe her. I cannot say that she shams until I have seen her walk."

The old woman listened attentively; a sly look on her face. A week, two, then a month passed and still Mme. Simon did not leave her chair. Her appetite was excellent, she gained flesh and joked with the other patients. She seemed to accept her lot as a well-earned rest after fifty years of labor as a charwoman.

Hector came every day and found her the same; always repeating:

"I can't move, my poor man, I can't!"

When Hector came home, his wife would ask with anxiety:

"How is Mme. Simon?"

"Just the same; absolutely no change," answered Hector dejectedly.

They dismissed the servant and economized more than ever. The money received from his chief had been spent. Hector was desperate and one day he called four doctors to hold a consultation. They examined Mme. Simon thoroughly, while she watched them slyly.

"We must make her walk," said one of the doctors.

"I can't, gentlemen; I can't!"

They took hold of her and dragged her a few steps, but she freed herself, and sank to the floor emitting such piercing screams, that they carried her back to her chair very gently.

They reserved their opinion, but concluded, however, that she was incapacitated for work.

When Hector brought the news to his wife, she collapsed.

"We had much better take her here, it would cost us less."

"In our own house! What are you thinking of?"

"What else can we do, dear? I am sure it is no fault of mine!"

The Man with the Dogs

His wife, even when talking to him, always called him Monsieur Bistaud, but in all the country round, within a radius of ten leagues, in France and Belgium, he was known as *Cet homme aux chiens*.* It was not a very valuable reputation, however, and "That man with the dogs," became a sort of pariah.

In Thierache they are not very fond of the custom-house officers, for everybody, high or low, profits by smuggling; thanks to which many articles, and especially coffee, gun-powder, and tobacco, are to be had cheap. It may here be stated that on that wooded, broken country, where the meadows are surrounded by brushwood, and the lanes are dark and narrow, smuggling is carried on chiefly by means of sporting dogs, who are broken in to become smuggling dogs. Scarcely an evening passes without some of them being seen, loaded with contraband, trotting silently along, pushing their nose through a hole in a hedge, with furtive

and uneasy looks, and sniffing the air to scent the custom-house officers and their dogs. These dogs also are specially trained, and are very ferocious, and can easily kill their unfortunate congeners, who become the game instead of hunting for it.

Now, nobody was capable of imparting this unnatural education to them so well as the man with the dogs, whose business consisted in breaking in dogs for the custom-house authorities. Everybody looked upon it as a dirty business, a business which could only be performed by a man without any proper feeling.

"He is a man's robber," the women said, "to take honest dogs in to nurse, and to make a lot of traitors out of them."

While the boys shouted insulting verses behind his back, and the men and the women abused him, no one ventured

---

*That man with the dogs.

to do it to his face, for he was not very patient, and was always accompanied by one of his huge dogs, and that served to make him respected.

Certainly without that bodyguard, he would have had a bad time of it, especially at the hands of the smugglers, who had a deadly hatred for him. By himself, and in spite of his quarrelsome looks, he did not appear very formidable. He was short and thin, his back was round, his legs were bandy, and his arms were as long and as thin as spiders' legs, and he could easily have been knocked down by a back-handed blow or a kick. But then, he had those confounded dogs, which intimidated even the bravest smugglers. How could they risk even a blow when he had those huge brutes, with their fierce and bloodshot eyes, and their square heads, with jaws like a vise, and enormous white teeth, sharp as daggers, and with huge molars which crunched up beefbones to a pulp? They were wonderfully broken in, were always by him, obeyed him by signs, and were taught not only to worry the smugglers' dogs, but also to fly at the throats of the smugglers themselves.

The consequence was that both he and his dogs were left alone, and people were satisfied with calling them names and sending them all to Coventry. No peasant ever set foot in his cottage, although Bistaud's wife kept a small shop and was a handsome woman, and the only persons who went there were the custom-house officers. The others took their revenge on them all by saying that the man with the dogs sold his wife to the custom-house officers, like he did his dogs.

"He keeps her for them, as well as his dogs," they said jeeringly. "You can see that he is a born cuckold with his yellow beard and eyebrows, which stick up like a pair of horns."

His hair was certainly red or rather yellow, his thick eyebrows were turned up in two points on his temples, and he used to twirl them mechanically as if they had been a pair of mustaches. And certainly, with hair like that, and with his long beard and shaggy eyebrows, with his sallow face, blinking eyes, and dull looks, with his dogged mouth, thin lips, and his miserable, deformed body, he was not a pleasing object.

But he assuredly was not a complaisant cuckold, and those who said that of him had never seen him at home. On the contrary, he was always jealous, and kept as sharp a lookout on his wife as he did on his dogs, and if he had broken her in at all, it was to be as faithful to him as they were.

She was a handsome and, what they call in the country, a fine body of a woman; tall, well-built, with a full bust and broad. hips, and she certainly made more than one exciseman squint at her. But it was no use for them to come and sniff round her too closely, or else there would have been blows. At least, that is what the custom-house officers said, when anybody joked with them and said to them: "That does not matter; no doubt, you and she have hunted for your fleas together."

It was no use for them to defend Madame Bistaud's fierce virtue; nobody believed them, and the only answer they got, was: "You are hiding your game, and are ashamed of going to seduce a woman who belongs to such a wretched creature."

And, certainly, nobody would have believed that such a buxom woman, who must have liked to be well attended to, could be satisfied with such a puny husband, with such an ugly, weak, redheaded fellow, who smelled of his dogs, and of the mustiness of the carrion which he gave to his hounds.

But they did not know that the man with the dogs had some years before given her, once for all, a lesson in fidelity, and that for a mere trifle, a venial sin! He had surprised her for allowing herself to be kissed by some gallant, that was all! He had not taken any notice, but when the man was gone, he brought two of his hounds into the room, and said:

"If you do not want them to tear your inside out as they would a rabbit's, go down on your knees so that I may thrash you!"

She obeyed in terror, and the man with the dogs had beaten her with a whip until his arm dropped with fatigue. And she did not venture to scream, although she was bleeding under the blows of the thong, which tore her dress, and cut into the flesh; all she dared to do was to utter low, hoarse groans; for while beating her, he kept on saying:

"Don't make a noise, by——; don't make a noise, or I will let the dogs fly at you."

From that time she had been faithful to Bistaud, though she had naturally not told anyone the reason for it, or for her hatred either, not even Bistaud himself, who thought that she was subdued for all time, and always found her very submissive and respectful. But for

six years she had nourished her hatred in her heart, feeding it on silent hopes and promises of revenge. And it was that flame of hope and that longing for revenge, which made her so coquettish with the custom-house officers, for she hoped to find a possible avenger among her inflammable admirers.

At last she came across the right man. He was a splendid sub-officer of the customs, built like a Hercules, with fists like a butcher's, and had long leased four of his ferocious dogs from her husband.

As soon as they had grown accustomed to their new master, and especially after they had tasted the flesh of the smugglers' dogs, they had, by degrees become detached from their former master, who had reared them. No doubt they still recognized him a little, and would not have sprung at his throat, as if he were a perfect stranger, but still, they did not hesitate between his voice and that of their new master, and they obeyed the latter only.

Although the woman had often noticed this, she had not hitherto been able to make much use of the circumstance. A custom-house officer, as a rule, only keeps one dog, and Bistaud always had half-a-dozen, at least, in training, without reckoning a personal guard which he kept for himself, which was the fiercest of all. Consequently, any duel between some lover assisted by only one dog, and the dog-breaker defended by his pack, was impossible.

But on that occasion, the chances were more equal. Just then he had only five dogs in the kennel, and two of them were quite young, though certainly old Bourreau* counted for several. After all they could risk a battle against him and the other three, with the two couples of the custom-house officer, and they must profit by the occasion.

So one fine evening, as the brigadier of the custom-house officers was alone in the shop with Bistaud's wife and was squeezing her waist, she said to him abruptly:

"Do you really want to have something to do with me, *Môssieu*† Fernand?"

He kissed her on the lips as he replied. "Do I really want to? I would give my stripes for it; so you see."

"Very well!" she replied, "do as I tell you, and upon my word, as an honest woman, I will be your commodity to do what you like with."

And laying a stress on that word *commodity*, which in that part of the country means strumpet, she whispered hotly into his ear:

"A commodity who knows her business, I can tell you, for my beast of a husband has trained me up in such a way that I am now absolutely disgusted with him."

Fernand, who was much excited, promised her everything that she wished, and feverishly, malignantly she told him how shamefully her husband had treated her a short time before, how her fair skin had been cut, and of her hatred and thirst for revenge. The brigadier acquiesced, and that same evening came to the cottage accompanied by his four hounds, with their spiked collars on.

"What are you going to do with them?" the man with the dogs asked.

"I have come to see whether you did

not rob me, when you leased them to me," the brigadier replied.

"What do you mean by 'robbed you?' "

"Well, robbed! I have been told that they could not tackle a dog like your Bourreau, and that many smugglers have dogs who are as good as he is."

"Impossible."

"Well, in case any of them should have one, I should like to see how the dogs that you sold me could tackle them."

The woman laughed an evil laugh, and her husband grew suspicious, when he saw that the brigadier replied to it by a wink. But his suspicions came too late. The breaker had no time to go to the kennel to let out his pack, for Bourreau had been seized by the custom-house officer's four dogs. At the same time, the woman locked the door; already her husband was lying motionless on the floor, while Bourreau could not go to his assistance, as he had enough to do to defend himself against the furious attack of the other dogs, who were almost tearing him to pieces, in spite of his strength and courage. Five minutes later two of the attacking hounds were totally disabled, with their bowels protruding, but Bourreau himself was dying, with his throat gaping.

Then the woman and the custom-house officer kissed each other before the breaker, whom they bound firmly. The two dogs of the custom-house officer that were still on their legs were panting for breath, and the other three were wallowing in their blood. And now the

---

*Executioner, hangman.
†Vulgar for Monsieur.

amorous couple were carrying on all sorts of capers, still further excited by the rage of the dog-breaker, who was forced to look at them, and who shouted in his despair:

"You wretches! you shall pay for this!" And the woman's only reply was, to say: "Cuckold! cuckold! cuckold!"

When she was tired of larking, her hatred was not yet satisfied, and she said to the brigadier:

"Fernand, go to the kennels and shoot the five other brutes, otherwise he will make them kill me to-morrow. Off you go, old fellow!"

The brigadier obeyed, and immediately five shots were heard in the darkness; it did not take long, but that short time had been enough for the man with the dogs to show what he could do. While he was tied, the two dogs of the custom-house officer had gradually recognized him, and came and fondled him, and as soon as he was alone with his wife, as she was insulting him, he said in his usual voice of command to the dogs:

"At her, Flanbard! at her, Garou!" The two dogs sprang at the wretched woman, and one seized her by the throat, while the other caught her by the side.

When the brigadier came back, she was dying on the ground in a pool of blood, and the man with the dogs said with a laugh: "There you see, that is the way I break in my dogs!"

The custom-house officer rushed out in horror, followed by his hounds, who licked his hands as they ran, and made them quite red.

The next morning the man with the dogs was found still bound, but chuckling, in his hovel that was turned into a slaughter-house.

They were both arrested and tried; the man with the dogs was acquitted, and the brigadier sentenced to a term of imprisonment. The matter gave much food for talk in the district, and is indeed still talked about, for the man with the dogs returned there, and is more celebrated than ever under his nickname. But his celebrity is not of a bad kind, for he is now just as much respected and liked as he was despised and hated formerly. He is still, as a matter of fact, the man with the dogs, as he is rightly called, for he has not his equal as a dog-breaker, for leagues round. But now he no longer breaks in mastiffs, as he has given up teaching honest dogs to "act the part of Judas," as he says, for those dirty custom-house officers. He only devotes himself to dogs to be used for smuggling, and he is worth listening to, when he says:

"You may depend upon it, that I know how to punish such commodities as she, when they have sinned! I was glad to see my dogs tearing that strumpet's skin and her lying mouth."

A King's Son

THE Boulevard, that river of life, was rushing along under the golden light of the setting sun. All the sky was red, dazzling red; and behind the Madeleine an immense, brilliant cloud threw into the long avenue an oblique shower of fire, vibrating like the rays from live coals.

The gay crowd moved along in this ruddy mist as if they were in an apotheosis. Their faces were golden; their black hats and coats were reflected in shades of purple; the varnish of their shoes threw red lights upon the asphalt of the sidewalks.

Before the *cafés,* men were drinking brilliantly colored drinks, which one might take for precious stones melted in the crystal.

In the midst of the consumers, two officers, in very rich uniforms, caused all eyes to turn in their direction on account of their gold braid and grand bearing. They were chatting pleasantly, without motive, rejoicing in this glory of life, in the radiant beauty of the evening. And they looked at the crowd —at the slow men and the hurrying women who left behind them an attractive, disturbing odor.

All at once, an enormous negro, clothed in black, corpulent, decorated with trinkets all over his duck waistcoat, his face shining as if it had been oiled, passed before them with an air of triumph. He smiled at the passers-by, he smiled at the venders of the newspapers, he smiled at the shining heavens, and the whole of Paris. He was so large that he towered above all their heads; and all the loungers that he left behind him turned to contemplate his back.

Suddenly he perceived the officers and, pushing aside the drinkers, he rushed toward them. When he was before their table, he planted upon them his shining, delighted eyes, and, raising the corners of his mouth to his ears, showed his white teeth, shining like a crescent moon in a black sky. The two men, stupefied, looked at this ebony giant without understanding his merriment.

Then he cried out, in a voice that made everybody at all the tables laugh:

"Good evenin', my Lieutenant."

One of the officers was chief of a battalion, the other was a colonel. The first said:

"I do not know you, sir; and cannot think what you can want of me."

The negro replied:

"Me like you much, Lieutenant Védie, siege of Bézi, much grapes, hunt me up."

The officer, much astonished, looked closely at the man, seeking to place him in his memory. Suddenly he cried:

"Timbuctoo?"

The negro, radiant, struck himself on his leg, uttered a most strident laugh, and bellowed:

"Yes, ya, ya, my Lieutenant, remember Timbuctoo, ya, good evenin'."

The officer extended his hand, laughing now himself with all his heart. Then Timbuctoo became grave. He seized the officer's hand and kissed it as the custom is in Arabia, so quickly that it could not be stopped. In a confused manner, the military man said to him, his voice rather severe:

"Come, Timbuctoo, we are not in

914

Africa. Be seated and tell me how you came to be here."

Timbuctoo swelled out his ample front and stammered, from trying to talk too quickly:

"Got much money, much, great rest'rant, good eat, Prussians come, much steal, much, French cooking, Timbuctoo chef to Emperor, two hundred thousand francs for me. Ah! ah! ah! ah!"

And he laughed, twisting himself and howling, with a perfect madness of joy in his eye.

When the officer who comprehended this strange language had asked him questions for some time, he said to him:

"Well, good-bye now, Timbuctoo; I will see you again."

The negro immediately arose, shook the hand that was extended to him, properly this time, and, continuing to laugh, cried:

"Good evenin', good evenin', my Lieutenant."

He went away so content that he gesticulated as he walked until he was taken for a crazy man.

The colonel asked: "Who was that brute?"

The commander responded: "A brave boy and a brave soldier. I will tell you what I know of him; it is funny enough.

*　　*　　*　　*　　*　　*　　*

"You know that at the commencement of the war of 1870 I was shut up in Bézières, which the negro calls Bézi. We were not besieged, but blockaded. The Prussian lines surrounded us everywhere, beyond the reach of cannon, no longer shooting at us but starving us little by little.

"I was then a lieutenant. Our garrison was composed of troops of every nature, the *débris* of cut-up regiments, fugitives and marauders separated from the body of the army. We even had eleven Turcos arrive finally, one evening, from no one knew where. They presented themselves at the gates of the town, harassed, hungry, drunk, and in tatters. They were given to me.

"I soon recognized the fact that they were averse to all discipline, that they were always absent and always tipsy. I tried the police station, even the prison, without effect. My men disappeared for whole days, as if they had sunk into the earth, then reappeared intoxicated enough to fall. They had no money. Where did they get their drink? How and by what means?

"This began to puzzle me much, especially as these savages interested me with their eternal laugh and their character, which was that of a great roguish child.

"I then perceived that they blindly obeyed the biggest one of them all, the one you have just seen. He governed them by his will, planned their mysterious enterprises, and was chief, allpowerful and incontestable. I made him come to my house and I questioned him. Our conversation lasted a good three hours, so great was my difficulty in penetrating his surprising mixture of tongues. As for him, poor devil, he made the most unheard-of efforts to be understood, invented words, gesticulated, fairly sweated from his difficulty, wiped his brow, puffed, stopped, and then began suddenly again when he thought he had found a new means of explaining himself.

"I finally divined that he was the son of a great chief, a sort of negro king in the neighborhood of Timbuctoo. I asked him his name. He responded something like Chavaharibouhalikhranafotapolara. It appeared simpler to me to call him by the name of his country: 'Timbuctoo.' And eight days later all the garrison was calling him that and nothing else.

"A foolish desire seized me of finding out where this ex-African prince found his drink. And I discovered it in a singular way.

"One morning I was on the ramparts studying the horizon, when I perceived something moving in a vine near by. It was at the time of the vintage; the grapes were ripe, but I scarcely gave this a thought. My idea was that some spy was approaching the town, and I organized an expedition complete enough to seize the prowlers. I myself took the command, having obtained the General's authorization.

"Three small troops were to set out through three different gates and join near the suspected vine to watch. In order to cut off the retreat of any spy; one detachment had to make a march of an hour at least. One man remained upon the wall for observation, to indicate to me by a sign that the person sought had not left the field. We preserved a deep silence, crawling, almost lying in the wheel-ruts. Finally, we reached the designated point; I suddenly deployed my soldiers, charging them quickly upon the vine, and found—Timbuctoo traveling along among the vine stocks on four paws, eating grapes, or rather snapping them up as a dog eats his soup, his mouth full, of leaves, even, snatching the bunches off with a blow of his teeth.

"I wished to make him get up; there was no longer any mystery and I comprehended why he dragged himself along upon his hands and knees.

"When he was planted upon his feet, he swayed back and forth for some seconds, extending his arms and striking his nose. He was as tipsy as any tipsy man I have ever seen.

"They brought him away on two poles. He never ceased to laugh all along the route, gesticulating with his arms and legs.

"That was the whole of it. My merry fellows had drunk of the grape itself. Then, when they could no longer drink and could not budge, they went to sleep on the spot.

"As for Timbuctoo, his love for the vine passed all belief and all measure. He lived down there after the fashion of the thrushes, which he hated with the hatred of a jealous rival. He repeated without ceasing:

" 'The th'ushes eat all g'apes, the d'unkards.'

* * * * * * *

"One evening some one came to find me. Off over the plain something seemed to be moving toward us. I did not have my glass with me, and could not distinguish what it was. It looked like a great serpent rolling itself along, or a funeral procession; how could I tell?

"I sent some men to meet this strange caravan, which soon appeared in triumphal march. Timbuctoo and nine of his companions were carrying a sort of altar, made of campaign chairs, upon which were eight cut-off heads, bloody and grimacing. The tenth Turco dragged a horse by the tail to which another was attached, and six other beasts still followed, held in the same fashion."

"This is what I learned. Having set out for the vine, my Africans had suddenly perceived a detachment of Prussian soldiers approaching a neighboring village. Instead of fleeing they concealed themselves; then, when the officers put foot to the ground at an inn to refresh themselves, the eleven merry ones threw themselves upon them, put to flight the uhlans who believed themselves attacked, killed the two sentinels, then the Colonel and the five officers comprising his escort.

"That day I embraced Timbuctoo. But I also perceived that he walked with difficulty; I believed that he was wounded. He began to laugh and said to me:

" 'Me get p'ovisions for country.'

"It seems that Timbuctoo had not made war for the sake of honor, but for gain. All that he found, all that appeared to him to have any value whatever, everything that glistened, especially, he plunged into his pocket. And what a pocket! An abyss that begun at the hip and extended to the heels. Having learned the word of a trooper, he called it his 'profound.' It was, in fact, his profound! He had detached the gold from the Prussian uniforms, the copper from their helmets, the buttons, etc., and thrown them all into his profound, which was full to the brim.

"Each day he cast in there every glistening object that fell under his eye, —pieces of tin or pieces of money,—

which sometimes gave him an infinitely droll figure.

"He counted on bringing things back like an ostrich, which he resembled like a brother,—this son of a king tortured by a desire to devour these shining bodies. If he had not had his profound, what would he have done? Doubtless he would have swallowed them.

"Each morning his pocket was empty. He had a kind of general store where he heaped up his riches. Where? No one could ever discover.

"The General, foreseeing the uproar that Timbuctoo had created, had the bodies quickly interred in a neighboring village, before it was discovered that they had been decapitated. The Prussians came the next day. The mayor and seven distinguished inhabitants were shot immediately, as it had been learned through informers that they had denounced the Germans.

*   *   *   *   *   *   *

"The winter had come. We were harassed and desperate. There was fighting now, every day. The starved men could no longer walk. The eight Turks alone (three had been killed) were fat and shining, vigorous and always ready for battle. Timbuctoo even grew stout. He said to me one day:

" 'You much hungry, me good food.'

"In fact, he brought me an excellent fillet. Of what? We had neither beeves, sheep, goats, asses, nor pigs. It was impossible for him to procure a horse. I reflected upon all this after having devoured my viand. Then, a terrible thought came to me. These negroes were born near a country where they ate men! And every day soldiers were falling all about them! I questioned Timbuctoo. He did not wish to say anything. I did not insist, but henceforth I ate no more of his presents.

"He adored me. One night the snow overtook us at the outposts. We were seated on the ground. I looked with pity upon the poor negroes shivering under this white, freezing powder. As I was very cold, I began to cough. Immediately, I felt something close around me like a great warm cover. It was Timbuctoo's mantle, which he had thrown around my shoulders.

"I arose and returned the garment to him, saying:

"'Keep it, my boy, you have more need of it than I.'

"He answered: 'No, no, my Lieutenant, for you, me not need, me hot, hot!'

"And he looked at me with suppliant eyes. I replied:

"'Come obey, keep your mantle; I wish it.'

"The negro arose, drew his saber which he knew how to make cut like a scythe, held in the other the large cloak that I had refused and said:

"'So you not take mantle, me cut; no mantle.'

"He would have done it. I yielded.

*   *   *   *   *   *   *

"Eight days later we had capitulated. Some among us had been able to get away. The others were going out of the town and giving themselves up to the conquerors.

"I directed my steps toward the Armory, where we were to reunite, when I met face to face a negro giant clothed in white duck and wearing a straw cap. It was Timbuctoo. He seemed radiant and walked along, his hands in his pockets, until we came to a little shop, where in the window there were two plates and two glasses.

"I asked him: 'What are you doing here?'

"He responded:

"'Me not suffer, me good cook, me make Colonel Algeie to eat, me feed Prussians, steal much, much.'

"The mercury stood at ten degrees. I shivered before this negro in white duck. Then he took me by the arm and made me enter. There I perceived a huge sign that he was going to hang up before his door as soon as I had gone out, for he had some modesty. I read, traced by the hand of some accomplice, these words:

"'MILITARY CUISINE OF M. TIMBUCTOO.
Formerly caterer to H. M. the Emperor. Paris Artist. Prices Moderate.'

"In spite of the despair which was gnawing at my heart, I could not help laughing, and I left my negro to his new business. It would have availed nothing to have him taken prisoner.

"You see how he has succeeded, the rascal, Bézières to-day belongs to Germany. Timbuctoo's restaurant was the beginning of revenge."

Mohammed Fripouli

"SHALL we have our coffee on the roof?" asked the captain.

I answered:

"Yes, certainly."

He rose. It was already dark in the room which was lighted only by the interior court, after the fashion of Moorish houses. Before the high, ogive windows, convolvulus vines hung from the gnat terrace, where they passed the hot summer evenings. There only remained upon the table some grapes, big as plums, some fresh figs of a violet hue, some yellow pears, some long, plump bananas, and some Tougourt dates in a basket of *alfa*.

The Moor who waited on them opened the door and I went upstairs to the azure walls which received from above the soft light of the dying day.

And soon I gave a deep sigh of happiness, on reaching the terrace. It overlooked Algiers, the harbor, the roadstead, and the distant shores.

The house, bought by the captain, was a former Arab residence, situated in the midst of the old city, among those labyrinthine little streets, where swarm the strange population of the African coasts.

Beneath us, the flat, square roofs descended, like steps of giants, to the pointed roofs of the European quarter of the city. Behind these might be perceived the flags of the boats at anchor, then the sea, the open sea, blue and calm under the blue and calm sky.

We stretched ourselves upon the mats, our heads resting upon cushions, and while leisurely sipping the savory coffee of the locality, I gazed at the first stars in the dark azure. They were hardly perceptible, so far away, so pale, as yet giving scarcely any light.

A light heat, a winged heat, caressed our skins. And at times the warm, heavy air, in which there was a vague odor, the odor of Africa, seemed the hot breath of the desert, coming over the peaks of Atlas. The captain, lying on his back, said:

"What a country, my dear boy! How soft life is here! How peculiar and delicious repose is in this land! How the nights seem to be made for dreams."

I looked at the stars coming out with a lazy, yet active, curiosity, with a drowsy happiness.

I murmured:

"You might tell me something of your life in the south."

Captain Marret was one of the oldest officers in the army of Africa, an officer of fortune, a former *spahi*, who had cut his way to his present rank.

Thanks to him, to his relations and friendships, I had been able to accomplish a superb trip to the desert, and I had come that evening to thank him before going to France.

He said: "What kind of a story do you want? I have had so many adventures during twelve years of sand, that I can't think of a single one." And I replied: "Well, tell me of the Arabian women." He did not reply. He remained stretched out with his arms bent, and his hands under his head, and I noticed at times the odor of his cigar, the smoke of which went straight up into the sky, so breezeless was the night.

And all of a sudden he began to laugh.

"Ah! yes, I'll tell you about a queer

affair which occurred in my first days in Algeria.

"We had then in the army of Africa some extraordinary types, such as have not been seen since, types which would have amused you, so much in fact, that you would have wanted to spend all your life in this country.

"I was a simple *spahi*, a little *spahi*, twenty years old, light-haired, swaggering, supple, and strong. I was attached to a military command at Boghar. You know Boghar, which they call the balcony of the south. You have seen from the top of the fort the beginning of this land of fire, devoured, naked, tormented, stony, and red. It is really the antechamber to the desert, the broiling and superb frontier of the immense region of yellow solitudes.

"Well, there were forty of us *spahis* at Boghar, a company of *joyeux*, and a squadron of Chasseurs d'Afrique, when it was learned that the tribe of the Ouled-Berghi had assassinated an English traveler, come, no man knows how, into the country, for the English have the devil in their bodies.

"Punishment had to be given for the crime against a European; but the commanding officer hesitated at sending a column, thinking, in truth, that one Englishman wasn't worth so much of a movement.

"Now, as he was talking of this affair with the captain and the lieutenant, a quartermaster of *spahis* who was waiting for orders proposed all at once to go and punish the tribe if they would give him only six men. You know that in the south they are more free than in the city garrisons and there exists between officer and soldier a sort of comradeship which is not found elsewhere.

"The captain began to laugh:

" 'You, my good man?'

" 'Yes, captain, and if you desire it, I will bring you back the whole tribe as prisoners.'

"The commandant, who had fantastic ideas, took him at his word.

" 'You will start to-morrow morning with six men of your own selection, and if you don't accomplish your purpose, look out for yourself.'

"The subofficer smiled in his mustache.

" 'Fear nothing, commandant. My prisoners shall be here Wednesday noon at latest.'

"The quartermaster, Mohammed Fripouli, as he was called, was a Turk, a true Turk, who had entered the service of France, after a life which had been very much knocked about and not altogether too clean. He had traveled in many places, in Greece, in Asia Minor, in Egypt, in Palestine, and he had been forced to pay a good many forfeits on the way. He was an ex-Bashi-Bazouk, bold, ferocious, and gay, with the calm gaiety of the Oriental. He was stout, very stout, but supple as a monkey and he rode a horse marvelously well. His mustache, incredibly thick and long, always aroused in me a confused idea of the crescent moon and a scimiter. He hated the Arabs with a deadly hatred, and he pursued them with frightful cruelty, continually inventing new tricks, calculated and terrible perfidies. He was possessed, too, of incredible strength and inconceivable audacity.

"The commandant said to him: 'Choose your men, my blade.'

"Mohammed took me. He had confidence in me, the brave man, and I was grateful to him, body and soul, for this choice, which gave me as much pleasure as the Cross of Honor later.

"So we started the next morning, at dawn, all seven of us, and nobody else. My comrades were composed of those bandits, those plunderers, who, after marauding and playing the vagabond in all possible countries, finish by taking service in some foreign legion. Our army in Africa was then full of these rascals, excellent soldiers but not at all scrupulous.

"Mohammed had given to each to carry ten pieces of rope about a meter in length. I was charged, besides as being the youngest and the least heavy, with a piece about a hundred meters long. When he was asked what he was going to do with all that rope, he answered with his sly and placid air:

"'It is to fish for the Arabs.'

"And he winked his eye mischievously, an action which he had learned from an old Chasseur d'Afrique from Paris.

"He marched in front of our squad, his head wrapped in a red turban, which he always wore in a campaign, and he smiled with cunning chuckles in his enormous mustache.

"He was truly handsome, this big Turk, with his powerful paunch, his shoulders of a colossus and his tranquil air. He rode a white horse of medium height, but strong; and the rider seemed ten times too big for his mount.

"We were passing through a long, dry ravine, bare and yellow, in the valley of the Chelif, and we talked of our expedition. My companions had all possible accents, there being among them a Spaniard, a Greek, an American, and two Frenchmen. As for Mohammed Fri-

pouli, he spoke with an incredibly thick tongue.

"The sun, the terrible sun, the sun of the south, which no one knows anything about on the other side of the Mediterranean, fell upon our shoulders, and we advanced at a walk, as they always do in that country.

"All day we marched without meeting a tree or an Arab.

"Toward one o'clock in the afternoon, we had eaten, near a little spring which flowed between the rocks, the bread and dried mutton which we had brought in our knapsacks; then after twenty minutes' rest, went out again on our way.

"Toward six o'clock in the evening, finally, after a long detour which our leader had forced us to make, we discovered behind a knob, a tribe encamped. The brown, low tents made dark spots on the yellow earth, looking like great mushrooms growing at the foot of this red hill which was burned by the sun.

"They were our game. A little further away, on the edge of a meadow of *alfa* of a dark green color, the tied horses were pasturing.

"'Gallop!' ordered Mohammed, and we arrived like a whirlwind in the midst of the camp. The women, terrified, covered with white rags which hung floating upon them, ran quickly to their canvas huts, cringing and crouching and crying like hunted beasts. The men, on the contrary, came from all sides to defend themselves. We struck right for the tallest tent, that of the *agha*.

"We kept our sabers in the scabbards, after the example of Mohammed, who galloped in a singular fashion. He sat absolutely motionless, erect upon his small horse, which strove under him madly to carry such a weight. And the tranquillity of the rider with his long mustache contrasted strangely with the liveliness of the animal.

"The native chief came out of his tent as we arrived before it. He was a tall, thin man, dark, with a gleaming eye, full forehead, and arched eyebrows.

"He cried in Arabic:

" 'What do you want?'

"Mohammed, stopping his horse short, replied in his language: 'Was it you who killed the English traveler?'

"The *agha* said in a strong voice:

" 'I am not going to be examined by you!'

"There was around us, as it were, a rumbling tempest. The Arabs ran up from all sides, pressing and surrounding us, all the time vociferating loudly.

"They had the air of ferocious birds of prey, with their big curved noses, their thin faces with high cheek-bones, their flowing garments, agitated by their gestures.

"Mohammed smiled, his turban crooked, his eye excited, and I saw shivers of pleasure on his cheeks which were pendulous, fleshy, and wrinkled.

"He replied in a thunderous voice:

" 'Death to him who has given death!'

"And he pointed his revolver at the brown face of the *agha*. I saw a little smoke leap from the muzzle; then a red foam of blood and brains spurted from the forehead of the chief. He fell, like a block, on his back, spreading out his arms, which lifted like wings the folds of his burnous.

"Truly, I thought my last day had come, such a terrible tumult rose about us.

"Mohammed had drawn his saber. We unsheathed ours, like him. He cried, whirling away the men, who were pressing him the closest:

" 'Life to those who submit. Death to all others.'

"And seizing the nearest in his herculean grasp, he dragged him to his saddle, tied his hands, yelling to us:

" 'Do as I, and saber those who resist.'

"In five minutes, we had captured twenty Arabs, whose wrists we securely bound. Then we pursued the fleeing ones, for there had been a perfect rout around us at the sight of the naked sabers. We captured about twenty more men.

"Over all the plains might be seen white objects which were running. The women were dragging along their children and uttering piercing cries. The yellow dogs, like jackals, barked around us, and showed us their white fangs.

"Mohammed, who seemed mad with joy, leaped from his horse at a bound and seizing the cord which I had bought:

" 'Attention!' he cried, 'two men to the ground.'

"Then he made a terrible and peculiar thing—a string of prisoners, or rather a string of hanged men. He had firmly tied the two wrists of the first captive, then he made a running knot around his neck with the same cord, which bound his neck. Our fifty prisoners soon found themselves fastened in such a way that the slightest movement of one to flee would strangle him as well as his two neighbors. Every gesture they made pulled on the noose around their necks, and they had to march with the same step with but a pace separating from one another, under the penalty of falling immediately, like a hare in a snare.

"When this strange deed was done, Mohammed began to laugh, with his silent laughter, which shook his stomach without a sound leaving his mouth.

" 'That's an Arabian chain,' said he.

"We began to twist and turn before the terrified and piteous faces of the prisoners.

" 'Now,' cried our chief, 'at each end fix me that.'

"A stake was fastened at each end of this ribbon of white-clad captives, like phantoms, who stood motionless as if they had been changed into stones.

" 'Now, let us dine!' said the Turk. A fire was made and a sheep was cooked, which we ate with our fingers. Then we had some dates which we found in the trees; drank some milk obtained in the Arab tents; and we picked up a few silver trinkets forgotten by the fugitives. We were tranquilly finishing our repast, when I perceived, on the hill opposite, a singular gathering. It was the women who had just now fled, nothing but women. They came running toward us. I pointed them out to Mohammed Fripouli.

"He smiled:

" 'It is the dessert!' said he.

" 'Ah! yes! the dessert.'

"They approached, running like mad women, and soon we were peppered with stones which they hurled at us without stopping their pace; then we saw that they were armed with knives, tent stakes, and old utensils.

" 'To horse!' cried Mohammed. It was time. The attack was terrible. They came to free the prisoners and tried to cut the rope. The Turk, understanding the danger, became furious and shouted: 'Saber them! Saber them! Saber them!' And as we stood motionless, disturbed by this new kind of charge, hesitating at killing women, he threw himself upon the advancing band.

"He charged all alone, this battalion of women, in tatters, and he began to saber them, the wretch, like a madman, with such rage and fury, that a white body might be seen to fall at every stroke of his arm.

"He was so terrible that the women, terrified, fled as quickly as they had come, leaving on the ground a dozen dead and wounded, whose crimson blood stained their white garments.

"And Mohammed, frowning, turned toward us, exclaiming:

" 'Start, start, my sons! They will come back.'

"And we beat a retreat, conducting at a slow step our prisoners, who were paralyzed by fear of strangulation.

"The next day, noon struck as we arrived at Boghar with our chain of hanged men. Only six died on the way. But it had often been necessary to loosen the knots from one end of the convoy to the other, for every shock half strangled ten captives at once."

The captain was silent. I did not say anything in reply. I thought of the strange country where such things could be seen and I gazed at the innumerable and shining flock of stars in the dark sky.

"Bell"

He had known better days, in spite of his misery and infirmity. At the age of fifteen, he had had both legs cut off by a carriage on the highway near Varville. Since that time he had begged, dragging himself along the roads, across farmyards, balanced upon his crutches which brought his shoulders to the height of his ears. His head seemed sunk between two mountains.

Found as an infant in a ditch by the curate of Billettes, on the morning of All Souls' day, he was, for this reason, baptized Nicholas Toussaint (All Saints); brought up by charity, he was a stranger to all instruction; crippled from having drunk several glasses of brandy offered him by the village baker, for the sake of a laughable story, and since then a vagabond, knowing how to do nothing but hold out his hand.

Formerly, Baroness d'Avary gave him a kind of kennel full of straw beside her poultry-house, to sleep in, on the farm adjoining her castle; and he was sure, in days of great hunger, of always finding a piece of bread and a glass of cider in the kitchen. He often received a few sous, also, thrown by the old lady from her steps or her chamber window. Now she was dead.

In the villages, they gave him scarcely anything. They knew him too well. They were tired of him, having seen his little, deformed body on the two wooden legs going from house to house for the last forty years. And he went there because it was the only corner of the country that he knew on the face of the earth—these three or four hamlets where he dragged out his miserable life. He had tried the frontier for his begging, but had never passed the boundaries, for he was not accustomed to anything new.

He did not even know whether the world extended beyond the trees which had always limited his vision. He had never asked. And when the peasants, tired of meeting him in their fields or along their ditches, cried out to him: "Why do you not go to some other villages, in place of always stumping about here?" he did not answer, but took himself off, seized by a vague and unknown fear, that fear of the poor who dread a thousand things, confusedly,— new faces, injuries, suspicious looks from people whom they do not know, the police, who patrol the roads in twos, and make a plunge at them, by instinct, in the bushes or behind a heap of stones.

When he saw them from afar shining in the sun, he suddenly developed a singular agility, the agility of a wild animal to reach his lair. He tumbled along on his crutches, letting himself fall like a bundle of rags and rolling along like a ball, becoming so small as to be almost invisible, keeping close as a hare running for covert, mingling his brown tatters with the earth. He had, however, never had any trouble with them. But this fear and this slyness were in his blood, as if he had received them from his parents whom he had never seen.

He had no refuge, no roof, no hut, no shelter. He slept anywhere in summer, and in winter he slipped under the barns or into the stables with a remarkable adroitness. He always got out before anyone was aware of his presence. He knew all the holes in the buildings that could be penetrated; and, manipulating his crutches with a surprising vigor, using them as arms, he would sometimes crawl, by the sole strength of his wrists, into the hay-barns, where he would remain four or five days without budging, when he had gathered together sufficient provisions for his needs.

He lived like the animals in the woods, in the midst of men without knowing anyone, without loving anyone, and exciting in the peasants only a kind of indifferent scorn and resigned hostility. They nicknamed him "Bell," because he balanced himself between his two wooden pegs like a bell between its two standards.

For two days he had had nothing to eat. No one would give him anything. They would, now, have nothing more to do with him. The peasants in their doors, seeing him coming, would cry out to him from afar:

"You want to get away from here, now. 'Twas only three days ago that I gave you a piece of bread!"

And he would turn about on his props and go on to a neighboring house, where he would be received in the same fashion.

The women declared, from one door to another:

"One cannot feed that vagabond the year round."

Nevertheless, the vagabond had need of food every day. He had been through Saint-Hilaire, Varville, and Billettes without receiving a centime or a crust of bread. Tournolles remained as his only hope; but to reach it he must walk two leagues upon the highway, and he felt too weary to drag himself along, his stomach being as empty as his pocket.

He set out on the way, nevertheless.

It was December, and a cold wind blew over the fields, whistling among the bare branches. The clouds galloped across the low, somber sky, hastening one knew not where. The cripple went slowly, placing one support before the other with wearisome effort, balancing himself upon the part of a leg that remained to him, which terminated in a wooden foot bound about with rags.

From time to time he sat down by a ditch and rested for some minutes. Hunger gave him a distress of soul, confused and heavy. He had but one idea: "to eat." But he knew not by what means.

For three hours he toiled along the road; then, when he perceived the trees of the village, he hastened his movements.

The first peasant he met, of whom he asked alms, responded to him:

"You here yet, you old customer? I wonder if we are ever going to get rid of you!"

And Bell took himself away. From door to door he was treated harshly, and sent away without receiving anything. He continued his journey, however, patient and obstinate. He received not one sou.

Then he visited the farms, picking his way across ground made moist by the rains, so spent that he could scarcely raise his crutches. They chased him away, everywhere. It was one of those cold, sad days when the heart shrivels, the mind is irritated, the soul is somber, and the hand does not open to give or to aid.

When he had finished the rounds of all the houses he knew, he went and threw himself down by a ditch which ran along by M. Chiquet's yard. He unhooked himself, as one might say to express how he let himself fall from between his two high crutches, letting them slip along his arms. And he remained motionless for a long time, tortured by hunger, but too stupid to well understand his unfathomable misery.

He awaited he knew not what, with that vague expectation which ever dwells in us. He awaited, in the corner of that yard, under a freezing wind for that mysterious aid which one always hopes will come from heaven or mankind, without asking how, or why, or through whom it can arrive.

A flock of black hens passed him, seeking their living from the earth which nourishes all beings. Every moment they picked up a grain or an invisible insect, then continued their search slowly, but surely.

Bell looked at them without thinking of anything; then there came to him— to his stomach rather than to his mind —the idea, or rather the sensation, that these animals were good to eat when roasted over a fire of dry wood.

The suspicion that he would be committing a robbery only touched him slightly. He took a stone which lay at his hand and, as he had skill in this way, killed neatly the one nearest him that was approaching. The bird fell on its side, moving its wings. The others fled, half balanced upon their thin legs, and Bell, climbing again upon his crutches, began to run after them, his movements much like that of the hens.

When he came to the little black body, touched with red on the head, he received a terrible push in the back, which threw him loose from his supports and sent him rolling ten steps ahead of them. And M. Chiquet, exasperated, threw himself upon the marauder, rained blows upon him, striking him like a madman, as a robbed peasant strikes with his fist and his knee, upon all the infirm body which could not defend itself.

The people of the farm soon arrived and began to help their master beat the beggar. Then when they were tired of beating, they picked him up, carried him, and shut him up in the woodhouse while they went to get a policeman.

Bell, half dead, bloody and dying of hunger, lay still upon the ground. The evening came, then the night, and then the dawn. He had had nothing to eat.

Toward noon, the policemen appeared, opening the door with precaution as if expecting resistance, for M. Chiquet pretended that he had been attacked by robbers against whom he had defended himself with great difficulty.

The policeman cried out:

"Come there, now! stand up!"

But Bell could no longer move, although he did try to hoist himself upon his sticks. They believed this a feint, a sly ruse for the purpose of doing some mischief, and the two men handled him roughly, standing him up and planting him by force upon his crutches.

And fear had seized him, that native fear of the yellow long-belt, that fear of the Newgate-bird before the detective, of the mouse before the cat. And, by superhuman effort, he succeeded in standing.

"March!" said the policeman. And he

marched. All the employees of the farm watched him as he went. The women shook their fists at him; the men sneered at and threatened him. They had got him, finally! Good riddance.

He went away between the two guardians of the peace. He found energy enough in his desperation to enable him to drag himself along until evening, when he was completely stupefied, no longer knowing what had happened, too bewildered to comprehend anything.

The people that he met stopped to look at him in passing, and the peasants murmured:

"So that is the 'robber'!"

They came toward nightfall to the chief town in the district. He had never been seen there. He did not ex-actly understand what was taking place, nor what was likely to take place. All these frightful, unheard-of things, these faces and these new houses, filled him with consternation.

He did not say a word, having nothing to say, because he comprehended nothing. Besides, he had not talked to anybody for so many years that he had almost lost the use of his tongue; and his thoughts were always too confused to formulate into words.

They shut him up in the town prison. The policemen did not think he needed anything to eat, and they left him until the next day.

When they went to question him, in the early morning, they found him dead upon the ground. Surprise seized them!

The Victim

THE north wind whistled in a tempest, carrying through the sky the enormous winter clouds, heavy and black, which threw, in passing, furious rainbursts over the earth.

A heavy sea moaned and shook the coast, hurrying upon the shore enormous waves, slow and dribbling, which rolled with the noise of artillery. They come in slowly, one after the other, as high as mountains, scattering from their heads in the wind the white foam that seems like the sweat of monsters.

The tempest rushed into the little valley of Yport, whistling and groaning, whirling the slates from the roofs, breaking down fortifications, knocking over chimneys, darting through the streets in such gusts that one could not walk there without keeping close to the walls, and lifting up children like leaves and throwing them into the fields beyond the houses.

They had brought the fishing boats to land, for fear of the sea which would sweep the whole coast at full tide, and some sailors, concealed behind the round wall of the breakwater, lay on their sides watching the anger of the heavens and the sea.

Then they went away, little by little, because night fell upon the tempest, enveloping in shadow the excited ocean and all the disturbance of the elements in fury.

Two men still remained, their hands

in their pockets, with back rounded under a sudden squall, woolen caps drawn down to the eyes, two great Norman fishermen, with rough beards for collars, with skin browned by the salt winds of the open sea, with blue eyes pricked out in the middle in a black dot, the piercing eyes of mariners who see to the end of the horizon like birds of prey.

One of them said:

"Come, let us go, Jeremy. We will pass the time at dominoes. I will pay."

The other still hesitated, tempted by the game and the drink, knowing well that he would get drunk if he went into Paumelle's and held back by the thought of his wife at home alone in their hovel.

He remarked: "It looks as if you had made a bet to get me tipsy every night. Tell me, what's the object, since you always pay?"

And he laughed at all the brandy he had drunk at the expense of the other, laughed with the contented laugh of a Norman who has the best of it.

Mathurin, his comrade, kept pulling him by the arm. "Come," he would say, "come, Jeremy. It is not the evening to go home without anything warm on the inside. What are you afraid of? Your wife will warm the bed for you!"

Jeremy responded: "Only the other evening I couldn't find the door—they almost had to go fishing for me in the brook in front of our house!"

And he laughed still at the memory of this vagary and went patiently toward Paumelle's *café*, where the illuminated glass shone brilliantly. He went, drawn along by Mathurin and pushed by the wind, incapable of resisting these two forces.

The low hall was filled with sailors, smoke, and noise. All the men, clothed in wool, their elbows on the table, were talking in loud voices to make themselves heard. The more drinkers that entered, the more was it necessary to howl into the uproar of voices and of dominoes hitting against the marble, with an attempt to make more noise still.

Jeremy and Mathurin seated themselves in a corner and commenced a game, and little glasses disappeared, one after another, into the depth of their throats.

Then they played other games and drank more glasses. Mathurin always turned and winked an eye to the proprietor, a large man as red as fire, and who laughed as if he knew about some good farce; and Jeremy guzzled the alcohol, balanced his head, uttered roars of laughter, looking at his companion with a stupid, contented air.

Finally, all the clients were going. And, each time that one of them opened the door to go out, a blast entered the *café*, driving in a whirlwind the smoke of the pipes, swinging the lamps to the end of their chains and making their flames dance. And they could hear suddenly the profound shock of an in-rolling wave, and the moaning of the squall.

Jeremy, his clothing loosened at the neck, took the pose of a tipsy man, one leg extended, one arm falling, while in the other hand he held his dominoes.

They were alone now with the proprietor, who approached them full of interest. He asked:

"Well, Jeremy, how goes it in the interior? Are you refreshed with all this sprinkling?"

And Jeremy muttered. "Since it

slipped down—makes it dry in there."

The *café* keeper looked at Mathurin with a sly air. Then he asked:

"And your brother, Mathurin, where is he at this hour?"

The sailor answered with a quiet laugh:

"Where it is warm; don't you worry."

And the two looked at Jeremy who triumphantly put down the double six announcing:

"There! the syndic."

When they had finished the game, the proprietor declared:

"You know, my lads, I must put up the shutters. But I will leave you a lamp and bottle. There's twenty sous left for it. You will shut the outside door, Mathurin, and slip the key under the step as you did the other night."

Mathurin answered: "Don't worry. I understand."

Paumelle shook hands with both his tardy clients, and mounted heavily his wooden staircase. For some minutes his heavy step resounded in the little house; then a loud creaking announced that he had put himself in bed.

The two men continued to play; from time to time a more violent rage of the tempest shook the door, making the walls tremble, and the two men would raise their heads as if some one was about to enter. Then Mathurin took the bottle and filled Jeremy's glass.

Suddenly, the clock, suspended over the counter, sounded midnight. Its hoarse ring resembled a crash of pans and the blows vibrated a long time, with the resonance of old iron.

Mathurin immediately rose, like a sailor whose quart is finished. He said:

"Come, Jeremy, we must break off."

The other put himself in motion with more difficulty, got his equilibrium by leaning against the table; then he reached the door and opened it, while his companion extinguished the light.

When they were in the street, and Mathurin had locked the door, he said:

"Well, good night, till to-morrow."

And he disappeared into the shadows.

Jeremy took three steps, extended his hands, met a wall which held him up, and then began to walk along stumblingly. Sometimes, a gust rushing through the straight street, threw him forward, making him run for some steps; then when the violence of the wind ceased, he would stop short, and having lost his poise, begin to vacillate upon the capricious legs of a drunken man.

He went, by instinct, toward his dwelling, as birds fly to their nests. Finally, he recognized his door and began to fumble to find the keyhole to place his key in it. He could not find it, and swore in an undertone. Then he struck upon it with his fist, calling his wife to come and aid him:

"Melina! Eh! Melina!"

As he leaned against the door in order not to fall, it yielded, flew open, and Jeremy, losing his balance, entered his house in a tumble, then rolled upon his nose into the room; he felt that something heavy had passed over his body and then fled into the night.

He did not move, perplexed with fright, astonished, in the devil of a fright, from the spirits of all the mysterious and shadowy things, and he waited a long time without daring to make a sound. But, as he saw that nothing more moved, a little reason came back to him, the troubled reason of vagary.

And he slowly sat up. Then he waited still a long time and finally said:

"Melina!"

His wife did not answer.

Then, suddenly, a doubt went through his obscure brain, a wavering doubt, a vague suspicion. He did not move; he remained there, seated on the floor in the dark, gathering his ideas, clutching his reflections as incomplete and uncertain as his legs.

He called again:

"Tell me who it was, Melina, tell me who it was. I will do nothing to you."

He waited. No voice came out of the shadow. He reasoned out loud now:

"I am drunk—all same! I am drunk! He made me drink like this now! He kept me from coming back home. I am drunk!"

Then he repeated: "Tell me who it was, Melina, or I'm going to do harm."

After having waited again, he continued, with the slow and obstinate logic of an intoxicated man:

"It was him kept me at that lazy Paumelle's; and other evenings too, so I couldn't come home. He's some 'complice. Ah! carrion!"

Slowly he got up on his knees. A sudden anger helped him, mingling with the fermentation of the drink. He repeated:

"Tell me who it was, Melina, or I'm going to beat you; I give you warning."

He was standing now, trembling with anger, as if the alcohol which he had in his body was inflamed in his veins. He took a step, hit against a chair, seized it, walked to the bed, touched it, and felt there the warm body of his wife.

Then, excited with rage, he cried:

"Ah! there you are, filth, and you wouldn't answer."

And, raising the chair which he held in his robust sailor's fist, he brought it down before him with exasperated fury. A scream arose from the bed; a terrified, piercing cry. Then he began to beat like a thrasher in a barn. Nothing moved now. The chair was broken in pieces. One leg remained in his hand and he hit with it until he gasped.

Then suddenly he stopped and asked:

"Will you tell me who it was, now?"

Melina did not answer.

Then, worn out with fatigue and stupid from his violence, he sat down again upon the floor, fell over, and was asleep.

When the day appeared, a neighbor, seeing the door open, entered. He perceived Jeremy snoring upon the floor, where lay the *débris* of a chair, and on the bed a pulp of flesh and blood.

The Englishman

THEY made a circle around Judge Bermutier, who was giving his opinion of the mysterious affair that had happened at Saint-Cloud. For a month Paris had doted on this inexplicable crime. No one could understand it at all.

M. Bermutier, standing with his back to the chimney, talked about it, discussed the divers opinions, but came to no conclusions.

Many women had risen and come nearer, remaining standing, with eyes fixed upon the shaven mouth of the magistrate, whence issued these grave words. They shivered and vibrated, crisp through their curious fear, through that eager, insatiable need of terror which haunts their soul, torturing them like a hunger.

One of them, paler than the others, after a silence, said:

"It is frightful. It touches the supernatural. We shall never know anything about it."

The magistrate turned toward her, saying:

"Yes, Madame, it is probable that we never shall know anything about it. As for the word 'supernatural,' when you come to use that, it has no place nere. We are in the presence of a crime skillfully conceived, very skillfully executed, and so well enveloped in mystery that we cannot separate the impenetrable circumstances which surround it. But, once in my life, I had to follow an affair which seemed truly to be mixed up with something very unusual. However, it was necessary to give it up, as there was no means of explaining it."

Many of the ladies called out at the same time, so quickly that their voices sounded as one:

"Oh! tell us about it."

M. Bermutier smiled gravely, as judges should, and replied:

"You must not suppose, for an instant, that I, at least, believed there was anything superhuman in the adventure. I believe only in normal causes. And, if, in place of using the word 'supernatural' to express what we cannot comprehend we should simply use the word 'inexplicable,' it would be much better. In any case, the surrounding circumstances in the affair I am going to relate to you, as well as the preparatory circumstances, have affected me much. Here are the facts:

"I was then judge of Instruction at Ajaccio, a little white town lying on the border of an admirable gulf that was surrounded on all sides by high mountains.

"What I particularly had to look after there was the affairs of *vendetta*. Some of them were superb; as dramatic as possible, ferocious, and heroic. We find there the most beautiful subjects of vengeance that one could dream of, hatred a century old, appeased for a moment but never extinguished, abominable plots, assassinations becoming massacres and almost glorious battles. For two years I heard of nothing but the price of blood, of the terribly prejudiced Corsican who is bound to avenge all injury upon the person of him who is the cause of it, or upon his nearest descendants. I saw old men and infants, cousins, with their throats cut, and my head was full of these stories.

"One day we learned that an Englishman had rented for some years a little villa at the end of the Gulf. He had brought with him a French domestic, picked up at Marseilles on the way.

"Soon everybody was occupied with this singular person, who lived alone in his house, only going out to hunt and fish. He spoke to no one, never came to the town, and, every morning, practiced shooting with a pistol and a rifle for an hour or two.

"Some legends about him were abroad. They pretended that he was a high personage fled from his own country for political reasons; then they affirmed that he was concealing himself after having committed a frightful crime. They even cited some of the particularly horrible details.

"In my capacity of judge, I wished to get some information about this man. But it was impossible to learn anything. He called himself Sir John Rowell.

"I contented myself with watching him closely; although, in reality, there seemed nothing to suspect regarding him.

"Nevertheless, as rumors on his account continued, grew, and became general, I resolved to try and see this stranger myself, and for this purpose began to hunt regularly in the neighborhood of his property.

"I waited long for an occasion. It finally came in the form of a partridge which I shot and killed before the very nose of the Englishman. My dog brought it to me; but, immediately taking it I went and begged Sir John Rowell to accept the dead bird, excusing myself for intrusion.

"He was a tall man with red hair and red beard, very large, a sort of placid, polite Hercules. He had none of the so-called British haughtiness, and heartily thanked me for the delicacy in French, with a beyond-the-Channel accent. At the end of a month we had chatted together five or six times.

"Finally, one evening, as I was passing by his door, I perceived him astride a chair in the garden, smoking his pipe. I saluted him and he asked me in to have a glass of beer. It was not necessary for him to repeat before I accepted.

"He received me with the fastidious courtesy of the English, spoke in praise of France and of Corsica, and declared that he loved that country and that shore.

"Then, with great precaution in the form of a lively interest, I put some questions to him about his life and his projects. He responded without embarrassment, told me that he had traveled much, in Africa, in the Indies, and in America. He added, laughing:

"'I have had many adventures, oh! yes.'

"I began to talk about hunting, and he gave me many curious details of hunting the hippopotamus, the tiger, the elephant, and even of hunting the gorilla.

"I said: 'All these animals are very formidable.'

"He laughed: 'Oh! no. The worst animal is man.' Then he began to laugh, with the hearty laugh of a big contented Englishman. He continued:

"'I have often hunted man, also.'

"He spoke of weapons and asked me to go into his house to see his guns of various makes and kinds.

"His drawing-room was hung in black, in black silk embroidered with gold. There were great yellow flowers running over the somber stuff, shining like fire.

"'It is Japanese cloth,' he said.

"But in the middle of a large panel, a strange thing attracted my eye. Upon a square of red velvet, a black object was attached. I approached and found it was a hand, the hand of a man. Not a skeleton hand, white and characteristic, but a black, desiccated hand, with yellow joints with the muscles bare and on them traces of old blood, of blood that seemed like a scale, over the bones sharply cut off at about the middle of the fore-arm, as with a blow of a hatchet. About the wrist was an enormous iron chain, riveted, soldered to this unclean member, attaching it to the wall by a ring sufficiently strong to hold an elephant.

"I asked: 'What is that?'

"The Englishman responded tranquilly:

"'It belonged to my worst enemy. It came from America. It was broken with a saber, cut off with a sharp stone, and dried in the sun for eight days. Oh, very good for me, that was!'

"I touched the human relic, which must have belonged to a colossus. The fingers were immoderately long and attached by enormous tendons that held the straps of skin in place. This dried hand was frightful to see, making one think, naturally, of the vengeance of a savage.

"I said: 'This man must have been very strong.'

"With gentleness the Englishman answered:

"'Oh! yes; but I was stronger than he. I put this chain on him to hold him.'

"I thought he spoke in jest and replied:

"'The chain is useless now that the hand cannot escape.'

"Sir John Rowell replied gravely: 'It always wishes to escape. The chain is necessary.'

"With a rapid, questioning glance, I asked myself: 'Is he mad, or is that an unpleasant joke?'

"But the face remained impenetrable, tranquil, and friendly. I spoke of other things and admired the guns.

"Nevertheless, I noticed three loaded revolvers on the pieces of furniture, as if this man lived in constant fear of attack.

"I went there many times after that; then for some time I did not go. We had become accustomed to his presence; he had become indifferent to us.

"A whole year slipped away. Then, one morning, toward the end of November, my domestic awoke me with the announcement that Sir John Rowell had been assassinated in the night.

"A half hour later, I entered the Englishman's house with the central Commissary and the Captain of Police. The servant, lost in despair, was weeping at the door. I suspected him at first, but afterward found that he was innocent.

"The guilty one could never be found.

"Upon entering Sir John's drawing-room, I perceived his dead body stretched out upon its back, in the middle of the room. His waistcoat was torn, a sleeve was hanging, and it was evident that a terrible struggle had taken place.

"The Englishman had been strangled! His frightfully black and swollen face seemed to express an abominable fear; he held something between his set teeth; and his neck, pierced with five holes apparently done with a pointed iron, was covered with blood.

"A doctor joined us. He examined closely the prints of fingers in the flesh and pronounced these strange words:

"'One would think he had been strangled by a skeleton.'

"A shiver ran down my back and I cast my eyes to the place on the wall where I had seen the horrible, torn-off hand. It was no longer there. The chain was broken and hanging.

"Then I bent over the dead man and found in his mouth a piece of one of the fingers of the missing hand, cut off, or rather sawed off by the teeth exactly at the second joint.

"Then they tried to collect evidence. They could find nothing. No door had been forced, no window opened, or piece of furniture moved. The two watchdogs on the premises had not been aroused.

"Here, in a few words, is the deposition of the servant:

"For a month, his master had seemed agitated. He had received many letters which he had burned immediately. Often, taking a whip, in anger which seemed like dementia, he had struck in fury, this dried hand, fastened to the wall and taken, one knew not how, at the moment of a crime.

"He had retired late and shut himself in with care. He always carried arms. Often in the night he talked out loud, as if he were quarreling with some one. On that night, however, there had been no noise, and it was only on coming to open the windows that the servant had found Sir John assassinated. He suspected no one.

"I communicated what I knew of the death to the magistrates and public officers, and they made minute inquiries upon the whole island. They discovered nothing,

"One night, three months after the crime, I had a frightful nightmare. It seemed to me that I saw that hand, that horrible hand, running like a scorpion or a spider along my curtains and my walls. Three times I awoke, three times I fell asleep and again saw that hideous relic galloping about my room, moving its fingers like paws.

"The next day they brought it to me, found in the cemetery upon the tomb where Sir John Rowell was interred—for they had not been able to find his family. The index finger was missing.

"This, ladies, is my story. I know no more about it."

The ladies were terrified, pale, and shivering. One of them cried:

"But that is not the end, for there was no explanation! We cannot sleep if you do not tell us what was your idea of the reason of it all."

The magistrate smiled with severity, and answered:

"Oh! certainly, ladies, but it will spoil all your terrible dreams. I simply think that the legitimate proprietor of the hand was not dead and that he came for it with the one that remained to him. But I was never able to find out how he did it. It was one kind of revenge."

One of the women murmured:

"No, it could not be thus."

And the Judge of Information, smiling still, concluded:

"I told you in the beginning that my explanation would not satisfy you."

VOLUME X

Sentiment

It was during the hunting season, at the country seat of the De Bannevilles. The autumn was rainy and dull. The red leaves, instead of crackling under foot, rotted in the hollows after the heavy showers.

The forest, almost leafless, was as humid as a bath-room. There was a moldy odor under the great trees, stripped of their fruits, which enveloped one on entering, as if a lye had been made from the steeped herbs, the soaked earth, and the continuous rainfall. The hunters' ardor was dampened, the dogs were sullen, their tails lowered and their hair matted against their sides, while the young huntresses, their habits drenched with rain, returned each evening depressed in body and spirit.

In the great drawing-room, after dinner, they played lotto, but without enthusiasm, as the wind made a clattering noise upon the shutters and forced the old weather vanes into a spinning-top tournament. Some one suggested telling stories, as they are told in books; but no one could think of anything very amusing. The hunters narrated some of their adventures with the gun, the slaughter of wolves, for example; and the ladies racked their brains without finding anywhere the imagination of Scheherazade.

They were about to abandon this form of diversion, when a young lady, carelessly playing with the hand of her old, unmarried aunt, noticed a little ring made of blond hair, which she had often seen before but thought nothing about.

Moving it gently about the finger she said, suddenly: "Tell us the history of this ring, Auntie; it looks like the hair of a child—"

The old maiden reddened and then grew pale, then in a trembling voice she replied: "It is sad, so sad that I never care to speak about it. All the unhappiness of my life is centered in it. I was young then, but the memory of it remains so painful that I weep whenever I think of it."

They wished very much to hear the story, but the aunt refused to tell it; finally, they urged so much that she at length consented.

"You have often heard me speak of the Sentèze family, now extinct. I knew the last three men of this family. They all died within three months in the same manner. This hair belonged to the last one. He was thirteen years old, when he killed himself for me. That appears very strange to you, doesn't it?

"It was a singular race, a race of fools, if you will, but of charming fools, of fools for love. All, from father to son, had these violent passions, waves of emotion which drove them to deeds most exalted, to fanatical devotion, and even to crime. Devotion was to them what it is to certain religious souls. Those who become monks are not of the same nature as drawing-room favorites. One might almost say, as a proverb, 'He loved like a Santèze.'

"To see them was to divine this characteristic. They all had curly hair, growing low upon the brow, beard crinkly, eyes large, very large, whose rays seemed to penetrate and disturb you, without your knowing just why.

"The grandfather of the one of whom this is the only souvenir, after many

935

adventures, and some duels on account of entanglements with women, when toward sixty, became passionately taken with the daughter of his farmer. I knew them both. She was blond, pale, distinguished looking, with a soft voice and a sweet look, so sweet that she reminded one of a madonna. The old lord took her home with him, and immediately became so captivated that he was unable to pass a minute away from her. His daughter and his daughter-in-law who lived in the house, found this perfectly natural, so much was love a tradition of the family. When one was moved by a great passion, nothing surprised them, and, if anyone expressed a different notion before them, of disunited lovers, or revenge after some treachery, they would both say, in the same desolate voice: 'Oh! how he (or she) must have suffered before coming to that!' Nothing more. They were moved with pity by all dramas of the heart and never spoke slightingly of them, even when they were unworthy.

"One autumn, a young man, M. de Gradelle, invited for the hunting, eloped with the young woman.

"M. de Santèze remained calm, as if nothing had happened. But one morning they found him in the kennel in the midst of the dogs.

"His son died in the same fashion, in a hotel in Paris, while on a journey in 1841, after having been deceived by an opera singer.

"He left a child of eleven years, and a widow, the sister of my mother. She came with the little one to live at my father's house, on the De Bertillon estate. I was then seventeen.

"You could not imagine what an as-tonishing, precocious child this little Santèze was. One would have said that all the powers of tenderness, all the exaltation of his race had fallen upon this one, the last. He was always dreaming and walking alone in a great avenue of elms that led from the house to the woods. I often watched this sentimental youngster from my window, as he walked up and down with his hands behind his back, with bowed head, sometimes stopping to look up, as if he saw and comprehended things beyond his age and experience.

"Often after dinner, on clear nights, he would say to me: 'Let us go and dream, Cousin.' And we would go together into the park. He would stop abruptly in the clear spaces, where the white vapor floats, that soft light with which the moon lights up the clearings in the woods, and say to me, seizing my hands: 'Look! Look there! But you do not understand, I feel it. If you comprehended, you would be happy. One must know how to love.' I would laugh and embrace him, this boy, who loved me until his dying day.

"Often, too, after dinner, he would seat himself upon my mother's knee. 'Come, Aunt,' he would say to her, 'tell us some love story.' And my mother, for his pleasure, would tell him all the family legends, the passionate adventures of his fathers, as they had been told a thousand times, true and false. It is these stories that have ruined these men; they never concealed anything, and prided themselves upon not allowing a descendant of their house to lie.

"He would be uplifted, this little one, by these terrible or affecting tales, and sometimes he would clap his hands and cry out: 'I, too; I, too, know how to love, better than any of them.'

"Then he began to pay me his court; a timid, profoundly tender devotion, so droll that one could but laugh at it. Each morning I had flowers picked by him, and each evening, before going to his room, he would kiss my hand, murmuring: 'I love you!'

"I was guilty, very guilty, and I have wept since, unceasingly, doing penance all my life, by remaining an old maid— or rather an affianced widow, his widow. I amused myself with this childish devotion, even inciting him. I was coquettish, enticing as if he were a man, caressing and deceiving. I excited this child. It was a joke to me, and a pleasing diversion to his mother and mine. He was eleven years old! Think of it! Who would have taken seriously this passion of a midget! I kissed him as much as he wished. I even wrote sweet letters to him that our mothers read. And he responded with letters of fire, that I still have. He had a belief all his own in our intimacy and love, judging himself a man. We had forgotten that he was a Santèze!

"This lasted nearly a year. One evening, in the park, he threw himself down at my knees, kissing the hem of my dress, with furious earnestness, repeating: 'I love you! I love you! I love you! and shall even to death. If you ever deceive me, understand, if you ever leave me for another, I shall do as my father did—' And he added in a low voice that gave one the shivers: 'You know what I shall do!'

"Then, as I remained amazed and dumfounded, he got up and, stretching himself on tiptoe, for I was much taller

than he, he repeated in my ear, my name, my first name, 'Genevieve!' in a voice so sweet, so pretty, so tender that I trembled to my very feet.

"I muttered: 'Let us return to the house!' He said nothing further, but followed me. As we were ascending the steps, he stopped me and said: 'You know if you abandon me, I shall kill myself.'

"I understood now that I had gone too far, and immediately became more reserved. When he reproached me for it, one day, I answered him: 'You are now too large for this kind of joking, and too young for serious love. I will wait.'

"I believed myself freed from him.

"He was sent away to school in the autumn. When he returned, the following summer, I had become engaged. He understood at once, and for over a week preserved so calm an appearance that I was much disturbed.

"The ninth day, in the morning, I perceived, on rising, a little paper slipped under my door. I seized it and read: 'You have abandoned me, and you know what I said. You have ordered my death. As I do not wish to be found by anyone but you, come into the park, at the place where last year I said that I loved you, and look up.'

"I felt myself becoming mad. I dressed quickly and ran quickly, so quickly that I fell exhausted at the designated spot. His little school cap was on the ground in the mud. It had rained all night. I raised my eyes and saw something concealed by the leaves, for there was a wind blowing, a strong wind.

"After that, I knew nothing of what I did. I shouted, fainted, perhaps, and fell, then got up and ran to the house. I recovered my reason in my bed, with my mother for my pillow.

"I at first believed that I had dreamed all this in a frightful delirium. I muttered: 'And he, he—Gontran, where is he—'

"Then they told me it was all true. I dared not look at him again, but I asked for a lock of his blond hair. Here—it —is—" And the old lady held out her hand in a gesture of despair.

Then, after much use of her handkerchief and drying of her eyes, she continued: "I broke off my engagement without saying why—and I—have remained always the—widow of this child thirteen years old."

Then her head fell upon her breast and she wept pensively for a long time.

And, as they dispersed to their rooms for the night, a great hunter, whose quiet she had disturbed somewhat, whispered in the ear of his neighbor:

"What a misfortune to be so sentimental! Don't you think so?"

Francis

WE WERE going out of the asylum when I perceived in one corner of the courtyard a tall thin man, who was forever calling an imaginary dog. He would call out, with a sweet and tender voice: "Cocotte, my little Cocotte, come here, Cocotte, come here my beauty," striking his leg, as one does to attract the attention of an animal. I asked the doctor what the matter was with the man.

"Oh! that is an interesting case," said he, "he is a coachman named Francis, and he became insane from drowning his dog."

I insisted upon his telling me the story. The most simple and humble things sometimes strike most to our hearts.

And here is the adventure of this man which was known solely to a groom, his comrade.

In the suburbs of Paris lived a rich, middle-class family. Their villa was in the midst of a park, on the bank of the Seine. Their coachman was this Francis, a country boy, a little awkward, but of good heart, simple and easily duped.

When he was returning one evening to his master's house a dog began to follow him. At first he took no notice of it, but the persistence of the beast in walking on his heels caused him finally to turn around. He looked to see if he knew this dog. No, he had never seen it before.

The dog was frightfully thin and had great hanging dugs. She totted behind the man with a woeful, famished look, her tail between her legs, her ears close to her head, and stopped when he stopped, starting again when he started.

He tried to drive away this skeleton of a beast: "Get out! If you want to save yourself— Go, now! Hou! Hou!" She would run away a few steps and then sit down waiting; then, when the coachman started on again, she followed behind him.

He made believe to pick up stones. The animal fled a little way with a great shaking of the flabby mammillæ, but followed again as soon as the man turned his back.

Then the coachman, Francis, took pity and called her. The dog approached timidly, her back bent in a circle, and all the ribs showing under the skin. The man smoothed these projecting bones and, moved by pity, for the misery of the beast, said: "Come along, then!" Immediately the tail began to move; she felt the welcome, the adoption; and instead of staying at her new master's heels, she began to run ahead of him.

He installed her on some straw in his stable, then ran to the kitchen in search of bread. When she had eaten her fill, she went to sleep, curled up, ringlike.

The next day the coachman told his master who allowed him to keep the animal. She was a good beast, intelligent and faithful, affectionate and gentle.

But immediately they discovered in her a terrible fault. She was inflamed with love from one end of the year to the other. In a short time she had made the acquaintance of every dog about the country, and they roamed about the place day and night. With the indifference of a girl, she shared her favors with them, feigning to like each one best, dragging behind her a veritable mob composed of many different models of the barking race, some as large as a fist, others as tall as an ass. She took them to walk through routes with interminable courses, and when she stopped to rest in the shade, they made a circle about her and looked at her with tongues hanging out.

The people of the country considered her a phenomenon; they had never seen anything like it. The veterinary could not understand it.

When she returned to the stable in the evening, the crowd of dogs made siege for proprietorship. They wormed their way through every crevice in the hedge which inclosed the park, devastated the flower beds, broke down the flowers, dug holes in the urns, exasperating the gardener. They would howl the whole night about the building where their friend lodged and nothing could persuade them to go away.

In the daytime, they even entered the house. It was an invasion, a plague, a calamity. The people of the house met at any moment, on the staircase, and even in the rooms little yellow pug dogs with tails decorated, hunting dogs, bulldogs, wolf hounds with filthy skin, vagabonds without life or home, beside some new-world enormities which frightened the children.

All the unknown dogs for ten miles around came, from one knew not where, and lived, no one knew how, disappearing all together.

Nevertheless, Francis adored Cocotte. He had named her Cocotte, "without malice, sure that she merited her name." And he repeated over and over again: "This beast is a person. It only lacks speech."

He had a magnificent collar in red leather made for her, which bore these words, engraved on a copper plate: "Mademoiselle Cocotte, from Francis, the coachman."

She became enormous. She was as

fat as she had been thin, her body puffed out, under which hung always the long, swaying mammillæ. She had fattened suddenly and walked with difficulty, the paws wide apart, after the fashion of people that are too large, the mouth open for breath, wide open as soon as she tried to run.

She showed a phenomenal fecundity, producing, four times a year, a litter of little animals, belonging to all varieties of the canine race. Francis, after having chosen the one he would leave her "to take the milk," would pick up the others in his stable apron and pitilessly throw them into the river.

Soon the cook joined her complaints to those of the gardener. She found dogs under her kitchen range, in the cupboards, and in the coal bin, always fleeing whenever she encountered them.

The master, becoming impatient, ordered Francis to get rid of Cocotte. The man, inconsolable, tried to place her somewhere. No one wanted her. Then he resolved to lose her, and put her in charge of a wagoner who was to leave her in the country the other side of Paris, beyond De Joinville-le-Pont.

That same evening Cocotte was back.

It became necessary to take measures. For the sum of five francs, they persuaded a cook on the train to Havre to take her. He was to let her loose when they arrived.

At the end of three days, she appeared again in her stable, harassed, emaciated, exhausted.

The master was merciful, and insisted on nothing further.

But the dogs soon returned in greater numbers than ever, and were more provoking. And as they were giving a great

dinner, one evening, a stuffed chicken was carried off by a dog, under the nose of the cook, who dared not dispute the right to it.

This time the master was angry, and calling Francis to him, said hotly: "If you don't kick this beast into the water to-morrow morning, I shall put you out, do you understand?"

The man was undone, but he went up to his room to pack his trunk, preferring to leave the place. Then he reflected that he would not be likely to get in anywhere else, dragging this unwelcome beast behind him; he remembered that he was in a good house, well paid and well fed; and he said to himself that it was not worth while giving up all this for a dog. He enumerated his own interests and finished by resolving to get rid of Cocotte at dawn the next day.

However, he slept badly. At daybreak he was up; and, preparing a strong cord, he went in search of the dog. She arose slowly, shook herself, stretched her limbs, and came to greet her master. Then his courage failed and he began to stroke her tenderly, smoothing her long ears, kissing her on the muzzle, lavishing upon her all the loving names that he knew.

A neighboring clock struck; he could no longer hesitate. He opened the door; "Come," said he. The beast wagged her tail, understanding only that she was to go out.

They reached the bank and chose a place where the water seemed deepest. Then he tied one end of the cord to the beautiful leather collar, and taking a great stone, attached it to the other end. Then he seized Cocotte in his arms and kissed her furiously, as one does when he is taking leave of a person. Then he held her right around the neck, fondling her and calling her "My pretty Cocotte, my little Cocotte," and she responded as best she could, growling with pleasure.

Ten times he tried to throw her in, and each time his heart failed him.

Then, abruptly, he decided to do it; and, with all his force, hurled her as far as possible. She tried at first to swim, as she did when taking a bath, but her head, dragged by the stone, went under again and again. She threw her master a look of despair, a human look, battling, as a person does when drowning. Then, before the whole body sank, the hind paws moved swiftly in the water; then they disappeared also.

For five minutes bubbles of air came to the surface as if the river had begun to boil. And Francis, haggard, excited, with heart palpitating, believed he saw Cocotte writhing in the slime. And he said to himself, with the simplicity of a peasant: "What does she think of me by this time, that beast?"

He almost became idiotic. He was sick for a month, and each night, saw the dog again. He felt her licking his hands; he heard her bark.

It was necessary to call a physician. Finally he grew better; and his master and mistress took him to their estate near Rouen.

There he was still on the bank of the Seine. He began to take baths. Every morning he went down with the groom to swim across the river.

One day, as they were amusing themselves splashing in the water, Francis suddenly cried out to his companion:

"Look at what is coming toward us. I am going to make you taste a cutlet."

It was an enormous carcass, swelled and stripped of its hair, its paws moving forward, in the air, following the current.

Francis approached it making his jokes:

"What a prize, my boy! My! But it is not fresh! It is not thin, that is sure!"

And he turned about, keeping at a distance from the great, putrefying body.

Then, suddenly, he kept still and looked at it in strange fashion. He approached it again, this time near enough to touch. He examined carefully the collar, took hold of the leg, seized the neck, made it turn over, drew it toward him, and read upon the green copper that still adhered to the discolored leather: "Mademoiselle Cocotte, from Francis, the coachman."

The dead dog had found her master, sixty miles from their home!

He uttered a fearful cry, and began to swim with all his might toward the bank, shouting all the way. And when he reached the land, he ran, all bare, through the country. He was mad!

The Assassin

THE guilty man was defended by a very young lawyer, a beginner, who spoke thus:

"The facts are undeniable, gentlemen of the jury. My client, an honest man, an irreproachable employee, gentle and timid, assassinated his employer in a moment of anger which seems to me incomprehensible. If you will allow me, I would like to look into the psychology of the crime, so to speak, without wasting any time or attempting to excuse anything. We shall then be able to judge better.

"John Nicholas Lougère is the son of very honorable people, who made of him a simple, respectful man.

"That is his crime: respect! It is a sentiment, gentlemen, which we of today no longer know, of which the name alone seems to exist while its power has disappeared. It is necessary to enter certain old, modest families to find this severe tradition, this religion of a thing or of a man, this sentiment where belief takes on a sacred character, this faith which doubts not, nor smiles, nor entertains a suspicion.

"One cannot be an honest man, a truly honest man in the full force of the term, and be respectful. The man who respects has his eyes closed. He believes. We others, whose eyes are wide open upon the world, who live here in this hall of justice, this purger of society, where all infamy runs aground, we others who are the confidants of shame, the devoted defenders of all human meanness, the support, not to say the supporters, of male and female sharpers, from a prince to a tramp, we who welcome with indulgence, with com-placence, with a smiling benevolence all the guilty and defend them before you, we who, if we truly love our profession, measure our legal sympathy by the size of the crime, we could never have a respectful soul. We see too much of this river of corruption, which catches the chiefs of power as well as the lowest scamp; we know too much of how it gives and takes and sells itself. Places, offices, honors brutally exchanged for a little money, or skillfully exchanged for titles and interests in industrial enterprises, or sometimes, simply for the kiss of a woman.

"Our duty and our profession force us to be ignorant of nothing, to suspect everybody, because everybody is doubtful; and we are taken by surprise when we find ourselves face to face with a man, like the assassin seated before you, who possesses the religion of respect to such a degree that he will become a martyr for it.

"We others, gentlemen, have a sense of honor, a certain need of propriety, from a disgust of baseness, from a sentiment of personal dignity and pride; but we do not carry at the bottom of our hearts the blind, inborn, brutal faith of this man.

"Let me tell you the story of his life.

"He was brought up, like many an-other child, to separate all human acts into two parts: the good and the bad. He was shown the good with an irresistible authority which made him only distinguish the bad, as we distinguish day and night. His father did not belong to the superior race of minds who, looking from a height, see the sources of belief and recognize the social necessities born of these distinctions.

"He grew up, religious and confident, enthusiastic and limited. At twenty-two he married. His wife was a cousin, brought up as he was, simple and pure as he was. His was the inestimable privilege of having for a companion an honest woman with a true heart, the rarest and most respectable thing in the world. He had for his mother that veneration which surrounds mothers in patriarchal families, that profound respect which is reserved for divinities. This religion he reflected somewhat upon his wife, and it became scarcely less as conjugal familiarity increased. He lived in absolute ignorance of double dealing, in a state of constant uprightness and tranquil happiness which made him a being apart from the world. Deceiving no one he had never a suspicion that any one would deceive him.

"Some time before his marriage, he had become cashier in the office of Mr. Langlais, the man who was lately assassinated by him.

"We know, gentlemen of the jury, by the testimony of Mrs. Langlais and of her brother, Mr. Perthuis, a partner of her husband, of all the family and of all the higher employees of the bank, that Lougère was a model employee, upright, submissive, gentle, prompt, and deferential toward his superiors. They treated him with the consideration due to his exemplary conduct. He was accustomed to this homage and to a kind of respect shown to Mrs. Lougère, whose worthiness was upon all lips.

"But she died of typhoid fever in a few days' time. He assuredly felt a profound grief, but the cold, calm grief of a methodical heart. Only from his pallor and from a change in his looks was one able to judge how deeply he had been wounded.

"Then, gentlemen, the most natural thing in the world happened.

"This man had been married ten years. For ten years he had been accustomed to feel the presence of a woman near him always. He was habituated to her care, her familiar voice upon his return, the good night at evening, the cheerful greeting of the morning, the gentle rustle of the dress so dear to the feminine heart, to that caress, at once lover-like and maternal, which renders life pleasant, to that loved presence that made the hours move less slowly. He was also accustomed to being spoiled at table, perhaps, and to all those attentions which become, little by little, so indispensable.

"He could no longer live alone. Then, to pass the interminable evenings, he got into the habit of spending an hour or two in a neighboring wine shop. He would drink a glass and sit there motionless, following, with heedless eye, the billiard balls running after one another under the smoke of the pipes, listening to, without hearing, the discussion of the players, the disputes of his neighbors over politics, and the sound of laughter that sometimes went up from the other end of the room, from some unusual joke. He often ended by going to sleep, from sheer lassitude and weariness. But, at the bottom of his heart and of his flesh, there was the irresistible need of a woman's heart and flesh; and, without thinking, he approached each evening a little nearer to the desk where the cashier, a pretty blonde, sat, attracted to her unconquerably, because she was a woman.

"At first they chatted, and he got into the habit, so pleasant for him, of passing the evening by her side. She was gracious and kind, as one learns in this occupation to smile, and she amused herself by making him renew his order as often as possible, which makes business good.

"But each day Lougère was becoming more and more attached to this woman whom he did not know, whose whole existence he was ignorant of, and whom he loved only because he was in the way of seeing nobody else.

"The little creature was crafty, and soon perceived that she could reap some benefit from this guileless man; she then sought out the best means of exploiting him. The most effective, surely, was to marry him.

"This she accomplished without difficulty.

"Need I tell you, gentlemen of the jury, that the conduct of this girl had been most irregular and that marriage, far from putting a check to her flight, seemed on the contrary to render it more shameless?

"From the natural sport of feminine astuteness, she seemed to take pleasure in deceiving this honest man with all the employees of his office. I said with all. We have letters, gentlemen. There was soon a public scandal, of which the husband alone, as usual, was the only one ignorant.

"Finally, this wretch, with an interest easy to understand, seduced the son of the proprietor, a young man nineteen years old, upon whose mind and judgment she had a deplorable influence. Mr. Langlais, whose eyes had been closed up to that time, through friendship for his employee, resented having his son in the hands, I should say in the arms of this dangerous woman, and was legitimately angry.

"He made the mistake of calling Lougère to him on the spot and of speaking to him of his paternal indignation.

"There remains nothing more for me to say, gentlemen, except to read to you the recital of the crime, made by the lips of the dying man, and submitted as evidence. It says:

"'I learned that my son had given to this woman, that same night, ten thousand francs, and my anger was stronger on that account. Certainly, I never suspected the honorableness of Lougère, but a certain kind of blindness is more dangerous than positive faults. And so I had him come to me and told him that I should be obliged to deprive myself of his services.

"'He remained standing before me, terrified, and not comprehending. He ended by demanding, rather excitedly, some explanation. I refused to give him any, affirming that my reasons were wholly personal. He believed then that I suspected him of indelicacy and, very pale, besought, implored me to explain. Held by this idea, he was strong and began to talk loud. As I kept silent, he abused and insulted me, until he arrived at such a degree of exasperation that I was fearful of results.

"'Then, suddenly, upon a wounding word that struck upon a full heart, I threw the whole truth in his face.

"'He stood still some seconds, looking at me with haggard eyes. Then I saw him take from my desk the long shears, which I use for making margins to certain registers, I saw him fall upon me with uplifted arm, and I felt something enter my throat just above the breast, without noticing any pain.'

"This, gentlemen of the jury, is the simple recital of this murder. What more can be said for his defense? He respected his second wife with blindness because he respected his first with reason."

After a short deliberation, the prisoner was acquitted.

Semillante

THE widow of Paolo Saverini lived alone with her son in a poor little house on the ramparts of Bonifacio. The town, built upon the side of the mountain, suspended in spots above the sea, overlooks, through a defile bristling with rocks, the lowest part of Sardinia. At its foot, on the other side, and almost entirely surrounding it, is a cut in the cliff, which resembles a gigantic corridor and serves as a port; it leads up to the first houses (after a long circuit between the two abrupt walls), the little Italian or Sardinian fishing-boats, and, every two weeks, the old, broken-winded steamer that plies between there and Ajaccio.

Upon the white mountains, the bunch of houses makes a spot whiter still. They have the appearance of nests of wild birds, fastened thus upon this rock, overlooking this terrible passageway where ships scarcely dare venture. The wind, without repose, harasses the sea, harasses the bare coast, which is nibbled by it until it has but little vegetation; it rushes into the defile, whose two sides it strips bare. The track of pale foam, fastened to black points on the innumerable rocks which pierce the waves, has the look of bits of cloth floating and palpitating upon the surface of the water.

The house of the widow Saverini, soldered to the edge of the cliff, had three windows opening upon this wild and desolated horizon.

She lived there alone, with her son Antoine and their dog Semillante, a great, thin beast with long, coarse hair, of a race that watches the herds. This dog served the young man for hunting.

One evening, after a dispute, Antoine Saverini was killed traitorously with a blow of a knife by Nicholas Ravolati who, the same night, went over to Sardinia.

When the old woman received the body of her child, which some passers-by brought to her, she did not weep but remained a long time motionless, looking at him. Then, extending her wrinkled hand upon the dead body, she promised revenge. She did not wish anyone to remain with her, and she shut herself up with the body and the dog.

The dog howled. She howled, this beast, in a continuous fashion, at the foot of the bed, her head extended toward her master, her tail held fast between her legs. She no more stirred than did the mother, who, hanging now upon the body, her eyes fixed, was weeping great tears while gazing at him.

The young man, upon his back, clothed in his coat of gray cloth, torn and bloody about the breast, seemed to be asleep. And there was blood everywhere: on his shirt, drawn up in the first moments, on his waistcoat, his trousers, upon his face, and his hands. Little clots of blood had coagulated in his beard and in his hair.

The old mother began to speak to him. At the sound of her voice, the dog was silent.

"Come, come," she said, "you shall be avenged, my little one, my boy, my poor child. Sleep, sleep, you shall be avenged, do you hear? It is your mother who promises! And she always keeps her word, does your mother, as you know well."

And gently she bent over him, gluing her cold lips to his dead mouth. Then Semillante began to groan again. She uttered a long, plaintive monotone, harrowing and terrible.

There they remained, the corpse, the woman and the beast, until morning.

Antoine Saverini was buried the next day, and soon no one spoke of him more in Bonifacio.

He had left no brother, no near relatives. There was no man to follow up the revenge. Alone, the mother thought of it, the old woman.

On the other side of the defile she saw, each morning and evening, a white spot on the coast. It was the little Sardinian village, Longosardo, where Corsican bandits took refuge when too closely pursued. They almost peopled this hamlet, opposite the shore of their own country, and awaited there the moment of returning, of going back again to the brakes. It was in this village, she knew, that Nicholas Ravolati had taken refuge.

All alone, the whole day long, seated before her window, she would look down there and think of vengeance. How could she do it without anyone to help, infirm as she was and so near death? But she had promised, she had sworn it upon his dead body. She could not forget, she must not delay. How should she accomplish it? She could not sleep at night; she had no repose, no ease; she sought obstinately. The dog slept at her feet, and, sometimes raising her head, howled to the distance. Since her master was no longer there, she often howled thus, as if she were calling him, as if her soul, that of an inconsolable beast, had preserved a remembrance of him that nothing could efface.

One night, as Semillante began to howl in this way, the mother suddenly had an idea, a savage, vindictive, ferocious idea. She meditated upon it until morning; then, rising at the approach of day, she betook herself to the church. She prayed, prostrate upon the floor, humbled before God, supplicating him to aid her, to sustain her, to give to her poor, spent body force that would be sufficient to avenge the death of her son.

Then she returned. She had in her yard an old barrel with the head knocked in, which caught the rain from the gutters. She emptied it and turned it over, making it fast to the soil by means of some stakes and stones; then she chained Semillante in this niche and went into her house.

Now she walked about constantly in her room, without repose, her eye fixed upon the coast of Sardinia. He was down there, was that assassin.

The dog howled all day and all night. The old woman carried her some water in the morning, in a bowl. But nothing more; no soup, no bread.

The day slipped away. Semillante, weakened from want of food, slept. The next day she had shining eyes and bristling hair; she pulled desperately at her chain.

Still the old woman gave her nothing to eat. The beast became furious, baying with raucous voice. The night passed away thus. Then, at the break of day, Mother Saverini went to the house of a neighbor and begged him to give her two bundles of straw. She took some old clothes that her husband had formerly worn and filled them full of the fodder, to simulate a human body.

Having stuck a stick in the ground before Semillante's niche, she bound the manikin to it, giving him the appearance of standing. Then she formed a head by means of a package of old linen.

The dog, surprised, looked at the straw man and was silent, although devoured with hunger.

Then the old woman went to the butcher's and bought a long piece of black pudding. She returned home, lighted a wood fire in her yard, and cooked this pudding. Semillante, excited, bounded about and frothed at the mouth, her eyes fixed upon the meat, the fumes of which entered her stomach.

Next the woman made a cravat for the straw man of this smoking sausage. She wound it many times about his neck, as if to make it penetrate him.

When this was done, she unchained the dog.

With a formidable leap, the beast reached the manikin's throat, and, her paws upon his shoulders, began to tear him to pieces. She fell back, a piece of her prey in her mouth, then leaped upon him again, sinking her teeth in the cords, snatching some particles of nourishment, fell back again, and rebounded enraged. She tore away the face with great blows of the teeth, tearing into shreds the whole neck.

The old woman, mute and motionless, looked on, her eyes lighting up. She rechained the beast, made him fast two days again, and repeated this strange operation.

For three months, she accustomed the dog to this kind of struggle, to a repast conquered by tooth and claw. She did not chain her now, but set her upon the manikin with a gesture.

She taught her to tear him, to devour him, even without anything eatable hung around his throat. She would give her afterward, as a recompense, the pudding she had cooked for her.

Whenever she perceived the manikin, Semillante growled and turned her eyes toward her mistress, who would cry: "Go!" in a whistling tone, at the same time raising her finger.

When she thought the right time had come, Mother Saverini went to confession and to communion one morning in ecstatic fervor; then, having clothed herself in male attire, so that she looked like a feeble, old man, she went with a Sardinian fisherman, who took her and her dog to the other side of the defile.

She had, in a sack of cloth, a large piece of pudding. Semillante had fasted for two days. Every few moments the old woman made her smell of the pleasand food and endeavored to excite her.

They entered into Longosardo. The Corsican went into a wine-shop. She presented herself at a baker's and asked where Nicholas Ravolati lived. He had taken his old trade, that of a carpenter. He was working alone at the back of his shop.

The old woman opened the door and called:

"Hey, Nicholas!"

He turned around; then, loosing the dog, she cried out:

"Go! go! Devour him! devour him!"

The animal, excited, threw herself upon him and seized him by the throat. The man extended his arms, clinched her, and rolled upon the floor. For some minutes he twisted himself, beating the soil with his feet; then he remained motionless, while Semillante dug at his neck until it was in shreds.

Two neighbors, seated before their doors, recalled perfectly having seen an old man go out of the shop, with a black dog at his side, which was eating, as he went along, something brown that his master gave him.

That evening, the old woman returned to her house. She slept well that night.

On the River

LAST summer I rented a cottage on the banks of the Seine, several miles from Paris, and I used to go out to it every evening. After a while, I formed the acquaintance of one of my neighbors, a man between thirty and forty years of age, who really was one of the queerest characters I ever have met. He was an old boating-man, crazy on the subject of boats, and was always either in, or on, or by the water. Surely he must have been born in a boat, and probably he will die in one, some day, while taking a last outing.

One evening, as we were walking along the edge of the river, I asked him to tell me about some of his nautical experiences. Immediately his face lighted up, and he became eloquent, almost poetical, for his heart was full of an all-absorbing, irresistible, devouring passion—a love for the river.

"Ah!" said he, "how many recollections I have of the river that flows at our feet! You street-dwellers have no idea what the river really is. But let a fisherman pronounce the word. To him it means mystery, the unknown, a land of mirage and phantasmagoria, where odd things that have no real existence are seen at night and strange noises are heard; where one trembles without knowing the reason why, as when passing through a cemetery,—and indeed the river is a cemetery without graves.

"Land, for a fisherman, has boundaries, but the river, on moonless nights, appears to him unlimited. A sailor doesn't feel the same way about the sea. The sea is often cruel, but it roars and foams, it gives us fair warning; the river is silent and treacherous. It flows stealthily, without a murmur, and the eternal gentle motion of the water is more awful to me than the big ocean waves.

"Dreamers believe that the deep hides immense lands of blue, where the drowned roll around among the big fish, in strange forests or in crystal caves. The river has only black depths, where the dead decay in the slime. But it's beautiful when the sun shines on it, and the waters splash softly on the banks covered with whispering reeds.

"In speaking of the ocean the poet says:

" 'Oh! what tragic tales of the vast, blue deep,—
    The vast blue deep prayerful mothers fear,—
    The sad waves tell, when at night, we hear,
Their ceaseless moanings in our sleep!'

Well, I believe that the stories the slender reeds tell one another in their wee, silvery voices are even more appalling than the ghastly tragedies related by the roaring waves.

"But as you have asked me to relate some of my recollections, I will tell you a strange adventure that happened to me here, about ten years ago.

"Then, as now, I lived in old mother Lafon's house and a chum of mine, Louis Bernet, who since has given up boating, as well as his happy-go-lucky ways, to become a State Councilor, was camping out in the village of C——, two miles away. We used to take dinner together every day, either at his place or at mine.

"One evening, as I was returning home alone, feeling rather tired, and with difficulty rowing the twelve-foot boat that I always took out at night, I stopped to rest a little while near that point over there, formed by reeds, about two hundred yards in front of the railway bridge. The weather was gorgeous; the moon shed a silvery light on the shining river, and the air was soft and still. The calmness of the surroundings tempted me, and I thought how pleasant it would be to fill my pipe here and smoke. The thought was immediately executed, and, laying hold of the anchor, I dropped it overboard. The boat, which was following the stream, slid to the end of the chain and came to a stop; I settled myself aft on a rug, as comfortably as I could. There was not a sound to be heard nor a movement to be seen, though sometimes I noticed the almost imperceptible rippling of the water on the banks, and watched the highest clumps of reeds, which at times assumed strange shapes that appeared to move.

The river was perfectly calm, but I was affected by the extraordinary stillness that enveloped me. The frogs and toads, the nocturnal musicians of the swamps, were voiceless. Suddenly, at my right, a frog croaked. I started; it stopped, and all was silent. I resolved to light my pipe for distraction. But, strange to say, though I was an inveterate smoker I failed to enjoy it, and after a few puffs I grew sick and stopped smoking. Then I began to hum an air, but the sound of my voice depressed me.

At last I lay down in the boat and watched the sky. For a while I remained quiet, but presently the slight pitching of the boat disturbed me. I felt as if it were swaying to and fro from one side of the river to the other, and that an invisible force or being was drawing it slowly to the bottom and then raising it to let it drop again. I was knocked about as if in a storm; I heard strange noises; I jumped up; the water was shining and all was still. Then I knew that my nerves were slightly shaken, and decided to leave the river. I pulled on the chain. The boat moved along, but presently I felt some resistance and pulled harder. The anchor refused to come up; it had caught in something at the bottom and remained stuck. I pulled and tugged but to no avail. With the oars I turned the boat around and forced her up-stream, in order to alter the position of the anchor. This was all in vain, however, for the anchor did not yield; so in a rage, I began to shake at the chain, which wouldn't budge.

I sat down discouraged, to ponder over my mishap. It was impossible to break the chain or to separate it from the boat, as it was enormous and was riveted to a piece of wood as big as my arm; but as the weather continued fine, I did not doubt but that some fisherman would come along and rescue me. The accident calmed me so much that I managed to remain quiet and smoke my pipe. I had a bottle of rum with me so I drank two or three glasses of it and began to laugh at my situation. It was so warm that it would not have mattered much had I been obliged to spend all night out of doors.

Suddenly something jarred slightly against the side of the boat. I started, and a cold sweat broke over me from head to foot. The noise was due to a piece of wood drifting along with the current, but it proved sufficient to disturb my mind, and once more I felt the same strange nervousness creep over me. The anchor remained firm. Exhausted, I seated myself again.

"Meantime the river was covering itself with a white mist that lay close to the water, so that when I stood up neither the stream, nor my feet, nor the boat, were visible to me; I could distinguish only the ends of the reeds and, a little further away, the meadow, ashen in the moonlight, with large black patches formed by groups of Italian poplars reaching toward the sky. I was buried up to my waist in something that looked like a blanket of down of a peculiar whiteness; and all kinds of fantastic visions arose before me. I imagined that some one was trying to crawl into the boat, which I could no longer see and that the river hidden under the thick fog was full of strange creatures that were swimming all around me. I felt a horrible depression steal over me, my temples throbbed, my heart beat wildly, and, losing all control over myself, I was ready to plunge overboard and swim to safety. But this idea suddenly filled me with horror. I imagined myself lost in the dense mist, floundering about aimlessly among the reeds and water-plants, unable to find the banks of the river or the boat; and I felt as if I should certainly be drawn by my feet to the bottom of the dark waters. As I really should have had to swim against the current for at least five hundred yards before reaching a spot where I could safely land, it was nine chances to ten that, being unable to see in the fog, I should drown, although I was a fine swimmer.

"I tried to overcome my dread. I determined not to be afraid, but there was something in me besides my will and that something was faint-hearted. I asked myself what there was to fear; my courageous self railed at the other, the timid one; never before had I so fully realized the opposition that exists between the two beings we have in us; the one willing, the other resisting, and each one triumphing in turn. But this foolish and unaccountable fear was growing worse and worse, and was becoming positive terror. I remained motionless, with open eyes and straining ears, waiting. For what? I scarcely knew, but it must have been for something terrible. I believe that had a fish suddenly taken it into its head to jump out of the water, as frequently happens, I should have fallen in a dead faint. However, I managed to keep my senses after a violent effort to control myself. I took my bottle of brandy and again raised it to my lips.

"Suddenly I began to shout at the top of my voice, turning successively toward the four points of the horizon. After my throat had become completely paralyzed with shouting, I listened. A dog was barking in the distance.

"I drank some more rum and lay down in the bottom of the boat. I remained thus at least one hour, perhaps two, without shutting my eyes, visited by nightmares. I did not dare to sit up, though I had an insane desire to do so; I put it off from second to second, saying: 'Now then, I'll get up,' but I was afraid to move. At last I raised myself

with infinite care, as if my life depended on the slightest sound I might make, and peered over the edge of the boat. I was greeted by the most marvelous, stupendous sight that it is possible to imagine. It was a vision of fairyland, one of those phenomena that travelers in distant countries tell us about, but that we are unable to believe.

"The mist, which two hours ago hung over the water, had lifted and settled on the banks of the stream. It formed on each side an unbroken hill, six or seven yards in height, that shone in the moonlight with the dazzling whiteness of snow. Nothing could be seen but the flashing river, moving between the two white mountains, and overhead a full moon that illuminated the milky-blue sky.

"All the hosts of the water had awakened; the frogs were croaking dismally, while from time to time a toad sent its short, monotonous, and gloomy note to the stars. Strange to say, I was no longer frightened; I was surrounded by a landscape so utterly unreal that the strangest freaks of nature would not have surprised me at all.

"How long this situation lasted I am unable to tell, for I finally dozed off to sleep. When I awoke, the moon was gone and the sky was covered with clouds. The water splashed dismally, the wind was blowing, it was cold and completely dark. I finished the brandy and lay listening to the rustling of the reeds and the murmur of the river. I tried to see, but failed to distinguish the boat or even my hands, although I held them close to my eyes. The darkness, however, was slowly decreasing.

Suddenly I thought I saw a shadow glide past me. I shouted to it and a voice responded: it was a fisherman. I called to him and told him of my plight. He brought his boat alongside mine and both began tugging at the chain. The anchor still would not yield. A cold, rainy day was setting in, one of those days that bring disaster and sadness. I perceived another boat, which we hailed. The owner added his strength to ours, and little by little the anchor gave way. It came up very slowly, laden with considerable weight. Finally a black heap appeared and we dragged it into my boat. It was the body of an old woman, with a big stone tied around her neck!"

Suicides

SCARCELY a day goes by without the newspapers containing an account like this:

"Tenants of No. 40 B —— street were startled Wednesday night by the report of two shots that proceeded from the apartment occupied by Mr. X ——. The door was burst open and he was found on the floor, in a pool of blood, his hand still grasping the revolver with which he committed suicide. Mr. X —— was fifty-seven years old and prosperous. He had everything to live for, and no reason can be ascribed for his tragic act."

What grief and secret despair, what burning sorrows lead these people, who are supposed to be happy, to end their lives? Financial troubles and love tragedies are hinted at, but as nothing really precise ever becomes known, these deaths are pronounced "mysterious."

A letter that was found on the table of one of these suicides, who wrote it during his last night on earth, with the loaded pistol within his reach, has come into our possession. We deem it interesting, though it reveals no great tragedy such as one usually expects to find at the bottom of these rash acts. It only tells of the slow succession of the little ills of life, of the inevitable disorganization of a solitary existence weaned from its illusions; it makes clear those tragic endings which no others but people of high-strung, supersensitive temperaments can understand.

This is the letter:

"It is midnight. When I finish this letter I intend to destroy myself. Why? I will endeavor to explain, not for those who read this, but for myself, in order to strengthen my failing courage and to convince myself of the now fatal necessity of my determination which, if not carried out to-night, could only be deferred.

"I was brought up by parents who believed in everything, and so I, too, believed. My dream lasted a long time. But now its last illusions have fled.

"The past few years have wrought a great change in me. The things that used to seem most alluring and desirable have lost their attraction. The true meaning of life has dawned upon me in all its brutal reality; the true reason of love disgusts me even with poetical sentiment.

"We are nothing but the eternal toys of illusions as foolish as they are charming, which reblossom as soon as, they fade.

"Getting on in years, I became resigned to the utter shallowness of life, to the uselessness of any effort, to the vanity of any hope, when suddenly tonight, after dinner, I viewed the futility of everything in a different light.

"Formerly I was happy. Everything charmed me; the women I met in the streets; the streets themselves; my own home; even the shape of my clothes was a subject of interest to me. But finally the repetition of these visions bored and annoyed me; I feel like a theater-goer seeing the same play night after night.

"During the last thirty years I have arisen at the same hour; have dined at the same place, eating the same things served at the same times by different waiters.

"I have tried to travel! But the sensation of forlornness that came over me in strange places deterred me. I felt so isolated and small on this immense earth that I hastened to return home.

"But the furnishings of my apartment, that have not been changed in thirty odd years, the worn places on the chairs which I recollect when they were new, even the odor of the place (for after a while each home acquires a distinctive atmosphere) gave me every night an awful, nauseating sense of melancholy.

"Does not everything repeat itself in an eternal, heartrending fashion? The way in which I put my key into the latch-hole, the spot where I find the match-box, the first glance I give the room after striking a light, all these little things make me desire to fling myself out of the window, so as to end for good and all the series of monotonous incidents which fill life and from which there is no escape.

"Every day when shaving in front of my little mirror I feel like cutting my throat; the same face with soap on its cheeks that stares at me has driven me many a time to cry out from sheer despondency.

"To-day I hardly care to meet the people whose society I used to enjoy, because I know too well what they are going to say and what I shall reply; the trend of their thoughts is as familiar as the drift of their arguments. Each brain is like a circus-ring around which gallops a poor, imprisoned horse. No matter what our efforts or dodges may be, we cannot escape from the circular ring, which has no unexpected turns, no door opening on the unknown. We must go around forever, through the same joys, the same jokes, the same beliefs, habits, disgusts.

"The fog was dreadful to-night. It covered the boulevard, dimming the gas-lights that shone like so many smoky candles. A heavier weight than usual oppressed me. My digestion was probably in bad shape. A good digestion is a great blessing. It gives to artists inspiration, to thinkers clear ideas, to young men amorous desires, and to everyone happiness.

"It lets us eat our fill and, after all, this is the greatest satisfaction. A weak stomach predisposes one to scepticism and unbelief, and incites bad dreams and morbidity. I have noticed it very, very often. Perhaps I would not care to die, to-night, if my digestion were perfect.

"When I seated myself in the chair in which I have sat every night the past thirty years, I glanced around and felt so depressed that I thought I should become distracted.

"I wondered how I could escape from myself? To be occupied appeared to me even more intolerable than to remain inactive. I had the idea of putting my old papers in order. I have intended to arrange them for a long time. For thirty years I have flung letters and bills together in the same drawer, and the confusion resulting therefrom has often caused me a great deal of trouble. But the mere idea of straightening out anything gives me such mental and physical distress that I never have had sufficient courage to undertake the odious task.

"So I sat down at my desk and opened it, intending to look over my old papers and to destroy some. At first I felt quite helpless before the heaps of yellowed leaves; but finally I extricated one of them.

"Never, if you value your life, dare touch the desk or the tomb that contains old letters! And if by chance you should open it, close your eyes so as to shut out the letters, lest a long-forgotten but suddenly recognized handwriting awaken a world of recollections; take the fatal pages and throw them into the fire, and when they are ashes stamp them into invisible dust or else you will be lost—as I have been—for the last hour.

"The first letters I picked out did not interest me. They were from men I meet once in a while, and for whom I feel no great interest. But all at once an envelope attracted my eyes. It bore my name written in a broad, firm hand; tears filled my eyes. Here was a letter from my dearest friend, the one in whom I used to confide in my youth, and who knew my hopes; he arose before me so clearly with his outstretched hand and good-natured smile, that a shudder ran through my frame. Yes, the dead come back, for I saw him! Our memory is a world far more perfect than the real universe, for it brings to life those who have gone forever.

"With misty eyes and trembling hands I read over all the letters, while my poor crushed heart throbbed with a pain so acute that I groaned aloud like a man whose limbs are being tortured.

"I went over my whole life, and it was like floating along a familiar river. I recognized people whose names long ago had been blotted from my mind. Only their faces had stamped themselves upon my memory. My mother's letters revived recollections of the old servants of our household, brought back all the little insignificant details that impress themselves on a child's brain.

"Yes, I even saw my mother as she looked in the gowns of years ago, with the changed appearance she would assume with each new style of hair-dressing she successively adopted. She haunted me most in a silk gown of some gorgeous pattern, and I remembered what she said to me one day, wearing that robe: 'Robert, my child, if you fail to hold yourself erect, you will be round-shouldered all your life.'

"On opening another drawer, I suddenly gazed on my love trinkets—a satin slipper, a torn handkerchief, several locks of hair, some pressed flowers, even a garter.

"My romances, whose heroines, if still living, must have white hair, arose before me with all the bitterness of loved things forever gone. Oh! the young brows shaded by golden hair, the clasped hands, the speaking glances, the throbbing hearts, the smile that promises the lips, and the lips that promise all—then the first kiss—long, unending, with no thought but of the immense ecstasy to come!

"I grasped with both hands the cherished tokens and I kissed them passionately. My harassed soul beheld each one of my loves at the moment of sweet surrender—and I suffered worse torments than those imagined in the descriptions of hell.

"A single letter remained. It had been written by me and was dictated fifty years ago by my teacher.

"It ran:

"'MY DEAR MAMMA:

"'I am seven years old to-day. As it is the age of reason, I want to thank you for having brought me into this world.
"'Your loving little son,
"'ROBERT.'

"This was the last. I had arrived at the very beginning of my life and I turned to face the prospect of the remaining years. I see nothing but a hideous and lonely old age with all its accompanying disablements—all is over, over, over! Nobody to care for me.

"The revolver lies here on the table. I am loading it— Never read over your old letters."

And this is the reason why so many men kill themselves, while one searches their lives in vain for the discovery of some hidden tragedy.

———————◆———————

A Miracle

DOCTOR BONENFANT was searching his memory, saying, half aloud: "A Christmas story—some remembrance of Christmas?"

Suddenly he cried: "Yes, I have one, and a strange one too; it is a fantastic story. I have seen a miracle! yes, ladies, a miracle, and on Christmas night."

It astonishes you to hear me speak thus, a man who believes scarcely anything. Nevertheless, I have seen a miracle! I have seen it, I tell you, seen, with my own eyes, that is what I call seeing.

Was I very much surprised, you ask? Not at all; because if I do not believe from your view point, I believe in faith, and I know that it can remove mountains. I could cite many examples; but I might make you indignant, and I should risk diminishing the effect of my story.

In the first place, I must confess that if I have not been convinced and converted by what I have seen, I have at least been strongly moved; and I am going to strive to tell it to you naïvely, as if I had the credulity of an Auvergnat.

I was then a country doctor, living in the town of Rolleville, on the plains of Normandy. The winter that year was terrible. By the end of November the snow came after a week of heavy frosts. One could see from afar the great snow clouds coming from the north, and then the descent of the white flakes commenced. In one night the whole plain was in its winding-sheet. Farms, isolated in their square inclosures, behind their curtains of great trees powdered with hoar-frost, seemed to sleep under the accumulation of this thick, light covering.

No noise could reach this dead country. The crows alone in large flocks outlined long festoons in the sky, living their lives to no purpose, swooping down upon the livid fields and picking at the snow with their great beaks. There was nothing to be heard but the vague, continued whisper of this white powder as it persistently fell. This lasted for eight days and then stopped. The earth had on its back a mantle five feet in thickness. And, during the next three weeks, a sky spread itself out over this smooth, white mass, hard and glistening with frost, which was clear blue crystal by day, and at night all studded with stars, as if the hoar-frost grew by their light.

The plain, the hedges, the elms of the inclosures, all seemed dead, killed by the cold. Neither man nor beast went out. Only the chimneys of the cottages, clothed in white linen, revealed concealed life by the fine threads of smoke which mounted straight into the frosty air. From time to time one heard the trees crack, as if their wooden limbs were breaking under the bark. And sometimes a great branch would detach itself and fall, the resistless cold petrifying the sap and breaking the fibers. Dwellings set here and there in fields seemed a hundred miles away from one another. One lived as he could. I alone endeavored to go to my nearest clients, constantly exposing myself to the danger of remaining in some hole in the winding-sheet of snow.

I soon perceived that a mysterious terror had spread over the country. Such a plague, they thought, was not natural. They pretended that they heard voices at night, and sharp whistling and cries, as of some one passing. These cries and the whistles came, without doubt, from emigrant birds which traveled at twilight and flew in flocks toward the south. But it was impossible to make this frightened people listen to reason. Fear had taken possession of their minds, and they listened to every extraordinary event.

The forge of Father Vatinel was situated at the end of the hamlet of Epivent, on the highway, now invisible and deserted. As the people needed bread, the blacksmith resolved to go to the village. He remained some hours chattering with the inhabitants of the six houses which formed the center of the country, took his bread and his news and a little of the fear which had spread over the region and set out before night.

Suddenly, in skirting a hedge, he believed he saw an egg on the snow; yes, an egg was lying there, all white like the rest of the world. He bent over it, and in fact it was an egg. Where did it come from? What hen could have gone out there and laid an egg in that spot? The smith was astonished; he could not comprehend it; but he picked it up and took it to his wife.

"See, wife, here is an egg that I found on the way."

The woman tossed her head, replying:

"An egg on the way? And this kind of weather! You must be drunk, surely."

"No, no, my lady, it surely was at the foot of the hedge, and not frozen but still warm. Take it; I put it in my bosom so that it wouldn't cool off. You shall have it for your dinner."

The egg was soon shining in the saucepan where the soup was simmering, and the smith began to relate what he had heard around the country. The woman listened, pale with excitement.

"Surely I have heard some whistling," said she, "but it seemed to come from the chimney."

They sat down to table, ate their soup first and then, while the husband was spreading the butter on his bread, the woman took the egg and examined it with suspicious eye.

"And if there should be something in this egg," said she.

"What, think you, you would like to have in it?"

"I know very well."

"Go ahead and eat it. Don't be a fool."

She opened the egg. It was like all eggs, and very fresh. She started to eat it but hesitated, tasting, then leaving, then tasting it again. The husband said:

"Well, how does it taste, that egg?"

She did not answer, but finished swallowing it. Then, suddenly, she set her eyes on her husband, fixed, haggard, and excited, raised her arms, turned and twisted them, convulsed from head to foot, and rolled on the floor, sending forth horrible shrieks. All night she struggled in these frightful spasms, trembling with fright, deformed by hideous convulsions. The smith, unable to restrain her, was obliged to bind her. And she screamed without ceasing, with voice indefatigable:

"I have it in my body! I have it in my body!"

I was called the next day. I ordered all the sedatives known, but without effect. She was mad. Then, with incredible swiftness, in spite of the obstacle of deep snow, the news, the strange news ran from farm to farm: "The smith's wife is possessed!" And they came from all about, not daring to go into the house, to listen to the cries of the frightened woman, whose voice was so strong that one could scarcely believed it belonged to a human creature.

The curate of the village was sent for. He was a simple old priest. He came in surplice, as if to administer comfort to the dying, and pronounced with extended hands some formulas of exorcism, while four men held the foaming, writhing woman on the bed. But the spirit was not driven out.

Christmas came without any change in the weather. In the early morning the priest came for me.

"I wish," said he, "to ask you to assist me to-night at a service for this unfortunate woman. Perhaps God will work a miracle in her favor at the same hour that he was born of a woman."

I replied: "I approve heartily, M. l'Abbé, but if the spell is to be broken by ceremony (and there could be no more propitious time to start it) she can be saved without remedies."

The old priest murmured: "You are not a believer, Doctor, but aid me, will you not?" I promised him my aid.

The evening came, and then the night. The clock of the church was striking, throwing its plaintive voice across the extent of white, glistening snow. Some black figures were wending their way slowly in groups, drawn by the bronze call from the bell. The full moon shone with a dull, wan light at the edge of the horizon, rendering more visible the desolation of the fields. I had taken four robust men with me, and with them repaired to the forge.

The Possessed One shouted continually, although bound to her bed. They had clothed her properly, in spite of her resistance, and now they brought her out. The church wase full of people, illuminated but cold; the choir chanted their monotonous notes; the serpent hummed; the little bell of the acolyte tinkled, regulating the movements of the faithful.

I had shut the woman and her guards into the kitchen of the parish house and awaited the movement that I believed favorable.

I chose the time immediately following communion. All the peasants, men and women, had received their God, resolving to submit to the severity of His will. A great silence prevailed while the priest finished the divine mystery. Upon my order, the door opened and the four men brought in the mad woman.

When she saw the lights, the crowd on their knees, the choir illuminated, and the gilded tabernacle, she struggled with such vigor that she almost escaped from us, and she gave forth cries so piercing that a shiver of fright ran through the church. All bowed their heads; some fled. She had no longer the form of a woman, her hands being distorted, her countenance drawn, her eyes protruding. They held her up until after the march of the choir, and then allowed her to squat on the floor.

Finally, the priest arose; he waited. When there was a moment of quiet, he took in his hands a silver vessel with bands of gold, upon which was the consecrated white wafer and, advancing some steps, extended both arms above his head and presented it to the frightened stare of the maniac. She continued to shout, but with eyes fixed upon the shining object. And the priest remained thus, motionless, as if he had been a statue.

This lasted a long, long time. The woman seemed seized with fear, fascinated; she looked fixedly at the bright vessel, trembled violently but at intervals, and cried out incessantly, but with a less piercing voice.

It happened that she could no longer lower her eyes; that they were riveted on the Host; that she could no longer groan; that her body became pliable and that she sank down exhausted. The crowd was prostrate, brows to earth.

The Possessed One now lowered her eyelids quickly, then raised them again, as if powerless to endure the sight of her God. She was silent. And then I myself perceived that her eyes were closed. She slept the sleep of the somnambulist, the hypnotist—pardon! conquered by the contemplation of the silver vessel with the bands of gold, overcome by the Christ victorious.

They carried her out, inert, while the priest returned to the altar. The assistants, thrown into wonderment, intoned a "Te Deum."

The smith's wife slept for the next four hours; then she awoke without any remembrance either of the possession or of the deliverance. This, ladies, is the miracle that I saw.

Doctor Bonenfant remained silent for a moment, then he added, in rather disagreeable voice:

"And I could never refuse to swear to it in writing."

The Accursed Bread

DADDY TAILLE had three daughters: Anna, the eldest, who was scarcely ever mentioned in the family; Rose, the second girl, who was eighteen; and Clara, the youngest, who was a girl of fifteen.

Old Taille was a widower, and a foreman in M. Lebrument's button-manufactory. He was a very upright man, very well thought of, abstemious; in fact a sort of model workman. He lived at Havre, in the Rue d'Angoulême.

When Anna ran away the old man flew into a fearful rage. He threatened to kill the seducer, who was head clerk in a large draper's establishment in that town. Then when he was told by various people that she was keeping very steady and investing money in government securities, that she was no gadabout, but was maintained by a Monsieur Dubois, who was a judge of the Tribunal of Commerce, the father was appeased.

He even showed some anxiety as to how she was faring, asked some of her old friends who had been to see her how she was getting on; and when told that she had her own furniture, and that her mantelpiece was covered with vases and the walls with pictures, that there were clocks and carpets everywhere, he gave a broad, contented smile. He had been working for thirty years to get together a wretched five or six thousand francs. This girl was evidently no fool.

One fine morning the son of Touchard, the cooper at the other end of the street, came and asked him for the hand of Rose, the second girl. The old man's heart began to beat, for the Touchards were rich and in a good position. He was decidedly lucky with his girls.

The marriage was agreed upon. It was settled that it should be a grand affair, and the wedding dinner was to be held at Sainte-Addresse, at Mother Lusa's restaurant. It would cost a lot certainly; but never mind, it did not matter just for once in a way.

But one morning, just as the old man was going home to breakfast with his two daughters, the door opened suddenly and Anna appeared. She was elegantly dressed, wore rings and an expensive bonnet, and looked undeniably pretty and nice. She threw her arms round her father's neck before he could say a word, then fell into her sisters' arms with many tears, and then asked for a plate, so that she might share the family soup. Taille was moved to tears in his turn and said several times:

"That is right, dear; that is right."

Then she told them about herself. She did not wish Rose's wedding to take place at Sainte-Addresse,—certainly not. It should take place at her house, and would cost her father nothing. She had settled everything, so it was "no good to say any more about it,—there!"

"Very well, my dear! very well!" the old man said, "we will leave it so." But then he felt some doubt. Would the Touchards consent? But Rose, the bride-elect, was surprised, and asked, "Why should they object, I should like to know? Just leave that to me, I will talk to Philip about it."

She mentioned it to her lover the very same day, and he declared that it would suit him exactly. Father and Mother Touchard were naturally delighted at the idea of a good dinner which would cost them nothing and said:

"You may be quite sure that everything will be in first-rate style, as M. Dubois is made of money."

They asked to be allowed to bring a friend, Mme. Florence, the cook on the first floor, and Anna agreed to everything. The wedding was fixed for the last Tuesday of the month.

II.

After the civil formalities and the religious ceremony the wedding party went to Anna's house. Among those whom the Tailles had brought was a cousin of a certain age, a M. Sauvetanin, a man given to philosophical reflections, serious, and always very self-possessed, and Mme. Lamonoois, an old aunt.

M. Sauvetanin had been told off to give Anna his arm, as they were looked upon as the two most important persons in the company.

As soon as they had arrived at the door of Anna's house she let go her companion's arm, and ran on ahead, saying, "I will show you the way," while the invited guests followed more slowly. When they got upstairs, she stood on one side to let them pass, and they rolled their eyes and turned their heads in all directions to admire this mysterious and luxurious dwelling.

The table was laid in the drawing-room as the dining-room had been thought too small. Extra knives, forks, and spoons had been hired from a neighboring restaurant, and decanters full of wine glittered under the rays of the sun, which shone in through the window.

The ladies went into the bedroom to take off their shawls and bonnets, and Father Touchard, who was standing at the door, squinted at the low, wide bed, and made funny signs to the men, with many a wink and nod. Daddy Taille, who thought a great deal of himself, looked with fatherly pride at his child's well-furnished rooms, and went from one to the other holding his hat in his hand, making a mental inventory of everything, and walking like a verger in a church.

Anna went backward and forward, and ran about giving orders and hurrying on the wedding feast. Soon she appeared at the door of the dining-room, and cried: "Come here, all of you, for a moment," and when the twelve guests did as they were asked they saw twelve glasses of Madeira on a small table.

Rose and her husband had their arms round each other's waists, and were kissing each other in every corner. M. Sauvetanin never took his eyes off Anna; he no doubt felt that ardor, that sort of expectation which all men, even if they are old and ugly, feel for women of a certain stamp.

They sat down, and the wedding breakfast began; the relatives sitting at one end of the table and the young people at the other. Mme. Touchard, the mother, presided on the right, and the bride on the left. Anna looked after everybody, saw that the glasses were kept filled and the plates well supplied. The guests evidently felt a certain respectful embarrassment at the sight of the sumptuousness of the rooms and at the lavish manner in which they were treated. They all ate heartily of the good things provided, but there were no jokes such as are prevalent at weddings of that sort; it was all too grand, and it made them feel uncomfortable. Old Madame Touchard, who was fond of a bit of fun, tried to enliven matters a little and at the beginning of the dessert she exclaimed: "I say, Philip, do sing us something." The neighbors in their street considered that he had the finest voice in all Havre.

The bride-groom got up, smiled, and turning to his sister-in-law, from politeness and gallantry, tried to think of something suitable for the occasion, something serious and correct, to harmonize with the seriousness of the repast.

Anna had a satisfied look on her face, and leaned back in her chair to listen,

and all assumed looks of attention, though prepared to smile should smiles be called for.

The singer announced, "The Accursed Bread," and extending his right arm, which made his coat ruck up into his neck, he began.

It was decidedly long, three verses of eight lines each, with the last line and the last line but one repeated twice.

All went well for the first two verses; they were the usual commonplaces about bread gained by honest labor and by dishonesty. The aunt and the bride wept outright. The cook, who was present, at the end of the first verse looked at a roll which she held in her hand with moist eyes, as if they applied to her, while all applauded vigorously. At the end of the second verse the two servants, who were standing with their backs to the wall, joined loudly in the chorus, and the aunt and the bride wept outright. Daddy Taille blew his nose with the noise of a trombone, old Touchard brandished a whole loaf half over the table, and the cook shed silent tears on to the crust which she was still holding.

Amid the general emotion M. Sauvetanin said:

"That is the right sort of song; very different to the pointed things one generally hears at weddings."

Anna, who was visibly affected, kissed her hand to her sister and pointed to her husband with an affectionate nod, as if to congratulate her.

Intoxicated by his success, the young man continued, and unfortunately the last verse contained words about the bread of dishonor gained by young girls who had been led astray from the paths of virtue. No one took up the refrain about this bread, supposed to be eaten with tears, except old Touchard and the two servants. Anna had grown deadly pale and cast down her eyes, while the bridegroom looked from one to the other without understanding the reason for this sudden coldness, and the cook hastily dropped the crust as if it were poisoned.

M. Sauvetanin said solemnly, in order to save the situation: "That last couplet is not at all necessary"; and Daddy Taille, who had got red up to his ears, looked round the table fiercely.

Then Anna, with her eyes swimming in tears, told the servants, in the falter- ing voice of a woman trying to stifle her sobs, to bring the champagne.

All the guests were suddenly seized with exuberant joy, and their faces be- came radiant again. And when old Tou- chard, who had seen, felt, and under- stood nothing of what was going on, and, pointing to the guests so as to emphasize his words, sang the last words of the refrain: "Children, I warn you all to eat not of that bread," the whole com- pany, when they saw the champagne bottles with their necks covered with gold foil appear, burst out singing, as if electrified by the sight:

"Children, I warn you all to eat not of that bread."

———————◆———————

My Twenty-five Days

I HAD just taken possession of my room in the hotel, a narrow apartment between two papered partitions, so that I could hear all the sounds made by my neighbors. I was beginning to arrange in the glass cupboard my clothes and my linen, when I opened the drawer which was in the middle of this piece of fur- niture, I immediately noticed a manu- script of rolled paper. Having unrolled it, I spread it open before me, and read this title:

"MY TWENTY-FIVE DAYS."

It was the diary of a bather, of the last occupant of my room, and had been left behind there in forgetfulness at the hour of departure.

These notes may be of some interest to sensible and healthy persons who never leave their own homes. It is for their benefit that I here transcribe them without altering a letter.

"CHÂTEL-GUYON, July 15.

"At the first glance, it is not gay, this country. So, I am going to spend twenty-five days here to have my liver and my stomach treated, and to get rid of flesh. The twenty-five days of a bather are very like the twenty-eight days of a reserviste; they are all de- voted to fatigue-duty, severe fatigue- duty. To-day, nothing as yet; I am installed; I have made the acquain- tance of locality and the doctors. Châtel-Guyon is composed of a stream in which flows yellow water, in the midst of several mountain-peaks, where are erected a Casino, houses, and stone- crosses. At the side of the stream, in the depths of the valley, may be seen a square building surrounded by a little garden: this is the establishment of the baths. Sad people wander around this building—the invalids. A great silence reigns in these walks shaded by trees, this is not a pleasure-station but a true health-station: you take care of your health here through conviction, but you cannot get cured, it seems.

"Competent people declare that the mineral springs perform true miracles here. However, no votive offering is hung around the cashier's office.

"From time to time, a gentleman or a lady comes over to a kiosk with a slate roof, which shelters a woman of smiling and gentle aspect and a spring boiling in a basin of cement. Not a word is exchanged between the invalid and the female custodian of the healing water. She hands to the newcomer a little glass in which air-bubbles quiver in the transparent liquid. The other drinks and goes off with a grave step in order to resume his interrupted walk under the trees.

"No noise in the little park, no breath of air in the leaves, no voice breaks through this silence. Inscribed over the entrance to this district should be: 'Here you no longer laugh; you nurse yourself.'

"The people who chat resemble mutes who open their mouths in order to simulate sounds, so much are they afraid of letting their voices escape.

"In the hotel, the same silence. It is a big hotel where you dine solemnly with people of good position, who have nothing to say to each other. Their manners bespeak good-breeding and their faces reflect the conviction of a superiority of which it would be difficult to give actual proof.

"At two o'clock, I make my way up to the Casino, a little wooden hut perched on a hillock to which one climbs by paths frequented by goats. But the view from that height is admirable. Châtel-Guyon is situated in a very narrow valley, exactly between the plain and the mountains. At the left I see the first great waves of the mountains of Auvergne covered with woods, exhibiting here and there big gray spots, their hard lava-bones, for we are at the foot of the extinct volcanoes. At the right, through the narrow slope of the valley, I discover a plain infinite as the sea, steeped in a bluish fog which lets one only dimly discern the villages, the towns, the yellow fields of ripe corn, and the green square of meadow-land shaded with appletrees. It is the Limagne, immense and flat, always enveloped in a light veil of vapor.

"The night has come. And now, after having dined alone, I write these lines beside my open window. I hear, over there, in front of me, the little orchestra of the Casino, which plays airs just as a wild bird sings all alone in the desert.

"From time to time a dog barks. This great calm does me good. Good night.

"*July* 16. Nothing. I have taken a bath, or rather a douche. I have swallowed three glasses of water and I have walked in the pathways of the park for a quarter of an hour between each glass, then half-an-hour after the last. I have begun my twenty-five days.

"*July* 17. Remarked two mysterious pretty women who are taking their baths and their meals after everyone else.

"*July* 18. Nothing.

"*July* 19. Saw the two pretty women again. They have style and a little indescribable air which I like very much.

"July 20. Long walk in a charming wooded valley as far as the Hermitage of Sans-Souci. This country is delightful though sad; it is so calm, so sweet, so green. Along the mountain-roads you meet the long wagons loaded with hay drawn by two cows at a slow pace or held back in descending the slopes by their straining heads, which are tied together. A man with a big black hat on his head is driving them with a slight switch, tipping them on the side or on the forehead; and often with an ample gesture, a gesture energetic and grave, he suddenly draws them up when the excessive load hastens their journey down the rougher descents.

"The air is good in these valleys. And, if it is very warm, the dust bears with it a light odor of vanilla and of the stable, for so many cows pass over these routes that they leave a little scent everywhere. And the odor is a' perfume, whereas it would be a stench if it came from other animals.

"July 21. Excursion to the valley of the Enval. It is a narrow gorge inclosed in superb rocks at the very foot of the mountain. A stream flows through the space between the heaped-up bowlders.

"As I reached the bottom of this ravine, I heard women's voices, and I soon perceived the two mysterious ladies of my hotel, who were chatting seated on a stone.

"'The occasion appeared to me a good one, and without hesitation I presented myself. My overtures were received without embarrassment. We walked back together to the hotel. And we talked about Paris. They knew, it seemed, many people whom I knew too. Who can they be?

"I shall see them to-morrow. There is nothing more amusing than such meetings as this.

"July 22. Day almost entirely passed with the two unknown ladies. They are very pretty, by Jove, one a brunette and the other a blonde. They say they are widows. Hum!

"I offered to accompany them in a visit to Royat to-morrow, and they accepted my offer.

"Châtel-Guyon is less sad than I thought on my arrival.

"July 23. Day spent at Royat. Royat is a little cluster of hotels at the bottom of a valley, at the gate of Clermont-Ferrand. A great deal of society there. A great park full of movement. Superb view of the Puy-de-Dôme, seen at the end of a perspective of vales.

"I am greatly occupied with my fair companions, which is flattering to myself. The man who escorts a pretty woman always believes himself crowned with an aureole,—with much more reason, therefore, the man who goes along with one on each side of him. Nothing is so pleasant as to dine in a restaurant well frequented, with a female companion at whom everybody stares, and besides there is nothing better calculated to set a man up in the estimation of his neighbors.

"To go to the Bois in a trap drawn by a sorry nag, or to go out into the boulevard escorted by a plain woman, are the two most humiliating accidents which could strike a delicate heart preoccupied with the opinions of others. Of all luxuries woman is the rarest and the most distinguished; she is the one that costs most, and which we desire most; she is, therefore, the one that we like best to exhibit under the jealous eyes of the public.

"To show the world a pretty woman leaning on your arm is to excite, all at once, every kind of jealousy. It is as much as to say: Look here! I am rich, since I possess this rare and costly object; I have taste, since I have known how to discover this pearl; perhaps even I am loved, unless I am deceived by her, which would still prove that others, too, consider her charming.

"But what a disgraceful thing it is to bring an ugly woman with you through the city! And how many humiliating things this gives people to understand!

"In the first place, they assume she must be your wife, for how could it be supposed that you would have an unattractive mistress? A real wife might be ungraceful; but then her ugliness suggests a thousand things disagreeable to you. One supposes you must be a notary or a magistrate, as those two professions have a monopoly of grotesque and well-dowered spouses. Now, is this not painful for a man? And then it seems to proclaim to the public that you have the odious courage, and are even under a legal obligation, to caress that ridiculous face and that ill-shaped body, and that you will, without doubt, be shameless enough to make a mother of this by no means desirable being,—which is the very height of ridicule.

"*July* 24. I never leave the side of the two unknown widows, whom I am beginning to know well. This country is delightful and our hotel is excellent.

Good season. The treatment has done me an immense amount of good.

"*July* 25. Drive in a landau to the lake of Tazenat. An exquisite and unexpected party, decided on at lunch. Abrupt departure after getting up from the table. After a long journey through the mountains, we suddenly perceived an admirable little lake, quite round, quite blue, clear as glass, and situated at the bottom of a dead crater. One edge of this immense basin is barren, the other is wooded. In the midst of the trees is a small house, where sleeps a good-natured, intellectual man, a sage who passes his days in this Virgilian region. He opens his dwelling for us. An idea comes into my head. I exclaim: 'Suppose we bathe?'

"'Yes,' they said, 'but—costumes?'

"'Bah! we are in the desert.'

"And we did bathe!

"If I were a poet, how I would describe this unforgettable vision of bodies young and naked in the transparency of the water! The sloping high sides shut in the lake, motionless, glittering, and round, like a piece of silver; the sun pours into it its warm light in a flood; and along the rocks the fair flesh slips into the almost invisible wave in which the swimmers seemed suspended. On the sand at the bottom of the lake we saw the shadows of the light movements passing and repassing!

"*July* 26. Some persons seemed to look with shocked and disapproving eyes at my rapid intimacy with the two fair widows! Persons so constituted imagine that life is made for worrying oneself. Everything that appears to be amusing becomes immediately a breach of good-breeding or morality. For them duty has inflexible and mortally sad rules.

"I would draw their attention with all respect to the fact that duty is not the same for Mormons, Arabs, Zulus, Turks, Englishmen, and Frenchmen; and that one will find very virtuous people among all those nations. As for me, I take a little off each people's notion of duty, and of the whole I make a result comparable to the morality of holy King Solomon.

"*July* 27. Good news. I have grown 620 grams thinner. Excellent, this water of Châtel-Guyon! I am bringing the widows to dine at Riom. Sad town! Its anagram constitutes an offense in the vicinity of healing springs: Riom, Mori.

"*July* 28. Hoity-toity! My two widows have been visited by two gentlemen who came to look for them. Two widows, without doubt. They are leaving this evening. They have written to me on fancy note-paper.

"*July* 29. Alone! Long excursion on foot to the extinct crater of Nackère. Splendid view.

"*July* 30. Nothing. I am taking the treatment.

"*July* 31. Ditto. Ditto. This pretty country is full of polluted streams. I am drawing the notice of the municipality to the abominable sink which poisons the road in front of the hotel. All the remains of the kitchen of the establishment are thrown into it. This is a good way to breed cholera.

"*August* 1. Nothing. The treatment.

"*August* 2. Admirable walk to Châteauneuf, a station for rheumatic patients where everybody is lame. Nothing

can be queerer than this population of cripples!

"*August* 3. Nothing. The treatment.

"*August* 4. Ditto. Ditto.

"*August* 5. Ditto. Ditto.

"*August* 6. Despair! I have just weighed myself. I have got fatter by 310 grams. But what then?

"*August* 7. 66 kilometers in a carriage in the mountain. I will not mention the name of the country through respect for its women.

"This excursion had been pointed out to me as a beautiful one, and one that was rarely made. After four hours on the road I arrived at a rather pretty village, on the border of a river in the midst of an admirable wood of walnut-trees. I had not yet seen a forest of walnut-trees of such dimensions in Auvergne. It constitutes, moreover, all the wealth of the district, for it is planted on the common. This common was formerly only a hillside covered with brushwood. The authorities had tried in vain to get it cultivated. It was scarcely enough to feed a few sheep.

"To-day it is a superb wood, thanks to the women, and it has a curious name: it is called—'the Sins of the Curé.'

"Now it is right to say that the women of the mountain district have the reputation of being light, lighter than in the plain. A bachelor who meets them owes them at least a kiss; and if he does not take more, he is only a blockhead. If we think rightly on it, this way of looking at the matter is the only one that is logical and reasonable. As woman, whether she be of the town or the country, has for her natural mission to please man, man should always prove that she pleases him. If he abstains from every sort of demonstration, this means that he has found her ugly; it is almost an insult to her. If I were a woman, I would not receive a second time a man who failed to show me respect at our first meeting, for I would consider that he had failed to appreciate my beauty, my charm, and my feminine qualities.

"So the bachelors of the village X—— often proved to the women of the district that they found them to their taste, and, as the curé was unable to prevent these demonstrations as gallant as they were natural, he resolved to utilize them for the profit of the natural prosperity. So he imposed as a penance on every woman who had gone wrong a walnut to be planted on the common. And every night lanterns were seen moving about like will-o'-the-wisps on the hillock, for the erring ones scarcely liked to perform their penances in broad daylight.

"In two years there was no room any longer on the lands belonging to the village; and to-day they calculate that there are more than three thousand trees around the belfry which rings for the offices through their foliage. These are 'the Sins of the Curé.'

"Since we have been seeking for so many plans for rewooding in France, the Administration of Forests might surely enter into some arrangement with the clergy to employ a method so simple as that employed by this humble curé.

"*August* 8. Treatment.

"*August* 9. I am packing up my trunks, and saying good-bye to the charming little district so calm and silent, to the green mountain, to the quiet valleys, to the deserted Casino from which you can see, almost veiled by its light, bluish mist, the immense plain of the Limagne.

"I shall leave to-morrow."

*   *   *   *   *   *   *

Here the manuscript stopped. I wish to add nothing to it, my impressions of the country not having been exactly the same as those of my predecessor. For I did not find the two widows!

A Lucky Burglar

THEY were seated in the dining-room of a hotel in Barbizon.

"I tell you, you will not believe it."

"Well, tell it anyhow."

"All right, here goes. But first I must tell you that my story is absolutely true in every respect; even if it does sound improbable." And the old artist commenced:

"We had dined at Soriel's that night.

When I say dined, that means that we were all pretty well tipsy. We were three young madcaps. Soriel (poor fellow! he is dead now), Le Poittevin, the marine painter, and myself. Le Poittevin is dead, also.

"We had stretched ourselves on the floor of the little room adjoining the studio and the only one in the crowd who was rational was Le Poittevin.

Soriel, who was always the maddest, lay flat on his back, with his feet propped up on a chair, discussing war and the uniforms of the Empire, when, suddenly, he got up, took out of the big wardrobe where he kept his accessories a complete hussar's uniform and put it on. He then took a grenadier's uniform and told Le Poittevin to put it on; but he objected, so we forced him into it. It was so big for him that he was completely lost in it. I arrayed myself as a cuirassier. After we were ready, Soriel made us go through a complicated drill. Then he exclaimed: 'As long as we are troopers let us drink like troopers.'

"The punch-bowl had been brought out and filled for the second time. We were bawling some old camp songs at the top of our voice, when Le Poittevin, who in spite of all the punch had retained his self-control, held up his hand and said: 'Hush! I am sure I heard some one walking in the studio.'

"'A burglar!' said Soriel, staggering to his feet. 'Good luck!' And he began the 'Marseillaise':

"'To arms, citizens!'

"Then he seized several weapons from the wall and equipped us according to our uniforms. I received a musket and a saber. Le Poittevin was handed an enormous gun with a bayonet attached. Soriel, not finding just what he wanted, seized a pistol, stuck it in his belt, and brandishing a battle-axe in one hand, he opened the studio door cautiously. The army advanced. Having reached the middle of the room, Soriel said:

"'I am general. You [pointing to me], the cuirassiers, will keep the enemy from retreating—that is, lock the door.

You [pointing to Le Poittevin], the grenadiers, will be my escort.'

"I executed my orders and rejoined the troops, who were behind a large screen reconnoitering. Just as I reached it I heard a terrible noise. I rushed up with the candle to investigate the cause of it and this is what I saw. Le Poittevin was piercing the dummy's breast with his bayonet and Soriel was splitting his head open with his axe! When the mistake had been discovered the General commanded: 'Be cautious!'

"We had explored every nook and corner of the studio for the past twenty minutes without success, when Le Poittevin thought he would look in the cupboard. As it was quite deep and very dark, I advanced with the candle and looked in. I drew back stupefied. A man, a real live man this time, stood there looking at me! I quickly recovered myself, however, and locked the cupboard door. We then retired a few paces to hold a council.

"Opinions were divided. Soriel wanted to smoke the burglar out; Le Poittevin suggested starvation, and I proposed to blow him up with dynamite. Le Poittevin's idea being finally accepted as the best, we proceed to bring the punch and pipes into the studio, while Le Poittevin kept guard with his big gun on his shoulder, and settling ourselves in front of the cupboard we drank the prisoner's health. We had done this repeatedly, when Soriel suggested that we bring out the prisoner and take a look at him.

"'Hooray!' cried I. We picked up our weapons and made a mad rush for the cupboard door. It was finally opened, and Soriel, cocking his pistol which was not loaded, rushed in first.

Le Poittevin and I followed yelling like lunatics and, after a mad scramble in the dark, we at last brought out the burglar. He was a haggard-looking, white-hired old bandit, with shabby, ragged clothes. We bound him hand and foot and dropped him in an arm-chair. He said nothing.

" 'We will try this wretch' said Soriel, whom the punch had made very solemn. I was so far gone that it seemed to me quite a natural thing. Le Poittevin was named for the defense and I for the prosecution. The prisoner was con-demned to death by all except his counsel.

" 'We will now execute him,' said Soriel. 'Still, this man cannot die without repenting,' he added, feeling somewhat scrupulous. 'Let us send for a priest.'

"I objected that it was too late, so he proposed that I officiate and forthwith told the prisoner to confess his sins to me. The old man was terrified. He wondered what kind of wretches we were and for the first time he spoke. His voice was hollow and cracked:

" 'Say, you don't mean it, do you?'

"Soriel forced him to his knees, and for fear he had not been baptized, poured a glass of rum over his head, saying: 'Confess your sins; your last hour has come!'

" 'Help! Help!' screamed the old man rolling himself on the floor and kicking everything that came his way. For fear he should wake the neighbors we gagged him.

" 'Come, let us end this'; said Soriel impatiently. He pointed his pistol at the old man and pressed the trigger. I followed his example, but as neither of our guns were loaded we made very little noise. Le Poittevin, who had been looking on said:

" 'Have we really the right to kill this man?'

" 'We have condemned him to death!' said Soriel.

" 'Yes, but we have no right to shoot a civilian. Let us take him to the station-house.'

"We agreed with him, and as the old man could not walk we tied him to a board, and Le Poittevin and I carried him, while Soriel kept guard in the rear. We arrived at the station-house. The chief, who knew us and was well ac-quainted with our manner of joking, thought it was a great lark and laugh-ingly refused to take our prisoner in. Soriel insisted, but the chief told us very sternly to quit our fooling and go home and be quiet. There was nothing else to do but to take him back to Soriel's.

" 'What are we going to do with him?' I asked.

" 'The poor man must be awfully tired!' said Le Poittevin, sympathiz-ingly.

"He did look half dead, and in my turn I felt a sudden pity for him (the punch, no doubt), and I relieved him of his gag.

" 'How do you feel old man?' I asked.

" 'By Jingo! I have enough of this,' he groaned.

"Then Soriel softened. He unbound him and treated him as a long-lost friend. The three of us immediately brewed a fresh bowl of punch. As soon as it was ready we handed a glass to the prisoner, who quaffed it without flinching. Toast followed toast. The old man could drink more than the three of us put together; but as daylight appeared, he got up and calmly said: 'I shall be obliged to leave you; I must get home now.'

"We begged him not to go, but he positively refused to stay any longer. We were awfully sorry and took him to the door, while Soriel held the candle above his head saying: 'Look out for the last step.'"

An Odd Feast

It was in the winter of—I do not remember what year, that I went to Normandy to visit my bachelor cousin, Jules de Banneville, who lived alone in the old manor, with a cook, a valet, and a keeper. I had the hunting fever and for a month did nothing else from morning until night.

The castle, an old, gray building surrounded with pines and avenues of tall oak-trees, looked as if it had been deserted for centuries. The antique furniture and the portraits of Jules's ancestors were the only inhabitants of the spacious rooms and halls now closed.

We had taken shelter in the only habitable room, an immense kitchen, which had been plastered all over to keep the rats out. The big, white walls were covered with whips, guns, horns, etc., and in the huge fireplace a brushwood fire was burning, throwing strange lights around the corners of the dismal room. We would sit in front of the fire every night, our hounds stretched in every available space between our feet, dreaming and barking in their sleep, until, getting drowsy, we would climb to our rooms and slip into our beds shivering.

It had been freezing hard that day and we were sitting as usual in front of the fire, watching a hare and two partridges being roasted for dinner, and the savory smell sharpened our appetites.

"It will be awfully cold going to bed to-night," said Jules.

"Yes, but there will be plenty of ducks to-morrow morning," I replied indifferently.

The servant had set our plates at one end of the table and those of the servants at the other.

"Gentlemen, do you know it is Christmas eve?" she asked.

We certainly did not; we never looked at the calendar.

"That accounts for the bells ringing all day," said Jules. "There is midnight service to-night."

"Yes, sir; but they also rang because old Fournel is dead."

Fournel was an old shepherd, well known in the country. He was ninety-six years old and had never known a day's sickness until a month ago, when he had taken cold by falling into a pool on a dark night and had died of the consequences.

"If you like," said Jules, "we will go and see these poor people after dinner."

The old man's family consisted of his grandson, fifty-eight years old and the latter's wife, one year younger. His children had died years ago. They lived in a miserable hut at the entrance of the village.

Perhaps Christmas eve in a lonely castle was an incentive, at all events we were very talkative that night. Our dinner had lasted way into the night and long after the servant had left us, we sat there smoking pipe after pipe, narrating old experiences, telling of past revels and the surprises of the morrow which followed our adventures. Our solitude had brought us closer together and we exchanged those confidences which only intimate friends can.

"I am going to church, sir," said the servant, reappearing.

"What, so soon!" exclaimed Jules.

"It lacks only a quarter of twelve, sir."

"Let us go to church too," said Jules. "The midnight service is very attractive in the country."

I assented and having wrapped ourselves up we started for the village. It was bitterly cold, but a clear, beautiful night. We could hear the peasants' wooden shoes on the crisp, frozen earth and the church bell ringing in the distance. The road was dotted here and there with dancing lights. It was the peasants carrying lanterns, lighting the way for their wives and children. As we approached the village, Jules said:

"Here is where the Fournels live, let us go in."

We knocked repeatedly, but in vain. A neighboring peasant informed us that they had gone to church to pray for their grandfather.

"We will see them on our way back," said Jules.

The service had begun when we entered the church. It was profusely decorated with small candles, and to the left, in a small chapel, the birth of Christ was represented by wax figures, pine brush forming a background. The men stood with bowed heads, and the women, kneeling, clasped their hands in deep devotion. After a few minutes Jules said:

"It is stifling in here, let us go outside."

We left the shivering peasants to their devotions and regaining the deserted road, we resumed our conversation. We had talked so long that the service was over when we came back to the village. A small ray of light filtered through the Fournels' door.

"They are watching their dead," said Jules. "They will be pleased to see us."

We went in. The low, dark room was lighted only by a smoking candle, placed in the middle of the large, coarse table, under which a bread bin had been built, taking up the whole length of it. A suffocating odor of roasted blood pudding pervaded every corner of the room. Seated face to face, were Fournel and his wife, a gloomy and brutish expression on their faces. Between the two, a single plate of the pudding, the popular dish on Christmas eve, out of which they would take turns in cutting a piece off, spread it on their bread and munch in silence. When the man's glass was empty, the woman would fill it out of an earthen jar containing cider.

They asked us to be seated and to "join them," but at our refusal they continued to munch. After a few minutes' silence Jules said:

"Well, Anthime, so your grandfather is dead!"

"Yes, sir, he died this afternoon."

The woman snuffed the candle in silence and I, for the want of something to say, added:

"He was quite old, was he not?"

"Oh, his time was up," she answered; "he was no earthly use here."

An invincible desire to see the old man took possession of me and I asked to see him. The two peasants suddenly became agitated and exchanged questioning glances. Jules noticed this and insisted. Then the man with a sly, suspicious look, asked:

"What good would it do you?"

"No good," said Jules; "but why will you not let us see him?"

"I am willing," said the man, shrugging his shoulders, "but it is kind of unhandy just now."

We conjectured all sorts of things. Neither of them stirred. They sat there with eyes lowered, a sullen expression on their faces seeming to say: "Go away."

"Come Anthime, take us to his room," said Jules with authority.

"It's no use, my good sir, he isn't there any more," said the man resolutely.

"Where is he?" said Jules.

The woman interrupted, saying:

"You see, sir, we had no other place to put him so we put him in the bin until morning." And having taken the top of the table off, she held the candle near the opening. We looked in and sure enough, there he was, a shriveled gray mass, his gray hair matted about his face, barefooted and rolled up in his shepherd's cloak, sleeping his last sleep among crusts of bread as ancient as himself.

His grandchildren had used as a table the bin which held his body!

Jules was indignant, and pale with anger, said:

"You villains! Why did you not leave him in his bed?"

The woman burst into tears and speaking rapidly:

"You see, my good gentlemen, it's just this way. We have but one bed, and being only three we slept together; but since he's been so sick we slept on the floor. The floor is awful hard and cold these days, my good gentlemen, so when he died this afternoon we said to ourselves: 'As long as he is dead he doesn't feel anything and what's the use of leaving him in bed? He'll be just as comfortable in the bin.' We can't sleep with a dead man, my good gentlemen!—now can we?"

Jules was exasperated and went out banging the door, and I after him, laughing myself sick.

Sympathy

He was going up the Rue des Martyrs in a melancholy frame of mind, and in a melancholy frame of mind she also was going up the Rue des Martyrs. He was already old, nearly sixty, with a bald head under his seedy tall hat, a gray beard, half buried in a high shirt collar, with dull eyes, an unpleasant mouth, and yellow teeth.

She was past forty, with thin hair over

her puffs, and with a false plait; her linen was doubtful in color, and she had evidently bought her unfashionable dress at a *hand-me-down* shop. He was thin, while she was chubby. He had been handsome, proud, ardent, full of self-confidence, certain of his future, and seeming to hold in his hands all the trumps with which to win the game on the green table of Parisian life, while she had been pretty, sought after, fast, and in a fair way to have horses and carriages, and to win the first prize on the turf of gallantry among the favorites of fortune.

At times, in his dark moments, he remembered the time when he had come to Paris from the country, with a volume of poetry and plays in his portmanteau, feeling a supreme contempt for all the writers who were then in vogue, and sure of supplanting them. She often, when she awoke in the morning to another day's unhappiness, remembered that happy time when she had been launched on to the world, when she already saw that she was more sought after than Marie G. or Sophie N. or any other woman of that class, who had been her companions in vice, and whose lovers she had stolen from them.

He had had a splendid start. Not, indeed, as a poet and dramatist, as he had hoped at first, but by a series of scandalous stories which had made a sensation on the boulevards, so that after an action for damages and several duels, he had become "our witty and brilliant colleague who, etc., etc."

She had had her moments of extraordinary good luck, though she certainly did not eclipse Marie P. or Camille L., whom men compared to Zenobia or Ninon de l'Enclos. Still her fortune caused her to be talked about in the newspapers, and brought about a revolution at certain *tables d'hôte* in Montmartre. But one fine day, the newspaper in which our brilliant and witty colleague used to write became defunct, having been killed by a much more cynical rival, thanks to the venomous pen of a much more brilliant and witty colleague. Then the insults of the former having become pure and simple mud-pelting, his style soon became worn out, to the disgust of the public, and the celebrated "Mr. What's-his-name" had great difficulty in getting on to some minor paper, where he was transformed into the obscure penny-a-liner "Machin."

Now one evening the quasi-rival of Marie P. and Camille L. had fallen ill, and consequently into pecuniary difficulties, and the prostitute "No-matter-who" was now on the lookout for a dinner, and would have been only too happy to get it at some *table d'hôte* in Montmartre. Machin had had a return of ambition with regard to his poetry and his dramas, but then, his verses of former days had lost their freshness, and his youthful dramas appeared to him to be childish. He would have to write others, and, by Jove! he felt himself capable of doing it, for he had plenty of ideas and plans in his head, and he could easily demolish many successful writers if he chose to try! But then, the difficulty was, how to set about it, and to find the necessary leisure and time for thought. He had his daily bread to gain, and something besides; his coffee, his game of cards and other little requirements, and the incessant writing article upon article barely sufficed for that, and so days and years went by, and Machin was Machin still.

She also longed for former years, and surely it could not be so very hard to find a lover to start her on her career once more, for many of her female friends, who were not nearly so nice as she, had unearthed one, so why should not she be equally fortunate? But there, her youth had gone and she had lost all her chances; other women. had their fancy men, and she had to take men on every day at reduced prices, and so day after day and months and years passed, and the prostitute No-matter-who had remained the prostitute No-matter-who.

Often, in a fit of despondency, he used to say to himself, thinking of. some one who had succeeded in life: "But, after all, I am cleverer than that fellow."

And she always said to herself, when she got up to her miserable, daily round, when she thought of such and such a woman, who was now settled in life: "In what respect is that slut better than I am?"

And Machin, who was nearly sixty, and whose head was bald under his shabby tall hat, and whose gray beard was half buried in a high shirt collar, who had dull eyes, an unpleasant mouth, and yellow teeth, was mad with his fellow-men, while the prostitute No-matter-who, with thin hair over her puffs, and with false plait, with linen of a doubtful color, and with her unfashionable dress, which she had evidently bought at a *hand-me-down* shop, was enraged with society.

Ah! Those miserable, dark hours, and the wretched awakenings! That evening he was more than usually wretched, as he had just lost all his pay for the next month, that miserable stipend which he earned so hardly by almost editing the newspaper, for three hundred francs* a month, in a brothel.

And she, too, that evening, was in a state of semi-stupidity, as she had had too many glasses of beer, which a charitable female friend had given her. She was almost afraid to go back to her room, as her landlord had told her in the morning that unless she paid the fortnight's back rent that she owed at the rate of a franc a day, he would turn her out of doors and keep her things.

This was the reason why they were both going up the Rue des Martyrs in a melancholy frame of mind. There was scarcely a soul in the muddy streets; it was getting dark and beginning to rain, and the drains smelt horribly.

He passed her, and in a mechanical voice she said: "Will you not come home with me, you handsome, dark man?"

"I have no money," he replied.

But she ran after him, and catching hold of his arm, she said: "Only a franc; that is nothing."

And he turned round, looked at her, and seeing that she must have been pretty, and that she was still stout (and he was fond of fat women), he said: "Where do you live? Near here?"

"In the Rue Lepic."

"Why! So do I."

"Then that is all right, eh? Come along, old fellow."

He felt in his pockets and pulled out all the money he found there, which amounted to thirteen sous,† and said:

---

*$60. ·   †Thirteen cents.

"That is all I have, upon my honor."

"All right," she said; "come along."

And they continued their melancholy walk along the Rue des Martyrs, side by side now, but without speaking, and without guessing that their two existences harmonized and corresponded with each other, and that by huddling up together, they would be merely accomplishing the acme of their twin destinies.

A Traveler's Tale

I.

THE car was full as we left Cannes. We were conversing; everybody was acquainted. As we passed Tarascon some one remarked: "Here's the place where they assassinate people."

And we began to talk of the mysterious and untraceable murderer, who for the last two years had taken, from time to time, the life of a traveler. Everyone made his guess, everyone gave his opinion; the women shudderingly gazed at the dark night through the car windows, fearing suddenly to see a man's head at the door. We all began telling frightful stories of terrible encounters, meetings with madmen in a flying-express, of hours passed opposite a suspected individual.

Each man knew an anecdote to his credit, each one had intimidated, overpowered, and throttled some evildoer in most surprising circumstances, with an admirable presence of mind and audacity.

A physician, who spent every winter in the south, desired, in his turn, to tell an adventure:

"I," said he, "never have had the luck to test my courage in an affair of this kind; but I knew a woman, now dead, one of my patients, to whom the most singular thing in the world happened, and also the most mysterious and pathetic.

"She was Russian, the Countess Marie Baranow, a very great lady, of an exquisite beauty. You know how beautiful the Russian women are, or at least how beautiful they seem to us, with their fine noses, their delicate mouths, their eyes of an indescribable color, a blue gray, and their cold grace, a little hard! They have something about them, mischievous and seductive, haughty and sweet, tender and severe, altogether charming to a Frenchman. At the bottom, it is, perhaps, the difference of race and of type which makes me see so much in them.

"Her physician had seen for many years that she was threatened with a disease of the lungs, and had tried to persuade her to come to the south of France; but she obstinately refused to leave St. Petersburg. Finally, the last autumn, deeming her lost, the doctor warned her husband, who directed his wife to start at once for Mentone.

"She took the train, alone in her car, her servants occupying another compartment. She sat by the door, a little sad, seeing the fields and villages pass, feeling very lonely, very desolate in life, without children, almost without relatives, with a husband whose love was dead and who cast her thus to the end of the world without coming with her, as they send a sick valet to the hospital.

"At each station her servant Ivan came to see if his mistress wanted anything. He was an old domestic, blindly devoted, ready to accomplish all the orders which she should give him.

"Night fell, and the train rolled along at full speed. She could not sleep, being wearied and nervous.

"Suddenly the thought struck her to count the money which her husband had given her at the last minute, in French gold. She opened her little bag and emptied the shining flood of metal on her lap.

"But all at once a breath of cold air struck her face. Surprised, she raised her head. The door had just opened. The Countess Marie, bewildered, hastily threw a shawl over the money spread upon her lap, and waited. Some seconds passed, then a man in evening dress appeared, bareheaded, wounded on the hand, and panting. He closed the door, sat down, looked at his neighbor with gleaming eyes, and then wrapped a handkerchief around his wrist, which was bleeding.

"The young woman felt herself fainting with fear. This man, surely, had seen her counting her money and had come to rob and kill her.

"He kept gazing at her, breathless, his features convulsed, doubtless ready to spring upon her.

"He suddenly said:

"'Madame, don't be afraid!'

"She made no response, being incapable of opening her mouth, hearing her heart-beats, and a buzzing in her ears.

"He continued:

"'I am not a malefactor, Madame.

"She continued to be silent, but by a sudden movement which she made, her knees meeting, the gold coins began to run to the floor as water runs from a spout.

"The man, surprised, looked at this stream of metal, and he suddenly stooped to pick it up.

"She, terrified, rose, casting her whole fortune on the carpet and ran to the door to leap out upon the track.

"But he understood what she was going to do, and springing forward, seized her in his arms, seated her by force, and held her by the wrists.

"'Listen to me, Madame,' said he, 'I am not a malefactor; the proof of it is that I am going to gather up this gold and return it to you. But I am a lost man, a dead man, if you do not assist me to pass the frontier. I cannot tell you more. In an hour we shall be at the last Russian station; in an hour and twenty minutes we shall cross the boundary of the Empire. If you do not help me I am lost. And yet I have neither killed anyone, nor robbed, nor done anything contrary to honor. This I swear to you. I cannot tell you more.'

"And kneeling down he picked up the gold, even hunting under the seats for the last coins, which had rolled to a distance. Then, when the little leather bag was full again he gave it to his neighbor without saying a word, and returned to seat himself at the other corner of the compartment. Neither of them moved. She kept motionless and mute, still faint from terror, but recovering little by little. As for him, he did not make a gesture or a motion, remained sitting erect, his eyes staring in front of him, very pale, as if he were dead. From time to time she threw a quick look at him, and as quickly turned her glance away. He appeared to be about thirty years of age, and was very handsome, with the mien of a gentleman.

"The train ran through the darkness, giving at intervals its shrill signals, now slowing up in its progress, and again starting off at full speed. But presently its progress slackened, and after several sharp whistles it came to a full stop.

"Ivan appeared at the door for his orders.

"The Countess Marie, her voice trembling, gave one last look at her companion; then she said to her servant, in a quick tone:

" 'Ivan, you will return to the Count; I do not need you any longer.'

"The man, bewildered, opened his enormous eyes. He stammered:

" 'But, my lady—'

"She replied:

" 'No, you will not come with me, I have changed my mind. I wish you to stay in Russia. Here is some money for your return home. Give me your cap and cloak.'

"The old servant, frightened, took off his cap and cloak, obeying without question, accustomed to the sudden whims and caprices of his masters. And he went away, with tears in his eyes.

"The train started again, rushing toward the frontier.

"Then the Countess Marie said to her neighbor:

" 'These things are for you, Monsieur, —you are Ivan, my servant. I make

only one condition to what I am doing: that is, that you shall not speak a word to me, neither to thank me, nor for anything whatsoever.'

"The unknown bowed without uttering a syllable.

"Soon the train stopped again, and officers in uniform visited the train.

"The Countess handed them her papers, and pointing to the man seated at the end of the compartment said:

" 'That is my servant Ivan, whose passport is here.'

"The train again started.

"During the night they sat opposite each other, both mute.

"When morning came, as they stopped at a German station, the unknown got out; then, standing at the door, he said:

" 'Pardon me, Madame, for breaking my promise, but as I have deprived you of a servant, it is proper that I should replace him. Have you need of anything?'

"She replied coldly:

" 'Go and find my maid.'

"He went to summon her. Then he disappeared.

"When she alighted at some station for luncheon she saw him at a distance looking at her. They finally arrived at Mentone."

II.

The doctor was silent for a second, and then resumed:

"One day, while I was receiving patients in my office, a tall young man entered. He said to me:

" 'Doctor, I have come to ask you news of the Countess Marie Baranow. I am a friend of her husband, although she does not know me.'

"I answered:

" 'She is lost. She will never return to Russia.'

"And suddenly this man began to sob, then he rose and went out, staggering like a drunken man.

"I told the Countess that evening that a stranger had come to make inquiries about her health. She seemed moved, and told me the story which I have just related to you. She added:

" 'That man, whom I do not know at all, follows me now like my shadow. I meet him every time I go out. He looks at me in a strange way, but he has never spoken to me!'

"She pondered a moment, then added:

" 'Come, I'll wager that he is under the window now.'

"She left her reclining-chair, went to the window and drew back the curtain, and actually showed me the man who had come to see me, seated on a bench at the edge of the side wall with his eyes raised toward the house. He perceived us, rose, and went away without once turning around.

"Then I understood a sad and surprising thing, the mute love of these two beings, who were not acquainted with each other.

"He loved her with the devotion of a rescued animal, grateful and devoted to the death. He came every day to ask me, 'How is she?' understanding that I had guessed his feelings. And he wept frightfully when he saw her pass, weaker and paler every day.

"She said to me:

" 'I have never spoken but once to that singular man, and yet it seems as if I had known him for twenty years.'

"And when they met she returned his bow with a serious and charming smile.

I felt that—although she was given up, and knew herself lost—she was happy to be loved thus, with this respect and constancy, with this exaggerated poetry, with this devotion, ready for anything.

"Nevertheless, faithful to her super-excited obstinacy, she absolutely refused to learn his name, to speak to him. She said:

" 'No, no, that would spoil this strange friendship. We must remain strangers to each other.'

"As for him, he was certainly a kind of Don Quixote, for he did nothing to bring himself closer to her. He intended to keep to the end the absurd promise never to speak to her which he had made in the car.

"Often, during her long hours of weakness, she rose from her reclining-chair and partly opened the curtain to see whether he were there, beneath the window. And when she had seen him, ever motionless upon his bench, she came back to lie down again with a smile upon her lips.

"She died one morning about ten o'clock.

"As I left the house he came to me, his countenance showing that he had already learned the news.

" 'I would like to see her, for a second, in your presence,' said he.

"I took him by the arm and we entered the house together.

"When he was beside the bed of the dead woman, he seized her hand and gave it a long and passionate kiss; then he went away like a man bereft of his senses."

The doctor again was silent. Then he resumed:

"There you have, certainly, the most singular railroad adventure that I know. It must also be said that men are queer lunatics."

A woman murmured in a low tone:

"Those two people were less crazy than you think. They were—they were—"

But she could speak no longer because she was weeping. As the conversation was changed to calm her, no one ever knew what she had intended to say.

———————

Little Louise Roque

MEDERIC ROMPEL, the postman, familiarly called by the country people "Mederi," started at his usual hour from the posthouse at Rouy-le-Tors. Having passed through the little town, striding like an old trooper, he cut across the meadows of Villaumes in order to reach the bank of the Brindelle, which led him along the water's edge to the village of Carvelin, where his distribution commenced. He traveled quickly, following the course of the narrow river, which frothed, murmured, and boiled along its bed of grass under the arching willow-trees. The big stones, impeding the flow of water, created around them a sort of aqueous necktie ending in a knot of foam. In some places, there were cascades a foot wide, often invisible, which made under the leaves, under the tendrils, under a roof of verdure, a noise at once angry and gentle. Further on, the banks widened out, and you saw a small, placid lake where trout were swimming in the midst of all that green vegetation which keeps undulating in the depths of tranquil streams.

Mederic went on without a halt, seeing nothing and with only one thought in his mind: "My first letter is for the Poivron family; then I have one for M. Renardet; so I must cross the wood."

His blue blouse, fastened round his waist by a black leathern belt, moved in quick, regular fashion above the green hedge of willow-trees; and his stick of stout holly kept time with the steady march of his feet.

He crossed the Brindelle over a bridge formed of a single tree thrown lengthwise, with a rope attached to two stakes driven into the river banks as its only balustrade.

The wood, which belonged to M. Renardet, the mayor of Carvelin, and the largest landowner in the district, consisted of a number of huge old trees, straight as pillars, and extended for about half a league along the left bank of the stream which served as a boundary for this immense arch of foliage. Alongside the water there were large shrubs warmed by the sun: but under the trees you found nothing but moss, thick, soft, plastic moss, which exhaled into the stagnant air a light odor of loam and withered branches.

Mederic slackened his pace, took off his black cap trimmed with red lace, and wiped his forehead, for it was by this time hot in the meadows, though not yet eight o'clock in the morning.

He had just recovered from the effects of the heat, and had accelerated his pace when he noticed at the foot of a tree a knife, a child's small knife. As he picked it up, he discovered a thimble, and then a needlecase, not far away.

Having found these objects, he thought: "I'll intrust them to the mayor," and resumed this journey. But now he kept his eyes open, expecting to find something else.

All of a sudden, he drew up stiffly as if he had run up against a wooden bar. Ten paces in front of him on the moss, lay stretched on her back a little girl, quite naked. She was about twelve years old. Her arms were hanging down, her legs parted, and her face covered with a handkerchief. There were little spots of blood on her thighs.

Mederic now advanced on tiptoe, as if afraid to make a noise; he apprehended some danger, and glanced toward the spot uneasily.

What was this? No doubt, she was asleep. Then, he reflected that a person does not go to sleep thus, naked, at half past seven in the morning under cool trees. Then she must be dead; and he must be face to face with a crime. At this thought, a cold shiver ran through his frame, although he was an old soldier. And then a murder was such a rare thing in the country—and above all the murder of a child—that he could not believe his eyes. But she had no wound—nothing save these blood drops on her legs. How, then, had she been killed?

He stopped when quite near her and stared at her, while leaning on his stick. Certainly, he knew her, as he knew all the inhabitants of the district; but, not being able to get a look at her face, he could not guess her name. He stooped forward in order to take off the handkerchief which covered her face; then paused with outstretched hand, restrained by an idea that occurred to him.

Had he the right to disarrange anything in the condition of the corpse before the magisterial investigation? He pictured justice to himself as a general whom nothing escapes, who attaches as much importance to a lost button as to a stag of a knife in the stomach. Perhaps under this handkerchief evidence to support a capital charge could be found; in fact if there were sufficient proof there to secure a conviction, it might lose its value if touched by an awkward hand.

Then he straightened up with the intention of hastening toward the mayor's residence, but again another thought held him back. If the little girl was still alive, by any chance—he could not leave her lying there in this way. He sank on his kness very gently, a yard away from her, through precaution, and stretched his hand toward her feet. The flesh was icy cold, with that terrible coldness which makes dead flesh frightful, and leaves us no longer in doubt. The letter-carrier, as he touched her, felt his heart leap to his mouth, as he said himself afterward, and his lips were parched with dry saliva. Rising up abruptly he rushed off through the trees to M. Renardet's house.

He hurried on in double-quick time, with his stick under his arm, his hands clenched, and his head thrust forward, and his leathern bag, filled with letters and newspapers, flapping regularly at his side.

The mayor's residence was at the end of the wood, which he used as a park, and one side of it was washed by a little lagoon formed at this spot by the Brindelle.

It was a big, square house of gray stone, very old. It had stood many a siege in former days, and at the end of it was a huge tower, twenty meters high, built in the water. From the top of this fortress the entire country around could be seen in olden times. It was called the Fox's Tower, without anyone knowing exactly why; and from the appellation, no doubt, had come the name Renardet, borne by the owners of this fief, which had remained in the same family, it was said, for more than two hundred years. For the Renardets formed part of that upper middle class which is all but noble and was met with so often in the provinces before the Revolution.

The postman dashed into the kitchen where the servants were taking breakfast, and exclaimed:

"Is the mayor up? I want to speak to him at once."

Mederic was recognized as a man of weight and authority, and it was soon understood that something serious had happened.

As soon as word was brought to M. Renardet, he ordered the postman to be sent up to him. Pale and out of breath, with his cap in his hand, Mederic found the mayor seated in front of a long table covered with scattered papers.

He was a big, tall man, heavy and red-faced, strong as an ox, and greatly liked in the district, though of an ex-cessively violent disposition. Very nearly forty years old, and a widower for the past six months, he lived on his estate like a country gentleman. His choleric temperament had often brought him into trouble, from which the magistrates of Rouy-le-Tors, like indulgent and prudent friends, had extricated him. Had he not one day thrown the conductor of the diligence from the top of his seat because the letter had nearly crushed his retriever, Micmac? Had he not broken the ribs of a gamekeeper, who had abused him for having passed through a neighbor's property with a gun in his hand? Had he not even caught by the collar the sub-prefect, who stopped in the village in the course of an administrative round described by M. Renardet as an electioneering tour; for he was against the government, according to his family tradition?

The mayor asked:

"What's the matter now, Mederic?"

"I have found a little girl dead in your wood."

Renardet rose up, with his face the color of brick.

"A little girl, do you say?"

"Yes, M'sieu', a little girl, quite naked, on her back, with blood on her, dead—quite dead!"

The mayor gave vent to an oath:

"By God, I'd make a bet 'tis little Louise Roque! I have just learned that she did not go home to her mother last night. Where did you find her?"

The postman pointed out where the place was, gave full details, and offered to conduct the mayor to the spot.

But Renardet became brusque:

"No, I don't need you. Send the

steward, the mayor's secretary, and the doctor immediately to me, and resume your rounds. Quick, go quick, and tell them to meet me in the wood."

The letter-carrier, a man used to discipline, obeyed and withdrew, angry and grieved at not being able to be present at the investigation.

The mayor, in his turn, prepared to go out. He took his hat, a big soft hat, and paused for a few seconds on the threshold of his abode. In front of him stretched a wide lawn in which three large patches were conspicuous—three large beds of flowers in full bloom, one facing the house and the others at either side of it. Further on, rose skyward the principal trees in the wood, while at the left, above the spot where the Brindelle widened into a pool, could be seen long meadows, an entirely flat green sweep of country, cut by dykes and monster-like willows, twisted drawf-trees, always cut short, having on their thick squat trunks a quivering tuft of branches.

To the right, behind the stables, the outhouses, and the buildings connected with the property, might be seen the village, which was prosperous, being mainly inhabited by raisers of oxen.

Renardet slowly descended the steps in front of his house, and, turning to the left, gained the water's edge, which he followed at a slow pace, his hands behind his back. He went on, with bent head, and from time to time he glanced round in search of the persons for whom he had sent.

When he stood beneath the trees, he stopped, took off his hat, and wiped his forehead as Mederic had done; for the burning sun was shedding its fiery rain

upon the ground. Then the mayor resumed his journey, stopped once more, and retraced his steps. Suddenly stooping down, he stepped his handkerchief in the stream that glided at his feet and stretched it round his head, under his hat. Drops of water flowed along his temples, over his purple ears, over his strong red neck, and trickled one after the other, under his white shirt-collar.

As yet nobody had appeared; he began tapping with his foot, then he called out: "Hallo! Hallo!"

A voice at his right answered: "Hallo! Hallo!" and the doctor appeared under the trees. He was a thin little man, an ex-military surgeon, who passed in the neighborhood for a very skillful practitioner. He limped, having been wounded while in the service, and had to use a stick to assist him in walking.

Next came the steward and the mayor's secretary, who, having been sent for at the same time, arrived together. They seemed scared, as they hurried forward, out of breath, walking and trotting in turn in order to hasten, and moving their arms up and down so vigorously that they seemed to do more work with them than with their legs.

Renardet said to the doctor:

"You know what the trouble is about?"

"Yes, a child found dead in the wood by Mederic."

"That's quite correct. Come on."

They walked on side by side, followed by the two men.

Their steps made no noise on the moss, their eyes were gazing downward right in front of them.

The doctor hastened his steps, interested by the discovery. As soon as they were near the corpse, he bent down to examine it without touching it. He had put on a pair of glasses, as you do when you are looking at some curious object; then he turned round very quietly and said, without rising up:

"Violated and assassinated, as we shall prove presently. The little girl, moreover, is almost a woman—look at her throat."

Her two breasts, already nearly full-developed, fell over her chest, relaxed by death. The doctor lightly drew away the handkerchief which covered her face. It was almost black, frightful to look at, the tongue protruding, the eyes bloodshot. He went on:

"Faith, she was strangled the moment the deed was done."

He felt her neck:

"Strangled with the hands without leaving any special trace, neither the mark of the nails nor the imprint of the fingers. Quite right. It is little Louise Roque, sure enough!"

He delicately replaced the handkerchief:

"There's nothing for me to do. She's been dead for the last hour at least. We must give notice of the matter to the authorities."

Renardet, standing up, with his hands behind his back, kept staring with a stony look at the little body exposed to view on the grass. He murmured:

"What a wretch! We must find the clothes."

The doctor felt the hands, the arms, the legs. He said:

"She must have been bathing, no doubt. They ought to be at the water's edge."

The mayor thereupon gave directions:

"Do you, Princèpe [this was his secretary], go and look for those clothes for me along the river. Do you, Maxime [this was the steward], hurry on towards Rouy-le-Tors, and bring on here to me the examining magistrate with the gendarmes. They must be here within an hour. You understand."

The two men quickly departed, and Renardet said to the doctor:

"What miscreant has been able to do such a deed in this part of the country?"

The doctor murmured: ·

"Who knows? Everyone is capable of that! Everyone in particular and nobody in general. However, it must be some prowler, some workman out of employment. As we live under a Republic, we must expect to meet this sort of miscreant along the roads."

Both of them were Bonapartists. The mayor went on:

"Yes, it could only be a stranger, a passer-by, a vagabond without heart or home."

The doctor added with the shadow of a smile on his face:

"And without a wife. Having neither a good supper nor a good bed, he procured the rest for himself. You can't tell how many men there may be in the world capable of a crime at a given moment. Did you know that this little girl had disappeared?"

And with the end of his stick he touched one after the other the stiffened fingers of the corpse, resting on them as on the keys of a piano.

"Yes, the mother came last night to look for me about nine o'clock, the child not having come home for supper up to even. We went to try and find her along the roads up to midnight, but we did not think of the wood. However, we needed daylight to carry out a search with a practical result."

"Will you have a cigar?" said the doctor.

"Thanks, I don't care to smoke. It gives me a turn to look at this."

They remained standing in front of the young girl's body, pale and still, on the dark background of moss. A big fly was walking along one of the thighs, it stopped at the blood-stains, went on again, always rising higher, ran along the side with his lively, jerky movements, climbed up one of the breasts, then came back again to explore the other. The two men silently watched this wandering black speck. The doctor said:

"How tantalizing it is, a fly on the skin! The ladies of the last century had good reason to paste them on their faces. Why has the fashion gone out?"

But the mayor seemed not to hear, plunged as he was in deep thought.

All of a sudden he turned around, surprised by a shrill noise. A woman in a cap and a blue apron rushed up through the trees. It was the mother, La Roque. As soon as she saw Renardet she began to shriek:

"My little girl, where's my little girl?" in such a distracted manner that she did not glance down at the ground. Suddenly, she saw the corpse, stopped short, clasped her hands, and raised both her arms while she uttered a sharp, heartrending cry—the cry of a mutilated animal. Then, she rushed toward the body, fell on her knees, and snatched the handkerchief that covered the face.

When she saw that frightful countenance, black and convulsed, she recoiled with a shudder, then pressed her face against the ground, giving vent to terrible and continuous choking screams, her mouth close to the thick moss.

Her tall, thin frame, to which her clothes clung tightly, was palpitating, shaken with convulsions. They could see her bony ankles and withered limbs covered with thick blue stockings, shivering horribly. Unconsciously she dug at the soil with her crooked fingers as if to make a grave in which to hide herself.

The doctor pityingly said in a low tone:

"Poor old woman!"

Renardet felt a strange rumbling in his stomach; then he gave vent to a sort of loud sneeze that issued at the same time through nose and mouth; and, drawing his handkerchief from his pocket, began to weep copiously, coughing, sobbing noisily, wiping his face, and stammering:

"Damn — damn — damned pig to do this! I would like to see him guillotined!"

But Princèpe reappeared, with his hands empty. He murmured:

"I have found nothing, M'sieu', le Maire, nothing at all anywhere."

The mayor, scared, replied in a thick voice, drowned in tears:

"What is it you could not find?"

"The little girl's clothes."

"Well — well — look again, and find them—or you'll have to answer to me."

The man, knowing that the mayor would not brook opposition, set forth again with hesitating steps, casting on the corpse horrified and timid glances.

Distant voices arose under the trees, a confused sound, the noise of an approaching crowd; for Mederic had, in the course of his rounds, carried the news from door to door. The people of the neighborhood, stupefied at first, had gone gossiping from their own firesides into the street, and from one threshold to another. Then they gathered together. They talked over, discussed, and commented on the event for some minutes, and they had now come to see it for themselves.

They arrived in groups, a little faltering and uneasy through fear of the first impression of such a scene on their minds. When they saw the body they stopped, not daring to advance, and speaking low. Then they grew bold, went on a few steps, stopped again, advanced once more, and soon formed around the dead girl, her mother, the doctor, and Renardet, a thick circle, agitated and noisy, which swayed forward under the sudden pushes of the last comers. And now they touched the corpse. Some of them even bent down to feel it with their fingers. The doctor kept them back. But the mayor, waking abruptly out of his torpor, broke into a rage, and, seizing Dr. Labarbe's stick, flung himself on his townspeople, stammering:

"Clear out—clear out—you pack of brutes—clear out!"

And in a second the crowd of sightseers had fallen back two hundred metres.

La Roque was lifted up, turned round, and placed in a sitting posture; she remained weeping with her hands clasped over her face.

· The occurrence was discussed among the crowd; and young lads, with eager eyes, curiously scrutinized the nude body of the girl. Renardet perceived this, and, abruptly taking off his vest, flung it over the little girl, who was entirely lost to view under the wide garment.

· The spectators drew quietly nearer. The wood was filled with people, and a continuous hum of voices rose up under the tangled foliage of the tall trees.

The mayor, in his shirt-sleeves, remained standing, with his stick in his hands, in a fighting attitude. He seemed exasperated by this curiosity on the part of the people, and kept repeating:

"If one of you comes nearer, I'll break his head just as I would a dog's."

The peasants were greatly afraid of him. They held back. Dr. Labarbe, who was smoking, sat down beside La Roque, and spoke to her in order to distract her attention. The old woman soon removed her hands from her face, and replied with a flood of tearful words, pouring forth her grief in rapid sentences. She told the whole story of her life, her marriage, the death of her man —a bull-sticker, who had been gored to death—the infancy of her daughter, her wretched existence as a widow without resources and with a child to support. She had only this one, her little Louise, and the child had been killed—killed in this wood. All of a sudden, she felt anxious to see it again, and dragging herself on her knees toward the corpse, she raised up one corner of the garment that covered it; then she let it fall again, and began wailing once more. The crowd remained silent, eagerly watching the mother's gestures.

But all of a sudden there was a swaying of the crowd, and a cry of "The gendarmes! The gendarmes!"

Two gendarmes appeared in the distance, coming on at a rapid trot, escorting their captain and a little gentleman with red whiskers, who was bobbing up and down like a monkey on a big white mare.

The steward had found M. Putoin, the examining magistrate, just at the moment when he was mounting to take his daily ride, for he posed as a good horseman, to the great amusement of the officers.

He dismounted along with the captain, and pressed the hands of the mayor and the doctor, casting a ferret-like glance on the linen vest which swelled above the body lying underneath.

When he was thoroughly acquainted with the facts, he first gave orders to get rid of the public, whom the gendarmes drove out of the wood, but who soon reappeared in the meadow, and formed a line, a long line of excited and moving heads all along the Brindelle, on the other side of the stream.

The doctor in his turn gave explanations of which Renardet took a note in his memorandum book. All the evidence was given, taken down, and commented on without leading to any discovery. Maxime, too, came back without having found any trace of the clothes.

This surprised everybody; no one could explain it on the theory of theft, since these rags were not worth twenty sous; so this theory was inadmissible.

The examining magistrate, the mayor, the captain, and the doctor set to work by searching in pairs, putting aside the smallest branches along the water.

Renardet said to the judge:

"How does it happen that this wretch should conceal or carry away the clothes, and should then leave the body exposed in the open air and visible to everyone?"

The other, sly and knowing, answered:

"Perhaps a dodge. This crime has been committed either by a brute or by a crafty blackguard. In any case, we'll easily succeed in finding him."

The rolling of a vehicle made them turn their heads. It was the deputy magistrate, another doctor, and the registrar of the court who had arrived in their turn. They resumed their searches, all chatting in an animated fashion.

Renardet said suddenly:

"Do you know that I am expecting you to lunch with me?"

Everyone smilingly accepted the invitation, and the examining magistrate, finding that the case of little Louise Roque was quite enough to bother about for one day, turned toward the mayor:

"I can have the body brought to your house, can I not? You have a room in which you can keep it for me till this evening."

The other got confused, and stammered:

"Yes—no—no. To tell the truth, I prefer that it should not come into my house on account of—on account of my servants who are already talking about ghosts in—in my tower, in the Fox's Tower. You know—I could no longer keep a single one. No—I prefer not to have it in my house."

The magistrate began to smile:

"Good! I am going to get it carried off at once to Rouy, for the legal examination."

Turning toward the doctor:

"I can make use of your trap, can I not?"

"Yes, certainly."

Everybody came back to the place where the corpse lay. La Roque, now seated beside her daughter, had caught hold of her hand, and was staring right before her, with a wandering listless eye.

The two doctors endeavored to lead her away, so that she might not witness the dead girl's removal; but she understood at once what they wanted to do, and, flinging herself on the body, she seized it in both arms. Lying on top of the corpse, she exclaimed:

"You shall not have it—'tis mine—'tis mine now. They have killed her for me, and I want to keep her—you shall not have her——!"

All the men, affected and not knowing how to act, remained standing around her. Renardet fell on his knees, and said to her:

"Listen, La Roque, it is necessary—in order to find out who killed her. Without this it could not be found out. We must make a search for him in order to punish him. When we have found him, we'll give her up to you. I promise you this."

This explanation shook the woman's mind, and a feeling of hatred manifested in her distracted glance.

"So then they'll take him?"

"Yes, I promise you that."

"She rose up, deciding to let them do as they liked; but when the captain remarked: "'Tis surprising that her clothes cannot be found," a new idea, which she had not previously thought of, abruptly found an entrance into her brain, and she asked:

"Where are her clothes? They're mine. I want him. Where have they been put?"

They explained to her that they had not been found, then she called out for them with desperate obstinacy and with repeated moans:

"They're mine—I want them. Where are they? I want them!"

The more they tried to calm her, the more she sobbed, and persisted in her demands. She no longer wanted the body, she insisted on having the clothes, as much perhaps through the unconscious cupidity of a wretched being to whom a piece of silver represents a fortune, as through maternal tenderness.

And when the little body, rolled up in blankets which had been brought out from Renardet's house, had disappeared in the vehicle, the old woman, standing under the trees, held up by the mayor and the captain, exclaimed:

"I have nothing, nothing, nothing in the world, not even her little cap—her little cap."

The curé had just arrived, a young priest already growing stout. He took it on himself to carry off La Roque, and they went away together toward the village. The mother's grief was modified under the sugary words of the clergyman, who promised her a thousand compensations. But she incessantly kept repeating: "If I had only her little cap."

This idea now dominated every other.

Before they were out of hearing Renardet exclaimed:

"You will lunch with us, Monsieur l'Abbé—in an hour's time?"

The priest turned his head round, and replied:

"With pleasure, Monsieur le Maire. I'll be with you at twelve."

And they all directed their steps toward the house, whose gray front and large tower, built on the edge of the Brindelle, could be seen through the branches.

The meal lasted a long time. They talked about the crime and everybody was of the same opinion. It had been committed by some tramp passing there by chance while the little girl was bathing.

Then the magistrates returned to Rouy, announcing that they would return next day at an early hour. The doctor and the curé went to their respective homes, while Renardet, after a long walk through the meadows, returned to the wood, where he remained walking till nightfall with slow steps, his hands behind his back.

He went to bed early, and was still asleep next morning when the examining magistrate entered his room. He rubbed his hands together with a self-satisfied air. He said:

"Ha! ha! Still sleeping? Well, my dear fellow, we have news this morning."

The mayor sat up on his bed.

"What pray?"

"Oh! Something strange. You remember well how the mother yesterday clamored for some memento of her daughter, especially her little cap? Well, on opening her door this morning, she found on the threshold her child's two little wooden shoes. This proves that the crime was perpetrated by some one from the district, some one who felt pity for her. Besides, the postman Mederic found and brought me the thimble, the scissors, and the needlecase of the dead

girl. So then the man in carrying off the clothes in order to hide them, must have let fall the articles which were in the pocket. As for me, I attach special importance to the wooden shoes, as they indicate a certain moral culture and a faculty for tenderness on the part of the assassin. We will therefore, if you have no objection, pass in review together the principal inhabitants of your district."

The mayor got up. He rang for hot water to shave with, and said:

"With pleasure, but it will take rather a long time, so let us begin at once."

M. Putoin sat astride on a chair, thus pursuing even in a room, his mania for horsemanship. Renardet now covered his chin with a white lather while he looked at himself in the glass; then he sharpened his razor on the strop and went on:

"The principal inhabitant of Carvelin bears the name of Joseph Renardet, mayor, a rich landowner, a rough man who beats guards and coachmen—".

The examining magistrate burst out laughing:

"That's enough; let us pass on to the next."

"The second in importance is ill. Pelledent, his deputy, a rearer of oxen, an equally rich landowner, a crafty peasant, very sly, very close-fisted on every question of money, but incapable in my opinion of having perpetrated such a crime."

M. Putoin said:

"Let us pass on."

Then, while continuing to shave and wash himself, Renardet went on with the moral inspection of all the inhabitants of Carvelin. After two hours' discussion, their suspicions were fixed on three individuals who had hitherto borne a shady reputation—a poacher named Cavalle, a fisher for club and cray-fish named Paquet, and a bull-sticker named Clovis.

II

The search for the perpetrator of the crime lasted all the summer, but he was not discovered. Those who were suspected and those who were arrested easily proved their innocence, and the authorities were compelled to abandon the attempt to capture the criminal.

But the murder seemed to have moved the entire country in a singular fashion. It left a disquietude, a vague fear, a sensation of mysterious terror, springing not merely from the impossibility of discovering any trace of the assassin, but above all from that strange finding of the wooden shoes in front of La Roque's door on the day after the crime. The certainty that the murderer had assisted at the investigation and that he was doubtless still living in the village, left a gloomy impression on every mind, and hung over the neighborhood like a constant menace.

The wood, besides, had become a dreaded spot, a place to be avoided, and supposed to be haunted.

Formerly, the inhabitants used to come and lounge there every Sunday afternoon. They used to sit down on the moss at the foot of the huge trees, or walk along the water's edge watching the trout gliding under the green undergrowth. The boys used to play bowls, hide-and-seek, and other games in certain places where they had upturned, smoothed out, and leveled the soil, and the girls, in rows of four or five, used to trip along holding one another by the arms, and screaming out with their shrill voices ballads which grated on the ear, disturbed the tranquil air with discord and set the teeth on edge like vinegar. Now nobody ventured into and under the towering trees, as if afraid of finding there some corpse lying on the ground.

Autumn arrived; the leaves began to fall. They fell day and night from the tall trees, whirling round and round to the ground; and the sky could be seen through the bare branches. Sometimes when a gust of wind swept over the tree-tops, the slow, continuous rain suddenly grew heavier, and became a hoarsely growling storm, which drenched the moss with thick yellow water that made the ground swampy and yielding. And the almost imperceptible murmur, the floating, ceaseless whisper, gentle and sad, of this rainfall seemed like a low wail, and the continually falling leaves, like tears, big tears shed by the tall mournful trees, which were weeping, as it were, day and night over the close of the year, over the ending of warm dawns and soft twilights, over the ending of hot breezes and bright suns, and also perhaps over the crime which they had seen committed under the shade of their branches, over the girl violated and killed at their feet. They wept in the silence of the desolate empty wood, the abandoned, dreaded wood, where the soul, the childish soul of the dead little girl must have been wandering all alone.

The Brindelle, swollen by the storms, rushed on more quickly, yellow and angry, between its dry banks, lined with thin, bare willow-hedges.

Renardet suddenly resumed his walks

under the trees. Every day, at sunset, he came out of his house, descended the front steps slowly, and entered the wood, in a dreamy fashion with his hands in his pockets. For a long time he would pace over the damp, soft moss; while a legion of rooks, rushing to the spot from all the neighboring haunts in order to rest in the tall summits, spread themselves through space, like an immense mourning veil floating in the wind, uttering violent and sinister screams. Sometimes they would perch on the tangled branches dotting with black spots the red sky, the sky crimsoned with autumn twilight. Then, all of a sudden, they would set off again, croaking frightfully and trailing once more above the wood the long darkness of their flight. Then they would swoop down, at last, on the highest tree-tops, and gradually their cawings would die away, while advancing night merged their black plumes into the blackness of space.

Renardet was still strolling slowly under the trees; then, when the darkness prevented him from walking any longer, he went back to the house, sank all of a heap into his armchair in front of the glowing hearth and dried his feet at the fire.

Now, one morning, an important bit of news was circulated around the district: the mayor was getting his wood cut down.

Twenty woodcutters were already at work. They had commenced at the corner nearest to the house, and they worked rapidly in the master's presence.

At first the loppers climbed up the trunk. Tied to it by a rope collar, they clung round it in the beginning with both arms, then, lifting one leg, struck the tree hard with the edge of a steel instrument attached to each foot. The edge penetrated the wood and remained stuck in it; and the man rose up as if on a step in order to strike with the steel attached to the other foot, and then once more supported himself till he could lift his first foot again.

With every upward movement was slipped higher the rope collar which fastened him to the tree. Over his loins hung and glittered the steel hatchet. He kept continually climbing in easy fashion like some parasite attacking a giant, mounting slowly up the immense trunk, embracing it and spurring it in order to decapitate it.

As soon as he reached the lowest branches, he stopped, detached from his side the sharp ax, and struck. Slowly, methodically, he chopped at the limb close to the trunk. Suddenly the branch cracked, gave way, bent, tore itself off, and fell, grazing the neighboring trees in its fall. Then it crashed down on the ground with a great sound of broken wood, and it slighter branches quivered for a long time.

The soil was covered with· fragments which other men cut in their turn, bound in bundles; and plied in heaps, while the trees which were still left standing looked like enormous posts, gigantic forms amputated and shorn by the keen steel axes of the cutters.

When the lopper had finished his task, he left at the top of the straight slender shaft of the tree the rope collar which he had brought up with him, descending again with spur-like prods along the discrowned trunk, which the woodcutters below attacked at the base, striking it with heavy blows which resounded through all the rest of the wood.

When the base of the tree seemed pierced deeply enough, some men commenced dragging, to the accompaniment of a signal cry in which all joined harmoniously, at the rope attached to the top. All of a sudden, the immense column cracked and tumbled to the earth with the dull sound and shock of a distant cannon-shot. Each day the wood grew thinner, losing its trees one by one as an army loses its soldiers.

Renardet no longer walked up and down. He remained from morning till night, contemplating, motionless, with his hands behind his back, the slow death of his wood. When a tree fell, he placed his foot on it as if it were a corpse. Then he raised his eyes to the next with a kind of secret, calm impatience, as if he expected or hoped for something at the end of this massacre.

Meanwhile, they were approaching the place where little Louise Roque had been found. At length, they came to it—one evening, at the hour of twilight.

As it was dark, the sky being overcast, the woodcutters wanted to stop their work, putting off till next day the fall of an enormous beech-tree. But Renardet objected to this, insisting that even at this late hour they should lop and cut down this giant, which had overshadowed and seen the crime.

When the lopper had laid it bare, had finished its toilet for the guillotine, and the woodcutters had sapped its base, five men commenced hauling at the rope attached to the top.

The tree resisted; its powerful trunk, although cut half-way through, was as rigid as iron. The workmen, altogether,

with a sort of regular jump, strained at the rope, stooping down to the ground, and they gave vent to a cry with lungs out of breath, so as to indicate and direct their efforts.

Two woodcutters stood close to the giant, with axes in their grip, like two executioners ready to strike once more, and Renardet, motionless, with his hand on the bark, awaited the fall with an uneasy, nervous feeling.

One of the men said to him:

"You're too near, Monsieur le Maire. When it falls, it may hurt you."

He did not reply and did not recoil. He seemed ready to catch the beech-tree in his open arms in order to cast it on the ground like a wrestler.

All at once, at the foot of the tall column of wood there was a shudder which seemed to run to the top, like a painful shiver; it bent slightly, ready to fall, but still resisted. The men, in a state of excitement, stiffened their arms, renewed their efforts with greater vigor, and, just as the tree, breaking, came crashing down, Renardet suddenly made a forward step, then stopped, his shoulders raised to receive the irresistible shock, the mortal blow which would crush him to the earth.

But the beech-tree, having deviated a little, only grazed against his loins, throwing him on his face five metres away.

The workmen rushed forward to lift him up. He had already risen to his knees, stupefied, with wandering eyes, and passing his hand across his forehead, as if he were awaking out of an attack of madness.

When he had got to his feet once more, the men, astonished, questioned him, not being able to understand what he had done. He replied, in faltering tones, that he had had for a moment a fit of abstraction, or rather a return to the days of his childhood, that he imagined he had to pass under that tree, just as street-boys rush in front of vehicles driving rapidly past, that he had played at danger, that, for the past eight days, he felt this desire growing stronger within him, asking himself whether, every time a tree was cracking, was on the point of falling, he could pass beneath it without being touched. It was a piece of stupidity, he confessed; but everyone has these moments of insanity, these temptations to boyish folly.

He made this explanation in a slow tone, searching for his words and speaking in a stupefied fashion.

Then he went off saying:

"Till to-morrow, my friends—till to-morrow."

As soon as he had reached his study, he sat down before his table, which his lamp, covered with a shade, lighted up brightly, and, clasping his hands over his forehead, began to cry.

He remained crying for a long time, then wiped his eyes, raised his head, and looked at the clock. It was not yet six o'clock.

"I have time before dinner."

And he went to the door and locked it. He then came back, and sat down before his table. He pulled out a drawer in the middle of it, and taking from it a revolver, laid it down over his papers, under the glare of the lamp. The barrel of the firearm glittered, and cast reflections which resembled flames.

Renardet gazed at it for some time with the uneasy glance of a drunken man; then he rose and began to pace up and down the room.

He walked from one end of the apartment to the other, stopped from time to time and started to pace up and down again a moment afterward. Suddenly, he opened the door of his dressing-room, steeped a towel in the water-jug and moistened his forehead, as he had done on the morning of the crime.

Then he began to walk up and down once more. Each time he passed the table the gleaming revolver attracted his glance, and tempted his hand; but he kept watching the clock, thinking:

"I have still time."

It struck half past six. Then he took up the revolver, opened his mouth wide with a frightful grimace, and stuck the barrel into it, as if he wanted to swallow it. He remained in this position for some seconds without moving, his finger on the lock; then, suddenly, seized with a shudder of horror, he dropped the pistol on the carpet, and fell back on his armchair, sobbing:

"I can't. I dare not! My God! My God! My God! How can I have the courage to kill myself?"

There was a knock at the door. He rose up in a stupefied condition. A servant said:

"Monsieur's dinner is ready."

He replied: "All right. I'm going down."

He picked up the revolver, locked it up again in the drawer, then looked at himself in the glass over the mantelpiece to see whether his face did not look too much troubled. It was as red as usual, a little redder perhaps. That was all. He went down, and seated himself before the table.

He ate slowly, like a man who wants to drag on the meal, who does not want to be alone with himself.

Then he smoked several pipes in the dining-room while the plates were being removed. After that, he went back to his room.

As soon as he was alone, he looked under his bed, opened all his cupboards, explored every corner, rummaged through all the furniture. Then he lighted the tapers over the mantelpiece, and, turning round several times, ran his eye all over the apartment in an anguish of terror that made his face lose its color, for he knew well that he was going to see her, as he did every night— little Louise Roque, the little girl he had violated and afterward strangled.

Every night the odious vision came back again. First, it sounded in his ears like the snorting that is made by a thrashing machine or the distant passage of a train over a bridge. Then he commenced to pant, to feel suffocated, and had to unbutton his shirt-collar and loosen his belt. He moved about to make his blood circulate, he tried to read, he attempted to sing. It was in vain. His thoughts, in spite of himself, went back to the day of the murder, made him go through it again in all its most secret details, with all the violent emotions he had experienced from first to last.

He had felt on rising up that morning, the morning of the horrible day, a little vertigo and dizziness which he attributed to the heat, so that he remained in his room till the time came for lunch.

After the meal he had taken a siesta, then, toward the close of the afternoon, he had gone out to breathe the fresh, soothing breeze under the trees in the wood.

But, as soon as he was outside, the heavy scorching air of the plain oppressed him more. The sun, still high in the heavens, poured out on the parched, dry, and thirsty soil, floods of ardent light. Not a breath of wind stirred the leaves. Beasts and birds, even the grasshoppers, were silent. Renardet reached the tall trees, and began to walk over the moss where the Brindelle sent forth a slight, cool vapor under the immense roof of trees. But he felt ill at ease It seemed to him that an unknown, invisible hand was squeezing his neck, and he could scarcely think rationally, having usually few ideas in his head. For the last three months, only one thought haunted him, the thought of marrying again. He suffered from living alone, suffered from it morally and physically. Accustomed for ten years past to feeling a woman near him, habituated to her presence every moment, to her embrace each successive day, he had need, an imperious and perplexing need of incessant contact with her and the regular touch of her lips. Since Madame Renardet's death, he had suffered continually without knowing why, had suffered from not feeling her dress brush against his legs every day, and, above all, from no longer being able to grow calm and languid in her arms. He had been scarcely six months a widower, and he had already been looking out through the district for some young girl or some widow he might marry when his period of mourning was at an end.

He had a chaste soul, but it was lodged in a vigorous Herculean body; and carnal images began to disturb his sleep and his vigils. He drove them away; they came back again; and he murmured from time to time, smiling at himself:

"Here I am, like St. Antony."

Having had this morning several besetting visions, the desire suddenly came into his breast to bathe in the Brindelle in order to refresh himself and reduce his feverishness.

He knew, a little further on, of a large deep spot where the people of the neighborhood came sometimes to take a dip in the summer. He went there.

Thick willow-trees hid this clear pool of water where the current rested and went to sleep for a little while before starting on its way again. Renardet, as he appeared, thought he heard a light sound, a faint plash which was not that of the stream or the banks. He softly put aside the leaves and looked. A little girl, quite naked in the transparent water, was beating the waves with both hands, dancing about in them a little, and dipping herself with pretty movements. She was not a child nor was she yet a woman. She was plump and well formed, yet had an air of youthful precocity, as of one who had grown rapidly, and who was now almost ripe. He no longer moved, overcome with surprise, with a pang of desire, holding his breath with a strange, poignant emotion. He remained there, his heart beating as if one of his sensual dreams had just been realized; as if an impure fairy had conjured up before him this young creature, this little rustic Venus born of the river foam, who was making his heart beat faster.

Suddenly the little girl came out of the water, and without seeing him came over to where he stood looking for her clothes in order to dress herself. While she was gradually approaching him with little hesitating steps, through fear of the sharp pointed stones, he felt himself pushed toward her by an irresistible force, by a bestial transport of passion, which stirred up all his carnality, stupefied his soul, and made him tremble from head to foot.

She remained standing some seconds behind the willow-tree which concealed him from view. Then, losing his reason entirely, he opened the branches, rushed on her, and seized her in his arms. She fell, too scared to offer any resistance, too much terror-sticken to cry out, and he possessed her without understanding what he was doing.

He woke up from his crime, as one wakes out of a nightmare. The child burst out weeping.

He said:

"Hold your tongue! Hold your tongue! I'll give you money."

But she did not hear him, she went on sobbing.

He went on:

"Come now, hold your tongue! Do hold your tongue. Keep quiet."

She still kept shrieking, writhing in the effort to get away from him. He suddenly realized that he was ruined, and he caught her by the neck to stop her from uttering these heartrending, dreadful screams. As she continued to struggle with the desperate strength of a being who is flying from death, he pressed his enormous hands on that little throat swollen with cries. In a few seconds he had strangled her, so furiously did he grip her, yet not intending to kill but only to silence her.

Then he rose up overwhelmed with horror.

She lay before him with her face bleeding and blackened. He was going to rush away when there sprang up in his agitated soul the mysterious and undefined instinct that guides all beings in the hour of danger.

It was necessary to throw the body into the water; but he did not; another impulse drove him toward the clothes, of which he made a thin parcel. Then, as he had a piece of twine, he tied it up and hid it in a deep portion of the stream, under the trunk of a tree, the foot of which was immersed in the Brindelle.

Then he went off at a rapid pace, reached the meadows, took a wide turn in order to show himself to peasants who dwelt some distance away on the opposite side of the district, and came back to dine at the usual hour, telling his servants all that was supposed to have happened during his walk.

He slept, however, that night—slept with a heavy, brutish sleep, such as the sleep of persons condemned to death must occasionally be. He opened his eyes at the first glimmer of dawn, and waited, tortured by the fear of having his crime discovered, for his usual waking hour.

Then he would have to be present at all the stages of the inquiry as to the cause of death. He did so after the fashion of a somnambulist, in a hallucination which showed him things and human beings in a sort of dream, in a cloud of intoxication, with that dubious sense of unreality which perplexes the mind at times of the greatest catastrophes.

The only thing that pierced his heart was La Roque's cry of anguish. At that moment he felt inclined to cast himself at the old woman's feet, and to exclaim: "'Tis I."

But he restrained himself. He went back, however, during the night, to fish up the dead girl's wooden shoes, in order to carry them to her mother's threshold.

As long as the inquiry lasted, so long as it was necessary to guide and aid justice, he was calm, master of himself, sly and smiling. He discussed quietly with the magistrates all the suppositions that passed through their minds, combated their opinions, and demolished their arguments. He even took a keen and mournful pleasure in disturbing their investigations, in confuting their ideas, in showing the innocence of those whom they suspected.

But from the day when the investigation came to a close, he became gradually nervous, more excitable than he had been before, although he mastered his irritability. Sudden noises made him jump up with fear; he shuddered at the slightest thing, trembled sometimes from head to foot when a fly alighted on his forehead. Then he was seized with an imperious desire for motion, which compelled him to keep continually on foot, and made him remain up whole nights walking to and fro in his own room.

It was not that he was goaded by remorse. His brutal mind did not lend itself to any shade of sentiment or of moral terror. A man of energy and even of violence, born to make war, to ravage conquered countries, and to massacre the vanquished, full of the savage instincts of the hunter and the fighter, he scarcely took count of human life. Though he respected the Church through policy, he believed neither in God nor in the devil, expecting consequently in another life neither chastisement nor recompense for his acts. As his sole creed, he retained a vague philosophy composed of all the ideas of the encyclopedists of the last century. He regarded religion as a moral sanction of the law, both one and the other having been invented by men to regulate social relations.

To kill anyone in a duel, or in a battle, or in a quarrel, or by accident, or for the sake of revenge, or even through bravado, would have seemed to him an amusing and clever thing, and would not have left more impression on his mind than a shot fired at a hare; but he had experienced a profound emotion at the murder of this child. He had, in the first place, perpetrated it in the distraction of an irresistible gust of passion, in a sort of sensual tempest that had overpowered his reason. And he had cherished in his heart, cherished in his flesh, cherished on his lips, cherished even to the very tips of his murderous fingers, a kind of bestial love, as well as a feeling of horror and grief, toward this little girl he had surprised and basely killed. Every moment his thoughts returned to that horrible scene, and, though he endeavored to drive away the picture from his mind, though he put it aside with terror, with disgust, he felt it surging through his soul,

moving about in him, waiting incessantly for the moment to reappear.

Then, in the night, he was afraid, afraid of the shadows falling around him. He did not yet know why the darkness seemed frightful to him; but he instinctively feared it, felt that it was peopled with terrors. The bright daylight did not lend itself to fears. Things and beings were seen there; there only natural things and beings which could exhibit themselves in the light of day could be met. But the night, the impenetrable night, thicker than walls, and empty, the infinite night, so black, so vast, in which one might brush against frightful things, the night when one feels that mysterious terror is wandering, prowling about, appeared to him to conceal an unknown danger, close and menacing.

What was it?

He knew it ere long. As he sat in his armchair, rather late, one evening when he could not sleep, he thought he saw the curtain of his window move. He waited, in an uneasy state of mind, with beating heart. The drapery did not stir, then, all of a sudden it moved once more. He did not venture to rise up; he no longer ventured to breathe, and yet he was brave. He had often fought, and he would have liked to catch thieves in his house.

Was it true that this curtain did move? he asked himself, fearing that his eyes had deceived him. It was, moreover, such a slight thing, a gentle flutter of lace, a kind of trembling in its folds, less than such an undulation as is caused by the wind.

Renardet sat still, with staring eyes, and outstretched neck. Then he sprang to his feet abruptly, ashamed of his fear, took four steps, seized the drapery with both hands, and pulled it wide apart. At first, he saw nothing but darkened glass, resembling plates of glittering ink. The night, the vast, impenetrable night stretched out before him as far as the invisible horizon. He remained standing in front of the illimitable shadow, and suddenly perceived a light, a moving light, which seemed some distance away.

Then he put his face close to the windowpane, thinking that a person looking for crayfish might be poaching in the Brindelle, for it was past midnight. The light rose up at the edge of the stream, under the trees. As he was not yet able to see clearly, Renardet placed his hands over his eyes. Suddenly this light became an illumination, and he beheld little Louise Roque naked and bleeding on the moss. He recoiled frozen with horror, sank into his chair, and fell backward. He remained there some minutes, his soul in distress; then he sat up and began to reflect. He had had a hallucination—that was all: a hallucination due to the fact that a marauder of the night was walking with a lantern in his hand near the water's edge. What was there astonishing, besides, in the circumstance that the recollection of his crime should sometimes bring before him the vision of the dead girl?

He rose up, swallowed a glass of wine, and sat down again. He thought:

"What am I to do if this came back?"

And it did come back; he felt it; he was sure of it. Already his glance was drawn toward the window; it called him; it attracted him. In order to avoid looking at it, he turned aside his chair. Then, he took a book and tried to read; but it seemed to him that he presently heard something stirring behind him, and he swung round his armchair on one foot.

The curtain still moved—unquestionably, it did move this time; he could no longer have any doubt about it.

He rushed forward and seized it in his grasp so violently that he knocked it down with its fastener. Then, he eagerly pressed his face against the glass. He saw nothing. All was black without; and he breathed with the delight of a man whose life has just been saved.

Then he went back to his chair, and sat down again; but almost immediately he felt a longing to look out through the window once more. Since the curtain had fallen, the space in front of him made a sort of dark patch, fascinating and terrible, on the obscure landscape. In order not to yield to this dangerous temptation, he took off his clothes, extinguished the lamp, and lay down, shutting his eyes.

Lying on his back motionless, his skin hot and moist, he awaited sleep. Suddenly a great gleam of light flashed across his eyelids. He opened them believing that his dwelling was on fire. All was black as before, and he leaned on his elbow in order to try to distinguish his window, which had still for him an unconquerable attraction. By dint of straining his eyes, he could perceive some stars, and he arose, groped his way across the room, discovered the panes with his outstretched hands, and placed his forehead close to them. There below, under the trees, the body of the little girl glittered like phosphorus, lighting up the surrounding darkness.

Renardet uttered a cry and rushed toward his bed, where he lay till morning, his head hidden under the pillow.

From that moment, his life became intolerable. He passed his days in apprehension of each succeeding night; and each night the vision came back again. As soon as he had locked himself up in his room, he strove to struggle; but in vain. An irresistible force lifted him up and pushed him against the glass, as if to call the phantom, and ere long he saw it lying in the spot where the crime was committed, lying with arms and legs outspread, just in the way the body had been found.

Then the dead girl rose up and came toward him with little steps just as the child had done when she came out of the river. She advanced quietly, passing straight across the grass, and over the border of withered flowers. Then she rose up into the air toward Renardet's window. She came toward him, as she had come on the day of the crime. And the man recoiled before the apparition—he retreated to his bed, and sank down upon it, knowing well that the little one had entered the room, and that she now was standing behind the curtain, which presently moved. And until daybreak, he kept staring at this curtain, with a fixed glance, ever waiting to see his victim depart.

But she did not show herself any more; she remained there behind the curtain which quivered tremulously now and then.

And Renardet, his fingers clinging to the bedclothes, squeezed them as he had squeezed the throat of little Louise Roque.

He heard the clock striking the hours; and in the stillness the pendulum kept time with the loud beating of his heart. And he suffered, the wretched man, more than any man had ever suffered before.

Then, as soon as a white streak of light on the ceiling announced the approaching day, he felt himself free, alone at last, alone in his room; and then he went to sleep. He slept some hours —a restless, feverish sleep in which he retraced in dreams the horrible vision of the night just past.

When, later on, he went down to breakfast, he felt exhausted as if after prodigious fatigue; and he scarcely ate anything, haunted as he was by the fear of what he had seen the night before

He knew, however, that it was not an apparition—that the dead do not come back, and that his sick soul, possessed by one thought alone, by an indelible remembrance, was the only cause of his punishment, was the only evoker of that awful image, brought back by it to life, called up by it and raised by it before his eyes, in which the ineffaceable resemblance remained imprinted. But he knew, too, that he could not cure it, that he could never escape from the savage persecution of his memory; and he resolved to die, rather than endure these tortures any longer.

Then, he pondered how he would kill himself. He wished for some simple and natural death which would preclude the idea of suicide. For he clung to his reputation, to the name bequeathed to him by his ancestors; and if there was any suspicion as to the cause of his death, people's thoughts might be perhaps directed toward the mysterious crime, toward the murderer who could not be found, and they would not hesitate to accuse him.

A strange idea came into his head, that of letting himself be crushed by the tree at the foot of which he had assassinated little Louise Roque. So he determined to have the wood cut down and to simulate an accident. But the beech-tree refused to smash his ribs.

Returning to his house, a prey to utter despair, he had snatched up his revolver, and then he did not dare to fire it.

The dinner bell summoned him. He could eat nothing, and went upstairs again. But he did not know what he was going to do. Now that he had escaped the first time, he felt himself a coward. Presently, he would be ready, fortified, decided, master of his courage and of his resolution; just now, he was weak, and feared death as much as he did the dead girl.

He faltered out to himself:

"I will not venture it again—I will not venture it."

Then he glanced with terror, first at the revolver on the table, and next at the curtain which hid his window. It seemed to him, moreover, that something horrible would occur as soon as his life was ended. Something? What? A meeting with her, perhaps! She was watching for him; she was waiting for him; she was calling him; and her object was to seize him in her turn, to exhibit herself to him every night so that she might draw him toward the doom

that would avenge her, and lead him to death.

He began to cry like a child, repeating:

"I will not venture it again—I will not venture it,"

Then, he fell on his knees, and murmured: "My God! my God!" without believing, nevertheless, in God. He no longer dared, in fact, to look out through his window where he knew the apparition was visible, nor at the table where his revolver gleamed.

When he had risen up, he said:

"This cannot last; there must be an end of it."

The sound of his voice in the silent room made a shiver of fear pass through his limbs, but, as he could not come to a decision, as he felt certain that his finger would always refuse to pull the trigger of his revolver, he turned round to hide his head under the bedclothes, and to plunge into reflection.

He would have to find some way in which he could force himself to die, to invent some device against himself, which would not permit of any hesitation on his part, any delay, any possible regrets. He began to envy condemned criminals who are led to the scaffold surrounded by soldiers. Oh! if he could only beg of some one to shoot him; if he could, confessing the state of his soul, confessing his crime to a sure friend who would never divulge it, obtain from him death.

But from whom could he ask this terrible service? From whom? He cast about for one among his friends whom he knew intimately. The doctor? No, he would talk about it afterward, most certainly. And suddenly a fantastic

Idea entered his mind. He would write to the examining magistrate, who was on terms of close friendship with him and would denounce himself as the perpetrator of the crime. He would in this letter confess everything, revealing how his soul had been tortured, how he had resolved to die, how he had hesitated about carrying out his resolution, and what means he had employed to strengthen his failing courage. And in the name of their old friendship he would implore of the other to destroy the letter as soon as he had ascertained that the culprit had inflicted justice on himself. Renardet could rely on this magistrate; he knew him to be sure, discreet, incapable of even an idle word. He was one of those men who have an inflexible conscience, governed, directed, regulated by their reason alone.

Scarcely had he formed this project when a strange feeling of joy took possession of his heart. He was calm now. He would write his letter slowly, then at daybreak he would deposit it in the box nailed to the wall in his office, then he would ascend his tower to watch for the postman's arrival, and when the man in the blue blouse came in sight, he would cast himself headlong on to the rocks on which the foundations rested. First he would take care to be seen by the workmen who were cutting down his wood. He would then climb to the parapet some distance up which bore the flagstaff displayed on *fête* days. He would smash this pole with a shake and precipitate it along with him.

Who would suspect that it was not an accident? And he would be dashed to pieces, having regard to his weight and the height of the tower.

Presently he got out of bed, went over to the table, and began to write. He omitted nothing, not a single detail of the crime, not a single detail of the torments of his heart, and he ended by announcing that he had passed sentence on himself—that he was going to execute the criminal—and begged of his friend, his old friend, to be careful that there should never be any stain on his memory.

When he had finished his letter, he saw that the day had dawned.

He closed it, sealed it, and wrote the address; then he descended with light steps, hurried toward the little white box fastened to the wall in the corner of the farmhouse, and when he had thrown into it the fatal paper which made his hand tremble, he came back quickly, shot the bolts of the great door, and climbed up to his tower to wait for the passing of the postman, who would convey his death sentence.

He felt self-possessed, now. Liberated! Saved!

A cold dry wind, an icy wind, passed across his face. He inhaled it eagerly, with open mouth, drinking in its chilling kiss. The sky was red, with a burning red, the red of winter, and all the plain whitened with frost glistened under the first rays of the sun, as if it had been powdered with bruised glass.

Renardet, standing up, with his head bare, gazed at the vast tract of country before him, the meadow to the left, and to the right the village whose chimneys were beginning to smoke with the preparations for the morning meal. At his feet he saw the Brindelle flowing toward the rocks, where he would soon be crushed to death. He felt himself reborn on that beautiful frosty morning, full of strength, full of life. The light bathed him and penetrated him like a new-born hope. A thousand recollections assailed him, recollections of similar mornings, of rapid walks, the hard earth which rang under his footsteps, of happy chases on the edges of pools where wild ducks sleep. At the good things that he loved, the good things of existence rushed into memory, penetrated him with fresh desires, awakened all the vigorous appetites of his active, powerful body.

And he was about to die? Why? He was going to kill himself stupidly, because he was afraid of a shadow—afraid of nothing. He was still rich and in the prime of life! What folly! All he wanted was distraction, absence, a voyage in order to forget.

This night even he had not seen the little girl because his mind was preoccupied, and so had wandered toward some other subject. Perhaps he would not see her any more? And even if she still haunted him in his house, certainly she would not follow him elsewhere! The earth was wide. the future was long.

Why die?

His glance traveled across the meadows, and he perceived a blue spot in the path which wound along-side of the Brindelle. It was Mederic coming to bring letters from the town and to carry away those of the village.

Renardet got a start, a sensation of pain shot through his breast, and he rushed toward the winding staircase to get back his letter, to demand it back from the postman. Little did it matter to him now whether he was seen. He hurried across the grass moistened

by the light frost of the previous night, and he arrived in front of the box in the corner of the farmhouse exactly at the same time as the letter-carrier.

The latter had opened the little wooden door, and drew forth the papers deposited there by the inhabitants of the locality.

Renardet said to him:

"Good morrow, Mederic."

"Good morrow, M'sieu' le Maire."

"I say, Mederic, I threw a letter into the box that I want back again. I came to ask you to give it back to me."

"That's all right, M'sieu' le Maire—you'll get it."

And the postman raised his eyes. He stood petrified at the sight of Renardet's face. The Mayor's cheeks were purple, his eyes were glaring with black circles round them as if they were sunk in his head, his hair was all tangled, his beard untrimmed, his necktie unfastened. It was evident that he had not gone to bed.

The postman asked:

"Are you ill, M'sieu' le Maire?"

The other suddenly comprehending that his appearance must be unusual, lost countenance and faltered:

"Oh! no—oh! no. Only I jumped out of bed to ask you for this letter. I was asleep. You understand?"

Said Mederic: "What letter?"

"The one you are going to give back to me."

Mederic now began to hesitate. The mayor's attitude did not strike him as natural. There was perhaps a secret in that letter, a political secret. He knew Renardet was not a Republican, and he knew all the tricks and chicaneries employed at elections.

He asked:

"To whom is it addressed, this letter of yours?"

"To M. Putoin, the examining magistrate—you know my friend, M. Putoin, well!"

The postman searched through the papers, and found the one asked for. Then he began looking at it, turning it round and round between his fingers, much perplexed, much troubled by the fear of committing a grave offense or of making an enemy for himself of the mayor.

Seeing his hesitation, Renardet made a movement for the purpose of seizing the letter and snatching it away from him. This abrupt action convinced Mederic that some important secret was at stake and made him resolve to do his duty, cost what it might.

So he flung the letter into his bag and fastened it up, with the reply:

"No, I can't, M'sieu' le Maire. From the moment it is addressed and sent to the magistrate, I can't."

A dreadful pang wrung Renardet's heart, and he murmured:

"Why, you know me well. You are even able to recognize my handwriting. I tell you I want that paper."

"I can't."

"Look here, Mederic, you know that I'm incapable of deceiving you—I tell you I want it."

"No, I can't."

A tremor of rage passed through Renardet's soul.

"Damn it all; take care! You know that I don't go in for chaffing, and that I could get you out of your job,

my good fellow, and without much delay either. And then, I am the mayor of the district after all; and I now order you to give me back that paper."

The postman answered firmly:

"No, I can't, M'sieu' le Maire."

Thereupon Renardet, losing his head, caught hold of the postman's arms in order to take away his bag; but, freeing himself by a strong effort, and springing backward, the letter-carrier raised his holly stick. Without losing his temper, he said emphatically:

"Don't touch me, M'sieu' le Maire, or I'll strike. Take care, I'm only doing my duty!"

Feeling that he was lost, Renardet suddenly became humble, gentle, appealing to him like a crying child:

"Look here, look here, my friend, give me back that letter, and I'll give you money. Stop! Stop! I'll give you a hundred francs you understand—a hundred francs!"

The postman turned on his heel and started on his journey.

Renardet followed him, out of breath, faltering:

"Mederic, Mederic, listen! I'll give you a thousand francs, you understand—a thousand francs."

The postman still went on without giving any answer.

Renardet went on:

"I'll make your fortune, you understand—whatever you wish—fifty thousand francs—fifty thousand francs—fifty thousand francs for that letter! What does it matter to you? You won't? Well, a hundred thousand—I say—a hundred thousand francs—a hundred thousand francs."

The postman turned back, his face hard, his eye severe:

"Enough of this, or else I'll repeat to the magistrate everything you have just said to me."

Renardet stopped abruptly. It was all over. He turned back and rushed toward his house, running like a hunted animal.

Then, in his turn, Mederic stopped, and watched this flight with stupefaction. He saw the mayor re-entering his own house and he waited still as if something astonishing was about to happen.

Presently the tall form of Renardet appeared on the summit of the Fox's Tower. He ran round the platform like a madman. Then he seized the flagstaff and shook it furiously without succeeding in breaking it; then, all of a sudden, like a swimmer taking a plunge, he dived into the air with his two hands in front of him.

Mederic rushed forward to give succor. As he crossed the park, he saw the woodcutters going to work. He called out to them, telling them an accident had occurred, and at the foot of the walls they found a bleeding body the head of which was crushed on a rock. The Brindelle surrounded this rock, and over its clear, calm waters, swollen at this point, could be seen a long, thin, red stream of mingled brains and blood.

THE END